THE
Wonderful World
OF
Disney Television

THE
Wonderful World
OF
Disney Television

A Complete History

BILL COTTER

NEW YORK

To Carol, whom I met at Disney,
and to Margot and Neal, who are growing up with Disney

Copyright © 1997 Disney Enterprises, Inc.

Library of Congress Cataloging-in-Publication Data

Cotter, Bill.
The wonderful world of Disney television :
a complete history / by Bill Cotter. — 1st ed.
p.   cm.
ISBN 0-7868-6359-5
1. Walt Disney Productions.   2. Television programs—
United States—Catalogs.   I. Title.
PN1992.92.W35C68   1997
016.79145'75'0973—dc21   97-17962
CIP

Designed by Jessica Shatan

FIRST EDITION
2 4 6 8 10 9 7 5 3 1

CONTENTS

AUTHOR'S NOTES

When I was near to finishing this book, someone asked me how long it took to write. My answer of forty years surprised him! Although the actual writing did not take forty years, my interest in the subject began at an early age. Watching *The Mickey Mouse Club* with one of my brothers is one of my earliest memories. The family photo album shows us wearing "Mouse Club" shirts and ears while eating meals off "Mouse Club" snack trays. For years I was jealous because his personalized "Mouse Club" towel lasted longer than mine. My childhood dream of going to Disneyland did not materialize until many years later when I started working for Walt Disney Productions. For someone who grew up watching the Disney shows, it was heaven.

That's where this book began; I helped form a film club for employees, which eventually screened most of the Studio's theatrical product. I was also fortunate to have access to the television library, and we used many of Walt's "behind-the-scenes" shows as filler in our club meetings. I took notes to introduce the films and guest speakers, supplementing with material from the Disney Archives. Eventually, the number of requests for information from other employees encouraged me to expand my notes into this book.

A few notes on the contents of this book are in order. With the exception of theatrical films aired on television, the credits are at least as complete as those given on the actual shows. In some cases, the volume of programming on The Disney Channel and the Studio's recent flurry of Touchstone Television series made it necessary to summarize the credits for those shows rather than list them by each individual episode. For all other shows, the air credits were taken both from the actual prints and from Studio records, and have been supplemented from other sources.

Cast credits are listed with the individual episodes, and production credits in the Appendix.

The information in the credits has changed over the years. Various unions and guilds involved with the series gradually negotiated additional credits for their members. Thus, when an episode from the early years of the anthology series was rerun later, it may have had additional credits. Also, many of the cast and crew members changed their names over the years. A "Ronnie Howard" would later be billed as "Ron," and many employees added "Sr." to their credits when their sons followed them into the business. I have left the names as they were on the actual credits.

Another notable point is that some of Disney's records on the early days of television are limited. The available files show that the staff was just concerned about completing the shows in time. Bill Walsh, for example, who was the producer of the Studio's earliest shows, kept almost no records on those labors, concentrating instead on his later efforts as a successful theatrical producer. In addition, when the Studio shut down their one-hour drama department in 1990, many of the files for recent projects were lost. I've tried to fill in these gaps, using materials from outside sources where possible.

During the time I worked on *The Wonderful World of Disney Television*, the Disney organization underwent several name changes. I have cited the name that was in use at whatever time an event took place, or the generic title of "Disney Studios." Anyone writing about Disney usually finds a need to distinguish between Disney, the company, and Disney, the man. I have tried to use "Disney" to denote the company and "Walt" to signify Mr. Disney, although I have left quoted comments in their original text.

More significantly than the name issue, the Studio began releasing a large number of adult-oriented television series such as *The Golden Girls* and *Empty Nest.* This trend continues today with *Home Improvement* and *Ellen.* In these cases, I've limited the space devoted to the credits and episode descriptions for those series. I have listed theatrical releases according to the dates they aired. Shows are covered up to the end of the 1995–96 season.

Finally, my thanks to those who encouraged me and assisted me on this project. I was able to spend time with many of the people listed in this book, discussing some of my favorite shows with them. There was another side benefit: I met my wife while we both worked at the Studio. Little did I know back in 1955 what lasting effects *The Mickey Mouse Club* would have on me! A *big* thanks must go to Dave Smith and his staff at the Disney Archives, especially Robert Tieman, along with Becky Cline and Collette Espino, who must have thought I was about to take up permanent residency in their reading room. A thanks to former Archives staff members Rose Motzko and Jennifer Hendrickson, who left before the book was finished. Thanks also to Disney employees (and dedicated enthusiasts) Stacia Martin and Mike Vaughn, who provided significant input over the years, to Chris Barat for his helpful suggestions on the animated series, to Caryl Merritt and Jane Shaffer of the Disney Channel, and to Jerry Edwards for his proofreading skills. Finally, sincere thanks to Wendy Lefkon and Monique Peterson at Hyperion for their help in getting this book edited and assembled.

Also, last but definitely not least, a very special thanks to my wife, Carol, for editing and proofreading the manuscript and for putting up with several years of my being glued to the TV or the computer.

Bill Cotter
March 1997

In the
Beginning

1

The Early Days and Disney's Specials

Walt studies the possibilities

In the 1940s, Walt Disney was best known as a successful producer of animated short subjects and features who had also made several live-action films. Despite his successes in these fields, however, he was still considered a relatively minor force in Hollywood at the time television first interested him. Walt had long been known as an innovator, and his career included many firsts, such as *Snow White and the Seven Dwarfs* (the first animated feature) and *Fantasia* (the first stereophonic soundtrack). Intrigued by the possibilities that television offered, Walt saw it more as a new avenue to explore than as a threat. Instead of ignoring television and hoping it would somehow go away, Walt decided to investigate the new medium's possibilities.

The Studio's earliest television effort began in late 1944. World War II had called a virtual halt to the fledgling television industry, but with the war drawing to a close, broadcasters began gearing up for the boom times they hoped were ahead. One of the first hurdles they faced was convincing the average American that television was something they couldn't live without. Disney became involved in a joint effort with RCA, the owners of the NBC network, to produce *The World in Your Living Room*, a film designed to extol the virtues of television.

While *The World in Your Living Room* would never be produced, the time and money involved had been well spent for Disney, as it had afforded the Studio with an in-depth look at all phases of broadcasting. Walt continued to track advances in the field, and in 1948, he went on record as believing television to be the best medium to exploit films. As more television sets were being bought by an increasingly interested public,

Walt began to look more closely into the feasibility of entering the television market.

As at other studios, there was heated debate at Walt Disney Productions over the pros and cons of siding with the fledgling television networks. Before making any public commitments, Walt decided he needed some impartial advice on the matter. He commissioned a study by an outside research firm, C. J. LaRoche, to find out if television was financially worth the effort and risks. The resulting report, "Television for Walt Disney Productions," was delivered in September 1950.

Testing the water

Despite the considerable doubts held by his brother Roy, who was the company's money man, Walt decided to take another of the gambles that marked his career. In early November 1950, the Studio publicly announced plans for its first venture into broadcasting. Instead of committing to a series, which would have been disastrous if it either failed in the ratings or hurt his theatrical market, Walt had decided to follow LaRoche's advice for a trial run. The result was *One Hour in Wonderland*, a special set for broadcast on Christmas day. The basis for the show was a look at the upcoming animated film *Alice in Wonderland*. It provided Walt with a method of testing television's potential impact on his theatrical business.

One of the first steps Walt took was to pick someone to head the television effort. He surprised everyone by selecting Bill Walsh, who was working as a press agent at the time. Walsh was probably the most surprised. Years later he commented that he never really did find out why Walt chose him for the job. "I kept bumping into him in the hall which is not a bad place—or in the parking lot. So

Walt in his strange way said 'You, you be the producer of TV.' And I always said 'Huh? But I don't have any experiences of a producer,' and Walt would always say 'Who does?' "

Following the suggestion that he needed a host, Walt decided to split the duty between himself and a proven star. Walsh suggested that they use one of his former clients, Edgar Bergen, the popular ventriloquist, who was also exploring the potential of television. At the time *One Hour in Wonderland* was announced, Bergen had already committed to a special for Thanksgiving, and columnists noted that all three networks were interested in his service. Bergen was so popular that some articles went so far as to categorize *One Hour in Wonderland* as a Bergen show, with some "help" from Disney. One writer spent more time describing how Bergen had new heads made for his dummies than on Walt's "contribution" to the show. However, most of the articles correctly noted that Bergen was a hired hand in what was very much a Disney production, and they correctly predicted that a major success was all but inevitable.

This success was not automatic, though, for a major snag cropped up shortly after the project was announced. The special was to have been aired on CBS, but much to the dismay of those broadcast executives, they could not guarantee the required number of stations specified in the contract. At the time, it was not uncommon for stations to belong to two networks, and NBC had convinced several of the stations it shared with CBS to air its programming on Christmas instead. As a result, Coca-Cola, the sponsor, decided to move the show to NBC, which "guaranteed" a total of sixty-two stations—if they liked the show enough! Luckily for all involved, the magical Disney name worked, and the stations quickly signed.

Thus, at 4 P.M. on Christmas day, Walt Disney Productions entered the broadcast age. The public, and the critics, reacted favorably, as seen in this quote from widely syndicated columnist John Crosby:

One Hour in Wonderland, the premiere showing of Disney's celebrated characters on television, must have struck despair into the hearts of most of the people who earn a living in the medium. There is nothing in television even remotely comparable to Mickey Mouse, Donald Duck, Dopey, Goofy, Pluto and the rest of them. And there isn't likely to be, ever.

The kiddies and the adults, too, could hardly ask for more of a Christmas afternoon. Mr. Disney captured 90 per cent of the available television audience, and he got in a nice plug for his upcoming movie. I hope he decides to do it again.

While audience popularity and critical reaction were important, it wasn't ratings alone that had drawn Disney into television. Walt was keenly interested in the exploitation value of television, but he needn't have worried. One industry observer commented "That telecast should be worth $1,000,000 at the box office to *Alice in Wonderland*. I think Disney has found the answer to using television both to entertain and to sell his product."

How to proceed?

With the success of the special, Walt was inevitably the object of serious interest by the networks. They immediately began lobbying him to consider future projects for a weekly series. All of the networks tried to sign Walt to a deal, but his heart was elsewhere: Disneyland.

The ABC executives weren't interested in Walt's dream park, which they kept comparing to Coney Island, and they gracefully declined his overtures to participate. Walt received the same reaction at NBC and CBS. No one, including his brother Roy, shared Walt's faith in Disneyland.

Walt could have simply gone ahead and signed for a weekly series without a tie-in to Disneyland, but he knew that if he did so, he would never be able to use the networks as a source of financing. There was another major point to consider. Walt and Roy had serious concerns about making a major commitment at that time. They knew they could not simply air a weekly version of the special and maintain viewer interest, but a weekly series seemed beyond the capability of the Studio. As in years past, the Studio had an ambitious film schedule to complete, and substantial additional staff would be required to produce the twenty-six episodes needed for a full season. Many within the company, including Roy Disney, were deeply concerned about the financial commitment. Although the special had been well received, its success might have been due in part to the first use of the Disney characters on the air, and they felt a series could fail.

Repeating the magic

Despite the doubts of Roy and other staffers, Walt was not about to give up on broadcasting, given the high visibility of the first special and his belief that it could serve as a valuable marketing tool for his theatrical efforts. After much internal debate, Walt eventually decided to produce another special to see if the results of One Hour in Wonderland could be duplicated. The next special was to be very similar to the first; it would also promote an upcoming film release and be aired on Christmas day. Disney found a sponsor in Johnson & Johnson, the pharmaceutical supply firm, which agreed to put up the $250,000 required. This figure attracted a great deal of attention, for it would be the most expensive hour of television ever produced up to then.

Of this money, the Studio was to receive $150,000, and the balance would buy time on a network and pay for publicity. Young & Rubicam, the ad agency for Johnson & Johnson, acted as a liaison between the sponsor, Disney, and the networks, taking a fee for delivering a finished product suitable for airing at the best possible time. With Disney signed the deal, they then needed to find a network to air the show.

CBS, which had suffered a loss of face (and revenue) when it lost the first Disney special to NBC, made a major effort this time to line up enough stations to interest Johnson & Johnson, which agreed in November to buy a 3 P.M. slot on Christmas day.

The second special, The Walt Disney Christmas Show, again followed the theme of a Christmas party at the Disney Studio, although this time Walt was confident enough in his own drawing power that he dispensed with a co-host. Instead of sharing the spotlight with Edgar Bergen again, this time there was to be no doubt it was Walt's show all the way.

A change in direction

Walt and Roy were still concerned about the possible negative impact television could have on the theatrical market, for they were very aware that the first two shows were little more than thinly disguised commercials. Any regular series would require new programming, which might imperil ticket sales at the theaters. Thus Walt sought to allay the fears and suspicions of theater owners by making it clear that his first allegiance was still to producing new films. The Studio would spend $20 million over three years on an ambitious slate of new projects to include three all-cartoon features, two all-live-action features, a minimum of six True-Life Adventure featurettes, and eighteen shorts per year.

The Studio did participate in several projects created by outside companies, such as a nine-minute segment about the making of Peter Pan that appeared on CBS's Omnibus on December 28, 1952, and an episode of Ed Sullivan's Toast of the Town in 1953 dedicated to Walt Disney.

Overall, though, Walt seemed to have turned his back on television. It wasn't just concern over the possibility of damaging the theatrical market; instead, Walt turned his energies toward a project he found much more interesting than television—the world's first themed amusement park. The next special wasn't until July 17, 1955, when Disneyland opened its gates. From this point on, the Studio's output of specials was almost nonexistent for the next two decades.

In the 1974–75 season, the Studio reached an agreement with NBC for a series of four specials titled both Saturday Night at the Movies with Disney and NBC All-Disney Saturday Night at the Movies. Each of these specials consisted of a theatrical release paired with a short subject, a move that was billed as re-creating the lost theatrical experience of showing short subjects before the main feature. NBC's hopes that Disney could help the ratings with material other than the traditional anthology series were quickly rewarded. The special proved very popular.

Following this group of specials, the next several years would see more of a concentration on new production rather than continuing the practice of raiding the film vaults. A large number of these shows featured the theme parks, continuing the Disney tradition of using one medium to promote another. This changed when Disney decided to bring one of its animated stars back into the spotlight.

Sport Goofy

In 1983, Disney began production on a series of specials featuring an old favorite, Goofy. This time, the hapless hero was cast as Sport Goofy, a role created for a successful series of promotions that began in 1980. That year, the Studio had cast Goofy in the role of a sporting superstar, using scenes from many of the original Goofy cartoons. Sport Goofy hit the television screen in a series of specials, which included thirty-minute cartoon compilations and several two-hour outings built around real-life sporting events. The title of the first special, Walt Disney's Mickey and Donald Present Sport Goofy, showed that the Studio wanted to make 100 percent certain that audiences knew this was a Disney show, for Mickey and Donald didn't even appear in the program!

Sport Goofy retired without fanfare in December 1984. Then, in 1987, he suddenly returned in another special, *An All New Adventure of Disney's Sport Goofy*, which featured the first new Goofy cartoon produced since 1965. Sport Goofy also appeared in ten specials made for the overseas market, all of which were thirty-minute animated compilations.

After this, Disney again all but stopped production of new specials. Occasionally, Disney would agree to air a theatrical release, but it wasn't until 1989 and a change in management that it became a regular practice once again.

2

Specials Descriptions

Each show aired as a special is listed here in alphabetical order. For syndicated specials and those shown on the Disney-owned KHJ/KCAL, the airdate listed is for the show's airing in Los Angeles. Many of the specials have also been aired on the anthology series, and those dates are included here as well.

ABSENT-MINDED PROFESSOR, THE

This 1961 theatrical release starring Fred MacMurray as a scientist who accidentally discovers an antigravity formula aired as a special with *Hurricane Hannah* on 11/01/75 on NBC. This film also aired on the anthology series in two parts on 9/09/79 and 9/16/79.

Production Notes:

- A "behind-the-scenes" look at the filming of this movie was featured in the anthology episode *Man in Flight*.
- In addition to the theatrical sequel *Son of Flubber*, the Studio also produced two television episodes, *The Absent-Minded Professor* and *The Absent-Minded Professor: Trading Places*.

ACTING SHERIFF   Airdate (30-minute format): 8/17/91 (CBS).

Cast: Robert Goulet (Sheriff Brent McCord), John Putch (Mike Swanson), Hillary Bailey Smith (Donna Singer), Ruth Kobart (Helen Munson), Diane Delano (Judith Mahoney), Art LaFleur (Captain Van Patten), Michael McManus (Fred), Daniel O'Shea (Harper), Page Leong (Anne Wong-Fowler), Barney Burman (Doug), Buck Herron (Burns), Lee Tergesen (Robbie).

When a small Northern California town needs a sheriff, Brent McCord, a B-movie actor who needs work, decides to apply for the job. His lack of knowledge about the law puts him at odds with the district attorney, and his inexperience lets a prisoner escape. Luckily, a loyal deputy helps catch the escapee and covers for McCord.

Production Note:

- This was the pilot for an unsold series. If it had been picked up as a series, the pilot would have been aired under its own title, *Heck Is for Heroes*.

ADVENTURES IN BABYSITTING   Airdate (2-hour format): 10/20/90 (ABC).

This 1987 theatrical release stars Elisabeth Shue as a babysitter who suffers a series of problems on the job, including getting involved with a stolen car ring.

ADVENTURES IN BABYSITTING   (TV version) Airdate (30-minute format): 7/07/89 (CBS).

Cast: Jennifer Guthrie (Chris Parker), Joey Lawrence (Brad Anderson), Courtney Peldon (Sara Anderson), Brian Austin Green (Daryl Coopersmith), Ariana Mohit (Brenda), Susan Blanchard (Mrs. Anderson), Dennis Howard (Mr. Anderson), Art Evans (Mr. Dukeman), Rocky Giordani (Vince), Jason Tomlins (Rick).

Unsold pilot based on the 1987 film of the same name that finds Chris Parker babysitting for Brad and Sara Anderson and Brad's friend Daryl. She takes her young charges with her to visit a friend who works in a convenience store. The store is robbed while they're inside, and Chris and the kids are taken hostage.

Production Note:

- This show aired as part of the *CBS Summer Playhouse* series of specials.

ADVENTURES OF HUCK FINN, THE
Airdate (2-hour format): 7/22/95 (ABC).

This 1993 theatrical release stars Elijah Wood, Courtney B. Vance, Robbie Coltrane, and Jason Robards in a retelling of Mark Twain's classic tales of life on the Mississippi River.

ALICE IN WONDERLAND
This 1951 animated theatrical release aired as a special on 12/24/88 on ABC.

ALIEN ENCOUNTERS FROM NEW TOMORROWLAND   Airdate: 2/27/95 (Syndicated).
Cast: Robert Urich (Host).

This promotional special for the new Alien Encounters attraction at Walt Disney World is based on the many claims that there is evidence of aliens visiting Earth. Two UFO investigators, Kevin Randall and Clifford E. Stone, discuss possible reasons why the government may be suppressing the truth. One such cover-up in 1947 is the possible crash of a UFO in Roswell, New Mexico, where the government first claimed it had found a flying saucer and then reversed itself.

ALL NEW ADVENTURE OF DISNEY'S SPORT GOOFY, AN   Airdate: 5/27/87 (NBC).
Voices: Jack Angel, Tony Pope (Goofy), Phil Proctor (Museum Curator), Will Ryan (Beagle Boys, Gyro Gearloose), Russi Taylor (Huey, Dewey, and Louie).

Today, Goofy is known as Sport Goofy, an acknowledged master in the world of athletic endeavor. This wasn't always the case, however. Once, the pressures of daily life had reduced him to a quivering mass as demonstrated in the following shorts: *Hold That Pose, Goofy's Glider, Lion Down, Mickey's Birthday Party, Goofy Gymnastics,* and *Sport Goofy in Soccermania.*

Production Notes:

• *Sport Goofy in Soccermania* was the first original Goofy cartoon produced since 1965.
• This show also aired on the anthology series on 1/01/89.
• The cartoon *Double Dribble* is seen during Goofy's dream sequence.

AMERICA ON PARADE
See: *Monsanto Night Presents Walt Disney's America on Parade.*

ANNA   Airdate (30-minute format): 8/25/90 (NBC).
Cast: Maria Charles (Anna Gemignani), Keith Diamond (Tony Morgan), Tom LaGrua (Ted Gemignani), Dennis Lipscomb (Al Lubinski), Bill Macy (Max Fetchick), Herb Edelman (Cop #1), Bob Drew (Cop #2), James Edgcomb (Policeman).

Anna, an elderly woman living in New York City, is determined to improve the world around her. Her optimistic view of the world suffers a setback when she's hit by a bus and then confined to a wheelchair. Anna's son, Ted, wants her to move in with him in New Jersey, but she doesn't want to leave New York. Ted tries to force her into moving by subletting her apartment to Tony, a young black actor. When the landlord points out that they can both share the apartment and thus help each other, Anna and Ted decide to give it a try.

Production Note:

• This was a pilot for an unsold series.

APPEARANCES   Airdate (2-hour format): 6/17/90 (NBC).
Cast: Scott Paulin (Ben Danzig), Wendy Phillips (Marie Danzig), Casey Biggs (Harry Trace), Matt McGrath (Troy Danzig), Heather Hopper (Katherine Danzig), Penny Fuller (Barbara Stilton), Ernest Borgnine (Emil Danzig), James Handy (Danny Halligan), Mariclare Costello (Rose), Robert Hooks (Wesley), Mimi Lieber (Teresa), Douglas Roberts (Father Rick), Andrew Robinson (Mort), Katie Marberi (Deanne), Marty Davis (Bartender), Steve Liska (Kenny Lutz), Anita Ortega (Araceli), Fia Porter (Doreen), Jerome Anson Blackwell (Funeral Attendant), Richard Camphius (Officer), Jon Greene (Joey Kinsella), Brandon Maciel (Small Boy), Mark Sussman (Coley), Dan Tullis, Jr. (Deputy #1).

Years ago, Ben Danzig was a football star, unconcerned about the business world. Now, he's running a business started by his father, Emil, and the problems at work are mounting. Ben also has problems at home. His wife, Marie, blames Emil for the death of one of their twin children in an accident. The Danzig's other son, Troy, now has to carry the burden of being the surviving twin.

Production Note:

• This was the pilot for an unsold series.

ARIZONA SHEEPDOG
This 1955 theatrical featurette aired with *The Three Lives of Thomasina* and *It's Tough to Be a Bird* on 12/14/74 as part of the *NBC All-Disney Saturday Night at the Movies* series.

BAR GIRLS   Airdate: 7/05/90 (CBS).
Cast: Joanna Cassidy (Claudia Reese), Marcy Walker (Melanie Roston), John Terlesky (Gabe), Tom O'Brien (Jack Gallagher), Michael Bowen (Troy), Lee Garlington (Shelly), David Wilson (Kyle), Stanley Kamel (Judge), Matthew Faison (Stan Kent), Peter Hansen (Preston), Alan Rosenberg (Miles), James A. Watson, Jr. (Walter), Elisabeth Moss (Robin), Anthony Brooklier (Burt), Eloy Casados (Ortega), Maria Cavaiani (Lynn), Joe Finn (Marshall), Jennifer Flavin (Escort Girl), John Rixey Moore (Grant), Toni Nero (Faith), Robert Reeder (Neighbor), Sharone D. Rosen (Process Server), Kim Scolari (Escort Girl #2), Stan Sells (Byron), Patricia Veselich (Vickie), Tim Wade (Bailiff), Melissa Young (Escort Girl #1).

Claudia Reese, the senior partner at a large law firm, faces several problems. The firm is in trouble, and the other partners decide to quit before it goes under. After a hard day at the office, during which she fires attorney Melanie Roston for botching a trial, Claudia is shocked when her husband tells her their marriage is over. With no husband and the prospect of no career, Claudia's life is at an all-time low. Claudia reluctantly decides to give Melanie another chance. She hires her and they start a new law firm, naming it "Bar Girls." Though the two women are mismatched, they prove to be an effective force when they join to handle a rape and incest case.

Production Notes:
- The show ends with the message "To be continued," but *Bar Girls* never returned to the air.
- This was the pilot for an unsold series.
- The show's creator, Louise Terry Fisher, was part of the team behind *L.A. Law*.

BAREFOOT EXECUTIVE, THE (TV VERSION)   Airdates (2-hour format): 11/11/95, 7/27/96 (ABC).
Cast: Jason London (Billy Murdoch), Eddie Albert (Herbert Gower), Michael Marich (Wayne Persky), Terri Ivens (Lisa), Jay Mohr (Matt), Ann Magnuson, Shannon O'Hurley, Alan Blumenfeld, Stanley DeSantis, Willie Garson, Vyonne DeCarlo, Julia Sweeney, Chris Elliott, Ellia English (Gwen), Richard Penn (Research Guy), Greg Wrangler (Crocker), Maria Von Hartz (Calhoun), Dorian Gregory (Doctor), Christine Romeo (Nurse), Bob Glouberman (Executive), Kyle Gass (Joe), Kathy Griffin (Mary), Monica Allison (Jane), Arik Levy (Young Executive), Julie Benz (Sexy Woman), Michael McLafferty (Sexy Man), Jenny Morris (Daughter), Grant Hoover (Son), Roy Fagen (Warm-up Comic), Alex Bookston (Studio Guard), Zaid Farid (Habitat Security Guard), Murray Rubin (Man in his fifties), Brian Evans (Mail Boy), Nathan Anderson (Danny), Scott Immergut ("Maui Medical" Producer), Jeffrey Lampert (Executive #1), Saige Spinney (Executive #2), Eddie (Archie).

This remake of the 1971 theatrical features Billy Murdoch, who works at the UBC television network. He wants to be a programming executive, but no one will take him seriously because he works in the mail room. Things change when he realizes that a chimp named Archie is somehow able to pick hit television series.

BEACHES   Airdates (2½-hour format): 12/08/91, 10/31/92 (CBS).
This 1988 theatrical release stars Bette Midler and Barbara Hershey in the story of two women whose friendship spans several decades.

BEAR COUNTRY
This 1953 theatrical release aired on 5/01/76 with *That Darn Cat!* as part of the *NBC All-Disney Saturday Night at the Movies* series of specials. It was also included in the anthology series episode *Yellowstone Story (and) Bear Country*.

BEAVER VALLEY
This 1950 theatrical release aired on 2/23/74 with *20,000 Leagues under the Sea* as part of the *NBC All-Disney Saturday Night at the Movies* series of specials. It was also included in the anthology episode *Beaver Valley (and) Cameras in Africa*.

BEDKNOBS AND BROOMSTICKS
This 1971 theatrical release starring Angela Lansbury as an amateur witch who battles the Germans during World War II first aired on 3/22/87 as part of the anthology series. It also aired as a special on 2/12/89 as part of NBC's *Sunday Night Movie* series.

BELIEVE YOU CAN . . . AND YOU CAN!
Airdate (30-minute format): 4/21/83 (Syndicated).

Cast: Morey Amsterdam (J. Fauntenoy Chiffenrobe), Heather O'Rourke (herself), Lance Sloan (Billy), Mary Ann Seltzer (Mom).

When her family is transferred from California to Minneapolis, young Heather O'Rourke heads to Disneyland, hoping to use the Park's magic to stop the move. When she tries to enter Fantasyland, the drawbridge in Sleeping Beauty Castle closes and blocks the way. Luckily, J. Fauntenoy Chiffenrobe, the official Fantasyland Problem Solver, arrives and explains this section of the Park has been closed for improvements. Fauntenoy magically transports her into the construction site and they take a tour of the new attractions. Heather spots some Disney characters having a party for "believers only," but they see her and put her on trial for spying. Heather is found not guilty, and her mother rushes to Disneyland with the good news that they don't have to move. The show closes with a scene of Walt Disney opening the original Fantasyland.

BEST OF COUNTRY, THE
Airdate (2-hour format): 1/27/95 (CBS).

Cast: Brooks & Dunn, Joe Diffie, Vince Gill, Faith Hill, Kathy Mattea, Tim McGraw, Pam Tillis, Lari White, John Anderson, Diamond Rio, Vince Gill, Rickey Skaggs, Marty Stuart, George Jones, Travis Tritt, Sam Moore, Clint Black, The Pointer Sisters, The Staple Singers.

Clint Black and Travis Tritt are the hosts of this salute to country music. In a tribute to the influences of rhythm and blues, Tritt and Sam Moore sing *When Something Is Wrong with My Baby*, Black and The Pointer Sisters perform *Chain of Fools*, and Marty Stuart and The Staple Singers join together for *The Weight*. In a second segment, the show looks at the legacy of veteran musician George Jones with performances of *Why, Baby Why* and *One Woman Man*. Black and Tritt then take a look at the southern roots of The Eagles, with featured performances by Vince Gill *(I Can't Tell You Why)*, John Anderson *(Heartache Tonight)*, and Diamond Rio *(Lyin' Eyes)*. Other singers in the program are Lari White *(Now I Know)*, Vince Gill *(South Side of Dixie)*, Faith Hill *(Take Me as I Am)*, Brooks & Dunn *(Little Miss Honky Tonk)*, Pam Tillis *(Mi Vida Loca)*, Tim McGraw *(Don't Take the Girl)*, Kathy Mattea *(Walking Away a Winner)*, John Anderson *(Bend Until*

It Breaks), and Joe Diffie *(Pick-Up Man)*. Clint Black also sings *Wherever You Go*.

Production Note:

• The program was filmed entirely on location in Nashville, Tennessee. The Ryman Auditorium was used for what the producers called "Grand Ole Opry material," and more contemporary acts were filmed at the Wildhorse Saloon.

BEST OF COUNTRY '92, THE: COUNTDOWN AT THE NEON ARMADILLO
Airdate (2-hour format): 12/10/92 (ABC).

Cast: Clint Black, Mary Chapin Carpenter, Billy Dean, Suzy Bags, Brooks & Dunn, Garth Brooks, Mark Chesnutt, Billy Ray Cyrus, Diamond Rio, Vince Gill, Alan Jackson, Alison Krauss, Lorrie Morgan, Mark O'Connor, Collin Raye, Sawyer Brown, Tom Scot, Ricky Van Shelton, Doug Stone, Pam Tillis, Aaron Tippin, Randy Travis, Steve Warner.

Clint Black and Mary Chapin Carpenter host this look at the Top 35 country western songs for the years. Many of the performers who made these songs famous repeat them for a live audience, with music videos and dance numbers substituting for those who couldn't appear. The songs are accompanied by the Bad Girl Dancers, a new dance team. The program also includes a special salute to Garth Brooks, the first country artist to reach #1 on the pop charts.

Production Notes:

• This special was filmed in Nashville before a live audience.
• The successful ratings for this special led to the syndicated series *Countdown at the Neon Armadillo*.

BEST OF DISNEY, THE: 50 YEARS OF MAGIC
Airdate (2-hour format): 5/20/91 (ABC).

Cast: Harry Connick Jr., Annette Funicello, Teri Garr, Daryl Hannah, Sandy Duncan, Neil Patrick Harris, Shelley Long, Dick Van Dyke, Barbara Walters, Bill Campbell, Jennifer Connelly.

This celebration of the Studio's move to Burbank fifty years ago begins as Mickey Mouse interrupts Michael Eisner's introduction to remind him of a screening. On their way to the theater, they're joined by dozens of Disney staffers—both live and animated. Celebrity guests then introduce highlights of Disney's film successes.

After several Studio employees reminisce

about their careers, Michael Eisner thanks everyone at the Studio who has helped make the dreams come true. He's surrounded by hundreds of employees in the Studio parking lot who close the show by using flash cards to make *The Mickey Mouse Club* logo.

Production Notes:

- The opening sequence was originally filmed for use in the Backlot Tour at the Disney-MGM Studios in Florida.
- Also seen in this show are Roger Ebert, Gene Siskel, Tom Hanks, Tony Anselmo, Clarence Nash, Florence Gill, Charles Fleischer, Cliff Edwards, Cheech Marin, Richard Mulligan, Bob Newhart, Bill Farmer, and Wayne Allwine.
- Although the Studio had planned on having 2,000 employees participate in the flash card segment, only 800 showed up for the weekend filming and the sequence was completed using Disney's film magic technicians.

BEST OF DISNEY MUSIC, THE: A LEGACY IN SONG—PART I Airdate: 2/03/93 (CBS).
Cast: Angela Lansbury (Host), Branford Marsalis, Lea Salonga, Brad Kave.

Angela Lansbury hosts this celebration of 60 years of Disney music. As Lansbury notes, Disney's tradition of using music to help tell stories dates back to *Snow White and the Seven Dwarfs*, in which each dwarf was introduced by his own musical theme. Lansbury continues to introduce clips from several films that demonstrate the power and beauty of Disney music. The show closes with the notice "To be continued . . ."

Production Note:

- A segment featuring the music of Modeste Moussorgsky was first aired as part of the episode *The Plausible Impossible* in 1956.

BEST OF DISNEY MUSIC, THE: A LEGACY IN SONG—PART II Airdate: 5/21/93 (CBS).
Cast: Glenn Close (Host), Placido Domingo.

This portion of the two-part tribute to Disney music begins with Glenn Close singing *A Dream Is a Wish Your Heart Makes* from *Cinderella*. Additional songs and clips from the film show how the music created the mood for the animation. Demonstrating how important the music is, the program shows clips from several films without their dialogue track, leaving the music to carry the

mood. The closing segment looks at *Pinocchio*, which features the song that became the symbol of everything Disney does: *When You Wish upon a Star*, winner of the Academy Award that year for Best Song.

BIG BUSINESS Airdates (2-hour format): 5/10/91, 7/10/92 (CBS).
This 1988 theatrical release stars Bette Midler and Lily Tomlin in dual roles as two sets of twins who are accidentally switched at birth.

BLACK HOLES: MONSTERS THAT EAT SPACE AND TIME Airdate (30-minute format): 11/79 (Syndicated).
Durk Pearson hosts this look at black holes, the mysterious space phenomena featured in the Studio's theatrical release *The Black Hole*. Scientists are divided about what black holes actually are. Some researchers theorize that black holes are so powerful they can distort the very fabric of time itself. Others claim a black hole could absorb a planet and collapse it into a minuscule ball smaller than a pinhead. The episode uses footage from several sources to show what black holes may consist of and how scientists are preparing to explore these stellar giants.

Production Notes:

- One of the contributors to this show was former astronaut Gordon Cooper, who was then employed as a vice president at Disney's WED Enterprises, the research and development facility that designs and builds the company's theme parks.
- This was originally planned as a 1-hour episode of the anthology series.

BLACK SHEEP Airdate (30-minute format): 6/30/94 (Fox).
Cast: Jason Bateman (Jonathan Kelley), Anthony Tyler Quinn (Eugene), Willie Garson (Anthony Guifoyle), Jeffrey Dean Morgan (Bobby Debeneke), Jana Marie Hupp (Sherry Geeghan), Larry Poindexter (Alex P. Keaton), Sarah Essex (Annalise), Cleto Augusto (Customer).

When the stock market collapses, Wall Street broker Jonathan Kelley suddenly finds himself without a job. He goes home to New Jersey, where he takes a job in his brother's auto repair shop while he tries to sort out his life.

Production Notes:

- This was an unsold pilot for the Fox network.

- The character of "Alex P. Keaton" is an inside joke by producer Michael Jacobs. It was the name of Michael J. Fox's character in the sitcom *Family Ties*. Viewers of that series might recall that Alex's dream was to become a stock broker.

BLAST TO THE PAST   Airdate: 5/20/89 (KHJ).

Cast: Jon "Bowzer" Bauman, Brian Beirne, Little Anthony.

This one-hour special is a salute to the music of the '50s and '60s. Host Jon Bauman transforms himself from a typical 1989 businessman into a '50s rock and roll lover, "Bowzer." He drives to Disneyland, which is celebrating the summer with the Main Street Hop, a gala affair with special parades and entertainment. Bowzer keeps getting lost on his way to a concert at Videopolis, and stops along the way to enjoy the sights and sounds of Disneyland. He finally does find Videopolis, but the show has ended and the stage crew is clearing away the equipment. Happily, Little Anthony spots him and the two join for a duet of '50s music.

BLOSSOM   Airdate (30-minute format): 7/05/90 (NBC).

Cast: Mayim Bialik (Blossom Russo), Michael Stoyanov (Anthony Russo), Joey Lawrence (Donny Russo), Richard Masur (Terry Russo), Barrie Youngfellow (Barbara Russo), Jenna von Oy (Six LeMuere), Debra Sandlund (Mrs. Young), Justin Whalin (William Zimmerman), Kelly Packard (Kimberly).

In this pilot for the series *Blossom*, viewers are introduced to the Russo family. The show centers on Blossom Russo, who is trying to cope with the pressures of being a teenager. As Blossom records a video diary entry, she is interrupted when she hears her parents arguing. Her mother feels that she and her husband are too busy for each other, and Blossom worries that they might split up. Things get worse when Blossom's parents mention that they have an appointment with the family lawyer. Blossom daydreams about her parents getting divorced, but when they come home, they are laughing and seemingly in love once again. Blossom wants to know what's going on, and her confused parents tell her that they have seen the lawyer only to update their wills.

Production Notes:

- At the time this pilot aired, NBC had not yet committed to the series.

- This episode answers an often asked *Blossom* trivia question: how did her friend Six get her name? As Six tells Blossom, her father said "that's how many beers it took" the night she was conceived.

BLUE BAYOU   Airdate (2-hour format): 1/15/90 (NBC).

Cast: Alfre Woodard (Jessica Filley), Mario Van Peebles (Jay Filley), Roy Thinnes (Barney Fortenot), Ashley Crow (Morgan Fortenot), Joseph Culp (Thomas Fortenot), Pamela Gidley (Deanie Fortenot Serulla), Carmen de Lavallade (Madam Frosine), Tai Kimbrough (Monique), Keith Williams (Nick Filley), Maxwell Caulfield (Phil Serulla), Elizabeth Ashley (Lolly Fortenot), Bibi Besch (Claire Goldanna), Carolyn Seymour (Raleigh McMain), Annabella Price (Karen Vernet), Cassie Yates (Rosemary Angeli), Mitchell Lichtenstein (Martin Vernet), Marco St. John (Morley Rickerts), Stan Sells (Foster Goldanna), Robert Parrish (Tony), William Watkins (Officer Michaels), Michael Audley (Judge Marton), Stocker Fontelieu (Judge Sevario), George Sanchez (Judge Murillo), Elliott Keener (Bud), Philip Parrish (Greg), Billie Jean Young (Coral), Janet Shea (Belle), Marie Kaposchyn (Pauline Gruder).

Lawyer Jessica Filley moves to New Orleans with her son, Nick, to get him away from gang pressures in Los Angeles. Soon, Jessica lands a job with the district attorney, Barney Fortenot. Claire, a friend of Barney's wife, dies under mysterious circumstances. Claire's children are convinced that her new husband, Foster, is responsible for her death. Barney turns the case over to Jessica, but tells her not to prosecute, because there are serious political considerations. Despite Barney's orders, Jessica begins probing into Claire's death. She loses the case, but Barney tells her not to worry too much—the testimony has exposed Foster and he's ruined. Jessica then realizes she's going to have to learn how the South operates if she's going to succeed.

Production Note:

- This was the pilot for an unsold series.

CAMEO BY NIGHT   Airdate: 7/12/87 (NBC).

Cast: Sela Ward (Jennifer/Cameo), Justin Deas (Detective Bellflower), Thomas Ryan (Sorry Eddie), Art LaFleur (Pinky), David Graf (Detective Kraxburger), Tim Jones (Detective Hudgins), Michael Greene (Captain Uroff), Russell Curry (Bob White), Stephen Shellen

(Larry Willard), George Kirby (Grubby), Mary Jo Deschanel (Mrs. Schwinn), Scott Coffey (Gordon Schwinn), Tim Thomerson (Damon Rhodes), Kaz Garas (Red), Christopher Jackson (Dagnol), Charles H. Hyman (Large Man), Bert Hinchman (Security Guard), Dennis A. Pratt (First Hood), Brian Brophy (Slick), Jeanine Jackson (Saleswoman), Louis Mauna (Mexican Boy), Howard Allen (Lab Man), Michael Francis Clarke (First Deputy), Peter S. Mitchel (Patron), Marte Post (Singer).

During the day Jennifer is a nondescript secretary working for the Los Angeles Police Department, but at night she becomes Cameo, a daring crimefighter. Her secret known only to a few trusted friends, after solving crimes Cameo leaves a card bearing her silhouette as her trademark. In her daytime persona, she uses the police computers and laboratories in her quest to bring criminals to justice.

Production Notes:

- This was the pilot for an unsold series.
- Justin Deas was also in the unsuccessful pilot *Waco & Rineheart*.

CAPTAIN RON   Airdate (2-hour format): 10/08/95 (NBC).
This 1992 theatrical release stars Kurt Russell, Martin Short, and Mary Kay Place in the story of a family that takes a holiday cruise skippered by a very disreputable captain.

CARTOON ALL-STARS TO THE RESCUE
Airdates (30-minute format): 4/21/90, 4/20/91.
Cast: Jason Marsden (Michael). Voices: Ross Bagdasarian, Jeff Bergman (Daffy Duck/Bugs Bunny), Townsend Coleman (Michaelangelo), Wayne Collins, Jim Cummings (Winnie the Pooh/Tigger), Joey Dedio, Paul Fusco (Alf), Danny Goldman (Brainy Smurf), Georgie Irene, Janice Karman, Aaron Lohr, Don Messick (Papa Smurf), Lorenzo Music (Garfield), Laurie O'Brien (Miss Piggy), Lindsey Parker, George C. Scott (Smoke), Russi Taylor (Huey, Dewey, and Louie/Baby Gonzo), Frank Welker (Baby Kermit/Slimer).
A peaceful morning in Corey's bedroom is ruined when someone steals her piggy bank. The Smurfs sound the alarm, and soon the room is full of animated characters from Saturday morning cartoons, all trying to catch the thief. They discover the thief is Corey's brother, Michael. Even worse, they discover he stole the money to buy drugs. Bugs Bunny uses a time machine to show Michael where he first went

wrong. Michael sees for himself the horrible effect drugs can have. Afterward, Corey tries to talk to Michael, but he refuses to listen and threatens her. Corey is tempted to try drugs herself, hoping this will make Michael like her again. Luckily, Michael spots her in time and makes her stop. He also realizes he must quit using drugs and goes to his parents for help.

Production Notes:

- The 1990 broadcast had the highest ratings ever for a Saturday morning program, attracting more than 30 million viewers.
- This show, which was a joint effort of many studios, used the characters from eight Saturday morning shows and several other animated series.
- Produced by the Academy of Television Arts & Sciences, the show was funded by McDonald's restaurants and Ronald McDonald Children's Charities. A free "Family Viewing Guide" was given away by McDonald's.
- Free videocassettes of the show were distributed to schools and video stores.

CBS ALL-AMERICAN THANKSGIVING PARADE, THE   Airdate (3-hour format): 11/26/92 (CBS).
Cast: Mark McEwen, Marilu Henner, Nicole Dubuc, Clark Duke.
This holiday special features parades in New York City, Disneyland, Toronto, and Honolulu. The program begins in New York, then switches between the different parades throughout the program. The Disneyland segments are hosted by Nicole Dubuc and Clark Duke, who introduce the new "The World According to Goofy Parade" honoring Goofy's 60th birthday. The scene then shifts to the "Happy Holidays" show at Sleeping Beauty Castle. A collection of toys comes to life, including Pinocchio, soldiers, ballerinas, and Russian dancers, set to music from *Pinocchio*, *Babes in Toyland*, and *Fantasia*. The parade returns with visitors from Mickey's Toontown, who provide a preview of the newest themed land.

Production Note:

- Production credits were not aired for the Disney portions of this show.

CBS EASTER PARADE, THE   Airdate: 3/30/86 (CBS).
Cast: Susan Howard, Ken Kercheval, Ana Alicia, Robby Benson.

This live Easter salute features two very different Easter parades, beginning with one on New York's Fifth Avenue. Susan Howard and Ken Kercheval introduce scenes of past parades, then host a fashion show, mime routines, and a funny hat contest.

The Walt Disney World portion of the show is hosted by Ana Alicia and Robby Benson. The parade there begins with the world's largest Easter egg and is followed by dozens of Disney characters.

Production Note:

• The Walt Disney World Easter Parade has been aired since 1985, usually under the title *Walt Disney World Happy Easter Parade.* This was the only airing of the Easter parade under a different format and title.

CELEBRATE THE SPIRIT! DISNEY'S ALL-STAR 4TH OF JULY SPECTACULAR
Airdate (2-hour format): 7/04/92 (CBS).

Cast: John Ritter (Host), Mary Chapin Carpenter, Billy Ray Cyrus, Celine Dion, Kris Kross, Los Lobos, Martina McBride, Shanice, Anna Chlumsky, Alisan Porter, Anisa Kintz, Tawana Nichols, Greg Kintz, Tracy and Stephanie Campbell, Edwin and Dorthea Mills, Zachary de Vries, President George Bush.

After singer Billy Ray Cyrus starts this holiday special with his hit song *Achy Breaky Heart* at the Magic Kingdom in Walt Disney World, host John Ritter greets the crowd at Epcot Center, with entertainment there and at the Magic Kingdom and Disney-MGM Studios. It also features several segments at Disneyland, home of the new *Fantasmic!* show on the Rivers of America, where giant animated figures and new lighting techniques are mixed with Disney music. Throughout the show, performers on both coasts honor several winners of President Bush's "Points of Light" program, which celebrates significant contributions made by Americans to their local communities. President Bush appears to explain the program and to wish the viewers a happy holiday.

CELEBRITY CELEBRATION ABOARD THE QUEEN MARY
Airdate: 4/15/90 (KCAL).

Cast: Melissa Manchester, Michael Feinstein, Witney Kershaw, John Moschitta, Jr., Wil Shriner, Fulton Burley (Stage Announcer), David James Alexander (Percival Hollingsworth), Jane Hebson (Glynnis Hollingsworth), Jay Meyer (Waiter), Michael

Jacobs (Groucho Marx), Gene Daily (Clark Gable), Jeff Briar (Stan Laurel), Bevis Faversham (Oliver Hardy), Robert B. Hendricks (Announcer).

The retired ocean liner RMS *Queen Mary* is the setting for this trip back in time to 1939, the year the famous vessel first set sail. Host Wil Shriner begins the show by describing the huge size of the ship, which was the fastest of its time. The ship's band leader then introduces Melissa Manchester, who sings several period songs.

Shriner takes the audience on a tour of the ship, followed by another musical segment as Michael Feinstein plays the piano in the Grand Salon.

Production Notes:

• Cast member Fulton Burley starred for many years in the Golden Horseshoe Revue at Disneyland.
• Fast-talking John Moschitta, Jr., was a regular on Disney's *Zorro and Son.*

CHIP 'N DALE RESCUE RANGERS TO THE RESCUE
Airdate (2-hour format): 9/30/89 (Syndicated).

Voices: Corey Burton (Zipper, Dale, Snout, Mole), Peter Cullen (Kirby, Muldoon), Jim Cummings (Monterey Jack, Fat Cat, Professor Nimnul), Tress MacNeille (Chip, Gadget), Alan Oppenheimer, Rob Paulsen, Maureen Schrum.

When Chip and Dale grab a ride on a police car chasing jewel thieves, they have no idea how big a caper they have stumbled onto. The two chipmunks are friendly with Plato, a police dog on the case, and they learn that he and Detective Don Drake suspect a famous villain, Clawdane, may be involved in the theft of a giant ruby.

CHRISTMAS IN DISNEYLAND
Airdate: 12/06/76 (ABC).

Cast: Art Carney (Gramps/Dr. Wunderbar), Sandy Duncan (Tour Guide), Glen Campbell (Grandpa Jones/Disneyland Visitor), Brad Savage, Terri Lynn Wood.

The holiday season is well underway at Disneyland, where the Park is being decorated by the Disney characters as the guests leave. A grumpy grandfather (Art Carney) is in a hurry to get back to work, but his grandchildren (Brad Savage and Terri Lynn Wood) plead with him to stay. They're overheard by Sandy Duncan, who, working as a Disneyland tour guide, mentions that the Park gives a prize to the biggest "disbeliever." Carney announces he'll only believe in the holidays if it snows, which seems impossible in Southern California. Then, with everyone wishing for a miracle, it snows on Main Street.

Production Note:

• The ice skating sequence was accomplished using special plastic sheets that covered the pavement. Plastic chips completed the illusion of snow. The same technique was used again in 1980 when a Coca-Cola commercial was filmed there.

CIRCUS OF THE STARS GOES TO DISNEYLAND   Airdate (2-hour format): 12/16/94 (CBS).

Cast: Harry Anderson (Host), Scott Baio (Ringmaster), Leslie Nielsen (Ringmaster), All-4-One, Tichina Arnold, Zachery Ty Bryan, Phyllis Diller, Debbe Dunning, Schae Harrison, A.J. Langer, Vicki Lawrence, David Leisure, Ashlee Levitch, Mario Lopez, Shemar Moore, Kelly Packard, Raspyni Brothers, Alfonso Ribeiro, Paul Rodriguez, Jenna von Oy, J.C. Wendel, Adam West, Adam Wylie, David Yost, Michael Castner (Interviewer), Rick Kirkham (Interviewer).

The 19th annual *Circus of the Stars* show is set at Disneyland, where celebrities from popular television series have gathered to perform a variety of circus acts. The hosts salute Give Kids the World, an organization that benefits children with life-threatening diseases.

COCKTAIL   Airdates (2-hour format): 5/06/91, 9/25/93 (ABC).

This 1988 theatrical release stars Tom Cruise, Bryan Brown, and Elisabeth Shue in the story of two bartenders and the problems they encounter in business and in their love lives.

COLOR OF MONEY, THE   Airdates (2½-hour format): 11/22/89, 6/08/92 (ABC).

This 1986 theatrical theatrical release, starring Paul Newman, Tom Cruise, and Mary Elizabeth Mastrantonio, is a sequel to *The Hustler.*

COMPUTER WORE TENNIS SHOES, THE (TV version)   Airdates (2-hour format): 2/18/95, 6/29/95 (ABC).

Cast: Kirk Cameron (Dexter Riley), Larry Miller (Dean Al Valentine), Jason Bernard (Professor Miles Quigley), Andrew Woodworth (Will Rafferty), Anne Marie Tremko (Sarah Matthews), Matthew McCurley (Norwood Gill), Jeff Maynard (Gozin), Charles Lane (Regent Yarborough), Paul Dooley (Senator Thatch), Dan Castellaneta (Alan Winsdale), Dean Jones (Dean Webster Carlson), Christine Hinojosa (Penelope), Eric Schaeffer (Rich Prentiss), Jeff Garlin (Agent Reese), Eddie Deezen (Agent Tucker), Norris Young (Rathouser #7), John Wesley (Dr. Freeman), Sean Gavigan (Professor Knowlton), Janet Rotblatt (Professor Goldstein), Adrian Ricard (Mrs. Weaver), Joe Minjares (Brazilian), Iqbal Theba (Sri Lankan), Darshanie Bruite (Princess Shmiri), John Petlock (Maitre d'), Paul Barselou (Regent Mears), Frank Bausmith (Gent), Renee Ridgeley (Mother), Josh Wolford (Boy), Lelia Goldoni (Woman at Hale Club), Jeffrey Lampert (Stage Manager), Peyton Reed (Policeman).

This television remake of the 1969 theatrical feature of the same name begins as Medfield College gets connected to the Internet. Notoriously poor student Dexter Riley tries to use the computer for research, but a lightning bolt hits and he receives a massive shock as the system wildly accesses the Internet. The next day, he races through a test at amazing speed, and soon finds himself winning all the prestigious College Knowledge contests. But Dexter's troubles worsen when his friends think he has become conceited and the government thinks he is a notorious computer hacker.

Production Notes:

• In a spoof of the long-running series of Disney theme park commercials, when Dexter is asked "You've just won, what are you going to do now?," he says he's going to go to the library.

• This was one of the *Disney Family Films* series of specials.

• After appearing in numerous Disney films, it's revealed for the first time that the fictitious school's full name is Chester Q. Medfield College.

COMPUTERS ARE PEOPLE, TOO!   Airdate (30-minute format): 5/23/82 (Syndicated)

Cast: Elaine Joyce (Hostess), Joseph Campanella (Narrator), Michael Iceberg (Musician).

This look at computer graphics provides a brief explanation of some of the techniques used in the Studio's theatrical release *Tron.* For several years, researchers have been using computers to create images once only accomplished through conventional animation.

Following a visit to a computer camp where children are studying programming instead of handicrafts, the show concludes with a sneak preview of scenes from *Tron*.

Production Notes:

- The associate producer of this show, Cardon Walker, is the son of E. Cardon Walker, former chairman of the board of Walt Disney Productions.
- This show was intended to promote interest in the theatrical release *Tron*.

CORPSE HAD A FAMILIAR FACE, THE
Airdates (2-hour format): 3/27/94, 8/28/94 (CBS).

Cast: Elizabeth Montgomery (Edna Buchanan), Dennis Farina (Detective Harry Lindstrom), Yaphet Kotto (Detective Martin Talbot), Audra Lindley (Monica), Branscombe Richmond (Rodriguez), Luanne Ponce (Jennifer Nicholson), Matthew Posey (Sam), David Spielberg (George), Lee Horsley (Ben Nicholson), Silvana Gallardo (Mrs. Sanchez), Kamar De Los Reyes (Puerto Rican), Carey Scott (Billy), Kevin Patrick Walls (Stephen Hollings), Ria Pavia (Desk Clerk), Hugh Gillin (Stanley), Michael Ray Miller (Sal), Steven Meek (Tom), Stephen Pizzo Jr. (Rookie), Rebecca Hahn (Cynthia), Anthony Turk (Desk Clerk), Jessica Cole (Marcia), Yavone Evans (Paula Nicholson), David J. Partington (Alan), Rene Fernandez (Sergeant), Andrea Naversen (TV Reporter), Bill Brinsfield (Bartender), Jeff Reynolds (Young Man), Paul James Kruse (Maintenance Man).

Edna Buchanan, a crime reporter for the *Miami Herald* newspaper, thinks she has seen and heard it all and nothing can affect her. This changes when she hears a story on her police scanner about a shooting in a tenement. While the police search for a suspected shooter, Edna finds herself trying to comfort the victim. When the shooter suddenly appears at a window, Edna interviews him to keep him there until the police can grab him, but the arrest is botched and he flees. Later, the police set a trap for the man and he is caught by Detective Harry Lindstrom. Edna and Harry meet and develop an interest in each other, even though he hates reporters. Meanwhile, Edna has been working on another story involving a missing 18-year-old girl, Jennifer Nicholson. Unknown to Edna, Jennifer's father, Ben Nicholson, has a long history of sexually abusing his daughter and is determined to find her. Edna discovers that Jennifer is hiding with her boyfriend, Stephen. Ben has followed Edna and tries to shoot Stephen, but Jennifer steps in the way, is shot and dies. The father then kills himself, leaving Edna with serious doubts about her role in the affair and whether she should remain a reporter.

Production Notes:

- This show was inspired by the life of a real journalist, Pulitzer Prize winner Edna Buchanan of Miami.
- The successful ratings for this special led to a sequel *Deadline for Murder: From the Files of Edna Buchanan* (see description under that title).

COUNTRY COYOTE GOES HOLLYWOOD, A
This 1965 theatrical featurette aired on 2/14/76 with *Old Yeller* and *Pecos Bill* as part of the *NBC All-Disney Saturday Night at the Movies* series of specials.

COUNTRY ESTATES   Airdate: 7/10/93 (ABC).

Cast: Tom Irwin (Sam Reed), Barbara Williams (Sarah Reed), Bruce A. Young (Henry Carver), Tina Lifford (Robyn Carver), Jason London (Adam Reed), Vinessa Shaw (Heather Calhoun), Patrick Y. Malone (Henry Carver, Jr.), Scott Bairstow (Oliver), Michele Kelly (Jiwanda Carver), Perry King (Sheriff Kurt Morgan), Clifton Powell, Brandon Douglas, Fred Applegate, Karen Landy (Connie Morgan), Michael Bryan French (Lt. Claude Prine), Jason Green (Lance Morgan), Joshua Green (Mace Morgan), Chance Boyer (Taft Flanders), Brecken Bronner (Sabrina), Simply Marvalous (Erna), Richard Partlow (Coach Jonas Creed), Jennie Kwan (Cheerleader #1), Natalie Strahl (Cheerleader #2), Timothy D. Stickney (A.J.).

This pilot for an unsold series was set in the newly built community of Country Estates. Unfortunately, life there is not the all-American dream, for the residents face a never-ending series of problems, including racism, seduction, and murder. When the Reed family moves in, they are trying to deal with the recent death of a son. Things get more complicated when their other son, Adam, becomes involved with the murder of a neighbor.

DARKWING DUCK PREMIERE, THE/BACK TO SCHOOL WITH THE MICKEY MOUSE CLUB   Airdate (2-hour format): 9/08/91 (Syndicated).

Cast: Fred Newman, Terri Misner, Josh Ackerman, Lindsey Alley, Rhona Bennett, Nita Booth, Mylin Brooks, Blaine Carson, JC Chasez, Tasha Danner, Dale Godboldo, Tony Lucca, Ricky Luna, Jennifer McGill, Terra McNair, Ilana Miller, Jason Minor, Matt Morris, Kevin Osgood, Keri Russell, Marc Worden. The Party: *Albert Fields, Tiffini Hale, Chase Hampton, Deedee Magno, Damon Pampolina.* Voices: *Christine Cavanaugh (Gosalyn Mallard), Jim Cummings (Darkwing Duck), Tim Curry (Taurus Bulba), Eddie Deezen (Hoof), Laurie Faso (Hammerhead Hannigan), Terry McGovern (Launchpad McQuack), Hal Rayle (Huge Jerk), Marcia Wallace (Clovis, Mrs. Cavanaugh).*

The newest Disney animated series, *Darkwing Duck,* and the return of The Disney Channel's *The Mickey Mouse Club* are both saluted in this syndicated special. It begins with *Darkly Dawns the Duck,* which tells the origin of Darkwing Duck. Next, *The Mickey Mouse Club* returns for a new season with several segments intended to make the return to school easier for viewers.

The show closes with a *Darkwing Duck* video, featuring clips of kids dancing and scenes from the series.

DATELINE: DISNEYLAND Airdate (90-minute format): 7/17/55 (ABC).

Cast: Art Linkletter, Bob Cummings, Ronald Reagan, the Mouseketeers, Fess Parker, Buddy Ebsen, Firehouse Five Plus Too, Dr. Heinz Haber.

Following many months of construction and at a cost of $17 million, Walt Disney's dream, Disneyland, has its opening day celebrated in this live broadcast. Hosted by Art Linkletter, Bob Cummings, and Ronald Reagan, it features many Hollywood personalities and politicians who have gathered to honor Walt and to enjoy the Park's attractions. The opening comments are by reporter Hank Weaver, who is sitting in a very busy newsroom as reporters rush to let the world know about Disneyland.

As the show closes, Walt thanks all of the workers who helped make his dream come true, then heads into Fantasyland with Linkletter to have some fun.

Production Notes:

- Unable to pay Art Linkletter his usual fee, Walt instead offered him the merchandising rights for film and camera sales at Disneyland for several years. Linkletter later recalled it as probably the best business deal he ever made.
- The announcer of the Disneyland series, Dick Wesson, also narrated several sequences in this show.
- The following celebrities are among those also seen in this show: Johnny Greene, Irene Dunn, Jack Whatia, Bonita Granville, Danny Thomas, Bobby Driscoll, Marjorie Raines, Margaret and Barbara Whiting,, Gail Storm, Ken Murray, Julie Bishop, Don Defore, Jeanne Crain, Frank Sinatra, Sammy Davis, Jr., Alan Young (the voice of Uncle Scrooge years later), and Jerry Colonna.
- This show was watched by an estimated 90 million viewers.

DAVY CROCKETT: GUARDIAN SPIRIT
Airdate: 1/13/89 (NBC).

Cast: Tim Dunigan (Davy Crockett), Gary Grubbs (George Russell), Garry Chalk (Major Benteen), Jeff Irvine (Lieutenant North), Henry Kingi (Indian Chief), Evan Adams (Indian Boy), Craig Brunanski (Guard #1), Bill Croft (Guard #2), David Longworth (Rider), Charlie Sam, Jr. (Indian Warrior).

The third of the new *Davy Crockett* episodes finds large numbers of Creek warriors gathering. The soldiers fear an attack on the army camp, but Davy explains that the Indians gather every year for a religious ceremony. Seeing this as a chance to destroy the Indian leadership, Major Benteen sends Davy and Russell to search for the meeting site. Deep in the woods, the two men spot an Indian boy engaged in a ritual to show that he has become a man.

Davy and Russell leave without interfering with the ritual and to avoid senseless slaughter on both sides, they tell Benteen they couldn't find the Creeks. Their trip back is interrupted when they spot a wolf heading toward the Indian boy and Davy is forced to kill it to save the youth. Davy and Russell take him back to the army camp, where Benteen threatens to kill the Indian if he doesn't tell him where the meeting is to be held. The army patrol is ambushed by Indians and Davy is blinded in the attack. Crockett has the boy take him to the Indian camp, for he hopes to convince the Indians that he couldn't have spotted the boy because of his blindness. The chief accepts the boy back into the tribe and Davy heads back to camp, revealing to Russell that he was faking blindness.

Production Note:

- The other *Davy Crockett* episodes aired on the anthology series.

DAYO   Airdate (2-hour format): 5/03/92 (NBC).

Cast: Delta Burke (Grace Connors), Elijah Wood (Dayo), Carlin Glynn (Margaret DeGeorgio), Charles Shaughnessy (Ben Connors), David Packer (Tony DeGeorgio), Ashley Peldon (Grace at age 5), Fred Dalton Thompson (Frank DeGeorgio), Caroline Dollar (Cory Connors), Bekka Eaton (Judith), Richard K. Olsen (Papa Louie), Michael Hunter (Man at the Park).

Grace Connors spends much of her time covering for her brother, Tony, at the family business. In a flashback, Grace recalls how at age 5, her father told her to give up her imaginary friend, whom she called Dayo, and she left him behind at an amusement park. Now, she visits the old rides that are in storage and Dayo reappears. No one else can see or hear Dayo, and Grace wonders about her own sanity.

Grace and her husband go on vacation, but when the business suffers, her father finally figures out that Grace is the brains behind the business, not Tony. Grace also realizes she doesn't want to go back to the business and decides, instead, to fulfill her old dream of opening up her own restaurant. Soon the new restaurant, named "Dayo's," is open for business. As Grace heads home, Dayo shows up for one last visit. He tells her that he is now the imaginary friend of another child who needs to learn self-pride, and Grace thanks him for his help in enabling her to put her problems behind her.

Production Note:

- Filming took place on location in Wilmington, North Carolina.

DEADLINE FOR MURDER: FROM THE FILES OF EDNA BUCHANAN   Airdate (2-hour format): 5/09/95 (CBS)

Cast: Elizabeth Montgomery (Edna Buchanan), Yaphet Kotto (Marty Talbot), Audra Lindley (Jean), Joe Flanigan (Scott Cameron), Jennifer Lewis (Denice Cooper), Richard Lineback (Billy Coleman), Matthew Posey (Sam), Saundra Santiago (Rosinha Zulueta), Liz Sheridan (Wendy Padison), Geno Silva (Teo Cruz), David Spielberg (George), Lewis Van Bergen (Johnny Cresta), Raymond Serra (The Man), Eddie Barth

(Mickey Rosen), Alley Mills (Julie Cresta), Dean Stockwell (Aaron Bliss), Heidi Mark (Bebe Quinn), Tracy Grant (Dionda Brown), Castulo Guerra (Orlando Zulueta), Thomas Mills (Lee Ray Pepper), David Jean Thomas (Prison Guard), Patrick Massett (Eric Wachtel), Evelyn Bakerges (Donna), Gary Kasper (Rosen Bodyguard), Mike Robelo (Francisco Sulliman), Casey Stengel (Newspaper Man).

This sequel to the special *The Corpse Had a Familiar Face* begins with the murder of mobster Johnny Cresta. Cresta has been trying to bring legalized gambling to Miami, which has upset people on both sides of the law. When Cresta's car breaks down one night, Orlando Zulueta, a tow truck driver, comes to his aid. Another car pulls up and someone machine-guns Cresta, his mistress, and Zulueta to death. Although it has all of the signs of a mob hit, reporter Edna Buchanan still feels something is wrong.

DEAD POETS SOCIETY   Airdates (3-hour format): 1/03/92, 11/21/92 (CBS).

This 1989 theatrical release starring Robin Williams as a professor in an exclusive boy's school was aired with 13 minutes of additional footage not included in the original release.

DEVIL AND MAX DEVLIN, THE

This 1981 theatrical release starring Elliott Gould as a man trapped into collecting souls for the Devil was first aired on the anthology series on 4/26/87. It aired as a special on 8/12/89 on ABC.

DICK TRACY   Airdate (2-hour, 15-minute format): 2/14/93 (ABC).

This 1990 theatrical release stars Warren Beatty in the title role of the famous comic-strip detective.

DICK TRACY: BEHIND THE BADGE— BEHIND THE SCENES   Airdate (30-minute format): 6/13/90 (Syndicated).

Cast: Warren Beatty, Madonna, Doug Drexler, John Cagilone, Jr., Ed O'Ross, William Forsythe, Jean Gould O'Connell, Richard Sylbert, Joel Marrow, Charlie Korsmo, Jeffrey Katzenberg.

This behind-the-scenes look at the 1990 theatrical release *Dick Tracy* begins with a recap of the film's plot. Big Boy, a notorious crime lord, wants to take over the other gangs in town, but to do so, he has to first do away with famed detective Dick Tracy. Tracy, the hero of a long-running comic strip, was the creation of artist Chester Gould. One of the trademarks of the strip was its outlandish villains, and this film has tackled the difficult chore of bringing them to life.

DISNEY AFTERNOON LIVE! AT DISNEYLAND   Airdate: 9/14/91 (KCAL).

Cast: Carl Bell (Host).

Disneyland is celebrating the success of *The Disney Afternoon* with special exhibits and shows, including chances for guests to meet the stars of their favorite Disney animated series. This special starts with a look at Walt's career and the early days of Disneyland, featuring clips from *The Disneyland Story* and *Dateline Disneyland*. Scenes of Walt Disney Imagineering show how the famous Disney attractions are designed, followed by a visit to Splash Mountain, Disneyland's new thrill ride.

Michael Eisner has declared this to be the "Disney Decade," when there will be ten years of constant improvements. Sketches of the upcoming Mickey's Toontown and proposals for a new Tomorrowland show that the Park will continue to excite visitors for many years to come.

DISNEY CHRISTMAS GIFT, A   Airdate: 12/20/83 (CBS).

Using the cartoon *The Clock Watcher* as a connecting link, this special features Donald Duck as a worker who wants to leave his job wrapping Christmas presents so he can enjoy the holiday. Flashbacks provide a look at how the Disney stars celebrated past holidays, beginning with *On Ice*.

The show includes sequences from *Pluto's Christmas Tree, Bambi, Peter Pan, The Three Caballeros, Toy Tinkers, Cinderella,* and *The Night before Christmas.*

Production Note:

- A different version of this show was aired on 12/04/82 as part of the anthology series. Both shows used scenes from *A Magical Disney Christmas*. This special has also been included in the syndicated anthology series.

DISNEY'S ALADDIN ON ICE   Airdate: 11/17/95 (CBS).

Cast: Kurt Browning (Aladdin), Kristi Yamaguchi (Jasmine), Erick Avari (The Mystic Traveler).

Disney took advantage of having the touring company from Walt Disney's World on Ice in Cairo, Egypt, to re-create the animated feature *Aladdin* on ice. Skating champions Kurt Browning and Kristi Yamaguchi star as Aladdin and Jasmine, with more than forty other skaters joining in. The show uses the music from the film to help tell the story, including *A Whole New World*, and Browning performs two energetic solo routines to *One Jump Ahead* and *Prince Ali*.

DISNEY'S ALL-STAR MOTHER'S DAY ALBUM   Airdate: 5/11/84 (CBS).

Over the years Disney films have included many memorable moments about mothers. This special, created from classic Disney animation, is a salute to all mothers—even those in the animal world. The show begins with a sequence from *Peter Pan* as Wendy sings *Your Mother and Mine* to remind her brothers and the Lost Boys about the mothers they left behind. The special features segments from *Daddy Duck, Lambert, the Sheepish Lion, Chicken in the Rough, Mickey and the Seal, Father's Day Off, Bambi, Pluto's Fledgling,* and *Donald's Nephews.*

Before the show concludes with a montage of clips from other Disney films, a very special mother is featured. Actually, it's the fairy godmother from *Cinderella*, who transforms a depressed girl into a fairy princess, thus helping her win the heart of the kingdom's handsome prince.

Production Note:

- This special was originally scheduled for 5/9/88 but was delayed due to a speech by the President.

DISNEY'S ALL-STAR VALENTINE PARTY   Airdate: 2/14/84 (NBC).

This show highlights the ageless wonder of love. The first story shows that the path to true romance is sometimes a rocky road, as in *Mickey's Rival*. A short sequence from *Bambi* shows how love can take you by surprise. Next, *Brave Little Tailor* features Mickey as a poor tailor who inadvertently volunteers to battle a giant. *Pluto's Heart Throb* is the story of a canine love triangle. In *Donald's Double Trouble*, his temper and uncouth manner have caused Daisy to end their relationship. *Cured Duck* again finds Donald's temper causing a rift between him and Daisy. Donald also runs into trouble in *Mr. Duck Steps Out*, for his nephews interfere with a date with Daisy.

DISNEY'S BEAUTY AND THE BEAST: THE BROADWAY MUSICAL COMES TO L.A.
Airdate: 4/13/95 (KCAL).

Cast: Tawny Little (Hostess), Kerry Kilbride (Host), John Corcoran, Cary Berglund, Robert T. McTyre, Linda Woolverton, Michael Eisner, Alan Menken, Gary Beach, Susan Egan, Terrence Mann, Robert Jess Roth, Tim Rice, Beth Fowler.

The premiere of the Los Angeles cast of *Disney's Beauty and the Beast: The Broadway Musical* is saluted in this live broadcast. The crowds are busy arriving for opening night, and John Corcoran is on duty at the entrance to get their reactions. Inside the theater, Cary Berglund provides a backstage tour of the production. Throughout the program, members of the cast and crew comment on the magic feeling of the show, mixed with clips of the play itself.

DISNEY'S *CAPTAIN EO* GRAND OPENING
Airdate: 9/20/86 (NBC).

Cast: Patrick Duffy (Host), Justine Bateman (Hostess), Belinda Carlisle, The Moody Blues, Robert Palmer, Starship, Gregg Burge, Jack Wagner (Announcer), Anjelica Huston, Michael Eisner.

Disney's newest 3-D film, *Captain Eo*, is about to open, and the crowds have been gathering at Disneyland in anticipation. The celebrations begin with a parade down Main Street U.S.A., where many of the film's crew and cast are seen in antique cars. Francis Coppola, the director, is shown rehearsing with star Michael Jackson and the dancers who appear in the film's climactic number. Famed director George Lucas is also seen working on the film.

Production Notes:

- The following celebrities are seen in the parade and crowd: Elliott Gould, Dorothy Hamlin, Ed Begley, Jr., Charles Bronson, Valerie Harper, Debbie Boone, Nell Carter, Dolph Lundgren, Lisa Hartman, Alfonso Ribeiro, Susan Sullivan, Dirk Benedict, Esther Williams, Judge Reinhold, John Ritter, Whoopi Goldberg, Alan Thicke, The Pet Shop Boys, Jack Nicholson, Debra Winger, Tommy Chong, Annette Funicello, Michele Lee, O.J. Simpson, Steven Bishop, Cheryl Ladd, Paul Rodriguez, John Stavros, Michael Warren, Jackie Collins, Sissy Spacek, Gene Anthony Ray, Ana Alicia, Dick Shawn, Garret Morris, Yakov Smirnoff, Margot Kidder, Richard Mull, Soleil Moon Frye, Joseph Campanella, Steven Furst, Elizabeth Montgomery, Robert Foxworth, Catherine Bach, Sarah Purcell, and Bruce Jenner.

- Disneyland remained open for an unprecedented 60-hour stretch. More than 157,000 people attended the event.

- The episode *Captain Eo Backstage* and The Disney Channel special *The Making of Captain Eo* both featured behind-the-scenes looks at the making of *Captain Eo.*

DISNEY'S CHAMPIONS ON ICE
Airdate: 3/09/96 (ABC).

Cast: Scott Hamilton (Host), Nicole Bobek, Surya Bonaly, Todd Eldredge, Chen Lu, Elvis Stojko, Ekaterina Gordeeva and Sergei Grinkov.

Michael Eisner dedicates this special to Sergei Grinkov, who died shortly after the show was taped. This was the last appearance of Grinkov and wife Ekaterina Gordeeva together. The show then finds Scott Hamilton boarding a train at Disneyland for Sun Valley, Idaho, where the featured skaters greet him at the station. They then performed in routines set to Disney music or based on classic films.

DISNEY'S CHRISTMAS FANTASY ON ICE
Airdates: 12/19/92, 12/24/93, 12/23/94 (CBS).

Cast: Brian Boitano, Kurt Browning, Peter and Kitty Caruthers, Ekaterina Gordeeva, Sergei Grinkov, Scott Hamilton, Nancy Kerrigan, Katarina Witt, Bronson Pinchot (Host/Jack Frost), Lindsey Rideway (Alice).

Disneyland is decorated for the Christmas holidays, and tourist Bronson Pinchot tells his niece, Alice, a story about the first time it snowed at Disneyland. Ready for a special holiday, Mickey and his friends visited Jack Frost and asked him to make it snow. Jack told them that they needed the six points of a snowflake to help cast the spell, so Mickey and his friends headed out to the different ice worlds to collect the points. In each world, they met championship figure skaters who performed for them and gave them the points they needed.

With the snowflake complete, the Disney characters got their wish and it snowed. After Bronson finishes the story, Alice wishes it will snow again—and it does.

Production Notes:

- The skating portion of this program was taped at the Sun Valley Resort in Sun Valley, Idaho.

- Brian Boitano does not appear in the repeat version of this program.
- It has yet to really snow at Disneyland.

DISNEY'S CHRISTMAS ON ICE   Airdates (CBS): 12/21/90, 12/27/91.

Cast: Peggy Fleming, Tai Babilonia, Randy Gardner, Gary Beacom, Judy Blumberg, Michael Seibert, Robin Cousins, Scott Hamilton, Caryn Kadavy, The Party, Rosalynn Sumners, Katarina Witt.

This special combines two winter traditions, Christmas and ice skating, with a Disney touch. Set in Squaw Valley, California, the show begins with Mickey and Minnie decorating Minnie's mountain cabin as their friends arrive to help. Then, the evening's hostess, Peggy Fleming, the 1968 Olympic gold medalist, begins the skating portion of the entertainment. Fleming is joined by skating champions Robin Cousins, Judy Blumberg, Michael Seibert, Katarina Witt, Scott Hamilton, Gary Beacom, Caryn Kadavy, Rosalyn Sumners, Tai Babilonia, and Randy Gardner. The grand finale features all of the cast members in *We Wish You a Merry Christmas.*

Production Notes:

- The show also featured clips from *On Ice, Pluto's Christmas Tree, Donald's Snow Fight,* and *From All of Us to All of You.*
- Announcer Hal Smith narrated the entire show in rhyme.
- The 12/27/91 version did not include The Party.

DISNEY'S COUNTDOWN TO KID'S DAY
Airdate: 11/21/93 (NBC)

Cast: Sinbad (Host), Gloria Estefan, Alan Jackson, Kris Kross, Celine Dion, Joey Lawrence, Marilyn Kentz, Caryl Kristensen, Harlem Boys Choir.

This special salutes Kid's Day, set by Congress as the third Sunday of November. It features celebrity appearances and glimpses at some of the 20,000 youngsters invited to Disney resorts in conjunction with the Children's Defense Fund. The program begins with the stars singing *It's a Small World* at each of the theme parks.

Michael Eisner welcomes the crowd, then introduces host Sinbad to read a congressional proclamation for Kid's Day. After a youngster translates the formal wording into "kids' language," the program ends with more songs and fireworks.

Production Note:

- This special marked the first time that all four Disney theme parks were featured in the same show.

DISNEY'S DTV DOGGONE HITS
See: *Disney's DTV Doggone Valentine.*

DISNEY'S DTV DOGGONE VALENTINE
Airdates (NBC): 2/13/87, 2/19/88 *(Disney's DTV Doggone Hits).*

Ludwig Von Drake opens the show by explaining that "DTV" is the combination of Disney animation and new musical soundtracks. Just like people, animals fall in love, and Disney animals have been featured in many memorable love scenes. Ludwig, Jiminy Cricket, and Mickey Mouse display the results by showing clips of Disney animals set to songs performed by various rock groups.

DISNEY'S DTV MONSTER HITS   Airdate: 10/30/87 (NBC).

Cast: Jeffrey Jones (Slave in The Magic Mirror).

This *DTV*-style music video salute to Halloween begins as the Slave in the Magic Mirror introduces his first co-host, Witch Hazel, who in turn introduces the first song, Michael Jackson's *Thriller.* More fun follows with Mickey, Donald, and Goofy, the first ghostbusters, seen in *Lonesome Ghosts,* matched to the theme to *Ghostbusters* by Ray Parker, Jr. The Halloween theme continues when Huey, Dewey, and Louie go out to *Trick or Treat,* set to *Bad Moon Rising* by Creedence Clearwater Revival. Mickey returns to star in *The Mad Doctor,* which leads into the comedy song *Monster Mash,* sung by Bobby "Boris" Pickett. The Slave salutes Disney's villains in a montage and ends the show by wishing the audience *Sweet Dreams,* sung by The Eurythmics.

DISNEY'S DTV ROMANCIN'
See: *Disney's DTV Valentine.*

DISNEY'S DTV VALENTINE   Airdates: 2/14/86, 9/07/86 *(Disney's DTV Romancin')* (NBC).

Voice Characterizations by: Tony Anselmo (Donald Duck), Corey Burton (Gruffi Gummi), Eddie Carroll (Jiminy Cricket), Mary Costa (Sleeping Beauty), Les Perkins (Mickey Mouse), Will Ryan (Pongo, Goofy), Judith Searle (Chip, Dale), Bill Shirley (Prince

Phillip), Lisa St. James (Dalmatian Puppies), Paul Frees (Ludwig Von Drake).

This musical special begins with animation clips and the song *It's in His Kiss*, then Ludwig Von Drake describes *DTV* as the best of Disney animation set to rock and roll. Next, Mickey Mouse introduces Donald Duck, who claims he's the screen's greatest lover. Donald tries to prove this amazing claim with clips from his cartoons set to Stevie Wonder's *I Just Called to Say I Love You*. Chip and Dale follow, with scenes from their television appearances and cartoons accompanied by *Dress You Up* by Madonna. A montage of black-and-white Mickey Mouse cartoons gets a new look when set to the sound of *Hey Mickey*, sung by Desiree Goyette. The Gummi Bears are next, along with clips of various other Disney bears, all to the tune of *Teddy Bear*, as sung by Elvis Presley. A segment from *Snow White and the Seven Dwarfs* and *Once upon a Wintertime* from *Melody Time* are used in the final sequence, which highlights *You Give Me Good Love* by Whitney Houston.

DISNEY'S FLUPPY DOGS   Airdate: 11/27/86 (ABC).

Voices: *Marshall Efron (Stanley), Carl Stevens (Jamie Bingham), Cloyce Morrow (Mrs. Bingham), Hal Smith (Dink, Haimish, Attendant), Lorenzo Music (Ozzie), Jessica Pennington (Claire), Michael Rye (Wagstaff), Susan Blu (Bink, Tippi).*

The Fluppy Dogs, a band of alien canines, have a magic key that opens doorways to other worlds. Their adventures take them to Earth, where they're spotted by J.J. Wagstaff, who discovers they can talk. Wagstaff, who is very wealthy and powerful, wants the dogs in his collection of exotic animals, but the Fluppys escape. The dogs hide in an animal shelter, not expecting that their leader, Stanley, will be adopted as a pet. Jamie Bingham, Stanley's new owner, promises to help free the other Fluppys. After numerous adventures, Jamie helps the Fluppys fly through the magic door that leads them back home.

Several months later, the dogs return for a visit. They liked Earth so much that they've brought dozens of their friends with them to share the adventure.

Production Notes:

- The dogs went through several namings during the production of this show. One model guide sent to potential licensees had them named by their

colors: Lavender "(loving, emphathetic, understanding, a good listener"); Blue ("honest, loyal, brave, protective"); Pink ("pretty, neat, style, savoir faire"); Yellow ("playful, fun, mischievous"); Green ("cool, calm, collected, artistic, easygoing"); and Peach ("kind, compassionate, shy"). A press release listed six dogs and brief descriptions: Silly Flup ("yellow"); Cuddle Flup ("violet"); Brave Flup ("blue and white, wears a bandanna"); Fanci Flup ("pink"); Shy Flup ("wears a bonnet"); and Cool Flup ("wears sunglasses"). They were later named as first described.

- This was a co-venture with Kenner Parker Toys, who released several Fluppy Dogs toys.
- This special was repeated on the anthology series on 8/30/87.

DISNEY'S GOLDEN ANNIVERSARY OF SNOW WHITE AND THE SEVEN DWARFS
Airdate: 5/22/87 (NBC).

Cast: *Dick Van Dyke, Jane Curtin, Sherman Hemsley, Linda Ronstadt.*

The show begins as Jane Curtin, playing the evil queen from *Snow White and the Seven Dwarfs*, once again asks her magic mirror who's the fairest in the land. The mirror, played by Sherman Hemsley, tells her it is still Snow White. That night, the dwarfs leave their mine and dance down Main Street U.S.A. at Disneyland. Dick Van Dyke is with them, and he sings a medley of songs from the film. Van Dyke then narrates a look at how the film *Snow White* came to be.

The *Snow White* premiere on December 21, 1937, was a gala affair. The magic of that night was only surpassed by the award of a special Oscar, presented to Walt by Shirley Temple. Linda Ronstadt closes the show as she sings *Some Day My Prince Will Come* at the Snow White Grotto at Disneyland.

Production Notes:

- Scenes are also included from *Cinderella, Mary Poppins, The Sword in the Stone, Sleeping Beauty* and *The Rescuers*.
- This show was also aired on the anthology series on 12/25/88.

DISNEY'S GOOF TROOP   Airdate (2-hour format): 9/05/92 (Syndicated).

This preview of the new *Goof Troop* series begins as Goofy gets a new job and returns to his hometown of Spoonerville with his teenage son, Max. He moves next door to his old friend, Pete, much to Pete's displeasure. While their kids get along great, Goofy soon drives Pete to the brink of insanity. The next segment of the program is a new music video, *Gotta Be Gettin' Goofy*, by rap artist The CEO, featuring clips from classic Goofy cartoons and new scenes from *Goof Troop*. The special concludes with the anthology episode *The Goofy Success Story*, which provides a look at Goofy's illustrious career.

DISNEY'S GREAT AMERICAN CELEBRATION   Airdate (2-hour format): 7/04/91 (CBS).

Cast: Robert Guillaume, Connie Sellecca, Barbara Mandrell, Sheena Easton, C&C Music Factory, The Kentucky Headhunters, Tevin Campbell, Tim Allen, The Party, Steven Banks, President George Bush, Bill Campbell, Jennifer Connelly.

This holiday special begins at Disneyland with guest acts from across the Park.

A parade down Main Street U.S.A. at Walt Disney World celebrates the 200th anniversary of the Bill of Rights. The theme for the parade is American traditions, with fanciful floats bringing back memories of picnics, baseball, and circuses. Also included in the parade are 101 live dalmatians, there to remind viewers of the upcoming rerelease of the 1961 animated classic.

DISNEY'S GREATEST HITS ON ICE   Airdates (2-hour format): 11/25/94, 12/28/95 (CBS).

Cast: Ekatarina Gordeeva and Sergei Grinkov, Scott Hamilton, Nancy Kerrigan, Marina Klimova and Sergei Ponomarenko, Michelle Kwan, Yuka Sato, Maia Usova and Alexander Zhulin, Katarina Witt, Paul Wylie.

Additional Cast—*Conductor: Denis LaCombe. Chimney Sweeps: Colin Beatty, Chris Beatty. Peter Pan Children: Cohen Duncan (Wendy), Amir Ganaba (Michael), Nicholas Johnson (John). Pirate Story Teller: Geoffrey Lewis. The Prince and Captain Hook: Michael Seibert. Vocal Soloists: Stephen Bishop, Kathy Fisher, David Pomeranz, Christina Saffran, Billy Vera, Mervyn Warren.*

Skaters bring Disney classics to life in a fanciful re-creation on ice of the Disney Studio in Burbank. The first film featured is *Cinderella*, with Ekatarina Gordeeva as Cinderella, Sergei Grinkov as Prince Charming and Nancy Kerrigan, Marina Klimova, and Katarina Witt as the stepsisters. Their skating is blended with clips from the film. Mickey

Mouse conducts while Scott Hamilton skates to music from Mickey's career. Disney's love songs are the focus of the next segment featuring Maia Usova, Alexander Zhulin, Marina Klimova, and Sergei Ponomarenko. Kerrigan closes the special with a routine from *Snow White and the Seven Dwarfs*.

Production Note:

• While this program supposedly was taped at the Disney Studios, it was actually filmed at Paramount because all of the Disney stages were booked.

DISNEY'S HALLOWEEN TREAT

This show first aired on the anthology series. It aired as a special on 10/29/83 on NBC.

DISNEY'S LIVING SEAS   Airdate: 1/24/86 (NBC).

Cast: John Ritter, Laura Branigan, Simon Le Bon, Dr. Robert Ballard, Scott Carpenter, Olivia Newton-John.

This special is a celebration of the opening of the Living Seas at Epcot. Host John Ritter begins the show by entering the pavilion's Seabase Alpha through a diving lock. He describes Disney's long history of interest in water, as illustrated in scenes from *Steamboat Willie, How to Swim, 20,000 Leagues under the Sea*, and *Swiss Family Robinson*.

Ritter then describes the new attraction as the show shifts to scenes from various films and cartoons.

The show concludes as Mickey Mouse, diving inside the main tank, waves goodbye to Ritter and the pavilion's first guests.

DISNEY'S MAGIC IN THE MAGIC KINGDOM   Airdate: 2/12/88 (NBC).

Cast: George Burns, Harry Anderson, Gloria Estefan and Miami Sound Machine, Morgan Fairchild, Markie Post, John Ratzenberger, Lance Burton, Dean Gunnarson, The Pendragons, Princess Tenko, Siegfried & Roy.

The opening of this special features magicians Siegfried & Roy, who make an elephant vanish. In its place, they produce the show's host, George Burns. After Burns does a comedy act, he tells the audience that Siegfried & Roy will make Sleeping Beauty Castle disappear before the show ends. After a series of magic routines by guest performers, Siegfried & Roy succeed, for the castle seemingly vanishes from sight. This feat is capped with a fireworks and light show.

Production Note:

- This show also aired on the anthology series on 7/23/89.

DISNEY'S MOST UNLIKELY HEROES

Airdate (30-minute format): 6/18/96 (ABC).

Cast: Roy E. Disney (Host), Don Hahn, Gary Trousdale, Kirk Wise, Alan Menken, Jason Alexander, Demi Moore, Kevin Kline.

Roy E. Disney begins the show talking about the heritage created by Walt and Roy O. Disney. Some of Roy's favorite heroes are the ones you would least expect, a tradition that dates back to Mickey Mouse. Clips from *Snow White and the Seven Dwarfs*, the 1939 version of *The Ugly Duckling*, *Pinocchio*, *Beauty and the Beast*, *The Lion King*, *Cinderella*, and *Aladdin* show some of Disney's past unlikely heroes.

Celebrities Sharon Stone, Nicolas Cage, Lindsay Wagner, Zachery Ty Bryan, John Travolta, Pat Sajak, Steve Young, Joan Rivers, Gilbert Gottfried, Robby Benson, Marilu Henner, Ben Savage, Alan Thicke, and Leonard Maltin all offer their votes for their favorite unlikely heroes.

DISNEY'S NANCY KERRIGAN SPECIAL: DREAMS ON ICE   Airdate: 2/15/95 (CBS).

Cast: Nancy Kerrigan, Scott Hamilton, Ekaterina Gordeeva and Sergei Grinkov, Paul Martini, Elvis Stojko, Paul Wylie, Maia Usova and Alexander Zhulin, Gordie Howe, Brian McKnight, 69 Boyz. Vocal Soloists: Maureen McGovern, Gary Stockdale, Billy Vera, Mervyn Warren.

This special begins as Nancy Kerrigan skates to *The Circle of Life* at Lake Placid and her family reminisces about the years leading up to her 1994 Olympic tryout. This is followed by a look at the musical influences in Nancy's past as Kerrigan skates on New York Street at the Disney-MGM Studios. Scott Hamilton and other skaters join to re-create moments from several Disney films.

Kerrigan's brothers join her to talk about their family street hockey games, and hockey great Gordie Howe visits with Lake Placid children at a practice game. Kerrigan watches Hamilton practice and they look back at their competitions in Lake Placid, along with those of other past skaters. The program ends as Kerrigan and her family talk about her commitment to skating.

Production Notes:

- Paul Martini was Nancy Kerrigan's skating partner for this show.
- While in Lake Placid for this show, Nancy Kerrigan also taped a brief segment for the *Wrong Side of the Tracks* episode of *Boy Meets World*.

DISNEY'S SPRING BREAK BLAST   Airdate: 4/23/95 (Syndicated).

Cast: Katie Wagner, James Wilder, Debbe Dunning, Mary J. Blige, Coolio, Crystal Waters.

Taped at Walt Disney World, this musical special features performers at locations across the Park. From Blizzard Beach, Crystal Waters sings *Gypsy Woman* and *100% Pure Love*. Other songs include Coolio's *Fantastic Voyage* and *Dial a Jam*, and Mary J. Blige with *Be Happy* and *I'm Going Down*.

DISNEY'S TALE SPIN: PLUNDER & LIGHTNING   Airdate (2-hour format): 9/07/90 (Syndicated).

Voices: Charlie Adler (Mad Dog), Jim Cummings (Don Karnage, Louie), Pat Fraley (Wildcat), Ed Gilbert (Baloo), Tony Jay (Shere Khan), Chuck McCann (Dumptruck), Janna Michaels (Molly Cunningham), Rob Paulsen, Sally Struthers (Rebecca Cunningham), Frank Welker, R.J. Williams (Kit Cloudkicker).

This pilot to the series *Tale Spin* begins as the evil Don Karnage hijacks a plane in midair to steal a strange jewel, but his gloating is interrupted when the gem is quickly stolen from him in turn. The new thief, Kit Cloudkicker, a young boy, escapes by hiding in Baloo's plane and tells him about the jewel. When Baloo and Kit go to get the jewel from its hiding place, they find that Karnage has kidnapped hostages. Kit tells Baloo the prisoners will be on Pirate's Island, Karnage's secret hiding place, and he reveals that he was once part of Karnage's gang. He leads Baloo to a secret entrance and they rescue the hostages just as Karnage returns to the island. They learn that he is building a superweapon and the jewel is needed to power it.

Karnage soon tries to invade the city, using his new weapon to fire lightning bolts at the gun crews. Kit steals the jewel from the lightning gun, then calls on the radio for help. Baloo crashes his plane into Karnage's ship and destroys the gun and saves the city.

DISNEY'S THE HUNCHBACK OF NOTRE DAME: FESTIVAL OF FOOLS Airdates: 6/23/96, 7/04/96 (KCAL).

Cast: Rick Dees (Host), All for One.

The first half of this special was aired on The Disney Channel as *The Making of The Hunchback of Notre Dame.* Then, host Rick Dees provides a behind-the-scenes look at the Festival of Fools stage show at Disneyland and a look at the world premiere of *Hunchback* at the Superdome in New Orleans.

DISNEY'S "THE LITTLE MERMAID: A WHALE OF A TALE" Airdates (30-minute format): 9/11/92, 9/10/93 (CBS).

Voices: Jodi Benson (Ariel), Samuel E. Wright (Sebastian), Edan Gross (Flounder), Ken Mars (King Triton), Jim Cummings.

After years in the doldrums, Disney's Feature Animation Division roared back to life with a vengeance with the 1989 release of *The Little Mermaid.* The film earned a very impressive $84 million and gave rise to the Studio's first television sequel to one of its animated films. In this preview episode, Ariel tries to keep her pet killer whale a secret from King Triton, who feels the animal would be better off in the wild. Ariel soon learns that a growing whale is not easily hidden.

DISNEY'S TOTALLY MINNIE Airdate: 3/25/88 (NBC).

Cast: Suzanne Somers (Director), Robert Carradine (Maxwell Dweeb), Elton John (Himself), Philip Michael Thomas (Himself), Vanna White (Herself), Jake (Maxwell's Dog). Featured Performers: *Tina Caspray, Mavis Vegas Davis, Peggy Holmes, Lise Lang, Thelma Smith, Andrea Wilson, Cheryl Yamaguchi.* Voices: *Russi Taylor (Minnie Mouse), Wayne Allwine (Mickey Mouse), Will Ryan, Tony Anselmo (Donald Duck).*

When Maxwell Dweeb realizes he's a total failure at meeting women, he decides to improve himself through a crash course at Minnie Mouse's "Center for the Totally Unhip." The center's director takes him on a tour, where they see television personalities giving lessons to Disney characters.

Production Note:

- This show was also aired on the anthology series on 5/07/89.

DISNEYLAND '59

See: *Kodak Presents Disneyland '59.*

DISNEYLAND PRESENTS: TALES OF TOONTOWN Airdate: 7/10/93 (Syndicated).

Cast: Jerry Hawkins (Spence Dempsey), Ray Joseph (The Gate Keeper), Steve Glaudini (The Toon Doctor), Dave Burkhart (Planning Commissioner). With the Voice Talents of: *Wayne Allwine (Mickey Mouse), Tony Anselmo (Donald Duck), Bill Farmer (Goofy).*

This look at Disneyland's newest theme land, Mickey's Toontown, begins as private detective Spence Dempsey leaves Toontown and looks back at the case he has just solved. Strange things were happening in Toontown, a new town that suddenly appeared next to Disneyland. Dempsey, with the help of many Toontown residents, discovered that Donald accidentally unleashed magic when he tried out Mickey's famous role, the sorcerer's apprentice.

Production Notes:

- This program was provided free by Disneyland to any station that wanted it. In exchange for airing this publicity for the theme park, the stations were able to sell 12 minutes of advertising and keep the money.
- Dave Burkhart, who played the part of the planning commissioner in an old newsreel, was the senior show producer for the Toontown project.

DISNEYLAND'S SUMMER VACATION PARTY Airdate (2-hour format): 5/23/86 (NBC).

Cast: Mindy Cohn, Kim Fields, Scott Valentine, Malcolm-Jamal Warner, Adam Ant, The Bangles, Chubby Checker and The Wildcats, Culture Club, Electric Light Orchestra, The Fabulous Thunderbirds, Fifth Dimension, Brenda Lee, Jay Leno, Kenny Loggins, Miami Sound Machine, Oingo Boingo, The Pointer Sisters, The Righteous Brothers, Paul Rodriguez, Jerry Seinfeld, Sha Na Na, Garry Shandling, Jack Wagner (Announcer).

Mindy Cohn, Kim Fields, Scott Valentine and Malcolm-Jamal Warner arrive on Main Street U.S.A. to host Grad Night, an annual party at Disneyland.

Production Note:

- Filmed over five nights, the show used 2,000 local high school students as extras.

DISNEYLAND'S 30TH ANNIVERSARY CELEBRATION

Airdates (2-hour format): 2/18/85, 8/11/85 (NBC).

Cast: John Forsythe, Drew Barrymore, Alabama, Debbie Allen, Peter Allen, Julie Andrews, Bobby Berosini's Orang-utans, Roy Clark, David Hasselhoff, Julian Lennon, Marie Osmond, The Pointer Sisters, Donna Summer, Harry Anderson, Mindy Cohn, The Cosby Kids, Kim Fields, Annette Funicello, John Moschitta, Tina Yothers.

This salute to Disneyland's 30th birthday begins with clips from *Dateline Disneyland* showing Ronald Reagan, Art Linkletter, and Walt Disney on the Park's opening day. Hosts John Forsythe and Drew Barrymore take a look at the Park's history during this special musical celebration, which ends with a new nighttime parade at Disneyland.

Production Note:

- This special, which required six nights of filming at Disneyland, was the first primetime appearance for Julian Lennon, son of late Beatle John Lennon.
- Former Mouseketeer Tommy Cole was one of the makeup crew for this special.

DISTINGUISHED GENTLEMAN, THE

Airdate (2-hour format): 12/10/95 (NBC).
This 1992 theatrical release stars Eddie Murphy as a con man who gets himself elected to the U.S. Congress.

DONALD DUCK'S 50TH BIRTHDAY

Airdates (CBS): 11/13/84, 10/29/85.

Cast: Dick Van Dyke (Host), Ed Asner, Bruce Jenner, Cloris Leachman, Kenny Rogers, Donna Summer, Andy Warhol, Henry Winkler, John Ritter, R2-D2, C3PO (Anthony Daniels).

In this celebration of Donald Duck's 50th birthday, Dick Van Dyke, John Ritter, Henry Winkler, Bruce Jenner, Clarence Nash (the voice of Donald), and others send Donald on a special tour across the country.

Production Note:

- Clarence Nash appears in a sequence following the show in which he discusses several books on Donald Duck.

DOWN AND OUT IN BEVERLY HILLS

Airdates (2-hour, 10-minute format, ABC): 11/06/88, 4/01/90.
This 1986 theatrical release stars Nick Nolte, Richard Dreyfuss, and Bette Midler in the story of a wealthy family that saves a vagrant from drowning. The Studio produced a television series based on this film.

DOWN AND OUT WITH DONALD DUCK

Airdates: 3/25/87, 4/29/88 (NBC).

Voices: Stan Freberg (Narrator), Tony Anselmo (Donald Duck, Daisy Duck, Huey, Dewey, Louie), Albert Ash (Ludwig Von Drake), Les Perkins (Mickey Mouse), Will Ryan (Pete, Goofy), Harry Shearer (Announcer).

This "duckumentary," done in the style of *60 Minutes*, traces the life of Donald Duck. As Donald's fame grew, so did his ego. While hosting a variety show, Donald cracked up and shot at the audience when they wouldn't behave. This led to a series of problems that caused Donald to seek psychiatric help from Ludwig von Drake. Von Drake used an insult machine as part of Donald's therapy, and after a long night of strange dreams, Donald realized the error of his ways and promised to be more lovable.

Production Notes:

- This episode used footage from the episode *A Day in the Life of Donald Duck* and the cartoons *Donald Gets Drafted, Donald's Golf Game, Donald's Nephews, The Riveter, Bellboy Donald, Donald's Crime, Sleepy Time Donald,* and *Chef Donald.*
- This special was rerun as part of the syndicated special *Going Bonkers.*

DREAM CALLED WALT DISNEY WORLD, A

Airdate (30-minute format): 9/19/82 (Syndicated).
This featurette promotes the many vacation thrills awaiting visitors to Walt Disney World. Each of the Park's themed lands is visited, with a special emphasis on those attractions not found at Disneyland.

Production Note:

- This show, which was originally released as a souvenir video at Walt Disney World, was aired without production credits.

DREAM IS ALIVE, THE: 20TH ANNIVERSARY CELEBRATION OF WALT DISNEY WORLD Airdate: 10/25/91 (CBS).

Cast: Michael Eisner, Garth Brooks, Amy Grant, Angela Lansbury, Tim Allen, Carol Burnett, Whoopi Goldberg, Goldie Hawn, Billy Joel, Steve Martin, Bette Midler, Eddie Murphy, Dolly Parton, Robert Williams, Robert Guillaume, Patti LaBelle, Park Overall, Sandi Patti, Regis Philbin, Kathie Lee Gifford.

Michael Eisner is trying to pick the perfect host for Walt Disney World's 20th anniversary, so he crosses the country, telling everyone he asks that they were his first choice for the job. The show includes guest appearances from numerous actors and musicians and concludes with a special re-reading of Roy O. Disney's Walt Disney World dedication plaque.

Production Notes:

- Park Overall from *Empty Nest* plays Michael Eisner's secretary, Laverne.
- Many of the stars listed in the credits are seen only in brief clips in a musical number.

DUCKTALES: THE MOVIE SPECIAL
Airdate (30-minute format): 8/01/90 (Syndicated).

Cast: Tracey Gold, Kadeem Hardison.

This preview of the film *DuckTales the Movie: The Treasure of the Lost Lamp* begins with Tracey Gold and Kadeem Hardison showing clips from past *DuckTales* adventures from television. They then show clips of the new film, which centers on Scrooge's search for an ancient treasure. The discovery of a genie in a hidden temple leads to unexpected trouble.

DUCKTALES: TIME IS MONEY Airdate (2-hour format): 11/25/88 (Syndicated).

With the Talents of: *Joan Gerber (Mrs. Beakley, Webra Walters), Don Hills, Chuck McCann (Duckworth), Terence McGovern (Launchpad McQuack), Haunani Minn (Sen-Sen), Hal Smith (Gyro Gearloose, Flintheart Glomgold), Russi Taylor (Huey, Dewey, Louie, Webbigail Vanderquack), Frank Welker (Bubba Duck, Big Time Beagle), Alan Young (Uncle Scrooge McDuck), Keone Young (Myng-Ho).*

After Scrooge McDuck buys an island from Flintheart Glomgold, his notorious rival, Flintheart learns it is full of diamonds. De-termined not to be outsmarted, Flintheart sends in the Beagle Boys, who blow the island into two parts so Scrooge's piece won't have the diamonds. Scrooge uses Gyro Gearloose's time machine to defeat the villains, but an accident leaves them in prehistoric times.

Production Note:

- This special was later aired on the *DuckTales* series in five parts: *Marking Time, The Duck Who Would Be King, Bubba Trubba, Gone with the Bin,* and *Ali Bubba's Cave.*

DUCKTALES: TREASURE OF THE GOLDEN SUNS Airdate (2-hour format): 9/18/87 (Syndicated).

Voices: Tony Anselmo (Donald Duck), Peter Cullen, Jim Cummings (El Capitan), Joan Gerber, Chuck McCann (Duckworth), Terry McGovern, Patty Parris (Skittles), Hal Smith, Russi Taylor (Huey, Dewey, Louie), Frank Welker, Stanley Wojno Jr., Alan Young (Uncle Scrooge McDuck).

This two-hour preview of Disney's new syndicated series, *DuckTales*, was shown later during the series in five parts: *Don't Give Up the Ship, Wrong Way to Ronguay, Three Ducks of the Condor, Cold Duck,* and *Too Much of a Gold Thing.*

DUMBO
This 1941 theatrical release was aired as a special on 9/17/78 as Part 2 of the show *NBC Salutes the 25th Anniversary of The Wonderful World of Disney* and again on 11/18/85, 9/14/86, and 10/30/88. The 1985 and 1986 versions included *Mickey and the Beanstalk* and *Lambert, The Sheepish Lion.*

EARTH*STAR VOYAGER
Aired as a special in two parts on 5/25/89 and 6/01/89 as part of the *Disney Family Classics* series, this show was first aired on the anthology series.

ENCINO MAN Airdate: (2-hour format): 9/16/95 (ABC).
This 1992 theatrical release stars Sean Astin, Brendan Fraser, and Pauly Shore in the story of a prehistoric man who comes to live in modern Los Angeles.

ENCINO WOMAN Airdate (2-hour format): 4/20/96 (ABC).
Cast: Jay Thomas (Marvin Beckler), Corey Parker (David Horsenfelt), Katherine Kousi

(Lucy), Ric Overton (Raji), John Kassir (Jean Michel), Annabelle Gurwich (Chris), Joel Murray (Mr. Jones), Chris Hogan (Roger), Elisa Donovan (Ivana), Suli McCullough (Marcus), Marissa Ribisi (Fiona), Jeffrey Ross (Mr. Smith), Clarence Williams III (Javier), Bobcat Goldthwait (Yogi Paxil), Michael Burger (Mike), Maty Monfort (Maty), Catherine Silvers (Susan), Kate Gibson (Model), Ashley Monique Clark (Kindergartner), Jackie Beat (Doorman), Calvert DeForest (Celeb), Terry Murphy (Reporter), Spencer Garrett (Bobby), Shawn Schepps (Brenda), Jeffrey Lampert (Dr. Lampert).

This *Disney Family Movie* is a female version of the 1992 theatrical release *Encino Man*. It begins as a major earthquake in Los Angeles uncovers a woman who was frozen in prehistoric times. She hides in the car of David Horsenfelt, a low-level advertising agency worker who has just been fired. Through a comedy of errors, Lucy helps David get his job back, and the two eventually fall in love and become the perfect suburban couple.

ERNEST GOES TO JAIL   Airdate (2-hour format): 8/07/94 (NBC).
This 1990 theatrical release stars Jim Varney as Ernest P. Worrell, who is a dead ringer for a notorious crime boss.

ERNEST GOES TO SPLASH MOUNTAIN
Airdate (30-minute format): 8/19/89 (KHJ).
Cast: Jim Varney (Ernest P. Worrell), Danny Breen (Skip Binkman), Sheryl Bernstein (Marjorie Hastings-Hardwicke), Bruce Gordon (Himself), Tom Miller (Cameron Chronomyer), Ralph Story (Himself).

Disneyland's newest attraction, Splash Mountain, is almost ready for its grand opening, but first, it needs to be tested. The brave volunteer for the first ride is Ernest P. Worrell, and a special news crew led by anchorman Ralph Story is standing by to record the moment for posterity.

ERNEST SAVES CHRISTMAS   Airdates (2-hour format): 12/14/91, 12/11/93 (ABC).
This 1988 theatrical release stars Jim Varney as a cabdriver who helps a retiring Santa Claus find a replacement.

ERNEST SCARED STUPID   Airdate (2-hour format): 11/05/94 (ABC).
This 1991 theatrical release stars Jim Varney again as Ernest P. Worrell, who this time almost causes the end of the world when he helps an evil troll escape from a grave.

ESCAPE TO WITCH MOUNTAIN (TV version)   Airdates (2-hour format): 4/29/95, 5/25/96 (ABC).
Cast: Robert Vaughn (Edward Bolt), Elisabeth Moss (Anna), Erik von Detten (Danny), Lynne Moody (Lindsay Brown), Perrey Reeves (Zoe Moon), Lauren Tom (Claudia Ford), Vincent Schiavelli (Waldo Fudd), Henry Gibson (Ravetch), Sam Horrigan (Xander), Bobby Motown (Skeeto), Kevin Tighe (Sheriff Bronson), Brad Dourif (Luther/Bruno), John Petlock (Butler), Beth Colt (Woman Officer), Daniel Lavery (Mr. Flynn), Jeffrey Lampert (Man on TV), Ray Lykins (Deputy).

This *Disney Family Movie* is based on the 1974 theatrical release. Witch Mountain State Park is a strange place, for it attracts a variety of people who travel there as if called by an inner voice. Two children meet there and learn they are from another dimension.

FAIREST OF THEM ALL, THE   Airdate (30-minute format): 6/03/83 (Syndicated).
Cast: Dick Van Patten (Host), Adrianna Caselotti, Harry Stockwell.

Walt Disney's precedent-setting 1937 theatrical release *Snow White and the Seven Dwarfs* is the subject of this salute at a party hosted by the Los Angeles Children's Museum. Dick Van Patten introduces several celebrities, including many of the animators who worked on the film.

Production Note:

- The following actors and actresses are featured in the show: Sally Struthers, Drew Barrymore, Ricky Schroeder, Shelley Duvall, Keith Mitchell, Paul Winchell, and Joseph Bottoms. Veteran Disney animators Ken Anderson, Ward Kimball, Frank Thomas, Eric Larson, Woolie Reitherman, and Ollie Johnston are joined by newcomers Glen Keane, John Lasseter, Cindy Whitney, and Phil Nibbelink. Also featured are Clarence Nash, the voice of Donald Duck, and Wayne Allwine of the Studio's Sound Effects Department.

FAMILY VALUES   Airdate (30-minute format): 12/26/95 (UPN).
Series Cast: Susan Ruttan (Melody Huck), David Lipper (Jimmy Huck), Christian Hoff (Johnson Huck), Rick Peters (Emory Huck), Matt Dotson (Lyle Huck), Jenna von Oy (Beebee Huck). *Guest Cast:* Kathryn Morris (Borgyork Grumm), Marianne Muellerleile

(Clerk), Catherine Alexandra Nagan (Victoria), Orlando Brown (Chuckie).

This was a pilot for an unsold series featuring a family that went out of its way to avoid work. In this episode, Johnson Huck annoys his brothers when he breaks with tradition and actually gets a job.

FATHER OF THE BRIDE Airdates (2-hour format): 12/27/94, 11/02/95 (ABC).
This 1991 theatrical release stars Steve Martin and Diane Keaton in the tale of a wedding that takes over the lives of everyone involved with it.

FIRE BIRDS Airdate (2-hour format): 1/11/93 (ABC).
This 1990 theatrical release stars Nicolas Cage, Tommy Lee Jones, and Sean Young as military helicopter pilots involved in a battle with drug lords.

FLIGHT OF THE NAVIGATOR
This 1986 theatrical release starring Joey Cramer is the story of a young boy who is missing for eight years, but when he's discovered, he hasn't aged a day. He then has to help a robot spaceship find its way home. It was aired on the anthology series in two parts on 1/03/88 and 1/10/88, and also aired as a *Disney Family Classic* special on ABC in two parts on 3/09/89 and 3/16/89.

FLORIDA'S DISNEY DECADE Airdate: 10/02/81 (Syndicated).
Cast: Susan Powell (Miss America 1981), Dick Van Dyke, Gene Burne (Narrator).
Walt Disney World opened on October 15, 1971, with only 10,000 guests in attendance, and Wall Street wags predicted failure. Now, ten years later, this special salutes the first decade of the world's most popular vacation destination.

Production Note:

- Disney purchased time on all three Orlando television stations at the same time to air this special, making it next to impossible for Orlando residents to miss this promotional piece.

40 YEARS OF ADVENTURES Airdates: 3/04/95, 3/05/95 (KCAL).
Cast: Wil Shriner (Host), George Lucas, Skip Lange, Susan Bonds, Tony Baxter, Michael Eisner.
This salute to Disneyland's new Indiana

Jones Adventure attraction begins with a look back at the opening of the Park, including clips from the opening special, *Dateline: Disneyland.* Celebrity guests, each attired in Indiana Jones–style hats, provide their thoughts on the ride as they enjoy an elaborate party in Adventureland.

Production Note:

- Celebrities interviewed at the opening party include Fran Drescher, Dennis Miller, Elliott Gould, Tony Danza, Meredith Baxter, Brad Savage, Clyde Kusatsu, Jenna von Oy, Lindsay Wagner, Joe Roth, Keenan Ivory Wayans, Arnold Schwarzenegger, John Stamos, Dean Cain, Jodie Sweetin, Taran Noah Smith, Dan Aykroyd, Lori Petty, Finola Hughes, Amy Hill, Bill Farmer, and Wayne Gretzky.

FREAKY FRIDAY (TV version) Airdates (2-hour format): 5/06/95, 3/02/96 (ABC).
Cast: Shelley Long (Ellen Andrews), Gaby Hoffman (Annabelle Andrews), Catlin Adams (Mrs. Barab), Sandra Bernhard (Frieda Debny), Andrew Bilgore (Mr. Sweet), Eileen Brennan (Principal Handel), Drew Carey (Stan Horner), Carol Kane (Librarian/Miss Futterman), Kevin Krakower (Herbie), Taylor Negron (Cary), Alan Rosenberg (Bill Davidson), Katherine Cortez (Mrs. Tarr), Joe Costanza (Construction Worker), E.J. de la Pena (Bully Kid), Mandi Douglas (Ninth Grader), John Dunbar (Teacher), John Carlos Frey (Miguel), Reagan Gomez-Preston (Heather), Peter Gregory (Joe), Jackie Hoffman (Coach Tyser), Andrew Keegan (Luke), Benjamin Lum (Master Lee), Gale Mayron (Salesgirl), Asher Metchik (Ben Andrews), Alyssa T. Poblador (Brynne), Cindy Ricalde (Seamstress), Danny Rimmer (Bully Kid), Natanya Ross (Jackie), Kate Sargeant (Gina), Marla Sokoloff (Rachel), Candy Trabucco (Miss Delia), Arsenio "Sonny" Trinidad (He Ho Lee), Thomas A. Woolen (Construction Worker).
Ellen Andrews is a single mother with a clothing business that is facing a sea of red ink. Things aren't much better at home, for she is always getting into arguments with her daughter, Annabelle. On Friday the 13th, both of them think "it would be nice to have her life" at the same time, and somehow they switch places with each other. Trapped in each other's bodies, they have to find a way to get through the day without anyone discovering their secret while they try to reverse the spell.

FUNNY, YOU DON'T LOOK 200: A CONSTITUTIONAL VAUDEVILLE   Airdate: 10/12/87 (ABC).

Cast: Richard Dreyfuss, Richard Belzer, Hamilton Camp, Emilio Estevez, Sir John Gielgud, Whoopi Goldberg, Bill Maher, Judd Nelson, Randy Newman, Rhea Perlman, Ally Sheedy, Jeffrey Tambor, Lily Tomlin, Bruce Vilanch, Lucy Webb, Henry Winkler, Miguel Alamo, The Beastie Boys, Lisa Bonet, Jill Eikenberry, Michael J. Fox, Goldie Hawn, Amy Irving, Marlee Matlin, Elizabeth Peña, Laurie Rubin, Steven Spielberg, Barbra Streisand, Michael Tucker, James Woods, Carmen Zapata, Jeffrey Kramer (Man Posting Bill of Rights), Jeramie Rain (Man on Bench), Patricia Gordon (Woman on Bench), Joseph Chander (Man on Bench), Eric Gilliom (Boy in Foxhole), Tim Haldeman (Man), Leigh Ann Orsi (Little Girl), Allen Hall (Rapper), Raymond Henderson (Rapper), Vernell Jones (Rapper), Carlos D. McGahee (Rapper), Reginald Singleton (Rapper), Anthony Singleton (Rapper). With the Voice Talents of: Wilford Brimley (Constitution), Royal Dano, Bill Farmer (Goofy), Eddie Carroll (Jiminy Cricket), Tony Anselmo (Donald Duck), Wayne Allwine (Mickey Mouse), S. Mark Jordan, Harvey Kalmenson.

This salute to the U.S. Constitution's 200th birthday features a medley of celebrities sharing their thoughts on freedom and liberty.

Production Notes:

- Most of the listed celebrities are seen in a brief opening number.
- As he gives a history lesson, Jiminy Cricket uses a blackboard as in his old appearances on *The Mickey Mouse Club*, and remarks, "I haven't done this in a long time!"

GOING BONKERS   Airdate (2-hour format): 9/04/93 (Syndicated).

Voices: Charlie Adler (Toon Siren), Tony Anselmo (Donald Duck), Michael Bell, Jeff Bennett (Jitters D. Dog), Earl Boen (Police Chief Leonard Kanifky), Rodger Bumpass (Grumbles Grizzly), Corey Burton, Nancy Cartwright (Fawn Deer), Jesse Corti, Jim Cummings (Bonkers D. Bobcat, Lucky Piquel), David Doyle (W.W. Wacky), Sherry Lynn (Marilyn Piquel), Frank Welker (Fall Apart Rabbit, Toots, Toon Radio), April Winchell (Dylandra "Dyl" Piquel).

This one-hour premiere of the new *Disney's Bonkers* series begins as a group of once popular cartoon characters discover that they're no longer in demand, for they have been replaced by muscle-bound movie stars.

Production Note:

- The first portion of this special is included in the *Disney's Bonkers* series as the episodes *Going Bonkers* and *Gone Bonkers*.

GOING TO MICKEY'S TOONTOWN

Airdate (30-minute format): 1/25/93 (KCAL).

Cast: Cary Berglund.

Host Cary Berglund gets a special tour of Toontown, the newest addition to Disneyland and learns that Walt Disney built it when Disneyland first opened so the cartoon characters had a place to live. After years of secrecy, the residents of Toontown have finally decided to open the gates to the public.

GOOD MORNING, VIETNAM   Airdates (2½-hour format, NBC): 2/24/91, 2/03/92.

This 1987 theatrical release stars Robin Williams as an irrepressible military radio announcer in Vietnam.

GOOF TROOP CHRISTMAS, A   Airdates: 12/05/92, 12/11/93 (Syndicated).

Voices: Nancy Cartwright (Pistol), Jim Cummings (Pete), Bill Farmer (Goofy), Dana Hill (Max), Rob Paulsen (P.J.), Frank Welker (Grizz, Waffles, Chainsaw), April Winchell (Peg).

This holiday special begins with a new *Goof Troop* story, *Have Yourself a Goofy Little Christmas*. With the holidays fast approaching, Goofy goes overboard on decorating, as usual. This prompts Pete to leave town before Goofy can blow out the power. Pete and his family head off to a ski vacation in Aspirin, Colorado, unaware that Goofy and Max are right behind them.

The second half of the 1992 version features *Up a Tree*, *The Art of Skiing*, and a behind-the-scenes look at some of Disney's animated classics.

The second half of the 1993 version features *On Ice*, *The Hockey Champ*, and *Toy Tinkers*.

GRAND OPENING OF EURO DISNEY, THE

Airdate (2-hour format): 4/11/92 (CBS).

Cast: Melanie Griffith (Hostess), Don Johnson (Host), Jose Carreras, Cher, Isabelle and Paul Duchesnay, Gloria Estefan and

Miami Sound Machine, The Gipsy Kings, Angela Lansbury, The Four Tops, The Temptations, Tina Turner, Pat O'Brien, Michel Vallete (Jules Verne), Steve Jones (Announcer).

The newest Disney theme park is ready for its grand opening. Hosts Don Johnson and Melanie Griffith are joined by Pat O'Brien and they look at some of the celebrities who attended a special party earlier that day. After a brief speech by Michael Eisner, a children's choir sings *When You Wish upon a Star* in French as the Sleeping Beauty Castle is lit and fireworks brighten the sky.

Production Note:

- When Euro Disneyland failed to attract the hoped for crowds, the ambitious expansion plans described in this show were put on hold.

GRAND OPENING OF WALT DISNEY WORLD, THE   Airdate (90-minute format): 10/29/71 (NBC).
Cast: Julie Andrews, Glen Campbell, Buddy Hackett, Jonathan Winters, Bob Hope, Chuck Hearn, Mark Donahue, Bobby Unser, Jackie Stewart, Mary Gregory.

The construction is over and Walt Disney World is ready to open. Julie Andrews and Glen Campbell host the celebration, which features guest stars performing across the Park.

HAND THAT ROCKS THE CRADLE, THE
Airdate (2-hour 15-minute format): 11/06/94 (ABC).
This 1992 theatrical release stars Rebecca De Mornay as a psychopathic woman who takes a job as a nanny.

HAPPY BIRTHDAY DONALD DUCK
Aired as a special on 4/04/79 on NBC, this episode was first broadcast on 11/21/56 as part of the anthology series under the title *At Home with Donald Duck*.

HERBIE DAY AT DISNEYLAND   Airdate: 7/11/74 (Syndicated).
Cast: Bob McAllister, Bob Crane, Helen Hayes, Keenan Wynn, Burl Ives, Binny Barnes, Fred MacMurray, The Kids of the Kingdom, Long Beach Band.

To promote the upcoming release of *Herbie Rides Again*, the Studio sponsors a contest featuring decorated Volkswagens. The program also features the opening of *America Sings at Disneyland*.

Production Note:

- The first "Herbie Day" was held on March 23, 1969, to promote *The Love Bug*. The promotion was so successful that the Studio held a new contest on June 30, 1974. The grand prize was a 1974 Volkswagen Beetle.

HOMEWARD BOUND: THE INCREDIBLE JOURNEY   Airdates (2-hour format): 10/01/94, 12/23/95 (ABC).
This 1993 theatrical remake of *The Incredible Journey* uses narration by Michael J. Fox, Sally Field, and Don Ameche to tell the story from the animals' point of view.

HONEY, I SHRUNK THE KIDS   Airdates (2-hour format, CBS): 11/26/91, 4/25/92.
This 1989 theatrical release stars Rick Moranis, Matt Frewer, Marcia Strassman, Thomas Brown, Jared Rushton, Amy O'Neill, and Robert Oliveri in the story of a scientist who accidentally shrinks his children and neighbors to microscopic size.

HORSE CALLED COMANCHE, A
Released theatrically in 1958 as *Tonka*, this film was aired on 1/29/77 with *Wonders of the Water World* as part of the *NBC All-Disney Saturday Night at the Movies* series of specials.

HURRICANE HANNAH
Aired on 11/01/75 with *The Absent-Minded Professor* as part of the *NBC All-Disney Saturday Night at the Movies* series of specials, this episode was first aired on the anthology series.

IN THE NICK OF TIME   Airdate (2-hour format): 12/16/91 (NBC).
Cast: Lloyd Bridges (Santa Claus), Michael Tucker (Ben Talbot), Allison LaPlaca (Susan Rosewell), A. Martinez (Charlie Misch), Jessica DiCicco (Aimee Misch), Cleavon Little (Freddy), Jenny Parsons (Melina Liviakis), Wayne Robson (Melvin), Audrey Webb (Sheila), Michael Lamport (Godfrey), Lucy Filippone (Sheila), Ken James (Ridley), Thomas Hauft (Figgus), Conrad Bergschneider (Louie), Matt Birman (Guard), Richard Blackburn (William), Steve Cliffe (Gang Member #1), Elvira Graham (Tough Chick), Ted Hanlan (Ward Santa), Phil Jarrett (Cop), Jamie Jones (Nick), Corey Macri (Gang Member #2), Martin Martinuzzi (Bartender), Adrian Paul (Interviewer), Bryan L. Renfro

(Folksinger), Jackie Richardson (Nurse), Roland Smith (Messenger), Thick Wilson (Street Santa).

The annual Christmas preparations at the North Pole are going well until one of the elves discovers that Santa's reign is about to end. According to the rules set down in a 1,200-year-old manuscript by the original Saint Nicholas, each Santa can only reign 300 years. Now, the current Santa has only one week to find a replacement or there won't be any more Santa at all.

INNOCENT MAN, AN   Airdate (2½-hour format): 3/13/94 (ABC).
This 1989 theatrical release stars Tom Selleck as a man who is framed as a drug dealer by two corrupt police officers.

IRON WILL   Airdate (2-hour format): 1/06/96.
This 1994 theatrical release stars MacKenzie Astin, Kevin Spacey, and David Ogden Stiers in the story of a boy who must endure a grueling dogsled race to earn money for his family.

IT'S TOUGH TO BE A BIRD
This 1969 animated theatrical release aired on 12/14/74 with *The Three Lives of Thomasina* and *Arizona Sheepdog* as part of the *NBC All-Disney Saturday Night at the Movies* series of specials.

JACK BENNY HOUR, THE   Airdate: 11/03/65 (NBC).
Cast: Walt Disney, Jack Benny, Bob Hope, Elke Sommer.
Walt Disney made an unusual guest appearance on this Jack Benny special. The Disney segment features Walt in his office being visited by Jack Benny. Jack tells Walt he wants to reward the crew of his latest show by taking them to Disneyland and returns the favor by offering Walt free publicity on the show.

JOURNEY OF NATTY GANN, THE   Airdate (2-hour format): 9/03/88 (ABC).
This 1985 theatrical releases stars Meredith Salenger and John Cusack in the story of a teenage girl who undertakes a perilous journey, accompanied by her pet wolf, to find her father. It also aired on the anthology series on 10/04/87.

JULIE ANDREWS HOUR, THE   Airdate: 11/22/72 (ABC).
Cast: Julie Andrews, The Young Americans,

Alice Ghostley, Donald O'Connor, Adriana Caselotti.

This episode of Julie Andrews's weekly variety series is a tribute to the music and animated characters made popular by Walt Disney.

JUNGLE BOOK REUNION   Airdate (30-minute format): 7/19/90 (Syndicated).
Cast: Downtown Julie Brown (Hostess), The Mouseketeers, The Disney Dancers, Michael Eisner.
Downtown Julie Brown is the hostess of this salute to the theatrical rerelease of *The Jungle Book.*

Production Note:

• Downtown Julie Brown was a hostess on MTV. This show spoofed that cable television network, calling itself JTV for "Jungle Television."

KNIFE AND GUN CLUB, THE   Airdate: 7/30/90 (ABC).
Cast: Dorian Harewood (Dr. Jack Ducette), Perry King (Dr. Matt Haley), Daniel Jenkins (Dr. Jeff Grail), Cynthia Bain (Nurse Nancy Gerson), Fran Bennett (Nurse Mary Falk), Judith Hoag (Dr. Annie Falk), Luis Ramos ("Figgy" Figueroa), Suzzanne Douglas (Ginny Ducette), Doug Savant (Dr. Barrow), John Finnegan (Mr. Warshawski), Ernie Lively (Ralph), Mindy Seeger (Lydia), Robert King (Dr. Scott), Laura Jacoby (Jill Durbin), Scott Colomby (Husband), Marcus Chong (George), Fabiana Udenio (Teresa Imperato), Harold Ayer (Mr. Beedle), Peggy Doyle (Mrs. Lewis), Julian Reyes (Henry), William Flatley (Security Cop), Greg McDaniel (Paramedic), Bill McIntyre (Driver), Elizabeth C. Rubino (Pregnant Woman), Robina Suwol (Tally Ryder), Bergen Williams (Parks).
Osler Hospital is in a rough, multiracial neighborhood. The emergency room, which has been nicknamed "The Knife and Gun Club" because of the high number of stabbing and gunshot victims, is run by two men who have been friends since medical school. Although the two men are very different personalities, Dr. Jack Ducette and Dr. Matt Haley are both dedicated to improving the quality of life of their patients.

Production Note:

• This was the pilot for an unsold series.

KODAK PRESENTS DISNEYLAND '59
Airdate (90-minute format): 6/15/59 (ABC).

Cast: Walt Disney, Art Linkletter, Ozzie Nelson, Harriet Nelson, David Nelson, Ricky Nelson, Julie Meade, Vice President Richard M. Nixon, Patricia Nixon, Julie Nixon, Tricia Nixon, Fred MacMurray, June Haver, Tim Considine, Roberta Shore, Annette Funicello, Chris Miller, Joanna Miller, Roy Williams, Meredith Willson, Adm. Charles C. Kirkpatrick, Stuart Nelson, Mildred Nelson, Nels Nelson, Kirk Nelson, Karl Nelson, Elliott Brothers Band, Robert Loggia, Tom Tryon, John Russell, Clint Eastwood, Rex Allen, Bobbie Diamond, Guy Williams, Gene Sheldon, Henry Calvin, Lawrence Welk, The Lennon Sisters, Chill Wills, Don DeFore, Sammy Tong, Marvin Miler, Kevin Corcoran, Tommy Kirk, Dennis Hopper, Jeffrey Hunter, Hedda Hopper, Mr. and Mrs. Roy Disney, Jon Provost and Lassie, Zasu Pitts, Mr. and Mrs. Edgar Bergen and family, Bob Cummings, Jock Mahoney, Wally Boag, George Putnam.

Disneyland Park has been open for four years and it's time to unveil all the newest additions. This live special opens with Walt Disney and Art Linkletter in front of Sleeping Beauty Castle, followed by visits to the Park's newest attractions.

Production Notes:

- This show can be considered a "lost" episode, as no known copies exist. It was broadcast live, and although it is believed to have been recorded on videotape, no copies have been located.
- The Studio does not possess a list of the credits for this show. It is known that the scenes of the new attractions were directed by Ham Luske.
- After the show aired, the Studio received numerous letters pointing out that they flew the Danish flag on the Matterhorn, not the Swiss.

KRAFT SALUTES DISNEYLAND'S 25TH ANNIVERSARY   Airdate: 3/06/80 (CBS).
Cast: Danny Kaye, Michael Jackson, The Osmonds, Adam Rich, Wally Boag, Sorrell Brooke, Bart Braverman, Danielle Brisebois, Ruth Buzzi, Peggy Cass, Quinn Cummings, Buddy Ebsen, Jamie Farr, Annette Funicello, Steven Furst, Fred Grandy, Linda Gray, Gregory Harrison, The International Children's Choir, Ted Lange, Richard Paul, Joan Prather, Kim Richards, The Royal Cavaliers Youth Band, Ronnie Schell, John Schneider, Judy Norton Taylor, Sal Viscuso, Robert Walden, Patrick Wayne, Anson Williams, Jo Anne Worley.

Disneyland's 25th birthday is hosted by Danny Kaye and features numerous cameo appearances by guest celebrities. Kaye, in the guises of foreign tourists and Park employees, introduces the various segments that provide a look at many of the popular attractions and shows.

Production Notes:

- This special later aired on the anthology series on 9/14/80 as *Disneyland's 25th Anniversary.*
- Many of the guest stars on this special donated their fees to charity, enabling underprivileged children to visit Disneyland.

KRAFT SALUTES WALT DISNEY WORLD'S 10TH ANNIVERSARY   Airdate: 1/21/82 (CBS).
Cast: Eileen Brennan (Aunt Angelique Lane), Larry Gatlin and the Gatlin Brothers Band, Dean Jones (Mr. Lane), Michele Lee (Mrs. Lane), Dana Plato (Daughter), John Schneider (Himself), Ricky Schroeder (Son).

This special follows the adventures of the Lane family as they visit Walt Disney World for a vacation.

LAST ELECTRIC KNIGHT, THE
Aired on 9/19/86 as a special on ABC to promote the series *Sidekicks,* this episode was first aired on the anthology series.

LEFTY   Airdate: 10/22/80 (NBC).
Carol Johnston is a champion gymnast despite a physical limitation that would have kept most other people from competing. Carol only has one arm, thus earning her the nickname "Lefty." This documentary begins with a look at Carol's life, including comments from her, her family, and her friends on how she has learned to minimize the effects of her disability.

Production Notes:

- This true story was planned as an episode of the anthology series when the producers saw Carol Johnston interviewed on a sports program. The Studio first made a featurette for the Walt Disney Educational Media Company, which won a CINE Golden Eagle Award.
- A 6-month shooting schedule was necessary to match Carol's competition timetable. On her first day of filming, she fell and tore two ligaments, causing an additional delay.

- This special was later repeated on 4/19/81 as part of the anthology series.
- This show was released theatrically overseas in 1981.

LT. ROBIN CRUSOE, U.S.N. Airdate (2-hour format): 12/11/76 (NBC).

This 1965 theatrical release starring Dick Van Dyke as a pilot stranded on a remote island aired as a special on 12/11/76 on NBC with the Academy Award–winning featurette *Nature's Half Acre*.

LIFE WITH MIKEY Airdates (2-hour format): 2/10/96, 8/03/96 (ABC).

This 1992 theatrical release starring Michael J. Fox and Christina Vidal is the story of a failing theatrical agent who turns a street urchin into a star.

LION KING, THE: A MUSICAL JOURNEY WITH ELTON JOHN Airdate (30-minute format): 6/15/94 (ABC).

Cast: Elton John, Tim Rice, Roy E. Disney, Jeffrey Katzenberg, Don Hahn, Ron Minkoff, Hans Zimmer, James Earl Jones, Jeremy Irons, Andreas Deja.

This special takes a look at the music from Disney's newest animated release, *The Lion King*. Composer Tim Rice wrote the music, and at his suggestion, Elton John was brought on board as the lyricist. The two men provide details on how they worked together on the film score.

Production Note:

- This special was an "infomercial," created and paid for by Disney. All of the commercials were for Disney films, videos, and theme parks. A special introduction by the cast of *Home Improvement* aired immediately before the special.

LION KING CELEBRATION, THE Airdates: 11/24/94, 12/09/95 (*A Roaring Good Time*) (KCAL).

Cast: Ross Crystal.

The first part of this program aired on The Disney Channel as *The Making of The Lion King*. *The Lion King Celebration* portion of the show includes interviews with cast members as they gather at the El Capitan theater in Hollywood for the film's premiere.

MAGIC OF ALADDIN, THE Airdate: 7/18/93 (Syndicated).

Cast: John Rhys-Davies (Host), Ron Clements, Glen Keane, Mark Henn, John Musker, Duncan Marjoribanks, Eric Goldberg, Andreas Deja, Alan Menken, Tim Rice, Lea Salonga, Brad Kane, Mike Davis, Steve Davison, Robert Ponce, Marilyn Soto.

Host John Rhys-Davies tells how Disney artists have created a new version of the ancient tale of Aladdin and the magic lamp, and the new *Aladdin* parade at Disneyland.

Production Note:

- An edited version of this special was used in the 1993 version of *Winnie the Pooh, and Christmas Too.*

MAKING OF DISNEYLAND'S INDIANA JONES ADVENTURE, THE Airdate (20-minute format): 7/18/95 (CBS).

Cast: Karen Allen, John Rhys-Davies, George Lucas, Skip Lange, Tony Baxter.

Karen Allen, who co-starred in *Raiders of the Lost Ark*, travels through the Indian jungle to the eerie Temple of the Forbidden Eye, recently discovered by Indiana Jones. Old newsreel footage tells the story of the discovery and the legend of Mara, the goddess who inhabits the temple. When Allen arrives at the temple, it's revealed that she is really at Disneyland. Her co-star from the film, John Rhys-Davies, gives her a tour of the exciting new thrill ride.

Production Note:

- This program was originally planned as a 30-minute special but was preempted for news coverage of the Oklahoma City bombing. It was later aired as the opening to *Indiana Jones and the Last Crusade*, as well as being shown on The Disney Channel.

MAKING OF THE NHL'S MIGHTY DUCKS, THE Airdate: 10/10/93 (KCAL).

Cast: Tom Murray (Host), Jack Ferreira, Pam Haynes, Jeff Krisch, Tony Tavares, Pierre Gauthier, Richard Green, Paul Kariya, Allan Bester, Stu Grimson, Ron Wilson, Dr. David Crouch, Blynn Deniro, Mike Laverty.

This look at Disney's "The Mighty Ducks" professional hockey team begins as the players take to the ice for the first time in public. Disney started putting the team together after Michael Eisner saw a new arena under construction in Anaheim and learned the owners didn't have a pro hockey team to play there. He decided to get a franchise, which was granted on December 10, 1992. The show provides a time line of the next steps in the team's brief history.

Production Note:

- An edited version of this special was shown on The Disney Channel as *The Making of The Mighty Ducks*.

MAKING OF TOY STORY, THE   Airdates: 12/02/95, 12/03/95 (KCAL).
Cast: Wil Shriner (Host).
This *Toy Story* special begins with *The Making of Toy Story* from The Disney Channel. It is followed by *To Infinity and Beyond!: A Toy Story Adventure*, an interactive funhouse based on the film.

MARRYING MAN, THE   Airdate (2-hour format): 6/23/96 (ABC).
This 1991 theatrical release stars real-life couple Kim Basinger and Alec Baldwin in the story of a man who is forced into a marriage and the problems that result when he can't decide if he should stay married or not.

MARY POPPINS
This 1964 theatrical release starring Julie Andrews and Dick Van Dyke was aired as a special as follows in a 3-hour format: 11/22/81 (CBS), 11/25/82 (CBS), 11/24/88 (ABC), 4/15/90 (ABC). It also aired on the anthology series on 5/03/87 and 4/15/90.

MICKEY AND NORA   Airdate (30-minute format): 6/26/87 (CBS).
Cast: Ted Wass (Mickey), Barbara Treutelaar (Nora), George Furth (Rip), Nancy Lenehan (Vivian), Cleavant Derricks (Marvin), Florence Stanley (Adele), Jessie Lawrence Ferguson (Colonel Ntsunge), Miriam Flynn (Betty).
After retiring from the CIA, ex-spy Mickey decides to settle down and enjoy a normal life, but no one will believe he has really left the espionage business. As a result, he and his wife, Nora, find themselves in some very unusual situations.

Production Note:

- This unsold pilot was aired as part of the *CBS Summer Playhouse*.
- CBS originally ordered six episodes, but canceled the order after the pilot was completed.

MICKEY'S CHRISTMAS CAROL   Airdates (NBC): 12/10/84, 12/22/85, 12/15/86, 12/04/87, 12/17/90 (*The Rescuers Down Under* version); 12/13/91 (*Fantasia* version, CBS); 12/01/93 (*The Nightmare before Christmas* version, CBS), 12/22/94 (*The Jungle Book* version, CBS); 12/21/95 (*The Hunchback of Notre Dame* version, CBS).
The show opens as Mickey and Donald discuss what Christmas means to them. This is followed by *Mickey's Christmas Carol*, a 1983 theatrical release nominated for an Academy Award for Best Short Subject.
Beginning in 1988, edited versions of this show were used to promote upcoming animated releases.

Production Note:

- Bridge sequences were produced with voice-overs by Wayne Allwine as Mickey Mouse and Clarence Nash as Donald Duck. Artwork was used similar to the title sequence from *Mickey's Christmas Carol*.

MIRACLE CHILD   Airdate (2-hour format): 4/06/93 (NBC).
Cast: Crystal Bernard (Lisa Porter), Cloris Leachman (Doc Betty), John Terry (Buck Sanders), Graham Sack (Lyle Sanders), Grace Zabriskie (Adeleine Newberry), George D. Wallace (Grandpa), Lexi Randall (Taffy Marshall), Gary Grubbs (John Marshall), Barnard Hughes (Judge), Becca Allen (Willa Marshall), Ryk O. (Cue Ball), Rick Galloway (English), Tom Chapman (Old Jack), Tom Archie (Sheriff Peak), Tim Goodwin (The Mailman), Brett Cipes (The Whittler).
Lisa Porter, a young widowed mother living in the city, feels that she can't raise her baby there properly. She decides the child would have a better life in Clements Pond, a small town near where she grew up. Lisa's troubles begin when she plans to leave the baby girl where she will be discovered by Doc Betty, a local physician, in hopes that the doctor will care for the child. A mishap has the town believing the baby is from heaven.

Production Note:

- This program was filmed on location in Gainesville, Florida.

MOM FOR CHRISTMAS, A   Airdates (2-hour format, NBC): 12/17/90, 12/22/91.
Cast: Olivia Newton-John (Amy Miller), Juliet Sorcey (Jessica Slocum), Doug Sheehan

(Jim Slocum), Carmen Argenziano (Sergeant Morelli), Aubrey Morris (Nicholas), James Piddock (Wilkins), Doris Roberts (Philomena), Elliot Moss Greenebaum (Chip Wright), Erica Mitchell (Stephanie Clark), Jesse Vincent (Teddy O'Neill), Brett Harrelson (Kendall), Steve Russell (Mr. Milliman), Gregory Procaccino (Detective Price), Ron Lautore (Fire Captain), Helen Whitelow, Justin DiPego, Kathy Lubow (Lora), Paula Ingram (Mrs. Garcia).

Teenager Jessica Slocum is upset that she doesn't have a mother to help her grow up. Strange things happen when she wins a free Christmas wish at a department store.

Production Notes:

- This special followed *Mickey's Christmas Carol* on 12/17/90.
- The show was filmed on location in Cincinnati.

MONSANTO NIGHT PRESENTS WALT DISNEY'S AMERICA ON PARADE   Airdate: 4/03/76 (Syndicated).
Cast: Red Skelton (Host), Jan Arvan, Francine York, Kate Murtagh, Arnold Soboloff, Basil Hoffman, The Kids of the Kingdom.

The Disney theme parks are celebrating the American bicentennial with America on Parade. Red Skelton hosts this look at the parade and its unique floats and costumes, all of which were designed to represent milestones in American history.

Production Notes:

- *Monsanto Night* was the title used for a series of specials sponsored by Monsanto during the 1970s. This was the 16th show in the series and was the only one with a Disney theme.
- Although this show included scenes of the parade from both Disneyland and Walt Disney World, the musical numbers were all filmed at Disneyland.

MOON-SPINNERS, THE
This 1964 theatrical release starring Hayley Mills aired on 11/26/76 in a 3-hour format with *Prowlers of the Everglades* as a "pre-Thanksgiving special." While it officially was part of the *NBC All-Disney Saturday Night at the Movies* series, it was run this time on a Wednesday.

MUPPETS CELEBRATE JIM HENSON, THE
Airdate: 11/21/90 (CBS).

Cast: Harry Belafonte, Carol Burnett, Ray Charles, John Denver, Steven Spielberg, Frank Oz.

As the Muppets work on a production number intended as a tribute to the late Jim Henson, they realize that they're not sure who Henson was. Some of them remember that he was "the guy down there" as they spot their puppeteers, but Fozzie decides they need to learn more about him. Clips from various Muppet productions follow, showing Henson's wide range of interests.

Production Note:

- David Gumpel and Girish Bhargava won an Emmy for Editing, Miniseries or Special (Multi-camera Production) for this special.

MUSICAL CHRISTMAS AT WALT DISNEY WORLD, A   Airdate: 12/18/93 (ABC).
Cast: Robert Urich (Host), Kathie Lee Gifford, Trisha Yearwood, Peabo Bryson, Andy Williams, Natalie Cole, Lea Salonga, Steven Curtis Chapman, Lorrie Morgan.

Entertainers gather at Walt Disney World for a holiday salute.

MYSTERIES OF THE DEEP
This 1959 theatrical featurette show aired as a special on 10/26/74 with *The Parent Trap* as part of the *NBC All-Disney Saturday Night at the Movies* series.

NATURE'S HALF ACRE
This 1951 theatrical featurette aired on 12/11/76 with *Lt. Robin Crusoe, U.S.N.* as part of the *NBC All-Disney Saturday Night at the Movies* series of specials.

NATURE'S STRANGEST CREATURES
Airdate: 3/08/75 (NBC).
This 1959 theatrical featurette aired as a special on 3/08/75 with *Pollyanna* as part of the *NBC All-Disney Saturday Night at the Movies* series.

NBC SALUTES THE 25TH ANNIVERSARY OF "THE WONDERFUL WORLD OF DISNEY"   Airdate (each in a 2-hour format)—Part 1: 9/13/78. Part 2: 9/17/78 (NBC).
Cast: Ron Howard, Suzanne Somers, Ed Asner, Valerie Bertinelli, Big Bird, Bill Bixby, Ray Charles, Scatman Crothers, Buddy Ebsen, Crystal Gayle, Melissa Gilbert, Don Haggerty, Phil Harris, Bob Hope, Bruce Jenner, Gavin

MacLeod, Fred MacMurray, Ricardo Montalban, Fess Parker.

This retrospective honoring the anthology series takes place over two nights. In the first part, hosts Ron Howard and Suzanne Somers look at the birth of the anthology series.

Part 2 begins with a look at the films that preceded *Dumbo*, then shows *Dumbo* in its entirety.

New Kids on the Block at Disney-MGM Studios: Wildest Dreams   Airdate: 1/25/91 (ABC).

Cast: Jonathan Knight, Jordan Knight, Joe McIntyre, Donnie Wahlberg, Danny Wood, Kareem Abdul-Jabbar, Khrystyne Haje, Mr. Olympia Lee Haney, Steve "Biscuit" Walker, Chick Hearn (Himself), Pam Hild (Marian), Mike Speller (The Director).

Framed as a documentary, this show features the band New Kids on the Block in a series of fantasies as they prepare for a concert at the Disney-MGM Studios Theme Park.

Newsies! Newsies! See All about It

Airdate (30-minute format): 3/28/92 (Syndicated).

Cast: Max Casella, Aaron Lohr, Arvie Lowe, Jr.

This preview of *Newsies*, Disney's newest musical feature, features three of its stars, Max Casella, Aaron Lohr, and Arvie Lowe. Between scenes from the film, fellow actors Christian Bale, David Moscow, Trey Parker, Marty Belafsky, Shon Greenblatt, Bill Pullman, and Ivan Dudynsky, film director and choreographer Kenny Ortega, and his assistant Peggy Holmes all comment on the experience.

Nikki, Wild Dog of the North

This 1961 theatrical release was aired on 10/16/76 with *The Great Locomotive Chase* as part of the *NBC All-Disney Saturday Night at the Movies* series of specials.

Old Yeller

This 1957 theatrical release first aired with *A Country Coyote Goes Hollywood* and *Pecos Bill* as part of the *NBC All-Disney Saturday Night at the Movies* series of specials on 2/14/76. It later aired on the anthology series in two parts on 11/09/80 and 11/16/80 and in a 2-hour format on 6/08/86.

The 1986 broadcast aired as a *Disney Summer Classic*, and was followed by a featurette on the making of *The Great Mouse Detective*.

Production Note:

- A behind-the-scenes look at the filming of this movie was featured in the anthology episode *The Best Doggoned Dog in the World*.

On Vacation with Mickey Mouse and Friends

Aired on 4/11/79 as a special on NBC, this episode first aired on the anthology series under the title *On Vacation*.

One Good Cop   Airdate (2-hour format): 10/31/93 (NBC).

This 1991 theatrical release stars Michael Keaton as a police officer forced to take drug money to care for the children of his murdered partner.

One Hour in Wonderland   Airdate: 12/25/50 (NBC).

Cast: Walt Disney, Edgar Bergen, Charlie McCarthy, Mortimer Snerd, Kathryn Beaumont, Bobby Driscoll, Hans Conried (Magic Mirror), The Firehouse Five Plus Two, Diane Disney, Sharon Disney.

The Studio's first experiment with television features a party to celebrate the upcoming animated release *Alice in Wonderland*. Walt hosts the program, which includes scenes from earlier films and a behind-the-scenes look at *Alice*.

Production Notes:

- The Firehouse Five Plus Two, a jazz group consisting primarily of Studio employees, released several successful records in the '50s.
- Sponsored exclusively by Coca-Cola, this show cost $100,000 to produce, a high sum for those days.

100 Lives of Black Jack Savage, The

The pilot to the series *Disney Presents The 100 Lives of Black Jack Savage* aired as a special on 3/31/91 on NBC.

One Magic Christmas   Airdate (2-hour format): 12/23/88 (ABC).

This 1985 theatrical release stars Harry Dean Stanton as the unlikely angel sent to help Mary Steenburgen when she begins to doubt her faith.

ONE MORE MOUNTAIN   Airdates (2-hour format): 3/06/94, 6/22/96 (ABC).

Cast: Meredith Baxter (Margaret Reed), Chris Cooper (James Reed), Larry Drake (Patrick Breen), Robert Duncan McNeill (Milt Eliot), Laurie O'Brien (Elizabeth Graves), Frances Conroy (Peggy Breen), Jean Kelly (Mary Graves), James G. MacDonald (Charles Stanton), Matthew Walker (George Donner), Don S. Davis (Franklin Graves), Jean Simmons (Sarah Keyes), Grace Johnston (Virginia Reed), Lachlan Murdoch (James Reed, Jr.), Joshua Silberg (Tommy Reed), Aline Levasseur (Patty Reed), Marie Stillin (Tamsen Donner), Byron Lucas (John Snyder), Pat Johnston (Mason), Bill Croft (Mr. Keseberg), Kathe Mazur (Mrs. Keseberg), Walter Marsh (Mitchell Forster), Molly Walsh (Eliza Williams).

Based on a true incident, this movie of the week begins as Margaret Reed, a woman pioneer, joins her husband, James, on a 2,000-mile trip to California in 1846. A total of 82 settlers start the trip as part of the infamous Donner Party, using advice from a faulty guidebook, but they are soon trapped in the wilderness.

OPERATION WONDERLAND   Airdate: 6/14/51 (NBC).

Cast: Walt Disney, James Melton, Kathyrn Beaumont, Winston Hibler, Don Barclay, Jerry Colonna, Ed Wynn.

This segment of the *Ford Festival* television series starts at the NBC studios in New York, where host James Melton says that his daughter asked him to find out everything he could about Walt Disney's new picture, *Alice in Wonderland*. Glad to oblige, he went to Burbank to meet with Walt and his staff for a special look at how the film was made. The rest of the segment is a flashback of Melton's trip.

Production Note:

- Although this 10-minute segment is based on Melton visiting the Studio, he didn't actually make the trip. Instead, a stand-in was used for his scenes, and the majority of the footage was filmed from Melton's point of view.

OUR PLANET TONIGHT   Airdate: 4/22/87 (NBC).

Cast: John Houseman, Morgan Fairchild, Rich Hall, Mitchell Laurance, Jay Leno, Don Novello (Father Guido Sarducci), Martha Quinn, Jim Stahl, John Standing, Jake the Dog (Freckles).

John Houseman and Morgan Fairchild host this spoof of television magazines.

Production Note:

- This pilot for an unsold series was created by the team responsible for the *Airplane!* and *Police Squad* movies.

OUR SHINING MOMENT   Airdate: 6/02/91 (NBC).

Cast: Cindy Pickett (Betty), Max Gail (John McGuire, Jr.), Jonathan Brandis (Michael "Scooter" McGuire), Seth Green (Wheels), Shawn Levy (J.J.), Luanna Ponce (Maureen), Don Ameche (John "Papa" McGuire, Sr.), Alec Burden (Father Hogan), Sonia Banman (Lois Jessel), George Catalano (Officer Harmsen), Mike Iacobucci (Teenage Boy), Bill Dow (Barney), Alvin Lee Sanders (Mr. Rahill).

In a series of flashbacks, Michael "Scooter" McGuire looks back at his childhood in the Midwest during the 1960s. He recalls how he was thrown out of school in 1963 and was too ashamed to go home. He hid in the park, where he was shocked to learn that his father had a secret; he had lost his job. Father and son soon came to share a bond that has lasted through the years.

OUTRAGEOUS FORTUNE   Airdates (2-hour format): 11/19/89, 7/26/92 (ABC).

This 1987 theatrical release stars Shelley Long and Bette Midler as two actresses who become romantically involved with a deadly spy.

PARENT TRAP, THE

This 1961 theatrical release starring Hayley Mills as identical twins first aired with *Mysteries of the Deep* on 10/26/74 as part of the *NBC All-Disney Saturday Night at the Movies* series of specials. It was also broadcast on 5/16/76, 5/06/79, and 4/05/87 as part of the anthology series. Most of the songs were edited from the 1979 and 1987 airings to fit a shorter time slot. It was also repeated as a special on 2/13/82 on CBS following *A Disney Valentine* and again on 5/18/89 as part of the *Disney Family Classics* series of specials.

Production Note:

- A behind-the-scenes look at the filming of this movie was featured in the episode *Titlemakers (and) Nature's Half Acre*.

PECOS BILL

First released theatrically in 1948 as part of *Melody Time*, this animated featurette aired with *A Country Coyote Goes Hollywood* and *Old Yeller* on 2/14/76 as part of the *NBC All-Disney Saturday Night at the Movies* series of specials.

PETE'S DRAGON   Airdate (2-hour format): 2/19/89 (ABC).

This 1977 theatrical release starring Helen Reddy, Jim Dale, Mickey Rooney, Red Buttons, Shelley Winters, and Sean Marshall is the story of how an orphan and his pet dragon change the lives of those in a small fishing village. It also aired on the anthology series on 9/21/86.

PLYMOUTH   Airdates (2-hour format, ABC): 5/26/91, 5/23/92.

Cast: Cindy Pickett (Addy Mathewson), Richard Hamilton (Mayor Wendell Mackenzies), Perrey Reeves (Hannah Mathewson), Matthew Brown (Jed Mathewson), Jerry Hardin (Lowell), James R. Rebhorn (Ezra), Ron Vawter (Percy), Robin Frates (Donna), Brent Fraser (Nathan Ridgefield), Anne Haney (Emily), John Thornton (Eugene Mathewson), Lindsay Price (April), Dale Midkiff (Gil Eaton), Fran Bennett (Debra), Sab Shimono (Hiro), Paul Linke (Ernie), James T. Callahan (Paddy), Carlos Gomez (Jimmy), Eugene Clark (Larry), Gary Farmer (Todd), Wendy Bowers (Bethany), Joseph Gordon-Levitt (Simon), Eric Chambers (Marshall), Jeanine Jackson (Young Woman), Erik F. Stabenau (Sean), Kyra Stempel (Rachel), Mark Phelan (Technician), Charles "Pete" Conrad, Jr. (Himself).

When Plymouth, a small logging town in the Pacific Northwest, is rendered unsafe by a toxic accident at the local UNIDAC factory, the town gets an unusual lease on life. UNIDAC is mining Helium-3 on the moon for fusion reactors on Earth and the residents of Plymouth volunteer to move there to run the operation in exchange for equity in the venture and a new town. After several years of preparation, the last of the Plymouth residents finally arrive on the moon and the town is complete again.

Production Note:

- This show was an $8 million pilot for an unsold series, making it a very expensive failure for Disney and its partners. It was intended for theatrical release in Europe.

POLLY—COMIN' HOME!   Airdate (2-hour format): 11/18/90 (NBC).

Cast: Keshia Knight Pulliam (Polly), Phylicia Rashad (Aunt Polly Harrington), Dorian Harewood (Dr. Robert Shannon), Barbara Montgomery (Mrs. Conley), Brandon Adams (Jimmy Bean), Vanessa Bell Calloway (Nancy Dodds), T.K. Carter (George Dodds), Ken Page (Mayor Warren), George Anthony Bell (Mr. Tarbell), Larry Riley (Reverend Gillis), Vickilyn Reynolds (Mrs. Tarbell), Anthony Newley (Dabney Mayhew), Celeste Holm (Miss Snow), Bilal (Cyrus), Geraldine Decker (Mrs. Beemer), Clark Johnson (Young Doctor), Barbara Perry (Mrs. Clayton), Matthew Dickens (Onlooker #1), Paul Kennedy (Onlooker #2), Ernie Lee Banks (Onlooker #3).

This musical sequel to the anthology episode *Polly* is set in Alabama in 1956. Everyone in town is glad to see Polly home from the hospital, and she can walk again. While she was away, there were some changes in town. Polly's actions help solve the town's problems.

POLLYANNA

This 1960 theatrical release starring Hayley Mills aired on 3/08/75 with *Nature's Strangest Creatures* as part of the *NBC All-Disney Saturday Night at the Movies* series of specials.

PRETTY WOMAN   Airdates (2½-hour format): 11/01/92, 10/17/93, 1/30/95, 5/11/96 (ABC).

This 1990 theatrical release stars Richard Gere and Julia Roberts in the story of a streetwalker and wealthy businessman who sweep each other off their feet.

PRINCE AND THE PAUPER, THE   Airdate: 3/26/94 (ABC).

Mickey and the Beanstalk Narrated by Corey Burton as Ludwig Von Drake.

This 1990 theatrical featurette casts Mickey Mouse in the dual roles of a lowly pauper and a lonely prince who trade places with each other. The episode concludes with a tale of Mickey, Goofy, and Pluto as Ludwig Von Drake narrates *Mickey and the Beanstalk*.

PROWLERS OF THE EVERGLADES

This 1953 *True-Life Adventure* aired on 11/26/75 with *The Moon-Spinners* as part of the *NBC All-Disney Saturday Night at the Movies* series of specials.

QUEEN: THE DAYS OF OUR LIVES
Airdate: 8/11/91 (Syndicated)

Cast: Queen (Freddie Mercury, Brian May, Roger Taylor, John Deacon), W. Axl Rose (Host), Elton John, Phil Collins, John Entwhistle, M. Hutchence, Jeff Beck, Cliff Richard, Mick Jagger, Bob Geldorf, Paul McCartney, Roy Thomas Baker.

W. Axl Rose of the rock group Guns N' Roses hosts this look at one of the music world's most successful groups, Queen. Using footage of old interviews and concerts, Rose and other music celebrities discuss the history of the group and how it created some of its biggest hits. In addition, the members of Queen look back on their careers.

Production Note:

• Disney produced this program to draw attention to Queen shortly after signing the group to Disney's new Hollywood Records subsidiary. Lead singer Freddie Mercury died of AIDS not long after this special aired.

REGIS AND KATHIE LEE: MOM'S DREAM COME TRUE   Airdate: 5/13/95 (Syndicated).

Cast: Kathie Lee Gifford, Regis Philbin.

Viewers of *Live! with Regis & Kathie Lee* had been asked to write in about the dreams special mothers in their lives might want to see fulfilled. Regis and Kathie Lee host a look at how some of those mothers had their wishes granted.

REGIS & KATHIE LEE: SPECIAL EDITION
Airdates: 9/03/88, 9/04/88 (Syndicated).

Cast: Regis Philbin, Kathie Lee Gifford, Mike Wallace, Barbara Walters.

This special promotes the addition of *LIVE! with Regis & Kathie Lee* to the Disney syndicated lineup.

RESTLESS SEA, THE   Airdate: 1/24/64 (NBC).
Narrated by Sterling Holloway, the show uses animation and time-lapse photography to explain some of the sea's deepest secrets.

Production Note:

• This show aired as part of the *Bell System Science Series* programs.

RETURN OF THE SHAGGY DOG, THE
Aired as a special in two parts on 4/13/89 and 4/20/89 as part of the *Family Classics* series of specials, this show was first aired on the anthology series.

ROARING GOOD TIME, A
See: *The Lion King Celebration.*

ROCK 'N' ROLL MOM
Aired as a special on 4/06/89 as part of the *Family Classics* series of specials, this show was first aired on the anthology series.

ROCKETEER: EXCITEMENT IN THE AIR
Airdate (30-minute format): 6/22/91 (Syndicated).

Cast: William Campbell (The Rocketeer), Dave Stevens, Joe Johnston, Timothy Dalton (Neville Sinclair), Jennifer Connelly (Jenny), Bill Winberg, Ken Brock, John Hall, Kinnie Gibson, Ken Ralston.

This special looks at Disney's 1991 theatrical release, *The Rocketeer*, hosted by the film's star, William Campbell. Rocketeer creator Dave Stevens discusses how he developed the comic book series on which the movie is based, followed by a behind-the-scenes look at the filming of the Rocketeer in flight.

ROCKETEER, THE   Airdates (2-hour format): 5/07/94, 3/16/96 (ABC).
This 1991 theatrical release stars Bill Campbell, Jennifer Connelly, and Alan Arkin in the story of a test pilot who discovers a rocket pack that lets him fly like a bird.

ROGER RABBIT AND THE SECRETS OF TOON TOWN   Airdate: 9/13/88 (CBS).

Cast: Joanna Cassidy, Tony Anselmo, Mel Blanc, Noel Blanc, Charles Fleischer, Lou Hirsch, Bob Hoskins, Gene Kelly, Christopher Lloyd, Mae Questel, Kathleen Turner, Dick Van Dyke, Friz Freleng, Chuck Jones, Ward Kimball, George Gibbs, Robert Watts, Ken Ralston, Robert Zemeckis, Steven Spielberg, Richard Williams.

This behind-the-scenes look at *Who Framed Roger Rabbit* is hosted by Joanna Cassidy, who co-stars in the film.

Production Note:

• The show was followed by a Diet Coke commercial featuring Roger and Eddie in the film's Ink and Paint Club.

RUTHLESS PEOPLE   Airdates (2-hour format): 2/05/89, 5/07/90 (ABC).
This 1986 theatrical release starring Danny DeVito, Bette Midler, Judge Reinhold, and

Helen Slater is the story of a greedy man who refuses to pay ransom to get his kidnapped wife back.

SANDY IN DISNEYLAND   Airdate: 4/10/74 (CBS).

Cast: Sandy Duncan, Ernest Borgnine, Ruth Buzzi, Ted Knight, John Davidson, Lorne Greene, The Jackson Five, Ken Loggins, Jim Messina, Doc Severinson, Marty Ingels, Alan Souse, Hank Sims (Announcer).

Sandy Duncan visits Disneyland where she is joined by a cast of celebrities and Disney characters in a variety of musical settings.

SHAGGY DOG, THE

This 1959 theatrical release starring Tommy Kirk, Fred MacMurray, Annette Funicello, and Kevin Corcoran was made in black and white and first aired on the anthology series. A colorized version was shown in two parts during the *Disney Family Classics* series of specials on ABC on 3/23/89 and 3/30/89.

SHAGGY DOG, THE (TV VERSION)

Airdates (2-hour format): 11/12/94, 6/24/95 (ABC).

Cast: Ed Begley, Jr. (Ron Daniels), Sharon Lawrence (Beth Daniels), Jon Polito (Detective Al), James Cromwell (Charlie Mulvihill), Jeremy Sisto (Trey Miller), Jordan Blake Warkol (Moochie Daniels), Sarah Lassez (Francesca), Natasha Gregson Wagner (Allison), Bobby Slayton (Coach Evans), Rick Ducommun (Officer Kelly), David Pasquesi (Officer Hanson), Scott Weinger (Wilby Daniels/The Shaggy Dog), Charles Dugan (Drunk in Cell), John C. Anders (Uniformed Officer), Gerry Del Sol (Uniformed Cop #2), Peyton Reed (Movie Usher), Ted David (Counter Person), Clare Salstrom (Girl #1).

This *Disney Family Film* remake of the 1959 theatrical release features Wilby Daniels, a teenager and would-be inventor, who finds himself cursed by a spell that turns him into a sheepdog. Wilby's problems begin when he is working in his father's museum and accidentally invokes a curse by Lucretia Borgia. Suddenly, and without warning, Wilby may turn into a dog at any time.

Production Notes:

- In a homage to *Lady and the Tramp*, Wilby is followed throughout the story by a cocker spaniel that fell in love with him while he was a dog.
- It took four real dogs, a mechanical du-

plicate, and computerized morphing to transform Wilby into a dog.

SHE STOOD ALONE   Airdate (2-hour format): 4/15/91 (NBC).

Cast: Mare Winningham (Prudence Crandall), Ben Cross (William Lloyd Garrison), Robert Desiderio (Andrew Gibson), Daniel Davis (Parker Ellsworth), Taurean Blacque (William Harris), Lisa Marie Russell (Marcia Davis), Kimberly Bailey (Sarah Harris), Monica Calhoun (Eliza Hammond), F. William Parker (Daniel Frost), H. Richard Greene (Dr. Rufus Adams), Joneal Joplin (Pardon Crandall), Harry Gibbs (Judge David Dagget), Frederic Cooke (Rev. Samuel May), Ronald William Lawrence (Frederick Olney), T. Max Graham (Sheriff George Cady), Wilson Bell (Charles), R.J. Lindsay (Whiton), Linda Kennedy (Sally Harris), Chris Anthony (Catherine Ann), Tracy Holliway (Amanda), Grady Smith (Sam Coit), Jim Deken (Clerk), Whit Reichert (Foreman), Michael Oppenheimer (Isaac Knapp).

In 1832, Prudence Crandall goes against the wishes of her strict Quaker father and opens a boarding school for girls. This isn't Prudence's only problem, for when she admits a black girl to the school, the town quickly turns against her.

Production Note:

- The show was aired as part of NBC's "Education 1st! Week."

SHIPWRECKED   Airdate (2-hour format): 2/29/92 (CBS).

This 1990 theatrical release starring Stian Smestad, Gabriel Byrne, and Louisa Haigh is the story of a young boy and girl who become involved with pirates in 1849.

SHOOT TO KILL   Airdates (2-hour format): 1/07/91, 5/13/91 (NBC).

This 1988 theatrical release starring Sidney Poitier, Tom Berenger, and Kirstie Alley is the story of a FBI agent and rugged guide who search for a young woman who was taken hostage deep in the wilderness.

SISKEL & EBERT: ACTORS ON ACTING

Airdate: 6/15/91 (Syndicated).

Cast: Gene Siskel, Roger Ebert.

The film critics interview Jodie Foster, Bruce Willis, and Michael Caine. They discuss different styles of acting, their proudest and lowest moments, and how much control performers have over their careers.

SISKEL & EBERT 500TH ANNIVERSARY SPECIAL, THE   Airdate: 6/03/89 (Syndicated).

Cast: Gene Siskel, Roger Ebert.

After fourteen years of working together, critics Gene Siskel and Roger Ebert celebrate a milestone with this show, their 500th episode.

Production Note:

• This was the first time Siskel and Ebert taped their show in front of a live audience.

SISKEL & EBERT: FUTURE OF THE MOVIES, THE   Airdate: 6/13/90 (Syndicated).

Cast: Gene Siskel, Roger Ebert, Steven Spielberg, George Lucas, Martin Scorsese.

Siskel and Ebert discuss new technologies and how they will impact movies. They are joined by famed filmmakers Steven Spielberg, George Lucas, and Martin Scorsese, who offer their thoughts on the direction of the industry.

SISKEL & EBERT HOLIDAY VIDEO GIFT GUIDE   Airdates (Syndicated): 11/28/87, 12/02/88, 12/01/89, 11/28/90, 11/30/91, 12/06/92, 12/06/93.

Cast: Gene Siskel, Roger Ebert.

Each year, the two film critics take time out from reviewing films to discuss the latest home electronic gadgets and video titles. Beginning the series in 1987, they critique interactive video games, hand-held cameras for kids, video recorders and disc players, new home video titles and publications. In following years, they are joined by celebrities who discuss their favorite video releases.

SISKEL & EBERT: IF WE PICKED THE WINNERS   Airdates (Syndicated): 3/16/89, 3/12/90, 3/15/91, 3/16/92, 3/15/93, 3/06/94, 3/25/95, 3/11/96.

Cast: Gene Siskel, Roger Ebert.

Film critics Gene Siskel and Roger Ebert show how they would vote for the Oscars if they were members of the Academy of Motion Picture Arts and Sciences. To make the show more entertaining, the two critics have kept their choices secret from each other.

SISKEL & EBERT SPECIAL, THE   Airdate: 5/21/90 (CBS).

Cast: Gene Siskel, Roger Ebert, Kathleen Turner, Danny DeVito, Garry Marshall, David Lynch, Clint Eastwood, Jack Valenti, Zalman King, Helen Mirren, Mel Gibson, Glenn Close, Franco Zeffirelli.

Film critics Siskel & Ebert take a look at current films and the careers of several Hollywood stars. Interviews with film industry leaders provide a number of differing viewpoints and predictions on what makes a film successful.

SISKEL & EBERT TALK ABOUT NEW BLACK CINEMA   Airdate: 6/05/92 (Syndicated).

Cast: Gene Siskel, Roger Ebert, John Singleton, Wesley Snipes, Whoopi Goldberg, Spike Lee.

Film critics Gene Siskel and Roger Ebert host this look at the rising importance of black filmmakers, both in front of and behind the camera.

SISTER ACT   Airdates (2-hour format): 2/13/95, 1/29/96 (NBC).

This 1992 theatrical release stars Whoopi Goldberg as a nightclub entertainer who is forced to go into hiding as a nun to escape from killers.

SNOW WHITE LIVE   Airdate (90-minute format): 1980 (HBO).

Cast: Mary Jo Salerno (Snow White), Richard Bowne (Prince Charming), Thomas Ruisinger (The King), Charles Hall (The Witch, The Mirror), Bruce Sherman (The Huntsman), Yolande Bavan (Luna), David Pursley (Chamberlain), Don Potter (Doc), Richard Day (Happy), Benny Freigh (Grumpy), Louis Carry (Sneezy), Jay Edward Allen (Bashful), Jerry Riley (Sleepy), Michael E. King (Dopey), Anne Francine (The Queen).

This stage production of *Snow White and the Seven Dwarfs* is taped in front of a live audience at Radio City Music Hall.

SOUNDS OF AMERICA, THE   Airdate: 2/17/61 (NBC).

Cast: Gene Nelson, Jacques d'Amboise, The Earl Twins (Jane Earl, Ruth Earl), The Ralph Brewster Singers, Dwight Marfield, Scott Lane.

This episode in the *Bell Telephone Hour* television series is set at Disneyland, which provides the backdrop as the entertainers re-create the feel of America's past. As the program begins, the performers tour Disneyland aboard a steam train, singing about the various attractions as they pass by. This includes a look at Fantasyland, the Grand Canyon Diorama, and Main Street U.S.A.

Production Notes:

- In order to film at the Park, the crew had to practice at night, and film on Mondays and Tuesdays when Disneyland was normally closed to the public. As a result, this one-hour program took six weeks to shoot.
- Jacques d'Amboise returned three decades later as a guest on The Disney Channel's version of *The Mickey Mouse Club.*

Splash Airdates (2-hour format): 11/09/86, 9/26/87, 2/03/96 (ABC).
This 1984 theatrical release, the first from Disney's Touchstone Pictures, stars Tom Hanks as a man who discovers the woman he loves (Daryl Hannah) is a mermaid.

Sport Goofy
The Studio produced a number of syndicated specials featuring Goofy as a sports star. Each of the specials is described in this chapter under their individual titles: *U.S. Junior Tournament World Junior Tennis Tournament #1–2, Walt Disney's Mickey and Donald Presents Sport Goofy #1–3, Walt Disney Presents Sport Goofy's Olympic Games Special; Walt Disney's Mickey, Donald and Sport Goofy: Getting Wet; Walt Disney's Mickey, Donald and Sport Goofy: Snowtime; and Walt Disney's Mickey, Donald and Sport Goofy: Happy Holidays.*

Stakeout Airdates (2-hour format): 10/28/90, 3/15/93 (ABC).
This 1987 theatrical release stars Richard Dreyfuss and Emilio Estevez as two police officers who have to watch a woman's house in the hope that her ex-boyfriend, an escaped killer, will return.

Steven Banks Show, The Airdates (30-minute format, Showtime): 1/12/91, 1/18/91, 1/22/91, 1/27/91, 2/06/91, 12/09/91, 12/28/91.
Cast: Steven Banks (Steven Brooks), David Byrd (Victor Ullman), Signy Coleman (Wendy Volster), Alex Nevil (Dennis), Dana Andersen (Martha), Christopher Collins (Mr. Troller), Michael Rider (The Cop), Christiane Carman (Melinda), Catherine Dent (Robin), Nancy Rubin (Sheila).
Stephen Brooks wants to be a rock star, but for now, he has to settle for being a copywriter at the Cutting Edge Catalogue Company. Stephen has a few other problems besides not being famous, though. When his landlord tries to remind him that his rent is due, the landlord's daughter bakes a cake and puts the rent request in icing just so Stephen will notice her. At work, Stephen must write ad copy for a strange electronic device without knowing what the device does. Perhaps worst of all, he's late for a much anticipated date.

Production Notes:

- This pilot for an unsold series was based on the one-man show, *Steven Banks' Home Entertainment Center,* which had aired on the Showtime cable network on 6/10/89.
- This was the first Touchstone Television product for cable.
- Early versions of the script placed Stephen at The Sharper Image, a real catalog company.

Strongest Man in the World, The
This 1975 theatrical release starring Kurt Russell as a student who invents a super strength formula was aired as a special on NBC on 5/01/82 after the anthology episode *A Disney Vacation.*

Swiss Family Robinson
This 1960 theatrical release starring John Mills, Dorothy McGuire, James MacArthur, Janet Munro, Tommy Kirk, and Kevin Corcoran as a family stranded on a remote island was aired as a special on ABC on 5/21/88. It also aired on the anthology series on 12/07/86, and in two parts on 3/12/89 and 3/19/89.

Tag Team Airdate: 1/26/91 (ABC).
Cast: Jesse Ventura (Bobby Youngblood), Roddy Piper (Rick McDonald), Phill Lewis (Ray Tyler), Raymond O'Connor (Harrigan), Robin Curtis (Lt. Carol Steckler), Mike Genovese (Hatch), Jennifer Runyon (Rita Valentine), Shannon Tweed (Leona), Sean Baca (Nick Phillips), Mark Ginther (Fred), Robert Hanley (Riker), Mark Lonow (Marty), Michael M. Vendrell (Barney), Kathy Kinney (Instructor), William L. Laster (Announcer), Joey Marella (Referee), Mr. Fuji (Mr. Saki), Randy Olea (Patrolman), Akio Sato (Soji Samurai), Pat Tanaka (Tojo Samurai).
Billy Youngblood and Rick McDonald, two professional wrestlers, are barred from the ring for life when they are framed by their conniving manager. After trying and failing at a series of different jobs, they decide to join the police force. There, they use wrestling techniques to subdue criminals.

Production Notes:

- Disney spent $2.5 million on this pilot, but the series was not picked up by the network.
- A real wrestling match was filmed at the Los Angeles Sports Arena for the opening scenes.
- Other episodes of the planned series were *Mad Dog, Code of Honor,* and *Friends and Neighbors.*

TAKING CARE OF BUSINESS   Airdate (2-hour format): 3/28/96 (ABC).
This 1991 theatrical release stars James Belushi and Charles Grodin in the story of a con man who assumes the identity of a real and successful businessman.

THAT DARN CAT!
This 1965 theatrical release starring Hayley Mills and Dean Jones was aired during the *NBC All-Disney Saturday Night at the Movies* series of specials along with *Bear Country.* It was later broadcast on the anthology series in a two-hour format on 1/13/80 and in two parts on 3/29/81 and 4/15/81.

THIS IS YOUR LIFE, DONALD DUCK
Aired as a special on 2/22/80 on NBC, this episode was first broadcast on 3/11/60 as part of the anthology series.

THREE FUGITIVES   Airdates (2-hour format): 1/05/92, 10/09/93 (ABC).
This 1989 theatrical release starring Nick Nolte, Martin Short, and Sarah Rowland Doroff is the story of a parolee who gets framed for a bank robbery and flees with his daughter and the real robber.

THREE LIVES OF THOMASINA, THE
This 1963 theatrical release was aired on 12/24/74 with *Arizona Sheepdog* and *It's Tough to Be a Bird* as part of the *NBC All-Disney Saturday Night at the Movies* series of specials.

THREE MEN AND A BABY   Airdates (2-hour format): 11/04/90, 3/10/91, 12/29/92 (NBC).
This 1987 theatrical release starring Tom Selleck, Steve Guttenberg, and Ted Danson is the story of three bachelors whose lives are changed when someone leaves a baby at their apartment.

THREE MEN AND A LITTLE LADY
Airdate (2-hour format): 2/13/94 (ABC).
This 1990 theatrical release is a sequel to *Three Men and a Baby.* This time out, the bachelors try to stop the baby's mother from marrying the wrong man.

THRILLS, CHILLS & SPIDERS: THE MAKING OF ARACHNOPHOBIA   Airdate (30-minute format): 7/15/90 (Syndicated).
Cast: Mark L. Taylor (Host), Frank Marshall (Director), Jeff Daniels, Harley Jane Kozak, John Goodman, Steven Kutcher (Supervising Entomologist), Jules Sylvester, Julian Sands.

This special on the making of *Arachnophobia* reveals the unusual techniques involved in working with bugs and other animals. The film's cast and crew discuss their experiences on the set, and animal specialists demonstrate how they get the animals to perform on cue.

TICKETS, PLEASE   Airdate (30-minute format): 9/06/88 (CBS).
Cast: Cleavon Little ("Bake" Baker), Marcia Strassman (Elaine), Joe Guzaldo (Ted), David Marciano (Sal Bernardini), Yeardley Smith (Paula Bennett), Barbara Howard (Ginger), Harold Gould (Jack), Bill Macy (Sam).

Each morning, thousands of commuters in the suburbs head to work in New York City on the train. Every night, they take the return ride home. One of the most popular cars on the trains is the bar car, where a group of regulars is seen sharing their commute together. In this episode, one of the commuters tries to cope with losing his job.

Production Notes:

- This unsold pilot was aired as part of the *CBS Summer Playhouse.*

TIN MEN   Airdate (2-hour format): 3/05/90 (NBC).
This 1987 theatrical release stars Richard Dreyfuss and Danny DeVito as two salesman who go to elaborate lengths to get the best of each other.

TO MY DAUGHTER, WITH LOVE
Airdates (2-hour format): 1/24/94, 6/26/95 (NBC).
Cast: Rick Schroder (Joey Cutter), Lawrence Pressman (Arthur), Khandi Alexander (Harriet), Megan Gallivan (Alice Cutter), Keith Amos (Tim), Ashley Malinger (Emily

Cutter), Linda Gray (Eleanor), Joseph Burke (Martin), Eric Hull (Mr. Lawrence), Nealla Gordon (Mrs. Lewiston), Georg Olden (Lou), Danny Perkin (George), Gail Hebert (Naomi), Danielle Campbell (Charlotte), Ashley Caldwell (Rachel), Kayla Crandall (Cynthia), Michelle Hasson (Teresa), Chris Mastrandrea (Ralph), Barbara Irvin (Clerk).

The happy life of Joey and Alice Cutter, and their 6-year-old daughter, Emily, is shattered when Alice dies suddenly. Joey has a hard time adjusting to his new single-parent duties, and his mother-in-law, Eleanor, is unhappy with how he raising Emily. She finally convinces Joey that Emily would be better off living with her and her husband, Arthur, when Joey loses his job.

Toast of the Town   Airdate: 2/08/53 (CBS).

Cast: Ed Sullivan, Walt Disney, Ted Sears, Ed Penner, Ward Kimball, Pinto Colvig, Frank Thomas, Beverly Jordan (Walt's Secretary).

This special edition of Ed Sullivan's variety show begins in New York. After reminiscing about meeting Walt Disney during the making of Snow White and the Seven Dwarfs, Ed mentions that it is Mickey Mouse's 25th anniversary. Wanting to see Walt again, he visited the Studio to salute the creator of the world's most famous mouse. Films of Ed's trip show his visit to California.

Production Notes:

- Disney made liberal use of artistic license in story session "reenactment," for Who's Afraid of the Big Bad Wolf was actually written by Frank Churchill. This was acknowledged by Ed Sullivan.
- Pinto Colvig's last name was misspelled as "Colveig" on the credits of this show.
- This program is also known as The Walt Disney Story.

Tough Guys   Airdate (2-hour format): 4/24/89 (NBC).

This 1986 theatrical release stars Burt Lancaster and Kirk Douglas as two aging criminals who decide to commit one last, and spectacular, crime.

Turner & Hooch   Airdates (2-hour format): 12/17/91, 5/02/92 (CBS).

This 1989 theatrical release stars Tom Hanks as a very neat and orderly detective who is assigned a very sloppy partner, who also happens to be large dog.

Turner & Hooch (TV version)

Airdates (30-minute format, NBC): 7/09/90, 8/04/91.

Cast: Tom Wilson (Scott Turner), Wendee Pratt (Emily Turner), Bradley Mott (Boney), Al Fann (Howdy), John Anthony (Derek), Beasley (Hooch), Michael Rich (Phil), Ivy Bethune (Mrs. Miller), Martin Casella (Policeman), Jack Evans (Clarence).

This unsold pilot was based on the 1989 theatrical release of the same name. This time, detective Scott Turner and his unlikely canine partner, Hooch, are assigned to investigate the thefts of strange objects around town. Turner eventually finds Derek, the young criminal behind the thefts, and takes him under his wing.

Production Notes:

- The episode title of this pilot was The Kid.
- NBC advertised the 7/09/90 airing as part of a "Two-Dog Night" theme, for they showed this pilot and another unsold pilot about a dog.

20,000 Leagues under the Sea

Airdates (2-hour format): 2/23/74 (NBC), 8/05/89 (ABC).

This 1954 theatrical release aired as a special on 2/23/74 with Beaver Valley as part of the NBC All-Disney Saturday Night at the Movies series of specials. The film also aired in edited form on 10/24/76, 11/04/79, and 2/15/87 as part of the anthology series.

Production Note:

- Behind-the-scenes looks at the filming of this movie were featured in the episodes Operation Undersea and Monsters of the Deep.

U.S. Junior Tournament World Junior Tennis Tournament   Airdate (2-hour format): 9/10/83 (Syndicated).

Cast: Dick Van Patten, Patti Van Patten, Vic Braden.

Sport Goofy joins hosts Dick and Patti Van Patten to salute the young tennis stars of the U.S. Junior Tournament.

U.S. Junior Tournament World Junior Tennis Tournament #2

Airdate (2-hour format): 12/03/83 (Syndicated).

Cast: Dick Van Patten, Patti Van Patten, Vic Braden, Stan Smith, Harry Hopman.

The International Tennis Foundation's Junior World Tennis Championship is set at Walt Disney World, where 128 of the world's best tennis players aged 14 and under have gathered to compete. Hosts Dick and Patti Van Patten are joined by Sport Goofy and several tennis pros to salute the young players.

WACO & RHINEHART   Airdate (2-hour format): 3/27/87 (ABC).

Cast: Charles C. Hill (Waco Wheeler), Justin Deas (Milo Rhinehart), Bill Hootkins (August Mirch), Bob Tzudiker (Ed Peavey), Kathleen Lloyd (Connie Stevik), Daniel Faraldo (Cooper), Eugene Butler (Victor Koury), Justin Lord (Shawcross), Carmen Argenziano (Varela), Nancy Stafford (Joyce), Talbot Simons (Fasil), Donald Gibb (Varela Leader), Eric Server (CHP Officer), Liz Georges (Angela), Chris Hendrie (FBI Agent #2), Mark Costello (FBI Agent #1), Vince McKewin (DC-3 Pilot), Victor Vidales (Perez), Charles Noland (Bishopson), Alma Beltran (Woman Worker), Sirri Murad (Mr. Farouk), Ann Fairlie (Mrs. Farouk), Creed Bratton (Agent Jones), Douglas Dirkson (Prison Officer), Duncan Gamble (Major Dentry), Rick Fitts (Armory Sergeant), Mary Petrie (Stewardress), Ted Gehring (Truck Stop Manager), Mitch Pileggi (Gate AP).

Two mismatched modern-day U.S. marshals, Waco Wheeler and Milo Rhinehart, travel the country as they are assigned to handle the more difficult cases of the Marshals' Service. In this pilot for an unsold series, they have to track down an international arms dealer, and also try to find the man who killed Milo's first partner.

Production Note:

- John DiAquino, who had starred as Varges in Disney's *Wildside*, was one of the actors tested for the role of Waco.

WALT DISNEY—A GOLDEN ANNIVERSARY SALUTE   Airdates (90-minute format, ABC): 10/25/73, 9/20/74.

Cast: Dean Jones (Host), Julie Andrews, Annette Funicello, Woolie Reitherman, Bill Walsh, Buddy Ebsen, Fred MacMurray, Ward Kimball.

In this tribute to Walt Disney, host Dean Jones takes a look at the Studio's history, which began in 1928 with the creation of Mickey Mouse.

WALT DISNEY CHRISTMAS SHOW, THE   Airdate: 12/25/51 (CBS).

Cast: Walt Disney, Kathryn Beaumont (Wendy), Bobby Driscoll (Peter Pan), Hans Conried (Slave in the Magic Mirror), Bill Thompson (Willoughby), Don Barclay (Dr. Miller and Santa Claus), Tommy Luske (Michael), Paul Collins (John).

The Studio's second television program opens in the children's ward of a large hospital as Dr. Miller entertains the patients by dressing as Santa Claus. This will be a special Christmas, for "Santa" has arranged, through the magic of television, for the children to attend a special party being held at the Disney Studio.

Production Notes:

- This show was sponsored by Johnson & Johnson and aired on CBS at the (now) unusual time of 3 P.M.
- Television sets were placed in children's wards in over fifty hospitals throughout the country. Johnson & Johnson distributed Disney toys and other gifts to these hospitals, and parties were held after the screening.

WALT DISNEY PRESENTS SPORT GOOFY'S OLYMPIC GAMES SPECIAL   Airdate (30-minute format): 6/08/84 (Syndicated).

This animated salute to the Olympics features Disney's greatest athlete, Sport Goofy. The action begins with *The Olympic Champ*, a look at the history of the Olympic games. As the narrator describes each of the sports, Goofy does his limited best to demonstrate the techniques involved.

WALT DISNEY STORY, THE
See: *Toast of the Town.*

WALT DISNEY WORLD CELEBRITY CIRCUS   Airdate: 11/27/87 (NBC).

Cast: Tony Randall, Allyce Beasley, Lisa Bonet, Tim Conway, Kim Fields, Malcolm-Jamal Warner, Jim Varney, The Andrews, The Berousek Bears, The Cristiani Elephants, The Dare Devil Cyclists, Robby Gasser and His Seals, Anthony Gatto, Denis Lacombe, Mark Lotz, The Rodriguez Family, Mark Watters, The Winn Family, Nicklaus Winn, Bello Nock the Clown.

Tony Randall is the host for a variety of circus acts performed throughout Walt Disney World. The show begins with a circus parade mixed in with units from the Main Street

Electrical Parade through Epcot. Mickey Mouse, acting as the ringmaster, introduces various circus acts.

WALT DISNEY WORLD JOURNEY INTO MAGIC   Airdate: 5/23/93 (Syndicated).

Cast: Tim Klein (Host), Ed McMahon (Himself), Scott Cassidy (Travel Writer), Kimberley Dockerby, Hank Duderstadt (Golfer), Chris Hurt, Martin Katz (Martin Meyers), Elaine Matthews, Mark Mazzerella, Chris Miles, Jonathan Sara, Kimber Taft (Kimber Meyers), Joretta Rodriquez.

This special takes a look at the many attractions at Walt Disney World, as seen through the eyes of three sets of visitors—the Meyerses, a harried businessman and his family; two honeymooners; and a golfer, there to write an article about his experiences.

WALT DISNEY WORLD OPENING SPECIAL, THE

See: *The Grand Opening of Walt Disney World.*

WALT DISNEY WORLD: 20 MAGICAL YEARS   Airdate: 5/11/92 (Syndicated).

Cast: Tim Klein, Roy E. Disney, Michael Eisner, Stephen Birnbaum, Scott Cassidy, Max Howard, Art Levitt.

This celebration of Walt Disney World's 20th birthday begins as Roy E. Disney rededicates the Park using the same words originally read by his father, Roy O. Disney. Michael Eisner starts the festivities, which include a variety of celebrations across the property. President George Bush then honors the more than 5,000 Points of Light program winners who have volunteered their time across America.

Production Note:

• Travel writer and guest star Stephen Birnbaum died shortly after taping his segments, and the show was dedicated to his memory.

WALT DISNEY WORLD 4TH OF JULY SPECTACULAR (1988 VERSION)   Airdate (2-hour format): 7/04/88 (Syndicated).

Cast: The Beach Boys, The Fat Boys, Tempestt Bledsoe, Mark Summers, Rita Moreno, Tommy Tune, Miss America Kaye Lani Rae Rafko, Willard Scott, Lee Greenwood, Sandi Patti, Carol Burnett, Bert Convy, Clifton Davis, Deidre Hall, Marc Price, Burt Reynolds, Jack Wagner (Announcer).

This holiday special begins with Mickey Mouse and his friends escorting a marching band through The Magic Kingdom. This year is Mickey's 50th birthday and Disney is celebrating in grand style. The newest attraction at Walt Disney World is Mickey's Birthday Land. Here, guests can see where Mickey and his friends live and work. Carol Burnett helps open the new land, along with visitors Cindy Williams and Nancy Reagan.

Production Notes:

• This syndicated special was sold on a barter basis to 145 stations and aired live on the East Coast.
• This was the first in an annual series of 4th of July specials.

WALT DISNEY WORLD 4TH OF JULY SPECTACULAR (1989 VERSION)   Airdate (2-hour format): 7/04/89 (Syndicated).

Cast: Willard Scott, Miss America Gretchen Carlson, Carol Channing, Janie Frickie, The New Kids on the Block, The Temptations, The Mouseketeers, Mark Price, The Mannequin Dancers, Sandi Patti.

Hosts Willard Scott and Miss America, Gretchen Carlson, introduce music and entertainment segments throughout Walt Disney World and Disneyland.

Production Note:

• This special was broadcast live on the East Coast.

WALT DISNEY WORLD 4TH OF JULY SPECTACULAR, THE (1990 VERSION)
Airdate (2-hour format): 7/04/90 (Syndicated).

Cast: Gladys Knight, Downtown Julie Brown, The New Kids on the Block, Charlie Korsmo, Teenage Mutant Ninja Turtles, Jermaine Jackson, Regis Philbin, Kathie Lee Gifford, The Disney Channel Mouseketeers, Samuel E. Wright, Sandi Patti.

Downtown Julie Brown is the host for this holiday-themed special. The show includes Mickey Mouse with a preview of Mickey's Starland; Disneyland's 35th anniversary parade, Party Gras; Charlie Korsmo, who played "The Kid" in *Dick Tracy*, introducing the new *Dick Tracy* stage show at the Disney-MGM Studios; and the Teenage Mutant Ninja Turtles.

WALT DISNEY WORLD HAPPY EASTER PARADE (1985 VERSION) Airdate: 4/07/85 (ABC).

Cast: Joan Lunden, Rick Dees.

Rick Dees and Joan Lunden host this live broadcast from Walt Disney World. In addition to the parade featuring Disney characters in Easter motif, the show also includes the Radio City Music Hall Rockettes, making a rare appearance outside New York City; magician Doug Henning; the world champion Detroit Tigers; George Burns at the Golden Horseshoe; The Oak Ridge Boys; and singer Jack Wagner.

Production Note:

- Singer and soap opera star Jack Wagner who appears on this show is not to be confused with the longtime "Voice of Disney," announcer Jack Wagner.

WALT DISNEY WORLD HAPPY EASTER PARADE (1986 VERSION)

See: *The CBS Easter Parade.*

WALT DISNEY WORLD HAPPY EASTER PARADE (1987 VERSION) Airdate (90-minute format): 4/19/87 (ABC).

Cast: Joan Lunden, Ben Vereen, Regis Philbin, Alan Thicke.

The Easter festivities begin as Ben Vereen joins the parade performers for *The Trolley Song.* In addition to the parade itself, the program includes Alan Thicke and the Disney characters aboard the cruise ship *Oceanic* for a trip to the Bahamas, and a salute to the 50th anniversary of *Snow White and the Seven Dwarfs.*

Production Note:

- One of the traditions of the Easter Parade programs is to have visitors to Walt Disney World introduce themselves at the commercial breaks. One of these segments this year featured former President Jimmy Carter and family.

WALT DISNEY WORLD HAPPY EASTER PARADE (1988 VERSION) Airdate (90-minute format): 4/03/88 (ABC).

Cast: Joan Lunden, Alan Thicke, Regis Philbin.

This annual special features Regis Philbin with visits to the new Norway pavilion at Epcot, the Disney-MGM Studios Theme Park, the new Grand Floridian Beach Resort, and IllumiNations, the nightly fireworks spectacular at Epcot. The program also includes *The Whole World Wants to Wish You Happy Birthday, Mickey Mouse,* a 60th-birthday tribute to Mickey, and a preview of Mickey's Birthdayland, Walt Disney's World's newest themed land.

WALT DISNEY WORLD HAPPY EASTER PARADE (1989 VERSION) Airdate (90-minute format): 3/26/89 (ABC).

Cast: Joan Lunden, Alan Thicke, Regis Philbin, Frankie Avalon, Scott Valentine.

The 5th annual broadcast of the Easter Parade begins with *I Love a Parade,* a musical number set in all of the Walt Disney World theme parks, including the new Disney-MGM Studios. The Florida portion of the program also features a visit to the new Disney-MGM Studios Theme Park. Meanwhile, Frankie Avalon is in California for Disneyland's "Blast to the Past" promotion, a salute to 1950s music.

WALT DISNEY WORLD HAPPY EASTER PARADE (1990 VERSION) Airdate (90-minute format): 4/15/90 (ABC).

Cast: Joan Lunden, Alan Thicke, Regis Philbin, Buster Poindexter, Howie Mandell, the Disney Channel Mousketeers.

The annual Easter outing begins with the 500-piece Walt Disney World Honor Band marching from Cinderella Castle down Main Street U.S.A. Buster Poindexter is at Disneyland for the Park's 35th birthday celebration, Party Gras. The program also includes a salute to the "Give Kids the World" foundation, which brings terminally ill children to Walt Disney World.

WALT DISNEY WORLD HAPPY EASTER PARADE (1991 VERSION) Airdate: 3/31/91 (ABC).

Cast: Joan Lunden, Alan Thicke, Regis Philbin, Howie Mandel, Betty White, Mary Kate and Ashley Olsen, Gen. H. Norman Schwarzkopf.

This version of the Easter Parade features Howie Mandel at the new Typhoon Lagoon water park; a preview of the Muppet*Vision 3-D show at the Disney-MGM Studios; a tour of the Disney-MGM backlot hosted by Betty White; and Regis Philbin with a look at the Park's Mickey Moo cow and other Mickey Mouse–shaped items. From Disneyland, Mary Kate and Ashley Olsen visit the new Afternoon Avenue, which features the stars of the Disney Afternoon cartoon series.

WALT DISNEY WORLD HAPPY EASTER PARADE (1992 VERSION) Airdate: 4/19/92 (ABC).

Cast: Joan Lunden, Regis Philbin, Robby Benson, Richard Mulligan, Terrence Smith, Sabine Marcon.

This year's Easter festivities include a visit to the Disney-MGM Studios Backlot Tour hosted by Richard Mulligan; the characters from *Adventures in Wonderland* partying at Typhoon Lagoon; and performances by the U.S. Army Field Band, the Lake Gibson High School band, and the visiting Sweet Adeleine Chorus and Barbershop Chorus groups. The program also includes a visit to Euro Disneyland and Disneyland, site of the new Fantasmic! water show.

WALT DISNEY WORLD HAPPY EASTER PARADE (1993 VERSION) Airdate: 4/11/93 (ABC).

Cast: Joan Lunden, Regis Philbin, Joey Lawrence, Mary Kate Olsen, Jodie Sweetin, Taran Noah Smith.

In addition to the festivities on Main Street U.S.A., this edition of the Easter Parade show features Taran Noah Smith from *Home Improvement* in a preview of Splash Mountain; Joey Lawrence in a high-speed roller-blade tour of Epcot and a Spring Break celebration at Typhoon Lagoon; and Mary Kate Olsen and Jodie Sweetin with a look at the taping of their series *Full House* on location at Walt Disney World.

WALT DISNEY WORLD HAPPY EASTER PARADE (1994 VERSION) Airdate: 4/03/94 (ABC).

Cast: Joan Lunden, Regis Philbin, Nancy Kerrigan, Antonio Sabato, Jr., The Boys Choir of Harlem, Bill Nye, Gladys Knight.

This edition of the annual Easter parade includes the *Beauty and the Beast* stage show at the Disney-MGM Studios; Nancy Kerrigan skating with the Genie from *Aladdin* at Cinderella Castle; the *Barbie's World* show at Epcot; a soap opera parody with guest star Antonio Sabato at Typhoon Lagoon; and previews of the Twilight Zone Tower of Terror, the All Star Resort and Wilderness Lodge hotels and Innoventions at Epcot.

WALT DISNEY WORLD HAPPY EASTER PARADE (1995 VERSION) Airdate: 4/16/95 (ABC).

Cast: Joan Lunden, Regis Philbin, Dave Chappelle, Jim Breuer, Kevin Bressard.

This year's Easter parade special features Dave Chappelle and Jim Breuer from the ill-fated series *Buddies* as the interviewers on Main Street U.S.A. The show also includes the new Mickey Mania parade, with floats and performers honoring Mickey's achievements over the years. For the Easter parade's grand finale, Regis Philbin and Joan Lunden lead the crowd in singing *Easter Parade.*

WALT DISNEY WORLD HAPPY EASTER PARADE (1996 VERSION) Airdate: 4/07/96 (ABC).

Cast: Joan Lunden, Regis Philbin, J.D. Roth, Brianne Leary, Joey Lawrence, Andy Lawrence, Matt Lawrence.

The 1996 edition of the Easter parade begins with the '50s-style dance number *At the Hop* and a medley of Easter songs as dozens of children in bunny ears launch colorful streamers across Main Street U.S.A. Other high points include Mary Poppins flying down into the parade; a visit to the new Disney Institute where guests are taking classes in making Easter baskets and topiary figures; the Lawrence brothers from *Brotherly Love* checking out the property's water parks; and the *Toy Story* parade at the Disney-MGM Studios.

WALT DISNEY WORLD VERY MERRY CHRISTMAS PARADE (1983 VERSION) Airdate: 12/25/83 (ABC).

Cast: Joan Lunden, Mike Douglas, Carol Lawrence.

Joan Lunden and Mike Douglas are the hosts for the first telecast of the gala Walt Disney World Very Merry Christmas Parade. The live one-hour special also stars Carol Lawrence, who provides a look at the holiday celebrations underway in Epcot Center.

Production Note:

• The show featured a dramatic plea by the 1973 Walt Disney World ambassador, Karin Cheatham, for the donation of a liver for Trine Engebretson, the daughter of the 1976 ambassador, Mary Ann Engebretson. The request was successful, and the girl was soon the healthy recipient of a donated organ.

WALT DISNEY WORLD VERY MERRY CHRISTMAS PARADE (1984 VERSION) Airdate (90-minute format): 12/25/84 (ABC).

Cast: Joan Lunden, Bruce Jenner, Regis Philbin, Joseph Campanella.

This live broadcast is essentially the same show as the 1983 show of the same name, with the main theme being the Florida theme park's festive holiday parade. It also provides a retrospective of Disney's early Christmas shows.

WALT DISNEY WORLD VERY MERRY CHRISTMAS PARADE (1985 VERSION)

Airdate (90-minute format): 12/25/85 (ABC).

Cast: Joan Lunden, Ben Vereen, Regis Philbin, Kevin Dobson.

This annual holiday special begins with Regis Philbin interviewing the crowd along the parade route. After Goofy stars in a musical show at Cinderella Castle, the Christmas parade starts with a marching band. Parade units then follow, based on Disney films.

WALT DISNEY WORLD VERY MERRY CHRISTMAS PARADE (1986 VERSION)

Airdate (90-minute format): 12/25/86 (ABC).

Cast: Joan Lunden, Ben Vereen, Regis Philbin.

This edition of the annual Christmas parade features a salute to the 50th anniversary of *Snow White and the Seven Dwarfs*, with remembrances from art director Ken Anderson, animator Ward Kimball, and Adriana Caselotti, the voice of Snow White. Snow White herself is seen as the grand marshal of the parade.

Production Note:

- This special aired around the world, including the Armed Forces Radio-Television Services.

WALT DISNEY WORLD VERY MERRY CHRISTMAS PARADE (1987 VERSION)

Airdate (90-minute format): 12/25/87 (ABC).

Cast: Joan Lunden, Alan Thicke, Regis Philbin.

This year's theme is a "Salute to America," and the first unit sets the mood as Mickey and Minnie Mouse appear with a replica of the Liberty Bell. Regis Philbin hosts a preview of coming additions to Walt Disney World.

WALT DISNEY WORLD VERY MERRY CHRISTMAS PARADE (1988 VERSION)

Airdate (2-hour format): 12/25/88 (ABC).

Cast: Joan Lunden, Alan Thicke, Regis Philbin, Sarah Purcell, Scott Valentine.

All across Walt Disney World, cast members get ready for the holidays to the sound of *We Need a Little Christmas.* The sixth annual Christmas show then continues with a preview of *Oliver and Company*, a visit to Disneyland, and previews of Mickey's Birthdayland, the Caribbean Beach Resort, and the Disney-MGM Studios Theme Park.

WALT DISNEY WORLD VERY MERRY CHRISTMAS PARADE (1989 VERSION)

Airdate (2-hour format): 12/25/89 (ABC).

Cast: Joan Lunden, Alan Thicke, Kermit the Frog, Regis Philbin, Joanna Kerns, Marc Price, Whitney Kershaw.

Previews of new attractions this year include Star Tours at the Disney-MGM Studios, Typhoon Lagoon water park, and a preview of *The Little Mermaid*, Disney's newest animated feature.

WALT DISNEY WORLD VERY MERRY CHRISTMAS PARADE (1990 VERSION)

Airdate (2-hour format): 12/25/90 (ABC).

Cast: Joan Lunden, Alan Thicke, Regis Philbin, Sarah Purcell, Jaleel White, Amy Grant.

As a special salute, many of those at Walt Disney World today are the families of troops in Saudi Arabia for Operation Desert Shield. Singer Lee Greenwood performs *I'll Be Home for Christmas* in tribute to the troops and some of them send taped messages back home.

WALT DISNEY WORLD VERY MERRY CHRISTMAS PARADE (1991 VERSION)

Airdate (2-hour format): 12/25/91 (ABC).

Cast: Joan Lunden, Regis Philbin, Mayim Bialik, Lee Greenwood, Sandi Patti.

Joan Lunden's new co-host for the annual holiday outing is Regis Philbin. A new Surprise Parade in honor of Walt Disney World's 20th Anniversary takes to the street with 40-foot-high floats of Disney characters. Historic film clips of Walt Disney World over the years, from Walt's original announcement of the project through today, are shown to the song *Through the Years*.

WALT DISNEY WORLD VERY MERRY CHRISTMAS PARADE (1992 VERSION)

Airdate (2-hour format): 12/25/92 (ABC).

Cast: Joan Lunden, Regis Philbin, Ed McMahon, Miss America Leanza Cornett, John Davidson, Richard Karn, Earl Hindman.

In addition to the parade activities, the program includes a visit to Mickey's Starland, where the characters are having problems decorating Mickey's house. Luckily, they get some help from Richard Karn and Earl Hindman from *Home Improvement*. The program also previews *Aladdin*, as well as Splash Mountain.

Production Note:

- This special won an Emmy Award for Outstanding Achievement in Costume Design.

WALT DISNEY WORLD VERY MERRY CHRISTMAS PARADE (1993 VERSION)
Airdate (2-hour format): 12/25/93 (ABC).

Cast: Joan Lunden, Regis Philbin, Kathie Lee Gifford, Robby Benson, John Davidson, Bill Nye.

The annual Christmas special gets underway as the Ohio State Marching Band begins the parade. Then, at the Disney-MGM Studios, Kathie Lee provides a behind-the-scenes look at the crew getting ready for her big holiday song number, *Winter Wonderland*. President Clinton greets viewers in a taped segment, reading *The Night before Christmas* to children at the White House.

WALT DISNEY WORLD VERY MERRY CHRISTMAS PARADE (1994 VERSION)
Airdate (2-hour format): 12/25/94 (ABC).

Cast: Joan Lunden, Regis Philbin, Jonathan Taylor Thomas, Nancy Kerrigan, Margaret Cho.

This annual Christmas special begins with a taped greeting from President and Mrs. Clinton. Then, Regis Philbin introduces the new "Honey, I Shrunk the Audience" show at Epcot and the Alien Encounter attraction in Tomorrowland. Other previews this year include the new Twilight Zone Tower of Terror attraction, a look at Disney's new film, *Pocahontas*, featuring animator Glen Keane, and the Lion King Celebration Parade at Disneyland.

WALT DISNEY WORLD VERY MERRY CHRISTMAS PARADE (1995 VERSION)
Airdate (2-hour format): 12/25/95 (ABC).

Cast: Joan Lunden, Regis Philbin, Ben Savage, Rider Strong, J.D. Roth, Brianne Leary, Jodi Benson, Richard White, Brad Kane.

This edition of the annual Christmas special features appearances by several singers who reprise their roles from recent animated films. Richard White from *Beauty and the Beast* sings *Gaston*, Brad Kane, the singing voice of Aladdin, performs *One Jump Ahead*, and Jodi Benson, Ariel from *The Little Mermaid*, sings *Part of Your World*. Joan Lunden gives a tour of the Disney Institute, Brianne Leary provides a behind-the-scenes look at the day's parades, and J.D. Roth interviews guests along Main Street U.S.A.

WALT DISNEY'S MICKEY AND DONALD PRESENTS SPORT GOOFY
Airdate (30-minute format): 5/27/83 (Syndicated). This compilation of Goofy sports cartoons includes *How to Play Baseball*, *How to Swim*, and *Tennis Racquet*.

WALT DISNEY'S MICKEY AND DONALD PRESENTS SPORT GOOFY #2
Airdate (30-minute format): 9/16/83 (Syndicated). This compilation of Goofy cartoons includes *How to Play Football*, *Goofy's Glider*, and *Get Rich Quick*.

WALT DISNEY'S MICKEY AND DONALD PRESENTS SPORT GOOFY #3: WINTER SPORTS
Airdate (30-minute format): 11/24/83 (Syndicated).

Another Sport Goofy outing begins with *Hockey Homicide*, followed by *Double Dribble*, *Aquamania*, and *The Art of Skiing*.

WALT DISNEY'S MICKEY, DONALD, AND SPORT GOOFY: GETTING WET
Airdate (30-minute format): 9/14/84 (Syndicated).

This animated special has a decidedly nautical flavor. *The Simple Things* features Mickey Mouse and Pluto in a day at the beach. *Chips Ahoy* pits Donald Duck against Chip and Dale, and Goofy tries to show his son how to water-ski in *Aquamania*.

WALT DISNEY'S MICKEY, DONALD, AND SPORT GOOFY: HAPPY HOLIDAYS
Airdate (30-minute format): 12/14/84 (Syndicated).

This animated special begins with Mickey and Pluto decorating their home for the holidays in *Pluto's Christmas Tree*. Donald Duck takes a job wrapping Christmas presents in *The Clock Watcher*.

Finally, Goofy stars in *How to Ride a Horse* from *The Reluctant Dragon*.

WALT DISNEY'S MICKEY, DONALD, AND SPORT GOOFY: SNOWTIME
Airdate (30-minute format): 11/30/84 (Syndicated).

Winter is the setting for this animated special. Pluto stars in the Oscar-winning *Lend a Paw*, followed by *Chip n' Dale*, and *How to Fish*.

WE'LL TAKE MANHATTAN
Airdate (30-minute format): 6/16/90 (NBC).

Cast: Jackée (Yvonne), Karin Bohrer (Cheryl Lee), Edan Gross (Rocky), Joel Brooks (Rigaletti), Fred Applegate (Burt), David Dunnard (Casting Director), Jean Speegle Howard (Mrs. Feinberg), Ossie Davis (Man in Subway), Stanley Kamel (Director), Louie Bonanno (Pedro).

Yvonne, a street-smart New Yorker, is determined to be a singer. First, however, she needs to find some way to pay her rent, for she's about to be evicted. She solves that problem by taking in a roommate, Cheryl, who wants to be an actress. Cheryl is new in town and quite naive, and Yvonne finds that she needs to teach Cheryl how to survive in the big city.

Production Note:

• Actress Jackée Harry now uses her last name for billing purposes.

WHAT ABOUT BOB?
Airdates (2-hour format): 2/20/94, 3/05/95, 11/25/95 (ABC). This 1991 theatrical release stars Bill Murray as a very annoying psychiatric patient who drives his doctor (Richard Dreyfuss) nuts.

WHITE FANG
Airdates (2-hour format): 1/04/92, 8/12/92 (CBS). This 1991 theatrical release starring Ethan Hawke is the story of a man who searches for gold during the Yukon gold rush of 1897, along with his pet wolf.

WHO FRAMED ROGER RABBIT
Airdate: 11/12/91 (2-hour 15-minute format), 12/12/92 (2-hour format) (CBS). This 1988 theatrical release starring Bob Hoskins, Christopher Lloyd, and Charles Fleischer combines humans and cartoon stars in a mystery set in old Hollywood. The 11/12/91 broadcast included additional footage not seen in the theatrical release.

WILD HEARTS CAN'T BE BROKEN
Airdate (2-hour format): 7/24/94 (NBC). This 1991 theatrical release stars Gabrielle Anwar as a young girl who takes a dangerous job riding a horse as it jumps from a tower to entertain crowds during the Depression.

WINNIE THE POOH, AND CHRISTMAS TOO
Airdates: 12/14/91 (*The Making of Beauty and the Beast* version, ABC); 12/11/92 (*The Making of The Muppet Christmas Carol* version, ABC); 12/08/93 (*The Making of Aladdin* version, ABC); 12/21/95 (*The Making of Toy Story* version, CBS).

Voices: Peter Cullen (Eeyore), Jim Cummings (Winnie the Pooh), John Fiedler (Piglet), Michael Gough (Gopher), Edan Gross (Christopher Robin), Ken Sansom (Rabbit), Paul Winchell (Tigger).

As Christmas draws near, Christopher Robin writes a letter to Santa that includes each of his friends' wishes. He then sets the letter free so the wind can carry it to the North Pole. Later, Piglet tells Pooh that the carefree bear forgot to tell Santa what he wanted for himself. Pooh and Piglet use a balloon to catch up to the letter, then head home to add Pooh's wish.

The 1991 version of the program continues with two Donald Duck cartoons, followed by a behind-the-scenes look at the making of *Beauty and the Beast*. The 1992 edition looks at the filming of *The Muppet Christmas Carol*. The 1993 version includes *The Making of Aladdin: A Whole New World*. The 1995 version includes *The Magic Earmuffs* and *The Making of Toy Story*.

Production Note:

• This was the first production from Disney's new Paris animation studio.

WINNIE THE POOH AND FRIENDS
This show first aired on the anthology series on 12/11/82. It was later repeated as a special on CBS on 8/30/83 with the cartoons *Chicken in the Rough*, *Chips Ahoy*, and *Up a Tree*.

WINNIE THE POOH AND THE BLUSTERY DAY
The 1968 animated theatrical featurette aired as a special on NBC in a 30-minute format as follows: 11/30/70, 12/01/71, 11/29/72, 11/28/73, 11/26/74, 12/01/78. It also aired on the anthology series on 3/05/89 with the cartoons *Working for Peanuts*, *Pluto's Sweater*, and *The New Neighbor*.

WINNIE THE POOH AND THE HONEY TREE
This 1965 animated theatrical featurette aired on NBC in a 30-minute format as follows: 3/10/70, 3/22/71, 3/14/72, 4/04/73, 3/26/74, 11/25/77. It also aired on the anthology series on 1/21/90, along with the cartoons *Springtime for Pluto*, *Donald's Garden*, and *Mickey's Parrot*.

WINNIE THE POOH AND TIGGER TOO

Airdates (30-minute format): 11/28/75 (NBC), 11/25/76 (ABC).

This 1974 animated theatrical featurette aired as a special in a 30-minute format on NBC on 11/28/75 and ABC on 1/25/76. It also aired in a one-hour format as a special on 11/26/88 (ABC) and on the anthology series on 3/16/86 and 11/15/87. The one-hour version of this show includes three cartoons: *Bee on Guard*, *Pluto and the Gopher*, and *In the Bag*.

WONDERFUL WORLD OF DISNEY, THE: 40 YEARS OF TELEVISION MAGIC

Airdate (2-hour format): 12/10/94 (ABC).

Cast: Kirstie Alley (Host), Debbie Allen, Bobby Burgess, Margaret Cho, Roy E. Disney, George Foreman, Tom Hanks, Hugh Hefner, John Hench, Stewart Jewell, Elton John, Ollie Johnston, Ward Kimball, Art Linkletter, James MacArthur, Ed McMahon, Cheech Marin, Dennis Miller, Hayley Mills, Fess Parker, Priscilla Presley, Michael Richards, Alan Shepard, Frank Thomas, Jim Varney, Stan Winston.

Forty years after the *Disneyland* anthology series began with the episode *The Disneyland Story*, celebrities offer their thoughts on what Disney television programs have meant to them. The program also includes numerous clips from the various Disney television series.

WONDERS OF THE WATER WORLD

Aired on 1/29/77 with *A Horse Called Comanche* as part of the *NBC All-Disney Saturday Night at the Movies* series of specials, this show was first shown on the anthology series.

The Cornerstone of the Empire

3

The Anthology Series

Much has been written about how Walt Disney created the concept for Disneyland while taking his young daughters to local amusement parks and carnivals. He knew there had to be a better way to entertain families, but unfortunately, his dreams would not come cheap. As the scope of his plans increased, so did the cost of the Park, and Walt found himself in a constant battle for financing.

Walt continued his work on the Park, but the estimated price tag of $7 million to buy the land and open the Park was far more than he could raise by himself. He was finally forced to come to the realization that the only way he could succeed was to find a wealthy outside partner. Luckily for Walt, he had a potential source of financing in television:

> Every time I'd get to thinking of television I would think of this Park. And I knew that if I did anything like the Park that I would have some kind of a medium like television to let people know about it. So I said "well here's the way I'll get my Park going. It's natural for me to tie in with my television." So it happened that I had sort of say whether we went into television or not. I had a contract that said I had complete say of what we produced. So I just sort of insisted that my Disneyland Park be a part of my television show.

Roy Disney began working on the task of sorting out the many offers the Studio had received, and over the following months there were several deals that almost succeeded in bringing Disney to the air. In order to counter criticism that a Disney series might be too self promoting, and to show the networks what they were bringing to the bargaining table, Walt had Bill Walsh, who had

helmed the two Christmas specials, prepare samples of possible shows. Walsh wrote to Walt on August 6, 1953, while Disney was in New York for meetings with the networks, and sent five dummy scripts for a proposed half-hour series to be titled *The Walt Disney Show*. Walsh also included ideas for eight more shows, and Walt was encouraged enough to have Walsh prepare thirty-three scripts for the series. Several of these scripts have been lost over the years, but those that survive show the Studio planned to use their existing animated product almost exclusively to fill the time slot, with very little new production or promotion of current Disney films. The first show, for example, was titled *Fables*, and would have featured the cartoons *The Ugly Duckling* and *Johnny Appleseed*.

Just in case the networks were not interested in *The Walt Disney Show*, the Studio prepared outlines for several other potential series. A Studio report dated September 30, 1953, lists the three additional shows as:

- *Mickey Mouse Club TV Show*, a proposed daily live show. This is one of the earliest mentions of using Mickey Mouse as the theme for a children's show.

- *The True Life TV Show*—a proposed half-hour series highlighting animals from around the world, following the format of the theatrical *True-Life Adventure* series.

- *The World of Tomorrow*—this series would have combined humorous animation with live action segments designed to educate viewers about the world around them.

Although the networks were definitely interested in discussing a television series with

Disney, they were all cool to the theme park concept. From the outset, Walt and Roy made it clear that the Park was an integral part of the package they were peddling—no support for Disneyland, no show. CBS showed the least interest, making it clear early on that despite their desire for a Disney TV show, they wanted no part of the highly speculative theme park. There was another stumbling block in dealing with CBS, for they wanted Walt to produce his series in color, but he had no faith in their color system. CBS and NBC had both developed their own independent methods of broadcasting in color, and the government had left it up to the marketplace to decide which would survive. If CBS could convince Walt to provide them with a color show, it would provide them with a powerful marketing tool to aid in sales of their system. Walt was invited by CBS executives to a special demonstration of their system, which used a rotating wheel inside each TV set to produce a primitive color picture. The results were fairly dismal, and Walt belittled the system, thus effectively ending the talks with CBS. ABC continued to express interest, but Disney decided to concentrate instead on making a deal with the far-larger NBC.

RCA, the parent company of NBC, was interested in attracting new viewers to NBC in the hope of selling them televisions. If NBC could create an entire new marketing group by introducing a series aimed at children, there was a very strong possibility this would result in additional sales of RCA televisions. The seriousness of Disney's interest can be judged by the fact that, for a time, Walt and Roy seriously considered the possibility of a merger with RCA. This was truly a major departure from their business dealings in the past, since they had very carefully steered clear of any partnerships since the disastrous loss of "Oswald," Walt's first cartoon success, to an early distributor. Walt's belief in Disneyland was so great that he considered risking his entire company to gain the money he so desperately needed.

Finally, a deal is struck

After months of negotiating, the time came when Walt and Roy decided they needed a final decision from NBC. Roy flew to New York in early 1954 for the showdown meeting, having received advance word that General Sarnoff, the head of RCA, was finally ready to sign the deal. As soon as Roy arrived,

though, the flight seemed to have been a complete waste of time, for RCA asked for yet more time to think things over. A disgusted Roy left Sarnoff's office, and by his telling, picked up the first phone he saw and called Leonard Goldenson, the head of ABC, asking him "Leonard, a couple of years ago you expressed an interest in working something out with us in television. Are you still interested?" Was ABC interested? Roy gleefully recalled the response from Goldenson: "Roy, where are you? I'll be right over." At long last, Walt would have his chance to build Disneyland.

Of course, it would take a great deal of effort to move from a statement of interest by ABC to getting a show on the air. Before Roy could finalize the financial arrangements with ABC, Walt needed to settle on the format for the series. Goldenson was interested in two series, one for adults and the second for children, so Walt prepared handwritten outlines for each. The first set of notes was for the now retitled adult-oriented series:

**Walt Disney
Presents
DISNEYLAND**

- Half hour T.V. show presenting Disney hits of the past—
- Something of the present
- And things to come

- Walt Disney to M.C. and present guest stars etc.—
- such as B. Goodman with Goodman shorts
- Ethel Smith with her shorts?
- (Fred) Waring
- Andrews Sisters
- Dennis Day
- Nelson Eddie (sic)
- F. Martin—Dina (sic) Shore
- Andy Russel—Carmen Miranda + Joe Carioca + possibly Marge/Gower (Champion)
- Edgar Burgen (sic)
- Roy Rogers etc.

- Special TV films to be produced such as
- HISTORY OF THINGS
     Fun with Facts
- MUSIC FOR THE LOW BROW
     You and Me
- WE CAN ALL DRAW
     It's a Cinch

- THE LOWDOWN ON ART
  A Good Cook's An Artist
- THE ORIGIN OF FABLES
  Aesop-LaFountain-Grimm

- Drawing Contests
- Story Contests
- Disneyland Contests
- Plenty of Prizes

- Give away ponies bred and raised in Disneyland
- Trips to Disneyland for winners and escorts
- One week stay at Disneyland hotel—
- Appearance on TV show for all winners

Walt's thoughts on using stars such as Benny Goodman and the others on this list reflects his continued hope that he could use his older product such as *Make Mine Music* and *Melody Time* to provide the framework for major portions of the series. This would have provided a relatively low cost per show, but later research would show that it would be necessary to make a major commitment to new production in order to fill the weekly slot. Thus, it would be the "Special TV films" that would come to dominate the series.

Although Walt's notes were only a very rough outline of what the series would be, they were enough to seal the deal with ABC. In addition to the *Disneyland* series, ABC's investment earned them the right of first refusal for any other product Disney might produce for television. This seemingly innocuous clause would be the basis for a major legal battle between Disney and ABC in just a few years.

The first rumors of the deal came in March 1954 and seemingly took many in the industry by surprise. After several weeks of speculation, the formal announcement of the ABC coup and the theme park was released on April 2, 1954. Robert E. Kintner, the president of ABC, proudly proclaimed that "Walt Disney is undoubtedly the greatest creative force in the entertainment field today. His entrance into TV marks a major and historical step forward for the industry. ABC is very proud of the privilege of working with the Disney organization, which will bring a new conception to television."

With the eyes of the world now turned toward the Studio to see what Walt would bring to television, the pressure was on to get the show into production.

Defining the show's format

The first major decision reached was settling on an anthology format for the series. The Studio knew they needed a format that allowed them to switch subjects from week to week in order to promote the Park or upcoming films, and an anthology show offered that freedom at little risk. Anthologies had done well so far, ranking as the top-rated series of 1949, 1950, and 1951.

In order to best promote the theme park, there needed to be a ready link between Disneyland the Park and Disneyland the series. This had been a major objective of Walt's all along, and the programming of the series soon reflected this desire. The series was split into several segments aligned with the themed lands in the Park.

A seemingly endless series of planning meetings were held to discuss possible formats and shows. It was a very busy time at the Studio, for all of this television effort was in addition to the effort underway for the theme park. Finally, though, the show began to crystallize. During a staff meeting on March 19, 1954, Walt described how he felt the show could both entertain the audience and be a promotional tool for the Studio:

> The format of the show is America. We can mingle fantasy, we can dream and be fantastic. There is no one over here telling us we cannot—I think this is part of America. We can show Frontierland and Main Street as part of that heritage.
>
> We may present something special for Thanksgiving, Christmas or Easter. We could have a guest day for everyone who has worked for us. Perhaps they could bring their children. One example, Benny Goodman and his child.

Another topic that day was how many shows the Studio could guarantee to deliver, as Card Walker felt they were in danger of falling behind on their commitment to ABC. Walt responded "Let's plug everything we can. For our benefit, have eighteen or twenty. We can do everything if we follow this format. I am thinking of four organizations or possibly five. One could be working on *20,000 Leagues*, another could be on *Lady* and we can pick up two units for the Disneyland show."

The "Disneyland show" Walt referred to was intended as the opening episode of the series, and was to promote both upcoming episodes and the Park. The tight timetable that all of this was being done under is seen when several of those at the meeting voiced their concerns about publicly revealing too much about the Park, for the agreement on the site in Anaheim had yet to be finalized.

By now it was clear to those involved at Disney that the main purpose of the show would be to promote the Park and other Disney ventures. The Studio had yet to clear these plans fully with ABC, and a meeting between the two was scheduled to finalize the schedule. There were countless details to work out, such as the amount of advertising to be carried in each show and where it should be placed. Walt and Card met again on April 22, this time with their advertising consultants, and they discussed how to interest the audience quickly at the start of each show by using a brief teaser of what was to come. This became a hallmark of the show, and served to whet the audience's appetite before the opening credits rolled—and before they might switch channels to another program.

Later that same day, the long-awaited meeting with the network was held, and Walt outlined his concept for the series' overall format. Each week would have a theme, and these would be tied to the themed lands being built at Disneyland. In addition to the shows using older Disney cartoons, there would be new episodes featuring American heroes, previews of upcoming films, and updates on the progress at Disneyland. Any concerns the Studio had over ABC accepting the format were quickly put to rest when ABC's Kintner replied "It is a very exciting concept. I think this would be great. I accept it."

The rest of the meeting went well, and an enthusiastic Kintner told Walt "I hope you have a large mail department," for he knew a wave of fan mail was inevitable. With close to carte blanche approval of their plans, the Studio team began the task of filming the shows for their first season.

The search for a host

One important item that still had not been resolved was who was to host the show. The Studio had considered using several different actors, and possibly avoiding an on-screen host entirely by simply tying the episodes together with narration. Walt announced his decision during a May 25, 1954, story meeting on a show intended to promote *Lady and the Tramp*:

I don't consider myself an actor or anything, but in trying to get hold of these things, I can introduce them, get them going. I'm myself, good or bad, I'm still myself; that will be the gimmick. It's the safest bet to get under way; then later we can develop ways and other people can take over. If we over-use me, I'll be the first to recognize it; I know my limitations. If it's right for me to be talking about it, if it's my business I can talk about it; if it's what we do here at the studio, the group, the individuals and the staff—it would be no problem to do that.

I stumped myself, worrying about being in too much of it. I haven't got a good voice to carry narration, got a nasal twang, I know. I'm not being immodest, just being practical. But I just think it's the way to get this thing off. We've been avoiding it, but I think I have got to do it until we've established other personalities that mean something to the audience. Like Peggy Lee. And tie her up with what she has done in this picture. She can carry the load since she has actually done things on the picture; she can really plug *Lady*. Unless we use someone like (Kirk) Douglas. Got to be an M.C. to get it going. It ties in with the whole thing. We've been selling the name and the personality.

Although Walt mentioned the possibility of handing the duties of hosting the series to someone else, he continued the role until his death. The closest he did come to giving up the central spot was in a number of the nature episodes, where Winston Hibler introduced the various segments. Even in those shows, though, Walt appeared long enough to welcome the audience, bring on Hibler, and then returned to describe next week's episode.

Although he was excellent in his role as host, and was enthusiastically received, Walt never enjoyed working in front of the camera, once saying "I'm as big a ham as anyone, but actually it's an ordeal for me to be in front of the cameras. They wanted me to smile, to be warm. All I could see was that cold eye of the camera and the glum faces of the crew staring at me." Looking back at the early episodes, one can detect Walt's nervousness, but his warm and friendly attitude contributed greatly to public acceptance not only of the show, but of all things Disney. To millions of Americans, he was seen each week as a friendly relative eager to share yet another new surprise.

"And now your host, Walt Disney"

The majority of Walt's introductions were done in a studio film set intended to represent his personal office. A fair bit of artistic license was taken with this, for while Walt's real office was in the Studio's Animation Building, the "window" of his television office had a nice view of the very same Animation Building. The various awards and mementoes seen on the set were real, for Walt felt more comfortable with his own items close at hand. A system was set up where each item used on the series was carefully noted as to the location in the real office and the television version, and the Studio moving crew became quite adept at emptying one office and setting up the other. This had to be done on very short notice, as Walt's busy schedule kept him from spending much time on the set. However, he still wanted his awards in his real office in case visitors stopped by, so each move was done at the last possible moment.

With Walt's time at a premium, he could not afford the time to film his introductions on a weekly basis. This would also not have been cost effective, for the office set needed to be prepared and the film crew standing by for each introduction. The solution was to film a number of introductions at the same time. Disney staffer Jack Bruner recalled at one point Walt filmed twelve to fourteen introductions over a three-day period, which evidently was a record.

At first, each of Walt's lead-ins was written by the same writers who had prepared that week's story. Walt didn't like this scheme, for he felt uncomfortable with the changes in speaking style he was presented with for each lead-in. He decided that he needed a personal writer who could make the lead-ins closer to something he would write himself if he had the time, with more humor and warmth to help him feel more comfortable on screen. He selected a former Studio employee, Jack Speirs, and convinced him to return to write the lead-in scripts. Speirs handled the task for several years, and when he later concentrated on nature film scripts for Winston Hibler, he was replaced as Walt's writer by Jack Bruner, who continued in that role until Walt's death. Despite the care with these scripts, and Walt's professed unease at appearing on camera, he also ad-libbed in many of the introductions, particularly when animals were involved. Staff members recalled one day when his lead-in was interrupted by an overly aggressive bear cub, which bit Walt. After some first-aid, Walt came back to the set, but he decided to do the lead-in his way—without the bear.

The temptation of color

Although the majority of television production at the time was in black-and-white, Walt felt strongly that color was the wave of the future. Although he had dismissed the CBS color system as being doomed to failure, his discussions with NBC had confirmed his own predictions that color broadcasting was inevitable. As far back as 1953 the Studio had indicated they planned to produce any potential series in color, but the deal with ABC unfortunately seemed to preclude this. Being the smallest of the networks, ABC had very few stations that could afford the cost of color transmission equipment. Despite Walt's best efforts to get ABC to pay for the cost of filming in color, the network refused, arguing that the first few years would never be shown in color and thus were not worth the additional cost.

Walt disagreed on this last point, so much so that he took yet another gamble by deciding to supply the additional money out of Studio funds. He had considerable experience with the periodic rerelease of the Studio's animated films to theaters, and wanted to make the shows reuseable as well, including their possible theatrical release overseas.

The show begins

On 10/27/54, after months of anticipation, the first episode was seen. *The Disneyland Story,* provided viewers with an explanation of both the new television series and the upcoming theme park, with a plug for the upcoming feature *20,000 Leagues Under the Sea* thrown in for good measure. Even before the series premiered, it was no secret that the Studio planned to heavily cross promote the theme park. As a Disney staffer noted in a *TV Guide* article about the upcoming opening of the Park, "By that time, there will be hardly a living soul in the United States who won't have heard about the Disneyland amusement park and who won't be dying to come see it. Yessir, television is a wonderful thing."

While it was intended to promote the Park further in future episodes, what followed was dictated more by time constraints in getting the show on the air than by programming choices. The next few shows made extensive use of existing product, such as the second episode, *Alice in Wonderland,* or promoted new films with heavy use of footage from those productions.

Even though these shows were done on a relatively low budget, they paid off handsomely for Disney. Although feature length films such as *Alice* were not part of the ABC deal, Walt knew that they would be tremendous audience draws. He also knew that using *Alice* on television didn't greatly damage the chance of reusing it in theaters, for the film had fared poorly at the box office and would not be released again for quite some time. Walt did have trouble convincing Roy to use films on the series, once joking "I got a few from him, though, by telling him I just wanted to use sections of them. I neglected to tell him how long the sections would be."

Operation Undersea is an excellent example of just how popular the series became as the season went on. Walt had been so confident that one of the networks would meet his terms that he had started production on this episode before striking a TV deal. Knowing that the behind-the-scenes footage was essential in selling the show to the public, he had sent a documentary crew out with the *20,000 Leagues* main unit. The show was run three times the first year, and rather than showing the expected decrease in ratings, the audience actually grew for each rerun. The episode also brought the Studio two Emmy Awards, one for Best Individual Show and one for Best Television Film Editing.

Up to this point, the series had consisted primarily of recycled theatrical product. The first truly new show ended up being the story of Davy Crockett.

"Born on a Mountaintop in Tennessee . . ."

One of Disney's biggest television hits, and now credited as television's first mini-series, *Davy Crockett* almost never made it to the air. The Studio researched a number of famous Americans to use in the Frontierland segments, but Walt rejected many of them as unsuitable. One point he stressed to his staff was that the subjects had to be heroes, telling them "I don't want any picked over heroes. There will be no outlaws or badmen glorified—no Jesse James or the Daltons." After months of research, the production team hadn't decided on a subject, but Walt was growing impatient and called a meeting to settle the matter. Knowing they needed a recommendation, the staff quickly picked one.

Bill Walsh admitted that their choice was a fortuitous accident, telling an interviewer "We were planning to do a series on American folk heroes—like Johnny Appleseed, Daniel Boone and Bigfoot Wallace. And the first one we pulled out, by dumb luck, was Davy Crockett."

The choice was far from unanimous, for Walt didn't share the team's enthusiasm. Walsh summed up Disney's reactions in a tale that insiders say is "classic Walt": "That's where we ran into the thing like Davy Crockett—because he wanted to do a series about legendary Americans like Davy Crockett—Bigfoot Wallace, Paul Bunyan, the guy who invented popcorn, Windwagon Smith and all those kind of legendary characters. Well, the first one we picked on was accidentally Davy Crockett, and Walt was not too thrilled by Davy Crockett—too much fighting Indians. After all, how many ways can you kill Indians, or learn anything new about it? So we did some (story) boards on Davy Crockett—and may I tell you, we put everything but the kitchen sink in those boards. Like there was fighting the Indians, Seminoles down in Florida, fighting tomahawk duels with Red Stick. Then he went to Congress and raised hell, then he fought Andy Jackson who was doing something bad to the Indians and Davy stalked out of Congress because Andy Jackson was stealing from the Indians and he didn't want to hear about it. In fact, he fought Andy tooth and nail. Then he went out west and had a lot of adventures going out west and he had a lot more Indian fights there. Then he got into trouble with the cowboys—early Texans—and then he got to the Alamo and then he lasted through the Alamo for 14 days—and last day of the Alamo they broke the joint wide open. He died as he had lived, swinging his rifle around and there was this pile of 17 dead Mexicans piling up in front of him. Walt looked at all of this, and he said—I'll never forget his classic line—'Yeah, but what does he *do?*' That's when Norman Foster fainted dead away."

Finally swayed to backing the Crockett project, Walt then took a personal interest in casting the shows. Veteran actor Buddy Ebsen was a leading candidate for the role of the frontier hero until Walt saw the science fiction film *Them!* Someone had suggested the star of that film, James Arness, as a potential Crockett, but a character actor in a minor role caught Walt's eye. The actor was Fess Parker, a lanky six foot, five inch actor who was born on a ranch near Ft. Worth, Texas. Parker signed a long-term contract with the Studio, making him the first adult actor to do so.

The Studio announced the signing of Carleton Carpenter as Davy's sidekick, Georgie Russel, but they had a change of heart and he was dropped just before filming was to begin. Buddy Ebsen, the original choice for Crockett, agreed to take the role of Russel and arrived at the North Carolina location the day before shooting began.

The Ballad of Davy Crockett

Besides Fess Parker, one of the most memorable aspects of the Crockett stories was the series' theme song, *The Ballad of Davy Crockett*. Bill Walsh remembered how the famous song came into being. When the editing was completed on the first episode, the Studio discovered that it was approximately five minutes shorter than they needed. "It was panic time again. Unless we padded the show", recalled Walsh, "we would run short. I finally decided we could pad it by using the original storyboard sketches as a prologue to the film. Walt liked the idea but thought that it needed something extra. Something like music. In a flash I was on the phone to Tom Blackburn, who had written the script. I told him we had to have a song to accompany the drawings. Could he write one?

"Tom nearly passed out. He stammered for a moment and said, 'Hell, I've never wrote a lyric in my life.' We told him it didn't matter; we needed a song—any song," Walsh continued. "He said, 'Okay, if you're that desperate.' He and George Burns, who composed the score, went down the hall. They came back in about twenty minutes and said, 'Well, this isn't much.' And they began, 'Born on a mountain top in Tennessee . . .' My first reaction was, 'That's supposed to be a song?' I thought it sounded pretty awful, but we didn't have time for anything else." Other versions of the story have the team needing two hours to write the song, but in either case, it was time well spent. In addition to helping fill out the first episode to the required length, the *Ballad of Davy Crockett* proved to be one of the most memorable pieces of music ever written for television. Interestingly, George Burns later recalled "The irony of it was that most people thought it was an authentic folk song that we had uncovered and updated."

Even before the first episode had aired, Walt decided to incorporate it in the remaining two episodes as well. He felt the song de-vice helped move the story along, remarking in a editing meeting that "This particular story will hit the adults more but the lyrics will pick it up for the kids. It's what I call a comic book approach, and you know how many adults still read comic books! These lyrics are important. They help to keep the story moving in the minds of children and also in the minds of some adults who will be wondering what's happening." Used throughout the Crockett episodes, the song would eventually have twenty verses.

The unexpected success of the three Crockett episodes took Walt by surprise. As Walt later acknowledged, "We had no idea what was going to happen on Crockett. Why, by the time the first show finally got on the air, we were already shooting the third one and calmly killing Davy off at the Alamo. It became one of the biggest over-night hits in TV history, and there we were with just three films and a dead hero!" Despite Davy's valiant death at the Alamo, the public clamored for more Crockett stories. Walt tried to resist, sticking to an oft-repeated dislike of repeating himself. In an interview on March 15, 1955, he apparently closed the door on any new Crockett stories, saying that "I didn't want to crawl into the hole of doing a series. There are too many good stories around. Besides, it was a matter of history. Everybody knows Davy Crockett died at the Alamo. I wasn't going to tamper with history."

Not long after the Crockett saga completed its run on television, Walt made an amazing announcement. The shows were so popular, he said, that the Studio would combine the episodes into one story and release it domestically as a feature film. Critics were astonished; no one had ever tried to have people pay to see something they had already seen for free. (There had been a film version of the popular television series *Dragnet* in 1954, but that was an all-new production, not reuse of television episodes.)

Reaction among theater owners to this plan was mixed at best. Some were happy to be able to cash in on the Crockett money machine, but others saw it as another threat by diminishing the uniqueness of the theatrical experience. S. D. Kane, the executive counsel of North Central Allied, a large distribution chain, scornfully remarked "Frankly, if I had a theatre and Mr. Disney asked me to play a picture which had been assembled from films shown on TV, I'd ask him how much he was going to pay me to run it."

Luckily, not everyone thought the concept

was ludicrous. *Davy Crockett, King of the Wild Frontier* was released in more than 1,300 theaters. It was an outstanding financial success, raking in $2.5 million at the box office. This was an unprecedented feat, particularly considering that the television episodes had already been seen by 90 million television viewers.

Tomorrowland, the forgotten land

While the anthology series was divided into four themes, there was not an even number of shows on each of them, and only one Tomorrowland segment was aired during the first season. It's not surprising that the Studio virtually ignored the Tomorrowland section of the show, for no one was quite sure exactly how to portray the future.

Despite the lack of attention given to the Tomorrowland segment, the Studio did place one show, *Rockets and Space*, into production. As part of the research for that episode, the Studio used the March 22, 1952, issue of *Collier's* magazine, which featured articles by space pioneers Wenrher von Braun, Willy Ley, and Heinz Haber. Ward Kimball, the Tomorrowland producer, was so impressed by these articles that he brought the three scientists aboard as special advisors. This was to be a major coup for Disney, as von Braun was later to become famous for his role with NASA on the American manned space program. The input of these scientists was virtually years ahead of its time, for the episode, which was aired as *Man in Space*, accurately foretold how man would break through Earth's gravity and achieve space flight. The Disney space shows came to feature multi-stage spaceships, reusable crafts similar to the space shuttle, and more amazingly, accurately predicted the steps needed to reach the moon. When Apollo 8 circled the moon, von Braun called Ward Kimball and remarked "Well, Ward, it looks like they're following our script."

With the Cold War in full swing there was tremendous interest in space travel, and *Man in Space* fit the public's needs perfectly. The ratings were so high that it was rerun just three months after the first broadcast. The repeat airing was just as successful, and it attracted a very important viewer. Impressed by the vision of Disney's experts, President Eisenhower called the Studio the same day and borrowed a print of the show to screen for his space experts at the Pentagon. On July 30, 1955 it was announced that America would place a satellite in Earth orbit. Eisenhower publicly credited the show with pushing the concept of space travel from science fiction to the possible, helping pave the way to get the necessary funding for America's fledgling space effort.

The public's interest in space continued unabated, and the Studio reran the show yet another time three months after the second broadcast. The ratings for that outing were also high, and the Studio released the show as a theatrical short subject in 1956. It's doubtful that any other television episode has been aired three times in six months then released theatrically, but once again, Disney had achieved the seemingly impossible.

Disneyland finished the first season as the number sixth rated series on the air, attracting an average of 39 percent of the viewers each week. The Nielsen ratings were not the only sign of success though. In addition to the two Emmy Awards earned by the episode *Operation Undersea*, the anthology series brought another honor to the Studio this season, winning an Emmy Award for Best Variety Series.

Crockett returns from the dead

In order to profit from last year's success with Davy Crockett, Disney finally gave in to public demand and decided to resurrect his hero, obviously setting the story before the fateful trip to the Alamo. A decision was made to rework a story already underway about Mike Fink, a legendary keelboater on the Mississippi River, and to incorporate Davy into the tale. Although there was no evidence that Crockett and Fink had ever met, one Studio staffer laughingly noted that there was no proof they hadn't.

The original Mike Fink story was reworked into a new story originally titled *Davy Crockett and the Rivermen*, which soon became two episodes, *Davy Crockett's Keelboat Race* and *Davy Crockett and The River Pirates*. Character actor Jeff York was signed to play Mike Fink, the self-styled "King of the River." Like Parker and Ebsen, York was a natural for the role, and Disney later used him in numerous television and film projects.

The two new Crockett episodes followed the pattern used for the original trilogy. They were filmed on location, this time along the Ohio River, and once again, edited and released theatrically after a number of successful airings on the anthology series. This film, also titled *Davy Crockett and The River Pirates*, did noticeably less business than the first, and an astute Walt realized that the Crockett craze was coming to an end.

Despite the success of *Man in Space* in the first season, the Studio only produced one Tomorrowland episode this year as well. *Man in Space* had aired late in the season and the ratings had taken the Studio by surprise, but the Studio was not ready to produce additional Tomorrowland segments in time to fully capitalize on its success. This was compounded by the fact that, once again, the Studio wasn't quite sure what the future should look like. The episode for this year, *Man and the Moon*, was very similar to *Man in Space*, and explained how a flight to the moon was possible and how a space station could be built in orbit.

When Walt retired Davy Crockett, he found himself with a rather gaping hole in the anthology schedule, for there was a noticeable lack of Frontierland episodes during the 1956–57 season. With Westerns gaining steadily in the ratings, this was a problem the Studio was determined to correct for 1957–58. The answer, not surprisingly, was to create a new series as close to the Crockett formula as possible. Once again the Studio set out to make a modern-day hero out of a plainspoken fur trapper, but this time out, the central character was a purely fictional one. The new hero was to be Andy Burnett, an explorer in a series of novels by Stewart Edward White. Aired under the blanket title *The Saga of Andy Burnett*, each episode followed Andy Burnett as he traveled west in the company of a band of mountain men.

The Studio tried to duplicate the Crockett formula in almost every detail. Andy, a taciturn and thoughtful man, was always downplaying his knowledge and skills, just like Davy Crockett. Like Davy, Andy dressed in buckskins and carried a rifle instead of a pistol. He had a sidekick, Joe Crane, who was somewhat like Crockett's pal Georgie Russel and somewhat like Crockett's one-time foe, Mike Fink. The latter point is not coincidental, for Crane was played by Jeff York, who had co-starred as Mike Fink. The actor who played Andy, Jerome Courtland, was tall (six feet, five inches), just like Fess Parker. And, to complete the cloning effort, Disney had the writers of *The Ballad of Davy Crockett*, George Burns and Tom Blackburn, come up with a theme song with much the same melody. Unfortunately, Andy never caught on with the viewers.

The only Tomorrowland episode this year was *Mars and Beyond*, and like its predecessors, it was also a ratings success. A large factor in this was that it aired just aired two months after the U.S.S.R. successfully orbited the world's first satellite, Sputnik I, and Americans turned toward Disney for a possible look at how America might respond.

ABC misses a very large opportunity

By this time, ABC was airing the anthology series, *The Mickey Mouse Club*, and *Zorro*. Even with four hours of Disney programming each week, however, the network wanted the Studio to produce additional series. Disney executive Donn Tatum recalled how a meeting on the subject with ABC led the Studio into an unexpected direction. "The idea for *The Shaggy Dog* was presented to ABC who were after Walt for a series. 'Please give us another series, please give us another series, please give us another series.' So they came out for their annual visit in the early part of the spring in order to talk about the plans for next year and Walt said, 'All right, you want another series, I'll give you one.' And he described *The Shaggy Dog* and Leonard Goldenson was there and Jim Aubrey who had just joined them was the top program man and before Walt finished Jim Aubrey looked at his watch and said 'Walt, I'm sorry I've got an appointment. I've got to leave.' It angered Walt and irritated him so, that a half-hour after they left he called a story meeting and said 'Let's make a picture out of it.' I told Aubrey once, 'Jim, we've got a shrine in our place to you. We keep a light there of undying pledge.' 'What do you mean?' I told him the story, I said 'Do you have any idea how many millions of dollars you made for us by getting up and leaving the meeting that day?' Then I gave him the grosses on *The Shaggy Dog*, and then *The Absent-Minded Professor*, and then *The Son of Flubber*."

Television is a medium of trends, and anytime one studio has a hit, you can count on the competition to quickly produce variations on that theme. This became obvious during the 1957–58 season, when Westerns were popular enough to take seven positions in the closely watched "Top 20" list. ABC was determined to share in the success, and thus Disney began receiving not-so-subtle pressure to increase the number of Frontierland episodes.

Walt definitely did not like having to give in to these demands. He complained about what he termed the "blankety blank Westerns," feeling they restricted the creative freedom he had enjoyed since starting the anthology series. Donn Tatum recalled how

Walt finally called a meeting with the network executives, making them wait in a conference room until he was ready for his grand entrance. He strode into the room, dressed in Western garb, threw his pistols on the table and said "Okay, you want Westerns, you're gonna have Westerns."

Despite a successful season, Walt was not entirely satisfied with how things were going. In May of 1959, he talked to an interviewer about possibly taking the show off the air, saying "I've had complaints from parents who ask me why we don't make new shows. Nobody wants to put up the money. I'd like to take them off the air and bring them back in three or four years. There would be a new audience then."

Part of this might have been posturing on Walt's part, for a legal storm was brewing over rights to both the anthology series and *Zorro*, a battle which would soon move into the courts. ABC and Disney began to argue over who owned the shows, and Walt might have been trying to engage the network in a game of wits. He singled out *Zorro* specifically, claiming "I'd just as soon quit it. I'd like to use Guy Williams in some features, anyway."

Several years later, after Walt moved the anthology series to NBC, he again went on record as to his feelings about the switch to Westerns. "They (the Disney westerns) made so much money for ABC that before long I found myself in a straitjacket. I no longer had the freedom of action I enjoyed in those first three years. They kept insisting that I do more and more Westerns and my show became loaded with Elfego Baca, the Swamp Fox, Texas John Slaughter, Daniel Boone. I found myself competing with *Maverick*, *Wyatt Earp* and every other Western myth. When I came up with a fresh idea in another field, the network executives would say no."

The western orientation of the anthology series was carried over into the 1959–60 season. A press release issued at the beginning of the season noted that eighteen of the twenty-six new shows to be produced that year would be from Frontierland, with the remaining eight split between Adventureland and Fantasyland.

The year unfortunately saw a serious deterioration in relations between the Studio and ABC. Walt and Roy had been increasingly unhappy with the deal they had struck with ABC, for they felt that the network was now benefitting far more from the arrangement than the Studio was. They wanted to see if they could sell their series to NBC or CBS,

but ABC balked at the possibility, claiming that the original deal had given it a seven-year exclusive commitment to the anthology series, *The Mickey Mouse Club* and *Zorro*. This effectively stopped negotiations with the other two networks. Donn Tatum described Roy as being incensed at ABC's actions. Visibly angered, Roy told Disney staffers he felt it was a breach of faith. On July 2, 1959, Disney filed a lawsuit against ABC, asking the court to invalidate the contracts between the two companies under provisions of the federal antitrust laws. Despite this battle between the two partners, Disney and ABC did agree to a separate contract for *Walt Disney Presents*, thereby keeping the anthology series on the air.

The series changed nights for the 1960–61 season to Sunday evening, marking the beginning of a television tradition that continues to this day. While the legal battles with ABC waged on, Walt appeared to show little interest in the anthology series, and the Western emphasis continued with repeats of *Davy Crockett* and new *Texas John Slaughter* stories. Disney produced four one-hour *Zorro* episodes and aired them on the anthology series to keep the character in the public's mind. The plan was to bring *Zorro* back as a weekly series once the ownership of the series was clear, but by the time the legal dust had settled Walt had realized that the time for *Zorro* had passed.

By this time, Walt had become re-interested in the anthology series, for the problems with ABC had escalated to the point where the relationship simply could not continue and he saw an end to the Westerns. Luckily, the legal issues were resolved in the Studio's favor, and Walt began to think seriously about moving to another network. The past success of the anthology series made it an attractive offering, but with only two networks to choose from, the Studio knew that it had to move very carefully during the negotiations. If anything happened to cause either NBC or CBS to reject the series, the Studio's bargaining power would be greatly reduced.

Right from the start, Walt decided to concentrate on the NBC network. One of the major reasons Walt wanted to move to NBC was their leadership in color broadcasting. His earlier discussions with CBS and NBC in the 1950s had not been forgotten, and although CBS had abandoned their incompatible color system, they still lagged behind NBC in the number of color-equipped stations. Walt felt that color was essential to making the best use of his products, and that since he was making his shows in color anyway, he was determined that the anthology series finally be broadcast in color.

Demonstrating his interest in moving to NBC, Walt made a personal pitch to a group of NBC executives to move the anthology series there and to broadcast in color. Afterward, he summed up his feelings when he told Donn Tatum and Card Walker "Fellas, I want this deal. If necessary I'll stand on my head in Macy's window."

Luckily for Walt, he never did end up on display in Macy's, for NBC was quick to see that advantage of teaming up with Disney, particularly as it might help parent company RCA sell more color televisions. In a rare move, RCA agreed to sponsor half of the episodes itself, proving the company's faith in the Disney name.

The move to Sundays at 7:30 PM on NBC for the 1961–62 season was proudly proclaimed in the trade press, with many newspapers dutifully carrying the word that Disney would soon be seen in color. The emphasis on color was so pronounced that the series received the new title *Walt Disney's Wonderful World of Color*, also known as *The Wonderful World of Color*. Ads began to appear urging people to be ready for this broadcasting milestone, and much to RCA's pleasure, sales actually began to increase even before the show began to air.

It was originally planned to re-create the original format of the "Disneyland" openings by dividing the series into four different themes. "We're going into the world and calling it *The Wonderful World of Color*," Walt said. "But within that, I break it down into *The Wonderful World of Fiction, The Wonderful World of Fantasy, The Wonderful World of Adventure* and *The Wonderful World of the Classics*." These individual titles were never used on the air, however.

Press releases noted that the series was to begin with a three-hour special, "including a two-hour film classic designed especially for color television," but this was eventually dropped for a special one-hour introduction instead. Knowing that he needed to quickly establish that his new series was indeed new, Walt created a new character, Professor Ludwig Von Drake, who was seen in the first and many other episodes. The good professor, who was related to Donald Duck, was a self-proclaimed expert on any subject that arose. However, his knowledge and explanations tended to blur over issues such as facts. In the first episode, *An Adventure in Color (and) Mathmagic Land*, Walt appeared to tell the viewers about some of the exciting new shows he was working on, then turned the show over to Von Drake for an explanation of the magic behind color television.

This season, by the way, did not include any of the Westerns that Walt had grown so tired of.

Other ventures with NBC

Just as the original deal with ABC had given them the right of first refusal for any proposed new Disney series, the contract with NBC included a similar arrangement. Over the years, Walt and NBC discussed several possible projects. At one point, Walt thought about producing a series to be called *Jimmy Dale, Alias the Grey Seal*. The main character was a private eye in Boston who was a master of disguise. After solving a crime, he always left his trademark, a grey seal, behind to let the police know he had cracked the case. Walt had bought the rights to all of the books in the series, but the network felt the concept was too far afield from what the public now expected of Disney and the project was dropped.

Another project that made it into the discussion phase was based on John Steinbeck's book *Travels with Charlie*. The format would have followed the book, featuring a man and his dog traveling and becoming involved with the people they meet. The project gained the attention of Du Pont, which was very interested in sponsoring the series. Donn Tatum tried to brush them off, feeling the timing wasn't right, but Walt was personally interested in the project and began negotiating with Du Pont and NBC. Tatum later remembered the initial reaction from NBC, saying "And NBC, of course, its hair was standing on end at the thought of putting Steinbeck and Disney together. And they actively promoted it and Walt and Steinbeck did have a discussion. It was very cursory. I think it became apparent to both of them that it wasn't going to work, and that was the end of it."

The anthology series began the 1963–64 season in a somewhat unusual fashion. At this time, the start of each new television season was a fairly rigid process. Each of the networks would agree to a starting week, and all of the new shows and episodes would be unveiled to the eager public in a controlled manner. Disney decided not to follow the rules this year, though, and began the

1963–64 season one week earlier than everyone else.

The first episode of the year was the old favorite, *Davy Crockett—Indian Fighter.* Unwilling to admit that they were breaking the unwritten rules governing the start of the season, NBC chose to officially list it as the last episode of the 1962–63 season, but the show did exactly what Disney—and NBC—had hoped it would. Tired of recent reruns, audiences turned to *Davy Crockett*, and followed that pattern the next two weeks as Disney repeated the rest of the original trilogy episodes. The new season was off to a great start.

The continued success of the Crockett episodes awoke interest in the possibility of producing new stories. Fess Parker proposed a new series or a film, but having escaped ABC, Walt wasn't interested in doing any more Westerns. Parker then went on to create a new series based on Daniel Boone, and it enjoyed several years of popularity. Today, many television viewers often confuse the two series, thinking that Disney had produced more than the five hours of Crockett episodes.

By the time the 1966–67 season began, Walt was spending less and less time on television. One of the reasons for this was his preoccupation with the new theme park being planned for Florida. Another, more ominous reason was Walt's failing health. No one outside of the immediate family knew it, but a lifetime of smoking had caught up with Walt. He checked into the hospital for a series of tests and it was discovered that he had lung cancer. Unfortunately, by the time the problem had been diagnosed, it was too late.

On December 15, 1966, Walt Disney died. The world was shocked, for there had been no hint of his illness to the press. The Disney staff was even more shocked, for the company suddenly found itself without a leader.

Walt's death was a major blow to the Studio, one that would be felt for many years to come, for despite all of Walt's innovations and dreams, he had never dealt with the subject of what would happen after his death. Realizing that he needed to take quick action, Roy Disney postponed his planned retirement and stepped in to steer the company through the massive Florida theme park project. Although Roy had agreed to head the company, he never considered himself as a replacement for Walt's role as a public spokesman and he continued to remain relatively unknown. For the 1967–68 season, the

Studio had to begin a search for a new host for the anthology series.

The search was no easier than when Walt had looked for a host back at the beginning of the series. In fact, the search was much harder this time, for any new host would certainly be compared to Walt. Studio executives began to argue over the benefits of introducing a new host, for they were unable to settle on anyone who would clearly be identified with the Disney organization. Donn Tatum remembered how the Studio dealt with this very touchy issue. "There was a great deal of consideration given to finding another person to assume that role as storyteller. At first, NBC's attitude was that we should try to find someone like Danny Kaye. But after considerable discussion and thought we agreed it was not the solution. We could not really continue Walt's program with somebody else being presented as the host. So what we finally did was in effect eliminate the personal introduction, knowing in our minds that there might be some programs where we would have to have a person introduce it."

With the decision made not to try to replace Walt, here's how the Studio described the changes to the series new opening titles to prospective advertisers:

The Wonderful World of Color will have a new format for introducing the weekly absence of Walt, whose emceeing did do very much to put set-buying and color-viewing in the big-profit column.

Ten new lead-ins will give a new pace and variety to the program. Each will be a one-minute set of quick scene cuts kaleidoscoping Disney motion pictures, television, the Florida project, Disneyland—the entire Disney world—plus random, candid cuts of Walt himself.

Walt's death proved to be a major problem, for after several years of high ratings in which the anthology series was comfortably rated in the top 20 most watched shows, a serious ratings drop occurred in both the 1967–68 and 1968–69 seasons. With audiences for the anthology series declining, the Studio was faced with a challenge. In order to reach a wider audience, and the profits that offered, they would either have to change the basic format of the anthology series or look for new programming opportunities.

There was a great deal of reluctance within the company to tamper with the anthology series, which had by this time had almost become an American tradition. While the ratings were not impressive, the show still provided an excellent opportunity to keep the Disney name in the minds of the viewing public. The continuing use of the anthology product in the overseas markets also allowed the Studio to turn a continual profit despite rising production costs. Also, even though it had been several years since Walt's death, there was a great deal of reluctance to change "his" show. Therefore, the decision was made to explore the possibility of producing a new series. Preliminary discussions with NBC showed an interest by the network in carrying a new half-hour series, and work began in earnest.

One of the first decisions the Studio reached was to build upon past success and use the story line from a successful theatrical release or television show rather than taking the risk of a new concept. The Studio decided the strongest candidate for a series was a spinoff based on *The Scarecrow of Romney Marsh*, the mini-series that had starred Patrick McGoohan. In addition to this possible dramatic series, there was a great deal of interest in a "contemporary family situation" comedy, possibly based on *The Absent-Minded Professor*, *The Shaggy Dog*, or the *Merlin Jones* films. Although there was a great deal of initial interest in following through with these plans, the project was eventually shelved. One of the major reasons given for this was the sheer volume of work the Studio was facing to build the new Walt Disney World complex, as the same executives were involved in both the television and theme park operations.

To its credit, the Studio did not turn it's back on the anthology series. During the audience testing for the potential new series it had been found that there was still enough interest to keep the show going. This same research showed that the public was particularly interested in animal stories, and the Studio responded by producing shows about geese, dogs, ostriches, cougars, falcons, and crows. They also scheduled a number of theatrical films featuring animals, and when the season was over, nineteen of the fifty episodes were about animals.

This scientific scheduling paid off, for *The Wonderful World of Disney* soared to number nine that season, gaining almost 24 percent of the available audience each week. Even more importantly, the series continued to do fairly well in the ratings for the next few years, which, not surprisingly, followed the same formula.

The Studio did make one change this year. The anthology series underwent another title change, becoming *The Wonderful World of Disney*.

Unfortunately for the Studio, the early renewals of past years were now seen to be working against the anthology series and the ratings began slipping once more. Entire seasons had been filmed well in advance of their eventual airdates, making it impossible to quickly change programming to reflect changes in public tastes. The Studio countered this to some degree by scheduling additional theatrical releases for the 1970–71 season, for these could be added to or dropped from the schedule relatively easily. The Studio was gratified to see the anthology series soar in the ratings. While Disney executives were quick to claim credit, saying it was due to the quality of the programming, at least part of the success was due to weak opposition programming. *The Wonderful World of Disney* became NBC's fourth-top-rated series of the 1972–73 season, placing in the Nielsen "Top 10" for four weeks.

Jubilant with the success, NBC renewed the series through the 1975–76 season, and exercised their options for the 1976–77 and 1977–78 seasons. This unprecedented order meant that Disney was assured that the anthology series was guaranteed another five years on the air. No other series had ever received such a guarantee.

After fifteen seasons of being aired at 7:30 every Sunday night, the anthology series was moved to a new time slot for the 1975–76 season when the Federal Communications Commission mandated the formation of a so-called "family hour" of programming. This time slot would pit Disney against a very formidable foe the next season when CBS scheduled their new series *60 Minutes* during the family hour. As Bob King, Disney's Director of Marketing Services, noted, "We really got surprised that *60 Minutes* absolutely devastated *The Wonderful World of Disney*. I admire those people for figuring out how to appeal to a very wide-range audience. Now, it's up to us to do better."

The Studio announced that a number of changes were being considered for 1977–78 to improve the series in order to combat *60 Minutes*, including programming yet more films. Unfortunately, the anthology series continued its downward spiral. Ron Miller admitted that the results were "very discouraging, very disappointing," commenting that "We set out this year to take *The Hardy Boys*" (the competition on ABC), "and we haven't done it. Maybe it's the charisma of young Shaun Cassidy. Or maybe we've become complacent." This was one of the first public admissions that the old formula needed some major revisions.

The 1979–80 season would prove to be a milestone of sorts for Disney. Hoping to show that the Studio was finally responding to the declining ratings, the anthology series was retitled *Disney's Wonderful World*. It was also announced that the series would return to a format very similar to the original *Disneyland* format, with each week having a different theme. Instead of naming the weeks after the theme park lands, though, the new show would feature "Animation Night," "Fantasy Night," "Adventure Night," and "Comedy Night."

Despite the change in title and the weekly themes, though, little else was to change this year, as the Studio continued to rely heavily on theatrical features and repeat broadcasts. Only ten new shows were scheduled, although some of those would be two-parters. The Studio didn't try to downplay this reuse of old product; instead, it tried to make it sound like a programming coup. Audiences weren't fooled and the ratings drop continued.

After eighteen years of airing the anthology series on NBC, all was not well. The relationship with NBC had been worsening for some time, for the years of declining ratings were catching up to the Studio. An article in the July 14, 1979, edition of *The Boston Globe* pointed out how the partners no longer were seeing eye-to-eye, saying that "NBC executives are tired of the Disney organization's arrogance, its hostility to press questions, its unwillingness to release its best-known films to television for even a single showing, and, above all for its contempt for television as a piddling source of revenue compared with the Disney entertainment parks and real estate." The article also claimed that NBC felt the declining ratings for the anthology series hurt the network's other Sunday shows, and as a result, impacted NBC in general.

Despite such criticism, the Studio refused to publicly acknowledge the growing rift. In fact, a Disney press release issued the same month claimed "Someone once said, 'All good things must come to and end.' But in the case of NBC's weekly series *Disney's Wonderful World*, the end isn't even in sight." In February 1980, though, Studio ex-

ecutives made their first acknowledgment that the anthology series was seriously in danger of being canceled.

As work began on the 1980–81 season, there was little hope at the Studio of returning the anthology series to its former greatness. Despite the Studio's best efforts to increase the ratings in the 1979–80 season, the ratings had only increased 4 percent, with the series only attracting 26 percent of the viewers. The series was preempted twelve times during the season, making this the low point of the series' run on NBC. Thus, it was no surprise when the end of an era was announced. The Studio's Quarterly report of December 31, 1980, paid relatively little attention to an announcement thought impossible just a few years before:

> In December, NBC decided not to continue with the Company's television Series *The Wonderful World of Disney* when the current television season ends in December 1981. We are presently discussing new plans and projects covering the entire spectrum of Disney entertainment with all three networks.

Negotiations were held with ABC and CBS to find a new home for the anthology series, for the Studio was desperately trying to find a way to maintain its television visibility. The Studio's efforts paid off when CBS agreed to pick up the anthology series for the 1981–82 season. As is customary, both parties praised each other, with glowing predictions about the successes sure to come. B. Donald Grant, the president of CBS Entertainment, stated "We are pleased to be opening up this relationship with a studio that has long been recognized as the world's leading producer of family entertainment." In turn, Ron Miller told reporters "We're excited about joining with CBS in this relationship and believe it will bring Disney to new heights in television programming." At the same time, though, both Disney and CBS did comment on the fact they hadn't agreed on a format for the series, and they weren't even sure the show would air weekly.

It was eventually decided to stick with the same anthology concept, despite the problems Disney had faced in recent years. There was one positive note, though. Retitled *Walt Disney*, the series was moved to Saturdays at 8 P.M., finally ending the one-sided competition with *60 Minutes*.

The agreement with CBS called for the Studio to provide twenty-two hours of programming, plus repeats. Eight of the hours were intended as pilots, and the Studio's annual report noted that this was one of the main reasons for the venture. CBS also insisted that the series not be a vehicle just for reuse of previously aired episodes, and thus the season opened with a number of films that had not yet been aired on television. Accordingly, the first episode would be *The Love Bug*, one of the Studio's biggest hits since Walt's death.

After the first twenty-three episodes had aired, however, the series suddenly seemed to lose momentum. The remainder of the year consisted of episodes from the ABC and NBC years, and not surprisingly, the ratings dropped accordingly. While it seems surprising that the Studio would take this approach after all of the work to keep the show on the air, part of the reason may be in a November 1981 announcement that would greatly change Disney's television presence. After months of studying the feasibility of the project, Disney and Westinghouse announced a new pay television service to be operated as a joint venture. Eventually to become "The Disney Channel," this project quickly gained a position of importance at the Studio, and the anthology series was treated like Cinderella. *Walt Disney* was keeping the Studio's name in the eyes of the public, but all of the energy was now being directed toward the pay service.

Going into the 1982–83 season, Disney intended once again to use the anthology series as a platform to test pilots for potential series, with an emphasis on sitcoms. One aspect of this plan called for the Studio's limited series *Small & Frye* and *Tales of the Apple Dumpling Gang* (later retitled *Gun Shy*), to run in the anthology time slot for several weeks. Once they had attracted audiences, they would be given their own time slots. Unfortunately, the anthology series faired so poorly this year that the Studio eventually decided the limited series would have a better chance of succeeding on their own.

In mid-December, CBS took the anthology series off the air for several weeks. When the show returned in January, it was moved to Tuesday nights in the hope that the new night would help attract the missing audiences. After just several weeks, it was painfully obvious that the anthology was doing just as poorly on the new day. The show was averaging number fifty in the ratings, and in some weeks, dropped as low as number sixty-four.

In February 1983, CBS canceled the series.

After twenty-nine years on the air, and a run on all three networks, Disney's famous anthology series had apparently run its course. On September 24, the last episode, *Walt Disney's Mickey and Donald*, aired and the anthology series was history.

The Eisner years begin

Nineteen-eighty-four was a dramatic year for Walt Disney Productions, one that would see the company dramatically transformed like never before. What happened has been well documented in countless newspaper and magazine articles, and in several books, for it became a textbook example of Wall Street maneuvering.

Since Walt's death, the company had remained in the hands of the Disney family and loyalists. Then, after a series of confrontations with his fellow board members, Roy E. Disney had stunned the industry by angrily resigning his seat. He now announced plans to use his considerable stock holdings in the company to launch a takeover battle, saying that he wanted to restore the Studio to its former glory. With this, the stage was set for an intricate series of battles that would threaten the very existence of the company itself. Sharp-eyed accountants began making estimates of the value of Disney's holdings, and rumors began spreading about the possibility of a hostile takeover.

When the dust settled, Walt Disney Productions was safe, but Ron Miller was no longer the president of the company. After an intensive search that had all of Hollywood wondering who would get the job, the Studio named Frank G. Wells from Warner Bros. as the new president, and Michael D. Eisner from Paramount as chairman. In September 1984, the new management team took the reigns of a very shaky Walt Disney Productions.

The first area Eisner and Wells turned to was revitalizing Disney's film division. Little attention was paid to television this season, and the only activity was the usual mix of specials that had been running for the past few years. In early 1985, though, rumors began to circulate that Disney might return to network television with a weekly series.

Each of the networks expressed interest in working with Disney, as the renewed success of the Studio's theatrical arm under Eisner and Wells had taken Hollywood by storm. Despite the dismal performance of the anthology series in its later years, network executives were convinced that a new version of the series could indeed succeed. Grant Tinker of NBC commented "I'd like to get Disney back. It would be the absolute perfect counter programming for CBS' *60 Minutes.*"

On May 3, 1985, the industry trade papers broke the news of *The Disney Sunday Movie,* the Studio's newest version of the anthology series. While it would indeed be slated against *60 Minutes,* the series was to air on ABC, not NBC. Disney didn't walk entirely away from NBC, though, agreeing to provide seven two-hour Specials during the next season.

One of the first problems the Studio needed to tackle to get the series underway was settling the issue of picking a host. It had long been felt that the anthology series had lost a significant public relations angle when Walt died and the show went on without a host, and the Studio began a search to correct this. Celebrities from several fields were considered, and actors Lloyd Bridges and Peter Graves were strong contenders for the role. Michael Eisner personally wanted Walter Cronkite, but the retired newsman was still tied to CBS for five years and thus unavailable. Finally, Disney executive Rich Frank suggested that Eisner follow in Walt's tradition and take the job himself.

Not comfortable with the thought of appearing on camera, and aware that he would be criticized for trying to fill Walt's shoes, Eisner protested at first, but finally accepted the challenge. He did give in to Jeffrey Katzenberg's suggestion to diet, losing fifteen pounds, and went for acting lessons and a new wardrobe. Eisner also announced that his salary for hosting the series, which the Studio was obliged to pay under union rules, would be donated to charity.

Despite the acting lessons, Eisner was still noticeably stiff and somewhat uncomfortable in the opening segments, just as Walt had been. In the 1986 annual report, he commented on how it felt to host the series. "The first one I did took me three days and sixty-two takes," he noted. "I shot as much film in the opening of my thing as the movie itself." For anyone that has not appeared on camera, it might be hard to understand the pressures such a challenge poses. Of course, Eisner's task was made even harder by the fact that no one, even Walter Cronkite, could have done the job as well as Walt.

The anthology series returned to the air in February 1986 as *The Disney Sunday Movie.* The series had the highest ratings in the 7–9 P.M. time slot that ABC had enjoyed for several years, with approximately 22 percent of the viewing public tuning in each week. When talking about the Studio's plans for the next season, Eisner made no secret of how he viewed the results thus far. "There is no more important project for us than *The Disney Sunday Movie,*" he said. "And there are a lot of reasons for that: the enormous audience that is seeing Disney, getting Disney back on television, creating what is Disney— the core Disney—from which all our lives flow out of. The fact of the matter is that since *The Disney Sunday Movie* has gone back on the air, our parks are exploding. I think people who grew up on Disney are thrilled there's a place during the week where they can sit down with their children and watch television together."

Once again, the famous Disney synergy machine was running at full speed. Eisner later reaffirmed his support for the series in the 1986 annual report:

The importance of *The Disney Sunday Movie* to the company goes far beyond its program ratings. The show's name and long history alone conjure up images of Disney's theme parks, reminding the American public of the fun and excitement they offer. In addition, the show consistently ranks among the top five in the ratings in Canada, an important market for Walt Disney World.

As the Studio approached the second season of the revived anthology series, they realized that something needed to be done to improve the ratings, which had failed to improve as much as hoped. Gary Barton, the executive in charge of *The Disney Sunday Movie,* admitted that they wanted to duplicate the feel of the old series, but the first season had shown that the plots needed updating. "Our shows are more sophisticated than what we watched as children," he said. "We want to make entertaining movies, but times have changed. Kids today, because they're exposed to more, are more sophisticated. I just hope we do it a well as they did twenty-five years ago." In an effort to keep viewers tuning in, the majority of programs for the 1987–88 season consisted of two-part stories. Less emphasis was placed on theatrical releases, as most of the shows this year were either produced for the anthology series or had been seen earlier on The Disney Channel.

In May 1988, Eisner once again spoke about the importance of television to the Studio. "Since Walt went on the air with *Disneyland,* television has always been the tent pole of our company," he said. "It keeps all of the people who love what Disney stands for current with our product. We had to get the Disney franchise back on the air, to carry the torch of Disney from one generation to the next."

After three seasons on ABC, it seemed as if the anthology series had finally succeeded in finding a permanent home. Then, in January 1988, came the surprising news that ABC's Business Affairs department had accidentally let the option to renew the series expire. After some intense negotiations, it was announced that the series would be moving once again to NBC.

With the change in networks, it was also planned to give the series, now titled *The Magical World of Disney*, a new look. NBC President Brandon Tartikoff explained "I wanted NBC to be the home of Walt Disney, but I wasn't interested in the anthology that is running on ABC." *The Disney Sunday Movie* had been rated fifty-ninth of the eighty-five shows in the prior season, and NBC wanted to take steps to improve the ratings. Tartikoff's answer was to suggest a programming concept called a "wheel," with different series rotating to make up the "spokes."

Several series have used this concept, with one of the most successful being the *NBC Mystery Movie*. That series featured *MacMillan and Wife*, *Columbo*, and *McCloud* among its spokes, and each of them proved popular enough to stand on their own. The plan this time was to launch several new programs under the "wheel" concept, and if any of them proved successful, spin them off as separate series. It was announced that *The Magical World of Disney* would have three spokes, as well as occasional specials.

The return—again— of Davy Crockett

When Walt began his original *Disneyland* series, his biggest hit that first year was Davy Crockett. The Crockett stories had served the Studio well over the years, always proving successful even after multiple reruns. Realizing this, Michael Eisner decided to resurrect the character and produce new Crockett stories as one of the spokes. The Studio hoped to capitalize on the successful name of the original episodes, but to bring a more contemporary touch to the screen. This was a risky gamble, for it was inevitable that the new stories would be compared to the originals. In fact, there was some immediate negative reaction to what looked like "tamper-ing" with a Disney classic, and some carping that the new management was reduced to merely copying Walt's old ideas.

The new Crockett episodes were modestly successful, and despite the initial predictions of doom from Disney loyalists, they held up well in comparison with the original stories. Despite this success, though, only five episodes were produced, as the ratings didn't justify the high production costs needed for the large casts required.

With work underway on the new Crockett shows, the Studio also began work on the second spoke. This time, Disney decided to adapt the successful 1961 film *The Absent-Minded Professor* as an ongoing comedy series. Instead of casting a new actor in the role of Ned Brainard, originally made famous by Fred MacMurray, Disney set the television version as a sequel. The third spoke would be an "action-adventure series," *Wild Jack*, featuring a hunting guide who found himself uprooted and thrown into the business world. Unfortunately, the spoke concept was quickly found to have been a failure and was quietly dropped. The series then reverted back to the same mixture of programming that had been the staple of the anthology series for so many years.

The honeymoon with NBC didn't last long, for a *TV Guide* listing of the ratings for all prime time series for 1989–90 placed *The Magical World of Disney* at a dismal number seventy-two. When the anthology ratings continued to decline, it was decided that the series would leave the air at the end of the 1989–90 season. On May 22, 1990, *The Magical World of Disney* was canceled by NBC.

The anthology series did gain a new lease on life, however. Disney announced that *The Magical World of Disney* was to continue airing each Sunday at 7 P.M., moving now to The Disney Channel. In doing this, the Studio continued to make television history, for the anthology series was now the only show that had been aired on three networks and cable. As Disney press releases proudly noted, prime-time's longest running series would continue.

Eisner spoke about the importance of keeping the anthology series on the air. "I would say *The Magical World of Disney* is our major league showcase," he said, "and will show our major league product, whether it is theatrical motion pictures as well as our major league Disney Premiere films produced totally for The Disney Channel. This is the place where we premiere our best."

These announcements were somewhat symbolic, though, for the Studio ceased production of new episodes for the series. Instead, programs and films that are aired at other times throughout the month are also broadcast under the anthology series banner, but new introductions with Michael Eisner as the "Voice of Disney" help keep the tradition alive. As of this writing, there are plans to bring the anthology series back to network television, though, maintaining the long legacy that started with *Disneyland* back in 1954.

4

Anthology Series Episode Descriptions

Each episode is listed here in alphabetical order. If a show aired under several different titles, the episode description is found under the original title, with cross references to any later titles.

A number of the episodes also aired as specials, and those dates are included here. The majority of the anthology episodes have also aired on The Disney Channel.

ABSENT-MINDED PROFESSOR, THE

Airdates—Part 1: 9/09/79, Part 2: 9/16/79. This 1961 feature film starring Fred MacMurray as a scientist who accidentally invents an antigravity formula first aired on 11/01/75 as a special. It later aired on the anthology series in two parts. The Studio also produced two television episodes based on the film. Each is described separately.

ABSENT-MINDED PROFESSOR, THE (TV VERSION) Airdates: 11/27/88, 5/21/89.

Cast: Harry Anderson (Henry Crawford), Cory Danziger (Gus), Mary Page Keller (Ellen Whitley), David Paymer (Oliphant), James Noble (Dr. Blount), Bibi Osterwald (Mrs. Nakamura), Tom Callaway, Stephen Dorff (Curtis), Jason Zahler (Greg), Dave Florek (Art), Erik Rondell (Student).

Henry Crawford, a professor at Medfield College, is absent-minded. His girlfriend, Ellen Whitley, becomes increasingly upset at Henry's habit of paying more attention to his science experiments than to her. Henry's troubles begin when he discovers a strange, gooey material that defies gravity—and several other laws of science. Henry sets out to share his discovery with Ellen, but she doesn't share his enthusiasm, and tells him their relationship is over.

Production Note:

- This show was based on the 1961 theatrical release of the same name. The Studio announced that the 1988–89 season would feature several episodes, but only this and a second episode, *The Absent-Minded Professor: Trading Places*, were ever produced.

ABSENT-MINDED PROFESSOR, THE: TRADING PLACES Airdates: 2/26/89, 8/20/89.

Cast: Harry Anderson (Henry Crawford), Mary Page Keller (Ellen Whitley), Ed Begley, Jr. (Dr. Jack Brooker), James Noble (Dean Blount), Richard Sanders (Dr. Dark), Ron Fassler (Hacker), Annette McCarthy (Ginnie Brooker), Gary Epp (Watchman), Thom Adcox (Student).

Professor Henry Crawford is visited by former roommate Jack Brooker, who is now working at the prestigious Rhinebloom Labs on a very secret project. Jack asks Henry to take his place there for a few days, claiming he's burned out from the workload. Jack confesses to Henry that he suspects the lab may be working on an illegal project. Afraid to act on his own and thereby risk his job, he had tricked Henry into trading places with the hope his friend would uncover the secret. The two men then decide to break into the lab to investigate for themselves.

Production Notes:

- This episode was a sequel to the episode *The Absent-Minded Professor* (see description under that title).
- As Henry and Jack fly to the lab in the flubber-powered Model T, they fly past a

Mickey Mouse "Buckle Up for Safety" billboard.

ADIOS EL CUCHILLO   Airdates: 11/06/60, 8/13/61.

Cast: Guy Williams (Zorro and Don Diego), Gilbert Roland (El Cuchillo), Henry Calvin (Sergeant Garcia), Gene Sheldon (Bernardo), Rita Moreno (Chulita), Rudolph Acosta (Carancho), Rudolpho Hoyos (Bandit), Vito Scotti (Chaco), Bern Hoffman (Trampa), George J. Lewis (Don Alejandro).

This is a continuation of the Zorro adventure begun in the episode *El Bandido*. Having previously suffered a setback and humiliation at the hands of Zorro (Don Diego), El Cuchillo leads his men back into Los Angeles where they begin to plunder the pueblo. One item of importance for the bandit leader is to have the embarrassing "Z" removed from his coat, a process observed by the waiting Zorro. Zorro playfully returns to the tailor shop where Cuchillo is just leaving—and leaves his mark on the newly repaired coat. Unfortunately for Zorro, his little prank may have been a serious mistake, because Cuchillo now becomes extremely anxious to win this series of battles.

ADVENTURE IN ART, AN   Airdate: 4/30/58.

Realizing that the Disney Studio is seen by many as an artistic trendsetter, Walt spends an hour discussing the various ways different people may interpret the same artistic piece. A book by American painter Robert Henri, *The Art Spirit*, is used throughout the show as a reference, and Walt reveals it has been an inspiration to him for many years.

Production Note:

- Marc Davis recalled that the four artists had gone out and painted an old oak tree on Barham Boulevard in Burbank on their own time. Fellow artist Art Riley had suggested the project and photographed it; Davis was surprised when it later ended up as part of the television series. This section of the show has been released as an educational short, *4 Artists Paint 1 Tree*.

ADVENTURE IN COLOR, AN (AND) MATHMAGIC LAND   Airdate: 9/24/61.

A new era in television begins for Walt Disney as he moves his show to NBC and begins broadcasting in color. To heighten the impact that color will portray in his shows, Walt discusses the early black-and-white days of the movies. The arrival of Technicolor, seen in clips from *Flowers and Trees* and *Fantasia*, allowed moviemakers to present their product in lifelike color.

The final portion of the program is a presentation of the 1959 theatrical release *Donald in Mathmagic Land*, in which the intrepid duck finds himself in a strange land where mathematical formulas and odd creatures abound.

Production Note:

- A new star joins the Disney family— Donald Duck's uncle, Professor Ludwig Von Drake. Von Drake's voice was created by veteran voice actor Paul Frees, who improvised much of the eccentric professor's dialogue.

ADVENTURE IN SATAN'S CANYON

Airdates: 11/03/74, 7/06/75, 4/16/78.

Cast: Richard Jaeckel (Jack Hughes), Larry Pennell (Dave Fletcher), David Alan Bailey (Rob).

Set in the mountains of the great Northwest, this is the story of Rob, a young sportsman, who is attempting to become an expert in the use of a kayak. When Rob fails to win an important competition, he dejectedly informs his coach, Ranger Jack Hughes, that he no longer has any interest in the sport. In reality, he is too afraid to continue. Several days later Hughes leaves on a trip to mark summer hiking trails and asks Rob to accompany him. While kayaking through a perilous area known as Satan's Canyon, Hughes is severely injured in an accident. With no other hope of rescue Rob must go for help, which lies on the other side of some dangerous rapids.

Production Notes:

- This show was filmed in Washington, Oregon, along Idaho's Snake River, and on California's Stanislaus River. Footage of the 1972 Olympics' kayak races in Munich is also shown.
- Richard Jaeckel both starred in and narrated this episode.

ADVENTURE IN THE MAGIC KINGDOM, AN   Airdates: 4/09/58, 5/28/58.

Tinker Bell's ability to make people fly is put to the test when she takes the audience on a tour of Disneyland. Using a sprinkle of pixie dust, she flies the viewers over the highways, passes the heliport, circles the Park, and settles in for a landing at Disneyland for a tour of the Park.

Production Notes:

- This show used portions of the 1956 theatrical release, *Disneyland, U.S.A.*
- An edited version of this show was used as a serial during the fourth season of *The Mickey Mouse Club.*

ADVENTURE IN WILDWOOD HEART
Airdates: 9/25/57, 12/18/57.
Walt opens the show in the Studio Morgue, the central area to store data that might be needed in future projects. All of the Studio's major films have benefited from the facts and pictures stored there, and he uses clips from several past productions to illustrate his point. Walt then introduces Winston Hibler, who tells how the Studio researched and filmed Felix Salten's story of *Perri*, soon to be seen in theaters as a *True-Life Fantasy.*

Production Note:

- This show, which took almost three years and 200 miles of film to produce, was filmed in the Unita mountain range in northeastern Utah.

ADVENTURE STORY, THE   Airdates: 3/20/57, 9/04/57.
Stating that everyone likes an adventure story, Walt presents a rather unusual one. It's not the story of any classic adventure known to the average historian—rather, it's the saga of the Goofy family's exploits throughout the ages.

Production Note:

- This show is also known as *The Goofy Adventure Story.*

ADVENTURES IN FANTASY   Airdates: 11/06/57, 5/21/58, 12/30/62.
The world of fantasy and its obvious artistic possibilities are the subjects of this episode, where various inanimate objects come to life and provide introductions to several cartoon sequences.

ADVENTURES OF BULLWHIP GRIFFIN, THE
Airdates—Part 1: 1/17/71, Part 2: 1/24/71, Part 3: 1/31/71 (includes *Project Florida*).
For the 1977–78 season the show was edited and presented in two parts. Part 1: 11/27/77, Part 2: 12/04/77.
Roddy McDowall, Suzanne Pleshette, Karl Malden, and Bryan Russell star in this 1967 theatrical release about a mild-mannered butler who must seek his fortune in the rough-and-tumble gold fields of Alaska. Project Florida is a preview of Walt Disney World, due to open in October 1971.

ADVENTURES OF CHIP 'N DALE, THE
Airdates: 2/27/59, 7/17/59, 6/03/62, 4/12/70, 7/14/74, 3/26/78 (Mixed Nuts), 7/27/80 (Misadventures of Chip 'n Dale, The), 7/26/81 (Misadventures of Chip 'n Dale, The).
The show opens with an unusual beginning—the set is empty except for a tape recorder. Walt has left a message explaining that since he couldn't be there in person, he's arranged for guest hosts—Chip and Dale. The two chipmunks have brought a book filled with stories of their exploits. Throughout the show, Dale keeps turning to the story of *The Lone Chipmunks*, and bullets, lassoes, and other dangers jump out of the book. Chip warns him to leave that story for later and, with a brief song and dance number, they introduce each of the stories.

Production Notes:

- After Walt's death, the opening was modified to provide a new narration explaining the presence of the guest hosts.
- Major portions of this episode were used in the show *Winnie the Pooh and Friends.*

ADVENTURES OF MICKEY MOUSE
Airdates: 10/12/55, 1/20/80 (Mickey's Greatest Adventures), 9/07/80 (Mickey's Greatest Adventures).
In this episode, Walt takes a look at the career of his longtime associate, Mickey Mouse. Cartoons include: *The Band Concert*, *Alpine Climbers*, *Squatter's Rights*, and *Mickey and the Beanstalk.*

Production Notes:

- The 1955 version of the show ends with the giant from *Mickey and the Beanstalk* still looking for Mickey, picking up the Studio roof and asking Walt if he's seen the mouse. This ending was omitted following Walt's death.
- Major portions of this show were used in the episode *Adventures with Mickey.*

ADVENTURES OF POLLYANNA, THE
Airdate: 4/10/82.
Cast: Shirley Jones (Aunt Polly), Patsy Kensit (Pollyanna), Edward Winter (Dr. Richard Chilton), Beverly Archer (Angelica), Lucille Benson (Mrs. Levelor), Nicholas

Hammond (Reverend Tull), Gretchen Wyler (Mrs. Emily Tarbell), John Randolph (Mr. Muller), Stacey Nelkin (Cora Spencer), John Putch (Johnny Muller), Roxanna Zal (Merilee), Rossie Harris (Jimmy Bean), Anne Haney (Miss Louella Best), Mitzi Hoag (Mrs. Muller), Barbara Cason (Mrs. Snow), Amy W. MacIntosh (Widow Jenn), Hap Lawrence (Iceman), David Haney (Homer Cocx), Pat Benson (Matella), James J. Collins (Tom Jenn).

The small town of Harrington is ruled by its wealthiest citizen, Polly Harrington. The powerful woman also dominates her niece, Pollyanna, who has come to live with Polly following the death of her parents. Aunt Polly wants her ward to pay more attention to her studies but Pollyanna would rather play with the local children, many of whom live in an orphanage supported by her aunt. The children decide to spy on a recent arrival in town, the Widow Jenn, for local gossip has it that there's something strange about the woman and the children want to learn the truth.

Production Notes:

- This show, which was based on the earlier theatrical release *Pollyanna,* was filmed as a pilot for a potential series. The network declined to pick up the series and no other episodes were produced. The Studio did redo the story again in the episode *Polly* and the special *Polly—Comin' Home.*
- The town of Harrington was the town-square set originally built for the theatrical release *Something Wicked This Way Comes.*

ADVENTURES WITH MICKEY   Airdate: Syndicated.

Over the years, Mickey Mouse has been involved in more adventures than the average mouse, as seen in *Mr. Mouse Takes a Trip, Magician Mickey, Squatter's Rights, Mickey's Trailer, Mickey and the Seal,* and *Alpine Climbers.*

Production Note:

- This show was an edited version of the episode *The Adventures of Mickey Mouse.*

ALASKAN ESKIMO

This is the second half of the episode *Behind the Cameras in Lapland (and) Alaskan Eskimo.*

ALICE IN WONDERLAND   Airdates: 11/03/54, 4/06/55, 1/09/57, 12/25/59, 12/20/64, 9/27/87, 2/25/90.

This animated version of Lewis Carroll's *The Adventures of Alice in Wonderland* and *Through the Looking Glass* was released theatrically in 1951.

Production Notes:

- In addition to Walt Disney, the 1954 and 1955 broadcasts featured James Algar and Winston Hibler.
- The following songs were cut from the television version in order to fit the one-hour format: *In a World of My Own* and *Very Good Advice.*
- *Alice* also aired as a special on 12/24/88. The 1991 anthology version was not edited.

ALL ABOUT MAGIC   Airdates: 1/30/57, 6/12/57, 10/23/60.

This hour is devoted to the art of magic, so Walt goes to the Studio basement, where the Magic Mirror from *Snow White and the Seven Dwarfs* is stored. In fact, the whole room is filled with magic props, such as an old standby, the "Magic Hat." Walt summons the Spirit of the Mirror and turns the show over to him, bowing to his greater experience.

ALL NEW ADVENTURE OF DISNEY'S SPORT GOOFY, AN

This show originally aired as a special on 5/27/87. It later aired on the anthology series on 1/01/89.

ALMOST ANGELS   Airdates—Part 1: 2/28/65, 4/19/70. Part 2: 3/07/65, 4/26/70.

The world-famous Vienna Boys Choir is the subject of this 1962 theatrical release, based on the story of a young boy who wants to join the choir.

Production Note:

- Production of this film began when Walt visited Europe on vacation in 1959. Impressed with the choir, he personally convinced the director, Dr. Ferdinand Grossman, to allow the group to be filmed for the first time in its history.
- The original plans called for a television show for the 1961–62 season to be titled *Franz and Tony of the Vienna Boy's Choir.* At some points the project was also titled *Born to Sing* (which was used as the foreign theatrical title), *Franz and Tony,* and *Franz and Peter.*

ALONG THE OREGON TRAIL   Airdates: 11/14/56, 2/20/57.

Cast: Fess Parker (John "Doc" Grayson), Jeff York (Hank Breckinridge), Sebastian Cabot (Bissonette), Iron Eyes Cody (Chief Many Stars), Kathleen Crowley (Laura Thompson), Phyllis Coates (Mrs. Martin), Morgan Woodward ("Obie" Foster), Roy Gordon (Judge Foster), Leslie Bradley (Spencer Armitage), David Stollery (Dan Thompson).

Walt begins the show by describing the famed Oregon Trail, a route favored by pioneers heading to the West. The journey was not an easy one, taking six months to cross from Kansas City to Oregon, but hundreds of wagon trains successfully completed the trip. The movie *Westward Ho the Wagons!* is the story of one such trip, and this behind-the-scenes look at its filming is hosted by Fess Parker, star of the film.

Production Note:

- Also seen in this episode are Mouseketeers Karen Pendleton and Paul Petersen.

AMBUSH AT LAREDO   Airdates: 11/14/58, 7/10/59.

Cast: Tom Tryon (Texas John Slaughter), Robert Middleton (Frank Davis), Norma Moore (Adeline Harris), Harry Carey, Jr. (Ben Jenkins), Judson Pratt (Captain Cooper), Robert J. Wilke (Outlaw #1), Edward Platt (Lease Harris), Leo Gordon (Outlaw #2), John Day (Private Jeff Clay), John Alderson (Sgt. Duncan MacGregor), Chris Alcaide (Outlaw #3), Robert Hoy (Ranger #2), Chuck Roberson (Ranger #1).

Part 2 of *The Tales of Texas John Slaughter* begins with the Texas Rangers tracking down the last of Frank Davis's gang. The Rangers' return to town is spoiled by the fact that Davis is out on bail and free to travel throughout Texas until his trial. Captain Cooper sends Slaughter and Ben Jenkins out to follow Davis, afraid that the gang leader will begin a new crime wave.

Production Note:

- This episode was edited into the 1960 foreign theatrical release *Texas John Slaughter*, along with scenes from the episode of that name.

AMBUSH AT WAGON GAP

This is Part 1 of *Westward Ho the Wagons!*

AND CHASE THE BUFFALO   Airdates: 12/11/60, 7/02/61.

Cast: Dewey Martin (Daniel Boone), Mala Powers (Rebecca Boone), Richard Banke (Squire Boone), Kevin Corcoran (James Boone), George Wallace (Mordecai), Brian Corcoran (Israel Boone), Kerry Corcoran (Jemina Boone), Alex Gerry (Judge Henderson), Whit Bissell (Governor Tryon), Ron Hayes (Cecil Calvert).

Part 2 of the story of Daniel Boone is set twelve years after Boone's first trip to Kentucky, with Daniel dreaming of returning there. The land around the Boone farm is becoming more populated all the time, with the inevitable problems that civilization can cause. Although the Boones attempt to remain neutral, they are nevertheless swept up in the politics of a tax rebellion.

ANDREWS' RAIDERS   Airdates—Part 1: 5/07/61, 8/28/66, 7/22/73. Part 2: 5/14/61, 9/04/66, 7/29/73.

The 1956 theatrical release *The Great Locomotive Chase* is presented in two parts, *Secret Mission* and *Escape to Nowhere*. This true story of a daring Union raid during the Civil War stars Fess Parker, Jeffrey Hunter, and Jeff York.

Production Notes:

- *The Great Locomotive Chase* also aired on 10/16/76 with *Nikki, Wild Dog of the North* as part of the *NBC All-Disney Saturday Night at the Movies* series of specials.
- The episode *Behind the Cameras with Fess Parker* is a behind-the-scenes look at the filming of this story.

ANDY BURNETT (mini-series)

Disney produced six episodes featuring this Easterner who wanted to become a mountain man: *Andy's Initiation; Andy's First Chore; Andy's Love Affair; Land of Enemies, The; White Man's Medicine;* and *Big Council, The.* Refer to each of these titles for the episode descriptions.

ANDY'S FIRST CHORE   Airdates: 10/09/57, 2/12/58.

Cast: Jerome Courtland (Andy Burnett), Jeff York (Joe Crane), Andrew Duggan (Jack Kelly), Slim Pickens (Old Bill Williams), Robert J. Wilke (Ben Tilton), Anthony Caruso (Bill Sublette), Robert Cornthwait (Sen. Tom Benton).

The second episode in *The Saga of Andy Burnett* begins with the Mountain Men teaching Andy to ride like an Indian and to use a bow and arrow. Jack Kelly joins the group, warning them that a band of men led by Bill Sublette is nearby. The Mountain Men become suspicious that the newcomers are attempting to learn the location of their private trapping grounds. Several encounters contribute to a growing dislike between the two groups, which increases when Andy outwits Sublette's men and is able to get several traps the Mountain Men desperately need.

ANDY'S INITIATION   Airdates: 10/02/57, 2/05/58.

Cast: Jerome Courtland (Andy Burnett), Jeff York (Joe Crane), Andrew Duggan (Jack Kelly), Slim Pickens (Old Bill Williams), Robert J. Wilke (Ben Tilton).

Set in 1820, the first part of *The Saga of Andy Burnett* begins with young Andy Burnett eating dinner in a Pittsburgh tavern. He befriends Joe Crane, a penniless Mountain Man who comes to Andy's aid when a gang of thugs attacks him. Crane recognizes Andy's rifle as one made by Daniel Boone, which was given to Gail Burnett, Andy's grandfather and a true pioneer. Despite such a heritage, Andy is heading west to become a farmer—a prospect that dismays Crane. He decides to "persuade" Andy to head into the mountains with him and "borrows" Andy's money so he doesn't have a choice.

Production Note:

- Jeff York also played the character of Joe Crane in several *Zorro* episodes, beginning with the episode *Zorro and the Mountain Man.*

ANDY'S LOVE AFFAIR   Airdates: 10/16/57, 2/19/58.

Cast: Jerome Courtland (Andy Burnett), Jeff York (Joe Crane), Andrew Duggan (Jack Kelly), Slim Pickens (Old Bill Williams), Britt Lomond (Capitan Paco Reyes), Adele Mara (Estrellita), Donald Lawton (Colonel Delgado).

The third segment in *The Saga of Andy Burnett* finds the Mountain Men arriving in New Mexico. The journey across the desert was long and hot, and now they must deal with the Spanish border patrol. The leader of the patrol, a reasonable man, agrees to take Jack Kelly to Santa Fe if the other men will stay in Taos until he returns. Unfortunately, they must go with Capitan Reyes, a

self-impressed officer who doesn't like Yankees.

Production Note:

- In addition to the uniforms worn by the soldiers in this episode, Disney used several of the sets from his *Zorro* series, which was also in production at the time.

ANTARCTICA—OPERATION DEEPFREEZE
Airdates: 6/05/57, 8/14/57.

The story begun in *Antarctica—Past and Present* continues with this update on the activities of Navy Task Force 43 and the efforts to explore the Antarctic for the International Geophysical Year. Walt introduces narrator Winston Hibler, who explains the scientific value of the studies being conducted in Antarctica and how the expedition spent their time on the ice.

Production Note:

- This episode was edited into the 1958 theatrical release *Seven Cities of Antarctica*, along with scenes from *Antarctica—Past and Present* and *To the South Pole for Science.*

ANTARCTICA—PAST AND PRESENT
Airdates: 9/12/56, 5/15/57.

This is the story of "Operation Deepfreeze," a navy expedition to the South Pole. Walt explains that Disney cameramen will travel with the navy crews to provide periodic reports throughout the year-long project. The remainder of the show is hosted by Winston Hibler, who presents a brief history of the region to be explored.

Production Notes:

- The Disney Studio served as a training base for the navy cameramen who were to make the trip, with lessons based on the problems encountered while filming the *True-Life Adventure* series.
- This episode, along with scenes from *Antarctica—Operation Deepfreeze* and *To the South Pole for Science*, was edited into the 1958 theatrical release *Seven Cities of Antarctica.*

APACHE FRIENDSHIP   Airdates: 2/19/60, 7/22/60.

Cast: Tom Tryon (Texas John Slaughter), Gene Evans (Loco Crispin), Regis Toomey (Mr. Howell), Betty Lynn (Viola Howell), Nora Marlowe (Mrs. Howell), Brian Corcoran

(Willie Slaughter), George Wallace (Gus), Don Haggerty (Trail Boss), James Edwards (Batt), Jay Silverheels (Natchez), Annette Gorman (Addie Slaughter).

Episode 10 in *The Tales of Texas John Slaughter* opens with John and his children discussing Viola Howell, whom John is thinking of marrying. Gus, the ranch foreman, joins in, convincing John that the children need a mother. Gathering his courage, John sets off for the Howell ranch. The trip to the Howells' is not all pleasure, for Mr. Howell and John must travel to Tombstone and testify at the trial of Loco Crispin, a killer apprehended by John.

APPLE DUMPLING GANG, THE   Airdates
(2-hour format): 11/14/76, 2/24/80, 11/02/80, 6/15/86. For the 1989–90 season the show was aired in two parts—Part 1: 8/06/89. Part 2: 8/13/89.
This 1975 theatrical release stars Bill Bixby, Don Knotts, and Tim Conway in a tale about three orphans who discover a huge gold nugget.

Production Note:

- This film inspired a theatrical sequel *(The Apple Dumpling Gang Rides Again)*, a made-for-television movie *(Tales of the Apple Dumpling Gang)*, and a television mini-series *(Gun Shy)*.

APPLE DUMPLING GANG RIDES AGAIN, THE   Airdates—Part 1: 9/25/82. Part 2: 10/02/82.
Cast: Tim Matheson, Tim Conway, Don Knotts.
This 1979 theatrical sequel to *The Apple Dumpling Gang* reunites Tim Conway and Don Knotts as two would-be desperados who become involved with a gang staging robberies from the safety of their prison cells.

Production Note:

- Bridger Military Prison used the cuartel sets still standing from the *Zorro* series.

ASK MAX   Airdate: 11/02/86, 7/12/87.
Cast: Jeff B. Cohen (Max Baxter), Gino DeMauro (Dennis), Cassie Yates (Jennifer Baxter), Ray Walston (Harmon), Glynn Turman (Lloyd Lyman), Mark L. Taylor (Braff), Kareem Abdul-Jabar (Himself), Deena Freeman (Pam), Christie Clark (Shelly Meyers), Ryan Lambert (Bully #1), Kreag Caffey (Coach), Tami Turner (Adrian), Byron Clark (Marcus), Walter Raymond (History Teacher), April Dawn (Student #1), Corki Grazer (Rider #1), Patrick Stehr (Student #2), Kat Sawyer-Young (Miss Hughes), Regina Leeds (Miss Phillips), Sean McFrazier (Basketball Player), Ed McReady (Carlyle), Vincent Joseph (Assistant Coach).

High school student Max Baxter likes Shelly Meyers, another student, but she barely knows he's alive. Shelly likes muscular athletes and it's unlikely that overweight Max can ever win her heart. However, Max is a child genius and he tries to use his knowledge of science to gain her admiration. He almost succeeds but his plan is discovered, making it even harder to get her to like him.

AT HOME WITH DONALD DUCK
Airdates: 11/21/56, 5/08/57, 5/20/62, 4/16/72, 11/07/76 *(Happy Birthday Donald Duck)*.
What should normally be a pleasant day—one's birthday—soon leads to problems in the Duck household. Donald decides to give his nephews a party for his own birthday, complete with cake and ice cream. As a special treat, he decides to show movies—all about himself.

Production Note:

- The show also aired as a special on 4/04/79 as *Happy Birthday Donald Duck.*

ATTA GIRL, KELLY!   Airdates—Part 1: 3/05/67, 5/14/72. Part 2: 3/12/67, 5/21/72. Part 3: 3/19/67, 5/28/72.
Cast: Arthur Hill (Evan Clayton), Billy Corcoran (Danny Richards), J.D. Cannon (Dr. Paul Durand), Beau Bridges (Matt Howell), James Olson (Chuck Williams), James Broderick (Cal Richards), Jan Shepard (Ruth Richards), Ted Hartley (Stuart MacIver), Alice Frost (Mrs. Dickens), Erik Holland (Jim Boyle), William Bramley (Oscar Gruber), William Boyett (Fred Wilson), Stuart Nisbet (Mr. Ferrara), Christopher Held (Mr. Oppenheim).

The story of a Seeing Eye dog is told in this three-part program. In *K for Kelly*, a 12-week-old puppy is given to Danny Richards. The boy has agreed to raise the puppy until she is old enough to begin her training as a Seeing Eye dog. In Part 2, *Dog of Destiny*, Kelly escapes from the training school and races back to Danny. The final episode, *Love Is Blind*, deals with the fact that the blind themselves must be trained.

Production Note:

- In the story, Danny is given a book on animal husbandry to help him develop an interest in other animals. The book was by "Dr. W. D. Retlaw." "Retlaw" is "Walter" spelled backward, and the "W. D.," of course, was for "Walt Disney."

ATTORNEY AT LAW   Airdates: 2/06/59, 5/15/59.
Cast: Robert Loggia (Elfego Baca), James Dunn (J. Henry Newman), Lynn Bari (Mrs. Simmons), Kenneth Tobey (Shorty), James Drury (Deputy Joe Monroe), Annette Funicello (Chucita Bernal), Grant Withers (Sheriff Wharton), Robert J. Stevenson (Simmons), Edward Colmans (Fernando Bernal), Gloria Castillo (Lolita Bernal).

In this fifth episode of the *Elfego Baca* series, Elfego's entry into the field of law proves to be an interesting one. He must defend Fernando Bernal, a former bank robber who may have returned to his old ways, and Elfego feels his client is being framed.

Production Note:

- This episode and *The Griswold Murder* were combined and released theatrically overseas in 1962 as *Six-Gun Law*.

AULD ACQUAINTANCE   Airdates: 4/02/61, 8/27/61.
Cast: Guy Williams (Zorro and Don Diego), Henry Calvin (Sergeant Garcia), Gene Sheldon (Bernardo), Suzanne Lloyd (Isabella Linares), Ricardo Montalban (Ramon Castillo), Ross Martin (Marcos Estrada), George J. Lewis (Don Alejandro).

Don Diego's plans to drive an old foe out of town go awry when the man realizes Diego is Zorro.

BABES IN TOYLAND   Airdates—Part 1: 12/21/69, 12/19/76. Part 2: 12/28/69, 12/26/76.
This 1961 theatrical release, starring Annette Funicello, Tommy Sands, and Ray Bolger, tells the musical tale of an evil banker determined to win the heart of a beautiful villager at any cost.

Production Note:

- The episode *Backstage Party* is a behind-the-scenes look at the making of this film.

BACKSTAGE PARTY   Airdate: 12/17/61.
Cast: Ray Bolger (Barnaby), Tommy Sands (Tom Piper), Annette Funicello (Mary Contrary), Ed Wynn (Toymaker), Tommy Kirk (Grumio), Kevin Corcoran (Little Boy Blue), Henry Calvin (Gonzorgo), Gene Sheldon (Roderigo), Mary McCarty (Mother Goose), Ann Jilliann (Bo Peep), Brian Corcoran (Wee Willie Winkie), Noah Beery (Gardener).

The television audience is invited to the Disney Studio for a special party to celebrate the completion of the new film, *Babes in Toyland*.

BALLAD OF HECTOR THE STOWAWAY DOG, THE   Airdates—Part 1: 1/05/64, 7/19/64, 4/25/71. Part 2: 1/12/64, 7/26/64, 5/02/71.
Cast: Guy Stockwell (Max Reiner), Craig Hill (Bill Mantel), Eric Pohlmann (Hugo Danzer), Walter Gotell (Benton), Edmund Hashim (Duke), Edward McCready (Adolph), Fortunio Bonanova (Inspector), John Stacy (Captain Willoughby), Henry Brandon (Circus Roustabout), Lina Volonghi (Mrs. Danzer), Paul Devlin (Crewmember), Stephen Levy (Crewmember), Stephen Chiu (Chinese Cook), Adelaide Ribeiro (Portuguese Singer), Mario Santos (Customs Officer), Jim Dolen (Captain Hall), Tony Doonan (Wireless Operator).

This story of a travel-loving Airedale is presented in two parts, *Where the Heck Is Hector?* and *Who the Heck Is Hector?* During his travels on a cargo ship, the dog becomes involved in a smuggling plot.

Production Note:

- This show, which was released theatrically overseas in 1967 as *The Million Dollar Collar*, has also been referred to as *Hector, the Stowaway Pup*.

BALLERINA   Airdates—Part 1: 2/27/66. Part 2: 3/06/66.
Cast: Kirsten Simone (Kirsten Holm), Astrid Villaume (Helga Sørenson), Paul Reichardt (Paul Sørenson), Henning Kronstam (Henning Tanberg), Jennifer Agutter (Ingrid Jensen), Ole Wegener (Sven), Eric Mork (Ballet Master), Edvin Tiemroth (Theatre Manager), Hans Schwarz (Trainer), Blandine Ebinger (Mme. Karova), Mette Honningen (Mette Sørenson). Featuring: *The Royal Danish Ballet.*

As graduation time draws near at a prestigious ballet school in Copenhagen, it appears that a promising young student is in danger of failing, much to the surprise of her teachers. Mette Sørenson was always a good student, so a teacher asks Mette's friend Kirsten, the company's prima ballerina, to help her pass.

Production Notes:

- Cast members Simone, Kronstam, and Honningen were members of the Royal Danish Ballet.
- *Ballerina* was released theatrically overseas in 1966 as *Ballerina: A Story of the Royal Danish Ballet.*

BANNER IN THE SKY   Airdates—Part 1: 2/17/63, 3/05/72. Part 2: 2/24/63, 3/12/72.
The 1959 theatrical release *Third Man on the Mountain* is presented in two parts, *To Conquer the Mountain* and *The Killer Mountain.* It stars Michael Rennie, James MacArthur, and Janet Munro in a tale about the conquest of a deadly Swiss mountain.

BAREFOOT EXECUTIVE, THE   Airdates—Part 1: 9/16/73, 4/02/78, 9/06/81, 8/27/89. Part 2: 9/23/73, 4/09/78, 9/13/81, 9/03/89.
Kurt Russell, Joe Flynn, and Harry Morgan star in this 1971 theatrical release about a chimp that can accurately predict hit series.

BARRY OF THE GREAT ST. BERNARD
Airdates—Part 1: 1/30/77. Part 2: 2/06/77.
Cast: Jean Claude Dauphin (Martin), Pierre Tabard (Julius), Maurice Teynac (Prior), Pascale Christophe (Simone), Roger Lumont (Dr. Bernay), Sacha Piteoff (Sergeant).
High in the Alps a young boy eagerly waits for the birth of a new litter of St. Bernard pups. Martin is an orphan who lives at the Hospice St. Bernard, a travelers' way station run by monks. The lad is assigned to Julius, the kennel leader who will train the puppies to serve as rescue dogs. When the pups arrive, one is more active than the others and is soon Martin's favorite. The boy names the dog Barry and stays close to him throughout the training. Tragedy strikes when Barry and Martin are caught in an avalanche.

Production Notes:

- A total of fifteen St. Bernards were used to perform Barry's various stunts.
- Location filming took place in the Simplon Pass, near Brig, Switzerland. The manufactured avalanche took place on a cliff previously used in the 1969 James Bond film *On Her Majesty's Secret Service.*

BASEBALL FEVER   Airdates: 10/14/79, 5/31/81, 9/17/83.
The all-American pastime is the subject of this animation program. Goofy provides an introduction to the sport's fundamental theories in *How to Play Baseball*, in which a series of painful disasters befall the hapless player. Other cartoons include *Slide, Donald, Slide, Goofy Gymnastics, Casey at the Bat,* and *Casey Bats Again.*

BATTLE FOR SURVIVAL   Airdate: 4/09/61.
The harsh world of nature is highlighted in this show, which makes wide use of time-lapse and close-up photography to bring this hidden story to the viewer. A seemingly simple subject, such as a wild oat seed or an ear of corn, takes on a new meaning when its entire life cycle is sped up.

BAYOU BOY   Airdates—Part 1: 2/07/71, 4/08/79. Part 2: 2/14/71, 4/15/79.
Cast: John McIntire (Father Boudreau), Mitch Vogel (Jeannot), Frank Silvera (Uncle Maxim), Jeanette Nolan (Aunt Louise), Percy Rodrigues (Charbot), Vito Scotti (Mr. Bob), Marcel Hillaire (M. Verret), Mike Lookinland (Claude), Paul Fix (Captain Pierre), Michael Ontkean (Alcide), Brad David (Philippe).
A murky and mysterious Louisiana bayou is the setting for this tale of a missing silver bell and the dangers two boys face in recovering it. Years earlier a hurricane had ripped the bell loose from a church steeple and hurled it into Dead Man's Bayou, where a giant alligator lies in wait for those who would dive for it.

Production Notes:

- Location filming took place at Caddo Lake, a swampy area on the Louisiana/Texas border. This location was also used in the episode *The Ghost of Cypress Swamp.*
- The alligator fight took place at the Disney studios in Burbank, where $12,000 was spent to re-create a section of the bayou in an on-set pond previously used for films such as *Lt. Robin Crusoe, U.S.N.*
- In 1979, the show was aired under the title *The Boy from Deadman's Bayou.*

BEAR COUNTRY

This is the second part of the episode *Yellowstone Story (and) Bear Country*. *Bear Country* was also seen in the episode *Rapids Ahead (and) Bear Country* and as part of the *NBC All-Disney Saturday Night at the Movies* series of specials on 5/01/76, when it aired as a co-feature to *That Darn Cat!*

BEARS AND I, THE   Airdates—Part 1: 2/01/76. Part 2: 2/08/76.

This 1974 theatrical release stars Patrick Wayne as an adventurer who saves three orphaned bear cubs from hunters and suspicious Indians.

BEAVER VALLEY (AND) CAMERAS IN AFRICA   Airdates: 12/29/54, 6/01/55 (Cameras in Africa [and] Beaver Valley), 8/24/55 (Cameras in Africa [and] Beaver Valley).

Walt introduces noted wildlife photographer Alfred Milotte, who has recently returned from an expedition to Africa where he and his wife, Elma, spent over two years filming the stories of the African lion and elephant. Milotte shows scenes of rampaging rhinos, a cheetah racing at over 80 miles an hour, and the animals of the Serengeti Plain. This footage was later used in the *True-Life Adventure* feature *The African Lion*, released in 1955. Part two of the program is *Beaver Valley*, another *True-Life Adventure*.

Production Notes:

- Repeat broadcasts of this episode were aired as *Cameras in Africa (and) Beaver Valley*.
- *Beaver Valley* also aired as a featurette on the *NBC All-Disney Saturday Night at the Movies* broadcast of 2/23/74.

BEDKNOBS AND BROOMSTICKS   Airdates (2-hour format): 3/22/87.

Angela Lansbury and David Tomlinson star in this 1971 theatrical release about an amateur witch who must use her mail-order magic course to stop a Nazi invasion during World War II. It also aired as a special on 2/12/89 in NBC's *Sunday Night Movie* series.

BEHIND THE CAMERAS IN LAPLAND (AND) ALASKAN ESKIMO   Airdates: 10/24/56, 6/26/57.

The *True-Life Adventure* crew heads for Lapland, a frigid area in northern Europe where huge herds of reindeer spend the winter in the lowlands. The annual migration to the summer pastures in the north has just begun, and the Lapland natives are preparing to move along with the herds. The Lapps are a nomadic people with a simple life that greatly depends on the reindeer, but they seem content with life even in this harsh environment.

Production Note:

- Part two of the program, *The Alaskan Eskimo*, won an Academy Award for Best Short Subject in 1953.

BEHIND THE SCENES WITH FESS PARKER
Airdates: 5/30/56, 8/01/56.

Cast: Fess Parker (James J. Andrews), Jeffrey Hunter (William A. Fuller), Jeff York (William Campbell), John Lupton (William Pittenger), Eddie Firestone (Robert Buffum), Kenneth Tobey (Anthony Murphy), Don Megowan (Marion A. Ross).

Walt introduces Fess Parker, who tells about the filming of *The Great Locomotive Chase*. Fess discusses the history of railroads and their importance for carrying troops and equipment during a war. He then tells of the true story on which the movie is based, a tale of twenty Union soldiers who traveled behind Confederate lines on a mission so vital that they were later honored with the first Congressional Medals of Honor.

Production Note:

- Wilbur Kurtz, who served as a technical adviser on the film, was married to Capt. William A. Fuller's daughter, and had served in a similar advisory capacity for *Gone with the Wind*.

BEHIND THE TRUE-LIFE CAMERAS (AND) OLYMPIC ELK   Airdates: 9/21/55, 11/23/55, 6/20/56.

In another behind-the-scenes visit to the *True-Life Adventure* series, Walt introduces James Algar, writer and director of the series. For a look at the filming of *Secrets of Life*, Algar takes viewers to the Everglades, where photographers Clare and Bill Anderson have been filming the local inhabitants. He then takes us to a desert where photographer Bob Crandall is documenting the lives of a colony of leaf cutter ants.

BEN AND ME (AND) PETER AND THE WOLF   Airdate: 11/15/64.

This show consists of two cartoon shorts. The first is the story of Amos, a Philadelphia church mouse who becomes involved with several important figures during the American Revolution.

The second part of the show, the story of Peter and the Wolf, was originally part of the theatrical release *Make Mine Music*.

BENJI THE HUNTED Airdates: 2/19/89. This 1987 theatrical release features canine star Benji as he tries to find his way home after being lost in a shipwreck. It was edited to fit in a one-hour format.

BEST DOGGONED DOG IN THE WORLD, THE Airdates: 11/20/57, 3/26/58, 2/12/61. Disney has just completed a movie based on the book *Old Yeller*. Dorothy McGuire, who stars in the film, tells the audience a few key stories about the movie. The remainder of the show is based on the 1955 theatrical featurette *Arizona Sheepdog*.

Production Note:

• Disney updated the 1961 version of the show to include scenes from his upcoming *101 Dalmatians* in place of the *Old Yeller* segment.

BEYOND WITCH MOUNTAIN Airdates: 2/20/82, 9/04/82.
Cast: Eddie Albert (Jason O'Day), Tracey Gould (Tia Malone), Andrew K. Freeman (Tony Malone), J. D. Cannon (Deranian), Noah Beery (Uncle Bene), Efrem Zimbalist, Jr. (Aristotle Bolt), Stephanie Blackmore (Dr. Adrian Molina), Peter Hobbs (Dr. Morton), Gene Dynarski (Lawrence), William H. Bassett (Lowell Roberts), James Luisi (Foreman), Hettie Lynee Hurtes (Reporter), Lola Mason (Lady Driver), Eric Aved (Gregory), Kirk Cameron (Boy).

This sequel to the films *Escape to Witch Mountain* and *Return from Witch Mountain* begins as Tony and Tia leave Witch Mountain hoping to find Uncle Bene. He has taken a hike outside their secret compound, and Tia has a feeling he is in trouble. Her fears are well founded, for Bene enters a "No Trespassing" zone monitored by hidden television cameras. He's spotted by Deranian, who has been searching for Tony and Tia ever since they escaped from his employer, Aristotle Bolt. Deranian almost traps Bene and the children, but they use their eerie powers to escape once more.

Production Note:

• This episode was a pilot for a proposed series.

BIG COUNCIL, THE Airdates: 3/12/58, 7/16/58.
Cast: Jerome Courtland (Andy Burnett), Jeff York (Joe Crane), Andrew Duggan (Jack Kelly), Slim Pickens (Old Bill Williams), Iron Eyes Cody (Mad Wolf), Abel Fernandez (Kiasak), John War Eagle (Matosuki), Ralph Valencia (Little Eagle), Jorie Wyler (Nitokeman).

The sixth (and final) chapter in *The Saga of Andy Burnett* series is a continuation of the story begun in *The Land of Enemies*. While Burnett and his friends are waiting for the Indian council to decide their fate, Mad Wolf is casting spells and calling demons to attack the Mountain Men. Chief Kiasak invites Burnett's group to enter a series of games and athletic competitions to be held before the council meets. He points out this may be their last chance to make friends with the same warriors sought out by Mad Wolf.

BIG RED Airdates—Part 1: 12/06/64, 2/15/70, 8/23/81. Part 2: 12/13/64, 2/22/70, 8/30/81. For the 1976–76 season the show was broadcast in a two-hour format: 11/09/75.

This 1962 theatrical release stars Walter Pidgeon and Gilles Payant in the story of a young boy who nurses an injured dog back to health.

Production Note:

• The episode *The Wetback Hound* is a behind-the-scenes look at the filming of this story, which was shot on location in the Canadian north woods.

BIG SWINDLE, THE Airdates: 10/03/65, 6/26/66.
Cast: Edmond O'Brien (Editor Crowley), Anne Francis (Adeline Jones), Roger Mobley (Gallegher), Harvey Korman (Brownie), Guy Raymond (The Shadow), John Lormer (Pete), Alan Hewitt (Chauncy Talbott), Arthur Malet (Sir James).

Part 2 of *The Further Adventures of Gallegher* finds the young newspaper copyboy helping Adeline Jones, the town's first female newspaper reporter. Adeline has been assigned to write a series of articles on confidence men, and the editor has decided to set a trap for the swindlers.

BIGFOOT Airdate (2-hour format): 3/08/87. The show was later aired in two parts—Part 1: 4/17/88. Part 2: 4/24/88.
Cast: James Sloyan (Dr. Zach Emerson),

Gracie Harrison (Laura Oneger), Joseph Maher (Jack Kendrix), Adam Karl (Kevin Emerson), Candace Cameron (Samantha "Sam" Oneger), Bernie White (Lazlo Whitefeather), Colleen Dewhurst (Gladys Samcoe), Dawan Scott (Albert), Jerry Chambers (Alice), Timothy Brown (Reporter #2), Lucy Butler (Reporter #1).

Zach Emerson and Laura Oneger are thinking about getting married, so they take their children, Kevin and Samantha, camping to get to know each other. The trip begins poorly. The two youngsters resent the possible marriage and constantly argue. The real trouble begins when Kevin and Samantha decide to go exploring and Samantha falls off a ledge and is knocked unconscious. When Kevin climbs down to try to help her, he is astonished to find that she has disappeared and strange footprints lead away from where she fell.

Production Note:

- The show was filmed on location near Big Bear, California.

BIRTH OF THE SWAMP FOX, THE

Airdates: 10/23/59, 4/29/60.
Cast: Leslie Nielsen (Lt. Col. Francis Marion), John Sutton (Gen. Banastre Tarleton), Joy Page (Mary Videaux), Tim Considine (Gabe), Dick Foran (Gabriel Marion), Richard Erdman (Sergeant Jasper), Myron Healey (Maj. Peter Horry), Jordan Whitfield (Oscar), John Alderson (Sergeant McDonald), Mary Field (Cathy), Louise Beavers (Dehlia), Chuck Roberson (Jenkins), Patrick Macnee (Dragoon Captain), Wilton Graff (General Lincoln), Yvette Vickers (Nina), J. Pat O'Malley (Dragoon Guard), Dabbs Greer (Storekeeper).

Francis Marion is the head of a small detachment of American troops attempting to free South Carolina from British rule under the command of Colonel Tarleton of the Green Dragoon cavalry.

Production Note:

- Patrick Macnee, cast as the unfortunate leader of the English guard party, later achieved fame as John Steed in the popular series *The Avengers*.

BISCUIT EATER, THE   Airdates—Part 1:

10/10/76. Part 2: 10/17/76.
This 1972 theatrical release stars Earl Holliman and Johnny Whitaker in the story of a young boy's efforts to turn a hapless hound into a prize-winning show dog.

Production Note:

- *The Biscuit Eater* has also been aired in syndication under the title *Tomorrow's Champions*.

BLACKBEARD'S GHOST   Airdates—Part 1:

11/20/82. Part 2: 11/27/82.
Dean Jones is the unlucky man who brings Capt. Edward "Blackbeard" Teach, played by Peter Ustinov, back to life in this 1968 theatrical release. Suzanne Pleshette co-stars as Jones's love interest.

BLUEGRASS SPECIAL, THE   Airdate:

5/22/77.
Cast: William Windom (Phil Wainright), Celeste Holm (Deirdre Wainright), Devon Ericson (Penny Wainwright), Davy Jones (Davey), James Gleason (Billy Joe), Shug Fisher (Harvey), Edward Faulkner (Dan), John R. McKee (Jerry).

The world of thoroughbred racing is explored in the story of Woodhill, a race horse with a growing reputation for being unruly and troublesome. One morning he's spotted by Penny Wainwright, a girl who dreams of being a jockey. She convinces her aunt that Woodhill is a potential winner, and the horse soon has a new owner.

Production Note:

- Davy Jones, a member of the popular 1960s singing group The Monkees, was previously a jockey in England.

BOATNIKS, THE   Airdates (2-hour format):

11/12/78, 6/02/91.
Robert Morse, Stefanie Powers, and Phil Silvers are among the stars of this 1970 theatrical release about an accident-prone coast guard ensign who becomes involved with jewel thieves.

BON VOYAGE   Airdates—Part 1: 1/11/70.

Part 2: 1/18/70. Part 3: 1/25/70.
This 1962 theatrical release is the story of the Willard family, their long-awaited trip to Europe, and the misadventures they encounter there. It stars Fred MacMurray, Jane Wyman, Michael Callan, Deborah Walley, Tommy Kirk, and Kevin Corcoran.

BOOMERANG, DOG OF MANY TALENTS

Airdates—Part 1: 9/22/68, 7/13/69. Part 2: 9/29/68, 7/27/69.
Cast: Darren McGavin (Barney Duncan), Patricia Crowley (Molly Graham), Darby

Hinton (Simon Graham), Lori Farrow (Janet Graham), Rusty Lane (F. M. Higbee), Russ Conway (Rancher), Hal Baylor (Hunter), Walter Sande (Harker).

Barney Duncan is a turn-of-the-century con man with a unique scam—he sells his dog, Boomerang, to unsuspecting victims and goes on his way. Just like an Australian boomerang, the dog returns to his owner each time.

Production Notes:

- Disney composer Mel Leven provided three songs performed by Darren McGavin: *Boomerang, A Single Man Goes Traveling,* and *Get Along You Turkeys.*
- Tiger, a cross-bred redbone hound, played the part of Boomerang, and also appeared in *Bristle Face, Those Calloways, Monkeys, Go Home!* and *Rascal* for Disney. For this role, he had a stand-in named Prince.

BORN TO RUN   Airdates—Part 1: 3/25/79. Part 2: 4/01/79.

Cast: Tom Farley (Matthew Boyd), Robert Bettles (Teddy Boyd), Andrew McFarlane (Doone Boyd), Mary Ward (Aunt Marian Castle), Julieanne Newbould (Cathy Castle), Alexander Archdale (Callant), Wyn Roberts (McGinnis), Kit Taylor (Paul Sanford), Gordon McDougall (Horace Weaver), Les Foxcroft (Loafer), Cul Cullen (Stranger #1), Rob Steele (Stranger #2), Nigel Lovell (Cantrell), Kenneth Laird (Hobart), Aileen Britton (Susannah), Alister Smart (Sergeant Meeker), Alan Cinis (Bruce McGinnis), John Meillon (Delaney).

First released theatrically overseas in 1977, this is the tale of a family of horse racers in Australia in 1911 who discover the racing sensation, Dandy Boy.

BOSTON TEA PARTY, THE
See: *Johnny Tremain.*

BOY AND THE BRONC BUSTER, THE
Airdates—Part 1: 3/18/73, 7/02/78. Part 2: 3/25/73, 7/09/78.

Cast: Earl Holliman (Cal Winslow), Strother Martin (Bartholomew "Buckshot" Blythe), Jacqueline Scott (Mary Thompson), Vincent Van Patten (Todd Thompson), Lonny Chapman (Lem Thompson), Lisa Gerritsen (Jenny Hutchins), Anthony Caruso (Marshal Brandon), Ken Swofford (Gentry), Larry D. Mann (Jesse Compton), Ross Elliott (Pat Hutchins), William Bryant (Rodeo Judge),

Scott Walker (Rodeo Cowboy), Ben Cooper (Deputy Harden), Frank Cady (Clothing Store Proprietor), Don Carter (Spencer), Ted Gehring (Brewster).

Cal Winslow is a drifter in the 1880s who is hired to break wild horses for Lem Thompson, an Arizona rancher. Intrigued by Cal's lifestyle, Lem's orphan nephew, Todd, runs away to follow him when the drifter leaves again for the rodeo circuit.

Production Note:

- This show was filmed on location in Santa Rita, Texas, and on Disney's Golden Oak Ranch.

BOY CALLED NUTHIN', A   Airdates—Part 1: 12/10/67, 8/15/71. Part 2: 12/17/67, 8/22/71.

Cast: Forrest Tucker (Turkeyneck), John Carroll (Sagebrush), Ronny Howard (Richie "Nuthin'" Caldwell), Mary La Roche (Carrie Brackney), Mickey Shaughnessy (Sheriff Hoop), Donna Butterworth (Laura-Kate Brackney), Sara Seegar (Mrs. Wampler), Richard Bakalyan (Shortie), Rafael Campos (Peewee).

Life out West with cowboys and Indians is what young Richie Caldwell is expecting when he leaves Chicago in the early 1900s to visit his uncle in the small town of Big Sun. His dreams abruptly end when he learns that civilization has changed the West from the tales he was fond of reading. He's also shocked to find his Uncle Lester's "ranch" to be a rundown shack and equally disreputable farm.

Production Note:

- Forrest Tucker sings the song *How Many Cows Can a Cowpoke Punch?* throughout the show.

BOY FROM DEADMAN'S BAYOU, THE
See: *Bayou Boy.*

BOY WHO FLEW WITH CONDORS, THE
Airdates: 2/19/67, 5/28/67, 4/15/73.

Cast: Christopher Jury (Himself), Margaret Birsner (Glider Pilot), Fred W. Harris (Sailplane Instructor), Milton O. Thompson (NASA Test Pilot).

Chris Jury is a California teenager who loves to spend time watching the graceful flights of the California condor, an endangered species. One day his bird-watching is interrupted by the arrival of a sailplane piloted by a woman who is attempting to earn an award for distance gliding. Soon he is an avid pilot himself.

Boy Who Stole the Elephant, The
Airdates—Part 1: 9/20/70, 5/30/71. Part 2: 9/27/70, 6/06/71.

Cast: David Wayne (Col. Rufus Ryder), June Havoc (Molly Jeffrys), Mark Lester (Davey), Dabbs Greer (Stilts), Parley Baer (Mayor Hancock), Whitney Blake (Helen Owens), James Westerfield (Sheriff Berry), Robert Emhardt (Cy Brown), Tom Drake (Mr. Corbett), Richard Kiel (Luke Brown), Betty Lynn (Lottie Ladare), Doris Singleton (Lizzie Ladare), Christopher Shea (Billy Owens), Susan Olsen (Lucy Owens), Ernestine Clark (Nana), Danny Rees (DeMarco), Walter Burke (Tinker), William Fawcett (Elmer), Hal Smith (Reb Canfield).

Col. Rufus Ryder runs a small traveling circus that never seems to make a profit, possibly due to Ryder's fondness for gambling. Davey is an orphan living with the circus who acts as the colonel's aide. Realizing he needs additional cash, Ryder asks Molly Jeffrys, owner of another small circus, for money to pay his debts. She instead loans him an elephant named Queenie, who can help work in the circus. Davey begins working with Queenie and soon the two are inseparable.

Production Note:

- Disney press releases stated that this episode was based on a real-life incident that occurred in Kentucky at the turn of the century.

Boy Who Talked to Badgers, The
Airdates—Part 1: 9/14/75. Part 2: 9/21/75. The show was also broadcast that season in a 2-hour format: 5/23/76.

Cast: Carl Betz (Will MacDonald), Salome Jens (Esther MacDonald), Christian Juttner (Benjy), Robert Donner (Burton), Denver Pyle (Ben as an Adult), Stuart Lee (John), Georgie Collins (Mrs. Gilman), Jim Roberts (Mr. Gilman), Chief Rufus Goodstriker (Joe), Joyce Doolittle (Mrs. Polanski), Robert Cruse (Farmer Pennyman), Robert Pulleyblank (Farmer Sawyer), Bill Berry (Deputy), Lyle Edge (Rider), Arnold Wilson (Minister), Frank D. Scott (Sexton).

Ben MacDonald is a small boy who not only is able to talk to animals but seems to prefer them to people, a trait not admired by his father, Will. Ben's mother and older brother are concerned by the growing prob-

lem between Ben and Will but are unable to bring the two closer together. The two finally learn to understand each other after Will hires a trapper to clear the farm of some pesky badgers, not knowing that one of them is Ben's closest animal friend.

Production Notes:

- This story was based on a real-life incident near Manitoba in 1870.
- Filming took place on location at Drumheller, Alberta, and near Calgary, Canada.

B.R.A.T. Patrol, The
Airdates (2-hour format): 10/26/86, 6/28/87.

Cast: Sean Astin, Tim Thomerson (Major D. Hackett), Jason Presson, Joe Wright, Dustin Berkovitz, Dylan Kussman, Nia Long, Brian Keith (General Newmeyer), Stephen Lee (Sergeant Phillips), John Quade (Knife Brunnell), Billy Jacoby, Dean Anthony (Card Checker), Lisa Dinkins (Desk Sergeant), Greg Finley (Joe), John H. Francis (Mr. Foster), Ira Heiden (Ray), Sgt. Anne C. Larson (Lieutenant), Marcus Mukai (Young Captain), John Putch (Corporal), Daniel Riordan (Harry), Lew Saunders (M.P.), Michael Tulin (Waiter), Jacob Vargas (Student #2), Ed Williams (Asst. Defense Secretary Atwood).

The B.R.A.T. Patrol is an unofficial club for a group of children living at the El Diablo Marine Corps base. They constantly run afoul of another group, the Junior Marines, which is led by the son of the base commander. The two groups are competing for the annual Youth Service Award, which is to be presented when the assistant secretary of defense visits the base, and this leads to some spirited arguments between them.

Production Notes:

- "B.R.A.T." stands for "Born—Raised and Trapped."
- This episode was filmed at the Marine Corps Air Station in El Toro, California.

Brand New Life (limited series)
After the pilot episode *Brand New Life: The Honeymooners* aired on *NBC Monday Night at the Movies*, Disney acquired the rights to that show and the five other episodes in the series: *Brand New Life: Above and Beyond Therapy; Brand New Life: I Fought the Law; Brand New Life: Private School; Brand New Life: Children of a Legal Mom;* and *Brand New Life: Even Housekeepers Sing the Blues.* The first four episodes were aired on the an-

thology series, but low ratings kept the final episode from being aired.

BRAND NEW LIFE: ABOVE AND BEYOND THERAPY Airdates: 10/01/89, 8/05/90.

Cast: Barbara Eden (Barbara), Don Murray (Roger Gibbons), Shawnee Smith (Amanda), Jennie Garth (Ericka), Byron Thames (Laird), Alison Sweeney, David Tom (Bart), Phillip R. Allen (Dr. Jason Pierce), John Hostetter, Gwil Richards, Preston Scott Lee (Randy), Trevor Edmond (Jeff), Jennifer Buchanan, Richard Stanley, Sheri Lynn (Elissa), Sonia Satra (Sara).

The first episode in the *Brand New Life* limited series begins as Barbara and Roger Gibbons attend Roger's 30th high school class reunion. One of his former classmates, Dr. Jason Pierce, a famous television therapist, asks the Gibbons to appear on his show. Roger doesn't trust Pierce, but the rest of the family successfully argue that they want to be on television.

Production Note:

- Chris Carter, the creator of this limited series, later created the cult series *The X-Files.* He also developed two failed pilots for Disney, *Cameo by Night* and *The Nanny,* which did not air.

BRAND NEW LIFE: CHILDREN OF A LEGAL MOM Airdates: 1/07/90, 8/12/90.

Cast: Barbara Eden (Barbara Gibbons), Don Murray (Roger Gibbons), Shawnee Smith (Amanda Gibbons), Byron Thomas (Laird Gibbons), Jennie Garth (Ericka), Alison Sweeney (Christy), David Tom (Bart), Todd Jeffries (Randy), Steven Gilborn (Professor Kratzman), Pat Crawford Brown (Mrs. Sayley), Dylan Tucker (Kirk), Kristin Pearcey, Ken Elks (Wes), Joseph Toohey, John Maucere, Terry Theriot.

Amanda brings a friend, Wes, home for a visit before he has to leave for college. At first, some of the family treat him differently because he is deaf, but they come to realize that he shares many of the same interests and problems they do.

Production Note:

- This episode aired in the anthology time slot, and was counted by NBC and Disney as being part of the series, but it featured all new titles and made no mention of Disney.

BRAND NEW LIFE: I FOUGHT THE LAW Airdate: 10/15/89.

Cast: Barbara Eden (Barbara), Don Murray (Roger Gibbons), Shawnee Smith (Amanda), Jennie Garth (Ericka), Byron Thames (Laird), Alison Sweeney (Christy), David Tom (Bart), Joseph Ruskin (Judge Smith), Christian LeBlanc (Marcus), Lou Hancock (Grandma Zora), John S. Ragin, Dylan Tucker (Kirk), Granville Ames, Tim Haldeman, Keely Christian, Anya Lund (Lady Judge), Gil Roscoe (Attorney), Cheryl T. Janecky (Susan), Gregory Littman (Bailiff #1), Debra Casey (Girl with Crew Cut), Janette Mateus (Dotray), Paul Harkins (Dino Brotviak), Mark Robman (Witness), Sonny Carver (Farnsworth), Julie Moran (Reporter), Dana Craig (Deputy), Michael A. Young (Bailiff #2).

The second episode in the *Brand New Life* limited series pits Barbara against an egotistical traffic court judge. The battle begins when her son receives a speeding ticket and finds himself in front of Judge Smith, an overbearing and sarcastic man who delights in tormenting those brought before him. Barbara protests Smith's actions and the judge retaliates by sending her to jail for contempt of court.

BRAND NEW LIFE: PRIVATE SCHOOL Airdate: 10/22/89.

Cast: Barbara Eden (Barbara), Don Murray (Roger Gibbons), Shawnee Smith (Amanda Gibbons), Jennie Garth (Ericka), Byron Thames (Laird Gibbons), Alison Sweeney (Christy), David Tom (Bart), Holly Fields (Tammy), Danny Nucci (D.J.), Mark Neely (Mark Benniger), Kristin Pearcey, Christiana Wu, Dylan Tucker (Kirk), Shiva Gordon, William Lucking (Bud McCray), Kerry Remsen (Assistant Casting Director), Bettina Devin (Alice), Edward Blanchard (Mr. Joseph), Jane Chung (Grandmother).

The third episode in this limited series finds the Gibbons family dealing with a number of weighty issues. Ericka learns that a 17-year-old classmate is pregnant and decides to celebrate by throwing a baby shower. The initial glow of excitement soon fades when Ericka and her friend both realize that having a baby is a major commitment and the carefree days of high school friendships are over.

BRAND NEW LIFE: THE HONEYMOONERS Airdate (2-hour format): 6/24/90.

Cast: Barbara Eden (Barbara McCray), Don Murray (Roger Gibbons), Shawnee Smith (Amanda Gibbons), Jennie Garth (Ericka McCray), Byron Thames (Laird Gibbons), Alison Sweeney (Christy McCray), David Tom

(Bart McCray), Lee Garlington, Elizabeth Savage, Brian Patrick, Stephanie Dicker, Eric Foster (Barlow Gibbons), Kate Benton, Chip Heller, Bernie Pock, Cynthia Ireland (Kelli Reynolds), Melinda Cordell (Mona Bacon), Oceana Marr (Instructor), Audree Chapman (Doctor), Jay Bradford (Reed), Gary Cohen (Ryan), Tony Pandolfo (Prosecuting Attorney), D. David Morin (Defense Attorney), Earl W. Billings (Judge), Annie O'Donnell (Defendant), Ross Borden (Tom), Lance Fenton (Pool Attendant), Dane Winters (Lifeguard), Richard E. Young (Judge at Wedding), Laurel Schaefer (Country Club Woman #1), Annie Waterman (Country Club Woman #2), Wendy Kim Sullivan (Country Club Woman #3), Mans P. Kjellin (Cook), Adrian Ricard (Nurse).

Barbara McCray, a divorced mother of three, is studying court reporting while working as a waitress to support her family. Her life unexpectedly improves when she meets Roger Gibbons, a wealthy widower, and the two begin dating. After only a month, they're engaged. Roger's children are thrilled with the news, but Barbara's family is worried about how the two families will get along.

Production Note:

- The first airing of this show was on 9/18/89 on *NBC Monday Night at the Movies*, and was not a Disney production. This was followed by four 1-hour episodes aired on the anthology series when Disney acquired the rights. This show was repeated as part of the anthology series on 6/24/90.

BRIDE OF BOOGEDY   Airdates (2-hour format): 4/12/87, 5/29/88.
Cast: Richard Masur (Carleton Davis), Mimi Kennedy (Eloise Davis), Tammy Lauren (Jennifer Davis), David Faustino (Corwin Davis), Joshua Rudoy (Ahri Davis), Leonard Frey (Walter Witherspoon), Howard Witt (Boogedy), Eugene Levy (Tom Lynch), Ray Girardin (Elmer), Alice Hirson (Mrs. Hooter), Karen Kondazian (Madeleinska Scott), Vincent Schiavelli (Lazarus), Jeff Abbott (Crowd Member #2), Annie Abbott (Crowd Member #3), Robert V. Barron (Mortician), Michael Bartholomew (Jonathan), Minda Burr (Mother), Bill Capizzi (Pizza Man), Kristin Clayton (Linda), Betty Cole (Crowd Member #1), Terrence Evans (Mechanic), Matthew Hurley (Brave Kid).*

This sequel to the episode *Mr. Boogedy* begins as a group of boys seated around a camp-

fire hears how the Davis family found themselves haunted by the evil spirit of Mr. Boogedy. Although the ghost was supposedly destroyed, Boogedy's spirit returns to terrorize the town and to take Mrs. Davis as his bride.

Production Note:

- The town-square set was built for the film *Something Wicked This Way Comes.*

BRIMSTONE, THE AMISH HORSE
Airdates: 10/27/68, 5/27/73.
Cast: Pamela Toll (Barbara Lansford), Wallace Rooney (Bishop Jonathon Lansford), Phil Clark (Eli Kreider), Robert Allen (Gordon Knight, Sr.), Michael Goodwin (Gordon Knight, Jr.), Abby Lewis (Mrs. Lansford), Tom Caldwell (Auctioneer).*

An accident cripples a championship steeplechase horse, Brimstone, who is then sold at auction to an Amish minister, Jonathon Lansford. He and his daughter, Barbara, hope to heal the horse enough for it to serve as a work horse and to pull their buggy.

Production Note:

- This episode was filmed on location in Pennsylvania.

BRISTLE FACE   Airdates—Part 1: 1/26/64, 4/20/69, 7/21/74. Part 2: 2/02/64, 4/27/69, 7/28/74.
Cast: Brian Keith (Lute Swank), Phillip Alford (Jace Landers), Jeff Donnell (Mrs. Jarkey), Wallace Ford (Emory Packer), Parley Baer (Sheriff Rad Toler), Slim Pickens (Newt Pribble), Barbara Eiler (Poor Woman), George Lindsey (Hermie Chadron), Sam Edwards (Bert Fogerty), Ray Teal (Justice Mackley), Robert McQuain (Sud Pribble), Paul E. Burns (Bailiff).*

Jace Landers is a 14-year-old orphan traveling throughout Tennessee with his only friend, a hound dog named Bristle Face. Their adventures begin when the two travelers interrupt their journey to stay with Lute Swank, a kindly shopkeeper who runs a small country store. Problems arise when Bristle Face attracts the attention of the local sheriff.

Production Notes:

- Bristle Face was played by two dogs. The main performer, Tiger, and his stand-in, Prince, were later paired together again in *Boomerang, Dog of Many Talents.*

- *Bristle Face* has also been aired in syndication under the title *Fox Hunter*.

BROTHER AGAINST BROTHER Airdates: 10/30/59, 5/06/60.

Cast: Leslie Nielsen (Lt. Col. Francis Marion), John Sutton (Gen. Banastre Tarleton), Dick Foran (Gabriel Marion), Joy Page (Mary Videaux), Richard Erdman (Sergeant Jasper), Tim Considine (Gabe), Myron Healey (Maj. Peter Horry), Edward Ashley (Captain Wall), Jordan Whitfield (Oscar), John Alderson (Sergeant McDonald), Parley Baer (Innkeeper), Mary Field (Cathy), Louise Beavers (Dehlia), Chuck Roberson (Jenkins), Patrick Macnee (Dragoon Captain).

The second of the Swamp Fox stories finds the Tories staging a series of raids on their patriot neighbors, often pitting longtime friends and relatives against each other. One such raid destroys the home of Gabriel Marion, the Swamp Fox's brother, but leaves standing the Videaux plantation. Although he's aware that Mary Videaux is his brother's fiancée, Gabriel joins a band of patriots headed for Mary's home with revenge in their hearts, for her parents are known Tories.

Production Note:

- Joy Page, who played Mary Videaux, was replaced after this episode by Barbara Eiler.

CALL IT COURAGE Airdates: 4/01/73, 3/06/77.

Cast: Evan Temarii (Mafatu).

The natives of the island of Hikueru tell a tale of the courage of a boy, Mafatu, and his dog, Tambu. Mafatu's father had been lost in the shark-infested ocean, and ever since, the boy has suffered from nightmares. Realizing that he must confront his fears before he can be judged a man, Mafatu takes Tambu with him and sets sail in a small outrigger canoe. The many dangers of the sea prove to be all too real when a storm forces him ashore on an island claimed by a savage tribe.

Production Notes:

- *Call It Courage* was filmed on location on Bora Bora, which served as the cannibal's island, and on Tahiti. Filming took over 8 months.
- The name Mafatu means "stout heart."

CAMERAS IN AFRICA (AND) BEAVER VALLEY

See: *Beaver Valley (and) Cameras in Africa.*

CAMERAS IN SAMOA (AND) THE HOLLAND STORY Airdates: 11/07/56, 7/10/57.

Winston Hibler narrates a behind-the-scenes look at Disney camera team Herbert and Trudi Knapp, who are in Samoa filming a segment of the *People and Places* series.

The show then takes a look at life in Holland. The dangers of living in an area separated from the sea by huge dikes are shown as a break in the protective wall is repaired.

CANDLESHOE Airdate (2-hour format): 6/22/86.

David Niven, Helen Hayes, and Jodie Foster star in this 1977 theatrical release about an American street urchin who holds the key to a missing fortune in England.

CAN'T BUY ME LOVE Airdate (2-hour format): 3/04/90.

Patrick Dempsey and Amanda Peterson star in this 1987 theatrical release about a nerdy high school student who achieves instant popularity when he pays an attractive cheerleader for dating lessons.

CAPTAIN EO BACKSTAGE Airdate (30-minute format): 5/15/88 (with *Justin Case* in a 2-hour format).

Cast: Michael Jackson, Whoopi Goldberg.

This behind-the-scenes look at the making of the 3-D film *Captain Eo* is an edited version of The Disney Channel special *The Making of Captain Eo*. It was aired on the anthology series following the episode *Justin Case*.

CAPTIVE STALLION, THE

This is Part 1 of *Comanche*.

CARLO, THE SIERRA COYOTE Airdates: 2/03/74, 8/04/74.

Cast: Jana Milo (Sally Watson), Steven S. Stewart (Chuck Watson), Hal Bokar (Driver), Dale Alexander (John Muir).

Carlo, a coyote, leaves his old home in the lowlands of California to escape human encroachment on his territory. He heads high into the mountains, into an area explored many years ago by naturalist John Muir. The old problem of coexisting with people resurfaces when a blizzard forces Carlo to enter the Watson camp in search of food. Chuck Watson scares away the hungry animal with a shotgun, and Carlo flees in fear of his life.

Production Note:

• Jana Milo was working as a secretary at the Studio when producer James Algar noticed her and cast her in this episode.

CARNIVAL TIME　Airdate: 3/04/62.
Ludwig Von Drake hosts this look at not one but two separate carnivals in what he "modestly" promises will be a spectacular TV event. His correspondents, Jose Carioca in Rio de Janeiro and Donald Duck in New Orleans, are standing by, ready to bring the highlights of each event to the viewer.

Production Notes:

• Ludwig and his co-stars sing three songs written by Disney composers Richard and Robert Sherman, who would later gain fame for *Mary Poppins, Carnival Time, It Gets You,* and *Carnival Samba.*

CASE OF MURDER, A　Airdates: 9/26/65, 6/19/66.
Cast: Edmond O'Brien (Editor Crowley), Roger Mobley (Gallegher), Harvey Korman (Brownie), Victoria Shaw (Katherine Van Raalte), Peter Wyngarde (Sir Richard Westerby), Liam Sullivan (Charles Van Raalte), James Flavin (Lieutenant Flynn), John Marley (Coachman), John Lormer (Pete).

Part 1 of *The Further Adventures of Gallegher* begins a new episode in the life of a newspaper copyboy who aspires to be a reporter. This story starts with Brownie, the paper's star reporter, writing critical reviews of Sir Richard Westerby's performance of *Hamlet* without even watching the play, just because Brownie has always disliked the actor. An outraged Westerby challenges Brownie to a duel of honor, and Crowley, the paper's editor, sees this as a means to raise the paper's circulation.

Production Note:

• *The Further Adventures of Gallegher* continues in the episode *The Big Swindle.*

CASE OF TREASON, A　Airdates: 1/22/60, 6/03/60.
Cast: Leslie Nielsen (Gen. Francis Marion), Robert Douglas (General Cornwallis), Barbara Eiler (Mary Videaux), John Sutton (Col. Banastre Tarleton), Myron Healey (Maj. Peter Horry), J. Pat O'Malley (Sergeant O'Reilly), Jordan Whitfield (Oscar), Hal Stalmaster (Gywnn), Donald Randolph (Mr. Videaux), Slim Pickens (Plunkett), George N.

Neise (Lieutenant Peters), Clarence Muse (Old Joseph).

Part 6 of *The Swamp Fox* opens with Marion and his men chasing Colonel Tarleton, whom they have "outfoxed" by causing one of his traps to backfire. The colonel races to the Videaux home for safety, unaware that Mary Videaux is actually Marion's fiancée and a spy for the patriots. When Marion enters the house searching for his foe, Mary pretends to be outraged and orders the rebels from the plantation. From his hiding spot Tarleton spots Mary and Marion sharing a secret kiss and begins to doubt her loyalty.

Production Note:

• The set for the city of Charleston was the cuartel from the *Zorro* series.

CASEBUSTERS　Airdates (aired with *My Town* in a 2-hour format): 5/25/86, 8/31/86.
Cast: Pat Hingle (Sam Donahue), Noah Hathaway (Jamie Donahue), Virginia Keehne (Allie Donahue), Gary Riley (Anthony "Ski" Zbrowski), Ebbe Roe Smith (Joe Bonner), Sharon Barr (Loretta Bonner), Thomas F. Duffy, Arthur Taxier, Nicholas Worth (Riker), Boyd Bodwell (Mullaney), Carlos Lacamara (Policeman #1), Sid Conrad (Jenkins), Eugene J. Collier (Policeman #2), Thomas Lew Mann (Thief), Tim Russ (Dixon).

Sam Donahue, a retired policeman, runs Sam's Security Service, a home protection company. When his grandchildren, Jamie and Allie, come for a visit, Allie announces that she wants to be a detective, just like him. Although Sam tells her that she's too young, Allie gets a chance to prove herself when she and Jamie catch a teenager breaking into a nearby house.

CASTAWAY COWBOY, THE　Airdates (2-hour format): 5/08/77. For the 1980–81 season the show was broadcast in two parts—Part 1: 3/15/81. Part 2: 3/22/81.
This 1974 theatrical release stars James Garner, Vera Miles, Robert Culp, and Eric Shea in the story of a cowboy who finds himself stranded on the Hawaiian island of Kauai in 1850.

CAT FROM OUTER SPACE, THE
Airdates—Part 1: 1/30/82. Part 2: 2/06/82.
A 1978 theatrical release, this is the story of an alien cat who is stranded on Earth when his spaceship is damaged. It stars Ken Berry, Sandy Duncan, Harry Morgan, and McLean Stevenson.

CAVALCADE OF SONGS   Airdates: 2/16/55, 6/22/55, 8/17/55, 9/16/62, 12/26/71.

Cast: Walt Disney, Firehouse Five Plus Two, Peggy Lee, Sonny Burke, The Mellomen.
The importance of music in motion pictures is this episode's theme as Walt discusses some of the more important tunes featured in his films over the years.

CHANDAR, THE BLACK LEOPARD OF CEYLON   Airdates—Part 1: 11/26/72, 6/10/73. Part 2: 12/03/72, 6/17/73.

Cast: Frederick Steyne (Sumana), Esram Jayasinghe (Dasa), Joe Abeywickrema (Father).
The lush jungles of Ceylon are home to a black leopard cub named Chandar, who falls into a pool of water and is rescued by Sumana, a holy man who loves to help animals. Chandar runs home to his mother and sister, not knowing that he and Sumana will meet again several years later.

Production Notes:

- Preproduction efforts on this show began in 1969, with actual filming lasting from July 1970 to August 1971. The $1 million project was briefly halted by an insurrection by local rebels against the government in early 1971.
- Narrator Ben Wright had been the speaking voice of Roger in *101 Dalmatians,* and would later return to the Studio for the role of Lord Grimsby in *The Little Mermaid.*

CHANGO, GUARDIAN OF THE MAYAN TREASURE   Airdate: 3/19/72.

Cast: Alonzo Fuentes (Ramon), Juan Maldonado (Uncle Carlos), Alex Tinne (Luis).
Two attendants, Carlos and his nephew Ramon, working at the ancient Mayan ruins of Tulum, pass the time by befriending a baby spider monkey, whom they name Chango. Although the animal continually gets into mischief, they let him have the run of the area. The monkey's curiosity leads to trouble when he explores the nearby camp of a group of archaeologists.

Production Note:

- The show was based on the book *Yucatan Monkey.*

CHARLEY AND THE ANGEL   Airdate (2-hour format): 10/16/77.
The Depression is the setting for this 1973 theatrical release about Charley Appleby, a hard-working man who doesn't make enough time for his family until an angel intervenes. It stars Fred MacMurray, Cloris Leachman, and Harry Morgan.

Production Note:

- This was Fred MacMurray's last acting role before he retired.

CHARLIE CROWFOOT AND THE COATI MUNDI   Airdates: 9/19/71, 7/23/72.

Cast: Edward Colunga (Charlie Crowfoot), Robert Keyworth (Tom Hardin), Dr. Emil Haury (Himself).
A young coati is shot and wounded by Tom Hardin, a rancher who dislikes the inquisitive animals. The coati is found by Charlie Crowfoot, an Indian working on an archaeological dig on Hardin's property. Charlie nurses the animal back to health and names it Cocoa. Later, Cocoa meets a pack of other coatis and leads them back to the digging site, which they promptly dig up even more, accidentally unearthing an ancient Indian tool that Charlie takes to the university for analysis.

Production Note:

- Location filming took place outside Phoenix, Arizona.

CHARLIE, THE LONESOME COUGAR   Airdates—Part 1: 11/02/69, 5/05/74, 7/01/79. Part 2: 11/09/69, 5/12/74, 7/08/79.
Ron Brown stars in this 1967 theatrical featurette about a lumberman who tries his best to raise an orphaned cougar kitten.

CHEROKEE TRAIL, THE   Airdates: 11/28/81, 6/19/82.

Cast: Cindy Pickett (Mary Breydon), Mary Larkin (Matty Maginnis), Timothy Scott (Wilbur Pattishal), David Hayward (Temple Boone), Victor French (Scant Luther), Richard Farnsworth (Ridge Fenton), Tina Yothers (Peg Breydon), Tommy Petersen (Wat Tanner), Buck Taylor (Laird), Murray McMurry (Cal Egan), Gene Ross (Grocer), Tom Williams (Mormon), Whitney Rydbeck (Bob Cochraine), Art Bradford (Charlie Bent), Roy E. Andrews (Cavalry NCO), Jeannie Linero (Painted Lady), Shan McCamey (Soldier), Richard Wright (Dillis), Bob Yothers (Arms Merchant), Skeeter Vaughan (Indian), Ben Hiller (Stage Driver #1).
Based on the novel by best-selling author Louis L'Amour, the episode features Mary Breydon, a widow who arrives at lonely

Cherokee Station, a rest stop on a stagecoach line in Colorado. She and her 8-year-old daughter, Peg, have come there to run the station, a fact which meets with extreme displeasure from the current manager, Scant Luther.

Production Notes:

- Shot as a pilot for a potential series that was not purchased by the networks, the story was later reworked for use on *The Disney Channel* as the series *Five Mile Creek*.
- Actor Richard Farnsworth had worked for the Studio years earlier when he was a stuntman on the *Texas John Slaughter*, *Daniel Boone*, *Elfego Baca*, and *Zorro* shows.

CHESTER, YESTERDAY'S HORSE   Airdate: 3/04/73.

Cast: Bill Williams (Ben Kincaid), Barbara Hale (Belle Kincaid), Russ McGubbin (Russ Benson), Jerry Gatlin (Bord Sullivan), Pete Logan (Announcer), Maynard Hadley (Tractor Salesman), Floyd Gibson (Balloon Operator), Jeff Tyler (Sliver Kincaid).

Chester, a Belgian draft horse used to haul timber in Oregon, has become a victim of technology. Russ Benson, the lumber boss, has decided to use balloons to carry the logs, so Chester is to be retired. Ben Kincaid and his son, Sliver, decide to take the horse to their farm to live out his days. However, during their trip a bridge collapses and the three are thrown into the river, requiring one of the balloons to lift Chester free. Ben is injured in the fall and then confined to a wheelchair, so the bills for Chester's upkeep soon become a problem.

Production Note:

- Chester, who weighed 2,200 pounds, was owned by writer Larry Lansburgh.

CHICO, THE MISUNDERSTOOD COYOTE

Airdates: 10/15/61, 9/02/62, 1/17/65, 4/18/76.
Cast: Bill Pace, Slim Sanford, Joy Hale.

Chico is a coyote pup who learns to fear humans when a hunter kills his family and takes the pup to sell as a "wild desert dog" to the owner of a shabby desert zoo. When Chico is accidentally poisoned, the owner puts him in a storeroom to recuperate. The coyote escapes and learns to survive on his own in the wild.

Production Note:

- This show was released theatrically overseas is 1962.

CHILD OF GLASS   Airdates (2-hour format): 5/14/78. For the 1979–80 season the show was broadcast in two parts—Part 1: 8/17/80. Part 2: 8/24/80.

Cast: Barbara Barrie (Emily Armsworth), Biff McGuire (Joe Armsworth), Anthony Zerbe (Amory Timmons), Nina Foch (Aunt Lavinia), Katy Kurtzman (Blossom Culp), Steve Shaw (Alexander Armsworth), Olivia Barash (Inez Dumaine), Denise Nickerson (Connie Sue Armsworth), Jack Rader (Sheriff Muncey), Irene Tedrow (Miss Merryweather), Lilyan Chauvin (Madame Dumaine), David Hurst (Jacques Dumaine), Sue Ann Gilfillan (Ludee Calhoun).

Alexander Armsworth is a teenager with a new home—and a problem. The Armsworths have moved into the "haunted" Dumaine estate, and Alexander soon begins receiving messages from the spirit of Inez Dumaine, a girl who died in 1862. She tells Alexander she cannot go to her final resting place until an old riddle is solved, and he must help her or be haunted for the rest of his life.

Production Note:

- Filming took place on location in Danville, Kentucky. The Studio bought an old barn and moved it over 10 miles to the filming site, then burned it.

CHRISTMAS AT WALT DISNEY WORLD

Airdate: 12/10/78.
Cast: Shields and Yarnell, Pablo Cruise, Andrea McArdle, Danielle Spencer (Cinderella), Avery Schreiber (Geppetto), Phyllis Diller, Allan Kinzie (Dancer), Penelope Sudrow, Holly Gagnier, Cathleen Ludwig, Vicki Firestone. Voices: Sterling Holloway (Sleeping Beauty Narrator), Joan Gerber (Evil Fairy), Dick Tufeld (Announcer).

Mimes Robert Shields and Lorene Yarnell visit Walt Disney World performing as their characters, the Clinkers, a robot couple. The trip almost ends in failure when they can't pass the metal detector test at the airport, but the clever robots ship themselves as baggage. Upon their arrival in Florida, they decide to tour Walt Disney World as "typical" tourists, affording the television viewer a guided tour as they go.

Production Note:

- This show aired on *The Disney Channel* with the episode *Disney on Parade* under the title *Happy Holidays at Walt Disney World*.

CHRISTMAS STAR, THE   Airdates (2-hour format): 12/14/86, 12/13/87.

Cast: Edward Asner (Horace McNickle), Rene Auberjonois (Mr. Sumner), Jim Metzler (Stewart Jameson), Susan Tyrrell (Sarah), Karen Landry (Clara Jameson), Alan North (Captain Whitaker), Philip Bruns (Lucky), Nicholas Van Burek (Billy Jameson), Vicki Wauchope (Trudy Jameson), Zachary Ansley (John Sumner), Fred Gwynne (Detective Waters), Peter Bibby (Jeremy), Lillian Carlson (Mrs. Thurgood), David Glyn-Jones (Night Watchman), Anthony Holland (Old Con), Frank Turner (Sad Sack Santa), Claire Brown (Mrs. Jerome), Renee D'Aoust (Waters Kid), Linda Darlowe (Harrington Mom), Lorraine Foreman (Mrs. Waters), Joseph Golland (Janitor), Russell Hunter (Old McNickle), Oliver Kearnes (Waters Kid), David Longworth (Con), Pamela Martin (Newscaster), Gordon McIntosh (Con), John Payne (Mr. Jerome), Roman Podhura (Barney), Enid Saunders (Salvation Army Lady), Raimund Stamm (Harrington Santa), Robyn Stevan (Waters Kid), William Taylor (Gate Guard), Don Thompson (Janitor), Jerry Wasserman (Desk Sergeant), Sid Williams (Brother Gerard), John Bolton (Child), Monica Fuhrmann (Child), Genesee Keevil (Child), Tiffinay Michas (Child), Toko Okada (Child), Nicole Roberts (Child), Brittany Wong (Child).

As Christmas nears, a group of convicts hears the story of the Christmas Star, which is said to shine only when there has been a great sacrifice. One of the convicts, Horace McNickle, doesn't pay much attention to the story. He is far too busy planning his upcoming jail break. McNickle has just learned that an old department store, the hiding spot for the money from his last robbery, will be torn down and the contents sold. Afraid the money will be lost, he escapes that night, dressed as Santa Claus.

CITY FOX, THE   Airdates: 2/20/72, 8/14/77.

Cast: Tom Chan and Family (Themselves), Jerry Jerish (Humane Society Officer).

An unexpected adventure in the city awaits a young fox named Rusty when he jumps aboard a passing rowboat on the Sacramento River to escape two pursuing dogs. Unwilling to swim to shore, the fox stays with the boat until it drifts ashore in San Francisco Bay.

Production Note:

- This episode took over 15 months to film.

COMANCHE   Airdates—Part 1: 2/18/62, 4/17/66, 8/29/71. Part 2: 2/25/62, 4/24/66, 9/05/71.

The 1958 theatrical release *Tonka* was aired as *Comanche* in two parts, *The Captive Stallion* and *The Lone Survivor of Custer's Last Stand*. It stars Sal Mineo, Philip Carey, Jerome Courtland, and Britt Lomond in the true story of the only survivor of the Indian attack at the Little Big Horn.

Production Notes:

- *Tonka* also aired as a special on 1/29/77 as *A Horse Called Comanche*, and it was serialized on *The New Mickey Mouse Club* under that title.
- This film had originally been planned as a continuing element of the anthology series. The episode titles announced were *White Bull and the Wild Stallion*, *Prairie Thunder in the Cavalry*, and *End of the Trail*.

COME FLY WITH DISNEY   Airdate: Syndicated.

Many Disney films and short subjects have dealt with the world of flight, and this episode joins the list. It begins with *Peter Pan* teaching Wendy, Michael, and John how to fly. In *Pedro*, originally released as part of *Saludos Amigos*, a young mail plane is called to duty when his parents are unable to fly. In *The Rescuers*, a very unusual aviator makes a most unusual landing. Goofy demonstrates his skills in a homemade craft in *Goofy's Glider*. Other aviation scenes include clips from *The Plastics Inventor*, *The Flying Gauchito*, *Dumbo*, and *Test Pilot Donald*.

COMPUTER WORE TENNIS SHOES, THE   Airdates—Part 1: 9/17/72, 1/27/80. Part 2: 9/24/72, 2/03/80. For the 1977–78 season the show was broadcast in a 2-hour format: 11/13/77.

Released theatrically in 1969, this is the story of Dexter Riley, a Medfield College student who accidentally absorbs the memory contents of a computer. It stars Kurt Russell, Cesar Romero, and Joe Flynn.

Production Notes:

- Originally planned as a two-part television story, *The Computer Wore Tennis Shoes* was released theatrically instead. It was followed by two theatrical sequels *(Now You See Him, Now You Don't* and *The Strongest Man in The World)* and helped establish Kurt Russell as a star.
- A made-for-television version of this story aired as a special in 1995.

CONCHO, THE COYOTE WHO WASN'T
Airdate: 4/10/66.
Cast: Delgado (Himself).

Concho, a coyote pup, narrowly escapes a group of bounty hunters and is rescued by Delgado, an old Navajo. The Indian takes him home and nurses him back to health, and Concho is soon roaming the reservation in search of adventure. On one of his forays he meets a band of wild pigs, which he takes back to Delgado's for a handout. The pigs return his hospitality by wrecking the place, and the Indian turns Concho outside to fend for himself.

COUNTRY COYOTE GOES HOLLYWOOD, A
Airdates: 12/19/65, 12/29/68, 9/05/76.
Also released theatrically in 1965, this is the tale of Chico, a coyote who hides aboard a moving van to escape a pack of dogs and dune buggy racers and, as a result, finds a whole new set of problems. The van is out of the desert before Chico can leave it, and the next stop is downtown Los Angeles. When the truck stops, a bewildered coyote heads for the only hills he can see: the Hollywood Hills, home of other coyotes, who give him lessons on how to survive with humans so nearby.

Production Notes:

- This show also aired as a special on 2/14/76 with *Old Yeller*.
- Major portions of the show were filmed in Griffith Park, a vast recreation area located just across the Ventura Freeway from the Studio. The fire sequence used scenes from a spectacular fire in the exclusive suburb of Bel Air, in which more than 450 homes were destroyed.

COYOTE'S LAMENT, THE
Airdates: 3/05/61, 2/12/67, 5/06/73.
The unfortunate fate of the coyote at the hands of humans and their dogs is the subject of this animated episode. Told from the coyote's point of view, the show features clips from many Disney short subjects. A quartet of coyotes sings a series of verses, each designed to tell the viewer about the injustices done to coyotes throughout the years.

Production Note:

- This episode was released theatrically overseas in 1968.

CRISLER STORY, THE (AND) PROWLERS OF THE EVERGLADES
Airdates: 2/27/57, 6/19/57, 8/12/60.
Narrator Winston Hibler tells about the problems the Crislers encountered in the filming of *The Arctic Wilderness*. The Crislers are a team of photographers sent to Alaska to film the annual fall caribou migration. *Prowlers of the Everglades*, a *True-Life Adventure* first released theatrically in 1953, ends the show with a look at the alligators that inhabit the Florida Everglades.

Production Note:

- *The Arctic Wilderness* was renamed and released as *White Wilderness*. It won an Academy Award in 1958.

CRISTOBALITO, THE CALYPSO COLT
Airdates: 9/13/70, 6/27/71, 1/23/77.
Cast: Roberto Vigoreaux (Chago), Walter Buso (Rodriguez), Charles A. Gibbs (Hernandez I), Jose de San Anton (Hernandez II), Delia Esther Quinones (Mama Dolores), Jackie Ross (Speedy).

Chago is an orphaned youth in Puerto Rico who is supporting himself as a fruit vendor. When he's offered a job as stable boy for a wealthy rancher, he gladly accepts and moves to the ranch. There, he meets Cristobalito, a Paso Fino Palomino who is a descendant of the horses ridden by the Spanish Conquistadors.

CRUSADING REPORTER
Airdates: 10/30/66, 7/02/67.
Cast: Dennis Weaver (The Sundown Kid), John McIntire (Whit White), Roger Mobley (Gallegher), Ray Teal (Sheriff Snead), Jeanette Nolan (Erm White), Larry D. Mann (Mayor "Genial Gene" Riggs), Bruce Dern (Turk), Peter Graves (Marshal Frank Neimeyer), Red Morgan (Stevie), Dennis Cross (Jake Powers).

Part 2 of *Gallegher Goes West* continues the story begun in the episode *Showdown with the Sundown Kid*. Although the Sundown Kid is now behind bars, the corrupt mayor of Brimstone is still in office. With the town's sheriff also in jail, Snead is appointed to the office until a replacement can be found. Snead and Marshal Neimeyer confront the mayor with proof of his guilt but the crafty politician refuses to resign, figuring he can withstand public criticism. The lawmen decide their only course of action is to force a recall election.

DAD, CAN I BORROW THE CAR?
Airdates: 4/09/72, 3/28/76, 12/30/79.
An expanded version of the 1970 theatrical featurette of the same name, this is a humorous look at America's love-hate relationship with the automobile. Merging live action and animation, this episode begins with an unusual trip on a highway where cars change shape and take on individual personalities. The scene then shifts to a hospital where a baby boy is spanked to "start his engine" and taken to the nursery in his first wheeled device—a simple cart. From this inauspicious beginning grows an ever-increasing infatuation with wheeled transportation—bicycles, skates, toy cars, and finally the automobile.

Production Note:

- This story was originally planned as a television episode but was instead first released theatrically.

DAILY PRESS VS. CITY HALL, THE
Airdates: 10/10/65, 7/03/66.
Cast: Edmond O'Brien (Editor Crowley), Anne Francis (Adeline Jones), Roger Mobley (Gallegher), Harvey Korman (Brownie), James Westerfield (Charles Mardis), Parley Baer (The Mayor), Maudie Prickett (The Maid), John Lormer (Pete), John Orchard (The Butler), Vaughn Taylor (Mr. Bildad), Tom Skerritt (Corky Mardis), Edward Platt (Judge).

The third part of *The Further Adventures of Gallegher* reteams the hopeful reporter with Adeline Jones, the town's first and only woman reporter. When the two are sent to cover a gas explosion, they learn that many of the town's gas pipes are made of a faulty material that leaks. Crowley, the editor, reviews past editions of the paper and finds a story telling how the mayor personally awarded a construction contract for the pipeline to the leader of the local political organization. The next edition of the paper carries a banner headline alleging that graft and corruption are behind both the contract and the faulty pipes.

DANIEL BOONE
Disney produced four episodes featuring this American pioneer: *The Warrior's Path; And Chase the Buffalo; The Wilderness Road;* and *The Promised Land.*

Refer to each of these titles for the episode descriptions.

Production Note:

- Longtime Disney actor Fess Parker later starred in a weekly version of *Daniel Boone* on NBC from 1964 to 1970. It was produced by 20th Century-Fox and should not be confused with the Disney version.

DAVY CROCKETT (mini-series)
In the 1954–55 season Disney aired three episodes about this American frontiersman: *Davy Crockett—Indian Fighter, Davy Crockett Goes to Congress,* and *Davy Crockett at the Alamo.*

Following the unprecedented success of these shows, two additional episodes were shown in the 1955–56 season: *Davy Crockett's Keelboat Race,* and *Davy Crockett and the River Pirates.*

Disney brought the frontier hero back to life for the 1988–89 season, producing five new episodes with an updated cast. The overall title for this new episodes was *The New Adventures of Davy Crockett,* and the individual episodes were *Davy Crockett: Rainbow in the Thunder, Davy Crockett: A Natural Man, Davy Crockett: Guardian Spirit, Davy Crockett: A Letter to Polly,* and *Davy Crockett: Warrior's Farewell.*

Refer to each of these titles for the episode descriptions. *Davy Crockett: Guardian Spirit* aired as a special.

Production Note:

- The original series received an Emmy Award for Best Action or Adventure Series of 1955.

DAVY CROCKETT AND THE RIVER PIRATES Airdates: 12/14/55, 2/22/56, 10/02/60, 9/13/64, 9/10/72, 9/19/76.
Cast: Fess Parker (Davy Crockett), Buddy Ebsen (George Russel), Jeff York (Mike Fink), Kenneth Tobey (Jocko), Clem Bevans (Captain Cobb), Irving Ashkenazy (Moose), Mort Mills (Sam Mason), Paul Newlan (Big Harpe), Frank Richards (Little Harpe), Hank Worden (Fiddler), Walter Catlett (Colonel Plug).

The fifth and final episode in the original Crockett saga finds Davy and Georgie out to clear the name of some Indian friends who have been accused of raiding boats traveling on the Ohio River. They recruit the aid of their friend, Mike Fink, and head upriver. Waiting for them is a gang of pirates led by the evil Harpe brothers, who have been impersonating the Indians to disguise the looting.

Production Notes:

- This episode was edited into the 1956 theatrical release of the same name, using additional footage from the episode *Davy Crockett's Keelboat Race.*
- Walter Catlett, who guest-starred as the villainous Colonel Plug, supplied the voice of J. Worthington Foulfellow in *Pinocchio.*
- The episode was nominated for an Emmy Award as the Best Single Program of the Year.

DAVY CROCKETT AT THE ALAMO
Airdates: 2/23/55, 5/11/55, 9/26/58, 9/22/63, 9/07/69, 9/08/74.
    Cast: *Fess Parker (Davy Crockett), Buddy Ebsen (George Russel), Hans Conried (Thimblerig), Kenneth Tobey (James Bowie), Don Megowan (William Travis), Nick Cravat (Bustedluck).*
    The concluding chapter of the original Crockett trilogy finds Davy and Georgie heading westward looking for new adventure. Sailing aboard a Mississippi River steamer, they meet a gambler named Thimblerig, who asks to join them when some of his victims discover he's a cheat. The trio sets course for Texas, where Davy intends to join the fight against the Mexican army led by Gen. Santa Anna.

Production Notes:

- Although Crockett was killed in this episode, Disney brought the Western hero back the next season in two additional episodes that were set earlier in his life. This episode was also used in the 1955 theatrical release, *Davy Crockett, King of the Wild Frontier,* using additional footage from the episodes *Davy Crockett—Indian Fighter* and *Davy Crockett Goes to Congress.*
- Southern California's Conejo Ranch was used for the Texas plains.

DAVY CROCKETT GOES TO CONGRESS
Airdates: 1/26/55, 4/27/55, 9/19/58, 9/15/63, 8/31/69, 9/01/74.
    Cast: *Fess Parker (Davy Crockett), Buddy Ebsen (George Russel), Basil Ruysdael*

(Andrew Jackson), William Bakewell (Tobias Norton), Mike Mazurki (Big Foot Mason), Helene Stanley (Polly Crockett), Jeff Thompson (Two Shirts), Henry Joyner (Swaney), Col. Campbell Brown (Bruno), Benjamin Hornbuckle (Henderson), Hal Youngblood (Opponent Political Speaker), Jim Maddux (First Congressman), Robert Booth (Second Congressman).
    The second episode of the Crockett trilogy finds Davy bored with his life. He and Georgie travel to a sparsely settled portion of Tennessee, hoping to resettle there with their families. Satisfied with the location, they go to a nearby town to file their claims. When Davy beats the town bully, Big Foot Mason, in a shooting match, the local judge asks Davy to become the town's lawman, as no one else has bested Mason to date. Crockett declines but is soon forced to change his mind.

Production Note:

- Together with the episodes *Davy Crockett—Indian Fighter* and *Davy Crockett at the Alamo,* this show was edited into the 1955 theatrical release, *Davy Crockett, King of the Wild Frontier.*

DAVY CROCKETT—INDIAN FIGHTER
Airdates: 12/15/54, 4/13/55, 9/12/58, 9/08/63, 8/24/69, 8/25/74.
    Cast: *Fess Parker (Davy Crockett), Buddy Ebsen (George Russel), Basil Ruysdael (Gen. Andrew Jackson), William Bakewell (Maj. Tobias Norton), Helene Stanley (Polly Crockett), Pat Hogan (Redstick), Eugene Brindel (Billy), Ray Whitetree (Johnny).*
    Reading from "Davy Crockett's Journal," Walt introduces the story of the American folk hero and unknowingly starts a national craze. The characters and plot of the show are introduced in a popular song *(The Ballad of Davy Crockett)* that was used throughout the Crockett TV episodes. In this outing, Davy arranges for a truce with the Indians.

Production Notes:

- This episode was edited into the 1955 theatrical release *Davy Crockett, King of the Wild Frontier,* along with scenes from *Davy Crockett Goes to Congress* and *Davy Crockett at the Alamo.*
- Chester Schaeffer was nominated for an Emmy award for Best Television Film Editing for this episode.

DAVY CROCKETT'S KEELBOAT RACE
Airdates: 11/16/55, 1/25/56, 9/25/60, 9/06/64, 9/03/72, 9/12/76.

Cast: Fess Parker (Davy Crockett), Buddy Ebsen (George Russel), Jeff York (Mike Fink), Kenneth Tobey (Jocko), Clem Bevans (Captain Cobb), Irvin Ashkenazy (Moose), Mort Mills (Sam Mason), Paul Newlan (Big Harpe), Frank Richards (Little Harpe), Troy Melton (Hank), Dick Crockett (Ben), Douglas Dumbrille (Saloon Owner).

The Crockett saga continues with Davy and Georgie ending a season of trapping and hunting, eager to bring the hides to market. Their plans for an easy sale are quickly thwarted when they try to ship the hides down the Ohio River, and the self-styled "King of the River," Mike Fink, attempts to charge them an outrageous price.

Besides having to beat Fink, Davy and his crew face another problem—a band of renegade Indians is being blamed for a series of attacks on passing boats.

Production Notes:

- This episode was included in the 1956 theatrical release *Davy Crockett and the River Pirates*.
- At the end of filming, both the *Bertha Mae* and the *Gullywhumper* were put into service at Disneyland, circling guests around Tom Sawyer's Island as the "Mike Fink Keelboats."

DAVY CROCKETT: A LETTER TO POLLY
Airdate: 6/11/89.

Cast: Tim Dunigan (Davy Crockett), Gary Grubbs (George Russell), Aeryk Egan (Aaron), Garry Chalk (Major Benteen), Jeff Irvine (Lieutenant North), Eric Bryant Wells (Volunteer), Jerry Wasserman (Soldier #1), Todd Shaffer (Hardin), Robin Mossley (Settler Father), Sheelah Megill (Settler Mother), Lalainia Lindberg (Settler Daughter), Terry Kelly (Matthew), Lorraine Forman (Sarah), John "Bear" Curtis (Rider), Buffalo Child (Brave), Beatrice Boepple (Esther), Ian Black (Soldier #2), Karen Becker (Squaw).

Continuing the new *Davy Crockett* stories, this fourth episode finds Davy missing his family. Visions of Polly have made Davy concerned about his wife and sons, but Major Benteen refuses his request for a leave. Benteen has learned that the Creeks are joining with the Cheyennes, and he decides to attack the Indians to prevent an Indian raid on the settlers. Davy finally convinces Benteen to let him take a letter to a peddler who will be passing near Davy's house, but the soldier warns him to be back in three days for the attack or face a court martial.

DAVY CROCKETT: A NATURAL MAN
Airdate: 12/18/88.

Cast: Tim Dunigan (Davy Crockett), Gary Grubbs (George Russell), Barry Corbin (Jimmy Crockett), Molly Hagan (Mary Ann Gibbons), Jeff Irvine (Lieutenant North), Rodger Gibson (Eyes Like Sky), Charles André (Zale), Stephen Dimopoulos (Hawkins), Don S. Davis (Will), R.G. Miller (Rider), Rob Morton (Wounded Soldier), Raimund Stamm (Sergeant), Frank C. Turner (Morton).

The second of the new *Davy Crockett* episodes almost ends in disaster when George Russell is attacked by a grizzly bear. Davy's gun misfires and he must save his friend by yelling loudly enough to scare away the bear. Davy then meets an uncle who vanished in an Indian raid 20 years earlier.

DAVY CROCKETT: RAINBOW IN THE THUNDER
Airdates (2-hour format): 11/20/88, 7/01/90.

Cast: Tim Dunigan (Davy Crockett), Gary Grubbs (George Russell), Cheryl L. Arutt (Young Ory/Delia O'Connor), Richard Tyson (Lute Newhouser), Samantha Egger (Ory Palmer), Matt Salinger (Young Andrew Jackson), Johnny Cash (Elder Davy Crockett), David Hemmings (President Andrew Jackson), Breanda Crichlow (Mary), Jill Gamley (Mrs. Palmer), Jeff Irvine (Lieutenant), Blu Mankuma (Butler), Freda Perry (Jess), Matt Walker (Woodrow Palmer).

The new *Davy Crockett* stories begin as Congressman Davy Crockett waits at the White House for a meeting with President Andrew Jackson. The President wants Davy's help in getting a new Indian affairs bill passed, and the two men reminisce about how they first met, which is seen in a series of flashbacks.

DAVY CROCKETT: WARRIOR'S FAREWELL
Airdate: 6/18/89.

Cast: Tim Dunigan (Davy Crockett), Gary Grubbs (George Russell), Ken Swofford (Callahan), Garry Chalk (Major Benteen), Jeff Irvine (Lieutenant North), Sherri Stoner (Amy), Prudence Wright Holmes (Mrs. Pickering), Lloyd Berry (Willard), Clem Fox (Medicine Man), Maggie O'Hara (Teenage Girl), Sonny Surowiec (Young Settler).

As the last of the new *Davy Crockett* episodes begins, an Indian medicine man stands on a hill overlooking the army camp and chants a spell. An earthquake strikes and the camp is soon full of rumors and fears about the powers of this strange man.

DAY IN THE LIFE OF DONALD DUCK, A
Airdates: 2/01/56, 5/09/56.

Cast: *Jimmie Dodd, Clarence Nash, the Mouseketeers, Roy Williams.*

Explaining that he's received many letters about Donald Duck, Walt relates a typical working day for the feathered star.

DAY OF RECKONING   Airdates: 1/08/60, 5/20/60.

Cast: *Leslie Nielsen (Gen. Francis Marion), John Sutton (Col. Banastre Tarleton), Barbara Eiler (Mary Videaux), Henry Daniell (Colonel Townes), Myron Healey (Col. Peter Horry), Rhys Williams (Professor Culpen), Dorothy Green (Mrs. Townes), Jordan Whitfield (Oscar), Sherry Jackson (Melanie Culpen), J. Pat O'Malley (Sergeant O'Reilly), James Anderson (Amos Briggs), Slim Pickens (Plunkett), Hal Stalmaster (Gwynn), Clarence Muse (Joseph).*

The fourth chapter in the saga of the Swamp Fox opens with Gen. Francis Marion relentlessly searching for Amos Briggs, the man who killed young Gabe Marion. His desire for revenge has caused him to ignore his men, and several of them begin to talk about deserting. Another of the rebel leaders convinces Marion to abandon the hunt until the men can capture some much needed supplies. Marion agrees, leading a small patrol on a dangerous ride against the Redcoats.

DEACON STREET DEER, THE   Airdates: 5/18/86, 8/17/86 (aired with *Fuzzbucket* in a 2-hour format).

Cast: *Bumper Robinson (Bobby), Eve Glazier (Jaynie), Mario Lopez (Hector), Sean De Veritch (Milton), Marissa Mendenhall (Lydia), Richard Mulligan (Shorty), John Finnegan, Ron Campbell, Kelly Minter, Marco Hernandez (Zopo), Walter Beery (Old Man), Viola Kates Stimpson (Mrs. Liebowitz), Louis P. Plante (Officer MacKechnie), Brandis Kemp (Cindy Crenshaw), Virginia Peters (Bag Lady), Ned Bellamy (Officer Nicholas), Billy Kane (Officer Schapers), Peter Ortel (Lorenzo), Tina Preston (Loud Woman).*

Two carnival workers accidentally strand a young deer in a large city when the animal's crate falls off their truck. Luckily, the deer is spotted by Bobby, a new boy in the neighborhood, who tries to help the scared animal.

DEACON, THE HIGH NOON DOG
Airdate: 3/16/75.

Cast: *Frank Keith (Abner), Paul Szemenyei (Jamie), C. Gordon Smith (Panamint).*

Deacon is a mongrel dog living with his master, Jamie, and Jamie's Uncle Abner during the late 1800s. His peaceful life in the Colorado Rockies is interrupted when Abner decides to send Jamie to school in the East. The dog chases Jamie's train into the desert where several misadventures befall him.

Production Notes:

- Deacon was played by Sean, a mongrel who previously appeared in Disney's *My Family Is a Menagerie* and *The Little Shepherd Dog of Catalina.*
- During the filming, Sean broke a hind leg, forcing a month-long halt in production when the Studio was unable to find a stand-in who resembled their multi-breed star.

DECEPTIVE DETECTIVE, THE
This is Part 2 of *Michael O'Hara the Fourth.*

DESERTER, THE
This is Part 1 of *Willie and the Yank.*

DESPERADO FROM TOMBSTONE
Airdates: 2/12/60, 7/15/60.

Cast: *Tom Tryon (Texas John Slaughter), Gene Evans (Loco Crispin), Regis Toomey (Mr. Howell), Betty Lynn (Viola Howell), Nora Marlowe (Mrs. Howell), Brian Corcoran (Willie Slaughter), George Wallace (Gus), Don Haggerty (Trail Boss), Annette Gorman (Addy Slaughter).*

Part 9 of *The Tales of Texas John Slaughter* finds John settled on his new ranch near Tombstone. One day he rides to the house of his neighbors, the Howells, with some good news. His children, who have been living in Texas with relatives, are on their way to join him. John finds new problems on his hands when Willie and his sister, Addy, find it hard to adapt to life on the frontier.

DEVIL AND MAX DEVLIN, THE   Airdate (2-hour format): 4/26/87.
This 1981 theatrical release stars Elliott Gould, Bill Cosby, Susan Anspach, and Adam Rich in the story of a man reluctantly forced to collect souls for the Devil. This film also aired as a special on ABC on 8/12/89.

DIAMOND IS A BOY'S BEST FRIEND, A
This is Part 1 of *Moochie of the Little League.*

DIAMONDS ON WHEELS Airdates—Part 1: 3/10/74. Part 2: 3/17/74. Part 3: 3/24/74.

Cast: Patrick Allen (Inspector Cook), George Sewell (Henry Stewart), Peter Firth (Robert Stewart), Spencer Banks (Charlie Todd), Cynthia Lund (Susan Stewart), Derek Newark (Mercer), Dudley Sutton (Finch), Barry Jackson (Wheeler), Christopher Malcolm (Jock), Maggie Hanley (Mrs. Stewart), George Innes (Inspector Timothy), Allan Cuthbertson (Ashley), Richard Wattis (Sir Hilary Stanton), Ambrosine Phillpotts (Lady Truesdale), Candace Glendenning (Elizabeth), Robin Langford (Peter Pitt), George Woodbridge (P. C. Andrew), Patrick McAlinney (Junkman), Andrew McCulloch (Billy), Arthur Hewlett (Benjy), Patrick Holt (Steward), John Savident (Steward), Mark Edwards (Whiteman), Edwin Richfield (Steward), Tom Bowman (Caretaker).

A million-dollar diamond robbery takes an unexpected twist when one of the gang decides to double-cross his partners and take the gems for himself.

Production Note:

- *Diamonds on Wheels* was released theatrically overseas in 1973.

DINOSAUR . . . SECRET OF THE LOST LEGEND Airdate: 1/08/89.
This edited version of *Baby . . . Secret of the Lost Legend*, a 1985 theatrical release, stars William Katt, Sean Young, and Patrick McGoohan in the story of scientists who discover living dinosaurs in Africa.

DISNEY ANIMATION: THE ILLUSION OF LIFE Airdate: 4/26/81.
Cast: Hayley Mills, Pearl Bailey. With the talents of: *The Andrews Sisters, Nelson Eddy, Stan Fidel, Betty Lou Gerson, Phil Harris, Richard O. Johnston, Peggy Lee, Freddy Martin and His Orchestra, Geraldine Page.*

Former Disney child star Hayley Mills returns to the Studio for a look at the techniques involved in producing animated films. Veteran animators Ward Kimball, Frank Thomas, Ollie Johnston, Milt Kahl, Marc Davis, and others illustrate their techniques throughout the program.

Production Note:

- This episode was nominated for an Emmy Award for Outstanding Children's Program, winning a certificate of honor.

DISNEY CHRISTMAS GIFT, A Airdate: 12/04/82.
This holiday salute opens as the Disney characters decorate Main Street U.S.A. at Disneyland, featuring Mickey Mouse as Santa Claus. Comprised of animated sequences from various Disney films, the show uses scenes of old Christmas cards and Disney toys as connecting footage.

Production Notes:

- A different version of this show was aired 12/20/83 as a special.
- Major sections of this show were also used in the earlier episode *A Magical Disney Christmas.*

DISNEY GOES TO THE OSCARS Airdates: 3/23/86, 3/01/87 (Disney Goes to the Academy Awards).
Cast: Tony Danza.
This show highlights Disney's outstanding success in winning Academy Awards. Host Tony Danza notes that of the 51 Oscars awarded to the Studio, a record 32 were personally awarded to Walt Disney.

DISNEY HALLOWEEN, A Airdate: 10/24/81.
The Slave in the Magic Mirror from *Snow White and the Seven Dwarfs* returns to host this look at some of the legends surrounding Halloween.

Production Note:

- A different version of this show aired on The Disney Channel under the same title.

DISNEY ON PARADE Airdates: 12/19/71, 7/02/72.
Disney on Parade is a multimedia presentation featuring Disney characters performing live on stage. This is a videotape of the first tour, filmed in Adelaide, Australia.

Production Note:

- This episode was aired on The Disney Channel as part of *Happy Holidays at Walt Disney World.*

DISNEY STORYBOOK, A Airdates—Part 1: 11/14/81. Part 2: 11/21/81.
Featuring classic Disney animation, the show begins with *Mickey and the Beanstalk* from the theatrical release *Fun and Fancy Free.* Next is *Dumbo,* the story of a tiny elephant with huge ears. The show concludes with the

story of another elephant, in *Working for Peanuts.*

Production Note:

- This show was broadcast in a 2-hour format as a special on 9/14/86 under the title *Dumbo.*

DISNEY VACATION, A Airdates: 5/01/82, 7/09/83.

Every year, people try to find someplace new to go on vacation. In this collection of Disney cartoons, unexpected adventures befall our travelers.

DISNEY VALENTINE, A Airdate: 2/13/82.

Footage from Disney films and cartoons provides a comical look at the subject of romance.

DISNEY'S ALL-AMERICAN SPORTS NUTS

Airdate: 10/16/88.

Cast: David Leisure, John Matuszak, Susan Ruttan, Martin Mull, Brian Boitano, Janet Evans, Teresa Ganzel, Bruce Jenner, Tommy Lasorda, Ray "Boom-Boom" Mancini, Pam Matteson, Willie Shoemaker, Bubba Smith, Jake Steinfeld, Danny Sullivan, James Worthy, The Fountain Valley High School Cheerleaders.

Martin Mull hosts this comedy look at sports. Scenes from *Gus* show some of the lighter moments of football, Disney style. This is followed by Goofy in *How to Play Baseball*, baseball bloopers, and several skits on other sports.

DISNEY'S FLUPPY DOGS

This episode originally aired as a special on 11/27/86. It later aired on the anthology series on 8/30/87.

DISNEY'S GOLDEN ANNIVERSARY OF SNOW WHITE AND THE SEVEN DWARFS

This show originally aired as a special. It later aired on the anthology series on 12/25/88.

DISNEY'S GREATEST DOG STARS

Airdate: 11/28/76, 5/03/81.

Cast: Dean Jones. With the talents of: Jack Albertson, Pearl Bailey, Pat Buttram, Tim Conway, Pat Crowley, Corey Feldman, John Fiedler, Ruth Gillette, George Givot, Earl Holliman, Clifton James, George Kirby, Tommy Kirk, Peggy Lee, George Lindsey, Fred MacMurray, Michael McGreevey, Dorothy McGuire, Keith Mitchell, Suzanne Pleshette, Larry Roberts, Mickey Rooney, Kurt Russell, George Spell, Bill Thompson, Dick Van Patten, Luis Van Rooten, Johnny Whitaker, Ilene Woods, Jo Anne Worley, Keenan Wynn.

Dean Jones is the host of this look at Disney's past canine stars and at the upcoming new release in which he stars, *The Shaggy D.A.*, a sequel to *The Shaggy Dog.*

Production Note:

- The concluding section in the 1976 airing is a preview of *The Shaggy D.A.* In the 1981 rerun, the show was edited to feature *The Fox and the Hound.*

DISNEY'S GREATEST VILLAINS Airdates: 5/15/77, 6/11/78, 10/26/80, 5/21/83.

Cast: Eleanor Audley (Stepmother, Maleficent), Kathryn Beaumont (Wendy), Hans Conried (Slave in the Magic Mirror, Captain Hook), Bobby Driscoll (Peter Pan), Verna Felton (Queen of Hearts), Eva Gabor (Miss Bianca), Betty Lou Gerson (Cruella De Vil), Billy Gilbert (Willie the Giant), Anita Gordon (The Singing Harp), Sterling Holloway (Cheshire Cat), Jim Jordan (Orville the Albatross), Junius Matthews (Archimedes), Clarence Nash (Donald Duck), Bob Newhart (Bernard), Jeanette Nolan (Ellie Mae), Geraldine Page (Madame Medusa), Bruce Reitherman (Mowgli), George Sanders (Shere Khan), Rickie Sorenson (Wart), Michelle Stacy (Penny), Karl Swenson (Merlin), Bill Thompson (Smee), Martha Wentworth (Madam Mim), Ilene Woods (Cinderella).

The Slave in the Magic Mirror is the host of this show, which is designed to point out that every hero needs a villain for balance. Without those dedicated to evil pursuits, there would be no heroes. Luckily, villains abound, as clips from numerous Disney films prove.

Production Note:

- This show is an edited version of the 1955–56 season episode entitled *Our Unsung Villains.* For the later reruns, the program was edited to feature scenes from current Studio films.

DISNEY'S HALLOWEEN TREAT Airdate: 10/30/82.

Long thought to be the favorite night for witches, ghosts, and goblins, Halloween is the theme for this look at magic in Disney films and cartoons.

Production Note:

- This show also aired as a special on 10/29/83.

DISNEY'S MAGIC IN THE MAGIC KINGDOM

This show originally aired as a special. It later aired on the anthology series on 7/23/89.

DISNEY'S OSCAR WINNERS   Airdates: 4/13/80, 2/22/81.

The many Academy Awards and nominations won by the Studio are highlighted in this retrospective hour.

DISNEY'S SPORTS SPECIAL   Airdate: Syndicated.

This Disney look at sports includes segments from *Bedknobs and Broomsticks, The Olympic Champ, Bambi, The Hockey Champ, Pinocchio,* and others.

DISNEY'S TOTALLY MINNIE

This episode originally aired as a special on 3/25/88. It later aired on the anthology series on 5/07/89.

DISNEY-MGM STUDIOS THEME PARK GRAND OPENING, THE   Airdate (2-hour format): 4/30/89.

Cast: Harry Anderson, Ashford & Simpson, George Burns, Joy, Monica and Leanna Creel, Walter Cronkite, Jane Fonda, John Forsythe, Estelle Getty, George S. Irving, Kate Jackson, Rue McClanahan, Ann Miller, Yves Montand, Willie Nelson, Buster Poindexter, The Pointer Sisters, Stefanie Powers, Tony Randall, John Ritter, Smokey Robinson, Mickey Rooney, Suzanne Somers, James Stewart, Dick Van Dyke, Ronald Reagan, Margaret Thatcher, Lech Walesa.

Walt Disney World's newest theme park, the Disney-MGM Studios, is almost ready to open. A host of celebrities provide viewers with a sneak preview tour of the new park.

Production Note:

- Choreographer Walter Painter won an Emmy award for this episode.

DISNEYLAND AFTER DARK   Airdates: 4/15/62, 7/01/62.

Cast: Walt Disney, Louis Armstrong, Bobby Rydell, Annette Funicello, Bobby Burgess, Monette Moore (Singer), Kid Ory (Trombone), Johnny St. Cyr (Banjo), Harvey Brooks (Piano), Alton Redd (Drums), Mike De Lay (Trumpet), Paul Barn (Clarinet), The Elliott Brothers Orchestra, The Dapper Dans (Barbershop Quartet), The Osmond Brothers, The Royal Tahitians (Dancers), Tony Paris (Musician).

The show begins as passengers board the Monorail at the Disneyland Hotel for a trip to Disneyland. The short ride provides a brief look at some of the many attractions in Tomorrowland and Frontierland, and then it's time to visit the rest of the Park after dark.

Production Notes:

- Released theatrically as a short subject overseas in 1962, and domestically in 1963, this was the network television premiere of the Osmond Brothers.
- Richard M. Sherman and Robert B. Sherman, who were later to write the music for *Mary Poppins,* wrote the title song for this episode.

DISNEYLAND AROUND THE SEASONS

Airdates: 12/18/66, 6/18/67.

This is a show that begins with a bang, as fireworks fill the sky over Disneyland. It's a special day at the Park: crowds have gathered to watch the dedication ceremonies for the newest attraction, It's a Small World. First seen at the 1964–65 New York World's Fair, this is a musical trip where more than 600 stylized dolls represent the children of the world.

Production Note:

- *Disneyland around the Seasons* was released theatrically overseas in 1967.

DISNEYLAND: FROM THE PIRATES OF THE CARIBBEAN TO THE WORLD OF TOMORROW   Airdates: 1/21/68, 6/09/68.

In the episode *The Disneyland Tenth Anniversary Show,* Walt provided a sneak preview of an upcoming attraction, The Pirates of the Caribbean. Marcia Miner, the 1967 Disneyland ambassador, hosts this look at how the Disney Imagineers go about the task of building such a unique ride.

Production Note:

- The announcer for this episode gave the title as *From Pirates of the Caribbean to Tomorrowland.*

DISNEYLAND GOES TO THE WORLD'S FAIR   Airdates: 5/17/64, 6/28/64.

The upcoming 1964–65 New York World's Fair is the topic of this show, which begins with an animated look at some past fairs and a look at Disney's exhibitions under construction.

DISNEYLAND SHOWTIME   Airdates: 3/22/70, 6/28/70.

Cast: The Osmond Brothers, Kurt Russell, E.J. Peaker, Peter Bruni (Mr. Gridley), Kids of the Kingdom, The Sound Castle, The Dapper Dans.

The opening of the Haunted Mansion at Disneyland is the setting for this musically oriented look at the Park.

DISNEYLAND '61 (AND) OLYMPIC ELK Airdate: 5/28/61.

The featurette *Gala Day at Disneyland*, released theatrically in 1960, is the basis for the first half of this show, with additional footage added to show the new attractions ready to greet Disneyland's guests.

Released theatrically in 1952, *Olympic Elk* is the story of the annual migrations of the elk herds in Washington.

DISNEYLAND STORY, THE   Airdate: 10/27/54.

In this, the opening show of the *Disneyland* television series, Walt presents a preview of the upcoming season, beginning with a brief tour of the Studio.

The second part of the show looks at the career of Mickey Mouse.

Production Notes:

- This show is also known as *What Is Disneyland?* The second part of the episode is titled *A Tribute to Mickey Mouse*, and later was used in the show *The Pre-Opening Report on Disneyland (and) A Tribute to Mickey Mouse.*
- Although the narration mentions *Sleeping Beauty* as the next animated feature, *Lady and the Tramp* was released next in 1955, followed by *Sleeping Beauty* in 1959.

DISNEYLAND 10TH ANNIVERSARY Airdates: 1/03/65, 5/30/65.

The arrival of Disneyland's "Tencennial" is a time for celebration at the Park, plus a look at some of the new attractions soon to open. Walt and Julie Reihm provide the tour.

Production Note:

- This program is also known as *The Disneyland 10th Anniversary Show.*

DISNEYLAND, THE PARK (AND) PECOS BILL   Airdates: 4/03/57, 8/21/57.

Cast: Roy Rogers and Trigger, The Smartest Horse in the Movies, The Sons of the Pioneers, Luana Patten, Bobby Driscoll.

Walt opens the show by mentioning the importance of American folklore, and promises to tell the story of the legendary Pecos Bill. First, however, he treats the audience to a helicopter ride to Anaheim and the Park. The remainder of the episode is the story of Pecos Bill, first seen in *Melody Time* and released as a short subject in 1954.

DISNEYLAND'S ALL-STAR COMEDY CIRCUS   Airdate: 12/11/88.

Cast: Rue McClanahan, Christopher Barnes, Kim Fields, Benji Gregory, Danny Ponce, Tina Yothers, Countess Vaughn, Ed Alonzo, Rudy Coby, Guzman-Camadi Duo, Bob Moore's Amazing Mongrels, Hans and Maureen Panter, Raspini Brothers, Dave "Captain Zoom" Smith, Bobby Berosini, Dian Parkinson, Richard Dysart.

In this special, featuring the stars from several NBC series, Rue McClanahan and Benji Gregory decide to form their own circuses.

DISNEYLAND'S 25TH ANNIVERSARY SHOW

This show originally aired as a special on 3/06/80 as *Kraft Salutes Disneyland's 25th Anniversary*. It later aired on the anthology series on 9/14/80 under this title.

DISNEYLAND'S 35TH ANNIVERSARY CELEBRATION   Airdate: 2/04/90.

Cast: Tony Danza, Charles Fleischer, Frank Oz (Miss Piggy), Dave Goelz (Gonzo), James Varney (Ernest P. Worrell), DJ Jazzy Jeff and the Fresh Prince, Brandon Maciel (Young Woody), Erinn Canavan (Ghost Girl), Chris Demetral (Dave), Billy O'Sullivan (Bob), Debbie Carman (Cinderella), Canela Cox (Teenage Girl #1), Laura Bridge (Teenage Girl #2), Anthony Daniels (Voice of C3PO), George Both (Young Ernest), Chris Kinkade (Cop), Woody Harrelson, Rhea Perlman, George Wendt, John Ratzenberger, Kelsey Grammer, Bebe Neuwirth, Art Linkletter, Bob Cummings, President Ronald Reagan.

Scenes of Disneyland over the years show how Disney has continued to improve "The Happiest Place on Earth."

DOG OF DESTINY

This is Part 2 of *Atta Girl, Kelly!*

DONALD AND JOSE, OLÉ! Airdate
(90-minute format): 1/23/82.
The program begins as Donald Duck opens a mysterious package from South America and discovers his friend, Jose Carioca, inside. Jose has come to visit Donald to tell him about South America, through a variety of Disney cartoons.

DONALD DUCK QUACKS UP
See: *Kids Is Kids.*

DONALD DUCK STORY, THE Airdates:
11/17/54, 4/20/55, 8/31/55.
Walt explains the creation of Donald Duck, using a scrapbook filled with highlights of Donald's career.

Production Note:

- This episode is also known as *The Story of Donald Duck.*

DONALD LOVES DAISY Airdate:
Syndicated.
This look at the world of romance, Disney style, features clips from numerous Disney cartoons.

DONALD TAKES A HOLIDAY Airdate:
Syndicated.
After many months of hard work, Donald Duck leaves on a well-deserved vacation. He encounters many trials and tribulations as seen in clips from Donald Duck cartoons.

DONALD'S AWARD Airdates: 3/27/57,
8/28/57, 9/09/62.
Walt opens the episode by talking about how happy he is to be part of the Studio "family," even though there is a problem child—Donald Duck. Donald has become so much of a problem that Walt has had to talk to him about it, promising him a good conduct medal if an entire week passes without a complaint about his behavior.

DONALD'S SILVER ANNIVERSARY
Airdates: 11/13/60, 9/17/61.
There's a festive air at the Studio: it's time to celebrate Donald's 25th year in show business. Walt reminisces about Donald's career, beginning in 1935 in *Orphan's Benefit* where a frustrated duck attempted to recite a poem before a very disrespectful audience.

Production Note:

- Although Walt describes *Orphan's Benefit* as Donald's first film, he had actually premiered earlier in 1934 as a bit player in *The Wise Little Hen.*

DONALD'S VALENTINE DAY SALUTE
Airdate: 2/10/80.
This holiday salute to love features a selection of cartoons and clips from animated features.

DONALD'S WEEKEND Airdates: 1/15/58,
8/27/58.
A typical weekend with Donald Duck is the setting for this episode as he heads home to see his nephews, who are visiting him. On the way home he stops for gas and a friendly attendant gives him passes to the circus, which Donald decides to use as a bribe to control the boys.

DONOVAN'S KID Airdates—Part 1:
1/07/79, 6/22/80. Part 2: 1/14/79, 6/29/80.
Cast: Darren McGavin (Timothy Donovan), Mickey Rooney (Old Bailey), Shelley Fabares (Grace Carpenter), Murray Hamilton (Henry Carpenter), Michael Conrad (Silas Rumford), Ross Martin (Mayor J. Calvin Stokes), Katy Kurtzman (Jamie Carpenter), Brenda Scott (Charity), Larry D. Mann (Larson), Larry Pennell (Shepherd), James Chandler (Ridgely), John Crawford (Thunder City Sheriff), Martin Kove (Kelso), Joe Higgins (Greenbush Sheriff), H.B. Haggerty (Sharkey), James Almanzar (1st Horseman), Alvy Moore (2nd Horseman), Dave Cass (Seaman Dodge), Richard Wright (Seaman #2), Hugh Hooker (Seaman #3), Don "Red" Barry (Sheriff at Stagecoach), Ralph Manza (Lou), Hanna Hertelendy (Frieda), Dick Winslow (Gambler #1), Warde Donovan (Gambler #2), Ken Del Conte (Jake), Wally K. Berns (Man), Bob Minor (Shotgun), Wayne Winton (Farmer), Daryle Ann Lindley (Lady at Ringside), David Mitchell (1st Ringsider), Rickie Layne (2nd Ringsider), Count Billy Varga (Referee), Lee Duncan (Bartender), Hector Morales (Hotel Manager), John Lawrence (Policeman), Jeri Lea Ray (Maid), Tom Lester (Photographer).
Con man Timothy Donovan, framed years ago for a crime actually committed by his wife's Uncle Henry, is finally returning to turn-of-the-century San Francisco where several surprises await him.

DOUBLE AGENT   Airdate (2-hour format): 3/29/87. The show was later aired in two parts—Part 1: 6/19/88. Part 2: 6/26/88.

Cast: Michael McKean (Warren Starbinder/Jason Star), John Putch (Abercrombie), Susan Walden (Sharon Starbinder), Christopher Burton (Russ Starbinder), Judith Jones (Meredith Starbinder), Lloyd Bochner (Special Agent Vaughn), Alexa Hamilton (Gerlinde Krueger), Savely Kramarov (Yurgi), Allan Kolman (Vlado), Big John Studd (Igor), Marguerite DeLain (June), Lois January (Dowager), Jane A. Johnston (Harriet), Patrick O'Brien (Eddy), Jean-Paul Vignon (Maitre d'), David Yanez (Vendor), Del Zamora (Willie).

Secret agent Jason Star meets Gerlinde Krueger as promised, but the woman tells him she doesn't have the set of circuit overlays he needs. She says she'll have them in two days, but Jason is killed in a massive explosion as he tries to leave. All this changes the life of Warren Starbinder, a mild-mannered veterinarian, who is Jason's twin brother. He is asked to take Jason's place.

DOUBLE SWITCH   Airdates (2-hour format): 1/24/87. The show was later repeated in two parts—Part 1: 9/13/87. Part 2: 9/20/87.

Cast: George Newbern (Bartholomew Holton/Matt Bundy), Elisabeth Shue (Kathy Shelton), Michael Des Barres (Simon), Peter Van Norden (Jake), Mariclare Costello (Mrs. Holton), John Lawlor (Mr. Bundy), Barbara Rhoades (Mrs. Bundy), Peter Van Norden (Jake), Alyson Croft (Emily Bender), Claude Knobler (Jason), Christopher Peters (Darryl), Betty Ramey (Secretary), Tom Breznahan (Greg), Mark Bringelson (Lone Man), Martin Casella (Lawyer), Tsutomu Carton (Valet), Lucinda Dooling (Costumer), Chris Drury (Roadie), Vicki Gabrielle (Stage Manager), Mark R. Gordon (Song Writer), Jeffrey Hornaday (Choreographer), Karen Michaels (Waitress), Rick Overton (Deejay), Lena Pousette (Princess Regina), John C. Reade (Bus Driver), Hal Riddle (Security Guard), Michele Russell (Hilary), Henry Sutton (Servant), Jason Tomlins (Soundsman), Marc Tubert (Director), Barry Wiggins (Person #3), Bradd D. Wong (Waiter), Ruth Zakarian (Mary Jo).

Matt Bundy is like many other teenagers—shy, and more afraid of the opposite sex than he wants to admit. Unlike most other teenagers, though, Matt is the exact double of a famous rock star, Bartholomew. Matt is a big fan of Bartholomew's, and he spends hours in his room imitating his hero. He later wins a contest impersonating Bartholomew, because the singer asks him to trade places.

DOWN THE LONG HILLS
This made-for-television movie originally aired on The Disney Channel. The film also aired on the anthology series in a 2-hour format on 5/24/87 and later in two parts on 8/21/88 and 8/28/88.

DUCK FLIES COOP   Airdate: 2/13/59.
Just like many other film stars, Donald Duck is more than a little temperamental and vain. When he doesn't show up for work one day, leaving behind a note vowing never to return, Walt decides to teach the wayward actor a lesson by replacing him.

DUCK FOR HIRE   Airdates: 10/23/57, 6/25/58, 11/25/79, 3/08/81, 7/17/82 (30-minute format).
Donald has decided to quit show business and leaves the Studio promising never to return. He goes to the Ajax Employment Agency and soon finds a job as a service station attendant. His first day on the job ends in disaster when he gets mad at his nephews and destroys their car, only to discover he had won it in a raffle.

Production Note:

• Following Walt's death, the show was modified to provide a new narration explaining Donald's quitting and subsequent return to the Studio. An edited version was aired in 1982.

DUCKING DISASTER WITH DONALD AND HIS FRIENDS
See: *Man Is His Own Worst Enemy.*

DUCKTALES VALENTINE!, A   Airdate: 2/11/90.
Uncle Scrooge's search for the lost temple of Aphroducky, the ancient goddess of love, has some unexpected results.

DUMBO   Airdates: 9/14/55, 12/21/55, 12/25/57, 12/29/63, 10/30/88. *Dumbo* also aired as a special in a 2-hour format: 9/17/78, 11/18/85, 9/14/86.
This 1941 theatrical release is the story of a circus elephant with huge ears who discovers he can fly. The 1955 airing carried the credit "Adapted for Television by: Ben Sharpsteen, Wilfred Jackson, Harry Tytle."

Production Notes:

- *Dumbo* was also included in the anthology episode *A Disney Storybook*.
- The 1978 version was part of the special *NBC Salutes the 25th Anniversary of The Wonderful World of Disney*. The other versions aired as two-hour specials on NBC.

EARTH*STAR VOYAGER
Airdates (each in a 2-hour format)—Part 1: 1/17/88. Part 2: 1/24/88.

Cast: Duncan Regehr (Capt. Jacob Brown), Brian McNamara (Capt. Jonathan Hays), Julia Montgomery (Dr. Sally Arthur), Jason Michas (Jessie "Beanie" Bienstock), Tom Breznahan (Huxley Welles), Margaret Langrick (Luz Sansone), Sean O'Byrne (Vance "Top Dog" Arthur), Peter Donat (Admiral Beasley), Henry Kingi (Shell), Lynnette Mettey (Priscilla), Ric Reid (Captain Forbes), Frank C. Turner (Willy), Dinah Gaston (Lani Miyori), Bruce Harwood (Dr. Leland Eugene), Bill Croft (Trager), John "Bear Curtis" (Whistlestick), Stephen Dimopoulos (The Crier), Nigel Harvey (Security Leader), Andrew Kavadas (Brody Arnold), Barry Kennedy (Lieutenant Matthews), Kevin McNulty (Commander Gardiner), Jennifer Michas (Jeannie), Stephen E. Miller (Lieutenant Krieger), Enid Saunders (Elderly Woman), Mike Stack (Crewman #1), Sandy Tucker (Mrs. Bienstock), Meredith Bain Woodward (Mrs. Hays).

In 2088, Earth is deteriorating, and a specially selected group of young academy cadets learn that they have been selected as the crew of the new space ship *Earth*Star Voyager*. It will be their job to find a new home for humanity.

Production Notes:

- Disney hoped to sell *Earth*Star Voyager* as a series, but the first part was aired against a major football game and it fared very poorly in the ratings.
- This show also aired as part of the *Family Classics* series of specials—Part 1: 5/25/89. Part 2: 6/01/89.

EL BANDIDO
Airdates: 10/30/60, 8/06/61.

Cast: Guy Williams (Zorro and Don Diego), Gilbert Roland (El Cuchillo), Henry Calvin (Sergeant Garcia), Gene Sheldon (Bernardo), Rita Moreno (Chulita), Rudolph Acosta (Carancho), Rudolpho Hoyos (Bandit), Vito Scotti (Chaco), Bern Hoffman (Trampa), George J. Lewis (Don Alejandro).

A group of Mexican bandits led by El Cuchillo ("The Knife") flees into Southern California to escape a band of pursuing soldiers. They decide to try their luck in Los Angeles despite the reputation of Zorro. As luck would have it, the local rancheros are storing a large supply of hides in a new warehouse and a silver shipment is ready to leave, providing the bandits with ample temptation.

Production Note:

- This story is concluded in the episode *Adios El Cuchillo*.

ELFEGO BACA (mini-series)
There were ten episodes produced about this former gunman who turned to law, first as a sheriff and then as an attorney: *The Nine Lives of Elfego Baca; Four Down and Five Lives to Go; Lawman or Gunman; Law and Order, Incorporated; Attorney-at-Law; The Griswold Murder; Move Along Mustangers; Mustang Man, Mustang Maid; Friendly Enemies at Law;* and *Gus Tomlin Is Dead*. Refer to each of these titles for the episode description.

ELFEGO BACA AND THE MUSTANGERS
This is the overall title for the episodes *Move Along Mustangers* and *Mustang Man, Mustang Maid*. Both shows are listed under their individual titles.

EMIL AND THE DETECTIVES
Airdates—Part 1: 9/11/66, 5/09/71. Part 2: 9/18/66, 5/16/71.

This 1965 theatrical release stars Walter Slezak, Bryan Russell, and Roger Mobley in a story of amateur detectives who stumble onto a bank robbery in Berlin.

Production Note:

- This film was serialized on *The New Mickey Mouse Club* under the title *The Three Skrinks*.

END OF THE TRAIL
Airdates: 1/29/61, 7/09/61.

Cast: Tom Tryon (Texas John Slaughter), Betty Lynn (Viola Howell), Onslow Stevens (General Miles), Harry Carey, Jr. (Corp. Ben Jenkins), Pat Hogan (Geronimo), Brian Corcoran (Willie Slaughter), Annette Gorman (Addie Slaughter).

The 13th episode of *The Tales of Texas John Slaughter* opens as a column of soldiers led by General Miles arrives in town to search for Geronimo, who has been terrorizing the civilian population. Miles is under heavy pressure from the government to end the attacks so he asks John for help. Slaughter agrees and rides to the army camp, where he meets his old friend, Ben Jenkins, who is now a corporal in the cavalry.

Production Note:

- This episode was released theatrically overseas in 1964 as *Geronimo's Revenge*, using footage from the episode of that name.

EPCOT CENTER: THE OPENING CELEBRATION   Airdate: 10/23/82.

Cast: Danny Kaye (Host), Drew Barrymore, Roy Clark, Marie Osmond, Eric Severeid, Alan Shepherd, The West Point Glee Club, The All-American Marching Band.

Despite poor weather, EPCOT Center has opened on schedule, and Danny Kaye is there to host the gala festivities commemorating the occasion. He begins by singing *And the Twenty-First Century Begins*, a musical look back at how Walt Disney first announced his plans for EPCOT and the massive construction project that followed.

Production Note:

- Originally planned to be aired as a special, the show was instead broadcast as part of the anthology series.

ERNEST GOES TO CAMP   Airdate—Part 1: 10/29/89. Part 2: 11/05/89.

This 1987 theatrical release stars Jim Varney. His character of Ernest P. Worrell saves a summer camp from extinction.

ESCAPADE IN FLORENCE   Airdates—Part 1: 9/30/62, 6/23/63, 6/22/69. Part 2: 10/07/62, 6/30/63, 6/29/69.

Cast: Tommy Kirk (Tommy Carpenter), Annette Funicello (Annette Aliotto), Nino Castelnuovo (Bruno), Clelia Matania (Aunt Gisella), Venantino Venantini (Lorenzo), Ivan Desny (Count Roberto), Odoardo Spadoro (Padrone), Carlo Rizzo (Uncle Mario), Renzo Palmer (Carabiniere), Richard Watson (Butler), Helen Stirling (Miss Brooks), Elisa Cegani (Felicia), Liana del Balzo (Countess della Scala), George Ehling (Gino), Ivan Triesault (Professor Levenson), Massimo Luigi (Mayor).

Tommy Carpenter, a student studying in Florence, makes the accidental acquaintance of another American, Annette Aliotto, by knocking her down as she enters an art store to sell one of her paintings. Trouble ensues when Tommy and Annette get caught in the middle of an art crime.

Production Notes:

- The story was based on the book *The Golden Doors.*
- This show was released theatrically overseas in 1963.

ESCAPE TO NOWHERE
This is Part 2 of *Andrews' Raiders.*

ESCAPE TO PARADISE (AND) WATER BIRDS   Airdate: 12/18/60.

Cast (Playing Themselves): John Mills, Dorothy McGuire, James MacArthur, Janet Munro, Sessue Hayakawa, Tommy Kirk, Kevin Corcoran, Cecil Parker, Andy Ho, Milton Reid, Larry Taylor, Sir Hercules and His Friends (Calypso Singers).

This behind-the-scenes look at the filming of *Swiss Family Robinson* takes place on location on the island of Tobago in the West Indies. The Studio has sent a crew there to film the story of a 19th Century family stranded far from civilization when their ship sinks. Since there is no motion picture industry located there, everything has to be imported to the island, including the animals. The second half of this show originally was seen in the episode *A Trip Thru Adventureland (and) Water Birds* and is described under that title.

ESCAPE TO WITCH MOUNTAIN   Airdates (2-hour format) 2/17/80, 10/12/80. For the 1981–82 season the show was aired in two parts—Part 1: 12/19/81. Part 2: 12/26/81.

This 1975 theatrical release stars Eddie Albert, Kim Richards, and Ike Eisenmann in the story of two orphans who discover that they are aliens stranded on Earth.

Production Note:

- This film, one of the Studio's most successful of the '70s, was originally planned as a two-part television episode for the 1975–76 season. It spawned a theatrical sequel and a made-for-television film.

EXILE   Airdates (2-hour format): 1/14/90, 7/22/90.

Cast: Christopher Daniel Barnes (Dave), Scott Bloom, Sarah Buxton, Alice Carter (Marian), Gino DeMauro (Larry), Kristin Dattilo, Chris Furrh, Stacy Galina (Jill), Christian Jacobs (Derf), Sherrie Krenn, Philip Linton, Mike Preston (Rupe Murphy), Markus

Redmond (Jackson), Michael Stoyanov, Kiersten Warren (Diana), Corey Feldman (Schenke), Christopher Lawford, Scott McGinnis, Kate Benton (Mrs. Anderson), Charlotte Carpenter (Newswoman), Anne Marie Gillies (Mrs. McCombs), Alan Koss (Mr. Anderson), Ann Walker (Mrs. D'Arienzo), Ken Zavayna (Mr. McCombs).

A diverse group of students plans to spend the summer in a small village in Malaysia. The last leg of the trip is on an ancient seaplane, and the disreputable pilot must land it near an island after the engine fails. When the pilot must leave them behind while he goes for help, the adventure takes a tragic turn.

Production Note:

- This unsold pilot was loosely based on William Golding's novel *The Lord of the Flies*.

FAMILY BAND, THE   Airdates—Part 1: 1/23/72. Part 2: 1/30/72.

Cast: Walter Brennan (Grandpa Bower), Buddy Ebsen (Calvin Bower), Lesley Ann Warren (Alice Bower), John Davidson (Joe Carder), Janet Blair (Katie Bower), Kurt Russell (Sidney Bower), Bobby Riha (Mayo Bower), Jon Walmsley (Quin Bower), Smitty Wordes (Nettie Bower), Heidi Rook (Rose Bower), Debbie Smith (Lulu Bower), Pamelyn Ferdin (Laura Bower), Wally Cox (Mr. Wampler), Richard Deacon (Charlie Wrenn), Steve Harmon (Ernie Stubbins), Goldie Jeanne Hawn (Giggly Girl), John Craig (Frank), Jonathan Kidd (Telegrapher).

Released theatrically in 1968 as *The One and Only, Genuine, Original Family Band*, this film stars Walter Brennan, Buddy Ebsen, Lesley Ann Warren, and John Davidson in the story of a family that upsets local politics in the emerging Dakota Territory in 1889.

FANTASY ON SKIS   Airdates: 2/04/62, 12/27/64.

Cast: Susie Wirth (Herself), Bruno (Himself).

Susie is a 9-year-old living in a ski lodge in Aspen, Colorado, and she has a dream. She hopes to win a race in the upcoming Ski Festival, but first she must save enough money to replace her wornout skis. She arranges to help deliver the mail from the lodge to the post office, and takes it with her as she skis to school.

Production Note:

- *Fantasy on Skis* was released theatrically as a short subject in 1975 with *Snowball Express*.

FARAWAY PLACES—HIGH, HOT, AND WET (SIAM)   Airdates: 1/01/58, 8/20/58. Husband-and-wife camera team Herbert and Trudie Knapp are featured in this look at how Disney crews prepare for, and carry out, some of the most difficult photo assignments available. The first sequence is set high in the Andes mountains in Peru, home of the former Inca empire. The next assignment is at sea level, for the Knapps have been sent to the Fiji Islands. A visit to Siam (now known as Thailand) concludes the episode.

Production Note:

- This episode included the 1954 theatrical release *Siam*, which was part of the *People and Places* series.

FEATHER FARM, THE   Airdate: 10/26/69.

Cast: Nick Nolte (Les), Mel Weiser (Shorty), Christine Coates (Nancy), Shirley Fabricant (Aunt Carrie).

It's 1915, and ostrich feathers are such a popular accessory to ladies' wardrobes that South African ostrich farms are unable to keep up with the demand. In response, a Boston socialite and her niece decide to open an ostrich ranch. Nancy and her Aunt Carrie buy three birds, hire two ranch hands, and head back to Boston, confident of success. Almost as soon as the owners leave, the hired help runs into trouble.

FERDINAND THE BULL AND MICKEY   Airdate: 1/18/83.

Heroes come in many different forms, and some of them never wanted to be heroes at all. Scenes from Disney films illustrate the perils these screen stars face, and the point is made that reluctant heroes are just as brave as those that crave adventure. The show opens with the Academy Award winning *Ferdinand the Bull* featuring a timid bull who is content to spend his days sitting in a field sniffing the flowers.

FIFTY HAPPY YEARS   Airdates: 1/21/73, 6/03/73.

Cast: Julie Andrews, James Baskett, Ray Bolger, Brian Bedford, Walter Brennan, Wally Brown, Alan Carney, Mary Costa, Brandon de Wilde, Buddy Ebsen, Verna Felton, Matthew

Garber, George Givot, Phil Harris, Sessue
Hayakawa, Andy Ho, Dean Jones, Brian
Keith, Tommy Kirk, Michele Lee, Peggy Lee,
James MacArthur, Fred MacMurray, James
Mason, Dorothy McGuire, Vera Miles, John
Mills, Janet Munro, Nancy Olson, Fess Parker,
Louis Prima, Elliott Reid, Milton Reid,
Tommy Steele, Terry-Thomas, David
Tomlinson, Peter Ustinov, Dick Van Dyke,
Kennan Wynn.

This nostalgic look at the works of the Disney Studio begins with the story of how Walt Disney created Mickey Mouse, and how his older brother, Roy, helped him create an entertainment empire unlike any other. The Studio's many firsts, such as *Snow White and the Seven Dwarfs*, the first full-length animated feature, and other milestones are described, with numerous clips from cartoons, television programs, and feature films to illustrate these highlights.

FIGHTING CHOICE, A   Airdates (2-hour format): 4/13/86, 8/09/87.
Cast: Beau Bridges (Thad Taylor), Karen Valentine (Meg Taylor), Patrick Dempsey (Kellin Taylor), Frances Lee McCain (Lawyer), Lawrence Pressman (Dr. Tobin), Danielle Von Zerneck (Susie Fratelli), Allan Arbus (Dr. Andreas Hellman), Alice Hirson (Judge E.L. Rosenstiel), Parker Jacobs (Harvey Taylor), Allen Williams (Dan Goodman), Philip Linton (Eli Rhodes), Robin Thomas (Dr. Gardner), Charles Lanyer (Dr. Leonard Faraday), Nina Henderson (Janet), Jeanne Hepple (Martha), Don Saroyan (Dick), Rick Biggs (Process Server), Damito Jo Freeman (Natalie), Jim Gatherum (Boy at School), Creed Bratton (Court Clerk), Marion Yue (Newscaster).

Kellin Taylor, a teenager who suffers from epilepsy, wants a dangerous operation that will cure him. When his parents object, he sues them to allow it.

FIGHTING PRINCE OF DONEGAL, THE
Airdates—Part 1: 10/01/67. Part 2: 10/08/67. Part 3: 10/15/67.
This 1966 theatrical release, set during the 16th-century civil war between England and Ireland, stars Peter McEnery and Susan Hampshire.

FIRE CALLED JEREMIAH, A   Airdates: 12/03/61, 7/22/62, 6/05/66.
Cast (playing themselves): Cliff Blake (Smoke Jumper), Carole Stockner (Fire Lookout), Roy Carpenter (Instructor), Randle

Hurst (Instructor), John Nash (Instructor), Tom Uphill (Dispatcher).

Fire lookout towers are lonely places, and Cliff Blake only has Frisky, a trained squirrel, to keep him company. Thus he's happy to learn he's been accepted as a trainee in the fire-jumper school, where he'll learn how to fight forest fires.

Production Note:
• This episode was released theatrically overseas in 1962.

FIRE ON KELLY MOUNTAIN   Airdates: 9/30/73, 6/26/77, 7/06/80, 8/21/82.
Cast: Andrew Duggan (Ed Jorgenson), Larry Wilcox (Phil Mallory), Anne Lockhart (Karen Jorgenson), Noam Pitlik (News Commentator), Ted Hartley (Jumper Captain), Paul Micale (Max), Frank Farmer (Smoke Jumper), Clay Tanner (Hank).

Phil Mallory is a new forest watcher who feels left out. Not far away, a major fire is burning, and a crew of other Forest Service employees is busy fighting it. Although he knows he must stay in his tower to look for other fires, Phil longs to fight fires rather than sit idle. He gets his wish when lightning strikes nearby and starts a small fire, prompting headquarters to send him out to investigate.

FLASH, THE TEENAGE OTTER   Airdates: 4/30/61, 6/14/70.
Despite the ever-increasing encroachment of humans on nature, wildlife continues to flourish, particularly in game preserves, and it's in one of these preserves that two young otters are born. Flash and Fleta begin their lives happily frolicking in a deserted mill pond under their mother's watchful eye.

Production Note:
• *Flash* was released theatrically overseas in 1964 and domestically in 1965.

FLIGHT OF THE GREY WOLF, THE
Airdates—Part 1: 3/14/76. Part 2: 3/21/76.
Cast: Jeff East (Russ Hanson), Bill Williams (The Sheriff), Barbara Hale (Mrs. Hanson), William Bryant (Mr. Hanson), Eric Server (Ed, The Deputy), Judson Pratt (Mr. Pomeroy), Sam Edwards (Amsel), Owen Bush (Tom), Joe Haworth (Josh), Jesse Martin (Hunter).

Russ Hanson has a special pet—a grey wolf he's raised from a cub. His parents run a kennel, and Grey, as the wolf is called, feels like he's one of the dogs. Everyone's life changes when a Doberman is left at the kennel and attacks Russ, who is saved when Grey challenges the vicious dog.

FLIGHT OF THE NAVIGATOR   Airdates—Part 1: 1/03/88. Part 2: 1/10/88.

This 1986 theatrical release starring Joey Cramer is the story of a young boy who is missing for eight years, but when he's discovered, he hasn't aged a day. He then has to help a robot spaceship find its way home. It also aired as a *Disney Family Classic* special on ABC in two parts on 3/09/89 and 3/16/89.

FLIGHT OF THE WHITE STALLIONS

Airdates—Part 1: 10/17/65, 11/11/73. Part 2: 10/24/65, 11/18/73.

Released theatrically in 1963 as *Miracle of the White Stallions*, this story of how the famed Lipizzan stallions were saved during World War II stars Robert Taylor, Lilli Palmer, Curt Jurgens, Eddie Albert, and James Franciscus.

FLY WITH VON DRAKE   Airdates: 10/13/63, 6/07/64.

Walt opens the show by commenting on our long interest in the subjects of flight and outer space. An animated sequence shows how some of the more fanciful speculators imagined life on Mars. Then, the science of manned flight gets the unique Ludwig Von Drake treatment as the self-styled expert attempts to trace the history of aviation and explain how planes and balloons can fly.

FOLLOW ME, BOYS!   Airdates—Part 1: 8/02/81. Part 2: 8/16/81.

This 1966 theatrical release stars Fred MacMurray and Vera Miles in the story of how one man changes the lives of many boys by forming a Boy Scout troop.

FOLLOW YOUR HEART

This is Part 1 of *The Horsemasters*.

FOOTLOOSE GOOSE, THE   Airdate: 3/09/75.

Cast: Brett Hadley (Tom Rank), Paul Preston (John Mackenna), Judy Bement (Sarah Armstrong).

Duke is a 2-year-old Canadian gander who falls in love with Duchess, a 2-year-old goose. Unfortunately, Duchess is part of a flock living at a Minnesota trout farm and her wings have been clipped, preventing her from joining Duke on his migration to Canada. The wild gander decides to stay with Duchess, and since geese usually mate for life, the two look for a nesting site. Although Duchess is land bound, Duke still ventures out for occasional flights around the area, and it's during one of these trips that disaster befalls him.

Production Note:

- The production company faced an unusual problem trying to identify which goose was which. Some were trained to walk toward the camera, others to fight with a wolverine, and some to fly on command. They solved their problem by punching small holes in the webbed feet of their stars, with special codes for each skill the goose was trained for. The small holes grew over with time.

FOR THE LOVE OF WILLADEAN

Airdates—Part 1: 3/08/64, 5/14/67, 6/09/74. Part 2: 3/15/64, 5/21/67, 6/16/74.

Cast: Ed Wynn (Alfred), Michael McGreevey (J.D. Gray), Billy Mumy (Freddy Gray), Roger Mobley (Harley Mason), John Anderson (Farmer Wills), Terry Burnham (Willadean Wills), Barbara Eiler (Mrs. Mason), Harry Harvey, Sr. (Sheriff), Peter Adams (Mr. Mason).

In Part 1, titled *A Taste of Melon*, the Mason family moves from Detroit to the countryside, and their son Harley becomes friends with Freddy and J.D. Gray. The boys have a club that they invite Harley to join, but J.D. starts to have second thoughts when Harley shows an interest in Willadean Wills, the object of J.D.'s affections.

In *Treasure in the Haunted House*, Part 2 of the story, J.D. and Harley are still trying to impress Willadean, and they dare each other to enter a supposedly haunted house. Harley doesn't realize that the house has already been visited by Freddy and J.D., or that the two brothers have installed a number of tricks to scare their victim.

FOUR DOWN AND FIVE LIVES TO GO

Airdates: 10/17/58, 4/10/59.

Cast: Robert Loggia (Elfego Baca), Robert F. Simon (Deputy Morgan), Lisa Montell (Anita Chavez), Nestor Paiva (Justice of the Peace), Leonard Strong (Zanaga Martinez), Charles Maxwell, Linc Foster (Jim Spears), Rico Alaniz (El Sinverguenza).

The second chapter in the story of Elfego Baca opens as Elfego wins election to the post of sheriff in Socorro County, New Mexico. Never one to use orthodox methods, Baca begins by sending letters to all of the wanted men in the area asking them to turn themselves in. If they don't, he'll come looking for them and will show no mercy. His reputation as a deadly shot is so widespread that only one man doesn't take advantage of the offer.

Production Note:

- This episode was combined with *The Nine Lives of Elfego Baca* and released theatrically overseas in 1959 under that title.

FOUR FABULOUS CHARACTERS   Airdates: 9/18/57, 8/13/58, 5/03/64.

The show is dedicated to the memory of four Americans who have become folk heroes, celebrated in song and story. Jerry Colonna begins with the story of Casey Jones, a railroad engineer, with a penchant for being on time that bordered on fanaticism.

The second story is about two famous characters, Henry Martin and Grace Coy, whose story concerns a feud that began so long ago no one even remembers why.

Mighty Casey of the "Mudville Nine" is next as the story of one of the world's most famous baseball players.

The final tale is that of John Chapman, better known as "Johnny Appleseed."

FOUR TALES ON A MOUSE   Airdates: 4/16/58, 7/23/58.

Past episodes have shown how Mickey Mouse began his career and rose to stardom, but this show tells how Mickey has helped other Disney performers with their careers. Mickey shares the spotlight with Donald Duck, Goofy, Pluto, and Minnie.

14 GOING ON 30   Airdates—Part 1: 3/06/88. Part 2: 3/13/88.

Cast: Steve Eckholdt (Harold Forndexter/Adult Danny), Daphne Ashbrook (Peggy Noble), Adam Carl (Lloyd Duffy), Gabey Olds (Danny O'Neil—age 14), Irene Tedrow (Aunt May), Patrick Duffy (Gentleman), Harry Morgan (Uncle Herb), Loretta Swit (Louisa Horton), Alan Thicke (Mr. Forndexter), Dick Van Patten (Principal Loomis), Rick Rossovich (Roy "Jackjaw" Kelton), Kit McDonough (Danny's Mom), Richard McGonagle (Danny's Dad), John Ingle (Mr. Thornby), Sal Viscuso (Mr. Lloyd), John "Bunky" Butler (Student #2), David Cobb (Beefy Jock), Debbie Evans (Police Officer), Amy Hathaway (Young Peggy), David Hess (Host), Rachel Jacobs (Odemeyer), Milt Jamin (Waiter), Judith Jones (Nagel), Andrew Potter (Student #1), Otis Sallid (Desk Sergeant), John Howard Swain (Maitre 'd #2), Barry Vigon (Maitre 'd #1), Ahmet Zappa (Student #3), Polo (The Master Blasters).

Fourteen-year-old Danny O'Neil has a crush on his teacher. He finds a way to get her attention when he uses a machine to change himself into an adult.

FOURTH ANNIVERSARY SHOW, THE
Airdate: 9/11/57.

Cast: Sharon Baird, Bobby Burgess, Lonnie Burr, Tommy Cole, Tim Considine, Kevin "Moochie" Corcoran, Jimmie Dodd, Bonnie Lynn Fields, Annette Funicello, Darlene Gillespie, Don Grady, Cheryl Holdridge, Linda Hughes, Tommy Kirk, Cubby O'Brien, Karen Pendleton, Lynn Ready, David Stollery, Doreen Tracey, Roy Williams, Jerome Courtland (Andy Burnett), Fess Parker (Davy Crockett), Guy Williams (Zorro).

Walt opens this celebration of four years on television by telling how the late Serge Prokofieff played his composition *Peter and the Wolf* for Walt and how that convinced him to make an animated short subject based on the musical work. In this musical piece, an instrument and musical theme are used to denote each of the characters, and the Disney animators had to match their work to the existing soundtrack. The second part of the show is the actual celebration. It begins with the jubilant arrival of the Mouseketeers, including the stars of the *Mickey Mouse Club* serials. They pester Walt with questions on what he has planned for future shows, and the surprised studio chief agrees to give them a special preview.

FRANK CLELL'S IN TOWN   Airdates: 4/23/61, 7/30/61.

Cast: Tom Tryon (Texas John Slaughter), Ralph Meeker (Frank Clell), Betty Lynn (Viola Slaughter), Brian Corcoran (Willie Slaughter), Jim Beck (Burt Alvord), Robert Burton (Mayor Clum), Michael McGreevey (Freddy), Raymond Bailey (Mark Morgan), Ernest Sarracino (Sam).

Part 16 of *The Tales of Texas John Slaughter* opens as Tombstone's store owners realize there is a price to pay for law and order. The sheriff, John Slaughter, has recently arrested a major criminal named Jimmy Deuce, prompting all of the other bandits and outlaws to flee in fear. With their departure, the economy suffers. Meanwhile, John's wife tries to convince him to resign, arguing that he's not needed any longer. John isn't convinced. He feels there will be a large number of decent citizens wanting to move to a crime-free Tombstone and a lawman will be needed to keep it that way. His theories are quickly put to the test when a seemingly peaceful man arrives in town, only to be identified as Frank Clell, a noted killer who claims he's looking to leave all of that behind him.

Production Note:

- This episode was combined with *A Trip to Tucson* and released theatrically overseas in 1966 as *A Holster Full of Law*.

FREAKY FRIDAY   Airdates—Part 1: 10/09/82. Part 2: 10/16/82.
This 1976 theatrical release stars Joe Foster and Barbara Harris in the story of a teenage girl and mother who mysteriously trade places with each other. A made-for-television version was aired as a special on 5/06/95 and 3/02/96.

FRIENDLY ENEMIES AT LAW   Airdates: 3/18/60, 9/09/60.
   Cast: Robert Loggia (Elfego Baca), John Kerr (Martin Dibler), Patricia Crowley (Patricia Kettrick), Barton MacLane (Rauls Kettrick), Robert Lowery (Wade Cather), Guinn Williams (Buffalo), Ray Teal (Frank Oxford), Roy Barcroft (Sheriff Bodie).
   In Part 9 of *Elfego Baca*, the frontier lawyer is offered a beautiful stallion by Frank Oxford, a cattleman who needs Baca's help. Oxford is from nearby Taota, a town run by the powerful Rauls Kettrick, and it's Kettrick who's the source of his problem. Fifty head of Oxford's cattle apparently wandered onto Kettrick's ranch, and Kettrick won't give them back. Other small ranchers are having the same problem, but there's only one lawyer in Taota, and he works for Kettrick.

FRIENDSHIP IN VIENNA, A
This made-for-television movie first aired on The Disney Channel. It also aired on the anthology series on 7/15/90.

FROM AESOP TO HANS CHRISTIAN ANDERSEN   Airdates: 3/02/55, 6/08/55, 8/10/55.
The age-old art of storytelling is featured as Disney presents an all-cartoon tribute to several classic tales.

Production Notes:

- *From Aesop to Hans Christian Andersen* was released theatrically overseas in 1958.

FROM ALL OF US TO ALL OF YOU
Airdates: 12/19/58, 12/25/60, 12/22/63 (*The Sword in the Stone* version); 12/24/67 (*Jungle Book* version); 12/20/70 (*Aristocats* version); 12/23/73 (*Robin Hood* version); 12/25/77 (*Pete's Dragon* version); 12/23/79 (*Corn Chips* version); 12/14/80 (*Aristocats* version).
Walt has asked for the help of several Disney stars in presenting a special holiday show. Tinker Bell, the hostess, starts things off by introducing Mickey Mouse and Jiminy Cricket. Jiminy announces he's arranged a special visit to the North Pole to see *Santa's Workshop*. The show continues with magical scenes from various animated shorts and films.

Production Notes:

- In subsequent years, the show's contents were edited to incorporate a plug for an upcoming theatrical release or an additional animated short subject.
- Major portions of this episode were later included in The Disney Channel's first yule celebration, *A Disney Channel Christmas*.

FROM THE PIRATES OF THE CARIBBEAN TO THE WORLD OF TOMORROW
See: *Disneyland: From The Pirates of the Caribbean to the World of Tomorrow*.

FROM TICONDEROGA TO DISNEYLAND
This is Part 2 of *Moochie of Pop Warner Football*.

FURTHER ADVENTURES OF GALLEGHER, THE
This is the overall title of three episodes in the continued story of Gallegher, a newspaper copyboy who aspires to be a reporter. The individual episode titles are *A Case of Murder; The Big Swindle;* and *The Daily Press vs. City Hall*. Refer to each of these titles for the episode description.

FURTHER REPORT ON DISNEYLAND, A (AND) TRIBUTE TO MICKEY MOUSE, A
See: *The Pre-Opening Report from Disneyland (and) A Tribute to Mickey Mouse*.

FUZZBUCKET   Airdates: 5/18/86, 8/17/86 (with *The Deacon Street Deer* in a 2-hour format).
   Cast: Chris Hebert (Michael Gerber), Phil Fondacaro (Fuzzbucket), Joe Regalbuto (Dad), Wendy Phillips (Mom), Robyn Lively (Stevie

Gerber), John Vernon (Principal), Fran Ryan, Deena-Marie Consiglio (Tina), David Katz (Boy #1), Wally Taylor (Cop), Judith Durand (Counselor), Paul Harper (Wino), Ernie Lively (Teacher #1), Roger Nolan (Teacher #2), Lily Mariye (Teacher #3), Ilana Martin (Girlfriend), Nancy McLoughlin (Mrs. Fielding), Hal Smith (Voice of Fuzzbucket).

Young Michael Gerber is upset with all the rules his parents have set for him, and he is also upset when they argue. The day before school starts, Michael meets a new invisible friend, Fuzzbucket, for the first time. Michael doesn't know it, but Fuzzbucket has come to help him and his parents get along better.

Production Note:

• This was the pilot for an unsold series.

GALLEGHER   Airdates—Part 1: 1/24/65, 7/25/65. Part 2: 1/31/65, 8/01/65. Part 3: 2/07/65, 8/08/65.
   Cast: Edmond O'Brien (Editor Crowley), Jack Warden (Lieutenant Fergus), Roger Mobley (Gallegher), Ray Teal (Detective Snead), Robert Middleton (Dutch Mac), Harvey Korman (Brownie), Philip Ober (Hade), Dean Fredericks (Zip Wyatt), Sean McClory (Officer Madden), Richard Derr (Mr. Dwyer), Donald Losby (Country Boy), Louis Quinn (Banjo), Bryan Russell (Jimmy, the Bootblack), Laurie Mitchell (Missy).

Told in three parts, *Gallegher* is the story of a newspaper copyboy who hopes to some-day become a reporter. The year is 1889, and Gallegher works for *The Daily Press*, a small paper that prides itself on its investigative reporting. Part 1 begins with Gallegher stumbling onto a bank robbery at the bank next door.

In Part 2, Gallegher is helping Brownie cover the trial of police chief O'Malley, who has been accused of collaborating with local criminals.

The third episode pits Crowley, the editor, against Gallegher when Gallegher sees a man in the bank whom he suspects of being a former train robber. The weary editor attributes Gallegher's suspicion to an overactive imagination and ignores the tip.

Production Notes:

• *Gallegher* was based on a short story written by Charles Dana Gibson, a real-life journalist. It was first published in *Scribner's Magazine* in the 1880s.
• *Gallegher* was released theatrically overseas.

• This show proved successful enough in the ratings to spawn several sequels. Each is described separately under the following titles: *The Further Adventures of Gallegher* (3 parts); *Gallegher Goes West* (4 parts); and *The Mystery of Edward Sims* (2 parts).

GALLEGHER GOES WEST
This is the third set of stories about a newspaper copyboy in 1889 who aspires to become a reporter. The four parts to this sequel are *Showdown with the Sundown Kid*, *Crusading Reporter*, *Tragedy on the Trail*, and *Trial by Terror*. Refer to each of these titles for the episode description.

GERONIMO'S REVENGE   Airdates: 3/04/60, 8/05/60.
   Cast: Tom Tryon (Texas John Slaughter), Darryl Hickman (Ashley Carstairs), Betty Lynn (Viola Slaughter), Brian Corcoran (Willie Slaughter), Allan Lane, Charles Maxwell (Johnson), James Edwards (Batt), Annette Gorman (Addie Slaughter), Don Haggerty (Wes), Jay Silverheels (Natchez), Pat Hogan (Geronimo), Bob Steele (Ben), Gregory Walcott (Henderson).

A domestic problem finds John Slaughter discussing responsibility with his son as Part 12 of *The Tales of Texas John Slaughter* begins. Willie Slaughter has broken his mother's prized organ, and a reluctant John begins to talk to him about it. This unwelcome chore is interrupted by the arrival of one of the ranch workers with news that a band of Apaches has killed five head of cattle without reason. John decides to visit his old friend Natchez, who is now chief of the Apaches.

Production Note:

• This episode was combined with footage from *End of the Trail* to create the foreign 1964 theatrical release *Geronimo's Revenge*.

GHOST OF CYPRESS SWAMP, THE
Airdate (2-hour format): 3/13/77.
   Cast: Vic Morrow (Tom Stone), Tom Simcox (Pa Bascombe), Jacqueline Scott (Aunt Louise), Noah Beery (Doc Manners), Louise Latham (Ma Landers), Shug Fisher (Sherman Prather), Jeff East (Lonny Bascombe), Cindy Eilbacher (Shirley Landers), Gavan O'Herlihy (Big Bob Landers), Jimmy Van Patten (Bucky Landers), Richard Wright (Morton Landers), James Almanzar (1st Searcher), Tom Waters (2nd Searcher).

Lonny Bascombe and his dog are hunting raccoons in the Great Cypress Swamp when they are suddenly attacked by Weakfoot, a black panther who is raiding the nearby farms. The dog is killed, and Lonny and his dad decide to track and kill the panther. Their hunt is unsuccessful and they lose one of their hounds, so Lonny stays behind to look for the dog while Pa returns home. Lonny's search is interrupted when he is attacked by a wild man living alone in the swamp.

Production Notes:

• Disney's publicity releases describe this show as the Studio's "first movie ever made especially for television." When the Studio couldn't locate trained panthers to use in this episode, they solved the problem by renting trained cougars and dyeing them black.

GHOSTS OF BUXLEY HALL, THE
Airdates—Part 1: 12/21/80. Part 2: 1/04/81.
Cast: Dick O'Neill (Gen. Eulace C. Buxley), Victor French (Sgt.-Maj. Chester B. Sweet), Louise Latham (Bettina Buxley), Rad Daly (Jeremy Ross), Monte Markham (Col. "Jumpin' Joe" Buxley), Ruta Lee (Ernestine Di Gonzini), Vito Scotti (Count Sergio Luchesi Di Gonzini), Rennee Jarrett (Emily Wakefield), Don Porter (Judge Oliver Haynes), Steve Franken (Virgil Quinby), Christian Juttner (Cadet Captain Hubert Fletcher), Tricia Cast (Posie Taylor), Guy Raymond (Ben Grissom), John Myhers (E. L. Hart), Joe Tornatore (Vincent), Stu Gilliam (Lt. Jim Rodney), John Ericson (George Ross), Tony Becker (Todd), Billy Jacoby (David Williams), Karyn Harrison (Waitress).

It's a sad day for Buxley Hall, a military academy founded in 1876 by Gen. Eulace Buxley and now run by his descendant, Col. Joe Buxley. The school is the victim of declining attendance and fiscal woes, and Joe Buxley has just made the sorrowful decision to merge with the Wakefield Academy for Girls, another private school facing the same problems. He hasn't counted on the ghosts of the school founders returning to foil his plans.

GIRL WHO SPELLED FREEDOM, THE
Airdates (2-hour format): 2/23/86, 12/21/86.
Cast: Wayne Rogers (George Thrash), Mary Kay Place (Prissy Thrash), Kieu Chinh (Phoen Yann), Kathleen Sisk (Laura Thrash), Margot Pinvidic (Mandy), Susan Walden (Suanna), Blu Mankuma (Turner), Jade Chinn (Linn Yann), Diana Ung (Kiev Yann), Linda Wong (Yieng Yann), Jasmin Tam (Ngor Yann), Wilson Lo (Chhoueng Yann), Raymond Lau (Hing Yann), Terry David Mulligan (Zack Coley), Tom Heaton (Buddy Brannan), Don Davis (Realtor), Don MacKay (Dr. Fitzroy), Robert Broyles (Jim), Janet Wright (Woman Neighbor), Shawn Clements (Billy), Gary Hetherington (Bill Johnson), Meredith Woodward (Elinor Howes), Garrick Jang (Thai Soldier), Keeman Wong (Thai Sergeant), Pat Lee (Thai Officer).

A Cambodian family's attempt to flee the terror of the Khmer Rouge regime ends in failure when they are captured and put in a refugee camp. The Yanns are luckier than many other Cambodians, however, because an American family sponsors their escape to the United States.

Production Note:

• This episode was nominated for an Emmy Award for Outstanding Children's Program.

GNOME-MOBILE, THE
Airdates—Part 1: 10/29/78. Part 2: 11/05/78.
This 1967 theatrical release stars Walter Brennan, Matthew Garber, and Karen Dotrice in the story of two children who discover a band of gnomes living in an endangered forest.

GOLDEN DOG, THE
Airdate: 1/02/77.
Cast: Paul Brinegar (Jock), Alan Napier (Archie).

The ghost of Whirlin' Henry Thomas looks down at his former partners with sadness. At one time they were all prospectors together, but now the two remaining men must be taught a lesson. Both Archie and Jock will have to learn that their friendship is more valuable than gold before Whirlin' Henry can rest in peace.

GOLDEN HORSESHOE REVUE, THE
Airdates: 9/23/62, 6/09/63.
Cast: Annette Funicello, Gene Sheldon, Wally Boag, Betty Taylor, Ed Wynn.

The Disneyland theme park is the setting for this episode, and Walt dresses as a sheriff for this special celebration in honor of the 10,000th performance of Frontierland's Golden Horseshoe Revue. The invited guests are already there, and the show features numerous musical and comedy sketches.

Production Note:

- This episode was also released theatrically in the United States in 1964 and overseas in 1963.

GOOFING AROUND WITH DONALD DUCK
See: *A Square Peg in a Round Hole.*

GOOFY ADVENTURE STORY, THE
See: *The Adventure Story.*

GOOFY SPORTS STORY, THE   Airdates:
3/21/56, 5/23/56, 8/29/56, 7/31/59, 7/30/72.
Walt introduces the narrator, Spyros Olympopolus, to demonstrate how many of the ancient sports practiced in foreign countries have evolved into the games we enjoy today. Spyros illustrates this by using Goofy, who has tried almost every form of exercise at one time or another.

Production Notes:

- Footage from this episode was also used in the show *Superstar Goofy.*
- This episode was released theatrically overseas in 1964.

GOOFY SUCCESS STORY, THE   Airdates:
12/07/55, 4/08/60.
This episode highlights Goofy's rise to stardom. It starts with a look at Hollywood, where talent scouts hide everywhere, all looking for the next superstar. Sitting high in a theater balcony, Goofy starts to laugh at a Mickey Mouse cartoon and finds himself "discovered." After that, it's a quick trip down easy street for the owner of the world's most unusual laugh.

Production Note:

- Jack Bailey was the narrator for this episode, which was released theatrically overseas in 1959.

GOOFY TAKES A HOLIDAY
See: *Holiday for Henpecked Husbands.*

GOOFY'S CAVALCADE OF SPORTS
Airdates: 10/17/56, 2/06/57, 12/31/57.
The wide variety of sports enjoyed today is demonstrated by Goofy as he attempts to participate in a number of athletic activities. Walt explains that many of these sports were derived from our earlier needs to stay physically fit to fight wars and find food, and they still are used today to test human endurance.

Production Note:

- Footage from this episode was also used in the show *Superstar Goofy.*

GOOFY'S SALUTE TO FATHER
See: *A Salute to Father.*

GO WEST, YOUNG DOG   Airdate:
2/20/77.
Cast: Frank Keith (Everett Stacy), Charles Granata (George McBride), Dennis Dillon (Ernie McBride), Donald Harris (Old Ben).

Dorsey is a dog in the 1880s with an unusual lifestyle. He lives aboard a mail train and helps the postal workers by picking up misplaced mail. Dorsey also thinks of himself as a watchdog, which gets him in trouble when the McBride brothers try to rob the mail car. They toss him from the train and he finds himself lost in the desert without food or water.

GRAVEYARD OF SHIPS
This is Part 2 of *The Mooncussers.*

GREAT CAT FAMILY, THE   Airdates:
9/19/56, 3/13/57, 12/24/61.
Opinions about cats are often divided. Some people love them, some hate them. Many people just fear them, for cats have gained a reputation that makes superstitious people reluctant to cross their paths. This look at the history of cats begins with the story of their ancestors in Egypt over 4,000 years ago.

Production Note:

- Portions of the made-for-television animation were used in the episode *Halloween Hall o' Fame* in 1977.

GREAT LOCOMOTIVE CHASE, THE
This 1956 theatrical release first aired as *Andrews' Raiders*. It also aired as a special under the original title in 1976.

GREAT MOMENTS IN DISNEY ANIMATION
Airdates: 1/18/87, 8/16/87.
Cast: Carol Burnett.

This salute to Disney animation begins as host Carol Burnett explains that the *I've Got No Strings* segment from *Pinocchio* is one of her favorite animated moments. Clips from *Alice in Wonderland, Fantasia,* and several short subjects are just a few examples of the Disney magic. Carol also describes the process of combining animation and live action using segments from *Song of the South, Mary Poppins,* and *Tron* as illustration.

GRETA, THE MISFIT GREYHOUND
Airdates: 2/03/63, 7/07/68, 7/13/75.
Cast: Tacolo Chacartegui (Shepherd).
Greyhound racing is a sport enjoyed by many, particularly if they've bet on the winning dog. These racing dogs are high strung and must be kept muzzled to prevent them from attacking each other instead of the mechanical rabbit that circles the track. Greta is one such dog, but unlike the others, she doesn't care to chase mindlessly after a mechanical lure. All Greta wants is some affection and attention from her master.

Production Notes:

- This episode was released theatrically overseas in 1966.
- Photographer Larry Lansburgh attached a 16mm camera to the mechanical rabbit at the racetrack to provide a unique viewpoint of the pursuing dogs.

GREYFRIARS BOBBY
Airdates—Part 1: 3/29/64, 1/05/75. Part 2: 4/05/64, 1/12/75.
This 1961 theatrical release stars Donald Crisp, Laurence Naismith, and Alex Mackenzie in the story of a Skye terrier who develops an undying devotion to his master.

GRISWOLD MURDER, THE
Airdates: 2/20/59, 6/12/59.
Cast: Robert Loggia (Elfego Baca), James Dunn (J. Henry Newman), Jay C. Flippen (Jeff Griswold), Patrick Knowles (Cyril Cunningham), Audrey Dalton (Mrs. Cyril Cunningham), Phillip Terry (Steve Shannon), Carl Benton Reid (Judge), Grant Withers (Sheriff), R.G. Armstrong (Jack O'Neil), Herbert Anderson (Charles Lowell Smith), Robert Kline (Lonny Griswold), Edward Colmans (Fernando Bernal), Annette Funicello (Chucita Bernal).
Chapter 6 in the story of Elfego Baca starts as Cyril Cunningham, a wealthy rancher, is accused of murdering another rancher, Drew Griswold. Local gossip has it that Griswold and Mrs. Cunningham were having an affair, and the authorities theorize that Cunningham killed the other man out of jealousy. Elfego believes the rancher is innocent and agrees to take his case, even though he must face his former law partner, who has just become the new district attorney.

Production Note:

- This episode was combined with *Attorney at Law* and released theatrically overseas in 1962 as *Six Gun Law.*

GUS
Airdates (2-hour format): 9/18/77. In later seasons the show was presented in two parts—Part 1: 10/21/79, 9/11/82. Part 2: 10/28/79, 9/18/82.
This 1976 theatrical release stars Edward Asner, Don Knotts, Gary Grimes, and Tim Conway in the story of a football team that seems doomed to another season without a win until they discover a mule that can kick field goals.

GUS TOMLIN IS DEAD
Airdates: 3/25/60, 9/16/60.
Cast: Robert Loggia (Elfego Baca), Alan Hale, Jr. (Bill Minters), Coleen Gray (Peggy Minters), Brian Corcoran (Ross Minters), Paul Birch (Sheriff Jim Wilson), Eddy Waller (Link Duffries), Richard Garland (Ben Palmer), Raymond Greenleaf (Judge Thomas Raine), Byron Foulger (Paul Sibley), Mickey Simpson.
Years ago a gunfighter named Gus Tomlin killed a man in Santa Fe, then fled town, never to be found. Interest in the case is reawakened when a prospector returns from a trip to Granite, a nearby small town, with the claim that he saw Tomlin there. The dead man's father wants to lead a posse there to hang Tomlin, but the sheriff convinces the angry townspeople to let Elfego bring him back for trial.

HACKSAW
Airdates—Part 1: 9/26/71, 7/09/72. Part 2: 10/03/71, 7/16/72.
Cast: Tab Hunter (Tim Andrews), Victor Millan (Cascade Joe), Ray Teal (The Rancher), Russ McCubbin (Dusty Trent), George Barrows (Olney Curtis), Christine Austin (Leona), John Prendergast (The Stranger), Susan Bracken (Sue Curtis).
Tim Andrews, a Canadian cowboy, agrees to take Olney Curtis and his daughter Susan on a fishing trip in the wilds of the Canadian Rockies. The trip becomes a horse roundup after Susan spots a wild stallion named Hacksaw and decides to capture him. Their initial attempt is foiled by a grizzly bear, which also scares Tim's horse into bolting.

HALLOWEEN HALL O' FAME   Airdate: 10/30/77.

Cast: *Jonathan Winters (The Watchman and Jack O'Lantern), Bing Crosby (Relating the Story of Ichabod Crane).*

It's Halloween Eve at the Disney Studios and a lonely watchman and his guard dog patrol the dark and deserted hallways. Entering a room full of props, the watchman begins to play-act several roles with them, only to have one of the props come to life. It's a jack-o'-lantern inside a crystal ball, and it argues with him about the history and true meaning of Halloween, using clips from several cartoons to prove its points.

HAMAD AND THE PIRATES   Airdates— Part 1: 3/07/71. Part 2: 3/14/71.

Cast: *Khalid Marshad (Hamad), Abdullah Masoud (Jumah), Khalifah Shaheen (Pirate Captain), Mubarak Buzaid (First Mate), Miriam Ahmed (Nurah), Slaiman Bin Salem (Ibrahim), Hilal Bin Rashid (Pearl Captain), Yousef Al Gaoud (Caretaker), Isa Jowder (Archaeologist), Abdullah Musalem (Inspector), Mansour Bin Mariyah (Abu Khamis), Officers and Men of HMS Yarnton, Courtesy of the Royal Navy.*

Hamad is an orphaned 12-year-old pearl diver on a small boat in the Persian Gulf whose life takes on new excitement when a sudden violent storm tosses him overboard. He's rescued by pirates who specialize in stealing artifacts, and they warn him not to interfere with their activities.

Production Notes:

- *Hamad and the Pirates* was originally intended to be a one-hour show entitled *The Boy from Bahrain*, but producer Roy E. Disney decided to expand it after viewing the initial results. This required a shooting schedule that lasted almost two years.
- This show was broadcast in two parts, *The Phantom Dhow* and *The Island of the Three Palms.*

HANG YOUR HAT ON THE WIND

Airdates: 11/29/70, 7/25/71.
This 1969 theatrical release stars Ric Natoli in the story of an American Indian boy who finds a valuable thoroughbred wandering in the desert.

HANS BRINKER OR THE SILVER SKATES

Airdates—Part 1: 1/07/62, 1/18/65. Part 2: 1/14/62, 4/25/65.

Cast: *Rony Zeander (Hans Brinker), Carin Rossby (Gretel Brinker), Gunilla Jelf (Hilda van Gleck), Erik Strandmark (Raff Brinker), Inga Landgre (Metje Brinker), Lennart Klefbom (Ludwig Schimmel), Claes-Håkan Westergren (Peter Bouman), Gunnar Sjoberg (Dr. Boekman), Ulf Palme (Mynheer van Gleck), Lauritz Falk (Kaps Bouman), Alf Kjellin (Frans Ruisdael).*

Set years ago in the rustic Dutch countryside near the Zuider Zee, this is the story of a young boy's determination to win a race and what that victory means to his family. The Brinker family is a poor but happy one. Raff, the father, works as a fisherman, but he hopes that his son, Hans, will aspire to something better. To that end, he has been slowly saving money for Hans's education. Raff's plans are ruined when he suffers a head injury and brain damage.

Production Notes:

- Filming took place near the scenic Dutch communities of Camperduin and Volendam, as well as at Rembrandt's home in Amsterdam. The filming of the winter scenes for the skating races took place in Sweden.
- *Hans Brinker* was released theatrically overseas.

HAPPY BIRTHDAY DONALD DUCK

See: *At Home with Donald Duck.*

HELP WANTED: KIDS   Airdates (2-hour format): 2/02/86, 6/07/87.

Cast: *Cindy Williams (Lisa Burke), Bill Hudson (Tom Burke), Chad Allen (Coop), Hillary Wolf (Mickey a.k.a. "Rat"), John Dehner (Cyrus Ludlum), Joel Brooks (Lee Sherbourne), Miriam Flynn (Helen Sherbourne), Billie Bird (Bea Ludlum), Carol Morley, Ebbe Roe Smith (Jesse Clay), Cecily Thompson, Joseph Chapman, Kenneth Kimmins, Hap Lawrence, Toni Attell (Welfare Worker), Arlene Banas (Lady with Clipboard), Bever-Leigh Banfield (Berri), Owen Bush (Attendant), Jack Galvin Clark (Man), Kellie Martin (Linda), Rick Overton (Photographer), Dorothy Patterson (Woman Passenger), Nicky Rose (Little Girl), Kathy Wagner (Tammy), Joan Welles (Receptionist), Fred D. Scott (Elderly Man), George Fisher (Bus Driver), Dion Zamora (Arnold).*

When Tom and Lisa Burke both lose their jobs in New York City, the only job Tom can find is in Arizona. They learn that Tom's boss expects his employees to be good parents, so the childless Burkes pay two youths to act as their children.

Production Note:

- This made-for-television movie inspired The Disney Channel's series *Just Like Family*, also starring Williams and Hudson as Lisa and Tom Burke.

HERBIE GOES BANANAS Airdates (2-hour format): 1/11/87, 1/22/89.
This 1980 theatrical release, the fourth in the *Love Bug* series, stars Cloris Leachman, Charles Martin Smith, Stephan W. Burns, Joaquin Garay III, and Harvey Korman in the story of Herbie's adventures in Latin America.

HERBIE RIDES AGAIN Airdates—Part 1: 10/10/81. Part 2: 10/17/81. For the 1985–86 season the show was broadcast in a 2-hour format: 7/27/86.
This 1974 theatrical release, a sequel to the 1969 hit *The Love Bug*, stars Helen Hayes, Ken Berry, Stefanie Powers, and Keenan Wynn as Herbie, the plucky Volkswagen, comes between an evil real estate developer and his plans to evict a kindly old woman from her home.

HERO IN THE FAMILY Airdates (2-hour format): 9/28/86, 7/19/87.
Cast: Christopher Collet (Benjamin Reed), Cliff De Young (Digger Reed), Annabeth Gish (Mrs. Reed), Darleen Carr (Jessie), Keith Dorman (Ralph), David Wohl (Dr. Loudon), Michael (Orville Starbright, the Chimp), M. Emmet Walsh (General Presser), Jay Brazeau (Zoo Guard), Bernard Cuffling (Galleria Manager), Don Davis (Capcom), Bill Dow (NASA Technician), Deryl Hayes (Security Man), Max Margolin (Student Council President), Alicia Michelle (Buffy), Stephen Miller (Security Man), Robin Mossley (Mr. Ozone Driver), Gordon McIntosh (Sonny Biker), William Nunn (Express Driver), Betty Phillips (Chairwoman), Andrew Rhodes (NASA Technician), Howard Storey (Guard at Gate), Raimund Stamm (Dempsey).
Benjamin Reed has a conflict with his dad, which is also causing him problems with his love life. His father, Digger Reed, is a famous astronaut, and the two have very different views on Benjamin's future. Things change when an accident in space causes Digger to trade brains with a chimpanzee.

HIGH FLYING SPY, THE Airdates—Part 1: 10/22/72, 6/05/77. Part 2: 10/29/72, 6/12/77. Part 3: 11/05/72, 6/19/77.
Cast: Stuart Whitman (Prof. Thaddeus Lowe), Darren McGavin (John Jay Forrest), Vincent Van Patten (Davey Stevens), Andrew Prine (Lieutenant Thomas), Shug Fisher (Captain Rob), Jim Davis (Colonel Porter), Jeff Corey (General McCellan), Roger Perry (Major Alfred Dark), Robert Pine (Lieutenant Carson), Larry D. Mann (Sheriff), John Smith (Reb Aeronaut), Don Carter (Johnny), Roy Roberts (James Whitfield), Arthur Space (Grandpa Clemens), John Zaremba (Balloon Judge), Jay Ripley (Confederate Soldier), John Flinn (Lieutenant Johnson), Voltaire Perkins (Chief Telegraph Operator), John Harper (Zeke), Roger Torrey (Burley Sergeant), Bryan O'Byrne (Telegraph Operator), William Bryant (General Magruder), Ken Del Conte (Third Reporter), Ken Swofford (Patrol Officer), Tom Lester (Photographer), Tom Lester (Traveling Photographer), Dick Farnsworth (Farmer), Marc Hannibal (Matthew).
Two rival aeronauts are drawn into the Civil War when the army decides to use balloons as observation posts.

HIGHWAY TO TROUBLE Airdate: 3/13/59.
When Huey, Dewey, and Louie identify the capital of California as Disneyland, a voice tells Donald he is a failure as the boys' teacher. In an effort to awaken their interest in geography, Donald Duck takes them on a trip across the country. They leave California and decide to stay overnight in Washington. Unfortunately, Donald has a series of troubles as seen in various clips from Donald Duck cartoons.

HIS MAJESTY KING OF THE BEASTS
Airdates: 11/07/58, 11/11/62.
Released theatrically in 1955 as the *True-Life Adventure* film *The African Lion*, this is the story of the animal that has become known as the king of the jungle.

HOG WILD Airdates—Part 1: 1/20/74, 8/06/78. Part 2: 1/27/74, 8/13/78.
Cast: John Ericson (Morris Melborne), Diana Muldaur (Martha Melborne), Clay O'Brien (Sterling Melborne), Nicholas Beauvy (Hank), Kim Richards (Sara Melborne), Shug Fisher (Ropejon), Walter Barnes (Tobias), Denver Pyle (Dr. Larson), Fran Ryan (Flora), Sam Edwards (Farmer), Don Knight (Red), Ted Gehring (Jud), William Lucking (Vern).

Morris Melborne is tired of city life in the 1880s, so he moves to Idaho to open a pig ranch and start life anew. His dreams are shattered when a large pig attacks and cripples him, requiring an expensive operation so he can walk again. Morris rejects the operation, deciding instead that the family must spend the money to keep the ranch running. He tells his son, Sterling, that he counts on him to take care of the ranch as well as his mother and sister.

HOLIDAY FOR HENPECKED HUSBANDS
Airdates: 11/26/61, 8/05/62, 12/05/76 (*Goofy Takes a Holiday*), 5/11/80 (*Goofy Takes a Holiday*), 7/05/81 (*Goofy Takes a Holiday*).
Like many other average men, Goofy would prefer to be out hitting golf balls rather than beating a rug, but it seems sometimes that life conspires against him. Forced to work instead of play, with the help of the "Spirit of Imagination," Goofy daydreams of a more adventurous life.

When his wife has given up on getting any work out of Goofy, she tells him he might as well go play golf instead. But by the time Goofy gets to the golf course, it's too dark to play.

HOLIDAY TIME AT DISNEYLAND   Airdate: 12/23/62.
Christmas time at Disneyland finds snow falling in front of Sleeping Beauty Castle. Walt attributes the unusual weather to movie magic, but Santa Claus complains it won't be good for the special holiday parade. An obliging Walt tells Tinker Bell to turn off the special effects and it stops snowing. Walt then offers the viewers a look at the holiday festivities and past entertainment events.

Production Note:

- Celebrities seen in this show include Prime Minister Nehru of India, the king and queen of Nepal, President Eisenhower, vice president Nixon, Prince Bernhard of the Netherlands, the shah and empress of Iran, Annette Funicello, and Roberta Shore.

HOLSTER FULL OF LAW, A   Airdates: 2/05/61, 7/16/61.
Cast: *Tom Tryon (Texas John Slaughter), Betty Lynn (Viola Slaughter), R.G. Armstrong (Billy Soto), Jim Beck (Burt Alvord), Robert Burton (Mayor Clum), Brian Corcoran (Willie Slaughter), Ross Martin (Cesario Lucero),*

Annette Gorman (Addie Slaughter), John Zaremba (Reverend).

Part 14 of *The Tales of Texas John Slaughter* involves an old enemy of John's, a rustler named Billy Soto. When John discovers forty head of his cattle missing, his first instinct is to find Soto and settle the debt himself. Viola argues that this is a bad role model for their son, and John agrees to ask the sheriff to handle the problem instead.

Production Note:

- *A Holster Full of Law* was combined with the episodes *Frank Clell's in Town* and *Trip to Tucson* and released theatrically overseas in 1966.

HORSE IN THE GREY FLANNEL SUIT, THE
Airdates—Part 1: 11/14/71, 3/20/77. Part 2: 11/21/71, 3/27/77.
This 1968 theatrical release stars Dean Jones, Diane Baker, and Ellen Janov in the story of an advertising executive who combines business and pleasure when he buys a champion jumping horse and uses it in a new ad campaign.

HORSE OF THE WEST, THE   Airdates: 12/11/57, 6/04/58, 5/26/63, 6/15/69.
Cast: *Rex Allen (Narrator), Sammy Fancher (Elena Vasquez), George Masek (The Cowboy), Jimmy Williams (The Trainer), Henny Penny Peake, the Quarter Horse Champion (The Bay Lady).*
This is the story of The Bay Lady, a quarter horse born on Rex Allen's ranch. The Bay Lady becomes the favorite filly of Elena Vasquez until the young horse is mistakenly shipped off the ranch to be sold at auction.

Production Note:

- Henny Penny Peake, the equestrian star of this show, was ranked as the #1 reined horse in the United States in 1964.

HORSES FOR GREENE   Airdates: 1/15/61, 6/18/61.
Cast: *Leslie Nielsen (Gen. Francis Marion), Barbara Eiler (Mary Videaux), Arthur Hunnicutt (Ezra Selby), Ralph Clanton (Captain Ball), J. Pat O'Malley (Sergeant O'Reilly), Jordan Whitfield (Oscar), Slim Pickens (Plunkett), James Seay (Captain Richardson), Charles Briggs (Folger).*
The eighth and final episode of *The Swamp Fox* finds Captain Richardson trying to instill some discipline in Marion's volunteer brigades. Marion stops the training long

enough to lead a daring raid to capture some much needed horses.

HORSE WITH THE FLYING TAIL, THE
Airdates: 3/10/63, 3/24/68, 8/21/77.
Cast: Bill Steincross (Captain of Team), Nautical (Himself).

The show begins at a stylish horse show, and a flashback tells the unlikely history of an award-winning horse. A Palomino is given the nickname Injun Joe after several raids for food on an American Indian village. Finally caught and broken for riding, Injun Joe spends his next few years working on a cattle ranch. There, he shows a natural talent for jumping fences, which leads to his purchase by members of the U.S. Equestrian team. Renamed Nautical, he wins a prestigious competition in Europe.

Production Notes:

- Based on a true story, this episode featured the coach of the U.S. equestrian team, Bertalan de Nemethy, and riders Hugh Wiley, Frank Shapow, and George Morris as themselves.
- Footage of the Queen Mother and Princess Margaret was included during the awards ceremony following the final competition.
- This 1960 theatrical release won an Academy Award for Best Short Subject.

HORSE WITHOUT A HEAD, THE
Airdates—Part 1: 9/29/63, 6/14/64, 7/23/67. Part 2: 10/06/63, 6/21/64, 7/30/67.
Cast: Jean Pierre Aumont (Inspector Sinet), Herbert Lom (Schiapa), Leo McKern (Roublot), Pamela Franklin (Marion), Vincent Winter (Fernand), Lee Montague (Mallart), Denis Gilmore (Tatave), Sean Keir (Bon-Bon), Loretta Parry (Melie), Michael Gwynn (Gendarme), Peter Butterworth (Zigon), Peter Vaughan (Police Sergeant), Jack Rodney (Pepe), Maxwell Shaw (Cesar), Jenny Laird (Madame Fabert), Maureen Pryor (Madam Douin), Robert Brown (Douin), Harold Goldblatt (Blache), John Bennett.

This story is presented in two parts, *The 100,000,000 Franc Train Robbery* and *The Key to the Cache.* When the famed Dijon-Paris mail train is robbed, the thieves hide the money inside an abandoned toy factory. The key to the factory falls into the hands of local children, who end up in a battle with the crooks for control of the factory.

Production Notes:

- The setting of this episode, a small French town named Montlhery, was actually a set built outside London. Press releases called the result of an 8-week construction project "the largest movie set Britain has ever seen."
- *The Horse without a Head* was released theatrically overseas in 1961, and was also serialized in the second season of *The New Mickey Mouse Club.*

HORSEMASTERS, THE
Airdates—Part 1: 10/01/61, 7/08/62, 6/04/67. Part 2: 10/08/61, 7/15/62, 6/11/67.
Cast: Annette Funicello (Dinah Wilcox), Tommy Kirk (Danny Grant), Janet Munro (Janet Hale), Tony Britton (Major Brooke), John Fraser (David Lawson), Donald Pleasence (Pinski), Harry Lockart (Vincenzo Lalli), Colin Gordon (Mr. Ffolliott), Anthony Nicholls (Hardy Cole), Jean Marsh (Andrienne), Lisa Mardon (Ingrid), Penelope Horner (Penny), Millicent Martin (Joan).

This two-part *(Follow Your Heart* and *Tally Ho)* story is set at England's Vallywood Riding School, a prestigious academy that specializes in training future instructors. In Part 1, Danny Grant prevents Dinah Wilcox from quitting when he helps her get over her fear of jumping. In Part 2, students help instructor Janet Hale keep her horse when she must auction it after winning a race.

Production Notes:

- *The Horsemasters* was released theatrically overseas in 1961.
- This was the first Disney film project for the Sherman brothers, who went on to write many of the Studio's musical scores.

HOUND THAT THOUGHT HE WAS A RACCOON, THE
Airdates: 9/20/64, 4/05/70, 10/09/77.
This 1960 theatrical release is the story of an abandoned puppy who is adopted by a raccoon.

HOW THE WEST WAS LOST
Airdates: 9/24/67, 7/15/73.
The vivid history of America's Old West is told through a series of cartoons by one of Donald Duck's ancestors, who's known as the "Oldtimer." He complains that modern civilization has ruined the West, replacing scenic beauty with concrete monstrosities.

This downtrend began when bands of settlers formed wagon trains and headed West, fighting nature and the Indians at every step.

HOW TO RELAX   Airdates: 11/27/57, 9/03/58, 7/07/63.

Our eternal desire to relax is illustrated by Goofy, who is first seen as a cave dweller making an unusual discovery—his thumb. Making this discovery led to an unfortunate invention called work. Ever since work was discovered, humans have attempted to discover a method of ensuring adequate leisure time.

Production Note:

- While vacationing in Hawaii, Goofy receives an inter-office memo telling him he has been fired. As an inside joke, it was marked as being copied to longtime Disney staffer Harry Tytle, who worked on this show and numerous others.

HUNTER AND THE ROCK STAR, THE

See: *Sultan and the Rock Star.*

HUNTING INSTINCT, THE   Airdate: 10/22/61.

Prof. Ludwig Von Drake is the guest host for this episode, for Walt feels this noted expert on everything can help shed some light on why humans are driven to hunt. The main thing Von Drake hunts for is his glasses. The professor has brought his assistant, Herman, the Bootle Beetle, to help demonstrate the finer points of hunting.

Production Notes:

- *The Hunting Instinct* was released theatrically overseas in 1962.
- Sequences from this episode were used in *Man's Hunting Instinct* (see description under that title).

HURRICANE HANNAH   Airdates: 12/16/62, 7/28/63.

Cast (playing themselves): Gordon E. Dunn (Chief District Meteorologist, Miami Weather Bureau), Cmdr. Joshua Langfur, U.S.N. (Airman), Lt. John Lincoln, U.S.N. (Meteorologist on Plane), Marilyn Lincoln (Airman's Wife), Allan Batham (Sailor), Michael Batham (Sailor).

When a weather satellite on a routine orbit spots an unusual cloud pattern in the Atlantic, it starts a far-ranging series of events on the ground. Gordon Dunn is the meteorologist in charge of the Hurricane Center in Miami, and he sends a specially equipped plane to investigate the storm. The plane radios back some ominous news: the storm is growing rapidly. Soon Hurricane Hannah forces the entire Caribbean into alert, but a small boat misses the warnings.

Production Note:

- This show aired on 11/1/75 with *The Absent-Minded Professor* as part of the *NBC All-Disney Saturday Night at the Movies* series of specials.

I CAPTURED THE KING OF THE LEPRECHAUNS   Airdates: 5/29/59, 8/28/59.

Cast: Pat O'Brien (Himself), Albert Sharpe (Darby O'Gill), Janet Munro (Katie O'Gill), Sean Connery (Michael McBride), Jimmy O'Dea (King Brian), Kieron Moore (Pony Sugrue), Jack MacGowran (Phadrig Oge), Denis O'Dea (Father Murphy), Farrell Pelly (Paddy Scanlon), J. G. Devlin (Tom Kerrigan), Nora O'Mahony (Molly Malloy), James Mageean (Roderic Rue, the Librarian).

This episode is a behind-the-scenes look at the filming of *Darby O'Gill and the Little People.* Walt has decided to make a movie about Ireland and leprechauns, and he visits actor Pat O'Brien to ask for advice on how to proceed. The first thing O'Brien tells him is that only Irishmen should approach the "Little People," but Walt is sure there won't be any problems, for he's half-Irish himself. Pat convinces Walt that the movie will only be successful if it features a live leprechaun.

Production Notes:

- The footage from *Darby O'Gill and the Little People* was directed by Robert Stevenson, with Harry Keller directing the footage filmed specifically for this episode.
- Sean Connery, who co-starred in the film, later achieved fame as James Bond, Agent 007.

IDA, THE OFFBEAT EAGLE   Airdates: 1/10/65, 7/18/65, 6/24/73.

Cast: Clifton E. Carver (Uncle Billy Kipp).

The story begins as a naturalist tags a young golden eagle for a wildlife survey. The metal band is stamped "I.D.A.," which stands for the Idaho Department of Agriculture. Soon after, the eagle loses a fight with a snake and falls into the turbulent waters of the Snake River, where she barely manages to survive a wild ride on a log. The bird finally manages to get aloft but crashes into the chimney of a cabin owned by a hermit named Uncle Billy.

I-MAN   Airdates (2-hour format): 4/06/86, 6/14/87, 7/02/89.

Cast: Scott Bakula *(Jeffrey Wilder)*, Ellen Bry *(Karen McCorder)*, Joey Cramer *(Eric Wilder)*, John Bloom *(Harry)*, Herschel Bernardi *(Bogosian)*, John Anderson *(Oliver Holbrook)*, Dale Wilson *(Rudy)*, Cindy Higgins *(Allison Holbrook)*, Charles Siegel *(Cabbie)*, Joseph Golland *(Meek Man)*, Ian Tracey *(Robbery Youth)*, Ted Stidder *(Dr. Allen)*, George Josef *(Guide Guard)*, Campbell Lane *(General)*, Terry Moore *(Distinguished Man)*, Lillian Carlson *(E.R. Nurse)*, Roger Allford *(ISA Agent #1)*, Anthony Harrison *(Curtain Guard)*, Don Davis *(Surgeon)*, Rebecca Bush *(Susan)*, Garwin Sanford *(Van Driver)*, Doug Tuck *(Paramedic)*, Brian Arnold *(Newscaster)*, Raimund Stamm *(Norman)*, Jane MacDougall *(Station Nurse)*, Nicholas von Zill *(Tardy Guard)*, Rob Morton *(Man on Barge)*, Tatoo *(Nolan, the Dog)*.

After a space shuttle retrieves a probe that holds a sample of another planet's atmosphere, cab driver Jeffrey Wilder is exposed to the gas when a NASA van crashes and he saves the driver. The van explodes and Jeffrey receives third-degree burns over 60 percent of his body, but somehow he recovers almost instantaneously. Realizing that he can't be killed, the government steps in and recruits Jeffrey as a secret agent.

Production Note:

• This was a pilot for a proposed series.

IN SEARCH OF THE CASTAWAYS
Airdates—Part 1: 10/01/78. Part 2: 10/08/78.
This 1962 theatrical release stars Hayley Mills and Maurice Chevalier in the story of a teenage girl who undertakes a risky trip to uncharted territory to rescue her missing father from cannibals.

IN SHAPE WITH VON DRAKE   Airdates: 3/22/64, 8/09/64, 7/26/70.
Prof. Ludwig Von Drake returns for another of his unique treatments of a favorite subject, sports. Von Drake illustrates his points with a series of Goofy cartoons.

IN THE LAND OF THE DESERT WHALES
This is Part 2 of *Three without Fear.*

INCREDIBLE JOURNEY, THE   Airdate (90-minute format): 10/23/77.
This 1963 theatrical release features two dogs and a cat who overcome tremendous obstacles to return home after being stranded hundreds of miles away. The story was remade by Disney as *Homeward Bound: The Incredible Journey* in 1993, with the animal stars "thinking aloud" via voice-overs.

INKY, THE CROW   Airdates: 12/07/69, 7/19/70, 6/29/75.
Cast: Deborah Bainbridge *(Carol Lee)*, Margo Lungreen *(Mrs. Lee)*, Willard Granger *(John Lee)*, Rowan Pease *(Mr. Fletcher)*.

Carol Lee is a 13-year-old who befriends a crow covered with yellow paint. She takes him home to clean him up and decides to keep him for a pet, not realizing that the crow has a mischievous nature.

INSIDE DONALD DUCK   Airdates: 11/05/61, 6/24/62, 6/20/65.
Walt has had to call Prof. Ludwig Von Drake for help, for Donald Duck has apparently cracked up. It seems that the stresses of modern living were too much for the star, and professional care is required. Von Drake rushes in and attempts to hypnotize Walt, who must set him straight as to who the real patient is.

INSIDE OUTER SPACE   Airdates: 2/10/63, 8/18/63.
Ludwig Von Drake is the guest host for this look at outer space, which begins with a brief history of our earlier beliefs and superstitions about what lies beyond Earth's atmosphere. People once feared the stars, thinking they were pieces broken off the moon. Later on, they started to study the skies, leading to conclusions that the earth was the center of the universe and was circled by the sun and other planets. Von Drake also takes a look at the moon and space exploration.

Production Note:

• This episode included footage from the short subjects *Mars and Beyond* and *Man in Space* as well as the television episode *Man and the Moon.*

ISLAND OF THE THREE PALMS, THE
This is Part 2 of *Hamad and the Pirates.*

IT'S TOUGH TO BE A BIRD   Airdates: 12/13/70, 6/20/71, 8/28/77.

Cast: Ruth Buzzi.

This is an extended version of the 1969 theatrical release that won an Academy Award for Best Cartoon Subject. The central character is M.C. Bird, who arrives amid a flurry of gunfire. He complains that humans are a constant problem for birds. He believes we both admire and hate birds for their ability to fly.

JIMINY CRICKET PRESENTS BONGO

Airdates: 9/28/55.

In an excerpt from the 1947 animated feature *Fun and Fancy Free*, Jiminy tells the story of Bongo, a lonely circus bear. Although he's the star of the show, poor Bongo is treated like a slave, kept locked away from the other animals. Longing for a more adventurous life, Bongo escapes to the forest. Quickly frightened by the night noises, he decides to head back to the circus. On his way, however, he meets and falls in love with a female bear named Lulubelle.

JOHNNY SHILOH   Airdates—Part 1: 1/20/63, 5/05/68. Part 2: 1/27/63, 5/12/68.

Cast: Brian Keith (Sgt. Gabe Trotter), Kevin Corcoran (Johnny Clem), Darryl Hickman (Lt. Jeremiah Sullivan), G.V. "Skip" Homeier (Captain MacPherson), Edward Platt (General Thomas), Regis Toomey (Mr. Clem), Rickie Sorensen (Rusty), Red Morgan (Sam), Eddie Hodges (Private Billy Jones), Hayden Rorke (Gen. Ulysses S. Grant), Dan Riss (General Wheeler), Don Harvey (Confederate Colonel), Henry Wills (Stark), Buck Taylor (Josh), Billy Williams (Blue Raider #1), Reg Parton (Blue Raider #2), Stacey Morgan (Blue Raider #3).

The year is 1861, and the Newark platoon of the Ohio Blue Raiders is practicing war games to prepare for battle in the Civil War. Their mascot, a 10-year-old drummer named Johnny Clem, achieves fame when he bravely sticks to his post during a fierce battle.

Production Notes:

- The real Johnny Clem died in 1937. He was a retired major general in the U.S. army.
- This show was released theatrically overseas in 1965.

JOHNNY TREMAIN   Airdates—Part 1: 11/21/58, 6/06/65, 2/02/75. Part 2: 12/05/58, 6/13/65, 2/09/75.

This 1957 theatrical release stars Hal Stalmaster, Luana Patten, Jeff York, and Sebastian Cabot in the story of a young silversmith who becomes involved with the Boston Tea Party, Paul Revere's ride, and the battle at Lexington. It was aired in two parts, *The Boston Tea Party* and *The Shot That Was Heard around the World*.

Production Note:

- This show incorporated footage from several short subjects that Disney purchased from Warner Bros.: *Give Me Liberty, Sons of Liberty,* and *Declaration of Independence.*

JOKER, THE AMIABLE OCELOT   Airdates: 12/11/66, 4/09/67, 5/07/72.

Cast: Robert Becker (Jim Benton), Jan McNabb (Nancy Conroy).

Jim Benton salvages an old car he finds in the desert, not realizing it contains an unexpected guest, for the car is the home of an ocelot and her kittens. One of the youngsters is trapped in the car when Jim tows it to his garage, where the cat frees itself and becomes friends with Jim and his other pets.

JOURNEY OF NATTY GANN, THE

Airdate—Part 1: 10/04/87. Part 2: 10/11/87.

This 1985 theatrical releases stars Meredith Salenger and John Cusack in the story of a teenage girl who undertakes a perilous journey, accompanied by her pet wolf, to find her father. It also aired as a special on 9/03/88.

JOURNEY TO THE VALLEY OF THE EMU, THE   Airdate: 1/22/78.

Cast: Victor Palmer (Wadjiri).

The Australian outback is the setting for this story of a dingo pup that loses its mother when the pair is discovered by cattle ranchers, who believe the wild dogs are killing their herds. The young dingo is befriended by an Aborigine boy named Wadjiri who is on a quest to prove he is an adult.

JUNGLE CAT, THE   Airdates: 4/12/64, 4/21/68, 6/02/74, 5/21/78.

Released theatrically in 1960 as a *True-Life Adventure*, this featurette studies the life of a family of jaguars.

JUSTIN CASE   Airdate (90-minute format): 5/15/88 (with *Captain Eo Backstage* in a 2-hour format).

Cast: George Carlin (Justin Case), Molly Hagan (Jennifer Spalding), Timothy Stack (Officer Swan), Kevin McClarnon (Officer Rush), Douglas Sills (David Porter), Gordon

Jump (Sheldon Wannamaker), Paul Sand (Cab Driver), Valerie Wildman (Woman in Black), Todd Susman (Aaron Slinker), Ron McCary (Simon Fresca), Philippe Denham (Paul Arkin), Richard McGonagle (Richard Weintraub), Jay Thomas (Delivery Man), Kenneth Tigar (Motel Manager), Kay Perry (Lucille Marposian), John Lavachielli (Cop), Dotty Colorso (Leggy), Reed McCants (Choreographer), Joe Mays (John Attaway), Lily Mariye (Commentator), Andrew Nadell (Newscaster), Nina Mann (Mona Fresca), Jerry Martin (Police Photographer), Stuart Tanney (Sign Painter).

When Jennifer Spalding applies for a job as a receptionist, she finds a body on the office floor and is very surprised to see the same man standing there next to her. The man, Justin Case, is a private detective. He tells Jennifer he has figured out that someone has killed him and he is a ghost. An astonished Jennifer says that she saw a woman in black leaving the scene, and Justin says he will hire her to help catch the killer, even if Justin is dead.

Production Note:

- *Justin Case* was the pilot for an unsold series.

JUSTIN MORGAN HAD A HORSE

Airdates—Part 1: 2/06/72, 8/12/79. Part 2: 2/13/72, 8/19/79.

Cast: Don Murray (Justin Morgan), Lana Wood (Kathleen), R.G. Armstrong (Squire Fisk), Gary Crosby (Bob Evans), Whit Bissell (Mr. Mays and Narrator), John Smith (Mr. Ames), E.W. Firestone (Matthew), James Hampton (Aaron), Mike Road (Dansforth), John Hubbard (Wellington).

Shortly after the Revolutionary War, Justin Morgan acquires a colt and decides to devote his time to developing its talents. He loses the horse to an unscrupulous businessman and tries to find a way to get him back.

Production Note:

- Work began on this story in 1965 but was halted following Walt Disney's death. Work was started again in 1971 when the Studio discovered its option on the story was about to expire.

K FOR KELLY

This is Part 1 of *Atta Girl, Kelly!*

KENTUCKY GUNSLICK   Airdates: 2/26/60, 7/29/60.

Cast: Tom Tryon (John Slaughter), Darryl Hickman (Ashley Carstairs), Betty Lynn (Viola Slaughter), Brian Corcoran (Willie Slaughter), Allan Lane (Johnny Ringo), Don Haggerty (Wes), Charles Maxwell (Ben Thompson), Jay Silverheels (Natchez), James Edwards (Batt), Pat Hogan (Geronimo), Annette Gorman (Addy Slaughter), Bob Steele (Ben), Gregory Walcott (Henderson).

Chapter 11 in *The Tales of Texas John Slaughter* opens as John leaves home for Tombstone to visit the land agent. His trip is interrupted by gunfire and he spots several men trying to kill a lone rider. He saves the man, only to find that it's Ashley Carstairs, a friend from Kentucky. Ashley is also a friend of Viola Slaughter, having once proposed to her before she accepted John's offer.

Production Note:

- Allan "Rocky" Lane, who played Johnny Ringo, starred in numerous "B" westerns and returned from semiretirement for this episode. He was also the voice of "Mr. Ed" in that television series. Bob Steele, another veteran cowboy star, had been working in westerns since the '20s at studios such as Republic and PRC.

KEY TO THE CACHE, THE

This is Part 2 of *The Horse without a Head.*

KIDNAPPED   Airdates—Part 1: 3/17/63, 3/21/71. Part 2: 3/24/63, 3/28/71. In later seasons the show aired in a 2-hour format: 7/10/82, 7/13/86.

This 1960 theatrical release stars James MacArthur and Peter Finch in a story of a young man who must reclaim his family estate from a corrupt uncle in 18th-century Scotland.

KIDS IS KIDS   Airdates: 12/10/61, 4/11/65, 4/06/75, 9/10/78 (*Donald Duck Quacks Up*), 1/06/80 (*Donald Duck Quacks Up*), 7/20/86 (*Donald Duck Quacks Up*).

Prof. Ludwig Von Drake hosts the show, sharing his vast knowledge on the subject of child psychology. He has been studying Donald Duck, whom he calls "Mister X" to protect his identity, and has decided to offer some advice on how to deal with Huey, Dewey, and Louie.

Production Notes:

- An edited version of this show was aired as *Mickey and Donald Kidding Around* and is described under that title.

- This show was released theatrically overseas in 1965.

KIDS WHO KNEW TOO MUCH, THE

Airdate (2-hour format): 3/09/80. For the 1982–83 season the show was presented in two parts—Part 1: 7/16/83. Part 2: 7/23/83.

Cast: Sharon Gless (Karen Goldner), Larry Cedar (Rizzo), Lloyd Haynes (Lt. Bill Boyd), David S. Sheiner (Frank Novack), Jared Martin (Sen. Nelson Dunning), Don Knight (Prescott), Rad Daly (Bert Hale), Dana Hill (Foxy Cooper), Christopher Holloway (T.J. Hoffman), Kevin King Cooper (Gus Jordan), Michael Dante (Ross), Jackie Coogan (Mr. Klein), Richard O'Brien (Commissioner Avery), John Milford (Green), Dave Shelley (Jack Gimble), Ben Aster (Premier Markov), Stanley Brock (Premier's Aide), Darrow Igus (Pinball), Erik Stern (Carl Davis), Mario Machado (TV Newscaster), H.B. Haggerty (Louie), Tom Lasswell (Bartender), Jackie Russell (Bert's Mom), Roger Mobley (Police Sergeant), Henry Slate (Studio Gate Guard), James E. Brodhead (Mayor of Los Angeles), William H. Bassett (Policeman), James Almanzar (TV Director), Ted Jordan (Ambulance Driver), Helen Boll (Jail Guard), Bill Quinn (Old Codger), Tony Ballen (Barker), Tracey Jackson (Receptionist).

Reporter Karen Goldner receives a mysterious message telling her to meet the caller at a nearby park if she wants a big story. When the caller is injected with a hypodermic needle, he staggers to a pond where 12-year-old Bert Hale is playing with a toy speedboat. Just before he dies, the stranger slips a note inside the boat, and two thugs try to steal it from Bert. Karen's arrival scares away the men, but they're determined to find the boy and get the message.

KILLER MOUNTAIN, THE

This is Part 2 of *Banner in the Sky.*

KILLERS FROM KANSAS Airdates: 1/09/59, 7/24/59.

Cast: Tom Tryon (John Slaughter), Lyle Bettger (Al Barko), Beverly Garland (Mrs. Barko), Norma Moore (Adeline Harris), Harry Carey, Jr. (Ben Jenkins), Judson Pratt (Captain Cooper), Don Haggerty (Outlaw #1), Christopher Dark (Reed), Robert Hoy (Jim), John Day (Clay), Lane Bradford (Outlaw #2), John Alderson (MacGregor).

John Slaughter and another Texas ranger are waiting in a bank to pick up the payroll when the Barko gang tries to rob it. The other ranger is killed and John is beaten unconscious, but before he passes out he pulls the hat off one of the thieves and discovers it's Mrs. Barko. The Barkos have robbed banks throughout the area, and in each robbery Mrs. Barko has slain bystanders in cold blood.

Production Notes:

- This episode was combined with *Showdown at Sandoval* and released theatrically overseas in 1961 as *Gunfight at Sandoval.*
- Veteran actor Slim Pickens had an unbilled role as a stagecoach driver.

KILLERS OF THE HIGH COUNTRY

Airdates: 10/16/59, 4/26/64, 5/20/76.

This episode tells the story of the mountain lions and their attempt to coexist with humans in their rapidly diminishing home in the Rocky Mountains. People are not their only worry, for as the story begins, two young cubs narrowly escape the claws of a Golden eagle. Chimbica and Tawny race for the safety of their den, where an angry mother helps drive away the hungry bird.

KILROY

There are four *Kilroy* stories, each of which is described separately. Because there were no individual titles, they are described as *Kilroy I* through *Kilroy IV.*

KILROY I Airdates: 3/14/65, 8/22/65, 5/11/69.

Cast: Celeste Holm (Mrs. Helen Fuller), Allyn Joslyn (Mr. Sam Fuller), Philip Abbott (Ed Barrett), Robert Emhardt (The Mayor), Bryan Russell (Billy Fuller), Warren Berlinger (Oscar Kilroy), Arthur Hunnicutt (Seth Turner), Marcus James (Pete), Mike Barton (Whitey), Dennis Rush (Freckles), Joie Russo (Porky).

Oscar Kilroy has just been discharged from the Marines, and he's decided to visit the parents of a buddy from the service. The Fullers live in the small town of Wilton Junction, and Kilroy decides he likes it there much better than his own home in Brooklyn. Although the Fullers are glad to help their son's friend, they soon begin to wonder if Kilroy is ever going to leave.

Production Note:

- Warren Berlinger won the title role following a screen test in which he competed against Pat Boone and John Gavin.

KILROY II   Airdates: 3/21/65, 8/29/65, 5/18/69.

Cast: Celeste Holm (Mrs. Helen Fuller), Allyn Joslyn (Mr. Sam Fuller), Philip Abbott (Ed Barrett), Robert Emhardt (The Mayor), Bryan Russell (Billy Fuller), Warren Berlinger (Oscar Kilroy), Cheryl Miller (Gladys Fuller), Tom Lowell (Harvey Wessup), Vaughn Taylor (Bank President), Marcus James (Pete), Mike Barton (Whitey), Dennis Rush (Freckles), Joie Russo (Porky).

Oscar Kilroy continues his stay in Wilton Junction and also his tendency to involve himself in other people's problems with unusual results. He decides to aid the boyfriend of Gladys Fuller, the daughter of his hosts, by helping him perfect a new burglar alarm system. Harvey, the would-be inventor, hopes that his system will earn him a promotion at his job in the local bank.

KILROY III   Airdates: 3/28/65, 9/05/65, 5/25/69.

Cast: Celeste Holm (Mrs. Helen Fuller), Allyn Joslyn (Mr. Sam Fuller), Philip Abbott (Ed Barrett), Robert Emhardt (The Mayor), Bryan Russell (Billy Fuller), Warren Berlinger (Oscar Kilroy), Chick Chandler (Ben Feeney), Philip Coolidge (Frank), Don Beddoe (Commissioner), Alvy Moore (Hal Dooley), Jess Kirkpatrick (Policeman).

Now that Kilroy has decided to stay in town, he needs a job. The mayor is pressured into finding the war hero a position, and the crafty politician decides to humiliate his sometime foe by making Kilroy a dogcatcher. The assignment is not very enjoyable for Kilroy, for he loves animals in general and dogs in particular.

KILROY IV   Airdates: 4/04/65, 9/12/65, 6/01/69.

Cast: Jack Oakie (Joe Kelsey), Joan Blondell (Rose Kelsey), Philip Abbott (Ed Barrett), Robert Emhardt (The Mayor), Bryan Russell (Billy Fuller), Warren Berlinger (Oscar Kilroy), Chick Chandler (Ben Feeney), Philip Coolidge (Frank), Alvy Moore (Hal Dooley), Maudie Prickett (Landlady), Elisabeth Fraser (Dog Buyer).

Reinstated as a dogcatcher, Kilroy puts an unusual plan into operation. Rather than taking his captures to the pound, he delivers them to Joe and Rose Kelsey, two retired vaudevillians who once had a famous dog act. The Kelseys agree to keep Kilroy's dogs at their remote farm and set to the task of training them to perform in a carnival act.

KING OF THE GRIZZLIES   Airdates—Part 1: 10/28/73. Part 2: 11/04/73. For the 1977–78 season the show aired in a 2-hour format: 9/25/77.

Moki is a Cree Indian working on a cattle ranch in the late 1880s. The ranch is owned by Colonel Pierson, who kills a grizzly and one of her cubs when the mother bear mauls one of his bulls. He misses a second cub, which escapes into the hills, and Moki decides to track down the bear.

Production Note:

- The grizzly bear that appeared in this episode stood 10 feet tall. Filming was halted when his coat began to thin during the warm summer weather, and the production shut down until the next year so his fur could regrow to match the scenes already shot.

KIT CARSON AND THE MOUNTAIN MEN   Airdates—Part 1: 1/09/77. Part 2: 1/16/77.

Cast: Christopher Connelly (Kit Carson), Robert Reed (Capt. John C. Fremont), Gary Lockwood (Bret Haskell), Ike Eisenmann (Randy Benton), Emile Genest (Basil LeJeunesse), Richard Jaeckel (Ed Kern), Val de Vargas (Tibor), Joaquin Martinez (Renni), Nick Ramus (Tioga), Ruben Moreno (Martinez), Gregg Palmer (Jim Bridger), Dub Taylor (Stableman), Geoff Parks (Jud), John Flinn (Toby), Rodolfo Hoyos (General Armijo), James Almanzar (Fur Trader).

A hunting party led by Kit Carson heads into the Green River Valley after a long winter of trapping. Besides Carson, the group consists of Basil LeJeunesse and two Delaware Indians, Renni and Tioga. A shooting match is being held in the valley, and the ten best marksmen will be able to join Capt. John Fremont on a survey party heading west to California.

Production Note:

- This fictitious adventure is based on the expeditions of John C. Fremont and Kit Carson.

LAND OF ENEMIES, THE   Airdates: 2/26/58, 7/02/58.

Cast: Jerome Courtland (Andy Burnett), Jeff York (Joe Crane), Andrew Duggan (Jack Kelly), Slim Pickens (Old Bill Williams), Iron Eyes Cody (Mad Wolf), Abel Fernandez (Kiasak), John War Eagle (Matosuki).

In the fourth installment of *The Saga of Andy Burnett,* Andy and his friends continue their journey to Taos, New Mexico. The experienced travelers among them are nervous, for they know they're now in Indian territory. Their fears prove to be well founded when they are taken prisoner by a band of Indians.

LAST ELECTRIC KNIGHT, THE Airdates: 2/16/86, 4/02/89.

Cast: Gil Gerard (Detective Sergeant Jake Rizzo), Ernie Reyes, Jr. (Ernie), Keye Luke (Mr. Lee), Nancy Stafford (Patricia Blake), Jason Hervey (Bobby), Clarence Landry (Old Man), Anthony Ponzini (Detective Kelly), Robert Mesa (Louie), Paco Vela (Fredo), Bruce Reed (Chichi), Joseph D'Angerio (Mark), Arthur Adams (Sergeant Cole), Don Cheadle (Cholo), Phil Diskin (Carter), Randy Polk (Chopper), Jo De Winter (Mrs. Niedermayer).

A young martial arts expert named Ernie claims to have unusual powers. He is put to the test when he has to save the life of his new foster father, detective Jake Rizzo.

Production Note:

- This was the pilot for the series *Sidekicks.* First aired as part of the anthology series, it was also repeated on 9/19/86 to preview the series.

LAST FLIGHT OF NOAH'S ARK, THE Airdates—Part 1: 10/31/81. Part 2: 11/07/81.

This 1980 theatrical release starring Elliott Gould is the story of a hapless pilot and his passengers who crash on an island inhabited by Japanese soldiers who don't know that World War II has ended.

LAW AND ORDER, INCORPORATED Airdates: 12/12/58, 5/01/59.

Cast: Robert Loggia (Elfego Baca), James Dunn (J. Henry Newman), Ramon Novarro (Don Esteban Miranda), Skip Homeier (Ross Mantee), Raymond Bailey (Arnold Bixby), Valerie Allen (Lucita Miranda), I. Stanford Jolley (Sheriff Adams), Jerry Oddo (Luis Vicente).

Part 4 of *The Nine Lives of Elfego Baca* opens as Elfego happily learns he has been made a partner in his law firm. He also learns that Don Esteban Miranda's problems proving rightful ownership of his land are not over, for the Southwestern Railroad has challenged his claim to title. Unfortunately, the papers that could prove his ownership are mysteriously missing.

LAWMAN OR GUNMAN Airdates: 11/28/58, 4/17/59.

Cast: Robert Loggia (Elfego Baca), James Dunn (J. Henry Newman), Ramon Novarro (Don Esteban Miranda), Skip Homeier (Ross Mantee), Valerie Allen (Lucita Miranda), Carl Benton Reid (Judge Hargraves), Clegg Hoyt (Bruiser), Joe Maross (Towne).

The third chapter of *The Nine Lives of Elfego Baca* involves Elfego in a plot by a crooked judge to steal the land of a wealthy local citizen. Judge Hargraves has Elfego arrested on a phony charge, and it is in jail that the lawyer learns of the plot to invalidate the deed of Don Esteban Miranda.

LEFTOVERS, THE Airdates (2-hour format): 11/16/86, 7/26/87.

Cast: John Denver (Maximillian Sinclair), Cindy Williams (Heather Drew), George Wyner (Gladstone), Pamela Segall (Jesse), Andrea Barber (Zoey), Matthew Brooks (Kim), Douglas Emerson (Harry), Jason Presson (Charlie), Jaleel White (Jake), Matthew Laurance, Henry Jones (Thorndike), Anne Seymour (Winifred Dewitt), Bernadette Birkett (Miss Parillo), Lucy Butler (Real Estate Lady), Allan David Fox (Assistant #2), Willie Garson (Gladstone's Assistant), Ed Hooks (Cab Driver), John Hostetter (Mr. Harmon), John Ingle (Commissioner), Dom Irrera (Mechanic), Carolyn Kennedy (Anchor Person), Enid Kent (Mrs. Wiggans), Richard McGonagle (Danny Scott), Georgie Paul (Woman #1), Bee-Be L. Smith (Nurse), Cynthia Szigeti (Woman #2), Richard Vidan (Surveyor), Charles Walker (Security Guard), Terry Wills (Mr. Wiggans).

The Hillsburg Home for Children is a rather unorthodox orphanage. Maximillian Sinclair, the director, is a carefree spirit who doesn't believe in rigid rules and likes the children to enjoy themselves. Max's boss, Mr. Gladstone, doesn't share his opinions. Max's worries are well founded, as Gladstone quickly tells Max that he's been turning down too many adoptions. Because of excessive costs, the home is to be closed. Gladstone's real reason is a secret plan to sell the orphanage site for land for development.

LEFTY

Lefty originally aired as a special on 10/22/80. It was later rerun on 4/19/81 as part of the anthology series.

LEFTY, THE DINGALING LYNX Airdates: 11/28/71, 7/24/77.

Cast: Ron Brown (Joel Barnes), Harrison Tout (Supervisor), Brooks Woolley (George), Elaine Ayres (Maude), Dean Melang (Snowplow Operator), James L. Wilson (Santa Claus), James Ponting (Ski Resort Employee), Dick Ross (Dog Derby Driver), Bill Thomas (Dog Derby Driver).

Forest ranger Joel Barnes adopts a lynx cub, which in turn adopts Joel's Irish setter, Brandy, as a substitute mother. Joel names the lynx Lefty because the animal seems to do everything backward, such as becoming friends with a dog, his natural enemy.

LEGEND OF EL BLANCO, THE Airdates: 9/25/66, 5/07/67.

Cast: Alfonso Romero (El Viejo), Jose F. Perez (Lopez), Assam (El Blanco).

This episode is based on an Aztec tale about El Blanco Magnifico, the legendary white horse of Hernando Cortez, the Spanish conqueror of Mexico. The legend states that the disappearance of the horse caused famine and drought to spread across the land and that conditions will only improve when the great stallion returns to Mexico.

LEGEND OF SLEEPY HOLLOW, THE

Airdates: 10/26/55, 10/30/57, 10/31/65, 1/25/76.

Animation is used to provide a brief biographical look at Washington Irving, who grew up in the Hudson River region of New York State. Of all his stories, Walt feels *The Legend of Sleepy Hollow* is the most famous. In the film *The Adventures of Ichabod and Mr. Toad*, Disney animators brought to life the character of Ichabod Crane, the eccentric schoolteacher who unfortunately makes an enemy of the town bully, Brom Bones, and is menaced by the terrifying Headless Horseman.

LEGEND OF THE BOY AND THE EAGLE, THE Airdates: 9/15/68, 3/30/69, 12/29/74, 4/22/79.

This 1967 theatrical featurette is based on a Hopi Indian legend over 500 years old about a young boy who turns into an eagle.

LEGEND OF TWO GYPSY DOGS, THE

Airdates: 3/01/64, 7/05/64, 8/25/68.

Jani and Elsa are two carefree dogs who have traveled together for several years across Hungary. Their trip brings them into contact with an old fisherman who uses a cormorant, a long-necked bird, to retrieve his catch. They later join up with a hawk and have several dangerous run-ins with hungry predators.

Production Note:

• Jani was a retriever, and Elsa a dachshund.

LEGEND OF YOUNG DICK TURPIN, THE

Airdates—Part 1: 2/13/66, 7/17/66. Part 2: 2/20/66, 7/24/66.

Cast: David Weston (Dick Turpin), Bernard Lee (Jeremiah), George Cole (William Evans), Maurice Denham (Fielding), William Franklyn (Tom King), Roger Booth (Lord Calmsden), William Mervyn (Lord Justice), Colin Blakely (1st Gamekeeper), Richard Pearson (Bailiff), Leonard Whiting (Jimmy), Peter Welch (Higgins), Harry Locke (Jailer), Richard Wattis (Shopkeeper), Donald Pickering (Sir John Burnside), Robert Brown (Big Man), Gladys Henson (Blind Annie), Toke Townley (Sad Willie), Simon Lack (Prosecuting Counsel), Duncan Lewis (Manservant), Paul Curran (Ship's Captain).

The criminal career of an 18th-Century English highwayman, Dick Turpin, begins as he poaches a rabbit to protest the placement of deadly traps on the estate of Lord Calmsden. He's caught and given a large fine with only 24 hours to pay. If he doesn't, he will forfeit all of his worldly possessions, including his prized mare, Bess.

Production Notes:

• This episode was based on the true story of Dick Turpin, who was hanged as a highwayman on April 7, 1739.
• *The Legend of Young Dick Turpin* was released theatrically overseas in 1965.

LIBERATORS, THE Airdate (2-hour format): 2/08/87. In the 1987–88 season the show was aired in two parts—Part 1: 6/05/88. Part 2: 6/12/88.

Cast: Robert Carradine (John Fairfield), Larry B. Scott (Bill Jackson), Cynthia Dale (Elizabeth Giddings), Renée Jones (Lilah), Bumper Robinson (Adam), Caryn Ward (Emily), James B. Douglas (Crocker Giddings), Denis Forest (Brandt), James Mainprize (Levi), Marsha Moreau (Angelica Giddings), Ken Pogue (Avery), Chris Wiggins (Flour Merchant), Tonya Williams (Jenny), Barry Edward Blake (Patroler), George Buza (Store Owner), Herb J. Chambers (Jacob), Alexander Chapman (Joseph), Gene Clark (Gabriel),

Warren Davis (Ticket Man), Michael Donaghue (Rudolph), Arlene F. Duncan (Amanda), Yohance Dyer (Matthew), Blain Fairman (Sheriff), Lorena Gale (Emily's Mother), Barbara Harris (Bill's Mother), Paul Horruzey (Young John), David W. Hudson (Boat Builder), David Hughes (Auctioneer), Patricia Idlette (Josie), Nicholas Kilbertus (Dinner Guest), Gene Mack (Fred), Paul Mayers (Young Black Man), Andrew Moodie (Emmanuel), Benjamin Newton (Young Bill), Sandi Ross (Mary), Donovan Spence (Joshua), Henderson Walcott (Jedidiah).

The story begins in Kentucky in 1849 as John Fairfield is forced by his uncle to beat Billy, a black slave who is his friend. Billy later convinces John to run to Canada to escape intolerance. The two set off together, with Billy acting as John's slave to fool the patrollers looking for runaways. When they meet more runaways, they decide to help them as well and head to an Underground Railroad way station in Ohio. Although there is no slavery in Ohio, slaves can still be sent back if caught. The group narrowly makes it, then are helped further by Levi, a Quaker who arranges for Billy and the other slaves to travel to Canada.

Production Note:

• This was the pilot for an unsold series.

LIBERTY STORY, THE Airdates: 5/29/57, 7/31/57.
Cast: Hal Stalmaster (Johnny Tremain), Luana Patten (Cilla Lapham), Jeff York (James Otis), Rusty Lane (Sam Adams).

The first part of this episode is excerpted from the 1957 theatrical production *Johnny Tremain*, featuring a young apprentice silversmith who becomes a member of the outlawed "Sons of Liberty." The second part of the show is the 1953 cartoon *Ben and Me*, which is told from the point of view of Amos, a church mouse.

Production Note:

• Walt mentions that the story of Johnny Tremain inspired him to add a new themed area to Disneyland. Named Liberty Square, it was to have re-created Boston in 1775, but it never got past the planning stage. There is, however, a Liberty Square at Walt Disney World.

LIFESTYLES OF THE RICH AND ANIMATED
Airdate (90-minute format): 8/18/91.
Ludwig Von Drake is the host of this look at the lives of famous cartoon stars. Three of Disney's biggest stars, Mickey, Donald, and Goofy, have been friends for years, and the cameras have captured many of their fun-filled moments together.

LIGHT IN THE FOREST, THE Airdates—
Part 1: 11/12/61, 5/15/66, 4/23/72. Part 2: 11/19/61, 5/22/66, 4/30/72.
This 1958 theatrical starring Fess Parker, James MacArthur, and Carol Lynley is the story of a white teenager kidnapped by Indians and later torn between the two cultures. Aired in two parts, *Return of the True Son* and *True Son's Revenge*, it was adapted for television by Mike Holoboff.

LIKE FATHER, LIKE SON Airdate: Syndicated.
This compilation of animated clips explores the special bond between fathers and sons. Examples are taken from *One Hundred and One Dalmations, Father's Lion, Bambi, Fantasia, Daddy Duck,* and others.

LITTLE DOG LOST Airdates: 1/13/63, 9/01/63, 8/17/69, 6/06/76.
Cast: Hollis Black (Carlson), Margaret Gerrity (Mother), Grace Bauer (Old Woman), Priscilla Overton (Katy), Dennis Yanglin (Bud), Norman Williams (Father), Champion Bundock's Rover Run Concerto, UD (Candy).
This is the story of Candy, a very young Welsh corgi puppy who is bought by a couple as a pet for their children, Bud and Katy. The parents begin training Candy almost at once and the dog seems to settle into the household without difficulty. Problems begin, however, when Candy is about 4 months old. The dog becomes terrified of brooms, associating them with punishment, and runs away from home.

LITTLE SHEPHERD DOG OF CATALINA, THE Airdates: 3/11/73, 5/29/77, 7/3/82.
Cast: Clint Rowe (Bud Parker), William Maxwell (Mark Mason), Joe Dawkins (Sam Hawkins), Robert O'Guin (Security Deputy Martin).
Champion Birkie of Scalloway is the name of Mark Mason's champion Shetland sheepdog, which he takes everywhere. He sets sail from Santa Catalina Island off Southern California and the Shetland has a prized spot on board the sailboat. The trip has barely begun when Birkie falls overboard, unknown to Mason.

LITTLE SPIES Airdate (2-hour format): 10/05/86. For the 1987–88 season the show aired in two parts—Part 1: 3/20/88. Part 2: 3/27/88.

Cast: Mickey Rooney (Jimmie Turner), Robert Costanzo (Bernie), Peter Smith (Jason), Candace Cameron (Julie), Adam Carl, Sean Hall (Clarence), Jason Hervey (Clint), Sarah Jo Martin (Kristi), Scott Nemes (Wendell), James Tolkan (Kennel Master), Jamie Abbott (Sponge), Kevin King Cooper (Spud), J.J. Hardy (Big Al), Laura Jacoby (Blister), Eric Walker (Scratch), Robin Pearson Rose (Jason's Mother), Alan Haufrect (Jason's Father), Art LaFleur (Sergeant Westwood), Charles Walker (Cop #2), Wayne Alexander (Father #2), Cher Bennett (Mother #2), Deirdre Kelly (Popcorn Girl), Juliet Sorci (Crying Girl), Nancy Parsons.

As a city dog pound employee is loading dogs into a truck bound for a science lab, he drops one of the dogs and it escapes. The worker knows he had better find the dog if he wants to keep his job, so he quickly gives chase. The unfortunate canine is also pursued by some local toughs, The Water Street Gang, but luckily it meets up instead with a friendlier group of children.

LITTLEST OUTLAW, THE Airdates—Part 1: 1/22/58, 5/24/64. Part 2: 1/29/58, 5/31/64.

This 1955 theatrical release is the story of Conquistador, a prize racehorse stolen from a Mexican general.

LONE SURVIVOR OF CUSTER'S LAST STAND
This is Part 2 of *Comanche*.

LONG LIVE THE RIGHTFUL KING
This is Part 3 of *The Prince and the Pauper*.

LOST ON THE BAJA PENINSULA
This is Part 1 of *Three without Fear*.

LOTS OF LUCK
This made-for-television movie first aired on The Disney Channel. An edited version aired on the anthology series on 5/28/89.

LOUIS L'AMOUR'S THE CHEROKEE TRAIL
See: *The Cherokee Trail*.

LOVE BUG, THE Airdate (2-hour format): 9/23/79. For the 1981–82 season the show was presented in two parts—Part 1: 9/26/81. Part 2: 10/03/81.

This 1969 theatrical release, the first in a series of films about Herbie, the Volkswagen with a mind of its own, stars Dean Jones, Michele Lee, David Tomlinson, and Buddy Hackett.

Production Note:

• The original screenplay was titled *Car-Boy-Girl.* When the Studio bought the rights in 1962, the contract included the option to produce a half-hour television series. *Herbie, The Love Bug* ran as a limited series on CBS.

MAD HERMIT OF CHIMNEY BUTTE, THE Airdates: 4/01/60, 9/23/60.

Walt tells the strange tale of the Mad Hermit of Chimney Butte, an angry recluse who shoots at anything that comes near his lonely cave. A peek through a telescope reveals that the hermit is none other than Donald Duck. The story unfolds through a series of Donald Duck cartoons.

MAGIC AND MUSIC Airdates: 3/19/58, 6/18/58, 5/19/63.

Cast: Walt Disney, Hans Conried

The Slave in the Magic Mirror, first seen in *Snow White and the Seven Dwarfs*, hosts the program, which is devoted to the Slave's favorite subject, the magic of music.

Production Note:

• For the 1958 airing of this show, the *Pastoral Symphony* was shown intact, including several black centaurettes since removed from the theatrical version of *Fantasia.* The repeat broadcast of 1963 was edited to remove these scenes.

MAGIC HIGHWAY U.S.A. Airdates: 5/14/58, 7/30/58, 7/29/62.

The importance of America's highways is the theme of this show, which begins with a look back at the early days of motoring. The first cars had to be driven on roads that barely deserved that name, for they were often little more than rutted cow paths. Each trip became an adventure, since fuel supplies and spare parts were few and far between. Another problem was the lack of useful maps or signposts, sometimes making a planned short drive into an all-day affair.

Production Notes:

• The show includes footage of the first cars to travel the unpaved Lincoln Highway, America's first cross-country route, in 1913. That film was in storage at the University of Michigan and had begun to decompose, requiring careful attention by the Disney technicians to make a permanent copy for future use at the school.

- Footage was also included from a short film produced by the Southern California chapter of the Horseless Carriage Club, parodying the efforts of early motorists.

MAGIC OF WALT DISNEY WORLD, THE
Airdates: 3/31/74, 8/18/74.
This expanded version of the 1972 theatrical featurette of the same name is a look at the new Disney complex located near Orlando, Florida. Walt Disney World opened in 1971 and has already hosted several million visitors from around the world.

MAGICAL DISNEY CHRISTMAS, A
Airdate: 12/05/81.
The Christmas holidays are celebrated through a series of animated clips, including scenes from *Lady and the Tramp*, *Toy Tinkers*, *The Three Caballeros*, *On Ice*, and others. The show concludes with an excerpt from the 1978 theatrical featurette *The Small One*.

Production Note:

- Portions of this show were later used in the episode *A Disney Christmas Gift*, aired first on 12/04/82 and as a special on 12/20/83.

MAGICAL WORLD OF DISNEY, THE
Airdate: 10/09/88.
Cast: Betty White, Johnny Cash, Dawnn Lewis, Countess Vaughn, Harry Anderson, Christopher Daniel Barnes, The Creel Triplets, Cassandra Peterson (Elvira), Charles Fleischer, Kate Jackson, Richard Mulligan, Steven Spielberg, Robert Zemeckis.

As the anthology switches networks and titles, the first episode of *The Magical World of Disney* begins with Michael Eisner talking about the 1961 premiere of *Walt Disney's Wonderful World of Color*. Now, after many years, Disney is returning to NBC.

MAGNIFICENT REBEL, THE   Airdates—
Part 1: 11/18/62, 7/14/63. Part 2: 11/25/62, 7/21/63.
Cast: Carl Boehm (Ludwig van Beethoven), Giulia Rubini (Countess Giulietta), Ivan Desny (Prince Lichnowsky), Peter Arens (Karl Amenda), Oliver Grimm (Blind Boy), Bruno Dallansky (Schuppanzigh), Erik Frey (Count Guicciardi), Peter Capell (Doctor), Erich Winn (French Colonel), Ernst Nadherny (Frank Joseph Haydn), Guido Wieland (Landlord), Gabriele Barth (Landlord's Daughter).

This life story of Ludwig van Beethoven opens in 1792 as the young composer arrives in Vienna to study with Franz Joseph Haydn. Beethoven's funds are limited and he must agree to give piano lessons in exchange for rent. He rises to prominence in musical circles only to learn that he is going deaf.

Production Notes:

- The original title for this episode, which was filmed on location in Vienna, was *The Ludwig van Beethoven Story*.
- This episode was released theatrically overseas in 1961.

MAJOR EFFECTS   Airdate: 12/16/79.
Cast: Joseph Bottoms (Major Effects), Hans Conried (Bigger Than Life), Derek Murcott (Animal Wizard), Mike Jittlov (Camera Wizard), Cyb Barnstable (Twin #1), Tricia Barnstable (Twin #2), Andy Romano (Prop Wizard), Tommy McLoughlin (Make-up Wizard), Bob Baker (Marionette), Lennie Weinrib (Voice Characterizations).

Although the narrator speaks of the show's star, Major Effects, as being a hero of superhuman proportions, a 100-year-old man appears instead. It's all a bit of special effects, explains the major, who is actually Joseph Bottoms, star of Disney's *The Black Hole*. Bottoms introduces a wizard known as Bigger Than Life, who endows him with magical powers so Bottoms can explain how the effects are produced.

MAN AND THE MOON   Airdates:
12/28/55, 6/13/56, 9/25/59 (Tomorrow the Moon).
Cast: Ward Kimball, Wernher Von Brown.
Ward Kimball, the show's director, starts off with a cartoon illustrating age-old legends and fantasies about the moon. Many of these stories involved fanciful ways to travel to the moon, predictions of the creatures that supposedly roamed its surface, or folktales about how the moon influenced events on Earth.

Production Notes:

- The broadcast of 9/25/59 was a special repeat aired as a "science special" in response to the enthusiastic reaction the first two airings received.
- This episode was released theatrically overseas.

MAN FROM BITTER CREEK, THE
Airdates: 3/06/59, 8/21/59.

Cast: Tom Tryon *(John Slaughter),* Stephen McNally *(Bill Gallagher),* Sidney Blackmer *(Sam Underwood),* Bill Williams *(Paul),* John Larch *(Frank Boyd),* Norma Moore *(Adeline Harris),* Grant Williams *(Mike),* H.M. Wynant *(Yancy),* Don Kelly *(Jed),* Edward Platt *(Lease Harris).*

The fifth episode in the life of Texas John Slaughter proves that even after resigning from the Texas rangers, John must fight to survive. Following his marriage to Adeline Harris, John buys a ranch and settles down. His tranquil life ends abruptly when Sam Underwood, a neighboring rancher, builds a dam that cuts off John's water supply.

Production Note:

- This episode was combined with *The Slaughter Trail* and released theatrically overseas in 1962 as *Stampede at Bitter Creek.*

MAN IN FLIGHT   Airdates: 3/06/57, 4/02/58, 3/26/61.
Cast (1961 version): Fred MacMurray *(Prof. Ned Brainard).*

There are two versions of this show, with the 1957–58 season version providing a more detailed look at past aviation concepts and experiments. For the 1961 airing, the show was modified to provide publicity for the theatrical release *The Absent-Minded Professor.* Both versions made extensive use of an educational short subject, *The History of Aviation,* which in turn includes numerous sequences from the theatrical feature *Victory through Air Power.*

Production Notes:

- The scenes from *Victory through Air Power* featured new narration written for this show.
- This episode was released theatrically overseas.

MAN IN SPACE   Airdates: 3/09/55, 6/15/55, 9/07/55, 9/18/59 (special repeat).
Cast: Ward Kimball, Willy Ley, Dr. Heinz Haber, Dr. Wernher Von Brown.

The first of the Tomorrowland shows is a look at how America is preparing for the challenge of space exploration. After a look at early experiments in rocketry, the show provides a look at the problems that must be overcome before mankind can travel safely in space.

Production Notes:

- *Man in Space* was very well received, prompting President Eisenhower to request the loan of a print for a screening at the Pentagon. He later credited the show with helping to further the progress of the American space program.
- A special repeat was aired during the 1959–60 season as a "Special Science Program."
- *Man in Space* was released theatrically in 1956.

MAN IS HIS OWN WORST ENEMY
Airdates: 10/21/62, 5/03/70, 5/09/76 *(Ducking Disaster with Donald and His Friends).*

Prof. Ludwig Von Drake hosts this look at the world's biggest problem—people. Von Drake reasons that if there weren't any people, there wouldn't be any problems. He also claims that people create problems because they don't stop to think. He illustrates this theory with the cartoons *Reason and Emotion, Chicken Little, How to Have an Accident in the Home, How to Have an Accident at Work,* and *Motor Mania.*

MAN ON WHEELS   Airdates: 3/26/67, 8/06/67.
This study of the wheel's effects on society is comprised of two short subjects that were first released theatrically. The first is *Donald and the Wheel,* in which Donald is seen as a cave dweller who invents the wheel. Walt narrates the second part of the show, *Freewayphobia,* which shows how motorists have to cope with modern highways.

MAN'S HUNTING INSTINCT   Airdate: 1/02/82.
Prof. Ludwig Von Drake is the guest host for this episode, which tries to shed some light on why humans are driven to hunt. Using several cartoons, the professor demonstrates the finer points of hunting.

Production Note:

- This episode made extensive use of footage from *The Hunting Instinct.*

MARS AND BEYOND   Airdates: 12/04/57, 6/11/58.
Cast: Dr. Ernst Stuhlinger, Dr. Wernher Von Brown.

Walt opens this look at how scientists are planning to explore the planet Mars by introducing an animated look at humankind's early thoughts on the universe. The segment includes a lighthearted look at how some "adventurers" described Martian creatures they claimed to have met or observed, and ends with a spoof of science fiction stories about unidentified flying objects.

Production Note:

- *Mars and Beyond* was released theatrically in 1957. The scenes of "Martian Creatures" were also used for the "in-flight movie" on the Mission to Mars attraction at Disneyland.

MARY POPPINS

This 1964 theatrical feature first aired as a special on 11/22/81. It also was rerun as a special on 11/24/88 and 4/15/90, and on the anthology series on 5/03/87 and 4/15/90.

MATCHMAKER, THE

This is Part 3 of *Willie and the Yank*.

MEDITERRANEAN CRUISE   Airdates: 1/19/64, 4/13/69.

Ludwig Von Drake hosts a combination animated and live-action look at several countries that border on the Mediterranean Sea.

MEET THE MUNCEYS   Airdate: 5/22/88.

Cast: Nana Visitor (Billie Muncey), Peggy Pope (Bernice Muncey), Carmine Caridi (Bud Muncey), Dan Gauthier (Bruce Muncey), Mark Neely (Freddie Vanderplas), Lee Weaver (Frank Munroe), D.D. Howard (Gabby Wilcox), William Glover (Edmund Haddy), Paddi Edwards (Jessie Burns), Joan Hotchkis (Cissy Vanderplas), Mary Jackson (Esther Lovell-Mingott), Linden Chiles (Lawyer), Jennifer Convy (Female Cop), Lee Moore (Maitre D'), Mark Roberts (Charles Vanderplas), Gyl Roland (Salesgirl), Kevin Telles (Kid), Huell Howser (Newscaster), Vanna White (Herself).

Billie Muncey has moved from New Jersey to Palm Beach, Florida, where she's working as a maid for Esther Lovell-Mingott, a wealthy old woman. When Esther dies, she leaves the bulk of her fortune, over $140 million, to a foundation, and shocks her family by naming Billie as the foundation's head. One of Esther's relatives, Cissy Vanderplas, refuses to accept the news and immediately begins trying to remove Billie from running the foundation.

Production Note:

- This was the pilot for an unsold series.

MENACE ON THE MOUNTAIN   Airdates—Part 1: 3/01/70, 8/02/70, 8/01/76. Part 2: 3/08/70, 8/09/70, 8/08/76.

Cast: Charles Aidman (Jed McIver), Patricia Crowley (Leah McIver), Albert Salmi (Poss Timmerlake), Mitch Vogel (Jamie McIver), Richard Anderson (Major Galt), Dub Taylor (Cicero Everhart), Eric Shea (Mark McIver), Dan Ferrone (Lieutenant Saunders), John Harper (Mr. Sykes), James Nusser (Ben Forrester), Jodie Foster (Suellen McIver), Gregg Palmer (Poss Bushwacker).

Jed McIver joins the Confederate Army during the Civil War. He tells his son, Jamie, to take care of his mother, Leah, his brother, Mark, and his sister, Suellen. The boy's first task is to find a way to pay the taxes due on their farm, and he decides to capture a mountain lion to collect a bounty. He succeeds, thereby angering Poss Timmerlake, the town bully, who had also wanted to earn the bounty. Poss and Jamie have another confrontation when Timmerlake tries to court Leah, even though Jed is still alive, and an angered Jamie orders the older man out of the house at gunpoint.

Production Note:

- This show was released theatrically overseas in 1972.

MERCIFUL LAW OF THE KING

This is Part 2 of *The Prince and the Pauper*.

MICHAEL O'HARA THE FOURTH

Airdates—Part 1: 3/26/72, 4/24/77. Part 2: 4/02/72, 5/01/77.

Cast: Dan Dailey (Capt. Michael O'Hara III), Michael McGreevey (Norman), Nehemiah Persoff (Artie Moreno), Jo Ann Harris ("Mike" O'Hara IV), William Bramley (Police Commissioner), James Almanzar (Rodriguez), Mike Henry (Fargo), Maggie Wellman (Wilma), Dave Willock (Store Manager), Tom Waters (Charley Grady), Mimi Saffian (Barbs), Maggie Wellman (Wilma), Robert Patten (Richard Caffey), James Lydon (John Stevens), Judson Pratt (Andy), Pete Renoudet (Stan), Walter Sande (John Parsons), Pat Delaney (Secretary #2), Maudie Prickett (Nosy Neighbor).

This comedy is presented in two parts, *To Trap a Thief* and *The Deceptive Detective*.

Capt. Michael O'Hara III has a problem. He would like someone to carry on the family tradition of having a police officer in the O'Hara family, but he never had a son. Instead, his daughter, who goes by the nickname "Mike," secretly hopes to become a detective and fulfill her dream. Unfortunately, her efforts are not always successful and her father doesn't pay much attention to her theories.

MICKEY AND DONALD
See: *Walt Disney's Mickey and Donald.*

MICKEY AND DONALD KIDDING AROUND   Airdate: 5/03/83.
Music: Buddy Baker.

Prof. Ludwig Von Drake hosts the show, explaining that he wants to share his vast knowledge on the subject of child psychology. He has been studying Donald Duck, whom he calls "Mister X" to protect his identity, and has decided to offer some advice on how to deal with Huey, Dewey, and Louie.

Production Note:

• This is an edited version of *Kids Is Kids.*

MICKEY MOUSE ANNIVERSARY SHOW, THE   Airdate: 12/22/68.
Cast: Dean Jones, Annette Funicello, Darlene Gillespie, Cubby O'Brien, Bobby Burgess, Don Grady, Sharon Baird, Tommy Cole, Lonnie Burr, Jay Jay Solari, Bonnie Fields, Dennis Day, Karen Pendleton.

Mickey Mouse has been a star for 40 years, and to celebrate that landmark, the Disney Studio has decided to throw a party. Dean Jones, star of numerous Disney pictures including *The Love Bug*, hosts this retrospective look at how Mickey came to achieve his unequaled success.

Production Note:

• An edited version of this episode was released theatrically overseas in 1970. The live-action sequences were deleted and additional animated clips were used instead, together with a new narration by Pete Renoudet.

MICKEY'S CHRISTMAS CAROL
This 1983 theatrical featurette first aired as a special on 12/10/84 and repeated on 12/15/86, 12/04/87, and 12/17/90. The anthology airings on 12/04/88 and 12/17/89 promoted the upcoming releases of *Oliver & Company* and *The Little Mermaid.*

MICKEY'S 50   Airdate (90-minute format): 11/19/78.
Cast: Johnny Carson, Dean Jones, Edgar Bergen, Rich Little, Jack Albertson, Elton John, Dick Clark, Bruce Jenner, Joe Namath, Steve Garvey, O. J. Simpson, Hans Conried, Shirley Jones, Kermit the Frog, Elliott Gould, LeVar Burton, Jodie Foster, Sterling Holloway, Roger Miller, Goldie Hawn, Dyan Cannon, Dick Van Patten, Alex Karras, Susan Clark, Gary Owens, Anne Murray, Charo, Roy Rogers, Dale Evans, Eva Gabor, Sally Field, Annette Funicello, Willie Nelson, Jan-Michael Vincent, Henry Winkler, Cheryl Ladd, Gene Kelly, Doc Severinsen, Burt Reynolds, Red Buttons, Ruth Buzzi, Ronnie Schell, Jo Anne Worley, Gerald Ford, Jonathan Winters, Lawrence Welk, Barbara Walters, Kenny Rogers, Reverend Billy Graham, Karen and Richard Carpenter, Mel Brooks, Anne Bancroft.

This star-studded birthday greeting to Mickey Mouse celebrates the amazing career of perhaps the world's best known celebrity. Although many of the performers appear only in brief cameos, several are included in longer segments that describe Mickey's career.

Production Note:

• The Studio lists Mickey's birthday as November 18, 1928, the day he made his screen debut in *Steamboat Willie* at New York's Colony (now Broadway) Theatre.

MICKEY'S GREATEST ADVENTURES
See: *Adventures of Mickey Mouse.*

MICKEY'S HAPPY VALENTINE SPECIAL
Airdate: 2/12/89.
Ludwig Von Drake is the host of this DTV-style look at love.

Production Note:

• Despite the title, this was not a special.

MICKEY'S 60TH BIRTHDAY   Airdates: 11/13/88, 6/25/89.
Cast: John Ritter (Dudley Goode), Jill Eikenberry (Mia Loude), Cheech Marin, Phylicia Rashad, Carl Reiner (Mel Fellini), Charles Fleischer, Michael Tucker, Jimmy Smits, Richard Dysart, Harry Hamlin, Corbin Bernsen, Blair Underwood, Justine Bateman, Tina Yothers, Michael J. Fox, Brian Bonsall (Andrew Keaton), Ted Danson, Kirstie Alley, Rhea Perlman, Woody Harrelson, Kelsey

Grammer, George Wendt, John Ratzenberger, Ed McMahon, Fred Dryer (Sergeant Hunter).

As Mickey gets ready for a special show to salute his birthday, a strange wizard in the mirror warns him not to use the sorcerer's hat from *Fantasia*. Mickey decides to wear the hat anyway, but his tempting of fate soon proves to be a mistake. When Roger Rabbit accidentally almost destroys the studio, Mickey uses the hat's magic to repair the damage. Outraged at being ignored, the wizard uses his powers to make everyone in the world forget what Mickey looks like.

MILLION DOLLAR DIXIE DELIVERANCE, THE   Airdates (2-hour format): 2/05/78, 5/27/79.

Cast: *Brock Peters (Zechariah), Christian Juttner (Timmy), Chip Courtland (Henry), Alicia Fleer (Jessica), Kyle Richards (Naomi), Christian Berrigan (Daniel), Joe Dorsey (Captain Guthrie), Kip Niven (Lieutenant Ames), Sonny Shroyer (Luke), Mary Nell Santacroce (Miss Carlyle), Ben Jones (Sergeant Bingham), Kenneth Daniel (Private Taggart), Grace Zabriskie (Widow Cummins), Ernie Brown (Denny), Stuart Culpepper (Ike), Richard Reiner (Poole), Kermit Echols (Farmer), Frank Rickman (Sentry), Henry Blankenship (Bartender), Mike Vines (Morgan).*

A Confederate officer puts a bold plan into operation in a desperate attempt to raise some much needed money to finance the South's battle in the Civil War. Captain Guthrie kidnaps five children from an exclusive Yankee boarding school and holds them hostage for a $1 million ransom.

Production Notes:

- The show was filmed during a 5-week period on location in Westville, Georgia. Volunteer "soldiers" from Civil War associations across the country provided authenticity for the battle scenes.
- A number of the performers in this show have ties to other Disney performers. Chip Courtland is the son of Jerry Courtland, formerly television's *Andy Burnett* and later a producer at the Studio, and Kyle Richards is the sister of Kim Richards (*Escape to Witch Mountain*).

MILLION DOLLAR DUCK, THE

Airdates—Part 1: 9/15/74, 9/30/79, 5/08/82. Part 2: 9/22/74, 10/07/79, 5/15/82. This 1971 theatrical release stars Dean Jones, Sandy Duncan, and Joe Flynn in the story of

a family that discovers their pet duck lays golden eggs.

MINADO, THE WOLVERINE   Airdates: 11/07/65, 7/31/66, 12/27/70.

Cast: *William Bacon III (Trapper).*

Minado is a young wolverine who sees his mother killed by a trapper, prompting the animal to avenge her death. The hunter drives two Indians from their log cabin and sets up camp there, so Minado builds a lair nearby and starts to torment the unsuspecting trapper.

Production Note:

- This episode was released theatrically overseas in 1978.

MISADVENTURES OF CHIP 'N DALE, THE
See: *The Adventures of Chip 'n Dale.*

MR. BOOGEDY   Airdates (2-hour format): 4/20/86, 9/14/86.

Cast: *Richard Masur (Carleton Davis), Mimi Kennedy (Eloise Davis), Benjamin Gregory (Ahri Davis), David Faustino (Corwin Davis), Kristy Swanson (Jennifer Davis), Howard Witt (Boogedy), John Astin (Neil Witherspoon), Katherine Kelly Lang (Widow Marion), Jaimie McEnnan (Jonathan), Kedric Wolfe (The Devil).*

The Davis family is excited about moving to the small New England village of Lucifer Falls to open a novelty shop. However, their excitement quickly turns to dismay when they have to battle an evil ghost known as Mr. Boogedy. The spirit has kept a woman and her child imprisoned in another dimension for almost 200 years.

Production Note:

- This episode was a pilot for a proposed series. The sequel episode *Bride of Boogedy* was produced as a second pilot.

MIXED NUTS
See: *The Adventures of Chip 'n Dale.*

MONKEYS, GO HOME!   Airdates—Part 1: 11/15/70. Part 2: 11/22/70. The show later was presented in a 2-hour format: 12/07/75. This 1967 theatrical release stars Dean Jones, Yvette Mimieux, and Maurice Chevalier in the story of an American farmer who uses chimps to pick his crops in France.

Production Note:

- The village of St. Prioust en Pegoustan in the film is the same set as El Cuartel de Los Angeles from *Zorro*.

MONKEY'S UNCLE, THE Airdates—Part 1: 11/26/67, 1/28/73. Part 2: 12/03/67, 2/04/73. For the 1979–80 season the show was presented in a 2-hour format: 3/02/80. This 1965 theatrical sequel to *The Misadventures of Merlin Jones* stars Tommy Kirk and Annette Funicello in a story about sleep learning and a contest for human-powered flight.

Production Note:

- This was Annette Funicello's last feature film for Disney.
- This film was serialized on *The New Mickey Mouse Club*.

MONSTERS OF THE DEEP Airdates: 1/19/55, 3/30/55, 7/27/55.

Cast: Kirk Douglas, Peter Lorre.

The show is devoted to strange creatures: Walt takes the viewer into his "Monster Room" at the Studio. The material stored here is used to provide details on creatures of all sorts, including many known only to the Disney artists.

Production Note:

- Kirk Douglas received an unusual payment for his appearance in this show: film copies of *Alice in Wonderland*, *Cinderella*, and *Peter Pan*.

MOOCHIE OF POP WARNER FOOTBALL Airdates—Part 1: 11/20/60, 9/03/61. Part 2: 11/27/60, 9/10/61.

Cast: Kevin Corcoran (Moochie Morgan), Dennis Joel (Hilliard Wood), Reginald Owen (J. Cecil Bennett), John Howard (Mayor Wood), Alan Hale, Jr. (Fred Preston), Francis Rafferty (Louise Morgan), Lumsden Hare (Croaker), Russ Conway (Monty Morgan), Annette Gorman (BB Preston), Norma Varden (Miss Devon), Harry O. Tyler (Mr. Green).

A follow-up to *Moochie of the Little League*, this two-part story (*Pee Wees Versus City Hall* and *From Ticonderoga to Disneyland*) opens as Moochie is trying to gain 8 pounds so he can join the Midget team in a Pop Warner Football League. At his present weight he would have to be a Pee Wee and there are no such teams in his town. Moochie's father and their next-door neighbor, Fred Preston, decide to form a team for the smaller boys.

Production Note:

- This show was serialized in the 1960s syndication of *The Mickey Mouse Club*.

MOOCHIE OF THE LITTLE LEAGUE Airdates—Part 1: 10/02/59, 4/15/60. Part 2: 10/09/59, 4/22/60.

Cast: Kevin Corcoran (Moochie Morgan), Reginald Owen (J. Cecil Bennett), Alan Hale, Jr. (Fred Preston), Frances Rafferty (Louise Morgan), Stuart Erwin (Lou Rosson), Jim L. Brown (Andy Clinton), Dorothy Green (Charlotte), Russ Conway (Monty Morgan), Lee Aaker (Chuck Taylor), Paul Bryar (Pete Dixon), Annette Gorman (BB Preston).

Presented in two parts, *A Diamond Is a Boy's Best Friend* and *Wrong Way Moochie*, the story begins as Moochie Morgan delivers newspapers along his route before heading to Little League practice. When Moochie's carelessness costs him a place in the game, he is forced to watch from the bench.

The team suffers a major setback when the boys learn the playing field has been sold and they'll soon be without a place to play.

Production Notes:

- The part of Marian Morgan, Moochie's sister, was played by Donna Corcoran, the real-life older sister of star Kevin Corcoran.
- This show was serialized in the 1960s syndication of *The Mickey Mouse Club*.

MOON PILOT Airdates—Part 1: 1/16/66, 2/21/71. Part 2: 1/23/66, 2/28/71. This 1952 theatrical release stars Tom Tryon, Dany Saval, Brian Keith, and Edmond O'Brien in the story of a reluctant astronaut who meets a beautiful girl from outer space.

Production Note:

- The episode *Spy in the Sky* is a behind-the-scenes look at the filming of this story.

MOONCUSSERS, THE Airdates—Part 1: 12/02/62, 8/04/63. Part 2: 12/09/62, 8/11/63.

Cast: Oscar Homolka (Urias Hawke), Kevin Corcoran (Jonathan Feather), Robert Emhardt (Mr. Wick), Rian Garrick (Dan Hallett), Joan Freeman (Besty Feather), Robert Burton (E. P. Hallett), Erin O'Brien-Moore (Mrs. Feather),

Dub Taylor (Fire Tender), Eddy Waller (Jeremy Weeks), Ted Jacques (Bill Stacey).

Set on Long Island, New York, in the 1840s, *The Mooncussers* is presented in two parts. In Part 1, *Graveyard of Ships*, a band of pirates is looking for unsuspecting ships they can lure to an untimely end on the shore. Mr. Wick, the pirate leader, orders his men to set a trap for the *Emily*, a clipper ship of the E. P. Hallett Line. The second part, *Wake of Disaster*, finds E. P. Hallett arriving in town to oversee the search for the pirates.

Production Note:

- This episode was released theatrically overseas in 1966.

MOON-SPINNERS, THE   Airdates—Part 1: 11/20/66, 8/20/67. Part 2: 11/27/66, 8/27/67. Part 3: 12/04/66, 9/03/67. For the 1981–82 season the show was presented in two parts—Part 1: 3/13/82. Part 2: 3/20/82 (90-minute format).
This 1964 theatrical release starring Hayley Mills, Eli Wallach, and Peter McEnery is the story of two tourists who become involved with jewel thieves on the island of Crete. It also aired as part of the *Saturday Night at the Movies with Disney* specials. It aired on 11/26/75 when it was co-featured with *Prowlers of the Everglades*.

MORE ABOUT THE SILLY SYMPHONIES
Airdate: 4/17/57.
Walt explains how the Silly Symphonies served as training for the animators and a chance to experiment with new techniques. The lessons learned in these early days would later be used in the production of full-length features such as *Snow White and the Seven Dwarfs* and *Fantasia*.

MOSBY RAIDERS, THE
This is Part 2 of *Willie and the Yank.*

MOTHER'S COURAGE, A: THE MARY THOMAS STORY   Airdate—Part 1: 12/03/89. Part 2: 12/10/89. The show later aired in a 2-hour format: 6/03/90.
Cast: Alfre Woodard (Mary Thomas), A.J. Johnson (Ruby Thomas), Leon (Lord Michael Thomas), Garland Spencer (Isiah Thomas/Age 11), Chick Vennera (Couch Pingatore), Larry O. Williams, Jr. (Isiah Thomas/Age 15), Jamey Sheridan (Brother Ted), Harry Lennix (Nero), WandaChristine (Sara), Shamon Ricks (Jojo), Lanei Chapman (Mary/Age 16), Barbara Robertson (Miss Day), Marty Higginbotham

(Mr. Davis), Ed Grennan (Mayor Daley), Moon Hi Hanson (Dr. Kim), Bernard Mixon (Ross), Rengin Altay (M.J.), Bob Kohut (LoBianco), Kent Martin (Grocery Store Manager), Darrell Echols (Store Clerk), Susan Ware (Mayor's Receptionist).

The true-life story of Detroit Pistons basketball star Isiah Thomas begins as his mother, Mary, thinks back about the struggle she had to raise him right. Mistreated by whites while working as a waitress, Mary moved to Chicago with her children. At first this seemed like a good idea, but years later, Isiah finds himself tempted to join a local street gang and his older brother, Michael, runs away from home.

Production Notes:

- This show was filmed on location on Chicago's West Side, where the real story took place. It ended with a 3-minute documentary featuring the real Thomas family in their Chicago home.
- The show won an Emmy Award for Individual Achievement for a Children's Program and a Christopher Award in the television specials category.

MOUNTAIN BORN   Airdate: 1/09/72.
Cast: Sam Austin (Jason), Walter Stroud (Benj), Jolene Terry (Martha).

Jason is an 11-year-old who lives with his widowed mother on an isolated sheep ranch high in the Colorado mountains. He hopes to someday be like his idol, Benj, the ranch foreman. Benj gives the boy the job of watching over a young lamb after Jason saves the animal from dying. This affords Jason his first real responsibility, and Benj helps him learn the ways of a shepherd.

Production Note:

- The episode's theme song was written and sung by Sam Austin, the 12-year-old star of the show.

MOUSEKETEER REUNION, THE   Airdate: 11/23/80.
Cast: Annette Funicello, Tim Considine, Paul Williams, Bonnie Lynn Fields, Johnny Crawford, Billie Jean Beanblossom, Dickie Dodd, Judy Harriet, Tim Rooney, Cheryl Holdridge, Mickey Rooney, Jr., Doreen Tracey, Larry Larsen, Eileen Diamond, Bonnie Lou Kern, Dennis Day, Mary Espinosa, Charley Laney, Ron Steiner, Linda Hughes, Mike Smith, Margene Storey, Don Underhill, Lynn Ready, Mary Sartori, Karen Pendleton, Cubby

O'Brien, Sharon Baird, Lonnie Burr, Sherry Alberoni, Tommy Cole, Darlene Gillespie, Bobby Burgess.

October 3, 1955, marked the beginning of *The Mickey Mouse Club*, one of the most popular children's series ever produced. One of the main features of the show was the Mouseketeers, a talented group of youngsters. Now, after a year-long search, the Studio has gathered together almost all of the original Mouseketeers to celebrate the show's 25th anniversary.

Production Note:

- This was the only episode of the anthology series to be taped or filmed in front of a studio audience.

MOUSEKETEERS AT WALT DISNEY WORLD, THE   Airdate: 11/20/77.

Cast: Jo Anne Worley (Miss Osborne), Ronnie Schell (Mr. Brown), Dennis Underwood (Mr. Harrison), Leslie Norris (The Clerk), The Mouseketeers: Billy "Pop" Attmore, Scott Craig, Nita Dee, Mindy Feldman, Angel Florez, Allison Fonte, Shawnte Northcutte, Kelly Parsons, Julie Piekarski, Todd Turquand, Lisa Whelchel, Curtis Wong.

The stars of *The New Mickey Mouse Club* arrive at Walt Disney World in Florida to do a live stage show, also hoping to enjoy the recreational aspects of the Vacation Kingdom. A series of problems follows as they explore the property.

MOVE ALONG, MUSTANGERS   Airdates: 11/13/59, 8/26/60.

Cast: Robert Loggia (Elfego Baca), Brian Keith (Shadrack O'Reilly), Arthur Hunnicutt (Elias O'Brien), Beverly Garland (Suzanna O'Brien), Barry Kelley (Sheriff Holman), Lillian Bronson (Rachel), Roger Perry (Luke Sawyer), James Coburn (James Carter), William Schallert (Deputy Denby), Robert Nichols (Pronto), John Maxwell (Pappy Sawyer), Skip Farrell (Josh Jordan), Robert Hoy (Sam Carter).

The seventh story of Elfego Baca involves the frontier lawyer and a group of Mustangers, a religious sect trying to establish a homestead despite the efforts of the region's cattlemen. The ranchers oppose any new settlers for fear they will lose the valuable grazing lands necessary to support their herds.

Production Note:

- This story is continued in *Mustang Man, Mustang Maid*. Both stories are referred to by the overall title *Elfego Baca and the Mustangers*.

MUPPET FAMILY CHRISTMAS, A

This episode was not produced by Disney, but was aired in the anthology time slot on 12/24/89 during Disney's abortive attempt to buy the Muppets. It had originally aired in 1987.

MUPPETS AT WALT DISNEY WORLD, THE

Airdate: 5/06/90.

Cast: Charles Grodin (Quentin Fitzwalter), Raven-Symoné.

Kermit the Frog leads his fellow Muppets to Paradise Swamp, where they meet with his friends and relatives. After singing *Knee Deep*, a song about swamp life, they realize they're near Walt Disney World and decide to visit it.

MUSIC FOR EVERYBODY   Airdates: 1/30/66, 6/07/70.

Prof. Ludwig Von Drake hosts this animated study of the importance music plays in people's lives.

Production Note:

- The show was set at the *Von Drake Bowl*, which was a spoof of the real-life Hollywood Bowl.

MUSTANG!   Airdates—Part 1: 10/07/73, 6/30/74, 7/03/77. Part 2: 10/21/73, 7/07/74, 7/10/77.

Cast: Charles Baca (Señor Delgado), Flavio Martinez (Julito), Ignacio Ramirez (Ruiz), Eloy Casados, Chico Morrison, Alfonso Cantu (Raton), Pete Gallegos, Tomas Sanchez, Lee Pacheco, The Pacheco Family.

Set during the 1880s, this is the story of Pechudo ("the proud one"), a wild mustang living in the southwestern United States and northern Mexico. His first three years are a constant battle with other animals and the local Indian tribes, but he survives to become the leader of his herd.

MUSTANG MAN, MUSTANG MAID

Airdates: 11/20/59, 9/02/60.

Cast: Robert Loggia (Elfego Baca), Brian Keith (Shadrack O'Reilly), Arthur Hunnicutt (Elias O'Brien), Beverly Garland (Suzanna O'Brien), Barry Kelley (Sheriff Holman), Lillian Bronson (Rachel O'Brien), Roger Perry (Luke Sawyer), James Coburn (Jack Carter), William Schallert (Deputy Denby), Robert

Nichols (Pronto), John Maxwell (Pappy Sawyer), Skip Farrell (Josh Jordan), Robert Hoy (Sam Carter).

Continuing the story begun in *Move Along Mustangers,* the eighth episode of the Elfego Baca mini-series again brings the Mustangers to the frontier lawyer asking for help in their battle with the cattlemen. The problems continue when Shadrack and Suzanna are refused service at a local store because, as the owner tells them, their business is not welcome. Shadrack tries to argue but is forcibly thrown out and a fight ensues. The store is demolished and Shadrack is taken to jail.

Production Notes:

- *Move Along Mustangers* and *Mustang Man, Mustang Maid* are also referred to by the overall title *Elfego Baca and the Mustangers.*
- DeForest Kelly of *Star Trek* fame has an unbilled part as Si Morgan, a shopkeeper who refuses to sell supplies to the Mustangers.

MY DOG, THE THIEF　　Airdates—Part 1: 9/21/69, 4/27/75, 7/22/79. Part 2: 9/28/69, 5/04/75, 7/29/79.

Cast: Dwayne Hickman (Jack Crandall), Mary Ann Mobley (Kim Lawrence), Elsa Lanchester (Mrs. Formby), Joe Flynn (P. J. Applegate), Roger C. Carmel (McClure), Mickey Shaughnessy (Foley), John van Dreelen (Travell), Charles Lane (Mr. Pfeiffer), Vaughn Taylor (Dog Catcher), Jim Begg (Baker).

Jack Crandall is a traffic reporter who is surprised to find a St. Bernard stowing away in his helicopter. His surprise is shared by his listeners, for when he spots the dog during a broadcast, he almost becomes hysterical. A bigger problem awaits, however, for his new pet is a kleptomaniac.

Production Note:

- *My Dog, the Thief* was released theatrically overseas in 1970.

MY FAMILY IS A MENAGERIE　　Airdates: 2/11/68, 6/08/75.

Cast: Ann Harrell (Sally Grant), Jack Garrity (Sheriff Eddie Patton), Kathy Thorn (Julie Morgan).

Sally Grant, widowed at an early age, inherits a small piece of land in Northern California. Wanting to start life anew, she closes her pet store and moves to the small town of Lakeside. Her past experience with animals serves her well when the sheriff asks her for help in capturing animals which have escaped from a travelling circus.

Production Note:

- Duke is the grandson of one of the dogs who starred in the episode *The Legend of Two Gypsy Dogs.* Along with the falcon and a raven used in this show, he was smuggled out of Hungary by trainer Hubert Wells.

MY TOWN　　Airdates (aired with *Casebusters* in a 2-hour format): 5/25/86, 8/31/86.

Cast: Glenn Ford (Lucas Wheeler), Meredith Salenger (Amber Wheeler), Mary Jackson (Mrs. McDaniel), Parker Jacobs (Tug Wheeler), Matt Norero (Billy Fisher), Laraine Newman (Cynthia Fisher), James Widdoes (Hal Fisher), Elya Baskin (Mr. Slovak), Richard Erdman (Fletcher Mays), Kate Mulgrew (Laura Adams), Jack Manning, Ellen Geer (Parent), Patrick Cranshaw (Elder Man), Critt Davis (Man #1), Don Perry (Man #2), Amy Lynne (Mary Lynn), Elizabeth Ward (Patty), Tom Bush (Bum), Ilana Martin (Laura).

Two children have to move to a small town to live with their uncle when their mother abandons them. There, they become involved in a suspected spy plot and a controversy over a sex education class.

Production Note:

- This was the pilot for an unsold series.

MYSTERY IN DRACULA'S CASTLE, THE　　Airdates—Part 1: 1/07/73, 7/01/73. Part 2: 1/14/73, 7/08/73. For the 1977–78 season the show aired in a 2-hour format: 9/11/77.

Cast: Clu Gulager (Keith Raynor), Mariette Hartley (Marsha Booth), Johnny Whitaker (Alfie Booth), Mills Watson (Noah Baxter), John Fiedler (Bill Wasdahl), James Callahan (Sheriff Wyndham), Scott Kolden (Leonard Booth), Gerald Michenaud (Morgan), Maggie Wellman (Jean Wyndham), Link Wyler (Patrolman), Pete Renoudet (Detective), Ben Wrigley (Grave Robber).

Marsha Booth takes her two children, Alfie and Leonard, on vacation to a small seaside town in California. She picks a quiet community, hoping to finish a novel she's working on, but the boys are not very happy. The town is too quiet for them and they're quickly bored, until Alfie decides to make his own horror movie. This brings them into contact with two jewel thieves who are hiding nearby.

Production Note:

- Sue Milburn, the winner of the 1970–71 Walt Disney Filmwriting Award, was in her junior year at New York University when she wrote a draft of the story that was developed into this show. Her prize was $2,500 plus 10 weeks employment at the Studio revising the script with the help of producer Bill Anderson.

MYSTERY OF EDWARD SIMS, THE

Airdates—Part 1: 3/31/68, 7/14/68. Part 2: 4/07/68, 7/21/68.

Cast: Roger Mobley (Gallegher), John McIntire (Whit White), John Dehner (Jason Gore), Warren Oates (John Blythe), John McLiam (Ephrem Killigrew), Michael Strong (Eldon Cain), Jeanette Nolan (Erm White), Jeanne Cooper (Della Martin), Ray Teal (Sheriff Snead), Stacey Maxwell (Darcy Killigrew), David Watson (William Killigrew), Wesley Lau (Mr. Parker), Byron Foulger (Henry Pederson).

Gallegher, the frontier reporter, returns for the tenth and eleventh installments of this Disney mini-series as he becomes involved in a land fraud. Someone named Edward Sims has sold land to a group of Cornish immigrants, who arrive in town hoping to settle there. They're dismayed to learn the land is valueless and more upset when Sims cannot be located.

Production Note:

- This was the last of the *Gallegher* stories.

NAPOLEON AND SAMANTHA

Airdate (2-hour format): 11/02/75. For the 1980–81 season the show was aired in two parts: Part 1: 6/21/81. Part 2: 6/28/81.

This 1972 theatrical release starring Michael Douglas, Will Geer, Johnny Whitaker, and Jodie Foster is the story of a boy who runs away to protect his unusual pet—a lion.

NASHVILLE COYOTE, THE

Airdates: 10/01/72, 8/26/73, 1/21/79.

Cast: Walter Forbes (Johnny Martin), William Garton (Harlan), Eugene Scott (Bluebelle's Master), Michael Edwards (Tug Captain), Vassar Clements, Tut Taylor, Randy Wood, Tom McKinney, Norman Blake, Peter Sayers (Nashville Losers), Chico (The Nashville Coyote).

Chico, a coyote who would like to be left alone to enjoy life in the desert near Barstow, California, finds himself in a strange new world when he's chased from his home by several dune buggy drivers. The frightened animal flees into a railroad yard and leaps aboard a passing freight train. The door slams shut and the surprised coyote's next stop is Nashville, Tennessee.

Production Notes:

- The narration for this episode was written in a form known as "talkin' blues," an outgrowth of old Elizabethan ballads.
- The show won an award from the Country Music Association, Inc., for Outstanding Contributions to Country Music in 1979.

NATURE'S BETTER BUILT HOMES

Airdates: 3/02/69, 6/25/72.

Cast (voices): Bill Thompson (J. Audubon Woodlore), Candy Candido, June Foray.

Some of the strangest structures in the world are the homes built by the animal community. Ranger J. Audubon Woodlore is the host for this look at animal residences, which features both animated sequences and clips from the *True-Life Adventure* series.

NATURE'S CHARTER TOURS

Airdates: 4/28/68, 6/01/75.

Cast (voices): Bill Thompson (J. Audubon Woodlore), George Walsh (narrator).

Ranger J. Audubon Woodlore hosts this story of migration, that often inexplicable phenomenon that lures animals across great distances and often against enormous dangers.

Production Notes:

- J. Audubon Woodlore's dialogue is all written in verse.
- The episode included footage from *Seal Island* and *White Wilderness*.

Nature's Strangest Oddballs Airdates: 3/29/70, 7/30/78.

The animal world is the latest recipient of the unique lecture style of Prof. Ludwig Von Drake, who opens the show in a display hall full of dinosaur exhibits. The professor notes that many of the animals have not changed greatly over the years. Live-action footage and animated sequences show these animals in their native surroundings.

Production Note:

• This episode made extensive use of footage from the 1959 theatrical featurette *Nature's Strangest Creatures*.

NEVER A DULL MOMENT   Airdate (2-hour format): 3/04/79.

This 1968 theatrical release stars Dick Van Dyke, Edward G. Robinson, and Dorothy Provine in the story of an second-rate actor who has to pull off the performance of his lifetime when he becomes involved in an art heist.

NEW ADVENTURES OF DAVY CROCKETT, THE

Disney brought the frontier hero back to life for the 1988–89 season, producing five new episodes with an updated cast. The individual episodes were *Davy Crockett: Rainbow in the Thunder; Davy Crockett: A Natural Man; Davy Crockett: Guardian Spirit; Davy Crockett: A Letter to Polly; Davy Crockett: Warrior's Farewell*. Refer to each of these titles for the episode descriptions. *Davy Crockett: Guardian Spirit* aired as a special.

NIKKI, WILD DOG OF THE NORTH

Airdate: Part 1: 9/27/64. Part 2: 10/04/64. This 1961 theatrical release is the story of a trapper, his wolf dog, and an orphaned bear in the Canadian Northwest.

NINE LIVES OF ELFEGO BACA, THE

Airdates: 10/03/58, 4/03/59.

Cast: Robert Loggia (Elfego Baca), Robert F. Simon (Deputy Sheriff Ed Morgan), Lisa Montell (Anita Chavez), Nestor Paiva (Justice of the Peace), Leonard Strong (Zangana Martinez), Charles Maxwell, Linc Foster (Jim Spears), Rico Alaniz (Fernandez).

The first chapter in the continuing story of Elfego Baca, a gunfighter who turned to the law, begins in 1884 as Elfego rides into Frisco, New Mexico. Elfego steps in to arrest a drunken cowboy when the sheriff is too afraid to act, which is not appreciated by the cowboy's friends. For the next 33 hours they fire a series of barrages at Elfego, even trying a dynamite blast to kill them. He survives the ordeal and becomes the new sheriff of Socorro, New Mexico.

Production Notes:

• This episode was based on an actual incident that occurred on November 18, 1884, when a group of Texas ranchers fired over 4,000 rounds into the hut from which Elfego Baca successfully held them off.

• One of the research items used in the preparation of the Elfego Baca stories was an autobiography written by the real Baca in 1944 when he ran for district attorney of Bernalillo, Sandoval, and Valencia counties in New Mexico.

• This episode was combined with *Four Down and Five Lives to Go* and released theatrically overseas in 1959.

NIOK   Airdates: 1/16/59, 9/11/59, 5/10/64.

This episode tells the story of the elephant, including several legends and tales that have developed about the huge beasts. The show is named after Niok, a 6-month-old baby Indian elephant that poses for the Disney animators. Niok happily spends his days at the Studio, where Walt helps feed the large baby with an oversized bottle.

Production Note:

• The sequence in Cambodia was released in 1957 as a theatrical short subject. The footage was shot near the ancient city of Angkor Wat.

NO DEPOSIT, NO RETURN   Airdates— Part 1: 11/06/82. Part 2: 11/13/82.

This 1976 theatrical release stars David Niven, Darren McGavin, Barbara Feldon, Kim Richards, and Brad Savage in the story of two runaways who befriend a pair of hapless thieves.

NORTH AVENUE IRREGULARS, THE

Airdate (2-hour format): 5/10/87.

This 1979 theatrical release starring Edward Herrmann, Barbara Harris, Susan Clark, Karen Valentine, Michael Constantine, and Cloris Leachman is the story of a small-town minister who bands together with local housewives to drive the mob out of town.

NOSEY, THE SWEETEST SKUNK IN THE WEST   Airdates: 11/19/72, 4/17/77.

Cast: Jane Biddle (Kim Walker), James Chandler (Ben Walker), Walter Carlson (Mr. Carmady), Lois Binford (Mrs. Carmady).

Ben Walker is an artist who lives with his daughter Kim in the desolate countryside of Red Rock County, Arizona, having quit his job in the city in order to paint western landscapes. The Walkers live in an old house trailer, enjoying the quiet pace of the area, and Kim spends many hours hiking through the countryside. On one of these trips she finds an orphaned baby skunk hiding in a tree. She takes it home and the curious animal scampers around the trailer, poking its nose into every opening it finds.

Not Quite Human

This made-for-television movie first aired on The Disney Channel. It also aired on the anthology series in two parts—Part 1: 12/20/87, 9/04/88. Part 2: 12/27/87, 9/11/88.

Not Quite Human II

This made-for-television movie first aired on The Disney Channel. It also aired on the anthology series on 4/01/90.

Not So Lonely Lighthouse Keeper, The   Airdates: 9/17/67, 5/19/68, 6/23/74.

Cast: Clarence Hastings (Capt. Moses Haskell, the Lighthouse Keeper), Ingrid Niemela (Mrs. Haskell).

Anacapa Island, located off the coast of Southern California, is uninhabited except for the lighthouse keeper and his wife. The light is a vital navigation beacon, warning ships of the dangers posed by Anacapa and several neighboring islands. Although only two humans live there, the island is far from empty.

Production Note:

* The episode was filmed on location on Anacapa Island, where an 85-foot-high lighthouse was being replaced by a smaller automated beacon.

Now You See Him, Now You Don't

Airdate (2-hour format): 10/26/75. In later seasons the show aired in two parts—Part 1: 10/15/78, 7/12/81. Part 2: 10/22/78, 7/19/81.
This 1972 theatrical release stars Kurt Russell, Cesar Romero, and Joe Flynn in the story of a college student who accidentally discovers the secret of invisibility.

Officer and a Duck, An   Airdate: Syndicated.

This program looks at Donald Duck's many appearances as a soldier during World War II. New dialogue is used with footage from *The Spirit of '43* as Donald decides to enlist after listening to a radio commercial extolling the virtues of today's army.

Production Note:

* This episode is slightly different than the home video release of the same title.

Old Yeller

This 1957 theatrical release first aired as a special. It also aired on the anthology series in two parts on 11/09/80 and 11/16/80 and in a 2-hour format on 6/08/86.

Omega Connection, The   Airdate (2-hour format): 3/18/79. In later seasons the show aired in two parts—Part 1: 8/03/80, 9/03/83. Part 2: 8/10/80, 9/10/83.

Cast: Jeffrey Byron (Luther Starling), Larry Cedar (Roger), Roy Kinnear (Bidley), Lee Montague (Vorg), Mona Washbourne (Aunt Lydia), David Kossoff (Professor Buchinski), Frank Windsor (McGuffin), Walter Gotell (Simmons), Nigel Davenport (Minton), Dudley Sutton (Goetz), David Battley (Peters), Julian Orchard (Driscoll), Kathleen Harrison (Elderly Lady), Percy Herbert (Ship's Captain), Don Fellows (General), Bruce Boa (Colonel), Wolfe Morris (Dr. Krause), Milos Kirek (Kaplan), Andre Maranne (Duvalier), Rita Webb (Cockney Woman), George Pravda (Kolenkov), Minah Bird (Narcotics Agent).

Luther Starling is a young American government agent visiting his friend Roger Pike in London, hoping for a relaxing vacation. His plans are suddenly changed when the two boys witness the kidnapping of Professor Buchinski, a scientist who had defected from an Eastern European nation.

On Vacation   Airdates: 3/07/56, 8/19/60, 7/28/68, 8/07/77 (On Vacation with Mickey Mouse and Friends), 6/29/86 (On Vacation with Mickey Mouse and Friends).

Jiminy Cricket hosts this animated look at Mickey, Donald, and Goofy as they go on vacation.

Production Notes:

* This episode also aired as a special on 4/11/79 under the title *On Vacation with Mickey Mouse and Friends.*
* Footage from *On Vacation* was used in *The Making of Mickey's Christmas Carol,* aired on The Disney Channel and released for home video.

One Day at Teton Marsh   Airdates: 11/08/64, 5/09/65, 5/03/70, 4/20/75.

This is a look at a day in the life of the animal inhabitants of Teton Marsh, located near the massive Grand Teton Mountains.

Production Note:

- Filming took place on location in Grand Teton National Park in Jackson Hole, Wyoming. To film this story of "one day" took the entire summer.

ONE DAY ON BEETLE ROCK   Airdates:
11/19/67, 6/02/68, 12/31/72.
Cast: The Robert Bennett family (themselves)

Sequoia National Park in California is the setting for this look at a seemingly quiet area that is actually teeming with wildlife. Beetle Rock, a granite formation, serves as the focal point, attracting numerous animals during the day.

Production Notes:

- This "one-day" story took 18 months to film.
- An edited version of this show was released to the educational market as *A Day in Nature's Community*.

101 PROBLEMS OF HERCULES, THE
Airdates: 10/16/66, 5/23/71, 4/04/76.
Cast: Harold Reynolds (Buckeye Jones), David Farrow (Sam), Elliott Lindsey (Capt. Bill Shriner), Kathe McDowell (Mrs. Shriner), Ray Barlow (Mort).

Sheepherding in the Old West is a strenuous job that requires a well-tuned team of men and sheepdogs. One example is Buckeye Jones, a herder who uses three dogs to help watch over a flock during the 1870s. Hercules is a Hungarian kuvasz; Boomer, an English sheepdog; and Lady is a Border collie. This seemingly mismatched trio has proven to work effectively as a team, enabling Jones to entrust the sheep to their care.

Production Note:

- This episode was based on a true story.

ONE LITTLE INDIAN   Airdates—Part 1:
9/26/76. Part 2: 10/03/76.
This 1973 theatrical release stars James Garner, Vera Miles, and Clay O'Brien in the story of a deserter from the U.S. Cavalry who flees on a most unusual mount—a camel.

100,000,000 FRANC TRAIN ROBBERY, THE
This is Part 1 of *The Horse without a Head*.

OPERATION UNDERSEA   Airdates:
12/08/54, 3/16/55, 6/29/55, 8/25/63, 4/04/71.
Walt tells how he became interested in the undersea world during the preparations for filming of Jules Verne's *20,000 Leagues under the Sea*, the Studio's latest live-action film. Several new film techniques had to be perfected, often under difficult conditions. Winston Hibler tells the story of this unusual film project.

Production Notes:

- This episode won an Emmy Award in 1954 for Best Individual Program of the Year. Editors Grant Smith and Lynn Harrison were also awarded an Emmy for Best Television Film Editing.
- Portions of this show were later used in the episode *Pacifically Peeking*.

OTTER IN THE FAMILY, AN   Airdates:
2/21/65, 4/06/69, 12/30/73.
Cast: Tom Beecham (Howard Blaine), Mable Beecham (Martha Blaine), Gary Beecham (Gary Blaine), Donald Cyr (Al Whitley), "Snoop" Beecham (Himself).

Gary Blaine is a 9-year-old boy living in northern Wisconsin, where he enjoys wandering through the countryside with his Labrador retriever, Tim. One day he finds a baby otter caught in a hunter's trap and frees it, taking the wounded animal home to care for it. The boy convinces his parents to let him keep the otter until it's well enough to survive by itself, but Tim doesn't care much for this intrusion that takes so much of Gary's time.

Production Note:

- Roy E. Disney first met the Beecham family during the filming of *Flash, The Teenage Otter*. Knowing they had a pet otter, he thought of them when work began on this story, and arranged to film the episode at their home.

OUR FRIEND THE ATOM   Airdates:
1/23/57, 4/24/57.
Dr. Heinz Haber, a noted scientist in the field of atomic energy, hosts this look at what may be an exciting new power source. Haber begins by comparing atomic energy to a genie in a bottle. Both are capable of doing either tremendous good or unbelievable evil, and it is up to humankind to develop safe controls over this largely unexplored science.

Production Notes:

- In 1956, Golden Press published *The Walt Disney Story of Our Friend the Atom* by Dr. Haber, incorporating artwork developed for the show. A paperback version was published by Dell Publishing for an older market.
- Disney had originally planned a show titled *Adam to Atom* on the subject of atomic energy. That show was canceled, but some of the material was incorporated in this episode.
- This episode was released theatrically overseas in 1958.

OUR UNSUNG VILLAINS   Airdates: 2/15/56, 6/10/60.

The Slave in the Magic Mirror hosts this tribute to Disney's villains, for he claims that without them, no one would need heroes.

OUTLAW CATS OF COLOSSAL CAVE, THE

Airdates: 9/28/75, 6/13/76.
Cast: Gilbert de la Peña (Paco), Jose Maierhauser (Joe Meyers).

A female bobcat looking for a safe den to give birth decides to move into Colossal Cave in Arizona. Soon, her two kittens are exploring the many passages in this unusual underground world. One of the cave's guides, Paco, finds them and manages to partially tame the animals.

Production Notes:

- Colossal Cave is a popular tourist attraction outside Tucson, Arizona, with over 39 miles of tunnels.
- Director Hank Schloss had planned to capture several bobcat kittens near Colossal Cave, but a local drought kept the wildlife up in the hills. He then tried to find a pair of 6-week-old kittens but was instead shipped two 6-day-old bobcats. They were taken to the Arizona-Sonora Desert Museum near Tucson until they were old enough for filming. The crew filmed everything that did not involve the kittens while the young cats grew and were trained.

OWL THAT DIDN'T GIVE A HOOT, THE

Airdates: 12/15/68, 7/06/69, 8/15/76.
Cast: David Potter (Johnny Fredericks), Marian Fletcher (Nora Fredericks), John Fetzer (Vic Fredericks), Hyde Clayton (Sam Miller).

Johnny Fredericks, a young boy taking photographs of wildlife near Salt Lake City, Utah, discovers an abandoned baby great horned owl. Johnny takes the animal home against his parents' advice and tries to raise it to maturity.

Production Note:

- Filming took place on location at Park City near Salt Lake City, Utah, over an 11-month period. When filming was completed, the owl they used had become so tame that it was kept as a pet by director Frank Zuniga.

PABLO AND THE DANCING CHIHUAHUA

Airdates—Part 1: 1/28/68, 6/23/68, 8/20/72. Part 2: 2/04/68, 6/30/68, 8/27/72.
Cast: Armando Islas (Pablo), Francesca Jarvis (Helen Gordon), Walker Tilley (Caretaker), Manuel Rivera (Manuel).

A young boy finds adventure in the desert as he searches for his missing uncle. Pablo's quest gets off to a bad start when he's caught trying to cross the border between Mexico and the United States, but he sneaks away while the border officials are examining the papers of Helen Gordon, an American tourist. Her pet Chihuahua follows him as he runs into the desert.

Production Notes:

- This episode, shot on location in Arizona, took two years to film. The production company had to plan for the normal growth of the young star so scenes shot over the 2-year span matched and didn't make his 6-inch change in height noticeable.
- This show was released theatrically overseas in 1969.

PACIFICALLY PEEKING   Airdate: 10/06/68.

Moby Duck, a new Disney animated character, makes his debut in this study of life on several Pacific Ocean islands. The show is presented as a "book," with each "chapter" relating to a specific topic.

Production Note:

- This was Moby Duck's only screen appearance, although he was featured in numerous Disney comic books. The character was to have been called Peg-Leg Duck.

PANCHO, THE FASTEST PAW IN THE WEST
Airdates: 2/02/69, 8/05/73.

Cast: Armando Islas (Manuel), Frank Keith (Sam Larrabee), Albert Hachmeister (Jack Kelso).

The year is 1880 and the setting is the Texas Panhandle, where a runaway orphan named Manuel and his dog, Pancho, are helped by Sam Larabee, a kindly peddler. The trio travels together, finding work wherever possible, just glad to be living free.

Production Note:

- Pancho was played by Hector, a Chesapeake Bay retriever who took his part so seriously that he bit a stunt man during the climactic battle scene, requiring eight stitches to close the wound.

PARENT TRAP, THE
This 1961 theatrical release first aired on 10/26/74 as a special. It was later broadcast on the anthology series on 5/16/76 in a 2-hour and 30-minute format and on 5/06/79 and 4/05/87 in a 2-hour format. Other special broadcasts in a 2-hour format were on 2/13/82 and 5/18/89. The 2-hour broadcasts were shortened by eliminating the majority of the musical sequences.

PARENT TRAP II
This made-for-television movie first aired on The Disney Channel. It also aired on the anthology series on 2/22/87, when it was followed by an edited version of The Disney Channel special On Location: Parent Trap II and previews of upcoming episodes.

PARENT TRAP III   Airdates—Part 1: 4/09/89, 9/10/89. Part 2: 4/16/89, 9/17/89.

Cast: Hayley Mills (Susan Evers/Sharon Evers), Barry Bostwick (Jeffrey Wyatt), Ray Baker (Nick), Patricia Richardson (Cassie McGuire), Christopher Gartin (David), Jon Maynard Pennell (Hawk), Joy Creel (Megan Wyatt), Leanna Creel (Lisa Wyatt), Monica Creel (Jessie Wyatt), Loretta Devine (Thelma), Richard Coca (Sergio), Robert P. Lieb (Shopkeeper), Nancy Fish (Judge Hickock), Tommy Morgan (Andy), Sharon Owens (Blair), John Cardone (Customs Official).

When Jeffrey Wyatt first meets Susan Evers, they both decide they don't like each other. Jeffrey has another problem to deal with, though, for his three daughters are coming home from a vacation and he has to tell them about his upcoming wedding. His plans change when his daughters enlist the help of Susan's twin sister to make Jeffrey fall in love with Susan instead.

Production Notes:

- This second sequel to the 1961 film *The Parent Trap* ignores the events and characters seen in *Parent Trap II*.
- This was the first of a number of episodes intended for the anthology series. The story continues in *Parent Trap Hawaiian Honeymoon*.
- The Creel sisters are identical triplets.

PARENT TRAP HAWAIIAN HONEYMOON
Airdates—Part 1: 11/19/89. Part 2: 11/26/89. The show also aired that season in a 2-hour format: 5/27/90.

Cast: Hayley Mills (Susan Wyatt/Sharon Evers), Barry Bostwick (Jeffrey Wyatt), John M. Jackson (Ray Devlin), Sasha Mitchell (Jack Surfer), Lightfield Lewis (Tim Harris), Glenn Shadix (Chuck Schtutz), Leanna Creel (Lisa Wyatt), Monica Creel (Jessie Wyatt), Joy Creel (Megan Wyatt), Jayne Meadows (Charlotte Brink), Nancy Lenehan (Mrs. Harris), Joe Mays (Ben Milton), Wayne Federman (Messenger), Al Acain (Cab Driver), Mike Ebner (Mr. Harris), Kamika Nakanelua (Keo), Steven Perry (Cop at Luau).

This sequel to *Parent Trap III* begins as Jeffrey learns that he has inherited a hotel in Hawaii. His family wants to see the place, but Jeffrey wants to go to Australia on his honeymoon. Susan sees this as her chance to get to know the triplets better, and when they realize this, they convince her and Jeffrey to take them to Hawaii. All their hard work is apparently for nothing, for when they arrive at the hotel, the family is shocked to learn that the place is a rundown dump.

PAUPER KING, THE
This is Part 1 of *The Prince and the Pauper.*

PEE WEES VS. CITY HALL, THE
This is Part 1 of *Moochie of Pop Warner Football.*

PEOPLE AND PLACES—TIBURON, SARDINIA, MOROCCO (AND) ICEBREAKERS
Airdates: 10/05/55, 4/18/56, 7/04/56.
This episode is comprised of several short subjects from the *People and Places* theatrical series.

Production Note:

- *Sardinia* was released theatrically in 1956. *Tiburon*, which took William N.

Smith four years to film, was planned for release as part of the *People and Places* series. The series was canceled, however, and the footage was only used in this show.

PEOPLE OF THE DESERT   Airdates: 4/10/57, 8/06/58.

Life in the desert is not easy, for the harsh climate can kill an unprepared traveler without warning. This show looks at two different cultures that have managed to survive in such areas, the first being the Navajo Indians. The *People and Places* theatrical release *The Blue Men of Morocco*, the second half of this episode, provides a look at these nomadic wanderers of the desert.

Production Note:

• *Navajo Adventure* was released theatrically in 1957.

PERILOUS ASSIGNMENT   Airdates: 11/06/59.

Cast: Michael Rennie, James MacArthur, Janet Munro, James Donald, Herbert Lom, Walter Fitzgerald, Laurence Naismith, Nora Swinburne, Lee Patterson, Ferdy Mayne.

This show takes a look at the many far-off locations where Disney crews have worked.

PERILS OF A HOMESICK STEER, THE

This is Part 2 of *Sancho, The Homing Steer.*

PETER TCHAIKOVSKY STORY, THE

Airdates: 1/30/59, 6/19/59.

Cast: Grant Williams (Peter Tchaikovsky as an adult), Rex Hill (Peter Tchaikovsky as a child), Lilyan Chauvin (Fanny Durbach), Leon Askin (Anton Rubinstein), Narda Onyx (Desiree Artot), Galina Ulanova and The Corps de Ballet of The Bolshoi Theatre.

When work began on the Studio's animated feature *Sleeping Beauty*, it was decided to use the music of Peter Tchaikovsky (from the ballet of the same name). Researchers working on the film began to note several interesting facts about Tchaikovsky's life and decided to produce a show about this famous composer.

Production Notes:

• This documentary is followed by previews of scenes from *Sleeping Beauty* narrated by Walt.
• Disney achieved a major first when he broadcast this episode, for it was simulcast in stereo.

• This episode was originally planned as a theatrical featurette and was released overseas in 1959.

PETE'S DRAGON   Airdate (2-hour format): 9/21/86.

This 1977 theatrical release starring Helen Reddy, Jim Dale, Mickey Rooney, Red Buttons, Shelley Winters, and Sean Marshall is the story of how an orphan and his pet dragon change the lives of those in a small fishing village. This broadcast used the foreign version of this film, which is shorter than the U.S. release. It also included previews of other shows for the season. *Pete's Dragon* was also aired on 2/19/89 as a special.

PHANTOM DHOW, THE

This is Part 1 of *Hamad and the Pirates.*

PIGEON THAT WORKED A MIRACLE, THE

Airdates: 10/10/58, 4/22/62, 1/09/66, 12/28/75.

Cast: Bradley Payne (Chad Smith), Winifred Davenport (Mrs. Smith).

Chad Smith is an active boy who receives a spinal injury while playing baseball, resulting in his being confined to a wheelchair. His mother encourages him to find a hobby and he picks pigeon racing, raising the birds in a small coop behind the house. He develops a special bond with one bird, that eventually encourages him to walk again.

Production Note:

• This episode was released theatrically overseas in 1962.

PLAUSIBLE IMPOSSIBLE, THE   Airdates: 10/31/56, 5/22/57, 10/09/60.

What is a "plausible impossible"? Walt explains it as something that is impossible in real life but can be convincingly portrayed in some manner. He opens a forthcoming book entitled *The Art of Animation* and shows examples of this technique that date back to the ancient Egyptians and Greeks.

Production Note:

• The *Art of Animation* book Walt refers to was only a prop and was not the book of the same title written by Bob Thomas.

PLUTO AND HIS FRIENDS   Airdate (30-minute format): 7/31/82.

Narrator: Gary Owens.

This salute to Mickey's faithful pal, Pluto, begins as Mickey and Pluto arrive at the

"Tailwagger Awards," a prestigious honor given to the most promising dog actor. Pluto is the winner, and the show shows a typical day in his life.

Production Note:

- The cartoon *Society Dog Show* was used for the *Tailwagger Awards* segment. Bridge animation was also used from the episode *On Vacation*.

PLUTO'S DAY   Airdates: 12/12/56, 8/07/57, 7/03/59, 4/06/80, 1/18/81.
Walt opens the show by displaying an award won by Pluto for being "the most promising dog actor," remarking that Pluto achieved his success by just being himself. To demonstrate this, Walt presents a typical day in Pluto's life.

POLLY   Airdates (2-hour format): 11/12/89, 9/09/90.
Cast: Keshia Knight Pulliam (Polly), Phylicia Rashad (Aunt Polly Harrington), Dorian Harewood (Dr. Shannon), Barbara Montgomery (Mrs. Conley), T.K. Carter (George Dodds), Vanessa Bell Calloway (Nancy Palmer), Brandon Adams (Jimmy Bean), Ken Page (Mayor Warren), Larry Riley (Reverend Gillis), Butterfly McQueen (Miss Priss), Brock Peters (Eban Pendergast), Celeste Holm (Miss Snow), George Anthony Bell (Mr. Tarbell), Tom McGreevey (Doctor), Michael Peters (Mr. Thurm), Vickilyn Reynolds (Mrs. Tarbell), William Thomas, Jr. (Manager), Lorraine Fields (Salesgirl #1).
Little Polly Whittier arrives in Harrington, Alabama, in 1955, where she has been sent to live with her Aunt Polly, the richest black woman in the county. Aunt Polly is very stern, and despite Polly's best efforts, refuses to warm up to her niece.

Production Notes:

- This was a musical remake of Disney's 1960 *Pollyanna*, with a black cast.
- This show led to the sequel *Polly— Comin' Home!*, aired as a special.
- The 9/09/90 airing was the last network episode of the anthology series.

POLLYANNA   Airdates—Part 1: 12/01/63, 10/29/67. Part 2: 12/08/63, 11/05/67. Part 3: 12/15/63, 11/12/67. For the 1980–81 season the show was aired in a 3-hour format: 5/24/81.
This 1960 theatrical release stars Hayley Mills, Jane Wyman, Richard Egan, and Karl

Malden in the story of a young orphan who brings new life to her new family and the local townspeople. It was adapted for television by Jack Bruner.

Production Note:

- This film also aired as a special on 3/8/75.

POP WARNER FOOTBALL
See: *Moochie of Pop Warner Football.*

POSTPONED WEDDING, THE   Airdates: 1/01/61, 8/20/61.
Cast: Guy Williams (Zorro and Don Diego), Annette Funicello (Constancia de la Torre), Henry Calvin (Sergeant Garcia), Gene Sheldon (Bernardo), Mark Damon (Miguel Serrano), Carlos Romero (Ansar), George J. Lewis (Don Alejandro).
The third hour-long episode of *Zorro* begins as Don Diego and Bernardo greet Constancia de la Torre, who has returned to the pueblo after a lengthy absence. When they last saw her she was a little girl, but she's now a beautiful 17-year-old. Constancia is glad to see them and Sergeant Garcia, but she gets nervous when the sergeant wants to inspect her luggage. She stalls him, but Bernardo knows something's wrong when he can barely lift a small bag. Zorro later discovers it full of jewels.

PRAIRIE (AND) SEAL ISLAND   Airdates: 11/10/54, 3/23/55, 7/06/55, 4/28/63.
Cast: James Algar, Winston Hibler.
James Algar describes some of the tricks the Disney photographers must use to capture the lives of animals in their native habitats. The next portion of the show features animals from the prairies of North America, detailing their lives through the seasons of a typical year.
Finally, Winston Hibler narrates the theatrical release *Seal Island* as the show moves northward to Alaska and the Pribilof Islands, the migratory home of the fur seal.

PRE-OPENING REPORT FROM DISNEYLAND, THE (AND) A TRIBUTE TO MICKEY MOUSE,   Airdate: 7/13/55.
With the opening of Disneyland only days away, Walt provides a final look at the many details necessary to ensure that the Park will be ready. He begins by showing the audience a large map of the site, then introduces Winston Hibler, who tells how Studio technicians went about designing and

building the unusual rides and shows about to open.

The second half of this show was originally aired as part of *The Disneyland Story* and is described under that title.

Production Note:

- This episode is also known as *A Further Report on Disneyland*.

PRESENT FOR DONALD, A Airdates: 12/22/54, 12/19/56, 12/26/65, 12/24/72. The show opens with Walt in his office, which is gaily decorated for the holiday season. He mentions a package that arrived for Donald Duck. Donald arrives to open the gift, which contains a movie projector and a reel of film. He's soon watching the story of Pablo, a strange penguin who tries to leave the cold weather of the South Pole in search of a warmer climate.

Production Note:

- This show consisted almost entirely of footage from the 1945 theatrical release *The Three Caballeros*. Although the 1954 credits list one of the characters as "Joe" Carioca, the correct name is Jose.

PRINCE AND THE PAUPER, THE Airdates—Part 1: 3/11/62, 8/12/62, 4/16/67. Part 2: 3/18/62, 8/19/62, 4/23/67. Part 3: 3/25/62, 8/26/62, 4/30/67.

Cast: Guy Williams (Miles Hendon), Laurence Naismith (Lord Hertford), Donald Houston (John Canty), Sean Scully (Prince Edward/Tom Canty), Niall MacGinnis (Father Andrew), Geoffrey Keen (Yokel), Walter Hudd (Archbishop of Canterbury), Paul Rogers (King Henry VIII), Dorothy Alison (Mrs. Canty), Jane Asher (Lady Jane Grey), Peter Butterworth (Will, the Knifegrinder), Reginald Beckwith (Landlord), Sheila Allen (Princess Mary), Derek Godfrey (Hugh Hendon), Geoffrey Bayldon (Sir Jeffrey), Nigel Green (The Ruffler), Charles Heslop (Old Gentleman), Diarmid Cammell (John Marlow), Richard O'Sullivan (Hugo), Meurig Wyn-Jones (Len), Andrew Faulds (Captain of the Guards), Katya Douglas (Princess Elizabeth), Martin Boddey (Waterman), Bruce Seton, Michael Ripper (Street Seller).

Mark Twain's timeless story of a poor English boy who trades places with a prince is told in three parts. *The Pauper King* opens in the year 1537 as two boys are born. One is Prince Edward Tudor, the only son of King Henry VIII; the other is Tom Canty, son of a thief. Years later the two are united by a strange twist of fate that affects all of England.

Production Note:

- This show won *TV Guide's* award for Best Dramatic Program of the Year, and was released theatrically overseas in 1962.

PROGRESS REPORT, A (AND) NATURE'S HALF ACRE Airdates: 2/09/55, 5/04/55. Work continues on the Disneyland theme park as Walt narrates the first half of this show, which provides a look at the construction progress.

Production Note:

- *Nature's Half Acre* was also included in the episode *The Titlemakers (and) Nature's Half Acre*, which aired during the 1960–61 season.

PROMISED LAND, THE Airdates: 3/19/61. *Cast:* Dewey Martin (Daniel Boone), Mala Powers (Rebecca Boone), Diane Jergens (Marybelle Yancey), William Herrin (Budd Yancey), Kevin Corcoran (James Boone), Anthony Caruso (Blackfish), Wally Brown (Cyrus Whittey), Dean Fredericks (Crowfeather), George Wallace (Mordecai), Stan Jones (Doc Slocum), Jean Inness (Sarah Watkins), Slim Pickens (Corporal Gass).

The fourth and final episode of Daniel Boone continues the story begun in *The Wilderness Road*. The wagon train is having a difficult time crossing the mountains, so Boone orders the settlers to dispose of any items not required to live, thereby angering many of the travelers. An Indian arrow kills one of the men, alerting Boone that his old enemy Crowfeather has returned.

Production Note:

- Co-star Kevin Corcoran was joined by two of his real brothers, Brian and Kerry, who also played the parts of Boone's children.

PROUD BIRD FROM SHANGHAI, THE Airdate: 12/16/73. The U.S. consul to Shanghai in 1881, Judge Owen Denny, brings a number of China's ring-necked pheasants home to Oregon, where he hopes they can adapt to life in the wild. He selects the strongest of the birds, which he names War Lord, and sets the pheasant free, along with three hens.

Production Note:

- This episode, which took over 9 months to film on location in Washington State, was based on a true story.

PROWLERS OF THE EVERGLADES
See: *The Crisler Story (and) Prowlers of the Everglades.*

RACE FOR SURVIVAL   Airdate: 3/05/78.
Cast: Bosco Hogan (Phil Garrison), Peter Lukoye (Kasuku), Saeed Jaffrey (Patel), Dick Thomsett (Airport Controller).

Game warden Phil Garrison is trapped in the wreckage of his small plane on the Mara Plains of East Africa. His greyhound, Smokey, escapes from the wreckage and sets off with a note from Phil that gives the plane's location and asks for help. While the dog is away, a tribe of friendly Masai warriors helps Garrison out of the plane, but Smokey doesn't know this and continues his search.

RAG, A BONE, A BOX OF JUNK, A
Airdate: 10/11/64.
Walt visits the office of Bill Justice and Xavier Atencio, who are working on the stop-motion animated titles for the movie *The Parent Trap.* This style of animation requires that each item be photographed, moved ever so slightly, and photographed again. When the film is run through a projector, the single frames appear to move, providing a unique form of entertainment.

RANGE WAR AT TOMBSTONE   Airdates:
12/18/59, 7/08/60.
Cast: Tom Tryon (Texas John Slaughter), Darryl Hickman (Ashley Carstairs), Betty Lynn (Viola Howell), Regis Toomey (David Howell), Jan Merlin (Robbie), James Westerfield (Ike Clanton), Nora Marlowe (Rachel Howell).

Part 8 of *The Tales of Texas John Slaughter* begins as John and his friend Ashley Carstairs are driving a herd of cattle to Tombstone, Arizona. En route, they come upon a deserted Conestoga wagon and stop to investigate, only to be taken prisoner by a young girl. Her name is Viola Howell, and her parents join her in accusing John and Ashley of being thieves. John disarms her and convinces them of their error, then agrees to escort them to Tombstone.

RANGER OF BROWNSTONE, THE
Airdates: 3/17/68, 8/11/74, 9/04/77, 8/05/79, 6/26/82.
Ranger J. Audubon Woodlore is trying to run his park as efficiently as possible, but somehow Humphrey, one of the bears, manages to continually disrupt the operation as seen in *Grin and Bear It, In the Bag, Hooked Bear, Rugged Bear, Grand Canyonscope,* and *Bearly Asleep.*

RANGER'S GUIDE TO NATURE, A
Airdates: 11/13/66, 4/11/76.
Walt takes a look at a specialized camps dedicated to the study of nature. It's run by Ranger J. Audubon Woodlore, who has written *Ranger Woodlore's Nature Guide.* Walt opens the book and the pages come to life in a combination of animation and live-action nature footage.

Production Note:

- Huey, Dewey, and Louie have children's voices rather than the Donald Duck–like voices used in the theatrical cartoons.

RAPIDS AHEAD (AND) BEAR COUNTRY
Airdate: 10/16/60.
Cast: Brian Keith (William "Bill" Dunn), John Beal (Maj. John Wesley Powell), James Drury (Capt. Walter Powell), R.G. Armstrong (Oramel Howland), Ben Johnson (George Bradley), L.Q. Jones (Billy "Missouri" Hawkins), Dan Sheridan (Jack Sumner), David Stollery (Andrew "Andy" Hall), Stan Jones (Seneca Howland), David Frankham (Frank Goodman).

The first part of the show deals with people and the second with animals. Each type of story required new and unusual photographic techniques, as demonstrated in a behind-the-scenes look at the filming of the theatrical release *Ten Who Dared.*

Production Notes:

- *Rapids Ahead* was narrated by Dick Tufield.
- The second half of this show was first seen in the episode *Yellowstone Story (and) Bear Country.*

RASCAL   Airdates—Part 1: 2/11/73. Part 2: 2/18/73.
This 1969 theatrical release stars Bill Mumy, Steve Forrest, and Pamela Toll in the story of a young boy and his father who are brought

closer together when the youngster adopts an orphaned raccoon.

REDCOAT STRATEGY   Airdates: 1/15/60, 5/27/60.

Cast: Leslie Nielsen (Gen. Francis Marion), Robert Douglas (General Cornwallis), John Sutton (Col. Banastre Tarleton), Barbara Eiler (Mary Videaux), Myron Healey (Col. Peter Horry), Henry Daniell (Colonel Townes), Dorothy Green (Mrs. Townes), J. Pat O'Malley (Sergeant O'Reilly), Jordan Whitfield (Oscar), Louise Beavers (Dehlia), Hal Stalmaster (Gwynn), Donald Randolph (Mr. Videaux), Slim Pickens (Plunkett), Eleanor Audley (Cook), Mary Field (Cathy), Clarence Muse (Old Joseph), George N. Neise (Lieutenant Peters), Robin Hughes (Dragoon Disguised as Patriot), Alan Caillou (Dragoon Disguised as Patriot).

Part 5 of the "Swamp Fox" story involves General Marion in a plot to capture a high-ranking British officer, Colonel Townes. An ambush forces the colonel's coach into a lake and the officer emerges ready for a fight. Marion declines Townes's challenge to a duel and informs him that he is to be taken to a colonial prison. Trouble ensues when Marion agrees to take Townes home first for dry clothes.

Production Note:

- Eleanor Audley, who appears in this episode, was the voice of the stepmother in *Cinderella* and of Maleficent in *Sleeping Beauty.*

RESCUE, THE   Airdate (2-hour format): 3/25/90.

This 1988 theatrical release is the story of a band of teenagers who stage a daring rescue mission when their fathers are stranded on a military mission deep within North Korea.

RETURN OF THE BIG CAT   Airdates—Part 1: 10/06/74, 5/18/75. Part 2: 10/13/74, 5/25/75.

Cast: Jeremy Slate (John McClaren), Patricia Crowley (Sophina McClaren), David Wayne (Grandpa Jubal), Christian Juttner (Leroy McClaren), Kim Richards (Amy McClaren), Ted Gehring (Hunk Purdy), Don Knight (J. C.), Geoff Parks (Lucas), Lonny Chapman (Frank Brannen), Bryan O'Byrne (Perc), Jeff East (Josh McClaren).

The McClaren family is trying to establish a foothold in the timber territory of Northern California during the 1890s. John and Sophina McClaren and their three children, Josh, Amy, and Leroy, are joined by Sophina's father, Jubal. The family's lifestyle is threatened when a vicious cougar returns to the area. The cat had attacked Amy two years earlier, frightening her so badly she hasn't spoken since.

Production Notes:

- Bear, the 130-pound cougar seen in this episode, was trained by Ron Oxley, who worked with the animal stars of *Gentle Ben* and *Daktari.*
- Filming took place on location at the Mammoth Lakes region of California.
- The show was released theatrically overseas in 1975.

RETURN OF THE SHAGGY DOG, THE   Airdate (2-hour format): 11/01/87.

Cast: Gary Kroeger (Wilby Daniels), Todd Waring (Moochie Daniels), Michelle Little (Betty Fielding), Cindy Morgan (Laura Wells), Jane Carr (Myra), Gavin Reed (Carl), K. Callan (Mrs. Fielding), James MacKrell (Mr. Fielding), Jack Ammon (Professor Plumkutt), Paul G. Batten (Officer No. 1), Lorena Gale (Officer No. 2), Gary Hetherington (The Director), Antony Holland (Minister), Don Mackay (Mr. Frampton), Betty Phillips (Cynthia), Leroy Schultz (Florist), Raimund Stamm (Raglin), Denalda Williams (Ellen), Bobby Porter (The Shaggy Dog).

This sequel to the 1959 film *The Shaggy Dog* begins as Professor Plumkutt dictates his will. His servants, Myra and Carl, are trying to get him to leave them his estate. Instead, he gives them his sheepdog, telling them it's a direct descendent of Lucrezia Borgia's dog. He also hands them a ring, saying it's his most valuable possession, but he dies before he can reveal its secret.

Production Notes:

- This film ignored the plot and characters of *The Shaggy D.A.*, an earlier theatrical sequel to *The Shaggy Dog.*
- *The Return of the Shaggy Dog* was also aired in two parts during the *Family Classics* series of specials on 4/13/89 and 4/20/89.

RETURN OF THE TRUE SON

This is Part 1 of *The Light in the Forest.*

RICHEST CAT IN THE WORLD, THE
Airdates (2-hour format): 3/09/86, 10/19/86.

Cast: Ramon Bieri (Oscar Kohlmeyer), Steven Kampmann (Merle Piggens), Caroline McWilliams (Paula Rigsby), Steve Vinovich (Gus Barrett), Jesse Welles (Louise Barrett), George Wyner (Victor Rigsby), Brandon Call, Kellie Martin, Palmer the Cat (Leo), J. A. Preston, Christina Cocek, Thomas Hill, Richard Kuss, Thomas Oglesby, Joel Bennett (Trooper), Richard Blum (Jailor), Bonnie Hellman (Mrs. Simms), Linda Hoy (Nurse), Deirdre Kelly (Woman with Cat), Frank Miller (Man with Skunk), Fred Morsell (Newscaster), Jordan Myers (Cabbie), John Otrin (Security Guard), Roger Rook (The Bailiff), Kevin Sifuentes (Delivery Boy), Kitty Swink (Minister's Wife), William Utay (Minister), Dan Woren (Policeman), Matthew Faison (Doctor).

When wealthy businessman Oscar Kohlmeyer dies, he surprises his staff by leaving his entire fortune to his cat, Leo. His relatives, Victor and Paula Rigsby, are furious. They discover they are next in line for the cash, and if anything happens to Leo, the money is theirs. Immediately, they begin to plot the cat's demise.

RIDE A NORTHBOUND HORSE
Airdates—Part 1: 3/16/69, 4/22/73. Part 2: 3/23/69, 4/29/73.

Cast: Carroll O'Connor (Shawnee), Michael Shea (Cav Rand), Ben Johnson (Will Parker), Dub Taylor (Purse), Andy Devine (Jim Demmer), Harry Carey, Jr. (Yonder), Edith Atwater (Mrs. Addy Mason), Jack Elam (Sheriff Eppes).

When bottomland fever claims the lives of his family, Cav Rand decides to sell all of his possessions to buy a horse. The orphan meets rancher Will Parker, who is preparing to leave on a cattle drive. Will has to help the boy when Cav is accused of being a horse thief.

Production Notes:

- The open ranch land used for location filming in this episode is now the community of Thousand Oaks, California.
- Carroll O'Connor starred as Archie Bunker in *All in the Family.*
- This show was released theatrically overseas in 1969.

RIDE A WILD PONY   Airdates—Part 1: 2/11/79. Part 2: 2/18/79.
This 1975 theatrical release set in Australia is the story of two children, one rich and one poor, who both claim ownership of the same horse.

RINGO, THE REFUGEE RACCOON
Airdate: 3/03/74.

Cast: William Hochstrasser (Night Watchman), The Foutz family (Family of Four), Chris Yuhl, Timothy Foutz (Surveyor), Greg Dietel (Surveyor), Freddie Orlando (Housemover), John Oldenkamp (Housemover), Charlie Miller (Man with Bell).

The building of a new shopping center accidentally changes the life of Ringo, a baby raccoon born on the site. His home in a hollow tree is demolished to make way for the new buildings, and a bewildered Ringo goes looking for someplace new to live.

ROB ROY   Airdates—Part 1: 10/03/56. Part 2: 10/10/56.
This story was released theatrically in 1954 as *Rob Roy, The Highland Rogue.* Footage from *The Mickey Mouse Club Newsreel* shows scenes of bagpipers preparing for a traditional Scottish celebration. Animated scenes from *So Dear to My Heart* illustrate a Scot's persistence in achieving a goal, no matter how difficult the effort may be. The rest of the episode tells the story of Rob Roy, a famous Scottish warrior.

ROBBER STALLION, THE   Airdates: 12/04/59, 6/24/60.
Cast: Tom Tryon (Texas John Slaughter), Darryl Hickman (Ashley Carstairs), Barton MacLane (John Scanlon), John Vivyan (Jason Hemp), Jean Inness (Bess Scanlon).

As Part 7 of *The Tales of Texas John Slaughter* begins, John rides to New Mexico to visit his friend, John Scanlon, intending to buy a herd of cattle to take back to Tombstone, Arizona. A nearby silver strike means that hundreds of hungry miners will soon descend upon the area, and John intends to supply their beef needs. He meets Ashley Carstairs, a young Easterner who is staying at the ranch, and takes a liking to him. Ashley is there to buy horses to take back to Kentucky, where he hopes to breed them with thoroughbreds to produce steeplechase racers.

Production Notes:

- This story is continued in the episode *Wild Horse Revenge.*
- Location filming took place in the desert near Apple Valley, California.

ROBIN HOOD Airdate (2-hour format): 4/27/86.
This 1973 animated feature aired with the cartoons *Mickey's Gala Premiere* and *Brave Little Tailor*.

ROCK 'N' ROLL MOM Airdate (2-hour format): 2/07/88.
Cast: Dyan Cannon (Annie Hackett), Michael Brandon (Jeff Robins), Telma Hopkins (Etta Sloane), Nancy Lenehan (Connie Orsini), Josh Blake (Nicky Hackett), Amy Lynne (Emma Hackett), Fran Drescher (Jody Levin), Alex Rocco (Jerry Weiss), Joe Pantoliano (Ronnie), Heather Locklear (Darcy X), Nina Blackwood (Video D.J.), Marie Cheatham (Janine), Waddy Wachtel (Himself), David Paymer (Boris), Jonathan Chapin (Emcee), Paula Hoffman (Shelley), Anne Rogers (Fritzie), John Hostetter (Johnny), Billy Elmer (Jelly Belly), Ian Fried (Albert), Chad Hayes (Engineer), Beverly Horn (Lucy), Alan Berger (Stage Manager), Niche Saboda (Emcee), Clay Wilcox (Eric), José Eber (Himself).

Annie Hackett, a typical suburban mother, loves rock and roll music. Her life changes dramatically when she sings in a local club, for a record executive hears a tape of the show and thinks that Annie might have a song for his hot client, Darcy X. The executive, Jeff Robins, buys the song, but when Darcy throws a temper tantrum, Annie is suddenly called on to record the song.

Production Notes:

• This was the pilot for an unsold series.
• This episode was also aired as part of the *Family Classics* series of specials on 4/06/89.

RUN, APPALOOSA, RUN Airdates: 10/22/67, 5/26/68, 4/28/74.
This 1966 theatrical release is the story of an Indian girl who raises a horse for competition in a famous local race, only to have to sell it when her family needs the money.

RUNAWAY ON THE ROGUE RIVER Airdates: 12/01/74, 7/20/75.
Cast: Slim Pickens (Bucky Steele), Willie Aames (Jeff Peterson), Denis Arndt (John Peterson).

Jeff Peterson and his father, John, are on a fishing trip in the Pacific Northwest. Meanwhile, a truck containing trained elephants suffers a flat tire and Bucky Steele, the owner, stops to fix it. He unloads the elephants so he can work and one, named Barney, wanders off into the woods. Jeff is amazed when he prepares to cast his line and snags an elephant.

Production Note:

• Location filming took place in Oregon. Shortly before filming was to begin, the trained elephant scheduled to appear in the show died and a substitute had to be found. The only one available was in Louisville, Kentucky, and had to be transported to Oregon. Producer Larry Lansburgh became friends with Bucky Steele, the animal's trainer, and used his name for Slim Pickens's character.

RUN, COUGAR, RUN Airdates—Part 1: 11/25/73. Part 2: 12/02/73. For the 1977–78 season the show was aired in a 2-hour format: 12/11/77.
This 1972 theatrical release stars Stuart Whitman in the story of Seeta, a mother cougar who is looking for a home for her three kittens.

RUN, LIGHT BUCK, RUN Airdates: 3/13/66, 7/10/66, 6/21/70, 8/10/75.
Cast: Al Niemela (Prospector).

A young pronghorn antelope panics during his first thunderstorm and runs away from his family, becoming tangled in a patch of vines. A prospector chances upon the unfortunate animal and frees him, naming the antelope "Light Buck" because of his light-colored coat.

RUSTY AND THE FALCON Airdates: 10/24/58, 5/13/62, 6/12/66.
Cast: Jerome Courtland (Narrator), Rudy Lee (Rusty), Jay W. Lee (Father), The Mellomen (Background Singers).

Rusty is a 12-year-old who lives in a Rocky Mountain mining town. The boy is lonely because few children his age live nearby, so he invents a number of secret games to play by himself.

One day he finds an injured falcon and takes it home to nurse it back to health. His parents reluctantly agree to let him keep the bird, not knowing that Rusty is studying falconry and plans to teach the falcon to hunt.

Production Notes:

• Location filming took place in Heber, Utah. The town was picked both for its scenic locale as well as the fact that local laws did not prohibit falconry, which is illegal in most areas of the United States.

- This episode was released theatrically overseas in 1966.

SAGA OF ANDY BURNETT, THE
(mini-series)
Disney produced six episodes featuring this Easterner who wanted to become a mountain man: *Andy's Initiation, Andy's First Chore, Andy's Love Affair, The Land of Enemies, White Man's Medicine,* and *The Big Council.* Refer to each of these titles for the episode descriptions.

SALTY, THE HIJACKED HARBOR SEAL
Airdates: 12/17/72, 7/15/79.
Cast: *John Waugh (Dr. John Stone), Doug Grey (Joey), Lance Rasmussen (Billy), Bud Sheble (Y.M.C.A. Counselor), Hal Stein (Mr. Hanson).*

Salty is a harbor seal pup born in Drake's Bay, California. Soon after birth he is examined by Dr. Stone, a biologist who is studying the area's seal colonies. In his early days, Salty seldom ventures far from his mother's side, but after he's weaned, he begins to travel further each day in search of adventure. On one of these trips Salty is caught in a fishing boat's nets and the crewmen decide to sell him. Their skipper orders them to free the animal as they enter San Francisco Bay, and the confused seal begins to explore the bay.

Production Note:

- Originally, the locale for Salty's trip was to be the Sacramento Delta region, with the seal stowing away on a river barge. Heavy rains flooded the area and the seals had to be placed in the pool of the Loma Mar, California, Y.M.C.A. for safety.

SALUDOS AMIGOS Airdate: 1/08/58.
This 1943 theatrical release is presented as a souvenir of the Disney staff's trip to South America, where they had gone to record the native customs, songs, and dances. It was adapted for television by Wilfred Jackson, Jack Speirs, George Gale, A.C.E., Samuel Horta, and Harry Tytle.

SALUTE TO ALASKA, A Airdates:
4/02/67, 8/13/67.
The Studio celebrates the 100th birthday of Alaska in this episode produced with the cooperation of the governor of Alaska. Animation and historic footage provide a look at Alaska's past, beginning with its discovery in 1741 by Capt. Vitus Bering.

Production Notes:

- Footage was used from the theatrical release *Seal Island.*
- This was the last episode to feature an original introduction by Walt Disney.
- This show was originally planned as a theatrical short subject to be titled *Alaska.*

SALUTE TO FATHER, A Airdates: 1/22/61,
6/16/63, 6/20/76 *(Goofy's Salute to Father),* 6/17/79 *(Goofy's Salute to Father),* 6/15/80 *(Goofy's Salute to Father).*
Walt opens the show by mentioning that most fathers are forgotten men, who receive only gaudy ties on Father's Day. To correct this oversight, this show is dedicated to fathers everywhere. Goofy has been selected as a typical father, and the episode shows how he spends a typical day.

SAMMY, THE WAY-OUT SEAL Airdates—
Part 1: 10/28/62, 5/05/63, 9/01/68. Part 2: 11/04/62, 5/12/63, 9/08/68. For the 1975–76 season the show was presented in a 2-hour format: 11/30/75, 4/05/76.
Cast: *Jack Carson (Harold Sylvester), Robert Culp (Chet Loomis), Patricia Barry (Helen Loomis), Elisabeth Fraser (Lovey Sylvester), Michael McGreevey (Arthur Loomis), Billy Mumy (Peter Loomis), Ann Jilliann (Rocky Sylvester), Renie Riano (Mrs. Crotty).*

Two brothers, Arthur and Petey Loomis, find an injured seal on the beach during their vacation and decide to adopt the animal. They name the seal "Sammy" and sneak it into their house, intending to care for it until it's well enough to care for itself. Now they must break the news to their parents.

Production Note:

- *Sammy, The Way-Out Seal* was released theatrically overseas in 1963.

SANCHO ON THE RANCHO . . . AND ELSEWHERE
This is Part 1 of *Sancho, The Homing Steer.*

SANCHO, THE HOMING STEER
Airdates—Part 1: 1/21/62, 6/10/62, 8/11/68. Part 2: 1/28/62, 6/17/62, 8/18/68.
Cast: *Bill Shurley (Ed Kerr), Rosita Fernandez (Maria), Arthur Curtis (Shiner), Stephen Akers, Bruce Arn Mace, Ginna Akers, Stuart A. Mace.*

This story is told in two parts, *Sancho on the Rancho . . . and Elsewhere* and *The Perils of a Homesick Steer.* Ed Kerr, a rancher in Texas, finds a baby longhorn steer at the side of its dead mother. He takes the animal home with him and his wife, Maria, agrees to help him care for it. They name the steer Sancho, which means "pet." Problems abound when their pet grows to maturity.

Production Note:

• This show was released theatrically overseas.

SAVAGE SAM   Airdates—Part 1: 10/02/66, 10/08/72. Part 2: 10/09/66, 10/15/72.
In this 1963 theatrical release, a sequel to *Old Yeller*, Tommy Kirk and Kevin Corcoran reprise their earlier roles in the story of a dog that helps free kidnapped settlers from a band of marauding Indians.

SAVE THE DOG
An edited 1-hour version of this Disney Channel film was aired on the anthology series on 2/05/89. To accommodate the shorter length, the parts of Billie Bird, Al Lewis, and James Gale were cut from the film.

SCARECROW OF ROMNEY MARSH, THE
Airdates—Part 1: 2/09/64, 8/16/64, 5/10/70. Part 2: 2/16/64, 8/23/64, 5/17/70. Part 3: 2/23/64, 8/30/64, 5/24/70. For the 1977–78 season the show was aired in two parts— Part 1: 6/18/78. Part 2: 6/25/78.
Cast: Patrick McGoohan (Dr. Christopher Syn/Scarecrow), George Cole (Mr. Mipps/Hellspite), Tony Britton (Simon Bates), Michael Hordern (Squire Thomas Banks), Geoffrey Keen (General Pugh), Kay Walsh (Mrs. Waggett), Eric Pohlmann (King George III), Patrick Wymark (Joe Ransley), Alan Dobie (Prosecutor Fragg), Sean Scully (John Banks/The Curlew), Eric Flynn (Lt. Philip Brackenbury), David Buck (Harry Banks), Percy Herbert (Head Jailer), Robert Brown (Sam Farley), Peter Welch (Stubbard), Jill Curzon (Kate Banks), Mark Dignam (The Bishop), Gordon Gostelow (Ben), Bruce Seton (Beadle), Alan McClelland (Second Jailer), Richard O'Sullivan (George Ransley), Simon Lack (Dragoon Corporal), Elsie Wagstaff (Mrs. Ransley).
When England's King George III tries in 1736 to raise money for the treasury by placing a heavy tax on all imports, the people respond by smuggling vast quantities of goods into the country. The heaviest activity takes place on the coast near Kent and Sussex, forcing the king to send a large concentration of troops there to enforce the law. This show of force meets with some unusual resistance. A mysterious figure dressed as a scarecrow has organized a formidable group.

Production Notes:

• The three-part version of this show contains a continuity error. In Part 1, Simon Bates, an American convicted of treason, arrives at Dr. Syns's church and is given shelter. He reappears later in that episode, then isn't seen in Part 2. In Part 3, the scenes of Bates arriving at the church are reused without any explanation as to why they are being repeated.

• The three episodes were combined and released theatrically overseas in 1963 under the title *Dr. Syn, Alias the Scarecrow.* It was later released theatrically in the United States in 1975.

SEARCHING FOR NATURE'S MYSTERIES
Airdates: 9/26/56, 12/26/56, 1/02/66.
Cast: Winston Hibler, Robert and Fanny Crandall, Donald Sykes, Dr. Tilden W. Roberts, Murl and Mildred Duesing, Stuart V. Jewell, John Nash Ott, Jr., Don Iwerks, Erwin L. Verity, George and Nettie MacGinnity.
Winston Hibler explains how Disney nature photographers have developed the tools and techniques used in productions such as *Secrets of Life.* Many of the special cameras were designed and built for specific tasks, including equipment used to photograph small animals such as ants.

SECRET MISSION
This is Part 1 of *Andrew's Raiders.*

SECRET OF BOYNE CASTLE, THE
Airdates—Part 1: 2/09/69. Part 2: 2/16/69. Part 3: 2/23/69. For the 1977–778 season the show was aired in a 2-hour format: 1/01/78 (*Spy-Busters*).
Cast: Glenn Corbett (Tom Evans), Alfred Burke (Kersner), Kurt Russell (Rich Evans), Patrick Dawson (Sean O'Connor), Patrick Barr (Lord Boyne), Hugh McDermott (Carleton), Patrick Westwood (Levick), Eddie Byrne (Bailey), Godfrey Quigley (Meister), Kevin Stoney (Enhardt), Shay Gorman (Headmaster), Niall Toibin (Kettering), Ernst Walder (Vollos), Robert Bernal (Sergeant Clune), Vincent Dowling (Maston), John

Horton (Stafford), J. G. Devlin (Muldoon), Nicola Davies (Kathleen), Gerry Alexander (Paddy), Eamon Morrissey (Hennessey), Declan Mulholland (Retchick), Mary Larkin (Mary), Paul Farrell (Groundskeeper).

Rich Evans, an American studying in Ireland, becomes involved in international intrigue when a dying man gasps out a warning for Rich's brother. The incident is seen by Russian agents, who kidnap Rich and his friend, Sean, hoping to learn what the dying man knew about an upcoming mission. The Russians surprise Rich by telling him his brother, Tom, is an American agent who has been assigned to meet a defecting scientist, and they want to learn the location of the meeting.

Production Note:

- This show was released theatrically overseas in 1969 under the working title *Guns in the Heather*.

SECRET OF LOST VALLEY, THE

Airdates—Part 1: 4/27/80. Part 2: 5/04/80.
Cast: Gary Collins (Ned Harkness), Mary Ann Mobley (Susan Harkness), Brad Savage (Adam Harkness), Eddie Marquez (Zane), Tom Simcox (Chief Ranger), Jackson Bostwick (Cal), Dave Cass (Donnie), Barry Sullivan (Dr. Seldon), Geoff Parks (Lab Technician), John Steadman (Old Packer), James Almanzar (Dave), Tom Waters (Wynn), Ruben Moreno (Village Elder), David Cadiente (A-Voh), Ceil Cabot (Mrs. Buckley), John Lupton (Detective), Patricia Van Patten (Miss Johnson), Henry Slate (Guard), Elven Havard (Intern), Linda Dangcil (Tribal Mom), George Jammal (Tribal Dad), Don Brodie (Camper), Peg Stewart (Camper's Wife), Warde Donovan (Reporter #1), Alfred Daniels (Reporter #2), Kay Elliot (Shopper #1), Riza Royce (Shopper #2), Ronald Gans (Bartender), Carson Sipes (David), Gerry Okuneff (Coach), John Starr (Newspaper Man).

Ned Harkness takes his wife, Susan, and their 12-year-old son, Adam, on a camping trip in the Lost Peak National Forest. Adam wanders off during a hike and is forced to spend the night in an abandoned cabin. The real danger begins when he meets a strange wild boy named Zane, member of an unknown tribe.

Production Note:

- Co-stars Gary Collins and Mary Ann Mobley, cast as husband and wife, were married to each other in real life.

SECRET OF OLD GLORY MINE, THE

Airdates: 10/31/76, 7/17/77.
Cast: Rowan Pease (Charlie Jackson), Barry Dowell (Pete Martin).

Years ago, Glory, Arizona, was a booming mining town, with hundreds of men working in the area's silver mines. Today, it's a ghost town with only one prospector left. Charlie Jackson still works the Old Glory, which was the largest mine back in the 1880s. His only neighbor is Agnes, his burro. Things change when a rural prospector moves into town.

Production Note:

- The "town" of Glory was built in the desert near Tucson, Arizona. It was later used in the episode *The Golden Dog*, where it was known as Last Chance.

SECRET OF THE POND, THE   Airdates—

Part 1: 10/05/75, 7/11/76. Part 2: 10/12/75, 7/18/76.
Cast: Moses Gunn (Sharbee), Anthony Zerbe (Sam White), John McLiam (Uncle Ben), Eric Shea (Joey Moncrief), Ike Eisenmann (Odie White), Rex Corley (Claude White), Robert Sampson (Joe Moncrief), Sam Vaugham (Storekeeper).

A pond in the backwaters of Virginia is the setting for a spoiled teenager's vacation. Joey Moncrief is anxious to spend his summer there, for he wants to hunt a deer and bring home a trophy to show his friends. His father drives him to the cabin where his Uncle Ben lives, and Joey immediately goes out to hunt. He soon meets a strange hermit who lives in the swamp.

Production Note:

- This was originally planned as a theatrical release titled *The Pond*.

SECRETS OF THE PIRATE'S INN

Airdates—Part 1: 11/23/69, 7/05/70, 4/14/74. Part 2: 11/30/69, 7/12/70, 4/21/74.
Cast: Ed Begley (Dennis McCarthy), Charles Aidman (Carl Buchanan), Jimmy Bracken (Scott Durden), Annie McEveety (Tippy Durden), Patrick Creamer (Catfish Jones), Paul Fix (Vern Padgett), Bill Zuckert (Sheriff Wiley), Fredd Wayne (Jim Durden), Anne Whitfield (Margaret Durden).

Dennis McCarthy has the sad duty of settling his brother's affairs following his untimely death. He stays at his brother's home, the Pirate's Inn in Calliou Bay, Louisiana, and soon begins searching for the legendary lost treasure of pirate Jean Lafitte.

Seeing Eye, The
This is Part 3 of *Atta Girl Kelly*.

Seems There Was This Moose
Airdates: 10/19/75, 6/27/76.
    Cast: Bob Cox (Pete), Ron Brown (Wally).
    A young moose begins life on the Olympic Peninsula of Washington State, where he finds both adventure and danger.

Shadow of Fear
Airdates—Part 1: 1/28/79. Part 2: 2/04/79.
    Cast: John Anderson (Abe Zook), Ike Eisenmann (Billy Stewart), Peter Haskell (Dave Bryant), Joyce Van Patten (Laura Stewart), Kip Niven (Jim), Lisa Whelchel (Robin Lapp), John McLiam (Isaac), Matt Clark (Ike), Charles Tyner (Hans), Tom Scott (Paul), Kurt Courtland (Amish Boy), Tasha Lee Zemrus (Amish Girl), Dermott Downs (Mark Swannenburg), William H. Bassett (Doctor), Pete Renoudet (Jacob), Peg Stewart (Ruth), Eddie Allen Bell (Lineman), Regina Waldon (Woman), Bill Murphy (Hunter).
    After his father dies, Billy Stewart becomes extremely introverted and unable to relate to other people. His only friends are his pets. This worries his mother so much she sends him to his great-uncle's farm in Pennsylvania's Amish country, hoping the change will do him good.

Shaggy D.A., The
Airdate (2-hour format): 9/24/78, 10/07/90 (colorized). In other seasons the show aired in two parts—Part 1: 3/23/80, 1/25/83. Part 2: 3/30/80, 2/01/83.
This 1976 theatrical sequel to *The Shaggy Dog* stars Dean Jones, Suzanne Pleshette, Tim Conway, and Keenan Wynn in the story of a cursed ring that turns a political candidate into a sheepdog as he tries to defeat his crooked opponent.

Shaggy Dog, The
Airdates (2-hour format): 1/29/78. For the 1980–81 season the show aired in two parts—Part 1: 9/28/80. Part 2: 10/05/80. For the 1987–88 season the movie was colorized and aired in two parts—Part 1:10/18/87. Part 2: 10/25/87.
This 1959 theatrical release starring Toomy Kirk, Fred MacMurray, Annette Funicello, Tim Considine, and Kevin Corcoran is the story of Wilby Daniels and how he becomes a sheep dog.

Production Notes:

- First planned as a television show, *The Shaggy Dog* was instead released theatrically and grossed over $9.5 million on its first release alone.
- The colorized version of *The Shaggy Dog* was also aired on 3/23/89 and 3/30/89 during the *Family Classics* series of specials.

Shipwrecked
Airdates (2-hour format): 1/05/92, 9/26/93.
This 1990 theatrical release starring Stian Smestad, Gabriel Byrne, and Louisa Haigh is the story of a young boy and girl who become involved with pirates in 1849. It also aired as a special on 2/29/92.

Shokee, The Everglades Panther
Airdates: 9/29/74, 9/03/78.
    Cast: Curtis Osceola (Sammy Osceola), The Miccosukee Tribe of Indians.
    A panther cub is separated from its mother in Florida's Everglades swamp and must learn to hunt and defend itself. Luckily, the lonely animal meets Sammy Osceola, an Indian boy, and the youth helps him survive. Sammy is also alone, for he is following an ancient tribal tradition that all boys must spend a summer alone in the swamp before they can be considered men.

Production Note:

- This show, which took over 6 months to film, was photographed entirely on location in Florida's Big Cypress Swamp and Everglades National Park.

Shot That Was Heard 'Round the World, The
This is Part 2 of *Johnny Tremain*.

Showdown at Sandoval
Airdates: 1/23/59, 8/07/59.
    Cast: Tom Tryon (Texas John Slaughter), Dan Duryea (Dan Trask), Beverly Garland (Mrs. Barko), Norma Moore (Adeline Harris), Harry Carey, Jr. (Ben Jenkins), Judson Pratt (Captain Cooper), Ann Doran (Mrs. Chadwick), Robert Foulk (Pitts), John Day (Clay), Robert Hoy (Jim), Henry Wills (Brown).
    Part 4 of *The Tales of Texas John Slaughter* begins as John is assigned the task of escorting Mrs. Barko to prison. She has refused

to explain why her gang was trying to join forces with Dan Trask, and John hopes he can discover the secret. He proposes a daring plan to his commanding officer, Captain Cooper.

Production Note:

• This episode was combined with *Killers from Kansas* and released theatrically overseas in 1961 as *Gunfight at Sandoval*.

SHOWDOWN WITH THE SUNDOWN KID
Airdates: 10/23/66, 6/25/67.

Cast: Dennis Weaver (The Sundown Kid), John McIntire (Whit White), James Gregory (Sheriff Dodds), Roger Mobley (Gallegher), Ray Teal (Detective Snead), Jeanette Nolan (Erm White), Peter Graves (Marshal Frank Neimeyer).

The story of Gallegher, the newsboy who wants to be a reporter, continues in Part 1 of *Gallegher Goes West*. Gallegher, following the advice of another newsman, Horace Greeley, has headed west. Gallegher travels to his next job on a stagecoach, where he meets another passenger, Mr. Tucker. When they arrive in town, Tucker narrowly saves Gallegher from being caught in a shootout, but the boy realizes Tucker is actually a wanted fugitive.

Production Note:

• The story continues in the episode *Crusading Reporter*.

SILVER FOX AND SAM DAVENPORT, THE
Airdates: 10/14/62, 1/01/67.

Cast: Gordon Perry (Sam Davenport).

This is the story of Domino, a silver fox that has stayed alive due to his superior speed and cunning nature. His luck almost runs out one day when he begins to tire and a pack of dogs almost catches up to him. Domino spots a wagon driven by farmer Sam Davenport and leaps aboard, hiding in a load of hay. The dogs lose his scent and the young fox stays hidden until Sam reaches his farm. When he jumps off the wagon, Domino is chased by Sam's hound, Heckla. He escapes, but not before Sam spots the valuable animal.

Production Note:

• This show was released theatrically overseas in 1964 and in the United States in 1972.

SKY HIGH #1   Airdate (2-hour format): 3/11/90.

Cast: Damon Martin (Jim Lincoln), Anthony Rapp (Wes Hansen), James Whitmore (Gus Johnson), Traci Lind (Dawn Harris), Annie Oringer (Sarah Harris), David Paymer (Vic), Ian Black (Heckler #2), Antony Holland (2nd Old Man), Franklin Johnson (1st Old Man), Cam Lane (Mr. Crawford), Larry Musser (Onlooker #3), Tom McBeath (Auctioneer), David McCulley (Bidder #1), Alan C. Peterson (Onlooker #1), Andrew Rhodes (Onlooker #2), James Stevens (Bidder #2), Dave "Squatch" Ward (Heckler #1), Jerry Wasserman (Ralph), Blu Mancuma (Detective Hiatt), Shirley Barclay (Woman on Ferry), John "Bear" Curtis (Frank), Larry Ewasher (Hank), Marcy Goldberg (Comic), Anna Hagen (Mary), Byron Lucas (Sal), Dwight McFee (Murphy), Chuck Perry (Pete), Silvio Rossi (Conductor), Wilf Rowe (Store Detective), Don Thompson (Manny).

Two teenagers in a small town, Jim Lincoln and Wes Hansen, dream about leaving town, for neither has much to keep him there. Their idle wishes are brought to fruition when they buy the contents of an old barn sight unseen and they find themselves the new owners of a mint condition 1917 Waco biplane.

SKY HIGH #2   Airdate: 8/26/90.

Cast: Damon Martin (Jim Lincoln), Anthony Rapp (Wes Hansen), Barney Martin (Willard the Rainmaker), Page Hannah (Cheryl), Heidi Kozak (Sally), Ismael Carlo (Jose), Michael Wren (Miguel), Randy Charach (Dealer), Ritch Hobden (Large Man), Rob Johnson (Attendant), Ganga Jolicouer (Girl), Stephanie Kirkland (Wife), Kim Kondrashoff (Bouncer), Armondo Anthony Leggio (Pepe), Howard Storey (Sheriff), Venus Terzo (Maria).

On their way to New Orleans, Jim and Wes meet two girls with car trouble. The girls, Cheryl and Sally, are on their way back to college, but when Wes fixes their car, they decide to stay long enough to enjoy a local carnival. Jim and Wes are arrested after a brawl with two con men and the girls have to bail them out. Jim wants to give up flying to stay with Cheryl, but when she goes back to college without him, he and Wes continue on toward New Orleans.

SKY'S THE LIMIT, THE Airdates—Part 1: 1/19/75, 8/26/79. Part 2: 1/26/75, 9/02/79.

Cast: Pat O'Brien (Abner Therman), Lloyd Nolan (Cornwall), Jeannette Nolan (Gertie), Ike Eisenmann (Three), Ben Blue (Ben), Alan Hale (Cholly), Richard Arlen (Grimes), Robert Sampson (Two), Huntz Hall (Hitchhiker), Ben Cooper (F.A.A. Representative), Bill Zuckert (Police Chief), Norman Bartold (Captain Willoughby).

Abner Therman III is picked up at his English boarding school by his father, who will take him to his grandfather's farm in California for the summer vacation. Abner and his grandfather establish a special relationship when they restore an old airplane. Despite the boy's father's objections, the grandfather teaches him to fly.

SKY TRAP, THE Airdate (2-hour format): 5/13/79. For the 1982–83 season the show was aired in two parts—Part 1: 7/30/83. Part 2: 8/06/83.

Cast: Jim Hutton (Joe Reese), Marc McClure (Grant Stone), Patricia Crowley (Florence Stone), Kitty Ruth (Marti Benson), John Crawford (Mark Sanders), Kip Niven (Buddy Phelps), Martin Kove (Hoover), Walter Barnes (Harry Shaughnessy), Dennis Fimple (Wilks), Bill Thurman (Sheriff), Allan Hunt (Customs Agent #2), William H. Bassett (Customs Agent #4), Alfred Daniels (Customs Agent #3), Elven Havard (Customs Agent #1), Art Scholl (Stunt Pilot), Chris Courtland (Stunt Pilot), Ted Janczarek (Stunt Pilot), Steven Hinton (Stunt Pilot), Charles Gyenes (Stunt Pilot), Tom Friedkin (Stunt Pilot), Dean Engelhardt (Stunt Pilot).

In an effort to stop drug smuggling, the U.S. Customs Service has begun to use planes to watch for other aircraft that may be carrying contraband into the country. One crew spots a low-flying plane near the Mexican border and suspects it belongs to the "Hawk," an infamous smuggler operating in the area. They force the plane to land and find several kilograms of marijuana, but the pilot escapes without a trace.

Production Notes:

- The sailplane used in this show belonged to producer Jerome Courtland, who became interested in the sport during the filming of *Diamonds on Wheels* in England. He flew a number of the aerial scenes, as did his son, Chris.

- Co-star Mark McClure learned to fly a sailplane and performed several of his own flying scenes. Chris Courtland did the rest; his father doubled for actress Kitty Ruth.

SLAUGHTER TRAIL, THE Airdates: 3/20/59, 9/04/59.

Cast: Tom Tryon (Texas John Slaughter), Sidney Blackmer (Sam Underwood), Bill Williams (Paul), John Larch (Frank Boyd), Norma Moore (Adeline Slaughter), Grant Williams (Mike), Harold J. Stone (Chisholm), H.M. Wynant (Yancy), Herbert Rudley (Judge), Don Kelly (Jed), Slim Pickens (Buck).

Part 6 of *The Tales of Texas John Slaughter* begins as John proposes to Sam Underwood, another rancher, that they combine their herds and take them to Arizona where they will command higher prices. Underwood agrees but doubts they can use the usual route, the Chisholm Trail, due to drought conditions. John plans to use a new trail he's scouted, one with plenty of water, but it passes through Comanche territory.

Production Note:

- This episode was combined with *The Man from Bitter Creek* and released theatrically overseas in 1972 as *Stampede at Bitter Creek.*

SMOKE Airdates—Part 1: 2/01/70, 5/22/82. Part 2: 2/08/70, 5/29/82. For the 1975–76 season the show was aired in a 2-hour format: 11/16/75.

Cast: Earl Holliman (Cal Fitch), Ronny Howard (Chris Long), Jacqueline Scott (Fran Fitch), Shug Fisher (Leroy), Andy Devine (Mr. Stone), Pamelyn Ferdin (Susie), Kelly Thordsen (Mr. Horn).

Not long after her husband is killed, Fran Long remarries in an attempt to rebuild her life. Cal Fitch, her new husband, finds that her son Chris resents the marriage, for the boy refuses to believe Cal can compare to his deceased father. The gap between the two narrows when Cal agrees to help Chris nurse an injured dog named Smoke.

Production Notes:

- Ron Howard's "dead" father in this episode was played by his real father, Rance Howard, in an unbilled cameo appearance. They had previously appeared together in *The Journey* with Yul Brynner and on *The Andy Griffith Show.*

- *Smoke* was released theatrically overseas in 1970.

SNOW BEAR   Airdates—Part 1: 11/01/70, 8/17/75. Part 2: 11/08/70, 8/24/75.

Cast: Steve Kaleak (Timko), Rossman Peetook (Akotak), Laura Itta (Oogala), Dan Truesdell (Jim Johnson), Noah Philips (Ramaluk), Paka (Queen of the Snow Bears).

After a hunter's trap separates Paka, a female polar bear cub, from her mother, the frightened animal is befriended by Timko, a teenage Eskimo boy. Timko plans to raise the bear and eventually trade her to a zoo for much needed supplies. The plan fails when Paka breaks out of her shed and destroys the village's meager stockpile of food, forcing the tribal elders to banish the bear from the village.

Production Note:

- The story developed from a research trip to Europe by Disney staffer Harry Tytle, who was scouting for animal acts to be presented at Disneyland. The planned animal show was canceled following Walt's death in 1966. A total of eight bears was needed to complete the show.

SO DEAR TO MY HEART   Airdates: 11/24/54, 1/02/57.

This 1949 theatrical release starring Bobby Driscoll and Burl Ives is the story of a young boy's efforts to raise a black lamb and exhibit it at the county fair. It was adapted for television by Bill Walsh and Al Teeter.

SOLOMON, THE SEA TURTLE   Airdates: 1/05/69, 8/31/75.

Cast: Dr. Archie Carr (Himself), Henry Del Giudice (Dr. Hamilton), Steve Weinstock (Mark), Arthur Holgate (The Skipper), Alvin Watts (The Seaman).

As the story begins, a green turtle waits in the Costa Rican surf until night, when it will be safe to crawl ashore and lay her eggs. She builds a nest and lays several dozen eggs, covers them from sight, and returns to the safety of the ocean. Two months later, the eggs have hatched and the young turtles try to make their own way to the water.

SON OF FLUBBER   Airdate (2-hour format): 3/16/80.

This 1963 theatrical sequel to *The Absent-Minded Professor* stars Fred MacMurray, Nancy Olson, Keenan Wynn, and Tommy Kirk as the miracle invention Flubber is used to control the weather.

SPACEMAN IN KING ARTHUR'S COURT, A   Airdate—Part 1: 2/27/82. Part 2: 3/06/82.

Released theatrically in 1979 as *Unidentified Flying Oddball*, this film was aired on television under its working title. It stars Dennis Dugan and Jim Dale in the story of an astronaut who is thrown back in time to the days of King Arthur and the Knights of the Round Table.

SPLASH, TOO   Airdates—Part 1: 5/1/88. Part 2: 5/8/88.

Cast: Todd Waring (Allen Bauer), Amy Yasbeck (Madison Bauer), Donovan Scott (Freddie Bauer), Rita Taggart (Fern Hooten), Noble Willingham (Karl Hooten), Dody Goodman (Mrs. Stimler), Mark Blankfield (Dr. Otto Benus), Barney Martin (Herb Needler), Doris Belack (Lois Needler), Timothy Williams (Harvey), Jana Marie Hupp (Buffy), Joey Travolta (Jerry), Kirk Fyson (Waiter), Roger Hewlett (Policeman #1), Russell J. McConnell (Policeman #3), Ralph Peduto (Policeman #2), Joseph O. Reed, Jr. (Wallace), R.A. Rondell (Bartender).

This made-for-television sequel to the 1984 theatrical release *Splash* finds a bored Allen Bauer on the island he shares with Madison, the mermaid. When he learns that his brother, Freddie, is in danger of losing the family business, Madison surprises him with the news that they can return to New York as long as she can spend time in the water.

Production Notes:

- This episode was filmed partly on location at Walt Disney World, where the *Living Seas* pavilion at Epcot was used as an aquarium and lab. It was the first film to use the facilities at the Disney-MGM Studios.
- This was the pilot for *Splash II*, an unsold series. It was originally planned as a theatrical sequel to the first *Splash*.

SPOONER

This made-for-television movie first aired on The Disney Channel. It also aired on the anthology series in two parts—Part 1: 4/22/90. Part 2: 4/29/90.

SPOT MARKS THE X

This film, which originally aired on The Disney Channel, was aired in a 2-hour format during the anthology series on 5/17/87. The movie was later shown in two parts—Part 1: 7/03/88. Part 2: 7/10/88.

SPY BUSTERS, THE
See: *The Secret of Boyne Castle.*

SPY IN THE SKY   Airdate: 4/01/62.
Cast: Tom Tryon (Capt. Richmond Talbot), Brian Keith (Maj. Gen. John Vannerman), Edmond O'Brien (McClosky), Dany Saval (Lyrae), Bob Sweeney (Senator McGuire), Kent Smith (Secretary of the Air Force).

This look at outer space begins with a preview of *Moon Pilot,* the Studio's next theatrical release. The film tells the story of Richmond Talbot, a reluctant volunteer in America's space program, and the strange girl who tries to help him become the first man in space. The second part of the show was first released theatrically in 1959 as *Eyes in Outer Space.* Following an animated look at past attempts to predict the weather, the program predicts that we will someday be able to launch satellites into orbit to control the weather.

SQUARE PEG IN A ROUND HOLE, A
Airdates: 3/03/63, 7/04/71, 2/22/76 *(Goofing Around with Donald Duck).*
Ludwig Von Drake has founded the "Research Institute for Human Behavior" to study humans' psychological makeup. He has selected Donald Duck for his testing, putting his bewildered patient through a series of personality and intelligence exams until he believes he has found a perfect career for his nephew.

Production Note:
• This show was released theatrically overseas in 1965.

STORM CALLED MARIA, A   Airdate: 11/27/59.
Cast (Playing Themselves): George Kritsky (Dam Superintendent), Walt Bowen (Telephone Lineman), Leo Quinn (Highway Superintendent).

The show looks at several famous storms, all of which caused great damage and, in some cases, death. It then shows the formation of a major storm named Maria, which moves from the coast of Japan toward California. Weather ships and planes follow the growing storm, hoping to learn enough about it to warn those in its path.

Production Note:
• George R. Stewart, author of the book this show was based on, was a professor of meteorology at the University of California. He is credited with creating the custom of giving human names to storms.

STORMY, THE THOROUGHBRED
Airdates: 3/14/56, 5/07/58, 3/31/63.
This 1954 theatrical release is the story of Stormy, a thoroughbred colt who is much younger than the other colts in his class and thus unlikely to ever win a race. The full theatrical title was *Stormy, the Thoroughbred with an Inferiority Complex.* Originally narrated by George Fenneman, the television version was narrated by Winston Hibler.

STORY OF DOGS, A   Airdates: 12/01/54, 5/25/55, 7/20/55.
Cast: Erdman Penner, Clyde Geronim, Wolfgang Reitherman, Frank Thomas, Milt Kahl.

The first part of the show is devoted to the Studio's upcoming animated feature film, *Lady and the Tramp.* In the second part of the episode, Walt produces a scrapbook that shows the progress of Pluto's career.

Production Note:
• A dog used as the model for Tramp was a stray found by a Studio animator. After the film was complete, he was moved to Disneyland, where he lived at the pony farm.

STORY OF DONALD DUCK, THE
See: *The Donald Duck Story.*

STORY OF ROBIN HOOD, THE   Airdates—
Part 1: 11/02/55, 12/26/58, 5/16/65 *(Robin Hood).* Part 2: 11/09/55, 1/02/59, 5/23/65 *(Robin Hood).*
This 1952 theatrical release starring Richard Todd, Joan Rice, and Peter Finch tells the story of how a gamekeeper's son became the legendary bandit, Robin Hood. It was adapted for television by Bill Walsh, Al Teeter, and Lee Chaney.

STORY OF THE ANIMATED DRAWING, THE
Airdates: 11/30/55, 4/25/56, 7/25/56.
This history of animation begins in 1906, when J. Stuart Blackton produced a short subject named *Humorous Phases of Funny*

Faces, using chalk drawings that were erased and redrawn for each frame of film. At that stage, the primary method of animation was to use cut-out figures or to redraw the entire scene each time, as in *Gertie the Dinosaur*.

More animation pioneers are profiled throughout the show.

Production Note:

- Portions of this episode were released as the educational featurette *The History of Animation*.

STORY OF THE SILLY SYMPHONY, THE
Airdates: 10/19/55, 4/11/56, 6/05/59.
Walt takes a look backward at the Silly Symphony cartoon series, explaining that many of the techniques used in the Studio's animated features were first perfected in those short subjects.

STRANGE MONSTER OF STRAWBERRY COVE, THE
Airdates—Part 1: 10/31/71, 8/06/72. Part 2: 11/07/71, 8/13/72. For the 1981–82 season the show was aired in a 2-hour format: 8/07/82.

Cast: Burgess Meredith (Henry Meade), Agnes Moorehead (Mrs. Pringle), Larry D. Mann (Halper), Parley Baer (Mayor), Skip Homeier (Harry), Bill Zuckert (Sheriff Wiley), Kelly Thordsen (Tiny), Annie McEveety (Tippy), Jimmy Bracken (Scott), Patrick Creamer (Catfish), Bob Hastings (Deputy Tom Martin), James Lydon (Jim Durden).

Elderly schoolteacher Henry Meade is ridiculed when he reports spotting a sea monster, an act that infuriates Mrs. Pringle, an influential town leader. She demands the school replace him, so three of his students decide to build a fake sea monster to save his job. Tippy, Catfish, and Scott pick a deserted spot near Strawberry Cove, where Meade thought he saw the monster, and begin gathering supplies for their project.

Production Note:

- Erin Moran, who later starred in television's *Happy Days*, appeared in an unbilled part.

STRONGEST MAN IN THE WORLD, THE
Airdates (2-hour format): 2/27/77, 11/11/79. This 1975 theatrical release stars Kurt Russell, Joe Flynn, Eve Arden, Cesar Romero, and Phil Silvers in the story of a college student who invents a formula that imparts great strength to anyone who takes it. The film also aired as a special on 5/01/82.

STUB, THE BEST COW DOG IN THE WEST
Airdate: 12/08/74.

Cast: Slim Pickens (Windy Bill), Jay Sisler (Himself), Mike Hebert (Tim—The Boy), Luann Beach (Luann Heath—Rancher's Daughter), Channing Peake (Himself).

A ranch owner and his daughter, Luann, help organize a search party to track down a wild Brahma bull that is endangering the area's prized cattle herds. Jay Sisler, another rancher, volunteers the use of his three Australian herding dogs, Stub, Queen, and Shorty.

Production Note:

- This show was an updated version of the 1956 theatrical featurette *Cow Dog*.

STUDENT EXCHANGE
Airdate—Part 1: 11/29/87. Part 2: 12/06/87.

Cast: Viveka Davis (Carole Whitcomb/Simone), Todd Field (Neil Barton/Adriano Fabrizzi), Mitchell Anderson (Rod), Heather Graham (Dorrie Ryder), Maura Tierney (Kathy), Gavin MacLeod (Vice Principal Donald E. Durfner), Lisa Hartman (Peggy), O.J. Simpson (Coach Seaver), Lindsay Wagner (School Principal), Moon Zappa (Murphy the Biker), Kim Walker (Kit), Virginia Keehne (Lucy Whitcomb), Ira Heiden (Simon), Rob Estes (Beach), Lee Garlington (Mrs. Whitcomb), David Selburg (Mr. Whitcomb), Nancy Lenehan (Mrs. Barton), Glenn Shadix (Mr. Barton), Lisa Mende (Tanning Salon Receptionist), Michelango Kowalski (Joe the Biker), Nancy Fish (Vera), Edward Edwards (Tony Gordon), "Flame" Harris-Metter (Roller Skating Waitress), Michael Ennis (Driving Instructor), Patricia Patts (Patricia), Philippe Simon (French Waiter), Robin Stober (Mrs. Beat), Ria Pavia (Student Pagley), Jack McGee (Cabbie), Alex Lende (Andre), Viva Vinson (Real Simone), Nick Bellazzi (Real Adriano).

Carole Whitcomb and Neil Barton are two nobodies, ignored by everyone else in high school. This changes when Carole intercepts a telegram saying that two exchange students will not be coming as planned and proposes that she and Neil take their place.

SULTAN AND THE ROCK STAR
Airdates: 4/20/80, 2/15/83 (*The Hunter and the Rock Star*).

Cast: Timothy Hutton (Paul Winters), Ken Swofford (George McKinzie), Bruce Glover (Alec Frost), Ned Romero (Joe Ironwood), Richard Paul (Al Mathews), Pat Delany (Mrs. Winters), Shug Fisher (Motel Owner), Brendan

Dillon (Hicks), Elven Havard (First Officer), Wayne Winton (Jake), John Lawrence (The Fisherman).

Sultan, a gentle Bengal tiger, is taken to Sportsman's Island by Alec Frost, a disreputable gamekeeper, and tortured in an attempt to make him vicious. Several days later, Sultan is turned loose to be the object of a hunting party led by the island's cruel owner, George McKinzie.

SUMMER MAGIC Airdates—Part 1: 12/05/65, 10/10/71, 8/22/76. Part 2: 12/12/65, 10/17/71, 8/29/76.
This 1963 theatrical release stars Hayley Mills, Burl Ives, Dorothy McGuire, and Deborah Walley in the story of a destitute family that must move to the country and live in a house they "borrow" from its unwitting owner.

Production Note:

- This story was originally planned as a three-part television story to be named after the original book it was based on, *Mother Carey's Chickens*.

SUNDAY DRIVE Airdate (2-hour format): 11/30/86. For the 1987–88 season the show was aired in two parts—Part 1: 7/31/88. Part 2: 8/07/88.
Cast: Tony Randall (Uncle Bill Franklin), Carrie Fisher (Franny Jessup), Audra Lindley (Aunt Joan Franklin), Hillary Wolf (Christine Elliott), Raffi Di Blasio (John Elliott), Ted Wass (Paul Sheridan), Claudia Cron, Norman Alden, James Avery, Charley Garrett, Chip Johnson, Lynette Mettey, Branscombe Richmond, William Utay, Chris Smith (Biker), Thomas F. Maguire (SFPD McSwain), Richard Wiley (Richard), John Achorn (Officer Penny), Larry Brand (Mike), Patricia L. Briody (Beth), Susan Bugg (Karen), Georgia Dell (Woman in Car), Art Frankel (Hotel Clerk), Nancy Lenehan (Receptionist), Sharon Madden (Redhead), Winifred Mann (Sally), Edward Markmann (Dock Man), Ron Orbach (Station Attendant), Stacey Lynn Shaffer (Waitress), Liz Sheridan (Hostess), James Terry (Dennis), Porthos (Bud the Dog).
According to a very bored pair of children, Sundays are the worst day of the week, and this is the worst summer ever. The children, a teenage girl named Christine and her brother, John Elliott, are staying with their relatives, Bill and Joan Franklin. Every Sunday, Uncle Bill insists on taking them for a long and boring drive and making a history lesson out of it. Things change dramatically one Sunday, though, when the Franklins make their usual stop for lunch. When they drive off, they're unaware they've taken an identical car that belongs to a stranger, and the children have been left behind.

SUPERDAD Airdate (2-hour format): 2/15/76. For the 1978–79 season the show was aired in two parts—Part 1: 11/26/78. Part 2: 12/03/78.
This 1973 theatrical release stars Bob Crane, Kurt Russell, and Kathleen Cody in the story of a father who tries his best to find a suitable husband for his daughter, even though she is already very much in love with her childhood sweetheart.

SUPER DUCKTALES Airdate (2-hour format): 3/26/89.
Voices: Hamilton Camp (Fenton Crackshell/Gizmoduck), Miriam Flynn (Gandra Dee), June Foray (Ma Beagle), Kathleen Freeman (Mrs. Crackshell), Joan Gerber (Mrs. Beakley), Chuck McCann (Duckworth, Burger Beagle, Bouncer Beagle), Terence McGovern (Launchpad McQuack), Hal Smith (Gyro Gearloose), Russi Taylor (Huey, Dewey, Louie), Frank Welker (Big Time Beagle, Baggy Beagle, Megabyte Beagle), Alan Young (Uncle Scrooge McDuck).
When the Beagle Boys trick Uncle Scrooge into moving his money bin, Scrooge hires a new accountant, Fenton Crackshell, to help count the money while they're moving it. Scrooge doesn't know it, but the Beagles have also tricked him into buying the land for his new bin from them. Their plan is to blast the bin off the mountain onto Ma Beagle's land below, which will make the money theirs.

Production Note:

- *Super DuckTales* was later aired on *DuckTales* in five parts: *Liquid Assets, Frozen Assets, Full Metal Duck, The Billionaire Beagle Boys Club,* and *Money to Burn.*

SUPERSTAR GOOFY Airdate: 7/25/76.
The show includes footage from several Goofy sports cartoons as the Studio celebrates the 1976 Olympics.

Production Note:

- This episode was originally released theatrically overseas in 1972.

SURVIVAL IN NATURE   Airdates: 2/08/56, 5/16/56, 8/08/56, 6/02/63.
Winston Hibler narrates this program about how animals must continually adapt to increase their chances for survival.

SURVIVAL OF SAM THE PELICAN, THE
Airdates: 2/29/76, 6/24/79.
   Cast: *Kim Friese (Rick Preston), Scott Lee (Peter Barnes), Bill DeHollander (Dave Weyburn).*
   Teenager Rick Preston is having a hard time trying to decide what to do with his life. He heads for the Florida Keys, hoping the area will provide a quiet place for him to think things over. There, he is offered a job by Pete Barnes, a salvage operator who is about to depart on a dive trip to a treasure ship. Rick declines, but Pete agrees to drop him on a secluded island, promising to return later to pick him up. Rick then meets Dave Weyburn, an officer with Florida's Fish and Wildlife Department, and agrees to participate in a survey of the local pelican population.

SWAMP FOX, THE (mini-series)
Disney filmed eight episodes based on the real-life American patriot known as the "Swamp Fox," Francis Marion: *The Birth of the Swamp Fox; Brother against Brother; Tory Vengeance; Day of Reckoning; Redcoat Strategy; A Case of Treason; A Woman's Courage; Horses for Greene.* Refer to each title for the episode descriptions.

SWISS FAMILY ROBINSON   Airdates: 12/07/86 (2-hour format). The show also aired in two parts—Part 1: 3/12/89. Part 2: 3/19/89.
This 1960 theatrical release stars John Mills, Dorothy McGuire, James MacArthur, Janet Munro, Tommy Kirk, and Kevin Corcoran in the story of a family stranded on a remote island. It also aired as a special on ABC on 5/21/88.

   Production Note:

   • The episode *Escape to Paradise (and) Water Birds* is a behind-the-scenes look at the making of this film.

TALE OF TWO CRITTERS, A   Airdate: 6/04/78.
This 1977 theatrical release, set in the Pacific Northwest, is the unusual story of a raccoon and bear who become close friends.

TALES OF TEXAS JOHN SLAUGHTER, THE
(mini-series)
There were 17 episodes filmed about the real-life gunman who was a Texas Ranger before he turned to ranching: *Texas John Slaughter; Ambush at Laredo; Killers from Kansas; Showdown at Sandoval; The Man from Bitter Creek; The Slaughter Trail; The Robber Stallion; Wild Horse Revenge; Range War at Tombstone; Desperado from Tombstone; Apache Friendship; Kentucky Gunslick; Geronimo's Revenge; End of the Trail; A Holster Full of Law; A Trip to Tucson;* and *Frank Clell's in Town.* Refer to each of these titles for the episode descriptions.

TALES OF THE APPLE DUMPLING GANG
Airdate: 1/16/82.
   Cast: *John Bennett Perry (Russell Donovan), Sandra Kearns (Millie Malloy), Ed Begley, Jr. (Amos Tucker), Henry Jones (Sheriff Homer McCoy), Arte Johnson (Theodore Ogilvie), Keith Mitchell (Clovis), Sara Abeles (Celia), William Smith (Monk Hardwick), Lew Brown (Leonard Sharp), Al Checco (Floyd Wilkins), Tom Bower (Timothy Burns), Judy Baldwin (Saloon Girl), Alice Borden (Widow Honeywell), Dee Cooper (Driver).*
   This remake of the 1975 theatrical feature *The Apple Dumpling Gang* opens as gambler Russell Donovan arrives in Quake City, California, and finds himself the unwilling guardian of two small children. He tries to decline, but the sheriff insists he care for Clovis and Celia until a proper home can be found for them. Sheriff McCoy even arranges for the release of two prisoners from his jail to help Donovan.

   Production Note:

   • This episode was intended as a pilot for a proposed weekly series. The network aired several episodes with a different cast as a limited series under the title *Gun Shy.* Refer to Chapter 8 on limited series for the episode descriptions.

TALLY HO
This is Part 2 of *The Horsemasters.*

TASTE OF MELON, A
This is Part 1 of *For the Love of Willadean.*

TATTOOED POLICE HORSE, THE
Airdates: 9/10/67, 1/02/72, 4/29/79.
   Cast: *Sandy Sanders (Capt. Martin Hanley), Charles Seel (Ben), George Swinebroad (J. P.*

Rollins), William Hilliard (Bill Churchill), Shirley Skiles (Pam Churchill).

Jolly Roger, a thoroughbred trotting horse from a fine background, can't resist the urge to break into a full gallop as he nears the finish line, thereby effectively rendering him useless as a trotter. Although his trainer, Pam Churchill, is an expert at working with difficult horses, she is unable to break him of the habit, and so reluctantly sells him.

Production Notes:

- This show was first released as a theatrical featurette in 1964.
- The equine star was Count Stevie C., a real-life champion trotter.

TENDERFOOT, THE Airdates—Part 1: 10/18/64, 6/27/65. Part 2: 10/25/64, 7/04/65. Part 3: 11/01/64, 7/11/65.

Cast: Brian Keith (Mose Carson), Brandon de Wilde (Jim Tevis), James Whitmore (Captain Ewell), Richard Long (Paul Durand), Rafael Campos (Juarez), Donald May (Phineas Thatcher), Christopher Dark (Pike), Judson Pratt (The Sergeant), Pedro Gonzalez-Gonzalez (Pablo), Carlos Romero (Commandante Maldonado), Angela Dorian (Señorita Margarita), Harry Harvey, Jr. (Corporal), Eddie Little Sky (Apache Indian).

Jim Tevis, new to the West, becomes a scout on Kit Carson's expedition, where he battles Indians.

Production Note:

- *The Tenderfoot* was released theatrically overseas in 1966.

TEN WHO DARED Airdates: 4/14/68, 8/04/68.

This edited version of the 1960 theatrical release stars Brian Keith, John Beal, and James Drury in the story of the 1869 expedition of Maj. John Wesley Powell along the previously unconquered Colorado River as it travels through the Grand Canyon.

Production Notes:

- The episode *Rapids Ahead (and) Bear Country* is a behind-the-scenes look at the filming of this story.
- This film was first planned as a television show for the 1956–57 season, *Powell of the Colorado.*

TEXAS JOHN SLAUGHTER Airdates: 10/31/58, 6/26/59.

Cast: Tom Tryon (Texas John Slaughter), Robert Middleton (Frank Davis), Norma Moore (Adeline Harris), Harry Carey, Jr. (Ben Jenkins), Judson Pratt (Captain Cooper), Robert J. Wilke (Outlaw #1), Edward Platt (Lease Harris), Leo Gordon (Outlaw #2), John Day (Private Jeff Clay), John Alderson (Sgt. Duncan MacGregor), Chris Alcaide (Outlaw #3), Robert Hoy (Ranger #2), Chuck Roberson (Ranger #1), Dabs Greer (Storekeeper).

The first episode in *The Tales of Texas John Slaughter* begins in 1870 as he rides into Friotown, Texas. He has barely started down the street when two men try to ambush him, forcing John to kill them in self-defense. Ben Jenkins, a member of the famous Texas rangers, explains that the attackers mistook John for him, for John wears a white hat similar to the distinctive headgear of the rangers. John declines an offer to join the rangers and instead buys a small herd of cattle and settles outside of town.

Production Notes:

- Roy Barcroft, who starred in the *Spin and Marty* serials on *The Mickey Mouse Club,* had an unbilled role as a man who rents a horse to Slaughter.
- This episode was combined with *Ambush at Laredo* and released overseas in 1960 as *Texas John Slaughter.*

THANKSGIVING PROMISE, THE Airdates (2-hour format): 11/23/86, 11/22/87.

Cast: Beau Bridges (Hank Tilby), Millie Perkins (Lois Tilby), Courtney Thorne-Smith (Sheryl), Ed Lauter (Coach), Anne Haney (Mrs. Sudsup), Beau Dremann (Alec), Bill Calvert (Jason Tilby), Jordan Bridges (Travis Tilby), Jason Bateman (Steve Tilby), Lloyd Bridges (Stewart Larson), Jason Naylor (Arnold), Jessica Puscas (Jenni Tilby), Joshua Bryant (Sam the Vet), Zero Hubbard (Jess), Tina Caspary (Girl #1), Scott Nemes (Boy #1), Kiblena Peace (Emily), Mark Clayman (Tommy), Dorothy Dean Bridges (Mrs. Aggie Larson), Allan Dietrich (Square Dance Caller), Lucinda Jany (Neighbor Lady), Leonard P. Geer (Old Man), Jeff Bridges (Cameo Role).

Young Travis Tilby suffers from a lack of self-image until Stewart Larson, a local farmer, hires Travis to raise a goose for Larson's Thanksgiving dinner. Travis feels important, because the goose, which his sister names Chester, was hurt by a hunter and needs his help to survive.

Production Note:

- The show featured three generations of the Bridges family.

THAT DARN CAT!

This 1965 theatrical release first aired on 5/01/76 as a special as part of the *NBC All-Disney Saturday Night at the Movies* series when it was featured with *Bear Country*. It also aired on the anthology series during the 1979–80 series on 1/13/80 in a 2-hour format. For the 1980–81 season it was aired as follows—Part 1: 3/29/81. Part 2: 4/05/81.

THIS IS YOUR LIFE DONALD DUCK

Airdates: 3/11/60, 6/16/68, 2/13/77, 2/01/81.

Jiminy Cricket has decided to imitate the popular program *This Is Your Life* and present a tribute to Donald Duck, but he hasn't counted on Donald's determination to spend the day quietly at home.

Production Note:

- This show also aired as a special on 2/22/80.

THOSE CALLOWAYS

Airdates—Part 1: 1/12/69, 11/10/74, 4/23/78. Part 2: 1/19/69, 11/17/74, 4/30/78. Part 3: 1/26/69, 11/24/74, 5/07/78.

This 1965 theatrical release stars Brian Keith, Vera Miles, Brandon de Wilde, and Walter Brennan in the story of a family that struggles to preserve a sanctuary for wild geese that migrate past their farm.

THREE LIVES OF THOMASINA, THE

Airdates—Part 1: 11/14/65. Part 2: 11/21/65. Part 3: 11/28/65. In later years the show aired in two parts—Part 1: 10/05/69, 8/20/78. Part 2: 10/12/69, 8/27/78.

This 1963 theatrical release stars Patrick Mc-Goohan, Susan Hampshire, Karen Dotrice, and Matthew Garber in the story of how a cat's apparent death brings a veterinarian and his daughter closer together.

Production Note:

- Originally planned as a two-part television show for the 1961–62 season, *Thomasina* was also shown as a special on 12/24/74 with *It's Tough to Be a Bird* and *Arizona Sheepdog* as part of the *NBC*

All-Disney Saturday Night at the Movies series.

THREE ON THE RUN   Airdate: 1/08/78.

Cast: Denver Pyle (Clay Tanner), Davey Davison (Betsy Tanner), Ron Brown (Ranger Harley Townsend), Peggy Rea (Mrs. Lacy), Brett McQuire (Scott), Donald Williams (Steve), D. Kenton Brine (Lee Roy).

Scott and Steve Tanner are talked into entering Icicle Valley's Annual Sled Dog Race with the hopes of defeating reigning champion Lee Roy Norris. If they win, they will repeat the earlier victories of their now deceased father.

Production Note:

- This story was shot on location in and near Leavenworth, Washington, and in the Wenatchee National Forest. Many of the actors were local residents, including Bozo, the grizzly bear, who was obtained from the Olympic Game Farm.

THREE TALL TALES   Airdates: 1/06/63,

4/21/63, 6/08/69, 12/21/75, 12/31/78.

Prof. Ludwig Von Drake provides a look at several "bigger-than-life" legends. Assisted by Herman, the Bootle Beetle, Von Drake begins with a brief look at several such stories, using special "dialect pills" to add authenticity to his presentation.

THREE WITHOUT FEAR   Airdates—Part 1:

1/03/71, 7/27/75. Part 2: 1/10/71, 8/03/75.

Cast: Bart Orlando (Dave Rodgers), Pablo Lopez (Pedro), Marion Valjalo (Maria), Claude Earls (Mr. Rodgers), Carol Lee Doring (Mrs. Rodgers), Juan Jose Ramos (Juan), Alex Tinne (Manuel), Earl Campus (Grunts), Anthony Cordova (Rider), Umberto Sandoval (Bartender), Ignacio Ramirez (Old Man in Bar).

Presented in two parts (*Lost on the Baja Peninsula* and *In the Land of the Desert Whales*), this adventure story begins as a private plane is forced to land along the desolate Baja California shoreline. The pilot is injured in the crash and Dave Rodgers, a vacationing American, must go for help. A scorpion bite almost kills Dave, but two Mexican orphans chance upon him and save his life. Maria and Pedro, who are fleeing from an evil guardian named Manuel, ask Dave for help in reaching their grandmother's home. Learning that Manuel is after a bag of pearls the orphans are carrying, Dave agrees to help.

TIGER TOWN (AND) STAR TOURS

Airdates: 12/28/86 (with *Star Tours*, 2-hour format), 8/14/88 (1-hour format).

This program begins with a preview of the new Star Tours attraction at Disneyland. The remainder of the program is *Tiger Town*, a Disney Channel film.

TIGER WALKS, A Airdates—Part 1: 3/20/66, 8/07/66, 9/02/73, 6/03/79. Part 2: 3/27/66, 8/14/66, 9/09/73, 6/10/79.

This 1964 theatrical release stars Brian Keith, Vera Miles, Pamela Franklin, and Sabu in the story of a small town's reaction to the escape of a circus tiger.

TIME FLYER

This made-for-television movie first aired on The Disney Channel as *The Blue Yonder*. It also aired on the anthology series on 2/09/86 and 8/02/87.

TITLE MAKERS, THE (AND) NATURE'S HALF ACRE Airdate: 6/11/61.

Cast: Tommy Sands (Himself), Annette Funicello (Herself), Hayley Mills (Sharon McKendrick and Susan Evers), Maureen O'Hara (Maggie McKendrick), Brian Keith (Mitch Evers), Charlie Ruggles (Charles McKendrick), Una Merkel (Verbena), Leo G. Carroll (Reverend Mosby), Joanna Barnes (Vicky Robinson).

The first half of this episode is a promotional piece for the upcoming theatrical release *The Parent Trap*. The second part of the show was originally aired under the title *A Progress Report (and) Nature's Half Acre*.

Production Note:

• This was the last original episode broadcast on ABC in black and white.

TOBY TYLER Airdates—Part 1: 11/22/64, 10/13/68, 8/12/73. Part 2: 11/29/64, 10/20/68, 8/19/73.

The 1960 theatrical release stars Kevin Corcoran, Henry Calvin, Gene Sheldon, and Bob Sweeney in the story of a young boy who finds adventure when he runs away with the circus. The full theatrical name is *Toby Tyler, or Ten Weeks with a Circus*. It was adapted for television by Jack Bruner.

Production Note:

• This film was serialized on *The New Mickey Mouse Club*.

TO CONQUER THE MOUNTAIN

This is Part 1 of *Banner in the Sky*.

TO THE SOUTH POLE FOR SCIENCE

Airdates: 11/13/57, 4/23/58.

The third in a series of looks at International Geophysical Year activities near the South Pole, this episode continues the story begun in *Antarctica—Past and Present* and *Antarctica—Operation Deepfreeze*. Set between November 1956 and February 1957, the show details the efforts of scientists to construct five bases in the frigid wasteland.

Production Note:

• This episode, combined with *Antarctica—Past and Present* and *Antarctica—Operation Deepfreeze*, was released theatrically as *Seven Cities of Antarctica*.

TO TRAP A THIEF

This is Part 1 of *Michael O'Hara the Fourth*.

TOMORROW THE MOON

This is an alternate title for *Man and the Moon* when it aired on 9/25/59 before the start of the 1959–60 season.

TOOT, WHISTLE, PLUNK, AND BOOM

Airdates: 3/27/59, 4/19/64.

Music, which is so important to proper storytelling, is merely a series of sounds, or so claims Professor Owl. He demonstrates this theory through a series of animated clips, including the Academy Award winning short, *Toot, Whistle, Plunk, and Boom*.

TORY VENGEANCE Airdates: 1/01/60, 5/13/60.

Cast: Leslie Nielsen (Gen. Francis Marion), John Sutton (Col. Banastre Tarleton), Henry Daniell (Colonel Townes), Barbara Eiler (Mary Videaux), Dick Foran (Gabriel), Tim Considine (Gabe), Myron Healey (Col. Peter Horry), Dorothy Green (Mrs. Townes), Jordan Whitfield (Oscar), Sherry Jackson (Melanie Culpen), J. Pat O'Malley (Sergeant O'Reilly), Rhys Williams (Professor Culpen), Louise Beavers (Dehlia), Slim Pickens (Plunkett), Mary Field (Cathy), Clarence Muse (Joseph), James Anderson (Amos Briggs).

The third part of the story of Francis Marion, the "Swamp Fox," opens as the patriot leader gathers information on the British activities from several of his informers. Although many people believe his fiancée, Mary Videaux, to be a Tory, she is actually one of his most valuable sources of information. In order to discover what she has learned, Marion must confront Mary as she visits the Townes, the local Tory leaders, and pretends to bully her as he questions her. Despite their best efforts at secrecy, Colonel Tarleton, the local military commander, begins to suspect Mary.

TRACK OF THE AFRICAN BONGO, THE
Airdate—Part 1: 4/03/77. Part 2: 4/10/77.

Cast: Johnny Ngaya (Kamau), Oliver Litondo (Njiri), Tony Parkinson (Himself), John Seago (Himself), Alexander Aron Mshiu (Himself), Charles Hayes (Jock McEwen), Andrew Warwick (Carlin), Shane Mwigereri (First Officer), Peter Pearce (Habib).

Set in the bamboo forests of Kenya, this is the story of Kamua, a young boy who spots a rare breed of African antelope, the bongo. His uncle, Njiri, a poacher, treats Kamua with scorn when he asks how much a bongo skin would be worth, for Njiri refuses to believe the boy saw one of the rare animals. Upset at this, Kamua decides to find someone who will pay him enough to let him buy a bicycle he's long admired.

Production Note:

• This show took over five years to produce, partially due to the difficulties encountered in finding bongos for use in filming. It was filmed on location in Kenya.

TRADING PLACES
See: *The Absent-Minded Professor: Trading Places.*

TRAGEDY ON THE TRAIL   Airdates: 1/29/67, 7/09/67.

Cast: John McIntire (Whit White), Beverly Garland (Mrs. Carlson), Harry Townes (Mr. Barlow), Ron Hayes (George Moran), Roger Mobley (Gallegher), Jeanette Nolan (Erm White), Bill Williams (Joe Carlson), Joe Maross (Mr. Hatfield), Ray Teal (Sheriff Snead), Darleen Carr (Laurie Carlson), Tim McIntire (Phin Carlson), Don Keefer (John Prentice), Walter Sande (Judge McManus), John Launer (Judge Hargraves).

Chapter 9 in the life of Gallegher, a frontier newsboy, features his adventures when he decides that owning a horse would let him become a more efficient salesman. He convinces the paper's owners to let him try, and carrying an old saddle, heads out to look for a suitable horse. Instead, he stumbles on a murder.

Production Notes:

• This story is continued in the episode *Trial by Terror.*
• This episode is also known as *Gallegher Goes West—Part 3.*

TRAIL OF DANGER   Airdates—Part 1: 3/12/78. Part 2: 3/19/78.

Cast: Jim Davis (Pop Apling), Larry Wilcox (Beech Carter), Robert Donner (The Sheep Boss), David Ireland (The Hand), Charles Hoagland (The Old Timer), Tom Hiler (The Ice Man).

Two weary trail hands reach the end of a tiring 80-mile trip and discover that no one is waiting for the 22 hungry horses they've been herding. Pop Apling, veteran of many prior rides, decides to take the herd to the railroad and sell them in exchange for the wages owed him.

Production Note:

• Larry Wilcox, who also appeared in the episode *Twister, Bull from the Sky,* later starred in the long-running series *CHiPs.*

TREASURE IN THE HAUNTED HOUSE
This is Part 2 of *For the Love of Willadean.*

TREASURE ISLAND   Airdates—Part 1: 1/05/55, 11/28/56, 4/29/62, 7/13/80, 4/17/82. Part 2: 1/12/55, 12/05/56, 5/06/62, 7/20/80, 4/24/82.
This 1950 theatrical release stars Bobby Driscoll and Robert Newton in Robert Lewis Stevenson's classic tale of a young boy who becomes involved with pirates and buried treasure. It was adapted for television by Bill Walsh and Al Teeter.

TREASURE OF MATECUMBE, THE   Airdate (2-hour format): 10/02/77.
This 1976 theatrical release stars Robert Foxworth, Joan Hackett, Peter Ustinov, and Vic Morrow in the story of adventurers searching for a missing treasure after the Civil War.

TREASURE OF SAN BOSCO REEF, THE
Airdates—Part 1: 11/24/68, 8/03/69, 6/05/82. Part 2: 12/01/68, 8/10/69, 6/12/82.

Cast: James Daly (Uncle Max), Roger Mobley (Dave Jones), Nehemiah Persoff (Captain Malcione), John van Dreelen (Dr. Lindquist), Antony Alda (Gus Donato), Carlos Romero (Raoul), Robert Sorrells (Cece).

Dave Jones travels to Italy for his vacation and becomes involved with international smugglers when he visits his uncle Max, who heads a government salvage team. The divers are exploring the sunken wreck of an ancient ship and Dave begins spending his days at the dive site. He spots the body of one of the divers and tells Max, who discovers that many of the valuable artifacts have been stolen.

TRIAL BY TERROR Airdates: 2/05/67, 7/16/67.

Cast: John McIntire (Whit White), Beverly Garland (Mrs. Carlson), Harry Townes (Mr. Barlow), Ron Hayes (George Moran), Roger Mobley (Gallegher), Jeanette Nolan (Erm White), Bill Williams (Joe Carlson), Joe Maross (Mr. Hatfield), Ray Teal (Sheriff Snead), Darleen Carr (Laurie Carlson), Tim McIntire (Phin Carlson), Don Keefer (John Prentice), Sylvia Field (Mrs. McManus).

The tenth *Gallegher* episode continues the story begun in *Tragedy on the Trail*. The night before Joe Carlson's trial, his daughter Laurie sees George Moran with a pocket watch that resembles one owned by the victim, Judge McManus. She tells Gallegher, who sneaks into the gunman's room and steals the watch to examine it. When Gallegher and the sheriff examine it, they find it is inscribed with the initials "C.E.D.," evidently eliminating the link to McManus.

Production Note:

- This story is also known as *Gallegher Goes West—Part 4.*

TRIBUTE TO JOEL CHANDLER HARRIS, A
Airdates: 1/18/56, 3/28/56, 6/27/56.

Cast: David Stollery (Joel Chandler Harris), Jonathan Hale (J. A. Turner), Sam McDaniel (Herbert), Harry Shannon (Mr. Wilson), Barbara Woodell (Mrs. Harris).

This show salutes American storyteller Joel Chandler Harris, famous for several works, including the Uncle Remus stories featured in *Song of the South*. A live-action re-creation of Harris's early years shows how he first became interested in writing. The episode ends with the *Tar Baby* sequence from *Song of the South*.

TRIBUTE TO MICKEY MOUSE, A

This sequence was included as the second half of *The Disneyland Story* and is described under that title. It was also used as the second half of *The Pre-Opening Report on Disneyland (and) A Tribute to Mickey Mouse.*

TRICKS OF OUR TRADE Airdates: 2/13/57, 7/03/57.

This episode takes a look at the science of animation, where there are many complex principles at work for every movement seen on the screen. Like many other sciences, animation techniques were developed both to solve specific problems and for general knowledge.

Production Note:

- An edited version of this show was released by Disney's educational division.

TRIP THRU ADVENTURELAND, A (AND) WATER BIRDS Airdates: 2/29/56, 5/02/56, 9/05/56.

The first portion of this show is a trip through the Adventureland section of Disneyland, with a special look at the popular Jungle Cruise attraction. The second part of the show is an edited version of the 1952 Academy Award winner, *Water Birds*. Winston Hibler narrates this look at the many types of birds that live in aquatic locales.

Production Note:

- *Water Birds* was also aired as part of the episode *Escape to Paradise (and) Water Birds.*

TRIP TO TUCSON Airdates: 4/16/61, 7/23/61.

Cast: Tom Tryon (Texas John Slaughter), Betty Lynn (Viola Slaughter), Joe Maross (Jimmy Deuce), Jim Beck (Burt Alvord), Brian Corcoran (Willie Slaughter), Peggy Knudsen (Nellie), Lane Bradford (Jace Caldwell), Annette Gorman (Addie Slaughter), Larry Blake (Drummer).

Episode 15 of *The Tales of Texas John Slaughter* portrays Slaughter as a sheriff who has become hated by the very people he has sworn to protect. Many of the residents of Tombstone feel he has become too harsh in enforcing the law, for Slaughter has killed a number of people who resisted his efforts to arrest them.

Production Note:

- This episode and *Frank Clell's in Town* were released theatrically overseas in 1966 as *A Holster Full of Law.*

TRUE SON'S REVENGE

This is Part 2 of *The Light in the Forest.*

TRUTH ABOUT MOTHER GOOSE, THE
Airdates: 11/17/63, 7/12/64, 12/25/66, 12/22/74.

Prof. Ludwig Von Drake and his assistant, Herman, host this look at Mother Goose, who is credited with creating many famous nursery rhymes, and several of the world's other well-known storytellers. The two co-hosts compete with each other to tell the stories, often with comedic results.

Production Note:

- The Mother Goose sequences were taken from the theatrical short subject *The Truth about Mother Goose*, an Academy Award nominee released in 1957.

20,000 LEAGUES UNDER THE SEA
This 1954 theatrical release first aired as a special on 2/23/74. An edited 2-hour version was later broadcast as part of the anthology series on 10/24/76, 11/04/79, and 2/25/87.

TWISTER, BULL FROM THE SKY   Airdates: 1/04/76, 8/31/80.
Cast: Larry Wilcox (Andy Holton), Willie Aames (Andy as a Boy), Keith Andes (Ed Holton), Denis Arndt (Pete Wiley, the Pilot), David Combs (Ranger), Wick Peth (Tourist), Jack Roddy (Jack Downs, the Rodeo Boss).

When a baby Brahma bull is rejected by its mother, young Andy Holton adopts the animal and raises it to become a championship bucking bull. Twister, the calf, grows to the impressive weight of 1,800 pounds and becomes well known throughout the rodeo circuit. During their flight to a rodeo, the plane develops engine trouble and Twister is dropped by parachute to save the crew.

2½ DADS   Airdates: 2/16/86, 8/10/86.
Cast: George Dzundza (Pete Seltzer), Richard Young (Frank Manley), Sal Viscuso (Chick Leone), Lenore Kasdorf (Arlene Kubick), Mary Kohnert (Kathleen), Billy Warlock (Danny Seltzer), Ricky Stout (Frank Jr.), Marissa Mendenhall (Dorothy), Shana O'Neil (Rose), Sharon Madden (Candy).

Three friends are forced to move in together when they all have financial problems and can't afford homes of their own. Frank Manley brings his son and daughter, both of whom are still grieving over the recent death of their mother. Pete Seltzer's wife has just left him and their three children. The third friend, Chick, is alone because his wife and daughter disappeared in Cambodia.

Production Note:

- This was an unsold pilot.
- The 2/16/86 edition aired with *The Last Electric Knight* in a 2-hour format.

TWO AGAINST THE ARCTIC   Airdates—
Part 1: 10/20/74, 6/15/75. Part 2: 10/27/74, 6/22/75.
Cast: Susie Silook (Lolly), Marty Smith (Joseph), Rossman Peetook (Father), Jerome Trigg (Grandfather), Vernon Silook (Uncle).

An ordeal in survival begins as two Eskimo children, Lolly and Joseph, accompany their father, Ningeok, on a hunting trip deep inside the Arctic Circle. Ningeok and two other hunters set up a base camp from which they intend to hunt for walruses. They then leave the children alone in the camp as they begin their search.

Production Note:

- The author of this story, Sally Carrighar, also wrote the books used for *One Day on Beetle Rock* and *One Day at Teton Marsh*.

TWO HAPPY AMIGOS   Airdates: 2/05/60, 6/17/60.
Jose Carioca travels from South America to visit Donald Duck. The show features several animated clips starring Jose and Donald, including *Saludos Amigos*, that shows how they first met.

UGLY DACHSHUND, THE   Airdates—Part 1: 11/03/68, 2/10/74, 2/19/78. Part 2: 11/10/68, 2/17/74, 2/26/78.
This 1965 theatrical release stars Dean Jones and Suzanne Pleshette in the story of pet owners who agree to raise an abandoned Great Dane puppy, mistakenly thinking that it can't take much more attention than their dachsunds.

UNDERGRADS, THE
This made-for-television movie first aired on The Disney Channel. It also aired on the anthology series on 3/02/86 and 1/25/87.

VALENTINE FROM DISNEY, A   AIRDATE: 2/08/83.
Clips from several animated films provide brief looks at some of Disney's most memorable romantic couples.

VARDA, THE PEREGRINE FALCON
Airdates: 11/16/69, 8/16/70.

Cast: Peter de Manio (Charlie Cypress), Noreen Klincko (Sally Cypress), Denise Grisco (Mary Ann Cypress).

Billed as following in the tradition of the Studio's *True-Life Adventures*, this is the story of Varda, a female falcon. The bird is captured by a Seminole Indian who tries to train her to hunt food for his family.

Production Note:

- A camera was mounted on a radio-controlled plane to provide a "bird's-eye view" for the flying scenes.

VON DRAKE IN SPAIN   Airdates: 4/08/62, 4/11/71.

Cast: Spanish Dancers: *Rafael de Cordova, Pedro Azorin, Oscar Herrera, Mariemma, Lola de Ronda, Farruco, Maria Angeles, Alicia Diaz, Maria Luisa Ejido, Manoli Vargas, Carmen Artea, Cancienes y Danzas de España and Seccion Femenina.* Guest Artist: *Jose Greco.*

Prof. Ludwig Von Drake returns to host a look at the colorful dances and customs of Spain. He claims to be an expert on the subject, stating that his real name is Prof. Ludwig Jose Antonio Pablo Rafael Seemore Von Drake. Discovering that he doesn't know as much as he thought, Von Drake uses animated and live-action films to provide additional facts about Spain.

Production Note:

- This episode was released theatrically overseas in 1965.

WACKY ZOO OF MORGAN CITY, THE
Airdates—Part 1: 10/18/70, 7/11/71. Part 2: 10/25/70, 7/18/71.

Cast: Hal Holbrook (Mitch Collins), Joe Flynn (Mayor Bernard Philbrick), Cecil Kellaway (Old Al Casey), Wally Cox (Becker), Mary LaRoche (Nancy Collins), Michael-James Wixted (Noah Collins), Anne Seymour (Maggie Hargrove), Michael McGreevey (Ralph), Christina Anderson (Jen Collins), Ian Wolfe (Reverend Hodgkins), George N. Neise (Councilman Thompson), Annie McEveety (Rosemary), Bill Zuckert (Policeman), Penny Marshall (Mayor's Secretary), Harriet MacGibbon (Mrs. Westerfield), Judson Pratt (Scott Shellog), J. Edward McKinley (Councilman Parson).

With Election Day growing near, the mayor of Morgan City, Bernard Philbrick, accepts the support of an influential ladies' group. The ladies will help with his campaign if the mayor agrees to close down the town's dilapidated zoo and let them use the site for a new museum. Sure that no one important cares about the zoo, he agrees, then appoints Mitch Collins, a city accountant, to run the zoo. Philbrick hasn't counted on Collins's children, who prompt their dad into working for the zoo's survival.

Production Note:

- The zoo scenes were shot in the abandoned former home of the Los Angeles City Zoo, which had recently moved to new quarters.

WAHOO BOBCAT, THE   Airdates: 10/20/63, 8/02/64, 5/04/69.

Cast: Jock MacGregor (Jed Morgan), Bill Dunnagan (Sam Baker), Lloyd Shelton (Harry Baker).

Florida's vast Okefenokee Swamp is the setting for this tale of an aging fisherman who befriends a bobcat that is hiding from a determined hunter. Tiger, the bobcat, has also begun to feel the effects of time and thus comes to rely on the kindness of Jed Morgan, a lifetime resident of the swamp.

Production Notes:

- Filming took place in the marshes of Florida's Withlacoochie River.
- This episode was released theatrically overseas in 1965.

WAKE OF DISASTER
This is Part 2 of *The Mooncussers.*

WALT DISNEY . . . ONE MAN'S DREAM
Airdate (2-hour format): 12/12/81.

Cast: Michael Landon, Mac Davis, Marie Osmond, Carl Reiner, Dick Van Dyke, Ben Vereen, Julie Andrews, Mikhail Baryshnikov, Walter Cronkite, Buckminster Fuller, Beverly Sills, Andy Warhol, Christian Hoff (Young Walt Disney), Charles Aidman (Mark Twain), Jan Hoff (Roy Disney), Lawrence Guy (Elias Disney), Frances Bain (Flora Disney), Kathlee MacNaighton (Ruthie).

The genius of Walt Disney and his refusal to listen to defeatists is the subject of this preview look at Epcot Center, which is under construction in Florida. Hosted by Michael Landon, it begins at the construction site, where crews are at work on the billion-dollar project, the largest ever undertaken by private industry.

Production Note:

- "Epcot" stands for "Experimental Prototype Community of Tomorrow."

WALT DISNEY WORLD'S 15TH BIRTHDAY CELEBRATION   Airdates (2-hour format): 11/09/86, 5/31/87.

Cast: Diahann Carroll, Ray Charles, The Charlie Daniels Band, Everly Brothers, Gladys Knight and the Pips, Emmanuel Lewis, The Monkees, Dolly Parton, Harry Shearer, Air Supply, Charlton Heston, Bea Arthur, Betty White, President Ronald Reagan, Sen. Edward Kennedy, Former Chief Justice Warren Burger, Jack Wagner (Announcer).

Bea Arthur and Betty White host this birthday celebration. During the program they describe World Showcase at Epcot, introduce film footage of Walt describing the Park in 1965, and show scenes of Roy O. Disney at the grand opening gala.

WALT DISNEY'S MICKEY AND DONALD

Airdate: 1/01/83 (30-minute format), 9/24/83 (1-hour format).
There's little doubt that Walt Disney's two biggest cartoon stars are Mickey Mouse and Donald Duck. This show salutes them with a look at several of their most popular cartoons.

WALT DISNEY'S WET AND WILD

Airdate: Syndicated.
The Disney characters have many different ways of getting wet. This show takes a look at some of the wettest scenes in Disney animation.

WALTZ KING, THE   Airdates—Part 1: 10/27/63, 8/01/71. Part 2: 11/03/63, 8/08/71.

Cast: Kerwin Mathews (Johann Strauss, Jr.), Senta Berger (Yetty Treffz), Brian Aherne (Johann Strauss, Sr.), Peter Kraus (Josef Strauss), Fritz Eckhardt (Tobias Haslinger), Vilma Degischer (Mrs. Strauss), Karl Lieffen (Stieglitz), Kai Fischer (Russiche Dame), Michael Janisch (Kosakenoffizier).

Johann Strauss, the "Waltz King" of Vienna, is determined that his son, Johann Strauss, Jr., will be a respectable citizen and not a musician, and thus insists that he be-come a lawyer. Despite his father's orders, Johann, Jr., decides to pursue a career in music, and it's soon apparent that musical talent has been passed from father to son. His father scares the music publishers into not buying his son's sheet music, and Schani is forced to give music lessons in exchange for food.

Production Notes:

- This story was shot on location in Strauss's home of Vienna, Austria.
- *The Waltz King* was released theatrically overseas in 1964.

WARRIOR'S PATH, THE   Airdates: 12/04/60, 6/25/61.

Cast: Dewey Martin (Daniel Boone), Mala Powers (Rebecca Boone), Richard Banke (Squire Boone), Eddy Waller (John Finley), Anthony Caruso (Blackfish), Dean Fredericks (Crow Feather), Don Dorrell (John Stuart), Alex Gerry (Judge Henderson).

The first episode of the *Daniel Boone* mini-series begins as Boone, a farmer in North Carolina, talks to a salesman named John Finley about Kentucky, where legend has it that the land is amazingly fertile and the forests are full of game. Finley claims that the dangerous trip to Kentucky can be made on the Warrior's Path, an old Indian trail used by hunting parties, and Daniel decides to move his family there.

WATER BIRDS

This is Part 2 of *A Trip thru Adventureland (and) Water Birds.* It was also aired as part of the episode *Escape to Paradise (and) Water Birds.*

WAY DOWN CELLAR   Airdates—Part 1: 1/07/68, 6/11/72. Part 2: 1/14/68, 6/18/72.

Cast: Butch Patrick (Frank Wilson), Sheldon Collins (Beans Emerson), Lindy Davis (Skeeter Martin), Frank McHugh (Constable Seely), Richard Bakalyan (Charlie), David McLean (Professor Wilson), Ben Wright (Ethan Marcus), Grace Lee Whitney (Velma), Frederic Downs (Mr. Hotchenfelter), Lou Byrne (Mrs. Wilson).

A football game leads to excitement and danger for three friends when they search for the ball after a bad pass. Frank Wilson, Skeeter Martin, and Beans Emerson discover the entrance to a secret tunnel hidden in the ruins of a burned-out church and follow it to a supposedly haunted house. They're surprised to learn that the house has recently been rented and they see the new tenant, Mr. Marcus, with some suspicious-looking men.

Production Note:

- A special 35mm camera was mounted on a football helmet and worn by Butch Patrick during the football game in order to provide a "player's-eye" view.

WELCOME TO THE "WORLD" Airdate: 3/23/75.

Cast: Lucie Arnaz, Lyle Waggoner, Tommy Tune, The Rhodes Kids, Scotty Plummer.

The grand opening of Walt Disney World's newest attraction, Space Mountain, provides the backdrop for this musical look at the Florida theme park.

WESTWARD HO THE WAGONS!

Airdates—Part 1: 2/19/61, 10/04/70. Part 2: 2/26/61, 10/11/70.

This 1956 theatrical release stars Fess Parker, Kathleen Crowley, Jeff York, and Sebastian Cabot in the story of wagon trains traveling along the Oregon Trail in 1844 en route to the Northwest Territory. It was aired in two parts, *Ambush at Wagon Gap* and *White Man's Medicine.*

Production Notes:

- This film was originally planned as a two-part television episode to be titled *Children of the Covered Wagon.*
- The episode *Along the Oregon Trail* is a behind-the-scenes look at the filming of this story.

WETBACK HOUND, THE Airdates: 4/24/59, 5/27/62 (*Big Red* version), 5/29/66 (*Lt. Robin Crusoe, U.S.N.* version).

Cast: Marvin Glenn (Himself), Warner Glenn (Himself).

This is the story of Paco, a dog from a fine line of mountain lion hunters. Paco meets with his owner's displeasure when he abandons a scent to chase after a deer. There is a bounty on mountain lions and Paco's skills are needed to earn a living for his owner.

Production Note:

- In its original 20-minute length, *The Wetback Hound* won an Academy Award in 1957 for Best Live-Action Short Subject. It was expanded for this television version.

WHAT IS DISNEYLAND? (AND) A TRIBUTE TO MICKEY MOUSE

See: *The Disneyland Story.*

WHEN KNIGHTHOOD WAS IN FLOWER

Airdates—Part 1: 1/04/56, 7/11/56, 4/07/63. Part 2: 1/11/56, 7/18/56, 4/14/63.

Released theatrically in 1953 as *The Sword and the Rose,* this film stars Glynis Johns, Richard Todd, and James Robertson Justice in the story of two noblemen who develop an interest in King Henry VIII's sister. It was adapted for television by Bill Walsh, Al Teeter, and Lee Chaney.

WHERE DO THE STORIES COME FROM?

Airdates: 4/04/56, 6/06/56.

Cast: Kirk Douglas, Ollie Johnston, Ward Kimball, Oliver Wallace

In response to an often asked question, Walt announces that he will attempt to explain just where the stories for the Studio's cartoons come from. He mentions that they can come from just about anywhere and provides four different animated examples.

Production Note:

- This episode made extensive use of "home movies" photographed by the Studio staff.

WHERE THE HECK IS HECTOR?

This is Part 1 of *The Ballad of Hector the Stowaway Dog.*

WHITE MAN'S MEDICINE Airdates: 3/05/58, 7/09/58.

Cast: Jerome Courtland (Andy Burnett), Jeff York (Joe Crane), Andrew Duggan (Jack Kelly), Slim Pickens (Old Bill Williams), Iron Eyes Cody (Mad Wolf), Abel Fernandez (Kiasak), John War Eagle (Matosuki).

The fifth episode of *The Saga of Andy Burnett* continues the story begun in *The Land of Enemies.* Andy has used a telescope lens to light a fire by focusing the sun's rays, thereby making the Indians think he is a friend of the sun god. He then convinces the chief to let them live.

Production Note:

- This story is continued in the episode *The Big Council.*

WHITE MAN'S MEDICINE

This is Part 2 of *Westward Ho the Wagons!*

WHIZ KID AND THE CARNIVAL CAPER, THE   Airdates—Part 1: 1/11/76, 7/16/78. Part 2: 1/18/76, 7/23/78.

Cast: Jack Kruschen (Abner Debney), John Colicos (Moroni), Jaclyn Smith (Cathy), Dick Bakalyan (Ernie Nelson), Eric Shea (Alvin Fernald), Clay O'Brien (Shoie), Kim Richards (Daphne "Daffy" Fernald), Ronnie Schell (Deputy Scurf), Ted Gehring (Moody), Richard O'Brien (Bernie Thorness), Eileen McDonough (Stephie), Hal Smith (Carnival Barker), Ed McCready (Carnival Barker), Milton Frome (Carnival Barker), John Lupton (Mr. Fernald).

Daffy Fernald loses her brother's toy rocket when it flies into a storm drain. She knows Alvin will be upset if he finds out, so she climbs into the dark tunnel to search for it. She spots a stranger, Ernie Nelson, and sees that he's carrying a gun. She races home and tells Alvin, but the would-be inventor refuses to believe her.

Production Notes:

- This is a sequel to the episode *The Whiz Kid and the Mystery at Riverton,* aired during the 1973–74 season.
- A carnival set for the show was built in an employee parking lot at the Studio. Located next to a freeway, it attracted crowds of passersby who thought it was a real carnival and asked to be admitted.

WHIZ KID AND THE MYSTERY AT RIVERTON, THE   Airdates—Part 1: 1/06/74, 5/19/74. Part 2: 1/13/74, 5/26/74.

Cast: Edward Andrews (Mayor Massey), John Fiedler (Charles Blackburn), Lonny Chapman (Fred Benson), Eric Shea (Alvin Fernald), Clay O'Brien (Shoie), Kim Richards (Daffy), Ted Gehring (Doyle Reager), Larry J. Blake (Police Chief), Lynn Borden (Miss Pinkney), Norman Bartold (Sam Preston), Judson Pratt (Sergeant O'Halloran), Claude Johnson (Mr. Fernald), Bebe Kelly (Mrs. Fernald), Maudie Prickett (Mrs. Hundley), George O'Hanlon (Herb Evans), Molly Dodd (Mrs. Blake), Hal Smith (Ed Haskins), Dick Wilson (Mr. Hodges), Brian Morrison (Shorty), Ed Prentiss (Commissioner), Rae Dawn Chong (Greta), Marshall Kent (City Engineer), Chuck Sullivant (Worm), Pete Renoudet (Reporter), Oliver Dunbar (Mrs. Barkley).

Alvin Fernald is a young inventor who wants to win an essay contest being held in his sixth grade class. The topic is city government, so he decides to get as much information as possible by talking to Mayor Massey. While waiting in City Hall, Alvin and his friend, Shoie, overhear the city treasurer discussing a crooked land deal with two other men.

Production Notes:

- The Studio later filmed a sequel, *The Whiz Kid and the Carnival Caper,* starring much of the same cast.
- This episode was based on the book *Alvin Fernald, Mayor for a Day.*

WHO THE HECK IS HECTOR?
This is Part 2 of *The Ballad of Hector the Stowaway Dog.*

WILD BURRO OF THE WEST   Airdates: 1/29/60, 11/10/63, 6/04/72.

Cast: Bill Keys (Andy), Bill Pace (Rustler), Jim Burch (Rustler).

Dusty is a small burro living a quiet life with her elderly master, a farmer in Mexico, until two men sneak onto the farm and steal her. They use the animal to help them rustle cattle. Dusty carries their water and other supplies, but the men are cruel and mistreat the burro, allowing her little water and feed. Tired of this mistreatment, Dusty strains to break free of the hobbles used to control her.

Production Note:

- Forest ranger Charles Draper, who assisted the crew of this episode, later quit his government job to work for the Studio on numerous nature shows.

WILD COUNTRY, THE   Airdates—Part 1: 2/23/75, 6/07/81. Part 2: 3/02/75, 6/14/81. This 1971 theatrical release stars Steve Forrest, Jack Elam, Ronny Howard, and Vera Miles in the story of a family and its struggle to survive in the rugged territory of Jackson Hole, Wyoming, during the 1880s.

WILD GEESE CALLING   Airdates: 9/14/69, 5/11/75.

Cast: Carl Draper (Dan Tolliver), Persis Overton (The Mother).

Filmed in the style of the *True-Life Adventures,* this is the story of Dan Tolliver, a 9-year-old boy who discovers a wounded Canadian gander. The bird has been shot by a hunter and is too weak to continue its annual migratory flight.

Production Note:

- *Wild Geese Calling* was released theatrically overseas in 1971.

WILD HEART Airdate: 3/10/68.

Cast: Andrew Penn (The Brother), Kitty Porteous (The Sister), Stanley Bowles (Ned, the Uncle).

Two Canadian children travel to Puget Sound to visit their aunt and uncle and become involved in a series of adventures with the area's animal residents.

WILD HORSE REVENGE Airdates: 12/11/59, 7/01/60.

Cast: Tom Tryon (Texas John Slaughter), Darryl Hickman (Ashley Carstairs), Barton MacLane (John Scanlon), John Vivyan (Jason Hemp), Jean Inness (Mrs. Scanlon), William Phipps (Gabe), Bing Russell (Arne).

Episode 7A of *The Tales of Texas John Slaughter* continues the story begun in *The Robber Stallion* as John vows to capture the wild mustang that stranded him in the desert. His friend, John Scanlon, warns him that Jason Hemp will continue to try to stop him, for Hemp wants to control the horse business in the area.

Production Note:

• Bing Russell is the father of longtime Disney star Kurt Russell.

WILD JACK (#1) Airdate: 1/15/89.

Cast: John Schneider (Jack McCall), Carol Huston (Constance Fielding), Richard Coca (Tony Cruz), E. Erich Anderson (Carver), James Karen (Stepfield), Mel Ferrer (Winston Fielding), Gary Epp (Officer), F. William Parker (Lawyer Moran), Arell Blanton (Fred), Mitchell Bobrow (Chet), David Caine (Guard), Ellen Albertini Dow (Elderly Woman), Holgie Forrester (Nurse), Erik Holland (German Businessman), Roy L. Jones (Security Guard), Norman Merrill (Ray), Ron Orbach (Manager), Jill Wakeman (Attendant).

The unexpected death of publishing magnate Winston Fielding stuns his family and business partners, not because he's dead, but because of his very unusual will.

Production Note:

• This was the first of three *Wild Jack* stories aired on the anthology series.

WILD JACK (#2) Airdate: 7/09/89.

Cast: John Schneider (Jack McCall), Carol Huston (Constance Fielding), Nathan LeGrand (Thorp Covington), Janet MacLachlan (Grace), Kevin Skousen (Marion Reynolds), Lory Walsh (Natalie Korda),

Thomas McTigue (Darien Blake), Richard Roat (Ferris Edgewood), Michael Wren (Maitre d'), Terry Bozeman (Jerome Rossiter), Jed Mills (Mechanic), Lydia Jade (Loomis Tuatu), Sandi Stutz (Older Woman).*

A lunch date with an old friend plunges Constance into intrigue when the other woman, Natalie, suddenly runs from the restaurant in terror after spotting two men there. Constance asks Jack to find Natalie, and he discovers that she is hiding from someone to escape a gambling debt.

WILD JACK (#3) Airdate: 7/16/89.

Cast: John Schneider (Jack McCall), Carol Huston (Constance Fielding), Jack Kehler (Dave), Charles Lucia (Jorgen Ellis), Janet MacLachlan (Grace), Kevin Skousen (Marion Reynolds), Cary-Hiroyuki Tagawa (Mr. Noh), Patricia Gaul (Betty), Richard Roat (Ferris Edgewood).

A hostile takeover bid may cost Constance her father's company, for the bid hinges on an important contract that has mysteriously disappeared. Unless it is found by the end of the week, Constance will lose control of the company as part of an elaborate takeover scheme.

WILDERNESS ROAD, THE Airdate: 3/12/61.

Cast: Dewey Martin (Daniel Boone), Mala Powers (Rebecca Boone), Diane Jergens (Maybelle Yancey), William Herrin (Buddy Yancey), Slim Pickens (Captain Gass), Kevin Corcoran (James Boone), Anthony Caruso (Blackfish), Wally Brown (Cyrus Whittey), Dean Fredericks (Crowfeather), George Wallace (Mordecai), Stan Jones (Doc Slocum), Jean Inness (Sarah Watkins).

The third story of Daniel Boone finds the frontier hero searching for his son, who was kidnapped by Indians.

WILLIE AND THE YANK Airdates—Part 1: 1/08/67, 8/23/70. Part 2: 1/15/67, 8/30/70. Part 3: 1/22/67, 9/06/70.

Cast: James MacArthur (Corp. Henry Jenkins), Nick Adams (Sergeant Gregg), Jack Ging (Lieutenant Mosby), Kurt Russell (Pvt. Willie Prentiss), Peggy Lipton (Oralee Prentiss), Jeanne Cooper (Ma Prentiss), Donald Harron (General Stoughton), James Callahan (Sam Chapman), Robert Sorrells (Private Starkey), Michael Pate (Captain Blazer), E.J. Andre (Uncle Ferd), Bob Random (Private Lomax), Michael Kearney (Homer Prentiss), Michael Forest (Gen. Jeb Stuart),

Steve Raines (Sergeant Maddux), John Crawford (Gen. Fitzhugh Lee).

This adventure story, set during the American Civil War, is presented in three parts: *The Deserter*, *The Mosby Raiders*, and *The Matchmaker*. A young Confederate private, Willie Prentiss, is assigned to guard duty at a lonely outpost on the Rappahannock River. He becomes friends with his Union counterpart, Cpl. Henry Jenkins, and the two spend their days talking to each other across the river.

This unusual friendship takes a new turn after Willie accidentally shoots his commanding officer and Jenkins helps him escape a court martial by disguising him as a Yankee.

Production Note:

- This story had originally been planned as a U.S. theatrical release, and was released theatrically overseas in 1967 under one of its working titles, *Mosby's Marauders*.

WIND IN THE WILLOWS, THE   Airdates:
2/02/55, 5/18/55, 8/03/55, 5/22/59, 5/02/65.
Walt devotes this hour to the British writer of children's tales, Kenneth Grahame. The creator of Mr. Toad and many other famous characters has long been a favorite of Walt's, who first used one of his stories in the 1941 film, *The Reluctant Dragon*.

WINNIE THE POOH AND A DAY FOR EEYORE   Airdate: 1/29/89.
This 1983 theatrical featurette finds Winnie the Pooh inventing a new game called "poohsticks" and discovering that Eeyore is upset because everyone has forgotten his birthday. The program also includes three cartoons: *The Big Wash*, *Honey Harvester*, and *Out on a Limb*.

WINNIE THE POOH AND FRIENDS
Airdate: 12/11/82, 8/30/83.
The 1974 theatrical featurette *Winnie the Pooh and Tigger Too* pits Winnie the Pooh and the other residents of the Hundred Acre Woods against Tigger, who has been driving them all crazy with his excessive bouncing.

WINNIE THE POOH AND THE BLUSTERY DAY
This episode first aired as a special on 11/30/70. It later aired on the anthology series on 3/05/89 with the cartoons *Working for Peanuts*, *Pluto's Sweater*, and *The New Neighbor*.

WINNIE THE POOH AND THE HONEY TREE
This episode first aired as a special on 3/10/70. It later aired on the anthology series on 1/21/90 with the cartoons *Springtime for Pluto*, *Donald's Garden*, and *Mickey's Parrot*.

WINNIE THE POOH AND TIGGER TOO
This episode first aired as a special on 11/28/75. It later aired on the anthology series on 11/15/87 with *Bee on Guard*, *Pluto and the Gopher*, and *In the Bag*.

WOMAN'S COURAGE, A   Airdates:
1/08/61, 6/04/61.
   Cast: *Leslie Nielsen (Gen. Francis Marion), Barbara Eiler (Mary Videaux), Arthur Hunnicutt (Ezra Selby), Sean McClory (Captain Myles), J. Pat O'Malley (Sergeant O'Reilly), Jordan Whitfield (Oscar), James Seay (Captain Richardson), Charles Briggs (Folger), Richard Lupino (Ensign Wilkes).*

The seventh episode of *The Swamp Fox* opens as Marion and his men flee from the British after freeing Mary Videaux from her captors in Charleston. She discovers a prison ship and launches a daring plan to save the captured patriots.

WONDERS OF THE WATER WORLD
Airdates: 5/21/61, 5/08/66.
The subject of this show is water and how it affects our lives.

Production Note:

- This episode was also aired on 1/29/77 with *A Horse Called Comanche* as part of the *NBC All-Disney Saturday Night at the Movies* series.

WORLD'S GREATEST ATHLETE, THE
Airdates—Part 1: 1/04/83. Part 2: 1/11/83.
This 1972 theatrical release stars Jan-Michael Vincent, Tim Conway, John Amos, Roscoe Lee Browne, and Dayle Haddon in the story of a college coach who discovers a boy in Africa who can outrun a cheetah, the fastest animal on land.

WRONG WAY MOOCHIE
This is Part 2 of *Moochie of the Little League*.

YELLOWSTONE CUBS, THE   Airdates:
9/19/65, 8/21/66, 1/04/70, 4/13/75.
This 1963 theatrical release, set in Yellowstone National Park, is the story of a mother bear's desperate search for her missing cubs.

YELLOWSTONE STORY (AND) BEAR COUNTRY Airdates: 5/01/57, 7/24/57.

The *True-Life Adventure* series required the Studio's crews to travel to far-off locations. In filming *Bear Country*, the photographers were sent to Yellowstone National Park in Montana, which is the subject of this episode.

Production Note:

- *Bear Country*, which won an Academy Award for Best Short Subject of 1953, was also aired as part of the episode *Rapids Ahead (and) Bear Country* and on 5/1/76 as a special with *That Darn Cat!*

YOU RUINED MY LIFE Airdates (2-hour format): 2/01/87, 8/23/87.

Cast: *Soleil Moon Frye (Minerva), Paul Reiser (Dexter Bunche), Mimi Rogers (Charlotte Waring), Allen Garfield (Howie Edwards), Edith Fields (Aunt Hermione), Yoshi Hoover (Yaki), Tony Burton (Moustache), Lisa Raggio (Lorraine), Ken Olfson (Mr. Arnold), Todd Susman (Jake), John Putch (Winston), Bill Gratton (Dean Harrison), Irwin Keyes (Reginald), Spencer Milligan (Detective), Lana Schwab (Waitress), Tammy Bass (Casino Woman), Nan Brennan (Marie), Jerry Clark Cleary (Doorman), Pepper Davis (Garage Master), Joseph Dickey (Reservation Clerk), Armand Farr (Eddie), Delynn Gardner (Female Dealer), S.A. Griffin (Casino Guard), Elven Havard (Policeman), Peter Lind Hayes (Congressman Riley), Mary Healy (Mrs. Riley), Thomas Hilliard (Security Guard), Lew Hopson (Trucker #1), Red McIlvaine (Maintenance Man), Maggie Peterson (Jennifer), Sly-Ali Smith (Pit Boss), Sylvie Strauss (Maid), Alison Sweeney (School Girl #1), Cecily Thompson (School Girl #2), Harry Woolf (Trucker #2).*

The staff of a Las Vegas casino is on "Minerva Alert." Some of the workers are happy, and others are terrified. Howie Edwards, the head of the casino, nervously greets the object of all this attention—his young niece, Minerva. She's been thrown out of yet another school and has come back to live at the casino.

Production Note:

- The casino used was Caesar's Palace.

YOUNG AGAIN Airdates (2-hour format): 5/11/86, 9/06/87.

Cast: *Lindsay Wagner (Laura Gordon), Robert Urich (Michael Riley—40), Jack Gilford (The Angel/Old Man), Keanu C. Reeves (Mick/Michael Riley—17), Jessica Steen (Tracy Gordon), Jason Nicoloff (Peter Gordon), Jeremy Ratchford (Todd Johnson), Peter Spence (Jeff), Jonathan Welsh (Jerry), Louise Vallance (Deborah), Vincent Murray (Ted), John Friesen (Coach), Marshall Perlmutar (Mr. Tyler), Barbara Kyle (Mrs. Ross), Les Carlson (Mr. Dillon), Leslie Toth (Steve Martini), Lisa Schrage (Girl #1 at Disco), Laura Sherman (Girl #2 at Disco), Barry Flatman (Newsman at Basketball Game), Warren van Evera (Bum), Michael Dolan (Assistant Coach), Valerie Boyle (Edith), Marla Lukofsky (Suzanne), Greg Spottiswood (Player #1), J.J. Stocker (Kid at Party), Ron Singer (Sam), Jeff Pustil (Roger the Doorman), Beth Amos (Landlady), Steve Brinder (Bus Driver—Country), Michael Copeman (Bus Driver—City), John Davies (Man #1 at Party), Ferne Downey (Woman #1 at Party), Barry Stevens (Man #2 at Party), Andrew Skelley (Other Boy at Party), Ron Rubin (Teenage Guy), David Peregrine (Romeo), Susan Bennet (Juliet).*

Michael Riley is feeling particularly old on his 40th birthday, for a teenage boy has just beaten him at basketball. That night, as he rides on a bus, he wishes out loud that he was 17 again. An elderly man warns Michael that he has forgotten about the problems of youth, but Michael pays little attention. That is, until the next bus stop, for when Michael gets off the bus he has somehow turned 17 again.

Production Note:

- The Madonna Ciccone who wrote two songs for this episode is now better known as Madonna.

YOUNG HARRY HOUDINI Airdate (2-hour format): 3/15/87. The show later aired in two parts—Part 1: 7/17/88. Part 2: 7/24/88.

Cast: *Wil Wheaton (Erich Weiss/Young Harry Houdini), Jeffrey DeMunn (Adult Houdini), Kerri Green (Calpernia), Barry Corbin (Elmore Johnson), Roy Dotrice (Sir Arthur Conan Doyle), J. Reuben Silverbird (John Parker), Ross Harris (Theo), Jose Ferrer (Dr. Tybolt Grimaldi), Phil Brock (Wesley Johnson), Michael Allredge (Yardbull), Seán McClory (Sean O'Casey), Lee de Broux (Marshall), Rita Zohar (Mrs. Weiss), J.C. Quinn (Slats), Michael Pniewski (Large Miner), Mark Lonow (Assistant), Byrne Piven (Rabbi Weiss), Tony Becker (Albert), Val*

Bettin (Dr. Allworth), Alan David Gelman (London Bobby), Oliver Muirhead (London Bobby), Billy McComb (Merlin), Arlee Reed (Policeman), Bob Stephens (Bartender).

As the program begins, an adult Harry Houdini is performing a trick for the Prince of Wales in London. Watching from the audience is Sir Arthur Conan Doyle, who later asks how the trick works. As they talk, Houdini looks back, remembering his childhood in Appleton, Wisconsin, in 1886.

YOUNG LONER, THE Airdates—Part 1: 2/25/68, 5/13/73. Part 2: 3/03/68, 5/20/73.

Cast: Kim Hunter (Freda Williams), Frank Silvera (Carlos), Edward Andrews (Bert Shannon), Butch Patrick (Bumper), Jane Zachary (Angie).

Bumper, a young crop picker, and Bert, his older friend, are riding in a old truck when they have an accident that injures Bert. Afraid of the police, Bumper leaves the area, unaware that he has suffered a head injury. He passes out and is later found by a sheep herder who takes him back to the ranch where he works.

YOUNG RUNAWAYS, THE Airdate (2-hour format): 5/28/78. For the 1979–80 season the show was aired in two parts—Part 1: 6/01/80. Part 2: 6/08/80.

Cast: Gary Collins (Lieutenant Phillips), Anne Francis (Mrs. Lockhart), Sharon Farrell (Mamma Doyle), Robert Webber (Fred Lockhart), Alicia Fleer (Rosebud), Chip Courtland (Eric), Tommy Crebbs (Joseph T.), Pat Delany (Katherine), Sonny Shroyer (C.L. Doyle), Dick Bakalyan (Jocko), Howard T. Platt (Bubba), Walter Barnes (Sergeant Abel), Barbara Hale (Mrs. Ogle), Lucille Benson (Grandma Hopkinson), Ken Jones (Mike), Poindexter (Louis), Jennifer Jason Leigh (Heather), Dermott Downs (Chuck), Steve Sherman (Pete), Kurt Courtland (Stanley), Dolores Sandoz (Miss Anderson), John Lupton (Benefactor), Newell Alexander (Doctor), Tim Pellegrino (Little Freddie), Daryn Sipes (Margaret Jean), Cynthia Mayberry (Girl Backpacker), Brad Wilkin (Boy Backpacker), Michael Warren (Officer #1), Robert Dunlap (Officer #2), Walt Davis (Officer #3), Dick Wieand (Cop).

Before beginning a trip to Alaska, C.L. Doyle and his wife leave two of their children at a foster home in Los Angeles, for the uncaring parents don't want to be burdened by the youngsters. Freddie and Margaret Jean are left behind, but the parents take their two older children, Rosebud and Joseph T., with them. Rosebud decides to find her brother and sister and runs away, taking Joseph T. with her.

Production Note:

- Six tons of tomatoes were used in a crash scene.

YOUR HOST, DONALD DUCK Airdates: 1/16/57, 7/17/57.

Donald Duck announces his plans for a special episode to be titled *The Duckland Four-in-One Show.* Several animated clips are shown as Donald travels through Adventureland, Frontierland, Tomorrowland, and Fantasyland.

ZORRO

In addition to the 78 half-hour episodes produced for the weekly *Zorro* series, there were also four hour-long episodes produced for the anthology series: *El Bandido; Adios El Cuchillo; The Postponed Wedding;* and *Auld Acquaintance.* Refer to each of these titles for the episode descriptions.

The Leader of the Band

5

The Mickey Mouse Club

Of all of Disney's television product, perhaps the most fondly remembered show is *The Mickey Mouse Club*. In addition to changing the general look of children's television programs and unleashing a merchandising phenomenon, it launched the careers of several Disney stars, including that of Annette Funicello, and helped reestablish Mickey Mouse in the minds of the American public. It also helped Walt realize the expansion of his theme park dream, Disneyland.

As with the *Disneyland* anthology series, the Club had its birth in Walt's need for more money to finance his theme park. The Studio had originally offered *The Mickey Mouse Club* to the networks as part of the efforts to secure financing for the Park. A September 30, 1953, summary of the proposed series provides an early look at the Club:

Mickey Mouse, the best known personality in the world, has an international boys and girls club. Club headquarters are located in fabulous Disneyland. Disneyland is everything a child has ever imagined, even in his wildest dreams. Located in a secluded spot in this land of fantasy is an island set aside exclusively for the Mickey Mouse Club International Headquarters.

Direct from this Mickey Mouse Club Headquarters, the Club presents THE MICKEY MOUSE CLUB TV SHOW!!!!!!

At this point the Studio was thinking of producing a live 15-minute series to be aired weekdays., but ABC turned down the Club due to concerns about the cost. When the theme park continued to grow in size, Walt went back to ABC in 1954 looking for more money. The network eventually put up a total of $2.5 million in exchange for a daily one-hour children's series.

The project begins

Walt, already burdened with the heavy demands of the theme park and anthology series projects, quickly realized he could not devote the same amount of time and energy to this new series. He immediately turned the reins over to a surprised Bill Walsh, who had previously helmed the Studio's first two television specials. Walsh, who ironically did not care much for children, found himself having to create the format for the biggest venture into children's television to that time.

Walsh quickly began work on the series. Although he received little credit for his role, Hal Adelquist, the head of the Story Department, was also instrumental in developing the format of the series. Somehow Adelquist managed to run afoul of Walt, and as his role diminished, Walsh increasingly molded the show as he saw fit. Walsh also received significant input from Walt, who would constantly jot down ideas for the show and circulate them around the Studio for comment.

Reading those notes now provides a fascinating look at how the show developed, for hardly any of the early ideas made it to the screen. For example, during the summer of 1954, Walt again suggested that the show be set at Disneyland, where the audience would "Enter club thru cave—up hollow tree to tree house." This tree house was to have been located on the "Mickey Mouse Club Island," which is now Tom Sawyer's Island, and it would have been open to park guests. Planning ahead, Walt also noted a plan to "Tour country with club show."

It was also initially planned that the show would have a live studio audience. This was considered a necessity by many, as all of the popular children's shows of the day used an audience. In one of his early notes on the show, dated December 8, 1954, Walt detailed his thoughts about how the audience would be used. Children were to be picked from the Park visitors, with several chosen to dress in costume as Disney characters and to participate in skits. Walt also made a brief mention of telling the story of children around the world. Interestingly, only this last item ever made it to the screen, in the form of a brief serial.

In addition to the plans for a live audience, it was also intended that the show should have an adult host. Walsh proposed using a master of ceremonies named Smee, noting he would have "eccentric makeup and costume to conceal his own human personality." He also proposed other cast members, including Ellsworth, "a talking Mynah bird, an impudent, Charlie McCarthy type of personality who makes rude remarks about the proceedings from time to time," and a genie in a bottle.

As the show continued to evolve, all of these ideas were eventually dropped. Finally, the format began to settle down, as seen in an important memo from Walt dated April 15, 1955. The abandoned audience was to be replaced in favor of using a core group of young performers, with Walt noting that "The talented kids . . . will be called Mouseketeers," thus coining a word that was to become famous to children across the country. The concept of using a host had been changed by then to using several adults in that role, with Walt calling these adults "Mooseketeers." He named Roy Williams as the "Big Mooseketeer," Jimmie Dodd as the "Musical Mooseketeer," and Tom Moore as the "Roving Mooseketeer" (Moore was later dropped, as were several others of Walt's casting ideas). Walt also announced that "The younger, less talented kids, who are still amateurs, are to be called Meesketeers."

The adults

Jimmie Dodd, who was the principal adult member of the cast, first came to Disney's attention when he wrote a tune called The Pencil Song for a proposed episode of the anthology series. That episode was never produced, but Walt liked the energetic songwriter and brought him aboard as a staff composer and lyricist. A veteran actor, Jimmie had been in productions as varied as the original version of Kidnapped, Easter Parade, The Flying Tigers, and television's Adventures of Superman.

Many of those involved with the show agree that Jimmie was instrumental in the success of The Mickey Mouse Club. His pleasant personality endeared him not only to the other cast members and crew, but more importantly, to the audience. Jimmie was categorized as everybody's favorite uncle—someone you were glad to welcome into your home every day. An important point for parents was Jimmie's rigid adherence to a strict moral code, making him an excellent role model for their children.

Jimmie's contributions to the show went much further than just a pleasant personality, of course. In addition to performing, Jimmie wrote many of the songs for the series, including the popular title song, The Mickey Mouse March. He also contributed regular observations on life and morality, which were to become known as "Doddisms."

The other main adult was Roy Williams, who was a very unlikely choice for a children's show. Roy had first begun to work for Disney on a part-time basis back in 1929 and had worked in a number of positions at the Studio over the years, including work on the Mickey Mouse comic strip and a lengthy period in the Story Department. A prolific cartoonist, Roy's drawing skills were often employed to comedic effect on The Mickey Mouse Club.

In addition to appearing on the show, Roy made a memorable contribution to The Mickey Mouse Club and to the theme parks—the "Mickey Mouse Club ears." These hats, which were originally designed only as part of the costumes for the Mouseketeers, were so popular that the Studio quickly began selling them at Disneyland and in retail outlets. Selling over 25,000 a day at their peak, the hats were based on a gag from the 1929 cartoon The Karnival Kid, where Mickey tips his ears to Minnie.

All but forgotten today is the third adult of the series, Bob Amsberry. He had achieved success as "Uncle Bob," the host of his own children's series airing in Portland, Oregon, and was a friend of George Bruns, the composer of The Ballad of Davy Crockett. Bob's new role on The Mickey Mouse Club would be much smaller than in Oregon, for he always took a back seat to Jimmie, Roy, and the Mouseketeers, and for some reason was never given on air acknowledgement or much publicity. Bob usually played small parts in scenes with the Mouseketeers, appearing until his untimely death in an automobile crash in 1957 at age 29. Following his death, the third adult role was quietly dropped from the cast.

The merry Mouseketeers

Of all of Walt's casting decisions, the most important by far was the Mouseketeers, the future young stars of the series. Despite the old adage in Hollywood against working with children and animals, Walt decided to make children the focus of the show, thereby hopefully increasing the show's appeal to young audiences. Not lost on Disney was the fact that this unknown group of children would also work for little money. In fact, the starting pay for Mouseketeers was to be $185 per week, a very low sum for television performers of the time.

One of the key elements the Studio looked for as it cast the show was young performers who seemed natural—just like "the kid next door." Walt wanted to avoid using known show business professionals, as he knew the show had a better chance of success if audiences related to the Mouseketeers. Bill Walsh noted that Walt also wanted to avoid dealing with the sticky problem of potential favoritism: "Walt was getting needled quite a lot by his peers about using their daughters and sons as Mouseketeers. Walt wouldn't do that. There was James Mason and Edgar Bergen—Candice wanted to be one—and they thought that the most glamorous thing that could happen to them was to be a Mouseketeer."

Walsh, who admitted he had no idea what to look for in potential Mouseketeers, went to Walt for direction. To find "the kid next door," Walt told Walsh "I don't want those kids that tap dance, or blow instruments while they're tap dancing, or skip rope or have curly hair like Shirley Temple's or nutty mothers and things like that—I just want ordinary kids." Walt also had very definite ideas on where to find these young stars, telling Walsh to go to schools at recess and watch the kids: "Watch what happens to you. You'll notice that you're watching one kid. Not any of the other kids, but sooner or later your gaze will always go back to this one kid. That kid has star quality maybe, but there's always a reason why you're watching one kid."

The search succeeded with admirable results, for even the Mouseketeers who had worked professionally gave the impression of innocence. The first season's Mouseketeers were Nancy Abbate, Sharon Baird, Billie Beanblossom, Bobby Burgess, Lonnie Burr, Tommy Cole, Johnny Crawford, Dennis Day, Dickie Dodd, Mary Espinosa, Annette Funicello, Darlene Gillespie, Judy Harriet, Dallas Johann (soon replaced by his brother, John Lee Johann), Bonnie Lou Kern, Carl "Cubby" O'Brien, Kareb Pendleton, Paul Petersen, Tim and Mickey Rooney, Jr., Mary Lynn Satori, Bronson Scott, Michael Smith, Ronnie Steiner, Mark Sutherland, Doreen Tracey and Don Underhill.

The business of show business

Of the twenty-eight Mouseketeers hired, some were quickly dismissed and now are all but forgotten. Several were fired for misbehaving, but others were let go during the course of the season due to problems with their on-screen efforts. The Studio enjoyed a great deal of flexibility in dealing with the Mouseketeers, having initially signed the young stars to very short-term contracts. All of the Mouseketeers knew that they could be let go at any time, which made for a great deal of competition. It also helped to avoid any tendency on the part of the children or their families to let their egos get in the way of their careers.

One area of dissent that the Studio did need to deal with was an intense dislike by many of the Mouseketeers of the *Mickey Mouse Club* ears. The male stars in particular hated wearing the hats, and tried to get out of wearing them by conveniently "losing" them. The Studio grew tired of having to replace them, and finally solved the problem by deducting a charge for lost ears from the Mouseketeer's paychecks. Bobby Burgess later recalled that the cost was $50, a considerable sum at the time, and that the losses quickly stopped.

The importance of teamwork

With the large number of children in the cast, it was obviously impossible to use them all at any one time. In addition, the Studio needed to send the youngsters to class during the school season, which would normally have cut severely into the production schedule. The solution was to break the Mouseketeers into different production teams.

There were three teams of Mouseketeers for the first year, denoted as the red, white, and blue teams. Originally, all three teams were supposed to have equal standing. However, as time went on, it was readily apparent to the production crew, and audiences, that some of the Mouseketeers were more talented than others, and it was inevitable that they be featured more prominently. Thus, the Red team became the first-line group of the Mouseketeers, with more and more air time devoted to this group. The ranks of the three teams were adjusted to move the best performers into the Red team, which came to be composed of Sharon, Bobby, Lonnie, Tommy, Annette, Darlene, Doreen, Cubby, and Karen. Eventually many of the White and Blue team Mouseketeers were all but ignored.

The daily format

While the search was underway for the Mouseketeers, work continued on refining the format of the show. A near final concept called for a specific theme for each day of the week as follows:

Monday—Travel Night
Tuesday—Participation and Improvement Night
Wednesday—Musical Night
Thursday—Pets and Hobbies Night
Friday—Surprises, Parties, and Contests Night

These themes were constantly being changed. For example, Wednesday was also known for a time as Stunt Night. As can be noted in these titles, the original plan was to air the show in the early evening, right after most families finished dinner. However, when the show's time period was eventually set for late afternoon instead of early evening, the now familiar schedule below was announced:

Monday—Fun with Music Day
Tuesday—Guest Star Day
Wednesday—Anything Can Happen Day
Thursday—Circus Day
Friday—Talent Round-up Day

The main title sequence

Each episode began with an animated opening sequence featuring Mickey Mouse and a host of Disney characters, directed by animator Bill Justice. As with all of his other efforts in the '50s, Walt continued to show amazing foresight in the filming of this sequence, for although the series was to be filmed in black and white for economic reasons, he had the opening titles made in color, just in case he ever wanted to later make episodes of the series itself in color. This would later allow the Studio to use the same titles for the 1970s version of the series. The titles ran a full three minutes, but most viewers have trouble recalling the long version of the opening credits as a shorter version was used near the end of the series and later in syndication.

After the main titles, the opening sequence ends as Donald tries to hit a huge gong. There were many different versions of this ending and they were shown on a random basis, helping to hold the viewer's interest until the last moment. As Walt described it, "There will be a little surprise about this each time. Sometimes Donald will hit it and sometimes he won't, and maybe the thing will just disintegrate." Years after the show ended, Bill Walsh noted that this plan worked, for Jimmie Dodd told him that he saw numerous drunks during his promotional tours, and they would go into bars at 5 P.M. to bet on what would happen to Donald when he tried to hit the gong. Poor Donald wouldn't have it easy, for among the problems he encounters:

- It swings over and hits him on the head
- It explodes and spins like a firework pinwheel
- It's a giant pie that splatters on him
- The gong is made of paper and he flies through it
- It shatters and falls in a small pile
- It spins and Donald is caught up in it
- One of Donald's nephews rushes in and hits it first
- Two nephews jump out and shoot him with water pistols
- He tries a cannon which hits him instead
- A goat smacks Donald as he bends to pick up the mallet
- The gong splits open, water spills out and floods the studio
- He hits the gong without a sound, only to have it ring in his ear
- He vibrates instead of the gong
- He hits a small musical triangle instead of the gong

The daily themes

As noted earlier, each day of the week had a specific theme. Right after Donald battled with the gong, an animated sequence with Mickey Mouse introduced the theme of that day's show. The daily animated introductions were also produced in color, but were never seen that way until they were used in the anthology episode *The Mouseketeer Reunion* in 1980.

Following Mickey's introduction, the opening segment of each show in the first season would be one of three series: *The Mickey Mouse Club Newsreel*, *Sooty* (an ill-tempered puppet from England), or an educational segment featuring Jiminy Cricket. The Newsreel was the most common of these, with more than 100 segments produced for the first season alone.

The second segment of the show was devoted to the Mouseketeers, and was the only place where the day's theme came into play. Each of the Mouseketeer segments began with the day's song, followed the all-important roll call. After a suitably placed commercial, the Mouseketeers returned for that day's skit or guest stars.

The third of the daily segments was devoted to serialized adventure stories, such as *Corky and White Shadow* and *The Adventures of Spin and Marty*. The serials were an important drawing card for the Club and are described in detail in later in this chapter.

The final segment in each show was the Mousekartoon, comprised of cartoons from the Studio's vaults. Many had not been shown anywhere since their initial theatrical releases, which may have been almost thirty years earlier. The cartoons had held up well despite the passage of time, and as the merchandise licensees and the Studio had hoped, helped introduce Mickey and the gang to a new generation of fans.

Now it's time to say goodbye . . .

One of the most fondly remembered segments of the Club was the closing segment. All of the Mouseketeers would gather at the Mickey Mouse Clubhouse (spelling intentional) to sing *The Mickey Mouse Club Alma Mater*. The song, which was sung slowly and somewhat reverently, seemed to show just how sad the Mouseketeers were to be done with the day's activities. Jimmie Dodd joined in with them, with his lines in italics below:

> Now it's time
> to say goodbye
> to all our family.
> M—I—C
> *See you real soon!*
> K—E—Y
> *Why? Because we like you!*
> M—O—U—S—E

With that, the lights would dim and the show was over.

The first season: 1955–56

Finally, after months of hard work, The Mickey Mouse Club premiered on October 3, 1955. The Studio needn't have worried about the reception the show was to receive, for it was an immediate ratings success. That first day, an astounding 44.9 percent of the TV sets in use were turned to the Club. This was not a one-time event, for while the ratings dropped the second day to "only" 39.6 percent, they climbed up again the next day to 48.8 percent. The fourth episode brought in an unprecedented 52.9 percent. What makes these ratings even more important was that the total number of sets in use had also climbed each day. A ratings report issued in March 1956 showed that the Club was being watched by 14,400,000 viewers. Surprisingly, it was found that one third of the viewers were adults.

The second season: 1956–57

The overwhelming success of the first season of *The Mickey Mouse Club* virtually guaranteed that the series would be renewed for a second year. Overall, the Club's format stayed pretty much the same, but there were some very important cast changes when it returned for the new year.

As noted previously, the Studio's decision to sign the Mouseketeers to short-term contracts allowed for a great deal of flexibility in recasting the show at any time. While several Mouseketeers had been quietly replaced during the first season, the Studio publicly announced at the end of filming for the season that they would be recasting many of the Mouseketeer positions. Thus, many of the Mouseketeers left the Studio unsure as to their future status. Of all the first season Mouseketeers, the only ones who would return were Sharon, Bobby, Tommy, Lonnie, Dennis, Annette, Darlene, Cubby, Karen, and Doreen.

The Studio generated a great deal of publicity by announcing that auditions would be held for new Mouseketeers, with hopeful performers once again inundating the casting crew with letters and resumes. When all of the hysteria was over, seven new Mouseketeers joined the cast: Sherry Allen, Eileen Diamond, Cheryl Holdridge, Charley Laney, Larry Larsen, John Joseph "Jay-Jay" Solari, and Margene Storey. Of these new additions, Cheryl quickly established herself as the most popular, and she was the only newcomer to gain one of the coveted positions on the Red team.

Jimmie's Doddisms

As noted earlier, the Studio had decided not to tamper with a proven formula and left the daily formats pretty well intact. One noticeable addition was a series of commentaries by Jimmie Dodd. Dubbed "Doddisms," they featured themes such as "Words to Grow By," explanations of "Proverbs," and encouragement to listen to parents. Jimmie wrote all of these sermonettes himself, and they reflected his own deep religious convictions. Happily, they didn't come across as lecturing, and would be included in the following seasons as well.

The third season: 1957–58

After two years on the air, there were some major changes in store this season for the Club. The biggest change was cutting the length of the show each day to thirty minutes from the prior one-hour format. While the Studio had been extremely fortunate in attracting advertisers thus far, the expense of producing a one-hour show had made it impossible thus far to turn a profit on the series.

Just as the ranks had thinned between the first and second seasons, there were fewer Mouseketeers returning this year. Veterans Sharon, Bobby, Lonnie, Tommy, Annette, Darlene, Cheryl, Cubby, Karen, and Doreen were teamed with new Mouseketeers Don Agrati, Bonnie Lynn Fields, Linda Hughes, and Lynn Ready. The new Mouseketeers received the standard Disney contracts, and were paid $185 per week, which would raise to $500 if all of the options were exercised during the five-year term of the deal.

The big winners this year were Tim Considine and David Stollery of *Spin and Marty* fame. The success of the serials led to new contracts for both of them, guaranteeing them $650 per week to start and $900 in the second year of the deal. Both actors were also to receive separate deals for a number of motion pictures, making them second only to Annette in terms of both work and salaries.

The Mouseketeers kept busy this year with a steady stream of personal appearances. One of the most highly publicized trips took Annette, Doreen, Tommy, and Jimmie on a swing through the East Coast in February 1958 to promote the films *The Light in the Forest* and *Cinderella*. A stop in Stratford, Connecticut, brought an unexpected result when the fans, upset that the Mouseketeers had to leave for another engagement, pelted their bus with snowballs and blocked its path. Extra police had to be called in before the Mouseketeers could safely escape the throng.

Other changes of the year

While it was never publicized, the Studio introduced several other format changes in ad-

dition to the cut to thirty minutes. The overall format for this season was:

1. Mickey Mouse Club March
2. Newsreels or Mouseketeers (daily theme days as in prior years, Mouseka-previews, Mousekartoons, Mousekatour to England)
3. Serials, Newsreel Specials, Encyclopedia
4. Doddism

In order to cut costs even further, the Studio quietly dropped Anything Can Happen Day and Circus Day, the two most expensive formats to produce, without public fanfare. While the three other daily themes survived, they were not used on the rigid schedule of prior years; thus, for example, while Fun with Music Day was usually aired during the third season on Monday, at times this season it could be found on a Wednesday or Thursday.

1958–59—the fourth and seemingly final season

The Club almost didn't have a fourth season, for Disney and ABC were unable at first to come to an agreement that would keep the show on the air. By this time, the two once-happy partners were involved in a series of legal skirmishes concerning the ownership of the anthology series and *Zorro*. A compromise agreement was reached that kept the Club going, but only by switching to thirty-minute episodes comprised solely of repeat material culled from the first three years.

The switch to reusing older material was not the only change for the year. One of the most dramatic results of this decision was the disbanding of the Mouseketeers, for all of their Club appearances this year were to be taken from the prior three seasons. By September 1958, the only cast members still working for Disney were Annette, Tim Considine, Tommy Kirk, and Kevin Corcoran, all of whom were working on films.

Dropping the Mouseketeers and switching to repeated material were not the only changes introduced this season. On Monday, Wednesday, and Friday the Club retained much the same look as in prior years, with each day using a daily theme featuring the Mouseketeers. The big change came with a totally new look created for Tuesday and Thursday, which received the new overall title of *Adventure Time*. These shows consisted solely of episodes from the serials, and Mickey Mouse and the Mouseketeers were noticeably absent.

See you real soon!

As could be expected, the use of all of this repeat material didn't go down well with audiences, and the ratings for the year showed a dramatic drop. ABC decided not to exercise their option for the 1959-60 season, and Disney executives agreed that the series had run its course. Finally, after four years on the air, it was time for the Mouseketeers to say goodbye "to all their company" one last time.

The Mickey Mouse Club Serials

One of the most popular segments of *The Mickey Mouse Club* was the daily serial. Serials were far from new, having been a major staple of theater programs in earlier years. Some children's television series also used serials, but none gave them the attention provided by Disney. Instead of merely editing old features into a serialized format as the other series generally did, Disney set up a special unit to begin production on serials for *The Mickey Mouse Club*.

The Disney serials took two forms. The majority were adventure stories such as *The Adventures of Spin and Marty* and *Annette*, and others were intended to be educational. While some of these, such as *What I Want to Be*, were original productions, Disney later decided to use footage from outside producers with new narration.

Each year of *The Mickey Mouse Club* is listed here in chronological order, with the serials appearing in alphabetical order.

First season: 1955–56

ADVENTURES OF SPIN AND MARTY, THE

Cast: Tim Considine (Spin Evans), David Stollery (Marty Markham), Roy Barcroft (Colonel Jim Logan), Harry Carey, Jr. (Bill Burnett), Lennie Geer (Ollie), J. Pat O'Malley (Perkins), B.G. Norman (Ambitious), Tim Hartnagel (Speckles), Roger Broaddus (Freddie), Jim Carlson (Pinky), Dale Hartleban (Biff), Brad Morrow (Louie), Dee Aaker (Russell the Muscle), Sammy Ogg (Joe Simpson), Pat Miller (Rick), Brand Stirling (Al), Stan Jones (Frank), Bucko Stafford (Gerald), Sammee Tong (George), Bill Waters (Spike), George Eldredge (Doctor Spaulding), Betty Hanna (Freddie's Mother), Connie Van (Joe's Mother), Tom Martin (Chauffeur).

The Triple R is a boys' summer ranch where the campers gain actual experience on a working ranch, including lessons in riding and other Western activities. Another season is beginning with the arrival of the campers, including Spin Evans, the most popular boy last year. Spin and the others are glad to be back, but one new camper proves to be an exception.

Production Notes:

- One of the scenes used in this serial was Tim Considine's screen test for the part of Marty. Considine wasn't fond of the role, disliking what he termed Marty's "snotty character." He wanted to play the "cool" character, Spin, and the producers obliged by enlarging that role.
- This serial was well received, with over 30,000 fan letters received—more than for the popular *Davy Crockett* mini-series. This response prompted the Studio to produce two sequels: *Further Adventures of Spin and Marty* and *The New Adventures of Spin and Marty*.

ANIMAL AUTOBIOGRAPHY

Using footage from the *True-Life Adventure* films, this serial explored life in the animal kingdom. Each episode discussed the evolution, habitat, and characteristics of a specific animal.

An additional set of episodes was aired during the second season.

BORDER COLLIE

Cast: Bobby Evans (Rob Brown), Arthur N. Allen (trainer), Alvy Moore (narrator).

Rob Brown begins training Scamp, a Scottish Border Collie, as a sheep dog, hoping to win a statewide dog show. Despite Rob's hard work, he discovers that Scamp prefers to do things his own way, making it doubtful whether the dog will ever be able to compete. With the help of an older trainer, and a great deal of patience, Rob finally breaks Scamp of his bad habits and decides the dog is ready to enter the contest.

CHRISTMAS 'ROUND THE WORLD

Cast: Alvy Moore (Narrator).

The Mouseketeers narrate scenes showing how Christmas is celebrated in different countries in this five-episode serial. An additional set of episodes was aired during the second season.

CORKY AND WHITE SHADOW

Cast: Darlene Gillespie (Corky Brady), Buddy Ebsen (Sheriff Matt Brady), Lloyd Corrigan (Uncle Dan), Buzz Henry (Durango Dude), Richard Powers (Sheriff Martin),

Chuck Courtney (Nevada Kid), Veda Ann Borg (Dolly Porter), Roger Broaddus (Freddy Porter), Harry O. Tyler (Gitt), Sandy Sanders (Pete), Bud Osborne (Chuck), Lane Chandler (Granville Sheriff), Stan Blystone (Storekeeper), Dan White (Jeff), Max Wagner (Man in Restaurant).

Corky Brady is the daughter of Matt Brady, the only lawman in the sleepy town of Beaumont, and she dreams of becoming a sheriff like her dad. She sees her chance when a band of outlaws led by the Durango Dude robs a bank in nearby Glen Forks, but her father refuses to let her help, claiming that it's too dangerous.

Production Notes:

- White Shadow was played by Harvey, a 145-pound German Shepherd, who had previously starred as "Chinook" in a series of films for Republic Pictures.
- Years after the serial was filmed, Darlene Gillespie had some less than kind words about her canine co-star: "He was an idiot. He was always fouling up takes. I bet you somewhere in the Disney studios there's a million feet of sound film of his trainer yelling 'Harvey! Goddamn it, come back here, Harvey!'"

ENGLISH CORRESPONDENT

Cast: Dick Metzger (Correspondent).
London is the setting for this serial, which takes a look at several tourist attractions, a unique school, and a boy with an unusual career.

ITALIAN CORRESPONDENT

Cast: Annette Funicello (Correspondent).
Mouseketeer Annette Funicello hosts this look at the home of her ancestors. Life in several Italian cities is mixed with profiles of several distinctly Italian careers.

JAPANESE CORRESPONDENT

Cast: George Nagata (Correspondent).
Japanese life is seen through the eyes of a young Japanese-American boy.
An additional set of episodes was aired during the second season.

LET'S GO SERIES

Cast: Alvy Moore (Narrator).
There are many unusual occupations, and this serial shows how several youngsters learn about some of them firsthand.

MEXICAN CORRESPONDENT

Cast: Gabriel Lopez (Correspondent), Andy Velasquez.
The scenic beauty of Mexico is spotlighted in this look at our neighbor to the south.

SAN JUAN RIVER EXPEDITION

Cast: Alvy Moore (Narrator), John Cunningham, Jim Lubach, Pug Mayfield, Frank Wright, Professor Lionel Francis Brady, Ruth Young, Horace S. Haskell, Donald B. Sayney, Harry B. Dahl.
An exciting trip down the San Juan River provides youngsters with more than just a thrill, for they learn about the Indians who once lived there and left their ancient markings. They also learn about more modern explorers and the dangers of floods.

WHAT I WANT TO BE

Cast: Alvy Moore (Reporter), Pat Morrow (Girl), Duncan Richardson (Boy), Virginia Hrubant (Instructor), John Lee Johann, Nancy Abbate, Karen Pendleton (Mouseketeers).
Alvy Moore, a reporter for the *Mickey Mouse Club Newsreel*, visits a school and asks for two volunteers to learn about the airline industry. He picks two 10-year-olds, and takes them to the headquarters of Trans World Airlines in Kansas City, Missouri, where they learn how TWA trains its flight crews.

Production Note:

- Initially, this was supposed to be an ongoing series. Additional segments were to feature doctors, railroad engineers, and FBI agents.

Second season: 1956–57

ADVENTURE IN DAIRYLAND

Cast: Herb Newcombe (Jim McCandless), Fern Persons (Mrs. McCandless), Annette Funicello (Herself), Sammy Ogg (Himself), Glen Graber (Jimmy McCandless), Mary Lu Delmonte (Linda McCandless), Ernst Zentner (Paulie), Kevin Corcoran (Moochie McCandless), Paul Grossenbacher (Leader of Singing Group), Clayton E. Streiff (Nels), John Craig (Veterinarian), William McKee (Square Dance Caller), Eric Borg (Bit), Lois Murray (Miss Ross).
Sammy Ogg (from *The Adventures of Spin and Marty* serial) and Mouseketeer Annette Funicello pack their bags for a trip to Wisconsin where they learn about dairy farming.

Production Note:

- This serial, which is also known as *The Dairy Story* and *Adventures in Dairyland*, was the first Disney appearance of Kevin "Moochie" Corcoran, who was to star in many of the Studio's television and theatrical productions.

ANIMAL AUTOBIOGRAPHY

This is the second set of episodes of this serial, which originally aired during the first season.

BOYS OF THE WESTERN SEA, THE

Cast: Kjeld Bentzen (Per), Anne Grete Hilding (Else), Lars Henning-Jensen (Mads), Nette Hoj Hansen (Birgit), Jens Konge Rasmussen (Jorgen), Bente Kas Hvalsee (Tine), Preben Lerdorff Rye (Vaerle), Einer Federspiel (Krae Brejning), Niels Jensen (Fredrik), Kai Holm (Pelican), Karl Stegger (Sheriff), Marie Niederman (Mother Karen), Poul Juhl (Grocer), Karl Jorgensen (Foreman), William Knoblauch (Man), Valso Holm (Man), Jorgen Kunz (Man).

Set on the western coast of Norway, this is the story of a small fishing village where the children must help their parents to survive. Although the harsh life of the villagers is a daily reality, the local boys often escape into a fantasy world of secret forts and "pirate attacks."

CHILDREN OF THE WORLD

Part 1—*Children of the Arctic*

Cast: Makaluk (Eskimo Boy).

This is the story of life in northern Alaska, as seen through the eyes of an Eskimo boy. The family lives in a primitive igloo made of sod and driftwood. The boy learns to hunt and fish, and eventually masters the art of harpooning from a fragile kayak.

Part 2—*Children of Siam*

Cast: Pok (Himself).

A small boy takes viewers on a tour of his homeland, Siam, which is now known as Thailand. Siam is often called the "Venice of the Orient" due to its numerous canals. Almost every family owns a boat of some kind, and children are taken to school on a special "school bus" barge.

CHRISTMAS 'ROUND THE WORLD

Cast: Annette Funicello (Narrator).

Throughout the world there are many ways in which people celebrate Christmas. Mouseketeers narrate scenes of some of the elaborate preparations that lead up to the big day, with explanations of local customs and costumes.

Five episodes on different countries had previously been seen in the first season.

DANISH CORRESPONDENT

Cast: Lotte Waver (Correspondent).

Life in Denmark is the theme of this serial, which centers on the nation's capital, Copenhagen. Included is a visit to the exciting amusement park, Tivoli, which is said to have influenced Walt Disney's plans for Disneyland.

EAGLE HUNTERS, THE

Cast: Kent Durden (Himself), Gary Hoffman (Himself), Tommy Kirk (Host).

Two boys from Carpinteria, California, participate in a hunt for Jupiter, a golden eagle. Aired in two parts, the story begins as the boys obtain a hunting permit to capture the bird. Once they capture the bird, Jupiter eventually learns to obey their commands.

Production Note:

- Never missing a chance to cross-promote another show, the Studio had one of the boys prominently wearing a *Davy Crockett* coonskin cap.

ENGLISH CORRESPONDENT

Cast: Dick Metzger (Correspondent), Robbie Serpell (Correspondent).

This is a continuation of the serial originally aired during the first season.

FIRST AMERICANS, THE

Cast: Tony Nakina (Host), Iron Eyes Cody (Narrator), John War Eagle, Karen Pendleton, Cubby O'Brien, Doreen Tracey, David Stollery.

The films *Westward Ho the Wagons!* and *The Vanishing Prairie* provide scenes about Indian lifestyles and history. This is the story of American Indian life in the prehistoric days.

FURTHER ADVENTURES OF SPIN AND MARTY

Cast: Tim Considine (Spin Evans), David Stollery (Marty Markham), Annette Funicello (Annette), B.G. Norman (Ambitious), Brand Stirling (Al), Roger Broaddus (Freddie), Tim Hartnagel (Speckles), Kevin Corcoran (Montgomery "Moochie" O'Hara), Melinda

Plowman (Peggy), Roy Barcroft (Colonel Jim Logan), Harry Carey, Jr. (Bill Burnett), Lennie Geer (Ollie), J. Pat O'Malley (Perkins), Sammee Tong (George), Joyce Holden (Helen Adams), Connie Gilchrist (Mrs. Markham), Sammy Ogg (Joe Simpson), Betty Hanna (Freddie's mother), Kelli Green (Speckles' Mother), James Horan (Speckles' Father), Tim Ryan (Jason), Charles Morton (Freddie's father), Robert J. Anderson (Terry Moore), Tom Hennesy (North Fork Counselor), Jesse B. Kirkpatrick (Meet Official), Ray Berwick (Meet Official), George de Normand (Starter), Robert B. Williams (Veterinarian), Bonnie Eddy (Lakeview Girl), George Eldridge (Doctor).

The second *Spin and Marty* serial begins as the campers return to the Triple R for another summer of Western fun. When Marty first arrives, it seems as if he's reverted to his haughty manners, but the others soon realize he is playing a joke on them. In addition to these returning boys, there are new campers. The youngest, Moochie, immediately finds ways to get himself in trouble.

Production Note:

- The success of the first serial prompted writer Jackson Gillis to suggest a theatrical sequel, but Walt decided to produce another serial for the Club instead.

JAPANESE CORRESPONDENT

Cast: George Nagata (Correspondent).

This is a continuation of the serial first aired during the first season.

JUNIOR SAFARI TO AFRICA

Cast: Annette Funicello (Hostess), Tommy Kirk (Host), Stephen Conrad Johnson (Camper).

Annette and Tommy use "home movies" sent from South Africa by Mickey Mouse Club fans as a backdrop for this look at life in the Kruger Game Park, an animal preserve.

MOUSEKATOUR TO SAMOA, A

Cast: Tommy Kirk (Host), Annette Funicello (Hostess).

Tommy Kirk and Annette Funicello introduce this look at the lifestyles, history, and customs of the South Pacific islands of Samoa.

MYSTERY OF THE APPLEGATE TREASURE, THE

Cast: Tim Considine (Frank Hardy), Tommy Kirk (Joe Hardy), Carole Ann

Campbell (Iola Morton), Donald MacDonald (Perry Robinson), Florenz Ames (Silas Applegate), Russ Conway (Fenton Hardy), Sarah Selby (Aunt Gertrude), Bob Foulk (Jackley), Arthur Shields (Boles), Charles Cane (Sergeant), Frances Morris (Landlady), Dan Sturkie (Detective), Bill Henry (Policeman), Mort Mills (Policeman), Brick Sullivan (Policeman), Jess Kirkpatrick (Policeman), Don Harvey (Policeman).

Frank and Joe Hardy are the sons of Fenton Hardy, a famous private detective. Finding everyday life at home in Bayport dull, the boys hope their father will let them work on one of his cases. Disappointed when he tells them his work is too dangerous for children, they become more determined than ever to solve a real mystery.

Production Notes:

- This show was based on the first in a long-running series of boys' adventure novels, *The Hardy Boys.*
- The sequel to this serial is *The Mystery of Ghost Farm*, aired during the 1957–58 season.

SECRET OF MYSTERY LAKE, THE

Cast: George Fenneman (Bill Richards), Gloria Marshall (Laney Thorne), Bogue Bell, R.P. Alexander, William Butler Quillin (Hermit).

When a naturalist enters the remote swamp territory of northeastern Tennessee, he finds unexpected adventure and mystery. The story takes place at Realfoot Lake in Tennessee, which suddenly came into being following an earthquake in 1811.

SIERRA PACK TRIP

Cast: Alvy Moore (Correspondent), Onis Brown (Guide), Glen Gallison (Fish Hatchery Worker).

Two students from John Muir High School are taken on a tour of Yosemite National Park by Onis Brown, a 72-year-old guide, so they can learn more about their school's namesake. The students get a brief history of the park and are then treated to a look at some of Yosemite's most spectacular features.

Third season: 1957–58

ADVENTURES OF CLINT AND MAC, THE

Cast: Neil Wolfe (Clinton "Clint" Rogers), Jonathan Bailey (Alistair "Mac" MacIntosh), Sandra Michaels (Pamela Gwendolyn Stuart),

John Warwick (Inspector MacIntosh, Mac's Father), Dorothy Smith (Mac's Mother), Bill Nagy (Clint's father), Mary Barclay (Clint's mother), Eric Phillips (Constable Hawkins), Maurice Durant (Smith), Oliver Johnston (Bookworm), Larry Burns (Skipper), Arthur Rigby (Inspector Atkins), George Woodbridge (Toby Jug), Evelyn Kerry (Old Lady), Edward Forsyth (Kurt), Gordon Harris (General Sir John Stuart), Ross Pendleton (General Gibson), Gibb McLaughlin (Store Clerk), Derek Aylward (Major Lovelace).

Filmed on location in England, this is the story of two boys who become involved with a dangerous band of thieves. A simple shopping trip plunges them into adventure when they agree to deliver a parcel to a stranger, unaware that it contains the original manuscript for *Treasure Island*, which was stolen from the British Museum.

Production Note:

• The Studio placed a hidden "plug" for one of its products in this serial. When the boys visit an open air market, a vendor tries to sell them a pair of boots "worn by Fess Parker in his role as Davy Crockett."

ANNETTE

Cast: Annette Funicello (Annette McCloud), Tim Considine (Stephen Abernathy), David Stollery (Mike Martin), Judy Nugent (Jet Maypen), Richard Deacon (Uncle Archie McCloud, Ph.D.), Sylvia Field (Aunt Lila McCloud), Mary Wickes (Katie), Jymme "Roberta" Shore (Laura Rogan), Doreen Tracey (Val Abernathy), Shelley Fabares (Moselle Corey), Rudy Lee (Olmstead "Steady" Ware), Steve Stevens (Drew Stafford), Sharon Baird (Kitty Blalock), Tommy Cole (Jimmy Smith), Doris Packer (Mrs. Helen Abernathy), Cheryl Holdridge (Madge Markham), Bonnie Lynn Fields (Pat Boren), Barry Curtis (Court Whitney), Ralph Dumke (Mr. Abernathy), William Benedict (Delivery Man), Amzie Strickland (Saleslady), Helene Marshall (Maid), Tom Mahoney (Haywagon Driver), Irving Bacon (Jim Maypen).

The story opens in the quiet town of Ashford as Annette McCloud unexpectedly arrives to stay with her relatives, Uncle Archie and Aunt Lila. It seems that the letter announcing her arrival was delayed, and Uncle Archie is not pleased to be sharing his home with a teenager. Aunt Lila, however, thinks it's a wonderful idea and immediately makes their surprise guest feel at home.

Production Note:

• This serial was originally planned to co-star Mouseketeer Darlene Gillespie in the part of Jet. The title was to have been *Annette and Darlene*, but Darlene was dropped when she began work on the film *Rainbow Road to Oz*, which was never produced.

MYSTERY OF GHOST FARM, THE

Cast: Tim Considine (Frank Hardy), Tommy Kirk (Joe Hardy), Carole Ann Campbell (Iola Morton), Sarah Selby (Aunt Gertrude Hardy), Russ Conway (Fenton Hardy), John Baer (Eric Pierson), Hugh Sanders (Mr. Binks), Bob Amsberry (Sam, the farmer), Andy Clyde (Lacey), Yvonne Lime (Gloria Binks), John Harmon (Bray), Paul Wexler (Fred), Tyler McVey (Police Chief), Florenz Ames (Silas Applegate), Gail Bonney (Prim Woman), Paul Birch (Banker).

This sequel to the serial *The Mystery of the Applegate Treasure* again features Frank and Joe Hardy, the teenage sons of detective Fenton Hardy. A year has passed since the boys solved their first big case and Joe is once again bored with life. Frank has become interested in girls, much to Joe's disgust, and refuses to play at detective games. Things change when Joe is sent on an errand to the countryside, for he discovers a "haunted" farm.

NEW ADVENTURES OF SPIN AND MARTY, THE

Cast: Tim Considine (Spin Evans), David Stollery (Marty Markham), Kevin Corcoran (Montgomery "Moochie" O'Hara), Annette Funicello (Annette), Darlene Gillespie (Darlene), J. Pat O'Malley (Perkins), Harry Carey, Jr. (Bill Burnett), Roy Barcroft (Colonel Jim Logan), B.G. Norman (Ambitious), Sammy Ogg (Joe Simpson), Tim Hartnagel (Speckles), Dennis Moore (Hank), Joe Wong (George), Bonnie Fields (Bonnie), Don Agrati (Don), Lynn Ready (Lynn), George Eldredge (Dr. Spaulding), James Horan (Speckles's Father), Hank Patterson (Pete Duggan), Thomas L. Mahoney (Specialty Dancer).

The third *Spin and Marty* serial begins as the campers return again to the Triple R for a summer of outdoor fun. Spin and Marty have spent the winter repairing an old car and happily arrive in it, only to see the car catch on fire. The other campers help extinguish the flames and the despondent mechanics vow to repair the damage later in the summer.

The car is almost forgotten when a wild stallion raids the corral and escapes with the ranch's horses.

Production Note:

- The Studio began work on a fourth *Spin and Marty* serial, but canceled the project when it was decided not to produce any new material for the Club's fourth season.

Fourth season: 1958–59

ADVENTURE IN THE MAGIC KINGDOM, AN

This was an adaptation of the *Disneyland* episode of the same name, which was aired during the 1957–58 anthology season.

6

The Mickey Mouse Club—
The Syndicated Series

After the last episode of *The Mickey Mouse Club* was aired in 1959, the Studio received thousands of letters protesting the show's cancellation. The volume of the letters eventually did have the desired effect, for the Studio could not ignore the potential of returning the Club to the air at a profit. Instead of incurring the costs and risks associated with producing new episodes, it was decided to examine the possibility of repeating the old shows.

Walt assembled a team to evaluate the possibility of editing and rerunning the original episodes, giving them instructions to keep their work low-key in case the plan was abandoned or deemed to be too expensive. Following months of work, the study indicated that the possibility of successfully returning the show to television was quite high, and work began in earnest on resurrecting the series.

The Studio faced several major obstacles, beginning with the question of who was going to broadcast the series. The bitter split between Disney and ABC was still relatively recent and precluded the possibility of them again becoming partners, and NBC and CBS did not share the Studio's enthusiasm for the project. This meant that the Studio would have to sell the show in syndication rather than make one sale to a network.

The 1962–63 season
As part of launching the syndication effort, the Studio began preparing a newly edited version of *The Mickey Mouse Club*. It should be remembered that the first two years of the series had been aired in a one-hour format, and with the consensus of the marketing staff that the new show needed to be limited to thirty minutes to succeed, it was necessary to alter the contents of the individual episodes.

Gone were low-rated segments such as *Sooty* and those sequences judged outdated, such as several of the Newsreels. Segments were taken from each year of the original broadcast, which at times led to a noticeable change in the ages of the Mouseketeers from day-to-day.

In order to help sell the series, former host Jimmie Dodd was called back into service and sent touring across the country, covering sixteen cities. While some would say that the show could have sold itself, Dodd's contribution cannot be minimized, for his public appearances attracted considerable press attention, with the desired increase in public awareness of the syndication package. Several of the Mouseketeers were also called back into duty, joining Jimmie or making appearances by themselves. Roy Williams performed a similar task on the West Coast, but his work at the Studio limited his availability for promotional purposes. Roy often appeared on the Los Angeles station airing the show, and on the weekends could be found signing autographs at Disneyland, using notepads that promoted the local segments.

A number of the stations airing the series decided to add their own locally produced segments to the show, usually featuring a host or hostess who would introduce local children from the audience. In some cases this led to shows with unusual lengths, such as forty-five minutes, and in others, the local stations replaced some of the Studio footage with their own. The Studio encouraged such efforts, feeling it would help to increase viewer interest, and prepared materials for local use. Initial plans noted that "*The Mickey Mouse Club* emcee in every market will be standardized through the use of a common Walt Disney character costume," but this was not enforced.

The marketing campaign was a success and the resultant sales were brisk. The series was placed on 119 stations for the first year, a figure which is made even more respectable when it is remembered that the show had only left the air three years earlier. As the Studio had hoped, audiences responded enthusiastically, with an estimated 12 million viewers tuning in daily.

The 1963–64 season

Despite the favorable reaction received during the first year of syndication, a number of stations declined to renew their contracts, complaining that the Studio's price was too high for what was essentially nothing more than repeats. Thus, when the second year began, the show was only seen on eighty-eight stations. With this smaller broadcast base, it was only natural that the ratings would drop. The decline in ratings showed a decrease to 10 million viewers, an amount not large enough to warrant cancellation, but still enough to cause concern at the Studio.

One of the major marketing efforts used to sell the show at this time was a long series of personal appearances by Jimmie Dodd across the country. Jimmie, who was still well known for his role in the series, continued to draw crowds wherever he went, and his enthusiasm helped to sell the series. Roy Williams also pitched in, for the Studio set up a "Mickey Mouse Club World Headquarters" inside the "Main Street Opera House" at Disneyland from June 1963 to September 1964. Roy continued to draw sketches and sign autographs, and all visitors were named as honorary Mouseketeers.

The 1964–65 season

The drop in sales between the first two years caused serious doubt as to the viability of offering a third season for sale. In order to combat complaints about the fact that the syndicated series was comprised totally of repeat material, Walt decided to produce new sequences with a more modern look in an attempt to attract a wider audience. To do so, the Studio added the a number of new segments for the third season of syndication, some of which can be traced back to the early plans for original Club:

- **Fun with Science:** Combining science with comedy, Julius Sumner Miller of El Camino College in California had come to the Studio's attention when he was profiled in *Life* magazine. Walt brought Miller to the Studio as a scientific consultant on *The Absent-Minded Professor*, tasked with providing an accurate look for the film professor's lab. For the syndicated version of *The Mickey Mouse Club*, Miller was cast as "Professor Wonderful," conducting a variety of experiments either in the "Mousekalab" or outdoors at Disneyland.

- **Marvelous Marvin:** A Disney press release offered the following description of this segment: "He is a master magician, a clever clown, an incomparable illusionist and contortionist, a man of many faces, funny disguises, and unusual voices—and naturally, many marvelous things happen when he is around the Mickey Mouse Club." Marvin was played by actor Bob Towner, a young man who was made up to look like an elderly handyman at the Studio.

- **Hub and Bub:** The same press release described them as: "The rollicking young comedy team of Hub and Bub contribute their own brand of hilarious fun on the Club during the season. When the zany pair are not cutting up with the regular and guest acts, they are up to their talents dancing, playing a dozen different musical instruments, clowning about, singing, and just being wonderfully goofy in general." Later in their careers to be billed as "Skiles and Henderson," the comedians were often the foils of Marvelous Marvin's tricks, and at times tried to assist Professor Wonderful or introduced guest stars. Their full names are Pete Henderson and Bill Skiles.

- **Guest Star Day:** New segments were filmed, featuring guests that the Studio claimed were personally picked by Walt Disney. The majority of these segments were filmed at Disneyland, providing yet another source of promotion for Disney. A number of segments from the original episodes were also used to supplement the newer entries.

- **Disneyland:** The Studio continued the past practice of promoting the theme park by filming a number of segments that featured Disneyland attractions and performers. Guest stars were sometimes used in these sequences.

The majority of the new scenes were directed by Bob Lehman, and instead of being shot directly on film and then edited, they were shot using video cameras and filmed using the kinescope method. This process, which uses a film camera focused on a video monitor, results in an image which is noticeably less sharp. However, it did allow the Studio to save substantially on the production costs by effectively eliminating the editing process. There was one problem, however, for any errors that occurred during filming were usually not edited out. If an experiment did not go as planned for Professor Wonderful, he had to quickly ad-lib and continue as if nothing had gone wrong.

In addition to his personal appearances promoting the series, Jimmie Dodd returned to the Studio to film introductions to these new sequences and often appeared in them. Dressed once again in Mouse ears and a "Jimmie" T-shirt, Jimmie was noticeably thinner than in the original series, often looking tired and drawn. However, he helped provide a needed continuity between the old and new segments. Shortly after filming his scenes for this season, Jimmie Dodd died on November 10, 1964, in Hawaii, where he was starting work on a new local children's series.

Unlike the first two years, the daily format was not as consistently followed during the final season. The concept of "themed" days was still used, but there was no consistency to what day of the week a sequence might be used on. Guest Star Day, for example, was sometimes on Tuesday, sometimes on Thursday, and in several weeks, both days. The Marvelous Marvin and Hub and Bub segments were generally used as filler, such as to conclude a week after a serial finished its run.

Despite these efforts, many stations decided against renewing their contracts for the series for this third year. Several programming buyers disagreed with Disney's decision to include science lectures in what was still widely perceived as a show for small children. Also, color was becoming more important to local stations, which had to compete for audiences against other broadcasters who had also purchased the expensive equipment required. Many other black-and-white series were being replaced, and within a few short years, they were to all but vanish from the airwaves as new series.

With fewer stations airing the show, it was inevitable that the ratings would drop even lower. And, as the ratings dropped, advertisers begin to demand lower rates to sponsor the series, thereby making the show even less attractive to the airing stations. Thus, after three years in syndication, it was decided

that *The Mickey Mouse Club* would once again be canceled. However, like a phoenix, it would make history years later by returning to television once again.

The 1975 syndication

During the late 1960s, it was often popular to attack Disney's work as being meaningless or childish, and audiences often turned away from the anthology series and theatrical product. In many college circles, to admit to being a Disney fan was unthinkable, and only the Disneyland theme park was still culturally acceptable to many. Then, in the '70s, a craze for nostalgia swept the country, often taking college campuses by storm. Mickey Mouse moved almost overnight from near obscurity to a cult hero, and the Studio found itself the surprised recipient of royalty income from items such as Mickey Mouse watches and shirts. Even more surprisingly, it was found that those merchandise items featuring the "old style" Mickey from the '30s were greatly outselling the more contemporary designs.

There was another important factor that was soon to come into play, for the former audiences of *The Mickey Mouse Club* were coming into the age of parenthood. Once again, the Studio began to receive letters asking for the return of *The Mickey Mouse Club*. Based on the popularity of Mickey Mouse on merchandising items, the Studio began to look into creating a new version of the show for modern audiences.

Although surveys showed potential audiences would be interested in an updated show, the Studio faced two problems. First, the cost of mounting a new series would be formidable, for the Studio chiefs knew they needed to maintain the overall quality of the first series, for there was bound to be comparison between the two. There was to be no network backing this time out, however, as the late afternoon time period during which the original series had aired was no longer controlled by the networks. The Studio would thus have to either move the show to the evening and thereby potentially lose the desired audience and sponsors, or syndicate the new series, thereby taking all of the financial risk involved.

The second reason why the Studio did not launch a new series was a surprising response to their surveys. A large percentage of those polled expressed strong interest in seeing the original series once again. This surprised many of the Studio executives, for black-and-white programs were generally of very little interest to viewers who had become accustomed to color. However, after looking at the poll results, they began to seriously explore the possibility of syndicating the original series. One of the aims of this effort was to test the market for the viability of producing a new series—if the original series could be relaunched at a relatively low cost but failed to succeed, it would still be less expensive (and less embarrassing) than watching a new version fail.

Despite their hopes for success, the Studio was not convinced the venture would be profitable, for major expenses were expected in trying to market the series. The Club's return began airing on January 20, 1975, with 110 stations signing up to air the series. Public response to the Club's return was enthusiastic, and word began to circulate that if the ratings were good enough, the Studio might produce a new color version for 1977.

While the ratings were good, the number of the stations airing the Club dropped in 1976 to eighty-three. A large portion of this was due to the series being in black-and-white, which was shown to deter modern audiences.

After two years in syndication, *The Mickey Mouse Club* was retired once again, this time to make way for *The New Mickey Mouse Club*. Since then, the series has been seen on The Disney Channel, and several episodes were released on home video.

The New Mickey Mouse Club

The success of the 1975 syndication of *The Mickey Mouse Club* took the Studio by surprise, for there had been serious doubts as to whether or not the series was too dated to be accepted by "modern" children. When the ratings showed these fears to be groundless, it was decided to explore the possibility of producing a new children's show. A small group was assembled to conduct a feasibility study of *The New Mickey Mouse Club*, as the series was quickly named, and they began work on the look and budget of the series.

The Daily Themes
Having decided early on to utilize many of the successful elements of the original series, the Studio again decided to split the week into five themed days. Several different proposals were evaluated, including the use of the themes from the original series. It was later decided that some new themes should be used, though, to better differentiate the new series from the old. The days were finally selected as: Monday—*Who, What, Why, Where, When, and How Day*; Tuesday—*Let's Go Day*; Wednesday—*Surprise Day*; Thursday—*Discovery Day*; and Friday—*Showtime Day*.

Once again, Walt Disney's foresight was found to be of value, for he had ordered that the opening credits of the original series be produced in color, even though the rest of the series was filmed in black and white. This allowed the Studio to reuse that footage, now thirty years old, to open their newest venture into television, this time with a new theme song that used electronic synthesizers to provide a distinctly different sound.

The Important Issue of Casting
The Studio recognized that the Mouseketeers would, of course, be an important part of the series. They also knew that it would be difficult, if not impossible, to duplicate the success of casting the original *Mickey Mouse Club*. Because of this, Disney launched a massive talent search, one designed to generate the maximum amount of publicity possible.

What exactly was the Studio looking for? Talent, of course, but more importantly that undefinable "something extra" that might produce the next Annette. There was one new requirement this time out, though—all of the Mouseketeers now had to be between the ages of seven and twelve. This was due to something that created a problem during the original series—puberty. As Martindale explained in an interview, "The boys' voices start changing, and we'd like the little girls to remain, well . . . little girls." This is an interesting contrast to the first series, for the Studio once took pains to point out in a press release that the stars of the *Spin and Marty* serials all had new voices one season.

There was another important item the Studio needed—ethnic variety. Sensitive to the criticism received about the racial make-up of the first series during the '70s syndication, Disney needed to make sure this version included a more representative mix of Mouseketeers. When the new Mouseketeers were finally picked, a press release made note that they were "from a wide variety of cultural and ethnic backgrounds."

Eventually, the selection process came to an end, and twelve happy applicants received the news that they were now Mouseketeers. They were Billy "Pop" Attmore, Scott Craig, Nita Dee, Mindy Feldman, Angel Florez, Allison Fonte, Shawnte Northcutte, Kelly Parsons, Julie Piekarski, Todd Turquand, Lisa Whelchel, and Curtis Wong.

There's one thing noticeably missing from this list—adults. While the first series had starred Jimmie Dodd, Roy Williams, and Bob Amsberry, it was decided that *The New Mickey Mouse Club* would star only the young

Mouseketeers. Co-producer Michael Wuergler told an interviewer, "We've done a lot of thinking and a lot of research into the fact that we don't have an adult host on the show, and we feel that in today's society, the kids can speak to their peers with a little more credibility than an adult." Another important reason was that all involved agreed that it would be difficult, if not impossible, to find someone who would as popular as Jimmie Dodd had been.

The casting choices soon proved to be a major problem. Disney had commissioned a marketing research firm to study audience reactions to the series. Their report stunned Disney with the findings that people simply didn't like the new series. In particular, the audiences felt the new Mouseketeers were "too distant," "too smily," and "too put-on." Mothers in the test groups said the new stars were "too professional and not 'friendly' like the old Mouseketeers," and everyone agreed the new series was just "too slick." The decision to forego an adult host also was to haunt the Studio, for the researchers commented that the new series had a "lack of an adult authority who could keep everything together and who could convert the elements into a happy family."

Unfortunately, by the time the Studio received this report, it was far too late to make any major changes to the series. Thus, facing a very uncertain future, *The New Mickey Mouse Club* took to the air with a special preview on January 14, 1977, and the regular episodes began on January 17.

Like their predecessors, the new Mouseketeers were slated for appearances at Disneyland as part of the Studio's overall marketing and publicity plan for the series. While they attracted crowds at each of these, they failed to catch on anywhere near the level of the original Mouseketeers. This did not go unnoticed at the Studio, which was beginning to have serious doubts about the project. After two seasons, the Studio finally gave up on tinkering with the format and canceled the series.

Today, with the show having been overlooked by The Disney Channel and unaired since it left the air in 1978, it is an almost forgotten piece of Disney television history. The series did earn a place in the history books, though, for *The All-New Mickey Mouse Club Album* was the top-selling children's record for 1977.

The New Mickey Mouse Club Serials

The New Mickey Mouse Club emulated its predecessor by featuring adventure serials.

This time, though, the serials were much less prominent and were not a daily part of the series. The majority of the serials were edited versions of feature films. Only one new serial, *The Mystery of Rustler's Cave*, was produced.

HORSE CALLED COMANCHE, A
Released theatrically in 1958 as *Tonka*, this serial was first aired in two parts on the anthology series as *Comanche*.

HORSE WITHOUT A HEAD, THE
This serial was first presented in two parts on the anthology series.

MISADVENTURES OF MERLIN JONES, THE
This 1964 theatrical release stars Tommy Kirk, Annette Funicello, and Leon Ames in the story of a college student who has an accident in the school lab and suddenly can read minds.

MONKEY'S UNCLE, THE
This 1965 theatrical release was first aired on the anthology series.

MYSTERY OF RUSTLER'S CAVE, THE
Cast: Kim Richards (Patty Bell), Robbie Rist (Stuart "Stewie" Withers), Christian Juttner (Chris Hollister), Bobby Rolofson (Doug Withers), Tony Becker (Brett Bell), Ted Gehring (Ted Nix), Lou Frizzel (Buzz), Bing Russell (Waco), Dennis Fimple (Charlie), Bob Hastings (Bus Driver), Lew Brown (Mr. Bell), Doug Finkle (Charlie), Pete Renoudet (Mr. Bill Logan), Bill Zuckert (Will, the Cook), Joan Wilkin (Sharon), Bill Erickson (Dan), Ben Cooper (Dan), Jack Lilley (Van Driver).

Three kids from the city arrive at the Circle B Ranch for a 2-week vacation. Patty Bell, who lives on the ranch, joins them for a tour, during which they stumble upon a major cattle rustling scheme. The kids find a secret cave at Apache Cliff which leads to a box canyon full of stolen cattle. They also discover the gang's ringleader. The kids finally help capture the rustlers as they try to leave with the stolen cattle.

THREE SKRINKS, THE
Released theatrically in 1965 as *Emil and the Detectives*, this film first aired in two parts on the anthology series.

TOBY TYLER
First released theatrically in 1960 as *Toby Tyler, or Ten Weeks With a Circus*, this film aired in two parts on the anthology series.

The Bold Renegade

8

Zorro

One of the more enduring heroes of modern literature and film has been Robin Hood, who has become famous for "stealing from the rich and giving to the poor." The Robin Hood legend, one of a skilled fighter who strives to overcome the unfair oppression of the people by a tyrant, is an easy one for fans to identify with. It's not surprising that there have been several variations on this theme, with one of the most successful being Zorro.

Zorro, which is Spanish for "fox," is the story of a masked rider who battles the unjust rulers of the pueblo of Los Angeles during the days of Spanish rule. His real identity is that of Don Diego de la Vega, the son of a wealthy landowner. Diego returns from his studies in Spain and discovers that Los Angeles is under the command of Capitan Monastario, a cruel man who relishes in the misuse of his power for personal gain. Knowing that he cannot hope to singlehandedly defeat Monastario and his troops, Diego resorts to subterfuge. He adopts the secret identity of Zorro, a sinister figure dressed in black, and rides to fight Monastario's injustice.

Zorro was created in 1919 by writer Johnston McCulley. The first Zorro story, *The Curse of Capistrano*, appeared that year in *All-Star Weekly*, which became *Argosy* magazine. More than sixty-five Zorro books and short stories were to follow, with an estimated 500 million readers around the world.

With that sort of reader interest, it was inevitable that the Zorro story be made into a film. In fact, there have been many filmed versions, beginning with Douglas Fairbanks Sr.'s portrayal of Zorro in the 1920 silent production *The Mark of Zorro*. Tyrone Power scored a huge hit with a 1940 remake of that film, and several other Zorro films and serials were also produced over the years.

Walt becomes interested in Zorro

In 1950, Johnston McCulley assigned the film and television rights to Zorro to Mitchell Gertz, a Hollywood agent. Gertz tried for several years to find the financing to produce a Zorro series, but to no avail. Then, in 1952, Walt Disney became involved in the Zorro legend when he was looking for a source of financing for his new theme park. He used his private research company, WED Enterprises, to license the rights to the Zorro stories from Gertz, planning to produce a number of episodes and use the resulting profits for developing the Park. The industry trade papers carried several stories in 1954 speculating that *Zorro* would be part of the packaging for ABC's investment in the Park, but the network instead settled on the *Disneyland* anthology series and it looked like the Zorro project was dead. However, when Walt later needed a new series to offer to ABC in exchange for more money for the Park, the Zorro series was reborn.

Casting the series

Walt immediately set to work on a search for someone to play Zorro, knowing full well that whoever he picked, comparisons to Tyrone Power were inevitable. This was a much sought after role, for Disney's success with *Davy Crockett* was not lost on a host of other actors who could only dream of being the Studio's next Fess Parker. More than twenty actors were tested for the part, including Hugh O'Brian, John Lupton, Jack Kelly, Dennis Weaver and David Janssen. On April 18, 1957, the Studio held a screen test for a relatively unknown actor, Guy Williams. When Walt saw the results, he knew he had found his Zorro.

Guy Williams, whose real name was Armando Catalano, was born on January 14,

1924 in New York. After school, he worked as a male model and came to the attention of MGM and then Universal-International Studios, who put him under contract in 1952. Although he appeared in films such as *Bonzo Goes to College, Mississippi Gambler,* and *I Was a Teenage Werewolf,* Williams's parts were relatively small and it looked like his hopes of becoming a leading man were in vain. By the time Disney found the six foot, three inch actor, Williams was almost ready to give up his acting career. Luckily for Williams, he was auditioned for the role of Zorro, and to his astonishment, he found himself the star of a network series.

Throughout his exploits, Diego could always count on the assistance of his faithful manservant, Bernardo. Bernardo, as played by Gene Sheldon, was mute and decided to help Diego by pretending to be deaf as well. This allowed Bernardo to secretly listen in on conversations and report back to Diego. Bernardo also came to the rescue several times by dressing as Zorro, which allowed Diego to be seen in the same place as Zorro, thereby eliminating suspicion that Diego might be the masked avenger.

Another important character was Sergeant Garcia, the second-in-command of the pueblo. Garcia, played by Henry Calvin, was a fairly comedic character, due in part to his rotund physique. He provided a welcome relief to the sinister commanders of the garrison, and as the series progressed, he developed a certain kinship with Zorro. While he tried his best to be a good soldier, Garcia could always be counted on to let his voracious appetite or appreciation of liquor to get the best of him.

Completing the regular characters on the series was Don Alejandro de la Vega, Diego's father, played by George J. Lewis. Alejandro was one of the wealthiest and most prominent of the citizens of Los Angeles. For most of the series, Alejandro didn't know that Diego was secretly Zorro, and his son's apparent cowardice caused friction within the family.

Besides his distinctive black costume and skill with his sword, Zorro relied on his trusty horse, Tornado, to aid in him in his battles. Tornado was played by Diamond Decorator, a seven-year-old quarter horse, with three stand-ins used to perform the horse's various stunts. One horse specialized in Tornado's dramatic rearing, as seen in the opening credits, one was used in fight scenes and the third for high-speed running.

Preparing for the series

While casting was underway, the Studio was also working on the logistics of turning back the clock to the early days of Los Angeles. In June 1955, workers started building the series' permanent sets, which included the buildings of the Pueblo La Reina de Los Angeles and the soldier's cuartel, or stockade. These were the Studio's first permanent sets, and cost more than $100,000 to construct. Disney also spent $35,000 on furnishings and $30,000 on additional props, helping to bring the preproduction costs to a total of $208,000. All of this was expensive, but the quality was obvious on the screen, helping to set the mood for the masked adventurer's heroics.

While the costs to get ready for the series were high, so were the costs for each episode. Disney set a budget of between $50,000 and $100,000 for each thirty-minute show, and the first season of thirty-nine episodes was to eventually cost $3,198,000. When Disney was studying the television marketplace in 1950, the average cost for a one-hour drama series was only $13,840—and here was Walt spending an average for $82,000 for a show only half as long. Once again, Walt was setting his own standards.

Even with these lofty budgets, Disney did try to contain costs where it wouldn't show on the air. One method was to shoot portions of up to four episodes at the same time if they used common sets. Guy Williams commented at the time that "(It's) a little confusing at times. Not remembering the dialogue, but remembering what led up to it. Sometimes I'm real blank and we have to go back and read scenes we've already filmed."

Williams also had to deal with a rigorous training schedule designed to turn the former model into a dashing hero. Although he had previously done some fencing, it was decided that Williams needed some intensive brushup work if he was to be convincing on the screen. The Studio hired Fred Cavens, the fencing coach who had earlier coached Douglas Fairbanks, Sr., and Tyrone Power for their Zorro outings, to tutor Williams and the rest of the cast.

In addition to the fencing classes, there were other lessons to attend. The part of Don Diego called for Williams to play the guitar as he serenaded young señoritas, but unfortunately, Williams could neither play the guitar nor sing. Despite a series of lessons from guitar instructor Vicente Gomez, Williams never mastered the skills required and his singing was dubbed by Bill Lee, who was also one of the singers of the series' theme song.

In addition to Don Diego's love songs, music played an important part throughout the series. Composer William Lava wrote a different musical theme for each of the show's main characters, similar to the technique used in *Peter and the Wolf*. These brief themes were played when the characters were on the screen, and they helped to set the mode for the action to follow. When the bumbling Sergeant Garcia entered a scene, for example, a lively piece of music in the background foreshadowed the events to come.

As soon as *Zorro* hit the air, children began imitating their new hero, pretending they were master swordsmen and scrawling "Z's" everywhere one looked. This juvenile vandalism was far-reaching—a popular news story of the time told how Williams discovered a large "Z" scratched into the paint on his new car.

Zorro enjoyed a very successful first season, averaging 35.7 percent of the viewing audience each evening, and an estimated 35 million viewers saw the show each week. Every series that went up against *Zorro* this year found itself canceled; on CBS, it was *Harbor Master* and *Richard Diamond*, and on NBC, *You Bet Your Life*.

The success of *Zorro* prompted the Studio to take a page from its *Davy Crockett* book. Portions of the first thirteen *Zorro* episodes were edited into the feature film *The Sign of Zorro*. The film only did moderate business domestically, but when released overseas, where the series had not yet aired, it achieved yet another success for Disney.

The second season

Having enjoyed a very successful first season, it was no surprise that *Zorro* was renewed for a second year. Like many other series, there would be a number of changes made in the look of the series to reflect viewer comments and economic realities. One of the first changes made was a move away from the first season's rigid format of using thirteen episodes for each story. As story editor Lowell S. Hawley noted at the time "Now we play stories for what they're worth. If a writer has material enough for three, four, or five episodes, we let it go at that."

The Studio also made a casting change for the second year in the hopes of attracting more woman viewers. One of the criticisms of the first season was Don Diego's lack of interest in the opposite sex, for he was always more interested in chasing yet another villain than in chasing women. Actress Jolene Brand was hired for the part of Anna Maria Verdugo, a local wealthy señorita. Anna Maria was set to appear in nine of the first thirteen episodes, allowing the Studio to assess audience reaction without having to commit to hiring Brand for the entire season. Evidently she didn't make a major impact, for the character was dropped and Don Diego went back to being his unromantic self.

The changes proved successful, for the ratings increased and *Zorro* moved ahead to take 38.9 percent of the audience each evening. The year saw the cancellation of two more series on NBC, *Ed Wynn* and *Steve Canyon*, and *Zorro* steadily outdrew CBS' *December Bride*. Overall, *Zorro* knocked five of the seven series to face it off the air.

The Studio also released another theatrical compilation of several episodes. *Zorro, The Avenger*, was only released overseas, and was not seen in the United States until it was eventually aired on The Disney Channel.

One other interesting Disney footnote concerns several of the second season episodes. Like many other young women, Annette Funicello developed a crush on Guy Williams, but unlike all the others, she was able to fulfill her fantasy. As a present for her sixteenth birthday, Walt cast her in several episodes as Anita Cabrillo, a new arrival in the pueblo with a mysterious past.

The battle with ABC begins

Unfortunately, Zorro was to come up against a foe even he could not hope to defeat—the American legal system. As noted earlier, Disney and ABC became locked in a bitter series of legal challenges over the ownership of the anthology series, *The Mickey Mouse Club* and *Zorro*. Unable to come to terms, Disney decided to pull *Zorro* off the air, despite the high ratings the series was sure to receive if were to return for a third season.

While the legal maneuvers went on, Disney aired four hour-long *Zorro* episodes on the anthology series to help keep public interest alive in the character. Walt kept Williams on full salary for two years, but by the time the legal issues were finally settled out of court, Walt decided that the public had moved on to other fads and there would be no point in resurrecting *Zorro*.

Despite this decision, Disney retained the

rights to *Zorro*, paying the Gertz estate $3,500 a year for the privilege. It wasn't until 1967 that the Studio finally relinquished their rights to *Zorro*.

Zorro in syndication

Like *The Mickey Mouse Club, Zorro* later returned to the air in syndication, beginning with the 1965–66 season. The original network run of the series had attracted an estimated 35 million viewers, and the demographics had been high in the desired age groups, making it relatively easy for Disney to sell the show in the syndicated market.

A total of forty-three stations signed up for the series, which began airing September 8, 1965, and Disney joined them in promoting the series. In addition to traditional print and television advertising, the Studio was able to tout the series and be paid for it at the same time! They created a new character, "Little Zorro," and used him in the daily Mickey Mouse comic strip which appeared in more than 100 newspapers across the country.

The first year of syndication went well and *Zorro* returned for a second year in syndication in 1966. There was serious thought given to starting production on new episodes, but a look at the costs involved soon quashed that idea.

Life after Zorro

After the last of the anthology *Zorro* episodes had aired, Walt lost interest in the character, and in 1967, the Studio decided not to renew its option and let the rights revert to the Gertz estate. With the syndicated run over, *Zorro* became just another canceled television series.

Following his role as Zorro, Guy Williams only appeared in one other Disney project, the television show *The Prince and the Pau-*per, then moved on to *Bonanza* and *Lost in Space*. After several years of playing an increasingly diminishing role in the latter series, Williams left show business and Los Angeles. He had appeared in Argentina several years earlier to promote *Zorro* and had enjoyed the public attention and lifestyle there. He moved to Buenos Aires and bought property in the country, opening a cattle ranch.

In 1982, word circulated yet again that Williams was to play Zorro once more. The Studio was starting work on a comedy version, *Zorro and Son*, and they were very interested in getting Williams to reprise his role as Don Diego and Zorro. At first, Williams indicated that he was indeed interested, but when he saw the scripts, he quickly decided to back out of the project. *Zorro and Son* did go ahead but without Williams, who had returned home to Buenos Aires.

It was there that he died alone, sometime in late April or early May, 1989, at age sixty-five. Neighbors noticed that they hadn't seen him for several days, and police found him dead of natural causes in his apartment. His passing received major coverage back in the United States, for it seemingly marked the end of an era.

Zorro wasn't finished yet, however. In addition to *Zorro and Son*, the masked avenger gained new audiences when the original episodes were screened repeatedly on The Disney Channel. After several runs in the original black-and-white format, the series gained a new generation of viewers when Disney successfully colorized the series, thereby making it more appealing to today's audiences. Thirty years after Zorro first rode to fight injustice, he continues to attract new fans, who once again love to make the "sign of the Z."

Zorro Episode Descriptions

Each of the episodes is described below in air-date order, divided by season.

Series cast: Guy Williams (Zorro and Don Diego), Henry Calvin (Sergeant Demetrio Lopez Garcia), Gene Sheldon (Bernardo), Don Diamond (Corporal Reyes), George J. Lewis (Don Alejandro).

First season: 1957–58

PRESENTING SEÑOR ZORRO Airdate: 10/10/57.

Guest Cast: Britt Lomond (Capitan Monastario), Jan Arvan (Don Ignacio Torres), Than Wyenn (Licenciado Pina).

The story of the masked rider in Old California opens as Don Diego de la Vega is returning to California from Spain, where he has been studying for several years. The Pueblo de Los Angeles is under the rule of a cruel dictator, Capitan Monastario.

To protect his true identity, Diego will become El Zorro—"The Fox." Zorro's first act is to save the life of Don Torres, whom Monastario plans to release and then kill, claiming the prisoner had escaped.

ZORRO'S SECRET PASSAGE Airdate: 10/17/57.

Guest Cast: Britt Lomond (Capitan Monastario), Romney Brent (Padre Felipe), Eugenia Paul (Señorita Elena Torres), Jan Arvan (Don Ignacio Torres), Pat Hogan (Benito).

Diego continues to develop his dual persona as Zorro by moving his horse Tornado to a secret cave beneath the hacienda, and he shows Bernardo a series of tunnels and hidden doors built into the house's walls. He then rides to the mission to check on the safety of Don Torres, who is hiding from Monastario.

ZORRO RIDES TO THE MISSION Airdate: 10/24/57.

Guest Cast: Britt Lomond (Capitan Monastario), Romney Brent (Padre Felipe), Jan Arvan (Don Ignacio Torres).

Don Torres's safety at the mission is imperiled when a peasant informs Monastario of his hiding place and the lancers ride to surround the church. Monastario tries to enter the mission but is blocked by Padre Felipe, who demands that the soldiers leave without violating the sanctuary of the church. Instead, the capitan forces the local Indians to build a road through a rocky area, vowing to continue the work until Torres surrenders.

GHOST OF THE MISSION, THE Airdate: 10/31/57.

Guest Cast: Britt Lomond (Capitan Monastario), Romney Brent (Padre Felipe), Jan Arvan (Don Ignacio Torres).

Monastario has a new plan to capture Don Torres. He claims a captured Indian was part of a plot to raid the mission, which enables the soldiers to occupy the church for its "protection" and hopefully then seize the fugitive. Hoping to drive Torres out of his hiding place, Monastario sends his men inside with orders not to let any food or water into the church.

ZORRO'S ROMANCE Airdate: 11/07/57.

Guest Cast: Britt Lomond (Capitan Monastario), Jan Arvan (Don Ignacio Torres), Eugenia Paul (Señorita Elena Torres), Madeleine Holmes (Dona Luisa Torres).

Following Don Torres's escape from the mission, Monastario and his men ride to the escapee's home hoping to find him hiding there. Diego also decides to visit to tell the family that Don Torres is safely on his way to Monterey, only to discover Torres hiding in the wine cellar. The fugitive had tried to see his family before leaving town, and now Diego must find a way to spirit Torres out from under Monastario's nose.

ZORRO SAVES A FRIEND   Airdate: 11/14/57.

Guest Cast: Britt Lomond (*Capitan Monastario*), Romney Brent (*Padre Felipe*), Eugenia Paul (*Señorita Elena Torres*), Madeleine Holmes (*Dona Luisa Torres*), Pat Hogan (*Benito*), Than Wyenn (*Licenciado Pina*).

Diego's claim of innocence in the escape of Don Torres backfires when Monastario decides that the women were the plotters and arrests them instead. The Torres women are taken into the cuartel and placed in the stockade for all the townspeople to see, and Monastario announces that they will be kept there until they sign a statement acknowledging Don Torres as a traitor.

MONASTARIO SETS A TRAP   Airdate: 11/21/57.

Guest Cast: Britt Lomond (*Capitan Monastario*), Than Wyenn (*Licenciado Pina*), Eugenia Paul (*Señorita Elena Torres*), Madeleine Homes (*Dona Luisa Torres*).

Don Alejandro's visit to inspect prison conditions at the cuartel produces an unexpected result when the Torres women assure him they've been well treated. He later learns that this is another one of Monastario's tricks. The wily commandante has told the prisoners that he captured Torres and will torture him if they complain to Don Alejandro.

ZORRO'S RIDE INTO TERROR   Airdate: 11/28/57.

Guest Cast: Britt Lomond (*Capitan Monastario*), Jan Arvan (*Don Ignacio Torres*).

Zorro rushes his wounded father to the secret cave where Tornado is stabled and tries to tend to his wounds, a task made more difficult by the fact that Alejandro has become delirious from infection. Monastario leads his men to the hacienda hoping to find Alejandro there, and Diego barely has time to doff his costume before the soldiers enter. Still wary of Diego, the capitan places him under arrest and orders his men to search the grounds for his quarry.

FAIR TRIAL, A   Airdate: 12/05/57.

Guest Cast: Britt Lomond (*Capitan Monastario*), Sebastian Cabot (*Judge Vasca*), Jan Arvan (*Don Ignacio Torres*), Than Wyenn (*Licenciado Pina*), William Schallert (*Innkeeper*).

Don Alejandro and Don Torres have surrendered to Monastario on advice from the governor, who has promised them a fair trial. The governor has sent Judge Vasca, known for his honesty, to Los Angeles to conduct the trial, but the capitan has other plans. He sends Garcia and a party of lancers northward to meet the judge and delay him. This will allow the capitan's henchman, Licenciado Pina, to conduct the trial in his absence and sentence the prisoners to death.

GARCIA'S SECRET MISSION   Airdate: 12/12/57.

Guest Cast: Britt Lomond (*Capitan Monastario*), Frank Yaconelli (*Pancho*), Nick Moro (*Pepe*).

The normally easy duty of raising the flag turns into a problem for Sergeant Garcia when he discovers that Zorro has substituted a flag with a large "Z" for the fort's flag and the flagpole has been greased to prevent the soldiers from removing it. Monastario publicly reprimands Garcia and then realizes he can profit from the situation by secretly ordering the sergeant to pretend he was thrown out of the service in disgrace. This, he hopes, will make the people of the village take Garcia into their confidence and thus unwittingly betray Zorro.

DOUBLE TROUBLE FOR ZORRO   Airdate: 12/19/57.

Guest Cast: Britt Lomond (*Capitan Monastario*), Romney Brent (*Padre Felipe*), Tony Russo (*Carlos Martinez*), Elvera Corona (*Pilar Fuentes*).

Two men's jealousy over a barroom dancer becomes a central point in Monastario's latest plot to discredit Zorro when he arrests Carlos Martinez for killing a man in a sword fight. The commandante realizes that Martinez bears a strong resemblance to Zorro, so he offers the prisoner his freedom in exchange for his impersonating Zorro. The offer is gladly accepted, for the alternative is death.

ZORRO, LUCKIEST SWORDSMAN ALIVE Airdate: 12/26/57.

Guest Cast: Britt Lomond (*Capitan Monastario*), Romney Brent (*Padre Felipe*), Than Wyenn (*Licenciado Pina*), Tony Russo (*Carlos Martinez*), Elvera Corona (*Pilar Fuentes*).

The capitan has another scheme to discredit Zorro by using Martinez, and he fakes the prisoner's death and buries a coffin full of rocks in his place. This will allow the fake Zorro to rob the villagers and then vanish, finally discrediting the masked rider.

FALL OF MONASTARIO, THE   Airdate: 1/02/58.

Guest Cast: Britt Lomond (Capitan Monastario), Lisa Gaye (Constancia), John Dehner (Viceroy), Than Wyenn (Licenciado Pina).

Monastario has seen through Diego's attempts to disguise his fencing ability and plans his arrest and trial. He confronts Diego with the charge that the latter is secretly Zorro, an accusation the young don tries to laugh off. This time, however, Diego's charm fails to sway the commandante, who orders Diego held in the jail until he can be tried.

SHADOW OF DOUBT   Airdates: 1/09/58, 7/10/58.

Guest Cast: Vinton Hayworth (Magistrado Carlos Galindo), Myrna Fahey (Maria Crespo), Robin Hughes (Esteban Rojas), Jack Elam (Gomez), Peter Daymond (Capitan Melindez), Charles Stevens (Josofat).

The entire pueblo is overjoyed at the downfall of Monastario and eagerly awaits the arrival of the new commandante, for his reputation is that of an honest and fair administrator. Capitan Melindez has barely arrived in town when he is assassinated by Esteban Rojas, a mysterious stranger who has also just arrived in the village. Rojas frames an elderly beggar for the crime but he has been spotted by Maria Crespo, a young girl who works at the inn.

GARCIA STANDS ACCUSED   Airdates: 1/16/58, 7/17/58.

Guest Cast: Vinton Hayworth (Magistrado Carlos Galindo), Myrna Fahey (Maria Crespo), Henry Willis (King's Messenger), Jack Elam (Gomez).

Sergeant Garcia is enjoying his temporary position as commandante until a replacement for the murdered Capitan Melindez can be found, and it appears his luck continues to improve when he receives a mysterious note from Zorro offering to surrender. The happy soldier reads that if he will travel alone into the hills, Zorro will give himself up.

SLAVES OF THE EAGLE   Airdates: 1/23/58, 7/24/58.

Guest Cast: Vinton Hayworth (Magistrado Carlos Galindo), Myrna Fahey (Maria

Crespo), Jack Elam (Gomez), John Doucett (Antonio Azuela).

The King's tax collector, Jose Morales, and his nephew are stopped by two outlaws while on their way to the pueblo. The conspirators threaten the men with death unless they cooperate, then seize Morales's official documents. The outlaws then tell him to return to the capital or they will kill his nephew, Domingo, whom they plan to hold hostage. As soon as Morales leaves, Domingo is seen to be another member of the criminal conspiracy. He gives the tax documents to one of the bandits, who rides into the pueblo to impersonate the uncle.

SWEET FACE OF DANGER   Airdates: 1/30/58, 7/31/58.

Guest Cast: Vinton Hayworth (Magistrado Carlos Galindo), Julia Van Zandt (Magdalena Montez), Edward Colmans (Don Francisco Montez), Henry Wills (Castro).

A quiet day in the pueblo is abruptly changed when a stranger is killed by an arrow, apparently the victim of an Indian attack. Diego helps Sergeant Garcia inspect the body for clues and finds another mysterious eagle feather, this time on the fake Indian arrow. This is Diego's first clue to a conspiracy by a mysterious figure known only as the Eagle.

ZORRO FIGHTS HIS FATHER   Airdates: 2/06/58, 8/07/58.

Guest Cast: Vinton Hayworth (Magistrado Carlos Galindo), Peter Brocco (Barca), Joan Shawlee (Barmaid), Noel de Souza (Paco).

A peaceful protest by a group of peons upset with taxes turns violent when one of the Eagle's men throws a rock through the magistrado's window. Galindo uses this as an excuse to order severe measures against the peasants, a move that upsets Don Alejandro. The other landowners want to set up vigilante posses to punish the peons, but Alejandro argues on the side of reason.

DEATH STACKS THE DECK   Airdates: 2/13/58, 8/14/58.

Guest Cast: Vinton Hayworth (Magistrado Carlos Galindo), Miguel Landa (Don Ramon Santil), Jim Bannon (Carlos Urista), Joan Shawlee (Barmaid).

Ramon Santil has just inherited his father's ranch and holdings, and some bad news. The magistrado tells him there's a high tax that must be paid at once or he will lose the land, and Ramon doesn't have the money to pay it.

In desperation, he sells all of his cattle to Carlos Urista, a recent arrival in town whom Diego suspects as another of the Eagle's men. Urista then invites Ramon to play cards, and soon the stranger has won back most of the money he just paid for the cattle. Diego tries to halt the game but is angrily turned away by Ramon, who proceeds to lose all of his money and the ranch.

AGENT OF THE EAGLE   Airdates: 2/20/58, 8/21/58.

Guest Cast: Vinton Hayworth (Magistrado Carlos Galindo), Anthony Caruso (Don Juan Ortega), George Keymas (Roberto), Sandy Livingston (Rosarita Cortez), Manuel Lopez (Franco Barbaroza).

Don Alejandro tells Diego he's received a letter from a friend in the capital telling him that the new commandante, Capitan Juan Ortega, has the reputation of being an honest and fair man. When Ortega arrives, he doesn't act that way. He treats Sergeant Garcia with contempt and is openly arrogant toward the civilians. The reason for this is revealed when Ortega meets the magistrado and informs him that the real commandante has been ambushed and murdered, on orders of the Eagle.

ZORRO SPRINGS A TRAP   Airdates: 2/27/58, 8/28/58.

Guest Cast: Vinton Hayworth (Magistrado Carlos Galindo), Anthony Caruso (Don Juan Ortega), George Keymas (Roberto).

The fake Ortega and the magistrado announce they have captured Zorro, and a cart holding a masked man is dragged into the town square. A public unmasking will be held at noon, and Diego fears that an innocent man will be charged with Zorro's "crimes." He also realizes it may all be a trap, so when he dons his costume and rides into the square to free the prisoner, he watches carefully for soldiers.

UNMASKING OF ZORRO, THE   Airdates: 3/06/58, 9/04/58.

Guest Cast: Vinton Hayworth (Magistrado Carlos Galindo), Anthony Caruso (Don Juan Ortega), Sandy Livingston (Rosarita Cortez).

The plans of the fake commandante and the magistrado go awry when Ortega spots Diego talking to Rosarita Cortez, a childhood friend who has recently returned from the capital. Ortega fears she will recognize him from her journey, for it was during that trip

that he murdered the real Ortega and assumed his identity. Bernardo overhears the two villains planning her death and notifies Diego.

SECRET OF THE SIERRA, THE   Airdates: 3/13/58, 9/11/58.

Guest Cast: Vinton Hayworth (Magistrado Carlos Galindo), Rodolfo Acosta (Perico), Laurie Carroll (Marya Montoya), Rudolfo Hoyos (Cuevas).

Another stranger with an eagle feather spells trouble for Zorro when Perico, a recent arrival, sees a gypsy girl trying to pay for a purchase with several gold nuggets. Diego and Alejandro realize that news of a gold discovery will cause a rush of "gold fever" and their peaceful way of life will be threatened, so they try to suppress the news.

NEW COMMANDANTE, THE   Airdates: 3/20/58, 9/18/58.

Guest Cast: Vinton Hayworth (Magistrado Carlos Galindo), Peter Adams (Capitan Arturo Toledano), Suzanne Lloyd (Raquel Toledano), Anthony George (Peralta).

The magistrado's plans to aid the Eagle may suffer a setback when a new commandante arrives in the pueblo. Unlike the fake Ortega, Capitan Toledano is loyal to the King and beyond corruption, yet he must be eliminated if the Eagle's plot is to succeed. Toledano's jealousy over his pretty wife, Raquel, is the key to the magistrado's newest scheme.

FOX AND THE COYOTE, THE   Airdates: 3/27/58, 9/25/58.

Guest Cast: Vinton Hayworth (Magistrado Carlos Galindo), Peter Adams (Capitan Arturo Toledano), Suzanne Lloyd (Raquel Toledano), Armand Alzamora (Figueroa).

Magistrado Galindo has smuggled a supply of weapons into the pueblo, intending to use them when the Eagle orders the overthrow of the government, but he has been unable to get a supply of gunpowder. The army has a large stockpile at the cuartel, and the magistrado decides to steal it for his use. As part of his plan, Galindo announces that a horse race will be held in the commandante's honor. Not only will this draw the capitan and most of his soldiers out of the cuartel, but he also hopes to win a substantial sum from the wagers that will be placed on the race.

ADIOS, SEÑOR MAGISTRADO   Airdates: 4/03/58, 10/02/58.

Guest Cast: Vinton Hayworth (Magistrado Carlos Galindo), Peter Adams (Captain Arturo Toledano), Armand Alzamora (Figueroa).

Capitan Toledano plans to interrogate two prisoners who were seized when the gunpowder was recovered. The prisoners warn Figueroa, one of the magistrado's men, that they will talk unless someone helps them escape. Instead, they are found dead in their cell the next morning. A doctor examines the bodies and suspects murder, but the magistrado announces that it was suicide.

EAGLE'S BROOD, THE   Airdate: 4/10/58.

Guest Cast: Charles Korvin (Jose Sebastian Varga—"The Eagle"), Peter Adams (Captain Arturo Toledano), Suzanne Lloyd (Raquel Toledano), Michael Pate (Salvador Quintana), Peter Mamakos (Enrique Fuentes).

With the death of the magistrado, the Eagle takes a more active role in his conspiracy to rule southern California. He sends two of his men, Quintana and Fuentes, to Los Angeles with a load of gunpowder for the weapons previously smuggled into the pueblo. The two men earn the wrath of the Eagle for suggesting that Zorro may upset the plan, and they fearfully head off on their mission.

ZORRO BY PROXY   Airdate: 4/17/58.

Guest Cast: Suzanne Lloyd (Raquel Toledano), Michael Pate (Salvador Quintana), Peter Mamakos (Enrique Fuentes).

The evil work of the Eagle takes a new turn when the commandante's wife, Raquel, visits Quintana and Fuentes and shows them an eagle feather, proving that she belongs to the conspiracy. She informs them the Eagle is furious over the loss of the gunpowder and that they must recover it if they hope to stay alive.

QUINTANA MAKES A CHOICE   Airdate: 4/24/58.

Guest Cast: Michael Pate (Salvador Quintana), Suzanne Lloyd (Raquel Toledano), Peter Mamakos (Enrique Fuentes).

Sergeant Garcia and the other soldiers are amazed one morning when every musket seems to misfire. When they check their gunpowder, they realize it has been replaced with charcoal. A search of the cuartel reveals that all of the gunpowder has been stolen, leaving the post defenseless. Unable to decide what to do, Garcia consults Diego, who learns that the only heavy load taken out of the cuartel was authorized by Raquel.

ZORRO LIGHTS A FUSE   Airdate: 5/01/58.

Guest Cast: Michael Pate (Salvador Quintana), Suzanne Lloyd (Raquel Toledano), Ted de Corsia (Espinosa).

Raquel's ambitious plans for her husband appear to end when she receives a letter from him. She had been promised by the Eagle that he would be made governor of California, but her husband wants her to join him in San Diego, for he plans to sail back to Spain. Realizing the Eagle will not let her go, she tries to sneak out of the pueblo, only to be caught by Quintana.

MAN WITH THE WHIP, THE   Airdate: 5/08/58.

Guest Cast: Kent Taylor (Carlos Murietta), Jack Kruschen (Jose Mordante), Steve Stevens (Rudolfo Martinez), Myrna Fahey (Maria).

Another agent sent by the Eagle arrives in the pueblo, this time smuggling jewelry to finance the conspiracy. Carlos Murietta, an Argentine who is contemptuous of the locals, particularly Sergeant Garcia, visits a tannery run by Jose Mordante. The two men discuss the disposition of the gems, including a famous piece known as "The Cross of the Andes," which were stolen from churches in Argentina.

CROSS OF THE ANDES, THE   Airdate: 5/15/58.

Guest Cast: Kent Taylor (Carlos Murietta), Mary Wickes (Dolores Bastinado), Jack Kruschen (Jose Mordante), Charles Wagenheim (Pasqual).

Expecting another shipment of jewels, Murietta goes to inspect the tannery where they will be stored. There, he spots Pasqual, a peasant who lives there, and whips the old man until he leaves. The shipment arrives accompanied by Dolores Bastinado, recently arrived in the pueblo, who attracts the attention of Sergeant Garcia.

DEADLY BOLAS, THE   Airdate: 5/22/58.

Guest Cast: Kent Taylor (Carlos Murietta), Mary Wickes (Dolores Bastinado), Paul Picerni (Pietro Murietta).

Determined to find the missing jewels, Diego and Bernardo visit a local padre in the hopes he can assist them in their quest, but the trip is to no avail. Later, when Carlos

Murietta complains to Sergeant Garcia about the missing trunk he had stored at the tannery, Diego is convinced more than ever that the jewels were hidden by Mordante before his death.

WELL OF DEATH, THE   Airdate: 5/29/58.

Guest Cast: Kent Taylor (Carlos Murietta), Mary Wickes (Dolores Bastinado), Bobby Crawford (Pogo Bastinado), Paul Picerni (Pietro Murietta).

Another shipment of stolen jewels arrives in the pueblo, and Dolores Bastinado unwittingly allows her brother, Pogo, to deliver the cargo to the Murietta brothers. The trunk slips and breaks open, and Pogo spots several of the gems. He realizes the men will try to kill him to protect their secret, but he is seized before he can flee.

TIGHTENING NOOSE, THE   Airdate: 6/05/58.

Guest Cast: Charles Korvin (Jose Sebastian Varga—"The Eagle"), Jay Novello (Juan Greco).

Don Alejandro convinces all of the landowners to sign a document pledging their loyalty to the government, for he has become worried by the growing signs of possible civil unrest. He leaves a copy in the hacienda and takes the original to the capitol, intending to present it to the governor. Alejandro has barely left when Diego receives some unwelcome news. A new administrator has arrived in the pueblo and announced his decision to use the de la Vega hacienda as his headquarters.

SERGEANT REGRETS, THE   Airdate: 6/12/58.

Guest Cast: Charles Korvin (Jose Sebastian Varga—"The Eagle"), Ralph Clanton (Señor George Brighton), Jonathan Hole (Alfredo).

An emissary from a foreign power has arrived in the pueblo to discuss plans to help the Eagle in his rebellion. George Brighton, the agent, warns Varga that there must not be any open resistance. His government wants an obedient colony, not one torn apart by internal battles. Varga promises to deliver control as planned, but he continues to worry about Don Alejandro and the other landowners who have pledged their allegiance to the King.

EAGLE LEAVES THE NEST, THE   Airdate: 6/19/58.

Guest Cast: Charles Korvin (Jose Sebastian Varga—"The Eagle"), Jay Novello (Juan Greco).

Diego overhears Varga telling his aide that the de la Vega hacienda is so comfortable he intends to make it his permanent headquarters. Knowing his father will soon return and would fight to the death to protect his home, Diego decides to try a risky plan to drive the Eagle out.

BERNARDO FACES DEATH   Airdate: 6/26/58.

Guest Cast: Charles Korvin (Jose Sebastian Varga—"The Eagle"), Henry Rowland (Count Kolinko), Jay Novello (Juan Greco).

Another stranger arrives in the pueblo and travels to the de la Vega hacienda, intending to meet with the Eagle. Diego recognizes the visitor as Count Kolinko, an ambassador from an Eastern European country that has long been interested in controlling California. Since the Eagle has left for the pueblo, Diego tries to convince Kolinko that he is also part of the conspiracy. He almost succeeds in gaining necessary details of the plot.

EAGLE'S FLIGHT, THE   Airdate: 7/03/58.

Guest Cast: Charles Korvin (Jose Sebastian Varga—"The Eagle"), Henry Rowland (Count Kolinko), Jay Novello (Juan Greco).

The Eagle sets into motion his plan to sieze control, and only Zorro and Bernardo can stop him.

Second season: 1958–59

WELCOME TO MONTEREY   Airdate: 10/09/58.

Guest Cast: Eduard Franz (Señor Gregorio Verdugo), Jolene Brand (Anna Maria Verdugo), Carlos Romero (Romero Serrano), Joseph Conway (Francisco Palomares), Lee Van Cleef (Antonio Castillo), Wolfe Barzell (Innkeeper).

The second season of *Zorro* opens with Don Diego and Bernardo visiting Monterey, California. They have been sent there by a group of Los Angeles investors to look over an import business. The visitors have barely arrived in town when two men burst into their room and demand the investors' money. Diego claims he doesn't have it and the men leave when the innkeeper investigates the disturbance. All they take is Diego's watch, but he suspects that a local businessman named Verdugo is involved.

ZORRO RIDES ALONE   Airdate: 10/16/58.

Guest Cast: Eduard Franz (Señor Gregorio Verdugo), Jolene Brand (Anna Maria Verdugo),

Wolfe Barzell (Innkeeper), Joseph Conway (Francisco Palomares), Ken Lynch (Pablo).

Diego continues his investigation into Señor Verdugo's business. He suspects Verdugo may be the leader of the robbers, so he sets a trap. Diego tells Verdugo the money is being sent via the Guadalupe Trail and should be arriving shortly, but a servant overhears him.

Horse of Another Color Airdate: 10/23/58.

Guest Cast: Eduard Franz (Señor Gregorio Verdugo), Jolene Brand (Anna Maria Verdugo), Wolfe Barzell (Innkeeper), Carlos Romero (Romero Serrano), Michael Forrest (Anastacio), Ken Lynch (Pablo).

Lieutenant Rafael Santos is ambushed on his way to Monterey and left for dead when the ambushers take his identification and uniform. One of them, a killer named Anastacio, puts on the uniform and rides to Verdugo's, where Diego is discussing the investment deal. The real soldier is not dead, however, and his beautiful white horse stands guard by his side.

Señorita Makes a Choice, The Airdate: 10/30/58.

Guest Cast: Eduard Franz (Señor Gregorio Verdugo), Jolene Brand (Anna Maria Verdugo), Carlos Romero (Romero Sorreno), Ken Lynch (Pablo).

After the Verdugos return to Monterey, Anna Maria enters their home and discovers that her father is missing. Pablo, their former servant, tells her the old man is being held hostage and will be killed unless she hands over 45,000 pesos believed to be in the house. Diego and Bernardo arrive and Pablo slips away, warning Anna Maria that her father will be killed if she tells anyone of the kidnapping.

Production Note:

- Dan Blocker, who is best known for his role as Hoss Cartwright in television's long-running series *Bonanza*, played an unbilled role as a blacksmith.

Rendezvous at Sundown Airdate: 11/06/58.

Guest Cast: Eduard Franz (Señor Gregorio Verdugo), Jolene Brand (Anna Maria Verdugo), Carlos Romero (Romero Sorreno), Ken Lynch (Pablo).

The kidnappers send word that Anna Maria must meet them if she wants proof her father is still alive, but Diego warns her it is a trick. A would-be suitor argues that she must go, so she agrees to go with him, Garcia, and Reyes. Diego was right, and the trap is sprung.

New Order, The Airdate: 11/13/58.

Guest Cast: Barbara Luna (Theresa Modesto), Perry Lopez (Joaquin Castenada), Ric Roman (Capitan Briones), Frank Wilcox (Luis Rico).

Before he returns home, Sergeant Garcia angers Theresa, a tamale vendor, when he tries to carry out the orders of the acting governor. Luis Rico has decided that all of the vendors must be removed from the plaza despite their objections, and Diego promises Theresa he will try to help. She shows her appreciation with hugs and kisses, thereby angering her boyfriend, Joaquin Castenada, who was watching. Joaquin starts to say something to her but is knocked aside by Capitan Briones, leader of a band of soldiers named "Especials."

Eye for an Eye, An Airdate: 11/20/58.

Guest Cast: Barbara Luna (Theresa Modesto), Perry Lopez (Joaquin Castenada), Ric Roman (Capitan Briones).

Joaquin and several followers begin a series of raids against the Especials, which culminates with the beating of Capitan Briones. The soldier issues a death order for Joaquin and sends his men after Theresa, intending to force her to reveal his hiding place. She asks Diego to hide her, and with Garcia's assistance, he protects her from the searchers.

Zorro and the Flag of Truce Airdate: 11/27/58.

Guest Cast: Barbara Luna (Theresa Modesto), Perry Lopez (Joaquin Castenada), Ric Roman (Capitan Briones), Frank Wilcox (Luis Rico), John Litel (Governor).

Capitan Briones escalates his campaign against Joaquin by ordering that a peon be whipped until he reveals the rebel's hiding place. Zorro uses his own whip to stop Briones, then frees the peon. Shortly after, the real governor returns and Rico explains that his harsh rule was only imposed to make the capital a well-run city. Rico then convinces the governor to offer the rebel a truce so he can explain his case, planning all the while to kill Joaquin as soon as the outlaw turns himself in.

AMBUSH   Airdate: 12/04/58.
Guest Cast: Barbara Luna (Theresa Modesto), Perry Lopez (Joaquin Castenada), Ric Ramon (Capitan Briones), Frank Wilcox (Rico), John Litel (Governor).

The broken truce has convinced Joaquin that Diego cannot be trusted and that, if not for Zorro, he would have been killed. When Diego and Bernardo ride to his camp to explain, the rebel leader orders his men to lock the visitors in leg irons until he can decide upon a suitable fate for them. Joaquin announces his plans to kill the governor the next day while he visits a local shrine. When he tries to ride there, however, Joaquin is accidentally captured by Sergeant Garcia.

PRACTICAL JOKER, THE   Airdate: 12/11/58.
Guest Cast: Jolene Brand (Anna Maria Verdugo), Richard Anderson (Ricardo del Amo).

Anna Maria Verdugo returns to Monterey from San Francisco and becomes the object of Ricardo del Amo's affection. This friend of Diego's is an incurable practical joker. Ricardo realizes that Diego is also attracted to Anna Maria and hopes to lessen the competition by having some fun at his friend's expense.

Production Note:

• This episode was the first screen credit for assistant director Ron Miller, who would eventually rise to head the Studio.

FLAMING ARROW, THE   Airdate: 12/18/58.
Guest Cast: Whit Bissell (Commandante Luis del Guerro), Jolene Brand (Anna Maria Verdugo), Yvette Dugay (Milana del Carmen), Richard Anderson (Ricardo del Amo).

Ricardo asks for Diego's help in winning Anna Maria's heart, for he feels Zorro is too much competition for the two men to overcome. If they can make it seem that Zorro is seeing another woman, Anna Maria will scorn him, thus dropping the field of suitors to a more manageable size. Ricardo plans to accomplish this by dressing as Zorro and serenading Anna Maria's cousin, Milana del Carmen.

ZORRO FIGHTS A DUEL   Airdate: 12/25/58.
Guest Cast: Jolene Brand (Anna Maria Verdugo), Richard Anderson (Ricardo del Amo).

Diego doesn't know that Ricardo has developed a hatred for Zorro. He makes matters worse when he substitutes a block of wood for a box of chocolates intended for Anna Maria. When she opens her present and Ricardo sees the wood, complete with a carved "Z," he decides to kill or unmask his foe.

AMNESTY FOR ZORRO   Airdate: 1/01/59.
Guest Cast: John Litel (Governor), Jolene Brand (Anna Maria Verdugo), Richard Anderson (Ricardo del Amo).

Ricardo leaves town but causes another problem for Diego before he goes. Still infatuated with Anna Maria, Ricardo tells her that Zorro would unmask himself if he really loved her. The problem is, Diego does love her, and thus begins to consider turning himself in. The governor offers the outlaw amnesty if he will surrender himself at a public ceremony.

RUNAWAYS, THE   Airdates: 1/08/59, 7/09/59.
Guest Cast: Tom Pittmann (Romaldo), Gloria Castillo (Buena), John Hoyt (Don Tomas Yorba), Arthur Batanides (Lazaro), Mack Williams (Padre).

Two indentured servants who wish to marry find that the law states they must have the permission of their masters. Buena, who works in the de la Vega hacienda, is told she is free to marry, but her boyfriend, Ronaldo, is not so fortunate. One of his co-workers also wants to marry Buena so he convinces their boss that Romaldo plans to run away after the ceremony.

IRON BOX, THE   Airdates: 1/15/59, 8/27/59.
Guest Cast: Harold J. Stone (Salvio), Marc Damon (Eugenio), Tige Andrews (Nava), Rebecca Welles (Moneta), Jerry Oddo (Crispin).

It is time to send the tax money to the governor, and Sergeant Garcia has a plan to thwart any attempt to steal the funds during the long journey. He orders the town blacksmith to build a huge iron box that requires a special key to open it. The money will be placed in the box and the key sent to the governor by a separate route.

GAY CABALLERO, THE   Airdates: 1/22/59, 9/03/59.
Guest Cast: Cesar Romero (Estevan de la Cruz), Patricia Medina (Margarita), Nestor

Paiva (Innkeeper), Howard Mendell (Don Marcos).

Diego's uncle, Estevan de la Cruz, arrives in Los Angeles for an unannounced visit and surprises the de la Vegas when he tells them he plans to be their house guest. Furthermore, he expects them to give a lavish party to welcome him. All of this angers Don Alejandro, but to head off a family dispute, Diego convinces his father that Estevan will leave soon.

TORNADO IS MISSING   Airdates: 1/29/59, 9/10/59.

Guest Cast: Cesar Romero (Estevan de la Cruz), Patricia Medina (Margarita).

Estevan again becomes a problem for Diego when he decides to earn some easy money. Los Angeles is preparing for its annual horse race and Estevan would like to win the prize money, but his horse seems unlikely to win. His luck changes when he comes across Zorro's horse, Tornado, grazing in a hidden field, and he captures the animal.

ZORRO VERSUS CUPID   Airdates: 2/05/59, 9/17/59.

Guest Cast: Cesar Romero (Estevan de la Cruz), Patricia Medina (Margarita), Howard Wendell (Don Marcos).

Still hoping to strike it rich during his visit to Los Angeles, Estevan shows a great deal of interest in a young woman when he learns she comes from a wealthy family. Don Alejandro accuses Estevan of only being attracted to Margarita because of her money, but the suitor denies the charges, forcing Diego to dress as Zorro in an attempt to frighten Estevan away.

LEGEND OF ZORRO, THE   Airdates: 2/12/59, 9/24/59.

Guest Cast: Cesar Romero (Estevan de la Cruz), Patricia Medina (Margarita), Howard Wendell (Don Marcos).

Estevan still hopes to marry the wealthy Margarita but he knows that Zorro will continue to oppose him. Don Alejandro suggests that if Estevan were to settle down and begin farming, Zorro would realize that his intentions are honorable. He gives the visitor a small plot of land and wishes him well in his endeavor.

SPARK OF REVENGE   Airdates: 2/19/59, 9/28/59.

Guest Cast: Robert Vaughn (Miguel Roverto), Neil Hamilton (Don Hilario), Richard Devon (Mauridio Alviso), Mark Sheeler (Tonio Alviso), John Zaremba (Magistrado).

Los Angeles is suffering from a severe drought and tempers are fraying as crops and animals die from the lack of water. Most of the landowners are helping their neighbors by allowing them access to the few wells and springs that have not yet dried up. Don Hilario is an exception to this policy, though, for he fears his own crops will suffer. A neighbor, Miguel Roverto, a peasant with a small farm, begins to steal needed water. The Alviso brothers, who work for Hilario, catch Roverto in the act and beat him severely, warning him never to return.

Production Note:

- Guest star Neil Hamilton later starred as Commissioner Gordon in the extremely popular series *Batman*.

MISSING FATHER, THE   Airdates: 2/26/59, 7/16/59.

Guest Cast: Annette Funicello (Anita Cabrillo), Carlos Rivas (Ruiz), Arthur Space (Gonzales), Penny Santon (Cresencia), Wendell Holmes (Storekeeper).

A mystery develops when a teenage girl arrives in the pueblo and asks for directions to a ranch no one has ever heard of. Anita Cabrillo has been studying at a boarding school, and she has come to visit her father, whom she has not seen in many years. Anita attracts a small crowd when she asks about Don Cabrillo, who is unknown in the city, and Diego offers to let her stay at his house until the mystery can be solved.

Production Note:

- Annette's appearance on *Zorro* was a birthday present from Walt Disney, who knew that the former Mouseketeer had a crush on Guy Williams.

PLEASE BELIEVE ME   Airdates: 3/05/59, 7/23/59.

Guest Cast: Annette Funicello (Anita Cabrillo), Carlos Rivas (Ruiz), Arthur Space (Rafael Gonzales), Wendell Holmes (Storekeeper), Greigh Phillips (Jose), Penny Santon (Cresencia).

Anita is still hoping to find her father, but Sergeant Garcia has decided she is nothing but a liar and wants to send her back to Spain. Only Diego believes her story, and he tells her she needs to supply some proof of her father's existence. She mentions a package of letters her father sent to her, and Diego asks to see them. Anita goes to her room but quickly returns without them, claiming they have been stolen. When Don Alejandro again voices his doubts about her story, he arranges for her to leave on the next ship.

BROOCH, THE Airdates: 3/12/59, 7/30/59.

Guest Cast: Annette Funicello (Anita Cabrillo), Carlos Rivas (Ruiz), Arthur Space (Rafael Gonzales/Don Miguel), Wendell Holmes (Storekeeper), Griegh Phillips (Jose), Penny Santon (Cresencia).

Don Alejandro remains firm in his wish to send Anita back to Spain and tells the girl to pack her bags. As she leaves, Alejandro stops her, for Anita is wearing a brooch that he once gave to the mission to be sold at a charity auction. When she tells him her father sent it to her in Spain, Alejandro finally believes her story about the missing man.

ZORRO AND THE MOUNTAIN MAN Airdates: 3/19/59, 8/06/59.

Guest Cast: Jonathan Harris (Don Carlos), Jeff York (Joe Crane), Jean Willes (Carlotta), Paul Richards (Hernando).

When a jovial mountain man, Joe Crane, arrives in the pueblo, he is threatened with arrest for traveling in Spanish territory without official permission. Sergeant Garcia warns him to leave town but changes his mind when Crane buys him a few drinks in the tavern. Not all of Crane's problems can be solved so easily, however, for when he kisses a passing barmaid, he angers Don Carlos Fernandez so greatly that the landowner attacks the visitor.

HOUND OF THE SIERRAS, THE Airdates: 3/26/59, 8/13/59.

Guest Cast: Jonathan Harris (Don Carlos Fernandez), Jeff York (Joe Crane), Jean Willes (Carlotta), Lloyd Corrigan (Sancho), Paul Richards (Hernando).

Thought to be hiding safely in the hills, fugitive Joe Crane instead has sneaked back into the pueblo hoping to recover his hunting rifle and the load of furs he gathered during the trapping season. He also wants to see Carlotta, the barmaid who accidentally started the fight between him and Don Carlos Fernandez.

MANHUNT Airdates: 4/02/59, 8/20/59.

Guest Cast: Jonathan Harris (Don Carlos Fernandez), Jeff York (Joe Crane), Jean Willes
(Carlotta), Lloyd Corrigan (Sancho), Paul Richards (Hernando).

Don Carlos Fernandez decides to draw Joe Crane into the open by laying claim to the mountain man's furs and burro. Diego tries to end the feud by offering to buy the goods, but Fernandez refuses. Only Crane's death will satisfy him now. When Crane hears that Fernandez has his furs, he reacts predictably and goes to the man's hacienda to fight for his possessions.

MAN FROM SPAIN, THE Airdate: 4/09/59.

Guest Cast: Everett Sloane (Andres Felipe Basilio), Gloria Talbott (Moneta), Nestor Paiva (Innkeeper), Robert J. Wilke (Capitan Mendoza).

Another problem looms for Zorro when an arrogant stranger arrives in the pueblo and demands the help of Don Alejandro. Felipe Basilio has been sent by the Spanish government to sell bonds to the local citizens in order to help finance the Spanish war effort, but he gets off to a bad start by interrupting Sergeant Garcia's birthday party and throwing his piñata into the trash.

TREASURE FOR THE KING Airdate: 4/16/59.

Guest Cast: Everett Sloane (Andres Felipe Basilio), Gloria Talbott (Moneta), Robert J. Wilke (Capitan Mendoza), Edgar Barrier (Don Cornelio).

Basilio has begun to enjoy his stay in Los Angeles despite Zorro's interference. He is surprised at how well his war bonds are selling, for the landowners have decided to help support the Spanish government as much as possible. In fact, he and Capitan Mendoza have been able to collect three large chests full of gold. Mendoza suggests that they steal some for themselves before shipping it to Spain, but Basilio has a better idea. He wants it all.

EXPOSING THE TYRANT Airdate: 4/23/59.

Guest Cast: Everett Sloane (Andres Felipe Basilio), Gloria Talbott (Moneta Esperon), Robert J. Wilke (Capitan Mendoza), Edgar Barrier (Don Cornelio Esperon).

Even with his stolen gold gone, Basilio plans to remain in Los Angeles as a wealthy man. He decides to do so in a way that will let him exert a hold over Moneta Esperon, the attractive daughter of a wealthy landowner. Basilio tells Garcia that Spanish law forbids citizens to possess items made in countries

Walt Disney introduces "The Adventures of Mickey Mouse."

Mickey Mouse stars in "The Plausible Impossible."

A scene from "Man and the Moon."

Walt Disney introduces "From Aesop to Hans Christian Andersen."

A scene from a segment of "From Aesop to Hans Christian Andersen."

Walt Disney introduces "The Story of Robin Hood—Part I."

Jiminy Cricket presents.

Goofy goofing around in "The Goofy Cavalcade of Sports."

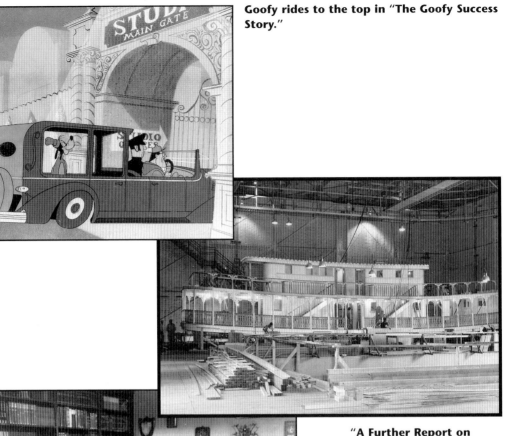

Goofy rides to the top in "The Goofy Success Story."

"A Further Report on Disneyland (and) A Tribute to Mickey Mouse."

Jiminy Cricket in "On Vacation."

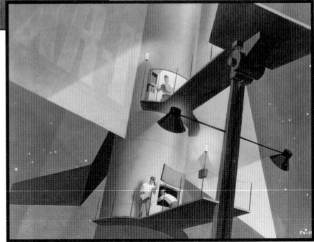

All in a day's work in "Man in Space."

"Dumbo," a story about a baby elephant, is presented by Walt Disney.

A cartoon baby and a mishandled bunny prove to be ideal subjects for Jiminy Cricket in an amusing animated lecture on "You—And Your Sense of Touch," on Walt Disney's *Mickey Mouse Club*.

Disney's Adventures of the Gummi Bears. Pictured from left to right are Tummi, Gruffi, Sunni, Cubbi, Grammi, and Zummi Gummi.

Donald Duck prepares to hit the gong on the *Mickey Mouse Club.*

A song for the *Mickey Mouse Club.*

Mickey leads this bright-eyed brigade of bears to the rousing music of the spirited "Mickey Mouse March" on the *Mickey Mouse Club.*

A model of New Orleans Square was made in intimate detail at WED Enterprises, the Disney arm which created attractions at Disneyland (now called Walt Disney Imagineering). Viewers were taken on a behind-the-scenes tour in this episode, titled "Disneyland—From the Pirates of the Caribbean to the World of Tomorrow."

Rare black beavers star in "The Wise One."

As a great and talented thespian, Donald Duck portrays one of the Three Musketeers in "Your Host, Donald Duck."

Professor Ludwig Von Drake may be a bit zany, but he isn't superstitious. Here he is holding an open umbrella in "The Truth about Mother Goose."

A skunk stalks his prey in "Wonders of the Water Worlds."

Goofy drives his vintage jalopy across a stage filled with comedy surprises during "Disney On Parade."

Holding a copy of *The Reluctant Dragon*, Walt Disney presents "Wind in the Willows."

Two Canada geese migrate south from Oregon to Mexico in "Wild Geese Calling."

Professor Ludwig Von Drake and Herman make a Christmas-week appearance in "Three Tall Tales."

A hound dog feeds his fawn friend in "The Wetback Hound."

In the Florida swamplands, Tiger scrambles up a log to escape a hunter and his dogs in "The Wahoo Bobcat."

Professor Ludwig José Antonio Pablo Rafael Seemore Von Drake demonstrates guitar playing, one of his many talents, in "Von Drake in Spain."

The life of peregrine falcons is explored in "Varda, the Peregrine Falcon."

A true camera addict, José Carioca, the Brazilian parrot, cautions a huge bear to smile as he snaps his photograph in "Two Happy Amigos."

A scene from "Twister, Bull from the Sky."

Walt Disney demonstrates stereophonic sound during "The Peter Tchaikovsky Story."

A helicopter view of the jungle riverboat ride at Disneyland in "A Trip thru Adventureland (and) Water Birds."

Dynamite blasting of hidden underground crevasses in "To the South Pole for Science."

A bongo is pursued in "The Track of the African Bongo."

Neither modest nor shy, Donald Duck interrupts his boss to remind him who the star of this show is in "The Story of Donald Duck."

Two bobcat cubs peer out from their hiding place in "Survival in Nature."

A burro fights a killer mountain lion in "Wild Burro of the West."

Walt Disney introduces "A Story of Dogs," which featured sequences from *Lady and the Tramp* and highlights from Pluto's career.

Paka, a lost polar bear cub, searches for her mother in "Snow Bear."

Harriet, a domesticated Great Horned Owl, becomes a peeping tom while trying to get home in "The Owl that Didn't Give a Hoot."

Shokee, a Florida panther cub, surveys his swampland home as his companion guides their dugout through the marshes in "Shokee, The Everglades Panther."

Walt Disney talks about the art of animation at the beginning of "The Plausible Impossible."

When bear cubs Tuffy and Tubby can't find their mother, they decide to poke around on their own and get into trouble in this scene from "Yellowstone Cubs."

Hector in a scene from "Pancho, the Fastest Paw in the West."

Brand-new Disney character Moby Duck talks about his Pacific Ocean tour as his boat slips away, pulling a seagull along with it, in "Pacifically Peeking."

Two silver foxes stalk their prey in "The Silver Fox and Sam Davenport."

Henry Becquerel, a French scientist, is credited with the accidental discovery of radioactivity in 1896, in a scene from "Our Friend the Atom."

that are at war with Spain. Those who do will forfeit their entire households to those who inform on the lawbreakers.

ZORRO TAKES A DARE   Airdate: 4/30/59.

Guest Cast: Everett Sloane (Andres Felipe Basilio), Gloria Talbott (Moneta Esperon), Robert J. Wilke (Capitan Mendoza), Edgar Barrier (Don Cornelio Esperon).

Humiliated by Zorro, Basilio gets his revenge by arresting Sergeant Garcia and hoisting him in the air in the public square outside the cuartel. A large sign dares Zorro to rescue Garcia, but Diego knows Basilio will have hidden lancers throughout the area. When night arrives, so does Zorro, using Bernardo to help create a diversion that draws the soldiers out of town.

AFFAIR OF HONOR, AN   Airdate: 5/07/59.

Guest Cast: Tony Russo (Avila), Booth Colman (Pineda).

Pedro Avila, recently arrived in the pueblo, earns a meager living by betting other men that he can beat them in a sword fight. He tries to talk Diego into betting, but Diego refuses, as Diego knows he must keep his skill a secret. This gives Avila and his friend Tony Pineda an idea about how to get rich. They plan to force Diego into a duel, then allow the frightened man to buy his way out of the situation.

SERGEANT SEES RED, THE   Airdate: 5/14/59.

Guest Cast: Joseph Calleia (Padre Simeon), Richard Reeves (Carlos).

Sergeant Garcia returns from escorting Padre Simeon on a trip from San Diego and is surprised to find that almost everyone in Los Angeles has contracted the measles. The doctor has placed the entire pueblo under quarantine and restricted residents to their homes. Even the soldiers cannot leave the cuartel.

INVITATION TO DEATH   Airdate: 5/21/59.

Guest Cast: Joan Evans (Leonar), George N. Neise (Capitan Felipe Arrellanos), John Litel (Governor), Douglas Kennedy (Manuel).

The governor of California is attacked during a visit to Los Angeles with his daughter and aide, and barely escapes with his life. Taken to the de la Vega house to recover, he is much too weak to travel for several days. The aide, Capitan Arrellanos, tells Diego he suspects the attack to be the work of the Rebatos, a group that wants to sever ties with the government in Spain.

CAPTAIN REGRETS, THE   Airdate: 5/28/59.

Guest Cast: Joan Evans (Leonar), John Litel (Governor), George N. Neise (Capitan Felipe Arrellanos).

Capitan Arrellanos refuses to help the Rebatos in their attempts to kill the governor. Instead, he chooses another plan designed to make him the head of the government. He asks the governor's daughter to declare her father too ill to continue in office. Furious at this request, Leonar refuses to cooperate. She then tells her father of the aide's plot.

MASQUERADE FOR MURDER   Airdate: 6/04/59.

Guest Cast: Joan Evans (Leonar), George N. Neise (Capitan Felipe Arrellanos), John Litel (Governor), Don Haggerty (Carmelo).

Capitan Arrellanos continues his attempts to rule California by hiring Carmelo, a recent arrival to the pueblo, to kill the governor. Diego and Bernardo overhear the plan but don't act at once, hoping instead to learn who the other conspirators are. The governor has begun to recover and spends his time sitting outside on the patio, which prompts Don Alejandro to give a party to celebrate his better health.

LONG LIVE THE GOVERNOR   Airdate: 6/11/59.

Guest Cast: Joan Evans (Leonar), George N. Neise (Capitan Felipe Arrellanos), John Litel (Governor), Douglas Kennedy (Manuel).

The recovering governor is beginning to become irritated by his confinement to the de la Vega home. At times it seems as if the only thing that can pacify him is a music box. Almost as soon as it begins to play, the governor falls asleep. Knowing that the Rebatos are still trying to kill the governor, Diego uses the box to lull him to sleep, then Bernardo moves him to safety.

FORTUNE TELLER, THE   Airdate: 6/18/59.

Guest Cast: Roxane Berard (Lupita), Alex Gerry (Don Sebastian), Paul Dubov (Gustavo), Kay Kuter (Hernando).

Don Sebastian, a friend of the de la Vegas, is growing impatient at the delay of the stage to Monterey, for he is carrying a purse full of gold and is afraid it may be stolen. While waiting in the tavern with Diego, he makes the mistake of mentioning the gold and is overheard by three crooked entertainers.

SEÑOR CHINA BOY   Airdate: 6/25/59.

Guest Cast: James Hong (Chinese Boy), Charles Horvath (John Vinson), Oliver Blake (Tomas Gregorio).

A Chinese boy escapes from a ship in San Pedro's harbor and tries to hide in Los Angeles. He is unable to seek help, for he speaks only his native language. Discovered hiding in a warehouse, he is arrested as a thief. The boy's only hope is a scribbled message he gives to Diego. Not knowing Chinese, Diego sends it to the mission, knowing Father Ignacio can translate it.

Production Note:

• Father Ignacio was played by Richard Deacon, best known for his role as Mel Cooley on *The Dick Van Dyke Show*.

FINDERS KEEPERS   Airdate: 7/02/59.

Guest Cast: Fintan Meyler (Celesta Villagrana), Richard Garland (Lopez), Rudolfo Hoyos (Montez).

Celesta Villagrana and her servant, Montez, are on their way to Los Angeles when a hooded robber stops them and steals her jewelry. The thief knocks the travelers to the ground then departs, leaving Celesta lying there unconscious. Bernardo rides by and sees a piece of jewelry glinting in the sunlight. He stops to pick it up but Celesta awakens and mistakes him for a thief. She screams, and Sergeant Garcia arrives in time to hear her accuse Bernardo, which leaves him no choice but to arrest the mute servant.

Additional
Series

10

The Mouse Factory

After *The Mickey Mouse Club* and *Zorro* both left the air, the Studio's only television series for many years was the anthology series. Disney did consider producing other series, but the company had come to increasingly concentrate its efforts on the theme parks, and the television division suffered.

When Walt Disney World opened its doors in 1971, some of the pressure throughout the Disney organization began to lessen, and people once again started to look more seriously at the possibility of getting another series on the air. One of these was veteran animator Ward Kimball.

Kimball returned to television to create a new series for the 1971–72 season. *The Mouse Factory*, which premiered on January 26, 1972, used Disney cartoons to provide a weekly theme. Each episode featured a celebrity host or hostess who would interact in skits with costumed characters from the theme parks, then introduce clips from classic Disney cartoons. *The Mouse Factory* was sold into syndication for airing on a weekly basis.

Episode Descriptions

Each of the episodes is described below in air-date order, divided by season. Episodes 1–17 were aired during the first season, and episodes 18–43 during the second season.

VACATIONS (Show #1)
This episode looks at a custom appreciated throughout the world—vacations. Although most workers look forward all year to their vacations, many of these respites from work end in disaster. Charles Nelson Reilly is the victim of several such holidays, and he agrees with Donald Duck that a nice safe picnic would be a better idea.

WOMEN'S LIB (Show #2)
Jo Anne Worley is the hostess for this look at how women have been improving their positions in life. For example, rather than facing her kitchen chores as drudgery, she dances through them, then watches the dancing hippos and ostriches from *Fantasia*.

FOLK TALE FAVORITES (Show #3)
Host Johnny Brown looks at many songs and stories that have been written about folk heroes. The show includes scenes from *The Tortoise and the Hare*, *Song of the South*, *Brave Little Tailor*, and *The Ugly Duckling*.

SPOOKS AND MAGIC (Show #4)
Phyllis Diller is the owner of a rooming house with some unwanted guests. The place is haunted by ghosts, and she decides to rid herself of the spooks by hiring Mickey, Donald, and Goofy, as seen in *Lonesome Ghosts*.

PHYSICAL FITNESS (Show #5)
Don Knotts, the unlikely proprietor of a physical fitness club, tries to explain his techniques to Goofy as seen in *No Smoking*. Knotts demonstrates his theories with the help of Donald Duck and Snow White.

GREAT OUTDOORS, THE (Show #6)
Hoping to prove that life in the great outdoors is not all it's reputed to be, Dom DeLuise hosts this spoof of recreational pursuits.

WATER SPORTS (Show #7)
Joe Flynn, star of several Disney movies, returns to the Studio for a look at some of the ways people enjoy life on or near the water. The show uses scenes from several Goofy cartoons.

Man at Work (Show #8)

Everyone needs a job and Donald Duck is no exception. Host John Byner comes to his assistance by opening an employment agency and sending Donald to a construction site that needs a steam-shovel operator.

Music (Show #9)

Former co-stars of the 1960s syndication of *The Mickey Mouse Club* (Hub and Bub), Canadian entertainers Skiles and Henderson arrive at *The Mouse Factory* to show how important sound effects and music can be. They begin by visiting the Sound Effects Department, where strange gadgets are used to create a wide variety of sounds. Clips from several cartoons are intercut with scenes of the hosts recreating the original sound effects.

Interplanetary Travel (Show #10)

Jonathan Winters appears in a variety of roles as he presents this spoof of space travel. His first character is that of Professor Eric Antiquity, the alleged inventor of rocket propulsion and the world's oldest astronaut. Antiquity now spends his days in a rocket-powered rocking chair, but he takes the time to show several old films from the early days of flight.

Production Note:

- Footage was also included from *Trip to the Moon* (from the Rocket to the Moon attraction at Disneyland).

Homeowners (Show #11)

Owning a home is not a simple thing. Host Jim Backus demonstrates this by showing how salesmen attempt to lure unsuspecting buyers with outrageous claims about the comfort and attractiveness of available properties. Very often these homes need repair, or one may suffer the same fate as Donald in *How to Have an Accident in the Home*.

Spectator Sports (Show #12)

Charles Nelson Reilly returns to host *The Mouse Factory*, this time to discuss the various types of sports one can enjoy by just watching. One of these is horse racing, as seen in *They're Off*, where several bettors try to defy the odds to find a winning system. Reilly also takes a look at basketball, boxing, and the modern decathlon.

Production Notes:

- It was originally planned for George Carlin to star in this episode.

- New soundtracks were provided for several of the cartoons, making them basically serve as backgrounds for Reilly's jokes.

Horses (Show #13)

Hostess Jo Anne Worley claims that horses are a cowboy's best friend. Although a horse's size may be intimidating, Worley claims it's easy to learn *How to Ride a Horse*, as seen in the Goofy cartoon.

Aviation (Show #14)

Mankind's interest in flight is the subject of this show, and host Johnny Brown sets the mood by dressing as a World War I flying ace. Footage from *Victory through Air Power*, *Flying Jalopy*, and *Goofy's Glider* provides just a few of the clips featured in this episode.

Back to Nature (Show #15)

Although civilization has its advantages, more and more people long to get back to nature. Host Wally Cox shows that nature, like the "good old days," isn't all it's reputed to be. He begins with an unusual form of entertainment, the "scorpion dance" from *The Living Desert* and square dancing from *Johnny Appleseed*, first seen in *Melody Time*.

Bullfighting to Bullfrogs (Show #16)

Host Pat Buttram, dressed as a matador, begins the show by talking of bullfights as he sells tacos. When the real matador enters the ring, he encounters *Ferdinand the Bull*, the most timid animal ever to be entered into the competition. Some of the other clips in this episode include scenes from *Baggage Buster*, *Bear Country* and *Two-Gun Mickey*.

Sports (Show #17)

Pat Paulsen teams up with Goofy for a look at the skills needed to master a variety of sports. Each demonstration presents its own set of problems, but Goofy valiantly continues to try, despite a steady dose of physical punishment.

Alligators (Show #18)

Host Johnny Brown describes alligators as having three parts—the eating part; the tail part; and the middle part, which keeps the eating part from eating the tail part. He goes on to describe how alligators have been featured prominently in a number of Disney films.

PAUL BUNYAN (Show #19)

Jim Backus serves as the host for this look at one of America's true folk heroes. The Disney cartoon *Paul Bunyan* begins with a storm washing a strange baby onto a beach in Maine. Paul is the biggest baby anyone has ever seen and the townspeople all pitch in to care for the boy, who grows to enormous height.

BULLFIGHTING (Show #20)

Just as baseball is known as "America's national pastime," so is bullfighting in Spain. Host Bill Dana explains that part of the excitement is generated by the sheer size of the bulls, which weigh over 1,000 pounds each. Although usually only the bravest of men will face these beasts, there are some exceptions as demonstrated by Goofy.

KNIGHTHOOD (Show #21)

Henry Gibson hosts the show in the costume of a court jester to set the mood for tales of brave knights and ladies in distress. Scenes are shown from *Knight for a Day*, *Sword in the Stone*, and *Ye Olden Days*.

PLUTO (Show #22)

Mickey's long-time pet and co-star is featured as John Astin hosts a tribute to Pluto. One of his earliest appearances was in *The Mad Dog*, where a problem with a bar of soap causes a dog catcher to mistakenly think Pluto has contracted rabies. Many other roles followed and Pluto established himself as a star in his own right.

Production Note:

- Pluto's first appearance was as an unnamed prison dog who searched for an escaped Mickey in *The Chain Gang*.

GOLIATH II (Show #23)

Veteran Disney star Kurt Russell presents a look at elephants in general and Goliath II in particular. His guest star is a two-year-old baby elephant. Scenes from several live-action films provide a quick study of elephant life in the wild, including the close family structure the animals enjoy.

MOUSE SHOW, THE (Show #24)

Although Mickey is undoubtedly the world's most famous mouse, the Disney Studio has also told the story of other mice. Dave Madden hosts a look at several of these perform-ers, beginning with *The Flying Mouse*. Other scenes feature mice from *Cinderella* and *The Country Cousin*.

CATS (Show #25)

Hostess Shari Lewis tries to convince her puppet friend Hush Puppy that cats aren't all bad, but the dog won't agree. Lewis decides to educate him by relating the history of cats, going as far back as ancient Egypt, where cats were thought of as gods.

Hush Puppy identifies with Pluto's treatment of the cats, so Lewis shows him scenes from Pluto cartoons.

BEN FRANKLIN (Show #26)

Host Wally Cox begins this look at Ben Franklin, one of colonial America's scientific and political leaders, by remarking that a man is only as good as his inspirations. Legend has it, he adds, that many of Ben's projects were successful due to a church mouse named Amos, as seen in *Ben and Me*.

MICKEY (Show #27)

Annette Funicello continues her long association with Mickey Mouse by hosting this look at his illustrious career. An early black-and-white cartoon, *The Barnyard Broadcast*, shows Mickey in a role that demonstrates the superstar's versatility. Another chapter in Mickey's story opened in 1935 with the introduction of color and he has continued to delight movie audiences ever since.

Production Notes:

- Mickey's vital statistics? Height 2 feet 3 inches, weight 13 pounds.
- A number of clips from black-and-white cartoons were tinted sepia for use in this episode.

LIONS (Show #28)

The proud "king of the jungle" is the subject of this episode, and host Henry Gibson begins by mentioning that not all lions are worthy of that title. He uses *Lambert, The Sheepish Lion* as an example, for Lambert is one of the most timid lions ever born. Other scenes include footage from *The Great Cat Family*, *The African Lion*, and *Lion Around*.

CONSCIENCES (Show #29)

Everybody has a conscience. The problem is, some people don't pay attention to it. Harry Morgan claims that mankind has been struggling with the battle between good and evil since the days of the cavemen. He uses *Donald's Better Self*, *Pinocchio*, and *Lend a Paw* as examples of such conflicts.

NOAH'S ARK (Show #30)
Over the years the Disney animators produced two very different versions of the story of Noah and his ark. Bill Dana introduces the earlier of the two, *Father Noah's Ark*, which was produced using conventional animation techniques. He then introduces the Studio's remade story of 1959. *Noah's Ark* was filmed using stop-motion animation and items such as erasers, corks, and paper clips.

HUNTING (Show #31)
Various types of hunting are explored as John Astin explains that men began to hunt for food and now sometimes hunt purely for sport. He demonstrates this with *The Fox Hunt*, *No Hunting*, and *Moose Hunters*.

SPORTS (Show #32)
In the not-so-distant past the only way to enjoy viewing a sporting event was to attend in person. Examples are seen in *Toby Tortoise Returns*, *Touchdown Mickey*, and *Tiger Trouble*.

TUGBOATS (Show #33)
The largest of ships needs the services of the lowly tugboat, claims host Dave Madden. In fact, the larger the vessel, the more it needs the help of a tugboat to safely dock and to navigate the crowded waters of modern harbors. Examples of this are shown from *Tugboat Mickey*, *Steamboat Willie*, and *Little Toot*, first seen in *Melody Time*.

AUTOMOBILES (Show #34)
Although cars have brought many pluses to modern living, they are not without their own unique problems. Host Ken Berry mentions how a tiny puncture in just one tire can place an entire car out of commission, as seen in *Donald's Tire Trouble*. Other complications are shown in *Mickey's Service Station* and *Susie, the Little Blue Coupe*.

TRAINS (Show #35)
One of Walt Disney's personal interests was trains, a hobby shared by many other Studio employees, including the producer and director of this show, Ward Kimball. As a result, the Studio produced several shorts about trains. Harry Morgan hosts this look at some of them, including *Mickey's Choo-Choo*, *Pigs Is Pigs*, and *The Brave Engineer*.

HOMES (Show #36)
Jim Backus hosts a look at how different homes serve the needs of different inhabitants as seen in *The Little House*, *Perri*, *Nature's Better Built Homes*, and *Building a Building*.

RELUCTANT DRAGON, THE (Show #37)
Cast as a wandering minstrel, Wally Cox cautions that not all stories about dragons are true. Usually depicted as flame-breathing and thoroughly despicable beasts, dragons have been blamed for everything from kidnapping damsels to causing droughts and famines. Cox decides to set the record straight by telling the story of *The Reluctant Dragon*.

WHEELS (Show #38)
The cartoon *Donald and the Wheel* serves as the core of this episode, and host Johnny Brown describes how the seemingly simple wheel is the basis for many of mankind's greatest inventions.

WINTER FUN (Show #39)
Kurt Russell begins the show by complaining that southern California is a nice place to live unless you like snow. Luckily, the Studio's special effects technicians can produce a storm on demand, thereby setting the mood for this animated look at winter sports.

PENGUINS (Show #40)
Annette Funicello returns for another visit to *The Mouse Factory*, bringing with her an Adelie dwarf penguin to introduce a series of cartoons starring this unusual bird.

ELEPHANTS (Show #41)
Host Nipsey Russell remarks that as a boy he used to think all elephants lived in circuses. He later learned that elephants live in many other places, but somehow those early memories remain with him. He then introduces *The Big Wash*, *Elmer Elephant*, and *Dumbo*.

MICKEY AND THE BEANSTALK (Show #42)
Puppeteer Shari Lewis tells the story of *Mickey and the Beanstalk*, first seen in

Fun and Fancy Free, to her friend Lamb Chop.

Dancing (Show #43)

Ken Berry, who is a talented dancer in his own right, hosts this look at how the Disney artists have captured several unusual dance routines on film. Scenes are included from *Mickey's Birthday Party, How to Dance, All the Cats Join In* (first seen in *Make Mine Music*), and *Woodland Cafe.*

The Limited Series

In addition to the Studio's regular series, Disney has also created several "limited" series. Each of these was produced with the advance knowledge that there would not be enough episodes made to fill a full season, although industry logic has it that several full seasons are needed to make a profit. Despite this apparent stumbling block, there are several reasons why the Studio would undertake projects that would seemingly never turn a profit.

In the early days of television, a network would generally commit to thirty-nine episodes of a new series, and the show would be aired as planned regardless of the ratings. When the switch from advertiser-owned series to producer-owned efforts came about, advertisers were then often free to switch their commercials to higher rated programs. This then made it impossible for the networks to earn a profit on low-rated series. As a result, they started to cancel shows that were rating failures, and for the first time, a series could be taken off the air before all of the episodes were produced or broadcast.

Taking a show off the air during the season meant, of course, that a replacement series was needed to fill the same slot. A producer could limit the potential loss for an unsold pilot if costs could be spread across several episodes. Likewise, if a network were to order a limited number of episodes instead of a full season, they could limit their own financial exposure, and assure viewers that a preset number of episodes would be aired. Thus, the limited series concept was born.

Disney experimented with several limited series between 1982 and 1985 although none of them did particularly well in the ratings. Each of the series is described below.

Meet Me at Disneyland

Marketing studies had shown that Disneyland was a success in attracting families to the Park, but weeknight attendance during the summer was lower than desired. The Studio hoped that they could somehow increase attendance all summer long and at a lower cost. The answer was to be *Meet Me at Disneyland*, a live show broadcast directly from Disneyland each week.

Each of the episodes is described below in airdate order.

MAIN STREET U.S.A.   Airdate: 6/09/62.
Cast: Walt Disney, Johnny Jacobs, Fred MacMurray, June Haver, The Firehouse Five, Ward Kimball, The Disneyland Band, Jimmy McHugh, Betty Taylor, Gene Jackson, Edward Graves, The Dapper Dans (Ronald G. Browne, Charles Beral, James Schamp, Gene Morford), The Four Cal-Quettes (Mary Ann Lucas, Muffy Cohen, Judy Hersh, Carol McConkey).

The first show in the series opens with a parade on Main Street U.S.A., where the Disneyland Band is playing *There Will Be a Hot Time in the Old Town Tonight*. Host Johnny Jacobs introduces the evening's guests, who pass by in the parade, followed by the arrival of The Firehouse Five in a firetruck with the siren blaring. The show includes lively musical numbers and performances.

PLAZA GARDENS   Airdate: 6/16/62.
Cast: Johnny Jacobs, The Elliott Brothers, Red Norvo, Mavis Rivers, Elliott Reid, The Four Preps (Glen Larson, Bruce Belland, Marv Ingram, Ed Cobb), Janet Leigh, Sandy Di Shell.

Johnny Jacobs opens the show at the Plaza Gardens where the Elliott Brothers and their

"Disneyland Date Nighters" are warming up. The Elliott Brothers are starting their sixth year at the Plaza Gardens, and they lead the group in a number of swing songs. The show also includes comedy, impersonations, and dance performances.

RHYTHM ON THE RIVER   Airdate: 6/23/62.

Cast: Johnny Jacobs, Ken Murray, Pamela and Janie Murray, Leo Diamond, Betty Taylor, Donnie Brooks, The Four Shamrocks, Frankie Carle, The Young Men of New Orleans (Harvey Brooks, Alton Redd, Mike Delay, Polo Barnes, Johnny St. Cyr), Monette Moore, Fulton Burley, The Excelsior Banjo Band, Judy Michaels, Tina Olsen, Toni Terry, Louis Prima, Seely Smith.

This show is set along the riverfront in Frontierland, beginning with *Waiting for the Robert E. Lee* performed by The Excelsior Banjo Band. Host Johnny Jacobs is joined by Betty Taylor from the Golden Horseshoe, who introduces the Disneyland group The Young Men of New Orleans. They play a number of tunes and then hop aboard the *Mark Twain* steamboat for more evening entertainment.

SWINGIN' THROUGH SPACE   Airdate: 6/30/62.

Cast: Johnny Jacobs, Annette Funicello, The Four Freshmen (Ross Barbour, Bill Comstock, Ken Albers, Bob Flanigan), Richard "Dick St. John" Gasling, Mary "Dee Dee" Sperling, Jimmy Dodd, Cubby O'Brien, The Space Men (Gary Howland, Walter Malzahn, Kay Bell, John A. Schmidt, Sonny Anderson), John Glenn (Space Man), Linda Albertano (Space Girl).

Tomorrowland is the site for this show, which begins as Johnny Jacobs greets the night's guests, who arrive in the miniature cars from the Autopia. One of the guests is Annette Funicello, who hosts the evening's festivities. Music from The Space Men provides a backdrop to scenes of dancers and the crowds throughout Tomorrowland.

THERE'S SOMETHING ABOUT A BAND
Airdate: 7/07/62.

Cast: Johnny Jacobs, Frank De Vol, Jack Smith, The Osmond Brothers, Owen Pope, "Big Fred," The Vonnair Sisters (Rene Von Euer, Sheila Von Euer, Sonya Jeanne Von Euer).

The show opens with scenes of Disneyland to tunes performed by the Disneyland Band.

Several musical and comedy segments follow as host Johnny Jacobs mingles with the crowd and talks to guests about their home towns.

TAHITIAN TERRACE SHOW   Airdate: 7/14/62.

Cast: Johnny Jacobs, Annette Funicello, Bill Skiles, Chief Tui Temakore, Vince Akina, Ernest Tavares, Freddie Tavares, Kaleimomi Nakea, Joan Ann Johnson, Henry Johnson Jr., Henry Keith Johnson, Arleen Keawe, Dolores Domasin (Orchid), William Ornelas, Rainbow Valentin, Michael Koaki Kauhi.

The blowing of a ceremonial conch shell opens this look at Polynesian dancers, beginning with the Royal Tahitians at Disneyland. Troupe member Henry Johnson describes some of the differences in dances between islands, and the group demonstrates some of the more popular dances.

FUN IN FRONTIERLAND   Airdate: 7/21/62.

Cast: Johnny Jacobs, Villa Fontana Violinists, The June Rudell Quintet (June Rudell, Don Beamsley, Jud Denaut, Bob Bain, Richard Cornell), Larry Verne, The Gonzalez Trio (Arturo G. Gonzalez, Roberto Gonzalez, Camelita Gonzalez), Brian Keith. Dancers: Antonia Armstrong, Deanna Garcia, Nanolo Reyes, Carmelo Casalenuovo. Zorro unit: Al Cavens, Buddy Van Horn, Gene Brent, Mark Post.

The emphasis this time is on Frontierland, and the show's first guests are the Gonzalez Trio, who perform a series of lively dance numbers. Johnny Jacobs introduces the Villa Fontana Violinists from Mexico City, who play several Mexican folk songs. After Zorro vanquishes a foe on the rooftops, Jacobs takes viewers aboard the Mine Train for an exciting ride through Rainbow Caverns and the Painted Desert.

MUSIC ON THE MALL   Airdate: 7/28/62.

Cast: Walt Disney, Johnny Jacobs, Harry James and His Orchestra, Dave Barry, Carol Lee, Joe Gilbert, Eddie Brown, Bill Munday (Guitar Player), The Osmond Brothers (Allan Osmond, Melvin Osmond, Merrill Osmond, Jay Osmond), Vivienne Wingo.

Johnny Jacobs introduces Dave Barry, who does a short comedy routine, then Jacobs takes viewers on a ride on the Douglas Moon Rocket. After returning to Earth, the show features Harry James and The Osmond Brothers.

FUN IN FANTASYLAND   Airdate: 8/04/62.

Cast: Johnny Jacobs, Ray Anthony and His "Book Ends" and Orchestra, Carl Ballantine (The Great Ballantine), Toni Harper, Vic Dana, Sandy Nelson, Diane Deveraux, Vikki Carr, Pat Hardin (Alice).

A parade of Disney characters passes through the arches of Sleeping Beauty Castle, where Alice from Wonderland joins Johnny Jacobs in introducing the show's guests. The show follows with music, magic, and comedy.

THIS WAS THE WEST   Airdate: 8/11/62.

Cast: Johnny Jacobs, Tex Williams, Cathy Taylor, Larry Verne, Dee Woolem, The Frontiersmen and Joanie (Hal Southern, Wayne West, High Busse, Billy Armstrong, Joanie Hall), Hollywood Square Dancers, Members of Drum and Feather Club, Truman Dailey (Indian Leader), Homer Garret (Square Dance Caller).

The evening begins with Johnny Jacobs riding on the Disneyland Railroad. His journey is interrupted when bandits stop the train, so he uses the time to introduce the show's guests, who are seated in the train's passenger car. Indian dancers perform as viewers tour Frontierland.

SWINGIN' AT THE MAGIC KINGDOM
Airdate: 8/25/62.

Cast: Johnny Jacobs, Frank Sinatra Jr., Ziggy Elman, Lucy Ann Polk, Gloria Wood, Rex Stewart, Chuck Cecil, The Elliott Brothers Band, Sandi Di Shell.

Johnny Jacobs hosts this celebration of swing music. The Elliott Brothers and their orchestra lead the evenings festivities with old favorites.

DIXIE ON THE DELTA   Airdate: 9/01/62.

Cast: Johnny Jacobs, Benny Goodman and His Band, Al Hirt and His Band, The Clara Ward Singers, The Hot Jazz Society Marching Band, Shelton Brooks, The Albert McNeil Choir, Voices of Hope, The Young Men from New Orleans and Kid Ory, Marvin Miller, The Elliott Brothers.

Tonight's show salutes jazz, and it opens at the river boat landing as the Mark Twain pulls away from dock.

Performers include the Hot-Jazz Society Marching Band, the Clara Ward Singers, and the Voices of Hope.

Production Note:

• Jack Benny was to have been a guest star on this episode but was unable to make it

at the last moment, requiring a last-minute rewriting of the script just before the show aired.

TALENT ON PARADE   Airdate: 9/08/62.

Cast: Johnny Jacobs, Attila Galambo, Kay Bell and the Spacemen, The Firehouse Five, The Clara Ward Singers, Inglewood Toppers Band, West Valley Youth Band, Long Beach Junior Concert Band.

The action starts on Main Street as the Seven Dwarfs march toward the camera to sound of *Heigh Ho*. Variations of that song are used throughout the show to introduce each of the acts. This final show features Disneyland performers.

Herbie, The Love Bug

When Disney decided to get back into the limited series arena in 1982, most of the Studio's new offerings were based on prior theatrical and television successes. One of these new series was *Herbie, The Love Bug*. The show had its beginnings in 1969, when the film *The Love Bug* became the highest grossing film of the year.

Series cast: Dean Jones (Jim Douglas), Patricia Hardy (Susan MacLane), Richard Paul (Bo Phillips), Claudia Wells (Julie MacLane), Nicky Katt (Matthew MacLane), Douglas Emerson (Robbie MacLane).

Each of the episodes is described below in airdate order.

HERBIE, THE MATCH MAKER   Airdate: 3/17/82.

Guest Cast: Larry Linville (Randy Bigelow), James Karen (Manager), Stanley Brock (Repossessor), Natalie Core (Mother Bigelow), Kipp Lennon (Raymond), Bryan Utman (Jason), Agatha Kincaid (Mrs. Gurney), Paul Tuerpe (Policeman), Kirk Cameron (Youngster).

Jim Douglas, once a famous auto racer, is now trying to make a living by running a driving school. His business isn't going well and the bank refuses to loan him money to buy new cars, so he must use Herbie, the Volkswagen with a mind of its own, to keep the school afloat. In this episode, Jim's life changes when Herbie helps rescue a hostage during a robbery.

Production Note:

• This show was originally planned as a special.

HERBIE TO THE RESCUE   Airdate: 3/24/82.

Guest Cast: Larry Linville (Randy Bigelow), Jay Varela (Mr. Diaz), Elvia Allman (Mrs. Farnstrom), Natalie Core (Mother Bigelow), Bryan Utman (Jason), Kipp Lennon (Raymond), Richard Caine (Father), Derek Barton (Policeman #1), Wyatt Johnson (Policeman #2), Blake Marion (Patrolman #1), Gerry Black (Patrolman #2), Wally K. Berns (Bagley), Johnny Graves (Boy).

Randy hasn't given up on marrying Susan, despite being left at the altar, so he launches a new campaign to rid himself of his competition, Jim Douglas. His plan is to offer Jim a loan to improve his driving school, then place enough red tape in the way that he can force Jim out of business. A gullible Jim accepts the offer, and his troubles begin.

MY HOUSE IS YOUR HOUSE   Airdate: 3/31/82.

Guest Cast: Larry Linville (Randy Bigelow), Andrea Howard (Diane Darcy), Alejandro Rey (Sergio), Mary Jo Catlett (Mrs. Thornton), Natalie Core (Mother Bigelow), Dennis Robertson (Cagey), Steve Jones (Mac), Bryan Utman (Jason).

With his wedding to Susan rapidly approaching, Jim takes her to the racetrack to meet his former racing friends. There, he introduces her to Sergio, an Italian racer who taunts him about giving up his racing days. Sergio also teases Jim about an old flame, Diane Darcy, who used to race with them, and Susan becomes jealous. Noticing this, Sergio tricks Susan into letting Jim race one lap "for old time's sake." While Jim is driving, Sergio then tries to romance Susan. Herbie sees this and goes wild, making Jim look like a maniac on the course. Susan then begins to worry about Jim's love of racing.

HERBIE, THE BEST MAN   Airdate: 4/07/82.

Guest Cast: Larry Linville (Randy Bigelow), Dick Bakalyan (Detective O'Brien), Natalie Core (Mother Bigelow), Lee Bryant (Elizabeth), Robert Lussier (Minister), Stu Gilliam (Policeman #1), James Emery (Policeman #2), Kathi Sawyer-Young (Miss Schaeffer), Elvia Allman (Mrs. Farnstrom), Bryan Utman (Jason), Wally K. Berns (Bagley), Lee Paul (Rainey).

The day before the wedding, Jim arrives at work and finds himself the guest of honor at a party. He doesn't know that Randy is still hoping to prevent the marriage, and has hired a private detective to find something that might change Susan's mind. When he learns that Jim's record is clear, he decides to place a stink bomb in Herbie to ruin the ceremony.

CALLING DOCTOR HERBIE   Airdate: 4/14/82.

Guest Cast: Dana Elcar (Warden), George Lindsey (Wally), Howard Platt (Larry), Warren Berlinger (Walker), Richard Bull (Dr. Williams), Bryan Utman (Jason).

When Jim and Susan decide they need a bigger car to carry the family, they must leave Herbie at the car lot as collateral on the loan. While they are away, Herbie has a temper tantrum and damages the car lot. Jim can't pay to repair the damage, so Herbie is impounded until Jim can raise the cash. Herbie then flees the lot when two car thieves try to strip him.

Small & Frye

This short-lived sitcom was about a detective who could shrink to six inches, though not when he wanted to. Chip Frye was the diminutive detective and Nick Small was the veteran gumshoe.

Small & Frye was added to the CBS schedule beginning March 7, 1983. The ratings were poor, averaging only 17 percent of the viewing audience each week, and it became clear that there was no chance of success as a full series. *Small & Frye* was dropped from the list of prospective series for the 1983–84 season.

Series cast: Darren McGavin (Nick Small), Jack Blessing (Chip Frye), Debbie Zipp (Phoebe Small), Bill Daily (Dr. Hanratty), Warren Berlinger (Eddie).

Each of the episodes is described below in airdate order.

FIDDLER ON THE HOOF   Airdate: 3/07/83.

Guest Cast: Kristoffer Tabori (Herman Pinkus), Ken Olfson (Freddie the Fence), J. J. Barry (Vinnie), Carolyne Barry (Miss Edwards), Dick Wilson (Bar Fly), Hal Smith (Stage Hand), Fuddle Bagley (Van Driver), Victoria Carroll (Waitress).

For her birthday, private detective Nick Small gives his daughter, Phoebe, tickets to a violin concert by Herman Pinkus, her former childhood friend. When they arrive at the theatre, they're dismayed to learn that the performance has been canceled. Someone has stolen Pinkus's prized Stradivarius violin, and without it, he lacks the confidence to perform. Nick and his partner, Chip Frye, set out to find the missing instrument, which they discover in the possession of a small-time thief.

ENDANGERED DETECTIVES Airdate: 3/14/83.

Guest Cast: Henry Gibson (Dr. Calder), Don Knight (Paulie), Bruce Glover (Frank), Vito Scotti (Angie), Robert Lussier (Health Inspector #1), Tom Scott (Health Inspector #2), Dick Wilson (Bar Fly), Maurice Sherbanee (Aide-de-Camp), Jason Evers (Mr. Ackly).

A scientist's suspicions about illegal chemical dumping place Nick and Chip on a case involving dead ducks and geese on a small pond. Dr. Henry Calder, a member of a group called "Pals of Fowl," has observed trucks from a nearby chemical plant dumping something into his favorite bird sanctuary, so he hires the detectives to stop the Ackly Chemical Co.

CASE OF THE STREET OF SILENCE, THE Airdate: 3/21/83.

Guest Cast: Sharon Farrell (Rita), John McCann (Man), Noel Conlon (Otis), Stu Gilliam (Florist), Victoria Carroll (The Waitress), Dick Wilson (Bar Fly), Joan Crosby (Sister #1), Merie Earle (Sister Rita), Jack Griffin (Cook).

When Nick is visited by a former girlfriend, he assumes she tracked him down out of past affection, but the lovely Rita has more sinister plans. She tells Nick her husband, Otis, is insanely jealous and that she has fled to begin a new life. Somehow, Otis has found her, so she asks Nick to hold a necklace for her until she's safe, then leaves. Outside, she tells her boyfriend that Nick has taken the bait.

SMALL & FRYE (pilot) Airdate: 6/01/83.

Guest Cast: Roddy McDowall (Professor Vermeer), Rue McClanahan (Miss Parsifal), Larry Storch (Waldo), Ken Mars (Grosso), Mike Gazzo (Wilmer), Stacey Shaffer (Miss Locket/Lulu Brown), Danny Dayton (Old Sailor).

A wounded man stumbles into the office and asks Nick and Chip to find his long-lost daughter before he dies. He hasn't seen Lulu since she was a child and can only supply an old photograph to aid in the search. Professor Vermeer spots some small writing on the picture, so Chip shrinks until he can read it. As a result of this clue, the detectives set off for the Melody of Love Orphanage, unaware that they're being followed by two killers.

Production Note:
• The original 1-hour pilot was cut to 30 minutes for this airing.

SCHLOCKY TOO Airdate: 6/08/83.

Guest Cast: Dana Elcar (Problems), Barney Martin (Pops Maloy), Tony Longo (Terry "The Tiger" Tyrell), Dick Wilson (Bar Fly), Ted Zeigler (Timekeeper), Bill Zuckert (Mailman), Victoria Carroll (Waitress).

To help a friend, Nick agrees to supervise a prize fighter, Tiger Tyrell, while his manager is trying to repay a gambling debt. Pops Maloy owes $15,000 to Problems, a loan shark, and wants to drop out of sight until he has the money, for Problems has threatened him. Later, when Pops tries to deliver $300 as a down payment, Problems takes him prisoner and demands that Tiger be ordered to throw his next fight.

CASE OF THE CONCERNED HUSBAND, THE Airdate: 6/15/83.

Guest Cast: Alex Rocco (Jacobi), Albert Salmi (Scar Tongue Malone), Tori Lysdahl (Boom Boom), Oliver Clark (Oliver), John Garwood (Man), Nancy Jeris (Millie), Gwen Watts Jones (Old Woman), Mel Carter (Jacobi's Assistant).

Nick's brother-in-law, Oliver, comes to him with a problem. Several weeks ago he went gambling and passed out after having a drink, and now someone is threatening to mail incriminating pictures of him and another woman to his wife. The detective agrees to help Oliver and takes Chip along to the scene of the gambling party, a run-down hotel. When they attempt to search the room, an elderly woman indignantly claims she lives there and has them thrown out.

Gun Shy

Gun Shy was directly based on the film *The Apple Dumpling Gang*, which was the Studio's biggest success of 1975. Like many other films that find their way to the small screen, it was difficult to maintain the momentum and uniqueness that had made the film so popular. *Gun Shy* averaged only 19 percent of the viewing public each week and was soon canceled.

Series cast: Barry Van Dyke (Russell Donavan), Tim Thomerson (Theodore Ogilvie), Keith Mitchell (Clovis, four episodes), Adam Rich (Clovis, two episodes), Bridgette Andersen (Celia), Henry Jones

(Sheriff Homer McCoy), Geoffrey Lewis (Amos Tucker), Janis Paige (Nettie), Pat McCormick (Colonel Mound).

Each of the episodes is described below in airdate order.

WESTERN VELVET   Airdate: 3/15/83.

Guest Cast: Bernard Fox (Sir Charles Wainright-Roberts), Pat McCormick (Colonel Mound).

The show begins as Clovis tearfully buries his pet snake and tells Donavan he wants a real pet, such as a horse. Donavan turns him down, telling him he's too young, then rides into town. He meets Sir Charles, a wealthy Englishman who wants to gamble, and soon has won the visitor's horse and boots. Sir Charles asks Donavan to hold the horse for collateral until he can obtain money from his office in the East, and the gambler reluctantly agrees.

PARDON ME BOY, IS THAT THE QUAKE CITY CHOO CHOO?   Airdate: 3/22/83.

Guest Cast: John Randolph (Phineas Richmond), Noble Willingham (Mr. Bender), Charles Napier (Carlton).

Donavan borrows money from a bank to pay Amos and Theodore's back taxes, not knowing this will place his life in danger. The problem begins when the inept outlaws catch a prowler on their land and haul him into town to be arrested. They learn he's a surveyor for the B&O Railroad, which plans to extend its line through town. A spokesman announces the only obstacle in the right-of-way is an unsightly shack, which turns out to be Amos and Theodore's home.

WHAT DO YOU MEAN "WE," AMIGO?
Airdate: 3/29/83.

Guest Cast: Lyle Waggoner (The Masked Stranger), Burton Gilliam (Jeremiah Jones), Royce D. Applegate (Luther Jones), Eric Server (Matthew Jones), Peter Miller (Mr. Taylor).

A family of robbers known as the Jones gang heads toward Quake City, planning to continue their protection racket that has worked well in other towns. In town, Clovis and Celia are busily reading a pulp novel about a hero known as The Masked Stranger to a nervous Theodore and Amos. The two robbers' worries about being captured by the Stranger give way to new worries when the Jones gang arrives, for they threaten to take over the town and drive out the competition.

Production Note:

- In one scene in a hotel room, a sketch of Fess Parker as Davy Crockett can be seen framed on the wall.

YOU GOTTA KNOW WHEN TO HOLD 'EM
Airdate: 4/05/83.

Guest Cast: Henry Polic II (Randy Turner).

Donavan is nervous about the pending arrival of another gambler, Randy Turner, for he had once lost his life's savings to the man. When Donavan and Turner meet again, the two men quickly begin a battle of wits and will to see who is the better card player.

READING, WRITING, AND ROBBING
Airdate: 4/12/83.

Guest Cast: Ruth Buzzi (Mrs. Mound), Mayf Nutter (Pecos Larry), Bill Cort (Mr. Barnett), Rex Holman (Sleazy).

There's a problem in Quake City, for frequent robberies of the stage line have left the railroad crews unpaid and they're threatening to walk off the job. The sheriff and Colonel Mound persuade Donavan to ride on the next stage in the hope he can prevent the robbery, but unknown to them, Theodore has a copy of the secret new route.

MAIL ORDER MOMMY   Airdate: 4/19/83.

Guest Cast: Delta Burke (Clementine).

Although Donavan tries his best to raise the children, he's not much of a housekeeper. Clovis and Celia decide they need a mother, and when Amos mentions he wants a mail order bride, they see a way to find Donavan a wife.

Zorro and Son

Disney agreed to produce *Zorro and Son*, a sitcom, as another limited series. The premise was that twenty-five years had passed since the last *Zorro* episode, and the masked avenger has had to slow down as age takes its toll. *Zorro and Son* benefited from the fact that most of the original exterior sets from *Zorro* were still standing on the Burbank lot. Unfortunately, the updated *Zorro and Son* failed to catch on with viewers, attracting only 13 percent of the viewing audience each week. After the five episodes were aired on CBS, the series quickly vanished from sight.

Series cast: Henry Darrow (Don Diego de la Vega/Zorro, Sr.), Paul Regina (Don Carlos de la Vega/Zorro, Jr.), Bill Dana (Bernardo),

Gregory Sierra (Capitan Paco Pico), Richard Beauchamp (Sergeant Sepulveda), Barney Martin (Brothers Napa and Sonoma), John Moschitta, Jr. (Corporal Cassette).

Each of the episodes is described below in airdate order.

ZORRO AND SON (pilot) Airdate: 4/6/83.

Guest Cast: Jack Kruschen (Commandante La Brea), Catherine Parks (Señorita Anita).

Twenty-five years after he first rode to avenge evil, Zorro has begun to slow down. Unwilling to abandon his crusade for justice, he now tries to outwit his foes rather than outfight them. However, when Brother Napa is arrested for selling wine before its time and is unjustly jailed, Zorro again takes up his sword to duel with the pueblo's evil commandante.

BEAUTY AND THE MASK Airdate: 4/13/83.

Guest Cast: Gina Gallego (Angelica), Vic Dunlop (Rapido Roberto), Pete Leal (Peasant/Prisoner), Ernie Fuentes (Peasant), Rita Rogers Aragon (Angelica's Mother).

Commandante Pico's plan to capture Angelica, a suspected gun runner, fails and the rebel reaches the monastery of Brother Napa. Don Carlos, who has been entertaining the children there, rushes to her rescue when Pico follows her and tries to take her back to town. Dressed as Zorro, Carlos takes her to his house, where he promises she'll be safe.

FISTFUL OF PESOS, A Airdate: 4/20/83.

Guest Cast: Pete Leal (Peasant), Don Diamond (Passenger #1), Danny Mora (Passenger #2), Thomas Rosales (Gomez).

Commandante Pico tries a new tactic to end Zorro's influence over the pueblo when he disguises himself in the characteristic black mask and begins robbing the peons. Unaware of this plot, Don Diego is dismayed when the people begin turning against him. When Bernardo discovers the reason, Diego decides to clear his name and avenge this injustice.

WASH DAY Airdate: 4/27/83.

Guest Cast: Catherine Parks (Señorita Anita), Pete Leal (Peasant).

When Bernardo tries to wash his costume, a gust of wind blows the clothes into the picnic lunch of Commandante Pico. The soldier arrests Bernardo and takes him to jail, hoping to prove that Don Diego is the masked rider. He sends for Diego and accuses him, but when Diego is forced to wear the costume, it has shrunk and no longer fits him. Pico tortures Bernardo to learn Zorro's identity and the faithful servant confesses that he is the masked rider in the hope of saving Diego.

BUTCHER OF BARCELONA, THE Airdate: 5/04/83.

Guest Cast: Dick Gautier (El Excellente), Catherine Parks (Señorita Anita), H.B. Haggerty (Capitan Jorge Mendez), Ralph Manza (Waiter), Michael Salcido (Prisoner).

Commandante Pico receives unwelcome news that a life-long rival, El Excellente, is due to arrive for an inspection of the pueblo. He is unaware that Zorro will also be unhappy about the visit, for El Excellente is guarded by Capitan Jorge Mendez, who hates the masked rider and has nearly captured him on several occasions. Diego fears that Mendez, a cruel and harsh man known as the "Butcher of Barcelona," will be named to run the pueblo.

Wildside

In trying to get its limited series on the air, Disney generally stuck to an area they knew well—comedy. With the exception of the early *Meet Me in Disneyland* series, each of the Disney limited series was a comedy, until the premiere of *Wildside*. Set in the turn-of-the-century town of Wildside in northern California, the series centered on an unlikely band of heroes who went by the name of the Wildside Chamber of Commerce.

The hour-long series aired during the 1984–85 season on ABC. Viewers were not interested enough to stay tuned, and *Wildside* lasted only six episodes.

Series cast: Howard Rollins (Bannister Sparks), William Smith (Brodie Hollister), J. Eddie Peck (Sutton Hollister), John DiAquino (Varges de la Cosa), Terry Funk (Prometheus Jones), Sandy McPeak (Governor J. Wendall Summerhayes), Meg Ryan (Cally Oaks), Jason Hervey (Zeke), Kurt Fuller (Elliott Throgmorton), Robin Hoff (Alice Freeze), Gerald Hiken (Father Crool), Jon Fong (Keye Ahn).

Each of the episodes is described below in airdate order.

WELL KNOWN SECRET Airdate: 3/21/85.

Guest Cast: Jack Starrett (General Wollack), Herta Ware (Mrs. Brinkenhoff), Liam Sullivan (Mr. Vick), Lynn Lowry (Estelle), Tommy Lamey (Parks Ritchie),

Robert V. Barron (Cook), Megan Wyss (Julietta), Daniel Bright (Brydon).

Robbing the bank in the town of Wildside proves to be a major mistake for the bandits, for they're quickly captured by the Wildside Chamber of Commerce. The leader of the bank robbers tells the Chamber members he takes his orders from a mysterious ex-Confederate general, who has vowed to take over the area. The general, who seems determined to accomplish his goal, quickly attacks the nearby town of Buzzard Forks.

Production Note:

- The town of Wildside used the Burbank sets originally built for the film *Something Wicked This Way Comes*.

DELINQUENCY OF A MINER Airdate: 3/28/85.

Guest Cast: Joshua Bryant (Pike), Timothy Scott, Harry Frazier (Hagen), Charles Knox Robinson (Bennett), Patrick Culliton (Pete Montana), Charles H. Hyman (Wiley), Gerald Hiken (Father Crool), Jeremy Ross (Reed), John Gallogly (Miner), Chuck Lindsly (Pass Guard), Wayne Van Horne (Gil Rawlings), Richard A. Lundin (Coach Driver).

The Wildside Chamber of Commerce is drawn into a murder case when the governor asks them to look into the man's death. The dead miner had been recruited to a mining camp by a newspaper advertisement, and the governor has reason to suspect something is wrong at the camp.

CRIMEA OF THE CENTURY, THE Airdate: 4/04/85.

Guest Cast: Paul Koslo, Jim Piddock, Jeff Pomerantz, Timothy Scott, Patrick Culliton (Pete Montana), Marta Kristen (Ellen Jonsen), Douglas Dirkson (Fester), Douglas Emerson (Markie Jonsen), Ami Foster (Sissy Jonsen), Owen Bush (Morgan), Peter Browne (British Consul).

A quiet day in Wildside takes an unusual turn when a uniformed band of renegade British soldiers, led by a bagpiper, arrives in town. The men's leader, Brigadier Troopshaw,

"late of the Crimea campaign," asks to stay for several days to rest his men. This is the beginning of a strange pattern of terror around the town, during which farmers are forced from their land and a gold mining camp is burned.

DON'T KEEP THE HOME FIRES BURNING Airdate: 4/11/85.

Guest Cast: Rick Hurst, Martin Kove (Ravenwood), Tracy Reed (Melissa), Timothy Scott, Tommy Lamey (Parks Ritchie), Sid Haig (Burnett), Robert Swan (Hayes), Travis McKenna (Andy Fussell), Tiny Welles (Darryl Fussell), Corky Greene (Tatum), David Wiley (Fire Captain).

The townspeople are being victimized by "insurance salesmen" who are running a protection racket and burning down the homes of those who refuse to pay. The governor asks the Chamber to help track down the men and their leader, Ravenwood, before the government is forced to declare martial law.

BUFFALO WHO? Airdate: 4/18/85.

Guest Cast: James Cromwell (Buffalo Bill Cody), Dee Dee Rescher (Annie Oakley), Alejandro Rey (Ambassador Pintadore), Will Sampson (Sitting Bull), Timothy Scott, Buck Taylor (Captain Angus Flint), Wayne Van Horn (Floyd Thorndike), Christopher Doyle (Mueller), Monty Stuart (Ross).

The arrival of Buffalo Bill Cody and his traveling show takes an unusual turn when a priest says Cody is an imposter. Cody laughs at the accusation, but when the priest mysteriously disappears, the Chamber starts to wonder what is going on.

UNTIL THE FAT LADY SINGS Airdate: 4/25/85.

Guest Cast: Stu Gilliam (Black Hostage), Geoffrey Lewis (Gunman), Jonathan Torp (Detective Sergeant Museliner), Clay Turner (Grosett), Paul Harper (Witz), Anne Mollinar (Fat Lady), Julianne Wilson (Idora).

A vengeful outlaw returns to town looking for Brodie with a pistol that's quicker than Brodie's quickest draw.

Animation!

12

Saturday Mornings and Disney Afternoons

For a company that built its name on animation, it's difficult to believe that it took Disney more than three decades to get an animated series on the air. Yet, that's exactly what happened.

The company had realized the potential benefits of a weekly series at least as far back as the 1967–68 season, when a production account was opened for a project known as *Disneyland A.M. Show-Survey*. The closest the Studio came to such a project was the syndicated *The Mouse Factory* during the 1971–72 and 1972–73 seasons. Several years later still, another project, *Saturday Morning A.M. Show*, was studied for the 1978–79 season, but like its predecessors, nothing ever came of it either. Finally, in 1985, the Studio altered the Saturday morning and syndicated animation markets.

Following is a listing by season of all of Disney's animated series:

1985–86
Saturday Morning series:
  Wuzzles, The (CBS)
  Disney's Adventures of the Gummi Bears
    (NBC)

1986–87
Saturday Morning series:
  Wuzzles, The (CBS)
  Disney's Adventures of the Gummi Bears
    (NBC)

1987–88
Syndicated series:
  DuckTales
Saturday Morning series:
  Disney's Adventures of the Gummi Bears
    (NBC)

1988–89
Syndicated series:
  DuckTales
Saturday Morning series:
  Disney's Adventures of the Gummi Bears
    (NBC)
  The New Adventures of Winnie the Pooh
    (ABC)

1989–90
Syndicated series:
  DuckTales
  Chip 'n Dale's Rescue Rangers
Saturday Morning series:
  Disney's Gummi Bears/Winnie the Pooh
    Hour (ABC)

1990–91
The Disney Afternoon series:
  Disney's Adventures of the Gummi Bears
  DuckTales
  Chip 'n Dale's Rescue Rangers
  Tale Spin
Saturday Morning series:
  The New Adventures of Winnie the Pooh
    (ABC)

1991–92
The Disney Afternoon series:
  DuckTales
  Chip 'n Dale's Rescue Rangers
  Tale Spin
  Darkwing Duck
Saturday Morning series:
  Darkwing Duck (ABC)
  The New Adventures of Winnie the Pooh
    (ABC)

1992–93
The Disney Afternoon series:
  Chip 'n Dale's Rescue Rangers
  Tale Spin

Darkwing Duck
Goof Troop
Saturday Morning series:
Darkwing Duck (ABC)
Disney's The Little Mermaid (CBS)
Goof Troop (ABC)
The New Adventures of Winnie the Pooh
(ABC)
Raw Toonage (CBS)

1993–94
The Disney Afternoon series:
Tale Spin
Darkwing Duck
Goof Troop
Disney's Bonkers
Saturday Morning series:
Disney's The Little Mermaid (CBS)
Marsupilami (CBS)

1994–95
The Disney Afternoon series:
Darkwing Duck
Goof Troop
Monday Mania: The Shnookums &
Meat Funny Cartoon Show
Tuesday–Thursday: Disney's Bonkers
Action Friday: Gargoyles
Disney's Aladdin
Saturday Morning series:
Disney's Aladdin (CBS)
Disney's The Little Mermaid (CBS)

1995–96
The Disney Afternoon series:
Goof Troop
Disney's Bonkers
Disney's Aladdin
Monday–Thursday: Gargoyles
Friday: The Lion King's Timon &
Pumbaa
Saturday Morning series:
Disney's Aladdin (CBS)
Disney's Sing Me a Story: With Belle
(syndicated)
The Lion King's Timon & Pumbaa (CBS)
The New Adventures of Winnie the Pooh
(ABC)

Disney's Wuzzles

The land of Wuz is a strange place, for it rains cowcats and frogdogs. These strange creatures are just some of the residents of Wuz, where all of the inhabitants are actually two animals in one. The main Wuzzles, as they prefer to be known, are Rhinokey (rhinoceros/monkey), Butterbear (butterfly/bear),

Moosel (moose/seal), Bumblelion (bumblebee/lion), Hoppopotamus (rabbit/hippopotamus), and Eleroo (elephant/kangaroo).

These stars were joined by a supporting cast of Wuzzles who were used as story needs dictated. Among them were Woolrus (lamb/walrus), Tycoon (tiger/raccoon), Piggypie (pig/porcupine), Pandeaver (panda/beaver), Skowl (skunk/owl), and Koalakeet (koala/parakeet). Some of these minor characters were seen in only one episode.

All good adventure stories need villains, and *Disney's Wuzzles* had them in the form of the "Creepasaurs," a gang of desperadoes determined to get the best of the Wuzzles. Chief among them are: King Croc (crocodile/bull), Flizard (frog/ lizard), and Brat (dragon/frog).

Each of the episodes is described below in airdate order.

BULLS OF A FEATHER
It's a beautiful day in Wuz for a picnic, until a swarm of flants (flying ants) ruins the fun. When Eleroo runs from them, he hits a banana pine tree and knocks an egg into his pouch. When a Brahma Bullfinch hatches, he thinks he is the baby's mother. Croc wants the bird for its valuable feathers, but the Wuzzles stop him and get the bird back to the real mother.

HOORAY FOR HOLLYWUZ
When the Wuzzles put on the play "Cinderwuzzle," Hoppo wants to be a star after playing the fairy godmother. She heads to Hollywuz, where she gets nowhere, but she writes home with stories of her "success." When the other Wuzzles come to visit, they learn the truth, and Hoppo learns that friends are more important than fame or fortune.

IN THE MONEY
When Bumblelion finds two bags full of money, he starts letting it get the best of him. Meanwhile, Rhinokey is suspected of bank robbery, for the bags had fallen from his taxi. Luckily, the Wuzzles manage to get the money to the police and all is forgiven.

CROC AROUND THE CLOCK
A fierce storm hits Wuz and collapses Croc's roof. He persuades Butterbear to let him stay with her, but the unexpected visit seems to have no end. Croc keeps taking advantage of her, so the Wuzzles band together to give him a taste of his own medicine.

MOOSEL'S MONSTER

In this retelling of the boy who cried wolf, Moosel keeps telling stories about monsters, and the others don't believe him when a real monster with a toothache shows up at his house. After the monster helps save Wuz from a weakened dam, the others finally learn the truth.

KLUTZ ON THE CLUTCH

When Rhinokey enters the famed Wuz 500 auto race, his reckless driving almost kills Bumblelion, so he drops out of the contest. Eleroo takes over for him, but he doesn't stand a chance against Croc. The others convince Rhinokey to re-enter the race, and he narrowly wins.

BUMBLELION AND THE TERRIFIED FOREST

Bumblelion desperately wants to be a hero, and he gets his chance when he rescues Butterbear from Transylvia, the wicked witch of the terrified forest. Butterbear discovers the witch needs help, for her pet has become a monster. The Wuzzles help her get the butterberries needed to cure her pet, and also rescue Hoppo, who is lost in a castle.

ELEROO'S WISHDAY

An annual tradition calls for each Wuzzle to give three wishes to the wishing well, and the one who was the least selfish gets their wishes. Eleroo wins, with unanticipated results, for Croc tries to trick him out of his wishes. When Eleroo finally decides that he wants to fly, it causes problems for both the birds and his friends.

GHOSTRUSTLERS

A swarm of humbugs drive everyone crazy with their noise, so the Wuzzles call in an exterminator. They decide to camp out while he's at work, but all of the campgrounds are full. Instead, they stop in Wuzzle Gulch, a ghost town rumored to have a gold mine.

PEST OF A PET, A

Rhinokey's practical jokes annoy his friends, so they give him a mockingbirddog, which repeats everything he says. The bird is so irritating that Rhinokey finally tries to hide from his new pet. After his friends tell him why they did it, he feels ashamed and runs away. But when a flock of mockingbirddogs take over the town, Rhinokey acts as a "pied piper" and leads the noisy birds away.

MAIN COURSE, THE

A cruise on Moosel's chugboat turns into a series of problems. The Wuzzles are attacked by Pi-Rats, and escape to an island run by pigmice. Hoppo unknowingly is about to be sacrificed, but luckily, Bumblelion arranges for their rescue.

CLASS DISMISSED

Butterbear is asked to set the guest list for a big social event, but she's worried that her friends won't fit in. Brat wants to go to the party, and Croc bets Butterbear that she can't make a gentleman of Brat before the big event. She agrees to the bet, and also decides to invite her friends. The party is a success, despite Croc's efforts to sabotage the evening.

WHAT'S UP, STOX?

The discovery of a money tree disrupts island life. Croc steals it, and each Wuzzle tries by itself to get it back. They fail, and the tree is ruined. The Wuzzles learn that greed is bad, for if they had cooperated, they could have saved the tree.

Disney's Adventures of the Gummi Bears

After years of studying the lucrative Saturday morning children's market, Disney finally decided to enter it for the 1985–86 season. The Studio tried two shows that year, one of which was *Disney's Adventures of the Gummi Bears.*

The six Gummi Bears were Gruffi Gummi, leader of the remaining Gummi Bears; Zummi Gummi, a scatter-brained magician and the Gummi historian; Cubbi Gummi, the youngest and most mischievous of the clan; Sunni Gummi, a teenager with a somewhat flighty personality; Tummi Gummi, a rather chubby and slow-witted bear; and Grammi Gummi, the oldest Gummi Bear.

Each episode is listed in the order aired for each season.

First season: 1985–86

NEW BEGINNING, A

Cavin, a page at Dunwyn Castle, accidentally discovers the underground home of the Gummi Bears. He helps them rediscover their proud heritage and, in turn, they help him stop Duke Igthorn from destroying the castle with a giant catapult.

SINISTER SCULPTOR, THE
Da Vini, an evil magician, is posing as an artist and freezing live animals into statues, which he passes off as fine sculpture. When four of the Gummies are frozen, their friends must find a way to thaw them out safely.

ZUMMI MAKES IT HOT
The Gummiberry Juice supply is threatened when something cuts off the water supply needed to make more juice. The Gummies trace the problem back to an ancient Gummi pumping station that happens to be deep in ogre country.

SOME DAY MY PRINTS WILL COME
The Gummies accidentally activate an old Gummi dragon decoy and wake up a sleeping dragon. Luckily, the dragon is friendly, but the knights at the castle don't know that and they set off to slay her.

CAN I KEEP HIM?
When Cubbi's toy flute summons a flying serpent, he and Sunni learn they can control it with music. Unfortunately, Igthorn gets control of the flute.

GUMMI IN A GILDED CAGE, A
A band of flying Carpies take Sunni to their mountain home and force her to sing for their king. Gruffi, Zummi, and Cubbi must use an ancient Gummi flying machine to save her.

ORACLE, THE
When the Duke asks an oracle for advice on defeating the Gummies, the voice he hears is Tummi, who has some fun with him and the ogres. The Duke discovers the deception, though, which places Tummi in danger.

WHEN YOU WISH UPON A STONE
After Cavin is beat up by a bully, he sets off to find the mysterious Wishing Stone so he can wish himself bigger. He must use his wits to defeat the giant that guards the stone, and in the process, learns that size is not important.

GUMMI BY ANY OTHER NAME, A
Sunni uses a magic hat to make her look like her idol, Calla, and the Duke kidnaps the fake princess while the ogres kidnap the real one. When the two prisoners meet, Calla learns about the Gummies and the new friends help each other escape.

LOOPY, GO HOME
Cubbi brings a wolf cub home against Gruffi's orders and hides the animal, but as it grows, it becomes harder to keep the secret. Cubbi realizes that he must teach the wolf to fend for itself before he can set it free.

A-HUNTING WE WILL GO
A dangerous wild pig is on the loose but no one believes the warnings. When King Gregor, Sir Tuxford, and Cavin go into the forest, it's up to Grammi, Sunni, and Calla to convince them of the danger.

FENCE SITTER, THE
A Brushprattle bird is devouring the Gummiberry crop but the bears can't decide on a plan to get rid of it. They try to vote on a plan, but Tummi has the deciding vote and can't make up his mind.

NIGHT OF THE GARGOYLE
The Duke sends a gargoyle disguised as a stone statue to the castle. Unless Zummi can find the spell to stop him, the "statue" will come to life and kill the king.

SECRET OF THE JUICE, THE
The Duke kidnaps Grammi to get the secret of Gummiberry Juice but she refuses to make it and is put into the dungeon. When the Gummies run out of juice, Sunni tries to make her first batch.

SWEET AND SOUR GRUFFI
Gruffi becomes too nice as the result of a spell, and saying "please" makes him a pushover. Unfortunately, saying "thank you" makes him obnoxious, and Zummi has to cure him before he destroys the cave.

DUEL OF THE WIZARDS
Wizard Dom Gordo is stuck in Dunwyn when Igthorn steals his magic transport key, so he starts blowing holes in Gummi Glen looking for the key. Gruffi and Zummi tell him to leave, starting a war of magic between Dom Gordo and Zummi.

WHAT YOU SEE IS ME
Trina, a blind shepherd, helps shelter Tummi. The Duke suspects she is hiding a Gummi, but she uses her blindness to defeat him.

TOADIE'S WILD RIDE
Toadie discovers the secret Quick Tunnel coaster and uses it to get a keg of Gummiberry Juice and a map to Gummi Glen.

Surrounded by the Gummies, he drinks the juice and is blasted back without the map and loses his memory.

BUBBLE TROUBLE

Sunni accidentally lets a baby dragon drink Gummiberry Juice and it gets explosive hiccups. The Duke steals the dragon to use as a weapon against the castle.

GUMMI IN A STRANGE LAND

After a Slumber Sprite puts Gruffi under a deadly spell, he sleepwalks into ogre territory and Grammi and Cubbi must protect him from exploding puffballs and sabre-toothed bunny rabbits.

LIGHT MAKES RIGHT

The Gummies discover a long-lost telescope that will allow them to reach other Gummies across the ocean. When the Duke captures it to use as a laser against the castle, the Gummies must destroy the device, even though that will keep them from a reunion with the other Gummies.

Second season: 1986–87

UP, UP AND AWAY

When a Gummi flying boat crashes on the island, the Gummies are surprised to find another Gummi on board. The newcomer, Chummi, offers to take them across the ocean to meet the other Gummies. Cubbi decides to take the trip but then decides to stay with his friends.

FASTER THAN A SPEEDING TUMMI

Disaster strikes when Tummi accidentally fills the glen with soap bubbles. He then uses a magic spell to move faster so he can clean up more quickly, but that also causes damage.

FOR A FEW SOVEREIGNS MORE

The Duke hires Flint Shrubwood, a bounty hunter, who promptly catches Cubbi. When the Duke refuses to pay as promised, Flint chains him up with Cubbi, and the two prisoners become unlikely allies to get free.

OVER THE RIVER AND THROUGH THE TROLLS

Cavin's grandfather, Gowan, is coming to visit, but trolls are attacking all travelers in the area. Cavin and the Gummies plan to trick the trolls but the scheme fails, and Zummi must reveal himself to Gowan to save him.

YOU SNOOZE, YOU LOSE

Everyone in Dunwyn is put to sleep for 1 hour after the Duke finds a powerful sleeping potion. It's then up to Calla, Cavin, and the Gummies to stop him.

CRIMSON AVENGER, THE

Cubbi dresses up as a super-hero but his ego causes Cavin and Calla to be imprisoned and Tummi to be hurt. Dismayed, Cubbi decides to undertake one last mission to right the wrongs.

HARD DAZED KNIGHT, A

Gruffi and Calla join forces to repair an ancient Gummi suit of armor and then use it to infiltrate the Duke's stronghold and remove a spell from King Gregor.

DO UNTO OGRES

Toadie wants some respect, but instead the Duke banishes him from Drekmore. He becomes friends with Sunni, and when she is captured by ogres, he uses a Gummi growth potion to become a giant and save her.

FOR WHOM THE SPELL HOLDS

Zummi wants to learn more about magic, so he opens a sealed section of advanced magic in the Great Book of Gummi. This awakens Zorlock the Wizard, who comes from the cavern with a pet monster to conquer the world.

LITTLE BEARS LOST

Someone is stealing things in Gummi Glen and Zummi and Grammi try to use magic to uncover the thief. The spell goes wrong and they are both shrunk to 1 inch in height.

GUESS WHO'S GUMMING TO DINNER?

Sunni invites Calla to dinner and forces the Gummies to follow "Gummi tradition" to excess to impress her. When she goes too far, they retaliate by acting silly during the meal.

MY GUMMI LIES OVER THE OCEAN

When Gruffi and Tummi are shipwrecked, they meet Gusto Gummi, a shipwrecked artist. Gruffi and Tummi want to build a bridge to safety, but Gusto wants to finish his greatest sculpture. To survive, they must work together to escape before the island sinks.

Third season: 1987–88

Too Many Cooks
Sir Paunch, the royal candy maker, wants to retire and Cubbi, Sunni, and Tummi try to duplicate his secret taffy recipe. The result is an explosion that covers the kingdom in candy.

Just a Tad Smarter
Toadie's cousin, Tadpole, ousts Duke Igthorn and orders the ogres to destroy every Gummiberry bush. The Gummies decide to help Igthorn regain power, figuring he is the lesser of two evils.

If I Were You
Igthorn gets a magic crystal and trades bodies with Tummi so he can steal Gummiberry Juice. He finds himself in the middle of Tummi's birthday party, where he hates the presents and events.

Eye of the Beholder
A beautiful woman, Marzipan, arrives in the kingdom and all of the men fall under her spell. Only Sunni knows that she's really a witch. Somehow she must convince the others of the truth before Marzipan marries Gregor.

Presto Gummo
Tummi wants to learn magic, and Cubbi convinces him he does have magic powers. Unfortunately, Tummi tries to use his "power" against Igthorn.

Tree Grows in Dunwyn, A
Calla gives her father a small tree as a gift, unaware that it holds a chest of stolen gold put there by trolls for safekeeping. The trolls takes the Gummies hostage and send Gruffi, Zummi, and Tummi into Dunwyn Castle to recover their treasure.

Day of the Beevilweevils
When a swarm of beevilweevils destroys all of the Gummiberry bushes, the Gummies must travel to South Gumpton for some new bushes. On the way, they must battle a band of mobile trees that are the sworn enemies of all Gummies.

Water Way to Go
Gusto and Sunni meet a mermaid and, jealous of Gusto's attention to the newcomer, Sunni convinces her that Gusto is planning to hurt her. The mermaid calls her pet sea serpent for protection, but Igthorn sees the creature as a chance to destroy the castle.

Boggling the Bears
Sunni makes friends with a boggle, a small creature that can take other forms but feels insignificant due to its size. The boggle fools the other Gummies by changing shapes and making them think the Glen is haunted. More boggles arrive and save Sunni from a wolf, which makes them feel better about themselves, so they leave.

Close Encounters of the Gummi Kind
Gusto builds a Gummi replica to fool the ogres, but it's spotted by the residents of Dunwyn, who all set out to catch a Gummi and become famous.

Snow's Your Old Man
Chillbeard, son of the Lord of Winter, brings a freak snowstorm to the Glen in Spring. When the Gummies try to steal the magic ram's horn that he uses to control the weather, it goes out of control and puts the kingdom in danger.

Knights of Gummadoon, The
Years ago, the "Knights of Gummadoon" fought against greedy humans. They then entered their castle, which reappears only every 100 years. They return now and mistakenly think Cavin is a thief, so they throw him into the dungeon.

Mirthy Me
Cubbi's practical jokes endanger the Glen by attracting Giggalin, a mischievous sprite who encourages Cubbi to try bigger pranks. The Gummies are soon at each other's throats until they realize Giggalin is behind it, and they decide to teach him a lesson.

Gummi Dearest
A newly hatched griffin mistakes Gruffi for its mother, while the mother thinks that Cubbi is her new baby.

Fourth season: 1988–89

Magnificent Seven Gummies, The
The Gummies must journey to the land of Shang-Wu to help save the people there from a dragon.

Music Hath Charms
Igthorn uses magical bagpipes to entrance everyone in Dunwyn. Grammi, who has tem-

porarily lost her hearing, is the only hope of saving everyone.

DRESS FOR SUCCESS
Sunni enters a fashion contest and everyone laughs at her costume. Later, she uses it in a plan to stop Igthorn from taking over the kingdom.

KNIGHT TO REMEMBER, A
The ghost of Sir Gallant, a Gummi knight, needs Cubbi's help in completing his unfinished quest of destroying the dreaded doomsday clock.

GUMMIES JUST WANT TO HAVE FUN
Grammi feels young again when her old friend, Nogam, visits the Glen.

COLOR ME GUMMI
King Gregor spots one of Gusto's paintings and Cavin says he painted it to keep the Gummies a secret. Gregor then wants Cavin to paint his portrait, so Gusto must do it in secret.

THERE'S NO PLACE LIKE HOME
Sunni thinks the Glen is too run down, so she takes Cubbi and Tummi on a search for a new home.

HE WHO LAUGHS LAST
Cavin's grandfather, Sir Gowan, vows to prove that the Gummies exist, but his quest puts them in peril.

TUMMI'S LAST STAND
Cubbi finds an old Gummi training camp and convinces Tummi to go through the obstacle course to toughen up.

OGRE BABY BOOM
Grammi finds a baby ogre and takes it home, hoping that raising it in the Gummi way will make it grow up right.

WHITE KNIGHT, THE
Cavin sees his hero, Sir Victor, plotting with Igthorn. The boy is crushed, unaware that the two men are brothers and Igthorn is blackmailing Victor.

GIRL'S KNIGHT OUT
Calla enters the annual squires' tournament in disguise, for no women are allowed to enter. The ruse works all too well, for she must now defeat the dreaded Dark Knight.

GOOD NEIGHBOR GUMMI
Gruffi is stuck in bed with a broken leg, but he must find a way to rid the Glen of a band of barbarians who have set up camp there.

TOP GUM
Cubbi flies using a set of homemade wings, but he is followed back to the Glen by a race of aviators who kidnap the others.

GUMMIES AT SEA
Tummi discovers the Gummarine, an ancient submersible. Igthorn hijacks it and sets out to capture Gregor at sea, so Tummi must save the day.

CRIMSON AVENGER STRIKES AGAIN, THE
Someone is running around in the Crimson Avenger costume. To his surprise, Cubbi discovers that it's Toadie.

Fifth season: 1989–90

ROAD TO URSALIA, THE
Gruffi accidentally destroys the Great Book of Gummi, so he and Cubbi must journey to Ursalia, the far-off capital of the ancient Gummies, to get a replacement.

LET SLEEPING GIANTS LIE
The Gummies celebrate the annual "Festival of the First Snow." Sunni thinks that it's a foolish event until she learns it helps protect them from a sleeping giant.

GUMMI A DAY KEEPS THE DOCTOR AWAY, A
Tummi helps a medicine show salesman by adding Gummiberry Juice to his elixir. When everyone gets super strength, the Duke forces the salesman to make more for him.

LIFE OF THE PARTY
Igthorn courts the powerful Lady Bane, for he wants to combine forces with her to conquer Dunwyn. Luckily, Cubbi and Sunni ruin the courtship by messing up the Duke's dinner party.

BRIDGE ON THE RIVER GUMMI
Gruffi decides to build a beautiful bridge, but Igthorn uses it to bring a new weapon to Dunwyn. A sad Gruffi must destroy his most impressive work ever.

MY KINGDOM FOR A PIE
Tummi vows to forgo food for a day to demonstrate his willpower. He is then cap-

tured by Igthorn, who tempts him to betray the others by offering him mounds of goodies.

World According to Gusto, The
Cubbi decides to be more carefree like Gusto and moves in with him. It's not long before they both learn the value of having rules.

Ogre for a Day
When Zummi transforms Cavin into an ogre so he can sneak into Drekmore to spy on Igthorn, the Duke puts him in charge of kidnapping the king. Cavin races off with the king with the real ogres in close pursuit.

Gummi is a Gummi's Best Friend, A
Gruffi finds a stone statue of Zummi and thinks that Zummi has accidentally changed himself into stone.

Princess Problems
A visiting princess, Princess Marie, is a royal brat and causes so much trouble that war looms between the two kingdoms.

Never Give a Gummi an Even Break
Grammi frees a captive Gummi from a side show and takes him to the Glen, unaware that the newcomer is really an elf in disguise. Once in the Glen, the elf begins his plan to capture the real Gummies.

Beg, Burrow, and Steal
Cubbi uses a Gummi device called the Mole to dig for buried treasure. The machine is captured by trolls who plan to drill into the castle to steal the crown jewels.

Return to Ursalia
The Gummies return to Ursalia and Sunni makes friends with Buddi, a bear cub from the remote Barbic Woods. Their friendship is threatened when the Barbic bears want to use a magic horn to destroy all humans.

Sixth season: 1990–91

Gummi's Work Is Never Done, A
After an argument, Gruffi and Grammi trade jobs to prove they work the hardest. Everyone suffers, but things get worse when the Duke tricks Grammi into finishing an old woodcutting machine which he wants to use as a weapon.

Friar Tum
Tummi joins a band of monks when he can't find a way to say no to their invitation to enter the order. He eventually finds the strength both to quit and to save them from some trolls.

Tuxford's Turnaround
Cubbi damages a secret Gummi door in Dunwyn and needs time to make repairs. Igthorn is trying to invade, but Sir Tuxford manages to get the Gummies the time they need while also battling the Duke.

Toadie the Conqueror
Igthorn finds a magic suit of armor that makes the wearer invincible, but it only fits Toadie. Using the suit, Toadie conquers Dunwyn then turns on the Duke. Zummi leads the others in a plan to get control back from Toadie.

Zummi in Slumberland
Zummi tries to memorize all of his spells but he works so hard that he ends up talking in his sleep and invoking strange combinations of spells.

Patchwork Gummi
The Gummies find an ancient patchwork quilt that highlights major Gummi milestones. Sunni wants to be depicted on the quilt but loses it to Lady Bane, who uses the quilt's magic against Dunwyn.

Thornberry to the Rescue
Sir Thornberry comes to visit Gummi Glen, but he accidentally frees a monster spider who captures the other Gummies and intends to eat them.

Once More, the Crimson Avenger
Cubbi dons his crime-fighter costume once more when he tires of the others laughing at his mistakes. He makes friends with Milton, a human boy who was being ridiculed by his friends for believing in the Crimson Avenger.

Recipe for Trouble, A
The Gummies are tired of Grammi's cooking, for the results are almost inedible. When the rest of the group is captured by gnomes, Grammi uses her food as weapons.

Queen of the Carpies
Sunni accidentally becomes the queen of the Carpies, a flock of evil birds that decide to raid the Glen. She stops them, but learns that being a leader isn't all fun.

TRUE GRITTY

When Ursalia runs out of water, Cubbi volunteers to help his friend Gritty get more water. Gritty becomes obsessed with driving off a flock of shepherds and endangers the Gummies.

KING IGTHORN—PART 1

The Gummies believe that Igthorn has left the castle for good and, thinking that it is finally safe to do so, they invite the Great Gummies to come back from across the sea. Igthorn returns with a rare termite that he uses to destroy the Glen. The Duke uses his new strength to capture Dunwyn and make himself king.

KING IGTHORN—PART 2

Zummi races to Ursalia for help as Igthorn sets a trap for the Great Gummies. Working in secrecy, the Gummies set the knights free and help retake the castle.

TUMMI TROUBLE

Igthorn buys a love potion to use on Lady Bane but instead she falls for Toadie. Meanwhile, Tummi falls in love with Lady Bane. She convinces him to steal the Great Book of Gummi, then announces that she will marry Toadie.

ROCKING CHAIR BEAR

Sunni is tired of being treated like a kid until Lady Bane drains her youth so she can stay young. Gusto, Gruffi, and Zummi are captured while trying to stop Lady Bane and Sunni must find a way to save them.

TRADING FACES

Igthorn disguises himself as Sir Victor, the White Knight, and sneaks into Dunwyn. The Gummies have to decide which Sir Victor is the real one if they are to save the kingdom.

MAY THE BEST PRINCESS WIN

Calla has to visit the bratty Princess Marie. The two girls try to embarrass each other, but when they are captured by a villainous nobleman, they must to work together to escape.

WINGS OVER DUNWYN

Igthorn catches giant birds to use as weapons against Dunwyn, planning to use them to fly his army over the castle walls.

RITE STUFF, THE

The young Gummies go to Ursalia to watch Buddi's test of bearhood but Ursa is outraged that they brought Cavin, a human, with them. The test goes awry when Ursa, Gruffi, and Thornberry are captured and the youngsters have to save them.

DuckTales

At first, *DuckTales* was intended as a 1-hour network series. However, when Bob Jacquemin, the head of the Studio's newly formed syndication unit, learned of the series, he realized that it had the potential to be his first hit. After intense internal lobbying, Jacquemin convinced Michael Eisner to let him have *DuckTales*, and in doing so, he virtually reinvented television animation.

One of the first decisions announced was that Donald Duck would play a very minor role in the series, for the emphasis this time was going to be on Uncle Scrooge and the nephews. To explain his absence, it was shown that Donald had enlisted in the Navy and was at sea, having left the nephews with Scrooge. The Studio created some new additions to the Disney stable. Among these were Launchpad McQuack, Mrs. Beakley, Webbigail ("Webby") Vanderquack, Doofus, Duckworth, Fenton Crackshell, and Bubba Duck.

DuckTales had a special 2-hour premiere in most markets on September 18, 1987, with the first regular episode airing on September 21.

Each of the syndicated episodes is listed below in order of the original airdate. Additional *DuckTales* episodes aired as specials or on the anthology series.

First season: 1987–88

TREASURE OF THE GOLDEN SUNS

The series opens with a special 2-hour episode. Donald joins the Navy and leaves Duckburg, while Huey, Dewey, and Louie stay behind with Uncle Scrooge. The boys must prove themselves innocent of stealing an expensive model ship and help Scrooge find a lost treasure ship. The scene then shifts to the Andes and later Antarctica where other adventures await the ducks. This episode was later shown in five parts: *Don't Give Up the Ship*, *Wrong Way to Ronguay*, *Three Ducks of the Condor*, *Cold Duck*, and *Too Much of a Gold Thing*.

SEND IN THE CLONES

Magica de Spell transforms the Beagle Boys into look-a-likes for the nephews. The imposters arrive at Scrooge's mansion just as a television interviewer prepares a profile on Scrooge.

Sphinx for the Memories
The spirit of an ancient Middle-Eastern ruler attempts to take over Donald's body.

Where No Duck Has Gone Before
Gyro's props for a science fiction television show accidentally launch the cast into space.

Armstrong
A "perfect" robot worker in Scrooge's money bin decides he would rather be the one in charge, forcing Scrooge and the boys to fear for their lives.

Robot Robbers
The Beagle Boys steal giant construction robots and take over the city. Scrooge and Flintheart must join forces to stop the Beagle Boys before the city is destroyed.

Magica's Shadow War
Magica de Spell brings her shadow to life in another plot to steal Scrooge's dime, but with unplanned results.

Masters of the Djinni
An evil Djinni transports Scrooge and Flintheart back in time so he can enjoy life giving orders for a change.

Hotel Strangeduck
When Scrooge buys an old castle and opens it as a hotel, he must deal with what seems to be the ghost of the former owner.

Lost Crown of Genghis Khan, The
Scrooge and the boys discover an abominable snowwoman. More importantly, they also discover the value of honesty.

Duckman of Aquatraz
Flintheart frames Scrooge for an art theft and the hapless duck is sent to Aquatraz, the toughest prison of them all.

Money Vanishes, The
The Beagle Boys steal an invention from Gyro and use it to transport Scrooge's money to their hideout—with unexpected results. It seems that money is not the only thing being transported.

Sir Gyro de Gearloose
Gyro, bored with life, goes back in time to the days of King Arthur and the Round Table in the medieval kingdom of Quackalot. His skills are needed there to defeat the evil Black Knight.

Dinosaur Ducks
Scrooge learns a lesson about love when he tries to capture a baby dinosaur and must risk his mission to save Webby from savages.

Hero for Hire
Launchpad screws up one time too many and is fired. His attempt to become "The Webbed Wonder," a hero for hire, provides the Beagle Boys with another chance to steal Scrooge's fortune.

Super Doo!
Doofus finds a stolen energy crystal from outer space that gives him super powers. He doesn't know it, but the aliens who lost the medallion are determined to get it back.

Maid of the Myth
A tribe of Vikings from the land of Valhalla attack Duckburg and take Mrs. Beakley prisoner. Scrooge's rescue effort leads to Mrs. Beakley's participating in a chariot race with Thor, the thunder god.

Down and Out in Duckburg
A long-forgotten debt costs Scrooge his fortune, but he learns a valuable lesson in the process.

Much Ado about Scrooge
A search for a lost play takes Scrooge to a haunted island, where another adventurer plots to steal the manuscript.

Top Duck
Launchpad learns that his family is proud of him—despite his series of crashes.

Pearl of Wisdom, The
Scrooge is pitted against an evil smuggler when he searches for a pearl with magic powers. The owner is granted ultimate wisdom, but no one expects the results.

Curse of Castle McDuck, The
A return to his ancestral home in Scotland forces Scrooge to face old fears and a ghostly hound. He defeats the hound, only to learn a shocking secret about one of his ancestors.

Launchpad's Civil War
Launchpad discovers a hidden band of Civil War soldiers. He also learns a famous ancestor was a fraud.

Sweet Duck of Youth
To avoid getting older, Scrooge sets out on a search for the Fountain of Youth. His search takes the ducks to the eerie Okeefedokie Swamp, where a hermit and the ghost of a Conquistador wait for unsuspecting visitors.

Earth Quack
Fears of earthquakes bring Scrooge and the boys to a strange land far underground, where a race of unusual creatures is trying to create the biggest earthquake of all—right underneath the money bin.

Home Sweet Homer
Scrooge and the boys travel back in time to ancient Greece, where they meet Homer and the evil sorceress Circe.

Bermuda Triangle Tangle
Scrooge's search for his missing ships leaves him a prisoner in the mysterious Sargossa Sea, home of the evil Captain Bounty.

Micro-Ducks from Outer Space
Miniature ducks from outer space are the unwitting cause of Scrooge and his helpers' being shrunk after a plea for assistance in ending a famine. The ducks must travel through a now giant-sized Duckburg, where everyday objects have become potential dangers.

Back to the Klondike
Scrooge returns to the site where he earned his first fortune and reawakens an old love affair with Glittering Goldie, the dance-hall girl who had stolen both his fortune and his heart. He must battle with Dangerous Dan, an old rival, for both Goldie and a fortune in gold.

Horse Scents
Scrooge and Flintheart Glomgold both enter horses in the famed Ken-ducky Derby. If Flintheart wins, he'll finally be the richest duck in the world, so he's not leaving anything to chance.

Scrooge's Pet
A lemming escapes with the only copy of the combination to Scrooge's impenetrable new vault.

The following four shows made up a four-part story titled *The Firefly Fruit Contest.*

Drain on the Economy, A (Part 1 of 4)
Scrooge loses his fortune to the Beagle Boys just when he needs it to win a contest with Flintheart for a miraculous new type of light-producing fruit.

Whale of a Bad Time, A (Part 2 of 4)
Scrooge must dump his fortune at sea to avoid being lost himself.

Aqua-Ducks (Part 3 of 4)
A search of the ocean floor reveals a secret race of underwater beings.

Working for Scales (Part 4 of 4)
Scrooge wins the prize when his fortune is found to be the largest in the world.

Merit-Time Adventure
A sea serpent is attacking ships in Duckburg Harbor and Scrooge wants to stop it. The boys become overconfident while at sea and Webby must save them.

Golden Fleecing, The
A search for the legendary golden fleece brings the adventurers into contact with the Harpies, guardians of the treasure.

Ducks of the West
Is it the ghost of Jesse James that's stealing oil from Scrooge's Texas wells?

Time Teasers, The
Gyro invents a device that can freeze time, but when the Beagle Boys steal it, they're thrown back in time—with Scrooge's fortune!

Back Out in the Outback
A report of wool-destroying U.F.O.s sends Scrooge on an expedition to his sheep ranch in Australia.

Raiders of the Lost Harp
When he ignores a warning on an ancient Trojan tomb, Scrooge awakens an ancient monster that almost destroys Duckburg.

Right Duck, The
Launchpad is chosen to fly a mission into space, where he accidentally starts a war between Mars and Earth.

SCROOGERELLO
A fever causes Scrooge to dream that he is the central figure in a Cinderella-style story.

DOUBLE-O-DUCK
Launchpad looks just like a foreign spy, and agrees to help capture an international counterfeiting ring.

LUCK O' THE DUCKS
A leprechaun and Scrooge engage in a battle of wits which leads to Ireland, where Scrooge schemes to discover the secret of the Golden Caverns, storage place of the leprechauns' fortune.

DUCKWORTH'S REVOLT
Duckworth must change his personality to save the boys from space invaders.

The following two episodes were aired together in a 30-minute format.

MAGICA'S MAGIC MIRROR (EPISODE 1)
Magica de Spell uses a trick mirror to force Scrooge to give up his "Old #1 Dime," planning to use his good luck charm to increase her power.

TAKE ME OUT OF THE BALLGAME (EPISODE 2)
Duckworth's attempts at coaching the nephews' baseball team lead to disaster.

DUCK TO THE FUTURE
Scrooge travels to the future to see what will become of the boys, but Magica strands him there in her latest plot to get his lucky dime.

JUNGLE DUCK
A quest for the legendary "silver buzzard" brings Scrooge to Africa, where he finds the missing heir to a fortune living as a wild duck in the jungle.

LAUNCHPAD'S FIRST CRASH
Scrooge and Launchpad reminisce about how they first met.

DIME ENOUGH FOR LUCK
Magica tricks Gladstone Gander, the world's luckiest duck, into helping her steal Scrooge's lucky dime.

DUCK IN THE IRON MASK
Dewey suffers an identity crisis. He's tired of being mistaken for his brothers and asserts his independence, only to learn a lesson

about teamwork during an adventure in the tiny country of Monte Dumas.

UNCRASHABLE HINDENTANIC, THE
A rash bet and a faulty blimp almost cause Scrooge to lose $1 million to Flintheart Glomgold.

STATUS SEEKERS, THE
Scrooge must shun his friends to join a snooty club. Once he becomes a member, he realizes how much he misses his friends and family.

NOTHING TO FEAR
Magica brings everyone's worst fears to life, and the heroes must learn to confront their personal demons.

DOCTOR JEKYLL AND MR. McDUCK
A strange spell turns Scrooge into a spendthrift. Searching for an antidote, the boys take him to London, where they meet the notorious Jack the Tripper.

ONCE UPON A DIME
Scrooge tells the boys how he earned his fortune.

SPIES IN THEIR EYES
Donald is accused of being a traitor and the nephews and Scrooge must clear his name despite overwhelming evidence against him.

ALL DUCKS ON DECK
Donald tells the boys he's an important crewmember on his ship, but they learn the truth. The boys try to help Donald get promoted, but their plans didn't count on the Phantom Blot stealing a secret bomber.

DUCKY HORROR PICTURE SHOW
Scrooge's attempt to revive an old theater almost fails when real monsters show up for a horror festival.

TILL NEPHEWS DO US PART
Uncle Scrooge almost marries a gold digger, but the boys help save him.

Second season: 1988–89
The following new episodes were produced for this season, and aired along with repeats of those produced for the first year.

TIME IS MONEY
Scrooge goes back in time to prove ownership of a valuable island, but he goes too

far. He accidentally brings Bubba, a cave-duck, and his pet triceratops, Tootsie, back to the present. Once home, Gyro warns Scrooge to return Bubba to his own time or risk changing history. This episode was first shown as a syndicated special on 11/25/88 and was later aired in five parts: *Marking Time, The Duck Who Would Be King, Bubba Trubba, Ducks on the Lam* (also known as *Gone with the Bin*), and *Ali Bubba's Cave.*

SUPER DUCKTALES

Scrooge hides his fortune in a lake, but the Beagle Boys discover the secret. Gyro builds a robot guard, but it becomes overprotective and won't let Scrooge near the money. This episode was first shown on the anthology series as *Super DuckTales* on 3/26/89 and was later aired in five parts: *Liquid Assets, Frozen Assets, Full Metal Duck, The Billionaire Beagle Boys Club,* and *Money to Burn.*

Third season: 1989–90

The following new episodes were produced for this season, and aired along with repeats of those produced for the first two years.

LAND OF TRALLA LA, THE

Scrooge unwittingly devastates a peaceful valley by the seeming innocuous act of dropping a bottle cap.

ALLOWANCE DAY

The boys try to trick Scrooge into giving them their allowance early, with unexpected consequences.

BUBBEO AND JULIET

Bubba becomes involved in an unusual romance when he falls in love with a neighbor.

GOOD MUDDAHS, THE

Webby is kidnapped by the Beagle Babes, cousins of the crooks, who want the famed Sowbuggian Crown Jewels.

MY MOTHER THE PSYCHIC

Fenton's mother has an accident and suddenly can predict the future. Scrooge and Flintheart try to use her to beat the stock market.

METAL ATTRACTION

A robot maid almost destroys Scrooge's fortune and Gizmoduck.

DOUGH RAY ME

The nephews misuse Gyro's new matter duplicator, and Duckburg ends up buried in money and in danger of exploding!

BUBBA'S BIG BRAINSTORM

Gyro invents a thinking cap for Bubba, but no one foresees another change in the caveduck's personality.

BIG FLUB, THE

Fenton rushes a new product to market and then has to deal with some unusual side effects.

CASE OF MISTAKEN SECRET IDENTITY, A

When Duckburg believes Launchpad is really Gizmoduck, the flyer is happy with the attention until an emergency develops.

BLUE COLLAR SCROOGE

Scrooge suffers amnesia and gets a job in one of his own factories.

BEAGLEMANIA

The Beagle Boys end up working for Uncle Scrooge when they win a TV show's rock-and-roll contest.

YUPPIE DUCKS

When the boys are left in charge of the money bin, they inadvertently lose all of Scrooge's fortune in bad business deals.

BRIDE WORE STRIPES, THE

Ma Beagle pretends she is married to Uncle Scrooge in an attempt to get half of his fortune.

UNBREAKABLE BIN, THE

Gyro's unbreakable glass sheathing on the money bin turns out to be breakable—and Magica de Spell knows the secret.

ATTACK OF THE FIFTY-FOOT WEBBY

An accident turns Webby into a giant, and a circus owner tries to kidnap her.

MASKED MALLARD, THE

Scrooge's attempts to improve his public image lead to him acting as a superhero, but someone else is framing him for a series of crimes.

DUCKTALES VALENTINE!, A: AMOUR OR LESS

Scrooge finds the submerged temple of Aphroducky, the goddess of love, but gets more than he bargained for when Aphro-ducky comes to retrieve Cupid's love arrows.

Fourth season: 1990–91
The following new episodes were produced for this season, and aired along with repeats of those produced for the first three years.

DUCKY MOUNTAIN HIGH
Scrooge and Flintheart battle for gold in Canada, with Flintheart turning to the local Beagle Boys for an extra edge.

ATTACK OF THE METAL MITES
Flintheart's scientists invent tiny bugs that can eat Scrooge's money.

DUCK WHO KNEW TOO MUCH, THE
Fenton feigns an ailment to take a vacation, but he doesn't count on Scrooge's checking into the same hotel.

NEW GIZMO-KIDS ON THE BLOCK
Mrs. Crackshell accidentally shrinks Gizmoduck's super suit, and the nephews have trouble controlling it.

SCROOGE'S LAST ADVENTURE
Fenton loses Scrooge's money in a computer, and the two ducks enter the machine to get it back.

GOLDEN GOOSE, THE (2 parts)
Scrooge sets chase after the Golden Goose—the world's "ultimate treasure"—and the world barely escapes being turned into solid gold in the process.

The New Adventures of Winnie the Pooh
The New Adventures of Winnie the Pooh joined the ABC Saturday morning line-up for the 1988–89 season and was an immediate hit. For the 1989–90 season, Winnie and friends were combined with the Gummi Bears to create *Disney's Gummi Bears/Winnie the Pooh Hour*, also on ABC on Saturday morning. The format returned to just *The New Adventures of Winnie the Pooh* for the 1990–91 through 1992–93 seasons. The series left the ABC schedule then, but returned with repeats of prior years for the 1995–96 season. *The New Adventures of Winnie the Pooh* won an Emmy award for Best Animated Program, Daytime, for both the 1988–89 and 1989–90 seasons.

The characters from this series have also been seen in prime time on the special *Winnie the Pooh, and Christmas Too.*

The episodes of this series were each composed of a number of different *Pooh* cartoons. The order of the cartoons was changed from year to year in order to keep the series looking fresh. Each of the individual cartoons is described here in alphabetical order.

ALL'S WELL THAT ENDS WISHING WELL
Tigger's greed causes an unexpected result when he overwishes for his birthday.

APRIL BOOH
Tired of a string of April Fool's jokes, Pooh and friends decide to track down the culprit responsible for these pranks.

BABYSITTER BLUES
Christopher Robin and the gang take advantage of a new babysitter until Roo steps in.

BALLOONATICS
A borrowed balloon carries Pooh and friends across the woods—and toward a meeting with their consciences.

BIRD IN HAND, A
Rabbit and friends try to save a kidnap victim but end up needing help themselves.

BUBBLE TROUBLE
Pooh is trapped inside a very big and very strong bubble.

BUG STOPS HERE, THE
Christopher Robin's science project escapes and the residents of the 100 Acre Wood don't want to turn the fleeing bug in.

CAWS AND EFFECT
When Pooh is left guarding Rabbit's garden, a flock of crows take advantage of his lack of wit.

CLEANLINESS IS NEXT TO IMPOSSIBLE
Christopher Robin must clean up his room. When he does, Pooh and the others end up under the bed, where they meet a sinister creature named Crud.

CLOUD, CLOUD, GO AWAY
Tigger insults a small cloud and it turns dark, stormy—and angry.

DONKEY FOR A DAY
Piglet decides that everyone must join together to cheer up the ever depressed Eeyore.

Easy Come, Easy Gopher
Gopher decides to build the biggest and best tunnel ever.

Eeyi Eeyi Eeyore
When Eeyore tries to grow a plant, his friends pull a joke and make him think that he has grown a Piglet.

Eeyore's Tail Tale
Somehow Eeyore has lost his tail and it's up to Tigger to find it.

Fast Friends
Tired of his slowness, Pooh's friends work on speeding him up until they realize they miss the old Pooh.

Find Her, Keep Her
Rabbit falls in love with a baby bird, but after he raises it, he realizes he must set it free to be with the other birds.

Fish out of Water
The woods are invaded by strange mutton-head trout, which begin to force Pooh's friends from their homes.

Friend, In Deed
Pooh, thinking that Rabbit is planning to move away, goes to incredible lengths and expense to keep his friend from leaving.

Gone with the Wind
Piglet takes refuge in his house to escape a strong wind that blew him across the 100 Acre Wood, then refuses to come back out.

Good, the Bad, and the Tigger, The
Tigger accidentally destroys Christopher Robin's toy train. Pooh is blamed for the damage and Tigger can't bring himself to confess the truth.

Goodbye, Mr. Pooh
His friends are shocked to learn that Pooh is leaving the woods.

Great Honey Pot Robbery, The
When a Heffalump and a Woozle steal honey pots, Winnie the Pooh gets blamed. His friends learn the truth, but then have to battle the biggest, meanest Woozle in the world.

Groundpiglet Day
Something has changed all of the seasons in the woods.

Grown, But Not Forgotten
When he is invited to a "grown up" party, Christopher Robin turns to his friends for advice on how to act.

Home Is Where the Home Is
Christopher Robin runs away from home after breaking a valuable family heirloom.

Honey for a Bunny
Rabbit needs honey to repay a debt to Pooh, but how to get it? Tigger's suggestions make a simple task very complicated.

How Much Is That Rabbit in the Window?
Rabbit runs away and ends up in the window of a secondhand toy store.

Invasion of the Pooh Snatcher
Tigger convinces everyone that Pooh has become the victim of a fierce jagular.

King of the Beasties
Tigger appoints himself King of the Beasties to protect his friends from the feared jagular.

Knight to Remember, A
Piglet's imagination places him on a chess board, along with some very familiar looking pieces.

Lights Out
Rabbit borrows Gopher's helmet and loses it, which causes a chain reaction as everyone searches for it.

Luck Amok
A broken mirror unleashes a wave of bad luck on everyone in the 100 Acre Wood.

Magic Earmuffs, The
The gang uses a pair of "magic" earmuffs to let Piglet overcome his fear of ice skating.

Masked Offender, The
Tigger's attempts to become a superhero result in more harm than good.

Me and My Shadow
Piglet must gather the courage to search the woods for his lost shadow.

Monkey See, Monkey Do Better
The arrival of a new toy gorilla makes everyone think that Christopher Robin doesn't love them anymore.

MONSTER FRANKENPOOH, THE
Tigger's assistance creates a monster from one of Piglet's usually dull stories.

MY HERO
Tigger is so grateful to Piglet for saving his life that he decides to become his servant. Unfortunately, Tigger's efforts put Piglet in danger.

"NEW" EEYORE, THE
Eeyore tries to become more popular by acting like Tigger.

NO RABBIT'S A FORTRESS
Determined to protect his garden, Rabbit cuts himself off from everyone else in the 100 Acre Wood.

NOTHING BUT THE TOOTH
When Pooh thinks he's lost his sweet tooth, he battles a band of pack rats to get it back.

OH BOTTLE!
A note in a bottle makes everyone think that Christopher Robin is in great danger.

OLD SWITCHEROO, THE
Tigger vows to save his buddy Roo from a terrible fate—a bath.

OWL FEATHERS
Owl is worried—if he keeps losing feathers, he won't be able to fly.

OWL IN THE FAMILY
Owl misses his family so Pooh arranges for a reunion, unaware that some crows will also attend.

OWL'S WELL THAT ENDS WELL
Owl wants to sing with the morning birds but unfortunately he can't sing at all.

PARTY POOHPER
Rabbit spends so much time getting ready for a big party that he forgets to invite the guests.

PAW AND ORDER
Pooh becomes the sheriff of a prairie dog town and must face Nasty Jack, the local villain.

PIGLET WHO WOULD BE KING, THE
Piglet's search for the perfect gift for Pooh takes him to the land of the Piglies, where he's made king against his will.

PIGLET'S POOHETRY
Piglet holds a poetry party but Tigger decides to improvise.

POOH DAY AFTERNOON
An offer to dog-sit soon teaches Christopher Robin and his friends a valuable lesson about responsibility.

POOH MOON
Pooh decides to investigate outer space in his never-ending quest for honey.

POOH OUGHT TO BE IN PICTURES
Piglet's fear of a movie monster makes him the laughingstock of the 100 Acre Wood, but when Pooh's life is threatened, he conquers his fears.

POOH SKIES
Pooh is convinced that he has poked a hole in the sky, so he convinces Gopher to help him build a tower to fix the damage.

PRIZE PIGLET
When Piglet is mistaken for a star runner, a special race is held to showcase his talents.

RABBIT MARKS THE SPOT
Everyone gets wrapped up in a hunt for buried pirate treasure.

RABBIT TAKES A HOLIDAY
When Rabbit takes a holiday, his friends mistakenly make a mess out of his house and garden.

RATS WHO CAME TO DINNER, THE
A band of thieving pack rats invades the 100 Acre Wood.

ROCK-A-BYE POOH BEAR
Piglet has a nightmare and becomes determined to stay awake so it can't come true.

SHAM POOH
Pooh loses his appetite and Owl suggests that he might be an imposter—a prospect that confuses and upsets Pooh!

SHOVEL, SHOVEL, TOIL AND TROUBLE
Gopher decides to use modern technology in his digging efforts.

SORRY, WRONG SLUSHER
Christopher Robin and his friends try to save themselves from the Slusher, a fiend who waits in the dark.

STRIPES
A bath washes away both Tigger's stripes and his self-confidence.

THERE'S NO CAMP LIKE HOME
Piglet, Pooh, and Tigger battle Heffalumps and Woozles for control of the woods. When Piglet and a baby Heffalump are put in danger, both sides join forces to save them.

THINGS THAT GO PIGLET IN THE NIGHT
Something mysterious has moved into the woods, and everyone is hearing strange noises.

THREE LITTLE PIGLETS
Pooh has a very different version of the old fairy tale.

TIGGER, PRIVATE EAR
Tigger becomes a private detective, but since there are no crimes to solve, he starts inventing some.

TIGGER GOT YOUR TONGUE?
Things are disappearing all over the 100 Acre Wood, and when Tigger loses his voice, his friends try to find the thief.

TIGGER IS THE MOTHER OF INVENTION
Tigger invents a machine to help his overworked friends, but in typical Tigger fashion, the results are not what he planned.

TIGGER'S HOUSEGUEST
Tigger accidentally makes friends with a very hungry termite that is devouring everything in sight.

TIGGER'S SHOES
Rabbit tries to cure Tigger's bouncing by using a pair of heavily weighted shoes.

TO BEE OR NOT TO BEE
Pooh is forced into a confrontation with a very tricky bee.

TO CATCH A HICCUP
Piglet seems doomed by a very persistent case of the hiccups.

TO DREAM THE IMPOSSIBLE SCHEME
Gopher is worried that his grandfather's visit may cause damage to the 100 Acre Wood.

TRAP AS TRAP CAN
When a Heffalump tries to teach his son how to trap, everyone in the 100 Acre Wood is suddenly in danger.

UN-VALENTINE'S DAY
Tired of exchanging Valentine's Day gifts, everyone decides to put on a play instead.

UP, UP, AND AWRY
Pooh decides flying would be much easier than walking and has great fun at it until he is arrested for breaking the law of gravity.

VERY, VERY LARGE ANIMAL, A
Everyone joins in to make Piglet realize that his small size is not a problem.

WHAT'S THE SCORE, POOH?
The gang joins in for a strange game that stumps all who try to understand the rules.

WHERE, OH WHERE HAS MY PIGLET GONE?
Pooh always loses things, but this time he manages to misplace Piglet.

WISE HAVE IT, THE
Too many candles on Pooh's birthday cake make his friends think he is older than they knew.

WISHING BEAR, THE
Pooh makes one wish too many and wears out the wishing star!

Chip 'n Dale's Rescue Rangers

Chip and Dale weren't the only stars of *Chip 'n Dale's Rescue Rangers.* The rest of the Rescue Rangers were: Gadget—the brains of the outfit, Monterey Jack—the brawn of the operation, and Zipper—a housefly.

The Rangers found themselves in battles with opponents such as: Fat Cat—the self-styled kingpin of animal criminals, Professor Nimnul—a somewhat typical mad scientist, and Sewernose de Bergerac—an alligator who lived in the sewers.

A total of 65 episodes were produced, and the series was syndicated for the 1989–90 season.

Each of the episodes is described below in production order.

PIRATSY UNDER THE SEA
The Rangers are captured by a strange band of Pi-Rats, a band of villainous rodents living inside a sunken galleon.

ADVENTURES IN SQUIRRELSITTING
When they accidently destroy a squirrel family's home, the Rangers agree to babysit while

the mother cleans up. No one expects the results.

FLASH, THE WONDER DOG
Fat Cat plans to ruin the reputation of Flash, a canine television star, by framing him for a series of crimes. When the Rangers step in to help, they learn that Flash is a hero only on the small screen.

POUND OF THE BASKERVILLES, THE
The Rangers become involved in the search for a missing will that will establish who is to be the next lord of Baskerville Manor.

RISKY BEESNESS
Scientist Irweena Allen uses a swarm of trained bees in her bid to become a rock star.

OUT TO LAUNCH
When Chip and Dale are accidentally launched into orbit, Gadget must rush to build a rocket to save them.

DALE BESIDE HIMSELF
An alien visitor changes himself to look like Dale, and other aliens threaten to destroy Earth unless he can be found.

PARENTAL DISCRETION RETIRED
Monterey's father, Cheddarhead Charlie, helps the Rangers stop Fat Cat's latest plan, but his dislike for planning almost ruins the day.

CATTERIES NOT INCLUDED
The Rangers are pitted against Professor Nimnul, who is stealing cats to power his giant static electricity generator.

THREE MEN AND A BOOBY
When an eccentric egg collector steals a rare Booby Bird egg and kidnaps the mother, the Rangers fly into action.

KIWI'S BIG ADVENTURE
The Kiwis, a band of flightless birds, steal the Ranger's plane and worship it as a god, hoping that it will somehow allow them to fly.

LAD IN THE LAMP, A
Monterey is tricked by an evil genie into trading places, unaware that Fat Cat wants to use the magic lamp in his latest crime wave.

BEARING UP BABY
A young boy is saved from drowning by Humphrey the bear, but the Rangers mistakenly think the bear is dangerous.

CARPETSNAGGERS, THE
Professor Nimnul returns with a strange flying doghouse, using his aircraft and magic carpets to rob houses across the city.

LUCK STOPS HERE, THE
Gadget is captured by an unlucky inventor who thinks she's a good luck charm.

BATTLE OF THE BULGE
Fat Cat is using Jamaican fruit bats to steal cargo from planes in mid-air, but the Rangers are slowed down in stopping him when Monterey goes on an exercise kick.

GHOST OF A CHANCE
When the Rangers follow Fat Cat to the Tower of London, they meet a ghostly ancestor of Monterey, who is cursed to remain there until he overcomes his cowardice.

ELEPHANT NEVER SUSPECTS, AN
A series of peanut thefts is traced to a pair of homesick pandas who plan to build a digging machine powered by peanut oil, and head home to China.

FAKE ME TO YOUR LEADER
Professor Nimnul's plan to enlarge bugs to enslave the city is foiled when Zipper grows to giant size.

LAST TRAIN TO CASHVILLE
Fat Cat is planning to use a toy train to rob a bank.

CASE OF STAGEBLIGHT, A
A crazed villain living beneath an opera house tries to kill an opera star so he can take his place.

CASE OF THE COLA CULT, THE
A strange band of cola worshippers almost manages to break up the Rangers.

THROW MUMMY FROM THE TRAIN
An evil archaeologist uses a magic ring to bring a mummy back to life.

WOLF IN CHEAP CLOTHING, A
A wolf cub asks the Rangers to find his missing father. They do, but no one is ready for

the shock that he's a were-man, turning human during the full moon!

ROBOCAT
Fat Cat programs a robotic cat for evil so he can rob a local mansion, and the Rangers must overcome the deadly program to save a little boy.

DOES PAVLOV RING A BELL?
Professor Nimnul has programmed a rat and guinea pig to follow a set of mazes, planning to use them in his latest scheme to rob the city.

PREHYSTERICAL PET
Scientists discover a baby dinosaur and think he has somehow survived all of these years alone. The Rangers discover that he is really a visitor from space.

RESCUE RANGERS TO THE RESCUE
The pilot episode, which was first aired as a special, was repeated for the series in five episodes.

CREEP IN THE DEEP, A
Captain Finn, an evil anchovy, has taken control of Captain Nemo's "Nautilus" and is using it to drive mankind from the sea.

NORMIE'S SCIENCE PROJECT
Professor Nimnul's nephew, Normie, uses a strange invention to disrupt his school's science fair, for it brings inanimate objects to life through sound.

SEER NO EVIL
When the predictions of a fortune teller start coming true, Chip is particularly worried about the last of them, for she has foreseen his getting crushed by an elephant.

CHIPWRECKED SHIPMUNKS
Monty and Dale are overcome with greed when they discover a treasure chest full of gold. They come to their senses when the Rangers are threatened by the villainous Pi-Rats and a hurricane.

WHEN MICE WERE MEN
Each year a small village celebrates the running of the bulls, but an evil bull is threatening them and stealing their cattle. Monty agrees to help them, but the Rangers discover that Monty himself needs help.

CHOCOLATE CHIPS
A crazed candymaker is using zombie slaves to steal the world's supply of chocolate.

LAST LEPRECHAUN, THE
The Rangers are captured by the last leprechaun in the world. The other leprechauns have been enslaved by the queen of the banshees, and by using the magic pot of gold, the Rangers are able to free the captives.

WEATHER OR NOT
Professor Nimnul invents a weather machine and uses it to rob banks across the city.

ONE-UPSMAN-CHIP
A series of practical jokes backfires when one of them results in Dale's being captured by Fat Cat.

SHELL SHOCKED
The Rangers interrupt their vacation at the beach to help some crabs recover their missing shells.

LOVE IS A MANY SPLINTERED THING
Monty has to make a difficult choice when he has to decide between an old friend and the Rangers.

SONG OF THE NIGHT 'N DALE
The Rangers accidentally fly into a remote Himalayan valley, where they help save the land from developers.

DOUBLE 'O CHIPMUNKS
The rest of the Rangers indulge Dale in his fantasy of being a secret agent, unaware that he has become involved in a real case.

GADGET GOES HAWAIIAN
A vacation in Hawaii takes a strange turn when Gadget is kidnapped by a mouse that looks just like her.

IT'S A BIRD, IT'S INSANE, IT'S DALE
A meteorite gives Dale superhuman powers and he goes overboard in trying to be a hero.

SHORT ORDER CROOKS
A sneak visit to a nearby kitchen for a late snack brings the Rangers into contact with bank robbers.

MIND YOUR OWN CHEESE AND Q'S
When cheese vanishes all over the city, the Rangers follow a trail to Rat Capone's secret hideout under a dairy.

Out of Scale
Professor Nimnul returns with his ray gun, but this time he's shrinking things.

Dirty Rotten Diapers
Gadget shows a surprising domestic side when she unveils a plan to solve crimes without resorting to violence.

Good Times, Bat Times
A witch sends a bat out to help trap the Rangers, but the would-be assistant falls in love with Dale and joins forces with the heroes.

Pie in the Sky
A super magnet foils the Rangers when they try to help a sparrow find her way to San Juan Capistrano.

Le Purrfect Crime
Reports that dogs are being driven out of Paris lead the Rangers to Europe. There, they discover that Fat Cat's French cousin is behind the strange events.

When You Fish upon a Star
Monty has been telling the Rangers about a wonderful vacation spot, but when they get there, the island definitely does not live up to its reputation.

Rest Home Rangers
Professor Nimnul invents a ray that causes things to age rapidly. Unfortunately, Monty gets caught in the evil beam and the Rangers need to search for a cure.

Lean on the Property, A
Buildings are falling over all across town, but the Ranger's efforts to solve the case are hampered by a visit from Monterey's mother.

Pied Piper Power Play, The
Professor Nimnul captures mice from across the city, planning to use them to run a generator needed for his next crime.

Gorilla of My Dreams
A trained gorilla's pet kitten is stolen by Fat Cat and the Rangers set out to retrieve the missing feline.

S. S. Drainpipe, The
The Rangers cross paths once more with Rat Capone.

Zipper Come Home
An upset Zipper is befriended by bugs, unaware that they plan on sacrificing him to their god.

Puffed Rangers
Someone is stealing the toys out of cereal boxes, and the Rangers head to Hong Kong to solve the mystery.

Fly in the Ointment, A
In a spoof of the movie *The Fly*, Zipper and Professor Nimnul get caught in an experiment gone wrong and switch heads with each other.

Chorus Crime, A
The Rangers help Canina LeFur, a famous star, recover her special dancing shoes.

They Shoot Dogs Don't They?
Canina LeFur asks the Rangers for help again when she thinks that her stand-in is trying to kill her.

Tale Spin

Another of the initial entries in the Disney Afternoon lineup was *Tale Spin*, a series built around the popular character Baloo. This amiable bear was first seen in the 1967 theatrical release *The Jungle Book*. For *Tale Spin*, all of *The Jungle Book* was gone except the characters of Baloo, Shere Khan, and Louie the ape.

Disney produced 65 episodes of *Tale Spin*, which debuted on The Disney Afternoon on 9/10/90 along with *DuckTales*, *Disney's Adventures of the Gummi Bears*, and *Chip 'n Dale's Rescue Rangers*. Like Disney's other syndicated animated series, it had been previewed on The Disney Channel, with the first screening there being on 5/05/90.

Each episode is described in the original order as aired on The Disney Afternoon.

From Here to Machinery
When Baloo loses an endurance contest to a new robot, Shere Khan quickly places an army of robots into action as his newest pilots.

It Came from beneath the Sea Duck
A submarine invasion of Cape Suzette by air pirates and a giant squid make a simple babysitting job much harder than Kit expected.

TIME WAITS FOR NO BEAR
Rebecca tries to put Baloo on a tight schedule to make him a better pilot, but the carefree bear has other ideas.

MOMMY FOR A DAY
Molly enlists Kit in a dangerous mission to return a strange animal to its mother. Rebecca and Baloo chase after them, for an evil hunter has vowed to capture the animal.

I ONLY HAVE ICE FOR YOU
When Baloo loses his pilot's license, Rebecca decides to learn how to fly. Unfortunately, she learns from a very strange instruction manual, and Baloo must step in to save her and his beloved plane.

MOLLY CODDLED
Rebecca takes an instant liking to a doll she finds hidden aboard the Sea Duck, unaware that it contains the secret of a missing treasure.

POLLY WANTS A TREASURE
A stowaway parrot puts Baloo and Kit in danger when Don Karnage discovers that the bird knows the way to a treasure cache.

VOWEL PLAY
Baloo accidentally puts Cape Suzette in danger when Rebecca accepts a skywriting assignment, for spies are using the messages to pass secrets. Baloo's inability to spell adds a new twist to their messages.

IDOL RICH, THE
Baloo plans to regain title to the Sea Duck by earning a reward for returning a valuable missing idol. Unfortunately, Colonel Spigot of the gloomy land of Thembria also has plans for the idol.

STORMY WEATHER
Kit runs away to join an air circus after Baloo complains about his cloudsurfing. When Baloo discovers Kit must perform a serious of dangerous stunts, he rushes into action to save his friend.

BEARLY ALIVE
Baloo sets off on a very dangerous flight when he gets the mistaken impression that he is ill and about to die.

HER CHANCE TO DREAM
Rebecca falls in love with a sea captain, but Baloo and Louie think there is something strange about her dream man.

ALL'S WHALE THAT ENDS WHALE
Baloo still wants to buy back the Sea Duck, and he finally earns the money when he returns a trained whale to an aquarium. When he later sees how the whale is being mistreated, he must decide if the plane is that important to him.

GOLDEN SPROCKET OF FRIENDSHIP, THE
After Baloo talks Sergeant Dunder into doing his work for him, he begins to feel guilty about misleading the not-unlikeable Dunder.

FOR A FUEL DOLLARS MORE
Rebecca's new scheme to earn money starts Baloo running a mid-air refueling service. This puts him in direct conflict with Louie, who starts his own service, and the two friends almost end up killing themselves—and Rebecca.

BAD REFLECTION ON YOU, A
(2 PARTS)
Baloo's self-confidence leads to disaster when Shere Khan uses him as bait to tempt Don Karnage into the open. Karnage tricks Baloo into crashing, and Kit must find a way to restore Baloo's confidence.

ON A WING AND A BEAR
Baloo is having trouble passing the test to renew his pilot's license. It takes an encounter with air pirates to show the test examiner that Baloo has what it takes in the air.

STAR IS TORN, A
Baloo lets his heart take control of his brain when he falls for a beautiful movie star. He throws caution to the winds and starts performing very dangerous flying stunts to impress her.

TOUCH OF GLASS, A
Rebecca is blinded by the good manners and apparent charm of two newcomers, unaware that they plan to use her as a pawn in an insurance scam.

Bigger They Are, The Louder They Oink, The

A search for truffles leads Baloo, Rebecca, and Kit into a dark and dangerous jungle, where hungry animals and angry pygmies wait for unsuspecting travelers.

Spy in the Ointment, A

A stranger's claim that he is a spy embroils Rebecca in what she thinks is foreign intrigue.

Balooest of the Blue Bloods, The

When Baloo gets word that he has inherited a fortune, he quits his job to live a life of luxury. That life may be a short one, for his new servants are determined to kill him for his fortune.

Baloo Switcheroo, A

A strange idol causes Baloo and Kit to exchange bodies with one another. By the time the confusion is sorted out and they are returned to normal, each of them comes to better understand the other.

Whistlestop Jackson, Legend

Rebecca hires a legendary flyer to draw attention to her business, unaware that Shere Khan will stop at nothing to settle an old score with the man.

Double or Nothing

Baloo's latest attempt to get rich almost succeeds. He manages to parlay $50 into $10,000, only to discover that a gang of thieves wants the money very badly indeed.

Feminine Air

Baloo isn't happy working for a woman, but when he's forced to enter a race disguised as a female, he gains new respect for the opposite sex.

Last Horizons

Baloo's attempt to become a famous adventurer almost leads to disaster when he unwittingly leads a savage horde of panda invaders to Cape Suzette.

Flight of the Snow Duck

Molly and Wildcat are imprisoned in Thembria for having an imagination. Luckily, they are able to use that very same imagination to escape on a very strange aircraft they saw in a children's book.

Save the Tiger

After Baloo saves his life, Shere Khan feels indebted to him and indulges his every whim. When Baloo takes advantage of the situation, Shere Khan launches a surprising plan to escape his debt of honor.

Old Man and the Sea Duck, The

An accident leaves Baloo with amnesia and unable to fly. Everyone tries to help him recover his memory, but it takes a special guardian angel to do the trick.

War of the Weirds

Baloo tries to play a hoax on Rebecca by sending a radio message that he is about to fly to Mars using a secret fuel. The message almost brings disaster to Cape Suzette when others hear the message and want the fuel.

Captains Outrageous

A membership test for a secret club brings Baloo, Kit, and Wildcat into conflict with Don Karnage.

Plunder and Lightning

The premiere 2-hour episode, first aired as a special and described earlier in this book, was also aired during the regular series in four parts.

Time Bandit, The

Baloo tries to convince Rebecca that payday has come early and is soon arrested for his efforts.

For Whom the Bell Klangs—Part 1

Baloo promises to give up hunting for treasure—until he and Louie meet a lovely archeologist who is looking for a lost city.

For Whom the Bell Klangs—Part 2

The search for the lost city is imperiled by Klang, an evil adventurer who wants a deadly weapon that is hidden there.

Citizen Khan

Imprisoned by Khan's men, Baloo tries to convince them that Wildcat is their leader in disguise.

Gruel and Unusual Punishment

Hoping to lose a few pounds, Baloo heads off to a fat farm. Unfortunately, he gets lost and finds himself in a deadly Thembrian prison-camp instead, thinking all the while it's a health spa.

Jolly Molly Christmas, A
Baloo gets deeper and deeper into trouble when he tries to convince Molly that Santa Claus is real. Just as Baloo is ready to give up, Santa appears to save the day.

My Fair Baloo
Baloo tries his best to fit in at a society ball but fails miserably. He more than redeems himself, however, by saving the guests from the mobster Owl Capone and a crash on a deserted island.

Waiders of the Wost Tweasure
Baloo and an old rival compete in a race, unaware that they are pawns in a deadly plan.

Flight School Confidential
Kit gets angry when Baloo tells him he is too young to fly, so he runs away to take flying lessons in Thembria. Kit soon learns that the flight school hides a terrible secret.

Bringing Down Babyface
The police believe that Baloo helped a deadly criminal escape from jail, and he must track down the villain to avoid going to jail himself.

Jumping the Guns
Don Karnage steals the *Sea Duck* and uses it to capture the guns that protect Cape Suzette.

In Search of Ancient Blunders
Baloo and Wildcat must deal with a needy archeologist, a mummy, an upside-down pyramid, and Don Karnage.

Louie's Last Stand
Baloo joins forces with Louie when one of Khan's men decides to take over Louie's island and nightclub.

Sheepskin Deep
Unable to go to his grade school reunion because he never graduated, Baloo decides to finally earn his diploma.

Pizza Pie in the Sky
An attempt to deliver pizzas by airplane results in another monetary setback for Baloo.

Baloo Thunder
To clear a friend's name, Baloo must recover a stolen secret helicopter.

Bullethead Baloo
Baloo tries to impress Kit and his friends by impersonating "Bullethead," a comic book hero who flies with a jet pack.

Destiny Rides Again
Baloo's hopes for a quiet weekend are dashed when he listens to a fortune teller's predictions of doom.

Mach One for the Gipper
The return of an old rival pits Baloo in a contest to decide who is the fastest pilot alive.

Stuck on You
A super sticky glue makes strange allies of Baloo and Don Karnage, who must reluctantly join forces if they are to get unstuck from each other.

Sound and the Furry, The
A treacherous mechanic is using strange little animals to wreck airplanes so she can fix them.

Road to Macadamia, The
In a setting straight from a Bob Hope–Bing Crosby "Road" movie, Baloo and Louie try to save a kingdom from an evil advisor.

Ransom of Red Chimp, The
Louie's aunt is kidnapped by Don Karnage, but the rescue attempt is complicated when she falls in love with her kidnapper—who can't wait until he is rid of her.

Your Baloo's in the Mail
Baloo mis-mails Rebecca's winning sweepstakes ticket and tries his best to get it to its destination before the deadline.

Paradise Lost
A hunter tricks Baloo into flying him into a remote valley full of dinosaurs.

Incredible Shrinking Molly, The
Molly is accidentally hit by a shrinking ray and her friends must also miniaturize themselves so they can save her.

Bygones
Rick Sky, a famous military pilot, returns years after he was lost on a secret mission. Only Baloo can help prove that the man wasn't a traitor or a coward.

Flying Dupes

Baloo and Spigot are tricked into delivering a bomb to the Thembrian High Marshall.

Darkwing Duck

The 1991–92 season saw the debut of *Darkwing Duck*, the story of Drake Mallard, an average citizen who created a secret identity for himself as a costumed crime fighter. It replaced *Disney's Gummi Bears* in the daily line-up for the season beginning 9/09/91.

In addition to the daily episodes aired in syndication, *Darkwing Duck* had the unusual distinction of also appearing each week on ABC. It was the first series ever to simultaneously air new episodes in syndication and on a network. Thirteen episodes were produced for ABC, which aired them at 9:00 A.M. on Saturdays beginning on 9/07/91. A total of 91 episodes were produced.

Each of the syndicated episodes is listed below in order of the original airdate, followed by the episodes produced for ABC.

Beauty and the Beet

Scientist Reginald Bushroot turns himself into a half-duck, half-plant creature that can to control all plant life.

Getting Antsy

Lilliput is shrinking buildings so his loyal army of ants can loot them for him.

Night of the Living Spud

Bushroot tries to grow a bride for himself but accidentally creates a vampire potato instead.

Apes of Wrath

SHUSH assigns Darkwing to find a missing scientist and he discovers she has become the leader of a band of gorillas.

Dirty Money

Someone is wiping all the ink off money in St. Canard.

Duck Blind

When Darkwing is blinded by Megavolt, he is forced to let Gosalyn, Honker, and Launchpad carry on for him.

Comic Book Capers

When a comic book company publishes a book starring Darkwing, everyone gets into the act trying to write the perfect story.

Water Way to Go

Darkwing looks for missing SHUSH agents in Oilrabia, where Steelbeak is creating heavy rain in the desert.

Paraducks

A visit to the past finds Darkwing unsure if he should stop a crime there and thus possibly change history.

Easy Come, Easy Grows

Bushroot is behind a bizarre plot involving counterfeit money trees.

Revolution in Home Appliances, A

Megavolt brings electrical appliances to life as part of his newest scheme to plunder the city.

Trading Faces

Gosalyn and Darkwing find their minds in each other's bodies, as do Honker and Launchpad. This makes it that much more difficult to thwart Steelbeak's plan to stop the Earth's rotation.

Hush, Hush Sweet Charlatan

Darkwing agrees to star in a movie, unaware that director Tuskernini plans to use some dangerous stunts to get rid of the crime fighter.

Can't Bayou Love

Two Cajun crooks make Darkwing the quarry of a hunting expedition.

Bearskin Thug

A camping trip goes awry when the gang stumbles on Steelbeak's plan to turn trees into missile silos.

You Sweat Your Life

Drake goes undercover to investigate a health farm that may hold the secret to missing gold.

Days of Blunder

Quackerjack, disguised as a psychiatrist, convinces Darkwing he is in the wrong line of work.

Just Us Justice Ducks—Part 1

Darkwing faces his worst threat ever when Negaduck, Megavolt, Quackerjack, Bushroot, and Liquidator team up to take over St. Canard.

JUST US JUSTICE DUCKS—PART 2

Darkwing realizes he can't fight the five crooks together, so he reluctantly accepts help from Gizmoduck, Neptunia, Steggmutt, and Morgana.

DOUBLE DARKWINGS

Jambalaya Jake, the Cajun crook, returns with a special zombie formula to enslave Darkwing, but it's Launchpad who falls into his clutches instead.

ADUCKYPHOBIA

Moliarty uses a giant spider to catch airplanes in huge webs, but when Darkwing tries to stop him, a spider bite gives him four extra arms.

WHEN ALIENS COLLIDE

Two aliens arrive on Earth and Darkwing befriends the wrong one. If the crime fighter doesn't act quickly, the Earth will be history.

JURASSIC JUMBLE

A dinosaur-loving scientist has plans to bring back his favorite creatures, even if it means destroying life as we know it.

CLEANLINESS IS NEXT TO BADLINESS

The mad cleaning woman, Ammonia Pine, almost wipes Darkwing out when she joins forces with Steelbeak.

SMARTER THAN A SPEEDING BULLET

An alien visitor arrives for some superhero training, but the classes almost prove to be the end of Darkwing.

ALL'S FAHRENHEIT IN LOVE AND WAR

When Isis Vanderchill tries to freeze her face to keep it young forever, she must seek out massive amounts of heat to stay warm enough to be comfortable.

WHIFFLE WHILE YOU WORK

Darkwing and Quackerjack must do battle inside a video game.

GHOUL OF MY DREAMS

Nodoff, the evil ruler of the dream world, plans to put everyone in St. Canard to sleep so he can rule that city as well.

The following two episodes were originally aired as the 1-hour series premiere.

DARKLY DAWNS THE DUCK—PART 1

Taurus Bulba steals an energy weapon from Gosalyn's grandfather.

DARKLY DAWNS THE DUCK—PART 2

Taurus tries to kidnap Gosalyn to learn how the weapon operates, but Darkwing goes into action.

ADOPT-A-CON

Binkie Muddlefoot signs Drake up to help rehabilitate a convict, never suspecting that Tuskernini will become her new neighbor.

TOYS CZAR US

Quackerjack kidnaps children to run his secret toy factory.

SECRET ORIGINS OF DARKWING DUCK, THE

Sometime in the future, two children hear a strange story of how Drake Mallard became Darkwing Duck.

UP, UP, AND AWRY

Darkwing asks Launchpad and Gizmoduck for help in creating his own super-powered suit, but the results are less than super.

LIFE, THE NEGAVERSE, AND EVERYTHING

Darkwing discovers an alternate universe where the villains are the heroes!

DRY HARD

A new foe arrives on the scene when a crooked businessman falls into a vat of contaminated water and emerges as the Liquidator, able to control all liquids.

HEAVY MENTAL

Both sides are after a ray that can give people incredible psychic powers.

DISGUISE THE LIMIT

Negaduck frames Darkwing and everyone in St. Canard is after him, so he uses a new ray to disguise himself, unaware of the consequences.

PLANET OF THE CAPES

Darkwing visits the planet Mertz, where everyone is a superhero except one poor fellow who is tired of always being rescued.

DARKWING DOUBLOON

Drake tells Gosalyn about pirate hero Darkwing Doubloon, with the characters of *Dark-*

wing Duck filling in the roles of the history lesson.

IT'S A WONDERFUL LEAF
Bushroot plans to ruin Christmas by making Christmas trees steal the presents.

TWITCHING CHANNELS
Megavolt's newest invention lets him steal things through people's television sets, but when Darkwing tries to stop him, the super hero is sucked inside a set and discovers he is a cartoon character in a human world.

DANCES WITH BIGFOOT
Gosalyn must come to the rescue when Darkwing is kidnapped by animals who plan to sacrifice him to a volcano.

TWIN BEAKS
Darkwing and Launchpad become involved in a strange case involving Bushroot, intelligent cows, and mutant cabbages.

INCREDIBLE BULK, THE
Bushroot's experimental plant food turns Darkwing into a huge mutated hero.

MY VALENTINE GHOUL
When Darkwing and Morgana have an argument, Negaduck, stolen diamonds, and a love potion all meet unexpectedly.

DEAD DUCK
Morgana is the only one who can help Darkwing when he becomes a ghost.

DUCK BY ANY OTHER NAME, A
When Launchpad is caught in his Darkwing decoy costume, Tuskernini thinks he has discovered the crime fighter's true identity.

LET'S GET RESPECTABLE
Darkwing tries a publicity campaign to improve his popularity, but Negaduck takes advantage of this to start a crime wave.

IN LIKE BLUNT
Darkwing must team up with retired SHUSH agent Derek Blunt to stop a thief from auctioning off a list of agents.

QUACK OF AGES
A trip to the past takes an unexpected turn when Darkwing and Launchpad are accused of being sorcerers and are sentenced to death.

TIME AND PUNISHMENT
Gosalyn's unexpected trip to the future reveals a terrible fate for St. Canard, for Drake has become the dreaded Darkwarrior Duck, a cold and ruthless dictator.

STRESSED TO KILL
Quackerjack and Megavolt join forces and make everyone in St. Canard so relaxed that they don't care they are being robbed.

DARKWING SQUAD, THE
J. Gander Hooter has Darkwing form a squad of agents, but they are so disorganized that they do more harm than good.

INSIDE BINKIE'S BRAIN
A blow on the head turns Binkie into the Canardian Guardian, a would-be superhero. Unfortunately, she is ill-prepared to do battle with Megavolt, who seems to cross paths with her at every turn.

HAUNTING OF MR. BANANA BRAIN, THE
Gosalyn accidentally unleashes Paddywhack, a villain who lives for practical jokes.

SLIME OK, YOU'RE OK
Bushroot turns Gosalyn into a slime creature with a tremendous appetite.

WHIRLED HISTORY
Gosalyn dreams about her favorite television hero, Astroduck, but in so doing, she learns that there are no shortcuts in life.

U.F. FOE
Aliens have kidnapped Launchpad to make him their king, but Darkwing's efforts to rescue his friend are slowed when the aliens remove the crime fighter's brain!

STAR IS SCORNED, A
Darkwing's television producer has some very strange plans for the show's hero, including making Bushroot the star of the show.

QUIVERWING QUACK, THE
Gosalyn is tired of being treated like a little girl, so she becomes Quiverwing Quack, the newest superhero in St. Canard.

JAIL BIRD
Negaduck invites the rest of the Fearsome Five to his hideout, where he sucks out their powers to turn himself into Mega-Negaduck.

DIRTYSOMETHING
Ammonia Pine's dirty sister, Ample Grime, arrives in town and the two begin arguing over how to control the city.

KUNG FOOLED
Darkwing learns that his old martial arts teacher has given up his vow of poverty and become a greedy businessman.

BAD LUCK DUCK
Negaduck finds a way to bring inanimate objects to life, and Darkwing has to overcome a curse of perpetual bad luck to stop him.

ABC episodes—first season: 1991–92

THAT SINKING FEELING
The evil Professor Moliarty plans to plunge the world into eternal darkness so he and his moles can rule the planet.

FILM FLAM
Tuskernini finds a way to bring movie villains to life.

NEGADUCK
Megavolt uses an energy ray to split Darkwing into two beings, but the new arrival shows some very evil tendencies.

FUNGUS AMONGUS
Darkwing has to combat a plan to create mushroom pizzas that are hungry for a duck dinner.

SLAVES TO FASHION
Tuskernini uses old movie costumes and a hypnotic gas to enslave the wealthy patrons of a charity ball.

SOMETHING FISHY
Neptunia, a mutated fish, uses her powers over the creatures of the sea to flood St. Canard.

TIFF OF THE TITANS
FOWL agent Steelbeak convinces Gizmoduck that Darkwing is a villain who needs to be brought to justice.

CALM A CHAMELEON
A woman discovers how to use the powers of chameleons to turn herself into any object she desires.

BATTLE OF THE BRAINTEASERS
Evil aliens shaped like hats take control of anyone who wears them, and only Gosalyn and Honker stand between them and world conquest.

BAD TIDINGS
FOWL is using a strange machine on the moon to create tidal waves.

GOING NOWHERE FAST
Darkwing gets the power of super speed during a battle with Negaduck, only to discover that he is rapidly aging every time he moves.

BRUSH WITH OBLIVION, A
Evil painter Splatter Phoenix has discovered a way to enter paintings.

MERCHANT OF MENACE, THE
It looks like Herb Muddlefoot might be a criminal mastermind in disguise, so Drake Mallard goes undercover to investigate his neighbor.

ABC episodes—second season: 1992–93

MONSTERS R US
Darkwing, Gosalyn, and Launchpad have to fight for their lives when they are turned into monsters.

INHERIT THE WIMP
A time machine brings some of Darkwing's ancestors to the present, and he is surprised to find they are not the heroes he thought them to be.

REVENGE OF THE BRAINTEASERS, TOO
The alien hats return with another plan to enslave the Earth, and Honker and Gosalyn must find a new way to stop them.

STAR CROSSED CIRCUITS
A new supercomputer turns against Darkwing and he can't find a way to shut it off.

STEERMINATOR
FOWL turns Taurus Bulba into a cyborg and sends it after Darkwing, who is recovering from an accident and is in no condition to fight.

FREQUENCY FIENDS
Gosalyn's subconscious is accidentally turned into three energy creatures who quickly terrorize St. Canard.

Paint Misbehavin'

Splatter Phoenix returns with her paint that brings things to life, but Darkwing's efforts to stop her are thwarted by a small problem with another would-be hero—Gosalyn.

Hot Spells

Lucifer tricks Gosalyn into opening the gates to Hell and then lures Darkwing inside.

Fraudcast News

A newscaster can't find any crimes to report on, so she decides to become a super villain and stir up some business.

Clash Reunion

Darkwing realizes that Megavolt is a former classmate, and just in time. It seems that Megavolt has plans to destroy the class reunion.

Mutancy on the Bouncy

Gosalyn discovers that Darkwing's latest foe is really a hero, and that a respected member of the community is really a villain.

Malice's Restaurant

Negaduck plans to exploit the grand opening of Morgana's new restaurant in his latest evil plot.

Extinct Possibility

Darkwing, Launchpad, and Gosalyn must travel back in time to defeat a band of evil dinosaurs.

Goof Troop

Goof Troop starred Goofy, who along with Mickey Mouse, Donald, and Pluto comprised what some called Disney's "Big Four" of animation.

Goof Troop began in syndication with the 1992–93 season. Additional episodes were also created for ABC, which aired the series on Saturday mornings. In addition to the stories seen on *Goof Troop* itself, another episode, *Have Yourself a Goofy Little Christmas*, was aired as part of the special *A Goof Troop Christmas*.

A total of 78 episodes were produced. The syndicated episodes are listed first in airdate order, followed by the ABC episodes.

Fatal Subtraction

Convinced that he'll be grounded for life for a bad report card, P.J. tries to cram all of the fun for the rest of his life into one day.

Unreal Estate

Hoping to save a few bucks, Pete hires Goofy to fix up a vacation cottage.

You Camp Take It with You

Goofy and Pete take the boys camping, only to meet a bear who is out with his cub as well.

Midnight Movie Madness

Seeing a horror movie makes the kids convinced that a killer is hiding in the house.

Counterfeit Goof

Goofy gets a job hanging wallpaper, only to end up involved with a band of counterfeiters.

O, R-V, I N-V-U

Pete uses Max in a scheme to create the ultimate recreational vehicle.

Meanwhile, Back at the Ramp

Goofy tries desperately to win an award to impress Max, going as far as trying the world's tallest skateboard ramp.

Close Encounters of the Weird Mime

A messed up science project results in the world thinking that aliens have invaded!

Slightly Dinghy

Max drags the others into a scheme to recover a sunken treasure, planning on using the money to buy video games.

Cabana Fever

Pete heads off to a deserted island for a vacation far away from Goofy, unaware that his hapless neighbor is locked in the luggage.

Where There's Smoke, There's Goof

The city of Spoonerville has a new fireman—Goofy.

Date with Destiny

When Max thinks he will be taken away from Goofy unless his dad gets married, Pete steps in as a matchmaker.

Hot Air

Goofy and Max take Pistol to an air show, where she unleashes terror in the skies.

Take Me Out of the Old Ball Game

Goofy and Pete both decide their sons are going to be the next baseball superstars, but the boys have other ideas.

Wrecks, Lies & Videotape

Max is sure that he can win the "America's Most Painful Home Videos" contest with a tape of his dad, but Pete steals it and wins the prize.

Max-imum Protection

A burglar is stalking the neighborhood and Max tries to convince Goofy to buy an elaborate security system.

Goofin' Hood & His Melancholy Men

Goofy tells Max about a family ancestor, hoping it will provoke an interest in history.

Leader of the Pack

Max goes into battle against a gang that won't let him eat at their hangout.

Inspector Goofy

Hoping to put a competitor out of business, Pete gets Goofy a job as a city inspector, never thinking that he himself might get a visit from the energetic new civil servant.

Shake, Rattle & Goof

Max and P.J. try to become rock stars, only to discover that the public is wild about Goofy and his ukelele.

Terminal Pete

Pete mistakenly thinks he is going to die and gives away all of his possessions, only to then discover he is going to live.

Fool's Gold

Goofy and Pete both sink to new lows in a madcap hunt for buried gold.

Cat's Entertainment

Pete steals Goofy's cat, planning to use it in a series of cat food commercials.

Waste Makes Haste

A recycling project gets out of hand when Goofy and Pete both search for a millionaire's accidentally discarded treasure.

Ungoofables, The

Goofy uses the family album to tell the story of Elliot Goof, G-Man.

All the Goof That's Fit to Print

Pete decides to start his own newspaper, reasoning that he could then have all of the free advertising he wants.

To Heir Is Human

Pete cons his own son into running the car lot so he can go fishing.

Hallow-Weenies

Max and P.J. dare each other to enter a spooky old mansion on Halloween, unaware that a bunch of spooks have set up house inside.

Tub Be or Not Tub Be

Pete tries to get P.J. to help him race in Spoonerville's annual bath tub race.

Major Goof

Another of Pete's practical jokes backfires, this time resulting in Goofy, Max, and P.J. being chosen for a secret mission.

Goof of the People, A

Upset at the pollution caused by a chemical plant, Goofy decides to run for mayor.

Goof under My Roof

Pete makes the amazing discovery that he owns half of Goofy's property and takes advantage of the situation by forcing Goofy to act as his servant.

The following two episodes were first seen in the Special *Disney's Goof Troop*. The title for the two segments is *Forever Goof*.

Everything's Coming Up Goofy (Segment 1)

Goofy gets a new job and moves back to his old home town, Spoonerville, where he buys a house next door to his old friend, Pete.

Good Neighbor Goof (Segment 2)

Both Goofy and Pete order their sons to stay away from each other, but the boys have other ideas.

Goodbye, Mr. Goofy

One of Pete's plans goes wrong and it looks like Goofy will lose his house.

Lethal Goofin'

Max and P.J. become part of the school's Safety Patrol, only to discover that the school bullies have a secret leader.

Frankengoof

Goofy inherits both the scary old Frankengoof castle and a monster that looks more than a little like Pete.

E=MC Goof
A mixed up job application results in Goofy's being hired as a rocket scientist.

Pete's Day at the Races
Pete decides to get rich by selling 50 percent shares in a race horse to as many people as will buy them.

In Goof We Trust
Everyone in Spoonerville knows that Goofy is honest, so Pete decides to try to use that to his advantage at the car lot.

And Baby Makes Three
A series of misunderstandings makes P.J. and Pistol think that Peg is going to have a baby.

Incredible Bulk, The
Pete tricks Goofy into stepping into the ring with Bulk Brogan, the world's champion wrestler.

Mrs. Spoonerville
Pete goes all out to win a contest for clean houses, despite the fact that he is a slob.

For Pete's Sake
Pete becomes convinced that someone is out to kill him—especially Goofy.

Big City Blues
Max and P.J. sneak away to the big city, leaving a worried set of fathers behind looking for them.

Rally Round the Goof
Pete won't enter a road rally without his good luck charm—Goofy.

Window Pains
Peg takes a job washing windows to earn extra money to buy Pete a present, but he somehow ends up in competition against her.

Nightmare on Goof Street
A pair of con artists get their hands on Pete's house as part of a remodeling scheme, and a desperate Pete turns to Goofy for help.

Where There's a Will, There's a Goof
A strange clause in a will requires Goofy and Pete to act like long lost brothers if they hope to claim the inheritance.

Winter Blunderland
Pete plans to pass off Goofy as "Bigfoot" to gain publicity for his car lot, but the real Bigfoot happens to be in the area.

Gymnauseum
Afraid that he is going to lose Peg to another car salesman, Pete embarks on an extremely ambitious exercise campaign.

Come Fly with Me
A computer, a fly, and Pete all combine for a strange twist on the horror movie *The Fly*.

As Goof Would Have It
Pete uses a picture of Goofy to trick a diet food company into thinking their product has done wonders for him.

Calling All Goofs
When Pete tricks Goofy into spending the money he had saved to go to a family reunion, Peg decides to use her husband's credit cards to bring all of the Goofs to Spoonerville.

Buddy Building
Max and P.J. find their friendship put to the test when a new kid in town starts spending a lot of time with one of them.

Dr. Horatio's Magic Orchestra
Pete accidentally buys a mechanical band that plays the one song in the world that he can't stand.

Goofs of a Feather
After Pete goes hunting and apparently kills a duck, the fowl's family moves in and takes over the house.

Goof Fellas
Goofy and Pete see an attempted killing and are put into a witness relocation program. Unfortunately, Goofy seems unable to keep a low profile!

Good, the Bad & the Goofy, The
Goofy accidentally makes the police think that Pete is the ringleader of a band of robbers.

Educating Goofy
Max is horrified to learn that Goofy has decided to go back to school—his school.

PEG O' THE JUNGLE

Peg longs for the sentimental Pete that she married, so Goofy concocts a plan to unveil the "real" Pete.

PARTNERS IN GRIME

Goofy ends up as partners with Pete in a questionable catering business.

PIZZA THE ACTION, A

Pete tricks Goofy into taking over a failing pizza franchise.

TO CATCH A GOOF

Pete's new diet, Goofy's ninja training, and a burglar all combine for an adventure that soon involves both families and the police.

GUNFIGHT AT THE OKIE DOKIE CORRAL

Another look at the Goof family album reveals the story of Mopalong Goofy, a cowboy ancestor.

ABC episode descriptions

QUEASY RIDER

Max takes Goofy's old motorcycle for a ride and ends up in trouble with a band of bikers.

MAX-IMUM INSECURITY

The boys have to work to clear their names after being framed for shoplifting.

PUPPY LOVE

Max uses a series of stunts to impress a new girl at school, only to find out that she likes him just as he is.

GREAT EGG-SPECTATIONS

Max wants a pet, but when he finds a strange egg, he gets more than he bargained for. When the egg hatches, Max is the proud owner of a baby dinosaur.

THREE RING BIND

Pistol sets a band of animals free from a dilapidated circus, but the ringmaster has other plans.

PISTOLGEIST

One of Pistol's books may be haunted and it's up to the boys to save her.

BRINGIN' ON THE RAIN

A little thing like a drought isn't going to stand in Pete's way. To keep his garden beautiful, he merely taps into Goofy's water line.

TALENT TO THE MAX

Max becomes convinced that his magic act will propel him to fame and fortune, even though P.J. tries to tell him he stinks.

TEE FOR TWO

Peg wants to save a miniature golf course from a greedy developer who is planning on bulldozing the place. The developer? Pete.

GOOFIN' UP THE SOCIAL LADDER

Peg's efforts to sell some high class real estate take a strange twist when Goofy and the gang get involved.

SHERLOCK GOOF

Another ancestor is featured, this time a detective in Victorian England.

FROM AIR TO ETERNITY

P.J. is afraid to let Pete know that he is afraid of heights.

CLAN OF THE CAVE GOOF

Goofy tells Max about their ancestor, caveman Goof, who accidentally invented fire, the wheel, and the leisure suit.

Disney's The Little Mermaid

When the animated feature *The Little Mermaid* brought in a very impressive $84 million at the box office, it virtually resurrected Disney's Feature Animation Division. It also introduced one of Disney's most popular heroines, Ariel, and left audiences wanting more of the strong-willed mermaid. *The Little Mermaid* became the first Disney animated feature to be turned into an animated series.

Set in the days before the film, *Disney's The Little Mermaid* joined the CBS Saturday morning line-up for the 1992–93 season after a special premiere episode during prime time. Two more seasons followed for a total of 31 episodes.

Each of the episodes is listed below in order of the original airdate.

First season: 1992–93

WHALE OF A TALE

Ariel tries to keep her pet killer whale a secret from King Triton, who feels the animal would be better off in the wild. Unfortunately, Ariel soon finds that a growing whale is not easily hidden. This episode was aired on prime time.

GREAT SEBASTIAN, THE
Sebastian volunteers to act as a peace envoy between King Triton and the Sharkanians, a nearby savage race. The Sharkanians appear receptive to the peace offerings, but they have a hidden motive for their friendliness.

STORMY
Ariel rides a wild giant seahorse that carries her into a dangerous wilderness.

URCHIN
Urchin, a young merboy anxious for friendship, falls in with a criminal gang led by the Lobster Mobster.

DOUBLE BUBBLE
Ariel babysits for visiting twins, but the youngsters are kidnapped by Lobster Mobster and Shrimp.

MESSAGE IN A BOTTLE
A note from a prisoner leads Ariel into an adventure with a friendly sea monster.

CHARMED
Disobeying her father yet again, Ariel ends up in danger when she puts on a strange bracelet. It gets stuck on her wrist and she has to enter a strange cavern to look for the key.

MARRIAGE OF INCONVENIENCE
Sebastian and Urchin almost unleash a war when they try to prevent a planned marriage between Ariel and a prince from another kingdom.

EVIL MANTA, THE
Ariel accidentally unleashes a creature that makes everyone hate one another. Note: This episode was retitled *In Harmony* for home video release.

THINGAMAJIGGER
A human boot, lost during a sea battle, is mistaken for a secret weapon.

RED
A sorceress transforms King Triton into a young boy and Ariel has to take care of him.

BEACHED
Ariel and her sister Arista, left alone in the palace as punishment for disobeying their father, have to stop two crocodiles from plundering the treasury.

TRIDENT TRUE
When Urchin borrows King Triton's powerful magic trident and loses it, the powerful weapon soon comes into the possession of the Evil Manta.

EEL-ECTRIC CITY
Ariel and her sister Allana visit a night club, unaware of an approaching deadly current.

Second season: 1993–94
The following new episodes were produced for this season, and aired along with repeats of those produced for the first year.

RESIGNED TO IT
Sebastian gets mad at King Triton and resigns, but finds he can't succeed in a series of new jobs.

CALLIOPE DREAMS
Ariel's lack of musical skill awakens a sea monster when she tries to play an underwater calliope.

SAVE THE WHALE
Ariel has to rescue her former pet whale, Spot, who has been captured by a human promoter and forced to perform in a show.

AGAINST THE TIDE
A creature with a reputation for causing bad luck needs to be protected from Ursula.

GIGGLES
A spell makes Ariel cause sea quakes every time she laughs.

WISH UPON A STARFISH
Ariel wants to learn how to dance, and a hearing-impaired mermaid wants to sing. The two girls join forces to look for a magic starfish that can grant their wishes.

TAIL OF TWO CRABS
A rival crab who is always getting the best of Sebastian drops in for a visit.

METAL FISH
Ariel has to save Hans Christian Andersen when he becomes trapped underwater in a submarine.

T'ANK YOU FOR DAT, ARIEL
Sebastian is upset at being small until a spell makes him grow larger, for something goes wrong and he keeps getting bigger.

Third season: 1994–95
The following new episodes were produced for this season, and aired along with repeats of those produced earlier.

SCUTTLE
Ariel's first meeting with Scuttle doesn't go well, but things improve when they join forces to save Prince Eric's ship.

KING CRAB
A visit from Sebastian's parents poses a little problem for the crab, for he has been telling them that he's the ruler of Atlantica.

ISLAND OF FEAR
When a mad scientist kidnaps Sebastian for use in an experiment, the plucky crustacean joins forces with the scientist's assistant to escape.

LAND OF THE DINOSAURS
The discovery of dinosaurs frozen in ice proves too much of a temptation for Ariel. When she uses King Triton's trident to set them free, they promptly run amuck.

HEROES
Ariel learns a lesson when she discovers that Apollo, a war hero, isn't everything he is said to be.

BEAST WITHIN, THE
A bite from a werewolf-like Howling Hairfish turns Flounder into one of the creatures himself.

ARIEL'S TREASURES
A nasty spell by Ursula turns Ariel's prized collection of human artifacts into deadly weapons.

LITTLE EVIL, A
Ariel meets the Evil Manta's son, Little Evil, and tries to be his friend.

Raw Toonage

Hoping to attract a different demographic group, the Studio unveiled *Raw Toonage* as part of the CBS Saturday morning line-up for the 1992–93 season. *Raw Toonage* was promoted as having an edge, with promotional clips suggesting that viewers would be treated to something new and different from Disney. Evidently, it was too different. The series was canceled after 12 of the original 13 episodes had been completed.

Each of these segments is described below.

Host sequences
Each of the animated host sequences is described below in production order. As two of the sequences were never completed, not all of the episodes actually featured a weekly host.

BONKERS
Bonkers demonstrates his skills as a delivery boy as he tries to take a huge yacht across town.

DON KARNAGE
The pirate leader from *Tale Spin* lectures on how to be a pirate, with a surprise visit from Captain Hook.

GOOFY
Goofy presents a guide to the Olympics as only he can.

GOSALYN & LUDWIG
Gosalyn from *Darkwing Duck* enlists the help of Ludwig Von Drake to create a monster. Unfortunately, Ludwig ends up turning himself into a monster carrot.

JITTERS
Jitters demonstrates what it's like to be a cartoon stand-in for the series from The Disney Afternoon.

LAUNCHPAD
Launchpad McQuack from *DuckTales* goes over the basic rules of flight, with a particular emphasis on Rule #4—"Always Carry a Parachute!"

LUDWIG
Ludwig explains "Cartoon Physics" by demonstrating various animation gags including incredible examples of stretching, shrinking, and strength.

MARSUPILAMI
Marsupilami puts Maurice on a diet and fitness program so the gorilla can take on a bully.

SCROOGE MCDUCK
The world's richest duck proudly shows off the virtues of his overzealous super security system by trying to break into his money bin—and gets repeatedly trashed for his trouble.

SEBASTIAN

The crustacean co-star of *The Little Mermaid* desperately tries to get to a performance but has to dodge Chef Louie (also from the film) along the way. Note: This sequence was later used on *The Shnookums & Meat Funny Cartoon Show.*

The following host segments were not completed.

BALOO AND BUCKY BUG

A relatively unknown comic book star, Bucky Bug, tries to take over the airwaves during Baloo's show.

FLOUNDER

Flounder, while being chased by a shark, is desperately searching for Ariel to help him. Instead he bumps into Sebastian, who suggests that he tell the shark some jokes.

He's Bonkers

One of the main segments of *Raw Toonage* was *He's Bonkers*, a series of short cartoons featuring a new Disney character, Bonkers D. Bobcat. Overly energetic and somewhat short on brains, Bonkers was cast in different roles throughout the series.

In real life, Bonkers enjoyed an unusual "career" of his own. When *Raw Toonage* failed to capture enough of an audience to stay on the air, Bonkers moved on to his own series, *Disney's Bonkers.*

The *He's Bonkers* shorts produced for *Raw Toonage* are described here in alphabetical order. They were later combined with new footage for reuse on the *Disney's Bonkers* series. In addition, two shorts that were not completed are listed at the end of the aired episodes.

BONKERS IN SPACE

Jitters is accidentally jettisoned into space when Bonkers tries to impress Fawn while working on an outer-space service station.

DOGZAPOPPIN'

Bonkers is determined to deliver a package to his boss, but a ferocious watchdog is just as determined to stop him.

DRAINING CATS AND DOGS

Bonkers and Jitters are plumbers who try to fix Fawn's broken water pipes and end up flooding the house.

GET ME A PIZZA (HOLD THE MINEFIELD)

A black-and-white look back at World War I finds Bonkers bravely delivering a pizza to the men in the trenches.

GET ME TO THE CHURCH ON TIME

Bonkers takes Jitters on a mad dash to his own wedding, with stops for a flat tire and a ride through a car wash on bicycles.

GOBBLE, GOBBLE BONKERS

Jitters agrees to let Bonkers take one of his prized turkeys to Thanksgiving dinner, unaware that his pet is on the menu.

QUEST FOR FIREWOOD

A prehistoric setting finds Bonkers looking everywhere for firewood, but without a tree in sight.

SHEERLUCK BONKERS

Back in Victorian days, fearless detective Sheerluck Bonkers searches for Fawn's missing necklace, which she had wanted to present to the queen.

SKI PATROL

When Grumbles has an accident on the ski slope, he finds the cure is worse than the disease when Bonkers is his ambulance driver.

SPATULA PARTY

Bonkers will do anything to impress his new neighbor, Fawn Deer, when she asks to borrow a spatula.

TRAILMIX BONKERS & THE PONY EXPRESS

Pony Express rider Trailmix Bonkers must deliver an important package and outsmart a notorious bandit, Grumbles the Kid.

The following two shorts were not completed.

INDIANA BONKERS AND THE TEMPLE OF FAWN

The spirit of an ancient Egyptian princess needs Bonkers to locate her stolen radio.

PLA-TOON

Another attempt to impress Fawn Deer finds Bonkers enlisting in the army.

Totally Tasteless Video

These segments did not follow any set pattern or format. In general, they were spoofs of other cartoons, movies, or news events. They are listed here in production order.

ALL POTATO NETWORK

A parody of special-interest cable channels, including one where every show features potatoes, including the crime series *Spudsky and Hutch.*

BADLY ANIMATED MAN

A parody of animated superheroes as seen in all-too-many children's series features a hero with a very limited range of motion and emotion.

FROG PRINCE OF BEL AIR

The story of a freeloading frog who is rescued from the obscurity of a pet store by a wealthy little girl.

Note: This sequence was not completed.

REFRESHMENT STAND, RAMBONES, TOTZILLA, BLAMMO!

A cartoon parody of motion picture trailers includes a preview of *Blammo!,* a movie without any characters or plot—just a lot of explosions.

CRO MAGNUM, P.I.

The story of a stone-age detective who has to investigate the theft of some early inventions, including the wheel and fire.

DOGGIE SCHNAUZER

A sit-com parody about a canine surgeon who has to operate on a patient who swallowed a dishwasher.

MY NEW SHOES

A music video about an amazing pair of high-tech shoes.

NIGHTMARE ON ROCKY ROAD

A boy who wishes that the whole world was made of ice cream has to face the evil Freddie Scooper, a Freddy Kruger-esque villain who wants to turn him into ice cream as well.

PORKERS' COURT, THE

Three little pigs sue a slumlord, a big bad wolf, in an updated version of the old classic.

POULTRYGEIST

A family discovers that they have built their dream house on the site of a destroyed fast food chicken franchise.

ROBIN HOOF

An iconoclastic send-up of the Robin Hood legend in '50s animated design, much like the *Fractured Fairy Tales* series by Jay Ward. The star of this one is a clever cow.

YOU THINK YOU KNOW EVERYTHING, DON'T YOU?

A game show for snooty super-intellectuals gets a canine contestant.

Marsupilami

The animated series *Raw Toonage* didn't last long on the air, but it was notable for providing new opportunities for some seldom seen animated stars and for bringing two new Disney characters to life. The series actually came into being when the Studio realized they had two new and exciting characters, but they didn't have a place to use them.

One of these characters was a very unusual jungle cat, Marsupilami.

When *Raw Toonage* was canceled after only one season, Disney still had faith that Marsupilami could attract viewers, so just as with Bonkers D. Bobcat, they decided to next create another new series, *Marsupilami*, described later.

BATHTIME FOR MAURICE

Marsupilami decides that Maurice needs a bath, but the ape will have nothing to do with it. Maurice finally does get in the water, only to find piranhas, crocodiles, and a giant waterfall awaiting him.

FEAR OF KITES, A

Marsupilami must retrieve his kite from the roof of a hotel, but Norman the bellman is determined to stop him.

HAIRY APE, THE

Norman traps Maurice by inviting him to a fake party, a party that Marsupilami is determined to crash.

HOT SPOTS

A heat wave, a watering hole, and Norman all combine to make trouble for the jungle residents.

JUNGLE FEVER

A stubborn cold bedevils Maurice, so Marsupilami sets out to find a cure, no matter what the cost.

Mars Meets Dr. Normanstein

Marsupilami and Maurice stumble onto the lab of the evil Dr. Normanstein, who happens to be looking for a brain for his new monster, Apenstein.

Mars vs. Man

When Norman destroys the jungle to build a condo complex, Marsupilami sets things right by tricking Norman into destroying the complex.

Prime Mates Forever

Maurice falls in love and turns to Marsupilami for some help in the art of love.

Puck Stops Here, The

An overactive air conditioner lets Marsupilami and Maurice enjoy a game of ice hockey inside Norman's hotel.

Romancing the Clone

Norman promises tourists that they can have their picture taken with Marsupilami, then has to impersonate him. His plan goes awry when the real Marsupilami falls in love with the copy.

Safari So Good

Norman takes his aunt on a safari and she decides she wants a photo of Marsupilami over her mantle. Norman decides the real Marsupilami would look better there and goes hunting.

Someone's in the Kitchen with Mars

While searching for their stolen fruit basket, Marsupilami and Maurice cause trouble for the thief, Chef Norman.

Treasure of Sierra Marsdre, The

Norman talks his way onto Marsupilami's treasure expedition, unaware that the treasure map they're following is a fake drawn by Marsupilami as part of a game.

Wannabe Ruler

Maurice and Norman battle to become the new ruler of the Wannabe tribe, but a series of accidents results in Maurice being named king.

Witch Dr. Is Which?

Witch Doctor Norman tries to become "the happiest of them all" by making Marsupilami miserable though a series of nasty spells.

Young and the Nestless, The

A look at the first time Norman battled Marsupilami, back when they were children, and Norman shows how little things have changed over the years.

Disney's Bonkers

In addition to the new episodes created for *Bonkers*, there were 4 episodes created by combining several of the *He's Bonkers* segments from *Raw Toonage*. This brought the total number of episodes to 65.

Bonkers was added to The Disney Afternoon line-up for the 1993–94 season and continues in repeats as of this writing.

Each of the episodes is listed below in order of the original airdate.

Going Bonkers

Part 1 of the pilot episode was later aired under this title. Famous Wackytoons star Bonkers D. Bobcat is fired when his popularity drops and he somehow finds himself on the Hollywood Police Department, Toon Division.

Gone Bonkers

Part 2 of the pilot episode was later aired under this title. Bonkers and his new partner, Detective Lucky Piquel, search for missing toons who have been kidnapped by a crazed villain known as the Collector.

In the Bag

Bonkers tries to help Lucky with an upcoming inspection, but they are sidetracked by reports from the Mad Hatter and the March Hare about missing tea cups.

Hear No Bonkers, See No Bonkers

Crooks are turning toons invisible, and then charging a high price to restore them to normalcy.

Out of Sight, Out of Toon

Lucky catches a rare flu from Bonkers and turns into a tiny toon.

Is Toon Fur Really Warm?

Hoping to impress his daughter, Lucky promises that Skunky Skunk, her favorite toon, will come to her birthday party, unaware that the toon may have accidentally killed someone on his show.

CALLING ALL CARS
Ma Parker, a crooked toon tow truck, is helping steal cars to finance her entry into a monster truck rally.

FALL-APART BOMB SQUAD
When a toon bomb terrorizes the city, the police department puts Fall-Apart Rabbit on the bomb squad.

IN TOONS WE TRUST
Bonkers doesn't believe that an old friend is robbing jewelry stores, but this loyalty may cost Bonkers his job.

NEVER CRY PIG
The Three Big Pigs, who are definitely not the famous Three Little Pigs, may be mixed up in a shady real estate deal.

HAMSTER HOUSEGUEST
A mouse and hamster, ex-partners on a cartoon show, are still chasing each other, and almost destroy the city in the process.

CHEAP SHEEP SWEEP, THE
Someone is kidnapping toons and "sheep dipping" them to sell them as novelty sheep.

DAY THE TOON STOOD STILL, THE
When Pops, the keeper of toon time, retires unexpectedly, the toon world is thrown into chaos.

WEATHER OR NOT
Bonkers is determined to find some missing toon weather reporters.

BASIC SPRAINING
Bonkers heads off to the police academy, unaware that it's being run by criminal mastermind Mackey McSlime.

ONCE IN A BLUE TOON
After he accidentally lands Lucky in the hospital, Bonkers tries his best to act responsibly and peacefully. He also has to stop a toon monster from eating everything in sight.

LUNA-TOONS
When aliens invade the Earth, no one panics because they think the aliens are just toons.

TIME WOUNDS ALL HEELS
An ex-con returns to town and vows vengeance on Lucky and his family.

POLTERTOON
A pesky ghost moves into Lucky's house just as the Chief and his wife are arriving for dinner.

HAND OVER THE DOUGH
A toon spokesman is behind the sabotage at a bakery.

RUBBER ROOM SONG, THE
The Bully Boys sing *The Rubber Room Song*, as all the toons in the room dance madly to the beat. Note: This episode comprised the cartoons *Ski Patrol*, *Bonkers in Space*, and *Draining Cats and Dogs* from *Raw Toonage*.

TUNE PIG
Singer Julio Calamari is using a kidnapped pig to supply his magnificent singing voice.

NEW PARTNERS ON THE BLOCK
Lucky gets a long-awaited job with the FBI and Bonkers gets a new partner, Officer Miranda Wright.

WITLESS FOR THE PROSECUTION
Miranda, the only witness to a major crime, has to hide at Bonkers's apartment until she can testify at the trial.

BOBCAT FEVER
Bonkers is temporarily incapacitated by Cheryl Germ, a toon virus, as part of Al Vermin's latest plot.

WHAT YOU READ IS WHAT YOU GET
Lillith DuPrave, the owner of a sleazy tabloid, is using a toon typewriter to make her stories come true.

DO TOONS DREAM OF ANIMATED SHEEP?
A toon sheep steals Bonkers's dreams, so Ludwig Von Drake invents a dream projector to help solve the case.

TRAINS, TOONS, AND TOON TRAINS
Bonkers and Miranda become involved in intrigue aboard a train as they transport a toon prisoner.

QUIBBLING RIVALRY
Miranda's reporter sister, Shirley Wright, comes to town for her story, "Toons: Threat or Menace?," and makes Bonkers look bad in her reports.

Toon That Ate Hollywood, The
A stolen invention is being used to suck the humor out of toons, including Bonkers.

Springtime for the Iguana
Bonker talks his friend, Roderick Lizard, into working on a monster film, but Roderick is framed for arson when someone burns up the set.

Casabonkers
An old girlfriend involves Bonkers and Miranda in this spoof of *Casablanca* as the police search for the famous Maltese Beanie.

Tokyo Bonkers
Bonkers and Miranda travel to Japan, where they accidentally turn a prisoner over to a toon gang.

Love Stuck
Someone is kidnapping the contestants from a toon version of the *Dating Game* show.

When the Spirit Moves You
A toon ghost takes over the station and the police must use an old movie trick to drive him out.

Of Mice and Menace
A rogue toon elephant steals Dumbo's magic flag and Bonkers unwittingly takes in his gang as roommates.

Toon for a Day
A knock on the head makes Sergeant Grating think he is toon beaver Bucky Buzzsaw.

Stork Exchange, The
The storks that deliver baby toons are all missing. Lillith DuPrave has kidnapped them and is using them to deliver weapons to her customers.

Dog Day AfterToon
Fired from his cartoon series, a toon pit bull turns to a life of crime. He starts by holding a bank full of people hostage as he demands a new series.

Fistful of Anvils, A
Bonkers tells Miranda's nephew a story of the wild west, featuring Trailmix Bonkers.

29th Page, The
The clue to a missing fortune is hidden on the 29th page of a book, but what book?

Cartoon Cornered
Sergeant Grating learns a new respect for toons when he is trapped in a toon universe at Wackytoons Studio with a vengeful killer who is searching for him.

Good, the Bad & the Kanifky, The
When the chief is demoted, he finds himself working alongside Bonkers and Lucky.

I Oughta Be in Toons
A human is trying to become the most famous toon in the world, and he starts by kidnapping Mickey Mouse.

Frame That Toon
Two different cases unexpectedly come together as Bonkers and Lucky search for a missing toon saxophone.

Wooly Bully, A
A formerly heroic toon elephant goes on a crime spree when he is fired from his television series.

Stay Tooned
When some evidence goes missing, Bonkers has everyone suspecting one another of the crime.

O Cartoon! My Cartoon!
Poor Fall-Apart Rabbit is the recipient of several surprises as Bonkers does his own version of Walt Whitman's poem *O Captain! My Captain!* Note: This episode comprised the cartoons *Get Me a Pizza (Hold the Minefield), Spatula Party,* and *Sheerluck Bonkers* from *Raw Toonage.*

Color Me Piquel
Two black-and-white toons are stealing color from their more modern counterparts.

Stand-In Dad
Lucky has to masquerade as the host of a children's television show, and in so doing, discovers that Marilyn feels neglected.

Cereal Surreal
Someone is stealing the prizes out of cereal boxes and framing toon spokesmen Slap, Sniffle, and Plop for the crime.

If
Bonkers tells another poem, Rudyard Kipling's *If,* and Jitters again suffers the consequences. Note: This episode comprised the theatrical short *Petal to the Metal* and the

cartoons *Dogzapoppin'* and *Trailmix Bonkers* from *Raw Toonage.*

DIMMING, THE
Lucky heads off to an old resort hotel for a quiet vacation so he can work on his horror novel. Unfortunately, the hotel just might be haunted.

TOON WITH NO NAME
The cast members of one of Bonkers's old films are disappearing one by one.

GET WACKY
Wacky Weasel, the worst criminal in toon history, escapes from prison and heads for a showdown with Bonkers.

FINAL REVIEW, THE
Bonkers and Lucky are assigned to protect a television critic who has been receiving death threats.

GOLDIJITTERS AND THE THREE BOBCATS
Jitters and Bonkers take the place of Goldilocks and the three bears in an unusual retelling of the classic tale. Note: This episode comprised the cartoons *Quest for Firewood, Gobble, Gobble Bonkers,* and *Get Me to the Church on Time* from *Raw Toonage.*

SEEMS LIKE OLD TOONS
Marilyn goes to Toon Camp, only to discover that it's a rundown animation studio.

MIRACLE AT THE 34TH PRECINCT
Bonkers is called into action when Santa is missing, and Lucky is asked to fill in for the big guy.

COMEBACK KID, THE
Two toon con men trick Bonkers into making a film with Lucky so they can cover their attempts to steal a diamond.

GREATEST STORY NEVER TOLD, THE
Fake toon reporters frame Lucky for a crime he didn't commit.

FALL-APART LAND
Lucky and Fall-Apart Rabbit become unlikely partners in a strange theme park.

IMAGINE THAT
Bonkers and Lucky try to stop a toon pencil from covering the city with graffiti.

FINE KETTLE OF TOONS, A
The Chief thinks that Lucky and Bonkers aren't working hard enough, so he teams up with Fall-Apart to check things out.

STRESSED TO KILL
When Lucky's stress level reaches a new high, Bonkers is determined to find a way to calm him down.

Marsupilami

First shown in *Raw Toonage,* Marsupilami returned in his own series.

Marsupilami was added to the CBS Saturday morning line-up for the 1993–94 season. When it was canceled after one season, Shnookums and Meat moved on to their own series. The Disney Channel later combined elements from *Raw Toonage* and *Marsupilami* and aired them under the single name of *Marsupilami.* Each of the original *Marsupilami* episodes is described here in airdate order.

WORKING CLASS MARS
An employment agency sends Norman two new secretaries—Marsupilami and Maurice.

HAIRY APE, THE
See episode description under *Raw Toonage.*

NORMZAN OF THE JUNGLE
Norman uses a book of jungle chants to control Maurice, forcing the ape to battle with his best friend, Marsupilami.

BATHTIME FOR MAURICE
See episode description under *Raw Toonage.*

HOLE IN MARS
Norman tries to con Marsupilami on the golf course, but he didn't count on anyone using a talented tail as a golf club.

TREASURE OF SIERRA MARSDRE, THE
See episode description under *Raw Toonage.*

WIZARD OF MARS, THE
A storm carries Marsupilami out of the jungle and into a strange land very much like Oz.

PUCK STOPS HERE, THE
See episode description under *Raw Toonage.*

MAR-SUP-DU-JOUR
Eduardo, a suave jaguar, decides to have a Marsupilami morsel for dinner.

ROMANCING THE CLONE
See episode description under *Raw Toonage*.

TOUCAN ALWAYS GET WHAT YOU WANT
Eduardo returns and tries again to devour Marsupilami, who promptly flees. The escape is imperiled when Marsupilami and Maurice discover a baby toucan who needs help in learning how to fly.

FEAR OF KITES, A
See episode description under *Raw Toonage*.

MARS' PROBLEM PACHYDERM
Marsupilami finds that trying to help build self-confidence in a neurotic elephant isn't going to be as easy as he thought.

MARS MEETS DR. NORMANSTEIN
See episode description under *Raw Toonage*.

STEAMBOAT MARS
Marsupilami and Maurice take a cruise on a river boat, unaware that Norman, the skipper, is a poacher.

SOMEONE'S IN THE KITCHEN WITH MARS
See episode description under *Raw Toonage*.

HEY! HEY! THEY'RE THE MONKEYS!
When he invites three homeless monkeys to stay with him, Marsupilami doesn't know that his houseguests want to move in permanently—right after they evict him.

PRIME MATES FOREVER
See episode description under *Raw Toonage*.

THORN O' PLENTY
Marsupilami pulls a thorn from Eduardo's paw, then has to find a way to let the jaguar repay his act of kindness before he drives him crazy.

WITCH DR. IS WHICH?
See episode description under *Raw Toonage*.

SPOTLESS RECORD, A
Eating a bad berry causes Marsupilami's spots to vanish, and only Stuie the neurotic elephant knows the cure. Unfortunately, the pachyderm is too scared to help.

MARS VS. MAN
See episode description under *Raw Toonage*.

CROPSY TURVY
Marsupilami invents a tale of a jungle monster to scare Stuie and Maurice, never suspecting that the real monster is nearby.

SAFARI SO GOOD
See episode description under *Raw Toonage*.

ROYAL FOIL
A vacation in London finds Marsupilami and Maurice tricked into stealing the crown jewels for Norman.

JUNGLE FEVER
See episode description under *Raw Toonage*.

Shnookums & Meat episode descriptions

KUNG-FU KITTY
Poor Shnookums the cat. His humans have bought a new guard dog, Meat, and the cat is decidedly unhappy with this turn of events. Worried about his own survival, the cat learns the art of Kung-Fu from a book and decides to show the dog who's boss.

I.Q. YOU TOO!
In a battle of wit and will, Shnookums and Meat each use a series of brain-enhancing devices in an attempt to make themselves smarter than the other one.

NIGHT OF THE LIVING SHNOOKUMS
Shnookums lets Meat think he has died from one of the dog's tricks, then comes back to haunt him.

SOMETHING'S FISHY
A tiny fish in a bowl gets tired of living in danger due to the constant battles between the cat and the dog, so he forces himself to evolve into a dinosaur to seek his revenge.

JINGLE BELLS, SOMETHING SMELLS
When Shnookums and Meat accidentally knock out Santa Claus with the smell of their Christmas stockings, they have to take his place and deliver toys around the world.

Sebastian episode descriptions

KING OF THE BEACH
Sebastian's job as a lifeguard is made next to impossible by a bird protecting her nest.

ROOM SERVICE

Sebastian the bellhop has his claws full when the chef checks into the hotel.

CRAB SCOUTS

Sebastian is the leader of a patrol of crab scouts out to explore the surface world. Unfortunately, his attempts to teach them about survival keep going awry.

TV JEEBIES

Television executives try to create a series for Sebastian, but his co-star in each is Chef Louie, who keeps trying to make a meal out of the hapless crustacean.

BASIC INSTING

A fish hook stuck on his shell attracts a near-sighted scorpion to Sebastian, who doesn't know the hook is there.

BOY AND HIS CRAB, A

Desperate to escape crab-hunting season, Sebastian convinces a boy that he's a dog.

CRABBY HONEYMOON, A

Sebastian finds himself having to help two newlyweds on their honeymoon at Niagara Falls.

FLAMBE, BOMBE

See *Sebastian*, under *Raw Toonage* host sequence.

IN THE PINK

Pinky Desmond, the former star of *The Pinky and Porkchop Show*, wants to revive her career by replacing a missing puppet with Sebastian. This episode was not completed.

Disney's Aladdin

The outstanding success of the 1992 theatrical release *Aladdin* led to the creation of a small-screen version titled *Disney's Aladdin.* Here, Aladdin and Jasmine have postponed their wedding, and Iago returns as a reluctant hero.

Disney's Aladdin was added to The Disney Afternoon line-up for the 1994–95 season, with additional episodes created for Saturday morning on CBS.

Episode descriptions

A total of 65 syndicated episodes were produced. An additional 13 episodes were aired on CBS during the 1994–95 season, with 8 more added to the 1995–96 line-up. Each of these is listed in airdate order.

Syndicated episodes

AIR FEATHERED FRIENDS

Aladdin suspects that thieves are behind the strange whirlwinds bedeviling Agrabah.

BAD MOOD RISING

The ruler of Quarkistan has the power to control the weather through his emotions.

TO CURE A THIEF

Aladdin gets tired of Abu's stealing everything in sight and sets out to cure his friend's larcenous tendencies.

DO THE RAT THING

While trying to prove her independence, Jasmine finds herself turned into a rat.

NEVER SAY NEFIR

A prankish imp is causing problems, not the least of which is a rampaging pink rhino.

GETTING THE BUGS OUT

A mechanical dragonfly leads the gang into battle against crazed Greek inventor Mekanikles.

VAPOR CHASE, THE

Abis Mal tries to conquer Agrabah using smoke demons that are hidden inside a magical powder.

GARDEN OF EVIL

The Sultan regrets a promise made 20 years ago when the time comes for the debt to be repaid.

MUCH ABU ABOUT SOMETHING

Abu is the unlikely hero who stops a dinosaur from destroying a neighboring kingdom.

MY FAIR ALADDIN

Aladdin's loss of self-confidence gives Mekanikles a chance to unleash a plan to turn the desert into glass.

SOME ENCHANTED GENIE

When Abis Mal steals Genie's lamp, he searches for his lost home and falls in love with a Genie from a bottle.

WEB OF FEAR
A cave-in reveals a band of spiderlike creatures, who promptly kidnap Jasmine.

MUDDER'S DAY
Aladdin and company find themselves captured by the al-Muddi, elementals who plan to use them as food.

PLUNDER THE SEA
Mekanikles returns with another invention. This one is a mechanical sea monster!

STRIKE UP THE SAND
When Sadira, a street urchin, sets her sights on Aladdin, she gets some unusual help from magical scrolls that allow her to command sand monsters.

I NEVER MECHANISM I DIDN'T LIKE
Mekanikles builds a robot with hypnotic powers to enslave Aladdin and the residents of Agrabah.

FOWL WEATHER
Iago almost meets his match when he butts heads against a determined female parrot.

FORGET ME LOTS
Amnesia causes Jasmine to hate Aladdin and to think she is the dreaded Scourge of the Desert.

SCARE NECESSITIES
Jasmine gets a gift that is not what it appears to be.

SANDSWITCH
Sadira casts a spell that makes everyone think she's engaged to Aladdin; everyone, that is, except Aladdin's animal friends.

LOST AND FOUNDED
When Abis Mal travels through time he changes Agrabah's history, which may mean that Princess Jasmine will cease to exist.

MOONLIGHT MADNESS
A night that starts as a quiet date for Aladdin and Jasmine turns into a treasure hunt.

FLAWED COUPLE, THE
Abis Mal and Mekanikles team up to defeat Aladdin, but they soon find that their own egos are more dangerous than he is.

RAIN OF TERROR
When Iago agrees to take control of the world's weather for a weekend, he doesn't know that Malcho, a flying snake, has plans for using the weather to control the world.

DUNE QUIXOTE
Sadira tries to snare Aladdin with another spell, but when it fails, he thinks he is a hero named Dragonslayer.

DAY THE BIRD STOOD STILL, THE
Hit by a spell intended for the Sultan, Iago is slowly turning into stone.

OF ICE AND MEN
The gang has a hot time when they travel to the frigid North.

OPPOSITES DETRACT
A visiting dragon plunges Aladdin and his friends into another adventure.

CAUGHT BY THE TALE
Abis Mal tricks a group of children into searching for treasure for him.

ELEMENTAL, MY DEAR JASMINE
Saleen, an undersea magician, decides life above water would be more interesting, especially if she can entrap Aladdin.

SMOLDER AND WISER
Aladdin's efforts to stop Abis Mal from using a fiery imp against Agrabah are made harder when he is struck by a spell that makes him clumsy.

GAME, THE
Two wizards use Aladdin and his friends as pawns in a deadly game.

SNOWMAN IS AN ISLAND
Genie is taken prisoner by a Yeti, a strange creature living in a land of snow and ice.

ANIMAL KINGDOM, THE
Aladdin finds himself in a strange valley where the animals can speak.

POWER TO THE PARROT
Things become very strange when Iago gets Genie's powers for a day.

SANDS OF FATE, THE
Unless the gang can break a loop in time, the world will be doomed to repeat itself for eternity.

CITADEL, THE
The evil sorcerer Mozenrath decides to force Aladdin to capture a Thirdak, a beast that lives on magical energy.

POOR IAGO
Years of greed take their toll on Iago, and he decides to repent by becoming totally good.

SECRET OF DAGGER ROCK, THE
Mozenrath decides to torture Aladdin if he can't get control of Genie by using a crystal designed to imprison magical beings.

IN THE HEAT OF THE FRIGHT
Aladdin and his friends must do battle with Mirage, a villainess with the head of a cat, who is the ruler of the strange dimension of Morbia.

SEVEN FACES OF GENIE, THE
Abis Mal tries to blow up Genie with a new bomb, but it somehow splits his intended victim into seven parts, each reacting to a different emotion.

WIND JACKALS OF MOZENRATH, THE
Mozenrath plans to use wind demons to enslave the desert kingdoms.

CLOCKWORK HERO, A
Mekanikles discovers that being a parent is harder than he expected when he builds himself a son.

MISSION: IMP POSSIBLE
Golden silk is the object of Nefir Hassanuf's criminal plot.

STINKER BELLE
An arranged marriage in a nearby kingdom faces problems when the groom's advisor tries to kill him and the bride decides she would rather marry Aladdin.

SHADOW OF A DOUBT
Mirage disguises herself as a visiting Sultana and sets forth a plan to destroy Agrabah using the shadow of a magic obelisk.

SMELLS LIKE TROUBLE
The gang returns to Odiferous for the annual cheese festival, but lizards with bad breath are ruining the festivities.

WAY WE WAR, THE
The citizens of Agrabah go to war against a neighboring country, unaware that the conflict has been arranged by an unscrupulous arms dealer.

NIGHT OF THE LIVING MUD, THE
A band of al-Muddi mud monsters threatens the palace until the Genie comes up with a novel plan to freeze them solid.

EGG-STRA PROTECTION
Abis Mal has unleashed a dangerous Gryphon.

HEADS, YOU LOSE
Aladdin is asked to help a wizard reunite his disembodied head and the rest of his body.

LOVE BUG, THE
Mechanical termites created by Mekanikles imperil the rain forest home of Thundra, the Rain Bird.

WHEN CHAOS COMES CALLING
Mirage tricks Chaos, a powerful creature who loves surprises, into stirring things up in Agrabah. One of his tricks is to create evil duplicates of Aladdin and the Genie, who battle their good counterparts.

ARMORED AND DANGEROUS
When the Sultan dons a suit of armor to defeat the pillaging Dominus Tusk, a spirit living in the suit turns him evil.

SHARK TREATMENT
Saleen turns Aladdin into a shark when he tries to recover a fabulous gold statue that has been lost at sea.

BLACK SAND
Zombies created from a strange black sand are taking the place of palace dwellers.

LOVE AT FIRST SPRITE
Creatures known as Sprites spirit Aladdin and his friends away to the clouds, but the trip then takes an unexpected deadly turn.

VOCAL HERO
Amim D'Moolah turns the Sultan into a statue, with the only cure being the toenails of the feared griffin.

LOST CITY OF THE SUN, THE
Mozenrath enslaves the Sprites to help him find a legendary lost power.

AS THE NETHERWORLD TURNS
Iago endangers the gang when his greed leads him into a misadventure with the dead, who are led by Ayam Aghoul.

SEEMS LIKE OLD CRIMES—PART I
A magic stone has disappeared and Aladdin is asked to find it. A flashback sequence shows how Aladdin and Abu first met.

SEEMS LIKE OLD CRIMES—PART II
The magic stone has turned Aladdin's friends into creatures bent on his destruction.

FROM HIPPSODETH WITH LOVE
Hippsodeth surprises everyone by announcing that she is in love with the only man to ever defeat her—the Sultan.

DESTINY ON FIRE
Aladdin returns to Agrabah only to discover that everyone in Agrabah has been turned into strange blobs.

RETURN OF MALCHO, THE
The winged serpent returns, determined to take his revenge on Iago.

CBS episodes—1994–95

RAIDERS OF THE LOST SHARK
A shark that can swim on land devours most of Agrabah before Aladdin joins forces with a determined sea captain.

SNEEZE THE DAY
When Genie comes down with a cold that confuses his powers, Aladdin has to defeat Machina, a crocodile-headed giant, to get the only cure.

PROPHET MOTIVE, THE
Aladdin and his friends get help from Fasir, a strange fortune-teller, when they have to stop Abis Mal from stealing a powerful talisman.

THAT STINKING FEELING
Jasmine tries to use Prince Uncouthma from Odiferous to make Aladdin jealous.

BEAST OR FAMINE
An evil Shaman who controls a race of sand dwellers wants to add Genie's power to his own.

SPICE IS RIGHT, THE
When Aladdin and Iago uncover a buried treasure of rare spice, but that in turn unleashes the spirit of Ayam Aghoul, who wants Jasmine as his next dead wife.

HERO WITH A THOUSAND FEATHERS, THE
Iago accidentally brings an ancient—and evil—fire creature back to life.

WITCH WAY DID SHE GO?
Sadira accidentally frees the Ancient Witches of the Sand, who convince her to join them in conquering Agrabah.

SEA NO EVIL
Iago and Abu sidetrack an important message meant for Aladdin.

SULTAN WORTH HIS SALT, A
The Sultan leads the rescue party when Jasmine is kidnapped by the female army of Queen Hippsodeth.

GENIE HUNT
Genie is stalked by a Mukhtaar, a bounty hunter who never gives up.

LOST ONES, THE
Someone or something is stealing the children of Agrabah.

EYE OF THE BEHOLDER
Mirage tests Aladdin's feelings for Jasmine by turning her into a snake.

CBS episodes—1995–96

HUNTED, THE
Genie is forced to trust the Mukhtaar when all of his friends vanish, but it turns out that the Mukhtaar is working with Mozenrath.

RIDERS REDUX
When Aladdin can't stop some magical gold thieves, Jasmine asks for help from the famous Riders of Ramond.

BOOK OF KHARTOUM, THE
Mozenrath gets some bad advice from the living magic book of Khartoum, which unleashes an evil wizard of unbelievable power.

While the City Snoozes
The gang returns to the city late one night and discovers that Mirage has enslaved all of the inhabitants in a deadly sleeping spell.

Two to Tangle
Mozenrath's body is wearing out, so he takes over Aladdin's, and only a legendary elixir can save the day.

Ethereal, The
Ethereal, a creature who has caused disasters at Atlantis, Babylon, and Pompeii, sets her sights on Agrabah.

Shadow Knows, The
Ayam Aghoul is stealing people's shadows, and Aladdin and Jasmine must get theirs back by sundown or live forever in the netherworld.

Great Rift, The
An evil sorceress, Queen Dalukah, and her three wizard brothers use black magic to create a terrible monster known as The Great Rift as part of a plan to take over Agrabah.

Gargoyles

After years of series featuring characters that could generally be described as "warm and fuzzy," Disney took a decidedly different approach for the series *Gargoyles*. Instead of chipmunks, ducks, or mice, the new series introduced a race of clawed, winged creatures that were sworn to protect humans at any cost.

Gargoyles was added to The Disney Afternoon for the 1994–95 season and aired once per week under the billing of "Action Friday." *Gargoyles* did well in the ratings the first season and was expanded to 4 days each week for 1995–96. A spin-off of *Gargoyles*, titled *The Goliath Chronicles*, was added to the ABC Saturday morning schedule for the 1996–97 season, with repeats of the original episodes continuing on The Disney Afternoon.

Fans of *Star Trek: The Next Generation* are sure to have noticed that most of the cast members from that series provided voices for *Gargoyles*.

A total of 65 episodes were produced and are listed here in airdate order.

Year 1: 1994–95

Awakening, The (five parts)
The first episode in the series shows how the Gargoyles were turned to stone for 1,000 years, and how they were brought back to life in New York City. There, they are tricked by Xanatos into stealing information to construct the Steel Clan, deadly robotics Gargoyles.

Thrill of the Hunt, The
Xanatos forms a group of mercenaries called The Pack and sends them into battle against the Gargoyles.

Temptation
Demona tricks Brooklyn into believing that humans and Gargoyles can never coexist.

Deadly Force
Elisa is almost killed when Broadway plays with her gun and accidentally shoots her.

Enter Macbeth
Shakespeare's tragic hero reappears on the scene, having used magic to stay alive all these years.

Edge, The
Xanatos uses an armored suit to make people think that the Gargoyles are behind a series of crimes.

Long Way to Morning
Demona seriously wounds Goliath, and Hudson has to protect him until the sun rises the next morning and they can be healed by the spell that turns them to stone.

Her Brother's Keeper
Elisa's brother puts his own life in danger when he ignores her warning and becomes Xanatos's personal pilot.

Reawakening
Demona and Xanatos team to create Coldstone, a monster created from the remains of dead Gargoyles.

Year 2: 1995–96

Leader of the Pack
Xanatos sends a robot duplicate of himself to break The Pack out of prison.

METAMORPHOSIS

Elisa's brother, Derek, and two other humans are somehow mutated into animal-like creatures and become the villains Talon, Fang, and Claw.

LEGION

A revived Coldstone is struggling for control of the personalities of the Gargoyles he was built from, and Goliath tries a virtual reality trip inside his mind to help him.

LIGHTHOUSE IN THE SEA OF TIME, A

Macbeth takes Broadway hostage while he tries to gain possession of Merlin the Magician's spells and Broadway discovers the beauty of the written word.

MIRROR, THE

Demona's plan to use a mysterious creature named Puck to destroy all humans backfires when he turns them all into Gargoyles instead.

SILVER FALCON, THE

One of Elisa's police investigations brings her and the Gargoyles into contact with an old but still deadly gangster, Dominic Dracon.

EYE OF THE BEHOLDER

Xanatos proposes to Fox, a member of The Pack, but his engagement gift turns her into a werefox and he must turn to Goliath for help in curing her.

VOWS

Demona uses a time travel device to transport her, Goliath, and Xanatos back to 975 A.D., where Xanatos establishes his future fortune and Demona tries again to destroy the castle and Gargoyles.

CITY OF STONE, THE (FOUR PARTS)

Demona casts a spell that turns all of the humans in New York to stone. The Gargoyles and Xanatos must join forces to save them.

HIGH NOON

Demona and Macbeth bring Coldstone back to life, unaware that they are pawns in a plot to steal several magical talismans.

OUTFOXED

Goliath is forced to help save Halycon Renard's life and airship from his own daughter, Fox.

PRICE, THE

Xanatos thinks that he has discovered a fountain of youth, but when his assistant Owens tests it with his hand, he discovers it turns those that bathe in it into stone.

REVELATIONS

Former FBI agent Matt Bluestone has been trying for years to unmask The Illuminati, a secret group said to run the world, and they offer him membership if he will bring them a Gargoyle.

DOUBLE JEOPARDY

When Xanatos and Sevarius create Thailog, a clone of Goliath, he turns the tables on them by escaping with $20 million of Xanatos's money.

UPGRADE

The Pack becomes much more dangerous when they are altered into new and more deadly weapons of destruction.

PROTECTION

Elisa poses as a crooked cop to get inside Dracon's protection racket.

CAGE, THE

Goliath kidnaps Sevarius and tries to make him turn Derek and the other mutants back into humans again.

AVALON (THREE PARTS)

A messenger from the past summons the Gargoyles to the mystical isle of Avalon, home of the Gargoyle eggs and their young.

SHADOWS OF THE PAST

A visit to original site of the castle almost drives Goliath crazy when he starts hearing voices from his past.

HERITAGE

The Gargoyles meet a descendent of King Oberon who refuses to believe in his own heritage and thus refuses to fight an evil sorcerer.

MONSTERS

The Gargoyles have to save the famous Loch Ness Monster from one of Sevarius's experiments.

KINGDOM
Brooklyn and Talon both discover that becoming the leaders of their groups will not be as easy as they thought.

GOLEM
While in Prague, the Gargoyles must stop Renard from bringing a strange clay creature back to life.

SANCTUARY
Demona tries to get Macbeth's fortune for Thailog, unaware that the cloned Gargoyle is quite willing to kill her to get it.

M.I.A.
A stop in London reveals two Gargoyles who somehow blame Goliath for the death of their friend in World War II.

GRIEF
Xanatos's latest quest for immortality involves the spirit of a long-dead Egyptian god.

HOUND OF ULSTER, THE
An Irish drifter helps Bronx free the other Gargoyles from a banshee's trap.

WALKABOUT
A biologically engineered creature in Australia at first threatens to destroy the world, but the Gargoyles help him and Dingo from The Pack see the error of their ways and they become new superheros.

MARK OF THE PANTHER
In Nigeria to visit her mother, Elisa is surprised to learn that her mother's friend can turn into a panther when their lives are threatened.

PENDRAGON
King Arthur arrives on the scene looking for the fabled sword Excalibur.

EYE OF THE STORM
Goliath becomes the fanatical protector of everything in sight when he dons the mysterious Eye of Odin.

NEW OLYMPIANS, THE
Descendants of ancient Greek gods tell Elisa that she can never leave their hidden island.

GREEN, THE
A trip to Central America reveals four Mayan Gargoyles protecting the rain forest.

SENTINEL
An alien guardian who uses Easter Island as his base mistakes the Gargoyles for evil invaders.

BUSHIDO
Traitors in Japan capture the visiting Gargoyles and threaten to expose them to the outside world.

CLOUD FATHERS
The Gargoyles and the Mazas are helped by an ancient Indian spirit in another battle with Xanatos.

ILL MET BY MOONLIGHT
A battle ensues when Oberon returns to Avalon intent on reclaiming his role as leader of the kingdom.

FUTURE TENSE
Puck creates an illusion of a miserable Xanatos-controlled future to trick the Gargoyles into giving him the time-travel device, the Phoenix Gate.

GATHERING, THE (TWO PARTS)
Queen Titania and King Oberon arrive with plans to bring Xanatos's new son back to Avalon, for the baby has magical powers.

VENDETTAS
The ghost of an ancient foe and a human with a strange weapon are both stalking the Gargoyles.

TURF
Gang warfare breaks out when a new mobster decides he wants control of Dracon's territory.

RECKONING, THE
A massive battle ensues when Thailog creates clones of the Gargoyles and pits them against the originals. Surprisingly, Demona comes to the rescue.

POSSESSION
Xanatos creates robots to hold two of Coldstone's personalities but needs help with the transfer.

HUNTER'S MOON, THE (THREE PARTS)
Demona's ancient enemies, The Hunters, set their sights on the other Gargoyles.

The Shnookums & Meat Funny Cartoon Show

Even though Shnookums and Meat had appeared in two failed series, *Raw Toonage* and *Marsupilami*, the Studio still thought there was a future for the battling cat and dog. They became the title stars of *The Shnookums & Meat Funny Cartoon Show*, which was added to The Disney Afternoon line-up for the 1994–95 season. Unlike other series in the line-up which appeared on a daily basis, this one would only appear once a week, on what the Studio dubbed "Manic Monday." The rest of the week was shared with *Disney's Aladdin*.

The third time proved not to be the charm in this case, for *The Shnookums & Meat Funny Cartoon Show* lasted only one season and the animal co-stars finally were retired.

In addition to the adventures of Shnookums and Meat, the series also included *Pith Possum, Super Dynamic Possum of Tomorrow*, and *Tex Tinstar, The Best in the West*. Each of these segments is described below, with the episodes listed in airdate order.

Weight for Me

When their owners decide the pets are too fat, the animals order special exercise chairs that work too well, for they end up muscle-bound. A stay in the sauna then leaves the pets as thin as snakes.

Ow, Hey!

Meat gets hit on the head once too often and Shnookums rushes him to the vet, but the cat gets hurt himself in the process.

Buggin Out

The pets have fleas and mix up some bug spray, but it makes the bugs bigger and they take over the house.

Poodle Panic

Shnookums and Meat are upset to learn that their owner has agreed to housesit Toulose, a sickly looking poodle who has had the same cold for 6 years.

Cabin Fever

When an earthquake strikes the house, the pets are trapped in the wreckage. After 4 days pass, they hallucinate about a giant hotdog that leads them to a world full of food.

Pain in the Brain

When the pets knock their brains out, they try to clean them before putting them back in their heads.

Step Ladder to Heaven

Killed in another fight, the pets try to argue their way into heaven when they learn they're supposed to go to "that hot place" for their past wrongdoings.

Kung-Fu Kitty

See episode description under *Marsupilami*.

I.Q. You Too!

See episode description under *Marsupilami*.

Something's Fishy

See episode description under *Marsupilami*.

Night of the Living Shnookums

See episode description under *Marsupilami*.

Jingle Bells, Something Smells

See episode description under *Marsupilami*.

What a Turkey!

Their owner has bought a live turkey home for Thanksgiving and Meat tries to get Shnookums to help him save the bird. Shnookums is more interested in eating his annual turkey dinner.

Pith Possum, Super Dynamic Possum of Tomorrow

When Peter Possum, a copy boy for the Weakly World Horsefeather, was turned into a super possum during a lab experiment, he became crime fighter Pith Possum.

Phantom Mask of the Dark Black Darkness of Black, The

The Easter Bunny is insane and turns himself into a huge carnivorous beast. Pith uses an exploding carrot to defeat his oversized foe.

Darkness on the Edge of Black

Dr. Paul Bunion is using robots to steal lumber. Doris sneaks into his hideout and Pith tries to rescue her. Obediah saves the day by pulling the plug on the robot controls.

Night of Darkness

A villain in a bug suit is stealing baby supplies. His wife is a termite and they have several thousand children, so he turned to crime to support them.

DARKNESS, IT IS DARK!, THE
Dr. Paul Bunion kidnaps Obediah and uses a new robot to terrorize the city. Alone in his lair, Pith can't make any of the gadgets work without Obediah's help.

RETURN OF THE NIGHT OF BLACKER DARKNESS
Two criminals disguised as Pith and Obediah unleash a crime wave across town and the heroes get all of the blame.

HAUNT OF THE NIGHT OF BLACKER DARKNESS
Pith finally gets a date with Doris, but a series of crimes finds him needing to slip away from dinner one time too many.

BRIDE OF DARKNESS
Shirley Pimple, who looks like an angelic child, tries to destroy the city with an army of termites.

SON OF THE CURSED BLACK OF DARKNESS
Super Water Buffalo, a new hero in town, stages crimes so he can solve them and make Pith look bad. It's part of a plan to get the town to let him guard their valuables.

LIGHT OF DARKNESS, THE
While attending the 3rd annual superhero convention, Pith is the only hero willing to stand up against Dr. Paul Bunion.

RETURN OF THE DARK MASK OF PHANTOM BLACKNESS
The annual Possum Day parade is ruined when a giant flying lizard carries Pith and Obediah off to Dr. Paul Bunion's lair.

DARK OF THE DARKER DARKNESS
A faulty new weapon makes Pith think that he is a dance instructor, a stand-up comic, and finally a band leader.

DARK QUEST FOR DARKNESS
Pith's 96-year-old grandmother makes an unexpected visit and races out in the Possummobile to fight crime.

LIGHT OR DARK MEAT?
Pith and Obediah go on a vacation cruise, unaware that the captain is really Dr. Paul Bunion in disguise.

Tex Tinstar, The Best in the West
This 13-part serial featured Tex Tinstar, sheriff of Bonehead, in a battle against The Wrong Riders, a band of villains led by Wrongo, a creepy black figure dressed in a long cape.

FISTFUL OF FOODSTAMPS, A
Wrongo arrives in town and announces that he has a score to settle with Tex. He captures the lawman and unleashes an elaborate death trap.

FOR A FEW FOODSTAMPS MORE
The villains have stolen the entire town and kidnapped bank examiner Percy Lacedaisy to get the combination to the safe.

GOOD, THE BLAND, AND THE WIGGLY, THE
Wrongo tries to beat the combination out of Percy, but stops long enough to capture Tex and set up another intricate trap.

LOW PANTS DRIFTER
Tex escapes Wrongo's trap by using Percy as an anchor to stop a runaway wagon. Percy goes over the edge of a cliff and Tex tries to pull him up with Floyd, a joke-telling rattlesnake.

STALE RIDER
The Wrong Riders turn to Krusty Rustnuckle, the most talented (and smallest) safecracker in the West to open the safe, then accidentally knock his head off.

LOATHSOME DOVE
The Wrong Riders find Krusty's head, but put it back on backwards.

MAGNIFICENT ELEVEN
Tex challenges Wrongo to a fair fight, but the villain cheats, of course, and ties him to a sunken ship as sharks approach.

SADDLESORES, SAGEBRUSH, AND SEAWEED
Floyd arrives in a submarine and saves Tex from the sharks.

SLAP-HAPPY TRAILS
Krusty stops to open the safe, but everyone is worried about the animals out there in the night.

MY SPINE HURTS

When morning arrives Tex and Chafe discover that Krusty was eaten by coyotes during the night. Even worse, a huge meteor is plunging toward Earth.

VINYL FRONTIER, THE

The meteor strikes and carries them all toward the Sun.

HEY, CAREFUL. THAT'S MY CEREBELLUM.

Tex lassoes the moon and pulls them out of the Sun's flames, but Percy is lost in space. When the heroes get back to Earth, they're captured by hungry coyotes.

THERE ARE SPIDERS ALL OVER ME!

Percy finally comes crashing back to Earth and smashes into the coyotes. The heroes escape, but the coyotes then set their eyes on Wrongo.

The Lion King's Timon & Pumbaa

Just as with *The Little Mermaid*, the overwhelming success of the film *The Lion King* led to an new animated series. Each episode starts with a *Timon & Pumbaa* cartoon, which can take place anywhere in the world. These are then followed by another *Timon & Pumbaa* cartoon or either a *Rafiki's Fable* or *The Laughing Hyenas*. *The Lion King's Timon & Pumbaa* joined The Disney Afternoon lineup for the 1995–96 season, but only on Friday afternoons. It was also added to the CBS saturday morning line-up, with different episodes created for that version. The series was renewed for the 1996–97 season.

Each of the syndicated episodes is described in airdate order, followed by the CBS episodes.

EPISODE #1 (9/08/95)   TIMON & PUMBAA: BOARA BOARA

A relaxing day at the beach turns nasty when Pumbaa is kidnapped by natives who want to make him their king.

TIMON & PUMBAA: SASKATCHEWAN CATCH

Timon and Pumbaa agree to help a flying squirrel snare a mate if she will get them some tasty beetles from a high tree.

EPISODE #2 (9/15/95)   TIMON & PUMBAA: KENYA BE MY FRIEND?

An argument between Timon and Pumbaa results in their finding two new best friends, Bampuu the Warthog and Monty the Meerkat.

RAFIKI FABLES: GOOD MOUSEKEEPING

A tiny mouse wants to be as tall as a giraffe and able to fly like a bird and swim like a fish.

EPISODE #3 (9/22/95)   TIMON & PUMBAA: NEVER EVERGLADES

Pumbaa's paternal instincts take over when he hatches an abandoned alligator egg.

THE LAUGHING HYENAS: COOKED GOOSE

The hyenas get sent on a series of wild goose chases by the cheetahs.

EPISODE #4 (9/29/95)   TIMON & PUMBAA: HOW TO BEAT THE HIGH COSTA RICA

Timon and Pumbaa discover a suitcase of stolen money and try to return it to the rightful owner.

TIMON & PUMBAA: SWISS MISSED

The jungle schedule gets thrown off when Timon persuades the local timekeeper to adopt a Hakuna Matata lifestyle.

EPISODE #5 (10/06/95)   TIMON & PUMBAA: UGANDA BE AN ELEPHANT

Pumbaa decides he wants to be an elephant when he hears Timon praising a pachyderm.

TIMON & PUMBAA: TO KILIMANJARO BIRD

Timon and Pumbaa are forced to babysit Earl the eagle when they get caught stealing his food.

EPISODE #6 (10/13/95)   TIMON & PUMBAA: FRENCH FRIED

After catching an elusive snail, the guys decide he's too cute to eat.

THE LAUGHING HYENAS: BIG TOP BREAKFAST

When a circus monkey falls out of a plane, the hyenas decide he would make a very tasty meal.

Episode #7 (11/03/95)   Timon & Pumbaa: Pain in Spain, The
Pumbaa finds himself taking the place of a bull who is too old for bullfighting anymore.

Timon & Pumbaa: Frantic Atlantic
Irving, the world's most annoying penguin, makes a cruise that is definitely not a trip on the Love Boat.

Episode #8 (11/10/95)   Timon & Pumbaa: Tanzania Zany
Timon and Pumbaa get an unwanted visit from Fred, a meerkat with a fondness for practical jokes.

Timon & Pumbaa: Guatemala Malarkey
This parody of *Raiders of the Lost Ark* finds the guys in a search for a valuable idol.

Episode #9 (11/17/95)   Timon & Pumbaa: Back Out in the Outback
Timon's visit to Australia finds him mistaking a land crab for a giant bug.

Timon & Pumbaa: Gabon with the Wind
Trapped by the cheetahs, Timon agrees to help them catch Pumbaa in exchange for his life.

Episode #10 (11/24/95)   Timon & Pumbaa: Timon's Time to Go
Timon eats a poisonous bug but finds himself turned away from Meerkat Heaven.

Timon & Pumbaa: Law of the Jungle
Timon incurs the wrath of the animal authorities when he accidentally breaks a jungle taboo.

Episode #11 (12/01/95)   Timon & Pumbaa: Be More Pacific
Pumbaa rescues a beached whale and discovers it's a magic whale, able to grant wishes.

Timon & Pumbaa: Going Uruguay
Timon agrees to help a termite ruler search for his lost kingdom, planning all the while to eat the subjects when they find them.

Episode #12 (12/22/95)   Timon & Pumbaa: Yosemite Remedy
Timon takes things into his own hands when the buddies are robbed by a raccoon and the Vulture Police can't help.

Rafiki Fables: Sky Is Falling, The
A falling meteor is seen as a sign that Timon and Pumbaa shouldn't be friends any more.

Episode #13 (12/29/95)   Timon & Pumbaa: Mozam-Beaked
The guys will stop at nothing to get rid of a pesky woodpecker.

Timon & Pumbaa: Ocean Commotion
Timon and Pumbaa have to save Speedy the Snail from a couple that wants to use his shell for an earring.

CBS episode descriptions

Episode #1 (9/16/95)   Timon & Pumbaa: Brazil Nuts
Timon and Pumbaa discover an all-you-can-eat buffet run by two pythons, not suspecting it may be a trap.

Timon & Pumbaa: South Sea Sick
Timon leaps into action as a nurse when Pumbaa is taken ill.

Video: Lion Sleeps Tonight, The
Something in the shadows seems to be very interested in Timon and Pumbaa as they sing the popular song.

Episode #2 (9/23/95)   Timon & Pumbaa: Yukon Con
Quint and gold fever come between Timon and Pumbaa when they visit the Yukon.

Timon & Pumbaa: Doubt of Africa
The two friends try to help a tigress learn how to catch her own prey.

Episode #3 (9/30/95)   Timon & Pumbaa: Russia Hour
When Timon accidentally injures Pumbaa's uncle Boaris, a ballet dancer, Pumbaa must take his place to dance Swan Lake.

Timon & Pumbaa: You Ghana Join the Club
A band of squirrels declares a patch of jungle off-limits, so Timon and Pumbaa turn to Leo the Lion for help.

Episode #4 (10/07/95)   Timon & Pumbaa: Rocky Mountain Lie
Timon gets trapped in a series of lies when he tries to cover up the disappearance of Pumbaa's new bug friend.

TIMON & PUMBAA: AMAZON QUIVER
A panther tries to trap Timon and Pumbaa, resulting in a series of wild chases.

EPISODE #5 (10/14/95) TIMON & PUMBAA: MADAGASCAR ABOUT YOU
Timon must help Pumbaa escape from an arranged marriage.

TIMON & PUMBAA: TRUTH OR ZAIRE
Timon and Pumbaa pretend to be baby gorillas to escape Congo Quint.

VIDEO: YUMMY YUMMY YUMMY
The 1960s song is the background to a bug-catching contest.

EPISODE #6 (10/21/95) TIMON & PUMBAA: MOJAVE DESERTED
The friends begin to regret saving a rabbit's life, for he insists on waiting on them hand and foot.

RAFIKI FABLES: BEAUTY AND THE WILDEBEEST
Horrible Herman the ugly wildebeest loves the lovely gazelle Lara.

EPISODE #7 (10/28/95) TIMON & PUMBAA: DON'T BREAK THE CHINA
Timon and Pumbaa help a lost Panda look for his parents, expecting a big Chinese meal as a reward.

LAUGHING HYENAS, THE: CAN'T TAKE A YOLK
The hyenas set their sights on a not-so-defenseless ostrich egg.

VIDEO: STAND BY ME
Poor Pumbaa—everything but the kitchen sink falls on him as Timon sings the song.

EPISODE #8 (11/04/95) TIMON & PUMBAA: UNLUCKY IN LESOTHO
Timon seems very unlucky on just the day he tries to join Ned the elephant's Good Luck Club.

RAFIKI FABLES: RAFIKI'S APPRENTICE
Rafiki's nephew, Nafu, appears in a take-off of The Sorcerer's Apprentice.

EPISODE #9 (11/11/95) TIMON & PUMBAA: MOMBASA-IN-LAW
Pumbaa has to pretend to be Timon's wife when Timon's mother drops in for a visit.

LAUGHING HYENAS, THE: TV DINNER
This parody of the Wild Kingdom television series finds the hyenas trying to get on a TV show that promises big meals to the stars.

EPISODE #10 (11/25/95) TIMON & PUMBAA: MANHATTAN MISHAP
A trip to Manhattan goes very wrong when Timon and Pumbaa are stranded on an island with a very hungry castaway.

TIMON & PUMBAA: PARAGUAY PARABLE
An anteater tricks Timon and Pumbaa into a ant-eating contest so they'll find his food for him.

EPISODE #11 (12/09/95) TIMON & PUMBAA: LET'S SERENGETI OUT OF HERE
Timon and Pumbaa are held in "protective custody" by Dr. Happy, an animal lover determined to save them from any harm.

SIMBA: CONGO ON LIKE THIS
A new predator is in the neighborhood, and it just might be Simba.

EPISODE #12 (12/16/95) TIMON & PUMBAA: OKAY BAYOU?
The friends travel through a dangerous bayou with a possum as their tour guide.

SIMBA: SHAKE YOUR DJIBOUTI
Timon teaches Simba how to protect all of them from an escapee from Dr. Happy's lab.

Disney's Sing Me a Story: With Belle

When the Federal Communications Commission mandated that television stations increase the amount of educational programming aired each week, beginning with the 1995–96 season, Disney responded with this "edu-tainment" series. The setting for the series is Belle's Book and Music Shop, which is run by Belle, the heroine from Beauty and the Beast. Footage from the animated film is used in the opening credits of the series, but Belle is played here by a live-action actress who entertains visiting children, with an educational song linked to a cartoon.

Disney's Sing Me a Story: With Belle was syndicated beginning with the 1995–96 season.

Series cast: Lynsey McLeod (Belle), Kerry Anne Bradford, Hampton Dixon, Jennefer Jesse, Shawn Pyrfrom, Kirsten Storms, Natalie Trott, Julie VanLue, Cyndi Vicino (Inez), J.J. Ward.

Each of the episodes from the first season is described below.

OVERCOMING FEAR
Belle explains that it's okay to be afraid sometimes. Cartoons: *Lambert, the Sheepish Lion, Brave Little Tailor.*

WORKING TOGETHER
The children discover that it's easier to clean up the shop when everyone works together. Cartoons: *Morris, the Midget Moose, Babes in the Woods.*

FOLK HEROES
Belle shows that heroes come in all different shapes and sizes. Cartoon: *Paul Bunyan.*

EVERYONE'S SPECIAL
The children learn that size isn't important when only the smallest of them can help Belle recover a missing key. Cartoon: *Goliath II.*

VALUING WHAT'S WORTHY
A rummage sale makes the children learn that people see value in objects differently. Cartoons: *Susie, the Little Blue Coupe, The Little House.*

FEELING LIKE AN OUTCAST
The children learn that being different from each other makes everyone special. Cartoons: *Ferdinand the Bull, Elmer Elephant.*

STICK TO IT (DON'T GIVE UP)
The children learn the importance of not giving up easily. Cartoons: *Mail Dog, The Brave Engineer.*

BEST FRIENDS
Everyone learns that even best friends can disagree. Cartoons *Goofy and Wilbur, The Pelican and the Snipe.*

EVERYBODY NEEDS A FRIEND
A visit from the village baker demonstrates the value of friendship. Cartoons: *Pluto's Fledgling, Little Hiawatha.*

TAKING RESPONSIBILITY
Carroll refuses to admit that he broke Belle's prized bust of Bach. Cartoons: *Little Toot, In Dutch.*

REAP WHAT YOU SOW
The children learn that they must work to get what they want. Cartoons: *The Wise Little Hen, Three Little Pigs.*

TAKING THE EASY WAY OUT
When the children try to put together a bicycle, they try to take some short cuts to get the job done faster. Cartoons: *The Big Bad Wolf, The Grasshopper and the Ants.*

STEADY EFFORT
One of the children gives up on her music lesson because it's too hard. Cartoons: *The Tortoise and the Hare, Pedro.*

FEELING LEFT OUT (LONELINESS)
Harmony is glad to get accepted in a new club until she learns that her friends aren't welcome there. Cartoons: *The Ugly Duckling, The Cold-Blooded Penguin.*

SIBLING RIVALRY
One of the children is tired of having her sister follow her everywhere. Cartoon: *Pluto's Kid Brother.*

WONDERFUL WORLD OF MUSIC
The children can't decide which instruments they want to learn to play. Cartoon: *Music Land.*

PROBLEM SOLVING (INGENUITY)
Belle shows the children that thinking about their problems often leads to solving them. Cartoon: *Mickey and the Beanstalk.*

Disney Takes
to Cable

13

The Disney Channel

In 1981, an inventory of the Disney film vaults showed that the Studio had 250 feature films, 456 cartoons, and 27 years' worth of television programming safely stored away. Other than the material shown in recent years on the anthology series, much of this inventory represented a virtually untapped resource.

This changed when Jim Jimirro, head of the company's division that found additional markets for existing products, approached senior management with a daring suggestion: that Disney create its own cable television network.

The Disney Channel began broadcasting on April 18, 1983. Since then, there have been many series, specials, and films on it. Each of these is described below.

The Disney Channel Series

ADVENTURES IN WONDERLAND
Cast: Elisabeth Harnois (Alice), Reece Holland (March Hare), Armelia McQueen (Red Queen), Patrick Richwood (White Rabbit), John Robert Hoffman (Mad Hatter), Harry Waters, Jr. (Tweedle Dee), Robert Barry Fleming (Tweedle Dum), Wesley Mann (Caterpillar), Richard Kuhlman (Cheshire Cat), John Lovelady (Dormouse).

Based on Lewis Carroll's books and Disney's 1951 animated film, this series is designed to teach language skills and vocabulary. Each episode begins in Alice's bedroom, where she steps through the looking glass into Wonderland. Once there, she and her friends explore the English language.

ANIMALS IN ACTION
Hosts: Thayne Maynard, Keith Shackleton.

This nature series showcases animals in the wild, with an emphasis on the fragile balance between mankind and nature. Each episode features film of the animals in the wild and studies their behavior and habits, with an emphasis on different behaviors or physical characteristics.

AVONLEA
Cast: Sarah Polley (Sara Stanley), Jackie Burroughs (Hetty King), Patricia Hamilton (Rachel Lynde), Mag Ruffman (Olivia Dale), Zachary Bennett (Felix King), Gema Zamprogna (Felicity King), Lally Cadeau (Aunt Janet King), Cedric Smith (Uncle Alec King), Michael Mahonen (Gus Pike), Harmony Cramp (Cecily King), Barbara Hamilton (Mrs. Bugle), Maja Ardal (Mrs. Potts), Elva Mai Hoover (Mrs. Lawson), John Friesen (Archie Gillis), Roger Dunn (Bert Potts), Gillian Steve (Clemmie Ray), Tara Meyer (Sally Potts), Marc Worden (Edward Rae), Michael Longstaff (Rupert Gillis), Janet Amos (Mrs. Spry), Tyler Labine (Alphie Rugle), Francois Klanfer (Theatre Manager), Frances Hyland (Nanny Banks), Robert Collins (Blair Stanley), Joel Blake (Andrew King), Miklos Perlus (Peter Craig), Susan Cox (Peg Bowen), James O'Regan (Constable Jeffries), Valentina Cardinalli (Jane Spry), Amy Stewart (Nelly Shatford), James Mainprize (Mr. Bartholomew), Rex Southgate (Mr. Heinrich), Eric Fink (Mr. Stewart), Paul LaRocque (Chauffeur), Jennifer Inch (Maid), Lloyd Bochner (Mr. Cameron), Colleen Dewhurst (Marilla Cuthbert), Zoe Caldwell (Miss Lloyd), Marilyn Lightsone (Miss Stacey), R.H. Thomson (Jasper Dale), Fiona Reid (Mrs. Craig), Malcolm Stoddard (Malcolm), John Gilbert (Wellington Campbell), Alexander Abraham (W.O. Mitchell), Peter Coyote (Romney Penhallow), Madeline Kahn (Pidgeon Plumtree), Michael York (Ezekiel Crane), Thomas Peacock (Duncan McTavish), Elizabeth Sheppard

(Lisa), J. Winston Carroll (Leo), Miklos Perlus (Peter Craig), Andrew Gillies (Roger King), Kyle Labine (Davey Keith), Ashley Muscroft (Dora Keith), Don Francks (Abe Pike), Joseph Bottoms (Edwin Clark), Christopher Lloyd (Alistair Dimple).

The Disney Channel's first hour-long original weekly dramatic series is based on stories by Lucy Maud Montgomery, who wrote the books on which the mini-series *Anne of Green Gables* and *Anne of Avonlea* were based.

BIG BANDS AT DISNEYLAND

Host: *Peter Marshall.*

This series features famous big band orchestras performing at Disneyland. Each show is taped before a live audience at Plaza Gardens.

COLLEGE BOWL '87

Cast: *Dick Cavett (Host), Jim McKrell (Announcer).*

This series is based on the original *College Bowl*, which ran on radio from 1953 to 1957 and on NBC from 1959 to 1970. In this version, 16 college teams compete in a battle of wits.

Production Note:

- The finale was aired 6 months after the series was taped. To keep the winning team's identity secret, the players agreed to forfeit the $10,000 prize if they disclosed the results.

COMING ON!

Host: *Jimmy Aleck.*

Performers from 24 colleges across the country are featured in this variety series. Host Jimmy Aleck, joined by guest hosts and hostesses from each college, presides over a veritable parade of singers, comedians, jugglers, and other entertainers.

CONTRAPTION

Host: *Ralph Harris.*

This series features children ages 7 to 12 competing on a giant game board. The board is divided into themed stations: "Books," "Animals," "Heroes & Villains," and "Magic." At each station, the players have to answer questions based on Disney films. The object of the game is to collect Contraptiles, and the winner is the player with the biggest pile at the end of the game.

DANGER BAY

Cast: *Donnelly Rhodes (Grant "Doc" Roberts), Susan Walden (J.L. Duval), Christopher Crabb (Jonah Roberts), Ocean Hellman (Nicole Roberts), Michele B. Chan (Dr. Donna Chen), Hagan Beggs (Dr. George Dunbar), Deborah Wakeman (Joyce Carter), Michael Fantini (Adam Berman).*

This adventure series features a family living on a small island in Danger Bay, a scenic waterway on the Pacific Northwest coast of Canada. Doc Roberts, the father, is the curator-veterinarian at the Vancouver Aquarium, and his work brings him into contact with the other residents of the area, both human and animal. His children, Jonah and Nicole, help their father at work, and they also find time to get into many adventures of their own.

DISNEY CHANNEL DISCOVERIES

This title was used as an umbrella for films from outside sources.

DISNEY CHANNEL PREVIEW

The Disney Channel aired several versions of this monthly preview of upcoming programming.

DISNEY FAMILY ALBUM

Narrated by: *Buddy Ebsen.*

This series salutes many of the people who have helped make the Disney name so popular. Each show highlights the career of a famous Disney personality or group.

DISNEY STUDIO SHOWCASE

This was the umbrella title used for a series of specials.

DISNEY'S LEGENDS AND HEROES

This "series" was actually a combination of serialized adventure episodes from the anthology series and *Zorro* episodes.

DR. JOYCE BROTHERS PROGRAM, THE

Cast: *Dr. Joyce Brothers.*

Popular psychologist Dr. Joyce Brothers hosts this talk show series, which features celebrity guests and responses to viewer questions. Each episode also features a guest comedian who provides a lighter look at the problems of the world.

DONALD DUCK PRESENTS

This series is composed of animated shorts, edited into 30-minute compilations.

DTV

DTV is Disney's version of MTV, the music-video cable channel. Each episode of *DTV* features clips of Disney animation set to popular music. *DTV* was so popular that several prime-time network specials were aired.

DUMBO'S CIRCUS

Live Action Animators: *Sharon Baird (Lionel), Caleb Chung, Joe Giamalva, Frank Groby, Patty Maloney, Ron Mangham, Norman Merrill, Jr., Serafin Rocha, Mark Sawyer, Van Snowden.* **With the Voice Talents of:** *Phillip Baron, Jim Cummings (Lionel), Walker Edmiston, Ron Gans, Katie Leigh (Dumbo), Patty Maloney, Ron Mangham, Patricia Parris, Will Ryan (Barnaby), Mark Sawyer, Hal Smith.*

Dumbo, the elephant who discovered he can fly, is the star attraction of this traveling circus. Each episode finds Dumbo and his pals in a musical adventure, with an educational theme carefully woven into the story.

EDISON TWINS, THE

Cast: *Andrew Sabiston (Tom Edison), Marnie McPhail (Annie Edison), Sunny Besen-Thrasher (Paul Edison), Judith Norman (Mrs. Edison), Robert Desrosiers (Mr. Edison).*

Sixteen-year-old twins Tom and Annie Edison use science to help them solve mysteries, often despite the "help" of their younger brother, Paul. In later years, the twins go on to college, where they continue to solve mysteries. Each episode includes an animated epilogue that explains the scientific principles featured in that show.

EMERALD COVE

Cast: *Rhona Bennett (Nicole "Niki" Williams), J.C. Chasez (Clarence "Wipeout" Adams), Dale Godboldo (Bobby Johnson), Tony Lucca (Jeff Chambers), Ilana Miller (Cindy "Mac" MacNamara), Keri Russell (Andrea McKinsey), Marc Worden (Will Jenkins), Rus Blackwell (Benny), David Shelton (Sebastian), Cassidy Ray Joyce (Maria), Blain Carson (Blake), Ricky Luna (Rick), Matt Morris (Matt Harper), Terri Misner (Deborah Chambers), Dah-Ve Chodan (Alex Morgan), Josh Ackerman (Joshua Q. Anderson), Kari Goetz (Susie Winters), Jennifer McGill (Melody), Todd Rulapaugh (Brian Malloy).*

This updated version of the '60s beach movies centers on a group of surfers, musicians, and party lovers. Many of the episodes are centered on the band High Density trying to get a job playing at a local club. Other continuing themes are the problems the teenagers encounter while trying to sort out their love lives over the summer and what to do about college.

ENCHANTED MUSICAL PLAYHOUSE

Cast: *Marie Osmond (Velveteen Rabbit/ Fairy), Joshua Tenny (Little Boy), Janey Swenson (Nana), Nina Sherman (Ballerina), Teri Waite (Baby Doll).*

This was the overall title for a series of musicals based on popular fairy tales. The four episodes were *The Velveteen Rabbit* (starring Marie Osmond), *The Steadfast Tin Soldier* (with Shields and Yarnell), *Ferdinand the Bull* (starring Paul Williams) and *Petronella.*

EPCOT AMERICA! AMERICA!

Host: *Lloyd Bridges.*

Aired twice each week, this series is based on CBS's *On the Road* series with Charles Kuralt, with correspondents traveling the country looking for stories about the American people. Back at Epcot, the audience in the "Future Choice Theater" votes in opinion polls, and computers are used to provide instant tabulations of the results.

EPCOT MAGAZINE

Cast: *Michael Young (Host), Frank Berry (Ideas Tipster, The Three-Minute Gourmet), Marjabelle Stewart (Queen of Manners), Paul Nelson (The Dollar Stretcher), Marilyn Hencken (The Mad Planter), Judi Missett (Jazzercise Instructor), Patty Fox (Fashion Correspondent).*

Like many of the other magazine shows that sprang up during the early '80s, this series covers a wide variety of topics. The basic framework of each show is a number of tips on the subjects of the day. In addition to the regular cast, the series also features a celebrity Tipster of the Week.

EYES AND EARS

Host: *Jim McKrell.*

This was a short-lived series previewing upcoming programming on The Disney Channel. First aired in 1983.

FIVE MILE CREEK

Cast: *Louise Caire Clark (Maggie Scott), Rod Mullinar ("Gentleman Jack" Taylor), Jay Kerr (Con Madigan), Liz Burch (Kate*

Wallace), Michael Caton (Paddy Malone), Priscilla Weems (Hannah Scott), Martin Lewis (Sam Sawyer), Gus Mercurio (Ben Jones), Peter Carroll (Charles Withers), Tony Blackett ("Backer" Boman).

Just like California, Australia had its own gold rush in the 1860s. Would-be prospectors flocked to the gold fields, and businesses grew up around the mining camps. Among the new businesses were stage coach lines, with many smaller firms competing against the biggest name in the industry, Cobb & Co. This series features life at one of the stage coach stations, Five Mile Creek, located 40 miles north of Sydney.

Production Note:

- This series was based on a novel by Louis L'Amour. It followed the format first set in the anthology episode *The Cherokee Trail*.

GOOD MORNING, MICKEY!
This series is composed of animated shorts, which were edited into 30-minute compilations. At one point, two different episodes were aired daily.

GOOD MORNING, MISS BLISS
Cast: Hayley Mills (Carrie Bliss), Dennis Haskins (Principal Richard Belding), Joan Ryan (Tina Palladrino), Max Battimo (Mikey Gonzales), Dustin Diamond (Samuel "Screech" Powers), Mark-Paul Gosselaar (Zack Morris), Heather Hopper (Nicki Coleman), Lark Voorhies (Lisa Turtle), T.K. Carter (Mylo Williams).

Disney and NBC made television history with the April 12, 1988, announcement that they would jointly produce a new situation comedy series, *Good Morning, Miss Bliss*. The series, based on a pilot originally aired on NBC on July 11, 1987, was the first such project between a broadcast network and a national cable service. Former Disney child star Hayley Mills, in her American television series debut, starred as Carrie Bliss, an unorthodox 8th grade teacher who likes to make her students experience their lessons.

HAPPY TRAILS
Cast: Roy Rogers, Dale Evans.

The Channel aired a number of films starring Roy Rogers and wife Dale Evans. *Happy Trails* features Rogers and Evans introducing each film and reminiscing about their careers.

HOLLYWOOD LIVES
Cast: Danielle Harris, Incubus (Brandon Boyd, Mike Einziger, Alex Katunich, Jose Pasillas), Joe Loera, Brandy Norwood, Devin Oatway, Tamara Ruth, Brian Gross, Jamie Kennedy, Biance Lawson, Poppi Monroe.

Filmed over a period of 7 months, this series follows the lives of several hopeful actors, models, singers, and other performers as they try to make it big in show business.

JIMINY CRICKET THEATRE
This is an umbrella title used for short subjects acquired from outside sources. The shorts themselves were not produced by Disney and thus are not described in detail.

JUST LIKE FAMILY
Cast: Cindy Williams (Lisa Burke), Bill Hudson (Tom Burke), Gabriel Damon (Coop Stewart), Grace Johnston (Emily Stewart), Dan Hedaya (Uncle Lucky), Patrick B. McCormick (Jake Crawford), Lu Leonard (Jinx Crawford), Shonda Whipple (Muffy Crawford), John Fiedler (Zane Huxley), Benjamin Lum (Mr. Shimokawa), Al Lohman (TV Announcer), Bob Yanez (Water Man), Kenneth Mars (Bud Holstein), Ann Wedgeworth (Lu Holstein), Jim Doughan (Stuart), Vernon Joyce (TV Announcer), Jaclyn Bernstein (Brandy), Lisa Ball (Peggy), Lynne Stewart (Nevada Nellie).

This series is based on the anthology episode *Help Wanted: Kids*. Tom and Lisa Burke leave New York City for a new job. As soon as they get to their new home, they receive an unwelcome surprise when Jake Crawford, Tom's new boss, asks them where their children are. The childless Burkes discover that the company insists that all executives have children—after all, children's clothing is its business.

JUST PERFECT
Cast: Christopher Barnes (Trent Beckerman), Jennie Garth (Crystal), Sean Patrick Flanery (Dion), Judith Jones (Shelly), Shon Greenblatt (Jinx), Linda Rae Jurgens (Mom), Danny Sullivan (Dad), Dallas Alinder (Mr. Harmon), Neil Billingsley (Dave), James Eric (Coach), Rene L. Moreno (Roger), Francesca Jarvis (Grandma), Debbie Bartelt (Mrs. Fletcher), Stephen Nathenson (Gardner), Gary Clarke (Mr. Hamilton), Jan Ryder (Instructor), Robert Donahue (Quinn), Brett Bollinger (Kid), Marion Gibson (Woman), Henry Max Kendrick (Willie), Don Champlin (Officer), Jerome Zelle (Leader), Blaine

Etcheverry (Punk), Stan Freitag (Cop #1), Rick Hoffman (Mugger), Barney (Bodie).

Trent Beckerman, possibly the world's tidiest teenager, finds his orderly life in turmoil when he has to take care of his grandmother's dog, Barney, for 3 weeks. Barney is a St. Bernard who has never seen the inside of obedience school. The dog tears up the house, and Trent is so busy cleaning up after him that his schoolwork begins to suffer.

KIDS, INCORPORATED

Cast: Ryan Lambert (Ryan), Martika Marrero (Gloria), Stacy Ferguson (Stacy), Devyn Puett, Rahsaan Patterson (Kid), Renee Sands (Renee), Richie Shoff, Kenny Ford Jr., Kimberly Duncan, Joseph Conrad, Tiffany Robbins, Cory Tyler, Leilani Lagmay, Love Hewitt, Sean O'Riordan (Club Owner), Connie Lew, Moosie Drier (Riley), Eric Balfour, Anastasia Horne, Haylie Johnson.

Disney acquired the rights to this syndicated series about young rock stars then produced additional episodes for The Disney Channel. Each episode features the group as they work in The P*lace, a local club, and the problems the teenagers face with everyday life.

MATCH POINT

Cast: Brian Krause (Barton Cummings), Renee O'Connor (Robin), Anthony Palermo (Jason Stroud, Jr.), Evan Richards (Tim Runkle), Kristin D'Attilo (Bonnie Stafford), Zero Hubbard (Joel), Marisol Cassidy (Theresa Gonzales), Crystal Justine (Francie Wheeler), Nels Van Patten (Delerue), Danny Sullivan (Casey Turner), Diana Baines (Holly Turner), Michael Waltman (Mr. Runkle), Linda Applequist (Mrs. Runkle), Larry Soller (Mr. Cummings), Linda Jurgens (Mrs. Cummings), Sandy Gibbons (Mr. Metcalf), Byron K. Judge (Dr. Muncie), Verda Forester (Mrs. Muncie), Christopher Wilson (Jeff), Tom Tucker (Doug), Toby Goodwin (Boy), Mark Wilson (Mr. Stroud), Frazier Bain (Kid).

The Match Point tennis camp is a summer retreat for young players from across the country. The season begins as the campers arrive and owners Holly and Casey Turner get them started on a summer of lessons and fun.

MICKEY MOUSE CLUB, THE

Cast and seasons they appeared: Josh Ackerman (1–7), Christina Aguilera (6–7), Lindsey Alley (1–7), Rhona Bennett (4–7), Nita Booth (4–7), Mylin Brooks (3–5), Brandy Brown (1–3), Blain Carson (4–5), J.C. Chasez (4–7), Braden Danner (1), Tasha Danner (4–5), Nikki DeLoach (6–7), T.J. Fantini (6–7), Albert Fields (1–3), Dale Godboldo (4–7), Ryan Gosling (6–7), Tiffini Hale (1–3, 7), Chase Hampton (1–3, 7), Roque Herring (1–2), Tony Lucca (4–7), Ricky Luna (3–7), Tate Lynche (6–7), DeeDee Magno (1–3), Jennifer McGill (1–7), Terra McNair (4–5), Ilana Miller (3–7), Jason Minor (3–5), Terri Misner (4–6), Matt Morris (4–7), Fred Newman (1–6), Kevin Osgood (2–5), Damon Pampolina (1–3), Mowava Pryor (1–3), Keri Russell (4–6), Britney Spears (6–7), Justin Timberlake (6–7), Marc Worden (3–7).

When The Disney Channel began broadcasting, the very first show aired was an episode of *The Mickey Mouse Club.* While the show was popular with younger audiences, Channel executives felt that it had become dated over the years, particularly as it was in black-and-white. Their answer to this problem was to create a brand-new version of the Club, one geared toward contemporary audiences.

Like prior versions, this show features serials, aired as follows:

• First season: Match Point, Teen Angel
• Second season: The Secret of Lost Creek, Teen Angel Returns
• Third season: My Life as a Babysitter, Just Perfect
• Fourth season: Secret Bodyguard
• Fifth through seventh seasons: Emerald Cove

Each of the serials is described separately in this chapter.

MOUSERCISE

Cast: Kellyn Plasschaert, Steve Stark, Garett Pearson (Coach).

Based on a successful children's record of the same name, *Mousercise* is themed toward healthy living through education and exercise. The setting is the *Mickey Mouse Health Club,* where hostess Kellyn Plasschaert is joined by young exercisers and Disney characters for segments on exercise, health, safety, and nutrition.

MOUSETERPIECE THEATER

Host: George Plimpton.

This compilation of animated short subjects is patterned after Alistair Cooke's *Masterpiece Theater* series on PBS. Host George Plimpton, comfortably seated in an overstuffed armchair, offers droll comments about the Disney cartoons seen in each episode.

My Life as a Babysitter

Cast: *Jim Calvert (Nick Cramer), Kelli Williams (Kelly), Shane Meier (Ben), Michele Abrams (Jennifer Edwards), Sean Patrick Flanery (Mitch Buckley), David Kriegel (Lucas Labowsky), Amanda Foreman (Lindsay), Lara Lyon (Michelle), Thom Adcox (Augie), Jane Galkoway (Ms. Marlowe), Marcia Reider (Mrs. Kramer), Maureen Eastwood (Mrs. Fitzsimmons), Micheala T. Nelligan (Sandy Coburn), Jeffrey Olson (Coach), Jaime Ballard (Alyssa), Joyce Cohen (Mrs. Edwards), Marvin Payne (Mr. Edwards).*

Nick Cramer and Mitch Buckley have always been rivals, first in sports and now with girls. Mitch always seems to win, but as they start their senior year in high school, Nick is determined to finally outdo him. They spot Jennifer, a new girl in school, and make it a contest to get her to ask them for a date, agreeing that they can't ask her out first.

New! Animal World

Cast: *Bill Burrud (Host).*

Bill Burrud, who had hosted an older series, *Animal World*, returns with this updated version that focuses on different animal species around the world. Each episode includes quizzes based on the animals seen in that show.

Prairie Home Companion with Garrison Keillor, A

Host: *Garrison Keillor.* **Guests:** *Chet Atkins (Guitarist), John Bayless, Beausoleil, Boys of the Lough, Eric Bye, Judy Carmichael, Chanticleer, Michael Clooney, James Dapogny's Chicago Jazz Band, Bob Elliott and Ray Goulding (Comedians), The Everly Brothers (Singers), Henderson Forsythe, Alasdair Fraser, Emmylou Harris (Singer), John Hartford, Kim Hunter, Doc Lawson Trio, Leo Kottke (Guitarist), Doyle Lawson and Quicksilver, Bobby McFerrin, Brownie McGhee, The Minnesota Chorale, Dave Moore, Karen Morrow (Comedienne), The New Grass Revival, Frank Patterson, Red Clay Ramblers, Jean Redpath, The St. Paul Chamber Orchestra, Ricky Skaggs and Family, Ralph Stanley and The Clinch Mountain Boys, Vern Sutton, Taj Mahal, Robin and Linda Williams (Folk Singers).*

Garrison Keillor's long-running radio series *A Prairie Home Companion* comes to television in a joint production with Minnesota Public Radio. Broadcast live from St. Paul, Minnesota, the program features life in the fictitious town of Lake Wobegon in Mist County, Minnesota.

Scheme of Things, The

Cast: *James MacArthur, Mark Shaw, Nan Lynn Nelson, Dave Garrison.*

This series examines the world of science. Hosts James MacArthur and Mark Shaw provide the framework for a variety of field reporters who, in turn, narrate filmed stories on a wide number of subjects.

Secret Bodyguard

Cast: *Ernie Reyes, Jr. (Ernie), Heather Campbell (Brittany Belmont), Stephen Burton (Rick), Johnny Moran (Kevin), James O'Sullivan (Mr. Belmont), Ernie Reyes (Uncle Benny), Michael Ensign (Niles), Ellen Dunning (Linda), Irene Y.L. Sun (Aunt Edith), John Fujioka (Akira), Steve Messina (Joe), Scott Coker (First Thug), Kevin Ruby (Second Thug), Martin Katz (Mr. Erkel), Bill Dunnam (Coach Little), Peggie Howerton (Mrs. Miller), Joseph Svezia (Middle Bouncer), Alan Litvak (Right Bouncer), Jim Mohr (Old Bum), Mary M. Egan (Old Crone), Mhari Frothingham (Reporter), Martin Rodriguez (Tall Hood), Tom Callos (Ugly Hood), Marc Williams (Fat Hood), Ted Deasy (Party D.J.), Dante (Slash), Jason Sutliff (Buddy), Steve Tom (Mr. Fisher), Glenn Morshower (Announcer).*

Brittany Belmont, a rich teenager, wants to attend a regular high school so she can be with others her own age. Her father wants to shelter her and doesn't approve at first, but he finally comes up with a novel plan. Mr. Belmont hires a teenage martial arts expert, Ernie, to act as her bodyguard, but with strict instructions that Brittany not know of the job.

Secret of Lost Creek, The

Cast: *Shannen Doherty (Jeannie Fogel), Jody Montana (Travis Hathaway), Scott Bremner (Robert Fogel), Florence H. French (Adelaid Murchison), Ruth Hale (Augusta Murchison), Dabbs Greer (Henry "Grandpa" Fogel), Marjorie Hiltion (Hettie "Grandma" Fogel), Don Shanks (Charlie Little Elk), Christa Denton (Camie), Shawn Phelan (Russy), Darrin Wheaton (Hardy), Jesse Bennett (P.T. Butler), Jay Clegg (Driver), Marvin Payne (Blackbeard, the Prospector), Chad Chiniquy (Mark), Kim Christianson (Marci), Mitch Masoner (Burly Man), Tiffany Soter (Girl), Michael Weathered (Boy), Frank Gerrish (Leon), Michael Ruud (Dwight), David Tibbetts (Lukey), Christopher Scott (Roy), Duane Stephens (Deputy Jack).*

Jeannie Fogel and her brother Robert have been sent to spend the summer in the small town of Lost Creek in the Sierras. Both are sure they'll be bored, but when Jeannie stumbles across clues leading to a lost treasure and Robert becomes convinced he has spotted Bigfoot, their vacation takes on new excitement.

STEVE ALLEN'S COMEDY ROOM

Cast: Steve Allen, Bill Maher (Announcer), Joe Baker, The Terry Gibbs Sextet.

This comedy series, hosted by Steve Allen, features both veteran comedians and newcomers. The guests include Shelley Berman, Red Buttons, George Gobel, Louis Nye, Jack Carter, Dick Shawn, Shecky Greene, Mort Sahl, and Sid Caesar. Between acts, the show also features the music of a 17-piece orchestra led by Terry Gibbs.

STEVE ALLEN'S MUSIC ROOM

Cast: Steve Allen, Bill Maher (Announcer), Terry Gibbs Band.

Well-known composers and lyricists visit host Steve Allen in this series of musical performances and interviews.

STILL THE BEAVER

Cast: Jerry Mathers (Theodore "Beaver" Cleaver), Barbara Billingsley (June Cleaver), Tony Dow (Wally Cleaver), Janice Kent (Mary Ellen Cleaver), Kipp Marcus (Ward "Kip" Cleaver), John Snee (Oliver Cleaver), Kaleena Kiff (Kelly Cleaver), Ken Osmond (Eddie Haskell), Eric Osmond (Freddie Haskell), Frank Bank (Clarence "Lumpy" Rutherford).

This revival of the popular 1957–63 television series *Leave It to Beaver* features many of the original cast members. Now grown, Beaver and Wally Cleaver are back with their All-American mom, June. Hugh Beaumont, who had played their father, Ward, had died in 1982 and his part was not recast. The series followed a made-for-television movie of the same name that had aired on CBS in the 1982–83 season.

TEEN ANGEL

Cast: Adam Biesk (Dennis Mullen), Jason Priestley (Buzz Gunderson), Renee O'Connor (Nancy Nichols), Sasha Jenson (Jason), Shano Palovich (Waitress), Don Champlin (Mr. Peters), Wendy Kravitz (Sheila), George Gray III (Rick), Ria Pavia (Joan), Rene L. Moreno (Wayne), Caroline Gilshian (Carolyn), Leslie Stevens (Girl in Mini), Doug Cotner (Mr. Mullen), Paul Mancuso (Greg), Marian Gibson (Mrs. Gilroy), Tony DeBruno (Dr. Schoenkopf), Miranda Kent (Pammy), Kim Christianson (Barbie), Leslie Wright (Judy), Kathryn Geith (Old Hag), Andy Hill (Coach), Mark Wilson (Mr. Rhoades), Kenneth Bridges (Mr. Nichols), Dave Adams (Man in Car), Jean Fowler (Mrs. Mullen).

After waiting 30 years, fledgling angel Buzz Gunderson finally gets his first assignment. The one-time biker is assigned as the guardian angel to Dennis Mullen, a teenager who is enamored with the lifestyle of the '50s. Buzz needs to create a miracle to become a full angel, but it looks like he will have a tough time succeeding, for Dennis refuses to believe he is an angel.

TEEN ANGEL RETURNS

Cast: Jason Priestley (Buzz Gunderson), Robin Elaine Lively (Cindy Boone), Scott Reeves (Brian), Jennie Garth (Karrie Donato), Randy Oglesby (Rodney "Hotrod" Boone), Michael Flynn (Mr. Donato), Eric Bruskotter (Kelvin Donato), Ken Page (Chubby), Ivan Crossland (Mr. Peters), Tiffany Michelle Soter (Judy), Micaela T. Nelligan (Waitress), Tim Eisenhart (Mr. Henderson), Nancy Borgenight (Mrs. Henderson), Michael D. Weatherred (Jeff Henderson), Jesse Bennett (Mr. Duffy), Karl Wilson (Coach), Bob Bedore (Jerk), Kim Christianson (Trendy Girl), Christopher Scott (Mack), Marcia Reider (Teacher), Michael Ruud (Biker), John Mylerberg (Hot Rod), S. Bryce Chamberlain (Businessman), Tracey Lee Harrison (Teenager).

Guardian angel Buzz Gunderson returns to Earth to help Cindy Boone, the daughter of his best friend, Rodney "Hot Rod" Boone. The Boones' '50s-style gas station is threatened by a greedy developer named Donato, and his children constantly harass Cindy. Buzz also learns that he has to help Cindy with her love life.

VIDEOPOLIS

This weekly series features southern California teenagers dancing to rock music, live performances by popular recording artists, and music videos. A troupe of 12 dancers joins host Randy Newman at Videopolis at Disneyland, with remote segments from across the country. The series debuted on 2/05/88 with a 1-hour premiere but a 30-minute format.

TEEN WIN, LOSE OR DRAW

Cast: Marc Price (Host), Chase Hampton, Brandy Brown (Announcers).

Marc Price hosts this teen-oriented version of the popular syndicated game show *Win, Lose, or Draw*. Contestants and celebrity guests try to guess objects or well-known phrases based on clues from their team members.

WALT DISNEY WORLD INSIDE OUT
(original version)
Host: *Scott Herriott.*

This series looks at the events happening throughout Walt Disney World. It features host Scott Herriott in irreverent interviews and comedy skits, as well as comments from Park visitors. A trademark of the series is a bright red couch with a yellow Mickey Mouse pattern, which is seen with Herriott in such unusual places as an airliner and a monorail.

WALT DISNEY WORLD INSIDE OUT
(second version)
Cast: *Brianne Leary, George Foreman, J.D. Roth.*

The second version of this series has a slightly more serious style than its predecessor. Once again, series hosts provide a look at what is happening at Walt Disney World and previews of upcoming events. Boxing champion George Foreman is featured in the segment "George's Corner," in which he offers his viewpoint on different parts of the property.

WELCOME TO POOH CORNER
Cast: *Sharon Baird (Eeyore), Al Berry, Joe Giamalva, Frank Groby, Patty Maloney, Ronald Mangham, Laurie Mann (Narrator), Norman Merrill, Jr., Peter Risch, Mark Sawyer, Larry Thomas.* **Voices:** *Phil Baron (Piglet), Kim Christianson, Robin Fredericks (Kanga), Ronald K. Gans (Eeyore), Diana Hale, Will Ryan (Tigger, Rabbit), Hal Smith (Pooh, Owl).*

Sophisticated costumes are used to bring Winnie the Pooh and A.A. Milne's other popular characters to life in this daily children's series. A new system, called Puppetronics, enables the performers inside the costumes to have extensive control over their characters' features, which makes them seem very lifelike. Each episode includes a lesson for viewers, in which the characters explain a safety lesson or moral.

WISH UPON A STAR
Cast: *Joyce Little, Sharon Brown.*

This series offers children age 7 to 12 the chance to act out their fantasies. Viewers write in with their wishes, and the most interesting ones are put on the air. Some of the wishes granted are running away with the circus, diving with a dolphin, being a major league baseball player, dancing like Fred Astaire, and planet hopping with Captain Kirk.

WONDERFUL WORLD OF DISNEY, THE
Episodes from all years of the anthology series were aired under this title.

YOU AND ME, KID
Cast: *Sonny Melendrez, Toni Attell, Celeb Chung, Mitchell Young Evans, Gary Schwartz, Ricci Mann.*

This series features parents and their children participating in a number of activities together. Host Sonny Melendrez is joined by the *You and Me Players* in segments that include *Let's Go!* (exercise), *You and Me Theater* (creative drama), *Famous and 1/2* (celebrities and their children), *Musical Moments* (songs and dance), *Ssh!* (listening and observation skills), and *Mime Your Own Business* (pantomime).

The Disney Channel Specials

ACADEMY OF TELEVISION ARTS AND SCIENCES HALL OF FAME
When the Academy of Television Arts and Sciences established a branch at the Disney-MGM Studios Theme Park, the Academy's annual award ceremony was moved there as well. In each annual broadcast, new inductees are honored by peers and colleagues, with a film montage honoring their careers.

1993 Inductees: Dick Clark, Agnes Nixon, Phil Donahue, Mark Goodson, John Chancellor, Bob Newhart, Jack Webb.

1994 Inductees: Alan Alda, Joseph Barbera, Howard Cosell, Barry Diller, Fred Friendly, William Hanna, Oprah Winfrey.

ALADDIN: INSIDE THE MAGIC
Ever since opening day, *Aladdin* has been drawing large crowds. This special features interviews with some of the cast and crew as they enjoy this success.

ANIMATION FROM AROUND THE WORLD
Host: *John Canemaker.*

This episode showcases animation from Hungary, Sweden, the Soviet Union, Canada, Great Britain, China, and the U.S.A. The animation styles seen include traditional cel animation, stop motion, and paper cut-outs.

The show also includes a look at some of the world's best animated commercials.

Production Notes:

- This program aired as part of the *Disney Showcase* series of specials.

ANNE MURRAY IN DISNEY WORLD

Cast: Anne Murray, Julio Iglesias, Patti LaBelle, Andrea Martin, Paul Janz, Teenage Mutant Ninja Turtles, El Bethel Temple of Jesus Choir.

This musical special begins with Anne Murray singing in front of the Castle at Walt Disney World at night. After her hit song *Snowbird*, she talks about the fun she had taking a tour of the Park with crew members' children when they first arrived, and she shows some of the high points of their day. Patti LaBelle joins her on stage to sing *If You Ask Me To*, then Anne and Patti do a joint medley of their hits.

ART OF DISNEY ANIMATION, THE

Cast: John Lithgow, Glen Keane, Roy E. Disney, Burny Mattinson, Cheech Marin, Billy Joel, Richard Mulligan, Bill Berg, Dan Hansen, Barry Cook, Penny Coulter, Donald Towns, Mike Gabriel.

John Lithgow hosts a look at the magical feel of classic Disney animation. Lithgow then discusses several highlights of Walt's animation career, including such milestones as sound, color, and feature-length animation.

ASHFORD AND SIMPSON: GOING HOME

Cast: Nickolas Ashford, Valerie Simpson, Roberta Flack, Cissy Houston, Phyllis Hyman, Ben E. King, Patti Labelle, Paul Schaffer, Stevie Wonder.

Singers Nickolas Ashford and Valerie Simpson, who have been married for 14 years, talk about how they have worked together for so many years. They are seen writing a song at their home in Connecticut and then singing it in a recording studio. The show concludes with a performance in their nightclub in New York City.

BACKSTAGE AT DISNEY

Cast: John Culhane.

John Culhane visits the Studio for a sneak preview of upcoming films. Early work on *Who Framed Roger Rabbit* shows a much different version than what finally appeared on the screen. The show also includes a look at *Something Wicked This Way Comes*.

Production Note:

- This program aired as part of the *Disney Studio Showcase* series of specials, which first aired in 1983.

BACKSTAGE DISNEY: THE AMERICAN ADVENTURE

Cast: Lloyd Bridges, Marty Sklar, Randy Bright, Rick Rothschild, Dave Feiten, Bob Zalk, Karyl Gonzales.

This look at the host pavilion of Epcot, The American Adventure, begins with a visit to Walt Disney Imagineering. Marty Sklar talks about the history of Imagineering, formerly known as WED Enterprises. Randy Bright discusses the creation of The American Adventure.

BACKSTAGE DISNEY: THE MAIN STREET ELECTRICAL PARADE

Cast: Michael Young, Bob Jani, Ron Miziker, Jack Muhs, Jerry Hefferly, Ken Dresser, Don Dorsey, Vini Reilly, Troy Barrett, Barnette Ricci, Dennis Despie, Bob Gault, Brad Russo.

One of the most popular entertainment events at the Disney parks has been the Main Street Electrical Parade. Bob Jani, the parade's creator, begins this special with a look at how the project began. The prototype was an electric whale on the lakes at Walt Disney World, which eventually led to an electric water pageant.

BACKSTAGE PASS: DISNEY'S BEAUTY AND THE BEAST GOES TO BROADWAY

Cast: Robby Benson.

This behind-the-scenes look at the mounting of the Broadway production begins with Linda Woolverton, who wrote the film and adapted it for the stage, and composer Alan Menken, who had gone to Michael Eisner and Jeffrey Katzenberg several times trying to get them interested in a Broadway project. They finally agreed, and picked *Beauty and the Beast* as the Studio's first Broadway show.

BE OUR GUEST: THE MAKING OF DISNEY'S BEAUTY AND THE BEAST

Cast: David Ogden Stiers (Host), Don Hahn, Alan Menken, Paige O'Hara, James Baxter, Glen Keane, Kirk Wise, Linda Woolverton, Robby Benson, Roger Allers, Andreas Deja, Angela Lansbury, Nik Ranieri, Jerry Orbach, Will Finn, David Pruiksma, Bradley Michael Pierce, Brian McEntee, Gary Trousdale.

Host David Ogden Stiers tells the tale of how the film *Beauty and the Beast* came to the screen. There have been many stories created around the theme that beauty is more than skin deep, and Disney took the best of each for this film. Don Hahn, the film's producer, discusses the mixing of all of these elements into a workable story.

BEE GEES, THE: GOING HOME

Cast: The Bee Gees (Maurice Gibb, Barry Gibb, Robin Gibb).

This episode of the *Going Home* series of specials features The Bee Gees. Barry, Maurice, and Robin Gibb are seen during their sold-out 1989 Australian tour, their first tour in more than a decade. In addition to performing, the brothers discuss growing up, and their careers both as a group and as solo acts.

BEHIND THE SCENES: LOVE LEADS THE WAY

Cast: Delbert Mann, Jimmy Hawkins, Gary Graver, Ernest Borgnine, Patricia Neal, Ralph Bellamy, Eva Marie Saint, Ron Bledsoe, Ned Myrose, Arthur Hill, Susan Dey, Glynnis O'Connor, Timothy Bottoms.

This 30-minute special looks at the filming of *Love Leads the Way*, a made-for-cable film starring Timothy Bottoms as a newly blind man who must adjust to life with a Seeing Eye dog.

Production Note:

• This program is also known as *Eyes & Ears in Production: Love Leads the Way.*

BEHIND THE SCENES WITH D3: THE MIGHTY DUCKS

Cast: Joshua Jackson, Aaron Lohr, Ty O'Neal, Kenan Thompson.

This look at the newest *Mighty Ducks* film begins at the Studio, where the hosts look at highlights from the past two films. Members of the cast then talk about the filming and answer questions from fans.

BEYOND TRON

Cast: William Katt.

Host William Katt looks at how Disney has taken risks over the years. The tradition has remained alive as, in 1982, the Studio gambled on a very unusual film, *Tron*. Just as in Walt's early *Alice* cartoons, live actors would be placed in a world drawn by artists. This time, however, the artists would be using computers in place of traditional animation tools.

Production Note:

• This program aired as part of the *Disney Showcase* series of specials.

CANDLELIGHT CHRISTMAS CEREMONY, A

Cast: Howard Keel (Narrator).

Taped at Disneyland, this special showcases one of the most popular holiday events staged at the Park each year. More than 1,000 choristers are joined by Disney employees to form a "Living Christmas Tree" in front of the Main Street train station. Before a capacity crowd, guest star Howard Keel narrates the Nativity Story as the performers sing a variety of Christmas carols and hymns.

CAROLE KING: GOING HOME

Singer and composer Carole King is featured in concert in New York City. Between looks back at her career, she performs several of her hits, including *I Feel the Earth Move, Natural Woman, Jazzman,* and *It's Too Late.* She also sings songs with a New York feel, such as *Up on the Roof,* and some of the material she has written for other performers.

CELEBRATING WALT DISNEY'S SNOW WHITE AND THE SEVEN DWARFS: THE ONE THAT STARTED IT ALL

Cast: Ward Kimball, Roy E. Disney, Marc Davis, Charles Solomon, Frank Thomas, Ollie Johnston, Adriana Caselotti, Ed Jones, Bruno George, Bob Lambert, Don Johnson, Chris Elliot, Michael J. Fox, Betty White.

Walt Disney made history in 1937 with the release of the world's first full-length animated film, *Snow White and the Seven Dwarfs.* This special salutes both that achievement and the restoration of the film to its original glory.

CELEBRITY KNOCKOUTS AT WALT DISNEY WORLD

Cast: Stuart Hall (Host), Jenny Agutter, The Fat Boys, Yvonne Goolagong, Meatloaf, Gil Gerard, Chantal Contouri, Eddie "The Eagle" Edwards.

This special, taped at Walt Disney World and produced in conjunction with The British Broadcasting Company, features celebrities competing in humorous sporting events.

CHICAGO ON THE GOOD FOOT

Cast: James Cotton, The Legendary Blues Band, Koko Taylor, Big Twist and the Mellow

Fellows, Jimmy Ellis, Junior Wells, The Art Ensemble of Chicago, The Victory Travelers.

This musical special features blues and gospel singers at a variety of locations in Chicago, including the Park West Club. It was produced in conjunction with National Public Radio, which simulcast it in stereo.

Production Note:

- This program aired as part of the *Disney Showcase* series of specials.

COMING YOUR WAY

Cast: Annette Funicello.

This show takes a look at the making of movie trailers, those previews of coming attractions seen in theaters and on television. Specialized companies have emerged to carefully edit a film's best moments into a format that can often influence its success.

Production Note:

- This program aired as part of the *Disney Studio Showcase* series of specials, which first aired in 1983.

CONVERSATION WITH BETTY WHITE, A

Veteran actress Betty White begins the program by discussing *The Golden Girls*, praising her co-stars on the series. Using clips from *The Mary Tyler Moore Show*, she compares her character on that show, Sue Ann Nivens, to her *Golden Girls* character, Rose Nylund, and to herself.

CONVERSATION WITH BOB HOPE, A

The world-famous comedian reminisces about his career as he answers questions for an audience at the Disney-MGM Studios Theme Park. He begins by commenting on the changes that have taken place at the Park since he presided over the ground breaking ceremony four years earlier. He also talks about participating in the opening ceremonies for Walt Disney World in 1971 and reminisces about Walt. Hope and Disney are seen together in newsreel footage from 1945 as Hope presents Walt with the *Look* magazine award for the Studio's contribution to the war effort.

CONVERSATION WITH CAROL, A

Cast: Carol Burnett, Peter Matz, Liz Dorsey.

Comedienne Carol Burnett takes the stage to answer questions from the audience about her versatile and successful career. Her replies and anecdotes are combined with clips from her hit television variety series.

CONVERSATION WITH GEORGE BURNS, A

Veteran comedian George Burns takes a retrospective look at his life and career, reminiscing about the days he worked with wife Gracie Allen and other comedians such as Jack Benny, Walter Matthau, and George Jessel. Personal observations, such as the fact that his favorite role was in *The Sunshine Boys*, for which he won an Academy Award, are mixed with clips from old television shows and movies.

Production Note:

- George Burns won an Emmy Award for Individual Achievement—Informational Programming/Performance for this special.

DISKIDS

Cast: Marcus Reed, Natasha Pierce, Jason Piazza.

Three teenagers enjoy a romp through Disneyland as the show cuts between their antics and classic Disney cartoons.

Production Note:

- The Disney Channel aired several of these specials. The Studio later aired a series of these shows on KCAL-TV under the title *K-CAL Kids*, in both 30-minute and 60-minute formats.

DISNEY CHANNEL CHRISTMAS, A

Hosted by Jiminy Cricket, this holiday special takes a comedic and nostalgic look at the Christmas season. In addition to clips from numerous cartoons with Christmas themes, the show includes *Christmas Morning*, a segment featuring clips of toys and Christmas decorations, and a look at *Mickey's Christmas Carol*. Jiminy Cricket ends the show with a special version of *When You Wish upon a Star*.

Production Note:

- This program featured major segments of the anthology episode *From All of Us to All of You*.

DISNEY CHANNEL SALUTES THE AMERICAN TEACHER, THE

Host: First Lady Barbara Bush.

This half-hour Special launches a new series of interstitials by the same name, which salute top teachers from across the country. The first group of shows features 31 teachers, who were selected from almost 300 entrants. The interstitials, which eventually ran for 2 years, led to the creation of Disney's American Teacher Award, which was presented in the special *The Walt Disney Company Presents the American Teacher Award.* First aired in 1989.

DISNEY HALLOWEEN, A
Long thought to be the favorite night for witches, ghosts, and goblins, Halloween is the theme of this look at magic in Disney films and cartoons.

DISNEY STUDIO SHOWCASE
This is the title given to a collection of films produced by outside production companies under the supervision of Disney's feature film division and several others acquired from outside sources. Many of the episodes were also later aired as specials on the Channel without the *Disney Studio Showcase* distinction. The individual episodes were *Animation from around the World, Backstage at Disney, Beyond TRON, Chicago on the Good Foot, Coming Your Way, Future Tense, The Great American Dreamobile, Hansel and Gretel/Vincent, A Matter of Survival, Mind's Eye: The Experience of Learning, The Movie Show, Odds & Ends, Red Riding Hood, Seeing Spots, So You're Afraid to Fly, Twentieth Century Fads, Where Did All My Money Go?* and *Where the Toys Come From.* First aired in 1983. Each of the episodes produced for Disney is described under its own name.

DISNEYLAND SPORTACULAR: SPORT GOOFY—USTA NATIONAL JUNIOR TENNIS CHAMPIONSHIP
Cast: Dick Van Patten, Patti Van Patten, Vic Braden, Randy Rosenbloom.

This special features Sport Goofy as he hosts a group of young tennis champs between the ages of 12 and 14. The show opens with Dick Van Patten at the Disneyland Train Station, where Goofy leads 128 of the nation's best young tennis players off the train for a parade down Main Street.

DISNEYLAND STORY, THE
Host: Harry Anderson.

This look at the history of Disneyland opens in the early morning hours before the Park guests have arrived. Host Harry Anderson boards the Disneyland Railroad for a trip back through time. As he talks about the past, a montage of early Disneyland scenes

and Disney films is seen outside the train window, including *Steamboat Willie*, the 1928 cartoon that launched Walt's entertainment empire.

DISNEY'S ROOTIN' TOOTIN' ROUNDUP
This special, hosted by an animated character named Saddlesore Sam, features several Disney cartoons about the Wild West. The program includes *The Legend of Coyote Rock, Donald's Gold Mine, Two Gun Goofy, Pecos Bill* (originally seen in *Melody Time*), *Dude Duck, The Brave Engineer, Little Hiawatha, Pueblo Pluto*, and *The Lone Chipmunks.*

DISNEY'S SALUTE TO MOM
See: *Tribute to Mom, A.*

DISNEY'S ACADEMY AWARD WINNERS
The many Academy Awards and nominations for animated and live-actions successes won by the Studio are highlighted in this retrospective hour.

DISNEY'S COYOTE TALES
As three coyotes sit on a hill howling down at the town below them, the youngest, Junior, says he is tired of being a coyote. Instead, he would like to be a human, for it looks like they have all the fun. Through a series of animated clips, his father, Pappy, tells him that humans and everything about them are strange.

Production Note:

- The animation of the three coyotes together was first used in the anthology episode *The Coyote's Lament.*

DISNEY'S "THE HUNCHBACK OF NOTRE DAME" FESTIVAL OF FUN MUSICAL SPECTACULAR
Cast: All 4 One, Jodi Benson, Peabo Bryson, Judy Kuhn, Lebo M, Paige O'Hara, Regina Troupe, Carmen Twillie, Samuel E. Wright.

For the world premiere of *The Hunchback of Notre Dame*, Disney created a special stage show and parade held in New Orleans, Louisiana. The parade, comprising huge floats with a Mardi Gras theme and dozens of performers, leads to the Superdome. There, a live stage show featuring musical highlights from Disney animated classics entertains the crowd as they wait for the newest Disney film to begin.

DISNEY'S YOUNG MUSICIANS SYMPHONY ORCHESTRA (1992 VERSION)

Host: *Dudley Moore.*

A talented group of 65 classical musicians, with an average age of 11, have gathered for a 1-week summer camp at Mount St. Mary's College in Los Angeles. There, they have sessions with composers Henry Mancini, John Williams, Herb Alpert, Louie Bellson, Ray Brown, and Jerry Goldsmith. This is followed by the musicians performing in concert at the Ambassador Auditorium in Pasadena, California.

DISNEY'S YOUNG MUSICIANS SYMPHONY ORCHESTRA (1993 VERSION)

Host: *Dudley Moore.*

The 1993 version of this program features 76 musicians, all age 12 or under. While in Los Angeles, they are taught by Doc Severinsen, Henry Mancini, and Branford Marsalis. After Severinsen opens their concert performance with Leonard Bernstein's *Candide Overture*, the program continues with numerous musical compositions.

DISNEY'S YOUNG MUSICIANS SYMPHONY ORCHESTRA (1995 VERSION)

This edition features Beethoven's Seventh Symphony, Mozart's Overture to *Figaro*, Rachmaninoff's *Rhapsody on a Theme of Paganini, 18th Variation*, Manuel de Falla's *Danza Ritual del Fuego*, and selections by Bizet, Straus, and Vivaldi. Guest artists include classical guitarist Christopher Parkening and the Pacific Chorale Children's Chorus.

DISNEY'S YOUNG PEOPLE'S GUIDE TO MUSIC: GREATEST BAND IN THE LAND, THE

Cast: *Rachel Worby, Charles Fleischer (Roger Rabbit), Pittsburgh Symphony Orchestra.*

This is the first of two specials featuring Roger Rabbit and the Pittsburgh Symphony Orchestra. Roger, who claims to be a virtuoso with the kazoo, tries to lead the orchestra during a concert for children. Rachel Worby, the conductor, steps in instead to teach him and the audience about real musical instruments.

DISNEY'S YOUNG PEOPLE'S GUIDE TO MUSIC: A TUNE FOR A TOON

Cast: *Rachel Worby, Charles Fleisher (Roger Rabbit), Pittsburgh Symphony Orchestra.*

The second *Disney's Young People's Guide to Music* Special features the Pittsburgh Symphony Orchestra. Guest conductor Roger Rabbit assists Rachel Worby in conducting the orchestra as she explains the musical pieces being performed. The theme this time is tunes and melodies, and the songs include Tchaikovsky's *Pas De Deux* and *Waltz Serenade for Strings*, plus *American Salute* and *Can-Can*.

DONALD'S 50TH BIRTHDAY

The illustrious career of Disney's cantankerous star, Donald Duck, is seen in clips from many of his cartoon and film appearances. Even though Donald has been entertaining audiences for 50 years, he remains a star with modern audiences, as seen in a music video set to rock music.

DTV^2: THE SPECIAL

Cast: *Nina Peoples (Hostess).*

Another outing of rock music set to clips of classic Disney animation, this program features the music of Huey Lewis, Elton John, and other performers. The songs include *1,2,3, Come On, Let's Go*, and *Heart and Soul*.

FALLING FOR THE STARS

Cast: *Richard Farnsworth, Betty Thomas, Robert Conrad, Buddy Ebsen, Hill Farnsworth.*

This look at the unusual careers of stuntmen and stuntwomen is hosted by actor Richard Farnsworth, who had worked as a stuntman on Disney projects like *Davy Crockett*, *Savage Sam*, and *Texas John Slaughter*.

FANTASIA: THE CREATION OF A DISNEY CLASSIC

Cast: *Michael Tucker, Roy E. Disney, Carl Fallberg, Joe Grant, Frank Thomas, Ron Haver, John Culhane, Ward Kimball, Marc Davis, Ollie Johnston, Ken Anderson, Leonard Maltin, Pete Comandini, Terry Porter.*

This tribute to the 50th anniversary of *Fantasia* looks at the creation of the film that many hail as Walt Disney's masterpiece.

FESTIVAL OF FOLK HEROES

This special comprises animated featurettes about American folk heroes, including *Johnny Appleseed, Casey at the Bat*, and *The Saga of Windwagon Smith* among others.

FLEETWOOD MAC: GOING HOME

Mick Fleetwood, lead singer of Fleetwood Mac, hosts this look at the group's long-running success. Recently discovered footage of their *Rumours* tour includes the songs *Don't Stop, Over My Head, Rhiannon,* and *I'm So Afraid.*

FOR OUR CHILDREN: THE CONCERT

Hosts: Mayim Bialik, Kadeem Hardison, Neil Patrick Harris, Ashley and Mary-Kate Olsen, Jason Priestley, Baby Sinclair.

Recorded live at the Universal Amphitheatre in Universal City, California, this is a benefit concert for the Pediatric AIDS Foundation.

FROM DISNEY, A SUPER HALF TIME

Narrated by: John Harlan.

This special looks at the preparations behind the half-time show for Superbowl XVIII, held on January 22, 1984. The Walt Disney World Entertainment Division began work on the project more than 2 years before the event.

FROM DISNEY, WITH LOVE

This animated tribute to love begins with a look at Disney girls. All Disney girls are special, no matter their size, for love is blind. This is amply demonstrated by the mismatched lovers in the hippo and alligator ballet sequence from *Fantasia.*

FUTURE TENSE

This special, a science fiction view of the future, comprised the outside acquisitions *Prairie Sun, The Solitaire Creature,* and an animated short, *Fun with Mr. Future.*

Production Note:

- This program aired as part of the *Disney Showcase* series of specials.

GOING HOME

This series of specials showcases popular singing acts as they perform in concert. Each show includes scenes of the concert and interviews with the singers and their families. The individual shows are described in this chapter under their full titles: *Ashford and Simpson: Going Home; Bee Gees, The: Going Home; Carole King: Going Home; Judy Collins: Going Home; Loretta & Crystal: Going Home; The Manhattan Transfer: Going Home; Paul McCartney: Going Home;* and *Ringo Starr: Going Home.* Other episodes of

the *Going Home* specials were acquired products and are not listed here.

GOOFY'S GUIDE TO SUCCESS

Animated character Paddy O'Riley tries to help Goofy find a job, using scenes from some of Goofy's many and varied roles.

GREAT AMERICAN DREAMMOBILE, THE

Cast: Anson Wilson, Len Frank.

While not all motorists are in love with their cars, many drivers are. A staff of researchers is devoted to finding out what makes one car a success while another fails, and to predict the trends in car design.

Production Note:

- This program aired as part of the *Disney Showcase* series of specials.

HANSEL AND GRETEL/VINCENT

Cast: Michael Yama (Stepmother/Wicked Witch), Andy Lee (Hansel), Alison Hong (Gretel), Jim Ishida (Father), Joe Ranft (Puppeteer), David Konigssberg (Voice of Dan).

This episode consists of two short films by Tim Burton. The first, *Hansel and Gretel,* is a retelling of the classic fairy tale about a boy, a girl, a witch, and a gingerbread house. The second film, *Vincent,* is the story of a young boy who thinks he is Vincent Price.

Production Note:

- This program aired as part of the *Disney Showcase* series of specials.

HAPPY BIRTHDAY MICKEY

This birthday salute to Mickey Mouse includes a montage from many of his early films. The clock turns back even further with a look at Walt Disney's early Alice comedies. The show then follows Mickey's amazing career over the years, including his first screen appearances, the transition to color, and his roles in *Fantasia* and *The Mickey Mouse Club.*

HAPPY HOLIDAYS FROM WALT DISNEY WORLD

This 90-minute special is composed of the anthology series episodes *Christmas at Walt Disney World* and *Disney on Parade.* First aired in 1983.

HERE COMES SAM: THE MAKING OF AN OLYMPIC SYMBOL

Cast: Billy Mills, Bob Moore.

Olympic gold medalist Billy Mills hosts this look at the effort behind creating Sam the Eagle, the official symbol of the 1984 Summer Olympics.

HERE'S TO YOU, MICKEY MOUSE

Cast: Mark Linn-Baker, Soleil Moon-Frye.
This special honors Mickey Mouse's 60th birthday on November 18, 1988.

HOLIDAY SPLENDOR

Cast: Carol Lawrence, Ryan Kelly, Nicole Chingoon, Karyn & Bobby Williams, The Epcot Center World Dancers.

This musical show on international holidays and traditions opens at the American Gardens Amphitheatre in Epcot Center. Hostess Carol Lawrence explains some of the different ways in which people celebrate the holiday season.

INTERNATIONAL CIRCUS STARS OF TOMORROW

Cast: Ben Vereen, Mark David, Nickolaus Winn.

Ben Vereen hosts the international circus competition known as "Le Cirque De Demain" in Paris, France. Performers from around the world have gathered to showcase their talents, many of which have taken years to develop. While many are already successful circus stars, some are newcomers hoping that their appearances will launch them to stardom.

IT ALL STARTED WITH A MOUSE: THE DISNEY STORY

Cast: Ken Anderson, Richard Williams, Frank Thomas, Tony Anselmo, Marc Davis, Ward Kimball, Ken O'Connor, Jimmy Macdonald, Roy E. Disney, Jane Sinclair Kinney, Joe Grant, Dick Jones, Shamus Culhane, Brian Sidley, Claude Coats, Rich Frank, John Taylor, Michael Eisner, Jeffrey Katzenberg.

Many of the men and women who worked with and for Walt Disney talk about their favorite memories of the man. These personal observations are intermingled with clips from Disney films, television episodes, and cartoons. In addition, a look at Walt's background and career highlights shows how he came to be a major force in the entertainment industry.

JIMINY CRICKET: STORYTELLER

Jiminy Cricket hosts this animated look at several famous stories.

Production Note:

- This special was released overseas on home video as *Jiminy Cricket's Fabulous Fables, Fairy Tales, and Other Wonderful Stuff.*

JUDY COLLINS: GOING HOME

Cast: Judy Collins, Kris Kristofferson.

This installment of the *Going Home* series of specials features folk singer Judy Collins. The concert portion of the show was taped at the Wheeler Opera House in Aspen, Colorado, where she was joined by singer Kris Kristofferson. The concert footage is mixed with interviews in which Collins discusses her childhood and her love of music.

KALEIDOSCOPE CONCERTS

Cast: Caren Glasser and Craig Taubman, Gary Lapow, Red Gammer, Parachute Express, Larry Groce, Linda Arnold, Rosenshontz (Gary Rosen, Bill Shontz), Glenn Bennett.

These concerts for children feature popular recording acts performing for live audiences. Each concert was broadcast in both a 30-minute and 1-hour format. First aired in 1988.

KRAG, THE KOOTENAY RAM

Cast: William Berry (Scotty), Ronald Rosvald (Client), Paul Jolicoeur (Dog Handler).

High in the Canadian Rockies, Krag, a newborn big horn sheep, must quickly learn to fight numerous enemies if he is to survive. Krag grows up to become king of his tribe, but he must still battle to protect his herd.

LAKE WOBEGON COMES TO DISNEY

Host: Garrison Keillor. Guests: Chet Atkins (Guitarist), Philip Brunelle (Conductor), Johnny Gimble, Prudence Johnson, Peter Ostroushko, Jean Redpath.

Garrison Keillor brings his popular radio series *A Prairie Home Companion* to the World Theatre in St. Paul, Minnesota, to celebrate the theater's grand reopening after a lengthy refurbishment.

Production Notes:

- In addition to this and several other specials featuring Keillor, the Channel also aired the series *A Prairie Home Companion with Garrison Keillor.*
- This show is also known as *A Prairie Home Companion Comes to Disney.*

LAKE WOBEGON LOYALTY DAYS

Cast: Garrison Keillor, Minnesota Orchestra with Philip Brunelle.

Subtitled *A Recital for Mixed Baritone and Orchestra*, this Garrison Keillor Special includes the segments *The Young Lutheran's Guide to the Orchestra, Sons of Knute: Loyalty Oath, A New Monologue,* and *The Radio Announcer.* The program was taped in front of a live orchestra at Orchestra Hall in Minneapolis.

LIFESTYLES OF THE RICH AND ANIMATED

Ludwig Von Drake is the host of this look at the lives of famous cartoon stars. Three of Disney's biggest stars, Mickey, Donald, and Goofy, have been friends for years, and the cameras have captured many of their fun-filled moments together.

LOCATION: ANNE OF AVONLEA

Cast: Kevin Sullivan, Megan Follows, Dawn Greenhalgh, Ed Hanna, Lee Wildgen, Lionel Purcell, David McAree.

This special provides a look at the filming of the mini-series *Anne of Avonlea.* Kevin Sullivan, the writer, producer, and director of *Anne of Avonlea,* talks about the original *Anne of Green Gables* and this sequel. Actress Megan Follows speaks about the problems of doing period films in the face of modern intrusions.

LORETTA & CRYSTAL: GOING HOME

Cast: Loretta Lynn, Crystal Gale.

Sisters Loretta Lynn and Crystal Gale appear at Nashville's Grand Ole Opry, the first time they have been on stage together in 15 years.

LUDWIG'S THINK TANK

Ludwig Von Drake hosts this look at learning. As he notes, everyone can learn something every day—even an expert on as many subjects as he is. To prove his point, he uses six Disney educational shorts, each of which is described below.

HAROLD AND HIS AMAZING GREEN PLANTS

A young boy learns how seeds become plants, getting a very unusual education from the plants themselves.

SCROOGE MCDUCK AND MONEY

The world's richest duck gives his nephews an education about money.

WALT DISNEY PRESENTS ADVENTURES IN MUSIC: TOOT, WHISTLE, PLUNK, AND BOOM

A wise owl teaches a classroom full of birds about the basic principles of musical instruments.

WINNIE THE POOH DISCOVERS THE SEASONS

Winnie the Pooh and the other residents of the 100 Acre Wood discuss the seasons and their effects on the plants and other animals around them.

COMETS: TIME CAPSULES OF THE SOLAR SYSTEM

This historical overview looks at how scientists have come to understand comets.

DONALD IN MATHMAGIC LAND

Voices: Clarence Nash (Donald Duck), Paul Frees (Narrator).

Donald Duck learns that mathematical principles are found in a surprising variety of everyday areas. Several examples are given of how mathematics can be found in many unexpected places, including music and sports.

Production Note:

- This special used footage of Ludwig from *Symposium on Popular Songs* and several television episodes.

MAGIC KINGDOM CELEBRATION—LIVE!

Cast: John Sebastian, The Miami Sound Machine, Brenda Carlisle, Wil Shriner, Frank Olivier, Stacy Ferguson, Ryan Lambert, Martika Marrero, Rahsaan Patterson, Renee Sands, Kids Incorporated, Chief Justice Warren Burger.

Wil Shriner is the host for this 15th birthday celebration broadcast live from Walt Disney World.

MAGIC KINGDOM YULETIDE SPECIAL, A

Cast: Christian Bolta, Paul Bryant, Dena Drotar, Cathy Haller, Wendy Hildyard, Rick Lewis, Donna Miller, Bobby Miranda, Lee Munn, Marc Oka (Kids of the Kingdom).

The show opens with the Kids of the Kingdom and Disney characters singing Christmas carols. Scrooge McDuck complains that he doesn't like Christmas and wants them to stop. Mickey Mouse then uses his "special holiday magic" to help change Scrooge's mind.

MAKING OF A GOOFY MOVIE, THE

Cast: Jenna von Oy.

This behind-the-scenes look at *A Goofy Movie* includes a look at Goofy's film career, which began with his debut as Dippy Dawg in 1932's *Mickey's Revue*. There's also a visit to Disney's animation studio in France, where much of the film was produced.

MAKING OF BLACK ARROW, THE

This is a look at the making of *The Black Arrow*, set in Great Britain's unruly past. A visit to the set in Spain shows the movie magicians hard at work as they turn back the clock and create scenes of castles and villages that have long since been destroyed.

MAKING OF DISNEY'S CAPTAIN EO, THE

Cast: Whoopi Goldberg (Hostess), George Lucas (Executive Producer), Francis Coppola (Director), Michael Jackson (Himself/Captain Eo), Angelica Houston (Herself/Witch Queen), Dick Shawn (Himself/Space Commander), Michael Eisner, Tony Cox (Hooter), Debbie Carrington (Geex), Cindy Sorenson (Geex), Gary DePew (Major Domo), Jeffrey Hornaday (Choreographer), John Napier (Theatre and Costume Consultant), Vittorio Storaro (Lighting and Photographic Consultant).

A behind-the-scenes look at the making of this attraction.

Production Note:

- An edited version of this special aired on the anthology series as *Captain Eo Backstage*.

MAKING OF DISNEY'S RETURN TO TREASURE ISLAND, THE

This look at Disney's epic mini-series shows the cast and crew at work on location in several countries, including Wales, England, and Jamaica. Cast members talk about the challenge of living up to the memories of Walt Disney's original *Treasure Island*, and the crew describes some of the work required to re-create the period sets and costumes.

MAKING OF FIVE MILE CREEK, THE

This special shows how The Disney Channel re-created the Australian frontier for the making of *Five Mile Creek*, a weekly adventure series featuring life along a stagecoach route.

MAKING OF HONEY, I SHRUNK THE KIDS, THE

Host: Rick Moranis.

Rick Moranis, star of the 1989 theatrical hit *Honey, I Shrunk the Kids*, hosts this behind-the-scenes look at how the film was made.

MAKING OF POCAHONTAS, THE: A LEGEND COMES TO LIFE

Host: Irene Bedard.

Irene Bedard, the speaking voice of Pocahontas, hosts this look at the first Disney animated feature to be based on a real person.

MAKING OF RUDYARD KIPLING'S THE JUNGLE BOOK, THE

Host: Patrick Van Horn.

In 1967, Disney released the animated film *The Jungle Book*. This program is a behind-the-scenes look at the new live action version, *Rudyard Kipling's The Jungle Book*.

Production Note:

- An edited version of this special was aired in 1994 as part of *Mickey's Christmas Carol*.

MAKING OF THE BLUE YONDER, THE

Cast: Annette Handley, Mark Rosman, Susan Landau.

This behind-the-scenes look at the filming of *The Blue Yonder* features interviews with producers Annette Handley and Susan Landau, who discuss some of the many details necessary to re-create the Virginia towns and countryside of 1927 for the film.

MAKING OF THE DISNEY-MGM STUDIOS THEME PARK, THE

Cast: Fred Newman

This behind-the-scenes program features Fred Newman from *The Mickey Mouse Club* as a detective investigating the building of the newest Disney theme park, Disney-MGM Studios.

MAKING OF THE HUNCHBACK OF NOTRE DAME, THE

Host: Jason Alexander.

The making of Disney's 34th animated feature begins with a look back at some of the Studio's past successes and awards. *Beauty and the Beast* was the first animated film nominated for an Academy Award for Best Picture, and many of the team responsible for that success have reunited for *Hunchback*.

Producer Don Hahn and directors Gary Trousdale and Kirk Wise discuss their roles on the project.

MAKING OF THE LION KING, THE
Host: Robert Guillaume.

Robert Guillaume, the voice of Rafiki in *The Lion King*, hosts this look at the creation of the film from a nature preserve, where Disney animators had gone to study real animals as models.

MAKING OF THE LITTLE MERMAID, THE
Host: Alyssa Milano.

Actress Alyssa Milano hosts this look at Disney's animated feature.

MAKING OF THE MIGHTY DUCKS, THE
Cast: Tom Murray (Host).

The Mighty Ducks professional hockey team began when Michael Eisner saw a new arena under construction in Anaheim and learned the owners didn't have a pro hockey team to play there. He obtained a franchise from the National Hockey League and then traveled to Quebec City, Canada, with team executives to select the team's first players at the annual hockey owners meeting.

Production Note:

• This was an edited version of the special *The Making of the NHL'S Mighty Ducks.*

MAKING OF THE THREE MUSKETEERS, THE
Cast: Chris O'Donnell (Host), Charlie Sheen, Kiefer Sutherland, Oliver Platt, Joe Roth, Roger Birnbaum, Stephen Herek, John Mollo, Rebecca De Mornay, Ned Dowd, William W. Wilson III, Paul Weston, David Harris, John F. Link, Bob Anderson, Michael Wincott, Dean Stemler, Michael Kamen.

Chris O'Donnell hosts this special look at the filming of *The Three Musketeers*, an action swashbuckler based on the novel by Alexander Dumas. Producer Joe Roth discusses both the characters from the book and the actors who filled the roles in this new telling of a classic tale.

MAKING OF THE UNDERGRADS, THE
This behind-the-scenes look at The Disney Channel film shows the cast and crew at work on location in Canada, including interviews with Art Carney and Chris Makepiece.

MAKING OF TOY STORY, THE
Annie Potts narrates this look at the making of *Toy Story*.

MANHATTAN TRANSFER, THE: GOING HOME
Cast: Tim Hauser, Janis Siegel, Alan Paul, Cheryl Bentyne, The Manhattan Transfer Band (Alex Blake, Frank Colon, Yaron Gershovsky, Ralph Humphrey, Wayne Johnson, Don Roberts).

The second concert in the *Going Home* series of specials includes footage of a concert at the Paul Masson Winery in Saratoga, California. Among the songs featured are *Birdland, Boy from New York City, Java Jive, Operator,* and *Gloria.*

MATTER OF SURVIVAL, A
Cast: Linda Blair.

This episode consists of two acquired animal films, *Primarily Primates* and *Keepers of the Wild*. The first deals with a San Antonio shelter for wild animals abandoned by their owners, and the latter is a look at state-of-the-art zoos such as the San Diego Wild Animal Park.

Production Note:

• This program aired as part of the *Disney Showcase* series of specials.

MICHAEL ICEBERG IN CONCERT FROM DISNEYLAND
Cast: Michael Iceberg.

This evening performance at Tommorrowland Terrace in Disneyland features Michael Iceberg, a musician who performs on his own synthesizer creation, the Iceberg Machine.

MICKEY GOES TO MOSCOW
Cast: Roy E. Disney, Patty Disney, Art Levitt.

The spirit of international cooperation takes an unusual turn when Mickey Mouse goes to Moscow to celebrate a special Russian nationwide Disney animation festival.

MICKEY MOUSE CLUB FIRST ANNIVERSARY SPECIAL
Cast: Fred Newman, Mowava Pryor, Joshua Ackerman, Lindsey Alley, Mylin Brooks, Brandy Brown, Albert Fields, Tiffini Hale, Chase Hampton, Ricky Luna, Dee Dee Magno, Jennifer McGill, Ilana Miller, Jason Minor, Kevin Osgood, Damon Pampolina, Marc Worden, Tommy Cole, Sharon Baird,

Don Grady, Sherry Alberoni, Bobby Burgess, Annette Funicello.

This 1st anniversary salute to The Disney Channel version of *The Mickey Mouse Club* begins as the cast members welcome several of the original Mousekeeters. The original stars join their contemporary counterparts in a variety of performances.

MICKEY MOUSE CLUB STORY, THE

The 40th anniversary of *The Mickey Mouse Club* is saluted in this collection of interviews, film clips, and rare home movies of the Mouseketeers.

MICKEY: REELIN' THROUGH THE YEARS

Cast: Zachery Ty Bryan, Bradley Pierce (Kirk), Dan Frischman (Joe), Charlotte Rae (Beryl), Andreas Deja, Ward Kimball.

When Zachery Ty Bryan from *Home Improvement* gives a friend a tour of the Studio, they discover a film can marked *Runaway Brain*. They learn that it's the newest Mickey Mouse cartoon and head off to screen it.

MICKEY'S NUTCRACKER

Cast: Bidalia Albanese, Denise Anderson, Tracy Bardens, Arik Basso, Kym Berry, Mark Bunker, Mark Devine, Phil Dominquez, Jill Foley, Tamara Harrison, Claudia Isola, Paul Kozlowski, Derick La Salla, Rachel Miller, Jane Oshita, Tracy Ray, Raymond Rodriguez, Michi Scott, Bill Wiley.

This live stage show features the Disney characters in their version of Tchaikovsky's *Nutcracker*.

MIND'S EYE, THE: THE EXPERIENCE OF LEARNING

Cast: Alvin Sargent (Host), Bruce Jenner, Oliver Reed, Harvey and Chris Korman, Dr. Richard Held, Dr. Moses Albalas, Dr. Arnold Scheibel, Dr. Norman Geschwind, Dr. Jerry Block, Dr. Eva Newbrun, Dr. Paul Satz, Dr. Albert Galabunda, Carol Murray.

This documentary looks at how the eye-to-brain connection works, and what happens when something goes wrong.

Production Note:

• This program was aired as part of the *Disney Showcase* series of specials.

MIRACLES OF SPRING—A TRUE-LIFE ADVENTURE

Walt Disney's famous *True-Life Adventure* series is showcased in this look at the pho-

tographers who captured scenes of animal life from across the world. Clips from many of the award-winning featurettes show some of the many animals and locales featured over the years.

MMC IN CONCERT

Cast: Josh Ackerman, Lindsey Alley, Rhona Bennett, Nita Booth, J.C. Chasez, Dale Godboldo, Tony Lucca, Ricky Luna, Jennifer McGill, Ilana Miller, Keri Russell, Marc Worden.

Cast members from *The Mickey Mouse Club* gather to promote their new album. The songs performed include *Real Talk* (Rhona), *Cool Love, Hanging on for Dear Life* (Jennifer), *I Want Your Love* (Nita), *Merry-Go-Round* (Matt), *Goodbye* (Rhona), and *Flavor* (entire cast).

MMC ROCKS THE PLANET

Cast: Fred Newman, Terri Misner, Josh Ackerman, Lindsey Alley, Rhona Bennett, Nita Booth, Mylin Brooks, Blain Carson, J.C. Chasez, Tasha Danner, Dale Godboldo, Tony Lucca, Ricky Luna, Jennifer McGill, Terra McNair, Ilana Miller, Jason Minor, Matt Morris, Kevin Osgood, Keri Russell, Marc Worden.

The cast of *The Mickey Mouse Club* appears in a live concert to benefit the Nature Conservancy and the World Wildlife Fund.

MOVIE SHOW, THE

Cast: Charles Champlin, Chantal Westerman.

Two noted entertainment critics use film clips and interviews to provide a brief history of filmed entertainment.

Production Note:

• This program was aired as part of the *Disney Showcase* series of specials.

MUPPETS TAKE TO THE HIGH SEAS, THE: THE MAKING OF MUPPET TREASURE ISLAND

Host: Clive Revill.

This behind-the-scenes look at the Muppet's latest film includes interviews with members of the cast and crew.

NATIONAL FAMILY SAFETY TEST, THE

Cast: Cindy Williams, Bill Hudson, Edan Gross (Child Psychologist), James F. McMullen.

Cindy Williams and Bill Hudson host this family-oriented look at safety, which features questions for the studio and home audiences.

NEW VAUDEVILLIANS, THE

Host: Peter Scolari.

This variety show includes performances by acrobats, comedians, jugglers, magicians, clowns, and various artists.

NEW VAUDEVILLIANS TOO

Host: Ed Begley Jr.

This variety show includes musicians, jugglers, ventriloquists, and musicians.

NEW VAUDEVILLIANS III

Host: Harry Anderson.

This variety show includes performances by numerous artists.

ODDS & ENDS

This special consisted of four acquired films: *Cooperage, Spartree, Nails,* and *Ballet Robotique.*

Production Note:

- This program aired as part of the *Disney Showcase* series of specials.

ON LOCATION: PARENT TRAP II

Cast: Hayley Mills, Stuart Krieger, Tom Skerritt, Carrie Kei Heim, Bridgette Andersen, Rona Maxwell, Peter Stein.

This look at the filming of *Parent Trap II* begins as its star Hayley Mills discusses the 3 weeks of filming in Tampa. She then recalls her past Disney roles, beginning at age 13 in *Pollyanna,* and talks about working with Walt Disney. First aired in 1986.

PARTY ALL NITE CONCERT, THE: GRAD NITE AT WALT DISNEY WORLD

Cast: Jon Secada, P.M. Dawn, Shai.

Each year graduating high school seniors gather at Walt Disney World for a night-long party. The fun this year includes performances by Jon Secada, P.M. Dawn, and Shai.

PARTY, THE: IN CONCERT

Cast: The Party (Albert Fields, Deedee Magno, Chase Hampton, Damon Pampolina, Tiffini Hale).

This musical special features concert footage and behind-the-scenes looks of The Party's nationwide "Tilyadrop" tour. The former Disney Channel Mouseketeers talk about the tour and their careers.

PAUL MCCARTNEY: GOING HOME

Cast: Paul McCartney, John Hurt (Narrator).

Former Beatle Paul McCartney is seen in concert in Philadelphia, Pennsylvania, and Rio de Janeiro, Brazil, during his 1990 World Tour.

Production Note:

- This special won the 1991 CableAce Award for Outstanding Music Special.

POP QUIZ

This was a pilot for a proposed monthly series that would have offered viewers an opportunity for self-assessment by posing questions in the monthly magazine and on the air.

PRAIRIE HOME COMPANION, A: THE SECOND ANNUAL FAREWELL PERFORMANCE

Host: Garrison Keillor. *Guests:* Chet Atkins (Guitarist), Rich Dworsky, The Everly Brothers (Singers), Vince Giordino and the Nighthawks (Jazz Band), Tom Keith, Leo Kottke (Guitarist), Kate MacKenzie, Karen Morrow (Comedienne), Dan Rowles, Butch Thompson (Pianist), Robin and Linda Williams (Folk Singers).

Garrison Keillor ends his *A Prairie Home Companion* radio series with a live broadcast from Radio City Music Hall in New York City. It includes a new chapter in the radio drama *Buster the Show Dog,* featuring Rich Dworsky, Tom Keith, Kate MacKenzie, and Dan Rowles.

PRAIRIE HOME COMPANION, A: THE THIRD ANNUAL FAREWELL PERFORMANCE

Host: Garrison Keillor. *Guests:* Richard Dworsky, Johnny Gimbel, Emmylou Harris (Singer), Tom Keith, Kate MacKenzie, Dan Rowles, Robin and Linda Williams (Folk Singers).

Garrison Keillor's 13-city tour is highlighted in this musical special, which is seen during his visit to Dallas.

PRESIDENTIAL INAUGURATION CELEBRATION FOR CHILDREN, THE

Cast: Markie Post (Host), Emmylou Harris, Jim Henson's Muppets, Fred Rogers, Diane Ferlatte, Raffi, Parachute Express, The Cast from Adventures in Wonderland.

Markie Post hosts this celebration of the inauguration of President Bill Clinton.

PRESIDENTIAL INAUGURAL CELEBRATION FOR YOUTH, THE

Cast: *Will Smith (Host), Boyz II Men, Clarence Clemons, Celine Dion, Jay R. Ferguson, The Joffrey Ballet, L.A. Youth Ensemble Theatre, Kenny Loggins, The Mickey Mouse Club, Vanessa Williams.*

Bill Clinton joins host Will Smith for this celebration of Clinton's inauguration the next day as President of the United States.

PRETTY GOOD NIGHT AT CARNEGIE HALL, A

Cast: *Garrison Keillor.* **Guests:** *Chet Atkins (Guitarist), Kate MacKenzie, Butch Thompson, Robin and Linda Williams (Folk singers).*

Taped in front of a live audience, this special includes another performance by The Hopeful Gospel Quartet (Keillor, Robin and Linda Williams, MacKenzie).

RED RIDING HOOD

Cast: *Allison Gregory (Red), Jeff Kober (Wolf), Dorothy Bennett (Red's Mother), Gregory Niebel (Hunter), Marilyn Korones (Grandmother).*

This is the classic story of Little Red Riding Hood on her way to grandmother's house, presented in a highly stylized format.

Production Note:

• This program aired as part of the *Disney Showcase* series of specials.

RICK NELSON: A BROTHER REMEMBERS

Cast: *David Nelson, Harriet Nelson, Tracy Nelson, Gunnar Nelson, Matthew Nelson.*

Clips of interviews, concerts, and television shows featuring Rick Nelson are introduced by his brother, David. The program begins with a look at their parents' careers as a band-leader and singer, and Harriet Nelson talks about their early days together. After the family starred in a radio show, the famous television program *The Adventures of Ozzie and Harriet* began in 1952.

RINGO STARR: GOING HOME

Former Beatle Ringo Starr goes back to Liverpool, joined by his son, Jason, and stepfather, Harry. He visits his old home and The Cavern, a replica of the nightclub where The Beatles were discovered. Concert footage from performances at The Liverpool Empire and the Greek Theatre in Los Angeles show Ringo performing some of his greatest hits.

ROCK 'N TOONTOWN

Cast: *Craig Taubman, Breanne O'Donnell (Rachel Lewis), Tahj Mowry (Jason Jaffe).* **Dancers:** *Ken Arata, Lana Bensinger, Christian Buenaventura, Taryn Francis, Shaun-Paul Kalinsky, Charles Klapow, Amber Kolar, John Reid, Alexaundria Simmons, Cammy Vincent, The Craig N Company Band (Robert Aguilar, Joel Bennett, Troy Dexter, Gary Griffin, Michael Turner).*

Singer Craig Taubman stars in this special to promote his new Disney children's record Rock 'n Toontown.

ROOTS OF GOOFY, THE

Host: *Gary Owens.*

This story of Goofy's ancestors begins with a musical segment featuring clips of Goofy in many of his different roles. Host Gary Owens explores Goofy's family tree, which goes way back to the days of the cavemen.

SAMANTHA SMITH GOES TO WASHINGTON . . . CAMPAIGN '84

Cast: *Samantha Smith, Governor Reubin Askew, Senator George McGovern, Senator Ernest Hollings, Reverend Jesse Jackson, Senator Alan Cranston, Senator John Glenn.*

Samantha Smith, the 11-year-old girl who achieved international recognition for her correspondence with Soviet Premier Yuri Andropov, takes a look at the American political process as the 1984 Presidential election nears. Before leaving to interview the candidates, she polls her fellow 6th grade classmates at the Hardy School in Manchester, Maine, to see what they want her to ask them.

SEBASTIAN'S CARIBBEAN JAMBOREE

Cast: *Sam Wright, Autumn Hoff (Tanya Terry, Reporter).* **Featured Children:** *David Boers, Leslie Boers, Tara Lynn Boers, Kheli Bracy, Sanjay Chadeesingh, T.J. Clark, Misty Hagan, Michael Johnson, Matt Morris, Mariah Parsons, Laura Stonebraker, Coriann Yarckin.* **Band:** *Glenn Barclay, Jim Braswell, Jim Coleman, Carlos Del Torro, Cullen Douglas, Eric Neal.*

Sebastian, the musical crab from *The Little Mermaid*, and his partner, Sam Wright, perform a concert at Walt Disney World, entertaining a crowd of children at Typhoon Lagoon.

Production Note:

• Sam Wright was the voice of Sebastian in *The Little Mermaid*.

Sebastian's Party Gras

Cast: Sam Wright. ***Featured Children:***
*David Boers, Rebecca Bromberg, Jeffrey
Bruckner, Sanjay Chadeesingh, T.J. Clark,
Brianna Hagle, Otiga Ogubi, Mariah Parsons,
Jennifer Pena, Kelly Stalcup, Nicholas Wood.*
Dancers: *Jim Braswell, Sy Byram, Jim
Coleman, Eric DeNard, Cullen Douglas, Lisa
Fernandez.* ***Voices:*** *Kenneth Mars (King
Triton), Will Ryan (Seahorse).*

Sebastian, the musical crab from *The Little
Mermaid,* is preparing for a new concert with
his friend, Sam Wright (the voice of Sebastian), at Walt Disney World.

Seeing Spots

Award-winning commercials from the 1982
Cannes Film Festival provide an interesting
look at marketing techniques from around
the world.

Production Note:

- This program aired as part of the *Disney
  Showcase* series of specials.

Simply Mad about the Mouse

This compilation of music videos featuring
new interpretations of classic Disney music
performed by contemporary artists was originally released on home video and later aired
on The Disney Channel in 1992.

Smithsonian Salutes Disney Music, The

Performers: Judith Blazer, Jason Graae,
Mark Jacoby, Mary Testa, Fairfax Chorale
Society Chorale.

The Smithsonian Institution, founded in
1846, has been called America's Attic, for the
facility is best known for its imposing collection of artifacts. In addition to these col-
lections, though, the Smithsonian has many
special events, such as this salute to Disney's
musical legacy.

Snow White: Singin', Dancin', Heigh Ho

Cast: Colleen Bartl (Snow White), Melissa
Boyer (Grumpy), Michelle DeCuir (Dopey),
Yvette Dieppa (Sneezy), Mark Griffin (Doc),
Christina Lagmay (Sleepy), John LaLonde
(Prince), Michael Lockett (Happy), Theresa
Rodriguez (Bashful), Bill Wiley (Witch).
Dancers: Brynne Becker, Kevin Calvin, Betsy
Chang, Ray Garcia, Jill Getman, Debra
Harris, John D. Harvey, Brett Heine, Raeleen
Juliano, Joseph McKee, Jeanne O'Connell, Ray

Rodriguez, Cynthia Sarmiento, Bob
Woodward.

The story of Snow White and the Seven
Dwarfs is seen in a live-action stage show
taped at Disneyland. In addition to the songs
made famous in the 1937 film, this version
features elaborate dance numbers and colorful costumes created for the stage.

So You're Afraid to Fly

Many people have a fear of flying. The show
looks at the possible causes of this sometimes disabling affliction and how people
work to overcome it.

Production Note:

- This program aired as part of the *Disney
  Studio Showcase* series of specials, which
  first aired in 1983.

Strange Companions

Cast: Doug McClure (Archie Anders),
Michael Sharrett (David), Mark Dusay (Mae
Corbin), Ted Stidder (Barnaby), Lloyd Berry
(Sam), Virginia Harrison (Claire).

Archie Anders, a crusty bush pilot, takes
off to count whooping cranes during their annual migration. Archie is unaware that
David, a runaway from an orphanage, has
stowed away until a sudden storm results in
a crash landing. The two travelers find themselves trapped in the wilderness.

Production Note:

- This show was originally announced as a
  2-hour episode of the anthology series for
  the 1980–81 season.

Time for Grandparents, A

Cast: Meredith MacRae, Anson Williams,
Aleen Cummings, Sam Goldman, Madie
Raye, Oak Gibson, Allison Mullavey.

Meredith MacRae and Anson Williams
host this look at how older people can still re-
late to today's young. It also shows how they
pass on family traditions and crafts to
younger generations.

Too Smart for Strangers

Cast: Joe Giamalva, Ron Mangham, Mark
Sawyer, Patty Maloney, Frank Groby, Sharon
Baird, Norman Merrill, Jr., Peter Risch. **With
the Voice Talents of:** Hal Smith (Pooh, Owl),
Will Ryan (Rabbit), Phil Baron (Piglet), Ron
Gans, Kim Christianson.

The cast of *Welcome to Pooh Corner* hosts
this program designed to warn young children to be cautious about strangers.

TRIBUTE TO MOM, A
A magic locket in the Disney Archives contains the spirit of all Disney mothers, and it provides an animated look at some of the most memorable ones.

TRISHA YEARWOOD: THE SONG REMEMBERS WHEN
Band Members: *Dave Pomeroy, Eddie Bayers, Matt Rollings, Billy Walker, Jr., Paul Franklin, Brent Mason, Rob Hajacos, Thom Flora, Lisa Silver.*

Filmed on location at the Tennessee Performing Arts Center in Nashville and at the Belle Meade Mansion, this Special features singer Trisha Yearwood as she performs *Wrong Side of Memphis, Mr. Radio, You Say You Will, Down on My Knees, Walk Away Joe,* and *I Will Never Marry.*

TWENTIETH CENTURY FADS
Recorded history shows that fads have existed for hundreds of years. This episode looks at some of the more modern ways that people are spending their time, efforts, and money.

Production Note:

- This program aired as part of the *Disney Showcase* series of specials.

VACATIONING WITH MICKEY AND FRIENDS
Cast: *Gary Owens.*

Gary Owens, owner of the Let's Get Away from It All Travel Agency, suggests a series of trips designed to relieve the stress of everyday life. His customers include Goofy, Mickey, Minnie, Donald, and Pluto.

VIDEOPOLIS: STARTRACKS
Host: *Jonathan Prince.*

These music Specials are based at Videopolis in Disneyland, with celebrity interviews.

VIDEOPOLIS SUPERSTAR SPECIAL
This 1-hour special from Videopolis, hosted by Jonathan Prince, features Debbie Gibson, The Jets, Nia Peeples, Shanice Wilson, Tina Yothers, and Michael Damian.

WALT DISNEY COMPANY PRESENTS THE AMERICAN TEACHER AWARDS, THE
The interstitial series *The Disney Channel Salutes the America Teacher* had showcased outstanding teachers in 5-minute segments for 2 years. Disney continued its commitment to the concept of promoting educators with this series of specials.

WALT DISNEY WORLD: A DREAM COME TRUE
This special looks at the 15 years since Walt Disney World opened. The program also includes previews of the upcoming Disney-MGM Studios Theme Park and Pleasure Island.

WALT DISNEY WORLD: PAST, PRESENT, AND FUTURE
Cast: *John Lithgow (Host), Corey Burton, Brandy Brown, Natalie Gregory, Raquel Herring.*

This 20th anniversary salute to Walt Disney World shows how the Park has progressed from Walt Disney's early plans through to the new attractions now being designed and built. Archival footage of the early days is combined with interviews of the original designers. Guest stars, including members of The Disney Channel's *Mickey Mouse Club*, host looks at some of the attractions and live shows that entertain guests from around the world.

WAPATULA
Cast: *Stephen James (Jack Crowley), Virginia Knowles (Carolanne Scott), Abb Dickson (Abner Dupree), Darryl McCullough (Stan Stu), Marya Small (Fawn Grabowski), Charlie Dell (Leo Thorn), Linda Hoy (Mayor Margaret Moody), Tom McFadden (Alton "Buck" Rogers), Bill Wiley (Sheriff Gridlock), Beverly Archer, Dean Dittman, Ken Embree, Carmen Filipi, Billie Jackman, Carole King, Alan Koss, Ken Lesco, Shane McCabe, Kevin McLaughlin, Harris Nelson, Annie O'Donnell, Chuck Olsen, Tony Papenfuss, Ron Ross, Ben Slack, John Steadman, Toru Tanaka, David Willis, Harry Woolf.*

This was a pilot for a proposed series for the Channel. The show centers around a myopic newscaster working at a small-town television station, who hopes to make it to the big time—a national network position. In this episode, the town's water supply is threatened by a local eccentric.

WHAD' YA KNOW?
Host: *Michael Feldman.*

The Disney Channel produced a series of four 30-minute specials based on National Public Radio's *Whad' Ya Know?* series. Michael Feldman, who starred in the radio version as well, hosts these comedy quiz shows, which combine skits, celebrity interviews, call-in quizzes, and a Town of the Week.

WHALE'S TOOTH, THE

Cast: Evan Temarii (Tato), Fabian Mataihau (Ratu Wassili), Etau Teraitepo (Ratu Salua).

Ratu Salua, the chief of a small tribe on the island of Mali, gives his young son, Tato, his first outrigger canoe. While Tato is out sailing, the island is attacked and a prized talisman, a whale's tooth, is stolen. Tato spots the smoke from the attack and tries to return home but the canoe mast breaks and he is carried away by a strong current.

WHERE DID ALL MY MONEY GO?

Sequences at a bowling alley, roller rink, ice cream parlor, and video game arcade and in Hawaii show how easy it is to spend money without realizing it. Many teenagers are growing up without an appreciation of the need to budget their funds wisely, as illustrated by the free-spending youths featured in this episode.

Production Note:

• This program aired as part of the *Disney Showcase* series of specials.

WHERE THE TOYS COME FROM

Cast: Sab Shimono (Kenji, the Designer), Erin Young (Robin), Jon Harvey (Peepers), Larry Wright (Zoom).

Toy designers of the world are kept constantly challenged by the need to make their products stand out over the competition. This episode examines the steps involved in designing a toy and bringing it to market.

Production Note:

• This program aired as part of the *Disney Studio Showcase* series of specials, first aired in 1983.

WHO'S IN CHARGE HERE?: THE RONN LUCAS SPECIAL

Cast: Ronn Lucas, Richard Jamison (Mr. Richards), Diana James (Receptionist), Raf Mauro (Salesman), Sam Allen (Body Guard).

Ronn Lucas is a ventriloquist with a problem. Somehow one of his dummies, Buffalo Billy, has gotten an interview with a television executive, who takes his silence as a negotiating ploy. By the time Ronn arrives at the studio, the executive has agreed to give Billy $1 million to star in a special.

WISE ONE, THE

Cast: Dehl Berti (Joseph Running Bear), Rick Romancito (Tshon).

The Canadian Northwest is the setting for a battle of wits between an Indian trapper and a wily beaver. The beaver has managed to outwit the trapper each hunting season, but it also has had to deal with predators.

The Disney Channel Films

ANNE OF AVONLEA: THE CONTINUING STORY OF ANNE OF GREEN GABLES

Cast: Megan Follows (Anne Shirley), Colleen Dewhurst (Marilla Cuthbert), Dame Wendy Hiller (Mrs. Harris), Frank Converse (Morgan Harris), Jonathan Crombie (Gilbert Blythe), Patricia Hamilton (Rachel Lynde), Marilyn Lightstone (Miss Stacey), Schuyler Grant (Diana Barry), Rosemary Dunsmore (Katherine Brooke), Kate Lynch (Pauline Harris), Genevieve Appleton (Emmeline Harris), Susannah Hoffman (Jen Pringle), Kathryn Trainor (Essie), Rosemary Radcliffe (Mrs. Barry), Charmion King (Aunt Josephine Barry), Robert Collins (Mr. Barry), Morgan Chapman (Minnie May Barry), Mag Ruffman (Alice Lawson), Les Carlson (Mr. Lawson), Jacqueline Blais (Mrs. Harrison), Kay Hawtrey (Mabel Sloane), Bruce McCollough (Fred Wright), Anna Ferguson (Mrs. Boulter), Miranda de Pencier (Josie Pye), Zack Ward (Moody Spurgeon), David Fox (John Blythe), David Hughes (Thomas Lynde), Trish Nettleton (Jane Andrews), Rod Heffernan (Harry Inglis), Jennifer Inch (Ruby Gillis), Sheila Harcourt (Christine Stewart), Arlene Meadows (Soprano at Wedding), Brigit Wilson (Tillie Boulter), Ian Heath (Anthony Pye), Fraser Chapman (Tommy Bell), James O'Regan (Mr. Pye), Patty Carroll Brown (Avonlea Townswoman), Chick Roberts (Avonlea Townsman), Martin Donlevy (Jerry Buote), Nuala Fitzgerald (Mrs. Tom Pringle), Meg Hogarth (Mrs. James Pringle), Carolyn Hetherington (Mrs. Walter Pringle), Lynne Gorman (Mrs. John Pringle), Maxine Miller (Mrs. Albert Pringle), Robert Gailbraith (Mr. Pringle), Molly McNeil (Myra Pringle), Fiona McGillivray (Hattie Pringle), Juno Mills-Cockell (Jimsie Pringle), Autumn Smith (KLC Girl), David Foley (Lewis Allen), Michael Fletcher (Minister), Louise Nicol (Miss Kerr), Ingrid Bauer (Miss MacKay), Fred Booker (Mr. McTavish), Charles Joliffe (Alex McGuiness), Janice Bryan (Maid at Mrs. Pringle's), Dora Dainton (Maid at Maplehurst), Gladys

O'Connor (Maid at Maplehurst), Joe Franklin
(Issac Kent), Glori Gage (Elvira Evans),
Marilyn Boyle (Gossip at Ball), Araby
Lockhart (Gossip at Ball), Lionel Purcell (Cab
Driver), Blair Purcell (Wagon Driver), Richard
Cryer (Shepherd), Hudson Sullivan (Diana's
Baby).

This 4-hour mini-series, a sequel to *Anne
of Green Gables*, finds Anne teaching in
Avonlea but considering an offer to teach at
an exclusive school in Kingsport. Marilla
tries to convince her to take the job, but at
first, Anne feels too attached to her friends in
Avonlea to leave town.

Production Notes:

- This was the first of the "Avonlea" films
produced for The Disney Channel.
- The filming of this series was showcased
in the Special *Location: Anne of Avonlea*.

BACK HOME

Cast: Hayley Mills (Peggy Dickinson),
Hayley Carr (Rusty Dickinson), Adam
Stevenson (Charlie Dickinson), Brenda Bruce
(Beatie), Jean Anderson (Grandmother
Dickinson), Rupert Frazer (Roger Dickinson),
Josh Drobnyk (Skeet), Michael Clark (Uncle
Bruno), Mary Ellen Ray (Aunt Hannah),
Christine Moore (Ambulance Driver), Juliette
Fleming (Beth), Vaughan Sivell (Harry), Sarah
Wynter (Mrs. Hatherley), Joanne Byett (School
Prefect), Carol Gillies (Miss Bembridge),
Brenda Kempner (Miss Bullivant), Jill Meager
(Miss Collins), Louise Cann (Schoolgirl), Anna
Madeley (Schoolgirl), Rachel West
(Schoolgirl), Katie Aldridge (Schoolgirl),
Carmel Momen (Schoolgirl), Sophia Colley
(Schoolgirl), Jessica Dean (Schoolgirl), George
Clark (Lane), Peter Hughes (Lawyer), Mac
MacDonald (Mitch), Colin Rix (Policeman).

The German bombing of London during
World War II led to the evacuation of many
children to the United States, where they
were raised in safety by friends and relatives.
When the war ends, young Virginia Dickinson is among the many children who return
home to a country and families they barely
remember.

BACK TO HANNIBAL: THE RETURN OF
TOM SAWYER AND HUCKLEBERRY FINN

Cast: Raphael Sbarge (Tom Sawyer),
Mitchell Anderson (Huckleberry Finn), Megan
Follows (Becky Thatcher Newman), William
Windom (Judge Thatcher), Ned Beatty ("The
Duke of Bridgewater"), Paul Winfield (Big Jim

Watson), Graham Jarvis (Pruitt, the Hannibal
Prosecutor), George O. Petrie (Judge
Cochran), Shea Farrell (Lyle Newman), Hank
Woessner (Willie Dawes), Joseph Bova ("The
King of France"), Zachary Bennett (Marcus),
Mark Dakota Robinson (Henry), Kenny Davis
(Allie Karcher), Val Saffron (Aunt Lucille),
T. Max Graham (Steven Carswell), Burt
Marshall (Wesley), Robert Crowley (Fowler),
Grady Smith (Keith Blevins), Eric Cole
(Wainright), Ralph Seeley (Ringland), Terry
Sneyd (Samuel Biggs), Addison Myers (Gene),
Brad Holiday (Deputy), Harry Gibbs (Chicago
Judge), Elias Eliadis (Chicago Prosecutor),
James Anthony (Sheriff), Larry McKeever
(Preacher), Holmes Osborne (Dockhand),
Whit Reichert (Bailiff #1), Sweeney LaBarge
(Bailiff #2), Tim Snay (Jake), Read James
(Hugh), Hollis Huston (Ben), Cynthia Harness
(Young Woman), Dorothy Farmer Davis
(Older Lady), Len Pighini (The Man), Tina
Chappel (Carla).

This adventure of Huckleberry Finn and
Tom Sawyer is set several years after their
times together on the river. Now grown, the
two men have drifted apart over the years and
no longer feel much friendship for one another. This changes when they must join together to save Big Jim Watson, an old friend
from their youth, who is falsely accused of
murder.

BEJEWELLED

Cast: Emma Samms (Stacey Orpington),
Denis Lawson (Alistair Lord), Jean Marsh
(Barbara Donaldson), Jerry Hall (Imelda B.),
Frances De La Tour (Beatrice), John Bird
(Eustace), Chris Langham (Cop), Trevor
Peacock (Crook), Jade Magri (Eloise), Aeryk
Egan (Marvin), Dirk Benedict (Gordon
Thringsby), Paris Jefferson (Linda), Bob
Dysinger (Janitor), Miranda Forbes (Fat Lady),
Serretta Wilson (Lola), Roy McReady (Mr.
Dinsdale), Jolyon Baker (Commercial Actor),
Thomas Lockyer (Commercial Director), Eric
Richard (Dog Catcher).

This comedy begins as Stacey Orpington
travels to London to display her family's
jewels in a local museum. Her boyfriend,
Gordon Thringsby, has some strange ideas
about security. He decides she should use a
hat box to transport the jewels, explaining
that no one would suspect what is hidden
inside. Unfortunately, several other people
on Stacey's flight have identical hat boxes,
and when she arrives in London, a mishap
causes everyone to unknowingly switch
boxes.

BLACK ARROW

Cast: Oliver Reed (Sir Daniel Brackley), Fernando Rey (Earl of Warwick), Benedict Taylor (Richard Shelton), Stephan Chase (Black Arrow), Georgia Slowe (Lady Joanna), Donald Pleasence (Oates), Roy Boyd (Will Lawless), Aldo Sanbrell (Scar), Carol Gotell (Hannah), Robert Russell (Appleyard), Frank Brana (Sykes), Ralph Brown (Yardley).

During England's War of the Roses, supporters of the warring factions chose the emblems of their leaders: the red rose of the House of Lancaster, and the white rose of the House of York. One wearer of the white rose is Sir Daniel Brackley, a corrupt nobleman who oppresses the people under his care. When one of Brackley's men tries to burn a peasant's house for not paying his taxes, he is killed by a mysterious archer dressed in black. The stranger, who calls himself Black Arrow, sends a warning to Brackley to stop his wave of terror.

BLUE YONDER, THE

Cast: Peter Coyote (Max Knickerbocker), Huckleberry Fox (Jonathan Knicks), Dennis Lipscomb (Finch), Joe Flood (Leary), Mittie Smith (Helen Knickerbocker), Frank Simons (Young Henry Coogan), Art Carney (Henry Coogan), Stu Klitsner (Mr. Knicks), Morgan Upton (Police Captain), Bennett Cale (Dooley), Cyril Clayton (Drunk), Charles Adams (Newsstand Man), Gretchen Grant (Mrs. Knicks), Doug Morrison (Barber), Jerry Landis (Doctor), Jo Mohrbach (Nurse), Eric Barnes (Radio Announcer), Art Scholl (Finch's Pilot), Scott Devenney (Coach), Stephen Prior (Little League Boy), Lew Horn (Gas Station Owner), Hugh Gillin (Mrs. Macdonald), Edith Fields (Mrs. MacDonald), Howard Goodwin (Driver #1), Crane Jackson (Driver #2), Ted Sawyer (Baseball Boy #1), Tommy Rosenkranz (Baseball Boy #2), Jimmy Powell (Baseball Boy #3).

Young Jonathan Knicks is fascinated by stories about his grandfather, Max, who was lost trying to become the first pilot to cross the Atlantic. Jonathan likes to spend time with Max's old assistant, Henry, who tells him about his grandfather's exploits and inventions. Henry, who has heart trouble, has spent his last days building a time machine from Max's old plans. He intends to use it to go back in time to stop Max's fatal flight, but when the old man's illness worsens, Jonathan decides he must take the trip instead.

Production Note:

• This film aired on the anthology series under the title *Time Flyer* on 2/09/86.

CHIPS, THE WAR DOG

Cast: Brandon Douglas (Danny Stauffer), Ned Vaughn (Mitch Wilson), Paxton Whitehead (Rutherford P. Smythe), Ellie Cornell (Kathy Lloyd), Robert Miranda (Sergeant Rust), William Devane (Colonel Charnley), Coby Scheldt (Jim Hastings), Juli Morser (Mrs. Maddie Hastings), Sheridan Gayr (Peggy), Luke Rossi (Jimbo), Dick Arnold (Farmer Steele), Lyn Tyrrell (Mrs. Steele), Robert Munns (Sheriff), Gary Taylor (Bob Stauffer), Corey Gunnestad (Teen in Uniform), Sara Hickcox (Girlfriend), Jason Connelly (Teenager #1), Ronald E. Lynch, Jr. (Teenager #2), Krisha Fairchild (DFD Woman), Ted D'Arms (Senator Browne), Dan Angst (Boot Camp Doctor), Michael Manuel (Osterholt), Landon Wine (Torres), Bill Walters (Basic Training Soldier), Robert Davenport (Dog Bath Soldier), Evelyn Perdue (Mrs. Browne), Harris D. Smithe (Kennel Soldier), Michael Blain-Rozgay (Mail Sergeant), Julie Pahl (WAC), William Dore (Veterinarian), Alfred Hollmann (Mess Cook), Tom Francis (Soldier #1), Brian Keilor (Demonstration Soldier), Robert Hardwick (Senator #1), Glen Mazen (Senator #2), Donald Riley (Narrator), Peter Lohnes (Captain Bridges), Stefan Enriquez (Chateau Soldier), Will McGarrahan (O'Keefe), Steven Zediker (Radioman), John Gliessman (Sergeant Mead), Marty Lewis (Command Post Sergeant), Charles Kahlenberg (The General), Vilas (Chips). **Stunts:** Gary Pike, Robert Brown, Gary Edelen.

Chips, a German Shepherd, is a dog who can't seem to stay out of trouble. When he scares chickens, an angry farmer vows to kill him. The year is 1943, and when his owners see a newsreel asking people to donate their dogs to the war effort, they realize this is a way to save the dog. Soon, Chips is aboard a train on his way to boot camp. Even then, though, he can't stay out of trouble.

Production Notes:

• This film is based on a true story. The real Chips was one of four dogs assigned to guard President Roosevelt during a historic meeting in Casablanca.
• The cartoon *Donald Gets Drafted* is seen when the family goes to the movies.

CHRISTMAS VISITOR, THE

Cast: Dee Wallace Stone (Elizabeth O'Day), John Waters (Patrick O'Day), Charles Tingwell (Max Bell), Bill Kerr (Trevor Watson), Nadine Garner (Sarah O'Day), Grant Piro (Angus Watson), Andrew Ferguson (Ned O'Day), Francis Bell (Sharkey), Christopher Stevenson (Jamie), Kim Gyngell (Hungry Bill), David Ravenswood (Mr. Gullett), Maggie Millar (Mrs. Gullett), Francine Ormrod (Penelope Gullett), Bruce Kilpatrick (Adam McKimmie), Callie Gray (Pip McKimmie), Christine Keogh (Heather McKimmie), Neil Melville (Mr. Potts), Martin Redpath (Sergeant Gibbs), Rosie Sturgess (Miss Daly), John Henwood (Tom Murchie), John Bishop (Railworker), David Lee Page (Stockman), Bruce Cowl (Trader), James Wright (Father Menzies), Bill Medley (Governor's Nephew).

In Australia in 1891, 8-year-old Ned O'Day is worried that he won't get anything for Christmas since his family is poor. His mood changes when he spots a man he thinks is Father Christmas, unaware that he is actually Max Bell, a wanted criminal.

DANNY, THE CHAMPION OF THE WORLD

Cast: Jeremy Irons (William Smith), Robbie Coltrane (Victor Hazel), Samuel Irons (Danny Williams), Cyril Cusack (Doc Spencer), Michael Hordern (Lord Claybury), Lionel Jeffries (Mr. Snoddy), Jean Marsh (Miss Hunter), Jimmy Nail (Rabbetts), Ronald Pickup (Captain Lancaster), John Woodvine (Tallon), William Armstrong (Springer), Ceri Jackson (Mrs. Clipstone), James Walker (Vicar), Phil Nice (Postman), Anthony Collin (Wheeler), Jonathan Davis (Sergeant Enoch Samways), Jonathan Leigh (Sidney), Richard Cubison (Inspector), John Grillo (Mr. Parker), Andrew MacLachlan (The Duke).

As the summer of 1955 draws to a close in England, the residents of a rural community find themselves having to deal with an obnoxious newcomer, Victor Hazel. Hazel has bought up a great deal of the local land for use in massive pheasant hunts, but he still needs one more parcel to complete his plans. Unfortunately for Hazel, the land is owned by William Smith, a fiercely independent man who vows to hang on to his property no matter how much money Hazel offers.

Production Note:

• This film was based on a novel by Roald Dahl.

DISNEY'S RETURN TO TREASURE ISLAND

Cast: Brian Blessed (Long John Silver), Christopher Guard (Jim Hawkins), Ken Colley (Ben Gunn), Reiner Schöne (Van Der Brecken), Deborah Poplett (Señorita Isabella), Artro Morris (Reverend Morgan), Bruce Purchase (Trelawney), Peter Copley (Dr. Livesey), Richard Beale (Captain Smollett), Charlotte Mitchell (Mrs. Hawkins), John Tordoff (Gadney), Tony Osoba (Joe), Geoffrey Greenhill (Hockley), Willoughby Goddard (Sir Solomon Pridham), John Hallam (Captain Parker), Forbes Collins (Gridley), Jean Faulds (Miss Macphail), Mark Colleano (Moxon), Declan Mulholland (Cook), Roy Pattison (Baker), Roger McKern (Jake), Graham McTavish (Ned), Eddie Blackstone (Bill), Stephen Lyons (Richards), Roy Heather (Simpson), Phil Rowlands (Roberts), Alan Haider (Spanish Captain), Hubert Tucker (Tom the Coachman), Martyn Colborn (Beadle). **Stuntmen:** Brian Bowes, Terry Cade, Gerry Crampton, Terry Forrestal, Nick Hobbs, James Lodge, Val Musetti, Doug Robinson, Peter Lloyd (Abed Jones), Aixa Moreno (Conchita), Don Pickering, Chris Godwin, Nicke Brimble.

Ten years after the events seen in the theatrical release *Treasure Island*, Jim Hawkins is plunged back into piratical adventure when Long John Silver shows up one night looking for his treasure map. Jim is later reunited with old friends Ben Gunn and Captain Smollett on a trip to Jamaica both to save Silver from hanging and to search for his fabled treasure.

DOWN THE LONG HILLS

Cast: Bruce Boxleitner (Scott Collins), Bo Hopkins (Jud), Michael Wren (Cal), Don Shanks, Ed Bruce, Buck Taylor, Thomas Wilson Brown (Hardy Collins), Lisa MacFarlane (Betty Sue Powell), Jack Elam (Bill Squires), David Cass (Mr. Andy), Peggy Matheson (Mrs. Andy), Beverly Rowland (Mrs. Bregman), Michael Ruud (Wagon Master), Corky Randall (Bystander), Roy J. Cohoe (Indian Chief), Richard J. Martin (War Chief), Fenton Quinn (Guard).

The story begins as Hardy Collins travels west to meet his dad, who has gone ahead to Fort Bridger. Hardy is traveling with his dad's prized horse, Red, and the animal attracts the unwelcome attention of two men who spend the night with the wagon train. One of the men tries to trade for Red, but Hardy turns him down. That night, the boy discovers that his horse is missing.

Production Note:

- This film also aired on the anthology series in a 2-hour format on 5/24/87 and later in two parts on 8/21/88 and 8/28/88.

ERNEST GREEN STORY, THE

Cast: Morris Chestnut (Ernest Green), CCH Pounder (Daisy Bates), Gary Grubbs (Mr. Loomis), Tina Lifford (Mrs. Green), Avery Brooks (Reverend James Lawson), Ruby Dee (Mrs. Wilson), Brian Mitchell (Thurgood Marshall), Omar Gooding (Marcus), James Harper (Governor Faubus), Wayne Tippit (Principal Matthews), Monica Calhoun (Minnijean Brown), Suli McCullough (Terrance Roberts), Lisa Marie Russell (Elizabeth Eckford), Tico Wells (Jefferson Thomas), Jacqueline Shaw (Thelma Mothershed), Jason Pratt (Scott Green), Ossie Davis (Grandfather), Sonny Shroyer (Coach Snell), Governor Griffin (Dennis Letts), Katherine Bernhardt (Mrs. Gaines), Jerry Leggio (Mayor Mann), John Boyd West (Starkey), Missy Crider (Charlene Talbot), Sarah Boss (Rhonda), Francis Kemp (Grace Lorch), Robert Alexander (Lionel), John Hickman (Mr. Prior), Anitra Lovelace (Gloria), Rashan Serino (Carlotta), Toya Stokes (Melba), Mark W. Johnson (Emmett Moody), Tommy Sanders (Governor's Aide Smiley), Jackie Stewart (Reverend Matcher), Moses Peace (Minnijean's Father), Harry Hood (TV Reporter). **Stunt Coordinator:** Ousan Elam.

Filmed on location in Little Rock, Arkansas, this story is set in 1957, 3 years after the United States Supreme Court ruling against "separate but equal" school facilities. Ernest Green and 8 other black high school students decide to enroll in the segregated Central High School, hoping that attending the better school will help them get into college.

FOUR DIAMONDS, THE

Cast: Christine Lahti (Dr. Burke/Sorceress Raptenahad), Kevin Dunn (Charles Millard/Charles the Mysterious), Jayne Brook (Irma Millard/Hermit of the Lagoon), Michael Bacall (Tony), Sarah Rose Karr (Stacy), Adilah Barnes, Catherine E. Coulson, Tom Guiry (Christopher Millard/Squire Millard), Leland Baxter Neal (Simon), Jason Mason (John), Dan

Kremer (Knight #1), Don Nau (Knight #2), Eric Jewett (Surgeon), Brett Jones (Black Cavalier), Al Jones (Stunt Coordinator), Casey O'Neill (Chris Millard Stunt Double), Deanna Esmaeel (Utility Stunt #1), Jerry Bestpitch (Utility Stunt #2), Nancy Thurston (Utility Stunt #3).

When teenager Christopher Millard has to undergo a grueling set of medical treatments because he has cancer, he compensates by writing a story about a medieval youth who is sorely tested by an evil sorceress. No matter how hard the young squire attempts to pass her tests, the sorceress keeps coming up with harder and harder tests. The parallels to Chris's own struggle are seen as his family members take the place of the heroic characters in his story and his doctor becomes the sorceress.

Production Note:

- This film was based on a true story.

FRIENDSHIP IN VIENNA, A

Cast: Edward Asner (Opah Oscar), Stephen Macht (Franz Dornenwald), Jenny Lewis (Inge Dornenwald), Kamie Harper (Lise Mueller), Rosemary Forsyth (Fraulein Pappenheim), Jane Alexander (Hannah Dornenwald), Jean Simmons (Narrator), Ferdinand Mayne (Father Bernard), Jeff Kizer (Gustl), John Cameron Mitchell (Tommi Lowberg), Kenna Kendall (Mitzi), John Hartley (Herr Mueller), Jeremy Gagan (Herbert Lowberg), Helen Bourne (Marianne Lowberg), Claire Sawyer (Gerda), Zoe Tahir (Susi), Luisa Bradshaw-White (Herte), Natasha Bell (Anni), Robert Mackey (SA Officer), Richard Jaromy (Heinz), Kati Marton (Frau Mueller), Andras Marton (Yugoslavian Consul), Ildiko Pesci (Frau Krausse), Aniko Safar (Frau Werner), Laszlo Dozsa (Man in Church), Peter Kertesz (SA Officer #2), Zoltan Gera (Building Manager), Robert Revesz (Heinz' Friend), Zsuzsa Manyai (Princess Jasmine), Csaba Pethes (Princess Jasmine's Assistant), Magdi Darvas (Frau Vollmer).

Tensions run high in Vienna in 1938, for the city is divided about the rising influence of the Nazi party. Two young girls, Lise and her best friend, Inge, are caught up in the rising emotions, for Lise is Christian and Inge is Jewish.

GONE ARE THE DAYES

Cast: Harvey Korman (Charlie Mitchell), Susan Anspach (Phyllis Daye), Robert Hogan (Harry Daye), Nate Esformes (Papa Delgado),

Joe Cortese (Frank Delgado), Victoria Carroll, Bibi Besch (District Attorney), Joshua Bryant, Mary Jo Catlett (Marge), Sharee Gregory (Melissa Daye), David Glasser (Ricky Daye), Justin Lord (Don), Steven Hirsch (Joe), Elizabeth Savage (Nurse #1), Ted Gehring (Cook), Beatrice Colen (Estelle), Eldon Quick (Seymour), Lawrence Kerr (Nick Delgado), Jim Boeke (Seth), Rodney Kageyama (Manager of Restaurant), Raymond Guth (Farmer #1), Daniel Greene (Larry), Mickey Jones (Mad Dog), Olaf Pooley (Grand Master), Hap Lawrence (Brother #1), Phil Rubenstein (Brother #2), Robert Snively (Brother #3), Michael Cornelison (Newscaster), Beau Starr (Big Man), Julius Harris (Man #1), John Dresden (Man #2), Twyla Littleton (Girl #1), Lynn Herring (Girl #2), Joan Leizman (Nurse #2), Hettie Lynne Hurtes (TV Newscaster), Tad Horino (Waiter), Austin Kelly (Vagrant), Greg Finley (Forest Ranger), Dirk Dahl (Mike), Kirk Scott (Purser), Morris Buchanan (Bailiff).

A mob shooting has unexpected repercussions for the Daye family, who are accidental witnesses to the crime. Nick Delgado, one of the assassins, is shot and captured, and the Dayes reluctantly agree to testify against him for the government. When Nick's mobster father, Papa Delgado, sends his other son, Frank, to silence the Dayes, the government assigns Charlie Mitchell, a grizzled veteran agent, to protect the Dayes until the trial.

GOOD OLD BOY: A DELTA BOYHOOD

Cast: Richard Farnsworth (Grandpa Percy), Ryan Francis (Willie Morris), Gennie James (Rivers Applewhite), Douglas Emerson (Spit McGee), Devin Ratray (Bubba), Kevin Joseph (Henjie), Ben Wylie (Billy), Dule Hill (Robert E. Lee), Jordan Marder (Buster), Dixie King-Wade (Mamie), Caryn West (Margaret Morris), Richard Council (Ray Morris), Maureen O'Sullivan (Aunt Sue), Anne Ramsey (The Hag), Curtis Caine, Jr., Ritchie Montgomery, Georgia F. Wise, Hayden Petkovsek, Jim Frasier, Leonard Wylie, Hugh Breland, James Rowan, Sage Guido, T. Waring Bennett, Anne Willis Ratray, Jamie Browning, Joey Bonnette, Joey Martin, Ian Arata, Todd Braley, Noah Saterstrom, Richard & Christopher Luckey.
Narrated by: Ralph Waite.

The quiet pace of life in Yazoo City, Mississippi, during World War II changes when 12-year-old Willie Morris and his friends hear the story of a local monster called the Yazoo. While they're trying to decide if the monster is real or not, they also hear that a wave of crimes in the area might be the work of river pirates. Willie, though, thinks that a woman said to be a witch is the real culprit.

GOODBYE, MISS 4TH OF JULY

Cast: Louis Gossett Jr. (Big John Creed), Chris Sarandon (George Janus), Chantal Contouri (Olympia Janus), Chynna Phillips (Alma), Mitchell Anderson (Henderson Kerr), Conchata Ferrell (Mrs. Bixby), Ed Lauter, Walker Edmiston, Ned Vaughn, Roxana Zal (Niki Janus), Kai Wulff (Peter Getner), E'lon (Jimmy Washington), Phil Diskin (Mr. Stamos), Andrew R. Stahl (Earl Whatley), Richard Speight Jr. (Young Klansman), Andy Rice (Soldier), George Roberts (Mayor Kerr), Charlie Riddle (Sheriff), Jackie Wright Miller (Woman at Station), Tim Powell (Reverend Bob Cotter), Dan Owenby (Billy Ray Odum), Patrick Cobble (Billy), Andrew Cobble (Eugene), Danny Dill (Judge), Mark Slagle (Prosecutor), Peggy Shipe (Nominator), Harriet Sumner (Woman), Robert Mausolf (Station Master).*

When the Janus family moves from Greece to Montgomery, West Virginia, in 1916 to escape political unrest, they find that life in their new home has its own set of problems. American customs seem confusing, and not everyone in town is glad to see the newcomers move in.

GREAT EXPECTATIONS

Cast: Jean Simmons (Miss Ada Havisham), John Rhys-Davies (Joe Gargery), Ray McAnally (Mr. Jaggers), Anthony Calf (Philip "Pip" Pirrip), Kim Thomson (Estella Havisham), Adam Blackwood (Herbert Pocket), Anthony Hopkins (Abel Magwitch), Sean Arnold (Compeyson), Niven Boyd (Orlick), Susan Franklyn (Biddy), Martin Harvey (Young Pip), Charles Lewson (Mr. Wemmick), Rosemary McHale (Mrs. Joe Gargery), Frank Middlemass (Uncle Pumblechook), John Quentin (Mr. Wopsle), Owen Teale (Mr. Drummle), Frank Thornton (Mr. Trabb), Preston Lockwood (Mr. Hubble), Eve Pearce (Mrs. Hubble), P.J. Davidson (Sergeant), Maria Charles (Sarah Pocket), Madeleine Moffatt (Georgina Pocket), Gerald Campion (Mr. Raymond), Hilary Mason (Mrs. Fagge), Shirley Stelfox (Mrs. Camilla), Henry Power (Young Herbert Pocket), John Savage (Urchin), Desmond Barrit (Jagger's Client), Martino Lazzeri (Sneak), Simon Warwick (Mr. Startop), Charles Pemberton (Mr. Philbran), Carolyn Jones (Molly), Angela Ellis (Mrs. Pocket), Arthur Hewlett (Aged P.), Jonathan Newth (Matthew Pocket), Paul Reynolds (The*

Avenger), Jonathan Stevens (Mr. Finch), Sarah Crowden (Mrs. Skiffkins), Jeffrey Gardiner (Vicar), Christine Moore (Ophelia), John Quarmby (Fat Partygoer), Stephanie Schonfeld (Clara), Frank Moorey (Doctor), John Sharp (Judge), Peter Gorey (Clerk of Court), Peter Spraggon (Customs Officer).

Charles Dickens's classic novel from 1860 begins as Pip, a young boy, befriends Abel Magwitch, an escaped convict. As Pip grows up, his life becomes intertwined with those of Magwitch and an eccentric neighbor, Miss Havisham. Pip learns that someone has set up a trust fund for him, and at first it seems as if Miss Havisham might be his benefactor. As time passes, though, he learns to his horror that it was Magwitch who has been supporting him.

HEIDI

Cast: Jason Robards (Grandfather Tobias), Jane Seymour (Fraulein Rottenmeier), Patricia Neal (Peter's Grandmother), Sian Phillips (Frau Sesemann), Lexi Randall (Klara Sesemann), Noley Thornton (Heidi), Jane Hazelgrove (Dete Roogen), Andrew Bicknell (Herbert Sesemann), Benjamin Brazier (Peter), Basil Hoskins (Sebastian), Michael Simkins (Doctor), Soo Drouet (Sonja), Edward Highmore (Herr Kandidat), Kate Isitt (Brigitte), John Quentin (Pastor), Daniel Flynn (John), Annemarie Burke (Adelheid), Catherine Punch (Tinette), Roger Ashton-Griffiths (Churchman), Heidi Ackerman (Cook), Richard Bates (School Teacher).

This film is based on the famous 1880 novel of a young orphan girl who eventually helps her grandfather cope with the death of her parents. After being raised in the city for years, Heidi is sent to life with her grandfather in his remote mountain cabin. The two of them have just started understanding each other when an unscrupulous cousin strikes a deal that forces Heidi to return to the city.

LANTERN HILL

Cast: Marion Bennett (Jane Stuart), Sam Waterston (Andrew Stuart), Patricia Phillips (Robin Stuart), Zoe Caldwell (Mrs. Kennedy), Sarah Polley (Jody Turner), Colleen Dewhurst (Hepzibah), Vivian Reis (Aunt Irene), Joyce Campion (Violet Titus), Florence Patterson (Justina Titus), Sharry Flett (Lillian Morrow), Glori Gage (Evelyn Morrow), Dora Dainton (Aggie), Robert Benson (William Kennedy), Juno Mills Cockell (Phyllis Kennedy), Jillian Cook (Gertrude Kennedy), James Mainprize (Frank Price), Judy Sinclair (Mary Price),

Valerie Boyle (Cook), Durward Allen (Superintendent), Esther Hockin (Mrs. Stanley), Ann Farquhar (Cecily Stanley), Alyson Court (Agnes Ripley), Dorion Davis (Schoolgirl), Denise Fergusson (Mrs. Simpson), Ellen Dubin (Charlotte Simpson), Gillian Steeve (Little Schoolgirl), Noam Zylberman (Poultry Boy), Gareth Bennett (Owen Meade), Zachary Bennett (Jimmy-John Mende), Dan MacDonald (Dr. Arnett), Paul Jolicoeur (Milkman), Jack Mather (Train Conductor), Jason St. Amour (Train Cook), Des Ellis (Jim), Jane Dingle (Jim's Wife), James O'Regan (Policeman #1), Paul LaRocque (Policeman #2), Robert McKenna (Ticket Seller), Charles Hayter (Station Master).

Young Jane Stuart receives a surprise when she learns that her supposedly dead father is actually alive. Jane's mother had told the girl that her father had died when Jane was a baby. In reality, the parents had separated after the husband was falsely implicated in the death of another woman.

LITTLE KIDNAPPERS, THE

Cast: Charlton Heston (James MacKenzie), Bruce Greenwood (Dr. Willem Hooft), Patricia Gage (Grandma MacKenzie), Dan MacDonald, Leah Pinsent (Kirsten MacKenzie), Charles Miller (Davy MacKenzie), Leo Wheatley (Harry MacKenzie), Richard Donat (Hans Hooft), Amos Crawley (Jan Hooft), Eileen Pedde (Mrs. Hooft), Deborah Allen (Mrs. Cameron), Erin Kuttner (Jean Cameron), Nicola Lipman (Mrs. MacNeill), Gay Hauser (Mrs. Thompson), Sten Eirik (Mr. Sinclair), John Dunsworth (Mr. Fraser), Wally McKinnon (Militia Captain), Ewan Clark (Searcher), Faith Bowyer (Baby Hooft).

Two boys orphaned by the death of their father in the Boer War in South Africa are sent to live in Nova Scotia with their grandfather. James Mackenzie takes in the two boys, Davy and Harry, but he warns them to stay away from a Boer family that lives nearby. Things get worse between the families when the Boers announce plans to build a house on a hill that James claims as his own, and he threatens to kill anyone who sets foot on the hill.

LITTLE RIDERS, THE

Cast: Paul Scofield (Grandpa Pieter Roden), Noley Thornton (Joanne Hunter), Rosemary Harris (Grandma Juliana Roden), Malcolm McDowell (Captain Kessel), Benedick Blythe (Lieutenant Karl Braun), Luke Edwards (Paul

Petersen), Derek de Lint (Dirk Petersen), Renee Soutendijk (Beatrix Hunter), Huib Broos (Jacob), Niven Boyd (Sergeant Borken), Christopher Villiers (2nd Lieutenant Muller), Frederik de Groot (Father Hugo), Michiel Nooter (Frederick), Hidde Maas (Dr. Van Renesse), Karin Meerman (Mrs. Van Renesse), Wim Serlie (Hans Keer), James Delaney (Lucas Keer), Genio de Groot (Green Policeman), Reinout Bussemaker (Ulrich), Baruch Schwartz (German Soldier), Adriaan Adriaansen (Man with Broom), Jeff Harding (Michael Hunter), William Sutton (American Airman #1), Chip Bray (American Airman #2).

When the Nazis invade Holland in 1940, young Joanne Hunter and her mother are visiting from America. Joanne's mother is killed in a bombing attack and Joanne must stay with her grandparents as the Nazis occupy the village.

LOOKING FOR MIRACLES

Cast: Greg Spottiswood (Ryan Delaney), Zachary Bennett (Sullivan Delaney), Joe Flaherty (Arnold "Chief" Berman), Patricia Gage (Grace Gibson), Patricia Phillips (Mrs. Effie Delaney), Noah Godfrey (Theodore "Ratface" Kowalski), Paul Haddad (Paul), Dean Hamilton (Babe), Hugh Thompson (Mo), Eric Fink (Floyd), Elliot Hurst (Myron), Thor Bishopric (Billy Tisser), Mary Durkan (Aunt Maureen), Mag Ruffman (Nurse Blanche), Michael Ribinoff (Moose), Darlene Heaslip (Gretta), Beverley Cooper (Connie), Marilyn Boyle (Wealthy Matron), Lynn Gormann (Wealthy Matron), Mia Anderson (Wealthy Matron), Vivian Reis (Wealthy Matron), Shane Skillen (Knuckles), Trevor Buttenham (Camper), Jonathan Bishop (Kid on Diveboard), Michael Maybee (Police Officer), Araby Lockhart (Chief's Secretary), Les Carlson (Principal), Howard Jerome (Mr. Schultz), Richard Horgan (John Schultz), Dora Dainton (Registrar's Assistant), Jack Jessop (Photographer), Les Rubie (Storekeeper), Patrick Sisam (Rich Kid), Ted Hanlan (Ryan's Stunt Double), Debbie Kirby (Grace's Stunt Double), Gary Shessman (Stunt Performer), Douglas Macey (Stunt Performer).

Desperate to earn money for college, Ryan Delaney takes a job as a summer camp counselor even though he knows nothing about camping and is only 16 years old. Ryan resents having to take his younger brother, Sullivan, along for the summer, but agrees to so their single mother can go to work.

Production Note:

- Greg Spottiswood won an Emmy as Outstanding Performer in a Children's Special for his role in this film.

LOTS OF LUCK

Cast: Martin Mull (Frank Maris), Annette Funicello (Julie Maris), Fred Willard (A.J. Foley), Polly Holliday (Lucille), Mia Dillon (Jesse Foley), Tracey Gold (Cindy Maris), Jeremy Licht (David Maris), Christina Nigra (Trish Maris), Hamilton Camp (Joe), Dick O'Neill (Mr. Wilson), Vincent Schiavelli (Skinny), Frederick Long (Fatty), Joseph Chapman (Mr. Ardle), John Terry Bell, Lonnie Burr (Shopkeeper), Sheila Cluff, Anita Dangler, Stephanie Edwards (Newswoman), Dick Patterson (TV Host), William Edward Phipps, Erin Patricia Boyd, Gloria Camden, Keith Coburn, Adele Corey, Keith L. Johnson, Frank Killmond, Matthew Licht, Anne Marie McEvoy, Bill McLean, Henry Proach, Ann Romeo, Robert Ruth, Sandra Sexton, William Schreiner, Helen Siff, Jack Riley (Marvin).

Frank Maris has a simple dream. All he wants to do is open his own auto repair shop to escape the depressing machine shop he toils in every day. Unfortunately, he doesn't have any money saved, and thus his dream appears impossible. The unexpected happens when his wife, Julie, discovers she is a winner in the preliminary drawing for the state lottery. If she wins the second drawing, they'll be $1 million richer.

Production Notes:

- An edited version of this film aired on the anthology series on 5/28/89 in a 1-hour format.
- This was Annette's first film for Disney since *The Monkey's Uncle* in 1965.

LOVE LEADS THE WAY

Cast: Timothy Bottoms (Morris Frank), Eva Marie Saint (Dorothy Eustis), Arthur Hill (Mr. John Frank), Glynnis O'Connor (Lois Coleman), Susan Dey (Beth), Gerald Hiken (Jack), George D. Wallace (Director at Blind Institute), Michael Anderson, Jr. (Hank), Stephen Young (Mike McShane), Ralph Bellamy (Senator William Christl), Ernest Borgnine (Senator A. Brighton), Patricia Neal (Mrs. Jessie Frank), Pilot (Buddy), Richard Roat (Proprietor), Richard Speight, Jr. (Jimmy), Paul Klapper (Veterinarian), Terri Gardner (Secretary), Bill Ewin (Mailman), Eugene Pidgeon (Nate), Chip Arnold (Bus Driver),

Ray Hill (Cliff), John Brown (Mr. Tyler), David Cobb (Carnes).

When Morris Frank suffers a head injury in 1927, he is permanently blinded and unable to continue working as an insurance salesman. He is accepted into an experimental program in Switzerland that trains guide dogs to help the blind and spends many difficult hours working with his new canine companion, Buddy. While the dog helps Morris navigate through town safely, Morris is not prepared for the resistance he encounters when he tries to bring the dog into offices and on the bus.

Mark Twain & Me

Cast: Jason Robards (Mark Twain/Samuel Clemens), Talia Shire (Jean Clemens), R.H. Thomson (Albert Paine), Fiona Reid (Mrs. Quick), Douglas Campbell, Chris Wiggins, Amy Stewart (Dorothy Quick), Anna Ferguson (Arabella), Chapelle Jaffe (Sarah Hardwig), Colin Fox (Dr. Quinard), Susan Coyne (Miss Hobby), Bunty Webb (Minnie), Jenny Turner (Mrs. Woods), Brian Paul (Ship's Purser), Corinne Conley (Saleswoman), Michael Polley (Orchestra Leader), James Mainprize (Concierge), Lee Macdougall (Porter), Roy Lewis (Carriage Man), John Shepherd (Oxford Dean), Doug Hughes (Reporter #1), John Bayliss (Reporter #2), Jank Azman (Reporter #3), Kelly Spalding (Schoolgirl #1).

Based on an actual event, this is the story of a long-lasting friendship that begins between 72-year-old Mark Twain and 11-year-old Dorothy Quick when they meet in 1908 while returning from England. Twain has been feeling old lately, and he sees something he likes in Dorothy. He encourages her to write and names the surprised girl as his "manager."

Mother Goose Rock 'n' Rhyme

Cast: Harry Anderson, Brian Bonsall, Elayne Boosler, Bobby Brown, Shelley Duvall, Art Garfunkel, Terri Garr, Dan Gilroy, Woody Harrelson, Debbie Harry, Cyndi Lauper, David Leisure, Little Richard, Los Trios (Neill Gladwin, Stephen Kearny), Howie Mandel, Cheech Marin, Van Dyke Parks, Katey Segal, John Santucci, Garry Shandling, Paul Simon, Jean Stapleton, Stray Cats (Brian Setzer, Lee Rocker, Slim Jim Phantom), Ben Vereen, ZZ Top (William F. Gibbons, Joe M. Hill, Frank L. Beard), Pia Zadora. **Stunts:** Ousaum Elam, Donna Evans, Allen Michael Lerner, Paula Marie Moody, Robert C. Pfeiffer, Brian J. Williams.

The stories of Mother Goose are brought to life in this all-star musical production. Celebrities sing and dance in fanciful settings based on the stories that have entertained children for centuries.

Night Train to Kathmandu, The

Cast: Pernell Roberts (Professor Harry Hadley-Smythe), Eddie Castrodad (Prince Johar), Milla Jovovich (Lily McCloud), Kavi Raz (Professor Dewan Godbothe), Tim Eyster (Andrew McCloud), Robert Stoeckle (Jeff McCloud), Jan Pessano (Maureen McCloud), Beecey Carlson (Siabhan), Ric Stonebeck (Brother Arjoon), Emile Homaty (Shri Nan), Tad Horino (Holy One), Santos Pant (Ravi), Gopal Raj Pant (Priest), Gopal Raj Bhutani (Lootan), Cochise Ochoa (Photographer).

American teenager Lily McCloud becomes involved in the strange tale of a vanishing city while traveling through Nepal with her family. She befriends a runaway teenager, Johar, when he climbs aboard their train, only to later discover that he is a prince from a city that only can be seen every 40 years. While an unscrupulous scientist tries to track Johar back to the city, Lily helps the prince get home before it vanishes again. If he doesn't make it in time, Johar will die.

Nightjohn

Cast: Beau Bridges (Clel Weller), Carl Lumbly (Nightjohn), Lorraine Toussaint (Delie), Bill Cobbs (Old Man), Kathleen York (Callie Weller), Gabriel Casseus, Tom Nowicki, Joel Thomas Traywick (Jeffrey Weller), Allison Jones (Sarny), John Herina (Homer Weller), Patty Mack (Evelyn), Deborah Duke (Lethe), Danny Nelson (Reverend Osee Rush), Monica Ford (Egypt), Gerald Brown (Joseph), Robin McLamb-Vaughn (Sarny's Mother), Alecia I. Gainey (Sarney, Age 4), Steven Sutherland (Alan Bowen), Shannon Eubanks (Fanny Bowen), John P. Ford III (Arthur Waller), John Herina (Homer Waller), Jordan Williams (James G. Weller), Bill Gribble (Tom—Slave Trader), Bruce Evers (Patroller #1), James Mayberry (Patroller #2), Antwan Isaac (Young Man).

In the 1830s, white slave owners made it illegal for slaves to learn how to read as a means of keeping them under control. A young black slave, Sarny, risks the wrath of Clel Weller, the plantation owner, when she pays another slave to teach her.

NOT QUITE HUMAN

Cast: Alan Thicke (Dr. Jonas Carson), Robyn Lively (Becky Carson), Robert Harper (Durks), Joseph Bologna (Gordon Vogel), Jay Underwood (Chip Carson), Brian Cole (Jake Blocker), Brandon Douglas (Scott Barnes), Lili Haydn (Jenny Beckerman), Sasha Mitchell (Bryan Skelly), Greg Monaghan (Coach Duckworth), Lonny Price (Mr. Sturges), Casey Scott (Paul Fairgate), Kristy Swanson (Erin Jeffries), Bob Anthony (Mr. Burley), Gene Blakley (Principal Gutman), Marcia Darroch (Ms. Buzzi), Aaron Peterman (Bartlett), Billie Shepard (Vogel's Secretary), Judy Starr (Dr. Sondra Stahl), Pat Willoughby (Greta).

Dr. Jonas Carson, who works for a toy company, builds the ultimate tot doll when he builds a lifelike android in his lab at home. He names the robot teenager Chip and sends him off to high school, reasoning that if Chip can survive that, he can survive anything.

NOT QUITE HUMAN II

Cast: Alan Thicke (Dr. Jonas Carson), Jay Underwood (Chip Carson), Robyn Lively (Becky Carson), Greg Mullavey (Dr. Phil Masters), Katie Barberi (Roberta), Dey Young (Professor Victoria Gray), Scott Nell (Brandon), Mark Arnott (Moore), Mike Russell (Miller), Ty Miller (Austin), Eric Bruskotter (Rick), Bob Sorenson (Walter), Doug Cotner (Mel), Nanette Varela (Party Girl #1), Holly Robertson (Party Girl #2), Kari Kulvinskas (Tiffany), Karon Kearney (Hostess). **Stunts:** Christine Baur, Doug Coleman, Lane Leavitt, Tom Ficke, Vaughn Schafer.

The adventures of Chip, the android, continue as he heads off to college. There, a team of researchers working on creating their own android have created a computer virus intended to slow down any potential rivals. Chip unknowingly is infected with the virus, which will cause him to self-destruct within 5 days.

OLD CURIOSITY SHOP, THE

Cast: Peter Ustinov (Grandfather), James Fox (Single Gentleman), Julia McKenzie (Mrs. Jarley), Adam Blackwood (Dick Swiveller), Christopher Ettridge (Sampson Brass), William Mannering (Kit Nubbles), Sally Walsh (Little Nell Trent), Tom Courtenay (Quilp), Cornelia Hayes O'Herlihy (Mrs. Quilp), Michael Mears (Skinflete), Brian McGrath (Schoolmaster), Martin Wimbush (Codlin), Alan Shearman (Short), Frank Thornton (Mr. Witherden), Anne White (Sally Brass), Jean Marlow (Mrs. Jintwin), Timothy Watson (Fred Trent), Alwyne Taylor (Mrs. Nubbles), Ricci Harnett (Tom), Wesley Murphy (Tame Constable), Brian De Salvo (Debtor Gentleman), Helen Norton (Bessy), John Rogan (Warncliffe), Birdy Sweeney (Crossing Sweeper), Doreen Keogh (Mrs. George), Daphne Neville (Mrs. Simmons), Stewart Permutt (Jowl), Bronco McLoughlin (George), Alan Barry (Groves), Hamish McColl (List), Oliver Maguire (Stout Gentleman).

Charles Dickens's classic novel, first published in 1841, is brought to life in two parts. A young girl, Nell Trent, and her grandfather, who runs an antique store, are pursued across the countryside by Quilp, a determined villain who is convinced that the grandfather is hoarding a fortune.

OLLIE HOPNOODLE'S HAVEN OF BLISS

Cast: Dorothy Lyman (Mom), James B. Sikking (The Old Man), Jason Adams (Randy), Daphne (Fuzzhead, the Dog), Cameron Johann (Flick), Ross Eldridge (Schwartz), Jean Shepherd (Narrator/Ralph as a Man/Mr. Scott), Jerry O'Connell (Young Ralph), Bill McDonald (Cop), Marjorie O'Neill-Butler (Clerk), Edward Logan (Johnson), W. Clapham Murray (Archie), Frank T. Wells (Zudoc), Peter Gerety (Gertz), Robert T. Colonna (John), Arnie Cox (Ace), Leslie Harrell (Mrs. Kissel), Dorothy Chiesa (Animal Shelter Assistant), Martin Rayner (Chauffeur), Annabelle Weenick (Colette), John William Galt (Grannie), Peyton Park (Gas Station Attendant), Desmond Dhooge (Ollie).

Told from the point of view of Ralph, a teenager, this comedic story begins as the family leaves for the same cabins on a lake that they go to every year. There are delays on the road at unusual curio shops, the car overheats, they get lost and encounter traffic problems. When they finally arrive at the lake, they learn that the fish have stopped biting, and it rains through their entire vacation.

ON PROMISED LAND

Cast: Joan Plowright (Mrs. Appletree), Judith Levy (Olivia), Norman D. Golden II (Jimmy "Jim Jam" Ween), Carl Lumbly (Floyd Ween), John Jackson (Albert Appletree), Juanita Jennings (Martha Ree Ween), Ken Sagoes (Bob Henry), Patty Mack (Sweet Mary), Elizabeth Omilami (Sally Mae), Tom

Nowicki (Joseph Appletree), Rhoda Griffis (Ellen Appletree), Bill Coates (Mr. Turner), Robert Benedetti (Mr. Baines), Carol Mitchell-Leon (Marva), Wayne Brady (Eli James).

For years, the Ween family has been living on land owned by the Appletree family. The Weens are black, and the Appletrees are white, and it seems that no matter what Floyd Ween does, there is always one more condition that must be met before the land will be his.

PARENT TRAP II

Cast: Hayley Mills (Sharon Ferris/Susan Corey), Tom Skerritt (Bill Grand), Carrie Kei Heim (Nikki Ferris), Bridgette Andersen (Mary Grand), Alex Harvey (Brian Corey), Gloria Cromwell (Florence), Judith Tannen (Jessica Dintuff), Janice Tesh (Irene), Duchess Tomasello (Mrs. Blazey), Daniel Brun (Steve), Antonio Fabrizio (Bruce), Ted Science (Chris), Margaret Woodall (Florist), Leonard Altobell (Walter Elias), Dorothy Keller (Lillian Elias), Terri Keever (Crystal).

In this sequel to the 1961 film *The Parent Trap*, young Nikki Ferris is upset about having to move from Tampa to New York City, where her mother, Sharon, has a new job waiting. Nikki is also unhappy about having to go to summer school to improve her grades. At school, she meets another reluctant student, Mary Grand, and the two quickly become friends.

PERFECT HARMONY

Cast: Peter Scolari (Derek Sanders), Darren McGavin (Roland Hobbs), Catherine Mary Stewart (Nancy Hobbs), Moses Gunn (Zeke), Justin Whalin (Taylor Bradshaw), Eugene Byrd (Landy Allen), David Faustino (Paul Bain), Casey Ellison (Orville), Richie Havens (Scrapper Johnson), Cleavon Little (Reverend Clarence Branch), Jeff B. Cohen (Ward), Devin Ratray (Shelby), Sky Ashley Berdahl (Marc), Wallace K. Wilkinson (Mayor Frank Macy), Dan Biggers (Doctor), Sharlene Ross (Woman #1), Yvette Jones Smedley (Woman #2), Mary Nell Santacroce (Miss Stoddard), John Huckenstein (Caretaker), Whitney L. Mosley (Little Girl), Marcus Williams (Belly Flop Boy).

Set in South Carolina in the '50s, the film begins as Derek Sanders arrives to be the new music teacher and choirmaster at the prestigious Blanton Boys Academy. Hailing from Massachusetts, Derek quickly comes to find that things are done differently down South.

SAVE THE DOG

Cast: Cindy Williams (Becky Dale), Katherine Helmond (Maude), Tom Poston (Doctor Crowley), Charlotte Rae (Dotty Schnidt), Billie Bird, Al Lewis, Tony Randall (Oliver Bishop), Tracy Fell (Suzanne Bidwell), Joey Hartdegen (Oliver's Assistant), Rick Stokes (Bill Gantz), Denise Merriweather (Ad Agency Executive), Bethlyn Weidler (Skating Waitress), Chris Kinkade (Medic #1), Starla Benford (Medic #2), Dee Macaluso (Diane Weegerman), Vernon Grote (Norton Bullnock), James Keller (Coach), Paul Menzel (Car Lot Manager), Jordan Burton (Kid with Bike), Ellen Blain (Sissy Kesky), Randy Means (Officer Kesky), J. David Moeller (Desk Sergeant), Julius Tennon (Arresting Officer), Alice Finney (Cat Lady), James Gale (George), China Kelly (Zombie Mommie), John Hussey (Detective Brock), Robert Rymill (Preppy), Allen Damron (Guitarist in Plaza), Remy Ramirez (Girl Lost in Plaza), Melanie Haynes (Mother in Plaza), Jerry Young (Glenn Yabbo), Brent Duncan (Party Guy #1), Lou Perry (Party Guy #2), Carrie Wood (Girl in Cake), Norma Jo Thomas (Guard), Mushroom (Petey).

Stretched for cash, actress Becky Dale schedules an audition for a role in a dog food commercial. Unfortunately, her dog, Petey, is seriously ill and she needs to raise $500 for surgery that day or the dog will be put to sleep. She gets a job as a courier, but a series of mishaps results in a traffic accident and her being arrested as a thief.

SPIES

Cast: David Dukes, Shiloh Strong, Gail Strickland, Jensen Daggett, Robert Duncan McNeill, Matthew Steer, Karen Salt, Cloris Leachman (Pamela Beale), Eric Paisley (Mr. Mills), John Bennes (Kovacs), Lou Criscuolo (Mayor), Chris Nubel (President Roosevelt).

During 1942, young Harry Prescott uses a shortwave radio to keep track of how World War II is going. One day he hears a strange broadcast that convinces him that Nazi spies have landed near his home on Long Island, New York. Determined to track them down, he gets help from Ned and Flo Carter, two orphaned children who were evacuated from England. Their search for the spies pays off when they uncover a plan to assassinate President Franklin D. Roosevelt.

SPOONER

Cast: Robert Urich *(Harry Spooner/Michael Norlon),* Jane Kaczmarek *(Gail Archer),* Paul Gleason *(Dean Roland Hyde),* Keith Coogan *(D.B. Reynolds),* Barry Corbin *(Principal Bennett Haskin),* Eric Christmas *(Joe Settles),* Rick Lenz *(Sheriff Reynolds),* John Wesley *(Marshall Ed Weston),* Brent Fraser *(Shane O'Connor),* Kate Barneri *(Caroline),* Robert King *(Coach Milton),* Vince McKewin *(Len Spervals),* Mark Phelan *(Deputy Bradley),* Bo Sabato *(Ron Fisher),* Bill Boyett *(State Police Captain),* Conrad Bachmann *(Warden Holt),* Seth Foster *(Harvey Warlow),* Steve Zanotti *(Tucker),* Henry Priest *(Tim Broden),* Jon "Jake" Jacobmeier *(Referee #1),* Jim Townsend *(Referee #2),* Eric Welch *(Billy Adams),* Brandi Burkett *(Marie),* Skip O'Brien *(Foreman),* Diane Defendorf *(Teller),* Phil Culotta *(Fighter),* Patrick Day *(Student #1),* Hal Sparks *(Student #2).*

When Michael Norlon, a convicted forger, escapes from prison in Montana, he decides to assume the identity of Harry Spooner, a recently deceased teacher. He then gets a job as an English teacher in Utah, and agrees to coach the wrestling team as well.

SPOT MARKS THE X

Cast: Mike the Dog *(Capone),* Barret Oliver *(Ken Miller),* Natalie Gregory *(Kathy),* Richard B. Shull *(Dodge),* Vic Dunlop *(Beevis),* Jerry Wasserman *(Elvis),* Geoffrey Lewis *(Dirty Jerry),* David Huddleston *(Doc Ross),* Frances Flanagan *(Joan Miller),* Dale Wilson *(Bob Miller),* Pat Armstrong *(Stolen Purse Woman),* Gary Chalk *(Cop on Bridge),* Don Davis *(Mr. Haskell),* Duncan Fraser *(Caretaker),* Antony Holland *(Lost Wallet Man),* Bobby Holt *(Larry),* Kim Kondrashoff *(Willy),* Dwight Koss *(Norrit),* Brian Linds *(New Recruit),* Andrew Markey *(Ashcroft),* Dwight McFree *(Shelter Worker),* Kevin McNulty *(Shelter Worker),* Mavor Moore *(Saul Frobel),* Tony Morrelli *(Arresting Cop),* Ruth Nichol *(Beautician),* Margot Pinvidic *(New Neighbor),* Doreen Ramus *(Dodge's Secretary),* Alvin Lee Sanders *(Dwyer),* LeRoy Schultz *(Party Man),* Bryant "Smitty" Smith *(Snack Bar Guy),* Raimund Stamm *(Cop in Park),* Ian Sullivan *(Neal),* William Taylor *(Jail Guard),* Doug Tuck *(Lost Watch Man).*

A gang of thieves fleeing from a bank robbery must bury their loot when the police catch up to them. The hiding place is deep in a forest and the gang is afraid they won't be able to find it again. The gang leader, Doc Ross, is counting on his dog, Capone, to find the money later after he's released from jail, and he quickly becomes a model prisoner to earn a fast parole. Unfortunately, his plan goes awry when the dog is accidentally given up for adoption.

Production Note:

• This film also aired on the anthology series in a 2-hour format on 5/17/87. The movie was later shown in two parts— Part 1: 7/03/88, Part 2: 7/10/88.

STILL NOT QUITE HUMAN

Cast: Alan Thicke *(Dr. Jonas Carson/Bonus),* Jay Underwood *(Chip Carson),* Christopher Neame *(Dr. Frederick Barrigan),* Betsy Palmer *(Aunt Mildred),* Adam Philipson *(Kyle Roberts),* Rosa Nevin *(Officer Kate Morgan),* Kenneth Pogue *(Bundy),* Robert Metcalfe *(Dr. Filmore),* Sheelah Megill *(Miss Prism),* Jerry Wasserman *(Tourist Man),* Carol Mann *(Tourist's Wife),* Stephen E. Miller *(Sergeant Murphy),* Debelda Williams *(Airport Guard),* Drew Reichelt *(Trucker),* Michael Rogers *(Photographer),* Frances Flanagan *(Photo Woman),* Bobby L. Stewart *(Policeman),* Cavan Cunningham *(Doorman),* Gwyneth Harvey *(Woman in Car),* Robert Thurston *(Technician),* David Hay *(Autograph Man),* Veena Sood *(Autograph Woman).*

Dr. Jonas Carson, the scientist who created Chip the android, is kidnapped by a rival robotics scientist, Dr. Barrigan, who wants to build an army of lifelike robots. Barrigan replaces Jonas with an android double, but Chip quickly discovers the substitution and disables the robot. Aided by his new friend, Kyle Roberts, Chip then searches for Jonas.

TIGER TOWN

Cast: Roy Scheider *(Billy Young),* Justin Henry *(Alex),* Ron McLarty *(Buddy, Alex's Father),* Bethany Carpenter *(Nancy, Alex's Mother),* Lindsay Barr *(Peanut Vendor),* Dave Bokas *(Crusty Man),* Chris Bremer *(Loud Kid),* Katie Delozier *(Little Girl),* Jack Fish *(Stadium Guard),* Noah Moazezi *(Eddie),* Gerald L. Monford *(Lunch Room Kid),* Leon Smith *(Druggist),* Ralph Valatka *(Hot Dog Vendor),* Whit Vernon *(Mr. Cullen),* Von Washington *(Souvenir Vendor),* Larry Williams *(Bus Driver),* Al Ackerman *(Sportscaster),* Sparky Anderson *(Tigers Manager),* Ernie Harwell *(Radio Announcer),*

Ray Lane (Radio Announcer), Mary Wilson (Soloist).

Midway through the season, the Detroit Tigers are in last place by sixteen games. One of the players, Billy Young, is about to retire, never having won a pennant. It doesn't look as if he ever will, for both Wilson and the Tigers are in a slump.

Production Notes:

- Filmed on location in Detroit, this was the first film made for The Disney Channel.
- *Tiger Town* won the National Cable Television Association's Award for Cable Excellence for Best Dramatic Feature Film of 1984.

UNDERGRADS, THE

Cast: *Art Carney (Mel Adler), Chris Makepeace (Dennis "Jody" Adler), Jackie Burroughs, Len Birman (Verne Adler), Alfie Scopp (Hobo), Lesleh Donaldson (Kim Barrett), Dawn Greenhall (Ellen Adler), Angela Fusco (Carol), Nereen Virgin (Polly Harris), Adam Ludwig (Professor Sickmier), Ron James (David Finnegan), Peter Spence (Steve Holmes), Wendy Bushell (Karen), Gary Farmer (Castro), Pat Patterson (Cabbie), Gordon Jocelyn (University President), Barbara Kyle (Advisor), Ron Singer (Al), Elena Kudaba (Mrs. Bonhoffer), Patricia Idlette (Nurse), Jacqueline McLeod (Woman #1), Susan Jay (Cashier #1), Myra Fried (Cashier #2), Hrant Alianak (Zook), James Kidnie (Butch), Ken Camroux (Detective), Eric Keensleyside (Mugger), Lee J. Campbell (Mugger), Ray Stancer (Rabbi), Jesse Collins*

(Jeff), Chris Owen (Allan), Nancy Roberts (Joni), Peter Sturgess (Sidney).

Mel Adler, age 68, astonishes his family by announcing that he wants to go to college and get his degree. He enrolls along with his grandson, Jody, and begins classes. Mel discovers that graduating will be a harder proposition than he thought, for the classwork and long hours tire him out.

WHIPPING BOY, THE

Cast: *Truan Munro (Jemmy), Nic Knight (Prince Horace), Karen Salt (Annyrose), Andrew Bicknell (King), Christopher M. Ohrt (Ambassador), Mathilda May (Betsy), Kevin Conway (Hold-Your-Nose-Billy), Vincent Schiavelli (Cutwater), George C. Scott (Blind George), Jean Anderson (Queen Mum), Michael Kausch (Peckwit), Nigel Betts (Walter), Nicholas Amer (Lord Chancellor), Georg Tryphon (Painter), Jane Hazelgrove (Mrs. Chestney), Danny Newman (Smudger), Tony Bluto (Song Seller), Frank Middlemass (Mr. Walrus), Andrea Mason (Molly), Michael Sweeney (Nips), Angus Wright (Cavalry Officer).*

During medieval times, it was forbidden to strike a member of royalty, so the spoiled young prince of Brattenburg orders his men to kidnap Jemmy, a street urchin, so he can take the prince's place during punishment. Later, Prince Horace's bad behavior almost starts a war and he is forced to flee from the castle. He joins up with Jemmy, who was trying to escape at the same time, and the two boys find themselves involved with a band of outlaws in the countryside.

Aiming for the Mainstream Market

14

Touchstone Television and the Studio's Bid for the Big Time

For all of the years that Disney has been on television, by the early 1980s the company had a noticeable lack of presence on the networks other than an occasional Special. All of this would change dramatically when Michael Eisner assumed the helm of the company, for as he noted in late 1984 while describing his priorities, "We have to be back on network television."

One of the first things Eisner did was to get the anthology series back on the air in 1985. In addition to Disney-produced series and films, the Studio also announced plans in 1986 to syndicate shows produced by other parties. The new Buena Vista Television unit syndicated a number of outside series in addition to the Disney product.

At the same time the Studio was in full gear trying to create a prime-time hit. Series such as *The Ellen Burstyn Show, Harry,* and *Down and Out in Beverly Hills* all failed to succeed. Realizing that the Studio needed to attract proven performers in the field, Disney joined up with producers Paul Junger Witt, Tony Thomas, and Susan Harris to create the hugely successful sitcom *The Golden Girls.* Since that point in time, Disney's Touchstone Television division has become one of the predominant suppliers of network programming.

In addition to Touchstone's prime-time series, the company also created a significant number of daytime and syndicated series. Each of these is described below in chronological order.

Daytime / Syndicated Series

1986–87 season

SISKEL & EBERT & THE MOVIES
Disney lured film critics Gene Siskel and Roger Ebert, stars of the very popular *Siskel*

& Ebert at the Movies series produced by Tribune Entertainment, with a lucrative 5-year deal. The format remained much the same, and even the name didn't change much. This syndicated series began airing 9/18/86 and continues today. When the deal was first announced, there was a great deal of skepticism that the critics would not be free to negatively review any Disney films. A number of less-than-biased reviews afterwards helped quell that controversy. Several *Siskel & Ebert* specials have been produced.

1987–88 season

WIN, LOSE, OR DRAW
Win, Lose, or Draw was created by actor Burt Reynolds and long-time game show host Bert Convy. The series was basically an adaption of the old party game Charades, and had two teams of three players each, with two celebrities and a contestant on each team. The players had one minute to give clues to a secret phrase by sketching on a large tablet, without using symbols, letters, numbers, or verbal clues. If the other team members guessed correctly, the contestant received a cash prize. If not, the other team was allowed to guess.

Buena Vista took the unusual route of selling the series to both a network and the syndicated market at the same time. Vicki Lawrence hosted a daytime version, which aired on NBC, and Bert Convy hosted a syndicated evening edition. The series debuted on 9/07/87, both on NBC and in syndication. It aired until the 1989–90 season.

1988–89 season

LIVE! WITH REGIS & KATHIE LEE
This daily talk show stars Regis Philbin and Kathie Lee Gifford as they interview guests and freely comment on current events. It began as a local program titled *The Morning*

Show on WABC-TV in New York City. Disney bought the rights to the series and renamed it so that it could be syndicated in time slots other than just in the morning. The show was syndicated from 9/03/88 to 10/04/91. On 10/07/91, it became part of the ABC network daily programming line-up.

1990–91 season

CHALLENGERS, THE
Dick Clark hosted this syndicated game show based in part on current events. As a result, this meant that each episode had to be timely and thus there were no reruns. This 30-minute format show aired from 9/30/90 to 8/30/91, with a preview episode on 8/27/90.

1993–94 season

CRUSADERS, THE
Reporters/hosts: *Mark Hyman, William La Jeunesse, Howard Thompson, Carla Wohl.*
Field reporters: *Katrina Daniel, Silvia Gambardella, Sandra Gin, Mark Hyman, Douglas G. McConnell, Diana Nyad, Randy Paige, John "Apollo" Payne, Brooke Skulski, Howard Thompson, Carlo Wohl, Ted Wayman.*

This syndicated series featured investigative reporters who provided on consumer-oriented issues. Each episode featured three major stories plus shorter segments from the field. There were plans to turn the weekly program into a daily series, but ratings never improved to justify the additional costs.

MIKE & MATY
Cast: *Michael Burger, Maty Monfort.*
This daily talk show starred Michael Burger, a former cruise ship entertainer and sitcom-warmup comic, and Maty Monfort, a Spanish-speaking hostess from the Univision network. As might be expected from their backgrounds, Maty was the voice of reason and Michael provided comic relief. Michael Kearney, the world's youngest college graduate at age 10, was later added as a correspondent. Network affiliates felt it bore too close a resemblance to *Live! with Regis & Kathie Lee*, and it was canceled after one season.

1994–95 season

JUDGE FOR YOURSELF
This syndicated program combines a talk show with courtroom drama. Moderated by attorney Bill Handel, each episode featured a trial setting, complete with twelve audience members seated as a jury panel. After cameras recorded their deliberations, other audience members would discuss the "verdict." Home audiences could also vote via a 900 number.

1995–96 season

STEPHANIE MILLER SHOW, THE
This late-night syndicated talk show starred Stephanie Miller, a Los Angeles radio host and stand-up comedienne. Like many others who went up against the formidable *Tonight Show*, this series failed to attract enough of an audience to survive.

DANNY!
This syndicated talk show starred Danny Bonaduce, former child star of *The Partridge Family*. Now 35, Bonaduce had lived a checkered past with several run-ins with the law, making him an unusual choice to host a Disney series. However, he had been quite successful as an energetic radio host in Chicago, and Studio executives created this series for him. The show included a contest or game based on the topic of the day.

Prime-Time Series

The Ellen Burstyn Show
One of the Studio's earliest attempts to produce a mainstream television series was *The Ellen Burstyn Show*, a situation comedy that aired during the 1986–87 season. Burstyn, who had won the Academy Award for Best Supporting Actress in *Alice Doesn't Live Here Anymore*, was cast as Professor Ellen Brewer, a literature teacher at a college in Baltimore. Ellen was divorced from her second husband, having remarried after her first husband died. Not only did she have to deal with the problems of her own life, but she had to help her family members cope with their own unusual situations.
Series Cast: *Ellen Burstyn (Ellen Brewer), Megan Mullally (Molly Brewer), Jesse Tendle (Nick), Barry Sobel (Tom Hines), Elaine Stritch (Sydney Brewer), Winifred Freedman (Carrie).*
Each of the episodes is described below in airdate order.

ELLEN BURSTYN SHOW, THE (pilot)
Airdates: 9/20/86, 9/12/87.
Guest Cast: *Winifred Freedman (Carrie), Billy Wirth (Johnny), Maurice Davis (Baskin), Lydie Denier (Allegra).*

Ellen tries to teach one of her students, Tom Hines, to devote himself more to his school work than to his rock band. Meanwhile, she and Molly argue over letting the family dog give birth at home.

MONKEY BUSINESS   Airdate: 9/27/86.
Guest Cast: Jim Dale (Robert Waits).
Molly is excited about her new boyfriend, a famous anthropologist. Unfortunately, he's more interested in spending time with Ellen than with her.

WHERE THERE'S A WILL   Airdate: 10/04/86.
Guest Cast: Winifred Freedman (Carrie), Maurice Davis (Baskin), Matt Mulhern (Mikey), Maria Strova (Maria).
Tom, Ellen's problem student, moves in until he can find a place to live. The family isn't thrilled about this, but Tom quickly becomes a fixture.

GUEST LECTURER, THE   Airdate: 10/18/86.
Guest Cast: Eileen Heckart (Natalie Garrett), Maurice Davis (Baskin), Matt Mulhern (Mikey), Maria Strova (Maria).
Ellen's houseguest, Natalie Garrett, is a renowned author and Ellen looks forward to working with her idol. Her enthusiasm doesn't last long, however, for Natalie tears Ellen's work apart and suggests that one of Ellen's students give up writing and get a new career.

CRIME AND PUNISHMENT   Airdate: 10/25/86.
Guest Cast: (Sydney Brewer), Jack Gilford (Mr. Quigley), Stephanie Musnick (Customer #1), Manuel Santiago (Chauffeur).
Everyone is dismayed to learn that Nick is stealing toys from a five-and-dime store. While they recognize it's a plea for attention, they differ on how to react.

SYDNEY'S NIGHT OUT   Airdate: 11/01/86.
Guest Cast: Joe Sirola (Phillip Dolan), Bo Kaprall (UPS Man).
Sydney scares the family by staying out late on a date. When she finally gets home, she shocks Ellen and Molly by announcing that she's off to Barbados with her date.

READING BETWEEN THE LINES   Airdate: 11/08/86.
Guest Cast: Harvey Keitel (Franklin Tanner), Jack Hallett (Alan Marshall), Jeff

Brooks (Waiter), John Capodice (The Snuffer), Cherron Hoye (Coordinator), Roscoe Lee Browne (Dean Waldo Ray Morton).
When Ellen meets Frank Tanner, a self-made man, she quickly falls for him. Then, she makes the surprising discovery that despite his success, Frank is illiterate.

Production Note:

- This show was developed in cooperation with Project Literacy U.S. (PLUS), a group working to combat adult illiteracy.

FAMILY AFFAIR   Airdate: 11/15/86.
Guest Cast: Joe Guzaldo (Marc), Daniel A. Harrison (Boy in Closet), John Francis (Heckler), Courtney Peldon (Lily).
Molly's ex-husband complicates her life when he unexpectedly shows up for Nick's sixth birthday party.

MOLLY SINGS THE BLUES   Airdate: 8/08/87.
Guest Cast: Nick Apolloforte (Gaslight Johnny Tomorrow), Norman Steinberg (Club Manager).
After six years of being a single parent, Molly wonders if there's more to life. She tries to fulfill a life-long dream by getting a singing job, but soon begins to question her priorities.

WRITER, WRONGER   Airdate: 8/15/87.
Guest Cast: J.T. Walsh (Dan), Maurice Davis (Baskin), Lyne Thigpen (Pam James), Matt Mulhern (Mikey), Maria Strova (Maria).
The newest member of Ellen's writing class has had a lot of time to plan his next writing project. He's an ex-con, having served 5 years for manslaughter, and Ellen must cope with her unexpected reaction to his past.

BOX, THE   Airdate: 8/22/87.
Guest Cast: Joe Grifasi (Timothy Winnegrew).
The family finds a strange looking box in a phone booth and daydreams about its contents while waiting for the owner to claim it.

WRITES OF PASSAGE   Airdate: 9/05/87.
Guest Cast: Maurice Davis (Baskin), Matt Mulhern (Mikey), Maria Strova (Maria), Tino Juarez (Charlie), Andy Roa (Carlos).
Ellen faces a dilemma when Molly asks her to critique a short story she wrote for a magazine.

I'M DANCING FASTER THAN I CAN
Airdate: Unaired.

Guest Cast: Austin Pendleton *(Dr. Cauley), Maurice Davis (Baskin), Matt Mulhern (Mikey), Maria Strova (Maria).*

The Disney Archives does not have plot information available on this unaired episode. In an interview, Ellen Burstyn mentioned that her character became hooked on amphetamines.

Harry

Although *The Ellen Burstyn Show* had been a quick failure, Disney was not about to give up on its plans to become a factor in network programming. The 1986–87 season also saw the arrival of *Harry*, another half-hour sitcom. This one starred film actor Alan Arkin as Harry Porschak, a wheeler/dealer who ran the supply room in County General Hospital. Harry always had some shady scheme in motion, and everyone was convinced he was defrauding either the hospital or its patients.

The original plans for *Harry* called for 13 episodes, and ABC scheduled the series on Wednesday at 8:30 P.M. as a mid-season replacement during the 1986–87 season. Only four episodes were actually aired.

Series Cast: Alan Arkin *(Harry Porschak),* Holland Taylor *(Nurse Duckett),* Thom Bray *(Lawrence),* Matt Craven *(Bobby),* Barbara Dana *(Sandy Houston),* Kurt Knudson *(Wyatt Lockhart),* Richard Lewis *(Richard).*

Each of the episodes is described below in airdate order, followed by the unaired episodes in production order.

MEET HARRY PORSCHAK   Airdate: 3/04/87.

Guest Cast: William Bronder *(Delivery Man #1),* John Del Regno *(Lucas),* Margaret Shendal *(Nurse #1),* Zoaunne LeRoy *(Sister Helena),* Santos Morales *(Delivery Man #2).*

Lawrence, the head expediter, discovers paperwork that proves Harry has been selling hospital equipment without authorization. He gives the proof to Nurse Duckett, who sees this as her chance to finally have Harry fired.

HOW DO YOU SOLVE A PROBLEM LIKE NURSE DUCKETT?   Airdate: 3/11/87.
Nurse Duckett discovers a shortage of surgical gowns and launches a determined search for them. It so happens that Harry has been tie-dying the gowns and selling them as fashion items in a local boutique.

THIS IS THE ARMY, MR. PORSCHAK
Airdate: 3/18/87.

Guest Cast: Scott Thomson *(Dr. Chesterfield),* Felton Perry *(Lieutenant McKenzie).*

When the U.S. Army discovers that Harry faked his discharge papers more than 20 years ago, they send him to Alaska for a year to finish his enlistment. With Harry gone, Lawrence becomes the head of the supply room and mass confusion results.

GREAT RAT RACE, THE   Airdate: 3/25/87.
Guest Cast: Tom LaGrua *(Lucas).*

When a rat escapes from the hospital lab, Bobby finds it and makes it his pet. Lockhart wants him to return the rat, but Harry has other plans for Bobby's new pet.

HARRY'S BIG NIGHT   Airdate: Unaired.
Guest Cast: Richard Libertini *(Dr. Ezra Taklow),* Terrence McNally *(Dr. Wagner).*

When Sandy asks Harry to take her to the hospital fund-raiser dance, he says yes at first. Later, he feels he won't fit in with the doctors, so he backs out. Harry arranges for Dr. Wagner to take Sandy to the dance, then later discovers that Sandy turned him down for Harry.

MR. IMPERFECT   Airdate: Unaired.
Guest Cast: Paul Eiding *(Bartender),* John Achorn *(Dr. Gaglianella),* Ricky Reynolds *(Kevin).*

Devastated when he learns he made a math error on an invoice, Lawrence quits in shame. Harry and his co-workers don't really care that Lawrence has left until they learn he'll be replaced by a computer.

REBEL WITHOUT A CAUSE   Airdate: Unaired.

Guest Cast: Richard Libertini *(Dr. Ezra Taklow),* Patrick Collins *(Harold Boynton),* Andrew Bloch *(Mr. Arons),* Randolph Brown *(Patient #1),* Lenny Hicks *(Patient #2),* Carolsue Walker *(Patient #3).*

Harry is admitted to the hospital after he drops a box on his foot, and Nurse Duckett is assigned to care for him. Upset at the poor conditions in the patient wards, Harry tries to speak out in protest, but Duckett wears him down and he finally gives up.

Sidekicks

When the Disney anthology series returned to the air as *The Disney Sunday Movie* in

1985, Studio executives made no secret of the fact that they were using it in part as a platform to showcase pilots for potential new series. Of all the pilots eventually aired, only *The Last Electric Knight* ever led to an order for a series. *The Last Electric Knight* was the story of police detective Jake Rizzo and his young ward, Ernie, a martial arts expert.

The series, renamed *Sidekicks*, began with a repeat of *The Last Electric Knight*, then continued the story of Jake, Ernie, and Patricia Blake, the social worker assigned to watch over Ernie.

Series Cast: Gil Gerard (Detective Sergeant Jake Rizzo), Nancy Stafford (Patricia Blake), Keye Luke (Sabasan), Frank Bonner (Detective Marty Mooney), Ernie Reyes, Jr. (Ernie, The Last Electric Knight), Vinny Argiro (Captain Blanks).

Each of the episodes is described below in airdate order.

LAST ELECTRIC KNIGHT, THE

This episode, the pilot for *Sidekicks*, first aired on the anthology series. It was repeated as a preview on 9/19/86 to begin the series.

ARE THESE YOUR KICKS?   Airdates: 9/26/86, 12/27/86.

Guest Cast: Richard Kline (Detective Charlie Cheatham), Dick McGarvin (Teacher), Katy Boyer (Girl), Bob Coker (Officer), David Kerr (Tough One), Ernie Reyes Sr. (Detective).

Rizzo is a confirmed slob, which causes conflicts with Ernie, who is a compulsive cleaner. Ernie feels that he doesn't fit in and runs away, staying with Patricia while he tries to decide what to do next.

OPEN HOUSE   Airdates: 10/03/86, 1/24/87.

Guest Cast: Ed Hooks (Crook), Vonni Ribisi (Travis Houghton), Carlos Cervantes (Derelict), Holly Colburn (Mrs. Houghton), Gloria Dobson (Miss Harper), Burt Marshall (Cop), Eric Server (Mr. Houghton).

"Parents Night" at school is coming up and Ernie is worried about how Rizzo will act at the event. In fact, he's worried if Rizzo will even show up, for the cop is busily trying to solve a very important case.

I HATE THE NEIGHBORS   Airdates: 10/17/86, 6/27/87.

Guest Cast: John Chappell (Mr. Weby), Elaine Giftos (Binns), Mary Carver (Mrs. Dubois), Joy Garrett (Randy), Joe Renteria (Ortega), Mi Mi Green (Jenny Wilson), John W.

Smith (Steve), Robert Axelrod (Bingham), Christopher Irrizarry (Punk #1), Lenore Woodward (Old Lady).

Rizzo is getting tired of life in the city and decides to move to a small town in Montana to get away from it all. Ernie thinks they should face problems rather than run away from them, and he convinces their neighbors to hold a going away party for Rizzo.

MY DAD THE CROOK   Airdate: 10/24/86.

Guest Cast: Brion James (Marshall), Gerald Gordon (Dobbs), Byron Webster (Tocino), Ryan Lambert (Derrick), Vonni Ribisi (Travis Houghton), Michael Rich (Carlton), Tom Finnegan (Wally), Christopher McCarty (Jordon), Daniel Morong (Vendor).

The city is plagued by a major fencing operation, and Rizzo agrees to act as a crooked cop so he can infiltrate the gang involved. His act is too convincing, though, for Internal Affairs suspects him of accepting bribes and they suspend him.

DOWN AND OUT IN VAN NUYS   Airdate: 10/31/86.

Guest Cast: Geoffrey Lewis (John Maxwell), John C. Cooke (Shelly), Michael DeLano (Horse), Charles H. Hyman (Garth).

When Ernie saves John Maxwell from a mugging, he takes him home to recuperate, unaware that the man is an embezzler hiding from the police.

THRILL OF THE CHASE   Airdate: 11/07/86.

Guest Cast: Michael Richards (Arnie Plimpton), Michael C. Gwynne (Shaw), El DeBarge (Himself), Ann McCurry (Newscaster), Wendy Becker (Reporter), Scott Cooper (Reporter), Cecil Hill (Reporter), Ernie Reyes, Sr. (Dojoe).

Ernie becomes a local hero when he saves a woman from being mugged, and everyone wants to exploit him. Rizzo refuses to let the sudden fame go to Ernie's head and only allows him one public appearance.

CATHERINE THE NOT-SO-GREAT

Airdate: 11/14/86.

Guest Cast: Barbara Stock (Catherine), Granville Ames (Sweeney), Ismael "East" Carlo (Judge).

Attorney Catherine Sable convinces a court that Rizzo cannot positively identify her client as a thief. Rizzo surprisingly doesn't hold a grudge against her for this; in fact, he becomes quite smitten with her and the two begin dating.

MY DAD'S BIGGER THAN YOURS
Airdate: 11/22/86.

Guest Cast: Nicholas Pryor (Cunningham), David Hoskins (Jason), Vonni Ribisi (Travis Houghton), Roger Hampton (Evan), Marsh Munro (Waiter), Charles Walker (Harold), Kenneth White (Mr. Veitch).

A neighborhood bully picks a fight with Ernie, who promptly wins the battle. Unfortunately, the bully's father is a city councilman, and he vows to make life tough for Rizzo, both at work and at home.

BIRDS AND THE KILLER BEES, THE
Airdate: 11/29/86.

Guest Cast: Nicole Huntington (Karen), Judd Omen (Aguila), Melora Harte (Liz), Karen Lind (Miss Kilgallen), Grant Moran (Driver), Joey Paul (Worker #1), J.J. Wall (Flower Man).

While Rizzo is attempting to get evidence about a murder plot, he has to take time off the case to deal with Ernie, who needs to learn about the birds and the bees.

I REMEMBER MAMA, BUT DOES SHE REMEMBER ME?
Airdates: 12/13/86, 3/14/87.

Guest Cast: Magda Harout (Mama Rizzo), Gary Hudson (Coach Kite), Tak Kubota (Tak).

Rizzo's mother comes to visit, and she immediately begins to argue with him about almost everything they discuss. She also has trouble adjusting to her "instant grandson," Ernie.

GREY BELTS   Airdates: 12/20/86, 6/20/87.

Guest Cast: Henry Jones (Irwin), Gerrit Graham (Krawchek), Frances Bay (Sarah), Herta Ware (Mamie), Jim Doughan (Officer), Paul Keith (Mr. Becker), Angel Salazar (Thug #1).

Ernie's well-intended efforts to help his elderly neighbors defend themselves against muggings accidentally result in one of them being injured. Rizzo decides that he has to step in to help.

Production Note:

• With this episode, the series title changed to *Disney's Sidekicks*.

COUSIN WHO FELL TO EARTH, THE
Airdate: 1/03/87.

Guest Cast: Ricky Steamboat (Primo), Richard Sanders (Broadhead), Dan Gerrity (Denton), Lorin Jean Vail (Debby), Jay S. York (Wrestler).

An unexpected guest keeps Rizzo and Ernie busy. He wants to be a policeman, but he learned English from watching television crime shows and thinks they accurately portray police work.

BOY WHO SAW TOO MUCH, THE
Airdate: 1/10/87.

Guest Cast: Rick Hurst (Berglund), Robin Pearson Rose (Connie), Kenneth Lloyd (Jevin), Vonni Ribisi (Travis Houghton), Tim Russ (Uniformed Officer), Eric Server (Mr. Houghton).

Ernie is suspicious of activities at their neighbors', but Rizzo doesn't take him seriously. When Ernie and a friend think they see a kidnapping, they try to solve the case themselves.

JUST FOR KICKS   Airdate: 1/17/87.

Guest Cast: Katherine Moffat (Monica), Corky Nemec (Kyle), Vonni Ribisi (Travis Houghton).

When Rizzo is nearly killed on the job, he questions if he should try to raise a child. Meanwhile, Ernie's coach is trying to convince him to use his martial arts skills to help win soccer games.

KICKED UPSTAIRS   Airdate: 1/31/87.

Guest Cast: John McCook (Small), Gerrit Graham (Krawchek), James Emery (Whistler), Vonni Ribisi (Travis Houghton).

Rizzo gets a long-desired promotion, then finds out he will have to spend most of his time sitting at a desk.

EYE FOR AN EAR, AN   Airdate: 2/07/87.

Guest Cast: Robert Gray (Grant), Kyle Galyean (Doctor), Jeffrey Lampert (Computer Operator), Larry Scarano (1st Tough), Michael Grayson (Desk Sergeant), Mary Ingersoll (Reporter), Ernie Reyes, Sr. (Sergeant #1), Richard Lee Sung (Patusan Man).

When Rizzo is critically wounded by an ex-con, Ernie vows to track the man down and avenge the assault.

NEXT BEST THING TO WINNING, THE
Airdate: 2/14/87.

Guest Cast: Terence Knox (Tecket), Madison Arnold (Tommy), Gary Hudson (Coach Kite), Joan Chodorow (Office Worker), Steve Susskind (Mickey).

Ernie is kicked off the soccer team when he fails algebra. Rizzo visits his teacher to see how to help and learns the man is heavily in debt to a loan shark.

PATUSANI ALWAYS RINGS TWICE, THE
Airdate: 2/21/87.

Guest Cast: Clyde Kusatsu (Dr. Tosh), Eileen Saki (Mrs. Treong), Jason Miyashiro (Tasho), Lauren Narikawa (Mi Ling), Arell Blanton (Liquor Store Owner), Robert Schuch (Bandit #1), Duane Whitaker (Bandit #2).

When an aunt and uncle track Ernie down, the boy can't decide if he should stay with Rizzo or leave with his relatives.

PETTY CACHE   Airdate: 2/28/87.

Guest Cast: Lindsay Fisher (Heather), Michael Wren (Mosley), Joshua Cadman (Bates), Ed DeFusco (Jenkins), Nick Ferris (Manager), Ray O'Keefe (Bowler), Vonni Ribisi (Travis Houghton), Michael Grayson (Desk Sergeant), Art Koustik (Cab Driver).

Ernie and his friends form a secret club, then find a strange key. They try to find its owner, unaware that it leads to a missing $500,000.

WORST OF THE MOHICANS, THE
Airdate: 3/07/87.

Guest Cast: Paul Gleason (Fargo), James Staley (Mel), Casey Ellison (Geezelman), Vonni Ribisi (Travis Houghton), Jared Rushton (Brave #1), David Clover (Older Man), Tom LaGrua (Younger Man).

Rizzo takes Ernie and some friends camping. The trip turns serious when they come across a ring of car thieves operating in the woods.

PLAYING FOR KEEPS   Airdate: 6/06/87.

Guest Cast: John Dennis Johnston (Carson), André Gower (Eric), Daryl Bartley (Charlie), Vonni Ribisi (Travis Houghton), Robert Coker (Mr. Green), Midge Dial (Mrs. Green).

Ernie and his friends use a cave to play a fantasy game, unaware that burglars are using it to store stolen goods.

READ BETWEEN THE LINES   Airdate: 6/13/87.

Guest Cast: Michael Manasseri (Matt Gambrell), Beau Starr (Frank Gambrell), Shawn Harrison (Gang Leader), Robert Miano (Chaffee), Patrick St. Esprit (Payne), Rahsaan Patterson (Derrick), Ann Price (Female Attendant).

Ernie and Rizzo come to the aid of friends who signed a contract without being able to read it.

Production Note:

• This episode was developed as part of Project Literacy U.S. (PLUS), a nationwide campaign launched by Capital Cities/ ABC, Inc., and the Public Broadcasting Service to combat adult illiteracy.

Down and Out in Beverly Hills

One of the Studio's biggest theatrical successes in 1985 was the comedy *Down and Out in Beverly Hills*. The film featured the Whiteman family, wealthy residents of Beverly Hills who had grown distant from one another.

A television version of *Down and Out in Beverly Hills* follows, airing in 1987.

Series Cast: Hector Elizondo (Dave Whiteman), Tim Thomerson (Jerry Baskin), Anita Morris (Barbara Whiteman), Evan Richards (Max Whiteman), Eileen Seeley (Jenny Whiteman), April Ovitz (Carmen), Mike the Dog (Matisse).

Each of the episodes is described below in airdate order. Five episodes not aired in the United States are included here as well.

JERRY'S MISSION   Airdate: 4/26/87.

Guest Cast: Bruce Kirby (Maury Rodman), Michael Fairman (Henry Phelps), Felton Perry (Al), Susan Kellerman (Duchess), Deanne Mencher (Celia Rodman).

Dave learns a lesson about being overly concerned with material wealth when he discovers that his new friend is a slumlord.

SOMETHING MILD   Airdate: 7/25/87.

Guest Cast: Michael Shaner (Turk Black).

Under pressure to please her parents, Jenny turns to Jerry for advice. He tells her to be more interested in making herself happy, and that will, in turn, please others. However, after another family argument, Jenny runs away.

SKIN TIGHT   Airdate: 8/01/87.

Guest Cast: Jo DeWinter (Victoria), Bruce Kirby (Maury Rodman), Monte Landis (Channeler), Lee Lucas (Ventura).

Dave and Barbara are worried about her mother's negative outlook on life. They try to persuade her that a 3-week cruise would cheer her up, but mom has another plan—plastic surgery.

MAX BEDROOM　Airdate: 8/08/87.

Guest Cast: Danielle Brisebois (Ally).

When Max brings a girl home, it looks as though some of his growing pains have been eased, until he fails in the romance area.

ALTARED STATES　Airdate: 8/15/87.

Guest Cast: Gina Hecht (Julie Whiteman), Daniel Chodos (Rabbi Bob), Rick Lieberman (Charlie).

Dave's sister, Julie, arrives for a visit shortly after being dumped by her fiance, Charlie. Dave rationalizes and blames Charlie for the end of the relationship, despite Barbara's protests that Julie is part of the problem.

SHAPIRO'S CARMEN　Airdate: 8/22/87.

Guest Cast: Ray Buktenica (Dr. Adam Shapiro).

Carmen, the family maid, finds herself pursued by a newly divorced doctor who wants very much to be married again. Although Carmen isn't in love with him, she finds herself tempted by his proposal.

DANCING IN THE DARK　Airdate: 9/05/87.

Guest Cast: Debbie Barker (Jo Jo Blankenship), Martin Cassidy (Director), Ricky Stout (Scout).

Barbara starts to feel old when they attend a play starring an old girlfriend who is now a big star. Determined to spice up her life, Barbara takes Jerry's advice and tries to find a job as a dancer.

YOU OUGHT TO BE IN PICTURES　Airdate: 9/12/87.

Guest Cast: Bruce Kirby (Maury Rodman), Bill Morey (Dirk Stoner), Doug Warhit (Ted Byrd).

Lured by the glamour of Hollywood, Dave agrees to invest in a movie, but only if his favorite actor, Dirk Stoner, will star. But Stoner is much older than in his last picture and in no shape for a starring role.

FISTFUL OF DOLLARS, A　Airdate: Unaired.

Guest Cast: Doug Warhit (Ted Byrd), Patrick Cronin (Stan), Bert Rosario (Ruben), Sam Scarber (Bernard).

Dave faces bankruptcy when his business manager steals his money. Part 1 of 2.

FOR A FEW DOLLARS MORE　Airdate: Unaired.

Guest Cast: Doug Warhit (Ted Byrd), Bert Rosario (Ruben), Sam Scarber (Bernard), Timmy Capello (John Q. Public), Alisha Das (Narcissus).

Part 2 of the story begun in A Fistful of Dollars. Jerry helps Dave recover from the shock of being penniless.

JERRY JUMPS RIGHT IN　Airdate: Unaired.

Guest Cast: Paxton Whitehead (Derek), Jay Acovone (Eddie), Michael Francis Clarke (Lounge Guy #2), Jeanine Jackson (Lounge Girl), Ian Praiser (Lounge Guy).

Dave finds Jerry a job playing the piano on a cruise ship, but some of the passengers' song requests make Jerry want to jump overboard.

LEGEND THAT IS BARBARA, THE　Airdate: Unaired.

Guest Cast: J.E. Freeman (Mr. Creukshank), Joseph Cali (Gus), Jack Bruskoff (Dwight), Melinda Gardner (Stylish Woman), Larry Mintz (Mr. Bennett), Michael Stoneall (Stylish Man).

Barbara buys a share of a pizza parlor to prove she can handle a business, but doesn't know that her partner is in the Mafia.

JERRY STRIKES OUT　Airdate: Unaired.

Guest Cast: David Alan Grier (Edwin), Bert Rosario (Ruben), Julian Deyer (Keith), Marina Palmier (Juanita), Vanessa Paul (Grace).

When Jerry talks to Dave's employees, the result is an unexpected strike.

The Oldest Rookie

Disney added to the lengthy list of police shows with the 1987–88 offering *The Oldest Rookie*.

The series, which was first called *The Rookie*, featured Paul Sorvino as Ike Porter, the Deputy Chief of Public Relations for a large police force. Ike had worked his way up through the ranks to a job coveted by many other officers, by writing press releases and giving speeches.

When CBS first placed *The Oldest Rookie* on the schedule they were evidently not firmly convinced that the public would warm to the comedy action-adventure show, for only 14 episodes were ordered. A total number of 13 episodes aired.

Series Cast: *Paul Sorvino (Ike Porter), D.W. Moffett (Tony Jonas), Raymond J. Barry (Lieutenant Marco Zaga), Marshall Bell (Detective Gordon Lane).*

Each of the episodes is described below in airdate order, followed by the unaired episode.

AT THE END OF THE LONG ARM IS THE GLAD HAND Airdates: 9/16/87, 12/02/87.

Guest Cast: *Mark Blankfield (Ernie), Patrick Cronin (Chief Black), Bruce Gray (Bob), Geoffrey Lewis (Sergeant Harry Clark), Zoaunne Leroy (Lady), Dianne Turley Travis (Mrs. Gottlieb), Ron Gilbert (Mario), Sarah Abrell (Pamela), Joseph G. Medalis (Sergeant), Lisa Dinkins (Anchor Woman), Doug DuVal (Mechanic #1), Leslie Norris (Flight Attendant), Hartley Silver (Vendor), Jim Smith (Mechanic #2), Sylvia Walden (Secretary).*

After 25 years on the police force, Deputy Chief Ike Porter is questioning his value as a cop. He's the head of the public relations department, and his days are spent writing an endless series of press releases. Ike finally decides that he misses being a "real" cop, so he requests a transfer back to the streets.

GAME EFFORT, A Airdate: 9/23/87.

Guest Cast: *Keone Young (Bok Song), Sheldon Feldner (Bill Boyde), Kerry Yo Nakagawa (Korean), Janis Ward (Sexy Blonde), Dennis Bowen (Fireman Bob), Frank Miller (Security Agent), Cuba Gooding (Street Kid Leader), Victoria Dakil (Nurse).*

Ike and Tony see a pattern in a recent spate of muggings. When Ike's friend is fatally injured, Ike vows revenge.

HEARTBREAKERS Airdate: 9/30/87.

Guest Cast: *Mira Sorvino (Patty Porter), Linda G. Miller (Vanessa Murdoch), Steve Kramer (John Barnes), Austin Kelly (Hotchkiss), Jim Hudson (Dr. Storts), Judy Kain (Molly Garber), Alan David Gelman (Pete Garber), Gary Epp (Lomax), Gary Dean Sweeney (Manny), Tammi Cohen (Clerk), E.M. Margolese (Maitre'D), Alixe Branch (Martha), Jake Jacobs (Cop), Eddie R. White (Eddie).*

When Ike's niece, Patty, comes to visit after being away for many years, he's glad to see her—until he realizes that she's becoming very interesting in Tony. This romantic problem will have to wait, though, for Patty becomes a witness to an unusual mugging.

CEREAL KILLER, THE Airdate: 10/07/87

Guest Cast: *Sue Giosa (Esperanza), John Welsh (Sid Herzog), Laura Malone (Susan Channing), Richard Zobel (Pew), Howard Honig (Sleazy Man), J.J. Wall (Horton), Ed McCready (Jablonski), Ron Sloan (Kovacs), Richard Courtney (Mandrake), Madeline Taylor Holmes (Madam Arcati), Richard Livingston (Lance), Victor Contreras (Mireles), Matty Bolduc (Felipe), Mandie Smith (Linda), Shaun Hunter (Dewitt), Kenny Morrison (Officer Flynn), Ron E. Dickinson (Strangler), Erwin Fuller (Banker), Abigail Hanes (Madonna), Toni Attell (Actor #1), Lee Grodsky (Actor #2).*

The city is being stalked by a strangler whose modus operandi is to kill only during breakfast, thus earning him the moniker "the cereal killer." When the police can't find any clues, Ike and Tony are told to interview psychics to prove that the force is doing everything possible to catch the killer.

BLUE FLU Airdate: 10/14/87.

Guest Cast: *Paul Provenza (Andy Babcock), Patrick Cronin (Chief Black), David Selburg (Bradley), Rich Hebert (Teasdale), Brenda Bolte (Spooky), J.J. Wall (Horton), Ricardo Gutierrez (Sanchez), Lou Cutell (Mr. Crum), Eileen T'Kaye (Taylor), John Paul Gamoke (Man in Line), Amy Hill (Mrs. Henderson), Tim Bartell (Mickey).*

Ike and Tony are assigned to a murder case where the chief suspect is an old friend of Tony's, Andy Babcock. The detectives believe Andy's claims of innocence, but their investigation is slowed by an outbreak of "blue flu."

COMING FROM BEHIND Airdate: 10/21/87.

Guest Cast: *Lora Staley (Melinda Sullivan), Deborah Wakeham (Rhonda Roth), Thom Sharp (D.A. Roger McManus), Dana Gladstone (Morty), Zoaunne Leroy (Gladys), Don Dolan (Racetrack Trainer), J.J. Wall (Detective Horton), Raye Birk (Coroner), Scotch Byerley (Racetrack Groom), Tom Dugan (Burke), Robert Donavan (Club Owner), Christopher Darga (Cab Driver), Sharon Howard (Lady), Rafael A. Nazario (Maitre'D), David Austin (Club Manager), Eddie R. White (Eddie).*

Elated at solving a murder, Ike and Tony can only watch in shock when the suspect is released from custody due to their clerical error. Zaga demotes them and assigns two other detectives to supervise them as they try to recapture the killer.

Grand Theft Avocado   Airdate: 10/28/87.

Guest Cast: Stan Ivar (Arthur White), Robert Phalen (Walter Hawthorne), Brett Hadley (Chairman), Michael Eugene Fairman (Sergeant Brothers), Barry Dennen (Caplan), Robert Mackenzie (MacPhee), Patricia Lee Willson (Karen), Ron Barker (Bentley), Anne Gee Byrd (Woman), Michelle Reese (Mailroom Officer), Scott Cooper (Fruitstand Man), Mort Sertner (Fishbein), Robert Coker (Uniformed Officer), Eddie R. White (Eddie).

A seemingly simple produce theft brings Ike and Tony into a murder plot involving Arthur White, one of the city's richest men. White becomes worried about their investigation and orders the detectives killed.

Expert Witness   Airdate: 11/04/87.

Guest Cast: Fern Fitzgerald (Karen), Joe Dorsey (Aaron Wilder), H. Richard Greene (Getz), Shelly Kurtz (Detective Hewitt), Steve Susskind (Moe), Michael Yama (Store Owner), John Moskoff (Judge Maltz), Carinee Carroll (Judge Tucker), William Schreiner (Defense Attorney), Jane Frances (Minerva), Joey Gaynor (Santa Claus), Robert Balderson (Bailiff), Jerry Cerwonka (Inspector), Eddie R. White (Eddie).

Karen Korman, Ike's former secretary, has been receiving anonymous calls threatening her if she doesn't resign from her job. Ike suspects that the calls are coming from the police department's executive offices, so he has himself and Tony assigned there.

Ike and Son   Airdate: 11/18/87.

Guest Cast: Richard Portnow (Albert Moont), Diane Stilwell (Sylvie), Ron Dean (Agent Gardens), John Christy Ewing (Assistant D.A. St. Jean), Frances Bay (Mrs. Zimmer), William Hootkins (Dr. Harry Shelton), Nick Angotti (Detective Gordon), Fred Ottaviano (Red Frank), Randy Polk (Guy Good).

The police set up a fake pawnshop as part of a sting operation to catch petty thieves, and Ike and Tony are assigned to the case, posing as father and son. The case takes an unusual turn when evidence points to a connection with organized crime.

Internal Affairs Affair, An   Airdate: 11/25/87.

Guest Cast: Leah Ayres Hendrix (Nina Zaga), Paul Comi (Detective Crawley), Lynn Milgrim (Audrey Nelson), Ned Bellamy (Prisoner), Luis Contreras (Zono), Carole Ita White (Secretary), Whitney Rydbeck (Postman), Cheryl Checcetto (Ginny), Michael Hungerford (Detective Cooper), Don Maxwell (Detective Robertson), William Sherry (Hostage/Busboy), Bill Dearth (Guard), Hugh B. Holub (Clerk), John J. Flynn (Postal Supervisor), Martin Charles Warner (Supervisor), Ed Levey (Caterer), Eddie R. White (Eddie).

Lieutenant Zaga seems to be investigating Internal Affairs for a reason known only to him. When Ike and Tony are visited by two Internal Affairs officers who are investigating Zaga, they wonder what is going on within the force.

Come Fly with Me   Airdate: 12/16/87

Guest Cast: Nancy Dussault (Maureen Porter), Earl Boen (Gordon), Wayne Grace (Buzz), Jon Menick (Father Corcoran), Marte Boyle Slout (Mrs. Frieburger), John T. Olson (Singlemeyer), J.J. Wall (Detective Horton), Charles Gruber (Fitzwater), Ken Belsky (Kressel), Eddie R. White (Eddie).

Garbage dumped in a local field is attracting coyotes, and Ike and Tony are put on the case to track down the dumpers. When the detectives learn that the field is being used as a landing strip by drug smugglers, they set a trap for the criminals.

Best Men   Airdate: 12/23/87.

Guest Cast: Marilyn Jones (Stephanie Benton), Ian Blackman (Parker Hilles), Edward Bell (Maurice Dumas), Frank Schuller (Uncle Billy), Dave Nicolson (Pastor Tiddle), Tony Montero (Cudahy), Lynn Seibel (Hodel), Tom Tully (Joe Abodeely), Frederic Arnold (Elderly Man), Valery Pappas (Receptionist), Jason Riffle (Rick), Jeremy Riffle (Randy), Frank Holms (Fritz), Melissa Behr (Model), Kate Yurka (Belly Dancer), Debby Harris (Balloon Girl), Eddie R. White (Eddie).

A young woman asks the detectives for help in finding her missing fiance just before their wedding. The man turns up but with total amnesia, prompting Ike and Tony to search for the cause of his illness.

Yessir, That's My Baby   Airdate: 1/06/88

Guest Cast: Michael Greene (Mr. Jonas), Toni Sawyer (Mrs. Jonas), Barney Martin (Heindorf), Keith David (Walker), Michael McGrady (John Raft), Michelle Joyner (Doreen), Julie Payne (Frieda Spitzer), Rosalee

Mayeux (Gillian), Aixa Clemente (Manager), J.J. Wall (Detective Horton), Barbara Bingley (Kareema), Katherine Bingley (Kareema), Michael Dobo (Higgins), Doug Ford (Head Biker), Tom Fitzpatrick (Man #1), Ty Crowley (Man #2), Joseph Romeo (Sleazy Guy), Susan Ann Connor (Voltron Lady), Joe Gibb (Ewok #1), Michael Gilden (Ewok #2), Daureen Collodel (Yuppie Lady), Michael Porter (Yuppie Man), Phil Fondacaro (Gnome), Michael Franco (Laser Player), Leonard John Crofoot (Martian), June Stoddard (College Girl), Ryan Sands (Waiver).

When one of Tony's former girlfriends leaves a baby on his doorstep, the detective assumes the child is his so he quits the police force to care for the child. Ike helps Tony search for the baby's mother, who has run afoul of a band of drug dealers.

LUCK BE A LADY   Airdate: Unaired.

Guest Cast: Sandra Berhard (Enola), Audrie J. Neenan (Vera), Don Calfa (Oscar), Geoff Edwards (Himself), Michael Wren (Morales), Dennis Robertson (Crazy One), Mark Blankfield (Ernie), Keith David (walker), Ellen Crawford (Mrs. Schirrmer), Michael G. Hawkins (Trowbridge), Mark Bringelson (Alex), Kevin Pollak (Danny), J.W. Smith (Owner), Max Perlich (Gary Jr.), Byron Scott (Himself), Joseph Medalis (Sergeant Beaudine), Vincent Lucchesi (Man #1), Jan Rabson (Guy), Craig Schaefer (Patrolman), Antonin Hodek (Man #2), Carrie Snow (Lady), Kimmy Robertson (Girl), Don Woodard (Salesman), Michael Saccente (Party Animal), Howard Allen (Suspect), Kipp Lennon (Singer at Oscars), Matthew Davis (Boisterous College Kid), Eddie R. White (Eddie).

When the detectives lose a prisoner they are transporting, they're demoted back to street duty. They buy a lottery ticket and win $200,000, which launches them on a spending spree.

The Golden Girls (and) The Golden Palace

After several failures, the Studio finally had a hit series with *The Golden Girls*. The concept of *The Golden Girls* first came to light in 1984 at the annual NBC affiliates meeting. Actress Selma Diamond, starring then in the comedy *Night Court*, did a brief sketch called *Miami Nice* to test the audiences' reaction to a comedy about older women. The crowd liked it, and NBC executives were sufficiently encouraged to explore the idea fur-

ther. The eventual result, a sitcom about four women living together in Miami, was hailed by critics for showing that older women could still enjoy life—and, in a most un-Disney touch, enjoy their sex lives. The four women were Dorothy Zbornak, a retired New York City school teacher; her outspoken 80-year-old mother, Sophia Petrillo; Blanche Devereaux, who, like Will Rogers, never met a man she didn't like; and Rose Nylund, a sweet but extremely unsophisticated woman who always seemed one step removed from reality.

The casting of *The Golden Girls* was a major reason for the show's success, for the ensemble cast worked well together. Each of the actresses received a steady stream of Emmy nominations and awards, and *The Golden Girls* made history as being the only series where each of the stars won the coveted award.

NBC first asked for 6 episodes to be produced, but as the show developed, the network became excited enough about the concept that they gave Disney a commitment for 13 episodes before the first one was fully written. The series joined the NBC lineup for the 1985–86 season.

The second season saw the series continuing to do very well. The series brought in 14 Emmy nominations for 1986–87.

The 1987–88 season brought yet another batch of Emmy awards.

By the end of the 1988–89 season, the series was #5 in the ratings, had garnered 51 Emmy nominations (winning 10), won 3 Golden Globes awards, and was seen in 60 countries around the world. The 1990–91 season saw a major change to the production staff, with many of the original producers and writers leaving for other series. The show also entered the lucrative syndication market. *The Golden Girls* ended the year as #12 in the ratings and with a total of 65 Emmy nominations.

As the season unfolded, Bea Arthur did decide to leave the series, and *The Golden Girls* ended as Dorothy got married and left her friends behind. However, her friends were not quite done yet, for there were more stories to tell.

Welcome to The Golden Palace

Series cast: Beatrice Arthur (Dorothy Zbornak), Betty White (Rose Nylund), Rue McClanahan (Blanche Devereaux), Estelle Getty (Sophia Petrillo).

Even though *The Golden Girls* had come to an end, it looked as though only Bea Arthur had had enough of the series. Disney looked for a way to keep the show alive without Arthur's very important character. Their answer took Blanche, Rose, and Sophia and found them a new home at The Golden Palace, an art deco hotel in Miami Beach that had seen better days.

Disney took the new series to CBS, which was desperately looking for new shows for its own lineup. As a result, *The Golden Palace* ended up on the CBS schedule for the 1992–93 season on Friday at 8:00 P.M.

Each of the episodes is described below in airdate order, divided by season.

1985–86 season

GOLDEN GIRLS, THE (pilot) Airdates: 9/14/85, 12/28/85, 7/19/86.

Cast: Beatrice Arthur (Dorothy Zbornak), Betty White (Rose Nylund), Rue McClanahan (Blanche Hollingsworth), Estelle Getty (Sophia Petrillo), Charles Levin (Coco), Frank Aletter (Harry), F. William Parker (The Minister), Meshach Taylor (The Cop).

Blanche shocks her roommates by announcing that she plans to marry her new boyfriend, Harry. The ladies worry about what will happen to them and where they will live, but on the day of the wedding, it's Blanche who has a problem. It turns out the groom-to-be is a bigamist.

Production Notes:

- This episode won an Emmy Award for Outstanding Technical Direction/Electronic Camera Work/Video Control for a Series, and the Director's Guild of America award.
- Rue McClanahan's character was changed from Blanche Hollingsworth to Blanche Devereaux after this episode. It was later established that Hollingsworth was her maiden name.

GUESS WHO'S COMING TO THE WEDDING Airdates: 9/21/85, 1/04/86.

Guest Cast: Herbert Edelman (Stanley Zbornak), Lisa Jane Persky (Kate), Dennis Drake (Dennis), Kurt Smildsin (The Priest).

When Dorothy's daughter, Kate, decides to get married, Dorothy must deal with ex-husband, Stan. She doesn't want to see him again, but she also doesn't want to let her anger ruin the wedding.

ROSE THE PRUDE Airdates: 9/28/85, 3/15/86.

Guest Cast: Harold Gould (Arnie Peterson).

Rose's new boyfriend, Arnie, wants to take her on a romantic cruise, but she's worried about falling in love again. He finally convinces her to go, and she sees that love is something not to be afraid of.

TRANSPLANT Airdates: 10/05/85, 1/25/86.

Guest Cast: Sheree North (Virginia).

A visit from Blanche's sister, Virginia, is a tense time for all. The two women have never gotten along, for Blanche has always felt that Virginia was their parents' favorite daughter. Now, Virginia needs a kidney transplant, and Blanche can't decide what to do.

TRIANGLE, THE Airdates: 10/19/85, 3/22/86.

Guest Cast: Peter Hansen (Dr. Elliot Clayton).

Dorothy and Blanche both become involved with the same man, but they refuse to believe it's his fault. When they start arguing all the time, Rose forces him to confess to save the friendship.

ON GOLDEN GIRLS Airdates: 10/26/85, 4/05/86.

Guest Cast: Billy Jacoby (David), John Hostetter (The Policeman), Karl Wiedergott (Boy #1).

Blanche's 13-year-old grandson, David, visits, and everyone can't wait until he leaves, for the boy is a terror. They try to win him with kindness, but then realize he needs some discipline in his life.

COMPETITION, THE Airdates: 11/02/85, 4/12/86.

Guest Cast: Ralph Manza (Augustine Bagatelli).

The ladies become involved in a cut-throat bowling competition, with Blanche and Dorothy pitted against Sophia and Rose.

BREAK-IN, THE Airdates: 11/09/85, 4/19/86, 9/03/88.

Guest Cast: Christian Clemenson (The Salesman), Robert Rothwell (Lester).

After the house is burglarized, everyone is worried about the possibility of the thief returning. Rose is so worried that she buys a gun, not thinking of the consequences.

BLANCHE AND THE YOUNGER MAN
Airdates: 11/16/85, 7/05/86.
Guest Cast: Jeanette Nolan (Alma Lindstrom), Charles Hill (Dirk).
Blanche starts dating an aerobics instructor and goes overboard in her exercise regime, hoping it will make her more attractive to him.

HEART ATTACK, THE
Airdates: 11/23/85, 4/26/85.
Guest Cast: Ronald Hunter (Dr. Harris).
Sophia has an apparent heart attack, and while everyone waits for the paramedics to arrive, she tells the ladies about her vision of heaven.

STAN'S RETURN
Airdates: 11/30/85, 5/17/86.
Guest Cast: Herbert Edelman (Stanley Zbornak), Simone Griffeth (Chrissy).
Dorothy is flattered when her ex-husband, Stan, returns to rekindle their romance—until she learns that his new wife has left him.

CUSTODY BATTLE, THE
Airdates: 12/07/85, 5/31/86.
Guest Cast: Doris Belack (Gloria).
Dorothy and Sophia are always arguing, but when Sophia says she wants to live with her other daughter, Dorothy realizes how much her mother means to her.

LITTLE ROMANCE, A
Airdates: 12/14/85, 5/24/86.
Guest Cast: Brent Collins (Dr. Jonathan Newman), Billy Barty (Edgar Lindstrom), Tony Carreiro (The Waiter), Jeane Dixon (Herself).
Blanche is having a hard time deciding what to do about her newest boyfriend. Her friends want to meet him, but she doesn't want them to know that she's dating a midget.

THAT WAS NO LADY
Airdates: 12/21/85, 6/07/86.
Guest Cast: Alex Rocco (Glen).
When Dorothy learns that her new boyfriend is married, she cannot bring herself to end the relationship. Eventually, she decides the situation is not fair to his wife and drops him.

IN A BED OF ROSE'S
Airdates: 1/11/86, 6/14/86, 9/06/86.
Guest Cast: Priscilla Morrill (Lucille), Richard Roat (Al).

After Rose's date dies in her bed, she becomes convinced that she has "the kiss of death" and must never become sexually involved with a man again.

TRUTH WILL OUT, THE
Airdates: 1/18/86, 6/28/86.
Guest Cast: Christina Belford (Kirsten), Bridgette Andersen (Charley).
Rose's daughter, Kirsten, visits and asks to share in her father's estate, only to be told that Rose has squandered the money. In truth, there never was any estate and Rose is protecting her dead husband's image.

NICE AND EASY
Airdates: 2/01/86, 6/21/86.
Guest Cast: Hallie Todd (Lucy), Ken Stovitz (Ed).
Blanche thinks that her visiting niece, Lucy, is acting promiscuously and tells her to stop. The two women argue, and Blanche sees some of her own actions in a new light.

OPERATION, THE
Airdates: 2/08/86, 9/13/86.
Guest Cast: Robert Picardo (Doctor Revell), Anne Haney (Bonnie), Bill Quinn (The Priest).
After Dorothy is injured while taking tap dancing lessons, her recovery is made worse by Rose and Blanche's attempts to entertain her.

SECOND MOTHERHOOD
Airdates: 2/15/86, 7/12/86.
Guest Cast: Kevin McCarthy (Richard), Alan Blumenfeld (Lou), Terry Wills (Plumber).
Blanche likes her new boyfriend, but she doesn't like the way he ignores his children. She tries to overlook the problem, but it eventually causes them to split up.

ADULT EDUCATION
Airdates: 2/22/86, 8/09/86.
Guest Cast: Jerry Hardin (Professor Cooper), James Staley (Dean Tucker).
Blanche returns to college to finish a long-delayed degree, and her professor pressures her to sleep with him to get good grades.

FLU, THE
Airdates: 3/01/86, 7/26/86.
Guest Cast: Sharon Spelman (Dr. Richmond), Bill Cort (Dave), Ray Reinhardt (Harold), Marc Tubert (Raoul), Tony Carreiro (Tommy Cochran), Dom Irrera (The Waiter), Silvana Gallardo (The Emcee).
Everyone except Sophia is suffering from the flu, but that doesn't stop them from won-

dering who will win the annual health benefit award.

JOB HUNTING   Airdates: 3/08/86, 8/02/86.

Guest Cast: Richard Venture (Milton).

The grief center where Rose works is closed due to a lack of funds. She needs to get a new job, but soon finds that it's not going to be easy.

BLIND AMBITIONS   Airdates: 3/29/86, 8/30/86.

Guest Cast: Polly Holliday (Lily), Annie Abbott (Woman #1), Bill Gratton (Man #2), Stuart Fratkin (Man #3), Donna LaBrie (Stewardess).

A visit from Rose's recently blinded sister, Lily, is an uncomfortable time for all. Lily is having a hard time adjusting to her blindness, and the others don't know how to treat her.

BIG DADDY   Airdates: 5/03/86, 8/23/86.

Guest Cast: Murray Hamilton (Big Daddy), Gordon Jump (Leonard Barton), Peggy Pope (Gladys Barton), Gary Grubbs (Waiter), Tony Frank (Cowboy #1), Blake Emmons (Cowboy #2).

Blanche's father arrives with the amazing news that he is becoming a country western singer. Unfortunately, he can't sing.

WAY WE MET, THE   Airdates: 5/10/86, 9/20/86.

Guest Cast: Shirley Prestia (Zelda), Edan Gross (The Boy), Dom Irrera (The Produce Clerk).

The ladies take a look back at how they first met. Blanche had advertised at the local market for two roommates, and Dorothy and Rose answered the ad.

1986–87 season

END OF THE CURSE   Airdates: 9/27/86, 3/28/87, 8/27/88.

Guest Cast: Philip Sterling (Dr. Barensfeld), Vince Cannon (Dr. Parks), George J. Woods (The Man).

The onset of menopause sends Blanche into deep depression, and her friends urge her to get professional help.

LADIES OF THE EVENING   Airdates: 10/04/86, 3/07/87, 8/06/88.

Guest Cast: Phil Rubenstein (The Exterminator), Peter Jason (The Policeman), Rhonda Aldrich (Meg), Peter Gonneau
(Walter), Ton Swartz (John), Ron Michaelson (Carl), Cheryl Checcetto (Hooker #1), Mimi Kinkade (Hooker #2), Ursaline Bryant (Hooker #3), Jim Keily (Jail Guard), Ron Kapra (Desk Clerk), Suanne Spoke (Girl in Lobby).

Everyone is excited when Blanche wins tickets to Burt Reynolds's new movie and a special party afterwards, but they are arrested as hookers by mistake.

TAKE HIM, HE'S MINE   Airdates: 10/11/86, 12/27/86.

Guest Cast: Herbert Edelman (Stanley Zbornak), Lana Schwab (The Girl), Tom La Grua (Vinny).

Dorothy asks Blanche to date her ex-husband, Stan, so she can date a new boyfriend without Stan getting in the way. Stan and Blanche keep dating, though, and Dorothy starts to get jealous.

IT'S A MISERABLE LIFE   Airdates: 11/01/86, 4/04/87.

Guest Cast: Nan Martin (Frieda Claxton), Thom Sharp (Mr. Pfeiffer), Amzie Strickland (Lady at Funeral), Johnny Haymer (The Commissioner).

When Rose argues with a neighbor and tells her to drop dead, the lady does just that. Poor Rose is guilt stricken, for she is convinced she is responsible for the death.

ISN'T IT ROMANTIC?   Airdates: 11/08/86, 4/18/87.

Guest Cast: Lois Nettleton (Jean).

A visit from Dorothy's college friend, Jean, takes everyone by surprise when she reveals that she's a lesbian.

BIG DADDY'S LITTLE LADY   Airdates: 11/15/86, 4/25/87.

Guest Cast: David Wayne (Big Daddy), Sondra Currie (Margaret Spencer).

Blanche's father, Big Daddy Hollingsworth, returns for another visit and again has some surprising news. This time, he's here to get married, and Blanche is shocked to learn that her new stepmother is much younger than she is.

FAMILY AFFAIR   Airdates: 11/22/86, 7/30/88.

Guest Cast: Scott Jacoby (Michael Zbornak), Marilyn Jones (Bridget Nylund).

Dorothy's son, Michael, doesn't have a job, but he does have a new girlfriend—Rose's daughter, Bridget. Both Dorothy and Rose are upset with the relationship, but for different reasons.

VACATION   Airdates: 11/29/86, 6/06/87.

Guest Cast: Tom Villard (Rick), Stuart Pankin (Jacques de Courville), Stephen Lee (Winston Hardwick III), Keye Luke (Toshiro Mitsumo), Paul Rodriguez (Ramone).

Dorothy, Rose, and Blanche go on vacation to a Caribbean island, where they discover that their hotel is a run-down dump.

JOUST BETWEEN FRIENDS   Airdates: 12/06/86, 7/18/87.

Guest Cast: Reid Shelton (Andrew Allen).

After Dorothy is laid off from work, Rose finds her a job at the museum where she works. Unfortunately, the boss likes Dorothy's work better than Rose's, and the two friends begin to argue.

LOVE, ROSE   Airdates: 12/13/86, 7/04/87.

Guest Cast: Paul Dooley (Isaac Q. Newton), Colin Drake (Wilfred Whitney Cheswick).

Rose places a newspaper ad looking for a boyfriend, but when no one responds, Dorothy and Blanche invent a mystery man.

'TWAS THE NIGHTMARE BEFORE CHRISTMAS   Airdates: 12/20/86, 6/13/87, 12/26/87.

Guest Cast: Terry Kiser (Santa Claus), Craig Richard Nelson (Thurber), Teddy Wilson (Albert), Sam Anderson (Meyer), Buddy Daniels (Hare Krishna).

It looks like a bleak Christmas when the ladies are first taken hostage by a lonely Santa Claus, then stuck in a run-down diner.

SISTERS   Airdates: 1/03/87, 5/23/87.

Guest Cast: Nancy Walker (Angela).

Sophia has a surprise visitor—her sister, Angela, to whom she hasn't spoken in more than 30 years. Neither sister can recall what started the feud, but that doesn't stop them from continuing their battle.

STAN WHO CAME TO DINNER, THE   Airdates: 1/10/87, 5/30/87.

Guest Cast: Herbert Edelman (Stanley Zbornak), Rod Sabbe (Rob), Odil Sabbe (Bob), Steven Kramer (Dr. Stephen Deutsch), Mario Machado (Sportscaster Voice).

After Stan has surgery, he moves in with the ladies to recuperate. It's not long before he has worn out his welcome with his constant demands.

ACTOR, THE   Airdates: 1/17/87, 6/20/87.

Guest Cast: Lloyd Bochner (Patrick Vaughn), Janet Carroll (Phyllis Hammerow), Frank Birney (Stage Manager).

Dorothy, Blanche, and Rose all vie for a role in a community theater play, attracted by the leading man. None of them gets the part, but they all manage to bed the star.

BEFORE AND AFTER   Airdates: 1/24/87, 8/01/87.

Guest Cast: Deborah May (Liz), Rosanna Huffman (Stephanie), Nat Bernstein (Dr. Wallerstein), Tony Pope (The Doorman).

Rose suffers from a seizure and believes she died, went to heaven, and returned to life. This gives her a new outlook on life, and she announces plans to move out of the house.

AND THEN THERE WAS ONE   Airdates: 1/31/87, 6/27/87.

Guest Cast: Christopher Burton (Norman Henderson), Nat Bernstein (Emily's Father), Ray Combs (Bob Henderson), Ariana Richards (Lisa), Scott Curtis (Timmy).

Dorothy, Rose, and Blanche agree to babysit a group of children, but when the parents return to pick up their offspring, the ladies find they have one child left over.

BEDTIME STORY   Airdates: 2/07/87, 7/25/87.

Guest Cast: Randy Bennett (Stationmaster).

The ladies look back at some of the more memorable nights they have spent together, including a night without heat and a very long night spent on the benches of a dirty train station.

FORGIVE ME, FATHER   Airdates: 2/14/87, 7/11/87.

Guest Cast: John McMartin (Father Frank Leahy), Barney McGeary (Father Callahan), Charles Summers (Confessional Priest), Charles Erikson (Tony).

A date with a fellow teacher leaves Dorothy confused. She finds out that he's a priest, and is thinking of leaving the priesthood because of her.

LONG DAY'S JOURNEY INTO MARINARA   Airdates: 2/21/87, 8/08/87.

Guest Cast: Nancy Walker (Angela), Joe Alfasa (Tony), Esther Larner (Woman).

The ladies convince Sophia's sister, Angela, to move to Miami from Sicily, but soon are regretting it after a series of problems with the new arrival.

WHOSE FACE IS THIS, ANYWAY?
Airdates: 2/28/87, 8/15/87.

Guest Cast: Joseph Whipp (Dr. Taylor).

When Rose and Blanche become concerned about their age, they start thinking about getting face-lifts.

DOROTHY'S PRIZED PUPIL   Airdates: 3/14/87, 8/29/87.

Guest Cast: Mario Lopez (Mario), John Braden (Sam Burns), Danny Goldman (Man in Theatre), Chip Olcott (Burt Nesbitt).

While Dorothy is trying to keep one of her students from getting deported, Rose has to pay off a debt to Blanche by working as her maid.

DIAMOND IN THE ROUGH   Airdates: 3/21/87, 1/02/88.

Guest Cast: Donnelly Rhodes (Jake Smollens), Vince Trankina (Mr. Hinkley), Mike Muscat (Waiter), Glenn Shadix (Musician), Howard Witt (Hunter McCoy).

Everyone is interested in the same man, but Blanche is determined to win him over no matter what the cost.

SON-IN-LAW DEAREST   Airdates: 4/11/87, 8/22/87.

Guest Cast: Herbert Edelman (Stanley Zbornak), Deena Freeman (Kate), Jonathan Perpich (Dennis).

Dorothy's daughter, Kate, arrives for a visit with some bad news. Her husband, Dennis, has had an affair and she doesn't know what to do about it.

TO CATCH A NEIGHBOR   Airdates: 5/02/87, 9/05/87.

Guest Cast: Joseph Campanella (Al), George Clooney (Bobby), Barbara Tarbuck (Martha).

The police use the house to watch some jewel thieves, and the ladies begin to watch the police.

PIECE OF CAKE, A   Airdates: 5/09/87, 9/12/87.

Guest Cast: Alan Blumenfeld (Mr. Ha Ha), Lyn Greene (Young Dorothy).

The ladies look back at some of the more memorable birthdays they've enjoyed over the years.

EMPTY NEST   Airdate: 5/16/87.

Guest Cast: Paul Dooley (George Corliss), Rita Moreno (Renee Corliss), Jane Harnick (Jenny), Geoffrey Lewis (Chuck), David Leisure (Oliver).

George and Renee Corliss, the ladies' neighbors, are having problems with their marriage. Renee feels that George, a doctor, is spending too much time at work and doesn't care for her anymore.

Production Note:

• This episode was the pilot for the series *Empty Nest*.

1987–88 season

OLD FRIENDS   Airdates: 9/19/87, 3/26/88.

Guest Cast: Joe Seneca (Alvin Newcastle), Janet MacLachlan (Sandra), Jenny Lewis (Daisy).

Sophia befriends an elderly man, unaware that he suffers from Alzheimer's. Meanwhile, Blanche mistakenly gives away Rose's prized teddy bear, and Rose goes in search of her old friend.

Production Note:

• This episode won an Emmy for Outstanding Technical Direction/Electronic Camerawork/Video Control for a Series.

ONE FOR THE MONEY   Airdates: 9/26/87, 4/02/88.

Guest Cast: Sid Melton (Salvadore), Lyn Greene (Young Dorothy), Roy Stuart (Marty), Ed Balin (Russell), Ed Kerrigan (Dave), Starr Andreeff (Priscilla), Conrad Janis (Announcer).

In a series of flashbacks, the ladies recall various schemes they've shared over the years to earn money.

BRINGING UP BABY   Airdates: 10/03/87, 1/30/88.

Guest Cast: Parley Baer (Chester T. Rainey), Tom McGreevey (Veterinarian).

Rose has to take care of a pet pig to win $100,000, but the animal threatens to come between the roommates.

HOUSEKEEPER, THE   Airdates: 10/17/87, 3/05/88.

Guest Cast: Paula Kelly (Marguerite), Deborah Rose (Midge), Carl N. Ciarfalio (Black Crow).

When the new housekeeper is fired, everything starts going wrong for the ladies, who begin to wonder if she put a curse on the house.

NOTHING TO FEAR BUT FEAR ITSELF
Airdates: 10/24/87, 4/09/88.
Guest Cast: Meg Wyllie (Stewardess).

Each of the ladies has a secret fear. For Rose, it's speaking in public. Blanche worries about bald men, and Dorothy doesn't like to fly. All of them are put to the test when the ladies fly on a plane full of bald men to a funeral where Rose must deliver the eulogy.

LETTER TO GORBACHEV
Airdates: 10/31/87, 4/16/88.
Guest Cast: Allan Rich (Alexi), Jaclyn Bernstein (Linda), Cynthia Marie King (Nancy), Edwin Newman (Himself).

Rose writes a letter to Soviet Premier Gorbachev and he asks to meet her, thinking that she is a little girl.

STRANGE BEDFELLOWS
Airdates: 11/07/87, 4/23/88.
Guest Cast: John Schuck (Gil Kessler), Sarah Partridge (Secretary), Darwyn Carson (Reporter #1), David Westgor (Reporter #2).

Local politics become confused when a candidate for the city council says he had an affair with Blanche, but for some reason, she denies it.

BROTHERLY LOVE
Airdate: 11/14/87.
Guest Cast: Herbert Edelman (Stanley Zbornak), McLean Stevenson (Ted).

Stan's brother, Ted, goes on a date with Blanche, but it's Dorothy who really interests him.

VISIT FROM LITTLE SVEN, A
Airdates: 11/21/87, 6/04/88.
Guest Cast: Casey Sander (Sven), Yvette Heyden (Olga), Chuck Walling (Floyd).

Rose's cousin, Sven, stops in to visit on the way to his wedding, but decides he would rather marry Blanche.

AUDIT, THE
Airdates: 11/28/87, 6/18/88.
Guest Cast: Herbert Edelman (Stanley Zbornak), Tony Perez (Mr. Escobar), Richard Penn (Mr. Murray).

After a tax audit, Dorothy must hock a prized ring to keep from having to go to jail.

THREE ON A COUCH
Airdates: 12/05/87, 5/21/88.
Guest Cast: Philip Sterling (Dr. Ashley), Terry Wills (Carl), John C. Moskoff (Jerry).

Unable to settle an argument, the ladies decide to visit a family counselor. When they each describe the problem, the stories don't sound anything alike.

CHARLIE'S BUDDY
Airdates: 12/12/87, 6/25/88.
Guest Cast: Milo O'Shea (Buddy).

Rose becomes infatuated with one of Charlie's old friends and decides to move in with him.

ARTIST, THE
Airdates: 12/19/87, 6/11/88.
Guest Cast: Tony Jay (Laszlo), Monte Landis (Victor).

The ladies each pose nude for a sculptor, unaware that the others are also modeling for him.

BLANCHE'S LITTLE GIRL
Airdates: 1/09/88, 7/02/88.
Guest Cast: Shawn Schepps (Rebecca), Scott Menville (McCracken), Meg Wyllie (Edna), Joe Regalbuto (Jeremy).

Blanche and her daughter, Rebecca, try to become friends again after 4 years apart, but Blanche doesn't care at all for how Rebecca's fiancee treats her little girl.

DOROTHY'S NEW FRIEND
Airdates: 1/16/88, 7/16/88.
Guest Cast: Bonnie Bartlett (Barbara Thorndyke), Monty Ash (Murray Guttman), Brad Trumbull (Maitre D').

Dorothy's new friend, Barbara Thorndyke, comes between the ladies when she talks down to Rose and Blanche.

GRAB THAT DOUGH
Airdates: 1/23/88, 7/09/88.
Guest Cast: James MacKrell (Guy Corbin), Lucy Lee Flippin (Nancy), Kelly Andrus (Tiffany), Charles Green (Willard), Ken Smolka (Policeman), Craig Schaefer (Stage Manager).

The ladies head to Hollywood to compete on a game show, but the trip is a disaster.

MY BROTHER, MY FATHER
Airdates: 2/06/88, 8/13/88.
Guest Cast: Herbert Edelman (Stanley Zbornak), Bill Dana (Uncle Angelo).

Sophia convinces Stan and Dorothy to pretend they're still married when her brother, Angelo, a priest, comes to visit. Unfortunately, Angelo stays much longer than expected.

GOLDEN MOMENTS Airdates (1-hour format): 2/13/88, 5/14/88.
When Sophia announces she wants to live with her son to help raise his children, the ladies look back at events of the last 3 years together.

AND MA MAKES THREE Airdates: 2/20/88, 12/17/88.
Guest Cast: James Karen (Raymond), Frank Smith (Duncan), Steven M. Porter (Waiter).
Dorothy and her new boyfriend are tired of having Sophia tag along on their dates, but they can't bring themselves to tell her she's not welcome.

LARCENY AND OLD LACE Airdates: 2/27/88, 8/20/88.
Guest Cast: Mickey Rooney (Rocco).
Sophia's new boyfriend takes her on a very unusual date—he robs a bank and makes her drive the getaway car.

ROSE'S BIG ADVENTURE Airdates: 3/12/88, 7/23/88.
Guest Cast: George Coe (Al), Vito Scotti (Vincenzo), Don Woodard (Ernie).
When Rose urges her new boyfriend to be more adventurous, he decides to sail around the world in a small boat and invites her along.

MIXED BLESSINGS Airdates: 3/19/88, 12/31/88.
Guest Cast: Scott Jacoby (Michael), Virginia Capers (Greta), Lynn Hamilton (Trudy), Montrose Hagins (Libby), Hartley Silver (Justice of the Peace), Rosalind Cash (Lorraine).
Dorothy's son plans to marry a black woman, and Dorothy has problems accepting the relationship. She is shocked to learn the woman's mother is equally as upset.

MR. TERRIFIC Airdates: 4/30/88, 12/24/88.
Guest Cast: Bob Dishy (Mister Terrific), Lonny Price (Hastings), Jody Price (Jody), Don Woodard (Kolak), John Wheeler (Patron), Jim Hudson (Freddy), Raf Mauro (Bartender), Ron Kapra (Stage Manager).

Rose tries to improve a children's television series, but her suggestions get the star, Mr. Terrific, fired.

MOTHER'S DAY Airdates: 5/07/88, 9/10/88.
Guest Cast: Herbert Edelman (Stanley Zbornak), Lyn Greene (Young Dorothy), Sid Melton (Salvadore), Helen Kleeb (Margaret), Alice Ghostley (Mrs. Zbornak), Wesley Mann (Jacob), Terrence Evans (Sheriff), Geraldine Fitzgerald (Anna).
Another flashback show features the women recalling their favorite Mother's Days.

1988–89 season

YES, WE HAVE NO HAVANAS Airdates: 10/08/88, 1/21/89.
Guest Cast: Henry Darrow (Fidel Santiago), Ralph Ahn (Jim Shu), Magda Harout (Woman), John Achorn (Priest).
While Sophia and Blanche both vie for the attention of an elderly man, Rose becomes one of Dorothy's students as she tries to finally get her high school diploma.

DAYS AND NIGHTS OF SOPHIA PETRILLO, THE Airdates: 10/22/88, 3/11/89.
Guest Cast: Frances Bay (Claire), Nick DeMauro (Clerk), David Selburg (Store Manager), Allen Bloomfield (Abe), Ellen Albertini Dow (Mrs. Leonard), Darlene Kardon (Woman), Marian Wells (Wanda), Peggy Gilbert (Esther), The Dixie Belles (The Band), Don "Kokko" Burnaby (Sam).
The rest of the ladies are worried that Sophia will be bored on a rainy day, but she has a full schedule that would amaze them.

ONE THAT GOT AWAY, THE Airdates: 10/29/88, 5/20/89.
Guest Cast: John Harkins (Ham Lushbough), Tom Dahlgren (Major Barker), Nick Toth (Waiter).
Blanche meets an old schoolmate who is very special for an unusual reason. He's the only man to ever have turned her down.

YOKEL HERO Airdates: 11/05/88, 4/08/89.
Guest Cast: Jim Doughan (Ben), Doug Cox (Sven), John Moody (Len), James Lashley (The Driver), Valente Rodrigues (Fred), Richard Mulligan (Dr. Harry Weston).
Blanche and Dorothy help Rose become St. Olaf's "Woman of the Year" by spicing up her biography, then find they have to go there with her for the award dinner.

BANG THE DRUM, STANLEY Airdates: 11/12/88, 4/22/89.

Guest Cast: Herbert Edelman (Stanley), Ben Rawnsley (Dr. Jerry), William Denis (Dr. Cauley), Helen Duffy (Woman in Wheelchair), Matthew Brooks (Timmy).

Although Sophia isn't hurt when she is hit on the head by a ball at a baseball game, Stan convinces her to sue the team.

SOPHIA'S WEDDING—PART 1 Airdates: 11/19/88, 7/08/89.

Guest Cast: Jack Gilford (Max Weinstock), Raye Birk (Caterer), Sid Melton (Salvadore), Harbey J. Goldenberg (Preacher), Fritzi Burr (Ruth), Roland August, Richard Bernard, Scott Gale, Blake Gibbons, Tally Lauriti, Rick Le Fever, Samuel Lloyd, Jay Pennick, Eddie Powers, Quentin Tarantino (Elvis Impersonator).

For 40 years, Sophia has despised her late husband's business partner, Max. When she meets him again, she suddenly decides to marry him.

Production Note:

• Quentin Tarantino appeared in a small part in this episode as an Elvis Presley impersonator.

SOPHIA'S WEDDING—PART 2 Airdates: 11/26/88, 7/15/89.

Guest Cast: Jack Gifford (Max Weinstock), Don Maxwell (Fire Chief), William E. Green (Saxaphone Player).

After their honeymoon, Sophia and Max open a small restaurant, but the marriage is not to last long.

BROTHER, CAN YOU SPARE THAT JACKET? Airdates: 12/03/88, 5/29/89.

Guest Cast: Karl Wiedergott (Kenny), Matthew Faison (Father Campbell), Herta Ware (Ida), Teddy Wilson (Ben), Andre "Rosey" Brown (Bodyguard), Howard Goodwin (Auctioneer), Art Koustik (Dave), Stanley Wojno Jr. (Philip Starr).

Sophia gives Blanche's jacket to a charity thrift shop, unaware that it contains a winning lottery ticket.

SCARED STRAIGHT Airdates: 12/10/88, 5/27/89.

Guest Cast: Monte Markham (Clayton), Gwen E. Davis (Mildred), Nancy Priddy (Lois), Sharon Howard (Woman), Darryl Ferrera (Man), Steve Porter (Waiter).

Blanche tries to arrange dates for her brother, Clayton, not knowing that he's gay.

STAN TAKES A WIFE Airdates: 1/07/89, 6/03/89.

Guest Cast: Herbert Edelman (Stanley Zbornak), Elinor Donahue (Katherine), Tom Tarpey (Dr. Seymour), Wayne Chou (Orderly), Doug Franklin (Young Doctor), Freeman King (Bartender).

Dorothy has always been glad she divorced Stan—until she learns he's planning to marry a much younger woman. Suddenly, she begins seeing him in a whole new light.

AUCTION, THE Airdates: 1/14/89, 6/10/89.

Guest Cast: Tony Steedman (Jasper DeKimmel), Michael McManus (Sid LaBass), Colin Hamilton (Auctioneer), Renata Scott (Woman), Derek Loughran (Mime).

The ladies plan to buy a painting by a dying artist, thinking that his death will suddenly make the artwork much more valuable.

BLIND DATE Airdates: 1/28/89, 6/17/89.

Guest Cast: Ed Winter (John Quinn), Kristopher Kent Hill (Billy), Paul Tennen (Freddy), Alan Koss (Ernie), Lesley Glassford (Elaine).

Blanche has a date with a blind man and worries about how to make him think she is attractive.

IMPOTENCE OF BEING ERNEST, THE Airdates: 2/04/89, 8/14/89.

Guest Cast: Richard Herd (Ernie).

Rose's new boyfriend is unable to perform in bed, and she becomes convinced that she is the cause of his problem.

LOVE ME TENDER Airdates: 2/06/89, 6/24/89.

Guest Cast: John Fiedler (Eddie), Stefanie Ridel (Jackie), Shana S. Washington (Marla), Tom Simmons (Security Guard).

Dorothy keeps dating someone she doesn't love, possibly just to annoy Sophia. Meanwhile, Rose and Blanche are mistakenly arrested for shoplifting.

VALENTINE'S DAY Airdates: 2/11/89, 8/05/89.

Guest Cast: Sid Melton (Salvadore), Pat McCormick (Clerk), Tom Isbell (Young Man), Wayne C. Dvorak (Maitre D'), Michael Blue (Porter), Peter Elbling (Desk Clerk), Michael J. London (Edgar), Joe Faust (Raymond), John

Rice (Steve), John Harnagel (Mechanic), Julian Deyer (Waiter), Bill Dana (Papa Angelo), Julio Iglesias (Himself).

When none of them have a date on Valentine's Day, the ladies look back at how they've spent the day in years past.

Two Rode Together   Airdates: 2/18/89, 12/30/89.

Guest Cast: Freddie Jackson (Sam).

Dorothy takes Sophia to Walt Disney World hoping the trip will make the two of them feel closer, but Sophia is only interested in having fun on the rides.

You Gotta Have Hope   Airdates: 2/25/89, 7/01/89.

Guest Cast: Bob Hope (Himself), Douglas Seale (Seymour), Eadie Del Rubio, Milly Del Rubio, Elena Del Rubio (The Donatello Triplets), Andre "Rosey" Brown (Bodybuilder), June Claman (Phyliss), Linda L. Rand (Frieda), Daniel Rosen (Misha), Patrick Stack (Man in Locker Room).

For some reason, Rose is convinced that Bob Hope is her long-lost father. She makes matters worse by insisting that he will star in their upcoming charity show.

Fiddler on the Ropes   Airdates: 3/04/89, 7/22/89.

Guest Cast: Chick Vennera (Pepe).

After Sophia invests their money in a prize fighter, the ladies are amazed to learn he is really a violinist, not a boxer.

'Til Death Do We Volley   Airdates: 3/18/89, 8/26/89.

Guest Cast: Anne Francis (Trudy), Robert King (Jack), Jean Palmerton (Woman).

Dorothy hosts a reunion of her high school tennis team, with plans to finally avenge the practical jokes of one of her old classmates.

High Anxiety   Airdates: 3/25/89, 7/29/89.

Guest Cast: Jay Thomas (Sy Ferber), Nancy Black (Heather).

Dorothy and Blanche discover that Rose has been addicted to pain killers for 30 years.

Little Sister   Airdates: 4/01/89, 9/02/89.

Guest Cast: Inga Swenson (Holly), Jerry Hardin (Gary Tucker).

Rose's younger sister, Holly, visits and starts coming between Rose and her friends.

Sophia's Choice   Airdates: 4/15/89, 9/09/89.

Guest Cast: Ellen Albertini Dow (Lillian), Ron Orbach (Dan Cummings), Mark Morocco (Orderly), Stanley Ullman (John Gale), Margaret Wheeler (Woman #1).

Sophia and Rose help one of Sophia's friends escape from a nursing home.

Rites of Spring   Airdates: 4/29/89, 8/12/89.

Guest Cast: Lloyd Bochner (Sophia's Hairstylist), Herbert Edelman (Stanley Zbornak).

As they get ready for a beach party, the ladies look back at past efforts to lose weight and look beautiful.

Foreign Exchange   Airdates: 5/06/89, 8/19/89.

Guest Cast: Vito Scotti (Dominic), Nan Martin (Philomena), Flo DiRe (Gina).

Sophia shocks Dorothy with the news that she might have been switched at the hospital with another baby. Now, a couple claiming to be Dorothy's real parents are on their way to take her back to Sicily for an arranged marriage.

Production Note:

• This was the series' 100th episode.

We're Outta Here   Airdates (1-hour format): 5/13/89, 9/16/89.

Guest Cast: Herbert Edelman (Stanley Zbornak).

Someone wants to buy Blanche's house, which makes the ladies look back at some of the happy times they have spent together.

1989–90 season

Sick & Tired—Part 1   Airdates: 09/23/89, 4/07/90.

Guest Cast: Jeffrey Tambor (Dr. Stevens), Michael McGuire (Dr. Budd).

Dorothy is constantly in pain and exhausted, but no one can find a reason for her ailments.

Sick & Tired—Part 2   Airdates: 09/30/89, 4/14/90.

Guest Cast: Michael McGuire (Dr. Budd), Keone Young (Dr. Chang), Bibi Besch (Helen Budd), Glenn Walker Harris Jr. (Oliver), Eric Poppick (The Waiter), Richard Mulligan (Dr. Harry Weston), Park Overall (Laverne).

Unable to feel better, Dorothy visits Harry Weston, who recommends that she see a specialist. Finally, Dorothy learns that she has Chronic Fatigue Syndrome.

ACCURATE CONCEPTION, THE   Airdates: 10/14/89, 12/23/89, 9/01/90.
Guest Cast: Debra Engle (Rebecca), James Staley (Dr. Manning), Kelly Ann Conn (Receptionist).
Blanche's joy at hearing that her daughter, Rebecca, wants to have a baby turns to dismay when she learns that Rebecca is planning on artificial insemination.

ROSE FIGHTS BACK   Airdates: 10/21/89, 3/10/90.
Guest Cast: Chick Vennera (Enrique Mas), Beth Grant (Terry Franco).
When Rose learns that her late husband's pension has run out of money, she gets a job as a consumer affairs reporter on a local television station.

LOVE UNDER THE BIG TOP   Airdates: 10/28/89, 1/20/90.
Guest Cast: Dick Van Dyke (Ken), Mel Stewart (Judge), John Di Santi (Fisherman).
Dorothy's boyfriend announces that he is giving up the legal profession to become a circus clown.

DANCING IN THE DARK   Airdates: 11/04/89, 4/21/90.
Guest Cast: Harold Gould (Miles Webber), G.F. Smith (Gale), Mimi Cozzens (Lillian), John Ingle (Harv), Channing Chase (Elise), Edgar Justice (Mr. Morelli), Al Berry (Paul).
Feeling inferior to Miles, Rose decides to end their relationship.

NOT ANOTHER MONDAY   Airdates: 11/11/89, 5/12/90.
Guest Cast: Geraldine Fitzgerald (Martha), Jayson Kane (Maitre D'), Doug Cox (Young Man), Bonnie Urseth (Young Woman), Robert Neches (Bartender), Richard Mulligan (Dr. Harry Weston).
Sophia doesn't know what to do when a friend asks for help in committing suicide.

THAT OLD FEELING   Airdates: 11/18/89, 3/17/90.
Guest Cast: George Grizzard (Jamie).
Hoping to recapture part of the special relationship she shared with her late husband, Blanche proposes to his brother.

COMEDY OF ERRORS   Airdates: 11/25/89, 5/19/90.
Guest Cast: Oliver Clark (Roger), Linda L. Rand (Gloria), David Jay Willis (Comedian), Tom La Grua (Jimmy).
Dorothy tries to be a stand-up comic, but she hasn't counted on Sophia's heckling.

ALL THAT JAZZ   Airdates: 12/02/89, 6/02/90.
Guest Cast: Herbert Edelman (Stanley Zbornak), Scott Jacoby (Michael Zbornak), Stan Roth (Make-up Man), Chick Vennera (Enrique Mas).
Dorothy finally loses patience with her unemployed son and makes him realize he must take responsibility for his life.

EBB TIDE   Airdates: 12/09/89, 5/26/90.
Guest Cast: Sheree North (Virginia), Steven Gilborn (Howard), Paul Eiding (Peter), Brandis Kemp (Maddy).
Blanche travels home for her father's funeral and must come to terms with her sister after years of battles between them.

HAVE YOURSELF A VERY LITTLE CHRISTMAS   Airdates: 12/16/89, 8/11/90.
Guest Cast: Herbert Edelman (Stanley Zbornak), Matt McCoy (Father Avery).
The ladies help out a soup kitchen on Christmas, and are astonished to see Stan there as Santa Claus.

MARY HAD A LITTLE LAMB   Airdates: 1/06/90, 6/09/90.
Guest Cast: Julie McCullough (Mary), John Dennis Johnston (Merrill), Lorry Goldman (Fred).
The ladies try to help a pregnant teenager patch things up with her father, while also trying to cope with Blanche's pen pal, who has just been released from prison.

GREAT EXPECTATIONS   Airdates: 1/13/90, 6/16/90.
Guest Cast: Robert Mandan (Steven), Michele Pawk (Mary Ellen), Kay Sawyer-Young (Woman), Kathy Bendett (Nurse).
Blanche's boyfriend has a heart attack, but she is so afraid of death that she can't bring herself to visit him in the hospital.

TRIPLE PLAY   Airdates: 1/27/90, 6/23/90.
Guest Cast: Harold Gould (Miles Webber), Molly Hagan (Caroline), Ronnie Schell

(Thomas), Bill Cort (James), Lance Wilson-White (Delivery Boy).

Blanche manages to sell a car she doesn't own, and Rose meets her daughter's new boyfriend.

CLINTON AVENUE MEMOIRS   Airdates: 2/03/90, 7/07/90.

Guest Cast: Sid Melton (Salvador), Kyle Hefner (Young Salvador), David Correia (Mr. Hernandez), Flo Di Re (Young Sophia), Jandi Swanson (Young Dorothy).

Sophia's wedding anniversary brings back memories of her late husband, Sal.

LIKE THE BEEP, BEEP, BEEP OF THE TOM-TOM   Airdates: 2/10/90, 6/30/90.

Guest Cast: Robert Culp (Simon), Peter Michael Geotz (Dr. Stein), David Jay Willis (Orderly).

Blanche needs a pacemaker, which makes her think that her sex life has ended.

ILLEGITIMATE CONCERN, AN   Airdates: 2/12/90, 8/25/90.

Guest Cast: Mark Moses (David).

Blanche is shocked when a stranger arrives at her door, claiming to be her late husband's illegitimate son.

72 HOURS   Airdates: 2/17/90, 7/14/90.

Guest Cast: Tony Carreiro (Doctor), Peggy Walton-Walker (Receptionist).

Rose may have received tainted blood during a transfusion and must wait 72 hours for the results of an AIDS test.

TWICE IN A LIFETIME   Airdates: 2/24/90, 9/15/90.

Guest Cast: Harold Gould (Miles Webber), Eddie Bracken (Buzz), April Ortiz (Maria), Douglas Seale (Malcolm).

Rose's childhood boyfriend shows up and demands that she choose between him and Miles.

SISTERS AND OTHER STRANGERS   Airdates: 3/03/90, 7/28/90.

Guest Cast: Barbara Babcock (Charmaine), Marian Mercer (Magda).

Blanche's sister writes a sexy romance novel, and many of the characters resemble Blanche.

CHEATERS   Airdates: 3/24/90, 8/04/90.

Guest Cast: Jerry Orbach (Glen), Sam McMurray (Mr. Kane), Nancy Lenehan (Nun).

Dorothy becomes involved again with an old flame who used to cheat on her every chance he got.

MANGIACAVALLO CURSE MAKES A LOUSY WEDDING PRESENT, THE
Airdates: 3/31/90, 7/21/90.

Guest Cast: Howard Duff (Mangiacavallo), Stuart Nisbet (Doug), Tanya Louise (Jenny), Paul Collins (man), Jonathan Schmock (Waiter), Myles Berkowitz (Groom).

Sophia invokes a Sicilian curse on the grandson of a man who jilted her 70 years ago.

ALL BETS ARE OFF   Airdates: 4/28/90, 8/18/90.

Guest Cast: Michael Ensign (Donald).

Dorothy becomes addicted to gambling but refuses to admit that she has a problem.

PRESIDENT'S COMING, THE   Airdates (1-hour format): 5/05/90, 9/08/90.

Guest Cast: Herbert Edelman (Stanley Zbornak), Timothy Stack (Agent Bell), Harry Shearer (Voice of George Bush), Raye Birk, Alan Blumenfeld, Henry Darrow, Jack Gilford, Harvey J. Goldenberg, Kevin McCarthy, Pat McCormick, Jeffrey Webber, Roland August, Richard Bernard, Gale Scott, Blake Gibbons, Tally Lauriti, Rick LeFever, Samuel Lloyd, Jay Pennick, Eddie Powers, Quentin Tarantino (Elvis Impersonator).

As they talk about the President's upcoming visit to Miami, the ladies look back at some of the more memorable moments they have shared together.

1990–91 season

BLANCHE DELIVERS   Airdates: 9/22/90, 12/08/90, 7/13/91.

Guest Cast: Debra Engle (Rebecca), Ken Lerner (Doctor), Leila Kenzle (Tamara), John O'Leary (Mr. Ninervini), Marti Muller, Diane Racine.

Blanche must help her pregnant daughter, Rebecca, prepare for the ordeal of childbirth.

ONCE IN ST. OLAF   Airdates: 9/29/90, 12/22/90, 8/03/91.

Guest Cast: Don Ameche (Brother Martin), Scott Bryce (Dr. Warren), Michael Goldfinger (Attendant), Tom Henschel (Dr. Bob), Alicia Brandt (Dr. Tess), William Bumiller (Man).

Rose, who was adopted, has a surprise meeting with her natural father, who is now a monk.

IF AT LAST YOU DO SUCCEED   Airdates: 10/06/90, 1/26/91.
Guest Cast: Herbert Edelman (Stanley Zbornak).
After years of failed deals, Stan suddenly succeeds in business, and Dorothy finds herself attracted to him once again.

SNAP OUT OF IT   Airdates: 10/13/90, 12/29/90, 8/17/91.
Guest Cast: Martin Mull (Jimmy), Danny Breen (Emcee), Lenore Woodward (Mrs. Taylor).
Dorothy tries to help a reclusive man leave his apartment and rediscover the world.

WHAM BAM THANK YOU, MAMMY   Airdates: 10/20/90, 6/22/91.
Guest Cast: Ruby Dee (Mammy Watkins), Peggy Rea (Mrs. Contini), Richard McKenzie (Jack).
Blanche is shocked to learn that her father had an affair with her nanny.

FEELINGS   Airdates: 10/27/90, 4/20/91, 8/24/91.
Guest Cast: George Wyner (Dr. Norgan), Robert Costanzo (Coach Odlivak), Frank Hamilton (Father O'Mara), Christopher Daniel Barnes (Kevin).
Dorothy has to resist increasing pressure to pass a sports star who is ignoring his studies. Meanwhile, Rose suspects that her dentist took advantage of her while she was under anesthesia.

ZBORN AGAIN   Airdates: 11/03/90, 5/11/91, 8/31/91.
Guest Cast: Herbert Edelman (Stanley Zbornak), Siobhan Fallon (Abby), Dion Anderson (Mr. Percy), Stan Roth (Cop).
Stan pursues Dorothy, and she can't decide if she wants him to stop or not.

HOW DO YOU SOLVE A PROBLEM LIKE SOPHIA?   Airdates: 11/10/90, 3/30/91, 8/10/91.
Guest Cast: Kathleen Freeman (Mother Superior), Paul Willson (Arthur Nivingston), Lela Ivey (Sister Claire), Lyne Marie Stewart (Sister Anne).
Grief stricken after her favorite nun dies, Sophia decides to enter a convent.

MRS. GEORGE DEVEREAUX   Airdates: 11/17/90, 3/16/91, 8/10/91.
Guest Cast: George Grizzard (George Devereaux), Sonny Bono (Himself), Lyle Waggoner (Himself), Todd Jeffries (Policeman), Brad Kepnick (Maitre D').
Blanche sees the ghost of George, her husband, who has been dead for 9 years. Meanwhile, Dorothy is involved in a love triangle with Lyle Waggoner and Sonny Bono.

GIRLS JUST WANNA HAVE FUN BEFORE THEY DIE   Airdates: 11/24/90, 7/27/91.
Guest Cast: Cesar Romero (Tony), Harold Gould (Miles Webber).
Determined to have at least one last fling, Sophia does her best to seduce her newest suitor.

STAND BY YOUR MAN   Airdates: 12/01/90, 4/13/91.
Guest Cast: Hugh Farrington (Ted), Tom Nibley (Librarian), Andy Goldberg (House Boy).
Blanche gets a surprise when she decides to end an affair with a physically disabled man.

EBBTIDE'S REVENGE   Airdates: 12/15/90, 6/01/91.
Guest Cast: Brenda Vaccaro (Angela), Earl Boen (Father Salerno).
Dorothy's brother dies, and she must force his widow and Sophia to put aside a long-running rivalry.

BLOOM IS OFF THE ROSE, THE   Airdates: 1/05/91, 5/25/91.
Guest Cast: Harold Gould (Miles Webber), Mitchell Ryan (Rex), Don Mirault (Flight Instructor).
Rose's longtime relationship with Miles suffers when she keeps comparing him to her late husband. Meanwhile, Dorothy tries to make Blanche realize that her latest boyfriend is treating her unfairly.

SISTER OF THE BRIDE   Airdates: 1/12/91, 7/06/91.
Guest Cast: Monte Markham (Clayton), Michael Ayr (Doug), Lou Cutell (Irving), Mimi Cozzens (Susan Dodd).
Blanche is shocked to learn that her brother announces plans to marry another man.

MILES TO GO   Airdates: 1/19/91, 8/31/91.
Guest Cast: Harold Gould (Miles Webber), Mary Gillis (Gladys).
Miles reveals an amazing secret. Instead of being a college professor as he has claimed, he is really an ex-accountant for the mob, and is hiding for his life.

THERE GOES THE BRIDE—PART 1
Airdates: 2/02/91, 5/18/91.

Guest Cast: Herbert Edelman (Stanley Zbornak), Jack Yates (Cop), Toni Sawyer (Lois).

Stanley proposes to Dorothy, and she thinks it over for quite some time before finally accepting. Sophia violently opposes her making the same mistake twice and threatens never to speak to her again.

THERE GOES THE BRIDE—PART 2
Airdates: 2/09/91, 5/18/91.

Guest Cast: Herbert Edelman (Stanley Zbornak), Raye Birk (The Caterer), Meg Wyllie (Myra), Jack Blessing (Father Munroe), Marvin Mitchelson (Himself), Milt Oberman (Erroll), Cleto Augusto (Photographer), Debbie Reynolds (Truby).

With Dorothy planning to marry Stanley, the ladies look for a new roommate.

OLDER AND WISER   Airdates: 2/16/91, 6/15/91.

Guest Cast: Don Lake (Mr. Porter), Julius Harris (Mr. Lewis), Carol Bruce (Lucille), Bill Wiley (Smokey), Ellen Albertini Dow (Sarah).

Sophia gets a job as the recreation director in a retirement home but begins to push the residents too hard.

MELODRAMA   Airdates: 2/16/91, 6/29/91.

Guest Cast: Alan King (Mel Bushman), Tommy Hinkley (Andy), Jonathan Schmock (The Robber), Phil Forman (Bill).

Blanche decides she wants a commitment from her sometimes boyfriend, Mel Bushman.

EVEN GRANDMAS GET THE BLUES
Airdates: 3/02/91, 7/20/91.

Guest Cast: Debra Engle (Rebecca), Allison Robinson (Actress), Jonathan Schmock (The Director), Alan Rachins (Jason).

Feeling old, Blanche tries to convince her boyfriend that her grandchild is actually her child.

WITNESS   Airdates: 3/09/91, 6/08/91, 9/07/91.

Guest Cast: Harold Gould (Miles Webber), Barney Martin (Karl), Beth Grant (Louise), Marla Adams (Woman #1), Gloria Dorson (Mrs. Ward), Elise Ogden (Woman #2), Kristy McNichol (Barbara Weston).

Miles, who has been hiding in the Federal Witness Protection Program, decides to risk everything to be with Rose.

WHAT A DIFFERENCE A DATE MAKES
Airdates: 3/23/91, 8/17/91.

Guest Cast: Hal Linden (John), Sid Melton (Don the Fool), Nick Jameson (The Minstrel).

When Dorothy's high school boyfriend visits, Sophia is forced to confess that she kept the two apart for the prom.

LOVE FOR SALE   Airdates: 4/06/91, 9/07/91.

Guest Cast: Herbert Edelman (Stanley Zbornak), Bill Dana (Uncle Angelo), Lou Felder (Terry), Tom Seidman (Man).

Hoping to win her back, Stanley buys a date with Dorothy at a charity auction.

NEVER YELL FIRE IN A CROWDED RETIREMENT HOME   Airdates (1-hour format): 4/27/91, 9/14/91.

Guest Cast: Stanley Kamel (Herb), Richard Riehle (Detective Parres), Jeffrey Tambor, Herbert Edelman, McLean Stevenson, Tony Jay, Richard Herd.

When fire investigators name Sophia in a fire years ago at the retirement home, the ladies look back at the events that have followed since Sophia first moved in with them.

HENNY PENNY—STRAIGHT NO CHASER
Airdates: 5/04/91, 8/24/91.

Guest Cast: George Hearn (Frank Nann), David Jay Willis (Delivery Boy).

Dorothy somehow convinces Blanche and Rose to appear in an elementary school play.

1991–92 season

HEY, LOOK ME OVER   Airdates: 9/21/91, 12/21/91, 6/20/92.

Guest Cast: None.

When Rose has the film in an old camera developed, she is shocked to find a picture of her now deceased husband in bed with Blanche.

CASE OF THE LIBERTINE BELLE, THE
Airdates: 9/28/91, 12/28/91.

Guest Cast: Todd Susman (Marlowe), Tony Plana (Alvarez), Richard Roat (Kendall), Claudette Sutherland (Posey), Nicholas Kepros (Maitre D'), Zach Grenier (Vaczy), Leland Orser (Waiter), Gloria Cromwell (Gloria), Tim Haldeman (Man), Margery Nelson (Woman).

When the ladies attend a murder mystery weekend, the fun ends when Blanche is blamed for a real murder.

BEAUTY AND THE BEAST   Airdates: 10/05/91, 11/30/91, 7/04/92.

Guest Cast: Alisan Porter (Melissa), Edie McClurg (Nurse DeFarge), Barbara Alyn Woods (Woman), Robert Gould (Stage Manager).

Dorothy hires a nurse to look after Sophia after she sprains her ankles, and Sophia enjoys the attention so much she continues to feign injury. Meanwhile, Blanche pushes her niece into a beauty contest despite the girl's wishes.

THAT'S FOR ME TO KNOW   Airdates: 10/12/91, 12/28/91.

Guest Cast: Richard Stahl (Don).

Dorothy is shocked to learn that Sophia may have been married before the marriage to her father.

WHERE'S CHARLIE?   Airdates: 10/19/91, 3/28/92.

Guest Cast: Harold Gould (Miles Webber), Tim Thomerson (Stevie).

Rose becomes convinced that her dead husband, Charlie, is trying to contact her from beyond the grave.

MOTHER LOAD   Airdates: 10/26/91, 2/01/92, 7/11/92.

Guest Cast: Herbert Edelman (Stan Zbornak), Peter Graves (Jerry Scott), Meg Wyllie (Mrs. Scott), Steve Landesberg (Dr. Halperin).

Stan's therapist surprises everyone with the claim that Stan secretly is obsessed with Sophia. While Dorothy, Stan, and Sophia try to sort this out, Blanche ends up on the wrong end of a very protective mother.

DATELINE MIAMI   Airdates: 11/02/91, 1/18/92.

Guest Cast: Pat Harrington (John), Fred Willard (Bob), Lenny Wolpe (Arnie), Jesse Dabson (Myron), Lyn Greene (Young Dorothy), Richard Tanner (Young Stan), Margaret Reed (Pregnant Woman), May Quigley (Woman), Stan Roth (Policeman), Nick Ullett (Waiter).

The ladies look back at some of the worst dates they have had over the years.

MONKEY SHOW, THE—PART 1 & 2

Airdates (1-hour format): 11/09/91, 6/06/92.

Guest Cast: Herbert Edelman (Stan Zbornak), Bill Dana (Uncle Angelo), Dena Dietrich (Gloria), Steve Landesberg (Dr. Halperin), Dinah Manoff (Carol Weston), Ed Hooks (Stage Manager), Jonathan Schmock (Cop #1), Richard Reicheg (Man), Kay St. Germain (Woman), Matthew Saks (Cop #2), Don Seigel (Davey Cricket), Bryan Norcross (Himself).

While the ladies wait for the predicted arrival of a hurricane, Dorothy tries to help Stan get used to the idea of not seeing her again. He copes by having an affair with her sister, Gloria, who is visiting.

Production Note:

- The hurricane theme from this episode was carried over into Disney's other Saturday night series aired that night, with footage of a weather forecaster "reporting" on the storm's progress between episodes.

ROSE LOVES MILES   Airdates: 11/16/91, 3/21/92, 7/18/92.

Guest Cast: Harold Gould (Miles Webber), Bill Dana (Uncle Angelo), John P. Connolly (Mort), Harvey Vernon (Barry), Joe Mays (Maitre d'), David Pressman (Waiter), Phil Leeds (Guido).

When Dorothy takes a vacation, she leaves Blanche to keep an eye on Sophia, never thinking the result could be her mother taking a trip to Sicily.

ROOM SEVEN   Airdates: 11/23/91, 3/14/92, 7/18/92.

Guest Cast: Sid Melton (Sal), Roy Brocksmith (William), Gibby Brand (Man), Don Stark (Sheriff).

Blanche takes one last trip back to the family plantation before developers tear it down. Once there, she handcuffs herself inside, hoping to save the place.

FROM HERE TO THE PHARMACY

Airdates: 12/07/91, 4/04/92.

Guest Cast: Bruce Kirby (Bill), Ed Call (Security Guard), Sergia Simone (Woman).

A soldier returning from the Gulf War calls Blanche hoping to start where they left off, but she can't remember the man at all.

POPE'S RING, THE   Airdates: 12/14/91, 4/11/92.

Guest Cast: Harold Gould (Miles Webber), Steven Gilborn (Priest), Fred McCarren (Detective), Gene Greytak (The Pope).

Sophia shocks everyone by stealing the Pope's ring and refusing to give it back unless he personally blesses a sick friend.

OLD BOYFRIENDS   Airdates: 1/04/92, 4/18/92.

Guest Cast: Betty Garrett (Sarah), Ken Berry (Thor), Louis Guss (Marvin).

Sophia's new boyfriend insists that his sister go on every date. When Sophia complains, she is amazed to learn that the "sister" is really his wife.

GOODBYE, MR. GORDON   Airdates: 1/11/92, 5/23/92.

Guest Cast: James T. Callahan (Malcolm Gordon), Jack Bannon (Chuck), Phil Proctor (Ron), Jana Arnold (Pat), Kent Zbornak (Kent).

Dorothy's favorite high school teacher visits, but when he steals one of her stories and has it published as his own, she is forced to look at their friendship in a new light.

COMMITMENTS, THE   Airdates: 1/25/92, 6/13/92.

Guest Cast: Ken Howard (Jerry), Terry Kiser (Don), Biff Yeager (Bellboy).

Dorothy and Blanche decide to switch dates for a night, with the predictable result being that they finally realize they would have been better off staying with their original plans.

QUESTIONS AND ANSWERS   Airdates: 2/08/92, 5/16/92.

Guest Cast: Derek McGrath (Coordinator), Bill Erwin (Mr. Hubbard), Camila Ashland (Mrs. Hubbard), Merv Griffin (Himself), Alex Trebek (Himself), Johnny Gilbert (Himself), Raymond Forchion (Professor Bradley), David Leisure (Charlie Dietz).

When she hears that the game show *Jeopardy* will be taping in Miami, Dorothy pulls out all the stops to win a place as a contestant.

EBBTIDE IV: THE WRATH OF STAN   Airdates: 2/15/92, 5/30/92.

Guest Cast: Herbert Edelman (Stan Zbornak), Bill Dana (Uncle Angelo), Lane Davies (Peterson), Jackie Swanson (Tracy), Art Metrano (Judge), David Doty (Police Officer).

Dorothy and Stan are found guilty of being slumlords and are ordered to live in a decrepit building until they repair it.

JOURNEY TO THE CENTER OF ATTENTION   Airdates: 2/22/92, 5/30/92.

Guest Cast: Jane Dulo (Myrtle), Ann Nelson (Eva), Don Mirault (Ron), Warren Munson (Frank), Kevin Brief (Roger), Gregory White (Bartender).

Blanche takes Dorothy to her favorite bar to cheer her up, never thinking that Dorothy would become more popular than she.

MIDWINTER'S NIGHT DREAM, A—PARTS 1 & 2   Airdates [1-hour format]: 2/29/92, 8/15/92.

Guest Cast: Harold Gould (Miles Webber), Hank Brandt (Brent), Doug Ballard (Policeman), Marius Weyers (Derek), Neal Lerner (Rabbi), Tony Segreto (Himself), Kristy McNichol (Barbara Weston), Dinah Manoff (Carol Weston).

Sophia announces that she must perform three strange tasks before midnight or an ancient curse will doom Dorothy. Meanwhile, Dorothy and Miles find themselves strongly attracted to each other.

ROSE: PORTRAIT OF A WOMAN   Airdates: 3/07/92, 6/27/92.

Guest Cast: Harold Gould (Miles Webber), Tom Villard (Randy), Keone Young (Mr. Tanaka), Angelo Tiffe (Harry), Gloria Dorson (Lillian), Glen Vernon (Charles), Dylan Lawrence (Student), Robert Yacko (Don).

Blanche convinces Rose to give Miles a sexy picture of herself for a birthday gift. Dorothy gets an exciting job offer, only to find it's part of a tax scam.

HOME AGAIN ROSE—PART 1   Airdates: 4/25/92, 8/29/92.

Guest Cast: Jessica Lundy (Janet), Lou Wagner (Larry), Rudolph Willrich (Pete), Paul Solomon (Man), Mario Roccuzzo (Man #1), Kevin Cooney (Man #2), David Cromwell (Man #3), Robyn Faye Bookland (Sarah), Linden Chiles (Dr. Thompson), Audree Chapman (Nurse).

The fun of a high school reunion ends suddenly when Rose suffers a serious heart attack.

HOME AGAIN ROSE—PART 2   Airdates: 5/02/92, 9/05/92.

Guest Cast: Lee Garlington (Kristen), Jessica Lundy (Janet), Paul Collins (Dr. Shrewsbury), Audree Chapman (Nurse), Robyn Faye Bookland (Sarah).

Unable to be near Rose as she undergoes surgery, the ladies look back at their years together as they wait anxiously for word from the doctor.

ONE FLEW OUT OF THE CUCKOO'S NEST
Airdates (1-hour format): 5/09/92, 9/12/92.

Guest Cast: Leslie Nielsen (Lucas), Earl Boen (Reverend), Herbert Edelman (Stan Zbornak).

A practical joke takes an unexpected turn when Dorothy dates Blanche's uncle to make her jealous. Soon, to everyone's surprise, Dorothy and Lucas announce their engagement.

1992–93 season—*The Golden Palace*

Cast: Betty White (Rose Nylund), Rue McClanahan (Blanche Devereaux), Estelle Getty (Sophia Petrillo), Don Cheadle (Roland Wilson), Billy L. Sullivan (Oliver Webb), Cheech Marin (Chuy Castillos).

GOLDEN PALACE, THE (pilot)
Airdate: 9/18/92.

Guest Cast: Stephen James Carver (Brad), Lee Ryan (Man), Tom LaGrua (Thief).

Blanche, Rose, and Sophia pack up to move into their new investment, a Miami hotel, with grand plans to live a life of luxury. Once there, however, they discover that they have been cheated.

PROMOTIONAL CONSIDERATION
Airdate: 9/25/92.

Guest Cast: Bobcat Goldthwait (Gordon M. Cosay), Gibby Brand (Mr. McGowan).

The hotel's newest guest is in town to star on a local talk show. The topic? "Men Who Kill, and Are Set Free."

MILES, WE HARDLY KNEW YE
Airdate: 10/02/92.

Guest Cast: Harold Gould (Miles Webber), Mary Pat Gleason (Woman), Robert Beecher (Elderly Man), Marty Brinton (Man #1).

The ladies are shocked when old guest records show that Miles has been staying at the hotel for years, each time with a different woman.

ONE OLD LADY TO GO
Airdates: 10/09/92, 3/12/93.

Guest Cast: Anne Haney (Vivian), Margaret Cho (Fong), Michael Francis Clarke (Officer #1), Kelly Cinnante (Officer #2), Annie O'Donnell (Charlene).

The police are looking for a missing old lady and pick up Sophia by mistake.

EBBTIDE FOR THE DEFENSE
Airdates: 10/16/92, 6/11/93.

Guest Cast: Gregory Sierra (Rubin), Christopher Collins (Angel), Steve Hytner (Burrows).

A motorcycle gang arrives at the hotel, just as Roland learns that the hotel's insurance has been canceled. To make matters worse, the hotel is also hosting a convention of lawyers.

CAN'T STAND LOSING YOU
Airdates: 10/23/92, 6/18/93.

Guest Cast: Kim Fields (Trisha), Monte Landis (Mr. Ricchuitti), Monica Allison (Joanne), Sonya Hunt (Roy).

Blanche meddles in Roland's love life when she invites his ex-girlfriend for a visit.

SEEMS LIKE OLD TIMES—PART I
Airdate: 10/30/92.

Guest Cast: Beatrice Arthur (Dorothy), Bertila Damas (Beverly), Henry Polic II (Man #1), Kent Zbornak (Cab Driver).

Everyone is happy when Dorothy comes for a visit—until they learn that she plans to take Sophia home with her.

SEEMS LIKE OLD TIMES—PART II
Airdate: 11/06/92.

Guest Cast: Beatrice Arthur (Dorothy), Bertila Damas (Beverly), Carol Leifer (Meredith), Miguel Sandoval (Ramone), Jack Black (Cab Driver), Furley Lumpkin (Security Guard), Mark Kubr (Brick).

Unable to decide between staying with her friends or going with Dorothy, a very upset and confused Sophia runs away.

JUST A GIGOLO
Airdates: 11/13/92, 6/25/93.

Guest Cast: Barry Bostwick (Nick DeCarlo), Phil Proctor (Vincent Vale).

Blanche appears to be the only one who doesn't notice that her new boyfriend has an unhealthy interest in her money.

MARRIAGE ON THE ROCKS, WITH A TWIST
Airdates: 11/20/92, 7/02/93.

Guest Cast: Tim Conway (Milton), Harvey Korman (Bill), Bruce A. Young (George Wilson), Ja'net DuBois (Louise Wilson), Edward Penn (Man #1).

Two pranksters set Sophia up for a cruel practical joke. Meanwhile, Roland gets some unhappy news when he learns that his parents are planning to divorce.

CAMP TOWN RACES AREN'T NEARLY AS MUCH FUN AS THEY USED TO BE
Airdate: 12/04/92.

Guest Cast: Camille Ameen (Mrs. Smith #1), Arthur Eckdahl (Mr. Smith #2), Joyce

Meadows (Mrs. Pinkerman), Hoe Alaskey (Mr. Smith #3), Charles Napier (Mr. Smith #1).

When Blanche hangs a Confederate flag for the "Daughters of the Traditional South" banquet, a disgusted Roland walks out in protest.

It's Beginning to Look a Lot (Less) Like Christmas   Airdate: 12/18/92.

Guest Cast: Nick Toth (Dr. Norman Charles), Susan Norfleet (Wanda), Isaac Ocampo (Young Chuy).

Chuy's dislike of Christmas brings on a visit from the ghosts of Christmas Past, Present, and Future.

Rose and Fern   Airdates: 1/08/93, 7/09/93.

Guest Cast: Harold Gould (Miles), Hartley Silver (Man #1), Nanette Fabray (Fern).

Rose helps her new friend, Fern, plan her wedding—until she learns that the groom-to-be is her old boyfriend, Miles.

Runaways   Airdate: 1/15/93.

Guest Cast: Michael Fairman (Ernie Niles), Hansford Rowe (Mr. Seigel), Joely Fisher (Paula Webb), Charles Bouvier (Mr. Fisk), Alexander Folk (The Cop), David Jay Willis (Mr. Wormer), Reno Goodale (Mr. Frenchie).

Feeling unwanted, Sophia and Oliver run away together, only to end up under arrest when they pick the wrong place to hide.

Heartbreak Hotel   Airdates: 1/29/93, 7/16/93.

Guest Cast: Dick Van Patten (Taylor Michaels), Pamela Dunlap (The Love Doctor).

Blanche and Rose wage an all-out war for the affections of a hotel guest.

Señor Stinky Learns Absolutely Nothing about Life   Airdate: 2/05/93.

Guest Cast: Ricardo Montalban (Lawrence Gentry), Stephen James Carver (Brad, the Pool Guy), Josef B. Cannon (Josef), David Rottman (David), Bryan Ivie (Bryan), Andrew Smith (Andrew).

Blanche can't understand why another hotel owner is spurning her romantic advances. Chuy, meanwhile, can't understand why no one wants him on the hotel volleyball team.

Say Goodbye, Rose   Airdates: 2/12/93, 4/23/93.

Guest Cast: Eddie Albert (Bill Douglas), Bill Engvall (Matthew Devereaux), George Burns (Himself).

Rose falls in love with a hotel guest who reminds her of her late husband, but she is crushed when he checks out.

You've Lost That Livin' Feeling   Airdates: 2/19/93, 7/30/93.

Guest Cast: Bill Morey (Mr. Mitchelson), Eric Christmas (Mr. Davenport), Stephen Root (Mr. Tucker), Jeanne Mori (Marion Kim).

The girls get a restaurant critic who had previously panned Chuy's cooking to eat at the hotel again, but the man dies after the first course.

New Leash on Life, A   Airdate: 4/02/93.

Guest Cast: Ken Kercheval (Charlie Sardisco), Ja'net DuBois (Louise Wilson), Daryl Roach (Man #1).

Rose tries to save a greyhound from destruction after it loses one race too many.

Pro and Concierge   Airdate: 4/09/93.

Guest Cast: Georgie Cranford (The Kid), Robert Rockwell (Mr. Cochran).

Roland is considering taking a job at another hotel, which leads to some unexpected hostility from Rose.

Tad   Airdate: 4/16/93.

Guest Cast: Ned Beatty (Tad), Patrick Culliton (The Taxi Driver).

The arrival of Blanche's older mentally retarded brother, Tad, is a surprise to everyone, for Blanche has never mentioned his existence to anyone.

One Angry Stan   Airdates: 4/30/93, 8/06/93.

Guest Cast: Herbert Edelman (Stan Zbornak), Earl Boen (The Priest), Abraham Alvarez (Herb Jenkins), Jennifer Barlow (Bambi), Catherine MacNeal (Kimberle), Tony Pope (Announcer).

Blanche and Rose have to find a way to tell Sophia that Stan has died, but then everyone finds out he was pulling an elaborate tax scam and is very much still alive.

Sex, Lies & Tortillas   Airdate: 5/07/93.

Guest Cast: Brooke Theiss (Charlene), Adam Bisek (Benson), Robert Cavanaugh (Rick), Micah Dyer (Kid #1), Jep Hill (Kid #2).

Rose's granddaughter arrives for a visit and announces that she wants to share a room with her boyfriend. Meanwhile, Chuy has his heart set on making the biggest burrito in the world.

CHICKEN AND THE EGG, THE Airdates: 3/05/93, 5/09/93, 7/23/93.

Guest Cast: Dick Gautier (Bobby Lee), Amzie Strickland (Sylvia), Reno Goodale (Parking Valet), Cynthia Frost (Woman #1), Debra Engle (Rebecca).

Blanche thinks that she has met the man of her dreams until he tells her he wants to have children.

Empty Nest

With *The Golden Girls* soaring to success, it was inevitable that Disney would again turn to Witt-Thomas-Harris to repeat the magic. The veteran producers quickly came up with *Empty Nest*, a sitcom featuring a Miami doctor whose two daughters move back home after his wife dies.

Each of the episodes is described below in airdate order, divided by season.

1988–89 season

Series Cast: Richard Mulligan (Dr. Harry Weston), Kristy McNichol (Barbara Weston, 1988–93), Dinah Manoff (Carol Weston), David Leisure (Charley Deitz), Park Overall (Laverne Todd), Paul Provenza (Patrick Arcola, 1992–93), Lisa Rieffel (Emily Weston, 1992–93), Marsha Warfield (Dr. Maxine Douglas, 1993–94), Estelle Getty (Sophia Petrillo, 1993–94).

EMPTY NEST (pilot) Airdates: 10/08/88, 12/24/88.

Guest Cast: Grace Zabriskie (Eva), Robin Pearson Rose (Mrs. Fogal), Victor DiMattia (Rocco).

Harry has dinner every Friday with Eva Barrett, a co-worker. He thinks they are just friends, but she thinks they're dating and proposes to him.

CHECK ISN'T IN THE MAIL, THE Airdates: 10/22/88, 12/31/88.

Guest Cast: Adrian Zmed (Gary), Leo Geter (Dr. Ross), Ann Ryerson (Mrs. Bridges), Craig Richard Nelson (The Waiter).

Carol gets a call from her ex-husband and gets excited about the possibility of getting together again.

BARBARA GETS SHOT Airdates: 10/29/88, 4/22/89.

Guest Cast: Thom Sharp (Dr. Mitch Helperin), Londsay Parker (Jennifer), Mark Schiff (The Anesthesiologist), Ruth Silveira (The Nurse), Richard Fancy (The Lieutenant), Dean Fortunato (Cop), David Correia (Cop #2), John Demita (Cop #3), Jan Rabson (Cop #4).

When Barbara is shot in the butt, Harry takes it hard, for he is afraid of losing her.

FATAL ATTRACTION Airdates: 11/05/88, 4/08/89.

Guest Cast: Rue McClanahan (Blanche Devereaux).

While Blanche is busy trying to seduce Harry, Carol is becoming obsessed about her father's health.

FATHER OF THE BRIDE Airdates: 11/12/88, 3/11/89.

Guest Cast: Sam McMurray (Brent Wolcott).

Harry fixes Barbara up with an eligible surgeon and the two are soon engaged.

HARRY'S VACATION Airdates: 11/19/88, 4/29/89.

Guest Cast: Marcia Rodd (The Woman), Tommy Hinkley (The Bartender), Lela Ivey (Debbie), Abdul Salaam El Razzac (The Piano Player), Joe Hart (The Man).

Barbara and Carol think Harry's been working too hard since Libby died, so they buy him a vacation trip.

TINKERS TO EVERS TO TUCSON Airdates: 11/26/88, 5/6/89.

Guest Cast: Jason Bernard (Mr. Noack), Brandon Adams (Peter), Eva Charney (Michelle).

Laverne quits to be with her baseball player husband, Nick, who is being sent to Tucson. Harry makes a bet with Nick's manager that if Nick hits a home run, he can stay in Miami.

WHAT'S A FATHER TO DO? Airdates: 12/03/88, 5/27/89.

Guest Cast: Raye Birk (Albert), Tim Haldeman (The Waiter), Xavier Garcia (Esteban), Grace Albertson (The Woman).

Harry accidentally agrees to escort both daughters to two different social events, unaware that they are at the same time.

HARRY'S FRIEND Airdates: 12/10/88, 6/03/89.

Guest Cast: Donnelly Rhodes (Leonard), Edan Gross, (Jeffrey Millstein), Diane Racine (Mother), Claude Knobler (Rick).

Harry's old pal, Leonard Wilcox, moves to Miami and the two men start spending lots of time together. Harry then learns that Leonard is dating Carol and wants to end the relationship.

LIBBY'S GIFT   Airdates: 12/17/88, 6/10/89.
Guest Cast: William Gallo (The Delivery Man), Katie V. O'Neill (Katie), Lee Wilkoff (The Electrician), Estelle Getty (Sophia Petrillo).

Harry wants to spend his wedding anniversary alone, but then some delivery men bring an organ to the house.

CYRANO DE WESTON   Airdates: 12/31/88, 3/18/89.
Guest Cast: Christina Belford (Fran), Ed Hooks (Mailman).

Charley asks Harry for help in dating a classy lady, so Harry acts as Cyrano, writing love letters and mapping out dates, unaware that Charley's new lady is his own girlfriend, Fran.

FIRST TIME . . . AGAIN, THE   Airdates: 1/07/89, 5/20/89, 9/02/89.
Guest Cast: Barbara Babcock (Paula Conroy), Edan Gross (Jeffrey Millstein), Dierk Torsek (Mr. Millstein), Jarrett Lennon (Little Boy).

Harry is nervous about an offer to go on an overnight trip with his new girlfriend, for he's concerned about his sexual prowess.

FULL NEST   Airdates: 1/14/89, 6/17/89, 9/16/89.
Guest Cast: Brad Hall (Chuck).

Barbara moves back in with Harry and promptly drives him crazy. Carol tells them that they need someone to mediate their never-ending series of disputes and also moves back home.

HERE'S A HOWDY-DO   Airdates: 1/28/89, 6/24/89.
Guest Cast: Susan Anspach (Diane), Judith-Marie Bergan (Janet), Charles Levin (Stan), Jana Marie Hupp (Tracy), Nike Doukas (Liz), Whitby Hertford (Alec), Rand Stone (Jeff).

Harry starts to date a prominent child psychologist, but no one else likes her.

STRANGE BEDFELLOWS   Airdates: 2/04/89, 9/09/89, 12/30/89, 12/23/90.
Guest Cast: Betty White (Rose Nylund), Franc Luz (Eric), Edan Gross (Jeffrey Millstein), Tom Nibley (The Waiter).

Jeffrey Millstein, who is only 9, falls in love with Laverne and tries to woo her with flowers, songs, and candy.

TEARS OF A CLOWN   Airdates: 2/06/89, 7/22/89.
Guest Cast: Paul Sand (Poko), Ian Abercrombie (Captain Burke), Diana Webster (Mrs. Lundquist), Nancy Cartwright (Ann), Nicky Rose (Little Girl), Shaun Weiss (Little Boy).

Harry gets Carol a job in public relations, but she accidentally reveals that a clown is a psychiatric patient.

BLAME IT ON THE MOON   Airdates: 2/11/89, 8/05/89.
Guest Cast: Ray Buktenica (Alan), Greg Kean Williams (Brad), Katherine Cannon (Dr. Kenney), Michael Garfield (Doug).

A full moon brings romance: Harry starts dating another doctor, Barbara rekindles a flame with an ex-boyfriend, and Carol meets their neighbor, Alan, when Dreyfuss falls for his dog.

DUMPED   Airdates: 2/18/89, 7/01/89.
Guest Cast: Beatrice Arthur (Dorothy Zbornak), John Scott Clough (Jim Harker), Cynthia Steele (Mother #1), Mary Garripoli (Mother #2), Matthew Kenemore (Sick Kid), Christopher Chas Robin (Coughing Kid).

Barbara starts dating Dorothy's nephew, Jim Harker, but he dumps her. This is the first time Barbara has ever been dumped, and she takes it hard.

MORE THINGS CHANGE . . . , THE   Airdates: 2/25/89, 8/12/89.
Guest Cast: Linda Thorson (Janice Brattle), James Staley (Ted), Jane Galloway (Lucy), Tony Longo (Stan), Gregory Itzin (Frank).

When the medical building is sold, Harry learns that he must move his offices. He tries to reason with the new building manager, Janice Brattle, but she wants sex to see things his way.

MAN OF THE YEAR   Airdates: 3/04/89, 8/29/89.
Guest Cast: Harold Gould (Dr. Stanfield Weston), Peter Hobbs (Dr. Garrison), Kat Sawyer-Young (Woman Doctor), William Bogert (Doctor #1), Milt Oberman (Doctor #2), Marla Adams (Elna).

Harry is nominated as "Man of the Year" by his medical school, and his father, Stanfield Weston, comes to town to present the award.

MY SISTER, MY FRIEND   Airdates: 3/25/89, 8/26/89.

Guest Cast: Francis Guinan (Dr. Mitchell), Eva Charney (Miss Clark), Jake Jundef (The Boy).

Harry says that he will take the girls to Paris if they can stop arguing for a month.

LIFE IN THE DAY, A   Airdates: 4/01/89, 7/15/89.

Guest Cast: Richard Kind (Elton), Debra Engle (Mrs. Sexton), Bill O'Sullivan (Billy at 5), Michael Lee Owens (Billy at 7), Aeryk Egan (Billy at 11), Stephen Dorff (Billy at 14), Matthew Perry (Bill at 18).

Harry treats five boys, ranging from an infant to a teenager. Later, it's seen that they are all the same boy, William Sexton, who has come for his last visit at age 18.

1989–90 season

SETTLING   Airdates: 9/30/89, 12/23/89.

Guest Cast: Tom Isbell (Dan), Craig Stark (Jack).

Carol can't understand why her boyfriend would want to marry her, for he doesn't seem to be physically attracted to her.

HARRY SNUBS LAVERNE   Airdates: 10/14/89, 1/20/90.

Guest Cast: Dee Dee Rescher (Mrs. Swenson), Ariana Richards (Phoebe), Stuart Nisbet (The Emcee), Terres Unsoeld (Candy), Raffi Di Blasio (Casey), Udana Power (Mrs. Watson).

Harry gets so excited when he is elected to the Medical Center Hall of Fame that he forgets to mention Laverne in his acceptance speech.

ON THE INTERPRETATION OF DREAMS
Airdates: 10/21/89, 4/21/90.

Guest Cast: Ralph Seymour (Jimmy).

Harry keeps having the same strange dream, and Barbara and Carol volunteer to help him decide what it means.

BETWEEN A COP AND A HARD PLACE
Airdates: 10/28/89, 3/17/90.

Guest Cast: Joe Lindstrom (Joe), R.J. Williams (Timmy), Michael Bower (Josh).

Barbara must decide between loyalty to her partner or to her sister, who are dating each other, when she learns that he is cheating on Carol.

JUST YOU AND MY KID   Airdates: 11/04/89, 5/12/90.

Guest Cast: Robin Riker-Hasley (Janet Majors), Nicky Rose (Amanda), Justin Burnette (Eddie).

Harry is shocked when a patient asks him to be the father of her child.

RAMBO OF NEIMAN MARCUS   Airdates: 11/11/89, 5/26/90.

Guest Cast: Betty White (Rose Nylund), Luis Avalos (Lieutenant Valdez), Jordan Brady (The Delivery Boy).

Rose has an accident with Harry's car and insists on repairing it, no matter how long it takes.

YOU ARE 16 GOING ON 17 . . . AND I'M NOT   Airdates: 11/18/89, 6/02/90, 1/23/93.

Guest Cast: Brian Bloom (Jimmy), Jana Arnold (Lurlene).

When Carol sleeps with a much younger man, she becomes ashamed about it and starts to withdraw.

R.N. WHO CAME TO DINNER, THE
Airdates: 11/25/89, 6/09/90.

Guest Cast: Mayim Bialik (Laurie), Margaret Willock (Mrs. Kincaid), Chris Demetral (Billy).

Laverne moves in with the Westons after a fight with Nick and immediately starts to meddle in their lives.

GREEN EGGS AND HARRY   Airdates: 12/02/89, 7/07/90.

Guest Cast: Andrew Trebor (Andrew), Todd Cameron Brown (Terrence), Sydne Squire (Jane), G.F. Smith (Mr. Harrison), Mitchell Allen (Billy).

Harry can't bring himself to tell Carol that the children's book she just wrote is absolutely dreadful.

OVERDUE FOR A JOB   Airdates: 12/09/89, 6/16/90.

Guest Cast: Alan Rosenberg (Professor Brooks), Mary Catherine Wright (Miss Bingham), Catherine Parks (Mrs. Harte), Garette Ratliff (Demetrie).

Harry sees a pattern when Carol again quits another job after only a few days and urges her to determine why she keeps quitting.

CHRISTMAS STORY, A   Airdates: 12/16/89, 12/22/90.

Guest Cast: Ronnie Schell (Mr. Ritter), Lisa Borges (Caroler), Theresa Ring (Caroler).

Just as the family is leaving for a long-awaited ski trip, Dreyfuss disappears.

CHANGE OF HEART, A   Airdates: 1/06/90, 8/25/90.

Guest Cast: Ray Abruzzo (Dr. Leonard), Bill Cort (Dr. Bonham), Annie Barker (Jody), Audree Chapman (Nurse).

Harry overworks himself and ignores his doctor's orders to slow down.

HARRY'S CHOICE   Airdates: 1/13/90, 6/30/90.

Guest Cast: Kathleen Noone (Cookie).

When Barbara quits her job on the police force to sell real estate, Harry is thrilled—at first.

COMPLAININ' IN THE RAIN   Airdates: 1/27/90, 8/04/90.

Guest Cast: Christopher Rich (John), Jack Blessing (Evan Phillips), William Edward Phipps (Otto), Thomas Knickerbocker (Man on Phone), Jayson Kane (Secret Service Agent).

Rain spoils Carol's big picnic and Barbara decides to spend the time with her sister to get to know her better.

M.D. P.O.V.   Airdates: 2/03/90, 7/21/90.

Guest Cast: Debra Engle (Alexandra Hudson), Beth Grant (Helen), Steve Kahan (Daniel), Matthew Brooks (Roy), Elise Ogden (Mother).

Laverne convinces Harry to let a television show chronicle his day, but he regrets it when the health of one of his patients begins to seriously decline.

EVERYTHING BUT LOVE   Airdates: 2/10/90, 7/14/90.

Guest Cast: Cynthia Stevenson (Amy), Jana Arnold (Lurlene), Wayne C. Dvorak (Waiter), Adam Wylie (Boy).

Love is in the air when Charley meets Harry's young niece, Amy. However, the eternal playboy is unprepared for the response when he tells Amy that he loves her.

TIMING   Airdates: 2/12/90, 9/15/90.

Guest Cast: Barbara Babcock (Paula), John Mansfield (Tom), Michael Bower (Josh).

After Harry has a few dates with the same woman, he wants a serious relationship with her.

IT HAPPENED TWO NIGHTS; FOUR COSTUME CHANGES   Airdates: 2/17/90, 7/28/90.

Guest Cast: Christopher McDonald (Nick Todd), Ron Orbach (The Waiter), Garett Lewis (Garett), Charles Walker (Man), Mark Allen Taylor (Other Man), Kevin Scannell (Steve Marlowe).

Laverne has a fight with her husband, Nick, and tries to make him jealous by claiming that she is having an affair with Harry.

LOVE IS BLIND   Airdates: 2/24/90, 9/01/90.

Guest Cast: Edan Gross (Jeffrey Millstein), Michael Sabatino (Alan), Stan Roth (Waiter).

Barbara and Carol both have difficulty in trying to act naturally with a blind date.

GOODBYE, MR. DIETZ   Airdates: 3/03/90, 8/11/90.

Guest Cast: William Edward Phipps (Otto), Jim Doughan (Man at Party), Diane Stilwell (Liza), Shawn Southwick (Jamie), Lance Wilson-White (Pool Man), Deas Turner (Ginny).

After Charley uses the Westons' house for a wild party, Harry throws him out with orders never to return again.

LESSONS   Airdates: 3/10/90, 8/18/90.

Guest Cast: Michael Stoyanov (Darrell), Paul Regina (Michael), David Dunard (Vice Principal), Katherine James (Teacher), Diana Barrows (Student #1), Christian Hoff (Student #2), Rif Hutton (Cop).

Barbara goes undercover to catch a high school computer thief, but ends up losing her heart in the process.

TAKE MY MOM, PLEASE   Airdates: 3/24/90, 6/23/90.

Guest Cast: Liz Sheridan (Elspeth), Jennifer Salt (Linda), Hayley Tyrie (Erica), Fran Ryan (Mrs. Kramer).

One of Harry's patients tries to play matchmaker between Harry and her mother.

DID YOU EVER SEE A DREAM DYING?   Airdates: 4/14/90, 8/22/92.

Guest Cast: Christopher McDonald (Nick Todd), Elizabeth Lambert (Waitress), Al Berry (Customer), Bunny Summers (Nana Feldman), David Jay Willis (Joey's Owner).

Harry helps Nick buy a bar, but when things go wrong, Laverne is quick to blame him for interferring.

STILL GROWING AFTER ALL THESE YEARS   Airdates: 4/28/90, 12/01/90.
Guest Cast: Edan Gross *(Jeffrey Millstein),* Freddie Dawson *(Waiter),* Lindsay Parker *(Girl),* Pat Crowley *(Claire).*

For some reason, Harry feels that something is wrong with the seemingly perfect relationship with his latest girlfriend.

1990–91 season

FLAW IS BORN, A   Airdates: 9/22/90, 12/29/90.
Guest Cast: Brynn Thayer *(Dr. Lydia Gant),* Stanley Kamel *(Monsieur Gerard),* Tim Dunigan *(John Taylor),* Charles Stransky *(Professor),* Mitchell Allen *(The Boy).*

Harry becomes depressed while dating a brain surgeon, for her career seems far more important than his.

HARRY'S EXCELLENT ADVENTURE Airdates: 9/29/90, 3/30/91.
Guest Cast: Earl Holliman *(Mike Bradovitch),* Earl Boen *(Lou),* Debi A. Monahan *(Gina),* Robert Lesser *(Russel),* Billy Cohen *(Stevie),* Fred Sadoff *(Mort).*

Harry gives in to a twinge of mid-life crisis and heads to Pamplona for the running of the bulls.

THERE'S NO ACCOUNTING   Airdates: 10/06/90, 3/02/91.
Guest Cast: John Terlesky *(Bucky Barnes),* Janet Carroll *(Leah),* Allison Mack *(Gloria).*

"Love is blind" when Carol is attracted to Barbara's boyfriend by the very qualities that upset Barbara and Harry realizes his attractive girlfriend is actually quite a bore.

BARBARA THE MOM   Airdates: 10/13/90, 5/25/91.
Guest Cast: Christopher Castile *(Larry),* Sumer Stamper *(Annette).*

Barbara decides to see if she has any maternal instincts by babysitting for a friend.

TORTOISE AND HARRY, THE   Airdates: 10/20/90, 4/20/91.
Guest Cast: Brandon Bluhm *(Joey),* Debra Mooney *(Mrs. Bierman),* Jaclyn Bernstein *(Amanda).*

When a young patient suffers from depression, Harry tries every trick he knows to cheer up the boy.

MAD ABOUT THE BOY   Airdates: 10/27/90, 6/08/91.
Guest Cast: Mary Catherine Wright *(Miss Bingham),* Robert Lesser *(Russell),* Gregory Paul Martin *(Ian),* Michael McKean *(Dennis).*

Carol's choice in men seems to have hit a new low when she falls in love with someone whose life ambition is to give away free samples of cheese.

HONEY, I SHRUNK LAVERNE   Airdates: 11/03/90, 3/30/91.
Guest Cast: Nana Visitor *(Dr. Dawn Phelps),* Mary Pat Gleason *(Nurse Bradford),* Art Metrano *(Art),* John Apicella *(John),* Ed Call *(Ed).*

Harry complains to Laverne that she is making too many decisions for him and she responds by quitting.

BOY NEXT DOOR, THE   Airdates: 11/10/90, 5/28/91, 1/09/93.
Guest Cast: Candy Hutson *(Cindy),* Gloria Dorson *(Mrs. Hill),* Ashley Bank *(Kid #1),* Michael Melby *(Kid #2).*

Charley and Carol both feel lonely at the same time, and despite their past battles, become lovers.

FAMILY AFFAIR, A   Airdates: 11/17/90, 6/15/90.
Guest Cast: Mitchell Laurance *(Scott),* Cecelia Riddett *(Mother).*

Harry becomes convinced that Barbara's new boyfriend is really married, but she refuses to listen to him.

SOMEONE TO WATCH OVER ME Airdates: 11/24/90, 7/20/91.
Guest Cast: Fred Applegate *(Mr. Patrick),* Eddie Bracken *(Eddie),* Dena Dietrich *(Ursula),* Robert Goodman *(Norman),* Brandon Adams *(Georgie),* Marti Muller *(Nurse),* Susan Krebs *(Norman's Mom).*

Charley feels lonely and takes unusual steps to ensure visitors during a hospital stay.

HARRY KNOWS BEST   Airdates: 12/08/90, 6/29/91.
Guest Cast: Mayim Bialik *(Laurie),* Judith Marie Bergan *(Paula),* Kat Sawyer-Young *(Woman),* Stan Roth *(Photographer).*

Everyone seems to want Harry's advice, and he starts to worry about the possibility he might be wrong.

WHENEVER I FEEL AFRAID   Airdates: 12/15/90, 7/13/91.
Guest Cast: Timothy Carhart (Billy), Aaron Lustig (Officer Hitner), Ben Ryan Ganger (Jimmy), Jay Goldenberg (Attendant), Robert Gould (Customer).
Laverne is mugged and Harry tries to help her overcome the fear that it might happen again.

SHOT IN THE DARK, A   Airdates: 1/05/91, 7/20/91.
Guest Cast: Paul Sand (Avery), Channing Chase (Emcee).
The Westons end up with a houseguest after Barbara accidentally shoots Carol's new boyfriend.

SUCKING UP IS HARD TO DO   Airdates: 1/19/91, 7/06/91.
Guest Cast: Rebecca Bush (Anne), Patricia Gaul (Mrs. Moses), Paul Eiding (Mr. Hartman), Judy Baldwin (Michelle), May Quigley (Woman #1), Shuko Akune (Secretary), Whitby Hertford (Timmy).
When Barbara tries to get a promotion, she decides to take Carol's advice and puts on an elaborate scheme to flatter her boss.

MAN WHO GOT AWAY, THE   Airdates: 1/26/91, 7/27/91.
Guest Cast: Craig Bierko (Fred), Jeff Doucette (Sam), Jana Arnold (Lurlene).
Barbara tries her best to get a man to ask her out, but none of her usual tricks seem to work this time.

MENTOR, THE   Airdates: 2/02/91, 7/27/91.
Guest Cast: Danny Thomas (Dr. Leo Brewster), Harvey Jason (Dr. Wakefield), Elise Ogden (Mrs. Lasko).
Harry is thrilled when his mentor returns to town, but soon must face the sad task of informing the older doctor that it is time to retire.

Production Note:

• This was Danny Thomas's final television appearance, for he died shortly after filming this episode.

DOG WHO KNEW TOO MUCH, THE
Airdates: 2/09/91, 9/07/91.
Guest Cast: Tina Johnson (Mrs. Knox), John Christian Grass (Timmy).
Harry, Barbara, and Carol all use Dreyfuss as a sounding board while they try to come to better understand their feelings for each other.

GUESS WHO'S COMING TO DINNER
Airdates: 2/16/91, 9/14/91.
Guest Cast: Phil Hartman (Tim Cornell), Tracy Kolis (Paige), Kenneth Kimmins (Pete), Valorie Armstrong (Gayle), Lance Davis (Waiter), Jaclyn Bernstein (Nancy).
Harry's new girlfriend is only 28, and he arranges a dinner so the two families can get to know each other and get past the age difference.

ALL ABOUT HARRY   Airdates: 3/09/91, 8/03/91.
Guest Cast: Christine Ebersole (Laura).
Harry is shocked to learn that his newest girlfriend is a journalist and is writing about their love life.

DRIVE, HE SAID   Airdates: 3/16/91, 6/13/92.
Guest Cast: Eric Allan Kramer (Apartment Manager), Micole Mercurio (Saleswoman), Kenneth Danziger (Airline Clerk), Robert Gould (Party Guest), Don Sparks (Party Guest).
Harry and Charley set off on a frantic ride looking for a girlfriend Charley dropped 6 years ago.

LAST TEMPTATION OF LAVERNE, THE
Airdates: 3/23/91, 8/10/91.
Guest Cast: Henry Jones (Arnold), David Correia (Fire Marshall), Elise Ogden (Mrs. Lasko), Doris Roberts (Aunt Retha).
Laverne needs a loan, but her rich aunt will only give her the money if Laverne agrees to take the blame for an accident that was not her fault.

WHAT'S EATING YOU?   Airdates: 4/13/91, 8/17/91.
Guest Cast: Michael Goldfinger (Tony), Richard McKenzie (Mr. Davidson), Lynne Marie Stewart (Secretary).
Worried that Barbara may be getting an ulcer, Harry and Carol encourage her to vent her feelings instead of bottling them up.

CRUISE, THE   Airdates: 5/04/91, 8/24/91.
Guest Cast: Richard Burgi (Matthew), Peggy Pope (Myrna), Pearl Shear (Charlotte), Teresa Ganzel (Simba Katzman), David Jay Willis (M.C.).

A short Caribbean cruise seems too good to be true. For one thing, Carol gets a marriage proposal from the man of her dreams.

WAY WE ARE, THE   Airdates: 5/11/91, 8/31/91.
Guest Cast: Shirley Jones (Jean), Christopher Pettiet (Little Harry), Robin Lynn Heath (Little Jean), Tom Henschel (Bartender), Cory Danziger (Little Eric).

Harry looks forward to a reunion with his first sweetheart, until he learns that his competition from youth is also in town.

1991–92 season

50 MILLION MEN AND A BABY   Airdates: 9/21/91, 11/30/91, 5/23/92.
Guest Cast: Derek McGrath (Dr. Yardley), Ami Foster (Wanda), Denice Kumagai (Woman), Carol Rosenthal (Receptionist).

Laverne convinces Harry to help care for her niece's baby. Then Barbara announces that she wants to have a baby through artificial insemination.

ALMOST LIKE BEING IN LOVE   Airdates: 9/28/91, 12/21/91, 7/04/92.
Guest Cast: Angie Dickinson (Jackie Sheridan), Dabbs Greer (Mr. Sobel), Don Stark (Timmy).

Carol decides that she better get ready to move out as Harry is about to propose to his new girlfriend. Carol doesn't care much for the woman, but a confrontation is unnecessary when Harry's offer is rejected.

HER CHEATIN' HEART   Airdates: 10/05/91, 12/28/91.
Guest Cast: Christopher McDonald (Nick), Jesse Dabson (Tom), Robin Thomas (Will Comstick), John Towey (Sam Eckert), Gibby Brand (Table Guest), Frank Como (Ballplayer).

Laverne feels that there no longer is any romance in her marriage and is tempted to have an affair.

FOOD FOR THOUGHT   Airdates: 10/12/91, 1/18/92.
Guest Cast: Eddie Vélez (Joe), Don Lake (Moss), Glenn Shadix (Bud Larkin), Diane Racine (Woman), Michael Malota (Timmy).

Harry's refusal to give Carol more spending money makes her decide to finally earn her own money, so she buys a run-down catering business.

HARRY'S GOT A GUN   Airdates: 10/19/91, 6/20/92.
Guest Cast: Jon Polito (Slocum), Roger Hewlett (Cop).

After a robbery, Carol decides that they need guns for protection.

DREYFUSS AFFAIR, THE   Airdates: 10/26/91, 1/25/92.
Guest Cast: Jeffrey Tambor (Dr. Binder), Jack Bannon (Dr. Bolton), Ann Ryerson (Mrs. Peterson), Todd Jeffries (Chris), Allison Robinson (Susan), Andy Milder (Vet's Assistant).

Dreyfuss needs a delicate operation, but the vet is so upset about his pending divorce that he can't concentrate on the procedure.

COUNTRY WESTON   Airdates: 11/02/91, 5/09/92, 1/16/93.
Guest Cast: Garth Brooks (Himself), John Lage (Doug), Christine Cavanaugh (Kimberly), Rex Ryon (Rocky).

Barbara saves Garth Brooks from over-enthusiastic fans and is rewarded with a job as his chief of security.

WINDY   Airdates: 11/09/91, 6/06/92.
Guest Cast: Ann Guilbert (Mama Todd), Nancy Mette (Robin MacKenzie), Leland Orser (Don MacKenzie), Estelle Getty (Sophia Petrillo), Laura Waterbury (Verna), Bryan Norcross (Himself).

As a hurricane nears, Harry announces that he has bought his dream house. When the storm hits, everyone huddles together, and they realize how much the house means to them.

Production Note:

- The hurricane theme carried over into Disney's other Saturday night series aired that night.

TALK, TALK, TALK   Airdates: 11/16/91, 3/07/92.
Guest Cast: Nana Visitor (Margie), Debra Jo Rupp (Claire), Dee Dee Rescher (Dana), Ed "Kookie" Burns (M.C.), Nancy Marks (Renee), Kellye Worrel (Dolores), Robyn Faye Bookland (Jenny), Marsha Clark (Noah), Victoria Vitartas (Ed).

Harry becomes a celebrity when he saves a girl's life, but the fame gets to him and he realizes he is neglecting his patients.

LONELY ARE THE BRAVE Airdates: 11/23/91, 3/21/92.

Guest Cast: Tom La Grua (Rick), Gregory Itzin (Bill Wallace), Erika Flores (Luella), Mary Joan Negro (Dr. Walker), Jenny O'Hara (Mrs. Kravitz), David Doty (Man), Lou Cutell (Dr. Wilkens).

Carol is jealous that Barbara is a hero for saving a drowning man, unaware that Barbara feels very guilty about the whole affair.

IF YOU KNEW ANDY, LIKE I KNOW ANDY Airdates: 12/07/91, 4/04/91.

Guest Cast: Beau Gravitte (Dr. Andrew Elliot), Robert Hy Gorman (Daniel), Mindy Ann Martin (Diana).

Harry takes on a new associate and everyone likes him at first. As time goes on, however, he shows himself to be very self-centered and cold toward his patients.

MY NURSE IS BACK AND THERE'S GONNA BE TROUBLE . . . HEY-LA, HEY-LA Airdates: 12/14/91, 4/11/92.

Guest Cast: Barbara Billingsley (Winifred McConnell), Tony Longo (Male Passenger), Maureen Arthur (Nun), Tina Johnson (Rhoda), Biff Yeager (Businessman), Barbara Alyn Woods (Stewardess), Joe Shea (Stan), Patricia Everly (Mrs. Wasserman).

Harry's old nurse, Winifred, comes in to fill in for Laverne during her vacation. It's soon obvious that Winifred is trying to show up Laverne, for she wants her old job back.

SON OF A PREACHERMAN, THE Airdates: 1/04/92, 4/18/92.

Guest Cast: John McMartin (Reverend Chambers), Matthew Brooks (Alex), D. David Morin (Greg), Andrea Walters (Suzanne), Clarke Gordon (Judge).

Harry's friend asks him to show his 13-year-old son what it's like to be a doctor, but Harry worries that the boy is being pushed too hard.

EX-APPEAL Airdates: 1/11/92, 5/09/92.

Guest Cast: Kevin Kilner (Jerry Duvall).

When Carol starts dating Barbara's ex-boyfriend, a problem develops when he decides he wants to see Barbara again.

GREAT ESCAPE, THE Airdates: 1/18/92, 5/30/92.

Guest Cast: Richard Libertini (Lou Zinni), Jeff Doucette (Desk Clerk).

The girls are taken prisoner by an escaped convict and almost drive him crazy until he leaves in desperation.

MISMATCHMAKER, THE Airdates: 2/01/92, 4/25/92.

Guest Cast: Jerry Ohrbach (Arthur), Renee Taylor (Anne), Phil Leeds (Bunky), Patty McCormack (Fran), Valorie Armstrong (Louise), Phil Leeds (Bunky).

Harry's friend Arthur has separated from his wife so he moves in with the Westons.

RETURN OF AUNT SUSAN, THE Airdates: 2/08/92, 7/11/92.

Guest Cast: Lee Grant (Aunt Susan), Reva Rose (Nurse Matthews), Garret Pearson (Roberto).

The Westons' Aunt Susan returns after devoting her life to charity. Carol is in awe of her achievements and wants to go with Susan on her next crusade.

UNIMPORTANCE OF BEING CHARLEY, THE Airdates: 2/15/92, 6/27/92.

Guest Cast: Marian Mercer (Ursula Dietz), Richard Stahl (Fred Dietz), Gregg Daniel (Simms), Richard Reicheg (Captain).

Hoping to impress his parents, Charley tells them he is the captain of his ship.

SAYONARA Airdates: 2/22/92, 5/16/92.

Guest Cast: Charlotte Ross (Antoinette), Michele Abrams (Kelly), Omar Gooding (Jason), Maree Cheatham (Audrey), Vernée Watson-Johnson (Jill).

Nick Todd wants a divorce and Laverne tries to keep it a secret, but finally collapses in tears as Harry tries to comfort her.

DR. WESTON AND MR. HYDE Airdates: 2/29/92, 8/15/92.

Guest Cast: Betty White (Rose Nylund), Jay Johnson (George/Myra/Donald), Chuck McCann (Red), Tom La Grua (Rick), Dermot Crowley (Ogilvie), Karen Chase (Hoffman), Tony Segreto (Himself).

Harry's back goes out and his pain pills have a strong adverse reaction just as he has a meeting with the hospital board.

CHARLEY FOR PRESIDENT Airdates: 3/14/92, 8/29/92.

Guest Cast: Lane Davies (Eric Proust), Amzie Strickland (Mrs. Robinson), Frances Bay (Sylvia), Bill Wiley (Hetzel), Pat Crawford Brown (Melba), Elmarie Wendel (Agnes), Alex Nevil (Mailman).

Carol convinces Charley to run for president of the homeowners' association.

GOOD NEIGHBOR HARRY Airdates: 3/28/92, 7/18/92.

Guest Cast: Louise Lasser (Louise Polsky), Gregory Paul Martin (Ian), April Lindsey (Mrs. Wasserman).

Harry's new girlfriend becomes so dependent on him that she can't function without him.

FINAL ANALYSIS Airdates: 4/25/92, 9/05/92.

Guest Cast: Jack Carter (Grandfather), Barry Kivel (Dr. Grossman), Ann Nelson (Mrs. Grossman), Christopher Castile (Barry), Peggy Mannix (Didi), Michelle Watkins (Michelle), Kate Fuglei (Kate), Noreen Hennessy (Noreen), Lindsay Parker (Sally).

Carol feels guilty and abandoned when her therapist dies.

ROOTS Airdates: 5/02/92, 9/12/92.

Guest Cast: None.

Harry and the girls travel to England to accept a family heirloom.

1992–93 season

WHY DO FOOLS FALL IN LOVE? Airdates: 9/19/92, 12/26/92.

Guest Cast: Thom Sharp (Mr. Logan), Rider Strong (Philip Logan), Rhonda Aldrich (Jane).

Charley gets a death threat and Barbara agrees to act as his bodyguard.

TAKE MY GARAGE, PLEASE Airdates: 9/26/92, 11/28/92.

Guest Cast: Zachary Benjamin (Albert).

Carol announces that she is in love with Patrick Arcola, a would-be artist, and Harry is not pleased when they decide to move in together in the Weston garage.

R.N. ON THE REBOUND Airdates: 10/03/92, 1/16/93.

Guest Cast: David Gianopolous (Gibby), Matt McKenzie (Matt), Brady Bluhm (Matt).

Ever since her divorce, Laverne has spending been way too much time at the Westons' house, so Barbara fixes her up with a friend.

. . . OR FOREVER HOLD YOUR PEACE Airdates: 10/10/92, 3/06/93.

Guest Cast: Jerry Orbach (Arthur), Charlotte Booker (Karen), Cynthia Szigeti (Diana), Gregory Itzin (Judge Eckert).

Harry's friend falls in love with a woman he just met and announces plans to marry her. Harry tries to talk him into waiting until he knows her better, but then realizes he was wrong to meddle in the romance.

BOOMERANG AFFAIR, THE Airdates: 10/17/92, 4/03/93.

Guest Cast: Diana Muldaur (Sonya), Eric Allan Kramer (Sven), Paul B. Bryce (Brian Levant).

When Harry is dumped by his latest girlfriend, he wages a determined campaign to win her back.

CRUEL AND UNUSUAL PUNISHMENT Airdates: 10/24/92, 3/27/93.

Guest Cast: Perry Anzilotti (Mark Dossler), Tony Longo (Jake Carlson), Joshua Boyd (Steven), Richard Fancy (Congressman), Wendee Cole (Reporter #1), Charles Champion (Reporter #2), Michael Burger (TV Announcer).

Serving on jury duty makes Carol feel guilty about sending a man to prison, so she tries to atone by hiring an ex-convict.

IT'S NOT EASY BEING GREEN Airdates: 10/31/92, 6/12/93.

Guest Cast: Harvey Vernon (Virgil), Patrick Warburton (Cop), Shannon Cochran (Stacy), Jeremiah Birkett (Ruffian #1), Tim Griffin (Ruffian #2), Doren Fein (Brittany), Brady Bluhm (Little Boy), Zachary Benjamin (Little Kid), Nathan Watt (Caveboy), Stacy Chess (Little Girl), Elise Ogden (Judge), Richard Tanner (Man).

A series of misadventures befalls Carol and Patrick on Halloween, including a series of muggings.

DIRTY HARRY Airdates: 11/07/92, 1/30/93, 7/24/93.

Guest Cast: Geraldo Rivera (Himself), Danny Breen (Roger Maxwell), Christian Cousins (Larry Larson), Kimble Jemison (Scott), Michelle Watkins (Mrs. Larson).

Carol is picked to appear on the *Geraldo* talk show and convinces Harry to go with her.

TIMING IS EVERYTHING   Airdates: 11/14/92, 4/17/93.

Guest Cast: Katherine Gannon (Laura Kilmer), Louis Guss (Bellman), James Duane Polk (Delivery Man).

Harry and an old flame try to pick up where they left off 30 years ago, but they both come to realize too much time has passed by to start again.

THANKSGIVING AT THE WESTONS Airdates: 11/21/92, 7/03/93.

Guest Cast: Debi Monahan (Jody), Kristen Amber (Coreen), Jacqueline Alexander (Doreen).

As the Westons prepare for Thanksgiving dinner, they all look back at a dinner when the turkey caught fire.

BODY BEAUTIFUL, THE   Airdates: 12/05/92, 5/29/93.

Guest Cast: Kevin Scannell (Pete Stanley), Matt Levin (Pauley), Hector Elias (Inspector Lopez), Kevin Michaels (Jerome), Trish Ramish (Tracy).

Convinced that Patrick thinks she is too fat, Carol goes on a diet and exercise crusade.

OVERBOARD   Airdates: 12/12/92, 6/05/93.

Guest Cast: Robin Pearson Rose (Diane), Margaret Reed (Sister Sasha).

Charley joins a religious sect after suffering a near-death experience, only to learn that he is expected to give up sex.

EMILY   Airdates: 1/02/93, 4/24/93.

Guest Cast: Andrew Hill Newman (George), Gian-Carlo Scandiuzzi (Gianni), Richard Tanner (Male Singer).

Harry and Carol are surprised by the unexpected return of Harry's third daughter, Emily.

STING, THE   Airdates: 1/09/93, 6/19/93.

Guest Cast: Fred Applegate (McGraw), Dena Dietrich (Helen), Steven Flynn (Zack), Sam Zap (Floyd), Joseph Cousins (Little Boy), Stan Roth (Client).

Emily is stunned when the FBI asks for her help in arresting a diamond smuggler, because the smuggler is her boyfriend.

FRACAS IN VEGAS, THE   Airdates: 1/23/93, 6/19/93.

Guest Cast: Frances Bay (Agnes), Richard Stahl (Slim), Michael Warwick (Bill), Leah Lail (Melissa), Jimmy Lennon Jr. (Ring Announcer), Katy Bret (Woman), Joshua Boyd (Steven).

Charley wins tickets to a big prize fight and invites Harry along, but they end up in a rundown hotel and are robbed by two women they meet in a bar.

PARDON MY FLASHBACK   Airdates: 1/30/93, 6/23/93.

While Laverne tries to fix their cable television connection so they can watch the Super Bowl, the Westons look back at some of life's more unusual moments.

DOG DAY AFTERNOON   Airdate: 2/06/93.

Guest Cast: Debra Jo Rupp (Dr. Simmons), Richard Reicheg (Security Guard), Sid Melton (Man), Richard Karron (Representative).

Convinced that Dreyfuss has been avoiding her, Carol drags him off to an animal psychiatrist to see what is wrong.

MORE TO LOVE   Airdates: 2/13/93, 8/01/93.

Guest Cast: Bob Amaral (Danny), April Ortiz (Florence), Lisa Gorlitsky (Theresa), Robert Lesser (Dr. Perry Smith), Ellia English (Jennifer), Richard Tanner (Eddie).

Emily's date with an overweight man is ruined by his constant attempts to make himself the butt of jokes as a way of getting people to like him.

MY DAD, THE DOCTOR   Airdates: 2/20/93, 7/17/93.

Guest Cast: Robert Curtis-Brown (Dr. Dave Foley), Anita Barone (Cara), Michael Heintzman (Mr. McKeever), Taylor Fry (Little Girl), Don Gibb (Biker #1), Jaime Cardriche (Biker #2), Bill Reid (Biker #3), Jack Haley (Himself).

When Emily hurts her leg, she and her father have very different views on how to treat it.

LOVE AND MARRIAGE   Airdate: 2/27/93.

Guest Cast: David Rasche (Jack Trenton), Raye Birk (Judge Talmadge), Holly Fields (Little Carol), Candi Milo (Mrs. Ortiz), Teresa Ganzel (Sharon), Winston Rocha (Jorge), Jon Patrick Walker (Acid).

Carol's niece announces that she has dropped out of college to get married, and a depressed Carol can't decide if she wants to be in the wedding party or not.

ALL-AMERICAN BOY—NOT!, THE
Airdates: 3/20/93, 8/14/93.
Guest Cast: Adam LaVorgna (Rudy), David Correia (Arturo), Richard Gant (Sergeant Fletcher), Eric Christmas (Mr. Garrison), Liz Torres (Madame LePard), Alan Blumenfeld (Storekeeper), Michael French (Man).

Harry befriends a youngster at a street clinic, but the boy rewards his kindness by robbing the Westons.

TWO FOR THE ROAD   Airdates: 4/10/93, 9/04/93.
Guest Cast: Casey Sander (Patrolman), Vincent Ventresca (Cop).

Charley makes Carol think that Patrick is having an affair with Emily.

AUNT VERNE KNOWS BEST   Airdates: 5/01/93, 9/11/93.
Guest Cast: Joey Lawrence (Wade), Art Metrano (Elevator Repairman), Renee Humphrey (Kerry).

Laverne's nephew arrives in Miami for college and she doesn't know how to deal with her new houseguest.

MY MOTHER, MY SELF   Airdates: 5/08/93, 8/21/93.
Guest Cast: Marian Mercer (Ursula), Elise Ogden (Woman), Rockey Collins (Les).

When Charley learns that his parents are divorced, he starts thinking of Harry as a possible new father.

CHARLEY TO THE RESCUE   Airdates: 5/15/93, 9/11/93.
Guest Cast: Barbara Mandrell (Ellen), Tom Gallop (Alan Hardy), Fred Holliday (Club Host).

Charley surprises everyone when he comes to the aid of Emily, who is being harassed by an obnoxious comedian working on Charley's ship.

SURPRISE! SURPRISE!   Airdates: 5/22/93, 8/28/93.
Guest Cast: None.

Harry becomes convinced that everyone is planning a surprise party for his birthday.

1993–94 season

WHEN THE ROOSTER DIES   Airdates: 9/25/93, 12/04/93.
Guest Cast: Michael McGuire (Dr. Marty Fitzgerald), April Grace (Irene), Ruby Salazar (Pregnant Woman), Barbara Lux (Street Woman).

Harry has retired and sold his practice, and is ready for a long deserved vacation in Europe. Before he leaves, though, he finds himself working alongside Dr. Maxine Douglas, the perpetually overworked head of the inner city health clinic.

BYE-BYE, BABY . . . HELLO—PART I
Airdates: 10/02/93, 6/11/94.
Guest Cast: Paul Provenza (Patrick Arcola), Brian Reddy (Mr. Vogle), S. Marc Jordan (Mr. McCully), Kimberly Newberry (Female Patient), Ryan MacDonald (Mr. Jensen), Jake Price (Delivery Boy), Russ Fega (Arm Man), Julie Stein (Miss Hidalgo), Loni Anderson (Casey MacAfee).

Tired of Patrick's lack of responsibility, Carol tells him to move out. Not long after he leaves, she discovers that she is pregnant.

BYE-BYE, BABY . . . HELLO—PART II
Airdates: 10/09/93, 6/18/94.
Guest Cast: Paul Provenza (Patrick Arcola), Stephanie Dunnam (Diane), Courtney Peldon (Libby).

Patrick learns that he is going to be a father and offers to become more responsible, but Carol decides that she wants to raise the baby alone.

MAMA TODD, THE SEQUEL   Airdates: 10/16/93, 1/29/94.
Guest Cast: Ann Guilbert (Mama Todd), Trevor Goddard (Joe), Loni Anderson (Casey MacAfee).

Laverne's ex-mother-in-law arrives for a visit, unaware that Laverne and Nick are divorced.

MOM'S THE WORD   Airdates: 10/23/93, 3/12/94.
Guest Cast: Tony Carreiro (Mike), Stan Roth (Waiter), Debbie Gregory (Tracey).

Carol is worried about how her new boyfriend might react to the news that she is pregnant.

DIARY OF A MAD HOUSEWIFE　Airdates: 10/30/93, 3/19/94.
Guest Cast: Fred Stoller (Mr. Garrison), Marty Pollio (Mr. Finnegan).
Carol is depressed about her lack of maternal feelings, so Harry gives her a diary kept by her mother, Libby, just before Carol was born.

MOTHER DEAREST　Airdates: 11/06/93, 4/02/94.
Guest Cast: Marla Gibbs (Josephine Douglas), Annie Corley (Anita), Loni Anderson (Casey MacAfee).
Maxine's mother needs an operation or she will go blind, but she refuses to even consider the possibility.

NO VOLUNTEERS, PLEASE　Airdates: 11/13/93, 5/28/94.
Guest Cast: Kari Lizer (Doris), Peter Sands (Mr. Ellis), Mary Kane (Brenda).
Harry talks a friend into volunteering at the clinic, never dreaming of the problems that will result.

DAS BOOB　Airdates: 11/20/93, 6/04/94.
Guest Cast: None.
Chaos results when Harry and Charley set off for a sail in Harry's new boat.

GIRL WHO CRIED BABY, THE　Airdates: 11/27/93, 6/25/94.
Guest Cast: Jeanine Jackson (Rachelle), Jane Lynch (Tammy), David Cromwell (Dr. Rubenstein), Tom Nibley (Rachelle's Husband), J. David Krassner (Man).
After a series of false starts, Carol finally has real labor pains and her baby, Scotty, is born.

SUPERBABY　Airdate: 12/11/93, 7/02/94.
Guest Cast: Richard McKenzie (Rudnick), Geraldine Leer (Mrs. Stanford), Mark L. Taylor (Mr. Stanford), Harvey Vernon (Bundy).
Carol becomes convinced that she has brought the wrong baby home from the hospital. Surprisingly, she is right.

READ ALL ABOUT IT　Airdates 12/18/93.
Guest Cast: Megan Gallagher (Dr. Heather Cook), Eric Christmas (Mr. Garrison), Robert Costanzo (Mr. Millard), Jeannie Elias (Jane Walsh), Kimberly Cullum (Kid).
When Harry is misquoted in a newspaper story, it causes problems between him and his co-workers.

LOVE À LA MODE　Airdates: 1/08/94, 7/02/94.
Guest Cast: Marian Mercer (Ursula Dietz), Richard Stahl (Fred Dietz), Heidi Swedberg (Patty Olsen).
Charley announces that he is getting married, but when the engagement falls through, his parents show surprisingly little sympathy.

WHAT'S A MOTHER TO DO?　Airdates: 1/15/94, 7/23/94.
Guest Cast: Lisa Darr (Laurie), Anna Berger (Bella), Jack Kruschen (Heshy), Michael A. Nickles (Athlete), Rachael Fox (Mommy #1).
Carol drives the other mothers in her mother and child support group crazy by worrying about details like the chemical composition of the center's rug.

GESUNDHEIT　Airdate: 1/22/94.
Guest Cast: Bill Cobbs (Jerome), Irena Ward (Sandy), Jean Speegle Howard (Mildred), Gary Hudson (Drake).
When the baby starts sneezing, Carol becomes convinced that he is allergic to Dreyfuss.

UNDER THE GUN　Airdate: 1/29/94.
Guest Cast: John Reilly (Adam Blakely), Jonathan Carrasco (Oscar), Andrew Keegan (T.J.).
A boy carrying a gun for protection at school accidentally shoots Harry.

BROTHERLY SHOVE　Airdate: 2/05/94.
Guest Cast: Peter Scolari (Dieter Dietz), Philip Baker Hall (Jerod), Maureen Arthur (Mrs. Carlton), Dennis Bailey (Salesman).
Charley quits his job on the ship and goes to work at his brother's used car lot, but the job doesn't last long when his brother cheats him.

BALLAD OF SHADY PINES, THE　Airdates: 2/12/94, 8/13/94.
Guest Cast: Bill Dana (Nathan), Elmarie Wendel (Vivian), Ruth Engel (Sylvia), Phil Leeds (Milt), Sid Melton (Horace), Jean Sincere (Eileen), Paul B. Price (Plasterer), Lisa Robin Kelly (Jody).
When Sophia catches her boyfriend and Laverne together, she refuses to believe that he was the one making a pass.

HOG HEAVEN　Airdate: 3/05/94.
Guest Cast: Eric Allan Kramer (Sam), Don Gibb (Jake).

An old boyfriend's unexpected return has Laverne thinking about settling down again, but Harry is convinced that she would be better off without this particular roommate.

CHARLEY'S MILLIONS Airdates: 3/12/94, 9/10/94.

Guest Cast: Don Adams (Himself), Chuck McCann (Coach Biederbeck), Nita Talbot (Mrs. Koontz), Liz Sheridan (Mrs. Coover), Geraldine Leer (Bonnie), Paul B. Price (Mr. Gurman).

When a Belgian tourist dies and leaves her money to Charley, he invites all of his friends on a gala trip to New Orleans for Mardi Gras.

HALF THAT JAZZ Airdates: 4/09/94, 8/27/94.

Guest Cast: Eydie Gorme (Heckler), Steve Lawrence (Miles James), Mike Larsen (Stage Manager).

Harry tries to convince a jazz saxophonist to come out of retirement, but the man is an alcoholic and is afraid that he can't play while sober.

FOREIGN AFFAIR, A Airdate: 4/16/94.

Guest Cast: J.A. Preston (Roland), Marlon Archey (Frederick), Aixa Clemente (Dr. Baxter).

A foreign diplomat's marriage proposal has Maxine thinking about moving back to his native country.

LORDY, LORDY LANDLORDY Airdate: 4/23/94.

Guest Cast: Debra Jo Rupp (Danielle), Patricia Coleman (Mrs. Griffin), Jill Pierce (Woman), Garett Lewis (Stuart), Fred Applegate (Mr. Hackler).

When Laverne threatens a rent strike unless the landlord makes some improvements around the clinic, he responds by throwing them out.

DEVIL AND DR. WESTON, THE Airdate: 5/07/94.

Guest Cast: Audrey Meadows (Margaret Randall), Kari Lizer (Doris), Basil Langton (Edgar), Joy Claussen (Louise), John Petlock (George), Richard Tanner (Bartender).

A rich woman donates an X-ray machine to the clinic, but Harry soon learns she has her eyes on him in return.

ABSENCE MAKES THE NURSE GROW WEIRDER Airdates: 5/21/94, 8/20/94.

Guest Cast: Wendie Malick (Denise), Paul Willson (Dr. Barshilon), Molly Snee (Shea), Brittany Smith (Shanna).

Harry meets a nurse who is more interested in him than he is in her.

BEST FRIENDS Airdates: 5/21/94, 9/10/94.

Guest Cast: Morgan Fairchild (Zoe), Tracey Walter (Mr. Malloy), Richard Reicheg (Mr. Griswald), Paul B. Price (Waiter).

Carol is thrilled when Zoe, an old friend, returns to town, until Zoe starts dating Harry.

1994–95 season

LET'S GIVE THEM SOMETHING TO TALK ABOUT Airdate: 9/24/94.

Guest Cast: Todd Susman (Braxton), Grant Gelt (Timmy), Alton Butler (Phil), Caston Holmes (Scotty), Elizabeth Sandifer (Sparkle).

Carol's newest career attempt is as a newspaper reporter.

MRS. CLINTON COMES TO TOWN Airdate: 9/24/94.

Guest Cast: Ken Marshall (Agent #1), Kathe Mazur (Agent #2), Zsa Zsa Gabor (Herself), Gary Pagett (Guard #1), Caston Holmes (Scotty), Randy Polk (Mr. Funderburke).

Carol is determined to interview Hillary Clinton when the First Lady makes plans to visit the clinic.

JUST FOR LAUGHS Airdate: 10/01/94.

Guest Cast: Yeardley Smith (Sally), Bobcat Goldthwait (Bobcat), Jon Menick (Man #1), Adrian Ricard (Woman #1), Chip Lowell (Emcee), Jonathan Bourne (Stage Manager).

Charley's new act as a standup comic consists solely of insults aimed at Harry.

CHIP OFF THE OLD CHARLEY, A Airdate: 10/08/94.

Guest Cast: Christopher Daniel Barnes (Raymond), Sid Melton (Mr. Parker).

Carol and Sophia spot a musical genius on television who bears more than a passing resemblance to Charley, and they convince Charley he is the boy's father.

WOMAN WHO CAME TO DITHER, THE Airdate: 10/15/94.

Guest Cast: Kari Lizer (Doris), Ellen Albertini Dow (Mildred), Bibi Osterwald (Betty), John Apicella (Mr. Spaulding), Aaron Heyman (Mr. McCully), Charles C. Stevenson, Jr. (Fred), Mark Davenport (Delivery Man), Rodney Kageyama (Mr. Kobara), David Brisbin (Lempke).

Sophia doesn't like the new manager at the retirement home so she moves in with the Westons.

CAROL GETS A RAISE   Airdates: 10/22/94, 6/24/95.

Guest Cast: Todd Susman (Braxton), Nikki Tyler (Mother), Sheila Shaw (Mrs. Castillo), Carl Glissmeyer (Billy), Sydney DeBear (Leslie).

Carol tries to get a raise and ends up sleeping with her boss.

COURTSHIP OF CAROL'S FATHER, THE   Airdates: 12/03/94, 6/17/95.

Guest Cast: Carol Kane (Shelby), Christine Rose (Nan), Kevin Cooney (Leonard).

Carol meddles once again in Harry's love life and he ends up with two dates the same night.

TINKER GRANT, THE   Airdate: 12/03/94.

Guest Cast: Earl Boen (Withers), Vito Scotti (Mr. Tartaglia), Maria Pecci (Ana Maria), Addie Matthews (Mrs. Tartaglia), Michelle Beauchamp (Waitress).

Everyone at the clinic pulls out all the stops to impress a visiting official from a charitable foundation.

WOULD YOU BELIEVE . . .   Airdate: 12/17/94.

Guest Cast: Maureen Mueller (Rebecca), Sean Moran (Man).

Harry's interest in Charley's new friend almost ruins their friendship.

PARTLY CLOUDY WITH A CHANCE OF PAIN   Airdate: 12/17/94.

Guest Cast: Julius Carry (Bo), Jay Pennick (Doug), Cynthia Kania (Diner #1).

A television weatherman asks his viewers for help in getting a date with Maxine.

SINGLE WHITE MALE   Airdates: 1/07/95, 6/24/95.

Guest Cast: Douglas Sills (Hank), Gordon Jump (Bud), Barry Gordon (Earl), Lawrence LeJohn (Todd), David Shawn Michaels (Blond).

Charley is mortified to discover that his new housemate is gay.

DEAR AUNT MARTHA   Airdates: 1/14/95, 7/01/95.

Guest Cast: Pat Harrington (Mulvaney), D. David Morin (Kevin), Todd Susman (Braxton),

Mike Saccone (John), Andrew Philpot (Ron), Paul B. Price (Artiste), Sid Melton (Man).

Carol uses her new position as the newspaper's advice columnist to help find a new boyfriend.

GOODBYE CHARLEY   Airdate: 1/21/95.

Guest Cast: William Frankfather (Minister), Steve Gilborn (Funeral Director).

Carol tries to overcome Charley's fears that no one would miss him if he died by throwing a mock funeral for him.

FAMILY PRACTICE   Airdate: 1/28/95.

Guest Cast: Joanna Sanchez (Marta), Sabrina Wiener (Ana), Paul Langdon (Armando), Chris Taafe (Orderly), Melinda Simpson (Celina), Melissa Simpson (Gloria).

Maxine gets more than she bargained for when she agrees to care for a patient's four children.

GRANDMA, WHAT BIG EYES YOU HAVE   Airdate: 2/04/95.

Guest Cast: Leigh Taylor-Young (Gwen), Caston Holmes (Scotty), Guy Boyd (Al), Myra Turley (Arlene).

Harry is thrilled with his new girlfriend until he learns she is married.

FEELINGS, WHOA WHOA WHOA, FEELINGS . . .   Airdate: 2/25/95.

Guest Cast: Stephen Nichols (Matt), Caroline Aaron (Shannon), Rhonda Aldrich (Patty), Esther Scott (Security Guard), Aaron Heyman (Mr. McCully).

When a childhood friend of Laverne's arrives for a visit, he becomes embroiled in a love triangle with Laverne and Carol.

AND KEVIN MAKES THREE   Airdates: 3/04/95.

Guest Cast: D. David Morin (Kevin), Caston Holmes (Scotty), Carlos Lacamara (Ernesto), Teresa Velarde (Rosa), John Hamelin (Dark-Haired Man).

Carol feels jealous when Scotty seems to like her new boyfriend, Kevin, more than he likes her.

HARRY WESTON: MAN'S BEST FRIEND   Airdate: 3/18/95.

Guest Cast: Todd Susman (Braxton), Fred Sanders (Producer), Pat Musick (Angie), Jess Harnell (Vince), Brian Posehn (Painted Gut Guy), Donna Ponterotto (Brandy).

Charley's feelings get hurt when Carol's boss announces that Harry is his best friend.

EX-FILES, THE   Airdates: 3/18/95.

Guest Cast: D. David Morin (Kevin), Nancy Sorel (Julie), Beau Gravitte (Taggert), Mike Larsen (Pizza Guy), Victor Vitartas (Repo Man).

Carol feels threatened by her boyfriend's close ties to his ex-wife.

STAND BY YOUR MAN   Airdates: 3/25/95, 7/01/95.

Guest Cast: Stephen Nichols (Matt), Edie McClurg (Peggy), Al Fann (Ned), Vince Grant (Bud), Sid Melton (Man).

Laverne is torn between spending time with an old friend or Charley's attractive friend.

LIFE GOES ON—PART 1 & 2   Airdates (1-hour format): 4/29/95, 7/08/95.

Guest Cast: Kristy McNichol (Barbara Weston), Grace Zabriskie (Scarlett), Jim Haynie (Grit), Judith-Marie Bergan (Libby), D. David Morin (Kevin), Caston Holmes (Scotty), Ellis Williams (Inspector).

The series comes to an end as Carol and Laverne both get married, Harry accepts a teaching position in Vermont, and Barbara returns to help him pack up the family house.

Production Note:

- Although this episode was the series finale, two additional episodes were later aired during the summer.

MY PAL VALY-VAL   Airdate: 6/10/95.

Guest Cast: Valerie Lansburg (Valerie), Steve Rankin (Sam), Meagen Fay (Bridget).

Carol comes to the rescue when she spots a woman about to commit suicide.

REMEMBRANCE OF CLIPS PAST   Airdate: 6/17/95.

Everyone looks back at their good times together as Laverne gets ready to move home to Hickory.

Hard Time on Planet Earth

When Disney produced the science fiction series *Hard Time on Planet Earth*, the Studio took pains to emphasize the action-adventure aspect of the series over the science fiction content. The series featured an alien warrior from the planet Andarius, who had been raised from birth to fight for his planet in an intergalactic battle. When the war ended, he became a danger to the leaders of his planet, who transformed him into human form and sent him to Earth, where he would have to perform a series of good deeds before returning home.

CBS added the series as a mid-season replacement for the 1988–89 season.

After 3 weeks on the air, the series was attracting only 15 percent of the potential audience, and the first rumors began to circulate about cancellation. When the ratings didn't improve, the series was canceled.

Series Cast: Martin Kove (Jesse), Danny Mann (Voice of Control).

Each of the episodes is described below in airdate order.

HARD TIME ON PLANET EARTH (pilot)
Airdate: 3/01/89.

Guest Cast: Marita Geraghty (Karen), Roscoe Orman (Captain Ralston), Robert Schenkkan (DeSalvo), Michael G. Hagerty (Deputy #2), James Lashly (Deputy #1), Laura Malone (Woman Thief), Jeanne Bates (Clerk), Brian Brophy (Van Dyke), Don Draper (Jewelry Store Manager), David Dunard (Detective Smitts), Terrence Evans (Guard), Ann Gillespie (Beautiful Woman), Stephen Lee (Fast Food Junkie), Brendon McKane (Sheriff Sarandon), Dean R. Miller (Chicken Boy man), Howard Mungo (Cop #1), Minerva Perez (News Commentator), Juney Smith (Newsperson).

An alien warrior is transformed into human form and exiled on Earth until he proves himself worthy of returning home.

Jesse is accompanied by Control, a robotic parole officer, who manages to get the exile involved in a series of problems.

SOMETHING TO BANK ON   Airdate: 3/08/89.

Guest Cast: Jamie Rose (Dr. Laura Rowlands), Terry Kiser (Felix), Rod Arrants (Kohler), Gerry Gibson (Lieutenant Dan Lowery), Raymond O'Connor (Phil Marker), William Lanteau (Reinhardt), Marcia Brandwynne (Anchorwoman), Anthony DeFonte (Vendor), Hector Mercado (Pickett), Kent Stoddard (Bellman), Barry Dennen (Hotel Clerk), Catherine Paolone (Mrs. Rosetti), Timothy Blake (Ms. Yardley), Brad Kepnick (Young Man), Perry Anzilotti (Exerciser), Ed Levy (Salesman), Karen Todd (Model).

Jesse receives an instant lesson in Earthly economics when he finds that he has to pay for food.

LOSING CONTROL   Airdate: 3/15/89.
*Guest Cast: Robin Riker-Hasley (Sullivan),
Adam Arkin (Harry Newcomb), Anne
Wyndham (Ruth Newcomb), Christian
Clemenson (Herb Leavitt), Ken Jenkins
(Sergeant Burdick), Tim Eyster (Jonathan
Newcomb), Michael Faustino (Mark), Rich
Garcia (Alvarez), Jeremy Roberts (Man), Marc
Silver (Archie), Frantz Turner (Patrolman),
Ryan McWhorter (Boy), Malachi Pearson
(Son), Trish Doolan (Railroad Loader), Chuck
Sloan (Car Salesman).*

Jesse and Control misunderstand a comment that "Disneyland makes people feel
young again," and they decide to visit the
theme park to see this rejuvenation process
for themselves.

WAY HOME, THE   Airdate: 3/22/89.
*Guest Cast: Darcy Marta (Erin Parker),
Karen Landry (Sue Parker), James Hardy (Jim
Parker), Bill Sadler (Officer Rollman), Roger
Aaron Brown (Officer Stoff), Marcus Chong
(Tim), Charles Gruber (Taxi Driver), Barry
Doe (Cook), David Katz (Kid #2), Tony
Mangano (Punk #1), Julio Medina (Gardener),
Danny Oberbeck (Kid #1), Stephen Quadros
(Larry), Shane Tyler Ralston (Freak), Joe
Nesnow (Jogger), Keith Tellez (Punk #2).*

Jesse meets Erin, a runaway teenager, who
has been thrown out of her home for her wild
behavior.

ALL THAT YOU CAN BE   Airdate:
3/29/89.
*Guest Cast: Larry B. Scott (Corporal Curtis
Tillman), Jane Modean (Lieutenant Arlene
Michaels), Real Andrews (Deacon Powell),
Marshall Bell (Sergeant Stryker), Tim Ryan
(Corporal Vance Butler), Jon Stafford
(Hudson), Tony Colitti (Franco), V.C. Dupree
(Wright), John DiSanti (Sergeant Hurley),
Judyann Elder (Mrs. Tillman), Chico Brooks
(Toots), B'Nard Lewis (Jeweleryman), Linda
Lutz (Woman), Shana Washington (Vanessa
Tillman), Patricia Wilson (Nun), James Brown
III (Tommy), Eric Chambers (Strider #2),
Brent DeHart (M.P. #1), Jake Jacobs (Driver),
Julie Moran (TV Reporter).*

Tired of being out of work, Jesse decides to
enlist in the U.S. Army, where he soon whips
some problem recruits into shape.

BATTLE OF THE SEXES   Airdate: 4/05/89.
*Guest Cast: Sandahl Bergman (Daniel),
Paul Comi (Frank Russo), Mark Thomas
Miller (Mike Russo), Lycia Naff (Connie
Russo), Al Ruscio (Carlo Caretti), Stephen*

*Liska (Tom Caretti), Tom Silardi (Vic Caretti),
Rhonda Aldrich (Salesperson), Darren E.
Burroughs (Young Man), David Clover (Cop),
Julie Hayek (Lana), Rob Fitzgerald (Man),
Jonathon Hugger (Janitor), Paunita Nichols
(Bartender), Jim Raymond (Businessman).*

A female alien is sent to Earth with orders
to interrogate Jesse for some vital information and then kill him.

DEATH DO US PART   Airdate: 4/12/89.
*Guest Cast: Lise Hilboldt (Jane), Tim
Dunigan (Michael), Scott Jaeck (Lieutenant
Taylor), Jeff MacGregor (Himself), Jack Riley
(Minister), Scott Lincoln (Bobby), Vance
Colvig (Bruno), John Batis (Chauffeur), Bill
Dunham (Truck Driver), Jerome Front
(Waiter), Elaine Wilkes (Date #3/Masseuse),
Susannah Woodside (Date #1), Kelly Andrus
(Date #2), Kelly Miller (Date #4), Hank
Woessner (Bruno), John Batis (Chauffeur),
Jerome Front (Waiter), Bill Dunnam (Truck
Driver), Michael Scoggins (Bachelor #1),
James Casey (Bachelor #2).*

When Jesse is picked for *The Dating Game*,
he wins a date and becomes involved in a
scam aimed at lonely women.

HOT DOG MAN, THE   Airdate: 4/26/89.
*Guest Cast: Conchata Ferrell (Annie), Jacob
Vargas (Billy), Pamela Cuming (Sandra),
"Tiny" Lister, Jr. (John Henry), Tau Logo (Tao),
"Pistol" Pete Marquez (Mongo), Magic
Schwartz (Bullwhip), Ronnie Schell
(Announcer), Michael Canavan (Burns),
Malcolme Groome (Morrow), Emily Doyle
(Mount Fuji), Ursula Hayden (Babe), Peach
Janae (Vicky Victory), Becky Mullen (Sally),
Richard Epcar (Jake), Fran Montano
(Promoter), Bert Rosario (Fan #1), Wren
Brown (Visiting Broker), Christine Cattell
(Receptionist), Vance Colvig (Fan #2),
Raymond Davis (Ted), Dick Durock (Coach),
Mando Guerrero (Referee #2), Paige Price
(Concession Girl), Count Billy Varga (Referee
#1).*

Jesse takes a job selling hot dogs at a small
wrestling arena, where he mistakenly thinks
the wrestlers are trying to kill each other.

JESSE'S FIFTEEN MINUTES   Airdate:
5/03/89.
*Guest Cast: Rebecca Staab (Donna),
Gregory Wagrowski (Perry), Brad Lockerman
(Zach), Sandy Simpson (Fred Waterman), Stan
Ivar (Remy), Gregory Procaccino (Agent), Bill
Stevenson (Kiosk Operator), Julia Sweeney
(Gladys), Tom Alexander (Male Model),*

Dylan Arrants (Second Punk), Terri Berland (Woman #1), Tanya Coleridge (Marlene), Martha Hackett (Makeup Woman), George Kyle (Bouncer), Alex Lende (Man #1), Claudio Martin (Punk #1), Greg Rusin (Magazine Vendor), George Siegal (Reporter #1).

Jesse saves a model from muggers and then happily accepts her invitation to a swank industry party.

RODEO Airdate: 5/10/89.

Guest Cast: Grainger Hines (Travis Brady), Michael Alldredge (Buck McGrew), Christian Jacobs (Mark Brady), Greg Kean (Shelby), Michael J. Cutt (Joe Pierce), Art Bradford (Announcer), Charles Dierkop (Fan), Shelly Lipkin (Director), David Starwalt (Cop), Robert Balderson (Husband), Charles Bazaldua (Cook), Robert Devlin (Fan #2), Jim James (Serviceman), Josh MacDonald (Kid), R. Leo Schreiber (Customer).

Passing by a used car lot, Jesse spots a kidnapping attempt. He rushes in to save the victim, only to learn too late that it is all part of a television commercial.

NOT IN OUR STARS Airdate: 5/31/89.

Guest Cast: Sam McMurray (Dr. Cyrus Jordan), Lezlie Dean (Carrie Robbins), Paul Tuerpé (Coldstream), Richard Roat (Chancellor Payton), Cathy McAuley (Nurse), Lisa Mende (Bookstore Clerk), Danny Mann (Bus Passenger), Elizabeth Cox (Coed), Bill Dearth (Military V.I.P.), Mitch Ford (Jerry), Terri Hoyos (Cashier), Mark Sussman (Freshman).

Jesse is taken aboard a ship from his home planet and is told that he has been found innocent of the crime for which he was exiled, and that his vice commander betrayed him. He then wakes up, and realizes it was only a dream.

ALL AMERICAN, THE Airdate: 6/14/89.

Guest Cast: Doug Johnson (Bill Mitchner), Dave Shelley (Mr. Roberts), Charles Bouvier (Mr. Boothby), Caryn Richman (Janet Gleason), Vinny Argiro (Donut Vendor), Kristine Blackburn (Ginger), Daniel Jordan (Matt), Michael Stoyanov (Jojo), Alice Borden (Teacher), Kathy Christopherson (Rebecca), Tyrone Jackson (Chris), Laura James (Mrs. Tucci), Raymond Lynch (Detective), Patricia Tallman (Francis).

Jesse is surprised to spot a teenager with strength like his, so he gets a job at the boy's school to observe him. The boy finally admits that he is also an alien exile.

WALLY'S GANG Airdate: 6/21/89.

Guest Cast: Gordon Jump (Wally Banks), Brandon Bluhm (Timmy Hogan), Brad Kepnick (Bill Webber), Leon Russom (Merrick), Rick Lieberman (Mr. Hogan), Katherine Cannon (Mrs. Hogan), Greg Mortensen (Kevin), Patricia Sill (Karen), Eric Server (Harry), Clayton Landey (Galloway), Jeffrey Lampert (Executive), Chuck Picerni Jr. (Reed).

Wally, the host of a children's television show, tries to kill himself when the show is canceled. Jesse saves him and then gets a job on the show as the fix-it man.

The Nutt House

The 1988 theatrical release *Big Business*, which starred Bette Midler and Lily Tomlin, took place in large part in New York's Plaza Hotel. Logistically unable to film in the actual hotel, the Studio built an elaborate duplicate of the Plaza's ornate lobby on a soundstage in Burbank. When filming ended, Disney went looking for some way to use the $1 million set. Thus, Disney's *The Nutt House* was born.

The Nutt family had been running The Nutt House for several generations. Edwina Nutt, the elderly current owner, realized she must turn the reins over to a younger, more energetic Nutt. Unfortunately, the only remaining heir was Charles Nutt III, a jetsetting playboy who had shown no interest at all in the family business.

The Nutt House debuted on September 20, 1989 and immediately ran into trouble. The use of sight gags evidently didn't transfer well to the screen. The series was canceled on October 30, having attracted only 13.2 percent of television viewers.

In its effort to use its $1 million set, Disney lost more than $2 million on *The Nutt House.*

Series Cast: Cloris Leachman (Ms. Frick), Harvey Korman (Reginald J. Tarkington), Brian McNamara (Charles Nutt III), Molly Hagan (Sally Lonnaneck), Gregory Itzin (Dennis), Mark Blankfield (Freddy).

Each of the episodes is described below in airdate order.

NUTT HOUSE, THE (pilot) Airdate (1-hour format): 9/20/89.

Guest Cast: Cloris Leachman (Edwina Nutt), David Huddleston (Big Jake Herder), John deLancie (Norman), Ronny Graham

(Raymond), Peter Pitofsky (Peter the Bellhop), Candace Brough (Bimbo #1), Randi Brough (Bimbo #2), Robert Briscoe Evans (Man in Bed), Gloria Hayes (Maria), Jon Menick (Businessman), Garret Smith (Executive), Patti Tippo (Dixie).

For years, the Nutt House hotel has been losing money. Owner Edwina Nutt is in danger of losing it to Big Jake Herder, the owner of a large hotel chain. She sends for her grandson, Charles Nutt III, and he soon arrives to manage the hotel for her in an attempt to save it.

ACCIDENTAL GROOM, THE   Airdate: 9/28/89.

Guest Cast: Mark L. Taylor (Agent Flynn), Arthur Malet (Raymond), Scott Fults (Minister), Gloria Hayes (Maria), Patti Tippo (Dixie), Claudia Bloom (Young Woman), Matt Flynn (Astronaut), Rob Narita (Painter).

A visit from an immigration official uncovers the fact that Ms. Frick is an illegal alien, and unless she marries an American citizen, she will be deported.

FRICK CALLED WANDA, A   Airdate: 10/11/89.

Guest Cast: Beth Broderick (Gwen Goode), M. K. Harris (Hans), James O'Doherty (Grekko), Vali Ashton (Bride), Patti Haddon (Cocktail Waitress), Ivan Naranjo (Indian Chief), David Sederholm (Groom).

Tarkington is going through a bout of depression, feeling that he has grown old and unattractive. This changes when a pretty hotel guest starts spending more and more time with him.

21 MEN AND A BABY   Airdate: 10/18/89.

Guest Cast: Andrew Bloch (Coach Willis), Joycelyn O'Brien (Rosemary), Gloria Hayes (Maria), Patti Tippo (Dixie), Robert Gaylor (Sports Announcer).

A professional basketball team checks into the hotel before a big playoff game and demands quiet. That night, a crying baby wakes up the team and an irate Tarkington orders the baby and mother evicted.

SUITES, LIES, AND VIDEOTAPE   Airdate: 10/25/89.

Guest Cast: Lee Garlington (Angelica), Samuel Chew Jr. (Mayor), Angus Scrimm (Grim Reaper), Gloria Hayes (Maria), Patti Tippo (Dixie), Joe Costanza (Man in Robe), Henry Kaiser (Leo), Archie Kessell (President), Edwina Moore (Newswoman).

Once again, the hotel is empty, the money has run out, and the creditors have given Charles another deadline to pay his bills. He suggests that they get the President to stay at the hotel on an upcoming visit.

Unaired episodes

The following episodes were produced but were not aired: *The Reunion, To Tell the Truth, When Charles Met Sally, My Man Tarkington,* and *Nutt Cracker Suite.*

The following episodes were written but not produced: *Phantom of the Nutt House, Dennis and the Menace, I Can't Tark It Anymore.*

Carol & Company (and) The Carol Burnett Show

When *The Carol Burnett Show* ended in 1978 after 11 years on the air, Carol Burnett was a major television star. Over the years she considered working for Disney and a number of sitcom possibilities were discussed. Following a suggestion from Michael Eisner, she finally signed for *Carol & Company,* a comedy anthology series that debuted on NBC for the 1989–90 season.

At first, the only regular cast member was to be Burnett, with a different set of guest stars each week, but this was changed to add a repertory company of five performers. After two seasons, Burnett became disenchanted with the anthology format and convinced Eisner that the time was right for a return to a musical comedy/variety format. The result was *The Carol Burnett Show.*

Each of the episodes is described below in airdate order.

Series Cast (Carol & Company): Carol Burnett, Anita Barone, Meagen Fay, Richard Kind, Terry Kiser, Jeremy Piven (1989–90), Peter Krause (1990–91).

Series Cast (The Carol Burnett Show): Carol Burnett, Rick Aviles, Chris Barnes, Meagan Fay, Roger Kabler, Jann Karam, Richard Kind, Jessica Lundy.

1989–90 season—Carol & Company

BUMP IN THE NIGHT   Airdates: 3/31/90, 9/01/90.

Cast: Carol Burnett (Lois Carlyle), Anita Barone (Jennifer), Meagen Fay (Sylvia), Richard Kind (Paul Carlyle), Terry Kiser (Brian Beckworth), Jeremy Piven (Plumber), Meghan Geary (The Maid).

When Lois Carlyle discovers that her husband, Paul, has been cheating on her, she wants him dead. Luckily for Paul, she can't bring herself to kill him. Unluckily for Paul, one of Lois's friends tells her that many of the local wives use contract killers.

REUNION   Airdates: 4/07/90, 8/18/90.

Cast: Carol Burnett (Georgette Boswell), Swoosie Kurtz (Laurie), Richard Kind (Ernie), Terry Kiser (Roger), Frank Bonner (Frank), Eugene Clark (Joey), Phoebe Dorin (Barbara).

Georgette Boswell goes to her high school reunion, but not surprisingly, no one remembers her. This is because her former schoolmates knew her as George Boswell, before her sex change operation.

Production Note:

- Guest star Swoosie Kurtz won an Emmy award for her appearance in this episode.

MOTHER FROM HELL   Airdates: 4/14/90, 8/25/90.

Cast: Carol Burnett (Sheila Miller), Dorothy Lyman (Barbara), David Carlile (Photographer), Alexander Folk (Baliff), Anita Barone (Laura Miller), Meagen Fay (Judge), Richard Kind (Larry Schuster), Terry Kiser (Ben Birdwell), Jeremy Piven (Kenny Miller), Burt Reynolds (Man on Beach).

Sheila is a mother with a problem—her grown children won't move out. She's tried numerous tactics to make them leave, but since nothing has worked, she decides to sue them to get them out of her house and her life.

IN-LAWS SHOULD BE OUTLAWED   Airdates: 4/21/90, 8/18/90.

Cast: Carol Burnett (Janet Peters), Anita Barone (Kimberly Tremont), Meagen Fay (Frances Tremont), Richard Kind (Wayne Tremont), Terry Kiser (Howard Peters), Jeremy Piven (Barry Peters).

Barry Peters is dreading an event that has ruined many relationships—the first meeting of his prospective in-laws. Barry's fears are well founded, for his parents, Howard and Janet, are hardcore practical jokers.

BATTLE OF THE EXES   Airdates: 4/28/90, 12/22/90.

Cast: Carol Burnett (Dr. Elaine Daniels), Alex Rocco (Dr. Arthur Daniels), Anita Barone (Lisa), Meagen Fay (Betsy), Richard Kind (Carl), Jeremy Piven (Robert).

When her ex-husband, Arthur, starts dating a young girl, Dr. Elaine Daniels finds a way to repay him for her pain caused by their recent divorce by dating a younger man.

SOAP GETS IN YOUR EYES   Airdates: 5/05/90, 11/17/90.

Cast: Carol Burnett (Barbara Wellington), Robert Guillaume (Sam), Kenneth David Gilman (Rich), George Wyner (Jack), Julie Warner (Brooke).

Barbara Wellington, a fading soap opera queen, resents competition from Brooke, a young star. Barbara talks to Sam, a studio guard, who tries to make her understand that Brooke is a talented actress who must be reckoned with.

MYNA AND THE MESSENGER   Airdate: 5/12/90.

Cast: Carol Burnett (Myna Bouleray), Howie Mandell (The Messenger), Dennis Burkley (Bob), James Avery (Chain Man), Beth Broderick (Redhead), Tom Spiroff (Stick Man), Richard Brose, (Gladiator), Linda Doná (Candy), Roger Hewlett, (Toga Boy), Clive Rosengren (Centurion).

When Myna Bouleray learns that her church needs money for urgent repairs, she finds an unlikely ally in an angel. The angel helps her win the money at a casino, but Myna then decides to keep it for herself.

FABULOUS BICKER GIRLS, THE   Airdate: 5/26/90.

Cast: Carol Burnett (Babe Bicker), Robert Urich (Bobby), Carrie Hamilton (Baby Bicker), Anita Barone (Anita), Meagen Fay (Lola), Richard Kind (Richard), Terry Kiser (Terry), Jeremy Piven (Jeremy).

Babe Bicker and her daughter, Baby, have been trying for years to succeed as singers, but the two can't agree on the type of music to perform and their careers seem stalled. This changes when they team up with Bobby, and the new trio is a surprise hit.

KRUBER ALBERT   Airdate: 6/02/90.

Cast: Carol Burnett (Sally Trickelson), Glenda Jackson (Dr. Doris Kruber), Martin Ferrero (Fred).

Dr. Doris Kruber, a radio psychologist, specializes in giving advice to the lovelorn. Her self-assured world is threatened when Sally, a crazed listener, locks herself in the broadcast booth seeking revenge for Doris's bad advice.

1990–91 season—Carol & Company

GRANDMA GETS IT ON   Airdates: 9/22/90, 12/29/90.

Cast: Carol Burnett *(Lillian Praskin),* Anita Barone *(Hilary),* Meagen Fay *(Diane Briggs),* Richard Kind *(Mr. Chester),* Terry Kiser *(Harry Greenwood),* Owen Bush *(Old Man).*

Diane Briggs arrives at the Willow Heights Retirement Home in response to an urgent summons from Mr. Chester, the administrator. He tells Diane that her mother, Lillian, is causing trouble for the other residents and will have to leave unless she stops.

DIARY OF A REALLY, REALLY MAD HOUSEWIFE   Airdates: 9/29/90, 3/30/91.

Cast: Carol Burnett *(Dorothy Tibbet),* Anita Barone *(Motorcycle Mama/Didi/Madden),* Meagen Fay *(Barbara/Bank Machine Voice/Sergeant Howard),* Richard Kind *(Jack/Carl/Brannigan),* Terry Kiser *(Marvin Tibbet/Bank Guard/Steve),* Peter Krause *(Young Man/Manager's Voice/Plumber).*

Typical housewife Dorothy Tibbet sends her husband, Marvin, out to play golf with his boss, unaware that her life will soon change on what should be just another day of chores.

GOIN' TO THE CHAPEL   Airdates: 10/06/90, 3/30/91.

Cast: Carol Burnett *(Evelyn Sweets),* Anita Barone *(Patty),* Meagen Fay *(Madeline Lawrence),* Richard Kind *(Marvin's Voice),* Terry Kiser *(Chester Neff),* Peter Krause *(Policeman),* Lew Horn *(Alfred Sternbacker),* Jennifer Richards *(Brandi Sternbacker),* Ellen Gerstein *(Pregnant Woman).*

This episode features two stories set at a small wedding chapel in Las Vegas. In *Dummy Dearest,* Evelyn Sweet advertises that she'll marry any couple, never expecting to meet Madeline Lawrence, who wants to marry a ventriloquist's dummy.

The second story, *Being Out There,* finds the arrival of Chester Neff. He has seen Evelyn's picture and wants to marry her, having misunderstood her "I'll Marry Anyone" ad slogan.

GUNS AND ROSIE   Airdate: 10/13/90.

Cast: Carol Burnett *(Rosie),* Anita Barone *(Fran),* Meagen Fay *(Ida),* Richard Kind *(Burglar),* Terry Kiser *(Officer #1),* Peter Krause *(Officer #2).*

Three elderly women who are all nuts about guns hear a noise in their apartment and decide to investigate. They find a burglar in the bedroom and tie him up at gunpoint.

STIFF COMPETITION   Airdate: 10/20/90.

Cast: Carol Burnett *(Bonnie Knudsen),* Anita Barone *(Gina),* Meagen Fay *(Leona Whitewood/Gladys Borman),* Richard Kind *(Elliot Bradley),* Terry Kiser *(Jack Knudsen),* Elaine Giftos *(Judy Bradley),* Michael Eugene Fairman *(Taxi Driver #1),* Eddie Hailey *(Taxi Driver #2).*

When Elliot Bradley's wife dies, his girlfriend, Bonnie Knudsen, is overjoyed to hear the news. Bonnie sees this as a sign that she should leave her husband, Jack, and marry Elliot.

HERE'S TO YOU, MRS. BALDWIN   Airdates: 10/27/90, 3/09/91.

Cast: Carol Burnett *(Lisa Baldwin),* Meagen Fay *(Sheila Everett),* Peter Krause *(Patrick),* Doug McKeon *(Ray Baldwin),* Joe Lala *(Bartender),* Robert Trumbull *(Ed Weikel).*

Lisa Baldwin is anxiously waiting for her son, Ray, to come home from college for dinner. Her neighbor, Sheila, visits and tells Lisa that her tarot cards predict a new romance for her.

TRISHA SPRINGS ETERNAL   Airdates: 11/03/90, 7/06/91.

Cast: Carol Burnett *(Rosalind Burke),* Anita Barone *(Margo),* Terry Kiser *(Philip),* Peter Krause *(Sid),* Betty White *(Trisha Durant),* John DiSanti *(Frank),* Jim Ishida *(Mr. Yamato).*

Years ago, Trisha Durant pushed her friend, Rosalind Burke, out of the path of a falling mirrored ball at a school dance. Trisha has never let poor Rosalind forget that she was hit instead, and Rosalind is at her wit's end trying to avoid her ex-schoolmate.

MOM AND DAD DAY AFTERNOON   Airdates: 11/10/90, 4/13/91.

Cast: Carol Burnett *(Julia Miller),* Terry Kiser *(Frank Miller),* Peter Krause *(Kevin Miller),* John Cothran Jr. *(Mr. Doogan),* Marc Grapey *(Evan),* Valerie Spencer *(Bank Teller).*

Frank and Julia Miller's visit to the neighborhood bank to apply for a loan takes an unexpected turn when the bank is robbed.

DRIVING MISS CRAZY   Airdates: 11/17/90, 4/20/91.

Cast: Carol Burnett *(Dorothy Tibbet),* Anita Barone *(Babs/Cheryl/Myrna),* Meagen Fay *(Examiner/Cop #1),* Richard Kind

(Supervisor/Man #2/Phillip/Mrs. Birnbaum), Terry Kiser (Marvin/Man #1/Ryan), Peter Krause (Roy/Robert Barkeley).

After a long period of rest in an asylum, Dorothy Tibbet is released to try to fit back into mainstream society.

JINGLE BELLES, THE   Airdates: 11/24/90, 7/31/91.

Cast: Carol Burnett (Arlene Harvey), Meagen Fay (Gloria Clark), Richard Kind (Mel), Peter Krause (Marty), Bernadette Peters (Kate Benton).

Arlene Harvey and Kate Benton have been writing jingles for 15 years. They pitch a new jingle to Marty and Gloria, two advertising executives, but the audition proves unsuccessful.

TEACHER, TEACHER   Airdates: 12/01/90, 4/20/90.

Cast: Carol Burnett (Daisy Kornfeld), Anita Barone (Anita), Meagen Fay (Meagen), Richard Kind (Richard), Terry Kiser (Terry), Peter Krause (Peter Loomis), Pat Crawford Brown (Miss Underwood), Robert Urich (Mr. Carmen).

Stopped by a highway patrolman for speeding, Daisy Kornfeld recognizes him as a former student of hers. Hoping to take advantage of their relationship, she tries her best to talk her way out of the ticket.

SPUDNIK   Airdate: 12/08/90.

Cast: Carol Burnett (Veta Mae Klybocker), Nell Carter (Dakota Johnson).

Veta Mae Klybocker hears aliens through a potato. Following their instructions, she goes to an abandoned dock to meet them.

NO NEWS IS BAD NEWS   Airdates: 1/05/91, 7/20/91.

Cast: Carol Burnett (Christine Howard), Anita Barone (Susan Allen), Meagen Fay (Brandi Marshwynne), Richard Kind (Warren), Peter Krause (Riff Slade), Paul Napier (Harry Langhorn), Richard Karn (J.T.), Kelley Wright (Wendy).

Television journalist Christine Howard is dismayed when she meets her new boss, Susan Allen. Susan, who loves game shows, has decided to try a new format for the news broadcast in the hope of increasing the ratings.

TURNING TABLES   Airdate: 1/19/91.

Cast: Carol Burnett (Phoebe Zanisky), Anita Barone (Margery), Meagen Fay (Lucille),

Richard Kind (Glen Zanisky), Terry Kiser (Dwight Beckley), Peter Krause (Roger Engles), I.M. Hobson (Waiter), Terry Davis (Woman), Josef Powell (Pianist).

A busy restaurant is the setting for a look at how different couples handle their romantic problems in public.

THAT LITTLE EXTRA SOMETHING   Airdate: 1/26/91.

Cast: Carol Burnett (Aunt Wanda/Lady Simpleton), Anita Barone (Opportunity), Meagen Fay (Lady Turncoat), Richard Kind (Chives), Terry Kiser (Major Blowhard), Peter Krause (Constable Goodear), Paul Brett (Paul), Tim Conway (Surprise Audience Member).

This episode is a play within a play, as the cast tries to re-create the old days of live television. Their efforts are strained by Aunt Wanda, who, seated in the studio audience, thinks they want her in the show.

Production Note:

• Ret Turner and Bob Mackie won an Emmy award for Costume Design, Variety or Music Program, for this episode.

FALL FROM GRACE, A   Airdate: 2/02/91.

Cast: Carol Burnett (Grace Fitchel/Mother), Anita Barone (Ellen/Young Grace), Meagen Fay (Funny Grace), Richard Kind (Walter), Terry Kiser (Uncle Lou/Voice), Peter Krause (Mark), Danielle Clegg (Little Grace).

Grace Fitchel is such a sourpuss that her neighbor, Ellen, describes her as the "Bitch Goddess of Darkness." Grouchy Grace's life takes an unexpected turn when she is sucked into her clothes dryer while looking for a lost sock.

SUTURE SELF   Airdate: 2/09/91.

Cast: Carol Burnett (Dorothy Tibbet), Anita Barone (Clerk/Nurse Ferguson/Mrs. Tetrick), Meagen Fay (Mildred/Ida), Richard Kind (Mr. Hoffenrank/Dr. Payne), Terry Kiser (Marvin Tibbet/Mel), Peter Krause (Smitty/Male Officer), Neil Patrick Harris (Doogie Howser), William Woodson (Voice).

In the third show featuring harried housewife Dorothy Tibbet, she goes to the hospital to have a splinter removed from her foot. The staff confuses her with a Delores Talbot, who has a splintered tibia, and the doctor sends her out for a series of X-rays.

HIGH ON LIFE   Airdate: 2/16/91.

Cast: Carol Burnett (Margaret), Anita Barone (Mindy), Meagen Fay (Colleen),

Richard Kind (Herb Finley), Terry Kiser (Joe Genuzzi), Peter Krause (Alfred Finley).

Just before her wedding, Margaret learns that Joe Genuzzi, her window washer, is in love with her.

MOMMA NEEDS A NEW PAIR OF SHOES
Airdate: 3/02/91.

Cast: Carol Burnett (Helen), Anita Barone (Tina), Meagen Fay (Marjorie), Richard Kind (Alfred), Peter Krause (Leon), Mimi Cozzens (Gladys Klein).

Three daughters who have grown distant over time must face one another when their mother dies.

JEWEL OF DENIAL   Airdate: 3/09/91.

Cast: Carol Burnett (Samantha Diamond), Anita Barone (Cigarette Girl), Meagen Fay (Singer), Richard Kind (Bartender), Terry Kiser (Bernie Sisler), Jeremy Piven (Gigolo), Kevin Thompson (Mickey).

This spoof of film noir begins as Mickey, with a knife in his back, falls into the office of Samantha Diamond, private eye. Samantha's policeman boyfriend, Bernie Sisler, sees the body and arrests her for murder.

INTIMATE BEHAVIOR   Airdate: 3/16/91.

Cast: Carol Burnett (Carol), Anita Barone (Anita/Marie), Meagen Fay (Meagen/Jean Schloss), Richard Kind (Richard/Dr. Sidney Fine), Terry Kiser (Terry), Peter Krause (Peter), Hal Linden (Hal).

In a departure from the series' usual format, Carol Burnett and Hal Linden lead the cast in a series of sketches and musical acts that explore the theme of intimate behavior.

NOAH'S PLACE   Airdate: 4/13/91.

Cast: Carol Burnett (Patsy/The Head), Anita Barone (Cheryl), Meagen Fay (Beth Ann/Zena), Richard Kind (Henry Farrell/Trucker #1), Terry Kiser (Louie/Trucker #2), Jeremy Piven (Rodney/Glenn Hacket).

This episode includes two different stories, both set in "Noah's Place," a small desert cafe. The first segment features Patsy, the waitress, who hasn't seen her husband, Louie, for 2 years because he's a convict.

The second story is about Zena, a local desert scavenger who shows up with a live human head.

OVERNIGHT MALE   Airdate: 4/27/91.

Cast: Carol Burnett (Myrna Fallows), Meagen Fay (Eileen), Richard Kind (Milton

Pedvis), Christopher Reeve (Rex Atwater/Harvey), Tom Urich (Maitre D'), Mark W. Scott (Postal Worker).

Myrna Fallows spends her evenings dreaming about Rex, her fantasy perfect lover. Her dreams take a strange turn one night when Rex complains that she expects too much of him.

FOR LOVE OR MONEY   Airdate (1-hour format): 5/04/91.

Cast: Carol Burnett (Agnes Pringle), Anita Barone (Susannah/Dollface), Meagen Fay (Betty), Richard Kind (Lefty Malone), Terry Kiser (Elderly Gentleman/Victor Caruso), Peter Krause (Clarke), John Pinette (Slappy), John Hoffman (Steward), Gary Lahti (Ward).

With the passing of years, life has slowed for Agnes Pringle. However, the passage of time has not dimmed her memories of a romance with a dashing gigolo aboard a cruise ship in the '40s.

1991–92 season—The Carol Burnett Show

EPISODE #1   Airdate: 11/01/91.

- *Celebrity Double:* Needing work, Carol Burnett agrees to take a job as a celebrity impersonator—impersonating herself! **Cast:** Carol Burnett (Herself), Richard Kind (Bernie the Agent), Chris Barnes (Bowling Alley Owner), Roger Kabler (Peter Falk Look-alike), Jann Karam (Bowler #1), Rick Aviles (Bowler #2), Christie Sutherland (Carol Look-alike).
- *Meaningless Moments: Milking the Cow:* In Krugard, Norway, in 1286 B.C., a cavewoman discovers that cows give milk, much to her husband's displeasure. **Cast:** Carol Burnett (Helga), Chris Barnes (Grendo), Richard Kind (Himself), Roger Kabler (Grendo's Neighbor).
- *Losers Win:* A woman looking for her blind date falls in love with an incredibly bad night club performer. **Cast:** Carol Burnett (Carol), Martin Short (Pianist), Richard Kind (Bartender), Jann Karam (Single Woman), Rick Aviles (Waiter), Roger Kabler (Patron), Jessica Lundy (Patron), Chris Barnes (Patron), Meagen Fay (Patron).
- *Miss Abigail's Enchanted High Security Gingerbread Cottage:* Miss Abigail, the host of a children's show, is overly crazy about security and protection. **Cast:** Carol Burnett (Miss Abigail), Roger

Kabler (Alex), Meagen Fay (Amber), Chris Barnes (Mr. Happy Jeans), Richard Kind (Mister Duck).

- *Nathan Thurm: The Waltower Report:* During a talk show discussion about a lawsuit which alleges that a group is re-making black films for white audiences, a lawyer takes control of the interview and humiliates the show's hostess. **Cast:** Carol Burnett (Andrea Waltower), Martin Short (Nathan Thurm), Jeff Maynard (Gang Member), Roger Kabler (Gang member).
- *2001 Overture:* Two parents manage to survive their child's unusual orchestra recital. **Cast:** Carol Burnett (Proud Parent #1), Martin Short (Proud Parent #2), Meagen Fay (Woman's Voice).
- *Fair Weather Friends:* During a year-long assignment in Antarctica, a meteorologist is shocked to discover that the other man there is gay. **Cast:** Richard Kind (Bill), Chris Barnes (Thomas), Rick Aviles (Voice on Radio).
- Guest star B.B. King sings *I'm Movin' On.*

EPISODE #2 Airdate: 11/08/91.

- *The Hallelujah Shopping Network:* Two con artists posing as television evangelists set up their own home shopping channel, only to be arrested on the air for dealing in stolen goods. **Cast:** Carol Burnett (Sister Rhonda), Delta Burke (Sister Lola), Meagen Fay (Sister Ruth), Jann Karam (Caller #1), Roger Kabler (Caller #2), Richard Kind (Voice-over).
- *The Neck:* A new employee at a law firm is warned never to let her boss see any part of her neck. The boss tells her that it was a joke, then acts like a child when she takes off her scarf. She takes control of the company by making him play "Simon Says." **Cast:** Richard Kind (Mr. Jordan), Carol Burnett (Doris Newman), Roger Kabler (Man/Employee), Chris Barnes (Mr. Hederopeat), Jessica Lundy (Woman/Employee), Jann Karam (Employee), Rick Aviles (Employee).
- *Prom Date:* While comforting her daughter who has been stood up for the prom, a mother is shocked when the man who stood her up at her own prom 30 years ago finally arrives for the date. **Cast:** Carol Burnett (Emma), Delta Burke (Debby), Tony Roberts (Joseph), Roger Kabler (Barry).

- *The Star Trek Sketch:* The men on the *U.S.S. Enterprise* are somehow changed into women and the women into men, each retaining the other's characteristics. When the Klingons attack, Kirk tricks them into going through the same space cloud and the same thing happens to them. The happy result is that all agree not to fight. **Cast:** Richard Kind (Announcer/Koloth), Bill Prady (Kirk voice-over), Andrea Martin (Spock), Carol Burnett (Kirk), Linda Wallem (McCoy), Meagen Fay (Scotty), Rick Aviles (Uhura), Jessica Lundy (Chekov).
- *I-90 Diner Theater:* A truck stop diner is the unusual setting for a musical dinner show featuring more than fifty Broadway melodies in less than 5 minutes. **Cast:** Carol Burnett (Rose), Tony Roberts (Harry), Chris Barnes (Michael), Meagen Fay (Kathy), Jann Karam (Bus Girl), Richard Kind (Trucker #1), Rick Aviles (Trucker #2), Jessica Lundy (Trucker #3), Owen Rutledge (Trucker #4), Roger Kabler (Trucker #5), Steve Owsley (Eddie).

EPISODE #4 Airdate: 11/15/91.

- *Rock Out of That Rockin' Chair:* The Del Vecchio Triplets, at age 80, are still singing as rock stars. **Cast:** Carol Burnett (Viv Del Vecchio), Andrea Martin (Val Del Vecchio), Linda Wallem (Rue Del Vecchio).
- *The Good Son Hotline:* People can hire a service to pose as good sons over the phone. **Cast:** Meagen Fay (Mrs. Dreyfuss), Roger Kabler (Richard Dreyfuss), Chris Barnes (Good Son), Richard Kind (Good Son), Rick Aviles (Good Son), Roger Kabler (Announcer).
- *The Waltower Report: Bubblewrap:* A reporter has the strange assignment of interviewing a man garbed in bubblewrap. **Cast:** Carol Burnett (Andrea Waltower), Steven Wright (Mr. Bubblewrap/Raymond Dinozzi), Richard Kind (Announcer), Paul Miller (Director).
- *Ordinary People:* A screenwriter is the unsung hero when her own mother ignores her efforts and instead focuses on her husband's acting. **Cast:** Meagen Fay (Prudence Hall), Carol Burnett (Amanda Hall).
- *Miss Abigail's School Daze:* Some lectures about absurd dangers that may wait at school. **Cast:** Carol Burnett (Miss Abi-

gail), Roger Kabler (Alex), Meagen Fay (Amber), Chris Barnes (Mr. Happy Jeans), Richard Kind (Mister Fox).

- *Clown Shoes:* The owner of a clothing store for clowns is upset when his daughter announces plans to marry a clown. **Cast:** Andrea Martin (Lucy), Steven Wright (Jake), Jessica Lundy (Greta), Richard kind (Clown), Meagen Fay (Clown), Roger Kabler (Clown).
- *The Charwoman Comes Home:* Carol, appearing as her charwoman character, goes home to her rundown apartment to celebrate her birthday alone. **Cast:** Carol Burnett (Charwoman), Tom Scott (Sax Soloist).

EPISODE #5   Airdate: 11/22/91.
- Carol Burnett and Christopher Reeve perform *Row, Row, Row Your Boat.*
- *Family Moments: Thanksgiving Dinner:* An overworked doctor tries to resuscitate his Thanksgiving turkey. **Cast:** Richard Kind (Norman), Carol Burnett (Marcy), Jessica Lundy (Tricia), Roger Kabler (Jimmy), Meagen Fay (Terry), Chris Barnes (Harry).
- K.T. Oslin sings *You Call Everybody Darling.*
- *Terminator 3: Parents' Day:* The Terminator is back and is having marriage problems. He has to do all of the house work while his wife fights for freedom. **Cast:** Christopher Reeve (The Terminator), Carol Burnett (Sarah Terminator), Chris Barnes (Dr. Nathan Schiller), Ryan McWhorter (John), Richard Kind (Announcer).
- *New Way Home:* At a wedding reception in a small midwestern town, the mothers of the bride and groom toast each other, singing the song *New Way Home* together. **Cast:** Carol Burnett (Ruth), K.T. Oslin (Ellie).
- *Brief Encounter:* Two lonely souls meet in a British tea shop, each speaking only one word at a time. When he finally says a complete sentence, she loses interest and calls him a chatterbox. **Cast:** Carol Burnett (Hillary), Christopher Reeve (Rex).
- *The Moiseyev Dancers* perform with Burnett.

EPISODE #6   Airdate: 12/13/91.
- *Happy Birthday Stella #1:* It's Stella's 116th birthday and she has a hard time blowing out all of her candles. **Cast:**

Carol Burnett (Stella), Roger Kabler (Grandson), Jessica Lundy (Daughter), Chris Barnes (Nephew), Richard kind (Friend), Meagen Fay (Daughter #2).
- *Parental Guidance:* Two parents rely too heavily on their son for even the simplest of tasks. **Cast:** Carol Burnett (Joan Wilcox), Tony Roberts (Bob Wilcox), Chris Barnes (Bobby Wilcox).
- Bernadette Peters sings *I'm Flying* from *Peter Pan.*
- *Happy Birthday Stella #2:* She has blown out a few candles, but the guests are getting bored waiting for her to finish.
- *You're Mad:* A wife sings a rap song about her angry husband, and he responds in rap as well. **Cast:** Carol Burnett (Lois), Tony Roberts (Harold).
- *Boy Meets Girl:* An aggressive woman picks up a man in a bar for no-commitment sex, only to find out that their spouses are related. **Cast:** Carol Burnett, Chris Barnes, Richard Kind.
- *Happy Birthday Stella #3:* She finally blows out all the candles but forgets to make a wish, so she has to start all over again.
- *Bernadette at the I-90 Diner:* Another musical performance at the truck stop, this time featuring *Side By Side By Sondheim.* **Cast:** Carol Burnett (Rose), Tony Roberts (Harry), Bernadette Peters (Herself), Richard Kind (Trucker #1), Jessica Lundy (Trucker #2), Roger Kabler (Trucker #3).

EPISODE #3   Airdate: 12/27/91.
- *Friends:* Carol is an overly aggressive woman in a cocktail lounge who doesn't pay attention to what the men are trying to tell her. She sees romance where there is none and reacts angrily when the truth comes out. **Cast:** Carol Burnett (Carol), Chris Barnes (Chris), Richard Kind (Bartender), Roger Kabler (Brad).
- *The Elevator Man's Talk Show #1:* An elevator operator does a talk show for his security camera, and the celebrities that live in his building become guests as they ride. **Cast:** Richard Kind (Brooks/Announcer), Chris Barnes (Kenny Buchanan), Roger Kabler (Robert De Niro), Meagen Fay (Woman).
- *The Bitter Mrs. Mallorys:* A man's two ex-wives eat together the last Friday of every month just to pick on him. **Cast:** Richard Kind (Paul), Carol Burnett (Corinne Mallory), Meagen Fay (Laura

Mallory), Roger Kabler (The Busy Boy), Jessica Lundy (Jennifer Mallory).

- *Meaningless Moments in History: Noah:* Noah's wife is not happy on the ark, so she tricks Noah into tending the animals so she can have an affair with a stowaway. **Cast:** Chris Barnes (Noah), Carol Burnett (Noah's Wife), Richard Kind (Richard), Roger Kabler (Jedidiah).
- *The Elevator Man's Talk Show #2.* **Cast:** Richard Kind (Brooks/Announcer), Chris Barnes (Kenny Buchanan), Jessica Lundy (Kathleen Turner).
- *White and Simmons:* A salute to a couple celebrating their 60th year together in show business hides the fact that they were never romantically linked and actually hate each other. **Cast:** Carol Burnett (Mildred White/Lucinda), Robert Townsend (Calvin Simmons/Roderick), Jessica Lundy (Leeza Givvons), Jann Karam (Cigarette Girl), Rick Aviles (Patron), Chris Barnes (Waiter), Meagen Fay (Photo Girl), Roger Kabler (Patron), Richard Kind (Maitre D'), Tom Scott and Orchestra (Themselves).

Hull High

As work began at Disney on preparing possible shows for the 1990–91 season, one project that received Studio approval was a weekly comedy series based in a California high school.

If *Hull High* was successful it could benefit Disney's new Hollywood Records division, which helped make the project somewhat more appealing. The format eventually developed was a musical comedy, set in the fictitious Cordell Hull High School, which was located somewhere in southern California. Each week would find the students involved in a plot typical of those on other teen-oriented series, but with the additional twist of several elaborate musical numbers.

By the time the regular season started and the third episode of the series had aired, it was obvious that *Hull High* was doomed. The series ranked 86th of the 90 prime-time series aired so far that season and was only attracting 5.9 percent of the possible audience. The series was quickly yanked from the schedule, making it NBC's first cancellation of the season.

Series Cast: *Will Lyman (John Deerborn), Nancy Valen (Donna Breedlove), Mark Ballou (Mark Fuller), Marshall Bell (Jim Fancher), Kristin Dattilo (D.J.), Cheryl Pollak (Camilla*

Croft), Trey Parker (Rapper), Phillip DeMarks (Rapper), Carl Anthony Payne (Rapper), Bryan Anthony (Rapper), Roy Brocksmith (Mr. Kelm), Holly Fields (Michelle), Marty Belafsky (Louis Plumb), Jennifer Blanc (Straight Girl), April Dawn (Hip Girl), Adrian Ricard (Mrs. Hawes), Rowdy Metzger (Randy).

Each of the episodes is described below in airdate order, followed by the unaired episodes in production order.

EPISODE #1   Airdates: 8/20/90, 9/15/90.

Guest Cast: *Lawrence "G. Love E." Edwards (Rapper), Gary Grubbs (Joe Brawley), Deonca Brown (Amanda), Tony Perez (Rudy), Mavis Vegas Davis (Lady Janitor), Stogie Harrison (Coach Davis), Alejandro Quezada (Alfredo), Tyren Perry (Gail), Liz Imperio (Daphne), Michael Bower (Big Boy), Mark David (Student), George Perez (Boy), Ezra Sutton (Derek), Frank W. Vega (Byron).*

The school's new teacher, Donna Breedlove, can't figure out why her students are not paying attention. John Deerborn, another teacher, surmises the reason—she is so sexy that she is distracting the boys and making the girls jealous.

EPISODE #2   Airdate: 9/30/90.

Guest Cast: *George Martin (Mr. Dobosh), Harold Pruett (Cody), Rodney Eastman (Raymond Stoltz), Gary Grubbs (Joe Brawley), Joseph Ruskin (Mr. Slovak), Carl Steven (Michael), Janet Brandt (Old Lady), Anne Gee Byrd (Mrs. Cross), Nancy Fish (Miss Hollander), Charles Walker (Mr. Stubbs), Mary Valena Broussard (Girl), Lee Maddox (Cute Boy), Michael McNab (Paramedic), D.A. Pawley (Young Man).*

When one of the teachers is found dead in his classroom, Louis thinks he killed the man with a practical joke; Camilla tries to convince Mark to skip a class; Mr. Brawley has a less than perfect driver's education class.

EPISODE #3   Airdate: 10/07/90.

Guest Cast: *George Martin (Mr. Dobosh), Harold Pruett (Cody), Marvin Elkins (Coach Henke), Joseph Malone (Good Cop), Phil Rubenstein (Mr. Nukbaum), Nancy Fish (Miss Hollander), Troy Fromin (Stan Foley), Mary Pat Gleason (Mrs. Gompers), Bruce Scott (Bad Cop), Hue Anthony (Dennis), Michael Cudlitz (Schwartz), Lindsay Fisher (Cute Girl), Brandon McNaughton (Palmquist), Patrick J. Pieters (Recruit), Derek Stefan (Henderson).*

Mr. Deerborn has to decide if he should accept a student's challenge to a fight; D.J. joins the boys' wrestling team; Louis sets a trap to catch a thief.

EPISODE #4   Airdate: 10/14/90.

    Guest Cast: George Martin (Mr. Dobosh), Harold Pruett (Cody), Gary Grubbs (Mr. Brawley), Brian Matthews (Dr. Mackey), Lucy Vargas (Priscilla), Mark David (Mark), Micki Duran (Micki).

    Camilla and a young teacher are drawn to each other; Mr. Deerborn and Donna are nominated for the Most Popular Teacher award; two teachers battle over a prized parking spot.

EPISODE #5   Airdate: 12/23/90.

    Guest Cast: George Martin (Mr. Dobosh), Harold Pruett (Cody), Rodney Eastman (Weird Raymond), Hal Landon, Jr. (Gus), Ellen Albertini Dow (Mrs. Pace), Andrea Paige Wilson (Dana Cleeter), Natalie Barish (Mrs. Fisher), Emilio Borelli (Lyle), Mary Valena Broussard (Girl), Michael Cudlitz (Schwartz), Mavis Vegas Davis (Mavis), Kort Falkenberg (Mr. Fisher), Peggy Holmes (Waitress), Frank Noon (Mechanic), Dorit Sauer (Mindy Wellington), Ezra Sutton (Derek).

    A school ski trip results in chaos when the bus breaks down near a remote hotel.

EPISODE #6   Airdate: 12/30/90.

    Guest Cast: George Martin (Mr. Dobosh), Harold Pruett (Cody), Bruce Kirby (Theodore Wansley), Alan Weeks (Coach Barkley), Meg Wittner (Catherine Manning), Dick Enberg (Himself), Michael Cudlitz (Schwartz), Christopher Carter-Hooks (Carpenter), Christopher Melvin Brown (Eddie Thomas), Christie Clark (Shannon).

    Mark gets ready to play in the big homecoming game; Donna feels competition from John's ex-girlfriend; someone steals the school mascot.

EPISODE #7   Airdate: Unaired.

    Guest Cast: George Martin (Mr. Dobosh), Harold Pruett (Cody), Gary Bayer (Mr. Dryer), Anne Gee Byrd (Nurse Cross), Nancy Fish (Miss Hollander), Ruben Amavizca (Mr. Rodriguez), Chad Bell (Heavy Metal Kid #1), Yvette Cruise (Mrs. Rodriguez), Joe Farago (Newscaster), Michael Kopelow (Heavy Metal Kid #2), Dawn Radenbaugh (Shampoo Blonde), Ralph Segarra (Doctor), Nancy Simpson (Fancher's Sister), Nick Thiel (Stage Manager).

    One of Deerborn's old teachers turns up and reveals he's a fugitive from justice for past radical activities; Louis sees a beautiful girl but then can't find her again; Fancher has to deal with three babies.

EPISODE #8   Airdate: Unaired.

    Guest Cast: George Martin (Mr. Dobosh), Harold Pruett (Cody), Bryan Cranston (Mr. McConnell), Hue Anthony (Dennis), Melissa Chan (Judy), Patrick Y. Malone (Kyle), Rowdy Metzger (Randy).

    When Deerborn's students tell him that he has it easy, he makes them switch places with him.

Lenny

Disney's *Lenny* centered on Lenny Callahan, a blue-collar worker who worked several jobs trying to get ahead. This wasn't an easy task, for his family always seemed to find some way to complicate his life. CBS added *Lenny* to the 1990–91 season.

    Series Cast: Lenny Clarke (Lenny Callahan), Lee Garlington (Shelly Callahan), Peter Dobson (Eddie Callahan), Alice Drummond (Mary Callahan), Jenna von Oy (Kelly Callahan), Alexis Caldwell (Tracy Callahan), Eugene Roche (Pat Callahan).

    Each of the episodes is described below in airdate order.

LENNY (pilot)   Airdates: 9/10/90, 9/27/90.

    Guest Cast: Ken Kimmins (Dr. Thomas), Martha Jane (Mrs. Luby).

    Lenny has grown tired of working days at the gas company as a construction worker and nights as the doorman at a fancy Boston hotel. Finally, he's managed to save some money and decides to quit his night job, but then he gets the news that his father needs money for an operation.

THREE MEN AND THREE BABIES
Airdate: 9/19/90.

    Guest Cast: Ryan Francis (Tommy Shaw).

    When Shelly and Mary have a car accident, the Callahan men must care for little Tracy and Kelly.

OPPORTUNITY KNOCKS OUT   Airdate: 9/26/90.

    Guest Cast: Steve Vinovich (Mr. Evans), David Landsberg (The Veterinarian), Audree Chapman (Mrs. Green), John Drayman (The Waiter), James Eakle (Man with Cat).

    Lenny is being considered for a promotion, but his chances fade considerably when he knocks out his boss for making a pass at Shelly.

LOAN ARRANGER, THE   Airdate: 10/03/90.
Guest Cast: Kevin Scannell (Detective Joey Gannon), David Shawn Michaels (Bernie Weintraub), J.J. Wall (The Bartender).

Lenny has loaned money to his boss, Sal Lobrico, but is afraid to ask for the money back. Eddie's promise to get the money by leaning on Sal lands him in trouble when Sal is killed in an explosion.

YES VIRGINITY, THERE IS A GOD
Airdate: 12/15/90.
Guest Cast: Chance Quinn (Ant'ny), Art Metrano (Father), Eda Zahl (Mother), Bonnie Morgan (Daughter).

Lenny is having a bad day off. The refrigerator has died and they need to cook 50 pounds of chicken—quickly. Tracy says she doesn't believe in God; Eddie breaks the television; and Shelly finds a condom in Kelly's wallet.

CAREER DAY   Airdate: 12/22/90.
Guest Cast: Anne Haney (Sister Mary George), Bonnie Urseth (Sister Theresa), Tony Simotes (Dr. Anthony Scala), Donna Lynn Leavy (Betty McGruder), William Utay (Glen Nowell).

When an uncle dies and the family has to go to New York for his funeral, Tracy is very upset about missing a big dance recital.

MY BOYFRIEND'S BLACK AND THERE'S GONNA BE TROUBLE   Airdate: 1/05/91.
Guest Cast: Judith Hoag (Megan), Scott Lawrence (Bob), Henry Harris (Jim), Ann Weldon (Sarah), Martha Jane (Mrs. Luby), John Ingle (Priest).

Lenny's sister, Megan, announces that she's going to marry a black man. This is fine with Lenny, but Pat and Mary are shocked at the news.

G.I. JOE   Airdate: 1/12/91.
Guest Cast: Don Lake (Doctor), Lauren Tom (Nurse).

Lenny has stomach pains but keeps saying that he can't take time to see a doctor. Shelly finally insists that he go for tests, and the doctor tells them it's either a polyp or cancer.

LENNY GET YOUR GUN   Airdate: 1/26/91.
Guest Cast: Fred Applegate (Miles Swanson).

When their house is robbed, Pat boobytraps it to save what's left.

GASMAN COMETH, THE   Airdate: 2/02/91.
Guest Cast: Henry Cho (Nick Harimoto), Lou Bonacki (Charlie).

Lenny resents having to take a visiting Japanese consultant for a tour of the underground gas lines. It's soon obvious the visitor is unhappy as well, for both men are racially biased.

FINE ROMANCE, A   Airdate: 2/09/91.
Guest Cast: Fred Stoller (Bobby).

Lenny loans Eddie $200, not knowing that his brother is going to bet it on a fighter. Later, when Shelly says she feels the romance has gone out of their marriage, Lenny wants the money back to treat her to a night in a hotel.

COLD   Airdate: 2/16/91.
Guest Cast: Barry Shabaka Henly (Furnace Man).

A broken furnace and a lack of spare parts finds the Callahans moving into a cheap motel for 6 weeks.

FAMILY MATTERS   Airdate: 3/02/91.
Guest Cast: Fabiana Udenio (Agility Tortorici).

The family is invited for dinner at Lenny's parents' house and Shelly is not happy about having to go.

IT AIN'T THE HEAT   Airdate: 3/09/91.
Guest Cast: Bill Dana (Charlie Gold).

Pat announces that they're moving to Florida, but no one takes him seriously because he does this every year.

ONE OF OUR LUBY'S IS MISSING
Airdate: Unaired.
Guest Cast: Martha Jane (Mrs. Luby), Jack McGee (Larry Luby), Ron Canada (Sergeant Murphy), Brenda Klemme (Waitress), Tyler Reid von Oy (Lester Luby).

As the Callahans and their neighbors, the Lubys, get ready for their annual bowling contest, Lenny and Larry Luby agree that the loser will have to run down the street naked.

Blossom

Disney's *Blossom* began as a mid-season replacement for the 1990–91 season. The focus was on 14-year-old Blossom Russo, who lived with her father, Nick, and two brothers. Early episodes featured fantasy segments as Blossom tried to make up for her missing mother, who had abandoned the family. As the series progressed, it took on a more serious tone, dealing with plot elements such as date rape and teenage pregnancy.

Blossom continued on NBC until the 1994–95 season.

Series Cast: Mayim Bialik (Blossom Russo), Joey Lawrence (Joey Russo), Michael Stoyanov (Anthony Russo), Jenna von Oy (Six LeMuere, 1991–95), David Lascher (Vinnie Bonitardi, 1992–94), Portia Dawson (Rhonda Jo Applegate, 1992–93), Barnard Hughes (Buzz Richman, 1991–93), Samaria Graham (Shelly Russo, 1994–95), Courtney Chase (Kennedy, 1994–95), Kevin Jamal Woods (Frank, 1994–95), Finola Hughes (Carol, 1994–95), Ted Wass (Nick Russo), Harvey (Winston, the bulldog, 1994–95).

1990–91 season

BLOSSOM BLOSSOMS   Airdates: 1/03/91, 4/15/91, 5/24/93.

Guest Cast: Phylicia Rashad (Dream Mother), Jenna von Oy (Six LeMuere), Vonni Ribisi (Mitchell), Eileen Brennan (Agnes).

When Blossom gets her first period, she is upset that her mom is not there to help her through puberty.

MY SISTER'S KEEPER   Airdates: 1/07/91, 4/22/91.

Guest Cast: Eileen Brennan (Agnes), Jenna von Oy (Six LeMuere), Stephen Dorff (Bobby).

Blossom hits it off with Joey's new friend, Bobby. This makes Joey nervous, and he warns Nick that Bobby likes to score with all of his dates.

DAD'S GIRLFRIEND   Airdates: 1/14/91, 6/03/91.

Guest Cast: Rhea Perlman (The Godmother), Jenna von Oy (Six LeMuere), Debra Engle (Elaine), Jay Lambert (15-Year-Old Richard Gere), Eileen Brennan (Agnes).

The family is jealous of Nick's new girlfriend, Elaine.

WHO'S IN CHARGE HERE?   Airdates: 1/21/91, 5/27/91.

Guest Cast: Jenna von Oy (Six LeMuere), Nile Lanning (Stephanie), Little Richard (Justice of the Peace).

Blossom spots Anthony's new girlfriend, Stephanie, stealing a family heirloom, but she's afraid to tell him because he might get depressed and go back to drugs.

SEX, LIES, AND TEENAGERS   Airdates: 2/04/91, 6/10/91.

Guest Cast: Jenna von Oy (Six LeMuere), Brenda Strong (Diane), Johnny Galecki (Jason), Ryan Francis (Ricky), Tobey Maguire (Boy), Alitzah Weiner (Sheila), Phil Donohue (Himself).

Nick is upset because Blossom lies to him and he also realizes she's getting interested in sex.

I AIN'T GOT NO BUDDY   Airdates: 2/11/91, 6/17/91.

Guest Cast: Jenna von Oy (Six LeMuere), Penina Segall (Doris), Aimee Brooks (Adrian), Michael Landes (Bobby), Jason Strickland (Boy #1), Xavier Garcia (Boy #2), Estelle Getty (Sophia Petrillo).

Nick's divorce papers arrive but the kids don't know how to give them to him.

THANKS FOR THE MEMOREX   Airdates: 2/18/91, 8/15/91.

Guest Cast: Aaron Freeman (Young Anthony), Matthew Lawrence (Joey, Age 11), Andrew Lawrence (Joey, Age 2).

After Blossom converts the family's old movies to video, she tries to recapture the "good old days" by organizing a trip to the lake where they used to go together.

GEEK, THE   Airdates: 2/25/91, 8/19/91.

Guest Cast: Jenna von Oy (Six LeMuere), Chris Demetral (Fred Fogerty), Justin Whalin (Jordan Taylor), Alf (Himself).

Blossom is tricked into a date with the biggest geek at school, and she dreams that everyone laughs at her.

TOUGH LOVE   Airdates: 3/04/91, 9/02/91.

Guest Cast: David Knell (Mozart), Joely Fisher (Bambi), John Apicella (Mr. Fisher), Rex Ryon (Cop), Aaron Lohr (Student), Sonny Bono (Himself).

Nick throws Anthony out when he refuses to get a job.

SUCH A NIGHT   Airdates: 3/11/91, 8/12/91.

Guest Cast: Jenna von Oy (Six LeMuere), Billy Morrissette (Jeff).

Blossom wants to ask a boy out, but by the time she calls, he already has a date. Anthony tries to help a friend stay on the wagon and finds himself tempted to have a drink.

SCHOOL DAZE Airdates: 3/25/91, 8/26/91.

Guest Cast: Tasha Scott (Billie), Judith Marie Bergan (Dominique), Priscilla Morrill (Mrs. Whiting), Nicole Huntington (Wendy), Frank Como (Mike Henderson), Kris Newquist (Boy).

It's the start of the school year, and Blossom doesn't want to return to an all-girls private school. She would much rather go to a public school and meet boys.

PAPA'S LITTLE DIVIDEND Airdates: 4/08/91, 8/17/91.

Guest Cast: Nick Ullett (Maitre D'), Eric Poppick (Francois), Megan Gallagher (Arlene).

A former date of Nick's shows up with a baby, claiming that it's his child.

LOVE STINKS! Airdate: 4/29/91.

Guest Cast: Josh Hoffman (Bobby), Jane Leeves (Sheila), Josh Goddard.

Blossom is in love with her pen pal, but he has met a girl in school.

1991–92 season

SECOND BASE Airdates: 9/16/91, 12/30/91.

Guest Cast: Reggie Jackson (Himself), Justin Whalin (Jimmy).

Blossom fantasizes about her relationship with Jimmy, her steady boyfriend.

HERE COMES THE BUZZ Airdates: 9/23/91, 3/09/92.

Guest Cast: Tisha Campbell (Toni), Anne Gee Byrd (Linda).

Blossom's maternal grandfather, Buzz, comes to visit and Nick can't wait until he leaves, feeling the older man is a bad influence.

JOINT, THE Airdates: 9/30/91, 4/20/92.

Guest Cast: None.

Blossom finds a joint and brings it home with thoughts of trying marijuana for the first time.

I'M WITH THE BAND AIRDATES: 10/07/91, 5/25/92.

Guest Cast: Jeff Kahn (Bellhop), Stefanie Ridel (Melissa), Will Smith (Fresh Prince).

When Blossom and Six go to San Francisco for a band contest, they have so much fun that they almost destroy their hotel.

HONOR? Airdates: 10/14/91, 3/16/92.

Guest Cast: Chris Demetral (Dennis), Nick Ullett (Teacher), Joshua Goddard (Boy #1), Omar Gooding (Tyler), Jane Hait (Michelle), Cleandré Norman (Larry), Douglas Emerson (Boy #2).

Joey learns that cheating in class can be dangerous, and Blossom learns that an ex-boyfriend is spreading lies about her honor.

TO TELL THE TRUTH Airdates: 10/21/91, 3/30/92.

Guest Cast: Tisha Campbell (Toni), John Capodice (Interviewer), Jonathan Brandis (Stevie), Magda Harout (Honey #1), Kay Freeman (Honey #2).

Blossom can't decide if she should tell Six that they both like the same boy, and Anthony is worried that he will lose a job if they know he is a recovering addict.

INTERVENTION Airdates: 11/04/91, 6/22/92.

Guest Cast: Matt Levin (Frankie), Tommy Newsom (Himself), Tom Nibley (Waiter), Alex Nevil (Usher), Dorothy Reo (Mrs. Williams).

Anthony must force Joey into realizing that his friend is an alcoholic; Blossom and Nick both play hooky together so they can better understand each other.

RUN FOR THE BORDER Airdates: 11/11/91, 6/01/92.

Guest Cast: Sam McMurray (Sergio), Karla Montana (Anna), Joe Shea (Mr. Garduno).

Six blames herself when her father moves out of the house; Joey has language problems with his new girlfriend; Anthony arranges a family photograph with disastrous results.

ROCKUMENTARY Airdates: 11/18/91, 6/08/92.

Guest Cast: Neil Patrick Harris (The "Charming" Derek Slade), J.J. Wall (The Cop), Ryeland Allison (Reggie), Jodi Peterson (Fan #1), Megan McGinnis (Fan #2). Cameos: Mr. Blackwell, Jere Burns, David Cassidy, Dick Clark, Dreyfuss, David Faustino, Don King, Warren Littlefield, Dinah Manoff, Wolfgang Puck, Martha Quinn, Tori Spelling.

After watching too many rock videos, Blossom fantasizes about being the world's biggest rock star.

EXPECTATIONS Airdates: 11/25/91, 4/13/92.

Guest Cast: Susan Anton (Suzy), Portia Dawson (Bambi).

When Nick tells the family that he is bringing his newest girlfriend home to meet them, they all fantasize about her in very unflattering ways.

You Can't Go Home   Airdates: 12/02/91, 7/12/93.

Guest Cast: Gail Edwards (Sharon LeMeure), Ann Guilbert (Elizabeth).

Six has a hard time accepting that her mother might want to date; Anthony tries to help an elderly woman with amnesia.

This Old House   Airdates: 12/09/91, 12/28/92.

Guest Cast: Margaret Reed (Madolyn), Matthew Lawrence (Young Joey), Grant Gelt (Young Anthony), Autumn Winters (Young Blossom), Marissa Rosen (Young Six), Peggy Mannix (Real Estate Lady).

When Nick announces that he might have to sell the house, everyone looks back at their happy times there together.

It's a Marginal Life   Airdates: 12/16/91, 12/20/93.

Guest Cast: Chance Quinn (Skunk), Nicholas Guest (Jean-Claude), Quinn Cummings (Millie), Jesse Dabson (The Cop), Santa Claus (Himself).

Christmas is looking dismal: Nick has lost his job, Blossom burns the dinner, the boys blow up a Christmas tree, and someone has stolen the presents.

Test, The   Airdates: 1/06/92, 7/13/92.

Guest Cast: Gregg Daniel (The Proctor), Jason Marsden (Jimmy), Omar Gooding (Brad), Marjorie Harris (Teddi), Jake Price (Woody), Megan McGinnis (Susan).

Blossom freezes when she takes an important test at school; Nick tries to fix things around the house but makes matters worse; Anthony worries about becoming addicted to gambling.

Hot for Teacher   Airdates: 1/13/92, 12/14/92.

Guest Cast: Parker Stevenson (Scott Alexander), Damon Martin (Jack), Omar Gooding (Brad), Jodi Peterson (Carrie), Paige Pengra (Melissa), Erin Reed (Tammi).

Blossom has a crush on a substitute teacher; Joey courts a new love interest with Blossom's help.

Three O'Clock and All Is Hell
Airdates: 1/20/92, 7/20/92.

Guest Cast: Todd Susman (Todd), Debra Jo Rupp (Lucy), Don Lake (Cop #1), Don Stark (Cop #2), Danny Nucci (Lou), Kelly Packard (Taylor), Helena Apothaker (Donna), Reva Rose (Miss Kitchens).

Blossom makes a new friend but his girlfriend threatens to beat her up; Nick's old friend gets depressed and locks himself in the bathroom.

Losers Win   Airdates: 2/10/92, 6/15/92.

Guest Cast: Portia Dawson (Rhonda Jo Applegate), Gregg Daniel (Mr. Ross), Randy Josselyn (Chad).

Blossom chokes under pressure after joining the debate team; Joey becomes convinced that Six is his good luck charm; Anthony saves a centerfold's life.

Letter, The   Airdates: 2/17/92, 7/06/92.

Guest Cast: Portia Dawson (Rhonda Jo Applegate), James Pickens Jr. (Vinnie), Salt-N-Pepa (Rap Group).

The kids make a video letter for their mother's birthday; Nick undergoes a mid-life crisis and overexercises.

Wake Up Little Suzy   Airdates: 2/24/92, 8/31/92.

Guest Cast: Edward Winter (Coach), Brooke Theiss (Allison), A.J. Langer (Sherry), Nicki Vannice (Tricia), Megan McGinnis (Susan), Karyn Parsons (Hilary).

A slumber party goes awry when a rebellious girl decides to crash it; Joey worries about a threat from his girlfriend's father; Anthony has to date a rich woman who "bought" him at a charity auction.

You Must Remember This   Airdates: 3/02/92, 9/07/92.

Guest Cast: Leah Remini (Ellen), Debra Jo Rupp (Mrs. Robinson), Ryeland Allison (Billy), C+C Music Factory.

Blossom and Six are determined to get tickets to a big concert; Joey has his first babysitting job; Anthony tries to decide why a woman at work hates him.

House Guests   Airdates: 3/23/92, 5/31/93.

Guest Cast: Gail Edwards (Sharon LeMeure), James Madio (Silvio), Portia

Dawson (Rhonda Jo Applegate), Brenda Strong (Diane), Jonathan Schmock (Waiter), Joel Murray (Doug LeMuere).

Six and her mother move in while their house is being fumigated.

WHINES AND MISDEMEANORS Airdates: 4/06/92, 10/19/92.

Guest Cast: Lee Garlington (Samy), Dena Dietrich (Mrs. Ubermeyer), Jonathan Prince (Mr. Cunningham), Abraham Benrubi (Francis).

A series of lies lands Blossom in detention; Anthony and Joey both get in trouble with the police; Nick realizes that his small lies can be a bad example for the family.

DRIVER'S EDUCATION Airdates: 4/27/92, 11/30/92.

Guest Cast: Teri Copley (Glenda Dudley), Perry Anzilotti (Driving Examiner), Tiffani-Amber Thiessen (Ricki), Vendela Kirsebom (Fairy Godmother).

When Blossom fails her driver's test she cries until the examiner decides to pass her; Joey's woman boss sexually harasses him; Nick has a blind date with a woman he went to high school with.

SPRING FEVER Airdate: 5/04/92.

Guest Cast: Portia Dawson (Rhonda Jo Applegate), David Lascher (Vinnie Bonitardi), Barbara Tyson (Diane).

Anthony must lie to break a date to help a recovering alcoholic; Joey and Six spy on Blossom's date; Blossom decides to run away from home with the boy.

1992–93 season

RUNAWAY Airdates: 8/10/92, 8/02/93.

Guest Cast: None.

Continuing the cliffhanger ending of the second season, Blossom realizes that she is not ready to sleep with Vinnie.

DEAR MOM Airdates: 8/17/92, 8/09/93.

Guest Cast: None.

Blossom writes to her mother about the recent conflicts in her life, then faces a new dilemma when she sees Anthony drinking.

NO CURE FOR LOVE Airdates: 8/24/92, 8/16/93.

Guest Cast: Lisa Rieffel (Cybill).

Vinnie announces that he wants to see other people, a situation that makes Blossom

very moody. She finally shakes her depression and cures him of it by saying that she wants to start dating again too.

WHAT PRICE LOVE? Airdates: 9/14/92, 4/26/93.

Guest Cast: Cathryn de Prume (Kandy), Christine Joan Taylor (Patty).

Six feels slighted by Blossom's attention to Vinnie and she tells Blossom she doesn't want to be taken for granted.

JOEY CHRONICLES, THE Airdates: 9/21/92, 4/19/93.

Guest Cast: Billy O'Sullivan (Chucky), Jessica Hahn (Herself), Raye "Zap" Hollitt, Bobbie Phillips, Jill Pierce.

Joey has to write a paper for school with himself as the main character, but he has writer's block.

KIDS Airdates: 9/28/92, 1/25/93.

Guest Cast: Katherine Cannon (Doris), Andrew Hill Newman (Guy #1), David Pressman (Guy #2).

When Vinnie has a motorcycle accident and is knocked unconscious, Blossom fantasizes about their future life together.

ONLY WHEN I LAUGH Airdates: 10/05/92, 3/29/93.

Guest Cast: David Arquette, Bernie Allen, Jack Carter, Bill Dana, Slappy White, Rex Ryon.

Blossom and Six buy fake identification to get into a popular music club, then discover that it's "teen night" and they're "too old."

I KILLED CHICO BARRANCA Airdates: 10/12/92, 6/07/93.

Guest Cast: Tony Plana (Chico Barranca), Gail Edwards (Sharon LeMeure), Bonnie Morgan (Girl in Prison), Paul Eiding (Officer).

A baseball scout offers Joey $10,000 to skip high school and play winter season ball. Meanwhile, Blossom and Six are arrested for selling stolen goods at a garage sale.

ALL HALLOWS EVE Airdates: 10/26/92.

Guest Cast: Perry Anzilotti, John Christian Graas, A.J. Langer, Jonathan Schmock, Wayne Smith.

Joey is mistaken as a crazed prowler on Halloween. Nick, Anthony, and Buzz dress as a female rock band to win a costume contest prize, but their car breaks down at a very macho bar.

MAKING OF A PRESIDENT, THE Airdates: 11/09/92, 6/21/93.

Guest Cast: Jason Marsden, Lenny Wolpe, Phil Buckman, Omar Gooding, Timothy Leary (Himself), David Leisure (Himself), Megan McGinnis, Keith Morrison, Tommy Newsom (Himself), Angul Nigam, Jill Pierce.

Six convinces Blossom that running for class office would be a good way to meet boys.

MY GIRL Airdates: 11/16/92, 3/08/93.
Joey feels that he doesn't fit in with the rest of the family, so Anthony tells him that he was probably switched at birth.

FRAT PARTY, THE Airdates: 11/23/92, 3/15/93.

Guest Cast: Christopher Daniel Barnes, Brooke Alexander (Ms. Quigley), Alexander Enberg.

Blossom and Six go to a fraternity party and unknowingly drink some spiked punch.

LOSING YOUR . . . RELIGION Airdates: 12/07/92, 7/02/93.

Guest Cast: Alan King (Rabbi Hyman Greenblatt), Mark-Paul Gosselaar (Kevin).

When their class is assigned a project to study other religions, Blossom is told to find out what it's like to be raised Jewish, and Six studies Catholicism.

RUBY Airdates: 12/21/92, 7/19/93.

Guest Cast: Christopher Daniel Barnes, Frank Capp and Juggernaut (Army Corps Band).

In a flashback, Buzz he tells Blossom how he met his late wife, Ruby.

LAST LAUGH, THE Airdates: 1/04/93, 7/05/93.

Guest Cast: Gail Edwards (Sharon LeMeure), Steven Gilborn (Vice Principal), Carol Barbee, Gina Philips, Arsenio Hall (Himself).

Nick is upset when his new girlfriend, a stand-up comic, uses parts of his life in her act. Blossom and Six run into trouble when they make a controversial video about safe sex.

TIME Airdates: 1/11/93, 6/14/93.

Guest Cast: Mary Margaret Humes, Michelle Collins.

Blossom and Six worry about getting older and having life pass them by. Nick is having problems with his new girlfriend's five kids. Anthony proposes to Rhonda.

CAR WRECKS AND MARRIAGE Airdates: 1/18/93, 6/28/93.

Guest Cast: Gladys Holland (Genevieve LeChere), Monica Lauren Buck, April Storms.

Blossom lets Six practice driving in Nick's car and she crashes it into a wall.

MYSTERY TRAIN Airdate: 2/01/93.

Guest Cast: Michael J. Pollard, Keith Allison (Pete Weston).

Nick agrees to help an old friend find a job. Vinnie falls asleep in Blossom's room and narrowly escapes being caught by Nick. Out in the desert, Joey and Anthony think they have spotted a UFO.

BEST LAID PLANS OF MICE AND MEN, THE Airdates: 2/08/93, 7/19/93.

Guest Cast: Adam Biesk, Carol Ann Susi, Julie Anne Martin, Cathy Merriman, Erik Reo, Temre Sawyer, Carolyn Lawrence, The Party.

Nick gets a job at Disneyland and the rest of the family tag along to tease him. Blossom has a fight with Vinnie when she sees him kiss another girl, and Six falls in love with a guide on the Jungle Cruise.

STUDENT FILMS Airdate: 2/15/93.

Guest Cast: Susan Burrell.
Everyone shows films they made in school.

ALL DRESSED UP Airdates: 2/22/93, 8/30/93.

Guest Cast: Ashlee Levitch (Heather).

Blossom is mad at Vinnie, and tells him she doesn't want to go to the junior prom with him. Rhonda is jealous of Anthony's new partner, and Joey learns that his girlfriend is pregnant.

THRILL IS GONE, THE Airdates: 3/01/93, 9/06/93.

Guest Cast: Melissa Manchester (Maddy Russo), B.B. King (Himself).

Nick feels that the magic has gone out of his current relationship, and Blossom writes a letter about how the magic between her and Vinnie is no longer there.

YOU DID WHAT? Airdate: 4/12/93, 6/25/93.

Guest Cast: Terry Kaiser (Vito).

Nick announces they have money problems so Joey tries to make a fortune speculating in baseball cards. Blossom finds a job but Six takes it instead, and Anthony gets a job selling cosmetics by phone.

SITCOM   Airdates: 5/03/93, 7/26/93.
Guest Cast: Mitchell Whitfield, Todd Susman, Mary Hart (Herself), John Ratzenberger (Himself), Robert Stack (Himself), Vincent Ventresca, Rickey D'Shon Collins.

Nick's friend builds a sitcom around the Russo family and Six is picked to be the star.

HUNGER   Airdates: 5/10/93, 8/23/93.
Guest Cast: Stephanie Beacham, Jennifer Nash, T.C. Warner, Mary Margaret Humes, Michelle Collins.

Blossom is worried that Six has an eating disorder. Joey is seduced by an older woman, and Anthony finds himself becoming romantically involved with an old friend.

PARIS   Airdates: 5/17/93, 9/13/93.
Still upset about breaking up with Vinnie, Blossom is thinking about moving to Paris to be with her mother.

1993–94 season

BLOSSOM IN PARIS   Airdate (2-hour format): 9/24/93.
Guest Cast: Jacques Coltelloni (Laurent), Chantal Delsaux (Information Woman), Tom Gallop (Frank), Gerard Ismael (Immigration Officer), Stephen Root (Louie), Jonathan Schmock (Man in Hat), Eric Viellard (Robert), Victoria Wicks (Jacqueline Renaud), Jaclyn Bernstein (Elizabeth), Don Bloomfield (Customs Official), Nikki Cox (Cynthia), Kelli Kirkland (Mary), Megan McGinnis (Jennifer), Brittany Murphy (Wendy), Riff Regan (Susan), Jodi Peterson (Darlene), Erik Reo (Airport Clerk), Penina Segall (Karen), Aquilina Soriano (Sherry), Melissa Manchester (Maddy Russo).

Blossom's visit to Paris to get closer to her mom actually finds her getting close to Laurent, a friendly waiter who gives her a tour of the city.

TRANSITIONS   Airdates: 9/27/93, 5/30/94.
Guest Cast: Portia Dawson (Rhonda Jo Applegate).

The return home holds several surprises for Blossom, including the discovery that Six has begun drinking. Nick and Joey try to get closer together by going on a camping trip.

KISS AND TELL   Airdates: 10/04/93, 12/27/93.
Guest Cast: Melissa Manchester (Maddy Russo), Phyllis Diller (Mrs. Peterson), Don Novello (Father Guido Sarducci/God), Stephanie Ridel (Barbara Jenkins), Tony Pope (Voice-overs).

Maddy moves back to Los Angeles to be closer to her children and Blossom thinks her parents may get back together. When Joey promises to never touch women again if God would help him out of a jam, God promptly calls him to Heaven.

SIX AND SONNY   Airdate: 10/11/93.
Guest Cast: Gail Edwards (Sharon LeMuere), David Schwimmer (Sonny).

Six becomes involved in a relationship with a married ex-con and runs away after her mother orders her to stop seeing him.

BLOSSOM'S DILEMMA   Airdate: 10/18/93.
Guest Cast: Gail Edwards (Sharon LeMuere), David Schwimmer (Sonny), Cathryn de Prume (Veronica), Tom McCleister (Prison Guard), Bill Bixby (Cop's Voice).

Blossom tries to talk Six into giving up Sonny, but it takes his arrest and subsequent infatuation with a female prison guard for Six to come to her senses.

.38 SPECIAL   Airdates: 10/25/93, 6/06/94.
Guest Cast: Dick Martin (Frosty the Clown), Keith Allison (Pete Weston), Devon Gummersall (Jimmy Kelly), Jack Kenny (Vice Principal), David Reo (Musician).

Blossom doesn't know what to do when another student brings a gun to school. Meanwhile, Nick has to scrape together the cash to play at a club date, and Joey finds himself trying to help a drunk clown.

FIFTY-MINUTE HOUR, THE   Airdates: 11/01/93, 3/07/94.
Guest Cast: Portia Dawson (Rhonda Jo Applegate), Richard Roat (Dr. Samuelson), William Bumiller (Surgeon), Laura Harring (Nurse Delafuente).

In a story set 10 years in the future, Nick sees a psychiatrist to discuss his problems with the family.

TRUE ROMANCE   Airdates: 11/08/93, 7/11/94.
Guest Cast: Michael A. Nickles (Drake), Christina Belford (Nancy), Irena Ward (June), Hugh Hefner (Himself), Tawnni Cable

(Brenda), Barbara Moore (Ariel), Monique Noel (Claire).

Blossom tries to write a romance novel and fantasizes about herself as the star. Anthony is invited to the Playboy Mansion after his break-up with Rhonda.

LET'S TALK ABOUT SEX   Airdates: 11/15/93, 6/13/94.

Guest Cast: Blaire Baron (Barbara), Lisa Kelly (Agnes).

Everyone seems preoccupied with sex: Blossom discovers that Vinnie has slept with another woman; Nick learns that his girlfriend used to date Anthony; and Six tries to convince Joey to sleep with her.

BIG DOINGS—PART I   Airdates: 11/22/93, 4/16/94.

Guest Cast: Finola Hughes (Carol), Samaria Graham (Shelly Russo), Tori Spelling (Herself), Jay Kerr (Elrod), Edd Hall (Announcer), Erik Reo (Dealer).

Anthony goes to Las Vegas to forget Rhonda and has too much to drink.

BIG DOINGS—PART II   Airdates: 11/29/93, 4/23/94.

Guest Cast: Finola Hughes (Carol), Samaria Graham (Shelly Russo), Alaina Reed Hall (Esther), Ivory Ocean (Carl Lewis), John Apicella (Minister), Kent Shocknek (Himself), Mary Pat Gleason (Woman), John Mariano (Dave).

Anthony and Shelly decide they really do love each other and get married again, this time sober. Vinnie proposes to Blossom.

COPYCAT   Airdate: 12/13/93.

Guest Cast: Samaria Graham (Shelly Russo), Ellen Blain (Audrey), Jake Price (Chip), Fred Roggin (Himself).

A new girl at school starts driving Blossom crazy by copying everything she does.

GETTING LUCKY   Airdate: 1/10/94.

Guest Cast: Finola Hughes (Carol).

Blossom is having a hard time accepting Nick's girlfriend, Carol, and she makes sure everyone knows just how unhappy she is.

MEAT   Airdates: 1/24/94, 6/20/94.

Guest Cast: Samaria Graham (Shelly Russo), Lochlyn Munro (Evan Henderson), Marty Polio (Waiter).

When Nick fails a cholesterol test, Blossom reacts by deciding they will become vegetarians.

DOUBLE DATE   Airdate: 1/31/94.

Guest Cast: Samaria Graham (Shelly Russo), Ivory Ocean (Carl Lewis), Scott Wolf (Gordo McCain), Paul Wittenburg (Leslie), Cliff Dorfman (Billy).

Tony tries to get better acquainted with his new father-in-law, Carl; Joey gets a love letter from another guy; Six comes home from the rehab clinic.

BEACH BLANKET BLOSSOM—PART I
Airdate: 2/14/94.

Guest Cast: Angela Visser (Ethel the Mermaid), Avery Schreiber (Stubby the Henchman).

In a dream, Blossom and the gang are seen in a strange version of a 1960s beach movie.

BEACH BLANKET BLOSSOM—PART II
Airdate: 2/21/94.

Guest Cast: Angela Visser (Ethel the Mermaid), Avery Schreiber (Stubby the Henchman), Phyllis Diller (Herself), Fabian (Himself), Jimmy Walker (Himself), David Willis (Surfer), Ken Enomoto (Japanese Guy #1), Y. Hero Abe (Japanese Guy #2).

Blossom's beach movie dream continues.

LITTLE HELP FROM MY FRIENDS, A
Airdates: 2/28/94, 7/25/94.

Guest Cast: Finola Hughes (Carol), Mr. T. (Himself), Doren Fein (Kennedy), David Deluise (Randy).

Blossom agrees to babysit Carol's daughter, Kennedy, but then leaves Anthony to care for the youngster.

OUR FAVORITE SCENES   Airdate: 3/14/94.

Guest Cast: None.

The cast appear as themselves and introduce their favorite scenes from past episodes.

BLUE BLOSSOM   Airdate: 3/19/94.

Guest Cast: Samaria Graham (Shelly Russo), Neil Duncan (Graham), Michole White (Robin).

Blossom is depressed about her upcoming birthday; Anthony worries about meeting Shelly's cousin; Nick worries about Carol's ex-husband; Joey writes Hillary Clinton a letter.

SEX, LIES, AND MRS. PETERSON
Airdates: 4/02/94, 8/08/94.

Guest Cast: Phyllis Diller (Mrs. Peterson), Sarah Lee Jones (Barbara).

Blossom and Anthony fix up Buzz with Mrs. Peterson, who works with Anthony, but the kids almost manage to end the relationship before it begins.

SEVEN DEADLY SINS   Airdate: 4/09/94.
Guest Cast: Marty Polio (Waiter).
Two aliens hoping to learn about the Seven Deadly Sins select the Russo family as their test subjects. As they watch, they observe each of the sins in very short order.

NIGHT OF RECKONING   Airdate: 5/02/94.
Guest Cast: Melissa Manchester (Maddy Russo), Samaria Graham (Shelly Russo), Andrew Lawrence (Little Joey), Matthew Lawrence (Young Joey), Carla Montana (Rhonda).
Blossom persuades Nick into revealing what he was like as a teenager; Joey loses faith in Shelly as a mom; and Rhonda drops by for a visit.

LAST TANGO, THE   Airdates: 5/09/94, 8/22/94.
Guest Cast: Finola Hughes (Carol), Jonathan Del Arco (Raymondo), Steven Gilborn (Mr. Marnacki), Marguerite Moreau (Melanie).
Blossom approaches Vinnie's senior prom with trepidation, for he will be leaving soon for college in New Jersey.

GRADUATION   Airdates: 5/23/94, 9/05/94.
Guest Cast: Melissa Manchester (Maddy Russo), Terry Bradshaw (Coach Morton).
As Vinnie's graduation approaches, Blossom is thinking about breaking off their engagement so he will be free to go to school in New Jersey.

1994–95 season

NEW LIFE, A—PART I   Airdates: 9/26/94, 12/12/94.
Guest Cast: None.
Nick tells Blossom that Carol and Kennedy will be moving into the house. Anthony and Joey decide it's time to move out.

NEW LIFE, A—PART II   Airdates: 10/03/94, 12/19/94.
Guest Cast: None.
Blossom runs away to join Joey on the road with his baseball team.

PUPPY LOVE   Airdate: 10/10/94.
Guest Cast: Philip Angelotti (Richie), Lorna Scott (Mrs. Featherman), Elisa Donovan (Tanya).

Blossom learns that there should be more to a relationship than just a physical attraction; Shelly is pregnant; Kennedy adopts Winston, a stray bulldog.

YOUR NEW PLANET   Airdate: 10/17/94.
Guest Cast: John Caponera (Thunderclap Jackson), Bridget Sienna (Maid).
Blossom and friends tape a video greeting for Anthony and Shelly's pending arrival; Kennedy is running up huge phone bills; Nick becomes upset when Carol plans a big wedding.

WEDDING, THE   Airdates: 10/24/95, 5/29/95.
Guest Cast: Melissa Manchester (Maddy), Neil Duncan (Graham), Kevin Woods (Frank), John Apicella (Minister).
The days before Nick and Carol's wedding are hard on everyone.

WRITING THE WRONGS   Airdate: 10/31/94.
Guest Cast: None.
Blossom is not sure how to handle a humanities assignment to "express herself."

DIRTY ROTTEN SCOUNDREL   Airdate: 11/07/94.
Guest Cast: Elisa Donovan (Tanya Adams), Melanie Smith (Alex), Francesca Taylor (Lizzie Martin), Mark L. Taylor (Ralph Martin), Elise Ogden (Nancy Martin).
Blossom and Six fail in an effort to create designer T-shirts; Kennedy's friend almost destroys the house; Joey has to fend off an amorous woman coach.

GAME YOU PLAY TOMORROW, THE   Airdate: 11/14/94.
Guest Cast: Eric Allen Kramer (Wildman Boyette).
Blossom and Six find they've been accepted by different colleges.

BLOSSOM GUMP   Airdate: 11/21/94.
Guest Cast: Jenna Strom (Madonna), E'Cassanova (Michael Jackson), Bill Saluga (Paul), Liz Sheridan (Mrs. Walker), Frank Fowler (Reporter #1), Sid Melton (Reporter #2).
Blossom dreams that she is Forrest Gump, changing the lives of people around her.

OH BABY   Airdates: 11/28/94, 6/05/95.
Guest Cast: Phyllis Diller (Mrs. Peterson), Brian George (Shakir), Darion Basco (Gang

Kid), Chris Read (Dispatcher), Mason and Quinn Bowers (Baby).

Nick is surprised to find out that Carol was married twice before; Shelly goes into labor; Anthony is being held hostage by a wounded gang member.

MATING RITUALS   Airdate: 1/09/95.
Guest Cast: Michael Buchman Silver (David), Stephanie Dicker (Hayley), Sara Rue (Angie).
Blossom wears a daring outfit to a party and acts older than she really is.

HI-DIDDLY-DEE   Airdate: 1/16/95.
Guest Cast: Ian Abercrombie (Mr. Winters).
Blossom tries to get into an acting class taught by a famous actor and director, but is rejected when she disagrees with his direction.

KISS IS JUST A KISS, A   Airdate: 1/23/95.
Guest Cast: Christopher Daniel Barnes (Steve), Stephanie Dicker (Hayley), Andrew Mark Berman (Boomer).
Blossom wants to stay home to watch a movie with her date, but the whole family is there.

WHO'S NOT ON FIRST   Airdate: 2/06/95.
Guest Cast: Alex Trebek (Himself), Shelly Smith (Andrea), Bruce Hedgeman (Steve).
Nick throws out his back and Carol thinks it may be psychological. Joey has a dream that pits him against Albert Einstein on *Jeopardy*.

IT HAPPENED ONE NIGHT   Airdate: 2/13/95.
Guest Cast: Chris Mulkey (Dan), Charlie Heath (Fred).
Blossom is forced into a blind date, then discovers that he is gay. Six is stranded with Joey in a motel and they have to share the only bed.

MIND WITH A HEART OF ITS OWN, A   Airdate: 2/20/95.
Guest Cast: David Lascher (Vinnie), Holly Fields (Alyssa).
Vinnie misses Blossom and comes home with plans to transfer to UCLA.

DATE, THE   Airdate: 2/27/95.
Guest Cast: Jimmy Marsden (Josh).
Blossom is bruised when she has to jump out of a car to avoid having sex with a popular football star.

DEPARTURE, THE   Airdate: 3/06/95.
Guest Cast: None.
Anthony and Shelly announce they are moving to Rhode Island and the family tries to adjust to the news.

STAR IS BARED, A   Airdate: 3/13/95.
Guest Cast: Talia Shire (Herself), Ken Lerner (Danforth), Steven Lloyd Williams (Marty).
Actress Talia Shire's car breaks down and she becomes friendly with Blossom while getting help. Shire offers Blossom a part in her new film, but then Blossom discovers it requires nudity.

YOU SAY TOMATO   Airdate: 3/20/95.
Guest Cast: Gina Hecht (Ms. Teller), Kathleen McClellan (Sorel), Sid Melton (Mr. Koch).
An argument with a teacher may mean that Blossom won't graduate from high school; Joey daydreams about several careers, all of which manage to involve a beautiful assistant.

SO MANY MILESTONES, SO LITTLE TIME   Airdate: 5/22/95.
Guest Cast: Marguerite Moreau (Melanie).
Blossom gets her first real job; Joey becomes engaged to an old girlfriend; Carol discovers that she is pregnant.

GOODBYE   Airdate: 5/22/95.
Guest Cast: Jonathan Schmock (Mr. Johnson), Michael Monks (Mr. Phillips), Judy Kain (Mrs. Phillips).
Nick announces that he is going to sell the house to start a new life with Carol. Blossom and Six try to scare away prospective buyers, but their plan fails.

The Fanelli Boys

Brandon Tartikoff, head of NBC, posed the question "What if Danny DeVito, John Travolta, Harold Ramis, and Keanu Reeves moved in with their mother in Brooklyn?" With that, *The Fanelli Boys* was on its way to network television.
Series Cast: Joe Pantoliano (Dominic Fanelli), Ann Guilbert (Theresa Fanelli), Christopher Meloni (Frank Fanelli), Ned Eisenberg (Anthony Fanelli), Andy Hirsch (Joe Fanelli), Richard Libertini (Father Angelo).
Each of the episodes is described below in airdate order.

FANELLI BOYS, THE (pilot)   Airdate: 9/08/90.

Guest Cast: Vera Lockwood (Philamena), Melanie Chartoff (Becky Goldblume), Shirley Prestia (Nina Donatelli), Vito Scotti (Sicilian #1), Ralph Manza (Sicilian #2), Alix Elias (Sandra Chia).

Recently widowed Theresa Fanelli plans to sell her house in New York and move to Miami to be with her friends. Her four sons are now grown and ready to live without her—or so she thinks.

YOU CAN GO HOME AGAIN   Airdates: 9/12/90, 1/26/91.

Guest Cast: Wendie Malick (Becky Goldblume), Shelley Morrison (Mrs. Goldblume), Amzie Strickland (Emily Bartlet), Floyd Levine (Rabbi Birnbaum), Al Ruscio (Archbishop Mosconi).

When Theresa discovers that Anthony and Dom are living in the funeral home, she tells them both to move back home. They do, but have to share a room, which causes friction.

PURSUED   Airdate: 9/19/90.

Guest Cast: Chazz Palminteri (Tommy Esposito), Susan Berman (Donna Fanucci), Nick De Mauro (Eddie DeTucci), Paddi Edwards (Connie Fanucci), John La Motta (Joe Fanucci), John Mese (Lloyd Fanucci).

Unusual love affairs are the themes of this episode, which begins as Anthony's love life takes an unexpected turn. Dom also has a problem. He discovers his old friend, Tommy Esposito, is gay.

HEX, THE   Airdate: 9/26/90.

Guest Cast: Louis Guss (Nick Bartoni), Vera Lockwood (Philamena), Nicholas Mele (Pete), Dani Klein (Lisa), Harriet Medin (Grandmother), Cleto Augusto (Luigi), Kim Geraghty (Woman #1), Anita Gregory (Woman #2).

When Theresa starts dating Nick Bartoni, the boys become jealous, for they feel no one can replace their father.

HEART ATTACK   Airdate: 10/03/90.

Guest Cast: Raffi Di Blasio (Young Dom), Benny Grant (Young Anthony), Jacob Kenner (Young Frank), Nicholas Mele (Pete).

A heat wave finds Frank down in the basement looking for an old air conditioner. When he tells Theresa about all of the other things stored there, she tells him everything is there for a reason. Her explanation is cut short when she apparently has a heart attack.

TAKE MY EX-WIFE, PLEASE   Airdate: 10/10/90.

Guest Cast: Randee Heller (Viva Fontaine), Nicholas Mele (Pete), Donna Ponterotto (Waitress), Anthony Russell (Moe), Robert Gould (Eddie), Glen Mauro (Bobby Tozzalo).

The arrival of Don's ex-wife, Viva Fontaine, shakes Dom, who introduces her to Anthony as an ex–business associate from Las Vegas.

POETIC JUSTICE   Airdate: 10/24/90.

Guest Cast: Barbara Tyson (Miss Hollister), Anthony Russell (Vinnie), Gail Shapiro (Denise), Catya Sassoon (Valentina), B.T. Taylor (Student #1), Barbara De Santis (Student #2).

When Ronnie enrolls in a college poetry class, his brothers have a good laugh at his expense; that is, all except Frank, for when he meets the beautiful teacher, he decides he's also interested in poetry.

FATHER SMOKE   Airdates: 10/31/90, 12/29/90.

Guest Cast: Fabiana Udenio (Isabella Palladino), Brandi Burkett (Holly).

The boys are all surprised to see a strange girl wearing a bathrobe in their kitchen. The girl, Isabella Palladino, is visiting from Sicily and will be staying with them until her college dorm is ready.

TARNISHED ANGEL   Airdate: 11/07/90.

Guest Cast: Robert Stack (Kyle Hadley), Michele Abrams (Jennifer), Arthur Malet (Arthur).

Dom's new girlfriend, Jennifer Hadley, is very different from past ones. Not only is she intelligent, she's also wealthy.

TWO DOMS, THE   Airdate: 11/14/90.

Guest Cast: Bruce Kirby (Uncle Dom), Heather Hoper (Leslie), Tasha Scott (Margo), Danielle Koenig (Winnie).

As the family gathers items for a church rummage sale, a teenage girl helping them takes a great interest in Frank.

ITALIAN-AMERICAN GIGOLO   Airdate: 12/01/90.

Guest Cast: Cynthia Mace (Victoria Reid-Smith), Nicholas Mele (Pete), Nick De Mauro (Eddie DeTucci), Anthony Russell (Moe Dumbrowsky), Bren McKinley (Danielle), Kelly Miller (Candy), Loren Blackwell (Gary Cosay), Channing Chase (Woman), Kathy Karges (Venus De Tucci).

Dominic hears that Anthony will win an award as "Small Businessman of the Year," but since he is nominated and loses every year, Anthony refuses to believe he can win this time.

VERY FANELLI CHRISTMAS, A   Airdate: 12/08/90.

Guest Cast: Robert Stack (Kyle Hadley), Susan Berman (Donna Fanucci), Nick De Mauro (Eddie DeTucci), Wendie Malick (Becky Goldblume), Nicholas Mele (Pete), Shelley Morrison (Mrs. Goldblume), Shirley Prestia (Nina Donatelli), Gail Shapiro (Denise), Fabiana Udenio (Isabella).

This episode consists primarily of flashback scenes from prior episodes. As the Fanellis open their Christmas gifts, they reminisce about various events.

OH, MY PAPAS   Airdate: 12/15/90.

Guest Cast: Billy Cohen (Alex), Jana Marie Hupp (Tina), Nicholas Mele (Pete), Nick De Mauro (Eddie DeTucci), Jaclyn Bernstein (Sunshine Cadet).

Theresa wins two tickets to Rome in a raffle and takes Angelo with her.

ACCIDENTS WILL HAPPEN   Airdate: 1/05/91.

Guest Cast: Wendie Malick (Becky Goldbume), Aliz Elias (Christina Ferris), Daniel Riordan (LaCroix), Jimm Giannini (Usher), Will Leskin (Emcee), James Arone (Steve Wild), Don Marino (Mike), Lenny Citrano (Man).

In a plot similar to the Jack Lemmon–Walter Matthau film *The Fortune Cookie*, Dom tries to take advantage of Frank's injury at a hockey game by suing the team for a huge sum.

DOCTOR, DOCTOR   Airdate: 1/12/91.

Guest Cast: Estelle Getty (Dr. Newman), Vera Lockwood (Philamena), Debra Engle (Monica), Anthony Russell (Moe), Jim Ishida (Ken Takaguchi).

When the boys argue over several things at once, Father Angelo hires a family counselor to help them learn to get along better.

ROPE A DOPE   Airdate: 1/19/91.

Guest Cast: Art La Fleur (Kid Comforte), Gina Masterogiacomo (Bunny), Nick De Mauro (Eddie DeTucci), Robert Costanzo (Mario), J. J. Johnston (Fredo), Reddy Wilson (Butch).

Dom creates a problem spending family money on Kid Comforte, an aging prize fighter.

UNDERGRADUATE, THE   Airdate: 2/02/91.

Guest Cast: Shannon Wilcox (Mrs. MacKenzie), Hannah Cutrona (Amanda MacKenzie), Jack Murdock (Captain Smith), Meg Wyllie (Sarah), Lisa Alpert-Thames (Widow).

Ronnie has broken up with Becky, feeling that there is too big a difference in their ages. He soon has another "age" problem when the mother of his new girlfriend, Amanda, makes a pass at him.

WEDDING, THE—PART 1   Airdate: 2/09/91.

Guest Cast: William Windom (Ernie Shaw), Jessica Lundy (Lauren Shaw), Anthony Russell (Moe Dumbrowsky), Nick De Mauro (Eddie DeTucci), Teddy Wilson (Butch), Richard Zobel (Reporter), Jeff Silverman (Joe).

Theresa has a new boyfriend, Ernie, and the boys are jealous of the attention she shows him. As the episode ends, the brothers must also decide what to do about their newest applicant to the Knights of Sicily, Theresa, and her announcement that she is going to marry Ernie.

WEDDING, THE—PART 2   Airdate: 2/16/91.

Guest Cast: William Windom (Ernie Shaw), Jessica Lundy (Lauren Shaw), Nick De Mauro (Eddie DeTucci), Anthony Russell (Moe Dumbrowsky), Teddy Wilson (Butch), Nancy Sheppard (Woman).

The story continues as Theresa is admitted to the Knights of Sicily and Dom quits in protest. Later, when he goes to Theresa's room and finds Ernie there, he moves out of the house and refuses to attend the wedding.

Disney Presents The 100 Lives of Black Jack Savage

This action-adventure series was a joint venture between Disney and Stephen J. Cannell.

The basic format of the series centered around two very different types of pirates. The first was the ghost of a very traditional pirate, Black Jack Savage, who plundered the ships of the Caribbean during the 17th Century.

The second pirate was Barry Tarberry, a modern-day financier who came under the unwelcome attention of the government for his unscrupulous business dealings.

The basic premise of the two pirates's having to save 100 lives or suffer eternal damnation never saw completion, for the series failed to catch on in the ratings and was canceled after only 7 airings on NBC.

Series Cast: Daniel Hugh Kelly (Barry Tarberry), Stoney Jackson (Black Jack Savage—pilot episode), Steven Williams (Black Jack Savage—remaining episodes), Roma Downey (Danielle St. Claire), Bert Rosario (General Abel Vasquez), Steve Hytner (Logan "FX" Murphy).

Each of the episodes is described below in airdate order.

100 LIVES OF BLACK JACK SAVAGE, THE
(pilot)   Airdate (2-hour format): 3/31/91.

Guest Cast: Tobin Bell (Tony Gianini), Roya Megnot (Reya Montenegro), Sami Chester (Jean Paul), Veronica Lauren (Brigette), Ed Amatrudo (Diggs Munroe), W. Paul Bodie (Napoleon Bird), Joe Hess (Bobby Neusel), Marc Macaulay (Quick Cunningham).

The marauding ways of the notorious Black Jack Savage come to an end when the pirate is captured and hanged during the 17th century on the island of San Pietro. Many years later, when financier Barry Tarberry is arrested for insider trading and flees to San Pietro, these two men find themselves unlikely partners in adventure.

PIRATE STORY, A   Airdate: 4/05/91.

Guest Cast: Caroline Williams (Christy Lawton), Scott Bryce (David Morton), Kevin Quigley (Shoes), William Horne (Harmon Willow), Tom Schuster (Zack Philips), Monica Zaffarano (Ali Morton), Glenn Maska (Bud Lawton), Emiliano Diez (Colonel Mendez), Craig Parrish (Blue), Carly Rothlein (Baby Jennifer), Kristy Feil (Tricia), Omar Cabral (Aide), Julie Upton (Sue).

When a vacationing couple, Bud and Christy Lawton, stop their boat to help a man adrift on a raft, they are killed by modern-day pirates. The pirates then try to sink the Lawtons' boat, unaware that the couple's infant is still on board.

DAY IN THE LIFE OF LOGAN MURPHY, A
Airdate: 4/12/91.

Guest Cast: David Marciano (Hancock), Julius J. Carry III, Tom Nowicki (Mendez), Will Knickerbocker (Officer Hograth), Juan Cejas (McCreay), Matt Mearian (Convict #1), Ben Ferguson (Convict #2).

A sadistic drug smuggler named Hancock, who once owned Barry's castle, escapes from a Florida road gang and heads back to the island. It seems that Logan had accidentally tipped the FBI on where to arrest Hancock, and the man plans to kill him in revenge.

DEALS ARE MADE TO BE BROKEN
Airdate: 4/19/91.

Guest Cast: Mary Kay Adams (Marla Lance), Michael Chiklis (Otis), Roya Megnot (Reya Montenegro), Ismael (East), Carlo (Gustavo), Alexander Panas (Exorcist), Roberto Escobar (Ramon), Yolanda Arenas (Silda), John Archie (Villager), Elmer Bailey (Jail Guard), Parris Buckner (FBI Man), Omar Cabral (Guard), Scott Gallin (Larry), Francisco Padura (Room Service Kid).

Barry and Jack have a problem, for someone is impersonating Jack and terrorizing the local villagers. While they try to sort out this new development, Barry has to also deal with the unexpected arrival of his ex-wife, Marla Lance, the infamous "Witch of Wall Street."

LOOK FOR THE UNION LABEL   Airdate: 5/12/91.

Guest Cast: Vanessa Bell Calloway (Rene), Carlos Gomez (Julio), Carlos Cestero (Man #1), Guillermo Gentile (Sebastio), Julian Bevans (Father), Dorette Young (Mother), Bobby Rodriguez (Masseur), W. Lawrence Flakes (Policeman), Tara Anderson (The Blonde).

Jack asks Barry to help save a band of remote villagers from a gang cutting down the rain forest for ranching and the financier agrees, to impress Danielle. When the would-be helpers travel into the interior, they are quickly captured by the very people they are there to help.

NOT-SO-GREAT DICTATOR, THE
Airdate: 5/19/91.

Guest Cast: Badja Djola (Dictator Francoise Benoir), Galyn Görg (Luce), Tony Bolano (Commando #1), Steve Chambers (Commando #2), George Bustamante (Otto), Steve Carter (Hugo), George Lauzardo (Corporal DuBois), Rex Benson (Priest), Omar Cabral (Vasquez's Aide), Xavier Coronel (Military Officer), Raul Santidrian (Soldier).

A violent coup on another Caribbean island plunges Jack and Barry into adventure when the island's corrupt dictator, Francoise

Benoir, flees to San Pietro, along with his mistress, Luce.

FOR WHOM THE WEDDING BELLS TOLL
Airdate: 5/26/91.

Guest Cast: Paul Ben-Victor (Charlie Dilwig), Kimberly Beck (Connie), Lou Bedford (Icehouse Dilwig), Mark McCracken (Freddie), Dave Corey (Bronco), Rene Rokk (Mugger #1), Joe Camerieri (Mugger #2), Anthony Giaimo (Bartender), David Morano (Waiter).

A young couple, Charlie and Connie, arrive on the island to get married but end up quarreling when he asks her to sign a prenuptial agreement. Furious, Connie storms off and the despondent Charlie wanders the island at night. He eventually ends up at Barry's house, where he tries to shoot himself.

STAT

The main setting of *STAT* was the hospital Emergency Room, where a constant parade of strange patients and doctors kept the staff very busy. Dr. Tony Menzies, the senior resident on duty, had a light-hearted approach to medicine, which was in direct contrast to that of his partner, Dr. Elizabeth Newberry.

STAT was picked up by ABC as a summer replacement during the 1990–91 season. *STAT* started extremely well in the ratings, and the first episode was the #4 rated show for the week. The following weeks saw a drastic drop in viewership, and *STAT* died a quick death.

Series Cast: Dennis Boutsikaris (Dr. Tony Menzies), Alison LaPlaca (Dr. Elizabeth Newberry), Casey Biggs (Dr. Lewis "Cowboy" Doniger), Alix Elias (Jeanette Lemp), Ron Canada (Anderson "Mary" Roche).

Each of the episodes is described below in airdate order.

PSYCHOSOMATIC   Airdate: 4/16/91.

Guest Cast: Kurt Fuller (Mickey Weller), Alan Koss (Mr. Dougherty), Donna Ponterotto (Mrs. Dougherty), Jennifer Lewis (Felicia Brown), Talia Balsam (Rita Falco), Rudolph Willrich (Leland Fisk), Wren T. Brown (Ron Murphy), Dannel Arnold (Dr. Werner), Wayne Duvall (Paramedic #1), Duke Moosekian (Paramedic #2), Arva Holt (Nurse #1), Yuri Ogawa (Nurse #2), Cynthia Lea Clark (Nurse #3), Carol A. Payton (Nurse #4).

When the Dougherty family arrives, the staff doesn't know how to treat them. Mrs. Dougherty is very pregnant, but it's Mr. Dougherty who acts as if he's about to have a baby.

FANTASY   Airdate: 4/23/91.

Guest Cast: Gerrit Graham (Dr. Gus Rivers), David Opatoshu (Sidney Wolff), Allan Arbus ("Hesh" Cooper), Howard McGillin (Randall Forbes), Julio Oscar Mechoso (First Orderly), Anne Haney (Disturbed Woman), Lucille Bliss (Woman on Gurney), Jack Kutcher (Drunk Man), Eric Kohner (Paramedic #1), Arva Holt (Nurse).

Dr. Newberry needs to leave work on time for an important date, but when one of her patients almost dies, she worries that she was in too much of a hurry to be a good doctor.

LADYFINGER   Airdate: 4/30/91.

Guest Cast: Gerrit Graham (Dr. Gus Rivers), Jose Perez (Eddie Diaz), David Margulies (Leonard Sorkin), Robert Symonds (Cassidy), Angela Bassett (Dr. Willie Burns), Julio Oscar Mechoso (First Orderly), Wren T. Brown (Ron Murphy), Larry Hankin (Stan Malkowski), Maurice Benard (Jorge Rosario), George Wallace (Policeman), Carlos Lacamara (Second Orderly), Tony Rolon (Orderly C), Rita Gomez (Orderly D), Bill Miller (First Paramedic), Vance Colvig (Alzheimer's Patient), Robina Suwol (Upstairs Nurse), Marabina Jaimes (Nurse A).

When an accident victim loses a finger, the good news is that the doctors may be able to reattach it. The bad news is that someone has managed to misplace the finger.

WILDING, THE   Airdate: 5/07/91.

Guest Cast: Allan Rich, Allen Garfield (Dr. Harold Frohman), Loretta Divine (Tilda Barclay), Angela Bassett (Dr. Willie Burns), Wren T. Brown (Dr. Ron Murphy), David Bowe (Warren Neff), Dannel Arnold (Dr. Werner), Julio Oscar Mechoso (Julio Oscar), Carlos Lacamara (Orderly), Marabina Jaimes (Nurse).

The daily pressure and increasing work load begin to take their toll on the staff, and one of the doctors keeps misplacing his patients.

HIGH SOCIETY   Airdate: 5/14/91.

Guest Cast: David Margulies (Leonard Sorkin), Denis Arndt (Dr. Stanley Deardorf), Brynn Thayer (Katherine Faraday), Brian Smiar (Frank Resnick), Jana Marie Hupp (Sherry Fazio), Dannel Arnold (Dr. Werner), Julio Oscar Mechoso (Julio Oscar), Ann Weldon (Winona Booth).

When Dr. Menzies operates on a wealthy woman, she decides she wants him to be her personal doctor.

SAFE SMUGGLING   Airdate: 5/21/91.

Guest Cast: Peter Michael Goetz, Jose Perez (Eddie Diaz), Fausto Bara (Jose Ramos), Allan Arbus ("Hesh" Cooper), Savely Kramarov (Dimitri Ivanovich), Dannel Arnold (Dr. Werner), Ron Canada (Anderson "Mary" Roche), Adilah Barnes (Nurse Barnes), Michael Lewis (Paramedic #1).

The doctors are faced with a very unusual patient who has a most unusual problem. The man is a cocaine smuggler who has swallowed drugs to sneak them into the country.

Dinosaurs

When Disney announced plans in 1989 to buy Jim Henson Associates, Disney wanted to draw on Henson's expertise to jointly create new characters and shows. One of the first of the hoped-for joint projects was the situation comedy *Dinosaurs*. In *Dinosaurs*, the cold-blooded animal stars had all of the characteristics of modern humans; they spoke, lived in houses, worked for a living, and spent all too many hours watching television.

The series centered on the Sinclair family, led by Earl, a bombastic blue-collar worker, and his long-suffering wife, Fran. Their three children, Robbie, Charlene, and Baby, all kept Earl on his toes, as did his boss, B.P. Richfield.

High-tech costumes and oversized sets were used to bring the reptiles to life, making this a very difficult show to produce. Disney and Henson agreed that the characters had to be convincing, and no expense was spared to create the illusion of life. Earl's head, for example, had 23 servos and miniaturized motors. It also didn't help that all of these effects mean that it took approximately 65 hours to film every 23-minute episode.

Each of the episodes is described below in airdate order, divided by season. The episodes not aired on ABC are listed in production order following the 1993–94 season.

1990–91 season

MIGHTY MEGALOSAURUS, THE
Airdates: 4/26/91, 8/21/91.
Guest Performers: Arthur Rizzic: Brian Henson. Cavepeople: Teri La Porte, Michelan Sisti.

Earl Sinclair, a lowly tree pusher for 24 years, finally gets the courage to ask for a raise. After he is fired for his efforts, Earl learns he needs a job right away, for his wife has just laid an egg.

MATING DANCE, THE   Airdates: 5/03/91, 5/05/91, 12/25/91.

Guest Performers: Mel Luster: Bruce Lanoil, Jack Tate, Richard Portnow (Voice).
Cavepeople: Perry Anzilotti, Jeff Chayette, Julie Maddalena, Michelan Sisti.

Fran feels unwanted and unattractive, and Earl realizes he is going to have to do a mating dance to cheer her up. He finds that prospect definitely unattractive, but finally decides to do his best at it.

Production Note:

- John C. Mula, Kevin Pfeiffer, and Brian Savegar won an Emmy award for Art Direction, Series, for this episode.

HURLING DAY   Airdates: 5/10/91, 5/14/91, 8/28/91.

Guest Performers: Dinosaur Chief: Kevin Clash, Michelan Sisti, Harold Gould (Voice).
Caveman: Michelan Sisti.

When dinosaurs turn 72, they are thrown into a tar pit to make life easier for their relatives. Earl's mother-in-law, Ethyl, is about to have that birthday and Earl is counting the minutes until he can hurl her over the edge.

HIGH NOON   Airdates: 5/17/91, 9/04/91.

Guest Performer: Gary: Steve Landesberg (Voice).

When a Tyrannosaurus Rex takes an interest in Fran, Earl worries about having to fight to keep her. Since the new rival is nine times his size, Earl also starts to think about running for the woods.

HOWLING, THE   Airdates: 5/24/91, 9/11/91.

Male dinosaurs mark their passage into manhood by howling, but Robbie complains that the tradition is foolish and refuses to join in.

1991–92 season

Several episodes aired during the second season had been produced for the first year but were held for later airing. These episodes were *The Golden Child, Family Challenge, I Never Ate for My Father, Charlene's Tale, Endangered Species, Employee of the Month, When Food Goes Bad,* and *The Clip Show.*

GOLDEN CHILD, THE   Airdates: 9/18/91, 4/03/92.

Guest Performers: Elders: Tom Fisher, Jack Tate, Michael Dorn (Voice). The Doctor: David Greenaway, Tom Fisher, Sam McMurray.

When Baby Sinclair suddenly sprouts a horn, the Council of Elders pronounces him the long-awaited King of the Dinosaurs.

FAMILY CHALLENGE   Airdates: 9/25/91, 12/04/91.

Guest Performers: Insurance Agent: Bruce Lanoil, Jack Tate, Peter Bonerz (Voice); Buddy Glimmer: Sam McMurray (Voice).

After their television set is destroyed, Earl tries to trick the family into appearing on a game show so he can win a new one.

I NEVER ATE FOR MY FATHER   Airdates: 10/02/91, 4/10/92.

Guest Performers: Folksinger: Michelan Sisti, John Kennedy, Steven Banks.

Shocked when Robbie refuses to eat meat like the rest of the dinosaurs, Earl follows his son into the swamp, where he discovers a band of herbivores.

CHARLENE'S TALE   Airdates: 10/09/91, 5/22/92.

Guest Cast: None.

Charlene grows a longer tail, the sign of a sexually mature female, and Earl must come to grips with the fact that she is not his little girl any more.

ENDANGERED SPECIES   Airdates: 10/16/91, 1/29/92, 5/01/92.

Guest Performers: Grapdelites: Kevin Clash, Dave Goelz.

Earl buys two rare creatures called grapdelites and plans to barbecue them for an anniversary dinner. His plans change when Robbie discovers the grapdelites are nearly extinct.

EMPLOYEE OF THE MONTH   Airdates: 10/23/91, 7/03/92.

Guest Performers: Sparky: Hank Cutrona, Sally Struthers (Voice). Cavepeople: Paula Marshall, Michelan Sisti.

The thrill of winning the "Employee of the Month" award at work begins to pale when Earl learns that he has to bring his cantankerous boss home as part of the "honor."

WHEN FOOD GOES BAD   Airdates: 10/30/91, 5/29/92.

Guest Performers: General Chow: Dave Goelz, Tim Doyle (Voice).

Charlene's attempt at babysitting goes awry when she and Baby are taken hostage by some ill-mannered creatures living in the refrigerator.

CAREER OPPORTUNITIES   Airdates: 11/06/91, 6/12/92.

Guest Performers: The Job Wizard: David Greenaway, Jack Tate, Jason Alexander (Voice).

Earl is thrilled when the job wizard decrees that Robbie will also be a tree pusher, but Robbie is less than pleased at the news.

UNMARRIED . . . WITH CHILDREN
Airdates: 11/13/91, 6/05/92.

Guest Performers: Monica Devertabrae: Julianne Buescher, Suzie Plakson (Voice). Bob (DMV Worker): David Greenaway, Jack Tate, David Wohl (Voice).

When Fran's and Earl's marriage license expires, Fran finds herself tempted to follow the example of her friend Monica, the world's first divorcee.

HOW TO PICK UP GIRLS   Airdates: 11/20/91, 5/15/92.

Guest Performers: Spike: David Greenaway, Christopher Meloni (Voice).

Deciding that he needs help to attract the attentions of a beautiful dinosaur at school, Robbie asks his new friend, Spike, for advice.

SWITCHED AT BIRTH   Airdates: 11/27/91, 4/17/92.

Guest Performers: Gus Molehill: David Greenaway, Jack Tate, Jason Alexander (Voice). Glenda Molehill: Bruce Lanoil, Tom Fisher, Mimi Kennedy (Voice). Aubrey Molehill: Brian Henson (puppeteer and voice), Julianne Buescher. Solomon: Bruce Lanoil, Jack Tate, Michael Dorn (Voice).

The news that switched eggs may mean that Baby belongs to another family delights Earl when he discovers that the other family's baby is very well mannered.

REFRIGERATOR DAY   Airdates: 12/11/91, 7/10/92, 12/25/92.

Guest Performers: Richard: John Kennedy, Jack Tate, Thom Sharp (Voice).

Every year the dinosaurs celebrate the invention of the cornerstone of their life, the refrigerator.

WHAT "SEXUAL HARRIS" MEANT
Airdate: 12/18/91.

Guest Performers: Monica Devertabrae: Julianne Buescher, Suzie Plakson (Voice). Sexual Harris: Bruce Lanoil, Jack Tate, Jason Alexander (Voice). Senator Otto Lynch: Allan Trautman, Earl Hindman (Voice). Senator Mason Dixon: Steve Whitmire. Senator Teddy Wolfe: Mac Wilson, David Leisure (Voice). Senator Harold Heffer: Bruce Lanoil, Jack Harrell.

Fran's friend Monica is fired when she refuses to date her boss. Her decision to fight back inspires Charlene in a dispute with some boys at school.

FRAN LIVE   Airdates: 1/08/92, 6/26/92.
Guest Performers: Monica Devertabrae: Julianne Buescher, Suzie Plakson (Voice). Frank: John Kennedy, Michelan Sisti, Thom Sharp (Voice). Jerry: Bruce Lanoil, Jack Tate, Tony Shalhoub (Voice).

Fran's decision to take a job as a talk show host means that Earl has to cope with the pressures of having a working wife.

POWER ERUPTS   Airdates: 1/15/92, 9/11/92.
Guest Performers: Spike: David Greenaway, Christopher Meloni (Voice). Mr. Ashland: Kevin Clash, John Vernon (Voice). WESAYSO Scientist: Allan Trautman, William Schallert (Voice). WESAYSO Interviewer: Allan Trautman, Sam McMurray (Voice). Shopper: Julianne Buescher, Edie McClurg (Voice).

Robbie invents a potentially pollution-free source of energy, much to the dismay of the WESAYSO executives. Earl is torn between having to support his son and keeping his job.

CLIP SHOW, THE   Airdates: 1/22/92, 7/24/92.
Guest Cast: Paxton Whitehead (Archeologist), Jarrett Lennon (Kid), Bill Capizzi (Worker), Eileen Dunn (Miss Honeywell). Guest Performers: Mel Luster: Bruce Lanoil, Jack Tate, Richard Portnow (Voice).

An archeologist uses scenes from Sinclair family life to speculate on how the dinosaurs might have lived and why they became extinct.

NEW LEAF, A   Airdates: 2/05/92, 6/19/92.
Guest Performers: Spike: David Greenaway, Christopher Meloni (Voice).

Robbie and Spike discover a new plant that makes everyone feel happy and complacent.

LAST TEMPTATION OF ETHYL, THE
Airdates: 2/12/92, 7/17/92, 11/27/92.

Guest Performers: Louie: Allan Trautman, Buddy Hackett (Voice). Lucius: David Greenaway, Jack Tate, John Glover (Voice).

It looks as though Ethyl has died, so the family is astonished when she returns from the grave and appears on a television show extolling the benefits of the afterlife.

NUTS TO WAR—PART I   Airdate: 2/19/92.
This show was also combined with Part II and aired in a 1-hour format on 8/28/92.

Guest Performers: Spike: David Greenaway, Christopher Meloni (Voice). Monica Devertabrae: Julianne Buescher, Suzie Plakson (Voice). Elder in Chief: Allan Trautman, George Gaynes (Voice).

The dinosaurs-who-walk-on-two-legs declare war on dinosaurs-who-walk-on-four-legs when their rivals cut off the supply of pistachio nuts.

NUTS TO WAR—PART II   Airdate: 2/26/92.
This show was also combined with Part I and aired in a 1-hour format on 8/28/92.

Guest Performers: Spike: David Greenaway, Christopher Meloni (Voice). Monica Devertabrae: Julianne Buescher, Suzie Plakson (Voice). Sarge: Bruce Lanoil, Jack Tate, G.W. Bailey (Voice). General H. Norman Conquest: John Kennedy, Michelan Sisti, Jason Alexander (Voice). Narrator: Gary Owens. Bob Hack: Bruce Lanoil, Jack Tate, Fred Travalena (Voice).

Earl and Roy disguise themselves as USO girls and sneak into the army camp, hoping to convince Robbie to come home. Unfortunately, Robbie is caught up in the furor of battle and refuses to return.

SLAVE TO FASHION   Airdates: 3/20/92, 8/21/92.
Guest Performers: Mindy: Julianne Buescher, Star Townshend, Jessica Lundy (Voice). Fox Jacket: Allan Trautman, Tim Curry (Voice). Heather: Terri Hardin, Tom Fisher, Julia Louis-Dreyfus (Voice).

Charlene gets some bad advice from a talking coat as she tries to become more popular at school.

AND THE WINNER IS . . .   Airdates: 3/27/92, 8/14/92.

Guest Performers: Edward R. Hero: Allan Trautman, Jason Bernard (Voice).

The death of the chief Elder takes an unusual turn when Earl finds himself the unwilling opponent of B.P. Richfield in the election for a replacement.

LEADER OF THE PACK   Airdates: 4/24/92, 8/07/92.

Guest Performers: Lingo: Allan Trautman, Terri Hardin, Tom Fisher, Shaun Baker (Voice). Scabby: Bruce Lanoil, Pons Maar, Stephen Caffrey (Voice). Andre: Mak Wilson, Jack Tate, Sam McMurray (Voice). Crazy Lou: Julianne Buescher, Michelan Sisti, Ken Hudson Campbell (Voice). Pterodactyl: Kevin Clash, Tim Curry (Voice).

Using the old adage, "If you can't beat them, join them" for advice, Robbie joins a gang that has been beating him up.

WESAYSO KNOWS BEST   Airdates: 5/08/92, 7/31/92.

Guest Performers: Monica Devertabrae: Julianne Buescher, Suzie Plakson (Voice). Director: Bruce Lanoil, Jack Tate, Michael Richards (Voice).

Earl finds his loyalty to WESAYSO pushed to the limit when the company decides that Roy would make a better father for the Sinclair family.

1992–93 season

NATURE CALLS   Airdates: 9/18/92, 1/22/93.

Guest Performers: Dinosaur: Richard Simmons (Voice). Pteranodon: Sally Kellerman (Voice).

When Earl tries to toilet train Baby, the rebellious youngster flees into the woods.

DIRTY DANCING   Airdates: 9/25/92, 6/11/93.

Guest Performers: Sitcom Wife: Julianne Buescher, Jessica Lundy (Voice). Shelly: Bruce Lanoil, Jack Tate, Conchata Ferrell (Voice).

Fran has to explain the dinosaurs' mating dance to Robbie, who has started to move uncontrollably whenever a pretty girl passes by.

BABY TALK   Airdates: 10/02/92, 4/25/93.

Guest Performers: Larry: Bruce Lanoil, Pons Maar, Thom Sharp (Voice). Neighbor #3: Terri Hardin, Star Townshend, Kate McGregor-Stewart (Voice).

Baby starts repeating a dirty word he heard on television, and nothing his parents do to make him stop seems to work.

NETWORK GENIUS   Airdate: 10/16/92.

Guest Performers: Stu: Jason Alexander (Voice). Ted: Robert Picardo (Voice).

Earl is hired as a guinea pig for new television programming, but while his favorite programs succeed in the ratings, they are turning the viewers dumber.

DISCOVERY, THE   Airdate: 10/23/92.

Guest Performers: Thighs of Thunder: Julianne Buescher, Star Townshend, Suzi Plakson (Voice). Walter Sternhagen: Bruce Lanoil, Pons Marr, Thom Sharp (Voice). Elder Caveman: Michelan Sisti (Voice).

Earl discovers an uncharted new land, but the natives hold his family hostage to protect their secret.

LITTLE BOY BOO   Airdates: 10/30/92, 6/25/93.

Guest Performers: Wereman: Kirk Thatcher (Voice). Rabid Caveman: Bill Barretta (Voice).

Robbie's prank of telling scary stories to Baby backfires when Baby takes the stories far too seriously.

GERM WARFARE   Airdate: 11/06/92.

Guest Performers: Dr. Ficus: Bruce Lanoil, Pons Maar, Charles Kimbrough (Voice). Zabar: David Greenaway, Michelan Sisti, Dan Castellaneta (Voice).

When Baby comes down with the flu, his parents pay dearly for a doctor's advice and for ignoring Grandma Ethyl's sage advice.

HUNGRY FOR LOVE   Airdates: 11/13/92, 7/09/93.

Guest Performers: Wendy Richfield: Julianne Buescher, Michelan Sisti, Wendy Jo Sperber (Voice).

Robbie falls in love with a girl who is rumored to have eaten her past boyfriends.

LICENSE TO PARENT   Airdates: 11/20/92, 6/04/93.

Guest Performers: Bettleheim: David Greenaway, Michelan Sisti, Michael McKean (Voice).

When Earl has another battle with Baby, the Parent Patrol suspends his License to Parent.

CHARLENE'S FLAT WORLD   Airdates: 12/04/92, 6/18/93.
Guest Performers: Muse: John Kennedy, Leif Tilden, Robert Picardo (Voice). Judge: Steve Whitmire, Paxton Whitehead (Voice). Stenographer: Rickey Boyd, Pat Crawford Brown (Voice). Guy in Lab Coat: Mak Wilson, Michael McKean (Voice). Prosecutor: Julianne Buescher, Pons Maar, John Glover (Voice).

Charlene shocks everyone at school when she announces that the world is round.

WILDERNESS WEEKEND   Airdates: 12/18/92, 8/13/92.
Earl and his friends set out for a weekend of male bonding, unaware that a hungry monster is just waiting for the chance to devour them.

SON ALSO RISES, THE   Airdates: 1/08/93, 7/23/93.
Guest Performers: Clerk: Bruce Lanoil, Jody St. Michael, Robert Picardo (Voice).

Robbie challenges Earl for leadership of the Sinclair family, never suspecting the problems that await him when he wins.

GETTING TO KNOW YOU   Airdates: 1/15/93, 7/30/93.
Guest Performers: Mindy: Terri Hardin, Star Townshend, Jessica Lundy (Voice). Henri: Allan Trautman, Tim Curry (Voice).

Charlene joins the dinosaur version of a student exchange program and the Sinclairs find themselves hosting a noisy young bird.

GREEN CARD   Airdate: 1/29/93.
Guest Performers: Chief Elder: Mak Wilson, Joe Flaherty (Voice).

Roy refuses to join his friends in their distrust of the four-legged dinosaurs and marries Monica so she won't be sent into exile.

OUT OF THE FRYING PAN   Airdates: 2/05/93, 5/28/93.
Guest Performers: John: Allan Trautman, Sam McMurray (Voice). Leeza: Julianne Buescher, Elizabeth Collins (Voice). Myman: David Greenaway, Leif Tilden, Michael McKean (Voice). Sally: Julianne Buescher, Star Townshend, Suzi Plakson (Voice). Grown Baby: Bruce Lanoil, Jack Tate, Jason Alexander (Voice).

Baby stars in a television commercial and his newfound fame quickly goes to his head.

STEROIDS TO HEAVEN   Airdate: 2/12/93.
Guest Performers: Caroline Foxworth: Julianne Buescher, Star Townshend, Jessica Lundy (Voice). Dolf: Allan Trautman, Jack Tate, Sam McMurray (Voice).

Robbie wants to impress a girl at school so he thinks about using drugs to increase his athletic prowess.

HONEY, I MISS THE KIDS   Airdates: 2/19/93, 7/16/93.
Fran gets tired of being a housewife and volunteers for social work, leaving Earl to manage the household.

SWAMP MUSIC   Airdates: 2/26/93, 8/27/93.
Guest Performers: Howlin' Jay: Kevin Clash (Voice and Puppeteer). Sonny: Steve Whitmire (Voice and Puppeteer). Mudbelly: Mak Wilson, Julius Carry (Voice). Ty Warner: Bruce Lanoil, Pons Maar, John Polito (Voice).

Robbie tries to get a record contract for some swamp animals with their own strange brand of music.

IF YOU WERE A TREE   Airdates: 4/18/93, 9/03/93.
Guest Performers: Spirit of the Tree: David Warner (Voice). Kyle: Michael McKean (Voice).

A lightning bolt causes Earl's mind to trade places with a tree.

WE ARE NOT ALONE   Airdate: 5/02/93.
Guest Performers: UFO! Host/Announcer: Bruce Lanoil, Michelan Sisti, Jason Alexander (Voice).

Robbie poses as an alien invader so he can trick Earl into helping protect the environment.

CHARLENE AND HER AMAZING HUMANS   Airdates: 5/09/93, 8/20/93.
Guest Performers: Hank Hibler: Allan Trautman, Jack Tate, Jeffrey Tambor (Voice). Mindy: John Kennedy, Star Townshend, Jessica Tate (Voice). Cavelings: Ben Ganger, Alyssa McGraw, Tiffany Taubman.

Charlene uses cave children in a stage show, then finds herself pressured to improve the act at their expense.

CLIP SHOW II, THE   Airdate: 7/02/93.
Guest Cast: Paxton Whitehead (Sir David Tushingham), Bill Barretta (Nick), Cynthia

Mace (Myrna), John Hawkes (Andrew), Darcy Lee (Kathy), Jeffrey Lampert (Ted), Holly Atkinson (Julie), Rick Zieff (Guard). **Guest Performers:** Monica Devertabrae: Julianne Buescher, Suzie Plakson (Voice). Bob (Game Show Host): David Greenaway, Jack Tate, David Wohl (Voice). Sitcom Wife: Julianne Buescher, Jessica Lundy (Voice).

Archeologist Sir David Tushingham returns for another look at the life of the dinosaurs, using scenes from past episodes to illustrate his theories.

1993–94 season

MONSTER UNDER THE BED Airdate: 6/01/94.

Guest Performers: Decker: Rickey Boyd, Pons Maar, Thom Sharpe (Voice). Parish: Rickey Boyd, Michelan Sisti, Michael McKean (Voice).

His parents may scoff at Baby's fear of a monster under his bed, but there really is something down there.

EARL, DON'T BE A HERO Airdate: 6/08/94.

Guest Performers: Roy Hess: David Greenaway, Pons Maar, Sam McMurray (Voice). B.P. Richfield: Rob Mills, Steve Whitmire, Sherman Hemsley (Voice). Ed: Bruce Lanoil, Pons Maar, Michael McKean (Voice).

Earl becomes a superhero and sets out to right wrongs everywhere.

GREATEST STORY EVER SOLD, THE Airdate: 6/22/94.

Guest Performers: Roy Hess: David Greenaway, Pons Maar, Sam McMurray (Voice). B.P. Richfield: Steve Whitmire, Sherman Hemsley (Voice). Chief Elder: Allan Trautman, Tim Curry (Voice). Elder #3: Julianne Buescher, Suzi Plakson (Voice). Elder #2: Sam McMurray (Voice).

When the Elders come up with a new religion, Robbie questions their wisdom.

DRIVING MISS ETHYL Airdate: 6/29/94.

Guest Performers: Ethyl: Rickey Boyd, David Greenaway, Florence Stanley (Voice). Monster: Kevin Clash, Glenn Shadix (Voice). Ansel: Julianne Buescher, Pons Maar, Michael McKean (Voice).

Earl has a miserable chore to face: driving Ethyl to her high school reunion.

EARL'S BIG JACKPOT Airdate: 7/06/94.

Guest Performers: B.P. Richfield: Steve Whitmire, Sherman Hemsley (Voice). Winston: Allan Trautman, Tim Curry (Voice). Judge: Bruce Lanoil (voice and puppeteer). Roy Hess: David Greenaway, Pons Maar, Sam McMurray (Voice).

When Earl is injured at work, he loses his job. Luckily, he later wins big in court.

TERRIBLE TWOS Airdate: 7/13/94.

Guest Performers: Ethyl: Rickey Boyd, Florence Stanley (Voice). Dr. Herder: Michael McKean (Voice). Babysitter: John Glover (Voice).

Baby becomes one of the most feared creatures of all time—a 2-year-old.

CHANGING NATURE Airdate: 7/20/94.

Guest Performers: Ethyl: Rickey Boyd, Florence Stanley (Voice). Roy Hess: David Greenaway, Pons Maar, Sam McMurray (Voice). B.P. Richfield: Steve Whitmire, Sherman Hemsley (Voice). Bert: David Greenaway, Pons Maar, Thom Sharp (Voice). Bryant: John Kennedy, Michael McKean (Voice). Katie: Julianne Buescher, Joyce Kurtz (Voice).

The dinosaurs try to solve an environmental crisis of their own making, but their efforts lead them down the path to extinction.

Unaired Episodes

The following episodes were produced but not aired as part of the network series. They later were included in the syndication package.

INTO THE WOODS Airdate: Unaired.

Guest Performers: Roy Hess: David Greenaway, Pons Maar, Sam McMurray (Voice). Les: Bruce Lanoil, Tony Sabin Prince, Michael McKean (Voice).

An ancient ritual causes the boys to become trapped in a tar pit and Earl has to sacrifice his beloved television to save them.

SCENT OF A REPTILE Airdate: Unaired.

Guest Performers: Ethyl: Rickey Boyd, Florence Stanley (Voice). Mindy: Julianne Buescher, Star Townshend, Jessica Lundy (Voice). Ed: David Greenaway, Pons Maar, Thom Sharp (Voice). Ray: Rickey Boyd, Jack Tate, Glenn Shadix (Voice).

Charlene develops the scent that marks her as a mature dinosaur but isn't happy with the first boy it attracts—the school janitor.

Working Girl   Airdate: Unaired.

*Guest Performers: Monica Devertabrae:
Julianne Buescher, Suzie Plakson (Voice). B.P.
Richfield: Steve Whitmire, Sherman Hemsley
(Voice). Inspector: Allan Trautman, Tom
Fisher, Michael McKean (Voice). Elder: Allan
Trautman, Joe Flaherty (Voice). Chef: David
Greenaway, Pons Maar, Thom Sharpe (Voice).*

When the last tree falls and leaves a wasteland, Earl suddenly finds himself unemployed.

Variations on a Theme Park   Airdate: Unaired.

*Guest Performers: Roy Hess: David
Greenaway, Pons Maar, Sam McMurray
(Voice). B.P. Richfield: Steve Whitmire,
Sherman Hemsley (Voice). Ticket Guy: David
Greenaway, Pons Maar, Thom Sharpe (Voice).
Vendor: Julianne Buescher, Star Townshend,
Jessica Lundy (Voice).*

The family visits the new WESAYSO-
LAND theme park, only to discover they
can't leave.

Life in the Faust Lane   Airdate: Unaired.

*Guest Performers: Roy Hess: David
Greenaway, Pons Maar, Sam McMurray
(Voice). B.P. Richfield: Steve Whitmire,
Sherman Hemsley (Voice). Devil: Bruce
Lanoil, Pons Maar, Tim Curry (Voice). Hank:
David Greenaway, Michelan Sisti, Michael
McKean (Voice).*

Earl is jealous of Richfield's collection of
mugs. To get his own mug, he enters into a
pact with the devil.

Earl and Pearl   Airdate: Unaired.

*Guest Performers: Roy Hess: David
Greenaway, Pons Maar, Sam McMurray
(Voice). Pearl: Rickey Boyd, Tom Fisher, Susan
Norfleet (Voice).*

Roy falls in love with a singer at the Bucking Bronto bar.

Georgie Must Die   Airdate: Unaired.

*Guest Performers: Roy Hess: David
Greenaway, Pons Maar, Sam McMurray
(Voice). Jean-Claude: David Greenaway,
Michelan Sisti, Tim Curry (Voice). Brigitte:
Julianne Buescher, Pons Maar, Joyce Kurtz
(Voice). Evil Georgie: Allan Trautman, Jack
Tate, Edward Asner (Voice).*

Baby becomes infatuated with a children's
television program. The star, Georgie, is a
seemingly friendly cow who really has a
nasty disposition.

Singer & Sons

In keeping with the Studio's decision to concentrate on comedies instead of dramatic series, *Singer & Sons* was a half-hour sitcom
centered around a New York City delicatessen. The deli had been in the Singer family for 90 years, but the current proprietor,
Nathan Singer, was worried that he might
have to sell or close the business. Then his
black housekeeper, Sarah Patterson, offered
to have her sons run the place. The result was
Singer & Sons, a Jewish delicatessen run by
two black men.

Singer & Sons was a summer replacement
series for the 1989–90 season, and only 4
episodes were ordered by NBC, a practice
called a "short order."

*Series Cast: Harold Gould (Nathan Singer),
Esther Rolle (Mrs. Sarah Patterson), Bobby
Hosea (Mitchell Patterson), Tommy Ford
(Reggie Patterson), Fred Stoller (Sheldon
Singer), Arnetia Walker (Claudia James), Phil
Leeds (Lou Gold), Brooke Fontaine (Deanna
Patterson),*

Each of the episodes is described below in
airdate order.

Two Sons for Singer   Airdate: 6/09/90.

*Guest Cast: Peter Iacangelo (Delivery Man),
Alan Haufrect (Mr. Fricker), Anna Berger
(Mrs. Tarkasian), Geoff Elliott (Arthur), Susan
Isaacs (Dana), Jeremy Daies (Blade),
Shaundra Beri (Aletia).*

After Nathan agrees to hire Sarah's sons,
Mitchell and Reggie, to run the deli, tensions
run high because the two brothers don't like
each other.

Boxer Rebellion, The   Airdate: 6/13/90.

*Guest Cast: Dick O'Neill (Floyd Patterson),
Alex Henteloff (Al), Mary Pat Gleason
(Marilyn), Anna Berger (Mrs. Tarkasian),
Bunny Summers (Mrs. Drepner), Janet Brandt
(Mrs. Meltzer).*

Reggie becomes convinced that he was accidentally switched in the hospital at birth
and that his real dad is famous boxer Floyd
Patterson.

Once Bitten   Airdate: 6/20/90.

*Guest Cast: Anne-Marie Johnson (Felicity
Patterson), Wesley Thompson (Elliott*

Pierpont, Jr.), Mauri Bernstein (Vicki), Jeff Lippa (Customer #1), Chantal Rivera Batisse (Customer #2).

Mitchell hopes to reconcile with his ex-wife, Felicity, even though everyone tells him he should stay as far away from her as possible.

OURS'S NOT TO REASON WHY SHMY
Airdate: 6/27/90.

Guest Cast: Wanda DeJesus (Mary Garza), Vic Polizos (Sam Gianelli), Richard Portnow (Maurice), Larry Hankin (Preacher), Rich Marotta (Sportscaster's Voice), Jim Painter (Businessman).

Someone's robbing all of the shops in the neighborhood—all, that is, except the deli. Claudia thinks Reggie is the thief, because he has money for a change.

Herman's Head

The start of the 1991–92 season saw the premiere of *Herman's Head,* which was publicized as the first series to have five actors playing one role.

The series centered on the life of one Herman Brooks, a young writer trying to make his mark in the business world. Throughout each episode, the series looked inside Herman's brain, where four actors portrayed Herman's emotions as they battled each other to gain control of Herman to get their way.

Herman's Head landed a spot on the Fox network schedule, airing right after the popular *Married With Children.* The success of the show led to its renewal for the 1992–93 and 1993–94 seasons.

Series Cast: William Ragsdale (Herman Brooks), Hank Azaria (Jay Nichols), Jane Sibbett (Heddy Newman), Yeardley Smith (Louise Fitzer), Molly Hagan (Angel), Rick Lawless (Wimp), Ken Hudson Campbell (Animal), Peter MacKenzie (Genius), Jason Bernard (Paul Bracken).

Each of the episodes is described below in airdate order.

1991–92 season

HERMAN'S HEAD (pilot)   Airdates: 9/08/91, 12/08/91.

Guest Cast: Corinne Bohrer (Connie), Ed Winter (Mr. Crawford).

Jay breaks up with his girlfriend, Connie, and she comes to talk to Herman about it.

Before long, they start developing a relationship. Jay realizes his mistake and makes up with Connie before it's too late—for all of them.

LIES, LIES, LIES   Airdates: 9/15/91, 12/15/91.

Guest Cast: Stephen Lee (Brian), Julie Hayden (Wanda), Marsha Dietlein (Meredith), Tom LaGrua (The Landlord), Marla Phillips (The Girl).

When a pretty reporter interviews Herman for an article about his high school class, he brags just a bit about his "success." More lies follow as Jay's new girlfriend lies about her husband and Herman lies to his boss.

DAYS OF WINE AND HERMAN   Airdates: 9/22/91, 11/29/91, 7/12/92.

Guest Cast: Ed Winter (Mr. Crawford), Raymond Fitzpatrick (Mail Clerk), Mindy Rickles (Woman at Bar).

Invited to give a speech at a party celebrating Bracken's 20th anniversary with the company, Herman drinks too much and makes a fool of himself.

ISN'T IT ROMANTIC?   Airdates: 9/29/91, 12/29/91.

Guest Cast: Judy Prescott (Sarah), Sean Masterson (Maitre D'), Lou DiMaggio (Waiter), Pete Leal (Janitor).

Herman has a date with his dream woman and he takes her to a fancy restaurant. Louise, who is also there, has been stood up and she drinks too much. When Herman takes her home, his date is furious.

FATAL DISTRACTION   Airdates: 10/13/91, 1/26/92.

Guest Cast: Megan Mullally (Yvonne).

Herman meets a young woman at a bar and they have a passionate first night together. However, the fun ends the next day when he can't get rid of her.

HERMAN-ATOR   Airdates: 10/20/91, 2/06/92.

Guest Cast: Paul Regina (Ted Tatum), Denise Gentile (Woman Doctor).

After Herman punches out a man who is harassing Heddy, he learns the man is an executive at work. Heddy agrees to go out with the man to save Herman's job, but Herman decides that he must stand up to the man.

My Brother, Myself   Airdates: 10/27/91, 3/15/92.

Guest Cast: John Scott Clough (Stan Brooks), Grace Phillips (Jaclyn), Edan Gross (Little Herman), Joey Wright (Little Stan).

Herman's brother, Stan, comes to visit and as they talk, Herman recalls past abuses by his brother.

9 1/2 Hours   Airdates: 11/03/91, 4/26/92, 8/26/93.

Guest Cast: Robin Sachs (Simon).

Forced to work late due to Heddy's plotting, Herman is surprised when she drops by the office. They argue, then impulsively make love in Bracken's office.

Babbling Brooks   Airdates: 11/10/91, 1/09/92.

Guest Cast: Mia Cottet (Kiki), Kip Reynolds (The Clown).

Herman accidentally sickens a diabetic bear at the zoo with a donut. As he worries about the animal's fate, he talks too much.

Near Death Wish   Airdates: 11/17/91, 6/28/92.

Guest Cast: Richard McKenzie (Michael A. O'Connell), Christopher Grove (Jim Dorsey).

When Herman is almost killed in an elevator accident, he realizes he has nothing much to show for his life so far.

Bracken's Daughter   Airdates: 11/24/91, 5/24/92.

Guest Cast: Victoria Rowell (Susan Bracken), Linda Doucett (Woman).

Herman falls in love with Bracken's daughter, but the two lovers begin to worry about where their affair may take them.

Last Boy Scout, The   Airdates: 12/01/91, 3/29/92.

Guest Cast: Earl Boen (Bob Randall), John DiSanti (Uncle Harry), William Utay (Frank Keller), Janet Gunn (Dierdre), Nicole Sullivan (Young Woman), Victor Wilson (Man).

Herman buys a computer and then learns that it is stolen property.

Fear and Loathing in Manhattan   Airdates: 12/22/91, 5/31/92.

Guest Cast: Denis Arndt (Russell Boswell), Kevin Cooney (Senator Harris), Michael Goldfinger (Cop), Bella Pollini (Reporter).

Russell Boswell, Herman's idol, is an obnoxious journalist. Herman tries to help him uncover a corrupt senator's secrets, but when the investigation blows up, Herman is left holding the bag.

That's What Friends Aren't For   Airdates: 1/05/92, 4/12/92.

Guest Cast: Miriam Flynn (Dr. Nina Bergstrom), Sarah Essex (Amber), Pete Leal (Janitor).

When Herman agrees to share an apartment with Jay, the office takes up a pool to see how long they will last together.

To Err Is Herman   Airdate: 1/12/92.

Guest Cast: Liz Sheridan (Miss Cracknick), George O. Petrie (Mr. Waterton), Jordan Brady (Guy in Bar).

After Herman writes a harsh job performance evaluation of Bracken, he decides it is too strong and might cost both of them their jobs. He returns to the office to steal it back.

How to Succeed in Business without Really Dying   Airdates: 1/19/92, 7/26/92.

Guest Cast: Ed Winter (Mr. Crawford).

Herman is talked into going on an adventure article assignment with Jay. They go skydiving, but Jay chickens out on the plane.

Hard Times   Airdates: 2/09/92, 6/07/92.

Guest Cast: Teri Ann Linn (Jennifer), Mark St. James (Tony), Edan Gross (Little Herman), Shonda Whipple (Sally).

Herman meets a beautiful model but he is so worried about dating her that he can't perform in bed.

Kept Herman, A   Airdates: 2/16/92, 8/02/92.

Guest Cast: Deborah Adair (Victoria), Kathe Mazur (Secretary), Kimberly S. Newberry (Lawyer), Romy Rosemont (Jan), Eve Ahlert (Pat).

When Herman goes to work for a powerful woman executive who starts making sexual demands on him, he doesn't know what to do about it.

Herman Au Naturel   Airdates: 2/23/92, 8/23/92, 8/12/93.

Guest Cast: Ed Winter (Mr. Crawford), Brenda String (Dr. Paige Holland).

The entire office goes to the Bahamas for a seminar hosted by a sexy doctor. There, the staff learns the seminar will be held in the nude.

Sweet Obsessions   Airdates: 3/08/92, 6/14/92.

Guest Cast: George O. Petrie (Mr. Waterton), Michael Cutt (Bob Kelly), Kit Flanagan (Sally Wainright).

The office gets into a series of bets: Herman will give up sugar if Bracken stops smoking, and Heddy says she will give up men. Meanwhile, a cost-cutting specialist makes them worry about their jobs.

First Time for Everything   Airdates: 3/22/92, 7/19/92.

Guest Cast: Jack Kenny (Conventioneer #1), Michael Monks (Conventioneer #2), Randall Caldwell (Man in Bar).

On her 25th birthday, Louise asks Herman for help in finding a man so she can lose her virginity. Herman wants to be the one so honored, but he is so awkward that he scares her off.

Bracken Up Is Hard to Do   Airdates: 4/05/92, 7/05/92.

Guest Cast: Alaina Reed Hall (Margaret Bracken), Gina La Mond (Tina), Karen Lynn Scott (Bev), Christina Miles (Bernice).

When Bracken's wife throws him out of the house, he starts driving the staff crazy. Even worse, he moves in with Herman.

Guns 'n Neurosis   Airdates: 4/19/92, 11/29/92, 8/19/93.

Guest Cast: Ed Winter (Mr. Crawford), Peter Jason (Fritz), Christopher Daniel Barnes (Crawford's Son), Gigi Rice (Mrs. Crawford), Orlando Jones (Cop), Nick Angotti (Doctor).

After Herman is robbed, Crawford convinces him to buy a gun. Crawford then decides to test Herman by breaking into his apartment, but the test goes too well when Herman shoots.

Dirty, Rotten Scoundrels   Airdates: 5/03/92, 8/16/92.

Guest Cast: Marcia Cross (Princess Gillian), Carlos Carrasco (Carlos).

Jay asks Herman to help him get a story from a princess. When her bodyguard, Carlos, menaces them, Herman is torn between his desire to get the story and his feelings for the lonely princess.

Twisted Sister   Airdates: 5/10/92, 8/09/92.

Guest Cast: Jennifer Aniston (Suzie), Steve Hytner (Roger Harris), Taylor Fry (Little Suzie), Brad Devore (The Boy), Jack Mayhall (Bruce Shaw).

When Herman's sister comes to visit, he is shocked that she has grown up—especially when she sleeps with Jay!

1992–93 season

Stop Me before I Help Again   Airdates: 9/13/92, 11/06/92, 12/06/92.

Guest Cast: Diana Bellamy (Mrs. Peebles), Barbara Alyn Woods (Danielle), Robert Clothworthy (Frank).

Herman saves a choking woman by using CPR but soon finds himself being sued for breaking her ribs during the effort.

Sperm 'n' Herman   Airdates: 9/20/92, 12/27/92.

Guest Cast: Liz Vassey (Rebecca Woods), Kevin M. Richardson (Male Nurse), Jared Gillman (Boy Wimp).

An old girlfriend arrives and asks Herman to be the father of her baby—by artificial insemination.

Herman's Heddy   Airdates: 9/27/92, 1/10/93, 8/08/93.

Guest Cast: Drew Pillsbury (Harold Larson), Edward Roberts (Minister), Jill Pierce (Woman).

Herman decides to stop Heddy's upcoming wedding when he realizes he cares for her himself.

Intern-Al Affairs   Airdates: 10/04/92, 3/07/93.

Guest Cast: Ed Winter (Mr. Crawford), George O. Petrie (Mr. Waterton), Meredith Scott Lynn (Helene), Robin Curtis (Diane Shaw), Heather Elizabeth Parkhurst (Bobbie), Melanie MacQueen (Boring Woman).

When Herman tries to fire a substandard employee, she accuses him of sexual harassment.

Brackenhooker   Airdates: 10/18/92, 1/31/93.

Guest Cast: Debbi Morgan (Melodie), Julie Merrill (Woman at the Bar).

Herman can't arrange a date for Mr. Bracken, so he turns to an "expert" in the field of romance—Jay.

WATERTONGATE BREAK-IN, THE
Airdates: 10/25/92, 3/21/93.
Guest Cast: Ed Winter (Mr. Crawford), George O. Petrie (Mr. Waterton), Steve Hytner (Roger Harris).
Waterton's death plunges the company into turmoil and Herman is forced to join forces with Crawford to save everyone's job.

UNTITLED GIRLFRIEND PROJECT, THE
Airdates: 11/01/92, 6/27/93.
Guest Cast: Julia Campbell (Elizabeth), Maria Pecci (Sarah), Marti Muller (Maitre D'), David Gautreaux (Man), Christopher Darga (Waiter), Robert Curtis-Brown (Sean).
Herman falls for a woman with an unusually feisty attitude.

"C" WORD, THE Airdates: 11/03/92, 7/04/93.
Guest Cast: Julia Campbell (Elizabeth), Roxanne Beckford (Susan Bracken).
A problem develops with Herman's new relationship when Susan Bracken unexpectedly returns to town.

FRIENDS AND LOVERS Airdates: 11/08/92, 7/11/93.
Guest Cast: Julia Campbell (Elizabeth), Bobby Collins (Peter Jerry Parker), Rosanna Iversen (Greta).
Herman's undercover assignment as a dating show contestant causes problems in his relationship with Elizabeth.

SUBTERRANEAN HOMESICK BLUES
Airdates: 11/15/92, 7/18/93.
Guest Cast: Julia Campbell (Elizabeth), Robert Curtis-Brown (Sean).
Herman and Elizabeth move in together, but they quickly find that being together all the time presents some unexpected problems.

ONE WHERE THEY GO ON THE LOVE BOAT, THE Airdates: 11/22/92, 7/25/93.
Guest Cast: Julia Campbell (Elizabeth), Davy Jones (Himself), Amber Van Lent (Woman at Bar).
On a cruise to the Bahamas, Herman is surprised to see his ex-girlfriend, Elizabeth. Meanwhile Louise is busy chasing after Davey Jones from *The Monkees.*

FEARDOM OF SPEECH Airdates: 12/13/92, 4/04/93.
Guest Cast: Ed Winter (Mr. Crawford), Karen Lynn Scott (Carol Stevens), Tom McTigue (John Maxwell), Susan Diol (Hypnotist), Acey Dubow (Little Herman), Robert Lesser (Troy Michaels).
Herman must overcome a crippling fear of public speaking when he is asked to give a presentation at a company gathering.

CHARLIE BROWN FITZER, A Airdates: 12/20/92, 12/23/93.
Guest Cast: Elinor Donahue (Mrs. Fitzer), Richard Paul (Mr. Fitzer), Christine Cavanaugh (Martha Fitzer).
Herman and Heddy help Louise finally accept her unconventional parents.

ALL'S AFFAIR IN LOVE Airdates: 1/03/93, 6/20/93.
Guest Cast: Don R. McManus (John), Elizabeth Morehead (Diane).
Herman fixes Louise up with a blind date, unaware that the man is married.

OPEN ALL NIGHT Airdates: 1/17/93, 4/18/93, 9/02/93.
Guest Cast: Ed Winter (Mr. Crawford).
Everyone pitches in for a marathon all-night session to help Crawford meet a deadline to keep his job.

GALS-A-POPPIN' Airdates: 1/24/93, 5/30/93.
Guest Cast: Dawn Wells (Mary Ann), Gregory Martin (Phillip Decker), Carolyn Pemberton (Caroline Tate).
Heddy and Louise try to get back at their new boss, but it looks like Herman will be blamed for their antics.

ANATOMY OF A BLIND DATE Airdates: 2/07/93, 4/25/93, 9/09/93.
Guest Cast: Ria Pavia (Ellen), Kathleen Horrigan (Woman).
Herman lets Louise find him a blind date and soon wishes he hadn't.

MY FUNNY VALENTINE—HERMO
Airdates: 2/14/93, 6/06/93.
Guest Cast: Michael Feinstein (Himself), Lara Steinick (Julie), Claudette Sutherland (Mrs. Parisi), Anastasia Barzee (Margie), Leland Orser (Ralph), Monique Noel (Gigi).

A Valentine's Day party at his apartment leads to romance for everyone but Herman.

GOD, GIRLS, AND HERMAN   Airdates: 2/28/93, 6/13/93.
Guest Cast: Leslie Nielsen (God), Rebeccah Bush (Eve), Gary Cervantes (Miguel), Bruce French (Minister).
After he sleeps with a married woman, Herman asks God for advice.

LAYLA—THE UNPLUGGED VERSION
Airdate: 3/14/93.
Guest Cast: Julie Warner (Layla).
Jay's ex-girlfriend returns and a rift soon develops between Jay and Herman.

CAT'S IN THE CRADLE—HERMO
Airdates: 3/28/93, 8/01/93.
Guest Cast: Dakin Matthews (Mr. Brooks).
Herman's father is forced to retire and he comes to New York to visit Herman. When his son is too busy to spend any time with him, Mr. Brooks decides to take drastic steps to get his attention.

FIRED IN A CROWDED RESEARCH ROOM
Airdate: 4/11/93.
Guest Cast: Kristen Amber (Carli), Jacqueline Alexandra (Tina).
After he gets Heddy fired, Herman tries to undo the damage and save her career.

I WANNA GO HOME   Airdate: 4/25/93.
Guest Cast: Ed Winter (Mr. Crawford), Deborah Adair (Victoria), Corinne Bohrer (Connie), Jack Kenny (Conventioneer), Gina LaMond (Tina), Teri Ann Linn (Jennifer), Michael Monks (Conventioneer), Megan Mullally (Yvonne), Victoria Rowell (Susan Bracken), Brenda Strong (Dr. Holland).
A job offer in Ohio has Herman thinking about the experiences he has had since he first arrived in New York.

LOVE ME TWO TIMER   Airdates: 5/02/93, 8/29/93.
Guest Cast: Lita Ford (Herself), Anastasia Barzee (Margie).
Herman upsets his new girlfriend when he falls for a rock star.

LOVE AND THE SINGLE PARENT   Airdate: 5/09/93.
Guest Cast: Lisa Waltz (Carin), Bradley Pierce (Brad).

A woman's unruly son stands in the way of her relationship with Herman.

1993–94 season

HERM-APHRODITE   Airdates: 9/16/93, 12/09/93.
Guest Cast: Ed Winter (Mr. Crawford), Patrick Ewing (Himself), Kevin O'Brien.
Herman dresses as a woman to get a story from the female point of view.

THERE'S A FLY GIRL IN MY SOUP
Airdates: 9/23/93, 1/06/94.
Guest Cast: Karen Malina White (Rene), The Fly Girls: Laurie Ann Gibson, Jossie Harris, Deidre Lang, Lisa Thompson, Masako Willis.
Bracken's niece wants to be a dancer and Bracken decides that Herman is just the guy to talk her out of it.

WHEN HERMY MET CRAWFORD'S DAUGHTER   Airdates: 9/30/93, 1/30/94.
Guest Cast: Ed Winter (Mr. Crawford), Kathleen McClellan (Ellen Crawford).
Herman has a shock when he meets his new girlfriend's father—it's Mr. Crawford.

WHEN HAIRY MET HERMY   Airdate: 10/07/93.
Guest Cast: Jessica Steen (Heather), Morey Amsterdam (Buddy), Rose Marie (Sally).
Herman has a hard time accepting his new girlfriend's unshaven armpits.

OVER HERMAN'S HEAD   Airdates: 10/14/93, 3/31/94.
Guest Cast: Ann Guilbert (The Old Woman), Claudette Sutherland (Mrs. Parisi).
Herman wants the apartment over his, but he worries that he might have accidentally killed the previous occupant.

JAYBO AND WEESIE—A LOVE STORY
Airdate: 10/21/93.
Guest Cast: Debbie James (Jackie).
Louise surprisingly finds herself falling for Jay, even though she knows all too well about his womanizing past.

HERMO-TIVATED   Airdate: 10/26/93.
Guest Cast: Lane Davies (Dick Van Adams), Stephen Hytner (Roger Harris), Craig Benton (The New Guy), Bo Sharon (Craig Lumpin).
A motivational seminar has a drastic effect on Herman, who soon becomes an editor,

with a completely different personality to match.

JAY IS FOR JEALOUSY   Airdate: 11/04/93.

Guest Cast: Bobcat Goldthwait (Jealousy), Jennifer Aniston (Suzy), Kenneth Kimmins (Mr. Joffe).

Louise's relationship with Jay takes a new turn when she worries about his flirting with Herman's sister.

TROUBLE IN PARADISE   Airdate: 11/11/93.

Guest Cast: Michelle Johnson (Aurora).

A weekend with a beautiful supermodel doesn't go as planned for Herman when Jay and Louise show up and start arguing.

WHEN HERMY MET MAUREEN McCORMICK   Airdates: 11/18/93, 3/03/94.

Guest Cast: Maureen McCormick (Herself), Lynne Marie Stewart (Joan).

Herman is assigned to assist former *The Brady Bunch* co-star Maureen McCormick with a book project, which upsets Jay tremendously.

ACTOR PREPARES, AN   Airdates: 12/02/93, 3/17/94.

Guest Cast: Peter Dobson (Thomas Alan Edwards), David Bowe (Jack), Judith-Marie Bergan (Mary), Yasmine Bleeth (Linda).

Herman trades places with an actor who is preparing for his role as a researcher.

DECENT PROPOSAL, A   Airdates: 12/16/93, 5/26/94.

Guest Cast: Andrea Parker (Heather Brookshire), Kirsten Holmquist (Tawny).

Herman agrees to pretend he is married to Heddy to help her impress a girlfriend, but things go awry when the friend asks to stay with them.

WHEN HERMY MET CRAWFORD'S GIRLFRIEND   Airdates: 12/30/93, 6/02/94.

Guest Cast: Ed Winter (Mr. Crawford), Rena Sofer (Stephanie), Sean Moran (The Elevator Guy).

Crawford's new girlfriend is a lot younger than he is. When she takes Herman's advice to date someone her own age, Crawford starts acting like a very old man.

THREE ON A MATCH   Airdate: 1/13/94.

Guest Cast: Gilbert Gottfried (Bob).

A fire in the office building prompts everyone to reexamine their priorities in life.

YOU SAY TOMATO . . .   Airdates: 2/03/94, 6/16/94.

Guest Cast: Tia Riebling (Lauren), Peggy McIntaggart (The Playmate), Anthony Forkush (The Geek).

Herman falls in love with a Playboy playmate and tries to make his girlfriend over in her image.

ONCE MORE WITH FEELING   Airdate: 2/10/94.

Herman and Heddy try all evening for a romp in the sack but have to combat a never-ending series of interruptions.

HERM FROM IPANEMA, THE   Airdates: 2/17/94, 6/09/94.

Guest Cast: Bob Denver (Himself), Ed Winter (Mr. Crawford), Jocko Marcellino (Eddie), Cristina Lawson (The Waitress), Pete Schrum (The Fisherman).

Herman and the gang find themselves on a Caribbean island with Bob Denver of *Gilligan's Island* fame.

BEDTIME FOR HERMO   Airdate: 3/10/94.

Guest Cast: Debra Mooney (Herman's Mother), Kathleen Freeman (Mrs. Debusher), Steve Franken (Mr. Prescott), Edmund L. Shaff (Coach Nubbin).

Herman has a big meeting tomorrow and is too keyed up to sleep, which brings back memories of a particularly nasty high school teacher.

HERM IN THE TIME OF CHOLERA   Airdate: 3/24/94.

Guest Cast: Kari Coleman (Lil), Maureen Pierson (Kimberly), Kevin Stapleton (Scott).

Herman thinks he can just be friends with a new acquaintance until he sees her in action with her boyfriend.

ABSENCE MAKES THE HEAD GROW FONDER   Airdate: 4/07/94.

Guest Cast: Kim Gillingham (Sarah), Todd Kimsey (Todd).

Herman breaks up with his girlfriend, but not long after decides he wants her back again.

HEAD IN THE POLLS, A   Airdate: 4/14/94.

Guest Cast: Michelle Phillips (Sandra Clayton), Daniel McDonald (Roy), Nigel Gibbs (Reporter #1), Art Metrano (Reporter #2).

A woman politician takes an interest in Herman, but the relationship suffers when the press gets wind of it.

First Impressions   Airdate: 4/21/94.

Guest Cast: Mark Lonow (The Vice President), Roger Hewlett (The Big Guy), Jim Kratt (The Bouncer), Lawrence A. Mandley (The Doctor), Shannon Sturges (The Waitress), Jillian McWhirter (The Woman).

Herman is hit by a cab and is seriously injured. As his friends recall their first impressions of Herman, his brain characters take his place and we see their recollections.

Nurses

With the series *STAT* having lived a very short life, it might have been reasonable to think that Disney would stay clear of any new series set in a hospital. In fact, though, the Studio quickly put another hospital sitcom, *Nurses*, into development for the 1991–92 season.

The setting for this new show was the Community Medical Center, the same hospital where Dr. Harry Weston had his office in *Empty Nest*. This time, though, as the title implies, the emphasis was to be on nurses, specifically those working in the Three West ward of the hospital. In addition to the regular cast, the hospital had frequent visits from the casts of Disney's other Saturday night series.

Cast: Stephanie Hodge (Sandy Salter, 1991–93), Loni Anderson (Casey MacAfee, 1993–94), Arnetia Walker (Annie Miller), Mary Jo Keenen (Julie Moser), Ada Maris (Gina Valdez), Kenneth David Gilman (Dr. Hank Kaplan), Carlos LaCamara (Paco Ortiz), Jeff Altman (Greg Vincent, 1991–92), Florence Stanley (Dr. Amanda Riskin, 1991–92), Markus Flanagan (Luke Fitzgerald, 1992–93), David Rasche (Jack Trenton, 1992–94). *Beginning with the episode No Hiding Place, Kenneth David Gilman changed his billing to Kip Gilman.*

Each of the episodes is described below in airdate order.

1991–92 season

Son of a Pilot   Airdates: 9/14/91, 3/14/92.

Guest Cast: Matt McCoy (Harold Miller), David Packer (Larry Haber), Mary Pat Gleason (Off Duty Nurse), Richard Fancy (Dr. Moss), Naomi Serotoff (Patient).

The newest nurse, Julie, doesn't inspire her co-workers with confidence. Meanwhile, Sandy is shocked to learn that her ex-husband is planning to marry a very young patient.

Lesson in Life, A   Airdates: 9/21/91, 11/30/91, 6/27/92.

Guest Cast: Florence Stanley (Dr. Riskin), Allan Rich (Mr. Milner), D. David Morin (Dr. Eric Vaughn), Richard Fancy (Dr. Moss), Steven M. Gagnon (Dr. Bickman), Park Overall (Laverne Todd).

A patient helps Julie with her phobias; Laverne convinces Sandy to go on a date; Gina helps a patient and his brother reunite; and the doctors try to cure Greg's bad attitude.

This Joint Is Jumpin'   Airdates: 9/28/91, 12/21/91.

Guest Cast: David Kaufman (Dr. Kirby), Nancy Lenehan (Cheryl Pinson), Angela Paton (Mrs. Pinson), Dick Monday (Mr. Kroft).

A new doctor frames Greg for the theft of some missing drugs; Sandy gets mad at a patient who is ignoring her own mother; and Annie worries that she may be pregnant.

Coming to America   Airdates: 10/05/91, 3/21/92.

Guest Cast: William Marquez (Papa Antonio Cuevas), John O'Hurley (Dave Grady), Eric Pierpont (Dr. Monford), Eda Reiss Merin (Mrs. Chase), Anna Berger (Mrs. Garber), Jean Sincere (Mrs. King), Walt Beaver (Patient #1), Lucille Bliss (Patient #2).

Gina's father is coming to visit. Worried that he might disapprove of her life alone, she convinces Hank to pretend to be her boyfriend.

Reversal of Grandpa   Airdates: 10/12/91, 1/18/92.

Guest Cast: June Lockhart (Mrs. Farley), George D. Wallace (Grandpa), Tom Virtue (John Doe), Harry Johnson (Dr. Hinterman).

The staff take turns talking to an accident victim in the hope that he will come out of a coma.

Mother, Jugs, and Zach   Airdates: 10/19/91, 12/28/91, 7/04/92.

Guest Cast: Matt McCoy (Harold Miller), Jeri Lynn Ryan (Lisa Connors), Maxine Elliott (Mrs. Heston), Raymond McQueen (Zach), Randy Bennett (The Waiter), Richard Mulligan (Dr. Harry Weston).

Sandy must look after her ex-husband's new fiancee; Annie's son is getting into trouble at school; Gina sneaks a dog onto the floor to comfort a burn victim; and Julie helps a senile patient.

DEAD NURSE   Airdates: 10/26/91, 1/25/92.

Guest Cast: Peggy Pope (Adele), Christine Mitges (Beverly), Robert Firth (Man).

The death of a co-worker makes the staff think more closely about their own lives.

KIND, KONSIDERATE KARE   Airdates: 11/02/91, 6/13/92.

Guest Cast: Andrew Masset (Mr. Watkins), Elizabeth Austin (Wendy), Christopher Burgard (Roger), Chuck Mavich (Dennis).

A white supremacist is outraged when Annie saves his life; Greg falls in love with a patient; and the ladies have their revenge on an abusive construction worker.

BEGONE WITH THE WIND   Airdates: 11/09/91, 6/06/92.

Guest Cast: Betty White (Rose Nylund), Ralph Bruneau (Phil), Richard Fancy (Dr. Moss), Patrick Cronin (Mr. Crandall), Jacob Vargas (Luis), Louie Leonardo (Blood Monster), Naomi Serotoff (Mrs. Libbit), Ken Kallmeyer (Man), Bradley Michael Pierce (Jimmy), Bryan Norcross (Himself), Park Overall (Laverne Todd).

An approaching hurricane puts the staff to the test as they prepare to be swamped with accident victims.

Production Note:

- The hurricane theme from this episode was carried over into Disney's other Saturday night series aired that night.

INTERNA-AL AFFAIR TO REMEMBER, AN   Airdates: 11/16/91, 3/28/92.

Guest Cast: Brian McNamara (Steve), James T. Callahan (Mr. Taber), Stanley Kamel (Damone).

Sandy must decide if she wants to move to Minnesota with her new boyfriend; a patient confuses her medicine because she can't read; and Greg overacts in a training video.

SEIZE THE DATE   Airdates: 11/23/91, 4/11/92.

Guest Cast: Lane Davies (Abe Kaplan), Amy Yasbeck (Debbie), Stuart Pankin (Milton Float), Florence Stanley (Dr. Riskin).

Hank's brother visits and falls in love with Gina; Julie makes friends with a selfish patient; and a hospital administrator tries to prove Dr. Riskin isn't billing poor patients for their tests.

FRIENDS AND LOVERS   Airdates: 12/07/91, 5/23/92.

Guest Cast: Fred Willard (Dr. Robinson), Forry Smith (Man), Raymond McQueen (Zach), Florence Stanley (Dr. Riskin).

Annie asks Sandy to babysit, with some unexpected problems; Julie falls in love with a doctor who is really a psychiatric patient.

LOVE, DEATH, AND THE WHOLE DAMN THING   Airdates: 12/14/91, 7/11/92.

Guest Cast: Adam Arkin (Peter), Florence Stanley (Dr. Riskin).

Julie is horrified to learn that an ex-boyfriend has AIDS.

NO HIDING PLACE   Airdates: 1/04/92, 5/30/92.

Guest Cast: Larry Linville (Mr. Garrett), James Lashly (Mr. Thorne).

A patient takes the nurses hostage, blaming the hospital and doctors for his ill health.

SPHERE TODAY, GONE TOMORROW   Airdates: 1/11/92, 4/18/92.

Guest Cast: Jennifer Blanc (Amy).

Hank is worried that he might have cancer; Dr. Riskin thinks about resigning instead of battling the hospital's red tape any longer; and Sandy befriends a liver transplant patient.

TRUTH SHALL SCREW YOU UP, THE   Airdates: 2/01/92, 6/20/92.

Guest Cast: K Callan (Lila), Lisa Waltz (Gail), Therese Kablan (Didi).

Sandy's mother arrives for a visit and immediately starts to complain; Gina is upset to learn that Hank is dating other women.

MARRIED TO THE MOP   Airdates: 2/08/92, 7/18/92.

Guest Cast: Jack Carter (Eddie Stracken), Richard Burgi (Doug from Supply), Derek Mark Lochran (Performance Artist).

Paco becomes indebted to a mob boss; Gina tries to make Hank jealous by dating another man, unaware that he is gay.

EAT SOMETHING   Airdates: 2/15/92, 8/22/92.

Guest Cast: Lee Weaver (Reverend Curtis), Joe Alaskey (Trekker #1), John Hawkes (Trekker #2), Scott Lawrence (Trekker #3), Nick Toth (Trekker #4), Toni Sawyer (Woman).

When a patient is killed by an ambulance, Annie begins to question her faith in God. The death of a friend only makes matters worse, and her friends realize they must help her or Annie will quit.

CATCH A FALLEN STAR   Airdates: 2/22/92, 8/29/92.
   Guest Cast: Stephen Furst (Chet "Poofie" McGuire), Al Ruscio (Mr. Hamel), Mary Gillis (Mrs. Kellner), Sid Melton (Ben).
   The nurses try to make an actor realize that his show makes the medical profession look foolish; Julie helps a dying man see his brother; and Dr. Riskin tries to find out why a patient gets ill when his mother visits.

MOON OVER MIAMI   Airdates: 2/29/92, 8/15/92.
   Guest Cast: David Leisure (Charlie Dietz), Tim Thomerson (Colonel Calvin Carlton), Raye Birk (Mr. Eckworth), Caitlin Dulany (Randi), Tony Segreto (Himself), Rue McClanahan (Blanche Devereaux).
   The crew discusses some strange events seemingly triggered by full moons.

RUDE AWAKENINGS   Airdates: 4/25/92, 9/05/92.
   Guest Cast: George Coe (Rudy), Michael Canavan (Dana), Robert Yacko (Gorilla Man).
   When a patient comes out of a 38-year coma, Dr. Riskin shocks the staff by telling them she was once engaged to the man, and that they had a son.

EX-FACTOR, THE   Airdates: 5/02/92, 9/12/92.
   Guest Cast: Marius Weyers (Dr. Peter Pleckner), Janet Zarish (Joyce), Steven Elkins (Mitch).
   Gina realizes that Hank is still carrying a torch for his ex-wife; Greg is trapped in the elevator with a cannibal.

1992–93 season

SLIME AND PUNISHMENT   Airdates: 9/16/92, 11/28/92, 7/03/93.
   Guest Cast: Art Metrano (Mr. Warner), Raymond Serra (Officer Torres).
   High-flying financier Jack Trenton is convicted of insider trading, bribery, and fraud. Annie decides it's time to show the staff who is in charge, and Gina tells Hank their relationship is over.

IN MY NEW COUNTRY   Airdates: 9/16/92, 12/26/92.
   Guest Cast: Park Overall (Laverne Todd), David Wells (Mueller).
   Gina becomes an American citizen and decides to go after a slumlord, who just happens to be Jack Trenton; Hank and Luke have a series of confrontations; Laverne Todd checks in for an operation.

INSIDE INFORMATION   Airdates: 10/03/92, 1/23/93.
   Guest Cast: Jim Ishida (Mr. Watanabe), Paul Eisenhauer (Dr. Rumson).
   Jack overhears a tranquilized patient babbling about the stock market and tries to use the information for a new stock deal; Sandy tries to deal with depression; Hank tries to get back in Gina's good graces.

BAD BOY IN THE BUBBLE   Airdates: 10/10/92, 1/09/93.
   Guest Cast: Shishir Kurup (Dr. Rajid).
   Luke tricks Jack into believing that he has been exposed to a fatal toxic substance and must stay in a plastic bubble to survive.

JULIE GETS VALIDATED   Airdates: 10/17/92, 3/06/93.
   Guest Cast: Tom Hodges (Carl), Angela Paton (Mrs. Kerper).
   Julie becomes romantically involved with Carl, the hospital's dim-witted parking lot attendant.

ANNIE'S CHOICE   Airdates: 10/24/92, 3/20/93.
   Guest Cast: Eric Christmas (Mr. Ross).
   The staff wonders whom Annie will leave in charge when she goes on vacation; Jack tries his best to con an elderly patient out of a valuable watch.

PLAYING DOCTOR   Airdates: 10/31/92, 1/16/93.
   Guest Cast: Dinah Manoff (Carol Weston), Philip Baker Hall (Mr. Todd), Ellerine! (The Woman), Fred Sanders (Arfie), Bear (Dreyfuss).
   Gina is suspended for giving an indigent child medicine without a prescription; Sandy saves Dreyfuss from drowning.

DIRTY LAUNDRY   Airdates: 11/07/92, 1/30/93, 7/24/93.
   Guest Cast: Geraldo Rivera (Himself), Sid Melton (Sy).

When Geraldo Rivera checks into the hospital, Hank worries that he will become Geraldo's next exposé, and Jack is convinced that Geraldo is there to spy on him.

ILLICIT TRANSFERS   Airdates: 11/14/92, 1/23/93.
Guest Cast: John Ratzenberger (Mr. Hafner), Connie Sawyer (Mrs. Deangelis).
Jack tries to bribe the hospital administrator into transferring Annie to another floor; Sandy's new policy of total honesty causes problems with her co-workers; Hank is charged with sexism.

OUR FRED   Airdates: 11/21/92, 3/27/93.
Guest Cast: Peter Scolari (George Myrock).
Annie's husband, Fred, starts spending too much time with his new friend, Hank; one of Jack's former business partners is admitted to the hospital.

ONE PEQUENO, TWO PEQUENO
Airdates: 12/05/92, 4/24/93.
Guest Cast: Salma Hayek (Yolanda Cuevas).
Gina's younger sister, Yolanda, arrives for a visit and all of the men are soon chasing after her.

SOLITARY MAN   Airdates: 12/12/92, 5/29/93.
Guest Cast: David Wells (Mueller).
Luke wants to be left alone but has picked a bad day for it—the staff has planned a surprise party for his birthday.

CAUGHT SHORT   Airdates: 1/02/93, 4/17/93.
Gina borrows some money from an office betting pool and must go to elaborate lengths to pay it back before she is discovered.

IF I WERE A RICH MAN   Airdates: 1/09/93, 6/05/93.
Guest Cast: Macka Foley (Ned Cummings).
Jack tricks Hank into making a highly speculative land investment; the women become convinced that Luke posed for a nude calendar.

GROPES OF WRATH, THE   Airdates: 1/16/93, 6/12/93.
Guest Cast: Sharon Martin (Danielle), Blanche Rubin (The Elderly Lady).

The staff has to deal with the topic of sexual harassment; Jack doesn't like the results of his physical.

SUPERBOWL   Airdates: 1/30/93, 6/19/93.
Guest Cast: Eva La Rue (Cindy).
No one wants to go to Hank's Superbowl party; when they finally do go, it's a predictable disaster.

DEVIL AND THE DEEP BLUE SEA, THE
Airdates: 2/06/93, 8/14/93.
Guest Cast: Larry Cszonka (Himself), Rider Strong (Max), Marius Weyers (Worthington), Charles Alvin Bell (Schwartz).
Sandy is attracted to Jack after she accompanies him to a high-stakes gambling ship; Hank's spoiled son is admitted to the hospital and the staff soon wishes he would leave.

LOVE AND DEATH   Airdates: 2/13/93, 6/26/93.
Guest Cast: Tom Hodges (Carl), David Wells (Mueller).
Julie wants to break up with Carl, but when he surprises her by proposing, she accepts.

FAMILY OUTING   Airdates: 2/20/93, 8/07/93.
Guest Cast: William Daniels (Norm Kaplan), Paul Keith (Bill), Michael Winters (Roy), Calvin Remsberg (Judge Hamilton).
Someone is stealing food from the nurses' lounge; Hank learns that his father is gay.

WHEN HANK MET GINA   Airdates: 2/27/93, 7/31/93.
Hank and Gina rekindle their romance; Paco wins the lottery and dreams of quitting.

STING OF HEARTS   Airdates: 4/03/93, 8/28/93.
Guest Cast: Tony Plana (Rico Garcia), Dave Florek (Agent Forest), Todd Kimsey (Agent Oakes).
Hank is jealous of Gina's relationship with a salesman; Jack, meanwhile, is meeting with the same salesman to get inside information on his company.

WHAT ARE FRIENDS FOR?   Airdates: 4/10/93, 8/21/93.
Guest Cast: Patrick Warburton (Chuck).
Sandy doesn't know how to tell Annie that she doesn't like Annie's friend; Jack panics

when he thinks he accidentally killed an elderly patient.

SMOKIN' IN THE BOYS ROOM   Airdate: 5/01/93.

Guest Cast: Kathleen Freeman (Sister Mary Alma), Michael Monks (Construction Guy).

Jack has a secret hideaway in the hospital; Luke doesn't know how to deal with a strong-willed nun.

1993–94 season

JUMPIN' JACK FLASH   Airdate: 9/04/93.

Guest Cast: Fred Applegate (The Angel).

When Jack is accidentally electrocuted and dies, he escapes death by cheating an angel in a game of Monopoly.

EAGLE HAS LANDED, THE   Airdates: 9/25/93, 12/04/93.

Guest Cast: Richard Mulligan (Dr. Harry Weston), Leslie Jordan (Cooley Waits), Sid Melton (Leo).

The hospital is bought by a large corporation which brings in a new administrator, Casey MacAfee. Casey doesn't have any experience running a hospital, and she and the staff are soon at each other's throats.

SEND IN THE GOWNS   Airdates: 10/02/93, 12/11/93.

Guest Cast: Leslie Jordan (Cooley Waits), Doug Anderson (Note Finder #2), James Kline (Note Finder #1), Danny Lee Jordan, Peter Neushul (Note Finder #3).

Casey orders new hospital gowns to impress the owner, but they give the patients rashes and catch on fire.

INTRUDERS   Airdates: 10/09/93, 3/19/94.

Guest Cast: Nicholas Coster (Dr. Melnitz).

The staff is outraged when they learn that Casey has been spying on them with a surveillance camera; Jack impersonates a doctor to impress a surgeon.

JACK'S INDECENT PROPOSAL   Airdates: 10/16/93, 4/02/94.

Guest Cast: David Leisure (Charlie Dietz).

Desperate for additional funds for the hospital, Casey ponders Jack's offer to sleep with him for a million dollars.

BRING ME THE HEAD OF HANK KAPLAN   Airdates: 10/23/93, 5/28/94.

Guest Cast: Gregory Sierra (Vargas Cuevas), Al Rodrigo (Diego), Lillian Hurst (Mother).

Even though Gina's father has threatened to kill him, Hank decides the best defense is a good offense, so he arranges to meet the family.

SNOWBALL'S CHANCE   Airdate: 10/30/93.

Casey's Halloween party for the staff is marred by the theft of one of her pet snowball globes; Hank accidentally gives some valuable baseball cards to Paco, who won't give them back.

BRIDGES OF DADE COUNTRY, THE   Airdates: 11/06/93, 6/04/94.

Guest Cast: Richard Mulligan (Dr. Harry Weston), Robert Gossett (Winston Bowman), Julie Merrill (Dawn), Eddie Yansick (Stunt Waiter).

With her marriage a dull routine, Annie is tempted to have an affair with a very eligible patient; Paco and Jack throw a bachelor party for Hank; Jack ruins a date between Casey and Harry Weston.

NO, BUT I PLAYED ONE ON TV   Airdates: 11/13/93, 6/11/94.

Guest Cast: Chad Everett (Himself), Vince Edwards (Himself), Larry Linville (Himself), Amy Hill (Joanna Joyce), Neil Ross (Announcer).

Casey invites three actors who are famous for playing doctors on television to the hospital to help dedicate the new maternity wing; Jack saves a woman from choking but no one believes him.

TEMPORARY SETBACKS   Airdates: 11/20/93, 6/18/94.

Guest Cast: Dinah Manoff (Carol Weston), Estelle Getty (Sophia Petrillo), Lisa Rhianna Smith (Lydia).

Jack tries to show that his time in the hospital hasn't dulled his ability to scheme.

BIRTH OF A MARRIAGE, THE   Airdate: 11/27/93.

Guest Cast: Richard Mulligan (Dr. Harry Weston), Raye Birk (Chaplain), Robert Michael Barta (Baby).

Hank and Gina race the stork in an attempt to get married before the baby arrives. Casey agrees to another date with Harry; Jack is hurt at work but no one believes him.

SHIFT OF THE MAGI, THE   Airdate: 12/18/93.

Guest Cast: None.

When Casey's Christmas gifts for the staff are delayed at the factory, Jack surprisingly comes to the rescue; Gina is upset that Hank has to work on Christmas.

PACO GETS MACED   Airdate: 1/08/94.
Guest Cast: Kevin Crowley (Barry Fry).

Casey accidentally maces Paco and a disreputable attorney sees an opportunity to make a fortune by suing her and the hospital.

PARENTAL GUIDANCE SUGGESTED
Airdate: 1/15/94.
Guest Cast: Timothy Stack (Oscar), Billie Worley (John Trenton, Jr.), Brenna S. and Jordain T. Bobola (Juanita Kaplan).

Jack's son visits and announces that he is going to Guatemala with the Peace Corps, a decision that doesn't sit well with Jack.

MI CASA, SU CASA   Airdate: 1/22/94.
Guest Cast: Stephen M. Porter (Dale Rourke).

An argument with their apartment manager gets the Kaplans evicted; Casey bribes Paco into spying on Jack.

FLY THE FRIENDLY SKIES   Airdate: 2/05/94.
Guest Cast: Richard Belzer (Jesse Wilner).

Jack and Paco sneak off to Nassau on Jack's jet, only to be hijacked by a disgruntled ex-employee; Casey loses a contact lens but is too vain to wear her glasses.

DON'T HIT THE ROAD, JACK   Airdate: 2/12/94.
Guest Cast: None.

When Jack stops asking Casey out, she can't stand the rejection, so even though she doesn't like Jack she sets out to seduce him.

BURY THE HATCHETS   Airdate: 3/05/94.
Guest Cast: Gregory Sierra (Vargas Cuevas).

Gina's father arrives for a visit and gets off to a rocky start with Hank; Casey finds out that she has been tricked into a date with Jack.

NOTHIN' SAYS LOVIN' . . .   Airdate: 3/12/94.
Guest Cast: Bergen Lynn Williams (Ms. Gump).

A tour of duty in the hospital cafeteria finds Jack being pursued by the hospital chef, a very direct woman who can't believe Jack can bake better than she can.

SILENT PARTNER   Airdate: 4/09/94.
Guest Cast: Henry Darrow (Hector Lopez), Martha Victoria (Maria Lopez).

Jack tries to pass Paco off as a business partner to impress a Cuban businessman, but the man's wife ruins everything when she makes a pass at Paco.

ONE AFTER THE EARTHQUAKE, THE
Airdate: 4/16/94.
Guest Cast: Tom Mardirosian (Mr. Parry), Sid Melton (Leo), Steve Bridges (Torrance), Vanessa Marquez (Angelica).

A student nurse decides she wants to be like Casey; a hypochondriac can't accept turning 40; a man has a throat operation because he sounds like Jack Nicholson; Jack and Paco have a fight; Julie loses a patient.

BIG JACK ATTACK, THE   Airdate: 4/23/94.
Guest Cast: Joe Flaherty (Mr. Fortin), Mayor Robert E. Metivier (Himself), Ed McMahon (Detective Salisbury).

Jack's offer to take care of a corporate hatchet man is misunderstood when the man turns up dead.

ALL THE PRETTY CASEYS   Airdate: 5/07/94.
Guest Cast: Adam West (Mr. Greer), Cheryl Bricker (Phyllis Cage), Jean Kasem (Jean).

Casey quits to take a new job, only to realize that her new boss hired her only for her looks.

Pacific Station

When Disney's sitcom *The Fanelli Boys* failed after one season, the creators of that series quickly bounced back with another offering for the 1991–92 season. The series, titled *Pacific Station*, was set in a police station in Venice, California, where by-the-book detective Bob Ballard found himself with a very unusual new partner. The other officer, Richard Capparelli, was heavily into New Age philosophies, a trait that the other officers viewed with suspicion.

Series Cast: Robert Guillaume (Detective Bob Ballard), Richard Libertini (Detective Richard Capparelli), John Hancock (Deputy Commissioner Hank Bishop), Joel Murray (Captain Kenny Epstein), Megan Gallagher (Detective Sandy Calloway), Ron Liebman (Detective Al Burkhardt).

Each of the episodes is described below in airdate order.

PACIFIC STATION (pilot) Airdate: 9/15/91.

Guest Cast: Tom La Grua (Joey), Susan Angelo (Detective #2), Cliff Bemis (Uniformed Cop), Robert Covarrubias (Detective #1), Daniel Dicks (Boy Scout), Steven Ho (Delivery Boy).

Bob Ballard is dismayed to find that his new partner Richard Capparelli looks like a hippie. Things don't get any better when Capparelli mentions that he just got off psychiatric leave.

MAGNIFICENT OBSESSION Airdate: 9/22/91.

Guest Cast: Arthur Malet (Jimmy), Bert Rosario (Sandwich Guy), William Cort (Santini), Sharon Lee Jones (Woman), Albert Michel Jr. (Man), Robert Barry (Blind Man), Tudi Roach (Mailperson), E.E. Bell (Window Washer).

When Bob becomes obsessed with catching a slippery drug dealer, his wife finally throws him out of the house. After moving in with Capparelli, Bob becomes even more determined to catch his quarry.

MAN'S BEST FRIEND, A Airdate: 9/29/91.

Guest Cast: Timothy Black (Swampcat Rollin), Frances Bay (Celia Linder), Doug Cox (Driver), Marco Sanchez (Sandwich Vendor).

Capparelli's former partner blames Bob for breaking up the old team and seeks his revenge. Unfortunately for Bob, the ex-partner is a very determined police dog.

LOVE AND DEATH Airdate: 10/06/91.

Guest Cast: Kario Salem (Henri), Randee Heller (Charlotte), Tracey Walter (Venice Guy), Jodie Markell (Rebecca), Julian Christopher (George Fergus), Freeman King (Detective #1), Mark Goldstein (Worker), Michael Mitchell (Detective #2), Bari K. Willerford (Detective #3), Stephen Held (Officer).

When Bob is declared dead due to a bureaucratic error, Capparelli is assigned a new partner, Detective Calloway. He finds her so attractive that he loses interest in bringing Bob back to "life."

FRIEND OF THE DEVIL Airdate: 10/13/91.

Guest Cast: Brock Peters (Ray Taylor), Cliff Bemis (Officer Renfro), Marietta DePrima (Allison), Rudy Ramos (Carlos), Ronald Paul Ramirez (Benito), Patrick Allen Reynolds (Krishna), Matthew Linville (Timmy).

Capparelli becomes suspicious of Bob's former partner, who is spending a lot of time hanging around the station house.

MIATA ES SU ATA Airdate: 10/20/91.

Guest Cast: Alex Trebek (Himself), Arthur Malet (Officer Jimmy), Lee Chamberlin (Dr. Carlisle), Charles McDaniel (Officer Mahoney), Allen Bloomfield (Supply Cop #1), Arnold Johnson (Supply Cop #2), Harvey Vernon (Ed Vokovich).

When the department psychiatrist announces that one of the detectives is not fit for duty, everyone is surprised to learn that it's Bob and not Capparelli.

WAITING FOR THE OTHER GUMSHOE TO DROP Airdate: 10/27/91.

Guest Cast: Janet Carroll (Judy Epstein), Tracey Walter (Harley), Cliff Bemis (Officer Renfro), Shirley Prestia (Madame Zora), Bari K. Willerford (Team Captain).

A psychic spooks Capparelli by predicting that he'll be shot. Despite the possibility of impending doom, Capparelli and Bob must deal with a man threatening to jump off a bridge.

BOB'S SON Airdate: 12/20/91.

Guest Cast: Barbara Stock (Cory Fiedler), Leroy Edwards III (Keith Ballard), Ed Evanko (Host).

A visit to the station makes Bob's son decide to quit college and become a police office, much to his father's displeasure.

OPERATION! Airdate: 12/27/91.

Guest Cast: Gedde Watanabe (Ram Sha), William G. Schilling (Dr. Collins), Cliff Bemis (Officer Renfro), Rebecca Staab (Nurse).

Bob refuses to have his tonsils removed and confesses to Capparelli that he is terrified of hospitals. When he meets Capparelli's holistic healer, though, he starts to rethink his position.

MY FAVORITE DAD Airdate: 1/03/92.

Guest Cast: Robert Mandan (Bill DuPont), Pam Grier (Grace Ballard), Meredith Scott Lynn (Cassandra Feinberg), Monica Calhoun (Dawn Ballard), Robert Poole (Officer Wallace).

Capparelli notices that someone is following him. When he confronts her, he is surprised to learn why—she thinks he is her father.

WHOSE DAD IS IT, ANYWAY? Airdate: 7/13/92.

Guest Cast: Whitman Mayo (Woody Ballard), Jane Leeves (Edwina Burwell), Cliff Bemis (Officer Renfro). The 5th Precinct: Wendell Anderson, Rusty Coleman, Kevin Guillaume, Soloman Henderson, Kevin McDowell.

Bob is worried when his father disappears from the nursing home, but those worries fade when he finds him sharing an apartment with Capparelli.

ONE FOR THE ROAD Airdate: 8/31/92.

Guest Cast: Beth Howland (Sunshine Rosenstock), Monica Calhoun (Dawn Ballard), Gedde Watanabe (Fuji), Alex Dessert (John Wilkins), Cliff Bemis (Officer Renfro).

When Al is left a tidy sum in his aunt's will, he learns that the money will go to her dog if he dies. It sounds funny at first, but all clues point to a murder plot by the dog.

LAST ANGRY DETECTIVE, THE Airdate: Unaired.

Guest Cast: Alix Elias (Karen), Sandy Helberg (Heifetz), Sal Viscuso (Fred Savoy), David Kriegel (Pablo), Frantz Turner (Mr. Harris).

The detectives are assigned to catch a major graffiti vandal who only paints when he feels an earthquake is coming. When they catch him, he has just finished his biggest paint job ever.

Home Improvement

Disney's biggest television success of the '90s came with the creation of the situation comedy *Home Improvement*, which took to the airwaves for the 1991–92 season.

The series is essentially an expansion of a comedy skit titled *Men Are Pigs*, which had won star Tim Allen an ACE Award when it aired on the Showtime cable network.

Home Improvement is the story of Tim "The Tool Man" Taylor, the host of *Tool Time*, a local cable television series in Detroit aimed at would-be home builders and "do-it-yourself" enthusiasts.

A great deal of the humor is derived from the fact that Tim really doesn't know what he is doing but refuses to admit it. Much of Tim's time is spent in a battle of wills with his wife, Jill, and three sons. The series also features Tim's assistant, Al, and his all-wise

neighbor, Wilson, whose face is never fully revealed.

Home Improvement was added to the ABC Tuesday line-up in September 1991. Right from the start, the series was a success. It immediately climbed to the top of the ratings, and within 3 months it was the #4 rated show in the country. It ended the season as #6 and was the highest-rated new series of the year. This led to an early renewal for a second season, a trend that would be followed in future years.

Series Cast: Tim Allen (Tim Taylor), Patricia Richardson (Jill Taylor), Earl Hindman (Wilson), Taran Noah Smith (Mark Taylor), Jonathan Taylor Thomas (Randy Taylor), Zachery Ty Bryan (Brad Taylor), Richard Karn (Al Borland). Although Richard Karn was listed as a guest star for the first year, he appeared in each episode.

Each of the episodes is described below in airdate order.

1991–92 season

HOME IMPROVEMENT (pilot) Airdates: 9/17/91, 12/03/92, 7/28/92, 5/02/95.

Guest Cast: John Cothran Jr. (Handyman), Richard Karn (Al Borland), Pamela Denise Anderson (Lisa).

Upset when Jill announces that she has a job interview, Tim decides to comfort himself by "improving" the family washing machine.

MOW BETTER BLUES Airdates: 9/24/91, 4/14/92.

Guest Cast: Richard Karn (Al Borland).

When he is challenged to a riding lawn mower race, Tim is sure that he can win simply by installing a surplus jet engine in his mower.

OFF SIDES Airdates: 10/01/91, 12/31/91, 6/30/92.

Guest Cast: John Marshall Jones (Rick), Eric Christmas (Sir Harry Houdini), Richard Karn (Al Borland), Rudolph Willrich (Franco).

After a football game comes between Jill and her idea of a romantic evening, she finds herself tempted by the thought of having an affair with a younger man.

SATELLITE ON A HOT TIM'S ROOF Airdates: 10/08/91, 5/26/92.

Guest Cast: Sam McMurray (Rondall Kittleman), Richard Karn (Al Borland),

Pamela Denise Anderson (Lisa), Rocky Giordani (Man #2), Bari K. Willerford (Man #1).

Tim has several problems: not only does he have to install a satellite dish without knowing how to do it, but Jill's new co-worker has some very unprofessional thoughts about her.

WILD KINGDOM   Airdates: 10/15/91, 3/10/92, 8/11/92.

Guest Cast: Stephen Root (Exterminator), Richard Karn (Al Borland), Pamela Denise Anderson (Lisa), Adam Wylie (Jimmy), Rickey Collins (Cub Scout #1), Everett Wong (Cub Scout #2), Cody Burger (Cub Scout #3).

The discovery that there is a snake hiding somewhere in the Taylor house soon has the entire family in an uproar.

ADVENTURES IN FINE DINING   Airdates: 10/22/91, 12/24/91, 4/20/94.

Guest Cast: Richard Karn (Al Borland).

Tired of watching her sons eat like animals, Jill bets Tim that he can't teach them table manners.

NOTHING MORE THAN FEELINGS

Airdates: 10/29/91, 3/31/92, 10/21/92.

Guest Cast: Art La Fleur (Jim), Ron Taylor (Kyle), Richard Karn (Al Borland).

Tim makes a thoughtless comment about Jill during his show, then realizes, the hard way, that hurt feelings aren't easy to fix.

FLYING SAUCES   Airdates: 11/05/91, 3/24/92, 7/27/92.

Guest Cast: Richard Karn (Al Borland), Pamela Denise Anderson (Lisa), Mickey Jones (Pete), Gary McGurk (Dwayne), Casey Sander (Rock Lannigan).

When Randy and Brad pull one prank too many on Mark, Tim decides to teach them a lesson. He tries to convince them that they are really aliens from another planet.

BUBBLE, BUBBLE, TOIL AND TROUBLE

Airdates: 11/19/91, 4/21/92, 10/20/93.

Guest Cast: Richard Karn (Al Borland), Al Fann (Felix), Gary Bayer (Workman #1), Dorien Wilson (Workman #2).

Tim decides to prove his skills and impress Jill at the same time by enlarging the family bathroom, with the predictable disastrous results.

REACH OUT AND TEACH SOMEONE

Airdates: 11/26/91, 5/19/92.

Guest Cast: Richard Karn (Al Borland), Ja'net DuBois (Judith), Jennifer Nash (Greta Post), Carol Mansell (Rose).

Trying to prove that women can't handle tools as well as men, Tim arranges for an all-women audience for his show.

LOOK WHO'S NOT TALKING   Airdates: 12/10/91, 7/07/92.

Guest Cast: Richard Karn (Al Borland), Pamela Denise Anderson (Lisa).

Jill is petrified about having to give a speech, so Tim decides to relieve her pressure by taking care of the house for her—with a super-powered vacuum cleaner.

YULE BETTER WATCH OUT   Airdates: 12/17/91, 6/02/92, 11/23/92.

Guest Cast: Richard Karn (Al Borland), Pamela Denise Anderson (Lisa), David Warshofsky (Fireman #1), Gary Bayer (Fireman #2).

Tim gets carried away in competing with a neighbor as they decorate their houses for Christmas. Meanwhile, Brad and Randy have Mark convinced that Santa Claus is dead.

UP YOUR ALLEY   Airdates: 1/07/92, 5/12/92, 9/16/92.

Guest Cast: Richard Karn (Al Borland), Casey Sander (Rock), Mickey Jones (Peter), Gary McGurk (Dwayne), Lewis Dix Jr. (Roger), Sean Baca (Chuck), Nick Shields (Manager).

Tim's male ego suffers a shattering blow when Jill beats him at the bowling alley, in full view of his friends.

FOR WHOM THE BELCH TOLLS   Airdates: 1/14/92, 6/23/92.

Guest Cast: Christopher McDonald (Stu Cutler), Richard Karn (Al Borland), Pamela Denise Anderson (Lisa).

A visit from Tim's college buddy starts driving Jill crazy, for Tim begins to pick up his annoying—and disgusting—habits.

FOREVER JUNG   Airdates: 1/21/92, 5/06/92, 11/04/92.

Guest Cast: Richard Karn (Al Borland), Betsy Randle (Karen), Jessica Wesson (Jennifer Sudarsky).

Brad is worried about what Tim will say or do when he meets his girlfriend for the first time. Tim, on the other hand, is busy worrying about a battle of wits with Jill's friend Karen.

JILL'S BIRTHDAY   Airdates: 2/04/92, 6/16/92, 2/02/94.

Guest Cast: Richard Karn (Al Borland), Patrick T. O'Brien ("Ink" Ingram), Jeannine Renshaw (Joan), Gloria Dorson (Mrs. Chapman), Meghan Geary (Saleswoman #1), Sarah Pasquin (Saleswoman #2), Greg Harms (Cameraman).

Tired of last-minute birthday gifts, Jill makes it plain that she expects Tim to buy a personal gift this year. Unfortunately, he has no idea at all what to buy her!

WHAT ABOUT BOB?   Airdates: 2/11/92, 6/09/92.

Guest Cast: Richard Karn (Al Borland), Bob Vila (Himself), Aaron Freeman (Curtis), Pamela Denise Anderson (Lisa), Noble Willingham (Mr. Binford).

Hoping to outsmart noted home repair expert Bob Vila, Tim challenges him to a "Stump the Tool Man" call-in contest, then tries to rig the outcome with Jill's help.

BABY, IT'S COLD OUTSIDE   Airdates: 2/18/92, 8/04/92, 2/16/94.

Guest Cast: Richard Karn (Al Borland), Pamela Denise Anderson (Lisa), Jessica Wesson (Jennifer Sudarsky), Noble Willingham (Mr. Binford).

Jill has big hopes for a romantic Valentine's Day weekend, but Tim caves in to pressure from his sponsor to work overtime.

UNCHAINED MALADY   Airdates: 2/25/92, 7/14/92, 12/01/93.

Guest Cast: Richard Karn (Al Borland), George Foreman (Himself), Betsy Randle (Karen), Pamela Denise Anderson (Lisa).

Tim refuses to believe Jill's prediction that a chain letter could change his life. Meanwhile, he prepares for an on-air visit by boxing champ George Foreman.

BIRDS OF A FEATHER FLOCK TO TAYLOR   Airdates: 3/03/92, 9/02/92.

Guest Cast: Richard Karn (Al Borland), Jack Elam (Hick Peterson), Pamela Denise Anderson (Lisa), Earl Billings (Mike), Ernest Borgnine (Eddie Phillips).

After yet another argument with Jill, Tim turns to some unusual new friends for advice. He also has to offer advice himself, for Mark is having trouble building a birdhouse.

BATTLE OF WHEELS, A   Airdates: 3/17/92, 8/19/92.

Guest Cast: Richard Karn (Al Borland), Pamela Denise Anderson (Lisa).

Jill inadvertently challenges Tim's male turf when she sets up her pottery wheel in his garage; Al discovers that being the host of *Tool Time* is harder than it looks.

LUCK BE A TAYLOR TONIGHT   Airdates: 4/07/92, 7/21/92.

Guest Cast: Richard Karn (Al Borland), Tom Verica (Charlie), Amy Ryan (Robin), Raye Birk (Fred), Pamela Denise Anderson (Lisa).

A big poker night with the guys is spoiled when Jill's sister shows up and spends the evening complaining about her marriage.

AL'S FAIR IN LOVE AND WAR   Airdates: 4/28/92, 8/26/92.

Guest Cast: Richard Karn (Al Borland), Jennifer Nash (Greta Post), Jessica Wesson (Jennifer Sudarsky), Pamela Denise Anderson (Lisa), Pearl Shear (Older Woman).

Tim tries to give Al some pointers in the manly art of dating, but he has to rethink his tactics after a peek into Jill's diary.

STEREO-TYPICAL   Airdates: 5/05/92, 9/09/92, 3/16/94.

Guest Cast: Richard Karn (Al Borland), Gary McGurk (Dwayne), Casey Sander (Rock), Mickey Jones (Peter), Pamela Denise Anderson (Lisa), Janeen Rae Heller (Herself), John "Juke" Logan (Himself).

Tim goes all out and installs the ultimate home stereo, only to discover that the rest of the family isn't at all impressed with the results.

1992–93 season

READ MY HIPS   Airdates: 9/16/92, 12/09/92, 5/11/93.

Guest Cast: Casey Sander (Rock), Gary McGurk (Dwayne), Mickey Jones (Pete), Pamela Denise Anderson (Lisa), Jessica Wesson (Jennifer Sudarsky).

Tim doesn't pay attention to Jill's romantic overtures and spends one night too many with his male buddies.

RITES AND WRONGS OF PASSAGE
Airdates: 9/23/92, 2/10/93, 6/30/93.
Guest Cast: Will Nye (Angus McClain), Virginia Watson (Policewoman).
Brad starts acting up in school and at home, and Wilson tells Tim this is a sign that the boy is growing up.

OVERACTIVE GLANCE   Airdates: 9/30/92, 1/27/93, 5/18/93.
Guest Cast: Betsy Randle (Karen), Debbe Dunning (Kiki), Sheila Franklin (Barbara), Kevin Brief (Man #1), Bob Destri (Man #2), Mike Randleman (Man #3), Kavi Raz (Maitre D').
Tim bets Jill that he can stop staring at other women, then finds out just how addicted he is to ogling the opposite sex.

GROIN PAINS   Airdates: 10/07/93, 12/30/92, 1/16/94.
Guest Cast: Pamela Denise Anderson (Lisa).
Tim is determined not to let a little thing like a pulled groin muscle ruin a romantic interlude with Jill.

HEAVY MEDDLE   Airdates: 10/14/92, 3/31/93.
Guest Cast: Eileen Brennan (Wanda), Dion Anderson (Hank), Betsy Randle (Karen), Tony Carreiro (Dave), Jessica Tuck (Leslie), Tom Gallop (Bob).
Tim invites his friends over to work on his car, but much to his displeasure, Jill sees it as a chance to fix one of them up with her friend.

HAUNTING OF TAYLOR HOUSE, THE
Airdates: 10/28/92, 3/24/93.
Guest Cast: Jessica Wesson (Jennifer Sudarsky), Aaron Freeman (Curtis), Rider Strong (Danny).
Not surprisingly, Tim goes way overboard with his annual Halloween party.

ROOMIE FOR IMPROVEMENT   Airdates: 11/04/92, 3/10/93, 8/11/93.
Guest Cast: Mario Andretti (Himself), Michael Andretti (Himself), Debra Engle (Cynthia).
Tim moves in with Al to avoid catching chicken pox and the two men are soon driving each other crazy.

MAY THE BEST MAN WIN   Airdates: 11/11/92, 2/17/93.
Guest Cast: Vicki Lewis (Maureen Binford).
Tim gets two unwelcome pieces of news: Jill has decided to go back to work, and even worse, John Binford has appointed his daughter, Maureen, as Tim's new producer on *Tool Time.*

WHERE THERE'S A WILL, THERE'S A WAY
Airdates: 11/18/92, 4/07/93, 7/21/93.
Guest Cast: Jim Boeke (Phil), Wilson Raiser (Red).
Jill wants Tim to sign a will but he absolutely refuses to even consider it.

LET'S DID LUNCH   Airdates: 11/25/92, 6/02/93.
Guest Cast: Betsy Randle (Karen), Tony Carreiro (Dave).
Tim doesn't know what to do when a friend asks for his help in cheating on his girlfriend.

ABANDONED FAMILY   Airdates: 12/02/92, 5/26/93, 4/13/94.
Guest Cast: Vicki Lewis (Maureen Binford).
Jill's new job is taking too much time and Tim must start handling the domestic chores.

I'M SCHEMING OF A WHITE CHRISTMAS
Airdates: 12/16/92, 7/28/93, 12/22/93.
Guest Cast: The Manhattan Transfer (Cheryl Bentyne, Tim Hauser, Alan Paul, Janis Siegel), Vicki Lewis (Maureen Binford).
Brad and Randy go all out collecting money for a Christmas charity, but then decide they deserve some of the money for their hard work.

BELL BOTTOM BLUES   Airdates: 1/06/93, 4/28/93, 12/08/93.
Guest Cast: Casey Sander (Rock), Gary McGurk (Dwayne), Mickey Jones (Pete).
Tim installs the world's most sophisticated automatic closet; Brad gets into a fight after another boy teases him about Tim's hugging him in public.

HOWARD'S END   Airdates: 1/13/93, 4/21/93, 8/25/93.
Guest Cast: Pamela Denise Anderson (Lisa), Jessica Wesson (Jennifer Sudarsky).
Brad doesn't pay enough attention when he agrees to babysit his girlfriend's goldfish.

LOVE IS A MANY SPLINTERED THING
Airdates: 1/20/93, 6/09/93, 12/29/93.
Guest Cast: None.
Tim fails a compatibility test in a women's magazine and the Taylors worry about what holds their marriage together.

DANCES WITH TOOLS
Airdates: 2/03/93, 6/23/93, 10/27/93.
Guest Cast: Ann Miller (Mrs. Keeney), Dirk Lumbard (Don Green), Michael Pniewski (Andy Paxton), Gregg Daniel (Jerry Holcomb).
Tim surprises Jill with a special anniversary present—long sought-after ballroom dancing lessons.

YOU'RE DRIVING ME CRAZY, YOU'RE DRIVING ME NUTS
Airdates: 2/10/93, 7/07/93.
Guest Cast: Kevin Scannell (Officer John Lambert), Betsy Randle (Karen), Cleto Augusto (Marty).
When Tim and Jill get lost in a snowstorm, he refuses to admit that he needs directions and they keep ending up in the same gas station.

BYE, BYE, BIRDIE
Airdates: 2/17/93, 6/16/93, 1/19/94.
Guest Cast: Jessica Wesson (Jennifer Sudarsky).
Tim engages in a battle of wits with a very persistent woodpecker; Jennifer breaks up with Brad when he tries to copy her homework.

KARATE OR NOT, HERE I COME
Airdates: 2/24/93, 7/14/93, 3/09/94, 11/08/94.
Guest Cast: Pamela Denise Anderson (Lisa), Stuart Quan (Robert Cho), Greg Collins (Boy), Mary-Pat Green (Daphne), Perry Anzilotti (Mike), Ryan Tomlinson (Artie).
A shoving match at Mark's karate class escalates when first Jill and then Tim comes to his rescue after a bigger boy pushes him around.

SHOOTING THREE TO MAKE TUTU
Airdates: 3/03/93, 9/01/93, 5/04/94.
Guest Cast: None.
Jill wants Tim to take Mark to the ballet, a plan that doesn't please Tim at all, especially as he has tickets to a big basketball game.

MUCH ADO ABOUT NANA
Airdates: 3/17/93, 8/04/93.
Guest Cast: Polly Holliday (Nana Lillian), Paige Tamada (Tiffany).
Jill's mother arrives for a visit and the two women are soon bickering constantly.

EX MARKS THE SPOT
Airdates: 4/14/93, 8/25/93.
Guest Cast: Kathleen Garrett (Stacey Lewis).
An old girlfriend of Tim's wants to meet Jill, which is the furthest thing from what Tim wants.

TO BUILD OR NOT TO BUILD
Airdates: 5/05/93, 8/18/93, 3/23/94.
Guest Cast: Ann Guilbert (Wilson's Mother), Mickey Jones (Pete), Casey Sander (Rock), Gary McGurk (Dwayne), Pamela Denise Anderson (Lisa).
Tim and the boys start an elaborate plan to celebrate Mother's Day, but all Jill wants is a quiet dinner with the family.

BIRTH OF A HOT ROD, THE
Airdate: 5/12/93.
Guest Cast: Pamela Denise Anderson (Lisa), David Correia (Gus), Gene Weygandt (Jim Lester).
Upset at the amount of time Tim is spending on his car, Jill decides to do a few chores around the house herself. When that fails, she hires a repairman, who ends up working on Tim's car instead.

GREAT RACE, THE
Airdates: 5/19/93, 9/08/93, 2/23/94.
Guest Cast: Bob Vila (Himself), Betsy Randle (Karen), Pamela Denise Anderson (Lisa), Lamont Johnson (Paul), Michael Goldfinger (Ned), Shawn Shea (Stage Manager).
Tim challenges arch rival Bob Vila to a high-powered lawn mower race. Meanwhile, Brad and Randy talk Mark into swallowing a tadpole.

1993–94 season

MAYBE, BABY
Airdates: 9/15/93, 3/23/94.
Guest Cast: Debbe Dunning (Heidi).
Jill finds herself thinking about having another baby; Randy and Brad convince Mark that Jill had wanted a girl instead of a third boy.

AISLE SEE YOU IN MY DREAMS
Airdates: 9/22/93, 4/13/94.

Guest Cast: Sherry Hursey (Ilene Markham), David Graf (Chuck Norwood), Debbe Dunning (Heidi), Christopher Michael Moore (Jimmy Gruber), Isaiah Thomas (Himself).

Al goes head over heels when Jill introduces him to an eligible friend; Jill and Tim help Mark get revenge on Randy and Brad over a practical joke involving basketball star Isiah Thomas.

THIS JOKE'S FOR YOU   Airdates: 9/29/93, 3/30/94.

Guest Cast: Debbe Dunning (Heidi), Jimmy Lee Newman, Jr. (Jeremy Schmidt).

Tim is hurt when he overhears Randy making fun of him; Brad tries to impress a girl by reading *David Copperfield*, thinking that it's about the stage magician.

SEW, SEW EVENING, A   Airdates: 10/06/93, 7/06/94.

Guest Cast: Robert Picardo (Joe Morton), Mariangela Pino (Marie Morton), Debbe Dunning (Heidi).

Jill likes their new neighbors but Tim is desperate to avoid an upcoming dinner date with them; Randy signs up for home economics to meet girls.

ARRIVEDERCI, BINFORD   Airdates: 10/13/93, 7/13/94, 6/20/95.

Guest Cast: Debbe Dunning (Heidi), Mickey Jones (Pete), Gary McGurk (Dwayne), William Allen Young (Gus).

Tim's friend and sponsor, John Binford, dies of a heart attack, and Tim finds himself unable to acknowledge his loss.

CRAZY FOR YOU   Airdates: 10/27/93, 6/29/94.

Guest Cast: Mariangela Pino (Marie Morton), Debbe Dunning (Heidi).

A seemingly obsessed fan inundates Tim with flowers, candy, and notes—all of which makes for a very nervous Tim.

BLOW-UP   Airdates: 11/03/93, 4/27/94, 11/15/94.

Guest Cast: Robert Picardo (Joe Morton), Mariangela Pino (Marie Morton).

Tim has to get a picture of Jill blown up to poster size for a dinner in her honor, but he picks her driver's license picture, much to her dismay.

BE TRUE TO YOUR TOOL   Airdates: 11/10/93, 8/03/94.

Guest Cast: Joel Polis (Wes Davidson), Debbe Dunning (Heidi), Laura Pacheco (Secretary).

Tim doesn't know what to do when the new head of Binford Tools orders him to promote an inferior new saw on the air.

DOLLARS AND SENSE   Airdates: 11/17/93, 4/06/94.

Guest Cast: David Wohl (Salesman), Mickey Jones (Pete), Gary McGurk (Dwayne), Debbe Dunning (Heidi).

Tim tries to teach the kids something about investing their money by buying an expensive remote control car, but it's not long before they break it into pieces.

FROZEN MOMENT, A   Airdates: 11/24/93, 6/01/94.

Guest Cast: Debbe Dunning (Heidi), Sherry Hursey (Ilene Markham).

Tim goes all out for his annual family Christmas card photo, making the family dress in elf costumes and pose in his new "North Pole."

FEUD FOR THOUGHT   Airdates: 12/01/93, 6/15/94, 11/01/94.

Guest Cast: Lee Garlington (Joanie Graham), Michael Toland (Jack Graham), Natalie Core (Mrs. Grabowski), Bonnie Hellman (Pam Kendall), Tom Simmons (Hotel Clerk), Rebecca Balding (Leslie Morrison), Leigh Ann Orsi (Ashley).

Jill's school reunion gives her a chance to settle an old score with a classmate who once stole her boyfriend; the boys lock Al out of the house when he tries to babysit.

'TWAS THE BLIGHT BEFORE CHRISTMAS
Airdates: 12/15/93, 6/08/94, 12/20/94.

Guest Cast: Debbe Dunning (Heidi), Alan Fudge (Reverend Tanner).

Jill is upset with Brad's plans to go skiing on Christmas; Randy is accidentally helping a neighbor in a holiday decoration contest.

SLIP SLEDDIN' AWAY   Airdates: 1/05/94, 6/15/94, 12/27/94.

Guest Cast: John Voldstad (Bob), Francesca Roberts (Marge), Lowell Sanders (Buzz).

Tim's improvements to Randy's sled result in yet another trip to the emergency room.

DREAM ON Airdates: 1/12/94, 4/20/94, 1/17/95.

Guest Cast: Debbe Dunning (Heidi), Sherry Hursey (Ilene Martin).

Al betrays Ilene's confidence when he tells Tim about a dream she had: she saw Tim in tight shorts aboard a golden stallion.

REEL MEN Airdates: 1/16/94, 8/31/94.

Guest Cast: Mariangela Pino (Marie Morton), Sherry Hursey (Ilene Martin).

Tim and Al go ice fishing, but Tim's improvements to the fishing shed go terribly wrong.

COLONEL, THE Airdates: 2/09/94, 6/22/94.

Guest Cast: M. Emmet Walsh (The Colonel).

Jill's father arrives with his newly written memoirs, and Jill doesn't know how to tell him they stink.

ROOM FOR CHANGE Airdates: 3/02/94, 8/10/94.

Guest Cast: Debbe Dunning (Heidi).

New bedroom assignments result when Brad complains that Randy won't leave him alone; Tim plays a joke on Al using a "soundproof" booth on *Tool Time*.

EVE OF CONSTRUCTION Airdates: 3/09/94, 9/14/94, 5/16/95.

Guest Cast: Mariangela Pino (Marie Morton), Leigh Ann Orsi (Ashley), Kimberly Aiken, John Elway, Eric Hipple, Evander Holyfield, Sean Jones, Kenny O'Brien, Bill Pickel, Kelvin Pritchett, Jimmy Carter.

It's a race to see who can build a house the fastest; Tim gets help from sports stars while Jill and Al are assisted by Miss America.

TOO MANY COOKS Airdates: 3/16/94, 9/20/94.

Guest Cast: Debbe Dunning (Heidi), Angela Paton (Irma), Leigh Ann Orsi (Ashley), Anndi McAfee (Beth).

Tim finds himself the odd man out when he agrees to help Al host a cooking show.

IT WAS THE BEST OF TIMS, IT WAS THE WORST OF TIMS Airdates: 3/30/94, 9/07/94, 4/18/95.

Guest Cast: Debbe Dunning (Heidi), Al Fann (Felix), Alice Carter (Linda), Melissa Christopher (Nora), Amy Steel (Eve).

Tim upsets Jill by acting charming in front of her friends, but then reverting back to his true self when they're alone.

FIFTH ANNIVERSARY Airdates: 4/06/94, 8/17/94.

Guest Cast: Joel Polis (Wes Davidson), Debbe Dunning (Heidi), Lois deBanzie (Mrs. Binford), Jim Labriola (Butcher), Michael Andretti (Himself), Johnny Rutherford (Himself).

Tim goes all-out for a special *Tool Time* anniversary program, building the ultimate in "men's kitchens"; a look back at the first episode of *Tool Time* shows how much the characters have changed.

SWING TIME Airdates: 5/04/94, 8/24/94.

Guest Cast: Mickey Jones (Pete Bilker), Debbe Dunning (Heidi), Drake Bell (Little Pete), Victoria Principal (Les Thompson).

Tim invites K&B Construction foreman Les Thompson on Tool Time and is surprised to discover that Les is short for Leslie. When he challenges her to a "tool competition," she wins every category.

WHAT YOU SEE IS WHAT YOU GET Airdates: 5/11/94, 7/27/94.

Guest Cast: Sherry Hursey (Ilene Martin), Debbe Dunning (Heidi).

Jill is upset to learn that Tim would like her to have cosmetic surgery.

REALITY BYTES Airdates: 5/18/94, 7/20/94.

Guest Cast: Debbe Dunning (Heidi), Joanna Daniels (Molly Lauden). Special Appearance by NASA Endeavour Space Shuttle Crew: Colonel Richard O. Covey, Lt. Commander Kenneth D. Bowersox, Dr. Story Musgrave, Mr. Claude Nicollier, Dr. Jeffrey Hoffman, Lt. Colonel Thomas D. Akers.

When the Space Shuttle crew visits Tool Time with some of the tools they used in space, Tim tries to "borrow" one.

GREAT RACE II, THE Airdates: 5/25/94, 9/14/94.

Guest Cast: Bob Vila (Himself), Debbe Dunning (Heidi), Shashawnee Hall (Audience Member #1), Peg Dirolf (Audience Member #2), Laurie Faso (Audience Member #3).

Tim is upset when rival Bob Vila attracts more attention at a celebrity auction, so he challenges him to another race—even though his car isn't finished yet.

1994–95 season

BACK IN THE SADDLE SHOES AGAIN
Airdates: 9/20/94, 3/07/95.

Guest Cast: Debbe Dunning (Heidi), Mariangela Pino (Marie Morton).

When Jill gets laid off and decides to go back to college, Tim worries that he might lose her to a smarter man.

DON'T TELL MOMMA   Airdates: 9/27/94, 3/07/95.

Guest Cast: Tom LaGrua (Eddie McCormick), Daniel Bryan Cartmell (Scotty).

Tim gives Jill a hard time when she gets a tiny scratch on his car, but then has to find a way to explain his dropping a 3-ton steel beam on her car.

DEATH BEGINS AT FORTY   Airdates: 10/04/94, 7/04/95.

Guest Cast: Blake Clark (Harry), Jim Labriola (Benny), Debbe Dunning (Heidi), Al Fann (Felix).

Harry, the owner of Tim's favorite hardware store, has a heart attack and Tim starts worrying about his own mortality.

EYES DON'T HAVE IT, THE   Airdates: 10/11/94, 1/24/95.

Guest Cast: Debbe Dunning (Heidi), Anndi McAfee (Beth).

Mark isn't doing well at school, but when it's discovered that he needs glasses, he refuses to wear them in case he looks like a nerd.

HE AIN'T HEAVY, HE'S JUST IRRESPONSIBLE   Airdates: 10/18/94, 6/27/95.

Guest Cast: William O'Leary (Marty Taylor), Debbe Dunning (Heidi).

Tim's brother, Marty, arrives for a visit with the disturbing news that he's leaving his wife.

BORLAND AMBITION   Airdates: 10/25/94, 6/06/95.

Guest Cast: Sherry Hursey (Ilene Martin), Blake Clark (Harry), Jim Labriola (Benny), Debbe Dunning (Heidi).

Al becomes part owner of the hardware store and then drives everyone crazy with his "improvements."

LET'S GO TO THE VIDEOTAPE   Airdates: 11/08/94, 3/28/95.

Guest Cast: Tom LaGrua (Eddie), Debbe Dunning (Harry), Sherry Hursey (Ilene

Martin), Bill Saluga (Man #1), Ed Hooks (Man #2), Lowell Sanders (Man #3).

Tim gets into trouble when he accidentally videotapes himself making fun of Jill in front of his hardware store buddies.

QUIBBLING SIBLINGS   Airdates: 11/15/94, 5/09/95.

Guest Cast: Debbe Dunning (Heidi).

Jill thinks that Randy's constant battles with his brothers is his way of trying to get attention; Brad, meanwhile, has developed a serious crush on Heidi.

MY DINNER WITH WILSON   Airdates: 11/22/94, 6/20/95.

Guest Cast: James Cromwell (Fred), Julie Cobb (Francine), William Thomas, Jr. (Appraiser).

Wilson shocks everyone during Thanksgiving dinner when he announces his plans to sell his house and move out of town.

YE OLDE SHOPPE TEACHER   Airdates: 11/29/94, 5/23/95.

Guest Cast: Dick O'Neill (Art Leonard), Jim Labriola (Benny), Debbe Dunning (Heidi), Murray Rubinstein (Larry), Michael Kaufman (Frankie).

The man who inspired Tim's love of tools, his old shop teacher Mr. Leonard, guest stars on *Tool Time*, but the reunion isn't a happy one.

SOME LIKE IT HOT ROD   Airdates: 12/06/94, 6/13/95.

Guest Cast: Debbe Dunning (Heidi), Ben Gillespie (Mikey), Christopher Ogden (Steven), John Webb (Norman).

Tim's big chance to get his hot rod in a nationwide magazine is threatened when Jill leaves the car outside in a snowstorm with the top down.

'TWAS THE NIGHT BEFORE CHAOS
Airdates: 12/13/94, 7/18/95.

Guest Cast: Polly Holliday (Lillian), William O'Leary (Marty Taylor), Jensen Daggett (Nancy Taylor), Debbe Dunning (Heidi), M. Emmet Walsh (The Colonel).

Christmas at the Taylor house is far from peaceful: Tim's brother and his wife are visiting with their new twins, and Jill's parents are having some marital problems.

ROUTE OF ALL EVIL, THE   Airdates: 1/03/95, 4/25/95.

Guest Cast: Mariangela Pino (Marie Morton), Debbe Dunning (Heidi).

Brad gets a newspaper route to earn money, but his grades at school start to suffer.

Brother, Can You Spare a Hot Rod?
Airdates: 1/10/95, 4/04/95.

Guest Cast: Bruce McGill (Doug O'Brien), Jay Leno (Jay), Anndi McAfee (Beth), Larry Flash Jenkins (Bud), Laura Hill (Salesclerk).

Tim impulsively sells his hot rod to real-life car collector Jay Leno, then tries to come up with some way to get it back.

Super Bowl Fever
Airdates: 1/31/95, 8/08/95.

Guest Cast: Mickey Jones (Pete), Jim Labriola (Benny), Blake Clark (Harry), Murray Rubinstein (Harry), Dave Krieg (Himself), Kelvin Pritchett (Himself), Chris Spielman (Himself).

Tim goes through with his plans for a big Super Bowl party even though Jill is sick upstairs with the flu.

Bachelor of the Year
Airdates: 2/07/95, 5/16/95.

Guest Cast: Sherry Hursey (Ilene Martin), Debbe Dunning (Heidi), Jolie Jackunas (Christine), Dorothy Brooks (Shelly), Cecily Adams (Dana), Peg Dirolf (Woman #1), Rose Portillo (Woman #2), Lucy Liu (Woman #3), Sonia Jackson (Receptionist).

Fame goes to Al's head when he's named as one of the city's "Most Eligible Bachelors" in a magazine poll and women start chasing after him; unfortunately, part of his new popularity is due to an extra zero at the end of his salary in the article.

It's My Party
Airdates: 2/14/95, 5/30/95.

Guest Cast: Mark L. Taylor (Bert Russell), Francesca P. Roberts (Marge), Debbe Dunning (Heidi), Kimberly Cullum (Michelle), John Volstad (Bob), Andrew Amic-Angelo (Sherman), David Carter (Dancer Double).

Tim builds a dance floor for Randy's birthday party, but the sixteen coats of polish turn it into a slippery disaster.

House Divided, A
Airdates: 2/21/95, 8/15/95.

Guest Cast: Jim Labriola (Benny), Debbe Dunning (Heidi), Blake Clark (Harry), Ralph Manza (Sam).

Tim's work on a friend's house results in disaster when a gas leak leads to a huge explosion.

Production Note:
- The house that explodes is perhaps best known as the home of Darrin and Samantha Stephens in the long-running series *Bewitched*.

Naked Truth, The
Airdates: 2/28/95, 8/29/95.

Guest Cast: Jensen Dagget (Nancy Taylor), William O'Leary (Marty Taylor), Debbe Dunning (Heidi), Earl Billings (Mike), Johnson West (Stage Manager), Milton Canady (Construction Worker).

Things get awkward at home when Tim and his sister-in-law accidentally see each other naked.

Talk to Me
Airdate: 3/14/95.

Guest Cast: Jim Breuer (Jim), Dave Chappelle (Dave), Debbe Dunning (Heidi).

Tim invites two *Tool Time* guests to talk about their love lives and ends up making yet another dumb comment about Jill on the air.

No, No, Godot
Airdates: 3/21/95, 8/01/95.

Guest Cast: Max Gail (Officer Carl Keegan), Mike Grief (George), Jennifer Lyon-Buchanan (Woman in Audience), Randy Kovitz (Man in Audience), Sherry Hursey (Ilene Martin), Rif Hutton (Man at Arena), Robby Gordon (Himself), Derrick Walker (Himself), Clive Rosengren (Policeman), Raffi Di Blasio (Boy), Sam Whipple (Usher).

Tim and Al skip a night at the theater to go to a hockey game. They should have gone to the play, for they end up in jail for scalping tickets.

Tool Time After Dark
Airdates (1-hour format): 4/11/95, 9/05/95.

Tim eats too much Polish food and spends the night watching old episodes of *Tool Time* when he can't fall asleep.

Sisters and Brothers
Airdates: 5/02/95, 9/12/95.

Guest Cast: William O'Leary (Marty Taylor), Jensen Daggett (Nancy Taylor), Tudi Riche (Carrie), Debbe Dunning (Heidi), Keith Lehman (Cal Borland).

Family relationships take some new turns when Jill's sister visits to see what married life is like, Marty moves to town, and Al gets into a fight with his brother on *Tool Time*.

Production Note:
- This was the 100th episode of the series.

MARKED MAN, A   Airdates: 5/09/95, 7/25/95.

    Guest Cast: Blake Clark (Harry), Debbe Dunning (Heidi), Deb Selby (Herself), Steve Selby (Himself), Jay Lacopo (Customer).

    Mark steals an expensive pocket knife in a misguided attempt to impress his brothers.

WILSON'S GIRLFRIEND   Airdates: 5/23/95, 8/22/95.

    Guest Cast: Beth Dixon (Judith Haber), Michelle Williams (Jessica Lutz).

    Jill's efforts as a matchmaker pay off when Wilson gets his first date in 20 years; Tim tries to give his friend some dating pointers.

1995–96 season

TAYLOR RUNS THROUGH IT, A   Airdates: 9/19/95, 1/09/96.

    Guest Cast: Bonnie Hellman (Bonnie), Robert Gould (Minister).

    What should be a simple trip to a cousin's wedding gets the "Tim Taylor" touch when he combines it with an adventurous vacation.

FIRST TEMPTATION OF TIM, THE   Airdates: 9/26/95, 12/19/95.

    Guest Cast: Debbe Dunning (Heidi), Charlie Robinson (Bud Harper), Royce D. Applegate (Frank), Shirley Prestia (Waitress).

    Bud Harper, the new boss at *Tool Time,* wants Tim to get rid of Al.

HER CHEATIN' MIND   Airdates: 10/03/95, 12/26/95, 5/22/96.

    Guest Cast: Blake Clark (Harry), Jim Labriola (Benny), William O'Leary (Marty), Gretchen German (June Palmer), Joe Urla (Chris Harper), Stephanie Dunnam (Sharon), Ja'net DuBois (Carol), Terri Cavanaugh (Jane).

    Tim joins Jill's book club when he feels threatened by the amount of time she is spending with her friends.

JILL'S SURPRISE PARTY   Airdates: 10/17/95, 5/07/96.

    Guest Cast: Debbe Dunning (Heidi), Charlie Robinson (Bud Harper), Jensen Daggett (Nancy), Sherry Hursey (Ilene), Jim Labriola (Benny), William O'Leary (Marty), Mariangela Pino (Marie), Tudi Roche (Carrie), Tracy Letts (Henry).

    Tim throws a surprise party for Jill's birthday but the guest of honor doesn't show up.

ADVISE AND REPENT   Airdates: 10/24/95, 1/02/96, 6/25/96.

    Guest Cast: Debbe Dunning (Heidi), Mark L. Taylor (Bert Russell), Nancy Youngblut (Dana Russell), Beth Dixon (Judith), Kimberly Cullum (Michelle).

    Jill gets an "A" on a psychology paper and starts giving out free advice, never thinking of the consequences.

LET THEM EAT CAKE   Airdates: 10/31/95, 1/23/96.

    Guest Cast: Debbe Dunning (Heidi), Jarrad Paul (Jason), Angela Paton (Irma), Sherry Hursey (Ilene), Adam Consolo (Preston), Lea Moreno (Bridgett), Marla Sokoloff (Page), Gregory White (Announcer).

    Will *Tool Time* win an award or will it go to *Cooking with Irma* as usual?

LOOK, THE   Airdates: 11/07/95, 3/19/96, 7/30/96.

    Guest Cast: Debbe Dunning (Heidi), Charlie Robinson (Bud Harper), William O'Leary (Marty), Jim Labriola (Benny), Blake Clark (Harry), Shirley Prestia (Dolores), Vincent Guastaferro (Nick).

    Tim gets a "woman's look" from Jill when he spends way too much on basketball tickets.

ROOM WITHOUT A VIEW   Airdates: 11/14/95, 3/26/96, 7/09/96.

    Guest Cast: Debbe Dunning (Heidi).

    Tim builds Randy a new bedroom in the basement, but Randy doesn't want to admit that he's afraid to spend the night down there.

CHICAGO HOPE   Airdates: 11/21/95, 4/23/96.

    Guest Cast: Charlie Robinson (Bud Harper), Troy Evans (Mike McKewen), Michael Yama (Japanese Man #1), Rodney Kageyama (Japanese Man #2), Wesley Leong (Japanese Man #3).

    What should be a relaxing weekend in Chicago for Tim and Jill goes awry when Tim tries to secretly mix business with pleasure.

DOCTOR IN THE HOUSE   Airdates: 11/28/95, 4/23/96.

    Guest Cast: Debbe Dunning (Heidi), Jim Beaver (Duke Miller), Marcia Rodd (Barbara Burton), Janet MacLachlan (Dean Cummings), Walter Addison (Professor Garver), Ritchie Montgomery (Delivery Man).

Tim gets an honorary Ph.D. and lets it go to his head.

THAT'S MY MOMMA   Airdates: 12/05/95, 4/16/96.

Guest Cast: Bonnie Bartlett (Lucille Taylor), Dick O'Neill (Art Leonard), William O'Leary (Marty).

Tim's feelings are hurt when his visiting mother prefers to spend time with his old shop teacher, Mr. Leonard, instead of with him.

'TWAS THE FLIGHT BEFORE CHRISTMAS
Airdates: 12/12/95, 7/16/96.

Guest Cast: Debbe Dunning (Heidi), Sherry Hursey (Ilene), Connie Sawyer (Old Lady), Sydney Anderson (Attractive Woman), Marcy Goldman (Flight Attendant), Tom Poston (The Clerk).

Tim and Al get trapped in the airport from Hell as they try to get home in time for Christmas.

OH, BROTHER   Airdates: 1/09/96, 7/02/96.

Guest Cast: Debbe Dunning (Heidi), William O'Leary (Marty), Blake Clark (Harry), Jim Labriola (Benny), Kristin Clayton (Angela).

Tim hires his brother Marty to rebuild the *Tool Time* set and the two are soon at each other's throats.

HIGH SCHOOL CONFIDENTIAL   Airdates: 1/16/96, 4/09/96.

Guest Cast: Debbe Dunning (Heidi), Miguel Sandoval (Mr. Jennings), Milton Candy (Milton).

Randy does so well at school that he's moved up to high school, which Brad doesn't appreciate at all.

TANKS FOR THE MEMORIES   Airdates: 1/30/96, 6/18/96.

Guest Cast: Tim Grimm (Lt. Colonel McDougal), Vaughn Armstrong (Lt. Colonel Hall), Debbe Dunning (Heidi).

Tim thinks it will be easy to beat Jill in a tank-driving contest, never suspecting that she might have picked up a few pointers from her soldier father.

Production Note:

- This was a special episode created to launch *Home Improvement* in the syndication market. It was originally aired in 9/95 in syndication, then included in the network line-up.

VASECTOMY ONE, THE   Airdates: 2/06/96, 9/03/96.

Guest Cast: Debbe Dunning (Heidi), Blake Clark (Harry), Jim Labriola (Benny), William O'Leary (Marty), Caroline Williams (Dr. Kaplan), Gretchen German (June Palmer), Kristin Clayton (Angela).

Tim isn't at all happy when Jill asks him to get a vasectomy, especially when he finds out that the doctor is a woman.

FEAR OF FLYING   Airdates: 2/13/96, 8/13/96.

Guest Cast: Debbe Dunning (Heidi), Charlie Robinson (Bud Harper), Lt. Commander Kenneth D. Bowersox (Himself), Dr. Kathryn C. Thornton (Herself), Dr. Fred W. Leslie (Himself), Dr. Albert Sacco (Himself), Dr. Catherine G. Coleman (Herself).

Space shuttle astronauts agree to take Tim's special screwdriver on a mission, and Mark announces he wants to take flying lessons.

WHEN HARRY KEPT DELORES   Airdates: 2/20/96, 6/11/96.

Guest Cast: William O'Leary (Marty), Alan Jackson (Himself), Debbe Dunning (Heidi), Blake Clark (Harry), Shirley Prestia (Delores), Jim Labriola (Benny).

Tim's advice to Harry about a romantic dispute looks like it may be leading to divorce.

EYE ON TIM   Airdates: 2/27/96, 5/28/96.

Guest Cast: Debbe Dunning (Heidi), Rosalind Allen (Kelly Barnes), Dex Sanders (Nick).

Jill is right to worry that an attractive reporter is more interested in Tim than in her story about *Tool Time*.

BUD BOWL, THE   Airdates: 3/05/96, 6/18/96.

Guest Cast: Debbe Dunning (Heidi), Charlie Robinson (Bud Harper), Bever-Leigh Banfield (Jean Harper), Kristin Clayton (Angela), Andi Eystad (Jessica).

Tim wants Jill to let his boss win at bowling and an arguments develops when she refuses.

ENGINE AND A HAIRCUT, TWO FIGHTS
Airdates: 3/12/96, 8/06/96.

Guest Cast: Joseph Whipp (Kendall).

Brad and Tim disagree both about what engine to use in the car they're building and about Brad's drastic new haircut.

LONGEST DAY, THE   Airdates: 4/02/96, 6/04/96.

Guest Cast: Debbe Dunning (Heidi).

A routine medical test reveals the disturbing news that Randy may have cancer.

MR. WILSON'S OPUS   Airdates: 4/30/96, 8/20/96.

Guest Cast: Debbe Dunning (Heidi), Laura Bell Bundy (Sharon), Patrick Renna (Todd), David Brisbin (Principal Piersall).

Wilson lets it go to his head when he's asked to direct Randy's school play.

SHOPPING AROUND   Airdates: 5/07/96, 7/23/96.

Guest Cast: Debbe Dunning (Heidi), Bonnie Bartlett (Lucille), Dick O'Neill (Art Leonard), Vasili Bogazianos (Antonio).

Tim is shocked to see Mr. Leonard, who is dating Tim's mom, out with another woman.

ALARMED BY BURGLARS   Airdates: 5/14/96, 8/27/96.

Guest Cast: Debbe Dunning (Heidi), William O'Leary (Marty), Jim Labriola (Benny), Blake Clark (Harry), Jarrad Paul (Jason), Michael Milhoan (Officer Guidry).

After a burglary at Wilson's, Tim overreacts in typical fashion and installs the alarm system from Hell.

GAMES, FLAMES, AND AUTOMOBILES   Airdates: 5/21/96, 9/10/96.

Guest Cast: Debbe Dunning (Heidi), Sherry Hursey (Ilene), Wesley Thompson (Phone Man), James Hong (Dave).

Al sinks his life savings into a board game he invented, but faulty wiring may burn up the profits.

Good & Evil

Good & Evil began as an idea by Susan Harris, who had been responsible in large part for the creation and success of the Studio's *The Golden Girls* and *Empty Nest*. For 8 years, Harris had been developing a series based on two brothers, one totally good and the other evil. The two brothers were recast as sisters, and the series featured a large cast of characters, each with their own idiosyncracies.

A copy of the pilot script came to the attention of the National Federation for the Blind, which reacted in outrage at the portrayal of a blind character. They started a campaign against the character, the series, and the network, ABC. A 4-week picketing campaign outside ABC offices in New York, Chicago, Denver, and Washington succeeded in drawing significant media attention to the controversy. Despite the protests, the series went on the air.

When it was all over, only 11 of the 13 episodes that had been ordered were ever produced, and *Good & Evil* quickly vanished.

Series Cast: Teri Garr (Denise), Margaret Whitton (Genny), Mark Blankfield (George), Lane Davies (Dr. Eric Haan), Mary Gillis (Mary), Seth Green (David), Sherman Howard (Roger), Marian Seldes (Charlotte Sanders), William Shockley, Brooke Theiss (Caroline), Marius Weyers (Ronald).

Each of the episodes is described below in airdate order, followed by the unaired episodes in production order.

EPISODE #1   Airdate: 9/25/91.

Guest Cast: Lauren Tom (Wang), Paris Vaughn (Secretary), David Chung (Tensang), Clyde Kusata (Tensing), Stuart Quan (Tensung), Brian George (Doctor #1), Erick Avari (Doctor #2), Anne Meara (voice-over), Jerry Stiller (voice-over).

High in the Himalayas, three Sherpas discover a frozen body. It's Ronald, Denise's husband, who has been missing for 4 years. When he thaws out, he realizes that she had pushed him off a cliff and he sets off to seek revenge.

EPISODE #2   Airdate: 10/02/91.

Guest Cast: Eric Christmas (Mr. Thompson), Peter Iacangelo (The Pawnbroker), Robert V. Barron (Pap Fowler), Dean Hill (The Drunk).

Denise vows to use her secret information about Eric to make him stay with her; Charlotte's family thinks that her new friend, Harlan Shell, is only interested in her for her money.

EPISODE #3   Airdate: 10/09/91.

Guest Cast: Allan Kolman (Sergei), Irene Forrest (The Maid), Macka Foley (The Bartender), D.R. Starr (Duke).

Denise convinces Ronald that his fall was an accident, then keeps his return a secret until she can find a new way to get rid of him; Eric confesses to Genny that he took a dead man's identity to hide his own past.

EPISODE #4   Airdate: 10/16/91.

Guest Cast: James Lashly (Chuck), John Mariano (Zippy), Ronnie Schell (The Barker).

Eric saves Denise from choking but she continues to blackmail him; after Roger agrees to help Denise kill Ronald, he gets cold feet but then comes through.

EPISODE #5   Airdate: 10/23/91.
Guest Cast: Kelly Connell (The Hitman), Terry Funk (The Biker), Darwyn Carson (Press Member).

Ronald's fall from a ledge lands him in a giant jar of cleansing cream placed there for a ceremony, so Denise hires a hit man to do the job; Charlotte announces that the new company president is her lover, Harlan.

EPISODE #6   Airdate: 10/30/91.
Guest Cast: Troy Evans (Cal), Roy Brocksmith (The Minister), Robert Dorfman (Photographer), Mary Jackson (Aunt Chloe).

Formerly mute Caroline talks; Genny threatens to tell her mother that Denise has been embezzling money unless Denise calls off her pending marriage to Eric.

EPISODE #7   Airdate: Unaired.
Guest Cast: Roy Brocksmith (The Minister).

Denise and Ronald renew their wedding vows; everyone learns that Harlan took the corporate payroll when he left town; Harlan is found, but he is dead and the money is missing.

EPISODE #8   Airdate: Unaired.
Guest Cast: Tim Thomerson (Lieutenant Babcock), Bill Morey (Skipper), Monty Hoffman (Fisherman).

Upset at Harlan's death, Charlotte decides to come out of retirement to run the business again; Lt. Babcock arrives to investigate Harlan's death; Denise is arrested for the murder.

EPISODE #9   Airdate: Unaired.
Guest Cast: Tim Thomerson (Lieutenant Babcock), Kathy Kinney (Bonnie), Amy Hill (Matron).

Ronald helps Denise fabricate an alibi; Caroline dresses as Genny, hoping to trick George into having sex with her; Timmy is dead and Charlotte is standing over him holding a scythe.

EPISODE #10   Airdate: Unaired.
Guest Cast: Tim Thomerson (Lieutenant Babcock), Lee Garlington (Fang).

Denise takes everyone to see the body, but Timmy is gone; Timmy is later found hanging on Denise's office door; Lorraine tries to attack Charlotte in the stable.

EPISODE #11   Airdate: Unaired.
Guest Cast: James Lashly (Chuck), Jack McGee (Sid), Gina Mastrogiacoma (Janie), Sam Menning (Bum).

Charlotte leaves the stable in time, then promotes Roger to vice president; Genny discovers that George is sleeping with Caroline; Sonny agrees to represent Denise.

The Torkelsons (and) Almost Home

The Torkelsons, another Disney sitcom, was created by Lynn Montgomery, who had previously worked on *Carol & Company*. The premise for this series was an eccentric family living in the rural hamlet of Pyramid Corners in northeast Oklahoma. *The Torkelsons* was the story of Millicent Torkelson, a single mother trying to raise her five children alone after her husband, a wildcat oil worker, abandoned the family to seek his fortune.

The Torkelsons debuted on 9/21/91 on Saturday at 8:30 P.M. on NBC, between Disney's hits *The Golden Girls* and *Empty Nest*. Unfortunately, the new series started losing viewers from the very start, so much so that it was hurting the ratings of the rest of the evening's lineup.

Despite a track record that would have killed most series, Disney and NBC still saw some potential in *The Torkelsons*. A radical change of format and cast resulted in the new series *Almost Home*, which became a midseason replacement for the 1992–93 season.

Cast: Connie Ray (Millicent Torkelson), Olivia Burnette (Dorothy Jane Torkelson), Elizabeth Poyer (Ruth Ann Torkelson), Benj Hall (Steven Floyd Torkelson), Lee Norris (Chuckie Lee Torkelson), Rachel Duncan (Mary Sue Torkelson), Ernie Lively (J.W. Presley), William Schallert (Wesley Hodges), Michael Landes (Riley Roberts), Richard McGinagle (Howard Roberts), Lynn Milgrim (Lillian Roberts), Jeanine Jackson (Appliance Saleslady), Gil Roscoe (Tall Man), Skip O'Brien (Burly Guy).

Each of the episodes is described below in airdate order.

1991–92 season

FENCE NEIGHBORS   Airdates: 9/21/91, 11/24/91.
Barely able to stay one step ahead of the bill collectors, Millicent Torkelson reluctantly

decides to take in a boarder to help with the rent. Her daughter, Dorothy Jane, is upset at the news that she will have to give up her room.

COTILLION, THE   Airdates: 9/28/91, 2/02/92.
   Guest Cast: Ronnie Claire Edwards (Bootsie Torkelson), Michael Landes (Riley Roberts), Paige Gosney (Kirby Scroggins), Tanya Fenmore (Laine), Alyson Kiperman (Dreama), Nicki Vannice (Shawna).
   A big dance causes problems for Dorothy Jane when only one homely boy asks her for a date and a rich girl makes fun of her second-hand dress.

KISS IS STILL A KISS, A   Airdates: 10/05/91, 2/16/92.
   Guest Cast: Ronnie Claire Edwards (Bootsie Torkelson), Jeff McCracken (Reverend Langley Wilson), Katie Jane Johnston (Debra Jo).
   Dorothy Jane sets a plan in motion to match Millicent up with an eligible new bachelor. Meanwhile, Steven Floyd heads out on his first hay ride.

FOR LOVE OR MONEY   Airdates: 10/12/91, 1/26/92.
   Guest Cast: Ronnie Claire Edwards (Bootsie Torkelson), Michael Landes (Riley Roberts).
   When Millicent has to take a job to pay the bills, Dorothy Jane is thrilled to be put in charge of the house. However, the thrill doesn't last long when she has to deal with her younger siblings.

POETRY IN MOTION   Airdates: 10/19/91, 3/15/92.
   Guest Cast: Michael Landes (Riley Roberts), Doreen Fein (Nancy), Suzie Plakson (Verna).
   After Ruth Anne spreads copies of Dorothy Jane's sensual love poem all over town, Dorothy Jane is thrilled with the sudden attention she gets from the town's older boys.

AMERICAN ALMOST IN PARIS, AN
Airdate: 10/26/91.
   Guest Cast: Paige Gosney (Kirby Scroggins), Alyson Kiperman (Dreama), Lenny Wolpe (Leonard Wheeler).
   A foreign exchange trip to Paris offers Dorothy Jane a chance to escape dull old

Pyramid Corners, until she learns that the judges want to interview her family at home.

MEN DON'T LEAVE   Airdates: 11/02/91, 3/22/92.
   Guest Cast: Ronnie Claire Edwards (Bootsie Torkelson), Gregg Henry (Randall Torkelson).
   A surprise visit from Randall, Millicent's estranged husband, has the family thinking about a reconciliation. Dorothy Jane is concerned, though, about her father's reputation as a ladies' man.

RETURN TO SENDER   Airdate: 11/24/91.
   Guest Cast: Patty Duke (Catharine Jeffers), Ashley Peldon (Milly Jeffers), Dave Florek (Mr. Katsotis).
   A series of returned letters from Hodges to his granddaughter sparks the Torkelsons into arranging a surprise reconciliation between the two—with a surprising result.

THANKSGIVING SOMETHING   Airdate: 12/01/91.
   Guest Cast: Jeff McCracken (Reverend Langley Wilson), Michael Horse (David Blackwing), Remy Ryan (Jenny Blackwing).
   The Torkelsons share their Thanksgiving dinner with a Native American family from a nearby reservation.

SIGH IS STILL A SIGH, A   Airdate: 12/08/91.
   Guest Cast: Paige Gosney (Kirby Scroggins).
   Tired of having to obey his mother, a rebellious Steven Floyd runs away from home to look for his father.

EDUCATING MILLICENT   Airdate: 12/22/91.
   Guest Cast: Kevin Clash (Elmo), Paige Gosney (Kirby Scroggins).
   Unable to help her children with their homework, Millicent admits that she had dropped out of school. Dorothy Jane convinces her to study for a high school equivalency certificate.

I FOUGHT THE LAW   Airdate: 1/05/92.
   Guest Cast: Paige Gosney (Kirby Scroggins), Stephen Root (Sheriff Bobby), Ken Thorley (Burke Miller), Molly McClure (Gertrude Perkins), Lou Hancock (Elvira Grandy).
   Every year the Torkelsons sell homemade produce at a roadside stand, but this year the sheriff decides to close the stand down and Dorothy Jane goes to jail.

DOUBLE DATE   Airdates: 1/09/92, 6/20/92.
Guest Cast: Paige Gosney (Kirby Scroggins), John Calvin (Michael), Omri Katz (Jason), Mother Love (Kitty Drysdale).
Dorothy Jane is upset that she is not allowed to date, so she calls radio talk show host Kitty Drysdale for advice. Kitty sees this as a sign that Millicent can't accept her divorce.

ICE PRINCESS, THE   Airdate: 1/12/92.
Guest Cast: Paige Gosney (Kirby Scroggins), Michael Landes (Riley Roberts), Amy Hathaway (Callie Kimbro), Scott Campbell (Big Jock), Rachel O'Neill (Daisy).
Determined to attract boys, Dorothy Jane decides to use makeup, tight sweaters, and her feminine wiles as weapons in the war between the sexes.

SWEAR NOT BY THE MOON   Airdate: 1/19/92.
Guest Cast: Paige Gosney (Kirby Scroggins), Michael Landes (Riley Roberts), Rick Lieberman (Mr. Whitman), Vinessa Shaw (Meredith Reed), Shawn Phelan (Mercurio), Alyson Kiperman (Dreama), Danuel Pipoly (Benvolio), Ian Bohen (Capulet).
A school play sets the stage for romance when Dorothy Jane tries desperately to be cast in *Romeo and Juliet* with the school's heartthrob.

SAY UNCLE   Airdate: 2/16/92.
Guest Cast: Paige Gosney (Kirby Scroggins), Drew Carey (Herby Scroggins), Sara Rose Johnson (Young Dorothy Jane), Adam Wyle (Young Kirby).
Kirby's uncle falls in love with Millicent and won't take no for an answer.

LONG GOODBYE, THE   Airdate: 5/02/92.
Guest Cast: Paige Gosney (Kirby Scroggins), Gregg Henry (Randall Torkelson), Mother Love (Kitty Drysdale).
Dorothy Jane's father returns for a visit and offers her some advice on her love life, advice that Millicent warns may not be worth very much.

EGG AND I, THE   Airdate: 5/23/92.
Guest Cast: Paige Gosney (Kirby Scroggins), Noah Christopher (Greg), Kelsea Gibbs and Kassandra Gibbs (Jennie), Mother Love (Kitty Drysdale).
Dorothy Jane and Kirby learn something about adult responsibilities when they are given an egg to care for as a school project.

IT'S MY PARTY   Airdate: 5/30/92.
Guest Cast: Paige Gosney (Kirby Scroggins), Amy Hathaway (Callie Kimbro), Alanna Ubach (Willie), Nick Ayers (Bobby Joe).
Dorothy Jane forgos her friends in an attempt to attract a new crowd of wealthy teenagers.

AUNT POISON   Airdate: 6/13/92.
Guest Cast: Steven Gilborn (Dr. Euless), Wayne Tippit (Strickland), Patrick Reilly (Delivery Boy).
The death of Millicent's Aunt Jimmy brings a strange collection of inheritances to the Torkelson house.

Almost Home

1992–93 season

NEW MOON   Airdates: 2/06/93, 5/29/93.
Guest Cast: None.
When Millicent is unable to make the mortgage payment and loses the house, she accepts a job as a nanny for widower with two spoiled teenagers and moves her family to Seattle.

GIRLS AND BOY   Airdates: 2/13/93, 6/19/93.
Guest Cast: Joey Lawrence (Jeff Thornton), Peter Van Norden (Mel), James Gleason (Male Customer), Shirley Prestia (Female Customer), Kimberlee Corney (Megan).
Both Dorothy Jane and Molly have their hearts set on Dorothy Jane's new boss, the assistant manager at a fast-food restaurant.

SLEEPING WITH THE ENEMY   Airdate: 2/20/93.
Guest Cast: Erin Gray (Jennifer).
Molly is jealous when her father takes an attractive woman to a business dinner, for she doesn't want anyone taking the place of her deceased mother.

IS THAT ALL THERE IS?   Airdate: 2/27/93, 7/03/93.
Guest Cast: Ben Affleck (Kevin Johnson).
Dorothy Jane enjoys her new-found popularity when she starts dating a sports star at

school, but she soon finds herself wondering if it's worth staying in a boring relationship.

FOX AND THE HOUND, THE   Airdate: 3/06/93.

Guest Cast: Paxton Whitehead (Sir Reginald Harrington), Sarah Douglas (Lady Harrington), Jared Leto (Rick Aiken), Frank Birney (Captain).

When Brian takes Millicent to an important business dinner with a prospective customer, things go fine until the man makes a pass at her.

WINNER TAKE MILLICENT   Airdates: 3/20/93, 6/26/93.

Guest Cast: Christopher Rich (Jim Morgan).

When Brian's brother asks Millicent for a date, it awakens some old wounds between the brothers and some new feelings between Brian and Millicent.

TO JANE EYRE IS HUMAN   Airdate: 3/27/93.

Guest Cast: None.

Brian is upset with Molly's latest report card, so she plagiarizes from Dorothy Jane's book report in an attempt to impress her father.

DUELLING BIRTHDAYS   Airdate: 4/03/93.

Guest Cast: Marguerite Moreau (Kimberly), Stephanie Brown (Candice), Trish Ramish (Linda), Devon Gummersall (Party Boy).

Dorothy Jane and Molly both turn 16, but the two girls have very different plans for the night. The Torkelsons aren't planning a big celebration, but Molly hopes to enter a new social circle by throwing a massive bash.

TO DATE OR NOT TO DATE?   Airdate: 4/10/93.

Guest Cast: James Calvert (Patrick), Curnal Aulisio (Bill), Vincent Ventresca (Dave).

Dorothy Jane and Molly sneak out for a double date, only to discover that the boys want to play a game called strip trivia.

DANCE, THE   Airdate: 4/17/93.

Guest Cast: Alyson Hannigan (Samantha), Richard Panebianco (Craig Keets), James Gleason (Mr. Hacker), Jay Lambert (Tom).

When Gregory's tomboy friend, Sam, asks him to a "girls' choice" dance, he doesn't know how to react when she arrives at the front door. Samantha has become a "major babe."

YOU OUGHTA BE IN PICTURES   Airdate: 4/24/93.

Guest Cast: Christine Rose (The Director), Mark Shera (Paul), Linda Larkin (Kim), Wayne Federman (Assistant).

Chuckie Lee models for Brian's new catalog and the resultant attention goes to his head.

HOT TICKET   Airdate: 6/05/93.

Guest Cast: Alyson Hannigan (Samantha), Donal Logue (Tommy Tom), Peter Van Norden (Mel).

Gregory tells the girls he can get tickets to a popular sold-out concert, but then finds that he can't deliver on his promise.

BOWLING FOR DADDIES   Airdate: 6/12/93.

Guest Cast: Robert Costanzo (Big Bob Petrelli), Jacob Kenner (Bobby Petrelli).

Millicent and Brian both enroll in a father–son bowling tournament as part of their plans to forge tighter bonds with their sons.

Walter and Emily

When Disney's *The Torkelsons* failed to attract sufficient viewers, the cancellation message also contained some good news for the Studio. The replacement series for *The Torkelsons* was to be *Walter and Emily*, another Disney sitcom, which joined the NBC Saturday evening line-up midway during the 1991–92 season. The namesakes of *Walter and Emily* were Walter and Emily Collins, a married couple who had been arguing for almost 40 years.

Series Cast: Cloris Leachman (Emily Collins), Brian Keith (Walter Collins), Christopher McDonald (Matt Collins), Matthew Lawrence (Zack Collins), Edan Gross (Hartley).

Each of the episodes is described below in airdate order.

BIG TROUBLE   Airdate: 11/16/91.

Guest Cast: Rene Auberjonois (Mr. Norman), Sandy Baron (Stan), Shelley Berman (Albert).

Zack tells Walter that he wants to skip school because a bully is picking on him. Walter tries to teach Zack and Hartley how to box, but the next day, Zack is suspended for fighting at school.

TAKE THIS JOB   Airdate: 11/23/91.

Guest Cast: Sandy Baron (Stan), Shelley Berman (Albert), Peter Iacangelo (Ray), Peter Allas (Sal), Cynthia Frost (Waitress), Kyle-Scott Jackson (Customer).

Zack wants to go to London with his soccer team but Matt tells him he'll have to earn the money himself. Walter gets Zack a job at the coffee shop, but Zack goofs off and the owner asks Walter to fire him.

RISKS   Airdate: 11/30/91.

Guest Cast: Larry Hankin (The Man), May Quigley (Richie's Mom), Patrick Cupo (The Customer), John Altobello III (Richie).

Emily refuses to let Zack go jet skiing with Hartley, telling him that it is too dangerous. Instead, Matt takes Zack on a "safe" trip to watch a tennis match, but Zack is hit by a racket and needs dental work.

BEDTIME STORY   Airdate: 12/07/91.

Guest Cast: Dan Gilvezan (Jack Thompson), Richard Fancy (Dr. Grissom), Danny Dayton (Leo), Elizabeth Hanley (Mrs. Patterson), Beth Tegarden (The Model), Brandie Braverman (Mindy Patterson).

When Walter buys twin beds so he can sleep better, Emily becomes upset and a heated argument breaks out. Matt throws them out of the house and they check into a motel.

DUCKY   Airdate: 12/14/91.

Guest Cast: None.

Walter gives Zack his prized Ducky Medwick baseball card from 1932, explaining that it had been his father's. The card is now worth $1,200, but Walter feels it's even more valuable in memories.

PERFECT WOMAN, THE   Airdate: 12/21/91.

Guest Cast: Christine Mitges (Esther Skinner).

Emily sets up a blind date for Matt and is overjoyed when he falls in love. Her happiness quickly fades when Walter points out that if Matt gets married, they will have to move out.

AUNT JULIA   Airdate: 1/04/92.

Guest Cast: Marian Seldes (Aunt Julia).

A visit from Emily's sister, Julia, brings chaos to the Collins house. Among other problems, Julia makes Matt worry about dying young.

EXPOSED   Airdate: 1/11/92.

Guest Cast: Sandy Baron (Stan), Shelley Berman (Albert), Ilene Graff (Dr. Barbara Morris).

When Walter and his friends go to see an old-time stripper, Emily discovers their secret and isn't at all pleased by it. Meanwhile, Zack is depressed when he learns that Hartley is moving.

REMEMBER ME?   Airdate: 1/25/92.

Guest Cast: Amy Steel (Ginny), Duke Moosekian (Freddie), Andrew J. Lawrence (Andrew).

Zack's mother, Ginny, comes for a visit and brings Zack's half-brother, Andrew, along with her. Andrew tears up Zack's belongings, but Zack keeps quiet in the hope that his parents will get back together.

LABOR PAINS   Airdate: 2/01/92.

Guest Cast: Ariana Richards (Shelly Peters), Grant Gelt (The Kid).

When Emily discovers that her wedding ring is made of glass, Walter is also surprised, for he thought he had bought a real diamond.

DATE NIGHT   Airdate: 2/08/92.

Guest Cast: Bill Macy (Ray Nelson), Nancy Dussault (Claire Nelson), Maria Pecci (Alexandra), Deasa Turner (Brandy).

Walter and Emily spend an unpleasant evening with the Nelsons, a new couple in town. To avoid spending another evening with them, Walter and Emily decide to go out and leave Zack alone at home.

FALCON AND THE LEG MAN, THE   Airdate: 2/15/92.

Guest Cast: Steve Arlen (Jim Garvin), Lauren Woodland (Katie Tanner), Lee Ryan (Steve Tanner), Taylor Leigh (Joanne Garvin).

Emily is doing volunteer work for a professor and Walter becomes jealous when he asks her to go on a trip with him.

SIS   Airdate: 2/22/92.

Guest Cast: Liz Vassey (Megan Collins), David Schwimmer (Eddie), Scott Bryce (Dr. David Rees), Monty Hoffman (Firpo).

Walter and Emily's daughter, Megan, arrives for a visit, just after having been dumped by her latest boyfriend. Megan spends the day with Zack and Hartley, and Emily is horrified when Zack comes home with a tattoo.

Laurie Hill

There have been many attempts to create the perfect "dramedy," or dramatic comedy, but most of the shows were lucky to last a full season. Undaunted, Disney agreed to try the genre with its series *Laurie Hill* for the 1992–93 season. *Laurie Hill* centered on a busy woman pediatrician.

Series Cast: DeLane Matthews (Dr. Laurie Hill), Robert Clohessey (Jeff Hill), Eric Lloyd (Leo Hill), Kurt Fuller (Dr. Spencer Kramer), Ellen DeGeneres (Nurse Nancy MacIntyre), Doris Belack (Beverly Fielder), Joseph Maher (Dr. Walter Weisman).

Each of the episodes is described below in airdate order. Additionally, several episodes were produced but not aired, and are listed in production order.

Laurie Hill (pilot)   Airdate: 9/30/92.

Guest Cast: Myra Turley (Ruth Miller), Joe Mays (Ralph Miller), Jarrett Lennon (Justin Miller), Priscilla Morrill (Mrs. Wiseman).

Laurie and Jeff find themselves at odds when their son announces that he wants a toy gun as his birthday present. Laurie has another more serious problem at work, where a young patient is dying of AIDS.

Woman on the Verge   Airdate: 10/07/92.

Guest Cast: Doug Ballard (Mr. Korsch), Cynthia Mace (Susan Newmyer).

Laurie has a plumbing problem at home, and a patient has a plumbing problem of his own—a genital infection.

Crush   Airdate: 10/14/92.

Guest Cast: Jordan Bond (Tim Williams), Lee Garlington (Margaret), Paige Gosney (Lenny), R.C. Weaver (Teddy), W.G. "Snuffy" Walden (Announcer).

A young patient develops a serious crush on Laurie. Meanwhile, she is busily trying to sew a Halloween costume for her son.

Grasshopper   Airdate: 10/21/92.

Guest Cast: Christina Pickles (Mary), Macon McCalman (Bill), Rebecca Cross (Mrs. Halper), Carole Ita White (Mrs. Ferguson).

Laurie and Jeff think that Leo's trouble at school may be his teacher's fault.

Sick and Tired   Airdate: 10/28/92.

Guest Cast: Gill Baker (Woman #2), Kate Randolph Burns (Woman #1), Chasiti Hampton (Amy), Kenneth Stephens (Man).

After the family suffers an illness, the Hills realize they need to slow down and enjoy life while they still have a chance.

Babysitter, The   Airdate: Unaired.

Guest Cast: Mary Elizabeth Murphy (Lisa Banks), Barbara Niles (Overweight Sitter), Kelly McMahan (Smoker Sitter), T.C. Warner (Young Girl Sitter), Jaclyn Carmichael (German Sitter).

When Jeff is offered a full-time job, the family must search for someone to care for Leo. This makes Laurie realize how much time she is spending away from her family.

Birds and the Elephants, The   Airdate: Unaired.

Guest Cast: Hallie Todd (Ellen Maddox), Tuc Watkins (Kenny Maddox), Brittany Gregerson (Chelsea), Brenda Thomson (Dr. Panetti), Yvette Freeman (Nurse).

Laurie and Jeff agree that she should cut back on work so she can spend more time with Leo, but he would rather spend time with his friends.

Heart Thing, The   Airdate: Unaired.

Guest Cast: Christina Pickles (Mary), Macon McCalman (Bill), Monni Harmon (Young Mary), Jetta King (Young Laurie), Joey Lauren (Young Susan).

Laurie's mother ignores her medical advice and suffers a heart attack, which eventually brings the two women closer together.

Much Ado about Nancy   Airdate: Unaired.

Guest Cast: Hank Adams (Bruce), Chelsea Lagos (Becky McKinney), Ryan Thomas Johnson (Colin McKinney), Jodi Carlisle (Jean McKinney), Carel Eidel (John McKinney).

Things go wrong right from the start when Laurie sets up a blind date between Nancy and one of Jeff's friends.

Walter & Beverly   Airdate: Unaired.

Guest Cast: Tom Dahlgren (Bill Winters), Diana Chesney (Aunt Lillian), Debi Derryberry (Temp), Scott Sites (Delivery Guy).

Two of Laurie's co-workers end up feuding when one of them starts dating someone else.

Woops!

For the 1992–93 season, Disney came out with *Woops!*, a sitcom featuring the 6 survivors of a nuclear accident that devastated the world. They found their way to a strange, unspoiled farmhouse in a green valley. There, with an ample supply of canned food, an uncontaminated well, and a working generator, they tried to survive in this oasis. Each week would find them having to deal with life cut off from civilization, a life where they had to rely totally on each other. In typical sitcom fashion, most of the group were inept and bumbling, making their lives a never-ending series of mishaps and predicaments.

Series Cast: *Fred Applegate (Jack Connors), Lane Davies (Curtis Thorpe), Cleavant Derricks (Dr. Frederick Ross), Meagen Fay (Alice McConnell), Marita Geraghty (Suzanne Skillman), Evan Handler (Mark Braddock).*

Each of the episodes is described below in airdate order. Additionally, several episodes were produced but not aired, and are listed in production order.

WOOPS! (pilot)   Airdate: 9/27/92.
After an accidental nuclear war, 6 survivors gather together. Their first efforts to create a new society result in chaos, until a giant spider scares them into cooperating with each other.

IT'S A DIRTY JOB   Airdate: 10/04/92.
The survivors realize they will need to reproduce to repopulate the Earth, but no one likes anyone enough to consider having sex.

ROOT OF ALL EVIL   Airdate: 10/11/92.
The group has problems setting up a new monetary system.

DAYS OF WINE AND BERRIES, THE
Airdate: 10/18/92.
Mark becomes addicted to strange berries from a mutant bush.

RISE AND FALL OF ALICE MCCONNELL, THE   Airdate: 10/25/92.
Alice discovers a crystal that greatly enlarges her breasts, giving her the confidence to enter a beauty pageant with Suzanne.

ELECTION, THE   Airdate: 11/01/92.
Curtis and Mark campaign for the honor of maintaining the farm's power supply, for it seems the job comes with a private bedroom.

CURTIS UNGLUED   Airdate: 11/08/92.
Curtis loses his necktie, his only link to his past life as a stockbroker, and the shock causes him to snap.

DUMB LOVE   Airdate: 11/15/92.
Jack and Suzanne announce they are in love and will be moving into the barn together.

THANKSGIVING SHOW, THE   Airdate: 11/22/92.
The group finds a turkey just in time for Thanksgiving, but when it mutates to giant size, they might be the entrees on the holiday menu.

SAY IT AIN'T SO, SANTA   Airdate: 12/06/92.
Guest Cast: *Stuart Pankin (Santa Claus).*
Santa Claus arrives at the farm with the sad news that Mrs. Claus and the elves were killed during the war.

LITTLE PATHOLOGIST, THE   Airdate: Unaired.
Guest Star: *Jimmy Lee Newman Jr. (Little Frederick).*
A freak storm turns Frederick into a kid again.

NUCLEAR FAMILY, THE   Airdate: Unaired.
Guest Cast: *David Lascher (Kiefer).*
When the group discovers that a socially misfit boy is hiding in the barn, they do their best to reform him—and fail.

DAYDREAMS COME, AND ME WAN' GO HOME   Airdate: Unaired.
Alice makes the group hold a party to celebrate their first 6 months together and they all daydream about ways to kill her.

Where I Live

Where I Live joined the ABC line-up as a mid-season replacement for the 1992–93 season, airing on Friday at 9:30 P.M. The series, which featured a black cast, focused on 18-year-old Douglas St. Martin, played by Doug E. Doug, and his friends in Harlem.

Series Cast: *Doug E. Doug (Douglas Martin), Flex (Reggie Coltrane), Shaun Baker (Malcolm), Lorraine Toussaint (Marie Martin), Yunoka Doyle (Sharon Martin), Jason Bose Smith (Kwanzie), Sullivan Walker (James Martin). Note: Flex is the stage name of actor Mark Knox.*

1992–93 season

OCCUPANT   Airdates: 3/05/93, 8/03/93.
Guest Cast: *Tammy Townsend (Dontay).*
Reggie gets a basketball scholarship to college but is afraid to tell Douglas the news.

His concerns prove well founded, for when Douglas finds out, he thinks about quitting school to get a job.

ONE DEAD MOTHER   Airdates: 3/12/93, 8/10/93.

Guest Cast: Damian Cagnolatti (Kevin), Tara Thomas (Teddi).

Marie doesn't approve of a rap compact disc and throws it away. Douglas thinks she is a prude, but he is later shocked to learn that she performed nude in the musical *Hair*.

CURF ME? . . . CURFEW!   Airdates: 3/19/93, 8/17/93.

Guest Cast: Almayvonne (Vonzella), Senait (Felicia).

Doug tries to prove to his parents that he's too old for a curfew, but his efforts only end up stranding him far from home late one night.

MY FAIR FORWARD   Airdates: 3/26/93, 8/24/93.

Guest Cast: Almayvonne (Vonzella), Josef B. Cannon (Luther), Juliette Jeffers (Tina).

The newest member of the neighborhood basketball team turns out to be a woman.

DOUG GETS BUSY   Airdate: 4/02/93.

Guest Cast: Brent Jennings (Franklin), Wesley Thompson (Mr. Williams).

Douglas tries to run a T-shirt business. When it fails, he develops a new respect for his father and the problems he faces in earning money to support the family.

DONTAY'S INFERNO   Airdate: 4/06/93.

Guest Cast: Tammy Townsend (Dontay), Roxanne Beckford (Yvette), Mushond Lee (Wendell), Allan Dean Moore (Roger), Gina Ravarra (Robin), John E. Kay (Antoine).

Douglas is upset when Reggie starts spending time with Dontay, a new girl in town.

PAST TENSE, FUTURE IMPERFECT   Airdate: 4/09/93.

Guest Cast: None.

James returns from a visit to Jamaica and worries that the family is losing touch with the island's culture.

OPPOSITES ATTACK   Airdate: 4/16/93.

Guest Cast: Brent Jennings (Reverend Dulcey Bohannan), Rosemarie Jackson (Sharitha), Rana Mack (Gina), Michelle L. Simms (Monique), Bebe Drake-Massey (Old Lady).

A poorly chosen sexist remark by Doug causes him and his friends to lose their dates for the school dance.

MARRIED . . . WITH CHILDREN   Airdate: 4/23/93.

Guest Cast: Garcelle Beavais (Terry), Tracey Jones (Girl #1), Elizabeth Jean-Paul (Girl #2).

Marie wants to have another baby, but decides instead to seek fulfillment in a new job.

MALCOLM 2X   Airdates: 4/30/93, 8/31/93.

Guest Cast: None.

Malcolm needs to pass algebra, so he hires Sharon to tutor him. Problems arise when Douglas thinks something else is going on at their nightly sessions.

I LIVE WHERE?   Airdate: 5/07/93.

Guest Cast: Earl Billings (Zachary), Ernie Banks (Johnson), Sylver Gregory (Nikki), Michelle Simms (Monique), Marjean Holden (Karen), Darwyn Carson (Margie), Hugh Dane (Mover).

Doug decides he needs freedom, particularly in his love life, so he gets an apartment with Malcolm and Reggie.

SHIRT HAPPENS   Airdate: Unaired.

Guest Cast: Brent Jennings (Franklin), Lisa Marie Russell (Lichelle), Rawley Valverde (Clerk).

Doug tries to impress a girl from a wealthy part of town by buying her an expensive shirt and later returning it before he has to pay for it, but the plan fails when the shirt is accidentally ruined.

1993–94 season

BIG MON ON CAMPUS   Airdate: 11/06/93.

Guest Cast: Almayvonne (Vonzella), Iona Morris (Ms. Hall), Monica Calhoun (Kaiya Hawkins), Yolanda Snowball (Waitress), "Brownstone": Nichole Gilbert, Charmayne Maxwell, Monica Doby.

Afraid of failure, Douglas only signs up for easy courses at college. He later realizes the value of an education and decides to become a lawyer.

I AM NOT A ROLE MODEL   Airdate: 11/13/93.

Guest Cast: Almayvonne (Vonzella), Shirley Jo Finney (Teacher), Chante Frierson

(Monica), Crystal Grant (Dorinda), Mayah McCoy (Carolyn), Ahmed Stoner (Khalil).

Doug thinks it's funny to give Kwanzie some bad advice on how to treat girls until Kwanzie asks him to explain further in front of the whole class.

Big Easy, The   Airdate: 11/20/93.

Guest Cast: Vanessa Bell Calloway (Delia Franklin), Unique Jackson (Doo Wop Singer #1), Natasha Pearce (Doo Wop Singer #2), Kelli Ball (Doo Wop Singer #3).

Doug falls in love with an older neighbor.

Miracle on 134th Street   Airdate: Unaired.

Guest Cast: Almayvonne (Vonzella), Ron Taylor (Santa Claus), Joan Pringle (Joanne), Glenndon Chatman (Boy #1), Tracey Jones (Cynthia), Jossi B. Harris (Krystal), Hugh Dane (Al), Cynthia Calhoun (Joyce), Unique Jackson (Doo Wop Singer #1), Natasha Pearce (Doo Wop Singer #2), Kelli Ball (Doo Wop Singer #3).

Douglas has to choose between spending Christmas with his family or at a big basketball game.

Local Hero   Airdate: Unaired.

Guest Cast: Rawle Lewis (Ferrari), Malik Yoba (Fisher), Almayvonne (Vonzella), Lawrence A. Mandley (Reverend), Don Fullilove (The Man), Marlon Taylor (Kevin), Cynthia Calhoun (The Girl), Unique Jackson (Doo Wop Singer #1), Natasha Pearce (Doo Wop Singer #2), Kelli Ball (Doo Wop Singer #3).

Although his neighbors are happy that Reggie is about to play his first game for St. John's University, he learns that he has to sit out the game.

Cutters

This short-lived sitcom was set in Buffalo, New York, where Harry Polachek was having a hard time keeping his barbershop open. The series was a mid-season replacement for CBS during the 1992–93 season, appearing on Friday at 8:30 P.M. It lasted only 5 episodes.

Series Cast: Robert Hays (Joe Polachek), Margaret Whitton (Adrienne St. John), Julia Campbell (Lynn Fletcher), Ray Buktenica (Chad Conners), Julius Carry (Troy King), Robin Tunney (Deborah Hart), Dakin Matthews (Harry Polachek).

Each of the episodes is described below in airdate order.

Cutters (pilot)   Airdate: 6/11/93.

Guest Cast: Jan Sheldrick, Wil Albert, Nancy Linehan Charles, Julie Lloyd.

Joe persuades his sexist father, Harry, to tear down the wall between their barbershop and the beauty parlor next door as part of his plan to improve the business.

Where's Harry?   Airdate: 6/18/93.

Guest Cast: Henry Gibson, Peter Keleghan, West Stern.

Harry doesn't feel like he's fitting in at the new shop so he disappears, only to return after spending several days at a trendy beauty school where he has learned more modern techniques.

Give 'Til It Hurts   Airdate: 6/25/93.

Guest Cast: John Mahon, Chance Quinn, Fred Applegate, Sean Bradley, Stefanie Ridel.

Chad, one of the barbers, enjoys chasing after Lynn until he runs out of money. Meanwhile, Adrienne convinces Harry to give her son a talk about the birds and the bees.

Harry's Best Friend   Airdate: 7/20/93.

Guest Cast: Jessica Tuck, James T. Callahan, Art Kimbro, Barbara Brighton, Nancy Linehan Charles, Cindy Ballou, Christopher Halsted, Robin Goodrin Nordli.

Harry learns that his former best friend, Troy, is gay. Joe says he doesn't date his clients, but his resolve is put to the test when a make-over turns an ugly duckling into a beauty.

Hi There, Sports Fans   Airdate: 7/09/93.

Guest Cast: Cristine Rose, Wil Albert, Paul Cavonis, Robert Rothwell.

When the editor of a local women's magazine visits the shop, she thinks she has finally found a business that caters to a woman's point of view.

Disney Presents Bill Nye the Science Guy

When the Children's Television Act of 1990 mandated that stations must provide programming deemed educational and beneficial to children, it opened the opportunity for a unique collaboration between Disney and the PBS education television system. Geared toward fourth-grade students, *Disney Presents*

Bill Nye the Science Guy was created to present science as fun, exciting, and not just for scholars.

Disney Presents Bill Nye the Science Guy began airing on PBS and in syndication for the 1993–94 season with the following episodes:

- *Flight:* This episode demonstrates how birds and man-made objects are able to achieve flight.
- *Earth's Crust, The:* Bill uses a helicopter to descend into an active volcano. Actress Jenna von Oy guest stars.
- *Dinosaurs:* Robin Leach and John Ratzenberger join Bill for a look at the prehistoric creatures.
- *Skin:* Bill takes a look at the body's largest organ.
- *Buoyancy:* A hot air balloon ride, a floating car, and a scuba dive show different aspects of buoyancy.
- *Gravity:* The force that holds us on the Earth and the Earth in orbit is the subject of Bill's experiments.
- *Digestion:* A steam engine that runs on corn flakes is just one of the tools Bill uses to explain digestion.
- *Phases of Matter:* A tour of a steel mill reveals matter in three phases—solid, liquid, and gas.
- *Biodiversity:* Bill takes a look at the complexity of the food chain.
- *Simple Machines:* Basic mechanical principles are seen in roller coasters and bicycles.
- *Moon, The:* Astronaut Harrison Schmitt, the last man to walk on the moon, joins Bill to discuss our natural satellite.
- *Sound:* Bill visits rock group Soundgarden as they record their newest song.
- *Garbage:* Trips to landfills show how mankind generates vast amounts of non-biodegradable trash.
- *Structures:* Bill bungee-jumps off New York's Verrazano Narrows Bridge to demonstrate the principles of tension and compression.
- *Earth's Seasons:* Bill explains how the Earth's tilt and rotation create our seasons.
- *Light and Color:* A colorful look at light includes a turn on the dance floor to the song *Staying Alive.*
- *Cells:* This episode explores the complex world of DNA.
- *Electricity:* Bill visits Washington's Grand Coulee Dam and Nevada's Hoover Dam to show one of the ways electricity is generated.
- *Outer Space:* A visit to the Mt. Wilson observatory helps explain some of the bodies found beyond our atmosphere.
- *Eyeball, The:* Critics Gene Siskell and Roger Ebert give two "thumbs up" to Bill's explanation of how we see.
- *Magnetism:* The science of things that attract and repel includes the fact that the Earth is itself a giant magnet.
- *Wind:* Bill parachutes and visits a wind farm to explore wind.
- *Blood and Circulation:* Actor Sinbad joins Bill to talk about blood and the circulatory system.
- *Chemical Reactions:* Actress Candace Cameron visits for a look at different chemical reactions.
- *Static Electricity:* A trip to a giant Van De Graaf generator demonstrates what makes socks cling.
- *Food Web, The:* Actor Alfonso Ribeiro participates in a look at how all living things are linked in the food chain.

Following the successful reception of these episodes, the series has been renewed each season since. The additional episodes include: *Amphibians, Animal Locomotion, Archaeology, Architecture, Atmosphere, Balance, Birds, Bones and Muscles, The Brain, Climates, Communication, Computers, Deserts, Earthquakes, Energy, Evolution, Farming, Fish, Flowers, Forensics, Forests, Fossils, Friction, Genes, Germs, Heart, Heat, Human Transportation, Inventing, Insects, Invertebrates, Light and Color, Light Optics, Mammals, Marine Mammals, Momentum, Nutrition, Ocean Currents, Ocean Life, The Planets, Plants, Pollution, Populations, Pressure, Probability, Pseudoscience, Reptiles, Respiration, Rivers and Streams, Rocks and Soil, Space Exploration, Spiders, Spinning Things, The Sun, Time, Top 11 Videos (science music videos), Volcanoes, Water Cycle, Waves,* and *Wetland.*

Countdown at the Neon Armadillo

The success of the special *Best of Country '92: Countdown at the Neon Armadillo* led to this syndicated series. Set both at the 328 Club in Nashville, Tennessee, and at the Neon Armadillo nightclub on Pleasure Island at Walt Disney World, country western performers gathered each week to sing and talk about their careers.

Cameramen prepare to shoot a scene 30 feet beneath the waves of the Caribbean in "Operation Undersea."

Homo Sapiens, a new Disney character, with a siren in "Operation Undersea."

This cougar got more than he bargained for when he tried to hunt a large buck deer in "One Day on Beetle Rock."

The *USS Nespelen* in McMurdo Sound, Antarctica, in "Antarctica—Past and Present."

Tinker Bell takes viewers on a tour of Disneyland in "An Adventure in the Magic Kingdom."

A perched koala bear in "Nature's Strangest Oddballs."

Ranger J. Audubon Woodlore discusses bird migration in "Nature's Charter Tours."

A diving bell spider builds a home for itself in "Nature's Better Built Homes."

The great English writer Charles Kingsley is depicted here, telling his son about "water babies" in "More about Silly Symphonies."

Salty, a harbor seal pup, stars in "Salty, the Hijacked Harbor Seal."

Jiminy Cricket prepares to interview Daisy Duck about Donald Duck's conduct in "Donald's Award."

At the entrance to his cave atop desolate Chimney Butte, Mad Hermit (played by Donald Duck) dares anyone to interrupt his seclusion in "The Mad Hermit of Chimney Butte."

Walt Disney stands beside the first boat to plunge down the Colorado River through the Grand Canyon in "Rapids Ahead (and) Bear Country."

Ranger J. Audubon Woodlore lets Huey try his binoculars in "Ranger's Guide to Nature."

Disney artists Bill Justice (left) and Xavier Atencio show their vegetable characters in "A Rag, A Bone, A Box of Junk."

A ring-necked pheasant defends itself from a predator owl in "The Proud Bird from Shanghai."

Equipment is collected for an expedition of the South Polar region in "Antarctica—Past and Present."

A lonesome otter seeks friendship in "One Day at Teton Marsh."

A spectacular battle for leadership of a wild mustang herd in "Mustang!"

Cinderella Castle under construction at the Magic Kingdom in Florida. "Project Florida," a special progress report on the park, was aired at the end of "The Adventures of Bullwhip Griffin."

Papa Goofy tells son Goofy about their family history in "The Adventure Story."

A beaver works furiously on his dam in "One Day at Teton Marsh."

A little accident bound to happen in "An Adventure in Color—Mathmagic Land."

Disney artist Marc Davis's rendering of a tree in "An Adventure in Art."

Standing guard over a flock of geese is "Boomerang, Dog of Many Talents."

Professor Ludwig Von Drake and his companions, Donald Duck and José Carioca, cannot shake the rhythm of the celebrations in "Carnival Time."

Barry, a Saint Bernard rescue dog, comes to the aid of a little girl trapped in the Swiss Alps in "Barry of the Great St. Bernard."

Professor Ludwig Von Drake turns out jazzy rhythms in "Music for Everybody."

Mickey Mouse stars in "The Mouse Factory," a comedy series featuring celebrity hosts and Disney characters.

Ward Kimball, producer of "The Mouse Factory."

A pair of polar bear cubs frolics in the snow in "A Salute to Alaska."

An orphan wolverine seeks to avenge his mother's death by a trapper in "Minado, the Wolverine."

Using a model of Monstro, a giant whale, Walt Disney introduces "Monsters of the Deep."

Ringo, a raccoon whose home is displaced by a shopping center, searches for new digs in "Ringo, the Refugee Raccoon."

Scrooge scolds employee Bob Cratchit (played by Mickey Mouse) for using yet another precious piece of coal in "Mickey's Christmas Carol."

Birkie, a Shetland sheepdog, becomes stranded on Santa Catalina Island in "The Little Shepherd Dog of Catalina."

Waiting for the unsuspecting used-car buyer in "Dad, Can I Borrow the Car?," a comedic treatment of America's love affair with the automobile.

Clarence "Ducky" Nash, the voice behind Donald Duck, stars in "Donald Duck's 50th Birthday," which also features the talents of Dick Van Dyke, Ed Asner, Bruce Jenner, John Ritter, Kenny Rogers, Donna Summer, Cloris Leachman, Andy Warhol, and Henry Winkler.

Goofy is determined to play golf as he tries to sneak out of the house without attracting his wife's attention in "Goofy Takes a Holiday."

A pronghorn antelope easily outruns a hungry bobcat in "Run, Light Buck, Run."

Candy stars in "Little Dog Lost."

Chandar, a black Ceylonese leopard, befriends a Buddhist monk in "Chandar, the Black Leopard of Ceylon."

Herbie, the mischievous Volkswagen Bug, stars in "Herbie, The Love Bug."

A proud cat and her equally proud kittens walk through a medieval town in "The Great Cat Family."

Donald Duck, Mickey Mouse, Peter Pan, Jiminy Cricket, Cinderella, Snow White, Wendy Darling, and Chip 'n Dale sing and entertain in a special Yuletide show called "From All of Us to All of You."

Donald Duck and his two amigos celebrate Donald's 25th birthday in "Donald's Silver Anniversary."

Assam, a prized Kellogg Arabian, has the equine lead in "The Legend of El Blanco."

Donald Duck eavesdrops on a story conference in "A Day in the Life of Donald Duck."

Walt Disney and Miss Disneyland Julie Reihm point out new exhibits planned for the park when Disneyland celebrates ten years of service in "Disneyland 10th Anniversary."

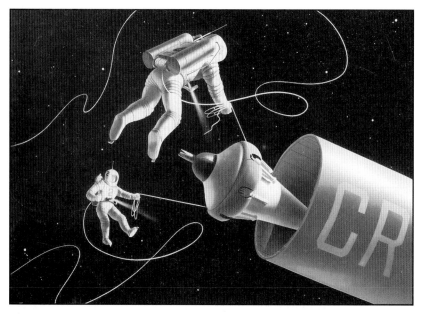

Crewmen 1,075 miles above the Earth work in "Man and the Moon."

Countdown began airing the week of 9/17/93.

Series Cast: *Carrie Folks, John Burke, Billy Dean.* **Countdown Dancers:** *Michael Clowers, Pauline Locsin, Brett Nugent, Mary Ann Oedy, Brigitte Snowden, Richard Villanueva, Karl Wahl, Paula Wise.*

Each of the episodes is described below in airdate order. Several performers returned with the same songs in multiple episodes as part of the weekly countdowns.

WEEK 1 (9/17/93)

Performers: Sawyer Brown, Tracy Byrd, Mark Chesnutt, Lorrie Morgan, Aaron Neville, Diamond Reo, Clay Walker, Vince Gill, Joe Diffie, Aaron Tippin, Wynonna, Billy Ray Cyrus, Dwight Yoakum, Garth Brooks.

WEEK 2 (9/24/93)

Performers: John Anderson, Sawyer Brown, Tracy Byrd, Pam Tillis, Aaron Tippin, Little Texas, Vince Gill, Clay Walker, Joe Diffie, Billy Ray Cyrus, Wynonna, Garth Brooks.

WEEK 3 (10/01/93)

Performers: Victoria Shaw, Billy Dean, Jess Leary, Doug Stone, Chris Ledoux, Mark Collie, Shawn Camp, Shania Twain, Toby Keith, George Strait, Clint Black, Brother Phelps, Wynonna, Vince Gill, Joe Diffie, Clay Walker, Tracy Byrd, Garth Brooks.

WEEK 4 (10/08/93)

Performers: Lorrie Morgan, Alison Krauss, Ricky Skaggs, Mark Chesnutt, Clay Walker, Steve Wariner, Toby Keith, George Strait, Wynonna, Garth Brooks, Joe Diffie, Vince Gill.

WEEK 5 (10/15/93)

Performers: David Gates, Billy Dean, Andy Childs, Toby Keith, Brother Phelps, Clay Walker, Steve Wariner, Garth Brooks, Suzy Bogguss, Reba McEntire, Clint Black, Joe Diffie, Vince Gill.

WEEK 6 (10/22/93)

Performers: John Anderson, Mark Chesnutt, Ricky Lynn Gregg, Lee Roy Parnell, Doug Supernaw, Pam Tillis, Brooks & Dunn, Suzy Bogguss, Joe Diffie, Reba McEntire, Toby Keith, Clint Black, Vince Gill, Clay Walker, George Strait.

WEEK 7 (10/29/93)

Performers: Sawyer Brown, Vince Gill, Toby Keith, Lorrie Morgan, Collin Raye, Doug Stone, Pam Tillis, Steve Wariner, Reba McEntire, Billy Dean, Billy Ray Cyrus, David Gates, Garth Brooks.

WEEK 8 (11/05/93)

Performers: John Berry, Sawyer Brown, Mark Chesnutt, Mark Collie, Ricky Skaggs, Lorrie Morgan, Alan Jackson, Clint Black, Collin Raye, Alabama, Suzy Bogguss, Brooks & Dunn, George Strait, Reba McEntire.

WEEK 9 (11/12/93)

Performers: Sawyer Brown, Victoria Shaw, Billy Dean, John Anderson, Lorrie Morgan, Clay Walker, Mark Chesnutt, Doug Stones, Tracy Byrd, Toby Keith, Vince Gill, Reba McEntire, Travis Tritt, Alan Jackson, Patty Loveless, Tracy Lawrence.

WEEK 10 (11/19/93)

Performers: Clint Black, Stephanie Davis, Gibson Miller Band, Wright and King Matthews, Lorrie Morgan, Aaron Neville, Collin Raye, Reba McEntire, Martina McBride, Garth Brooks, Lee Roy Parnell, Brooks & Dunn, Matthews, Wright & King, Alabama, Mark Chesnutt.

WEEK 11 (11/26/93)

Performers: John Anderson, Bobbie Cryner, Billy Ray Cyrus, Little Texas, Mark O'Connor, Collin Raye, Pam Tillis, Tracy Lawrence, Brooks & Dunn, Lee Roy Parnell, Martina McBride, Mark Chesnutt, Garth Brooks, Alabama.

Bakersfield P.D.

The story of *Bakersfield P.D.* began when Paul Gigante, a policeman in Washington, D.C., was forced to flee town to escape a scandal.

Paul took a job with the Bakersfield, California police department, where the small-town officers find their lives changed, for Paul was the first black officer on the force.

Bakersfield P.D. was part of the Fox line-up for the 1993–94 season.

Series Cast: *Ron Eldard (Detective Wade Preston), Giancarlo Esposito (Paul Gigante), Chris Mulkey (Denny Boyer), Tony Plana (Luke Ramirez), Jack Hallett (Captain Renny*

Stiles), Brian Doyle-Murray (Sergeant Bill Hampton).

Each of the episodes is described below in airdate order.

BAKERSFIELD P.D. (pilot) Airdates: 9/14/93, 9/18/93.

Guest Cast: Cynthia Bond (Deidre Gigante), Shaun Baker (Winston/Suspect #1), Tim Dezarn (Suspect #2), Rick Najera (Dispatcher), David Basulto (Tyron), Wendy Gordon (Newscaster), Abe Adams (Paulie Gigante).

When Washington, D.C., cop Paul Gigante moves to Bakersfield, California, he finds that he's the only black cop on the force. His partner, Wade Preston, is obsessed with black culture to the point of obnoxiousness.

IMPOSTER, THE Airdates: 9/21/93, 12/07/93.

Guest Cast: Allan Wasserman (Doctor Harbor), Laura Innes (Darcy Wilks), David Wiley (Walter Leeds), Flora Burke (Mrs. Carson), Jean Ford (Distraught Woman), Mark Wakefield (Tom Cruise Lookalike), Nick D'Egidio (Frank Sinatra Lookalike), Arlen B. Pantel (Bruce Springsteen Lookalike), Gregory Wolfe (Rod Stewart Lookalike).

The detectives' hunt for a con artist isn't helped by the police sketch artist, who would rather be drawing pictures of celebrities.

UNSOLVED MYSTERIES OF LOVE Airdates: 9/28/93, 1/04/94.

Guest Cast: Patrick Kilpatrick (Dwight), Marianna Elliott (Eden), Tom Towles (Riley), Sonia Jackson (Nurse), Christopher Michael Moore (Fireman).

Wade falls madly in love with the girlfriend of a burglary suspect. Stiles has his own problem—escaping the department's annual blood drive.

SNAKE CHARMER Airdate: 10/05/93.

Guest Cast: Diane Delano (Jessie), Marnie Crossen (Woman), Rolando Molina (Criminal).

Captain Stiles is forced to finally make a decision. He decides that he'll let Paul make his decisions for him.

POKER GAME, THE Airdates: 10/12/93, 10/28/93.

Guest Cast: William H. Macy (Russell), Todd Field (Lewis), Andrew Craig (Prisoner), Gwen Van Adam (Doug's Mother).

Paul is finally invited to the gang's poker game and happily ends the night by winning all the money.

BUST, THE Airdate: 10/19/93.

Guest Cast: Jenny Gago (Carmelina), Michael Kaufman (Chambers), Steve Fitchpatrick (Drug Dealer #1), Earl Billings (Drug Dealer #2), John Fleck (The Clown), Abe Adams (Paulie Gigante), Phil Forman (Dr. Glassboro).

Paul tells Wade in confidence why he moved to Bakersfield, unaware that his partner can't keep a secret.

EX-PARTNER, THE Airdate: 10/26/93.

Guest Cast: Bill Nunn (Troy Davis), W. Earl Brown (Mobster #1), Greg Germann (Hood), Nicholas Mele (Mobster #2).

A visit by Paul's former partner makes Wade feel jealous.

BAKERSFIELD MADAM Airdate: 11/02/93.

Guest Cast: Richard Bradford (Mayor Miller), Sherrie Rose (Kimberly), Sara Melson (Shauna), John Blevins (Guy), Charles Nolan (Fred).

A vice raid turns up a little black book that may contain the names of some influential customers.

CABLE DOES NOT PAY Airdate: 11/09/93.

Guest Cast: William H. Macy (Russell), Nancy Lenehan (Amy Baker), Allan Royal (President Childs), Kevin Page (Ken Fields), Lorna Scott (Operator #1), Christine Cavanaugh (Operator #2).

A disgruntled cable television customer holds the squad room hostage; Wade tries to get Paul to loosen up, both for their partnership and for Paul's own good.

GIFT, THE Airdate: 11/16/93.

Guest Cast: Joe Santos (Himself), Beth Grant (Donna Stiles), Lee Garlington (Judy Hampton), Mark Boone Junior (Ed), Norm Skaggs (Leo), John Bowman (The Perp).

When Joe Santos, co-star of the 1970s detective series *The Rockford Files*, has his car radio stolen while passing through town, the local boys in blue pressure him into helping them solve the crime.

PRESIDENT'S COMING, THE Airdate: 11/23/93.

Guest Cast: Willie Carpenter (Agent Wilder), Jeremy Roberts (Agent Ketron), Jim Haynie (Wallace), Janel Moloney (Sarah), Pat Crawford Brown (The Woman), Abe Adams (Paulie Gigante), Kristopher Logan (Brenner), Fred Pinkard (Chuck Lopez).

A presidential motorcade turns the department upside down, particularly when the police feel slighted by the Secret Service.

BULLET FOR STILES, A   Airdate: 11/30/93.
Guest Cast: Beth Grant (Donna Stiles), Jonathan Gries (Ray), Christine Estabrook (Mrs. Lester).

A paroled ex-con heads to Bakersfield seeking vengeance on the man who put him behind bars—Captain Stiles.

LUCKY 13   Airdates: 12/21/93, 8/25/94.
Guest Cast: Janel Moloney (Sarah), Melora Walters (Marnie Archer).

Suspended from the force, Denny is forced to sell underwear from his car.

ARMS AND THE MEN   Airdate: 7/07/94.
Guest Cast: Meagen Fay (Mrs. Selwyn), Tony Perez (Jerry Obstler), Karen Landry (Gail Boyer), Charles Noland (Fred), Anna Kerkorian (Opera Singer).

The city is up in arms when a severed limb is found in the city's water supply.

THERE GOES THE NEIGHBORHOOD
Airdate: 7/21/94.
Guest Cast: Brandon Maggart (Uncle Powell), Ramon Franco (Tom Tom), Shaun Baker (Zebra T), Jeff Norman (Cookie), Leslie Jones (Hakim), Tiny Ron (Indian), Jeanette O'Connor (Cousin Linda).

Denny isn't thrilled to hear that Paul is looking to buy a house in his neighborhood.

PSYCHIC AND THE C-CUP, THE   Airdate: 7/28/94.
Guest Cast: Jodie Markell (Brenda James), John Glen Bishop (Kyle Pruitt), Gloria Dorson (Shelly Krane), Jim Cody Williams (Roy).

The detectives turn to some unusual sources in their search for a missing psychic.

LAST ONE INTO THE WATER   Airdate: 8/18/94.
Guest Cast: Dan Castellaneta (Darian Ferguson), Tom Towles (Fireman Riley), Geraldine Farrell (Joanne Hibbler), Lorna Scott (Terry Croodell), Kathy Kinney (Mrs. Blaisher), John Voldstad (Suspect #1), Christopher Darga (Suspect #2), Patrick Dollaghan (Suspect #3), Rick Mansfield (Suspect #4), Tony Colitti (Suspect #5), Christopher Michael Moore (Fireman #1), Steve M. Porter (Max Davis), Doug Arnold (Prisoner).

Wade surprises Paul by revealing that he cares about people more than he admits. Denny gets an unexpected surprise after he picks an argument with the fire department.

The Sinbad Show

The runaway success of *Home Improvement* created a sudden new demand for stand-up comics. Disney joined in the frenzy and came up with *The Sinbad Show*, a new sitcom starring black comedian Sinbad (the professional name of comedian Sinbad Adkins).

The premise was that video game designer David Bryan decided that it was time to start acting more responsibly, and, in his case, have a family. Since he wasn't married and it didn't look like he would be in the near future, the answer to David's problem was to adopt two young children. The series thus focused on David's continuing attempts at both an adult social life and fatherhood.

The show was added to the Fox line-up for 1993–94 on Thursday night.

Series Cast: Sinbad (David Bryan), T.K. Carter (Clarence Hull), Salma Hayek (Gloria Contreras), Erin Davis (Zana Beckley), Willie Norwood (Little John/L.J. Beckley), Hal Williams (Rudy Bryan).

Production Notes:

- Salma Hayek was dropped after the fourth episode.
- Hal Williams was upgraded from guest star to the regular cast during the season.

Each of the episodes is described below, with the unaired episodes first and the regular episodes in airdate order.

PROMOTIONAL EPISODE   Airdate: Unaired.
Cast: Sinbad (David), Darryl Sivad (Marshall), Vanessa Bell Calloway (Sherry), Salma Hayek (Vivian), Lela Rochon (Denise), Erin Davis (Zane), Kyler Richie (Little John).

This was a brief test episode taped in May 1993. The part of Marshall was later dropped and the role of Little John recast before the series went into full production.

IN THE BEGINNING   Airdate: Unaired.
Regular Cast: Chaz Shepherd (Little John).
Guest Cast: Joan Pringle (Sherry), Edwina Moore (Woman #1), Michael Carrington (Voice Overs), Andrew Mark Berman (Steven), Lela Rochon (Denise), Nancy Lenehan (Marla).

In this version of the opening episode, two young orphaned siblings will have to be split up unless a home can be found for both of them.

PINCH SITTER   Airdate: Unaired.
Regular Cast: Chaz Shepherd (Little John).
Guest Cast: Andrew Mark Berman (Steven), Nancy Lenehan (Marla), Maggie Montgomery (Large Woman), Victoria Hoffman (Cindy), Mary Morrow (Sharon), Michael Carrington (Shaquile), Minnie Summers Lindsey (Mrs. Rhodes).

David learns how difficult it is to find a good babysitter.

SINBAD SHOW, THE (pilot)   Airdates: 9/16/93, 12/02/93.
Guest Cast: Wendy Raquel Robinson (Yvette), Lela Rochon (Denise), Lorraine Tousaint (Mrs. Alexandra Payton).

David Bryan, a foot-loose and care-free bachelor, meets two orphaned children and learns the authorities will have to split them up unless someone will adopt both of them.

TOOTH-FAIRY HAS LANDED, THE
Airdates: 9/23/93, 11/25/93.
When Zana loses a tooth and David tells her about the tooth fairy, L.J. tells David that he should be preparing her for the realities of life instead of making her believe in fairy tales.

PAR-TAY, THE   Airdates: 9/30/93, 1/20/94.
Guest Cast: Nancy Wilson (Louise Bryan), Rose Jackson (Ms. Page), Hal Williams (Rudy Williams), Terri J. Vaughn (Girl #1), Devika Parikh (Girl #2), Main Ingredient (Cuba Gooding, Sr., Tony Silvester, George Staley, Sr.).

David's parents want to take Zana and L.J. to Disneyland, but David will agree only if the kids have done their homework.

MY DAUGHTER'S KEEPER   Airdates: 10/07/93, 12/30/93.
Guest Cast: Vanessa Bell Calloway (Michelle Michaels), Terry Wills (Phil Coleman), Angelina Estrada (Woman), Eric Fleeks (Old Man).

David takes a class for working parents, but Clarence convinces him that the teacher's interest is more than professional.

PETTY LARCENY   Airdates: 10/14/93, 5/26/94.
Guest Cast: Sylver Gregory, Hal Williams (Rudy Bryan), Wendy Davis (Sandy), Don Dolan (Security Guard).

When David discovers that things are missing from the house, he accuses L.J. of taking them.

STRICTLY BUSINESS   Airdate: 10/21/93.
Guest Cast: Nancy Wilson (Louise Bryan), Natalia Venetia Belcon (Carey Lipton), Clifton Powell (Eddie Belk), Mari Morrow (Jasmine), Patty Toy (Hillary).

When an ex-girlfriend returns with a business proposition, David's parents warn that she is going to cause trouble.

DAVID'S VAN   Airdates: 11/04/93, 3/22/94.
Guest Cast: Nancy Wilson (Louise Bryan), Earl Billings (Car Salesman), Clifton Powell (Eddie Belk), Michole White (Roxanne), Ron O'Neal (Superfly), Yvonne Farrow (Chiffon), Rickey D'Shon Collins (Ziggy), Scott Randle (Ronnie).

David has a hard time dealing with the thought of trading in his car for a van, thinking that it will make him seem dull and unattractive.

DAVID GOES SKIING   Airdate: 11/11/93.
Guest Cast: Richard Frank (Mr. Lang), Clifton Powell (Eddie), Melissa DeSousa (Grace), Olivia Brown (Sharon), Rick Fitts (Chip), Hal Williams (Rudy Bryan), Amy Hunter (Glenda), Scott Randle (Ronnie).

David has a hard time enjoying his annual ski vacation when the kids keep calling him at the lodge.

SHADES OF ACCEPTANCE   Airdates: 11/18/93, 6/02/94.
Guest Cast: Nancy Wilson (Louise Bryan), Hal Williams (Rudy Bryan), Charles Brown (Joe), Tracy Douglas (Kathy), Jim Fyfe (Andre), William Hubbard Knight (Neil), Helena Reed (Marla), Christel Khalil (Crystal), Diahann Carroll (Mrs. Brooks), Robert Hooks (Mr. Brooks).

David enjoys making business connections at his new club until he discovers how bigoted some of the members are.

I COULDA BEEN THE MAN   Airdate: 12/09/93.
Guest Cast: Marques Johnson (Nelson Robinson), Shirley Hemphill (Mamie), Hal Williams (Rudy Bryan), Jeanine Michelle (Michelle), Christina Harley (Alexis), Tasha Smith (Chevette), Eartha Robinson (Porsche), Scott Randle (Ronnie), Adamah Taylor (Anthony).

David is upset when he learns that his father helped coach an old friend who is now a basketball star—and rich.

IT'S MY PARTY AND I'LL CRY IF I WANT TO   Airdates: 12/16/93, 6/26/94.

Guest Cast: Claudette Wells (Miss Davis), Deborah May (Buffy), Davida Williams (Frankie), Naya Rivera (Karen).

Zana wants her favorite television dinosaur at her birthday party and David does his best to accommodate her.

BREAKING THE PATTERN   Airdates: 1/06/94, 6/09/94.

Guest Cast: Nancy Wilson (Louise Bryan), Dawn Gardner (Donna Lee), Jamil Smith (Ernie), Jimmy Lee Newman (Chris), Rif Hutton (Mr. Lee), Candace Houston (Mrs. Lee).

L.J. gives in to temptation and invites his new girlfriend over when David is out of the house.

KEEP THE FAITH   Airdates: 1/13/94, 6/16/94.

Guest Cast: Nancy Wilson (Louise Bryan), Ken Page (Reverend Kingsley), Kym Whitley (Rose), Pamela Tyson (Norma), Michael Ralph (Peter), Lakesha Penn, Mara Brock (Angela), Charmaine N. Dixon (Katherine).

L.J. shocks David when he says he doesn't believe in God because his parents are dead.

DOG EPISODE, THE   Airdates: 1/27/94, 6/23/94.

Guest Cast: Lynn Manning (Donald), Marjean Holden (Gillian).

When the kids bring a large stray dog home with them, David is determined to find its owner.

MR. SCIENCE SHOW, THE   Airdates: 2/03/94, 7/07/94.

Guest Cast: Roxanne Beckford (Jackie Blanton), Lewis Dix (Roland Williams), Michael Ralph (Leon).

When the host of *It's Science Time*, a children's science show, comes down ill, David agrees to fill in for him.

BLACK HISTORY MONTH   Airdates: 2/10/94, 7/14/94.

Guest Cast: Sabrina Le Beauf (Alesia), Michael Ralph (Leon), Armelia McQueen (Miss Glidden), Leslie Redden (Pamela), Terrah (Linda), Marcus Paulk (Grady), Jeri Gray (Old Lady), Justin Cooper (Bus Driver).

Zana is cast as Rosa Parks in a school play but is afraid to speak on stage; L.J. doesn't want to work on his black history homework assignment.

TELETHON, THE   Airdates: 3/03/94, 7/28/94.

Guest Cast: Debbie Allen (Herself), Terry Bradshaw (Himself), Ice Cube (Himself), Jay Leno (Himself), Nancy Wilson (Louise Bryan), Pam Grier (Lynn Montgomery), Michael Ralph (Leon), Alan Toy (Henry).

David is thrilled to be asked to appear on a charity telethon until he learns he will only go on the air if someone else cancels.

NEIGHBORHOOD WATCH   Airdate: 3/10/94.

Guest Cast: Michael Ralph (Leon), Shashawnee Smith (Officer Lang), J.W. Smith (Chuck).

When L.J.'s bicycle and Rudy's stereo are stolen, David and Clarence decide to enroll in a neighborhood watch program, expecting to become crime fighters like David's hero Superfly.

LOVE LESSONS   Airdates: 3/17/94, 6/30/94.

Guest Cast: Rose Jackson (Miss Lauren Paige), Byron Stewart (Mercury Harris), Jimmy Lee Newman (Chris), Jamil Smith (Ernie), Marva Hicks (Rachel).

L.J. is doing poorly at school and David hires a tutor for him. It's not long before L.J. develops a crush on his teacher, but when she and David start dating, jealousy rears its ugly head.

CAN WE TALK?   Airdate: 3/22/94.

Guest Cast: Kenny "Babyface" Edmonds (Jerry), Alex Datcher (Sandra), Michael Ralph (Leon), Phil Proctor (Danny Brash), Shari Poindexter (Shari Warner), Jimmy Woodard (Man in Audience).

David and Clarence are tricked into having to defend their friendship on a television talk show.

FAMILY REUNION   Airdate: 3/31/94.

Guest Cast: Nancy Wilson (Louise Bryan), Lawanda Page (Aunt Lula Mae), Edye Byrd (Aunt Ruth), Lou Meyers (Uncle Luther), Michael Ralph (Leon), Montrose Hagins (Mama Saint), Michole White (Roxanne), Ernie Lee Banks (Uncle Bodell), Ellaraino (Pearl Lee), Cyrus Farmer (Tony), Senait (Gina), Tanya Brooks (Lulu).

David hosts the annual Bryan family reunion, which brings together a very unusual collection of relatives and friends.

ADOPTION—PART I   Airdate: 4/07/94.

Guest Cast: Kimberly Scott (Debra), William Allen Young (Curtis), Michael Ralph (Leon), Ellia English (Receptionist), Mary Valena Broussard (Palmer Girl).

David's adoption of L.J. and Zana runs into a snag when the new social services manager disapproves of the way he is handling the kids.

ADOPTION—PART DEUX   Airdate: 4/14/94.

Guest Cast: Nancy Wilson (Louise Bryan), Roger E. Mosley (Sergeant Al Beckley), Kimberly Scott (Debra), Michael Ralph (Leon), Bianca Taylor (Mrs. Beckley), Susan Beaubian (Vanessa), Anna Slotky (Lee), John Freeland, Jr. (Un-Hip Man).

It looks like L.J. and Zana will have to move to New Jersey with some distant relatives, but all ends well when everyone agrees that David can adopt the kids.

GIRLS UNDA-HOODZ   Airdate: 4/21/94.

Guest Cast: Michael Ralph (Leon), Michole White (Roxanne), Simbi Khali (Carmen), Kimberly Brooks (Micki), Patrice Chanel (Claudette), Trina McGee-Davis (Faith), Monique Peek (Bernice), Jeff Lee (Darnell), Tanya Brooks (Lulu).

David takes Zana to the beauty parlor and isn't happy with the results. A bigger problem awaits at home, though, for Clarence gave L.J. his first driving lesson and the car is in the living room.

Boy Meets World

The sitcom *Boy Meets World* began when series creator Michael Jacobs met with ABC executives to propose a series based on the viewpoint of a young boy.

The series centers on the trials and tribulations of Cory Matthews, an 11-year-old student who has to deal with the fact that his most-disliked teacher in the sixth grade, Mr. Feeny, is also his next-door neighbor.

Boy Meets World joined the ABC Friday line-up for the 1993–94 season. Positive reviews and audience reaction led to a renewal for the 1994–95 year. Cory advanced in age between years from 11 to 13, which allowed him to move to the same school as his older brother.

Series Cast: Ben Savage (Cory Matthews), William Daniels (Mr. Feeny), Betsy Randle (Amy Matthews), Will Friedle (Eric Matthews), Rider Strong (Shawn Hunter), Danielle Fishel (Topanga Lawrence; 1994–96), Lee Norris (Stuart Minkus; 1993–94), Lily Nicksay (Morgan Matthews), Alex Désert (Eli; 1995–96), Anthony Tyler Quinn (Jonathan Turner; 1994–96), William Russ (Alan Matthews).

Each of the episodes is described below in airdate order.

1993–94 season

BOY MEETS WORLD (pilot)   Airdates: 9/24/93, 12/24/93.

Guest Cast: Chauncey Leopardi (Nicholas), Cynthia Mace (Evelyn), Krystin Moore (Vanessa).

Cory gets detention for listening to a baseball game on the radio instead of Feeny's lecture on *Romeo and Juliet*.

ON THE FENCE   Airdates: 10/01/93, 12/31/93.

Guest Cast: DeJuan Guy (Ellis).

Cory takes a shortcut while painting Feeny's fence that results in even more work than he had planned.

FATHER KNOWS LESS   Airdates: 10/08/93, 1/21/94.

Guest Cast: Willie Garson (Lenny Spinelli), Thomas Brown IV (T.V. Announcer).

Alan and Feeny get into an argument when Feeny refuses to let Cory take a make-up test.

CORY'S ALTERNATIVE FRIENDS   Airdates: 10/15/93, 2/18/94, 7/01/94.

Guest Cast: Marla Sokoloff (Paige), Danielle Fishel (Topanga Lawrence), Megan Parlen (Barbara).

Cory decides to hang out with the school nerds when his friends make fun of his new haircut.

KILLER BEES   Airdates: 10/22/93, 3/04/94.

Guest Cast: DeJuan Guy (Ellis), Nikki Cox (Heather), Gisele MacKenzie (Loudspeaker Voice), Branelle Dahl (Contestant #5), Laurel Diskin (Contestant #6), Thomas Brown IV (Announcer Ed), Tom Kelly (Announcer John).

Cory bribes Feeny's star pupil so he can take his place in a spelling bee, for he has his eyes on the prize of bat boy at the World Series.

BOYS II MENSA   Airdates: 10/29/93, 3/18/94.

Guest Cast: Jane Carr (Mrs. Bertram), Marty York (Costumed Kid #1), Sam Horrigan (Costumed Kid #2), Dusty Gould (Costumed Kid #3).

When Cory gets a spectacular grade by cheating on a test, Feeny plans to enroll him in a class for gifted students.

GRANDMA WAS A ROLLING STONE   Airdates: 11/12/93, 4/22/94.

Guest Cast: Keri Russell (Jessica), Rue McClanahan (Bernice Matthews).

Cory becomes disappointed in his grandmother when she makes a promise she can't keep.

TEACHER'S BET   Airdates: 11/19/93, 4/08/94.

Guest Cast: Danielle Fishel (Topanga Lawrence), Lindsay Price (Linda).

Cory gets a new appreciation of teachers when he loses a bet with Feeny and has to teach class for a week.

CLASS PRE-UNION   Airdates: 11/26/93, 4/15/94.

Guest Cast: Jim Abbott (Himself), Danielle Fishel (Topanga Lawrence), Christine Healy (Jane), Marty York (Larry), Brittany English Stephens (Stephanie), Kristopher Kyer (TV Voice), Lisa E. Wilcox (TV Voice), Matt Kirkwood (TV Voice).

Feeny belittles Cory's career choice as a baseball player until Alan arranges for a surprise visit from New York Yankee pitcher Jim Abbott.

SANTA'S LITTLE HELPER   Airdates: 12/10/93, 7/15/94.

Guest Cast: Danielle Fishel (Topanga Lawrence), Tom LaGrua (Elf).

Shawn's father loses his job so Cory decides to make sure his friend gets a present for Christmas.

FATHER/SON GAME, THE   Airdate: 12/17/93.

Guest Cast: Danielle Fishel (Topanga Lawrence), Willie Garson (Lenny Spinelli).

Cory and Eric try to find a way out of a father–son baseball game.

ONCE IN LOVE WITH AMY   Airdates: 1/07/94, 6/10/94.

Guest Cast: Danielle Fishel (Topanga Lawrence).

Cory and Eric are surprised to learn that their mother has a secret interest in dancing.

SHE LOVES ME, SHE LOVES ME NOT   Airdates: 1/14/94, 6/24/94.

Guest Cast: Danielle Fishel (Topanga Lawrence), Krystee Clark (Nebula), Breanne O'Donnell.

Much to Cory's displeasure, Topanga develops a crush on Eric.

B-TEAM OF LIFE, THE   Airdates: 1/28/94, 7/08/94.

Guest Cast: Ahmad Stoner (Harris), Hugh Dane (Coach), Phil Proctor (T.V. Voice), Robert Clotworthy (T.V. Voice).

Cory doesn't take being rejected for the school basketball team very well.

MODEL FAMILY   Airdates: 2/04/94, 7/22/94.

Guest Cast: Danielle Fishel (Topanga Lawrence), Jason Marsden (Jason), Kelly Packard (Kelly), Stephanie Dicker (Erin), Matt Kirkwood (Photographer), Kristopher Kyer (Mall Announcer), Kathy Ireland (Alexis).

Eric falls in love with an older woman who convinces him he should be a male model.

RISKY BUSINESS   Airdates: 2/11/94, 7/29/94.

Guest Cast: Danielle Fishel (Topanga Lawrence), Thomas Brown IV (Sports Announcer), Trevor Denman (Track Announcer).

Cory and Eric learn that betting on the races is a risky proposition at best.

FUGITIVE, THE   Airdates: 2/25/94, 6/03/94.

Guest Cast: Danielle Fishel (Topanga Lawrence).

Shawn goes on the run when a prank goes awry and he worries about how his parents will react.

IT'S A WONDERFUL NIGHT   Airdates: 3/11/94, 8/05/94.

Guest Cast: Don Gibb (Tony), Jason Marsden (Jason), Kelly Packard (Kelly), Stephanie Dicker (Erin).

Cory and Shawn have to change their plans for a big night when Feeny fills in for their babysitter.

KID GLOVES   Airdates: 3/25/94, 8/12/94.

Guest Cast: Danielle Fishel (Topanga Lawrence).

Cory loses Alan's prized medal that he won in a boxing competition.

PLAY'S THE THING, THE   Airdates: 4/29/94, 8/19/94.

Guest Cast: Danielle Fishel (Topanga Lawrence), Ryan Tomlinson (Spear Carrier).

A less-than-masculine costume makes Cory drop out of the school production of *Hamlet*.

BOY MEETS GIRL   Airdates: 5/06/94, 9/02/94.

Guest Cast: Danielle Fishel (Topanga Lawrence), Breanne O'Donnell (Hilary), Gisele MacKenzie (Narrator Voice), Gil Stratton Jr. (TV Announcer).

Cory feels left out when Shawn starts spending time with a new girlfriend.

I DREAM OF FEENY   Airdates: 5/13/94, 8/26/94.

Guest Cast: Danielle Fishel (Topanga Lawrence), Janet Carroll (Nurse Jill), Juliette Jeffers (Karen Chase).

Cory feels guilty for wishing that Feeny would get sick when the teacher ends up in the hospital.

1994–95 season

BACK 2 SCHOOL   Airdates: 9/23/94, 12/02/94.

Guest Cast: Danny McNulty (Harley), Kevin West (Mr. Stimpleman), Lorna Scott (Nurse), Jonathan Charles Kaplan (Herbert), Blake Soper (Joey), Ethan Suplee (Frank), Luke Jackson (Lemke), Marguerite Moreau (Gail), Jeremy Wieand (Alvin), Christine Camille Wilson (Harley's Girl).

Cory's enjoyment of his move up to high school suffers when a bully picks on him and he learns that Feeny is the new acting principal.

PAIRING OFF   Airdates: 9/30/94, 12/30/94.

Guest Cast: Nancy Valen (Ms. Kelly), Jessica Wesson (Wendy), Marguerite Morea (Rebecca), Molly Morgan (Jacqueline), Hillary Tuck (Samantha), Hunter Garner (Peter).

When his friends all get girlfriends, Cory asks Eric for some advice on attracting the opposite sex.

NOTORIOUS   Airdates: 10/07/94, 1/20/95.

Guest Cast: Danny McNulty (Harley), Jason Marsden (Jason), Sydney Bennett (Desiree), Blake Soper (Joey), Jill Novick (Molly), Ethan Suplee (Frank), Bob Larkin (Janitor Bud), Joni Allen (Senior Girl #1).

Cory takes the blame for one of Shawn's pranks and is surprised that Feeny respects him for standing up for a friend.

ME AND MR. JOAD   Airdates: 10/14/94, 3/17/95.

Guest Cast: Sydney Bennett (Desiree), Jason Marsden (Jason).

A broken promise about a test finds Cory leading a walkout at school.

UNINVITED, THE   Airdates: 10/21/94, 6/09/95.

Guest Cast: Danny McNulty (Harley), Jonathan Charles Kaplan (Simon), Blake Soper (Joey), Ethan Suplee (Frank), Jessica Bowman (Jennifer), Phillip Glasser (Ubaldo), Luke Jackson (Alvin), Nick Banko (Boy #1), Joshua Wiener (Boy #2), Melissa DeLizia (Girl #1).

Cory tries to fit in with the most popular kids at school and learns a valuable lesson about friendship in the process.

WHO'S AFRAID OF CORY WOLF   Airdates: 10/28/94, 6/30/95.

Guest Cast: Don Calfa (Frank), Phyllis Diller (Madame Ouspenskaya).

Cory has a hard time dealing with the onset of puberty.

WAKE UP, LITTLE CORY   Airdates: 11/04/94, 5/26/96.

Guest Cast: Danny McNulty (Harley), Blake Soper (Joey), Bob Larkin (Janitor Bud).

Cory gets a new appreciation of the classics when he discovers that Shakespeare's works are still relevant today.

BAND ON THE RUN   Airdates: 11/11/94, 6/02/95.

Guest Cast: Mickey Dolenz (Norm), Rick Nielsen (Gordy), Billy Vera (Larry), Jhoanna Trias (Sonia), Jewelie Hull (Sherry), Rembrandt (Scream), Adam Scott (Senior), Matthew Stephen Lie (Thor), Andrew Fuentes (Flip).

Cory is relieved to learn that Topanga still likes him after he gets caught in a lie.

FEAR STRIKES OUT   Airdates: 11/18/94, 6/16/95.

Guest Cast: Danny McNulty (Harley), Blake Soper (Joey), Ethan Suplee (Frankie), Darlene Vogel (Katherine Thompkins), David Grieco (Donovan), Benny Grant (John).

Cory suffers a setback in his love life when he again takes advice from Eric.

SISTER THERESA   Airdates: 11/25/94, 6/23/95.
Guest Cast: Danny McNulty (Harley), Blake Soper (Joey), Danielle Harris (Theresa), Ethan Suplee (Frankie), Herschel Sparber (Delivery Guy).
Cory learns that it takes more than good manners to be a gentleman.

BEARD, THE   Airdates: 12/09/94, 7/07/95.
Guest Cast: Blake Soper (Joey), John Capodice (Chubbie), Lenny Wolpe (Car Dealer), Ethan Suplee (Frank), Haylie Johnson (Linda), Molly Morgan (Stacy), Joshua Wiener (Roy).
Cory finally develops some confidence with the fairer sex.

TURNAROUND   Airdates: 12/16/94, 12/29/95.
Guest Cast: Darlene Vogel (Katherine Thompkins), Natanya Ross (Ingrid), Marne Patterson (Allison), Jennifer Banko (Becky), Will Estes (Alex), Nick Banko (Boy).
A plan to take a popular girl to the school dance goes very much awry.

CYRANO   Airdates: 1/06/95, 7/14/95.
Guest Cast: Danny McNulty (Harley), Blake Soper (Joey), Ethan Suplee (Frankie), Mathea Webb (Gloria).
A love triangle develops when Cory tries to play Cupid.

I AM NOT A CROOK   Airdate: 1/13/95.
Guest Cast: Jonathan Charles Kaplan (Alvin), Shay Astar (Paula), Brandon Adams (Alex), Anndi McAfee (Jennifer).
Cory almost lets some new-found influence go to his head.

BREAKING UP IS REALLY, REALLY, REALLY HARD TO DO   Airdates: 1/27/95, 7/21/95.
Guest Cast: Jason Marsden (Jason), Jessica Wesson (Wendy), Katy Barnhill (Lori), Katie Jane Johnston (Bonnie), Musetta Vander (Dominique).
Sometimes it's easier to get into a relationship than to get out of it.

DANGER BOY   Airdate: 2/03/95.
Guest Cast: Monty Hoffman (Chubbie), Kathy Kinney (Rifkin), McNally Sagal (Trisha Stone), Heidi Lucas (Kim), Terry Crisp (Elvis), Mena Suvari (Laura), Phillip Simon (Rodique), Harley Zumbrum (Swindell).
Tired of being thought of as "good and safe," Cory opts for a new image.

ON THE AIR   Airdates: 2/10/95, 7/28/95.
Guest Cast: Jonathan Charles Kaplan (Alvin), Hillary Tuck (Sarah), Justin Thomson (Ludwig), Laurie Fortier (Jasmine), Grant Gelt (Spencer), Robin Leach (Himself).
A few mischosen words provide a valuable lesson about free speech.

BY HOOK OR BY CROOK   Airdates: 2/17/95, 8/04/95.
Guest Cast: Jason Marsden (Jason), Herschel Sparber (Uncle Mike), Terri Ivens (Torie).
Eric has to chose between his summer vacation plans and his personal integrity.

WRONG SIDE OF THE TRACKS   Airdates: 2/24/95, 8/11/95.
Guest Cast: Jason Marsden (Jason), Blake Soper (Joey), Ethan Suplee (Frankie), Kenny Johnston (Harley), Krystee Clark (Valerie), Becky Herbst (Jill), Shay Astar (Mindy), Nancy Kerrigan (Herself).
Cory helps Shawn realize that his actions are more important than his background.

POP QUIZ   Airdates: 3/10/95, 8/18/95.
Guest Cast: Blake Soper (Joey), Ethan Suplee (Frankie), Adam Scott (Griff), Susan Knight (Miss Gill), Laurie Fortier (Jasmine), Eric Balfour (Tommy).
Cory and Shawn take shortcuts with their homework and realize that it might have been smarter to study.

THRILLA IN PHILA, THE   Airdates: 5/05/95, 8/25/95.
Guest Cast: Robert Goulet (Himself), Leon White (Vader), Blake Soper (Joey), Yasmine Bleeth (Herself), Adam Scott (Griff), Ethan Suplee (Frankie), Jared Murphy (Matt), Charles Carpenter (Savage), Kelly Packard (Candy).
A few white lies make Cory seem more important than he really is.

CAREER DAY   Airdates: 5/12/95, 9/01/95.
Guest Cast: Jason Marsden (Jason), Blake Clark (Chet), Darlene Vogel (Katherine Thompkins), Peter Tork (Jedediah), Will Estes (Alex).

Cory discovers that a person's worth comes more from his actions than what he does for a living.

HOME   Airdates: 5/19/95, 9/15/95.
Guest Cast: Jason Marsden (Jason), Blake Clark (Chet), Darlene Vogel (Katherine Thompkins), Ivory Ocean (Policeman).
Shawn has to find somewhere to live when his parents abandon him.

1995–96 season

MY BEST FRIEND'S GIRL   Airdates: 9/22/95, 12/29/95.
Guest Cast: Blake Soper (Joey), Brittany Murphy (Trini), Ethan Suplee (Frankie).
It takes more trouble than he originally planned, but Cory and Topanga finally get together.

DOUBLE LIE, THE   Airdates: 9/29/95, 3/01/96.
Guest Cast: Erin J. Dean (Veronica), Lisa Wilcox (Kris).
Shawn and Jonathan both learn that lies can damage even a strong friendship.

WHAT I MEANT TO SAY   Airdates: 10/13/95, 5/24/96.
Guest Cast: Anastasia Horne (Christi).
Cory professes his love for Topanga but isn't prepared for her reaction.

HE SAID, SHE SAID   Airdates: 10/20/95, 5/31/96.
Guest Cast: Danny McNulty (Harley), Blake Soper (Joey), Amy Leland (Devon), Adam Scott (Griff), Ethan Suplee (Frankie), Carmen Filipi (Bum).
Shawn decides that it would be easier to run away than work harder at school.

HOMETOWN HERO   Airdates: 10/27/95, 6/07/96.
Guest Cast: Deborah Harmon (Connie), Bob Larkin (Janitor Bud), Jim Jansen (Dr. Sorrell), Michael Haniff (Tommy), Joey Gaynor (Crew Guy), Yolanda Gaskins (Sharon).
Cory takes the undeserved credit for saving the school from a fire.

THIS LITTLE PIGGY   Airdates: 11/03/95, 6/14/96.
Guest Cast: Richard Karn (Victor).
Shawn adopts an abandoned piglet but Topanga doesn't think he should keep his new pet.

TRUTH AND CONSEQUENCES   Airdates: 11/10/95, 6/21/96.
Guest Cast: Blake Soper (Joey), Kathy Trageser (Monique), Bob Larkin (Janitor Bud).
Cory and Shawn learn that sometimes there is a price to be paid for telling the truth.

RAVE ON   Airdates: 11/17/95, 6/28/96.
Guest Cast: Micky Dolenz (Gordy), Davy Jones (Reginald), Peter Tork (Jedidiah), Ethan Suplee (Frankie), Dave Madden (Madden), Veronica De la Cruz (Marisa).
Eric and Cory end up creating a very strange anniversary party for their parents.

LAST TEMPTATION OF CORY, THE   Airdate: 12/01/95.
Guest Cast: Brittany Murphy (Trini), Elisabeth Harnois (Missy), Gil Stratton (Announcer), Lindsey McKeon (Libby), Andrew Magarian (Bagwell).
Cory finds that quite a few other girls are interested in him now that he is dating Topanga.

TRAIN OF FOOLS   Airdates: 12/15/95, 7/05/96.
Guest Cast: Angela Visser (Rebecca-Alexa), Wendy Pitts (Janine), Brooke Theiss Genesse (Valerie), Wesley Jonathan (T.J.), Dawn Maxey (Lynn), Charisma Carpenter (Caterer).
A broken-down subway car makes for less than an enjoyable New Year's Eve.

CITY SLACKERS   Airdate: 1/05/96, 7/12/96.
Guest Cast: Blake Soper (Joey), Troy Evans (Ranger Mark), Ethan Suplee (Frankie), Julie Benz (Bianca).
Cory and Shawn slip away to the countryside, where they discover an unlikely friend—Mr. Feeny.

GRASS IS ALWAYS GREENER, THE   Airdates: 1/12/96, 7/19/96.
Guest Cast: Jim Jansen (Dr. Sorrell), Aeryk Egan (Brent), Marisa Theodore (Tara), Mena Suvari (Hilary).
Cory and Topanga have second thoughts and call off their relationship.

NEW FRIENDS AND OLD   Airdate: 1/19/96.
Guest Cast: Leon Allen White (Frankie, Sr.), Eliza Coyle (Melanie), Ethan Suplee (Frankie), Adam Wylie (Robert).
Cory and Shawn make a new friend at school, while Jonathan is busy getting reacquainted with an old girlfriend.

KISS IS MORE THAN A KISS, A   Airdates: 1/26/96, 4/19/96.

Guest Cast: Lindsay Ridgeway (Morgan), Anndi McAfee (Melissa), Adena Panella (Katie), Sadie Kratzig (Felicia), Shane West (Nick).

Cory finds that it will be harder getting over Topanga than he thought.

HEART IS A LONELY HUNTER, THE
Airdates: 2/02/96, 7/26/96.

Guest Cast: Brandon Maggart (Pat), Larisa Oleynik (Dana), Kimberly Scott (Sonja), Lindsay Ridgeway (Morgan), Danny Strong (Arthur).

Shawn gets some lessons on his love life from Cory and his other friends.

STORMY WEATHER   Airdates: 2/09/96, 8/02/96.

Guest Cast: Brandon Maggart (Pat), Larisa Oleynik (Dana), Rosalind Allen (Susan), John O'Hurley (Cal), Lindsay Ridgeway (Morgan), Matt Kirkwood (Stage Manager).

Eric's popularity as a weather reporter proves to be as fickle as the weather itself.

PINK FLAMINGO KID, THE   Airdates: 2/16/96, 8/09/96.

Guest Cast: Herschel Sparber (Uncle Mike), Maury Sterling (Eddie), Blake Foster (Danny).

Cory gets a new appreciation of Shawn's life as he videotapes his friend as a birthday present for Shawn's father.

LIFE LESSONS   Airdates: 2/23/96, 8/16/96.

Guest Cast: Lisa Akey (Brenda), Aaron Michael Metchik (Jake), Patrick Renna (Kyle), Ian Bohen (Denny), Anastasia Horne (Christy).

Cory and Shawn learn that Feeny was right about the importance of studying.

I WAS A TEENAGE SPY   Airdates: 4/26/96, 8/23/96.

Guest Cast: Tom Bosley (Himself), Pat Morita (Himself), Anson Williams (Himself), Lindsay Ridgeway (Morgan), Christopher Darga (Counterman), Don Sparks (Deputy).

When Cory gets an electric shock, he thinks he's back in the 1950s, where his talk about the future finds him labeled as a communist.

I NEVER SANG FOR MY LEGAL GUARDIAN   Airdates: 5/03/96, 8/30/96.

Guest Cast: Blake Clark (Chet), Bobbie Phillips (Louanne), Bobby Jacoby (Jeff), Frank Novak (Desk Sergeant), Cindy A. Lora (Anita).

Shawn finally succeeds in finding his missing father.

HAPPIEST SHOW ON EARTH, THE
Airdates: 5/10/96, 9/13/96.

Guest Cast: Andrew Keegan (Ronnie), Hillary Tuck (Kristen), Lindsay Ridgeway (Morgan), Staci Keanan (Dana), Debbe Dunning (Alexandra).

When Topanga wins a trip to Walt Disney World, Cory and Shawn follow her, then have to find her somewhere in the huge complex.

BROTHER, BROTHER   Airdates: 5/17/96, 9/13/96.

Guest Cast: Lindsay Ridgeway (Morgan).

Cory feels left out when Shawn and Topanga say they have plans for the summer and Eric announces he is going to leave home for college.

The Good Life

John Bowman is a middle-class working man who tries to get a piece of "the good life" for his family. He was the assistant manager at Honest Abe Security Products, a lock distribution warehouse in Chicago.

Thirteen episodes were filmed and the series was added to the NBC line-up as a mid-season replacement for the 1993–94 season.

Series Cast: John Caponera (John Bowman), Eve Gordon (Maureen Bowman), Drew Carey (Drew Clark), Jake Patellis (Paul Bowman), Shay Astar (Melissa Bowman), Justin Berfield (Bob Bowman), Monty Hoffman (Tommy Bartlett).

PAUL DATES A BUDDHIST (OR) THE ZEN COMMANDMENTS   Airdate: 1/03/94.

Guest Cast: Dah-ve Chodan (Lila), Paul Feig (Video Clerk), Ralph Ahn (Shaolin Priest), Foster (Kirby), Lynsey Barilson, Sheryl Bernstein, Ethan Glasser, Randy Rudy.

John gets a shock when his son, Paul, dates a Buddhist and decides to change to her religion.

MAUREEN'S PLAY (OR) SOMETHING OLD, SOMETHING NUDE   Airdate: 1/04/94.

Guest Cast: Laura Innes (Actress), Daniel O'Callaghn (King Arthur), Renee Parent (Attractive Woman), Foster (Kirby).

When Maureen's production of *Camelot* is a disaster, she creates her own play, *The Cycle of Womanhood*, a steamy tale that starts neighborhood tongues wagging.

GOOD LIFE, THE (pilot)   Airdate: 1/11/94.

Guest Cast: C.C. Pulitzer (Lynette), Donna Wilson (Motorcycle Girl), Foster (Kirby).

Hoping to teach Paul some responsibility, John tells his son he will have to work at the warehouse after school. Unfortunately, Paul screws up and the place is robbed.

JOHN HURTS HIS LEG (OR) TALES FROM THE CRIP   Airdate: 1/18/94.

Guest Cast: Ralph Ahn (Mr. Huang), Dave Adams (Dr. Madison), Max Goldblatt (Billy), Sean Babb (Frank), Andrew J. Ferchland (Andy), Tonya Offer (Heather), Richard Improta (Announcer), Adam West (Himself), Foster (Kirby).

John hurts his leg playing ball and is upset to find that he'll have to stay in a cast for the next 10 weeks.

STATUE, THE (OR) ROCK AND A HARD PLACE, A   Airdate: 1/30/94.

Guest Cast: Mario Rocuzzo (Charlie Donnetti), Marla Adams (Kate Donnetti), Foster (Kirby).

John and Drew don't know how to tell their boss they destroyed an expensive statue at his house.

CALENDAR GIRL (OR) SEX, LIES, AND FIRE SAFETY   Airdate: 2/01/94.

Guest Cast: Sherrie Rose (Phoebe), Foster (Kirby).

John, Drew, and Tommy decide that Paul is old enough to join them when they go to watch a model at work.

SHE SHOOTS, SHE SCORES (OR) WHY CAN'T WE ALL JUST GET ALONG   Airdate: 2/01/94.

Guest Cast: Ron Dean (Red O'Donnell), Bob Delegall (Charles Stowe), Cela Wise (Helen), Jack Kenny (Arty Guy), Art Chudubala (Kim), Dwayne L. Barnes (Tim), Foster (Kirby).

The star of Maureen's new commercial turns out to be an obnoxious bigot.

JOHN TAKES OUT MELISSA (OR) MISERY DATE   Airdate: 3/15/94.

Guest Cast: Foster (Kirby), Paul Feig (Waiter), Jeff Robinson (Donny), Richard Lee Jackson (David).

John realizes that he has to stop treating Melissa like a little girl.

JOHN FIGHTS THE SYSTEM (OR) RUBBLE WITHOUT A CAUSE   Airdate: 3/15/94.

Guest Cast: William Schallert (Judge Milligan), John Mulrooney (Officer Siminski), Jimmy Danelli (Criminal), Brandon Rane (Stoner Kid), Foster (Kirby).

John tries to fight a ticket for littering but runs afoul of a very strict judge.

BOB'S FIELD TRIP   Airdate: 3/22/94.

Guest Cast: J. Trevor Edmond (Mark), Eden Atwood (Miss Cole), Ramsey Krull (Smart Aleck Kid), Glynis K. McCants (Ice Cream Woman), Foster (Kirby).

John doesn't know how to explain his job to Bob's visiting school class without sounding boring.

MELISSA THE THIEF (OR) THE MINX STOLE   Airdate: 3/29/94.

Guest Cast: Taylor Fry (Jennifer), Philip Baker Hall (Mr. Humphreys), Monica Huart (Salesgirl), Nick Oleson (Arm Wrestling Opponent), J.J. Smith (Announcer Voice-over), Foster (Kirby).

When John discovers that Maureen has been shoplifting, he does his best to find a way to make sure she'll never do it again.

MOTHER IN LAW (OR) THREE MEN AND A LITTLE OLD LADY   Airdate: 4/05/94.

Guest Cast: Foster (Kirby), Betty Garrett (Phyllis), Robert Barry Fleming (Vendor), Lori Hall (Woman #2), Lynn Ann Leveridge (Woman #1).

John tries to get closer to his mother-in-law by taking her to a baseball game.

JOHN'S NEW ASSISTANT (OR) TOMMY, TOMMY, TOMMY'S IN LOVE   Airdate: 4/12/94.

Guest Cast: Becky Thyre (Mary-Lou), Robert Clohessy (Joe), Foster (Kirby).

Tommy is infatuated with John's new assistant, but Drew thinks she is hiding something about her past.

Monty

As radio talk shows, especially those with conservative hosts, became popular across the country, it was inevitable that someone would use the concept for a television series. This was the basis for *Monty*, a comeback attempt for actor Henry Winkler.

The series premise was that Monty Richardson was the ultra-conservative host of *Righttalk*, a cable television talk show on Long Island. This allowed Monty to come into conflict with a steady stream of guests with opposing viewpoints, as well as engaging in arguments with his more liberal family.

The Fox network decided to pick up the series and *Monty* was slotted as a mid-season replacement at 8:00 P.M. on Tuesday for the 1993–94 season.

Series Cast: Henry Winkler (Monty Richardson), Kate Burton (Fran Richardson), David Krumholtz (David Richardson), David Schwimmer (Greg Richardson), China Kantner (Geena Campbell), Tom McGowan (Clifford Walker), Joyce Guy (Rita Simon).

Each of the episodes is described below in airdate order. Additionally, several episodes were produced but not aired, and are listed in production order.

MONTY (pilot)   Airdate: Unaired.

Cast: Henry Winkler (Monty Richardson), Kate Burton (Fran Richardson), Noëlle Parker (Arlene Richardson), David Krumholtz (David Richardson), Cynthia Nixon (Vivian Campbell), Tom McGowan (Clifford Walker), Joyce Guy (Rita Simon). *Guest Cast:* Alan Blumenfeld (Jerry), Tim Russ (Man #1), Eda Zahl (Woman #1).

A major focus of this unaired pilot was Monty's problem in dealing with his daughter, Arlene, an avowed lesbian.

HERE COMES THE SON   Airdate: 1/11/94.

Guest Cast: Thora Birch (Ann Sherman).

Monty receives two shocks when his older son, Greg, returns home from 6 months in Europe. Greg decided to become a vegetarian chef instead of a lawyer; he also got engaged to a very unconventional woman.

SON ALSO RISES, THE   Airdate: 1/18/94.

Guest Cast: Charlotte Booker (Lillian Erickson), Erin J. Dean (Lisa Erickson).

When Monty discovers a condom in his younger son's room, he gets upset and makes teenage sex the subject of his next radio show.

EAST SIDE STORY   Airdate: 1/25/94.

Guest Cast: Haunani Minn (Janet Chow), Michelle Wong (Gong Chow).

David finally gets a date for the school dance but Monty ruins the evening when he has an argument with the girl's mother.

TWO COLD FEET   Airdate: 2/01/94.

Guest Cast: Julie Dretzin (Jill), Jim Labriola (Tommy), Hillary Danner (Sandra), Tom Chick (Beck), Bob Glouberman (Rappaport), Baillie Gerstein (Customer).

Monty's the only one happy to see the return of Greg's conservative ex-girlfriend, for he hopes this will lead to the end of Geena.

BABY TALK   Airdate: 2/08/94.

Guest Cast: Michael Tucci (Dr. Rubin), Sherilyn Wolter (TV Wife).

Monty's ill-chosen comments when Fran thinks she might be pregnant result in a trip to a marriage counselor.

PRINCIPAL'S INTEREST, THE   Airdate: 2/15/94.

Guest Cast: Marcus Giamatti (Principal Newell), Jason Bennett (Josh), Rae Ven Kelly (Tina), Ramsey Krull (Steve).

Monty heads for the school seeking justice when he discovers that the principal has been putting the moves on Fran.

WILD, WILD WILLY AND HIS O.K. CORRAL, OR THERE GOES THE G.L.A.A.D. AWARD   Airdate: Unaired.

Guest Cast: Max Wright (Wild, Wild Willy), Julie Payne (Sister Stigmata), Mark Roberts (Sweetback), Sarah Rush (Psychic), Joshua Cadman (Stagehand), Diane Racine (Vegetarian), Jane Kaczmarek (Nickerson).

Monty starts a slanderous campaign to knock a children's show off the air so he can get its time slot.

MY DAD COULD BEAT UP YOUR DAD   Airdate: Unaired.

Guest Cast: Micky Dolenz (Eli Campbell), Martha Hackett (Elenor), Vincent Ventresca (Reporter).

Monty surprises everyone, including himself, when he helps Geena in an argument with her father.

EGGHEADS   Airdate: Unaired.

Guest Cast: Harriet Sansom Harris (Mrs. King), Jack Black (Doug), Doris Grau (Elsa).

Monty and Geena both enroll in an adult education course to earn their high school diplomas and start cheating to earn better grades than each other.

BROTHER OF THE BRIDE, THE   Airdate: Unaired.

Guest Cast: Mary Beth Hurt (Adelaide), Annabelle Gurwitch (Lee), Nan Martin (Lois).

Monty doesn't know how to act when he learns that his sister is marrying another woman.

THOSE WHO CAN'T TEACH, TEACH GYM AT DAVID'S SCHOOL   Airdate: Unaired.
Guest Cast: Jason Marsden (Mark Cohen), Lee Arenberg (Coach Wilson), Patrick LaBrecque (Karl Strauss).

Monty tries to help David overcome his fear of wrestling class.

DEATH IN PLAINVIEW   Airdate: Unaired.
Guest Cast: Edie McClurg (God), Brian George (Dr. Nizam), Daniel Passer (Zimmer), Susan Knight (Manager), Pat Millicano (Bob).

A health scare makes Monty question his mortality and life style.

Thunder Alley

Thunder Alley is the name of Gil Jones's garage in Indiana. His daughter, Bobbi, has ideas on how to raise the children that differ greatly from those of the traditional and conservative Gil.

The series began its run as a replacement for the 1993–94 series, but right from the start it lost a considerable percentage of the lead-in audience. After 2 months on the air, the series was yanked for retooling.

The series returned to the air on 3/07/95, but ratings continued to be poor, and the series left the air before the end of the season.

Series Cast: Edward Asner (Gil Jones), Diane Venora (Bobbi Jones; 1993–94), Robin Riker (Bobbi Jones; 1994–95), Jim Beaver (Leland DuParte), Kelly Vint (Claudine Turner), Lindsay Felton (Jenny Turner), Haley Joel Osment (Harry Turner), Andrew Keegan (Jack Kelly).

Each of the episodes is described below in airdate order.

1993–94 season

PROTOTYPE, THE (pilot)   Airdate: 3/09/94.
Guest Cast: Ritch Brinkley (Walter), Wayne Wilderson (Mike).

Retired stock car racer "Wild" Gil Jones finds his life turned upside down when his recently divorced daughter moves in with her three children.

LOVE TRIANGLE, THE   Airdates: 3/16/94, 8/10/94.
Guest Cast: Ritch Brinkley (Walter), Nick Searcy (Brett), Barbara Stuart (Miss Crowe).

Gil develops an interest in Harry's teacher, not knowing that the boy has quite a crush on her as well.

CHORE PATROL   Airdate: 3/23/94.
Guest Cast: Ritch Brinkley (Walter), Nick Searcy (Brett), Claudette Nevins (Ellen).

Gil tries to bribe the children to do their chores but finds out there were a few flaws in his plan.

GIRL'S NIGHT OUT   Airdates: 3/30/94, 8/17/94.
Guest Cast: Angelina Fiordellisi (Rita), Wolf Larson (Clay), Ben Browder (Marcus).

Bobbi and a girlfriend go out for a night on the town, leaving Gil at home as a reluctant babysitter.

BLOODSUCKERS   Airdates: 4/06/94, 8/31/94.
Guest Cast: Richard Schiff (Pat Perkins).

Gil has fun at the kids' expense when someone brings a hearse in for servicing.

HAPPY ENDINGS   Airdates: 4/13/94, 8/24/94.
Guest Cast: Ritch Brinkley (Walter), Angelina Fiordellisi (Rita).

Claudine is turning 12, but it appears unlikely she'll get her birthday wish for her father to visit.

FISTFULL OF PHYLLIS, A   Airdate: 4/20/94.
Guest Cast: Sharon Madden (Mrs. Millman), Tina Hart (Phyllis Millman).

A problem with an annoying neighbor gets even worse when Jenny punches the woman's daughter.

AS A MANNER OF FACT   Airdate: 5/04/94.
Guest Cast: Ritch Brinkley (Walter), Nick Searcy (Brett), Jeremy Jackson (Danny).

Gil worries about how his grandchildren will act at an awards banquet.

1994–95 season

NEVER SAY DIE   Airdates: 9/14/94.
Guest Cast: Allen Garfield (Dr. Shapiro), Kathryn Kates (Nurse #1), Patricia Ayame Thomson (Nurse #3).

Gil tries to help Harry overcome his fears about having his tonsils removed.

SPEAK NO EVIL   Airdate: 9/21/94.
Guest Cast: Sam Anderson (Mr. Riley), David Brisbin (Mr. Mendelsohn), Brenda Song

(Brenda), E.J. De La Pena (E.J.), Dane Estes (Dane).

Gil's comments about formal education don't go over well with Harry's teacher.

EASY MONEY   Airdate: 9/28/94.

Guest Cast: Gloria Dorson (Mrs. Wilson), Carmen Filpi (Kookie).

Gil and Bobbi cross swords when he takes the kids out of school so they can go to the racetrack.

GET A JOB   Airdate: 10/05/94.

Guest Cast: William Thomas, Jr. (Job Counselor), Ryan Bollman (Instructor), Robert Neches (Training Tape Voice), Susan Bugg (Woman #1), Hanna Hertelendy (Woman #2).

Gil may regret telling Bobbi to get a job, for he ends up having to watch the kids all day.

FIRST DATE   Airdate: 10/12/94.

Guest Cast: Zachery Ty Bryan (Brad Taylor), Angelina Fiordellisi (Rita), Alexander Zale (Cashier), Mark Zecca (Announcer/Video Game).

Claudine is thrilled when she's asked out on a date, until she learns that her mother plans on driving them.

GIVE 'EM HELL, BOBBI   Airdate: 10/19/94.

Guest Cast: M.C. Gainey (Mr. Ohrt), Bertila Davis (Parent #1), Gregg Daniel (Parent #2), Marcus Toji (Mason Charter-Wells), Meghan Murphy (Patti).

Bobbi upsets the parents and players when she becomes the coach of Jenny's basketball team and tells them that winning is not everything.

SEX, LIES & POPCORN   Airdate: 10/26/94.

Guest Cast: Rob Roy Fitzgerald (Greg), Bertila Damas (Delores).

Things start getting out of hand when Bobbi tells a little white lie.

GARAGE SALE, THE   Airdate: 11/02/94.

Guest Cast: Chris Carrara (Rainbow/Stuart), Wesley Thompson (Customer #1), Jacqui Bakshy (Customer #2), Gloria Dorson (Gigi), Carmen Filpi (Older Man), Maxine Elliott (Older Woman).

Bobbi and Gil argue when they can't decide what to do about a valuable baseball card collection.

ACCIDENTALLY AT FIRST SIGHT   Airdates: 3/07/95, 5/30/95.

Guest Cast: Angelina Fiordellisi (Rita), Tony Carreiro (Peter Berlow).

The rest of the family doesn't agree with Bobbi's plans to date an attractive man she just met.

ARE WE THERE YET?   Airdates: 3/14/95, 5/27/95.

Guest Cast: Eileen Brennan (Irma), Dion Anderson (Guldie), Bryan Clark (Wrong Way Burdett), Randy Kovitz (Policeman).

Gil wants to spend a weekend alone but Harry has other plans and insists on tagging along.

BREAKING AWAY   Airdates: 3/21/95, 7/25/95.

Guest Cast: Angelina Fiordellisi (Rita), Dane Michael Estes (Robert), Timothy Trinidad (Kevin).

The children make it clear that Gil and Bobbi's help is not always welcome.

TROUBLE WITH HARRY, THE   (Airdates: 3/28/95, 6/06/95.

Harry becomes convinced that he is the cause of all of the family's problems.

WORKING MAN'S BLUES   Airdates: 4/04/95, 6/13/95.

Guest Cast: Matt Battaglia (Jack Crawford), Jordan Blake Warkol (Sam).

Tired of the kids acting up, Gil decides that it's time to lay down the law.

LITTLE ME TIME, A   Airdates: 4/11/95, 7/18/95.

Guest Cast: Angelina Fiordellisi (Rita), Kate Asner (Kate), Larry Gelman (Customer).

Bobbi complains that she is spending more time taking care of Gil than he is taking with the children.

I AM SPARTACUS   Airdate: 4/18/95.

Guest Cast: Angelina Fiordellisi (Rita).

Bobbi finally listens to Gil and tells the children they have to listen to her, but they don't seem to agree.

GUESS WHO'S COMING TO DINNER?   Airdates: 4/25/95, 6/27/95.

Guest Cast: Pat Crowley (Elizabeth), Bette Ford (Wanda), Angelina Fiordellisi (Rita), Gregory White (Maitre D').

A romantic dinner for two goes awry when Gil's family decides to help.

JUST A VACATION   Airdate: 5/02/95.
Guest Cast: Angelina Fiordellisi (Rita), Romy Rosemont (Mrs. Duffy), Kirsten Holmquist (Inga).

Bobbi has her heart set on giving her kids a great summer vacation.

BUZZ OFF, BUZZARD BOY   Airdate: 5/09/95.
Guest Cast: Bart Johnson (Buzzard Boy), Cliff Bemis (Enviro-Man), Brenda Song (Kathy), Ramsey Krull (Boy #1).

Upset with the way the children are acting, Bobbi finally realizes they'll just have to grow out of some of their behavior.

NO SWING SET   Airdates: 7/04/95.
Guest Cast: Anthony Russell (Delivery Guy).

This kids have their hearts set on an expensive gift but Bobbi can't afford it.

These Friends of Mine (and) Ellen

When *Laurie Hill* was canceled in 1992 after only five episodes had been aired, producers Carol Black and Neal Marlens were still under contract to Disney. They immediately set out to create a new series, and with the arrival of the 1993–94 season, they had succeeded in selling their newest project to ABC. Tentatively titled *The Ellen DeGeneres Show*, it featured a supporting cast member from *Laurie Hill*, but this time in a starring role.

The series centered on a single woman and her three best friends, a premise reflected in the show's new title, *These Friends of Mine*.

These Friends of Mine was a hit. The series later became *Ellen*, reflecting the change in emphasis from the group of friends to the main star.

Series Cast: Ellen DeGeneres (Ellen Morgan), Holly Fulger (Holly, 1993–94), Maggie Wheeler (Anita, 1993–94), Joely Fisher (Paige, 1994–96), David Anthony Higgins (Joe, 1994–96), Clea Lewis (Audrey, 1995–96), Jeremy Piven (Spence, 1995–96), Arye Gross (Adam Greene).

Each of the episodes is described below in airdate order.

1993–94 episodes

THESE FRIENDS OF MINE (pilot)
Airdates: 3/29/94, 8/02/94.
Guest Cast: William Bumiller (Roger), Matt Landers (Photographer), Giovanni Ribisi (Cashier), Dukek Moosekian (Man in Line), Lois Viscoli (Depressed Woman).

Ellen leaves a scathing message on Holly's answering machine, then must find some way to erase it before Holly can hear it. She also has to deal with a very bad picture on her new driver's license.

ANCHOR, THE   Airdates: 3/30/94, 8/16/94.
Guest Cast: Clea Lewis (Audrey), Lane Davies (Nate), Greg Germann (Rick).

A problem with the telephone causes a rift between Ellen and a friend; Holly stuffs her bra to attract men.

KISS IS STILL A KISS, A   Airdate: 4/06/94.
Guest Cast: Tony Carreiro (Jackson), David Higgins (Joe), Todd Waring (William), Tracy Tweed (Tara), Ann Talman (Beth), Jeff Weatherford (Teddy).

Ellen meets a new boyfriend through the personal ads; everything seems great until they kiss.

CLASS REUNION, THE   Airdate: 4/13/94.
Guest Cast: Don Lake (Bob), Greg Germann (Rick), Steven Flynn (Joe), Patty Toy (Engineer's Wife), John Mueller (Brad), Michael Chieffo (Bank V.P.), Brenda Varda (Lawyer), Jerry Sroka (Engineer).

Desperate to impress people at her class reunion, Ellen convinces Adam to pretend that they are married and are both successful doctors.

PROMOTION, THE   Airdate: 4/20/94.
Guest Cast: Alice Hirson (Lois), Sully Diaz (Maria), Cristine Rose (Susan), Rosie Taravella (Clerk), Gene Weygandt (Gallery Owner), Patrick Mickler (Officer).

Ellen's hopes of getting a promotion may be dashed by an ill-chosen remark about her boss, for it was made within range of a baby monitor.

HAND THAT ROBS THE CRADLE, THE
Airdates: 4/27/94, 9/13/94.
Guest Cast: Peter Krause (Tim), Brian Leckner (Karl), David Higgins (Joe), Wendel Josepher (Saleswoman), Daniel Edward Mora (Water Delivery Man).

Ellen suffers an identity crisis when she dates a much younger man.

GO-BETWEEN, THE   Airdates: 5/04/94, 9/06/94.

Guest Cast: David Higgins (Joe), Cristine Rose (Susan), Ryan Olson (Student #1), Jordan Bond (Student #2), Scott Sites (Flower Delivery Man), Sweeney McVeigh (Waiter).

Ellen convinces Adam to take her boss, Susan, to a wedding, then is amazed to discover the next morning that the date hasn't ended yet.

HOUSE GUEST, THE   Airdate: 5/24/94.

Guest Cast: Steven Gilborn (Harold), Dennis Burkley (Nestor), Joanna Daniels (Tracy), David Higgins (Joe), Christopher Darga (Officer), Jan Eddy (Big Ed), Charles Mavich (Roy), Molly Shannon (Woman), Jill Talley (Infomercial Woman), Michael Shamus Wiles (Bartender), Harland Williams (Ticket Taker), Jim Cody Williams (Biker #1), Dave Driver (Customer).

Tracy, Ellen's cousin, arrives in town from Missouri for a vacation and she and Ellen have to deal with problems such as polluted beaches and counterfeit theater tickets.

REFRIGERATOR, THE   Airdate: 8/09/94.

Guest Cast: Kurt Fuller (Dr. Collins), John Riggi (Manager), Steve Kehela (Jeff), Barry Wiggins (Herbert), Lisa Stahl (Delila), Don Stark (Repairman).

Ellen has problems getting her new refrigerator home when Adam fakes a back injury for an insurance claim and is unable to help her.

Production Note:

• This was the first episode aired under the series title *Ellen*.

SOFT TOUCH, THE   Airdate: 8/23/94.

Guest Cast: David Higgins (Joe), Steven Gilborn (Harold), Alice Hirson (Lois), John Bowman (Glenn), Steven Marcus (Agitated Man), Dorian Spencer (Young Man), Richard Hicks (Coffee Drinker), David Brisbin (Manager).

Ellen takes pity on a car salesman who was fired when she backed out of a deal.

BOYFRIEND STEALER, THE   Airdate: 8/30/94.

Guest Cast: David Higgins (Joe), Cristine Rose (Susan), Tommy Hinkley (Steve), Jimmy Danelli (Customer), John Mulrooney (Fight Fan #1), Don Yesso (Fight Fan #2), Amy Weinstein (Woman #1), Jo Brewer (Woman #2), Steve Albert (Fight Announcer).

Ellen is convinced that Holly's boyfriend is making passes at her but no one will believe her.

1994–95 episodes

DENTIST, THE   Airdates: 9/21/94, 1/18/95, 5/02/95.

Guest Cast: Andrea Parker (Joanna), Harley Venton (Dr. Dave Ellis), Blaire Baron (Waitress), Christine Romeo (Waitress), Martha Thompson (Sarah), Brian McGovern (Romantic Guy), Alicia Anne (Pretty Girl), Robert Gant (Dr. Garber).

Ellen becomes enfatuated with Paige's dentist; Adam decides his girlfriend isn't good enough for him.

SAINT ELLEN   Airdates: 9/28/94, 12/21/94, 4/25/95.

Guest Cast: Jane Carr (Glynnis), Patrick Bristow (Peter), Murray Rubinstein (Bill), Kathleen McMartin (Distressed Woman), Leonard Kelly-Young (Customer), Kymberly Newberry (Dignified Woman), Lisa Inouye (Clipboard Woman), Steve Houska (Waiter), Darla Haun (Beautiful Woman), John McCafferty (Barry).

Ellen develops a massive guilt complex when she crashes a society affair and wins a big-screen television there.

THIRTY MINUTE MAN, THE   Airdates: 10/05/94, 12/28/94, 5/09/95.

Guest Cast: William Ragsdale (Dan), Jerry Penacoli (Richard).

Ellen meets an interesting man at the bookstore, only to discover that he delivers pizza for a living and is seemingly without any ambition in life.

NOTE, THE   Airdates: 10/12/94, 5/31/95.

Guest Cast: Kenneth Timmins (Phil), Chad Einbinder (Bob), Helen Siff (Sharon), Paul Marin (Mr. Phillips), Dave Richardson (Ted), Gene Poe (Salesman), Andrea Leithe (Marion).

Ellen is shattered to learn that someone in her book club can't stand her.

FIX-UP, THE   Airdates: 10/19/95, 2/01/95, 8/30/95.

Guest Cast: Bradley Whitford (Doug), Alice Hirson (Lois), Jim Jackman (Man), Stephen James Carver (Detective #1), Garret Davis (Detective #2).

Determined not to like a blind date, Ellen is surprised to find that she actually finds him attractive. Unfortunately, that's the only thing about the date that goes well.

So Funny   Airdates: 10/26/94, 7/05/95.
   Guest Cast: Kathy Najimy (Theresa), Larry Poindexter (Don), Mary Otis (Flight Attendant), Milt Tarver (Passenger).
   Ellen becomes jealous of Adam's new friend.

Toast, The   Airdates: 11/09/94, 3/15/95.
   Guest Cast: Alice Hirson (Lois), Steven Gilborn (Harold), Matthew Letscher (Steven), Rebecca Staab (Cindy), Scott LaRose (Jack), Mark L. Taylor (Charles), Ryan Holihan (Billy), Nicki Vannice (Debbie), Gill Baker (Mrs. Thompson), J. Patrick McCormack (Reverend Engler).
   Ellen tries to organize her brother's wedding so she can prove to her parents that she can act responsibly.

Adam's Birthday   Airdates: 11/16/94, 4/19/95.
   Guest Cast: Bill Calvert (Patrick), Karen Maruyama (Kate), Brian Cousins (Billy), Patience Cleveland (Maisie), Patrick Cranshaw (Irving), Billye Ree Wallace (Polly), Chris Douridas (Chad), Jaime Hubbard (Melissa).
   When his birthday makes Adam feel that life is passing him by, he moves out of the apartment to start life anew.

Trainer, The   Airdates: 11/23/94, 3/08/95, 7/12/95.
   Guest Cast: Harry Shearer (Ted).
   Ellen tries to help Paige by acting as her manager's personal trainer, never expecting that she'll be offered the job full-time.

Mrs. Koger   Airdates: 11/30/94, 4/26/95.
   Guest Cast: Nick Bakay (Lloyd), Nita Talbot (Mrs. Koger), Marianne Muellerleile (Edna), Damian London (Funeral Director), Crystal Carson (Gwen), Matt McKenzie (Policeman), Rick Scarry (Man at Funeral).
   Ellen yells at a grouchy neighbor, then is devastated to learn that the old woman died just a few minutes afterwards.

Ellen's New Friend   Airdates: 12/07/94, 6/07/95.
   Guest Cast: Clea Lewis (Audrey Penney), Angela Dohrmann (Jessica), Andrew Shaifer (Party Guest).

Desperate to impress Audrey's influential friend, Ellen pulls out all of the stops in an effort to wangle an invitation to a big party.

Christmas Show, The   Airdates: 12/14/94, 7/19/95.
   Guest Cast: Eric Lutes (Greg), Kate Hodge (Stephanie), Connie Stevens (Paige's Mom), David Andrew Sederholm (Patrick), Jefrey Alan Chandler (Cookie Man), Molly David (Sweet Old Woman), Zachary Eginton (Bud), Jonathan Emerson (Lucky Customer), Laurel Green (Lorraine), Lisa Harrison (Bambi), Pat Lentz (Joanne), Mark McCracken (Richard), Joyce Sylvester (Cookbook Woman).
   Joe doesn't like Ellen's new employee, Stephanie, at first, but the two end up dating. Ellen, meanwhile, wishes she wasn't dating at all.

Ellen's Improvement   Airdates: 1/04/95, 4/05/95, 8/23/95.
   Guest Cast: Kate Hodge (Stephanie), Gregory Paul Martin (Roger), Peter Kim (Korean Man), Kim Kim (Korean Woman), Alex Trebek (Himself).
   Ellen decides that she and her friends need to become more cultured, so she drags them to an art gallery.

Apartment Hunt, The   Airdates: 1/11/95, 4/12/95.
   Guest Cast: Clea Lewis (Audrey), Kate Hodge (Stephanie), Ken Olandt (Alternate Juror #16), Ralph P. Martin (Tony), Marcia Mitzman (Debby), Joey Slotnick (Mr. Selman).
   Ellen tries to keep Audrey from moving nearby by spinning some outrageous yarns about her neighbors.

Spa, The   Airdates: 1/12/95, 4/04/95, 9/06/95.
   Guest Cast: Molly Cheek (Sylvia), Felicity Waterman (Lauren), Kimberly Russell (Tonya), Patrick Warburton (Brent), Patrick S. Harrigan (Customer).
   Wanting to be pampered, Ellen and Paige spend a weekend at a health farm, unaware that they will be put on a very strict diet.

Ballet Class   Airdates: 2/08/95, 6/14/95.
   Guest Cast: Patrick Bristow (Peter), Alice Hirson (Lois), Steven Gilborn (Harold), Elaine Hendrix (Maya), Spencer Rochfort (Jerry), Scott Fowler (Sam).
   The discovery that her parents took her out of ballet class because they thought she

wasn't graceful enough makes Ellen determined to become a ballerina so she can prove them wrong.

GUNS 'N ELLEN   Airdates: 2/15/95, 6/21/95.

Guest Cast: Clea Lewis (Audrey), Eric Allen Kramer (Detective Ryan), Steven Gilborn (Harold), David DeLuise (Robber in Hat), Jamie Marsh (Robber in Jacket).

A robbery convinces Ellen that she and her friends need lessons in self-defense.

SLEEP CLINIC, THE   Airdates: 2/22/95, 5/24/95, 9/06/95.

Guest Cast: Clea Lewis (Audrey), Paxton Whitehead (Dr. Whitcomb), Alice Hirson (Lois), The Andrae Crouch Singers.

A series of disturbing dreams about sex with Adam brings Ellen to a therapist, who makes things worse by telling her that it may mean she does care for Adam.

GLADIATORS   Airdates: 3/01/95, 8/30/95.

Guest Cast: Clea Lewis (Audrey), Dan Clark (Nitro), Lori Fetrick (Ice), Jackie Mari Roberts (Debbie), Mike Adamle (Himself), Raymond Forchion (Customer #2), W. Earl Brown (Customer #3), Jeffrey Lampert (Customer #1), Connie Needham (Waitress), Lee Reherman (Hawk), Jeff Sanders (Contestant).

Ellen is talked into competing on the *American Gladiators* sports show.

$5,000   Airdates: 3/22/95, 6/28/95.

Guest Cast: Patrick Bristow (Peter), Dann Florek (Mr. Woodruff), Brittany Ashton Holmes (Julie).

An unexpected windfall in the form of a tax refund poses several problems for Ellen.

THREE STRIKES   Airdates: 3/29/95, 7/26/95.

Guest Cast: Alice Hirson (Lois), Steven Gilborn (Harold), Clyde Kusatsu (Judge), Christine Elise (Rosie), Kate Benton (Psychotic Woman), Roger Eschbacher (Cop).

A protest about the killing of animals lands Ellen in jail.

THERAPY EPISODE, THE   Airdates: 5/03/95, 8/16/95.

Guest Cast: Alice Hirson (Lois), Steven Gilborn (Harold), Paxton Whitehead (Dr. Whitcomb), Michael White (Instructor).

A series of small lies lands Ellen in big trouble when she takes a therapist's advice and tries her best to tell the truth.

THIRTY KILO MAN—PART I   Airdates: 5/10/95, 8/02/95.

Guest Cast: Clea Lewis (Audrey), William Ragsdale (Dan), Alice Hirson (Lois), Patrick Warburton (Jack), Jerry Penacoli (Richard), Dean Fortunato (Man).

Ellen meets up with Dan, her ex-boyfriend who used to deliver pizza. She's surprised to learn that he's now in the import/export business, but she begins to worry about what it is that he imports.

THIRTY KILO MAN—PART II   Airdates: 5/17/95, 8/09/95.

Guest Cast: Clea Lewis (Audrey), William Ragsdale (Dan), Alice Hirson (Lois), Steven Gilborn (Harold), Patrick Warburton (Jack), Dean Fortunato (Man), Scotch Ellis Loring (Waiter).

Ellen wants to spend some time alone with Dan, but somehow they end up having dinner with Paige, Adam, and Audrey.

1995–96 episodes

SHAKE, RATTLE, AND RUBBLE   Airdates: 9/13/95, 12/13/95.

Guest Cast: Ruth Manning (Customer), Rick Fitts (Reporter), Maurice Chasse (Neighbor).

Ellen experiences two of the worst fears of all Los Angeles residents—an earthquake and a relative from back East who wants to move in.

THESE SUCCESSFUL FRIENDS OF MINE   Airdates: 9/20/95, 5/29/96.

Guest Cast: Jim Haynie (Jake), Hal Landon, Jr. (Bus Driver), Kevin Light (Contractor), David Wells (Mousey Man), Tommy Bertselsen (Kid), Sherlinda Dix (Lady), Paddi Edwards (Smoking Woman).

With her bookstore in ruins and her friends too busy with their own careers to help her rebuild it, Ellen takes a bus trip to get away from it all.

SHOWER SCENE, THE   Airdates: 9/27/95, 12/27/95, 6/05/96.

Guest Cast: Connie Britton (Heather), Judy Kain (Nurse), Rachel Davies (Mrs. Lowry), Fiona Hale (Grandmother), Dailyn Matthews (Pregnant Woman), Sandra Kinder (Saleslady), Colleen Wainright (Woman).

When she accidentally tapes over the only copy of Paige's sister giving birth to twins, Ellen cooks up a scheme to tape another birth and pass it off as the original.

BRIDGES OF L.A. COUNTY, THE
Airdates: 10/04/95, 1/17/96.

Guest Cast: Christine Taylor (Karen), Anthony Clark (Will), Kate Williamson (Mrs. Rogers), Brian George (Ranjit), Paul Bates (Kenny).

Ellen is upset with the way Spence has treated one of her book club members.

HELLO, I MUST BE GOING
Airdates: 10/18/95, 1/31/96.

Guest Cast: K.T. Vogt (Junker Woman), Shaun Toub (Foreign Man), Jay Johnston (Transition Guy), Jamie Kennedy (Tad).

Adam delivers two surprising bits of news. First, he's moving to London for a job there. Second, he's in love with Ellen.

TRICK OR TREAT, WHO CARES?
Airdates: 11/01/95, 6/12/96.

Guest Cast: Anthony Clark (Will), Kate Williamson (Mrs. Rodgers), Rachel Duncan (Little Girl), Ramon Choyce (Little Lawyer), Jimm Galeotta (Little Doctor).

Audrey talks Ellen into giving her a job at the bookstore but soon drives her crazy with her always perky attitude.

SHE AIN'T FRIENDLY, SHE'S MY MOTHER
Airdates: 11/08/95, 3/27/96, 9/04/96.

Guest Cast: Alice Hirson (Lois), Steven Gilborn (Harold), Doris Belack (Cora), Beverly Garland (Eva), Bruce Thomas (Mike), Mara Holguin (Katie).

Ellen doesn't know how to react when her mother tells her that she wants to be Ellen's best friend.

SALAD DAYS
Airdates: 11/15/95, 2/20/96, 8/28/96.

Guest Cast: Martha Stewart (Herself), Alice Hirson (Lois), Patrick Bristow (Peter), Pat Millicano (Randy), Jack Plotnick (Barrett), Stephanie Erb (Alien Denise).

After spending a day at the bookstore with Martha Stewart, Ellen decides that she can throw just as elegant a party as the famous writer.

MOVIE SHOW, THE
Airdates: 11/22/95, 4/10/96.

Guest Cast: Carrie Fisher (Herself), Jack Plotnick (Barrett), Michael Des Barres (Nigel), Michael Maynard (Colin), Michael Georgio (Dolly Grip), Matthew Sullivan (Salesman).

Ellen is starstruck when Paige arranges for a movie to be filmed at the bookstore.

WHAT'S UP, EX-DOC?
Airdates: 11/29/95, 4/17/96.

Guest Cast: Brian Doyle-Murray (Burt), Robert Lance (Man).

Spence is forced to finally admit to his father that he was thrown out of medical school.

ELLEN'S CHOICE
Airdates: 12/06/95, 4/24/96.

Guest Cast: Christine Taylor (Karen), Anthon Clark (Will), Vance DeGeneres (Erik), Brian George (Ranjit), Kate Williamson (Mrs. Rodgers), Paul Bates (Kenny), Lise Simms (Lesly), Bob Glouberman (Sean).

Ellen can't decide which members of her book club will appear on a television program.

DO YOU FEAR WHAT I FEAR?
Airdates: 12/20/95, 7/03/96.

Guest Cast: Alice Hirson (Lois), Steven Gilborn (Harold), Jamie Kennedy (Tad).

Ellen's parents give her a very unusual Christmas present—a burial plot.

HORSHACK'S LAW
Airdates: 1/03/96, 6/19/96.

Guest Cast: Elya Baskin (Sergei), Ron Palillo (Himself).

An invitation to John Travolta's birthday party results in bedlam when the gang starts acting silly in the limousine on the way there.

MORGAN, P.I.
Airdates: 1/10/96, 4/03/96, 7/10/96.

Guest Cast: Dan Gauthier (Detective Liston), Ron Canada (Detective Sutterman), Eric Menyuk (Jim Hogan).

Ellen hopes she can catch the thief who robbed the bookstore; Paige hopes she can catch one of the policemen for herself.

OH, SWEET RAPTURE
Airdates: 1/24/96, 6/26/96.

Guest Cast: Kathy Griffin (Peggy), Wayne Wilderson (Ronnie), Nick Toth (Earl), Lilian Sason (Mrs. Collins).

Audrey becomes a zealot about her new car and starts spending all of her time with other car owners instead of her friends.

WITNESS
Airdates: 2/07/96, 4/10/96.

Guest Cast: Anthony Clark (Will), Concetta Tomei (Professor Bass), Scott Mosenson

(Jodh), Stephanie Erb (Denise), Bari K. Willerford (Delivery Man).

Ellen turns a courtroom upside-down when she plays the part of a witness in a mock trial.

ELLEN: WITH CHILD Airdates: 2/24/96, 7/17/96.

Guest Cast: Dan Gauthier (Matt), Ebick Pizzadilli (Mia), Don Amendolia (Mr. Koundakian).

Paige wants to spend more time with her boyfriend, Matt, so Ellen agrees to babysit Matt's daughter. She then learns that the girl has a school project due the next day and hasn't even started it.

LOBSTER DIARY Airdates: 2/21/96, 5/22/96.

Guest Cast: Mary Tyler Moore (Herself), Paul Dooley (Thomas Kelsey), Tricia Leigh Fisher (Joanie), Wesley Thompson (Kevin Brown), Andy Houts (Brett).

Ellen goes to great lengths to liberate a 65-year-old lobster from a restaurant, only to discover that it's not easy getting rid of the crustacean.

TWO RING CIRCUS Airdates: 2/28/96, 8/07/96.

Guest Cast: Dan Gauthier (Matt Liston), Patrick Bristow (Peter), Jack Plotnick (Barrett), Judith Scarpone (Sydelle), Gregory White (Man), Bari K. Willerford (Delivery Man).

Matt's proposal to Paige at a hockey game is interrupted when he gets hit in the head by a puck, so Ellen tries her best to step in for him.

PENNY SAVED . . . , A Airdates: 3/13/96, 7/24/96.

Guest Cast: Barry Corbin (Jack Penney), Carol Kane (Lily Penney), Lawrence Hilton Jacobs (Himself).

Facing a financial pinch at the bookstore, Ellen plans to lay off Audrey until she discovers Audrey's parents are very wealthy and are willing to pay her to save their daughter's job.

TOO HIP FOR THE ROOM Airdates: 3/20/96, 7/31/96.

Guest Cast: Charlie Brill (Del Shapiro), Mitzi McCall (Rochelle Shapiro), Tera Hendrickson (Barb), Cynthia La Montagne (Lesly), Bodhi Pine Elfman (Surfer Dude), Paul Crowder (Trendy Man), Elizabeth Keener (Trendy Woman), Nicky Edenetti (Cabaret Singer), Loretta Palazzo (Guitar Woman), Abbie Jane (Piccolo Woman), Ruth Carlsson (Xylophone Woman), Happy Richard Hall (Drum Man), Venus Con Carne (The Garage Band).

Ellen hires a band to entertain at the bookstore, then learns that people are only coming there to laugh at them.

TWO MAMMOGRAMS AND A WEDDING Airdates: 4/03/96, 8/14/96.

Guest Cast: Janeane Garofalo (Chloe), Thea Vidale (Technician), Mina Kolb (Nurse), Michole White (Alyssa), Susan Powell (Salon Lady), Nancy Serrano (Art Student).

Ellen makes a new friend while the two of them are waiting to take a mammogram.

GO GIRLZ Airdates: 5/01/96, 9/04/96.

Guest Cast: Kathy Najimy (Lorna), Dan Gauthier (Matt), Alice Hirson (Lois), Steven Gilborn (Harold), Shae D'Lyn (Debbie), Timothy Elwell (Security Guy), Jonathan Stark (Gus).

Ellen throws a bachelorette party for Paige, but events go awry right from the start.

WHEN THE VOW BREAKS—PART 1 Airdates: 5/08/96, 9/11/96.

Guest Cast: Dan Gauthier (Matt), Patrick Bristow (Peter), Jack Plotnick (Barrett), Connie Britton (Heather), Ron Palillo (Himself), Ebick Pizzadilla (Mia), Gregory Sierra (General Colon), Jeff Dunham and Walter (Starky and Gus), Kimmy Robertson (Brandy), Greg Collins (Agent Chamberlain).

When Paige's wedding day starts to come apart, Ellen decides to step in to save the day.

TAPE, THE Airdate: 5/14/96.

Guest Cast: Brian McNamara (Jim), Earl Boen (Hubert), Elinor Donahue (Dolores), Dan Sachoff (Brian).

Anita entrusts a tape of her and her boyfriend having sex to Ellen, but Adam makes a mistake and gives Anita's parents a copy.

WHEN THE VOW BREAKS—PART 2 Airdates: 5/15/96, 9/11/96.

Guest Cast: Dan Gauthier (Matt), Patrick Bristow (Peter), Jack Plotnick (Barrett), Connie Britton (Heather), Ron Palillo (Himself), Ebick Pizzadilla (Mia), Kimmy Robertson (Brandy), Perry Anzilotti (Minister).

The misadventures of Paige's wedding day continue.

MUGGING, THE   Airdate: 5/21/96.

Guest Cast: Greg Germann (Rick), Mariska Hargitay (Dara), Willie C. Carpenter (Officer Wilson), Dave Florek (Officer), Edward Blanchard (Mugger), Rob Moore (Witness).

Adam refuses to come to the aid of a mugging victim.

Someone Like Me

With the success of *Blossom*, it was no surprise that Disney would create another sitcom built around a young girl. A mid-year replacement for the 1993–94 season, *Someone Like Me* starred Gaby Hoffman, who had gained positive reviews and public acceptance for her role in *Sleepless in Seattle*. Now, she was to star in her own series as Gaby Stepjak, an opinioned 11-year-old trying to deal with the pressures of daily life.

Series Cast: Gaby Hoffmann (Gaby Stepjak), Patricia Heaton (Jean Stepjak), Nikki Cox (Sam Stepjak), Raegan Kotz (Jane Schmidt), Matthew Thomas Carey (Neal Schmidt), Joseph Tello (Evan Stepjak), Anthony Tyler Quinn (Steven Stepjak).

Each of the episodes is described below in airdate order.

LYING GAME, THE   Airdate: 3/14/94.

Guest Cast: Andrew Lauer (Bobby), Krystin Moore (Marla).

When Gaby lies to her parents and stays out late, they decide to punish her by taking away her telephone privileges.

WHEN MOMS COLLIDE   Airdate: 3/28/94.

Guest Cast: Jane Morris (Dorie), Andrew Lauer (Bobby), Lorne Berfield (Perry Burke), Krystin Moore (Marla), Carlo Moretti (Barton).

Mrs. Schmidt angers Gaby's mother by bringing alcohol and a horror movie to her daughter's party, which is being held at Gaby's house.

GUY, THE   Airdate: 4/04/94.

Guest Cast: Ray Buktenica (Wardell), Bridget Brno (Nicole), Krystin Moore (Marla), Elan Rothschild (Rick), Stephen Samuels (Mitch), Dustin Voigt (Sean).

Gaby goes to her first dance and is swept off her feet by a handsome boy, but he already has a girlfriend.

EL PRESIDENTE   Airdate: 4/18/94.

Guest Cast: Ray Buktenica (Wardell), Krystin Moore (Marla), Elan Rothschild (Rick), Stephen Samuels (Mitch), Joshua Wiener (Brian).

Gaby gets a lesson in politics when her opponent in a school election unleashes a dirty campaign against her.

WHAT I DID FOR ART   Airdate: 4/25/94.

Guest Cast: Krystin Moore (Marla), Leslie Nielsen (Mr. Verdow).

Gaby thoroughly confuses her tradition-minded art teacher with her piece of "performance art."

SYMPATHY FOR THE DEVIL   Airdates: Unaired.

Guest Cast: Jane Morris (Dorie), Andrew Lauer (Bobby), Krystin Moore (Marla).

Gaby's mother forbids her to see her best friend, Jane, when she learns that Jane smokes.

Hardball

When the Fox network purchased the rights to National Football League games for the 1994–95 season, network executives wanted a sports-oriented comedy series to air afterward so sports fans would stay tuned. The result was the series *Hardball*, the story of a fictitious American League baseball team, the Pioneers.

Series Cast: Bruce Greenwood (Dave Logan), Mike Starr (Mike Widmer), Alexandra Wentworth (Lee Emory), Dann Florek (Ernest "Happy" Talbot), Joe Rogan (Frank Valente), Phill Lewis (Arnold), Steve Hytner (Brad), Chris Browning (Lloyd LaCombe), Gary Guercio (Hardball), Rose Marie (Mitzi), Adam Hendershott (Nelson).

Each of the episodes is described below in airdate order. Additionally, 2 episodes were produced but not aired, and are listed in production order.

HARDBALL (pilot)   Airdate: 9/04/94.

Guest Cast: Ashlee Levitch (Tonya), Mel Winkler (Slab Ennis), Eddie Velez (Diego Escobar), Nancy Valen (Jennifer), Charles Cyphers (Chuck), Christopher B. Duncan (Palmer), Dave Sebastian Williams (Sports Announcer), Jonathan Stark (Beefy Guy), Jack Kenny (Male Reporter), Terry Cain (Female Reporter), Frank Medrano (Heckler), Jim

Breuer (Pied Pioneer), Joel McKinnon Miller (Fan #1), Jimmy Danelli (Fan #2), Brian Levinson (Kid), Louis Lombardi (Pie Pioneer Heckler).

The Pioneers' new owner brings in no-nonsense manager "Happy" Talbot to improve the team; Dave finds out the girl he just slept with is Talbot's daughter.

MIKE'S RELEASE Airdate: 9/11/94.

Guest Cast: Fred Sanders (Pleasant Man), Christopher Darga (Male Reporter), Christopher B. Duncan (Palmer Atkins), Trenton Knight (Timmy), William Joseph Barker (Teenage Reporter), John Mulrooney (Cop).

Talbot fires Mike for being out of shape, but he has to reconsider when a series of errors results in Mike helping to apprehend a notorious fugitive.

BUTT WINNICK STORY, THE Airdate: 9/18/94.

Guest Cast: Joe Flaherty (Butt Winnick), Mary Ann Mobley (Peaches), Sally Hughes (Mrs. Emory), Charles Hutchins (Mr. Emory), Paul Eisenhauer (Umpire), Dave Sebastian Williams (Announcer).

The guys must play against a team led by Happy's arch-enemy, coach Butt Winnick; Frank strikes out when he tries to seduce Lee.

WHOSE STRIKE IS IT ANYWAY? Airdate: 10/02/94.

Guest Cast: Paul Feig (Agent #1), Tom McTigue (Agent #2), Dave Sebastian Williams (Reporter), Frank Medrano (Heckler), Shirley Prestia (Bird Woman).

Arnold panics when the team goes on strike and agrees to a very bad business deal.

FRANK BUYS AN ISLAND, MIKE PAYS THE PRICE Airdate: 10/09/94.

Guest Cast: Karla Tamburrelli (Carol Widmer), Christopher Darga (Reporter), Glen Chin (Mr. Sunga), James Keane (Umpire), Frank Medrano (Heckler), Justin Berfield (Kid).

Frank buys his own island, which doesn't go over well with the inhabitants; Mike's wife discovers that he has been making love to her as part of a scheme to improve his batting average.

LEE'S BAD, BAD DAY Airdate: 10/6/94.

Guest Cast: Philip Baker Hall (Beanball McGee), Alvy Moore (Old Hardball), Bill Wiley (Pickles McGerkin), Owen Bush (Wrong

Way Mulgrew), Dave Sebastian Williams (Male Anchor), Sally Ann Brooks (Female Anchor), Daniel Edward Mora (Spanish Anchor), Peter Cullen (Fox Announcer), Tom Drozdowski (Baseball Player).

Lee has her hands full when things go wrong during the annual Old-Timers' Day game.

MY NAME IS HARD B Airdate: 10/23/94.

Guest Cast: Judith Hoag (Barbara), Barry Bonds (Himself), Christopher Darga (Reporter), Dave Sebastian Williams (Male Anchor), Darcy DeMoss (Annie).

Team mascot Hardball loses his wife to a rival mascot.

SEE SPOT RUN Airdate: Unaired.

Guest Cast: Cress Williams ("Spotlight" Davis), Jennifer Nash (Sno Cone Girl), Christopher Darga (Male Reporter), Justin Berfield (The Kid), Jenna Cole (Female Reporter), Paul Eisenhauer (Umpire), Brent Corman (Kid #1), Chad Power (Kid #2), Dave Sebastian Williams (Sports Announcer).

The team hires a football pro as a publicity stunt but it turns out he plays better than some of the regular players.

ROOKIE, THE BATGIRL, AND THE COACH AND HIS WIFE, THE Airdates: Unaired.

Guest Cast: Patsy Pease (Gloria), Ashlee Levitch (Tonya), Roger Eschbacher (Man in Suit), Steve Kehela (Male Reporter), Frank Madrano (Heckler), Dave Sebastian Williams (Announcer), James Keane (Umpire).

When Nelson is injured, Lee hires a batgirl as his replacement; Happy strikes out in the romance field when his third wife files for divorce.

All-American Girl

Continuing the trend of casting stand-up comics in sitcoms, Disney cast Margaret Cho in *All-American Girl*, the first network series to feature an Asian cast. The major focus for the 1994–95 series was on Margaret Kim, a strong-willed daughter who argued a lot with her mother, a Korean immigrant who still valued her native heritage very strongly.

Series Cast: Margaret Cho (Margaret Kim), Jodi Long (Mom), Clyde Kusatsu (Dad), Amy Hill (Grandmother), Maddie Corman (Ruthie), Ashley Johnson (Casey), Judy Gold (Gloria), J.B. Quon (Eric Kim), B.D. Wong (Stuart Kim).

Each of the episodes is described below in airdate order.

Mom, Dad, This Is Kyle   Airdates: 9/14/94, 12/21/94.

Guest Cast: Christopher Burgard (Kyle), Tim Lounibos (Korean Man), Kennedy Kabasares (Lonnie Park).

After trying her best to defy her parents by dating a white guy, Margaret finally gives in and dumps him.

Submission: Impossible   Airdates: 9/21/94, 2/01/95.

Guest Cast: Garrett Wang (Raymond Han), Lisa Lu (Mrs. Han), Alvin Y.F. Ing (Mr. Han), Ralph Ahn (Grandpa Han), Gabe Dell, Jr. (Dakota).

Margaret bends over backward to act traditionally subservient to a Korean boy to please her mother.

Who's the Boss?   Airdates: 9/28/94.

Guest Cast: Catherine Lloyd Burns (Tipsy), Juanita Jennings (Carolyn), Benjamin Lum (Master), Sam Sako (Abzaad).

Ruthie isn't happy when Margaret is promoted and becomes her new boss.

Yung at Heart   Airdates: 10/05/94, 3/08/95.

Guest Cast: Sab Shimono (Sammy).

Margaret returns home from a shopping trip empty-handed but her grandmother brings home a marriage proposal.

Redesigning Women   Airdates: 10/12/94, 3/22/95.

Guest Cast: Ming-Na Wen (Amy), Elaine Kao (Tammy), Michael Lowry (Jack).

One night on the town with Margaret is all it takes to turn Stuart's quiet girlfriend into a wild woman.

Booktopus   Airdate: 10/19/94.

Guest Cast: Richard Fancy (Wallace), Tim Kelleher (Howard), Brian Reddy (Mr. Gordon).

The family bookstore faces severe competition when a large chain moves into the neighborhood.

Mommie Nearest   Airdate: 10/26/94.

Guest Cast: Michael Palance (Derek), Elise Ogden (Lisa), William Newman (Customer #1), William Medin (Customer #2).

Mother and daughter find a new way to clash when Margaret hires her for the department store.

Take My Family . . . Please   Airdate: 11/02/94.

Guest Cast: Tsai Chin (Auntie June), Dana Lee (Uncle Ken), Christopher Fuller (Billy), Bruce French (Mr. Wickes).

When mom and dad stop in at a karaoke bar and see Margaret on stage telling jokes about them, mom gets very upset and stops talking to her.

Exile on Market Street   Airdate: 11/16/94.

Guest Cast: Robert Firth (Officer), Robertson Dean (Rufino), Joseph Romanov (Club Employee).

Margaret rethinks her plans for law school after she is arrested.

Ratting on Ruthie   Airdate: 11/23/94.

Guest Cast: Deborah May (Sheila), Clifton Wells (Hal), Daniel Kim (Stan), Richard Herkert (Charlie), Marcy Kaplan (Jackie), Steve Fitchpatrick (Mike).

Margaret has to decide between being a boss and being a friend when Ruthie makes a mistake at work.

Educating Margaret   Airdate: 11/30/94.

Guest Cast: Alastair Duncan (Colin Whitaker), Susan Leslie (Classmate).

Things take a new turn at school when Margaret starts dating one of her professors.

Loveless in San Francisco   Airdate: 12/07/74.

Guest Cast: Joyce Van Patten (Emma), Dan Sachoff (Cyril), Eric Lutes (Grant), Dean W. Tarrolly (Cute Guy), Christopher James Williams (Waiter).

A drought in her love life finds Margaret looking for a cure—and an eligible doctor.

Malpractice Makes Perfect   Airdate: 12/14/94.

Guest Cast: Lisa Stahl (Beauty Contestant), Michelle Watkins (Nurse), Patricia Place (Older Woman), Robert Noble (Bartender).

Stuart decides to quit medicine after he makes a mistake until Margaret helps him put things in perspective.

Apartment, The   Airdates: 1/11/95, 8/23/95.

Guest Cast: Sharon Sharth (Sunshine).

Margaret moves into an apartment with Ruthie and Gloria to save money, then learns that Gloria likes to spend time at home in the nude.

Production Note:

- This episode was taped without a studio audience due to the nudity.

NOTES FROM THE UNDERGROUND
Airdate: 1/18/95.
Guest Cast: Billy Burke (Cody), Tom Kopache (Representative).
Margaret gets tired of her family's interference when she invites a date to the house.

VENUS DE MARGARET Airdates: 1/25/95, 8/16/95.
Guest Cast: Lance Guest (Leo), Christine Estabrook (Vivian).
Margaret gets a surprise when she learns that the statue she posed for in the nude will be put on public display.

NIGHT AT THE OPRAH, A Airdate: 2/15/95.
Guest Cast: Oprah Winfrey (Herself), Jana Marie Hupp (Lisa), Jack Black (Tommy), Elise Ogden (Dr. Marilyn Thorpe), Miguel Perez (Mitch), Joseph Rye (Simon), Cal Evans (Clutch).
The family appears on Oprah Winfrey's show for a makeover, but Oprah has to mediate when Margaret says she plans to quit college.

PULP SITCOM Airdate: 2/22/95.
Guest Cast: Quentin Tarantino (Desmond), Robert Clohessy (Average Tony), Andre Marquis (Mr. Roarke), Patrick Cranshaw (Mr. Vasin).
A video bootlegger turns the family's life upside down.

Production Note:

- Director and writer Quentin Tarantino was Margaret Cho's real-life boyfriend.

YOUNG AMERICANS Airdate: 3/15/95.
Cast: Margaret Cho (Margaret Kim), Amy Hill (Grandmother), Diedrich Bader (Spenser), Andrew Lowery (Jimmy), Sam Seder (Phil). Guest Cast: Mariska Hargitay (Jane), Vicki Lawrence (Phone Lady), John Terlesky (Tim), Arsenio "Sonny" Trinidad (Dr. Park).
This pilot for a proposed new series has Margaret moving in with three male roommates, described as a politically correct mechanic, a nerdy security guard, and a preppy law student.

Unhappily Ever After

This sitcom about a dysfunctional family comes from the creators of the popular series *Married . . . with Children*. This time out, they decided to focus on a family undergoing a messy divorce.

Unhappily Ever After was added to the new WB network line-up for the 1994–95 season and immediately proved itself to be one of the network's most popular series.

Series Cast: Stephanie Hodge (Jennie Malloy), Geoff Pierson (Jack Malloy), Kevin Connolly (Ryan Malloy), Nikki Cox (Tiffany Malloy), Justin Berfield (Ross Malloy), Joyce Van Patten (Maureen), Bobcat Goldthwait (Mr. Floppy), Allan Trautman ("Mr. Floppy" Puppeteer).

Each of the episodes is described below in airdate order.

1994–95 season

UNHAPPILY EVER AFTER (pilot)
Airdates: 1/11/95, 5/03/95, 6/21/95.
Guest Cast: Jessica Hahn (Miss Taylor), Dana Daurey (Amber), Brett Stimely (Larry), Ant (Barry), David O'Donnell (Chuck).
When his wife kicks him out of the house and tells him their marriage is over, Jack Malloy moves into a small apartment, where his only companion is Mr. Floppy, a stuffed bunny that happens to talk to him.

GIFT OF THE MAGNAVOX Airdates: 1/18/95, 3/08/95, 6/14/95.
Guest Cast: None.
Jack buys himself a new VCR but Jennie soon finds a way to con him out of it.

JACK'S FIRST DATE Airdates: 1/25/95, 3/29/95, 5/31/95.
Guest Cast: Allan Trautman ("Mr. Floppy" Puppeteer), Jessica Hahn (Miss Taylor), Ant (Barry).
Jennie sabotages Jack's date with an attractive teacher from Ryan's school.

BIGGER THEY ARE, THE HARDER THEY FALL, THE Airdates: 2/01/95, 4/05/95, 6/07/95.
Guest Cast: Steven Gilborn (Doctor), Betsy Monroe (Nurse Crenshaw), Thomas R. Meyers (TV Evangelist voiceover).
Jennie wants Jack to pay for breast implants so she can attract men.

JACK THE RIPPER Airdates: 2/08/95, 6/14/95, 8/16/95.

Guest Cast: Stephen T. Kay (Salesman).

When Jack hits Jennie's mother with his moped, it looks like she may sue him for what little material goods he has and he daydreams about killing her.

RUN Airdates: 2/15/95, 4/19/95, 6/28/95.

Guest Cast: Chelsea Lynn (Little Tiffany), Tommy Bertelsen (Little Ryan).

When Jack gets his hands on the family car he makes a run for Mexico and freedom.

DESCENT OF MAN, THE Airdates: 2/22/95, 4/12/95, 7/05/95.

Guest Cast: None.

Jack tries to teach the boys the finer points of being a man.

BOXING MR. FLOPPY Airdates: 3/01/95, 4/26/95, 6/21/95.

Guest Cast: Ant (Barry), Marne Patterson (Cindy), Benjamin Shelfer (Beau).

Ross cuts off Mr. Floppy's foot as a good luck charm and it seems to have a positive effect on everyone who possesses it.

DON JUAN DE VAN NUYS Airdates: 3/15/95, 5/24/95, 8/02/95.

Guest Cast: Quinn Duffy (Matt Cochran).

Jennie and Tiffany both set their sights on a good-looking handyman.

MISTRESS JENNIE Airdates: 3/22/95, 5/31/95, 8/09/95.

Guest Cast: Ant (Barry), Dana Daurey (Amber), Shonda Whipple (Chelsea), Benjamin Shelfer (Beau), James Cooper (Gavin).

Jennie learns that she is the "other woman," for her new boyfriend happens to be married.

DADDY'S LITTLE GIRL Airdates: 5/02/95, 7/12/95, 8/23/95.

Guest Cast: Bobcat Goldthwait (Forest Celebrity), Chelsea Lynn (Little Tiffany), Benjamin Shelfer (Beau), Nicole Nagel (Amazon Woman).

Jack refuses to let Tiffany spend a weekend at the lake with her boyfriend, so she finds a way to talk him into it.

GREAT DEPRESSION, THE Airdates: 5/10/95, 7/19/95, 8/30/95.

Guest Cast: Allan Trautman (Mr. Dunn), Dana Daurey (Amber), Ant (Barry), Andrea Bendewald (TV Newscaster), Tom Myers (TV Detective voice-over).

The school's spring dance is put into jeopardy when Tiffany is put in charge of the finances.

HOOP DREAMS Airdates: 5/17/95, 7/26/95.

Guest Cast: Allan Trautman (Mr. Dunn), Dana Daurey (Amber), Blake Soper (Billy Emery), Frank Lloyd (Righty), Greg Collins (Ed Moss).

Jack lets the kids down when he forgets to go to an event at the kids' school and goes to a basketball game instead.

1995–96 season

JACK MOVES BACK Airdates: 9/06/95, 10/18/95, 1/14/96.

Guest Cast: None.

Jack and Jennie agree that he should move back home for the sake of the children, so he and Mr. Floppy set up house in the basement.

ZIT COULD HAPPEN TO YOU Airdates: 9/13/95, 11/01/95, 1/14/96, 7/21/96.

Guest Cast: Ant (Barry), Dana Daurey (Amber), Shonda Whipple (Angora), Jamie Kennedy (Stoney), Scott Gurney (Dean Valentine), Momo Kimura (Japanese Kid), Dustin Voigt (Preppie Guy), Michael Dubrow (Buzzcut Guy).

When Tiffany gets a pimple and appears to have gained weight, she decides she belongs with the losers at school.

RAT, THE Airdates: 9/20/95, 12/17/95, 3/27/96, 7/28/96.

Guest Cast: None.

Jack is afraid to admit that he is terrified of a very large rat lurking in the basement.

ROCKY VI Airdates: 9/27/95, 12/06/95.

Guest Cast: Victoria Jackson (Susan), Diane Delano (Vic).

After a series of arguments with a neighbor, Jennie arranges for Jack to settle the matter through a fist fight.

ROCK STAR Airdates: 10/04/95, 12/27/95.

Guest Cast: Ian Patrick Jones (Ray Paul Jones), Sandy Sprung (Motel Manager).

Jennie sets her sights on a rock star she first developed a crush on 20 years ago.

DRIVING ME CRAZY   Airdates: 10/11/95, 12/13/95, 8/04/96.

Guest Cast: None.

Ryan and Tiffany get learners' permits and Jack almost suffers a breakdown when he tries to teach them how to drive.

TOUCH OF GLASS, A   Airdates: 10/25/95, 1/17/96, 6/12/96.

Guest Cast: Jamie Kennedy (Pony Burger Attendant).

Jennie becomes fanatical about protecting her new glass table top.

LINE IN THE SAND, A   Airdates: 11/08/95, 1/03/96, 9/01/96.

Guest Cast: Elisabeth Harnois (Patty), Ant (Barry), Dana Daurey (Amber), Dawn Landon (J.J.), Scott Matthew Bloom (Football Player), Donna D'Errico (Fantasy Girl #1), Kristen Williams (Fantasy Girl #2).

Tiffany crosses paths with a female bully at school. Meanwhile, Jack and Jennie can't agree where to go on vacation.

MAKING THE GRADE   Airdates: 11/15/96, 1/24/96, 7/14/96.

Guest Cast: Allan Trautman (Mr. Dunn), Jessica Hahn (Miss Taylor), Dana Daurey (Amber), Jamie Kennedy (Stoney), Richard Hoyt Miller (Mailman Pops), Tom Myers (Physics Teacher), Darcy Lee (French Teacher).

Jack and Jennie try to figure out where they went wrong when Ryan brings home an abysmal report card.

HONEY, I SCREWED UP THE KIDS FOR LIFE   Airdates: 11/22/95, 3/06/96, 8/18/96.

Guest Cast: Ant (Barry), Dana Daurey (Amber), Will Dimpflmaier (Mike).

When Tiffany announces plans to invite a boy up to her room, her parents use a videotape of Ryan's birth to illustrate the dangers of sex.

WHIZ KID, THE   Airdates: 11/29/95, 8/04/96.

Guest Cast: Kevin Scannell (Chipper Collins), Jeff Doucette (Coach), Ant (Barry), Dana Daurey (Amber), Benjamin Scott Shelfer (Beauregard Scott), Elisabeth Harnois (Patty), Michael Warwick (Nerd Boy).

Ryan achieves instant popularity when he agrees to take the urine test for members of the school football team.

HOT WHEELS   Airdates: 12/20/95, 3/20/96, 7/21/96.

Guest Cast: Gary Coleman (The Devil), Edmund Shaff (Insurance Guy), Derek Sellers (Valet).

A series of misunderstandings leads everyone to believe that the family car has been stolen.

PICNIC OF PAIN AND PERIL   Airdates: 1/10/96, 4/03/96, 7/03/96.

Guest Cast: Frank Lloyd (Righty), Craig Kvinsland (Jim), Benjamin Scott Shelfer (Bullhorn Voice).

Jennie wants the family to enjoy an old-fashioned picnic, but the event doesn't live up to her expectations.

METER MAID   Airdates: 1/31/96, 4/10/96.

Guest Cast: Judy Kain (Meter Maid), Eric Menyuk (Policeman), Murray Rubinstein (Guard), Don Gibb (Spike), Gunther Jensen (Murderer), Frank Lloyd (Rico).

A vengeful meter maid has Jack arrested after she loses an argument with Jennie.

IN THE STARS   Airdates: 2/07/96, 4/17/96, 6/19/96.

Guest Cast: Elisabeth Harnois (Patty), Ant (Barry), Dana Daurey (Amber), Mila Kunis (Chloe), Samantha Becker (Cute Girl), Shonda Whipple (Chelsea).

Jennie and Ryan both learn a lesson about controlling their own destinies when they believe a little too much in their horoscopes.

MR. NO   Airdates: 2/14/96, 4/24/96, 7/28/96.

Guest Cast: John Patrick White (Danny), Bobcat Goldthwait (Host), Ant (Barry), Dana Daurey (Amber), Priscilla Maye (Abbie).

Tiffany is attracted to a boy at school simply because he isn't attracted to her.

AGONY OF VICTORY, THE   Airdates: 2/21/96, 5/29/96, 8/11/96.

Guest Cast: Tommy Bertelsen (Little Ryan).

Jack starts feeling guilty about all of the years he has been cheating while playing basketball with Ryan.

ALL ABOUT JENNIE   Airdates: 2/28/96, 6/05/96, 8/18/96.

Guest Cast: Ant (Barry), Dana Daurey (Amber), Benjamin Shelfer (Beau), Gregory Polcyn (Lizard Agent).

Jennie becomes jealous when Tiffany is cast as Juliet in a school play and schemes to take her place.

Jack Writes Good   Airdates: 5/01/96, 6/26/96, 9/01/96.
Guest Cast: Allan Trautman (Mr. Pillow), Kent Irwin (Pierre), Diane Farr (Michelle).

Jack thinks that the children's book Mr. Floppy wrote is disgusting and sick. A look 30 years into the future shows that it's a big hit in France.

Girls Who Wear Glasses   Airdates: 5/08/96, 7/14/96, 8/25/96.
Guest Cast: Jackée Harry (Ms. Blake), Marcia Wilkie (Mrs. Finkelstein), J. Robin Miller (Agnes), Ant (Barry), Dana Daurey (Amber), Benjamin Shelfer (Beau), Aquilina Soriano (Sushi).

Tiffany is put into a class for overachievers and turns the class inside out when she lectures the other girls about their pitiful social lives.

Leaving Van Nuys   Airdates: 5/15/96, 7/10/96.
Guest Cast: Ant (Barry), Dana Daurey (Amber).

Summer vacation has barely started and the kids have driven Jack and Jennie to drink.

Getting More than Some   Airdates: 5/22/96, 8/11/96.
Guest Cast: Linda Malkiewicz (Crystal), Ant (Barry), Samantha Leavitt (Amanda), Matthew Z. Cox (Joey), Bobcat Goldthwait (Steve Courage, Stuntman).

Everyone is shocked when Ryan's new girlfriend comes to visit, for she brings her two children with her.

The George Wendt Show

After 11 years as supporting player Norm Peterson on the hit sitcom *Cheers*, George Wendt moved up to leading man status with his own series. The format for the 1994–95 sitcom on CBS was inspired by National Public Radio's *Car Talk* series, hosted by brothers Tom and Ray Magliozzi, which featured radio listeners calling in for automotive advice.

The series debuted as a mid-season replacement but failed to make much of an impression with viewers. When only 5 episodes had been aired, the series was pulled from the schedule.

Series Cast: George Wendt (George), Pat Finn (Dan), Mark Christopher Lawrence (Fletcher), Kate Hodge (Libby), Brian Doyle-Murray (Finnie).

Each of the episodes is described below in airdate order. Several episodes were produced but not aired, and are listed in production order.

Sweet Charity   Airdate: 3/08/95.
Guest Cast: George D. Wallace (Father McRudy), Cynthia Mason (Sister Borgnine), Scott Armstrong (Orphan).

A church charity casino-night proves to be too much temptation for Dan, who tries his best to break the bank.

Need for a Seed, A   Airdate: 3/15/95.
Guest Cast: Jessica Tuck (Tina), Dana Sparks (Mimi), Carol Ann Plante (Bernadette).

An attractive woman who likes cars also seems to have a romantic interest in both Dan and George.

Grave Concerns   Airdate: 3/22/95.
Guest Cast: George Wyner (Mr. Sinclair), Charlie Heath (Kevin), Paul Eiding (Jim), Lois Foraker (Karen).

George and Dan can't agree on what to do when a theme park wants to move their father's grave so it can expand into a neighboring cemetery.

Rash Behavior   Airdate: 3/29/95.
Guest Cast: Bernadette Birkertt (Pam), Lorna Scott (Mother), Doug Ballard (Ted), John Calvin (Steve), Jeffrey Lampert (Emcee), Michael Yama (Doctor).

George is lucky when he gets a date with a doctor, for he may need her professional attention when he gets a nasty rash.

Prom Night: The Return   Airdate: 4/05/95.
Guest Cast: Paul Wilson (Limo Driver), Jennifer Cox (Ashley), Andre Nemec (Greg), Randall Slavin (Philip), Richard Speight (Paul), Todd Waring (Teddy).

When George and Libby drive some teenagers to their prom, it makes them recall their own not very special night.

River Runs Through His Head, A   Airdate: 4/12/95.
Guest Cast: Larry Brandenberg (Sheriff), Michael Monks (Deputy), Ingo Neuhaus (Officer), Steven M. Porter (Bill), Jeris Lee Poindexter (Roger), Clayton Prince (Ed),

Connie Sawyer (Mrs. Landy), Will Ferrell (White Guy).

A fishing trip with the guys ends in a series of disasters, especially when two of them are mistakenly arrested as thieves.

AND HERE'S TO YOU, MRS. ROBERTSON
Airdate: Unaired.

Guest Cast: Beverly Archer (Eleanor Robertson), Marsha Dietlein (Carly), Stephen Burrows (Emcee).

Family relationships take an unusual turn when George's fiancee turns out to be Dan's girlfriend's mother.

MY BROTHER THE ALBATROSS   Airdate: Unaired.

Guest Cast: Eliza Coyle (Janet), Charles Cyphers (Mr. Blake), Debra Mooney (Mrs. Blake), Justin Jon Ross (Young Dan), Mikie Schadel (Young George), Brandy Sanders (Kiki), Trey Alexander (Waiter).

When Dan gets cold feet before the wedding, he leaves George the unpleasant chore of dealing with the jilted girlfriend.

Pride & Joy

This mid-season replacement for the 1995–96 season was the story of two families trying to get used to dealing with their young children. A large part of the show was the fact that each couple neither was financially secure nor really knew much about parenting.

Pride & Joy lasted 6 short weeks before it was placed on hiatus and production was halted. Four episodes later, it returned as reruns, but by then the series had already been canceled.

Series Cast: Julie Warner (Amy Sherman), Jeremy Piven (Nathan Green), Craig Berko (Greg Sherman), Caroline Rhea (Carol Green), Natasha Pavloví (Katya).

Each of the episodes is described below in airdate order.

PRIDE & JOY (pilot)   Airdates: 3/21/95, 6/27/95.

Guest Cast: Tom Virtue (Clown), Ping Wu (Delivery Man), Richard Chaim (Teenager).

Amy worries about returning to work and leaving her son in Greg's untrained hands.

MEANT TO BE   Airdates: 3/28/95, 6/20/95.

Everyone is shocked when Nathan admits he had a crush on Amy in college.

TERROR AT 30,000 FEET   Airdate: 4/04/95.

Guest Cast: Maggie Wheeler (Flight Attendant), Richard Poe (Herb), Zaid Farid (Security Officer), Peggy Roeder (Nun), Peyton Reed (Frenchman).

A plane ride turns into a test of endurance for everyone aboard when little Mel acts up.

ARE YOU MY MOTHER?   Airdate: 4/11/95.

Guest Cast: David Wohl (Bernard), Rose Abdoo (Wendy), Veanne Cox (Lisa).

Carol and Amy decide to take advantage of their mothering skills to launch their own line of baby food.

GENIUS   Airdates: 4/25/95, 7/04/95.

Guest Cast: Cynthia Mace (Mrs. Kluger), Susan Gibney (Donna), Preston Maybank (Jeffrey), Jack Laufer (Bruce), Chelsea Lynn (Vanessa), John Petlock (Raymond).

There's only one opening at a school for gifted children and each couple is sure that their child is the one who is going to get in.

BRENDA'S SECRET   Airdates: 5/02/95, 7/11/95.

Guest Cast: Peri Gilpin (Brenda), Jack Black (Man), Henriette Mantel (Nanny #1), Christin Hinojosa (Laughing Nanny), Denny Pierce (Messenger).

There's something strange about the new nanny; the couples suspect she is either a thief or a porn star.

Nowhere Man

In the science fiction–oriented dramatic series *Nowhere Man*, photographer Thomas Veil suddenly finds that he seemingly never existed. Everyone he has ever known claims never to have met him, causing Veil to go on a quest for the truth.

Audiences seemed to have a hard time understanding the elaborate plot twists and subterfuges employed through the series, and *Nowhere Man* was not renewed for a second season.

Series Cast: Bruce Greenwood (Tom Veil).

Each of the episodes is described below in airdate order.

ABSOLUTE ZERO   Airdates (90-minute format): 8/28/95, 1/08/96.

Guest Cast: Megan Gallagher (Alyson Veil), Ted Levine (Dave "Eddie" Powers), Bernie

McInerney (Father Thomas), Michael Tucker (Dr. Bellamy), David Brisbin (Driver), Mary Gregory (Mrs. Veil), John Hillard (Cop), Murray Rubenstein (Larry Levy), Rebecca Hayes (Woman #1), Heather Paige Kent (Woman #2), Alexandra Kenworthy (Woman #3), Mariah O'Brien (Nurse), Steve Restivo (Gino), Greg Wrangler (Husband), Jay Arlen Jones (Inmate), Lisa Rafel (Attractive Woman), Robert Kempf (Oscar).

Somehow, someone has erased photographer Tom Veil's existence clean. Within minutes, no one, not even his wife and mother, remembers anything about him. Veil is eventually brought to a psychiatric clinic where a Dr. Bellamy reveals that a secret organization has the power to engineer this baffling charade.

TURNABOUT   Airdates: 9/04/95, 12/04/95.
Guest Cast: Mimi Craven (Ellen Combs), George Del Hoyo (The Supervisor), Phil Reeves (Doctor Haynes), Tobias Anderson (The Monk).

While on the run, Veil uses Dr. Bellamy's credit card and is tracked down by his unknown pursuers. They think that he's Bellamy and order him to subject a young woman to the same brainwashing that Bellamy gave Veil.

INCREDIBLE DEREK, THE   Airdates: 9/11/95, 12/18/95.
Guest Cast: Mike Starr (Bert Williams), Zachery McLemore (Derek Bartholomew Williams), Tim DeZarn (Harry Corners), William Utay (Ira), Geoff Prysirr (Manor Deward), Don Burns (Earl), Michael E. Fetters (Pete), Curt Hanson (Cigar Smoker), Barbara Irvin (Norma), Victor Morris (Sergeant), Betty Moyer (Woman), George Rankin (The Man), Dylan Taylor (Ned).

Veil receives an ominous warning about his pursuers from a 10-year-old blind boy who seems to know all about them.

SOMETHING ABOUT HER   Airdates: 9/18/95, 12/25/95.
Guest Cast: Carrie Ann Moss (Karein Stolk), Raphael Sbarge (Dr. Moen), Kent Williams (Mr. Grey), Lindsey Blodgett (Young Girl), Todd Hermanson (Paramedic), Marilyn Hickey (Nurse #1), Tammie Andreas (Nurse #2), Russ Fast (Dr. Hamilton).

Veil is captured and drugged to make him think that he is in love with a young woman, for his captors hope he will trust her enough to reveal his secret to her.

PARADISE ON YOUR DOORSTEP
Airdates: 9/25/95, 1/01/96.
Guest Cast: Saxon Trainor (Dierdre Coltrera), Stephen Meadows (Paul), Zuma Bradley (Security Guard #3), Kelly Brown (Security Guard #2), Mario DePriest (Cory), Ian Hendry (Car Kid), Eric Hull (Roy), Mary Kane (Gardening Woman), Michael C. Lucas (Security Guard #1), Jay Pevney (Cabbie), Ted Roisum (Pilot), Burl Ross (Mowing Man), Marty Ryan (Customer), Mark Vincent (Master of Ceremonies).

While working in a photo lab, Veil is astonished to spot a picture of his wife. He follows a trail that leads him to town where everyone seems to have lost their identity at the hands of his pursuers.

SPIDER WEBB, THE   Airdates: 10/09/95, 3/25/96.
Guest Cast: Richard Kind (Max Webb), Kate Hodge (Nancy/Angie), Michael McGuire (Robert/Lenny), Nicholas Pryor (Phil), Sam Mowry (Mr. Simmons), Steve Restivo (Gino), Greg Wrangler (Alyson's Husband).

Veil is astonished when he sees *The Lenny Little Show* on television, for the characters on it are living out his own terrifying experience.

ROUGH WHIMPER OF INSANITY, A
Airdates: 10/23/95, 1/29/96.
Guest Cast: Megan Gallagher (Alyson Veil), Sean Whalen (Scott Hansen), Karen Moncrief (Pam Peterson), Jeanne Sanders (Carla), Bill Harper (Jimmy), Tracy LeRich (Cindy), Cheryl Hansen (Mrs. Fine), Michael Duvall (First Man), Rick Mullins (Second Man), Rod James (Elderly Man).

An eccentric computer hacker uncovers deleted files that can help Veil, then creates a virtual reality version of Alyson Veil.

ALPHA SPIKE, THE   Airdates: 10/30/95, 4/01/96.
Guest Cast: Bryan Cranston (Norman Wade), Jackson Price (Kyle), James McDonnell (Headmaster), Jennifer Banko (Vickie), Ivars Mikelson (Cigar Smoking Man), Marco Gould (Seth), Steve Lomax (Adam), Danny Stoltz (Brad), Giang Pham (Kid #1), Karen Rasor (Kid #2), Tony Melson (Kid #3), Jeremy Monlux (Kid #4).

Veil traces Dr. Bellamy's career back to a private school, where he discovers that the administration is programming the student body for an unknown purpose.

You Really Got a Hold on Me
Airdates: 11/06/95, 3/04/96.

Guest Cast: Dean Stockwell (Gus Shepard), Lesli Kay Sterling (Tina), Dinah Leffert (Mary), Shannon Day (Yuppie Woman), Steven Jacquith (Yuppie Man), Michael Scheinman (Yuppie Boy), Joe Ivy (Dr. Richards), Gene Freedman (Custodian), Cork Hubbert (Wino), James Fischer (Man), Vance Deadrick (Carny).

Veil's life is saved by a drifter who claims to also be on the run from the same organization.

Father
Airdates: 11/13/95, 4/22/96.

Guest Cast: Dean Jones (Jonathan Crane), Donna Bullock (Beth Crane), Joseph Carberry (Morris), Gary Rooney (Marty), Cody Hill (Johnny), Dennis Adkins (Doctor Hal), Grant Ouzts (Johnny's Teammate), Tyrone Henry (Umpire).

Veil travels back to his childhood home and is reunited with the man who betrayed him 20 years ago—his father.

Enemy Within, An
Airdates: 11/20/95, 5/27/96.

Guest Cast: Maria Bello (Emily Noonan), Raye Birk (Tobe Adler), James Lashly (Ed Durrant), Scott Parker (Doc Wilson), Linda Burden-Williams (Lillian), Jan Burrell (Hazel), Mayme Paul-Thompson (Mrs. Hardy), Randy Thompson (Mr. Hardy), Jeff Gorham (Mark), Peter Kjenas (Will), Dave Demke (Process Server), Aaron Bass (Guard #1), Ken Lodge (Guard #2), Robert Pete Randall (Delivery Man), Lev Liberman (Man in Crowd), Jim Lykins (Patron).

Veil is rescued from death by a Pennsylvania woman who is fighting to save her farm from a powerful and corrupt food conglomerate. For the first time, he may have found someone he can trust.

It's Not Such a Wonderful Life
Airdates: 11/27/95, 6/30/96.

Guest Cast: Megan Gallagher (Alyson Veil), Carol Huston (Sandra Wilson), Mary Gregory (Mrs. Veil), Willie C. Carpenter (Rick), W. Earl Brown (Roy), Joe Cronin (Alex), Edward Murphy (Sidewalk Santa), Scott Eisenhower (Photographer), Kaycheri Rappaport (Bailiff), Stephen Weyte (Father), John Kenower (Bumped Man), Brooke Cusick (Phonebooth Woman), Jim Garcia (Taxi Driver).

It looks like Veil may have a merry Christmas when he is found by federal agents who tell him that the group chasing him is "The Organization," political fanatics who are determined to control political policy.

Contact
Airdates: 1/15/96, 6/10/96.

Guest Cast: Joseph Lambie (Richard Grace), Robin Sachs (The Voice), Hank Cartwright (Hanks), Paul Fitzgerald (Joey), Michael Donovan (Security Guard), Shawna Schuh (Reporter), J.W. Crawford (Night Manager).

Someone from within the Organization contacts Veil, claiming he will help him if Veil will kill one of the group's leaders.

Heart of Darkness
Airdates: 1/22/96, 6/17/96.

Guest Cast: James Tolkan (Commander Quinn), Scott Coffey (Greer), Patrick Kilpatrick (C.W. Knox), J.R. Knotts (Jaxon), Derek Sitter (Recruit #1), Glen Baggerly (Recruit #3), Peter Paige (Recruit #4), William Harper (Jimmy), Charles Taylor Gould (Recruit #2), Peter Warnick (Guard), Danny Bruno (Crew Member #1), Terry Ward (Suited Man).

Veil infiltrates a group of political activists to get closer to a man who might be one of those seen in the "Hidden Agenda" photograph.

Forever Jung
Airdates: 2/05/96, 6/24/96.

Guest Cast: Leon Russom (Dr. Seymour), Melanie Smith (Young Pauline), Edith Fields (Older Pauline), Freda Foh Shen (Nurse Ellman), Paul Marin (Rudy).

Veil follows a lead to a nursing home in Minnesota. He discovers an apparent fountain of youth that disguises a horrible and deadly secret.

Shine a Light on You
Airdates: 2/21/96, 7/01/96.

Guest Cast: Dorie Barton (Helen Meyerson), Roy Brocksmith (Bud Atkins), Tom McCleister (Hank Bower), George Gerdes (Sheriff Wilkes), Bill Geisslinger (Dr. John Meyerson), David Meyers (Steven Weaver), Brian Boe (Manager), Chris Roccaro (Mrs. Thames).

Veil's search for an Organization scientist seems to have a strange ending when he is told the man was abducted by aliens.

Stay Tuned
Airdates: 2/19/96, 7/08/96.

Guest Cast: Chris DeYoung (Jim Hubbard), Karen Witter (Janet Cowen), Billy O'Sullivan (Michael), Maggie Hefferman (Elsie Marlowe), Bob Morrisey (Ed Marlowe), Abby Ribin

(Abigail), Betty Moyer (Sarah), Jordan Carlton (Robbie), Joanna Simmons (Barbara), Jeff McAtee (Ben), John Kenower (Officer Joe), Michele Mariana (Aunt Emaline), Brandon Sears (Daniel Marlowe), Blaine Browlow (Principal Hopper), Jay Pevney (Director), Matt Williams (Announcer), Dan Vhay (A.D.), Debbie Domby (Elsie's Neighbor), James Fischer (Passerby #1), Charles Bernard (Passerby #2).

Veil's contact within the Organization sends him to a small New York town, and he discovers another plot to control the community through mind control.

HIDDEN AGENDA   Airdates: 2/26/96, 7/15/96.

Guest Cast: Dwight Schultz (Harrison Barton), Robin Sachs (Alexander Hale), Anthony Guzman (Luis Borjes), Tracy Conklin (Sergeant Rock), William Earl Ray (Lieutenant Anson), Geoff Prysirr (Shadow One), Allen Nause (Shadow Two), Christine Calfas (Yolanda), Olga Sanchez (Angela), Jim Garcia (Ringo), Mark Homayoun (Spanish Guard), Michael Blain-Rozgay (Waiter), Fulvio Cecere (Sgt. Dirksen), Jon Bebe (Young Guard #1), Tim McKellips (Young Guard #2), Erin Cecil (Sobbing Woman).

Alexander Hale, Veil's informant in the Organization, tricks him into revealing details about the "Hidden Agenda" photograph.

DOPPLEGANGER   Airdates: 3/18/96, 7/22/96.

Guest Cast: Jamie Rose (Clare Hillard), Mia Korf (Jane Butler), Richard Penn (Detective Tanner), Laura Leigh Hughes (Lucy), Don Stewart Burns (Elmer), Barbara Kite (Mrs. Hilliard), Doug Baldwin (McClusky), Raissa Fleming (Rachel), Tracey LeRich (Jeanette), Brendan Quinlan (Bartender), David Cesana (Sniper).

Veil meets with another journalist from his Nicaraguan days and learns that another man has taken over his name, identity, and photographs.

THROUGH A LENS DARKLY   Airdates: 4/08/96, 7/29/96.

Guest Cast: Sydney Walsh (Laura), Sam Anderson (The Man), Jason Waters (Teenage Tom), Monica Creel (Teenage Laura), Trevor O'Brien (Young Tom), Julia Whelan (Young Laura), Joe Cronin (Commander), Kelly J. Ray (Cabbie), Dave Cascadden (Man #1), James Eikrem (Policeman), Louanne Moldovan (Wailing Woman).

Captured once again, Veil is subjected to a new technique that makes him relive his life in painful detail until he finally agrees to turn over the "Hidden Agenda" negative.

DARK SIDE OF THE MOON   Airdate: 4/15/96.

Guest Cast: Trevor Goodard (Mackie), Juliet Tablak (Margo), Dan Martin (Father Ray), Maurice Chasse (Bradley), Evan Matthews (Tiny), Jeff Gillis (Caps), Jan Brehm (Woman), Caton Lyles (Blaze), Louis Lotorto (Intern), Marvin Leroy Sanders (Bouncer), Josh Musselman (Attacker), Rob Middendorf (Sammy), Paul Cardona (Justin), George O'Mara (Samaritan), Johnny Useldinger (Vendor), Constance Frenzen (Nurse).

Veil is mugged by a street gang and they take the photos from him. He and the Organization both search for the gang, but the thieves are also after Veil seeking revenge for the death of one of their members.

CALAWAY   Airdate: 4/29/96.

Guest Cast: Jay Arlen Jones (Joe "J.C." Carter/Dr. Novik), Robert Cicchini (Michael Kramer), Bruce Gray (Dr. Gilmore), Don Alder (Dr. Madison), Robert Blanche (Security Guard), Brian Boe (Don), Paul Holstein (White Jacket Orderly), Mel Jones (Alan), Edmund Stone (Patient), Mark Tassoni (Dave), Wendy Westerwelle (Waitress), James Fischer (1st Orderly), Elisabeth Adwin (Nurse).

Veil returns to the Organization's hospital and is surprised to spot a former patient who believes he is one of the doctors.

ZERO MINUS TEN   Airdate: 5/06/96.

Guest Cast: Megan Gallagher (Alyson Veil), Murray Rubenstein (Larry Levy), Choppy Guilotte (Ben Dobbs), David Bodin (Doctor), Mark Vincent (Policeman #1), Stephen Rouffy (Policeman #2), Lenanne Sylvester (Vendor), Suzannah Mars (Nurse #1), Coletta Herbold (Nurse #2).

Veil wakes up in a hospital and is told that he has been in a coma since an automobile accident and his entire ordeal has been nothing but a nightmare.

MARATHON   Airdate: 5/13/96.

Guest Cast: Nicholas Surovy (Stanley Robman), Elsie Sniffen (Jenny Hsu), Barbara Lusch (Brenda), Oz Tortora (Sparky), Michael Behrens (Flannel), Gene Otis (Operative #1), Jim Steele (Operative #2), John Roemer (Specialist), Mark Schwahn (Technician),

Martin Ryan (Special Agent), Bill Wadhams (Rodman's Assistant), David Apple (Operator), Ross Huffman-Kerr (Bum).

Another study of the "Hidden Agenda" photograph leads Veil to a research facility under investigation by the FBI.

GEMINI   Airdate: 5/20/96.

Guest Cast: Hal Linden (Senator Wallace), Francis X. McCarthy (Robert Barton), Edward Edwards (Iverson), Alexandra Boyd (Wallace Aide), Kelly Laura (Wallace Secretary), David Angus MacDonald (Suit), Cheryl Yamaguchi (Female Passerby), Barbara Casement (Maid), Mark Friedrichsen (Uniform #2), Patrick Kelly (Hardhat), Dana Williams (FBI Operator).

Veil finally gets his hand on the unretouched "Hidden Agenda" photograph and learns that the victims were all members of a Senate committee investigating domestic terrorism.

Maybe This Time

Golden Girls veteran Betty White returned to Disney for this sitcom about a mother and daughter who ran a small neighborhood coffee shop together. Her co-star was singer-actress Marie Osmond. Osmond played Julia, a conservative mother who has just been divorced after 12 years. Hurt by this romantic downside, she decided to give up on men and concentrate instead on the family business and raising her daughter. This philosophy was totally at odds with that of her mother, for Shirley was a five-times widow who was always on the prowl for her next husband.

Series Cast: Marie Osmond (Julia), Betty White (Shirley), Ashley Johnson (Gracie), Amy Hill (Kay), Craig Ferguson (Logan).

Each of the episodes is described below in airdate order.

PLEASE RE-LEASE ME   Airdates: 9/15/95, 12/30/95.

Guest Cast: Elliott Reid (Henry), Alicia Brandt (Lorraine), Kelly Hu (Jennifer), James Wong (Robert), Derek Sage (Erich), Ric Stoneback (Customer).

Julia tries to prove that she can get a better deal on the rent than Shirley without having to flirt with the landlord.

MAYBE THIS TIME (pilot)   Airdate: 9/16/95.

Guest Cast: Shiloh Strong (Hunter), Sam McMurray (Greg), Ashley Gardner (Sherry), Catherine Lloyd Burns (Angela), Tony Carlin (Robert), Challen Cates (Gwyneth), Stacy Cortez (Jennifer), Ric Stoneback (David), Nicole Sullivan (Stephanie).

Although Julia is in no hurry to start dating again, Shirley is determined to play matchmaker.

GRACIE UNDER FIRE   Airdate: 9/23/95.

Guest Cast: Alan Young (Arthur), Bunny Summers (Farrah), Mia Korf (Brenda), Sarah Martineck (Morgan), Ebick Pizzadili (Cynthia), Keeira Lyn Ford (Jane), Dona Hardy (Brittany), Cynthia Lamontagne (Bethany).

Tired of all of Julia's rules and regulations, Gracie decides she would rather stay at Shirley's.

OUT, OUT, DAMN RADIO SPOT!   Airdate: 9/30/95.

Guest Cast: Mark Benninghofen (Morton), John Reilly (Flint), Ron Fassler (Al), Tara Charendoff (Emily).

Julia regrets it when Logan talks her into advertising the coffee shop on a popular but controversial radio talk show.

SNITCH DOGGY-DOGG   Airdate: 10/14/95.

Guest Cast: Pat Millicano (Lou), Andrew Hill Newman (Joe), Richard Schiff (Perlman), Lise Simms (Woman #1), Shelley Robertson (Woman #2), Lynn Daly (Woman #3).

Gracie gets in trouble for telling lies at school, but she's not the only one stretching the truth. Shirley asks Julia to lie to a health inspector, and Julia bends the truth to get her dog out of the pound.

BEASY BODY   Airdate: 10/28/95.

Guest Cast: Cloris Leachman (Beasy), Mary Ellen Lyon (Lauren), Rikki Dale (Wendy), Mathew Paul Botuchis (Johnny), Christopher James Miller (Brad).

When Logan's grandmother visits from Ireland, determined to help him find a wife, he tells her that he is engaged to Julia.

JULIA'S DAY OFF   Airdate: 11/04/95.

Guest Cast: Robert Kelker-Kelly (Brandon), Erin Williby (Lydia), Robert Machray (Herman), Don Perry (Quiet Man), Toshi Toda (Businessman #1), Jim Ishida (Businessman #2), Michael Hagiwara (Businessman #3), P.B. Hutton (Maryanne), Mike Randleman (Customer #1), Miriam Billington (Customer #2).

Julia takes Shirley's advice to relax and has a wonderful day off. Gracie skips school for the day and doesn't fare as well.

COACH JULIA   Airdate: 11/11/95.
Guest Cast: Julius Carry (Brock), Dane Cook (Kyle), Richard Speight, Jr. (Eddie).

Julia isn't happy with Kyle, the shop's new delivery boy, who is attending college on an athletic scholarship.

OTHER MOTHER, THE   Airdate: 11/25/95.
Guest Cast: Dane Cook (Kyle), Susan Wood (Kristi), Erin Williby (Lydia), Dane Cook (Kyle), Jordana Spiro (Chase).

When Julia meets her ex-husband's new and outgoing girlfriend, she tries to act like her to impress Gracie.

CATCH, THE   Airdate: 12/16/95.
Guest Cast: Todd Waring (Richard), Dane Cook (Kyle), Judith Jones (Lauren).

Julia gets up the courage to ask someone out, but Kyle lets Gracie do the dirty work for him when he takes a fancy to a customer at the diner.

JUDGEMENT DAY   Airdate: 12/23/95.
Guest Cast: Ethan Phillips (Douglas), Wendy Benson (Prudence Delaney), Michael Ensign (John Biddle), Patrick T. O'Brien (James Howell), David Wiley (Harold Dundin).

Julia volunteers to teach at Sunday school and Shirley tries to turn it into another attempt at matchmaking.

NICK AT NIGHT   Airdate: 1/06/96.
Guest Cast: Robert Cicchini (Nick), Ross Malinger (Nicky), Daniel Hagen (Bob), Sharisse Baker (Karen).

Gracie really likes her new boyfriend, but Julia definitely does not share the sentiment.

BREAK A LEG   Airdates: 1/13/96.
Guest Cast: Dick Van Patten (Jack), Julius Carry (Brock), Dane Cook (Kyle), Ross Malinger (Nicky), Clyde Kusatsu (Noriyuki), Dorie Barton (Wendy), Archie Kao (Takeshi), Otto Coelho (Delivery Man).

Five-time widow Shirley sets her sights on husband number 6, while Gracie is worrying about her first kiss.

LUCKY PUCK   Airdate: 1/20/96.
Guest Cast: Matt Battaglia (Bobby), Dane Cook (Kyle), Andrea Abbate (Casey), Sandra Purpuro (Angie), Marnie Brossen (Agnes), Susan Gainer (Kelly), Otto Coelho (Delivery

Man), Evan R. Press (Customer), Bill Small (Customer #2).

A hockey player becomes obsessed with Julia when he thinks she brings him good luck.

ACTING OUT   Airdate: 1/26/96.
Guest Cast: Ben Savage (Cory), Rider Strong (Shawn), William Daniels (Mr. Feeney), Dane Cook (Kyle), Ross Malinger (Nicky), Robert Cicchini (Nick), Ryan O'Donohue (Joey), Oliver Muirhead (Mr. Nichols), Andrew Amic-Angelo (Johnny), Joey Simmrin (Spencer), Rick Zieff (Alvin), Thomas Odell (Dudley), Mark Henderson (Customer).

Nicky enjoys acting in the school play until his classmates tease him about wearing tights.

STAND UP YOUR MAN   Airdate: 2/03/96.
Guest Cast: Dane Cook (Kyle), Robert Cicchini (Nick), Senta Moses (Felice), Bill Applebaum (Glenn), Bill Liblick (Himself), John Henson (Himself), Rick Zieff (Alvin), Lyndsay Riddell (Lisa), Ashley McDonogh (Tiffany), Jamie Olsen (Alanis), Leanna Nelson (Rachelle).

Julia meets up with a boy she stood up in high school and relives the guilt she has been hiding for 17 years over the incident.

ST. VALENTINE'S DAY MASSACRE
Airdate: 2/10/96.
Guest Cast: Dane Cook (Kyle), Ross Malinger (Nicky), Robert Cicchini (Nick), Lindsay Price (Veronica), Heidi Noelle Lenhart (Monique), Lyndsay Riddell (Lisa), Tony Sorensen (Sven).

Gracie reconsiders her decision to turn down Kyle's invitation for St. Valentine's Day.

WHOSE LIFE IS IT ANYWAY?   Airdate: 2/17/96.
Guest Cast: Lise Simms (Suzi), Dane Cook (Kyle), Ross Partridge (David), Christian Menard (Michael), Morgan Roth (Cindy), Miles Marisco (Howie), Jessica Cushman (Cathy), Richard Psarros (Bill), Sam Temeles (Ted).

A visit from an old friend shows how differently she and Julia have lived their lives and raised their children.

Brotherly Love

When it was apparent that *Blossom* had run its course and would be leaving the air at the end of the 1994–95 season, Disney executives set out to create a new vehicle for series co-star Joey Lawrence. The result was *Brotherly Love.* As the title hints, it is centered around a group of brothers, played by real-life brothers Joey, Matthew, and Andrew Lawrence.

Brotherly Love joined the NBC Sunday night lineup for the 1995–96 season.

Series Cast: *Joey Lawrence (Joe Roman), Matthew Lawrence (Matthew Roman), Andrew Lawrence (Andy Roman), Melinda Culea (Claire Roman), Michael McShane (Lloyd), Liz Vassey (Lou).*

Each of the episodes is described below in airdate order.

BROTHERLY LOVE (pilot)   Airdate: 9/16/95.
Joe Roman arrives in town to sell a business, and gets a family instead.

SUCH A BARGAIN   Airdates: 9/17/95, 11/05/95.
Guest Cast: *Chuck Bailey (Limo Driver), Mike Starr (Gus), Bryan Cranston (Russell).*
Matt goes way overboard to impress a pretty girl.

LIBERTY BELL SHOW, THE   Airdate: 9/24/95.
Guest Cast: *Hiram Kasten (Tour Guide), Tyler Layton (Debbie).*
Andy becomes convinced that he broke the Liberty Bell.

MIDSUMMER'S NIGHTMARE, A   Airdate: 10/01/95.
Guest Cast: *Shiri Appleby (Fairy #1), Shana Smith (Fairy #2), Dustin Voigt (Oberon), Jonathan Charles Kaplan (Ira Stolzer), Justine Johnston (Mrs. Maguire).*
Hoping to be more popular, Matt tries out for the school play, not expecting all of the teasing he then receives from Joe.

UPTOWN GIRL   Airdate: 10/08/95.
Guest Cast: *Joel Jordan (Johnny Romano), Ann Marie Lee (Mrs. Ford), Victor Raider-Wexler (Mr. Levenstein), Jonathan Charles Kaplan (Ira Stolzer), Mathea Webb (Christy).*
Joe falls in love with a woman from a wealthy family, which makes him think about his own meager existence.

COMIC CON, THE   Airdate: 10/25/95.
Guest Cast: *Tressa Goble (Nancy), Lisa Hyman (Helga), Dana Kaminsky (Comic Con Patron), Megan Cavanagh (Lotus), George Takei (Himself).*
Lloyd and Andy get ready for the high point of each year—a comic book convention.

SLEEPOVER SHOW, THE   Airdate: 10/29/95.
Guest Cast: *Jonathan Charles Kaplan (Ira Stolzer).*
Claire has quite a night dealing with Andy's fear of slumber parties.

WITCHCRAFT   Airdate: 10/30/95.
Guest Cast: *Tommy Bertelsen (Tin Woodsman), Derk Cheetwood (College Kid), Melanie Hutsell (Wilma), Laura Summer (Julie), Brant Van Hoffman (Missing Sock), John Kassir (The Cryptkeepr).*
Joey takes Andy to the mall for trick-or-treating and accidentally brings home the wrong kid who is dressed in the same costume.

BAIT AND SWITCH   Airdate: 11/12/95.
Guest Cast: *Joey Herman (Bill Fody), Randy Herman (Buck Fody).*
Lloyd tries to play Cupid between Joe and Lou; Matt looks for a way to defeat the school bully.

OUTBREAK!   Airdate: 11/19/95.
Guest Cast: *Michael Lowry (Josh), Sid Melton (Messenger).*
The whole family becomes infected when Andy comes home with chickenpox.

ROMAN HOLIDAY   Airdate: 12/18/95.
Andy wants all of the brothers together for Christmas but Joe has plans to fly back to California to see his mother.

ONCE AROUND THE BLOCK   Airdate: 3/04/95.
Guest Cast: *David Byrd (Alfred), Stephen Lee (Cop), Jonathan Charles Kaplan (Ira Stolzer), Gina Gallego (Lupe).*
The brothers sneak into a dance and see an attractive woman, only to discover it's their mother; someone brings the television Batmobile in for repairs and they decide to take it for a ride.

REMEMBER   Airdate: 3/11/96.
Guest Cast: *Nestor Carbonell (Eduardo), Adam Consolo (Lance), Jonathan Charles Kaplan (Ira Stolzer), Tom Kenny (Doug).*
The family isn't thrilled with Joe's decision to get back into motorcycle racing.

BIG BROTHERLY LOVE   Airdate: 3/18/96.

Guest Cast: Jimmy Briscoe (Jimmy), Billy West (Billy), Tom Arnold (Jack).

Joe is suspicious of a stranger who seems to have too much influence over the rest of the family.

BRIDE AND PREJUDICE   Airdate: 3/25/96.

Guest Cast: Melody Kay (Robin), Jeremy Linson (Dave), Michael Lowry (Josh).

Joe and Lou realize they are more than just a little interested in each other after Lou's boyfriend proposes.

DOUBLE DATE   Airdate: 4/01/96.

Guest Cast: Adam Consolo (Lance), Peter Krause (Tom), Lisa Reiffel (Amy).

A series of romantic misadventures makes the guys realize that you're sometimes better off with your current friends instead of looking for new ones.

If Not for You

If Not for You centered on two people who were drawn to each other from the moment they first saw each other across a crowded restaurant. The would-be lovers were Jessie Kent and Craig Schaeffer. It was indeed love at first sight, but there was just one problem: each of them was already engaged to someone else. The series was added to the CBS schedule as *One of Those Things* for the 1995–96 season, then switched back to its original title.

Series Cast: Elizabeth McGovern (Jessie Kent), Hank Azaria (Craig Schaeffer), Debra Jo Rupp (Eileen Richter), Jim Turner (Cal), Reno Wilson (Bobby Beaumont).

Each of the episodes is described below in airdate order.

IF NOT FOR YOU (pilot)   Airdate: Unaired.

Cast: Elizabeth McGovern (Jessie Kent), Hank Azaria (Craig Schaffer), Heidi Swedberg (Melanie McKee), Arabella Field (Paula Schaffer), Matthew Glave (Gary Schaffer). Guest Cast: Željko Ivanek (Elliot Gordon), Lauren Tom (Claire), Richard Schiff (Chernikov), Chris Hogan (Lance Richter), Raymond Ma (Waiter), Jack Ong (Wu), Deborah Tucker (Kate Mulkey), Leslie Caveny (Woman on Line).

After this pilot episode was completed, the producers decided to recast the supporting cast and reshot the first meeting of Jessie and Craig for the next episode.

DETOUR AHEAD   Airdate: 9/18/95.

Guest Cast: Kelly Coffield (Suzette), Peter Krause (Elliot), Jane Sibbett (Melanie), Wesley Leong (Waiter), Chris Hogan (Lance), Deborah Tucker (Kate).

Jessie and Craig are instantly attracted to each other when they exchange glances at a restaurant.

TAKING A SHOWER WITH MY TWO TRUE LOVES   Airdate: 9/25/95.

Guest Cast: Caroline Aaron (Nina), Kelly Coffield (Suzette), Peter Krause (Elliot), Jane Sibbett (Melanie).

Craig must pay in more ways than one when he gives Jessie an expensive gift.

KISS, THE   Airdate: 10/02/95.

Guest Cast: Peter Krause (Elliot), Jane Sibbett (Melanie).

When Craig gets a lunch invitation from Jessie's fiance, he sees this as a perfect chance to tell the truth about how he feels—a decision not shared by Jessie.

SNAP   Airdate: 10/09/95.

Guest Cast: Peter Krause (Elliot), Jane Sibbett (Melanie), Cress Williams (Ahmed), Josh Schaeffer (Chet), Cleandre Norman (Billy).

Jessie and Craig both discover that sometimes it's easier to get into a relationship than to end one when they try to call off their engagements.

DAY THE HALO CAME OFF, THE   Airdate: Unaired.

Guest Cast: Brian Doyle-Murray (Nestor), Peter Krause (Elliot), Jane Sibbett (Melanie).

When Jessie announces a 2-week break from their relationship to see how she really feels about him, Peter pulls out all the stops to get her back.

Land's End

Fred Dryer, who had starred in the long-running police series *Hunter*, returned to television in this first-run syndication action series as detective Mike Land. As the series began, Mike was a detective on the LAPD, but he retired to Cabo San Lucas in Mexico when his wife was killed by a drug dealer who then escaped justice. Along with his old buddy Willis P. Dunleevy, he sets up Cabo's first private detective agency.

Land's End aired in the 1995–96 season.

Series Cast: Fred Dryer (Mike Land), Geoffrey Lewis (Willis P. Dunleevy), Tim Thomerson (Dave "Thunder" Thornton), Pamela Bowen (Courtney Saunders), William Marquez (Chief Ruiz).

Each of the episodes is described below in airdate order. As *Land's End* was syndicated, the actual airdates vary by location. The airdates listed are the first day that the episode was available for broadcast.

LAND'S END (pilot)   Airdate (2-hour format): 9/18/95. Repeated in two parts—Part 1: 12/04/95, 4/14/96. Part 2: 12/11/95, 4/15/96.

Guest Cast: Bryan Cranston (Matt McCulla), Rena Riffel (Taffi Bishop), Castulo Guerra, Daniel Faraldo, Francis X. McCarthy, Steve Horn, Gary Cervantes, Mary-Margaret Humes (Rebecca), Robert Guy Miranda (Paulie Scully), E. Danny Murphy (Charlie), Guillermo Zapata (Hector Mendoza), Jed Curtis (Fat Morris), Ken Clark (Rich), Tracy Vaccaro (April), Norma Michaels (Judge), Kim Delgado (Jury Foreman), Andrew J. Marsh, Jr. (Bailiff), Carol Kierman (Secretary), Tony Capozzola (Himself), Dolores McCoy (Reporter #1), Marcy Goldman (Reporter #2), Mark Chaet (Reporter #3), Symba Smith (Sea Smith).

Detective Mike Land quits the LAPD after his wife is killed by a drug dealer. Land moves to Cabo San Lucas, and the dealer's girlfriend follows him with the evidence needed to convict the killer.

NIGHT EYES   Airdate: 9/25/95, 12/25/95.

Guest Cast: Maria Rangel (Luna), Guillermo Zapata (Hector Mendoza), Dan McVicar, Kenneth Martines, James O'Sullivan, Terri Hoyos, Margaret Medina.

The attempted murder of a Mexican rock star draws Mike into the case when a waiter is killed and Courtney's job is on the line.

PARENTNAPPING   Airdates: 10/02/95, 1/01/96.

Guest Cast: Juliana McCarthy (Susanne Foster), Rance Howard (Jeff Foster), Tony Carreiro (Archie), Mary Kay Adams (Mildred), Bert Williams, Sebastian Vellfrid (Amos Foster), Andriola Vellfrid (Sophia Foster), Eddie Zammit (Museum Guard).

Mike's first assignment as chief of security for the hotel is to find the missing parents of two young hotel guests.

LINE IN THE SAND, THE   Airdates: 10/09/95, 1/08/96.

Guest Cast: Don Swayze (Tom Boller), Daniel Abondano (Mendez).

An ex-con comes to Cabo looking for revenge against Mike for having put him in prison 16 years ago.

DAY OF THE DEAD   Airdates: 10/16/95, 1/15/96.

Guest Cast: Mary-Margaret Humes (Rebecca/Simone), Richard Yniguez (Mr. Logu), Fred Asparagus (Mr. Chavez).

Mike is so distracted by a woman who looks exactly like his dead wife that he neglects his job as security chief.

EL PERICO   Airdates: 10/23/95, 1/22/96.

Guest Cast: Abraham Alvarez (Commandante de Policia), Karen Kondazian (Commandante's Wife), Victor C. Contreras (Julio), Juan A. DeVoto (Felipe), Tia Texada (Corina), Robert Ridgely (Cha Cha).

Chief Ruiz turns to Mike for help when his superior officer comes to town and is promptly robbed.

BOUNTY HUNTER   Airdates: 10/30/95, 3/04/96, 7/01/96.

Guest Cast: Gary Grubbs (Walter Abbott/Joe Phillips), James Acheson (Sam Waters), Lorraine Morin (Mrs. Waters), Lou Casal (Carlo), Matt Gallini (Tomas), Gunther Jensen (Gosset).

Mike and Willis are duped into working for a crooked bounty hunter who is smuggling drugs.

WILLIS GETS LUCKY   Airdates: 11/06/95, 3/11/96, 7/08/96.

Guest Cast: Bobbie Eakes (Stephanie Wade), Ray Laska (Mullin), Armando Molina (Salesman), Richard Gross, Lee Arenberg, Jim Maniaci.

Willis doesn't know it but he has been kidnapped by a beautiful woman—he thinks he's on vacation with her.

WHAT ARE FRIENDS FOR?   Airdates: 11/13/95, 3/19/96, 7/22/96.

Guest Cast: William Lucking, S.A. Griffin (Agent Simmons), Able Schiro (Chad), Luis Cortez (Valdez), Roger Rignack (Store Clerk).

Willis is torn between his friendship with Mike and that of an old buddy from Vietnam who has been arrested for selling contraband.

CURSE OF WILLIS, THE   Airdates: 11/20/95, 3/25/96.

Guest Cast: Oliver Clark (Mr. Green), George Cheung (Japanese Man), Pedro Gonzalez-Gonzalez, Frank Roman, Perry D'Marco.

It looks like Willis has angered an ancient god of fishing by taking a medallion from a local shrine, for everyone in town starts having bad luck.

WHAT EVER HAPPENED TO MARIA ROSA? Airdates: 11/27/95, 4/01/96.

Guest Cast: Myriam Tubert (Maria Rosa), Richard Fancy (Allen Raffin), Karmin Murcelo (Louise #1), Wendy Girard (Louise #2), Marcelo Tubert (Fire Chief), Al Israel (Movie Operator), Chris Franco.

Mike and Willis don't have any clues to aid them in their search for the daughter of a famous actress from the '40s.

WINDFALL   Airdates: 12/18/95, 5/20/96.

Guest Cast: Julie Cobb (Leigh Breck), Ramon Gallegos (Valente Rodriguez), Ray Oriel (Armando Garcia), Ana Daniels (Mrs. Garcia), Sandra Reinhart (Betty), George Galvan (Realtor).

The FBI hires Mike and Willis to help catch a fugitive banker who has fled to Cabo with $500,000 in cash.

LONG ARM OF THE LAW   Airdates: 1/29/96, 5/27/96.

Guest Cast: Bonnie Burroughs (Cora Lucas), Gregory Scott Cummins (Terry), E.J. Callahan, Kevin West, Joe Lala, Robyn Rice, Lenny Rose.

Mike and the gang become involved in the search for a long-missing treasure that was hidden by a double-crossing crook.

FOOL'S GOLD   Airdates: 2/05/96, 6/03/96.

Guest Cast: Raymond O'Connor (Carl Granger), Deirdre Lewis (Lennie), Rudy Morino (Enrique), Jose Rey (Mandel).

Mike's car is stolen by two thieves who had hidden a chunk of gold in it before he bought it.

DR. AMORE   Airdates: 2/12/96, 6/10/96.

Guest Cast: Larry Storch (Bobby Forest), Tracy Vaccaro (April), Elizabeth Alvarez (Dancer), Alex Menses.

Willis agrees to take the job of investigating a local dance instructor who has quite a way with the ladies. Fred Dryer plays the dual role of "Dr. Amore."

RED CADILLAC   Airdates: 2/19/96, 6/17/96.

Guest Cast: Chuck McCann, Clifton Gonzalez-Gonzalez, Tom McCleister (Ari), Harold Canon Lopez, Don Calea, Louis Caracas, Luis Avalos, Michael Parise (Rolando), Odalys Nanin, Robert Ridgeley.

Two misfit thieves stumble into Cabo when they take a wrong turn on their way to Acapulco.

PIECES OF EIGHT IS ENOUGH   Airdates: 2/26/96, 6/24/96.

Guest Cast: Sergio Calderon, Gerard Ismael, Luis Avalos, Francois Guetery, Mary Pat Green (Florence), Tommy David (Carl).

Mike discovers that the murder of a local fisherman is tied to a plot by a wealthy treasure hunter and his partner.

GIRLS JUST WANNA HAVE FUN   Airdate: 4/22/96.

Guest Cast: Frank Converse (Robert Alexander, Sr.), Tom Frenahan (Robert Alexander, Jr.), Kaela Dobkin (Chrissy Michaels), Bo Jesse Christopher, Jennifer McDonald (Billie), Mark David, Michael Lexx, Amy Noelle Usher (Nicole), Sherri Giardina (Sherry).

A vacationing college student is assaulted and then stalked by her attacker.

WHO'S KILLING COLE PORTER?   Airdate: 4/29/96.

Guest Cast: Sid Sham (Sid Keyes), Ed Ames (Himself), Jeff Altman (Lou), Larry Brandenberg (Bruce), Johnny Williams (Joe), Lana Clarkson (Kay), Cheryl Richardson (Sherry), Hector Elias.

A talent competition for pianists takes a strange turn when one of the contestants is discovered unconscious in the ocean—tied to a floating piano.

MOTHERS BEHIND BARS   Airdate: 5/06/96.

Guest Cast: Toni Sawyer (Iris Land), Jean Speegle Howard (Dorothy Dunleevy), Don Calea (Julio), Leo Garcia (Sergeant Diaz), Irene Hernandez (Grandmother), Pierrino Mascarino (Alfredo), Louis Rivera (Warden), Sophia Santi (Hortense).

Mike and Willis have to free their mothers from a Mexican jail when the women are sentenced for a bank robbery they accidentally committed.

JENNY   Airdate: 5/13/96.
Guest Cast: Kim Lankford (Mother), Melissa Clayton (Jenny), Tony Carozzola.

Mike helps the terminally ill daughter of a high school friend during her visit to Cabo.

Misery Loves Company

This short-lived 1995–96 sitcom for the Fox network centered on New York University film professor Joe DeMarco. When his wife filed for divorce, he headed for his younger brother Mitch's apartment. Joe not only needed a place to live, but he also needed to figure out what went wrong with his love life.

Each of the episodes is described below in airdate order.

MISERY LOVES COMPANY (original pilot)
Airdate: Unaired.
Cast: Rick Rossovich (Mitch DeMarco), Dennis Boutsikaris (Joe DeMarco), Julius Carry (Perry), Stephen Furst (Larry). Guest Cast: Lorraine Toussaint (Nicky), Darlene Vogel (Jocelyn), Marla Sokoloff (Tracy), Wesley Jonathan (Connor), Phil Leeds (Jackie), Philip Angelotto (Mike), Kelly Perine (Roger), Steve Monroe (Billy).

This unaired version of the pilot used the same premise as the version that eventually made it on the air.

ADVICE AND DISSENT   Airdates: 10/01/95, 10/07/95.
Guest Cast: Kirsten Holmquist (Sasha), Dennis Rodman (Himself).

The guys don't know what to do when basketball star Dennis Rodman makes a play for one of their ex-wives.

UNEASY RIDER   Airdate: 10/08/95.
Guest Cast: M.C. Gainey (Scar), Don Gibb (Prussian Helmet Biker), Mickey Jones (Keebler Biker), Diane Delano (Melanie), Sandra Purpuro (Spike), Franc Ross (Butch), John Craig (Stock Clerk).

Joe runs into problems when he decides he needs a new image and tries to hang out at a tough biker bar.

THAT BOOK BY NABOKOV   Airdate: 10/15/95.
Guest Cast: Maria Bello (Kim), Rikki Dale (Girl in Pink Sweater), S.W. Fisher (Timmy), John Leone (Waiter), Michael Prozzo (Busboy).

Age difference becomes the topic of conversation when Joe thinks about dating one of his former students.

MISERY LOVES COMPANY (revised pilot)
Airdate: 10/22/95.
Guest Cast: Rebecca Glenn (Lisa), Phil Leeds (Jackie), Philip Angelotti (Mike), Kelly Perine (Roger), Steve Monroe (Billy).

When his wife files for divorce, Joe shows up at his brother Mitch's apartment looking for a place to live and for the meaning of life.

WITCHES OF EAST 6TH, THE   Airdate: Unaired.
Guest Cast: Tina Arning (Gretchen), Kathleen McClellan (Hildy), Kymberly Kalil (Bonnie), Andrew J. Ferchland (Jack), Herta Ware (Old Hildy), J. Patrick McCormack (Distinguished Man), Jeanne Determann (Old Gretchen), David Rosen (Kissyboy).

Joe and Mitch accept an invitation to a Halloween party from two beautiful women, but end up handcuffed in a hot tub while the women rob them.

Buddies

Buddies centered on two men who didn't let the fact that they were from different races get in the way of their friendship. Dave Carlisle and John Butler, friends since grade school, were partners in a videotaping business.

The show aired as a mid-season replacement for the 1995–96 season, but the series ran into problems. The producers weren't happy with the results of the pilot episode and then decided to abandon the second episode during production. ABC canceled *Buddies* after 4 episodes.

Series Cast: Dave Chappelle (Dave Carlisle), Christopher Gartin (John Butler), Paula Cale (Lorraine Butler), Tanya Wright (Phyllis Brooks), Richard Roundtree (Henry Carlisle), Judith Ivey (Maureen DeMoss).
Note: Paula Cale is the professional name of Paula Korologos.

Each of the episodes is described below in airdate order. Additionally, several episodes were produced but not aired, and are listed in production order.

BUDDIES (pilot)   Airdate: 3/05/96.
Guest Cast: Reed Rudy (Groom), Gary Bayer (Preacher).

The guys have major problems with a wedding video shoot and go to elaborate lengths to cover up their errors.

ROOM WITH A PYEW, A   Airdate: 3/13/96.

Lorraine wants John to talk her mother out of moving into the building, which suits Dave's father just fine. It seems he only wants "his kind" as neighbors.

REGARDING HENRY   Airdate: 3/20/96.

Guest Cast: Will Nye (Alex), Gary Bayer (Ray), Lee Ryan (Security Man).

Dave learns that spending time with Henry is a better birthday present than an expensive gift.

FAMOUS LAST WORDS   Airdate: 3/27/96.

Guest Cast: Arnold Johnson (Uncle Albert).

Lorraine is shocked to discover that John has taped one of their arguments; Dave's Uncle Albert wants his will taped.

LIGHTS, CAMERAS . . . YUCK!   Airdate: Unaired.

Guest Cast: JoAnn Willette (Gina Hampton), Eric Saiet (Richard Hampton), Amy Hill (Nurse), Arthur Rosenberg (Doctor).

John and Dave find out that taping a birth is not as easy as they thought.

MARRY ME . . . SORT OF   Airdate: Unaired.

Guest Cast: Vanessa Williams (Janice), Christina Solis (Pamela).

Dave gets in trouble when he tries to pass his girlfriend off as just a casual acquaintance so he can impress a beautiful client.

PET PEEVES   Airdate: Unaired.

John isn't happy to discover that the stars of a pet store video are spiders and tarantulas.

CONTENT OF THEIR CHARACTER, THE   Airdate: Unaired.

Guest Cast: Brent Jennings (Aaron), Stephanie Fudge (Stephanie)

The buddies mistakenly believe that their interracial friendship is standing between them and a job.

THERE GOES THE GROOM   Airdate: Unaired.

Guest Cast: Arnetia Walker (Sister Harris), Troy Winbush (Todd), Robert Barry Fleming (Steve), Hugh Dane (Junior), Prince Hughes (Tiny), Bari K. Willerford (Baby Brother).

Dave realizes that he is in danger of losing his girlfriend so he quickly proposes.

PSA STORY, THE   Airdate: Unaired.

Guest Cast: Kareem Abdul-Jabbar (Himself), Freda Foh Shen (Miss Maekawa), Dierk Torsek (Maitre D'), Dominic Hoffman (Marcel), Lee Reherman (Bus Boy), Eric Gordon (Spencer), Jeffrey Quittman (Rex).

The guys try to figure out how to get Kareem Abdul-Jabbar to star in a public service commercial.

JOHN, I'VE BEEN THINKING . . .   Airdate: Unaired.

Guest Cast: David DeLuise (Tom), Shaun Baker (Barry), Christopher James Williams (Eddie), Yvette Nelson (Pizza Babe).

After a night partying with the guys, John realizes just how important his wife is to him.

ENGAGEMENT HELL   Airdate: Unaired.

Dave gets cold feet and tries to find a way to delay his impending wedding.

WHACK & BLIGHT   Airdate: Unaired.

Guest Cast: Bill Harper (Walter).

Dave turns down a client who doesn't want to work with John because he is white.

APPENDIX

Production Credits

CHAPTER 2

Specials Descriptions

ACTING SHERIFF
Directed by: Michael Lembeck. Written by: Gary Murphy, Larry Strawther. Produced by: Tim Steele. Executive Producers: Larry Strawther, Gary Murphy. Director of Photography: Mike Berlin. Production Designer: Ed Laporta. Editor: Mike Gavaldon. Associate Director: Howard Ritter. Stage Managers: Paul Markoe, Kevin Sullivan. Original Music by: Ed Alton. Casting by: April Webster, C.S.A. Costume Designer: Tom Bronson. Key Costumers: Marcy Lavender, Bill Tiegs. Make-up: Ken Wensevic. Hair Stylist: Marina Hart. Set Decorator: Edward Joseph McDonald. Property Master: Frank Bellina. Script Supervisor: Susie Gunter. Production Coordinator: Paula Warner. Assistant to Executive Producers: Jacqueline Jannotta. Technical Director: Bob Holmes. Audio: Doug Nelson. Video: Tom Tcimpidis. Re-recording: Allen Patapoff, Craig Porter. Gary Murphy/Larry Strawther Productions in association with Touchstone Television.

ADVENTURES IN BABYSITTING   (TV version)
Executive Producers: Debra Hill, Lynda Obst. Co-Producer: David Simkins. Written by: Greg Antonacci, David Simkins. Based on Characters Created by: David Simkins. Directed by: Joel Zwick. Executive Producer: Greg Antonacci. Director of Photography: Mikel Neiers. Art Director: Herman Zimmerman. Editor: Ed Cotter. Unit Production Manager/First Assistant Director: Nick Smirnoff. Second Assistant Director: Susan Norton. Original Score by: Dan Foliart, Howard Pearl. *Just Can't Stop* Words and Music by: Barry Goldberg, Jay Gruska. Performed by: Percy Sledge. Casting by: Matt Casella. Casting Associate: Jeanne Troy. Costumers: Paul Lopez, Dawn Jackson. Property Master: Tracy Farrington. Make-up: Bob Ryan. Hair Stylist: Gail Rowell. Set Decorator: Deborah Siegel. Script Supervisor: Marilyn Bagley. Production Coordinator: Lark Bernini. Technical Coordinator: Erik Emi. Production Sound Mixer: Michael Ballin. Music Editing by: Segue Music/Chris Brooks. Post Production Sound by: Compact Sound Services. Acknowledgment: Marvel Entertainment Group, Inc. Antonacci Productions and Hill/Obst Productions in association with Touchstone Television.

ALIEN ENCOUNTERS FROM NEW TOMORROWLAND
Written and Produced by: Andy Thomas. Directed by: Andy Thomas. Co-Producer: Jeff Schedtel. Edited by: Andy Thomas. Production Manager: Jim Moroney. Talent Executive: Eileen Bradley. Camera: Mark Lynch, Melissa Lynch. Audio: Bill Byers. Cam Mate Technician: Warren Jones. Electrician: Pat Ayotte. Make-up: L.A. Johnson. Music: Scott Page-Pagter, John Valentino. Audio Post: Tim Carpenter. On-Line Editor: Joe Lewis. Graphics: Ron Clark. Thomas & Friends Productions in association with Walt Disney World Co.

ALL NEW ADVENTURE OF DISNEY'S SPORT GOOFY, AN
Narrated by: Stan Freberg. Written, Produced and Directed by: John Klawitter. Associate Producer: Lynn Jensen-Klawitter. Assistant Producers: Jason Walters, Christian

Roberts, Matthew Michaels. Design Elements: Lucy Weishaar. Art Director: John Jensen. Videotape Editors: Darryl Sutton, Phil Datry, Bill Waters. *Soccermania Featurette* Directed by: Matt O'Callaghan. Produced by: Stephen Hickner. Director of Animation: Matt O'Callaghan. Production Supervisor: Stephen Hickner. Narrated by: Chick Hearn. Music: John Debney. Story: Tad Stones, Michael Giaimo, Joe Ranft. Supervising Animators: Joe Lanzisero, Barry Temple, Chris Buck, Ed Gombert, Dan Jeup. *You Can Always Be Number One* Words and Music by: Dale Gonyea. A Happyfeets Production.

ANNA
Written by: Barry Fanaro, Mort Nathan, Kathy Speer, Terry Grossman. Directed by: Noam Pitlik. Executive Producers: Kathy Speer, Terry Grossman, Mort Nathan, Barry Fanaro. Director of Photography: Richard Brown. Art Director: Jane Fletcher. Editor: Michael L. Witzman. Associate Director: Gary L. Shaw. Stage Managers: Carun R. Shick, John J. Hill. Theme and Original Music by: Ed Alton. Casting by: Eileen Knight, C.S.A., Jennifer Jackson Part, C.S.A. Costume Designer: Tom Bronson. Costumers: Sherri Thompson, Richard E. Mahony. Make-up: Ken Wensevic. Hair Stylist: Ariel Bagdadi. Set Decorator: Richard DeCinces. Script Supervisor: Kathy Giangregorio. Production Coordinator: Christine Reedy. Property Master: Warren Shaffer. Assistants to the Executive Producers: Gail Haller, Alexandra Mulligan. Script Coordinators: Nancylee Myatt, Gordon R. McKee. Technical Director: Kenneth R. Shapiro. Audio: Steve Kibbons. Video: Jean Mason. Re-recorded by: Allen Patapoff, Craig Porter. Executive in Charge of Production for KTMB: Andrew J. Selig. KTMB in association with Touchstone Television.

APPEARANCES
Original Music Composed by: Joel McNeely. Edited by: Jim McElroy, Kelly Snyder. Art Director: Virginia E. Hildreth. Director of Photography: Isidore Mankofsky, A.S.C. Produced by: Frank Fischer. Written by: William Blinn. Directed by: Win Phelps. Executive Producer: William Blinn. Unit Production Manager: Nick Anderson. First Assistant Director: Arthur Anderson. Second Assistant Director: Cherylanne Martin. Casting by: Amy Lieberman. Costumes Designed by: Tom Bronson. Set Decorator: R. Lynn Smart. Key Costumers: Thomas S. Dawson, Charmaine Nash Simmons. Make-up: Jack Wilson. Hair Stylist: Gloria Montemayor. Property Master: Joe Olsen. Script Supervisor: Jon Michael. Production Coordinator: Dot Stovall. Location Manager: Marta Ball. Transportation Coordinator: Steve Hellerstein. Production Sound Mixer: Kenn Michael Fuller, C.A.S. Sound Editing by: Todd-AO/Glen Glenn Sound. Music Editing by: Thomas Milano. Echo Cove Productions in association with Touchstone Television.

BAREFOOT EXECUTIVE, THE   (TV version)
Music Composed and Conducted by: Philip Giffin. Film Editor: Andrew Mondshein. Production Designer: Peg McClel-

lan. Director of Photography: Russ Alsobrook. Producer: Irwin Marcus. Produced by: Joan Van Horn. Executive Producers: George Zaloom, Les Mayfield, Scott Immergut. Teleplay by: Tracy Newman, Jonathan Stark, Tim Doyle. Based on the Feature Screenplay by: Joseph L. McEveety. Story by: Lila Garrett, Bernie Kahn, Stu Billett. Directed by: Susan Seidelman. Unit Production Manager: Irwin Marcus. First Assistant Director: Ken Collins. Second Assistant Director: Kristi "Kat" Antunovich. Casting by: Allison Jones. Costume Designer: Tom Bronson. Set Decorator: Brenda Meyers-Ballard. Property Master: Frank Escobedo. Script Supervisor: Ira Hurvitz. Production Coordinator: Millie Crystal. Key Costumers: Dianne Kennedy, Michael Fitzpatrick. Make-up: Kathryn M. Kelly. Hairstylist: Carl Bailey. Location Manager: Jeff Spellman. Assistant to Executive Producer: Amy R. Baird. Production Sound Mixer: David Barr Yaffee, C.A.S. Music Editor: D.D. Stenehjem. Music Arranged and Orchestrated by: Stu Goldberg. ZM Productions.

BAR GIRLS
Produced by: Paul Pompian. Written by: Terry Louise Fisher. Directed by: Eric Laneuville. Executive Producer: Terry Louise Fisher. Original Score by: David McHugh. Director of Photography: Jack Whitman. Art Director: Ted Haworth. Editors: Janet Bartels, Barrott Taylor. Unit Production Manager: Jerry L. Ballew. First Assistant Director: Bob Engelman. Second Assistant Director: Gerry Keener. Casting by: Randy Stone, Holly Powell, C.S.A. Set Decorator: Linda Spheeris. Property Master: Dominic Belmonte. Key Costumers: Barbara Whitaker, Murray Lantz. Script Supervisor: Renate Schneuer. Make-up: Deborah Lamia Denaver. Hair Stylist: Kim Samson. Location Manager: Peter Rich. Production Coordinator: Susan McNamara. Sound Mixer: John Sutton III. Sound Editing by: Dimension Sound. Music Editing by: Steve McCroskey. Fisher Entertainment, Inc. in association with Touchstone Television.

BELIEVE YOU CAN . . . AND YOU CAN!
Produced by: Jack Sobel. Directed by: Lee Miller. Written by: Ron Friedman, Jack Sobel. Conceived by: Jack Sobel. Ad-lib Dialogue by: Morey Amsterdam. Associate Producer: Kimber Rickabaugh. Associate Director: Liz Plonka. Stage Managers: R.A. Clark, Anne Goodall. Assistant to the Producer: S. Dianne Reeves. First Production Assistant: Sharon Trojan. Music Director: Lenny Stack. Choreographer: Bonnie Cox. Lighting Director: Jeff Engel. Art Director: Michael Erickson. Costume Designer: Pete Menefee. Production Coordinator: Kevin O'Donnell. Talent Coordinator: Bridget O'Brien. Make-up: Diane Shatz. Production Accountant: Kelly Fein. Technical Director: Chuck Reilly. Cameramen: Sam Drummy, Ken Tamburri, Bob Highton, Kris Wilson. Audio: Mike Gannon, Ken Lay. Video: Mike Snedden, Pat Brennan. Production Executive: Eileen Barton. Technical Supervisor: Ron Stutzman. Video Tape Editor: Pam Marshall. Audio Rerecording: Kent Gibson. Snorkel Camera Sequence by: Paul Kenworthy. Theme Composed by: Lenny Stack. Production Associates: C. Alan Bogart, Susan Cowan, David Pitlik. The Voice of Disneyland: Jack Wagner. *Special Appreciation for Support and Assistance at Disneyland* WED Development: Raellen Lescault. Entertainment Division, Disneyland: Mike Davis, Doug McIntyre. Executive Supervisors for SFM Entertainment: Stanley H. Moger, Jordan Ringel. Executive Supervisor for Glendinning Associates: Doug John. Produced by: Free To Live Productions, Limited in association with SFM Entertainment, a Division of SFM Media Corporation, and Glendinning Associates, with the cooperation of Walt Disney Productions.

BEST OF COUNTRY, THE
Executive Producer: Ken Ehrlich. Directed by: Walter C. Miller. Co-Producer: Tisha Fein. Written by: Ken Ehrlich. Production Designer: Bruce Ryan. Lighting Designer: Bob Dickinson. Musical Director: Marty Stuart. Associate Producer: Renato Basile. Associate Director: Christine Clark Bradley. Script Supervisor: Kris Sheets. Script Coordinators: Jill Jackson, Paige Rabban Hadley. Talent Coordinators: Alicia Davis, Ali Gifford. Production Manager: Patricia Branan Wendell. Stage Managers: Garry Hood, Russ Nunnally, Cindy Sinclair. Music

Contractor: Harry Stinson. Band Coordinator: Robin Victor. Art Directors: John Janavs, Glenda Rovello. Production Assistants: Michelle Breger, C.A. Carson, Jason Franz, Joe Foster, Elizabeth Gwynne-Dyer, Ann McCarty, Steve Nation, William Saurel. Editor: Scott Reynolds. Operations Manager: Danny Wendell. Engineer in Charge: Gaylon Halloway. Technical Director: John B. Field. Lighting Directors: John Morgan, Ted Wells. Audio: Marc Repp. Camera Operators: Mike Breece, Larry Copeland, David Eastwood, Allen Fugua, Pat Gleason, Charlie Huntley, Ron Sheldon. Lighting Board Operator: Gil Samuelian. Monitor Mixer: Scotty Schenk. PA Mixer: David Kuhn. Wardrobe: Tammy Miller. Make-up: Linda Demith, Gina Giglio. Hair: Nanette Crafton. Music Clearance: Meryl Ginsberg. Executive in Charge of Production: Angela Fairhurst. Ken Ehrlich Productions. Touchstone Television.

BEST OF COUNTRY '92, THE: COUNTDOWN AT THE NEON ARMADILLO
Executive Producer: Don Weiner. Directed by: Gary Halvorson. Written by: Loree Gold. Associate Producer: Buck Allen. Talent Executive: Carla Patterson. Production Design by: Jeremy Railton & Associates. Lighting Designer: Kieran Healy. Choreographer: Anthony Thomas. Costume Design by: Vanessa Ware. Associate Director: Christopher A. Berry. Stage Managers: Ken Stein, Russell Nunnally, Jody Karlovic. Nashville Production Manager: Madeline Bell. Financial Coordinator: Rock Birt. Production Supervisor: Risa Thomas. Script Supervisor: Amy Storti. Segment Producers: Tony Imparato, Julie Fleischer. Production Coordinators: Raquel Navas, Alan Levi. Talent Coordinator: Jennifer Walton. Dancers: Leslie Benson, Raci Buchman, Diane Klimaszewski, Elaine Klimaszewski, Shawn Munoz, Anne Noelle, Mary Oedy, Chris Solari, Jeannie Thompson, Mic Thompson, Carol Tong. Staging Supervisor: Rodney Groth. Technical Supervisor: Paul Boykin. Engineer in Charge: Galen Holloway. Technical Director: Rich Goody. Video Control: Don Clagett. Video Tape Operator: Robert Britton. Camera Operators: Ed Fussell, Alan Fuqua, Hank Geving, Pat Gleason, Ronald E. Smith. 2nd Unit Camera Operator: Mike Breeze. Audio Mixer: Ken Raymer. Audio 2: Stan Ducus. 2nd Unit Audio: Kevin Lane. Audio Technicians: Andrew McHaddad, Shipley Landiss. PL Technician: Robin Midgett. Crane Operators: Frank Bess, Mike Gilbert, Norris Kemp, Steve McDonald, Brenda Smith. Utilities: Danny Barber, Dennis Cox, Marty Gilbert, Ray Perrin, Jim Robertson. Video Wall Technicians: Scott Stifle, Pete Pacione. Crew Chief: Paul Pigue. Stage Crew: Ken Aguilar, Tim Bolin, Jack Dedert, Dennis Harris, Jeff Hurley, Andre Nicks, Don Pitts, Troy Powers, Ora Rieve. Riggers: Ed Kish, Simon Franklin. Lighting Directors: Tom Beck, Dale Polanski. 2nd Unit Lighting: David Gossard. Varilite Technicians: Kevin Booth, David Haar, Tad Inferrera. Lighting Crew: Mark Billings, George Harvey, Dave Larringa. Follow Spot Operators: Brent Carpenter, Jonathan Friend, Zane Friend, Mike Hatchett, H. Joe Hooper, Mike Kane, Jamie Lupinetti, Curt Simmons, Clarence Swinton, Brent Thornton, Ed Toney. PA Mixer: Rick Schimer. PA Technicians: Larry Haley, Steve Smith, Tod Tillman. Propmaster: Chris Hill. Prop Assistants: Michael Sizemore, Robert Gentile. Make-Up/Hair: Melanie Conner, Mary Beth Felts, Wynn Gerlock, Penny Hester, Kim Hunter, Maria Smoot, Paige Simmons, Debra Smoot. Wardrobe Assistant: Kendall Kegley. Script P.A.: David Rumsey. Assistant to Anthony Thomas: Stephanie Clark. Craft Service: Melissa Lundgren. Production Secretaries: Nicole Cheney, Glenda Golemon. Production Assistants—Los Angeles: Victor Davis, Pete Fajkowski, Val Miller. Production Assistants—Nashville: Jamie Sue Amos, Boyer Barner, Tamera Brooks, Betsey Browning, Clay Callaway, Deidre Duker, Pamela Hamilton, Fonda Ong, John Rabasca, Stephen Rabasca, Lori Smith. Audience Coordinator: Brenda McClain. Editors—Los Angeles: Rich Uber, Mike Kaidbey, Mario Di Mambro, Michael Polito, Marty Rosenstock. Editors—Nashville: Roy Giorgio, Adam Weed, Eddie Hales. Nashville Convention Center Events Coordinator: Cindy Mills. Original Music by: Michael Boyd. Don Weiner Productions.

BEST OF DISNEY, THE: 50 YEARS OF MAGIC
Executive Producer: Don Mischer. Produced by: David J. Goldberg. Directed by: Don Mischer. Written by: Sara Lukinson,

Bill Prady. Co-Produced by: Phil Savenick. Supervising Producer: Harry Arends. Production Designer: Robert Keene. Lighting Designer: Bob Dickinson. Music by: Peter Matz. Field Producer: Kate Coe. Segment Producers: Bruce Bailey, Mark Governor, Kevin Miller, Bambi Moé, Bonnie Peterson, Jeff Savenick, Jim Savenick. Associate Director: Lesley Maynard. Stage Managers: Steve Burgess, Dency Nelson, Ken Stein, Mavis. Assistant to the Producers: Maureen Kelly. Production Supervisor: Nancy Kurshner. Production Coordinator: Brooke Karzen. Art Director: Jim O'Donnell. Set Decorator: Rochelle Moser. Production Assistants: Keith Elsner, Jane Schneider. Production Associates: Don Carroll, Kathleen Clark, Gavin Glennon, Chris May, Bill Romary, Lance Velazco, Matt Vlachos. Character Choreography by: Barnette Ricci. Additional Lighting: Ted Ashton, Bob Keys, George Reisenberger. Audio: David Demore, Jeff Fecteau, Sandy Fellerman, Joe Kendall, Dana McClure, Paul Sandweiss, Murray Siegel, Gar Smith. Video: Mark Sanford. Cameras: Ted Ashton, Dave Banks, Tom Geren, Larry Heider, Dave Hilmer, Bob Keys, Jeff Schaaf. Videotape Operators: Johnny Gooch, Bruce Solberg, Tim Wheeler. Videotape Editors: Robert P. Schneider, Mark West. Audio Post Mixer: David Fluhr. Make-up and Hair: Bob Schiffer. Wardrobe: Tom Bronson. Don Mischer Productions.

BEST OF DISNEY MUSIC, THE: A LEGACY IN SONG—PART I
Produced and Directed by: Don Mischer. Written by: Buz Kohan, Mark Saltzman. Line Producer: Nina Lederman. Co-Producers: Harry Arends, Phil Savenick. Music by: Glen Roven. Production Designer: Bob Keene. Lighting Director: Bob Dickinson. Associate Director: Javier Winnik. Editors: Robert P. Schneider, Rick Piccini. Segment Producers: Wayne Hudgins, Jim Savnick, Kevin Miller, Michael Pellerin, Mark Governor, Bruce Bailey. Associate Director: Bob Staley. Stage Managers: Michael Kelly, Rey Vincenty. Assistant to the Producers: Maureen Kelly. First Production Assistants: Deborah Kennedy, Belinda Lams, Julie Miller. Production Coordinator: Kerry Holmwood. Assistant Art Directors: Tom Buderwitz, Scott Murphy. Production Staff: Lydia Ash, Candy Cole-Capek, Eric Carpenter, Sarah Kleinberg, Steve Marschner, Scott Martin. Additional Production Staff: Doug May, Christiana Pillot, Franchie San Pedro, Fontelle Slater, Allen Stubblefield, Ernie Zayat. Technical Director: Kenneth Shapiro. Video: Bob Kaufmann, Mark Sanford. Cameras: David Eastwood, Bill Philbin, Marc Hunter, Bob Keys, Wayne Orr. Audio: Ed Greene, Toby Foster, Jamie Ledner. Tape Operators: Jon Aroesty, Tim Wheeler. Make-up: Robin Beauchesne. Hair: Linda Arnold. Wardrobe: Kenn Smiley. Don Mischer Productions.

BEST OF DISNEY MUSIC, THE: A LEGACY IN SONG—PART II
Produced and Directed by: Don Mischer. Written by: Buz Kohan, Mark Saltzman. Line Producer: Nina Lederman. Co-Producers: Harry Arends, Phil Savenick. Music by: Glen Roven. Production Designer: Bob Keene. Lighting Director: Bob Dickinson. Associate Director: Javier Winnik. Editors: Robert P. Schneider, Rick Piccini, Floyd Ingram. Segment Producers: Wayne Hudgins, Jim Savnick, Kevin Miller, Michael Pellerin, Mark Governor, Bruce Bailey. Associate Director: Bob Staley. Stage Managers: Michael Kelly, Rey Vincenty. Assistant to the Producers: Maureen Kelly. First Production Assistants: Deborah Kennedy, Belinda Lams, Julie Miller. Production Coordinator: Kerry Holmwood. Assistant Art Directors: Tom Buderwitz, Scott Murphy. Production Staff: Lydia Ash, Candy Cole-Capek, Eric Carpenter, Sarah Kleinberg, Steve Marschner, Scott Martin. Additional Production Staff: Doug May, Christiana Pillot, Franchie San Pedro, Fontelle Slater, Allen Stubblefield, Ernie Zayat. Technical Director: Kenneth Shapiro. Video: Bob Kaufmann, Mark Sanford. Cameras: David Eastwood, Bill Philbin, Marc Hunter, Bob Keys, Wayne Orr. Audio: Ed Greene, Toby Foster, Jamie Ledner. Videotape Operators: Jon Aroesty, Tim Wheeler. Make-up: Daniel Striepke. Hair: Susan Germain. Wardrobe: Kenn Smiley. Don Mischer Productions.

BLACK HOLES: MONSTERS THAT EAT SPACE AND TIME
Director: Chuck Staley. Producer: Phillip A. May. Executive Producer: Ron Miller. Writers: Philip A. May, Durk Pearson,

Sandy Shakocius. Technical Consultants: Durk Pearson, Sandy Shakocius. Special Animation: Mike Jittlov. Acknowledgments: British Broadcasting Co., Astronomy Magazine, N.A.S.A., MacGillivray Freeman Films, Sherman Grinberg Film Libraries, Gordon Cooper, Compact Video, Grass Valley Group, Inc. An SFM Media Corporation Presentation.

BLACK SHEEP
Supervising Producer: Mitchell Bank. Producer: Lori Jacobs. Written by: Michael Jacobs. Directed by: Matthew Diamond. Executive Producer: Michael Jacobs. Associate Producer: Brian J. Cowan. Director of Photography: Richard Hissong. Production Designer: John C. Mula. Edited by: Marco Zappia. Associate Director: Rae Kraus. Stage Manager: Lynn McCracken. Music by: Ray Colcord. Casting by: Cheryl Bayer, C.S.A. Set Decorator: Robinson Royce. Audio: J. Mark King. Video: Bob Snyder. Michael Jacobs Productions. Touchstone Television.

BLAST TO THE PAST
Produced by: Jon Bauman. Directed by: C.F. Bien. Written by: Jon Bauman. Associate Producer: Marilyn Jones. Post Production Supervisor: Mark Ruggio. Production Manager: Cal Brady. Field Camera: Peter B. Good. Field Audio: Larry Chung. Lighting Director: Dick Sulprizio. Production Coordinator: Melanie Steensland. Technical Director: Rick Ricksen. Audio: Fred Anzalone. Video: Phil Young. Cameras: Ron Price, Andy Weintraub, Diane Frierson, Carlos Lopez, Cliff Armstrong. Videotape: George Raquel. Audio Assistant: Lynda Bassett. Lighting Assistants: Don Anderson, Julie Ball. Stage Managers: Ridge Conlon, Jerry Vowels, Mike Scharfman. Make-up: David A. Langford. Engineering Supervisor: Jeff Koss. Maintenance: Jeff Kaner, Dave Mumby. Assistant Chief Engineer: Bob Morison. Production Assistants: Janelle Ricksen, Jackie Lugo, Kathy Flynn. Remote Truck: VTE. On-line Editor: Floyd Ingram. Assistant Editor: Ken Assessor. Acknowledgments: The Andersons, Brian Spaulding. *For Disneyland* Producer: Lisa Cappel. Line Producer: Dale Lanier. Tech Supervisor: Chris Robinson. Production Coordinators: Tim O'Day, Carri McClure. Entertainment Produced by Walt Disney Attractions Creative Entertainment. Executive Producer: Walt Baker. A Production of KHJ-TV, Inc.

BLOSSOM
Producer: Gilbert Junger. Written by: Don Reo. Directed by: Terry Hughes. Executive Producers: Paul Junger Witt, Tony Thomas, Don Reo. Production Designer: Edward Stephenson. Music by: George Aliceon Tipton. Casting by: Ellen Meyer, C.S.A. & Associates, Bonnie Shane. Costume Designer: Jane Ruhm. Associate Directors: Lex Passaris, Peter D. Beyt. Stage Managers: Tom Carpenter, Kent Zbornak. Production Coordinator: Gwen McCracken. Production Associate: Robert Spina. Art Director: Diane Yates. Post Production Manager: Richard J. Powell. Music Coordinator: Scott Gale. Production Assistant: Esther F. Himbaugh. Production Staff: Danny Filous, Bill Ghaffary, Jordan Goodman, Ray Kolasa, Ellen Moshein, Denise Porter, David Z. Sacks, Maria Schmidt, Dorothy Wong. Technical Director: O. Tamburri. Lighting: Alan Walker. Audio: Edward L. Moskowitz, C.A.S. Video: John O'Brien. Cameras: Jack Chisholm, Chester Jackson, Stephen A. Jones, Ritch Kenney. Property Master: Robert Devicariis. Gaffer: William Updegraff. Head Carpenter: Paul Wadian. Costumers: De Derderian, Richard Roach. Make-up: Art Harding. Hair Stylist: Joyce Melton Conroy. Technical Manager: Bill Conroy. Re-Recording: Craig Porter. Production Executive: David Amico. Executive in Charge of Production: Susan Palladino. Impact Zone Productions. A Witt/Thomas Production.

BLUE BAYOU
Original Score by: Stanley Clarke. Edited by: Laurel Ladevich, Kathleen Korth. Art Director: James Shanahan. Director of Photography: Thomas Neuwirth. Produced by: Christopher Morgan. Written by: Terry Louise Fisher. Directed by: Karen Arthur. Executive Producer: Terry Louise Fisher. Unit Production Manager: Robert J. Anderson. First Assistant Director: Paula Marcus. Second Assistant Director: Sandra M. Middleton. Casting by: Diane Dimeo, C.S.A. Casting Assistant:

Donnalyn Greenbaum. Set Decorator: Meredith Boswell. Costumes by: Enid Harris. Key Costumers: Murray Lantz, Sherry Thompson. Make-up: Carol Schwartz. Hair Stylist: Bette Iverson. New Orleans Casting by: Richard Castelman. Property Master: Daniel L. Stoltenberg. Script Supervisor: Linda "Bunky" Conklin. Location Manager: Bob Johnston. Technical Advisors: Staci A. Rosenberg, Roxie Wright. Assistant to Executive Producer: Stephanie Samuels. Production Coordinator: Allison Deen. Production Sound Mixer: Kenny Delbert. Music Editing by: Music Design Group. *Blue Bayou* Words and Music by: Roy Orbison, Joe Melson. Performed by René Walker. *Let It Go Tonight* Music by: Stanley Clarke. Lyrics by: Mark Mueller. Performed by: Charmaine Neville. Acknowledgment: City of New Orleans. Fisher Entertainment, Inc. in association with Touchstone Television.

CAMEO BY NIGHT
Produced by: Christopher C. Carter, John Ziffren. Written by: Christopher C. Carter. Directed by: Paul Lynch. Executive Producer: Lauren Schuler-Donner. Music by: Jay Ferguson. Director of Photography: James A. Contner. Art Director: Ed Richardson. Editor: Steven Kemper. Unit Production Manager: Richard Luke Rothschild. First Assistant Director: Anthony Brand. Second Assistant Director: Don Edward Wilkerson. Casting by: Peg Halligan. C.S.A. Costumes Designed by: Tom Bronson. Set Decorator: Daniel May. Propert Master: Barbara Adamski. Key Costumers: Bob Harris, Aida Swinson. Make-up: Scott H. Eddo. Hair Stylist: Paul Abascal. Location Managers: Ronald M. Quigley, Kevin McAteer. Script Supervisor: Sally J. Roddy. Production Coordinator: Nancy Rae Stone. Choreographer: Doug Rivera. Stunt Coordinator: Terry Leonard. Production Sound Mixer: Patrick Mitchell. Sound Editing by: Stephen J. Cannell Productions, Michael O'Corrigan. Music Editing by: Allan K. Rosen. Additional Editing by: Kevin Stitt. Lauren Schuler-Donner Productions in association with Touchstone Pictures.

CARTOON ALL-STARS TO THE RESCUE
Executive Producer: Roy Edward Disney. Producer: Buzz Potamkin. Written by: Duane Poole, Tom Swale. Voice Director: Hank Saroyan. *Wonderful Ways to Say No* Lyrics by: Howard Ashman. Music by: Alan Menken. Music Direction: Steve Tyrell. Art Directors: Don Morgan, Takashi. Animation Production at: Wang Film Productions Co., Ltd. Background Design: Alex Nino. Background Keys: Tim Barnes, Carol Grosvenor, George Taylor. Original Music: Richard Kosinski, Sam Winans, Paul Buckmaster, Bill Reichenback, Bob Mann, Guy Moon. Poster by: Barry Jackson. Associate Producers: Roy Allen Smith, Diane Steinmetz. Production Co-ordinator: Linda Loe. Production Assistants: Mark Low, Cynthia Wilbur. Animation Production Supervisor: Peter Aries. Storyboard: Adrian Gonzales. Storyboard: Adrian Gonzales. Storyboard Editor: Gary Goldstein. Supervising Animation Director: Karen Peterson. Animation Directors: Milton Gray, Mike Svayko, Bob Shellhorn, Marsh Lamore. Animation Dialogue Exposure: Erik Jan Peterson, Deborah & Cecil Broughton. Editor: Jay Bixon. Negative Cutting: Dennis Brookins. Additional Music: Richard Kosinski, Sam Winans, Paul Buckmaster, Bill Reichenback, Bob Mann, Guy Moon. *Wonderful Ways to Say No* Produced by: Steve Tyrell. Singing Direction: Janis Liebhart. Voice Track Recording by: Buzzy's Recording. Edited by: Larry Lance, Andy Morris. Digital Audio Post Production by: EFX Systems. Rerecording Mixers: Sherry Klein, C.A.S., Terry O'Bright. Sound Effects: Jeff Vaugh, C.A.S. Foley Walker: Ossama Khuluki. Mixing Assistant: Erin Hoien. Film to Tape Transfer by: The Post Group, Julius Friede. Video Post Production by: Laser Edit, Inc. Video Editor: Arden Rynew. Legal and Administrative Services: Jack Angeles, Lorna Bitensky, Dixon Dern, Scott Roth, Albert Spevak, Bill Terry, Jon Vein. For the Academy of Television Arts and Sciences: President: Lee Chaloukian. Executive Director: James L. Loper. Public Relations Committee: Cliff Dektar, Murray Weissman, Gene Walsh. Script Consultants: Stephen Bailey, Ph.D., Gordon Berry, Ph.D., Claudia Black, Ph.D., Jael Greenleaf, M. David Lewis, Ph.D., Corinne Rupert, Ph.D. Production Executives Committee: Bill Hanna, Mark Glamack, Lee Gunther, Margaret Loesch, Jean McCurdy, Phil Roman, Ken Spears, Michael Webster. Acknowledgments: Alien Pro-

ductions, Bagdasarian Productions, Columbia Pictures Television, Inc., DIC Enterprises, Film Roman, Hanna-Barbera Productions, Inc., Henson Productions, Inc., Marvel Productions, Ltd., Murakami-Wolf-Swenson Films, Southern Star Productions, Inc., The Walt Disney Company, Warner Bros., Inc., The American Academy of Pediatrics, Screen Actors Guild.

CBS ALL-AMERICAN THANKSGIVING PARADE, THE
Production credits were not aired for the Disney portions of this show.

CBS EASTER PARADE, THE
Executive Producer: Mike Gargiulo. Written by: Chuck Horner. Talent Coordinator: Ann Levack. Assistant to the Producer: Brenda Jimenez Rivera. Associate Directors: Stanley M. Faer, Joel Aronowitz. Production Supervisors: Gina Sappah, Arnold Boatner. Lighting Director: William Schelling. Fashion Consultants: Abbi Lindner, Sonia Duggan, Barrie Burgess, Madelin Guyon. *Parade Segments* Associate Producer: Bob Allen. Lighting: Todd Nichols. Production Co-ordinator: Jim Moroney. Parade Choreographers: Judy Lawrence, Jay Smith. Engineers in Charge: Mort Smith, Ivan Beltran. Remote Technical Supervisors: Fred Danichek, Marvin Kale. Technical Directors: Ron Resch, Phil Selby, Jeff Court. Audio: Gerry Jaick, Irv Elias. Videotape Editor: Mark Leoczko. Electronic Graphics: Nancy Villanueva. Production Assistants: Pamela Repp, George Callahan, Mike Grigaliunas. Stage Manager: Paul Shiers. Announcer: Hal Simms. Produced and Directed by: Mike Gargiulo.

CELEBRATE THE SPIRIT! DISNEY'S ALL-STAR 4TH OF JULY SPECTACULAR
Executive Producer: Don Weiner. Produced by: Michael Petok. Directed by: Gary Halvorson. Written by: Stephen Pouliot. Associate Producer: Drew Brown. Original Music by: Kevin Kiner. Art Director: Jimbo Marshall. Lighting Designers: Bob Dickinson, Todd Nichols. Talent Executive: Carla Patterson. Production Coordinator: Clay Newbill. Segment Producers: Tony Imparto, Kim Moses, Barnette Ricci. Associate Director: Chris Berry. Stage Managers: David Wader, Buck Allen, Virgil Fabian, Joe Hughes. Production Supervisor: Mary Braun. Script Coordinators: Rebecca Ancheta, Jennifer Stark. Talent Coordinator: Jennifer Walton. Location Coordinator: Amy Storti. Technical Directors: Keith Winikoff, Don Holt. Audio Mixers: Paul Sandweiss, Dana Mark McClure. Video: Keith Winikoff, Steve Berry. Cameras: Ted Ashton, Al Camoin, Van Carlson, Ken Dahlquist, Rocky Danielson, Tom Dasbach, Eddie Fussell, Dave Hilmer, David Irete, Dave Levisohn, Mark Lynch, Ron Smith. Edited by: Jerry Bixman. Segment Editor: Ron Andreassen. Additional Music by: Bruce Healey. Post Production Audio: Charles McDaniel, John Bickelhaupt. Main Title Design by: C. David Pina. Don Weiner Productions in association with Walt Disney Television.

CELEBRITY CELEBRATION ABOARD THE QUEEN MARY
Directed by: Rick Locke. Written by: Kathryn Stone Bookin. Executive Producers: Jack B. Lindquist, Susan Thomas Lee. Supervising Producer: John Alexander Lee. Producers: Allan W. Henderson, Chris L. Harding. Associate Producers: Maggie Probst, Pam Phillips. Editor: Lee S. Ollerton. Line Producer: Dale Lanier. Associate Producer: Syngehilde Schweikart. Stage Manager: John Marsh. Assistant to Producers: Stephanie Chaffin. Art Director: Seven Nielsen. Lighting Director: David Stoddard. Audio: Fred Aldous. Technical Director: Lee S. Ollerton. Technical Producer: Craig Wall. Original Music: Sam Cardon. *My Favorite Year* Segment Directed by: Allan W. Henderson, Lee S. Ollerton. Wardrobe Supervisor: Irmgard Terbrack. Make-up Artist/Hair Stylist: Karl Wesson. Choreographer: Carl Jablonski. Set Construction: Scenic Service Specialists, Inc. Q-Cards: Scot Walker, Mary Stel. Set Dresser: Bill Kirkpatrick. Production Assistants: Nicole Ludwig, Lori Mertz, Chris Otto. Video: Mark Sanford. Camera Operators: Sam Drummy, Tom Geren, Dean Hall, Lee S. Ollerton, Martin Metcalf, Jeff Winterroth. Crane Operators: Mike Boisclair, Steve Buff, Bob Lee. Utility: Dan Andresen, John Mayon. Audio Assistants: Art Hasmer, Sean Glen. VTR: Tom Young, Matthew Remund. Assistant Lighting Directors: Jeff Carr,

Kelly Mecham. Extra Casting & Coordination: Christine Papalexis, Kimberly Hahn. Ms. Manchester's Hair: Barron Matalon. Ms. Manchester's Make-up: Wayne Massarelli. Mobile Production Facilities: Coast to Coast Video, Inc. Post Production Audio: Matthew Nickel. Audio Production Facilities: L.A. East. Post Production Facilities: Video West. Post Production Audio: Bonneville Media Communications. Executive in Charge of Production: Jack Adamson. Acknowledgments: Tom Witherspoon, Staff and Crew of the Queen Mary. A Bonneville Producers Group Production. WCO Port Properties.

CHIP 'N DALE RESCUE RANGERS TO THE RESCUE
Produced by: Walt Disney Television Animation. Producers: Tad Stones, Alan Zaslove. Supervising Director: Alan Zaslove. Directors: John Kimball, Bob Zamboni, Rick Leon, Jamie Mitchell. Story Editors: Jymn Magon, Tad Stones, Mark Zaslove. Story by: Kevin Hopps, Tad Stones. Written by: Kevin Hopps, Jymn Magon, Julia J. Roberts, Tad Stones, Mark Zaslove. Assistant Producer: Maia Mattise. Key Layout Artists: Michael Spooner, Ed Wexler. Character Design: Toby Shelton, Kenny Thompkins. Prop Design: Rob Laduca, Terry Hudson. Overseas Animation Supervisor: Russell Mooney. Storyboard Design: Kurt Anderson, Jan Green, Larry Latham, John Norton, Frank Paur, Dave Schwartz, David Smith, Robert Taylor, Lonnie Thompson, Keith Tucker. Key Background Styling: Gary Eggleston, Bill Lorencz. Color Key Styling: Janet Cummings, Robin Draper, Debra Jorgensborg. Supervising Timing Director: David Brain. Timing Director: Rick Leon. Track Reading: Skip Craig. Script Coordinator: LuAnne Wood. Production Assistants: Jacaleen Cotter, Jeffrey Arthur. Production Archive Administrator: Krista Bunn. Art Coordinator: Karen Silva. Post Production Manager: Sara Duran. Post Production Coordinator: Barbara Beck. Talent Coordinator: Olivia Miner. Managing Editor: Rich Harrison. Supervising Editor: Cecil Broughton. Sound Effects Editors: Brian Baker, Rick Hinson, Mark Orfanos, Jerry Winicki. Assistant Editors: David Lynch, Thomas Needell, Craig Paulsen. *Chip 'n' Dale's Rescue Rangers* Theme Song Words and Music by: Mark Mueller. Music Composed and Conducted by: Glen Daum for Score Productions. *The Best of Everything* Words and Music by: Silversher and Silversher. Animation Production by: Walt Disney Animation Japan, Inc. and Sun Woo Animation.

CHRISTMAS IN DISNEYLAND
Produced and Directed by: Marty Pasetta. Written by: Buz Kohan. Associate Producer: Allan Baumrucker. Music Arranged and Conducted by: Jack Elliott, Allyn Ferguson. Choreographed by: Alan Johnson. Choral Direction and Special Musical Material by: Alan Copeland. Additional Special Musical Material by: Buz Kohan. Art Director: Ed Flesh. Costumes Designed by: Bill Hargate. Associate Director: Bob Bowker. Assistant to the Producer: Danette Herman. Assistant Art Director: Roger Speakman. Production Assistants: Debbie Ross, Tom Boles. Assistant Choreographer: Pam Barlow. Lighting Director: Jeff Engel. Staging Supervisor: Ray Brannigan. Audio: Larry Stephens. Video: Mark Sanford, Dean Terrell. Video Tape Editor: Bill Breshears. Stage Manager: Ted Ray. Make-up: Jerry O'Dell, Larry Abbott. Remote Facilities by: Compact Video Systems, Inc. A Pasetta Production, Inc.

CIRCUS OF THE STARS GOES TO DISNEYLAND
Executive Producer: Jack Wishard. Co-Executive Producer: Bunny Stivers. Produced by: Sid Smith. Co-Produced by: Timothy Kettle. Directed by: Sid Smith. Written by: Bunny Stivers, Turk Pipkin. Talent Executive: Sharon Olson. Associate Producer: Robin Howington. Art Director: Romain Johnston. Costume Designer: Pete Menefee. Musical Director: Tom Bahler. Choreographer: Betty Aidman. Act Producers: Phil Braverman, Rich De Michele, Turk Pipkin. Lighting Designers: Carl Gibson, Jeff Engel. Associate Director: Patricia Eyerman. Interviews Directed by: Timothy Kettle. Production Supervisor: Michael Dempsey. Post Production Coordinator: Sharon Taylor. Production Coordinator: Mark Wishard. Script Coordinator: Scott Dove. Rehearsal Footage: Adam Boster. Operations Management: Tom Ong. Technical Director: Bob Highton. Edited by: Woody Wilson. Audio:

Klaus Landsburg, Mike Abbott, Otto Svoboda. Video: Steve Berry. Stage Managers: Sandy Prudden, Mike Kelly, Gary Stella. Assistant Art Director: Everett Chase. Make-up Artist: Rhavan. Talent Coordinator: Brian Ahern. Additional Trainers: Les Chimes, Jan Dubsky, Tina Dubsky, Gina Rock. Production Staff: Joyce Jacalone, Kate Jones, Bonnie Morley. Production Associates: Bruce Chandler, Bill Gearty, Vonnie Hutchinson, Daniel Konate, Arthur Lew. *For Disneyland* Supervising Producer: Lisa Cappel. Line Producer: Gary Kurtz. Operations Manager: Tom Jacobsen. Promotions Manager: Scott Tanner. Executive in Charge of Production: Alan Baumrucker. Procter & Gamble Productions, Inc.

COMPUTER WORE TENNIS SHOES, THE (TV version)
Music Composed and Conducted by: Philip Giffin. Film Editor: Jeff Gourson. Production Designer: Peg McClellan. Director of Photography: Russ Alsobrook. Produced by: Joseph B. Wallenstein. Executive Producers: George Zaloom, Les Mayfield, Scott Immergut. Written by: Joseph L. McEveety, Ryan Rowe. Based on the Feature Film Written by: Joseph L. McEveety. Directed by: Peyton Reed. Coordinating Producer: Irwin Marcus. Unit Production Manager: Irwin Marcus. First Assistant Director: Linda Montanti. Second Assistant Director: Robin Holding. Casting by: Allison Jones. Costume Designer: Tom Bronson. Co-Producer: Michael Swerdlick. Set Decorator: Brenda Meyers-Ballard. Property Master: Cliff Bernay. Script Supervisor: Susan Bierbaum. Production Coordinator: Adam Salazar. Costumers: Emma Trenchard, Jay Caplan. Make-up: Kathryn M. Kelly. Hair Stylist: Cheri Ruff. Location Manager: Lisa Stewart. Music Arranged by: Stu Goldberg. Production Sound Mixer: David Barr Yaffee, C.A.S. Optical Effects by: Metrolight Studios. Acknowledgment: NASA. ZM Productions, Inc.

COMPUTERS ARE PEOPLE, TOO!
Directed by: Denis Sanders. Written by: Michael Bonifer, L.G. Weaver. Produced by: Michael Bonifer. Associate Producer: Cardon Walker. Computer Voices: Nancy Kulp, Billy Bowles. Camera: Ted Ashton. Music: Dan Kuramoto. Recordist: Larry Forkner. Sound: Steve Kibbons. Mixer: Larry Sullivan. Sound Mix Supervisor: Dan Kuramoto. Lighting: Joe Epperson, Mike Chaney. Video Engineers: Dick Caine, Alan Porter. Video Tape Editor: Joe Bella. Assistant Video Tape Editor: Cardon Walker. Research: Susan Champlin. Visual Consultant: Jodi McLaughlin. Production Assistants: Scott Cooper, Margie Hernandez, Steven Rogers, Jim Fanning. *The Juggler* Theme: Tom Seufert, Garth Hudson. Video Game Theme: David Garfield. Additional Music: Michael Iceberg. Additional Photography: Panos Productions, Telemation. Make-up: Robin Dee LaVigne. Hair Stylist: Frankie Bergman. Acknowledgments: University of Northern Colorado, Computer Camp Inc., John Whitney, Sr., Dr. James Blinn, Jet Propulsion Laboratory, The Ladd Company, Aladdin's Castle, Yoko Ichino, Fairlight Instruments, U.S.A. Flight Animation by: Evans and Sutherland. Monitor Graphics: General Electric-Calma. Post Production Supervisor: Arthur Swerdloff. Producers for S.R.S.: Arthur Swerdloff, Denis Sanders. *Panasonic Plane:* Robert Abel and Associates. *Caveman:* Computer Image. *Refractions:* Robert Conley and Cranston-Csuri. *Pillars:* Cranston-Csuri. *Times Square* Digital Effects. *Sunstone:* Ed Emschwiller and New York Institute of Technology. *The Juggler:* Information International. *Electronic Man:* Magi. *Carla's Island:* Nelson Max. *The Works:* New York Institute of Technology. *Euclidean Illusions:* Stan VanDerBeek and Cray Research. Video Synthesis: WTV. S.R.S. Productions in association with Walt Disney Productions.

CORPSE HAD A FAMILIAR FACE, THE
Music: Patrick Williams. Edited by: Robert Florio, A.C.E. Production Designer: Roy Amaral. Director of Photography: James Glennon. Producers: Terry Donnelly, Randy Sutter. Executive Producers: Debbie Blum, Tony Ganz, Doug Chapin, Barry Krost. Written by: Derek Marlowe, Dennis Turner. Suggested by the autobiography *The Corpse Had a Familiar Face* by: Edna Buchanan. Directed by: Joyce Chopra. Executive Producers: Robert M. Sertner, Frank Von Verneck. Casting by: Susan Glicksman, C.S.A. Unit Production Manager: Terry Donnelly. First Assistant Director: Cara Gaillanza. Second

Assistant Director: Keri L. McIntyre. Production Supervisor: Ted Babcock. Costume Designer: Shari Feldman. Costumes for Ms. Montgomery: Frances Hays. Costume Supervisor: Cheri Reed. Script Supervisor: Kate Hoogner. Stunt Coordinator: Terry James. Set Decorator: Linda Lee Sutton. Property Master: Brenton L. Lane. Gaffer: Derrick Kolus. Key Grip: David Donoho. Camera Operator: Casey Hotchkiss. Production Coordinator: Brian Tanke. Make-up/Hair for Ms. Montgomery: Bill Clift. Make-up: Karen Dahl. Hair: Lisa Marie Rosenburg. Sound Mixer: Randy Gable, C.A.S. Location Manager: Lynda Recht. Casting Assistant: Tammi Campbell. Title Song *Something Is Out There* Lyrics by: Arthur Hamilton. Music by: Patrick Williams. Performed by: Robin Wiley. Music Supervision: Terri Fricon. Songs Performed by: Dean Martin. Assistant Editors: Augie Hess, Tim Boettcher. Sound Effects: Rich Harrison. Music Editor: Susan Mick. Blum/Ganz Productions in association with Von Zerneck/Sertner Films.

COUNTRY ESTATES
Produced by: Kenneth R. Koch. Written by: Howard Gordon, Alex Gansa. Directed by: Donald Petrie. Executive Producers: Alex Gansa, Howard Gordon. Executive Producers: Paul Junger Witt, Tony Thomas. Director of Photography: Tim Suhrstedt. Production Designer: David Chapman. Editor: Kaja Fehr. Music by: Don Davis. Unit Production Manager: Richard Learman. First Assistant Director: Martha Elcan. Second Assistant Director: Gail Seely. Casting by: Nan Dutton, C.S.A., Michael Greer. Location Manager: Sondra West. Script Supervisor: Susan Bierbaum. Set Decorator: Clay Griffith. Sound Mixer: Kenneth Ross. Property Master: Nino Candido. Costume Supervisor: Dorothy Amos. Hair Dept. Head: Carol O'Connell. Make-up Dept. Head: Mark Bussan. Transportation Coordinator: Bob Bailey. Production Accountant: Stanley Mark. Construction Coordinator: Bob Blackburn. Sound Effects Supervisor: Anthony Mazzei. Executive in Charge of Production: Susan Palladino. A Witt-Thomas Production.

DARKWING DUCK PREMIERE, THE/BACK TO SCHOOL WITH THE MICKEY MOUSE CLUB
Produced by: Walt Disney Television Animation. *Darkly Dawns the Duck Credits* Supervising Producers: Tad Stones, Alan Zaslove. Producer: Alan Zaslove. Story by: Jan Strand, Tad Stones. Written by: Jymn Magon, Tad Stones. Dialogue Direction: Ginny McSwain. Animation Directors: Dale Case, John Kimball, Marsh Lamore, Rick Leon. Storyboard: Kurt Anderson, Lonnie Thompson, Hank Tucker, Roy Wilson. Storyboard Clean-up Artists: Jan Green, Paulette King. Art Director: Fred Warter. Key Layout Design: Fred Warter. Supervising Character Designer: Toby Shelton. Character Design: Kenny Thompkins. Prop Design: Terry Hudson, David Mink. Key Background Stylists: Paro Hozumi, Fred Warter. Color Key Stylist: Jill Stirdivant. Overseas Animation Supervisor: Dan Forster. Supervising Timing Director: Marlene Robinson May. Timing Director: Carole Beers. Assistant Producer: LuAnne Wood. Continuity Coordinators: Jim Finch, Kathrin Victor. Track Reading: Skip Craig. Post Production Manager: Sara Duran. Post Production Supervisor: Joseph Hathaway. Sound Dubbing Supervisor: Christopher Keith. Post Production Coordinators: Jeffrey Arthur, John Royer. Post Production Assistant: Nanci Battelle. Talent Coordinator: Lynne Batchelor. Production Assistants: Melinda Wunsch, Johanne Beaudoin. Script Coordinator: Susan McElroy. Archives Supervisor: Krista Bunn. Art Coordinators: Marjorie Warman, Jodey Kaminski, Karen Silva. Shipping Coordinator: Craig Simpson. Managing Film Editor: Rich Harrison. Supervising Editors: Cecil E. Broughton, MPSE, Charlie King, MPSE. Sound Editors: Rick Hinson, MPSE, David Lynch, Jerry Winicki. Dialogue Editors: Craig Paulsen, Andy Rose. Assistant Editors: Jenny Harrison, James N. Harrison. Theme by: Steve Nelson, Thom Sharp. Produced by: Steve Tyrell. Music by: Philip Giffin. Animation Production by: Walt Disney Television Animation (Australia) Pty, Limited, Walt Disney Animation (Japan) Inc. *Music Video Segment* Director: Bill Miller. Producer: Maria Sheehan. Editor: Michael Rothenberg. Composed and Performed by: Cliff Schwarz. Creative Director: Barry Rosenthal. *Back to School with the Mickey Mouse Club Credits* Executive Producer: Steve Clements. Supervising Producer: Jean Wiegman. Produced and Directed by: Joe

Carolei. Writing Supervised by: Alan Silberberg. Written by: Steve Clements, Hilary Rollins, Tim Grundmann, Stephen Winer. Co-Producer: Margie Friedman. Associate Producer: Bob Williams. Musical Performance Segments Produced by: Sarah Elgart. Music Producer: Dana Salyers. Choreography by: Myles Thoroughgood. Vocal Coach: Barbara Leventhal. Segment Directors: Maria Baltazzi, Jimmy Huckaby. Senior Segment Producers: Kevin Cronan, Jimmy Huckaby. Segment Producers: Bruce Anderson, Maria Baltazzi, Angela Wendkos. Associate Segment Producer: Jonathan Dowdell. Art Director: Randy Foster. Lighting Director: Nick Woolfolk. *Peace, Love and Understanding* Music Video Directed by: Joe Carolei. *Couple of Days Off* Music Video Directed by: David Seeger. Associate Directors: Kim Anway, Judi Elterman. Stage Managers: Gary Natoli, Rudi Corbett, Kelly Hernacki. Mouseketeer Casting by: Matt Casella. Set Designed by: Gerry Hariton, Vicki Baral. Lighting Designed by: Greg Brunton. Post Production Supervisor: Annie Court. Editor: Sam Patterson. Assistant Videotape Editor: Michael I. Coe. Camera Operators: Bill Akerlund, James Arminio, Neal Gallagher, Paul Klekotta, Mark Lynch. Technical Director: Pete Court. Video Control: Vince Vezzi. Audio Mixer: Jim Fay. Blue Wave Productions, Inc. in association with Steve Clements Productions. Walt Disney Television.

DATELINE: DISNEYLAND
Directed by: Stuart Phelps, John Rich. Produced by: Sherman Marks. Musical Director: Walter Schumann. Choreographer: Miriam Nelson. Executive Producer: Walt Disney.

DAVY CROCKETT: GUARDIAN SPIRIT
Produced by: Frank Fischer. Supervising Producer: Mark H. Ovitz. Developed by: William Blinn. Written by: Robert Sonntag, Deborah Gilliland. Directed by: Harry Falk. Executive Producer: William Blinn. Associate Producer: Frank Merwald. Original Score by: Joel McNeely. Director of Photography: Isidore Mankofsky, A.S.C. Art Director: Ian Thomas. Editor: Edward Salier. Unit Production Manager/Associate Producer: Justis Greene. First Assistant Director: Ken Collins. Second Assistant Director: Robert Petrovicz. Casting by: Peg Halligan, C.S.A. Costumes Designed by: Tom Bronson. Set Decorator: Chris August. Property Master: Grant Swain. Key Costumers: Christopher Ryan, Linda Lee Langdon. Make-up: Joanne Smith. Hair Stylist: Ian Ballard. Vancouver Casting: Sid Kozak. Location Manager: Janice Frome. Script Supervisor: Shelley Crawford. Production Coordinator: Catherine Howard. Stunt Coordinator: John Scott. Production Sound Mixer: Garry Cunningham. Sound Editing by: Stephen J. Cannell Productions. Music Editing by: Craig Pettigrew. Acknowledgments: The Province of British Columbia, Ministry of Parks, Golden Ears Provincial Park. Echo Cove Productions in association with Walt Disney Television.

DAYO
Music by: Lee Holdridge. Edited by: Christopher Holmes. Production Designer: Daniel Lomino. Director of Photography: Isidore Mankofsky. Produced by: Barry Bernardi, Ira Shuman. Written by: Bruce Franklin Singer. Directed by: Michael Schultz. Executive Producer: Steve White. Associate Producers: Ken Raskoff, Chris Defaria. Casting by: Francine Maisler. Unit Production Manager: Ira Shuman. 1st Assistant Director: Joel Tuber. 2nd Assistant Director: Ken Goch. Gaffer: David Jarrell. Camera Operator: Jeff Moore. Sound Mixer: Richard Van Dyke. Key Grip: Scott R. Davis. Set Decorator: Steve Davis. Prop Master: Robert M. Peck. Costume Designers: Marilyn Matthews, Patsy Rainey. Make-up: Kim Adrissi. Hair Dresser: Monique Desart. North Carolina Casting: Fincannon & Associates. Music Administration: Linda Koci. Location Manager: Steve Housewright. Production Coordinator: Carole J. Sanders. Assistant Editor: Jay R. Lawton. Sound Editors: Jeremy Hoenack, C.A.S., Joseph Zappala, Steve Jaskowiak. Rerecording Mixers: Jeremy Hoenack, C.A.S., Melissa Sherwood Hofmann, C.A.S., David Weishaar, C.A.S. Transportation Coordinator: Edward Flotard. Production Accountant: Jenny Fitzgibbons. Assistant to the Producer: Sara Mata. Casting Associate: Donna Lynn Greenbaum. Steve White Productions in association with Walt Disney Television.

DEADLINE FOR MURDER: FROM THE FILES OF EDNA BUCHANAN

Music by: Patrick Williams. Edited by: Robert Florio, A.C.E. Production Designer: Donald Light-Harris. Director of Photography: James Glennon. Executive Producers: Deborah Blum, Tony Ganz, Doug Chapin, Barry Krost. Producers: Terry Donnelly, Randy Sutter. Produced by: Carol Trussell. Written by: Les Carter, Susan Sisko. Based on Certain Characters Created by: Derek Marlowe, Dennis Turner. As Suggested by the Autobiography *The Corpse Had a Familiar Face* by: Edna Buchanan. Directed by: Joyce Chopra. Executive Producers: Robert M. Sertner, Frank von Zerneck. Acknowledgment: Edna Buchanan. Associate Producer: Ted Babcock. Casting by: Susan Glicksman, C.S.A., Fern Orenstein, C.A.S. Unit Production Manager: Terry Donnelly. First Assistant Director: Matthew Clark. Second Assistant Director: Robert Lorenz. Costume Designer: Tom Bronson. Set Decorator: R.W. Intlekofer. Property Master: Riley Morgan. Script Supervisor: Anne Melville. Location Manager: Marvin Bernstein. Production Manager: Adam Salazar. Costume Supervisor: Frances Hays. Costumer: Robert C. Stewart. Make-up/Hair for Ms. Montgomery: Billy Clift. Make-up: June Westmore. Hair Stylist: Lola M. Kemp. Production Sound Mixer: Richard I. Birnbaum, C.A.S. Sound Editing by: Rich Harrison. Music Editing by: Susan Mick. Title Song *Something Is Out There* Lyrics by: Arthur Hamilton. Music by: Patrick Williams. Performed by: Robin Wiley. Music Supervision: Terri Fricon. Krost/Chapin Productions and Blum/Ganz Productions and Von Zerneck/Sertner Films in association with Touchstone Television.

DICK TRACY: BEHIND THE BADGE—BEHIND THE SCENES

Produced by: Suzanne McCafferty. Written by: Rick Sublett. Directed by: Gayle Hollenbaugh. Narrator: Don La Fontaine. Editor: Kurt Tiegs. Online Editor: Keith Cook. Director of Photography: Daniel Yarussi. Title Design: Dale Herigstad. Title Animation: Kevin Rafferty. Cartoon Strip Animation Sequence: Ken Rudolph. Production Coordinator: Barbara Cole. Production Assistants: Gina Gennaro, Deborah Liekkio, Renee Siemann. Camera: Bruce Finn, Jose Luis Mignone, Daniel Yarussi. Camera Assistants: Echol Marshall, James Rapp, Ross Judd, Lance Fisher, Kevin Haggerty, Roy Hogstedt. Video Camera Operator: Kenneth Liston, Joseph Longo. Audio/Video Engineers: John H. Barbee, Gary Woods. Gaffer: Steven Hodge. Telecine Operator: Howard Cisco. Special Music Mix: Kevin Gilbert. Produced by Buena Vista Television Productions in association with ASTA Productions.

DISNEY AFTERNOON LIVE! AT DISNEYLAND

For Disneyland Producer: Lisa Cappel. Production Assistants: Robin Mensinger, Melissa Boyer, Cathryn Burroughs. Camera: Steve Ferrier. Editors: Barry Meyers, Paul Quade. *For KCAL-TV* Producer: Janelle Ricksen. Audio: Phil Kerns, Robin Hill. Post Production: Carlos A. Lopez, Greg Huson.

DISNEY CHRISTMAS GIFT, A

Prepared for Television by: Frank Brandt, Dennis Landa, Ed Ropolo, Tad Stones, V. Renee Toensing. With the Talents of: Bobby Driscoll, Verna Felton, Ilene Woods. Song *You Can Fly:* Sammy Cahn, Sammy Fain.

DISNEY'S ALADDIN ON ICE

Music by: Alan Menken. Lyrics by: Howard Ashman, Tim Rice. Produced by: Bill Bracken. Written by: Stephen Pouliot. Executive Produced and Directed by: Steve Binder. Executive Producer, Walt Disney's World on Ice: Kenneth Feld. Associate Producer: Chris Plourde. Principal Choreography: Sandra Bezic. Location Choreography: Michael Seibert. Production Designer: Jimbo Marshall. Lighting Designer: Simon Miles. Aladdin and Jasmine's Costume Designer: Jef Billings. Production Manager: John Foy. Production Supervisor: Sandy Broadway. Script Coordinator: Risa Thomas. Edited by: Ron Barr, Steve Binder. Art Director: Sharon Tanian. Associate Director: Allan Kartun. Stage Manager: Josh Berger. Production Associates: Jim Amerian, Caryn Santoro. Make-up and Hair: Magda Dajani. Engineer in Charge: Keith Winikoff. Camera Operators: Ted Ashton, Wayne Orr, Rick Robinson. Audio: Don Worsham. Technical Engineers: Charlie Fernandez, An-

drew Sabol. Post Production Audio: Ed Greene. Music Re-Mixer: Gary Lux. Macintosh Artist: Melody Welch. Character Graphic Imaging: Harri Paakkonen. DP Max Artist: Chris Love. *For Walt Disney's World on Ice* Adaptation: Jerry Bilik. Choreographer: Bob Paul. Costume Designer: Arthur Bocca. Production Designer: Robert Little. Show Manager: Mark Cox. *For Video Cairo* Producer: Nader Gohar. Production Manager: Hisham Gohar. Production Coordinator: Iman Farouk. Production Associates: Waleed Ezz, Caroline Adel. Helicopter Pilot: Ahmed Abbas. Produced by Walt Disney Television in association with Micawber Productions, Ltd. and Rodan Productions.

DISNEY'S ALL-STAR MOTHER'S DAY ALBUM

Prepared for Television by: Craig Murray, Robert L. Quinn, Q Productions. With the Voice Talents of: Verna Felton, Ilene Woods. *Father's Day Off* Music: Paul Smith. Production Coordinator for Disney: V. Renee Toensing. Additional Music by: John O'Kennedy.

DISNEY'S ALL-STAR VALENTINE PARTY

Prepared for Television by: Dennis Landa, V. Renée Toensing, Fausto Sanchez. *Mickey, She's Got a Crush on You* Song by: Michael and Patty Silversher. Music Video by: Jymn Magon. Narrated by: Rick Dees.

DISNEY'S *BEAUTY AND THE BEAST*: THE BROADWAY MUSICAL COMES TO L.A.

Senior Producer: Michael Waco. Producer: Suzan Jorgensen-Torgerson. Director: Melanie Steensland. Associate Director: Ed Parker. Writers: Michael Waco, Suzan Jorgensen-Torgerson, Elena Pearce, John Corcoran. Production Coordinator: Jay Alan Lavely. Chief Editor: Nancy Rosenblum. Chief Photographer: Ron Price. Editors: Shaka Armstrong, Mack McDermott, Carlos Lopez, Edward Lapple, Jason Lewis, Garry Ashton, Jeff Mills. Director, Graphic Production: Margaret Bassett. Logo Design: Mike Radogna. Animation Artist: Gil Haslam. Electronic Graphics: Alan Pfister. Cameras: Joel Fallon, Webb Webber, Robert Ashley, Xerro Ryan Covarrubias, David Cronshaw, Steve Medina, Bob Davis, Kris Smith, Steve Howell, Ron Wening, Brian Hollingsworth, Bob Berkowitz, Keith Dicker. Production Assistants: Celeste Sherman, Ngan Nguyen, Patty Soto. Technical Director: Bernd Bergman. Audio: Don Warsham, Greg Orrante. Videotape: Gene Lawrence, Doug Coffland. Video: Keith Buttleman. Lighting Director: Dick Sulprizio. Electricians: Randy Woods, Michael Lovelady. Production Associate: Susan Nakamura. Helicopter Pilot: Rob Marshall. Engineer in Charge: Arnold Tolbert. Microwave Transmission: Kris Smith. Stage Managers: Ridge Conlan, Frank Gervasi. Make-up: Kimberly Meyer. Engineering Coordinator: Debra Jackson. Sr. Vice President/Director of News: Bob Henry. KCAL-TV News.

DISNEY'S *CAPTAIN EO* GRAND OPENING

Produced and Directed by: Marty Pasetta. Written by: Buz Kohan. Associate Producers: Mick McCullough, Michael Petok. Special Musical Material: Earl Brown. Production Designer: Robert W. Rang. Choreographer: Walter Painter. Music Conducted and Arranged by: Lenny Stack. Talent Executive: Tisha Fein. Lighting Designers: Bob Dickinson, Michael Curry. Assistant to the Producer: Roberta Savold. Production Manager: Larry Cohen. Talent Consultant: Lillian Mizrahi. Production Assistant: Pat Germann. Transportation Coordinator: Rob Krueger. Associate Director: Mark Corff. Editor: Bruce Motyer. Stage Managers: Steve Burgess, Andi Copley, Terry McCoy, Dency Nelson, Greg Pasetta. Technical Directors: Gene Crowe, Terry Donahue. Audio: Doug Nelson. Production Associates: John Devine, Vickie LaBrie, Drew Ogier, Paige Rabban, Dru Rafkin, Steven Schillaci, John Wright. Staging Supervisors: John Bradley, Dennis Langston. For Disneyland: Production Supervisor: Del Shilling. Production Manager: Chris Robinson. Choreographer: Barnette Ricci. "The Making of" clips: Muffett Kaufman. Costumes: Jack Muhs. Art Designer: Clare Graham. Character Coordinator: Donna Tomlinson. Maintenance Coordinators: Keith Fulton, Dan Otrambo. Operations Coordinators: Bob Gault, Rory O'Leary, Ferril Onyett, Joe Pittaluga, Mark Taul. Acknowledgments: Horseless Carriage Club of Southern California,

Locke High School Band, Washington High School Band. Editing Facilities: The Editing Company. A Pasetta Production in association with Walt Disney Television.

DISNEY'S CHAMPIONS ON ICE

Executive Producers: Kimber Rickabaugh, Paul Miller. Directed by: Paul Miller. Written by: Stephen Pouliot. Music Adapted & Conducted by: Glen Roven. Choreographer: Sarah Kawahara. Production Designer: Rene Lagler. Lighting Designer: Greg Brunton. Costume Designer: Jef Billings. Talent Executive: Deena Esensten. Vocal Performances by: Maureen McGovern, Billy Vera, Carmen Carter, Mervyn Warren. Skating Ensemble: Kelly Abolt, Lisa Marie Allen, Darlin Baker, Bobby Beauchamp, John Brancato, Teresa Foy, Keith Green, Stephanee Grosscup, Natasha Kuchiki, Akop Manoukian, David Nickel, Susan Pereira, Ararat Zakarian. Associate Producer: Cisco Henson. Associate Director: Deborah Miller. Stage Manager: Henry Neimark. Assistant Choreographer: Jamie Isley. Script Supervisor: Sharon Nagata. Videotape Editors: Alan Carter, Stan Kellam. Production Manager: Lyn H. Rappaport. Production Coordinator: Michael Colbert. Set Decorator: Kristen Olenick. Research/Clip Clearance: Rene Baker Kibbler. Orchestrators: Joe Curiale, Larry Schwartz. Technical Director: Gene Crowe. Technical Supervisor: Ron Stutzman. Video Control: Paul Ranieri. Audio: Toby Foster, Gary Lux, Jamie Ledner. Camera Operators: Ted Ashton, Larry Heider, Barry Heidt, Bob Keys, Jeff Muhlstock, Ron Smith, Kevin Murphy. Videotape Operator: Andrew Sabol. Staging Supervisor: Keaton S. Walker. Gaffer: Vicki "Max" Brenner. Head Utility: Charlie Fernandez. Executive in Charge of Production: Ricky Kirshner. Rick Mill Productions.

DISNEY'S CHRISTMAS FANTASY ON ICE

Executive Producers: Kimber Rickabaugh, Paul Miller. Co-Producer: Sandra Bezic. Coordinating Producer: Marilyn Seabury. Directed by: Paul Miller. Written by: Bill Prady, Bruce Vilanch. Music Director: Tom Scott. Art Director: Rene Lagler. Lighting Design: Allen Branton, Simon Miles. Choreographers: Sandra Bezic, Michael Siebert. Costume Designer: Ret Turner. Music Supervisor: Nancy Severinsen. Associate Director/Stage Manager: Debbie Williams. Associate Producer: Bob Livengood. Talent Executive: Deena Esensten. Production Supervisor: Stephanie Chaffin. Production Coordinators: Tom Mahoney, Keith Taylor. Production Associates: Brad Bogart, Trisha Ricci, Tammy Karpenko. Make-up: Cheryl Ptak, Mary Resnick. Video: Mark Sanford. Audio: Paul Sandweiss, Jamie Ledner, Russell Dashiell. Louma Camera Operators: Bill Philbin, Hector Ramirez, Michael Boisclair, Brooks Guyer. Edited by: Stan Kellam. Assistant Editor: Stephen Berger. Computer Visual Effects by: Topix L.A. Acknowledgments: Chuck Webb & The Sun Valley Company, Nick Maricich, Rick Reay, Brent Gillette, Sawtooth National Recreational Area. RickMill Productions.

DISNEY'S CHRISTMAS ON ICE

Executive Producer: Don Ohlmeyer. Co-Executive Producer: Kenneth Feld. Supervising Producer: Linda Jonsson. Producer: Kim Moses. Directed by: Don Ohlmeyer. Written by: Barbara Allyn. Associate Producer: Mick McCullough. Skating Supervised by: Sandra Bezic. Lighting Designer: Kieran Healy. Production Designer: Jimbo Marshall. Associate Director: Ron Andreassen. Original Music Composed and Arranged by: Marc Ellis. Stage Managers: Ken Stein, Debbie Cole. Production Manager: Mark Rains. Script Supervisor: Pamela Lopez. Production Coordinator: Tracey Levine. Production Assistants: John Saade, Michael X Ferraro. Graphic Designer: Penelope Gottlieb. Technical Manager: Paul Boykin. Staging Supervisor: Ed Kish. Talent Coordinator: Bettina Ruckelshaus. Costume Designer: Jef Billings. Location Manager: Phil Casanta. Assistant Lighting Directors: Tom Beck, C.D. Simpson. Special Projections: XL Productions. Scenic Coordinator: Clay Newbill. Audio: Paul Sandweiss. Video: Steve Gaughen. Cameras: Billy Boatman, Richard Favazzo, D'Arcy Marsh, Hector Ramiriez, Mike Wimberly, Bunt Young. Editors: Ron Andreassen, Ron Barr. Paintbox: Laurie Resnick. Make-up: Barbie Gotschall. Hair: Luke O'Connor. *Sugar Is Sweet* Music Video Performed by: The Party. Directed by: David Seeger. Acknowledgment: Tahoe Star Entertainment. Ohlmeyer

Communications Company in association with Walt Disney Television.

DISNEY'S COUNTDOWN TO KID'S DAY

Executive Producer: Brad Lachman. Supervising Producer: Gregory Sills. Directed by: Louis J. Horvitz. Writers: Garry Bormet, Bruce Vilanch. Executive in Charge of Production: Tom Boles. Additional Segments Directed by: Gary Halvorson. Tokyo Segment Directed by: David Irete. Musical Director: George Duke. Talent Executive: Debi Genovese. Associate Producer: John Reed. Segment Producers: Rob Wilson, Dominic Orlando. Associate Director: Jim Tanker. Edited by: Jeff Palmer. Art Directors: Jimbo Marshall, John Shaffner, Joe Stewart. Lighting Designers: Simon Miles, John Rook, Kirk Witherspoon. Stage Managers: Ken Stein, Vince Poxon, Kelly Hernacki. Production Supervisor: Dorothy Wong. Assistants to Producers: S.M. Smith, Lisa McAlpin, Carole Scott. Post Production Coordinator: Joe Keaney, Jr. Talent Coordinator: Lisa Weisner. Production Coordinators: Ann Lauterio, April Corns. Production Assistants: Mark Pineiro, Gwen Balbuena. Technical Directors: Ken Shapiro, Alan Wells. Hair/Make-up: Christy Garran. Cameras: John Burdick, Hank Geving, Tom Gerren, Mark Hunter, Jay Millard, Bill Philbin, David Placos, Hector Ramirez. Brad Lachman Productions, Inc.

DISNEY'S DTV DOGGONE VALENTINE

Executive Producer: Andrew Solt. Produced by: Jim Milio, Susan F. Walker. Written by: Jim Milio, Andrew Solt, Susan F. Walker. Directed by: Andrew Solt. Associate Producer: Greg Vines. Post Production Supervisor: Kevin Miller. Edited by: Jim Milio, Kevin Miller, Susan F. Walker, Mark West. Additional Music by: John Debney. Voice Casting: Les Perkins. Voice Characterizations by: Wayne Allwine (Mickey Mouse), Albert Ash (Ludwig Von Drake), Eddie Carroll (Jiminy Cricket), Bill Farmer (Goofy), Maurice LaMarche (Radio announcer), Will Ryan (Pongo), Lisa St. James (Puppies), Russi Taylor (Minnie Mouse). Announcer: J.J. Jackson. Assistant Editors: Vickie Hilty, Kevin Fernan. Post-Production Audio: David Fluhr. Title Graphics: Jim House. Additional Graphics: Lee Scott. Production Associates: Laura Amelse, Darren Foreman. Production Executive: Rachelle Katz. An Andrew Solt Production.

DISNEY'S DTV MONSTER HITS

Executive Producer: Andrew Solt. Produced by: Phillip Savenick, Harry Arends. Written by: Phillip Savenick, Andrew Solt, Susan F. Walker. Directed by: Andrew Solt. Post-Production Supervisor: Kevin Miller. Associate Producer: Greg Vines. Edited by: Harry Arends, Donna Egan-Kaplan, Kevin Miller, Mark West. Director of Photography: Steve Gerbson. Unit Production Manager/1st Assistant Director: Ira Shuman. Additional Music by: John Debney. Production Consultant: Mark Hufnail. Voice Characterizations by: Wayne Allwine (Mickey Mouse), Tony Anselmo (Donald Duck), Bill Farmer (Goofy), June Foray (Witch Hazel), Maurice LaMarche. Voice Casting: Les Perkins. Announcer: Gary Owens. Title Graphics: Jim House. Assistant Editors: Vickie Hilty, Kevin Fernan. Post-Production Audio: Chris Haire, Doug Davey, Wilson Dyer. Additional Graphics: Lee Scott. Production Associates: Laura Amelse, Darren Foreman. Production Executive: Rachelle Katz. An Andrew Solt Production in association with Walt Disney Television.

DISNEY'S DTV VALENTINE

Produced by: Andrew Solt, Phillip Savenick. Directed by: Andrew Solt. Written by: Jim Milio, Phillip Savenick, Andrew Solt, Susan F. Walker. Co-Producers: Mark Hufnail, Harry Arends. Edited by: Harry Arends, Donna Egan-Kaplan, Kevin Miller. Associate Producer: Greg Vines. Additional Music by: John Debney. Videotape Editors: Mark West, John Neal. Assistant Editors: Daryl Baskin, Wayne Hudgins, Sidney Mandell. Music Clearance: Mitchell Leib. Announcer: Paul Frees. Voice Casting: Les Perkins. Post-Production Audio: Allen Patapoff. Title Graphics: Jim House. Additional Graphics: Lee Scott. Production Staff: Vickie Hilty, Chris Jarmick, James Photi, Vikki Prudden. Acknowledgment: Chuck Braverman. Production Executive: Rachelle Katz. An Andrew Solt Production.

Disney's Fluppy Dogs

Music by: Shirley Walker. Written by: Haskell Barkin. Produced and Directed by: Fred Wolf. Produced by: Walt Disney Television Animation. Associate Producer: Tom Ruzicka. Art Director: Ron Scholefield. Production Designers: Jill Colbert, Ed Gombert, Kevin Harkey. Storyboard Design: Larry Latham. Key Background Styling: Lisa Keene, Paro Hozumi. Key Color Styling: Debra Jorgensborg. Timing Directors: David Brain, Vincent Davis, Terry Harrison. Assistant Director: Randy Chaffee. Post Production Supervisor: Rich Harrison. Supervising Editor: Charlie King. Assistant Editor: Marc Orfanos. Post Production Coordinator: Ken Tsumura. Animation Supervisor: John Kafka. Animation Production by: TMS Entertainment, Inc.

Disney's Golden Anniversary of *Snow White and the Seven Dwarfs*

Produced by: Brad Lachman. Directed by: Louis J. Horvitz. Written by: Jack Burns, Daniel Helfgott. Coordinating Producer: Milt Hoffman. Art Director: Bob Keene. Music by: Michael Miller. Costumes Designed by: Tom Bronson. Choreographer: Barnette Ricci. Associate Producer: Steve Ligerman. Lighting Designers: Bob Dickinson, Michael Curry. Talent Executive: Vince Calandra. Associate Director: Emm-Jay Trokel. Script Supervisor: Pat Brannon Wise. Production Coordinator: Kent Weishaus. Talent Coordinator: Chief Lighting Technician: Vicki "Max" Brenner. Stage Managers: Peter Bright, Steve Ligerman. Technical Director: John B. Field. Audio: Gordon Klimuck, Larry Stevens, Bart Chiate. Video: John Palacio. Cameras: Sam Drummy, Dean Hall, Bill Philbin, Hector Ramirez. Edited by: David Foster, Floyd Carver. Sound Mixer: Jerry Clemans. *Some Day My Prince Will Come* Arranged and Conducted by: Jeremy Lubbock. Videotape Facilities by: PDS Video Productions, Inc. *For Disneyland* Production Supervisor: Del Shilling. Production Manager: Chris Robinson. Operations Coordinator: Dave Omel. Costuming: Andy Gordon. Character Coordinator: Lilia Illes. Maintenance Coordinator: Dan Otrambo. Brad Lachman Productions, Inc.

Disney's Goof Troop

Music video credits: Producer: Marian Sheehan. Director: Bill Miller. Set Designer: Brian Murphy. Editor: Michael Rothenberg. Choreographer: Diane Martel. Make-Up Designer: Jennifer Aspinal. Music Composed and Conducted by: Sam Winans, Barry Coffing.

Disney's Great American Celebration

Executive Producer: Brad Lachman. Producer: Garry Bormet. Coordinating Producer: Bill Bracken. Directed by: Michael Dimich. Written by: Garry Bormet, Bill Prady. "Abraham Lincoln," "Thomas Jefferson" Sketches Written by: Bill Prady, Steven Banks. Segment Directors: Michael Peters, Joe Carolei. Associate Producer: Mark Rains. Lighting Designers: Bob Dickinson, Simon Miles. Choreographer: Michael Peters. Production Designers: John Schaffner, Joe Stewart, Jimbo Marshall. Executive in Charge of Talent: Danette Herman. Music by: D'Vaughn Pershing, Timothy K. Mulholland, H.B. Barnum. Script Supervisor: Nancy Nash. Script Coordinator: Lori Margules. Editors: Michael A. Polito, Jerry Bixman, Skip Collector. Production Coordinators: Ann King, Amy Storti. Segment Producer: Julie Stein. Talent Coordinator: Marla Bradley. Production Assistants: Susan Youngman, Tom Cavanagh, Charles Gardner. Post Production Coordinator: Matt Purse. Production Choreographer: David Robertson. Production Staff: Marci Bokash, Chris Debeic, Kristan Kosh, Andy McWhirter, Brad Moore, Bill Romary, Scott Spreckman, Chip Swetnam, Tracy Wanek, Matt Waren, Brent Wilson. Associate Director: Greg Fera. Stage Managers: Jamie Batista, Michael Kelly, Peter Margolis, Keith Richmond. Technical Directors: Terry Donohue, Bill Moore. Audio: Doug Nelson, Don Worsham, Paul Sandweiss, Bill Bass. Post Production Audio: David E. Fluhr. Assistant Editor: Andrew J. Ralston. Acknowledgments: Chicago Gospel Festival, Chicago Fellowship Baptist Church Choir, Harborfest, Hawthorne California Elementary School, Irvine California High School Choir, Lake Taylor Virginia High School Marching Band, Life Choir, Mater Del High School, Mid Florida Dalmatian Club, Minneapolis Metropolitan Boys Choir, National Park Service—Mount Rushmore National Memorial, Shrine of Democracy Chorus, Sugar Foot, Swayze Dancers Studio, Tap America Project, West Angeles Church of God and Christ, Universal Dance Theatre, Yucca Valley Star Twirlers, Big Brothers of Greater Los Angeles, CBS News, Cox Cable, Creative Resource Group, Delta Airlines, Dreamlight Images, Fish Films, Integrated Media, KCAL-TV News, KFMB-TV News, Los Angeles SPCA and Glenn Winters Productions, Southeast Alabama Medical Center, Starlight Foundation/Los Angeles, Twentieth Century Fox, Volunteers of America, WAVY-TV, WUSA-TV. Brad Lachman Productions, Inc.

Disney's Greatest Hits on Ice

Produced by: Kimber Rickabaugh. Co-Producer: Sandra Bezic. Music Adapted and Conducted by: Glen Roven. Written by: Stephen Pouliot. Executive Produced and Directed by: Steve Binder. Associate Producer: Alma L. Ramirez. Choreographed by: Michael Seibert, Sandra Bezic. Production Designer: Charles Lisanby. Lighting Designer: Simon Mills. Costume Designer: Jef Billings. Talent Executive: Deena Esensten. Production Supervisor: Sandy Broadway. Production Manager: Cisco Henson. Production Assistant: Natasha Flint. Production Coordinator: Michael Cronin. Production Associates: Lazelle Free, Brad Gordon. Edited by: Ron Barr, Steve Binder. Opening Sequence Choreography: Brian Klavano, Jamie Isley. Art Directors: Arte Contreras, Keaton S. Walker. Music Recorded & Mixed by: Gary Lux. Music Coordinator: Mark Dillon. Staging Supervisor: John Bradley. Associate Director: Alan Kartun. Stage Manager: Josh Berger. Property Master: Ken Dawson. Make-up: Bob Ryan, Jim Scribner. Hair: Sylvia Surdu. Graphic Art: Carol Mackraine, Mark Dennison. Technical Director: Keith Winikoff. Audio: Paul Sandweiss. Camera Operators: Wayne Orr, Bill Philbin, Hector Ramirez. In Memory of Amy Sacks. Produced by Walt Disney Television in association with Rodan Productions.

Disney's Living Seas

Executive Producer: Gary Smith. Produced and Directed by: Ken Ehrlich. Written by: Buz Kohan, Ken Ehrlich. Associate Producer: Wenda Fong. Music Director: Dennis McCarthy. Film Portions: Stu Bernstein. Lighting Designer: John Rook. Production Coordinator: Jan R. Wirth. Assistant to the Producer: Syngehilde Schweikart. Production Assistant: Keith Henry. Production Staff: Joyce Lupo, Michael Canter, Bess Hopper, Robert Kinney. Associate Director: Wenda Fong. Stage Manager: Charles Gayton III. Technical Director: Terry Donohue. Audio: Don Worsham. Video Tape Operator: Bruce Solberg. Video Tape Editors: Mark West, Jill Stanton. Post Audio: Jerry Clemans. Camera Operators: Hank Geving, Ken Patterson, Melissa Wright. Gaffer: Steven Hetzer. New York Remote: Steve Hirsch, Joe Rosi, Skip Roessel. Main Title Design: C. David Pina. *If I Were a River* Written by: Laura Branigan. Produced by: Arif Mardin, Doug Morris. Additional Film Clips Supplied by: Can-Dive Services Limited, Capitol Records, Bill Delaney Films, Al Giddings/Ocean Images Inc., Golden Dolphin Productions Pty. Ltd., Johnson-Sea-Link Harbor Branch Foundation Inc., Bill Muller, New Horizons Pictures, Olivia Newton-John, The Oceanic Navigation Research Society, Charles Ira Sachs, Robert Rose, Sonat Subsea Services Inc., 20th Century Fox, UCLA Film, Television and Radio Archives, United Artists Corporation, Woods Hole Oceanographic Institution. For the Living Seas Pavilion: Tim Delaney, Kym Murphy, Allen Moyer, Matthew Sites, Aric Adolph. A Smith-Hemion Production.

Disney's Magic in the Magic Kingdom

Produced by: Brad Lachman. Directed by: Gary Halvorson. Written by: Hal Goldman, Garry Bormet, Bruce Vilanch. Coordinating Producer: Milt Hoffman. Art Directors: John Shaffner, Joe Stewart. Original Score by: Thomas Chase, Steve Rucker. Lighting Designer: Bob Dickinson. Costumes Designed by: Tom Bronson. Illusions by: John Gaughan. Illusion Design by: Jim Steinmeyer. Associate Producer: Kent Weishaus. Talent Executive: Vince Calandra. Talent Supervisors and Magic Consultants: Marcelli-Heller Management. Associate Director: Judi Elterman. Script Supervisor: Pat Brannon Wise. Production Coordinators: Paul Cockerill,

Michele Megan Dix, Kevin Gershan. Talent Coordinators: Chris Jardine, Debra L. Towsley. Chief Lighting Technician: Vicki Max Brenner. Stage Managers: Jon Hill, Steve Ligerman, Robert Ferkle. Technical Director: Terry Donohue. Audio: Gordon Klimuck, Bart Chiate. Video: Steve Berry, Dean Terrell. Cameras: Dean Hall, David Hilmer, Ken Patterson, Ron Sheldon, J. Barry Herron, Bob Keyes. Edited by: David Foster, Floyd D. Carver. Sound Mixer: Jerry Clemans. Television Facilities by: Greene, Crowe & Co. *For Disneyland:* Production Supervisor: Del Shilling. Production Manager: Chris Robinson. Operations Manager: Larry Nunez. Costuming: Andy Gordon. Character Supervisor: Donna Tomlinson. Maintenance Manager: Dave Burkhart.

DISNEY'S MOST UNLIKELY HEROES
Executive Producers: Dan Boothe, Stu Schreiberg. Producer: John Fuller. Directed by: Dan Boothe. Supervising Producer: Kellie Allred. Line Producer: Stacy Ryono. Director of Photography: Scott Kaye. Editor: Holly Howard. Additional Editing by: Brian Ross, John Fuller. Associate Producer: Seth Mellman. Production Manager: Renee Mendoza. Production Coordinator: Michele Bornheim. Talent Coordinators: Eileen Bradley, Fumi Kitahara. Graphic Design: Chris Williamson. Original Theme Music: Alan Ett. Sound: Doug Donald. Sound Mixer: Jim Corbett. Post Production Supervisors: Michael Cronin, Jerry Ferro, Joe Keeper. Gaffer: Brent Mazursky. Prop Master: Ron Shulem. Camera Assistant: Sharon Alley Blood. Make-up: Bob Schiffer. Production Assistants: Jim Amerian, Sheri Sedlik, Sarah Steinberg, Tom Demko, Greg Wolf. Executive in Charge of Production: John Bravakis. Produced by: Wrightwood Entertainment, Inc. in association with Walt Disney Television.

DISNEY'S NANCY KERRIGAN SPECIAL: DREAMS ON ICE
Executive Producers: Kimber Rickabaugh, Paul Miller. Co-Executive Producer: Jerry Solomon. Produced by: Mick McCullough. Written by: Stephen Pouliot. Directed by: Paul Miller. Music Composed & Adapted by: Glen Roven. Associate Producers: Cisco Henson, Javier Winnik. Choreographed by: Sarah Kawahara. Additional Skating Choreography: Mark Militano. Dance Choreography: Barry Lather. Art Director: Jimbo Marshall. Lighting Designer: Greg Brunton. Costume Designer: Jef Billings. Talent Executive: Deena Esensten. Production Supervisor: Sandy Broadway. Production Assistants: Natasha Flint, James Mottern. Assistant Choreographer: Jamie Isley. Edited by: Alan Carter, Stan Kellam. Technical Director: Ron Stutzman. Audio: Terry Kulchar, Jamie Ledner, Gary Lux. Camera Operators: Hank Geving, Alain Onesto, Bill Philbin, Ron Sheldon. Associate Director: Christine Clark Bradley. Stage Managers: Nancy Cohen, Hank Neimark. Acknowledgments: The New York Olympic Regional Development Authority; The Community of Lake Placid. RickMill Productions. Walt Disney Television.

DISNEY'S SPRING BREAK BLAST
Produced by: Gregory Sills. Written by: Peter Gaffney. Directed by: Milton Lage. Gregory Sills Productions in association with Walt Disney World.

DISNEY'S TALE SPIN: PLUNDER & LIGHTNING
Produced by: Walt Disney Television Animation. Supervising Producer: Jymn Magon. Producers/Directors: Larry Latham, Robert Taylor. Co-Producer: Mark Zaslove. Associate Producer: Ken Tsumura. Story Editor: Jymn Magon. Written by: Alan Burnett, Len Uhley, Mark Zaslove. Post Production Producer: Larry Latham. Dialogue Direction: Ginny McSwain. Animation Directors: Robert Taylor, John Kimball, Richard Trueblood, Bob Zamboni. Storyboard: Viki Anderson, Larry Eikleberry, Sharon Forward, Warren Greenwood, Bob Kline, John Norton, Frank Paur, David Schwartz, Lonnie Thompson, Hank Tucker, Wendell Washer, Roy Wilson. Assistant Producers: Donna Alcock, Barbara Donatelli, Stephanie Elliott, Beth Gunn. Key Layout Design: Kelly Day, Paul Felix, Carol Kieffer Police, Colette Van Mierlo. Character Design: Tom Owens, Toby Shelton, Kenny Thompkins. Computer Animation: Kelly Day, Michael Peraza. Prop Design: Terry Hudson, Marty Warner. Key Background Stylists: Greg Battes, Gary Conklin, James Gallego, Bill Lorencz. Color Key Stylists: Janet Cummings, Robin Draper, Marta Skwara. Supervising Timing Director: Bob Shellhorn. Timing Directors: Vincent Bassols, John Kimball, Marsh Lamore, Rick Leon, Bob Shellhorn, James T. Walker. Continuity Coordinators: Vonnie Batson, Jim Finch, Kathrin Victor. Post Production Manager: Sara Duran. Post Production Supervisor: Joseph Hathaway. Post Production Coordinator: Jeffrey Arthur. Post Production Assistants: Nanci Battelle, Wade Zia Nassir, John Royer. Track Reading: Christine Craig, Skip Craig. Production Assistants: Johanne Beaudoin, Michelle Pappalardo, Michelle Schlicht, Annamarie Solano, Yolanda Valdez, Jodi Wildman, LuAnne Wood. Talent Coordinator: Olivia Miner. Script Coordinators: Leona Jernigan, Anita Lish. Archives Supervisor: Krista Bunn. Art Coordinator: Karen Silva. Managing Editor: Rich Harrison. Supervising Editor: Cecil E. Broughton, M.P.S.E. Sound Editors: Jerry Winicki, Marc Orfanos, Rick Hinson, M.P.S.E., Brian Baker. Assistant Editors: Craig Paulsen, David Lynch, Thomas Needell, Jennifer Harrison. Foley Design: Ron Eng. Original Music Composed and Conducted by: Christopher L. Stone. *Spin It* Theme Words and Music by: Silversher and Silversher. Produced by: Robert Kraft. *I'm Gone, Home Is Where the Heart Is* and *Sky Pirates* Words and Music by: Silversher and Silversher. Animation Production by: *Walt Disney Animation (France) S.A.:* Layout: Bolhelm Bouchiba, Jean Duval, Vincent Massy, Pascal Pinon, James Baker, Nicolas De Crecy. Animation Director: Stephane Sainte-Foi. Line Producer: Sylvie Fauque. 2nd Producer Assistant: Ellenne Longa. Animators: Marc Eoche-Duval, Pierre Fassal, Dina Gellert-Nielsen, Arnold Gransac, Dominique Montfery, Jean-Christophe Roger, Pascal Ropars, Johnny Zeuten, Jean Luc Balester, Moran Caouissin, Bruno Galmetou, Nicolas Marlet, Catherine Poulain, Christophe Villez, Peter Hausner, Claude Montfort, Mireille Sarrault. Background Director: Pierre Pavloff. Assistant Background: Isabelle Bourelly, Vincent Miesser, Patricia Millereau, Nathalie Nicholas, Michel Pisson, Brigitte Reboux, Olivier Adam, Jean Paul Fernandez, Thierry Fournier, Didier Pinot, Colin Stimpson, Andrew MacNab, Mike Hirsh. Camera Coordinator: Serge Conchonnet. Artistic Director: Jean-Christophe Poulain. 1st Assistant Director: Isabelle Quenet. *Walt Disney Animation (Japan) Inc.* Animation Supervisor: Shigeru Yamamoto. Animation Directors: Takeshi Atomura, Ritsuko Notani. Directors: Saburo Hashimoto, Yukio Okazaki, Shigeru Kimiya, Yasumi Mikamoto, Rokoh Ogihara. Animator/Layout Artist: Tadakatsu Yoshida. Background Artist: Minoru Nishida. Animation Production by: Sun Woo Animation. Additional Production Facility: Hanho Heung-Up Co., Ltd.

DISNEY'S THE HUNCHBACK OF NOTRE DAME: FESTIVAL OF FOOLS
Produced by: Suzan Jorgensen-Torgerson. Director: Melanie Steensland. Coordinating Producer: Kathryn Lekan. Executive Producer: Bill Butler. Written by: Suzan Jorgensen-Torgerson. Participating Writer: Leo Quionones. Associate Producer: Susan Nakamura. Segment Producers: Kathryn Lekan, Mack McDermott. Field Producer: Janet Glenny, Regina Hamilton. Technical Director/EIC: Doug Ramsey. Associate Director: Ed Parker. Editors: Garry Ashton, L.J. Davenport, Jr., Paul Frazier, Edward Lapple, Mack McDermott. *Field Crew* Camera: Victor Smith, Chris Torgerson, John Vincent. Audio: Jamal Banks. *Remote Crew* Tape/EIC: Robert Berkowitz, Bryan Foster. Camera: Jeff Coppola, Bryan Foster, Jeff Haymes, Phil Kerns. Jib Camera: Brian Gedtke. Steadi-Cam: Bruce Green. Crane Camera: Kenny Rivenbark. Crane Arm: Scott Fishman. Audio Consultant: Paul Freeman. Audio Mixer: Jim Thomasson, Don Worsham. A2: Dave Fisher, Mark Weber. Lighting Director: Dick Soprizio. Spotlight Operators: Rodger Cole, Scott Dale, Jeremy Jenkins. Stage Manager: Ridge Conlan. Video: Randy Johnson. Videotape: Forrest Oden. Utility: Ian Bevan, Bill Eastham, Tim Garvey, Barry Vaniman. Electric: Jeffrey Smith. Grip: John Clement, Mike Nichols. Gaffer: Barbara Smith. Graphic Design Director: Claudio Mattia. Chyron Operator: Jackie Shearer. Make-up: David Langford. Cue Cards: Barry Grant, Mary Steck. Announcer: Toby Browning. Business & Legal Affairs: Hogo Rossiter, Editte Alsen. Acknowledgments: *Buena Vista Pictures Marketing* Kellie Allred, Arlene Ludwig, Charles Nel-

son, Sheri Sedlik, Elizabeth Wolfe *The Disney Channel, Disneyland Television Production* Lisa Cappel, Laurie Class, Gary Kurtz, Bruce McCoy, Chris Robinson, Laura Schaeffell, Del Schilling, Denise Thompson *Disneyland's The Hunchback of Notre Dame—Festival of Fools* Michael Bernard, Andrew Brothers, Tom Butsch, Tom Child, Mike Davis, Earle Greene, Sylvia Hase, Bruce Healey, Paulie Jenkins, Todd Larsen, Michael Maines, John Mensching, Coy Lee North, Blaine Rhea, Shigeru Yaji, Sayre Wiseman, Alan M-L Wager *Lumiere Film Production Co.* Toby Phillips, Thomas Smith *Dees Creations, Inc.* David Leonard, Craig Rogers. KCAL-9.

DISNEY'S "THE LITTLE MERMAID: A WHALE OF A TALE"
Produced by: Walt Disney Television Animation. Producer/Director: Jamie Mitchell. Written by: Peter S. Beagle. Art Directors: Ed Chernter, Ron Dias. Associate Director: Mircea Mantta. Dialogue Directors: Jamie Thomason, Meg McSweeney. Storyboard: George Goode, Lonnie Lloyd, Todd Kurosawa, Floro Dey, Holly Forsyth, John Dorman. Character Design: Len Smith. Key Layout Design: J. Michael Spooner. Assistant Producer: Traci M. Tolman. Character Animation: Ritsuko Notani. Prop Design: Tom Foxmarnick, Bob Pauley, Marty Warner. Color Key Stylist: Marta Skwara. Cel Painter: Marie Boughamer. Storyboard Revisions: Shawna Cha, John Fox. Timing Directors: Rick Leon, Russell E. Mooney, Brian Ray. Effects Consultant: Mark Dindal. Continuity Coordinators: Myoung Smith, Kathrin Victor. Post Production Manager: Cheryl Murphy. Sound Dubbing Supervisor: Christopher Keith. Post Production Coordinator: John Royer. *Just a Little You* and *You Got to Be You* Music by: Tom Snow. Lyrics by: Jack Feldman. Associate Producer Music: Bambi Moé. Music by: Dan Foliart. Songs Produced and Arranged by: Robby Merkin, Steve Gelfand. Supervising Editors: Sam Horta, John O. Robinson III. Post Production Sound Supervisor: Timothy J. Borquez. Picture Editor: Timothy Mertens. Music Editor: Brian F. Mars. Sound Editor: Michael Collom. Animation Production by Walt Disney Animation (Japan) Inc. Animation Supervisor: Shigeru Yamamoto. Director: Saburo Hashimoto. Animation Directors: Takeshi Atomura, Madoka Yasue, Hisashi Wada, Hiroshi Kawamata. Animators: Koichi Maruyama, Masaji Tada, Masaaki Kudo, Kiyomi Miyakawa, Mitsuko Ohtaku, Masumi Maeda, Miyuki Hoshikawa, Yoshihaki Matsuda. Background Supervisor: Masayoshi Banno. Background Artists: Michiko Taniguchi, Naomi Sakimoto, Kazushige Takato, Tachiko Kimura, Shuichi Hirowatari. Track Reading: Skip Craig. Production Assistant: Paul Fabela.

DISNEY'S TOTALLY MINNIE
Producers: Joie Albrecht, Scot Garen. Director: Scot Garen. Writers: Joie Albrecht, Scot Garen, Jack Weinstein. Associate Producer/Unit Production Manager: John Flynn. Choreographer: Kenny Ortega. *Totally Minnie* Animation by: FilmFair. Production Designers: Rhaz Zeizler, Aubrey Wilson. Original Music Composer: Bob Esty. Editors: Jack Weinstein, Jeff Neuman. Additional Sequences Edited by: Craig Shapiro. Online Editor: Brent Carpenter. Director of Photography: Richard Kooris. Director of Photography—Elton John: Daniel Pearl. Second Unit Photography: J. Michael McClary. Announcer: Don Pardo. Digital Graphics Designer: Jerry Pojawa. Art Directors: Kevin Adams, Thomas Megna, Joshua Ott. Synthesizer Programmer: Michael Bernard. Production Coordinator: David Combs. Assistants to the Producers: Terry Chupak, Nancy Hobson. Production Assistants: James Donadio, Diana Scoular, Michael Podolski. Key Grip: J.C. Cole. Gaffer: Roger Sassen. Sound: William Fiege, William Shaffer, Brad Gilderman. Script Supervisor: Diana Valentine-Stricklin. Hair & Make-up: Dina Ousley Carone, Annette Cordero, Judith Difray, Bruce Grayson, D. J. Plumb, Steve Reilly. Costume Designers: Dina Ousley Carone, Barbara Ingehart. Ms. Somer's Wardrobe Designed by: Leslie Hamel. Elton John's Suit Designed by: Bob Mackie. Party Dresses Designed by: Karen Okada. Music Clearance: Eric Greenspan. Garen/Albrecht Productions.

DISNEYLAND PRESENTS: TALES OF TOONTOWN
Director: Bruce Stuart Greenberg. Producer: Wayne A. Brown. Executive Producer: Lisa Cappel. Written by: Wayne A. Brown, Lisa Cappel. Associate Producer: Robin Mensinger.

Editors: Casey Sattler, Paul Jilbert, Jimmy Garcia. Unit Production Manager: Gary Kurtz. Production Coordinators: Melissa Boyer, Rhonda Hays. Technical Directors: Chris Robinson, Brent Thurston. Script Supervisor: Teresa McKnight. Lighting Director: Paul Jilbert. Steadicam Operator: Jimmy Garcia. Camera Operators: Jimmy Garcia, Paul Jilbert, John Bauer, Derek Arita. Art Director: Bryan Piette. Post Production Graphics: Casey Sattler. Make-up: Dave Langford, Ralph Wilcox. Costumes: Lynn Unfried. Wardrobe: Jesse Perez, Paul Tregor. Gaffer: Jon Griffin. Video Playback: John Clements. Key Grip: John Anderson. Grips: Dave Achilles, Calvin Richardson, Mary Roberts, Ken Wagner, Candy Wright. Electrics: Roger Cole, Dave Froeber, Diane Reifka, Fred Cutler, Terry Kerrigan, Jim Winters. Crane Arm Operator: Mike Machgan. Jimmy Bib Operator: Keith Dicker. Special Effects: Mickey Aronson. Production Assistants: Rony Cavalero, Loy McRosky, Tracy Jordan, Eric Uriate. Acknowledgments: Scott Tanner, Tom Elrod, Rich Irvine, Bryan C. Wittman, John Anello, Rob Boaz, Rick Dempsey, Gordon Foster, Bruce Healey, Tom Jacobson, Susie Lum, Ken Murphy, Emily Reed, Robyn Vossen, Dave Burkhart. Announcer: Bill Rogers. A Disneyland Promotions Production.

DISNEYLAND'S SUMMER VACATION PARTY
Executive Producer: Marty Pasetta. Produced by: Kenny Solms. Directed by: Marty Pasetta. Writing Supervised by: Kenny Solms. Written by: Ann Elder, Tom Perew. Art Director: Bob Keene. Music by: John Debney. Costumes Designed by: Ret Turner. Choreographer: Barnette Ricci. Associate Producer: Michael Petok. Lighting Designers: Bob Dickinson, George Reisenberger, Michael Curry. Talent Executive: Gus Schirmer. Talent Coordinator: Stephanie Zillgitt. Associate Director: Debbie Pasetta. Assistants to the Producer: Laura Lyons, Roberta Savold, Pamela Cantori. Production Coordinators: Mick McCullough, Larry Cohen. Production Manager: Kevin Berg. Transportation Coordinator: Rob Krueger. Film Segment Producers: Phil Savenick, Harry Arends. Clip Coordinator: Drew Brown. Assistant Choreographer: Roy Luthringer. Assistant Art Directors: Lynn Griffin, Kate Murphy. Gaffers: Vicki Max Brenner, Mike Boisclair. Stage Managers: Steve Burgess, Terri McCoy, Greg Pasetta, David Wader. Production Associates: Drew Oiger, Denny E. Ray, Steven Schillaci, Jamie Sweet. Staging Supervisors: Chuck Phillips, Bob Page. Staging Coordinator: Zola Burse. Technical Supervisor: Kevin Hayes. Technical Director: Gene Crowe. Audio: Doug Nelson. Video: Keith Winikoff. Edited by: Jim McQueen. Assistant Editors: Jerry Wade, Chuck Meyers. Post Production Sound: David Fluer. *For Disneyland* Production Supervisor: Bob MacKinnon. Production Assistant: Craig Smith. Entertainment Supervisor: Del Shilling. Production Manager: Darrel Dorr. Technical Services: Chris Robinson. Costuming: Pam Haynes. Show Services: Robert Mizusawa. Maintenance Coordination: Bob Nichols, Dan Otrambo, Brad Russo, George Cardwell. Security: Ike Isaacson. Participant Coordination: Chris Amador, Gail Brown, Charlie Almand. Executive in Charge of Production: Gregory Sills. A Pasetta Production in association with Walt Disney Television.

DISNEYLAND'S 30TH ANNIVERSARY CELEBRATION
Executive Producer: Marty Pasetta. Produced by: Kenny Solms. Directed by: Marty Pasetta. Writing Supervised by: Kenny Solms. Written by: Ann Elder, Martha Williamson, Mitzie & Ken Welch. Associate Producer: Gregory Sills. Lighting Director: Greg Brunton. Musical Director: Lenny Stack. Choreographer: Tony Stevens. Costumes Designed by: Ret Turner. Art Director: Bob Keene. Special Musical Material by: Ken & Mitzie Welch. Acknowledgments: USC Marching Band, Los Alamitos H.S. Band, Mater Dei H.S. Band, Santa Ana Winds. Documentary Supervisor: David Forman. Production Manager: Rikk Greengrass. Talent Coordinator: Paul Solomon. Assistants to the Producer: Susan Diamant, Debbie Pasetta. Associate Director: Marty Pasetta, Jr. Technical Supervisor: Kevin Hayes. Lighting Coordinator: Max Brenner. Gaffers: Ron Anderson, Lou Rogers. Stage Managers: Andi Copley, Barry Kaplan, Terri McCoy, Greg Pasetta, Vince Poxon, Sandy Pruden. Production Assistants: Kevin Berg, Larry Cohen, Bob Krueger, Mick McCullough. Assistant Art

Director: Lynn Griffin. Assistant Choreographer: Jude Van Wormer. Production Associates: George Boldizsar, Ken Fuchs, Bob Kelly, Nancy Nash, Robb Wagner. Make-up: Tommy Cole, Bob Ryan. Hair: Gail Rowell. Audio: Doug Nelson. Video Tape Operator: Bruce Solberg. Camera Coordinator: Ted Ashton. Video Tape Editor: Jim McQueen. Assistant Editors: Michael Kelly, Jerry Wade. Re-recording Mixer: Jerry Clemans. *For Disneyland* Production Supervisor: Bob MacKinnon. Production Assistant: Craig Smith. Entertainment Supervisor: Del Shilling. Production Manager: Darrel Dorr. Disneyland Choreographer: Barnette Ricci. Costuming: Pam Haynes. Art Designer: Clare Graham. Props: Marvin Rea. Parade Music: Jack Eskew. Dancer Coordinator: Linda Kimball. Character Coordinator: Donna Tomlinson. Show Services: Pat Denis. Technical Services: Chris Robinson. Maintenance Coordinators: Dave Burkhart, Bert Harrington, Dan Otrambo, Brad Russo, Ed Warshauer. Operations: Joe Pittaluga. Announcer: Jack Wagner. A Pasetta Production in association with Walt Disney Pictures Television.

DONALD DUCK'S 50TH BIRTHDAY
Produced and Directed by: Andrew Solt. Written by: Peter Elbling, Andrew Solt. Co-Producer/Segment Director: Phillip Savenick. Edited by: Larry Harris, Sarah Dalton Legon, Phillip Savenick. New Animation Supervisor: Sam Cornell. Production Coordinator: Greg Vines. Cameramen: Robert Jaye, Donald McQuaig, Theodore Ashton, John Monsour. New York Unit: Steve Gerbson. Associate Directors: Ira Shuman, Phillip Savenick. Donald Duck's Voice: Clarence Nash. Additional Music by: John Debney. Selected Background Music by: Paul J. Smith. Post-Production Sound: Ed Greene. Post-Production Coordinator: Richard Roberts. Studio Liaison: V. Renee Toensing. Animation Advisor: Tad Stones. Researchers: Karol Greene, Cheryl L. Wilkinson. Production Associates: Kevin Miller, Dominique Sumian. Animated Toy Sequence: Energy Productions. Announcer: John Harlan. Videotape Assistant: Rocco Zappia, Jr. *Happy, Happy Birthday to You* (Donald Duck Version) and *Can You Quack Like Donald Duck?* Words and Music by: Michael and Patty Silversher. *Goin' Quackers* Words and Music by: Will Ryan. Acknowledgments: PSA, SAS, Disneyland Entertainment Division. Post-Production Facilities: Complete Post, Inc. Production Executive: Larry Klingman. An Andrew Solt Production.

DOWN AND OUT WITH DONALD DUCK
Produced by: Joie Albrecht, Scot Garen. Directed by: Scot Garen. Written by: Joie Albrecht, Katharine Sloan, Scot Garen, Stan Freberg. Edited by: Mark Cole, Margareta Schiappa, Richard Roberts. Original Music by: Christopher L. Stone. Character Voice Casting by: Les Perkins. Celebrity Voices Were Impersonated. Post Production Supervisor: Tony Palermo. Production Coordinator: Rebecca Weinstein. On-line Editor: Spencer Willets. Assistant Editor: Craig Shapiro. Assistant to the Producers: Terry Chupak. Production Assistant: Patrick McGuire. Paint Box Artist: Vikki North. Music Clearance by: Mitchell Leib, Barry Enis. Garen/Albrecht Productions.

DREAM CALLED WALT DISNEY WORLD, A
This program was aired without production credits.

DREAM IS ALIVE, THE: 20TH ANNIVERSARY CELEBRATION OF WALT DISNEY WORLD
Executive Producers: Gary Smith, Dwight Hemion. Produced by: Steve Forrest. Directed by: Dwight Hemion. Written by: Buz Kohan. Associate Producer: Bill Bracken. "Baby Sinclair" Performed by: Brian Henson, Kevin Clash. Lighting Designer: John Rook. Production Designer: Romain Johnston. Associate Director: Allan Kartun. Stage Manager: Doug Smith. Production Manager: Cisco Henson. Music Arranged and Conducted by: Ian Fraser. Special Musical Material by: Larry Grossman. Executive in Charge of Talent: Vince Calandra. Script Supervisor: Jill Dove. Script Coordinators: Karen Grosso, Lori Margules. Production Coordinator: John Foy. Talent Coordinator: Sylvia O'Gilvie. Art Director: John Chichester. Costume Designer: Tom Bronson. Make-up/Hair: Bob Schiffer, Anita Polin. Technical Director: Gene Crowe. Audio: Ed Greene, Paul Sandweiss. Editor: Bruce Motyer. Clip Editor: John

Showalter. Audio Mixer: Doug Nelson. Post Production Coordinator: Matt Purse. Main Title Design by: C. David Pina.

DUCKTALES: THE MOVIE SPECIAL
Written and Directed by: Adam Small, Barbara Williams. Producers: Michael Doqui, George Zaloom, Les Mayfield. Line-Producer: Jean-Michel Michenaud. Production Managers: Carlos Torres, Leslie Jett. Director of Photography: Mark Zavad. Art Director: Jimbo Marshall. Editors: David Palmer, James Eaton, Fausto Sanchez. Post-Production Supervisors: Michael Matlock, Daniel R. Gillett. Unit Manager: Trish Ferdon. Talent Coordinator: Jamie Keyser. Assistant to the Producers: Jennifer Parsons. Re-Recording Mixers: Michael Perricone, C.A.S., Jim Henderson. Production Associates: Andrew Baird, Lisa Haskins. Musical Arrangement: Kevin Brandon. Gaffer: Rick Campbell. Audio: Jim Fay. Acknowledgments: Dennis Landa, Walt Disney Animators, Fax Bahr. Produced by Buena Vista Productions in association with ZM Productions, Inc.

DUCKTALES: TIME IS MONEY
Produced by: Walt Disney Television Animation. Producers: Bob Hathcock, Jymn Magon. Directors: Bob Hathcock, James T. Walker, Terence Harrison, Jamie Mitchell. Story Editor: Jymn Magon. Story by: Jymn Magon, Bruce Talkington. Teleplay by: Len Uhley, Jymn Magon, Bruce Talkington, Bruce Coville, Doug Hutchinson. Assistant Producer: Liza-Ann Warren. Art Director: Skip Morgan. Key Layout Stylists: Joe Pearson, Ed Ghertner. Storyboard Design: Viki Anderson, Ken Boyer, Robert Dranko, Paul Gruwell, Bruce Morris, Dale Schott, Robert Taylor, Frans Vischer, Wendell Walker. Key Background Styling: Fred Warter. Color Key Styling: Marta Skwara. Overseas Animation Supervisors: Mike Reyna, Bruce Pedersen. Supervising Timing Director: Dave Brain. Timing Directors: Brad Case, Joan Case, Rick Leon, James T. Walker. Track Reading: Skip Craig. Production Assistant: Scott Wolf. Script Coordinator: Leona Jernigan. Production Archive Administrator: Krista Bunn. Art Coordinator: Karen Silva. Post Production Coordinator: Sara Duran. Talent Coordinator: Olivia Miner. Managing Editor: Rich Harrison. Supervising Editor: Charlie King. Sound Effects Editor: Rick Hinson. Assistant Editors: Robert Martel, David Lynch. *DuckTales* Theme Composed by: Mark Mueller. Music Composed and Conducted by: Ron Jones. *Bubba Duck* Theme Words and Music by: Silversher and Silversher. Animation Production by: Wang Film Productions Co., Ltd., Cuckoo's Nest Studio.

DUCKTALES: TREASURE OF THE GOLDEN SUNS
Produced by: Walt Disney Television Animation. Supervising Producer: Fred Wolf. Associate Producer: Tom Ruzicka. Directors: Steve Clark, Terence Harrison, Alan Zaslove. Story Editor: Jymn Magon. Script Consultants: Tedd Anasti, Patsy Cameron. Story by: Jymn Magon, Bruce Talkington, Mark Zaslove. Teleplay by: Jymn Magon, Bruce Talkington, Mark Zaslove. Art Director: Brad Landreth. Associate Art Director: Skip Morgan. Key Layout Stylists: Ed Ghertner, Michael Peraza, Ed Wexler. Storyboard Design: Elizabeth Chapman, Rich Chidlaw, Thom Enriquez, Steve Gordon, Jan Green, Chuck Harvey, Rob LaDuca, Marty Murphy, Elyse Pastel, Hank Tucker, Monte Young. Key Background Styling: Gary Eggleston, Paro Hozumi, Lisa Keene. Color Key Styling: Jan Cummings, Debra Jorgensborg, Jill Stirdivant. Character Design: Ron Scholefield, Jill Colbert, Ed Gombert, Toby Shelton. Overseas Animation Supervisors: Sean Newton, Bill Wolf. Timing Directors: David Brain, Vincent Davis, Bob Zamboni. Dialogue Direction: Andrea Romano. Track Reading: Skip Craig. Production Manager: Olivia Miner. Assistant Director: Randy Chaffee. Post Production Coordinator: Ken Tsumura. Production Assistants: Barbara Brysman, Krista Bunn, Jacaleen Veber, LuAnne Wood, Judy Zook. Managing Editor: Rich Harrison. Supervising Editors: Robert S. Birchard, Charlie King, M.P.S.E. Sound Effects Editor: Marc Orfanos. Assistant Editors: Rick Hinson, Glenn Lewis. *DuckTales* Theme Composed by: Mark Mueller. Music Composed and Conducted by: Ron Jones. Additional Music by: Tom Chase, Steve Rucker. Animation Production by: TMS Entertainment, Inc.

ENCINO WOMAN
Music Composed by: David Lawrence. Film Editor: Duane Hartzell, A.C.E. Production Designer: Peg McClellan. Director of Photography: Russ Alsobrook. Producer: Irwin Marcus. Produced by: Jeffrey Lampert. Co-Executive Producer: Frank Isaac. Executive Producers: George Zaloom, Les Mayfield. Written by: Anne Joseph, Shawn Schepps. Directed by: Shawn Sheppes. Unit Production Manager: Irwin Marcus. 1st Assistant Director: Michael Daves. 2nd Assistant Director: Patricia Earnest. Casting by: Allison Jones. Costume Designer: Tom Bronson. Set Decorator: Brenda Meyers-Ballard. Property Master: Frank Escobedo. Script Supervisor: Ira Hurvitz. Production Coordinator: Millie Crystal. Key Costumers: Dianne Kennedy, Michael Fitzpatrick. Make-up: Kathryn M. Kelly. Hairstylist: Cheri Ruff. Location Manager: Jeff Spellman. Assistant to the Executive Producers: Amy R. Baird. Production Sound Mixer: David Barr Yaffee. ZM Productions.

ERNEST GOES TO SPLASH MOUNTAIN
Ernest Segments Provided by: Carden & Cherry Advertising, Inc. Producer: Sandra Moiseeff. Associate Producer: Jeffrey Shore. Production Coordinator: Allison L. Birnie. Director of Photography: Lester Wisbrod. Camera: L. David Irete, Dan Webb. Set Designer: Peter Van Stone. Stage Manager: D. Bernie Lawrence. Talent Coordinator: Patricia Kavanagh. Production Associates: John McAuley, Dan Phairse, Alene Richards. Audio: Dana Mark McClure, Laura Osborn. Video Control: Jon Palmer. Videotape Operator: Richard Strock. Grips: Paul Avery, Mark Claussen, Aaron Kaikko, John Olson. Utilities: Mike Martin, Peter Ney. Wardrobe: Julie Carnahan. Make-up/Hair: Jean Donielle, Christy Newquist. Props: Dennis Dimster, Max Jacobs. Graphic Art: Laurie Resnick. Videotape Editor: Ron Barr. Assistant Videotape Editor: Marty Rosenstock. Re-Recording Mixer: Peter Elliot Cole. Audio Assistant: Steve Michael. Additional Music: Richard Jennings. Acknowledgments: Vern, Dale Lanier, Greg Moiseeff, Tim O'Day, Bruce Williams. Executive Producers: John Cherry, Paul Abeyta, Peter Kaikko. A Production of RC Entertainment, Inc. Buena Vista Television.

ESCAPE TO WITCH MOUNTAIN   (TV version)
Music by: Richard Marvin. Film Editor: Duane Hartzell, A.C.E. Production Designer: Peg McClellan. Director of Photography: Russ Alsobrook. Produced by: Joan Van Horn. Executive Producers: George Zaloom, Les Mayfield, Scott Immergut. Teleplay by: Peter Rader. Based on the screenplay by Robert Malcolm Young and the book by Alexander Key. Directed by: Peter Rader. Coordinating Producer: Irwin Marcus. Unit Production Manager: Irwin Marcus. First Assistant Director: Richard Schroer. Second Assistant Director: Claudia Sills. Casting by: Allison Jones. Costume Designer: Tom Bronson. Set Decorator: Brenda Meyers-Ballard. Property Master: Cliff Bernay. Script Supervisor: Susan Bierbaum. Production Coordinator: Adam Salazar. Costumers: Emma Trenchard, Jay Caplan. Make-up: Kathryn M. Kelly. Hair Stylist: Cheri Ruff. Location Manager: Kevin Halloran. Production Sound Mixer: David Barr Yaffee, C.A.S. Visual Effects by: Royal Blue Images. ZM Productions.

FAIREST OF THEM ALL, THE
Produced by: Michael Bonifer. Written by: Michael Bonifer, L. G. Weaver. Directed by: Cardon Walker.

FAMILY VALUES
Produced by: Brian J. Cowan. Co-Executive Producer: Lance Reynolds. Executive Producer: Dale McRaven. Written by: Dale McRaven. Directed by: Jerry Cohen. Executive Producer: Ehrich Van Lowe. Based on the BBC Series *Bread* Created by: Carla Lane. Director of Photography: Donald Morgan. Art Director: Ken Johnson. Editor: Marco Zappia. Associate Director: Sam Orender. Stage Manager: Sal Baldomar. Music by: Ray Colcord. Casting by: Melinda Gartzman, C.S.A., Nora Kariya, Associate. Set Decorator: Robinson Royce. Property Master: David Glazer. Script Supervisor: Sandy Eustis. Production Coordinator: Greg Frampton. Costume Designer: Tom Bronson. Wardrobe Supervisor: Sara Markowitz. Key Costumer: Michael Fitzpatrick. Technical Director: Robert Bowen. Audio: Larry Stephens. Video: Eric Clay. Sweet Lorraine Productions, Inc.

FLORIDA'S DISNEY DECADE
Acknowledgments: Mid Florida Television, WFTV Channel 9, WDBO Channel 6, Orlando Area Chamber of Commerce, Orlando Magazine, Orlando Sentinel Star, Orange County Historical Museum, State of Florida Archives, State of Florida Photo Library, Tel-Air Interests, Inc.

40 YEARS OF ADVENTURES
Producer/Writer: Stephanie Keane. Director: Melanie Steensland. Associate Producers: Susan Nakamura, Ed Parker. Announcer: Janine Wolf. Technical Director: Bernd Bergman. On-Line Editor: Ed Lapple. Editors: Garry Ashton, Shaka Armstrong, Jeff Mills. Camera Operator: Simon Jarvis. Remote Audio: Andre Palai. Graphics: Mike Radogna. Electronic Graphics: John Shearer. Music: Peter Bohm. Acknowledgments: *Disney Channel* Chris Boehm, Christine Cascone, Jill Hansen-Schlauf. *Disney Studios* Dianne Kirschner. *Disneyland* Pam Baker, Debbie Barlow, Lisa Cappel, Jill Foley, Robert Gore, Gary Kurtz, Axel Kyster, Michael Levine, Barbara Mallory, Robin Mensinger, Laura Schaffell, Dathan Shore, Darryl Smith, Scott Tanner. KCAL-TV & Disneyland.

FREAKY FRIDAY   (TV version)
Music by: James McVay, Lisa Harlow Stark. Editor: Hank Van Eeghen. Production Designer: Peg McClellan. Director of Photography: Russ Alsobrook. Produced by: John Van Horn. Executive Producers: George Zaloom, Les Mayfield, Scott Immergut. Teleplay by: Stu Krieger. Based on the Book and the Screenplay by: Mary Rodgers. Directed by: Melanie Mayron. Project Consultants: Catlin Adams, Cynthia Mort. Vocals Performed by: Lisa Harlow Stark. Artistic Whistling by: James McVay. Coordinating Producer: Irwin Marcus. Co-Producer: Stu Krieger. Unit Production Manager: Irwin Marcus. First Assistant Director: Mary Beth Hagner. Second Assistant Director: Jason Saville. Casting by: Allison Jones. Costume Designer: Tom Bronson. Set Decorator: Brenda Meyers-Ballard. Property Master: Cliff Bernay. Script Supervisor: Susan Bierbaum. Production Coordinator: Millie Kline. Kid Coordinator: Barbara Bentree. Costumers: Emma Trenchard, Jay Caplan. Make-up: Kathryn M. Kelly. Hair Stylist: Cheri Ruff. Location Manager: Kevin Halloran. Production Sound Mixer: David Barr Yaffee, C.A.S. *Freaky Friday* Opening Sequence by: Broyles/Okun. ZM Productions, Inc.

FUNNY, YOU DON'T LOOK 200: A CONSTITUTIONAL VAUDEVILLE
Directed by: Jim Yukich. Written by: Jessica Teich, Judith Rutherford James, Christopher Chase, Richard Dreyfuss, Bruce Vilanch. Special Material Written by: Joie Albrecht, Scot Garen, Lorin Dreyfuss. Produced by: Judith Rutherford James, Richard Dreyfuss. Director of Photography: Tom Grubbs. Production Designer: Rhaz Zeisler. Editor: Jerry Behrens. Unit Production Manager/First Assistant Director: Paul Deason. Second Assistant Director: Kelly Wimberly. Music by: Hummie Mann. Music Supervisor: Gary Tigerman. Costumes by: Judy Swartz. Associate Producer: Christopher Chase. Disney Character Animation Produced and Directed by: Dave Michener. Production Manager: Stephen Hickner. Video Effects Editor: David Foster. Audio Effects Editor: Bob Manahan. Production Coordinator: Rosemary Mitchell. Film Clip & Still Research: Patricia Colvig. Script Supervisor/Assistant Editor: Theresa McKnight. Art Director: Thomas Megna. Visual Advisor: Ben Shedd. Casting: Vicki Hillman. Set Decorator: Joshua Ott. Production Sound Mixer: Chat Gunter. Make-up: Julie Hewitt. Hair Stylist: Medusah. Property Master: Barbara Benz. Assistant Property Master: Jeff Moore. Gaffer: Kerry Magness. Key Grip: David Butkovitch. 1st Assistant Camera: Paul Hughen. Production Secretary: David Combs. Craft Services: Spencer Hulme. Witness Research: William Schifrin. Post Production Facility: Pacific Video. Acknowledgments: Floyd Abrams, Sonny Aprile, The Honorable Robert Bork, The Honorable William Brennen, Patrick Buchanan, Congressman Barney Clark, Clark Clifford, The Constitutional Rights Foundation, Milton Friedman, Nat Hentoff, James Hutson, The Honorable Alex Kozin-

ski, Jack Langeth, Mark Taper Forum, Edmund S. Morgan, Benno Schmidt, Ron Steel, Congressman Gerry Studds, Assemblywoman Maxine Waters, Allen Weinstein. *Follow the Flag* by: Randy Newman. *Rap Goes to School* Lyrics by: Marie J. Parker, Phyllis C. Lumley, Mayme Brown. Music Composed by: Thomas C. Washington. "Project Pass is an inner-city, school-based project that teaches the Constitution through rock/soul rap numbers." Buena Vista Television. Constitution Productions, Inc.

GOING BONKERS
Produced by: Walt Disney Television Animation. Producer: Robert Taylor. Director: Robert Taylor. Story Editor: Karl Geurs. Written by: Marion Wells, John Behnke, Rob Humphrey, Jim Peterson. Dialogue Director: Ginny McSwain. Supervising Animation Director: Karen Peterson. Animation Directors: John Kimball, Mike Svayko, Rich Trueblood, Bob Zamboni. Timing Directors: Carole Beers, James T. Walker. Storyboard: Kurt Anderson, Viki Anderson, Sharon Forward, Lonnie Lloyd, David Prince, David Smith, Albert Ring, Kevin Wurzer. Layout Development: J. Michael Spooner. Key Layout Design: Derek Carter, J. Michael Spooner. Character Design: Shawn Keller, Alex Mann, J. Tom Owens, Jr., Kevin Wurzer. Background Development: Gary Eggleston. Key Background Stylists: Brooks Campbell, Gary Eggleston. Color Key Stylist: Janet Cummings. Prop Design: Marty Warner. Storyboard Revisions: Stark Howell, Phil Weinstein. Cel Painter: Marie Boughamer. Assistant Producer: Margot Pipkin. Continuity Coordinators: Vonnie Batson, Barbara Donatelli, Jim Finch, Kathrin Victor. Track Reading: Skip Craig. Music by: Mark Watters. Title Theme Written, Produced and Arranged by: Randy Petersen, Kevin Quinn. Assistant Producer Music: Bambi Moé. Animation Production by: Walt Disney Television Animation (Australia) Pty, Ltd. Animation Directors: Chris Bradley, Steven Trenbirth. Assistant Directors: Janey Dunn, Mickie Cassidy, Di Rudder. Animators: Gairden Cooke, Kang Zhu Lin, Andrew Collins, Dick Dunn, Helen McAdam, Mike Stapleton, Morris Lee, Steven Taylor, Wally Micati, Marek Kochout, Andrew Brooks, Peter Candeland, Paul Newell, Dwayne Labbe, Carol Seidl, Ariel Ferrari, Lily Dell, Mac Monks, Warwick Gilbert, Ty Bosco, Ian White, Marten Coombe, Alexs Stadermann, Kevin Peaty, Nilo Santillan, Georges Abolin, Troy Saliba, Mike Chavez, Henry Neville, Lianne Hughes, Josef Szekeres, Adam Murphy, Oscar Perez, Murray Debus, Dave MacDougall, Chris Derochie, Stephen Grant. Layout Supervisors: Alex Nicholas, John Hill. Layout Artists: Yosh Barry, Kevin Wotton, Steve Cooper, David Skinner, Kevin Spill, Nick Pill, Bruce Pedersen. Background Supervisor: Beverley McNamara. Background Artists: Barry Dean, Paul Pattie, Felice Ferrer, Jerry Liew, Helen Steele, George Humphrey, Milana Borkert. Ink and Paint Supervisors: Ruth Edelman, Angela Bodini, Robyn Drayton, Christine O'Connor, Liz Lane. Production Manager: Terry W. Smith. Production Management: Dan Forster, Robert Letteri, Carole Salter, Mark Evans, Charm Lee, Fernando Letteri, Jose Barrerios, Gary Page. Post Production Sound Supervisor: Timothy J. Borquez. Supervising Sound Editor: John O. Robinson III. Supervising Picture Editor: Sam Horta. Supervising Music Editor: Brian F. Mars. Sound Editors: Michael Geisler, Thomas Jaeger, Michael A. Gollom, Rick Freeman, Greg LaPlante, Kenneth Young, Timothy Garrity. Music Editors: Alex Wilkinson, William Griggs. Dialogue Editors: Craig Paulsen, Jennifer Mertens. Post Production Manager: Cheryl Murphy. Post Production Supervisor: Jeffrey Arthur. Sound Dubbing Supervisor: Christopher Keith. Talent Coordinator: Jamie Thomason. Production Assistants: Nanci Battelle, Johanne Beaudoin, Greg Chalekian, Leona Jernigan, Anita Lish, John Royer, Richard Salazar, Karen Silva, Craig Simpson, Steve Werner.

GOING TO MICKEY'S TOONTOWN
Producer: Barbara Zaneri. Director: Melanie Steensland. Associate Director: Ed Parker. Writers: Barbara Zaneri, Ed Parker. Camera Operators: Bryan Foster, Victor Smith. Remote Audio Mixer: Jamal Banks. Editor: Cliff Armstrong. Post Production Audio: Jeff Koss, Diane Frierson. Production Coordinator: Janelle Ricksen. Disneyland Stage Technicians: Mark Andrews, Kyle Takemori. Disneyland Production Co-

ordinator: Ed Baker. Disneyland Promotional Representative: Robin Mensinger. Executive Producer: Melanie Steensland.

GOOF TROOP CHRISTMAS, A
Produced by: Walt Disney Television Animation. Supervising Producer: Robert Taylor. Producer: Robert Taylor. Post Production Producer: Bob Hathcock. Written by: Jymn Magon. Dialogue Director: Ginny McSwain. Animation Directors: Mircea Mantta, Charles A. Nichols, Mitch Rochon, Richard Trueblood, Woody Yocum, Bob Zamboni. Storyboard: Jan Green, John Norton, Wendell Washer. Storyboard Revisions: Albert Ring, Phil Weinstein. Layout Styling and Development: J. Michael Spooner. Key Layout Design: J. Michael Spooner. Character Styling and Development: Alex Mann. Character Design: Alex Mann. Computer Graphics by: Kelly Day. Prop Design: Marty Warner. Key Background Stylist: Gary Eggleston. Color Key Stylists: Janet Cummings, Nancy Ulene. Supervising Timing Director: Marlene Robinson May. Timing Directors: Vincente Bassols, Brian Ray, James T. Walker. Assistant Producers: Lori Baio, Melinda Wunsch. Continuity Coordinators: Vonnie Batson, Myrna Bushman, Myoung Smith, Kathrin Victor. Track Reading: Skip Craig. Post Production Manager: Cheryl Murphy. Post Production Supervisors: Joseph Hathaway, Jeffrey Arthur, Regina Brittle. Sound Dubbing Supervisor: Christopher Keith. Post Production Coordinator: John Royer. Post Production Assistants: Nanci Battelle, Steve Werner. Talent Coordinator: Jamie Thomason. Production Assistants: Johanne Beaudoin, Laura Perrotta, Yolanda Valdez. Script Coordinator: Anita Lish. Supervisor of Production Art Services: Krista Bunn. Art Coordinators: John Hall, Karen Silva. Shipping Coordinator: Craig Simpson. Editorial Consultant: Sam Horta. Supervising Sound Editors: Brian F. Mars, Timothy J. Borquez. Sound Editors: Timothy M. Mertens, Michael A. Gollom, Gregory LaPlante. Dialogue Editor: Thomas Jaeger. Assistant Producer Music: Bambi Moé. Music by: Mark Watters. *Reindeer Rumba* Words and Music by: Randy Petersen, Kevin Quinn. *Animation Production by: Walt Disney Animation (France) S.A.* Directors: Paul Brizzi, Gaetan Brizzi. Layout Supervisor: Zoltan Maros. Layout: Bolhelm Bouchiba, Jean Duval, Vincent Massy, Richard Poulain. Background Supervisor: Pierre Pavloff. Backgrounds: Olivier Adam, Jean-Paul Fernandez, Helene Godefroy, Patricia Millereau, Vincent Misser. Artistic Director: Jean-Christophe Poulain. Animators: Jean-Luc Ballester, Bolhem Bouchiba, Sylvain Deboissy, Patrick Delage, Marc Eoche-Duval, Pierre Fassel, Bruno Gaumetou, Matias Marcos, Dominique Monfery, Catherine Poulain, Jean-Jacques Prunes, Jean-Christophe Roger, Stephane Sainte Foi, Yoshimi Tamura. Effects Animation: Thierry Chaffoin. Assistant Animation: Laurence Adam, Philippe Balmossiere, Valerie Braun, Antonio Campiglio, Jean Deleani, Jean Duval, Philippe Ferin, Dina Gellert, Pierre Girault, Thierry Goulard, Gontran Hoarau, Isabelle Lelubre, Gizella Maros, Lieve Miessen, Florence Montceau, Franck Pimenta, Daniela Tigano, Marc Tosolini, Xavier Villez, Karel Zilliacus. Inbetween: Nicolas Attie, Franck Bonay, Christophe Charbonnel, Heike Hoffman, Ivan Kassabov, Christine Landes, Pierre Leconte, Catherine Legendre, Ludovic Letrun, Antonnella Russo, Christiane Van Der Casseyen, Frederic Vervisch. Checking: Pierre Sucaud, Bernard Dourdent. Camera: Evariste Ferreira, Laurence Adde. Assistant Director: Raphael Vicente. Production Manager: Etienne Longa. Assistant to Background Supervisor: Claire Decarvalho.

GRAND OPENING OF EURO DISNEY, THE
Executive Producer: Don Mischer. Produced by: David J. Goldberg. Coordinating Producers: Geoff Bennett, Nina Lederman. Directed by: Don Mischer. Written by: Bob Waldman. Music Arranged and Composed by: Glen Roven. Lighting Designers: Bob Dickinson, John Rook, Todd Nichols. Clip Packages Produced by: Phil Savenick, Harry Arends. Land Tour Segments Directed by: Ron Andreassen, Allan Kartun, Liz Plonka, Chuck Vinson. Choreographer: Brian Rogers. Executive in Charge of Talent: Danette Herman. Production Designer: Terry Ackland-Snow. Costume Supervisor: Sue Lecash. Coordinating Director: Joe Novello. Technical Supervisors: Paul Boykin, Dan Johnson. Production

Managers: Jane Martin, Javier Winnik. Associate Directors: Allan Kartun, Liz Plonka, Ron Andreassen, Chuck Vinson. Assistants to the Producers: Maureen Kelly, Leslie Seage. 1st P.A.'s: Nancy Nash, Lori Margules, Amy Storti. Lighting Project Coordinator: Philippe LeClerq. Senior Production Coordinators: Didier Cornu, Jerome Debroise, Debi Giudice. Talent Coordinators: Candy Capek, Clement Sentilhes. Production Assistants: Roslyn Davis, Deanne Galosic. Stage Managers: Garry Hood, Dency Nelson, Chuck Vinson, Buck Allen, Rose Riggins, Simon Wallace, Yan Hervouet. Post Production Supervisor: Joanne F. Schnuckel. Orchestrations by: Joe Curiale, Larry Schwartz. Assistant Costumer: Frederica Jones. Field Producer for Pat O'Brien: Rhonda Martyn. Technical Director: Gene Crowe. Audio Mixers: Ed Greene, Roger Berry, Gerard Trevignon, Laurent Ballin, Andre Herring. Video Engineers: Mark Sanford, Mike Bloomfield, Chris Mathven. Camera Operators: Tom Arnold, Eric Atlan, Geoff Brown, Jean-Marc DeBois, Mike Dugdale, Peter Edwards, Paul Fitzgerald, Alex Gorsky, Larry Heider, Steve Jellyman, Bob Keys, Jean Yves Lemener, Bill Philbin, Jean Jacques Reverend, Ron Sheldon, Sepp Thoma, Keith Watts. Aerials: Yves-Marie Kerros, Michael Allwork. Editors: Ron Andreassen, Adrian Begon, Patrice Freymond, Dave Simpson, Clayton Parker, Lorenzo Dodi, Simon Thompson. Harry Artists: Guillaume De Viriey, Philippe Carluy. Clip Packages Edited by: Harry Arends, Phil Savenick, Adrian Begon, Jules Fuller, Malachy Coleman. Audio Assistants: Joseph Kendall, Jerome Isreal, William Sternberg, Mark Swinglehurst, Peter Vasey. Dolly Grips: Serge Grenier, Alain Benoist, Guy Plasson, Guy Masselier, Philippe Senie, Pierre Louis De Stefano, Gilbert Lucido. RF Engineer: Tony Heasman. Computer Countdown: Bruce Burmeister. Videotape Operators: Saul Connaughton, Lorenzo Dodi, Simon Thompson. Engineering Crew for CBS Coverage: Richard Dumar, Michaela Fishwick, Martin Hawkins, John Johnson, Keith Mayes, Jim McGlynn, Adam Ricketts, Simon Sanders, Roger Wedlake. Make-up: Annouchka, Marianne Jansson, Muriel Martin, Alex Mistral, Jocelyne Sevestre. Hair: Lucas Coulon, Valerie Florin, Laetitia Guenaou, Marc Villeneuve. Production Assistants: Lyn Harris, Don Carroll. *Grand Opening Marching Band* Director: Paul Nobel. Guest Conductor: Jim Christensen. Associate Director: Art Bartner. *Drill Team* Director: Kay Crawford.

GRAND OPENING OF WALT DISNEY WORLD, THE
Produced and Directed by: Robert Scheerer. Executive Producers: Ron Miller, Bill Walsh. Written by: Bill Walsh. Consultant: Jim Loren. Musical Director: Dave Grusin. *There's More* and *Wonderful World of Love* by: Billy Barnes. Choreographed by: Dee Dee Wood. Costume Designer: Pete Menefee. Choral Director: Earl Brown. Assistant to the Producer: Seagram Smith. Production Coordinator: Anne Menna. Assistant Choreographer: Ed Balin. Assistant Costume Designer: Judy Evans. Talent Coordinator: Bill Shepard. Musical Coordinator: Hal Hidey. Technical Supervisor: John Braislin. Production Supervisor: Harvey Plotnick. Associate Director: Zane Radney. Stage Manager: Bob Graner. Technical Director: Newt Bellis. Lighting Directors: Robert Boatman, Tom Schamp. Cameramen: Dean Hall, Webber Hall, Bob Hatfield, John Poliak, Gary Stanton. Video: Howard Duhamel, Pat Brennan, Jim Wilde. Audio: Marshall King. Video Tape Editor: Ted Watson. Make-up by: Bob Schiffer. Special Thanks to: Tom Garrison. Opening Day Ceremonies and Other Events Staged by: Walt Disney World Entertainment Division. Facilities Provided by: Wolper Video Center. A Division of the Wolper Organization.

HERBIE DAY AT DISNEYLAND
Directed by: Jack Scott. Executive Producer: Dick Stratton. Production Manager: Ray Green. Technical Director: John Westbrook.

IN THE NICK OF TIME
Executive Producer: Janet Faust Krusi. Produced by: Michael Jaffe. Co-Producers: John Danylkiw, Christine Sacani. Teleplay by: Rick Podell, Michael Preminger, Maryedith Burrell. Based on a story by: Jon S. Denny. Directed by: George Miller. Music by: Steve Dorff. Editor: Ron Wisman. Art Director:

Tony Hall. Director of Photography: Brian R. Hebb. Unit Production Manager: John Danylkiw. 1st Assistant Director: Elizabeth Scherberger. 2nd Assistant Director: Michael Johnson. Casting: Jeff Oshen. Camera Operator: Julian Chojnacki. Sound Mixer: Bruce Carwardine. Gaffer: Kevin Alanthwaite. Key Grip: Robert Daprato. 1st Assistant Art Director: Alta Louise Doyle. Set Decorator: Jaro Dick. Property Master: Jeff Foulis. Construction Coordinator: Don Vandewater. Location Manager: Victoria Harding. Wardrobe Designer: Lynne Mackay. Wardrobe Supervisor: Michael Clancy. Costumer: Christopher Hargadon. Make-up Artist: Donald Mowat. Hair Stylist: Bryan Charboneau. Production Coordinator: Shelley Boylen-Wakefield. Production Accountant: Lynn Lucibello. Script Supervisor: Mimi Wolch. 3rd Assistant Director: Cynthia Clayton. Transportation Coordinator: Neil Montgomerie. Canadian Casting: Jon Comerford, Brian Levy. Casting Associate: Donna Jacobson. Choreographer: Monique LaVoie. Stunt Coordinator: Rick Forsayeth. Assistant to Janet Faust Krusi: Jenny Jantzen. Assistant to Michael Jaffe: Lynn Josephson. Re-recording Mixer: Elius Caruso. Assistant Editor: Steve Humble. Dialogue Editor: Paul Williamson. Effects Editor: Brad Stephenson. Music Editor: Celia Weiner. Harry Operator: David Giles. Special Visual Effects: John Gajdecki/Visual FX. Stunts: Jamie Jones, Dwayne McLean, Larry McLean, John Stoneham Jr., Anton Tykodi. Model Maker: Walter Klassen. Produced by Spectator Films in association with Walt Disney Television.

JACK BENNY HOUR, THE
Executive Director: Irving Fein. Produced and Directed by: Ralph Levy. Written by: Sam Perrin, George Balzer, Al Gordon, Hal Goldman. Music Director: Dave Grusin. Choreographer: Paul Godkin.

JULIE ANDREWS HOUR, THE
Produced by: Nick Vanoff, William O. Harbach. Directed by: Bill Davis. Writing Supervised by: Frank Peppiatt, John Aylesworth. Written by: Jack Burns, Hal Goodman, Larry Klein, Jay Burton, George Bloom, Lila Garrett. Associate Producer: Albert J. Simon. Choreographer: Tony Charmoli. Music Directed & Conducted by: Nelson Riddle. Special Musical Material: Dick Williams. Musical Associate: Ian Fraser. Art Directors: Brian Bartholomew, Keaton S. Walker, Jim Tompkins. Costume Designer: Jack Bear. Miss Andrews' Make-up by: Joe Cranzano. Associate Director: Lee Bernhardi. Production Coordinator: Bonnie Burns. Assistant to Producer: Carol Warrian. Production Assistant: Nancy Heydorn. Assistant Choreographer: Richard Beard. Music Coordinator: Dick Priborsky. Talent Coordinator: Roy Gerber. Hairdresser: Lorraine Roberson. Unit Manager: John Monarch. Engineering Supervisor: Frank Genereux. Studio Supervisor: Jim Kussman. Technical Director: Ernie Buttelman. Lighting Director: Truck Krone. Audio: Doug Nelson. Senior Video: Hugo di Lonardo. Video Tape Editor: Nick Giordano. Cameramen: Jim Angel, Jim Balden, Dave Hilmer, Bob Kemp. Stage Managers: James Woodworth, Don Corvan. Make-up: Duane Fulcher. Founder and Director of The Young Americans: Milton C. Anderson. Young Americans Staged by: James Bates. A Jewel Production for ITC.

JUNGLE BOOK REUNION
Executive Producers: Eric Schotz, Kevin O'Donnell. Director: Eric Schotz. Writer: Kevin O'Donnell. Segment Director: Bill Davis. Editor: Sam Patterson. Associate Producers: Bradley Anderson, Robert Lihani. Assistant Director: Brad Kreisberg. Production Manager: Clay Newbill. Lighting Director: Todd Nichols. Production Coordinator: Jim Campbell. Gaffer: Rick Campbell. Stage Manager: Josh Berger. Camera Operators: Bob Van Dorn, Kenny Rivenbark, Steve Suggs, David Treiber. Technical Director: Jeff Court. Audio: Eric Bourgoujian, Jim Fay, Don Youngs. Music Composer: Eric Allaman. Art Director: Jimbo Marshall. Graphic Design: Eddie Pasquarello. Choreographer: Miles Thoroughgood. Assistant Editor: Tom Heckbert. Audio Mixer: Roy Pahlman. Production Assistants: Andrew Baird, Trish Weinstock, Nancy Parrish, Laura Broome. Set by: Ray Productions of Orlando. Produced by: Buena Vista Productions in association with LMNO Productions.

KNIFE AND GUN CLUB, THE
Produced by: Harvey Frand. Teleplay by: Bo Trigorin, Allison Hock. Story by: Bo Trigorin. Directed by: Eric Laneuville. Executive Producers: Bruce Sallan, David Sontag. Original Music by: John Tesh. Director of Photography: John J. Connor. Production Designer: Leslie Parsons. Editor: Steve Polivka. Unit Production Manager: Richard H. Prince. First Assistant Director: Allan Wertheim. Second Assistant Director: Wendy Ikeguchi. Casting by: Mary V. Buck, C.S.A., Susan Edelman, C.S.A. Costumes Designed by: Tom Bronson. Set Decorator: Bruce Gibeson. Property Master: Jack Marino. Key Costumers: Richard E. Mahoney, Dawn Jackson. Make-up: Don Cash. Hair Stylist: Lisa Meyers. Production Coordinator: Lark Bernini/Script Supervisor: Patience Thoreson. Technical Advisor: Ruth Ekholm, R.N. Location Manager: Elaine S. Lipton. Main Title Design: Castle/Bryant/Johnsen. Sound Mixer: Joe Kenworthy. Sound Editing by: Echo Sound Services. Music Editing by: Jamie Gelb. The IndieProd Company in association with Touchstone Television.

KODAK PRESENTS DISNEYLAND '59
Produced by: Bill Walsh.

KRAFT SALUTES DISNEYLAND'S 25TH ANNIVERSARY
Executive Producers: Gary Smith, Dwight Hemion. Produced by: Buz Kohan, Phil May. Directed by: Dwight Hemion. Written by: Buz Kohan, Marty Farrell. Associate Producer: Rita Scott. Special Musical Material: Larry Grossman. Musical Director: Dennis McCarthy. Choreographer: Alan Johnson. Costume Designer: Bill Hargate. Assistant to the Producers: Wenda Wong. Talent Consultants: Gus Schirmer, Carole Propp. Assistant Choreographer: Charlene Painter. Production Assistants: Jane Greene, Suellen Wagner, Greg Palmer. Music Arrangements: Billy Byers, J. Hill, Dennis McCarthy. Dance Arrangements: Lenny La Croix. Associate Director: Rita Scott. Technical Director: Gene Crowe. Lighting Consultant: George Riesenberger. Audio: Ed Greene, Mike Gannon. Video: Mark Sanford, Tom Weber. Video Tape Editor: Andy Zall. Cameramen: Joe Epperson, Larry Heider, Bob Keys, Wayne Orr. Stage Supervisors: Ray Brannigan, C.B. Chisam. Stage Managers: Ted Ray, Mike Erwin, Charles Gayton III. Make-up: Greg Nelson, Larry Abbott. Hairdresser: Irene De'Atley. Wigs by: Roselle Friedland. Film Montage by: Roy Brewer, Jr. Technical Facilities provided by: Hollywood Video and Ruxton, Ltd. Acknowledgment: All the Disneyland Employees. A Smith-Hemion Production in association with Walt Disney Productions.

KRAFT SALUTES WALT DISNEY WORLD'S 10TH ANNIVERSARY
Executive Producers: Gary Smith, Dwight Hemion. Produced by: Buz Kohan, Phil May. Directed by: Dwight Hemion. Written by: Buz Kohan, Phil May. Associate Producer: Michael B. Seligman. Associate Director: Wenda Fong. Stage Manager: Charles Gayton III. Special Music Material: Larry Grossman. Music Arranged and Conducted by: Ian Fraser. Art Director: Roy Christopher. Costumes Designed by: Ret Turner, Pete Menefee. Choreographer: Alan Johnson. Production Supervisor: Penelope Harrison. Assistants to the Producers: Sharon Taylor, Suellen Wagner. Production Assistant: Terrell Greene. Casting: Gus Schirmer. Music Arrangements: Bill Byers, Chris Boardman. Lighting: Fred McKinnon. Technical Director: John B. Field. Audio: Ed Greene, Tom Durell. Video: John Palacio. Video Tape Editors: Andy Zall, Kevin Fernan. Camera: Larry Heider, Wayne Orr, Bill Philbin. Make-up: Ralph Gulko, Sheryl Shulman. Hairdresser: Jan Cook. A Smith-Hemion Production.

LEFTY
Executive Producer: William Robert Yates. Produced by: James E. Thompson, Gina Rester. Written by: Gina Rester. Directed by: James E. Thompson. Cinematographers: William Moffitt, Wayne Threm, Don Cirillo, Kevin O'Brien, Michael Scott. Film Editor: David Arnold. Second Unit Director: John Cosgrove. Sound: Michael Moore, John Glascock. Gaffer: Don Robinson. Music: Frank Denson. *Song for Lefty* Music: Frank Denson. Lyrics: Alan Godfrey-Freeman. Sung by: Cindy Fee. Creative Consultant: David Arnold. Acknowledgments: Cal

State Fullerton Athletic Department, KIPS Gymnastics Center, NBC Sports Announcers Charlie Jones and Nancy Thies. This program is recommended by the National Education Association. A DBA Entertainment, Inc. Production in association with Walt Disney Productions.

LION KING, THE: A MUSICAL JOURNEY WITH ELTON JOHN
Executive Producers: Dan Boothe, Stu Schreiberg. Produced by: Stu Schreiberg. Directed by: John Jopson. Associate Producer: Eric Van Wagenen. Line Producer (U.K.): Elizabeth Flowers. Director of Photography (U.K.): Adrian Wilde. Art Director (U.K.): Caroline Greville-Morris. Edited by: Jeff Caldwell. Camera: Larry Gaudette, Bowden Hunt. Camera (U.K.): John Simmons, Jeff Baynes. Sound: Bill Kennedy. Sound (U.K.): Tim Fraser. Make-up: Suzi Pannenbacker. Production Coordinator: Troy Norton. Post Production Coordinators: Bart Astor, Sean Linderman. Telecine Supervisor: Renee Stauffer. Telecine Colorist: Mike Sowa. Sound and Music Mixed by: Tom Davis. Music and Clip Clearance: Greg Philippi. Production Assistants: Chris Freeland, Kelli Mayman. Original Songs from *The Lion King* Written by: Tim Rice, Elton John. Original Score Composed by: Hans Zimmer. *Circle of Life* Performed by: Carmen Twillie. African Vocals Performed by: Lebo M. *I Just Can't Wait to Be King* Performed by: Jason Weaver, Laura Williams. *Be Prepared* Performed by: Jeremy Irons. *Hakuna Matata* Performed by: Nathan Lane, Ernie Sabella, Jason Weaver, Joseph Williams. *Can You Feel the Love Tonight* Performed by: Nathan Lane, Ernie Sabella, Sally Dworsky, Joseph Edwards, Kristie Edwards. Executive in Charge of Production: John Bravakis. The Wrightwood Group, Incorporated in association with Walt Disney Television.

LION KING CELEBRATION, THE
Producers: Barbara Zaneri, Melanie Steensland. Writer: Barbara Zaneri. Editors: Cliff Armstrong, Carlos Lopez, Diane Frierson, Jeff Koss, Greg Katz, Garry Ashton. Camera: Victor Smith. Audio: Jose Smith. Graphic Design: Lindsay Braverman, Mike Henn. Electronic Graphics: Alan Pfister. Production Coordinator: Susan Nakamura. Acknowledgment: Disneyland's Promotions and TV Productions Departments. Producer, Television Projects: Lisa Cappel. Producer, TV Production: Gary Kurtz. Production Coordinator: Melissa Boyer. A Production of The Wrightwood Group, Inc.

MAGIC OF ALADDIN, THE
Aladdin: The Making of a Whole New World Producers: Dan Boothe, Stu Schreiberg. Director: Stephen Kroopnick. Written by: John Culhane. Coordinating Producer: Stacy Ryono. Associate Producer: Joanie Burton. Director of Photography: Larry Gaudette. Editors: Jeff Caldwell, Dave Hogan. Associate Director: Wendy Dawson. Production Designer: Jimbo Marshall. Unit Production Manager: Ken Malquist. Sound: Doug Donald. Post Production Audio: Cary Coppola, C.A.S., Alan Porzio. Tape Operators: Jim Brown, Jon Van Wye. Art Director: Greg Hart. Prop Master: Nick Farrell. Gaffer: Rick Campbell. Electric: Pat Meng, Larry Shure, Pat Knowles. Grip: John Hatchett, Dennis Hus. Make-up: Diane Mackey, Anita Polin. Wardrobe: Michelle Fisher. Teleprompter: Dave Schmidt. Graphics: Vikki North. Production Assistants: Vanessa Ioppolo, Lori Turchin, Julie York. *The Magic of Aladdin* Special Appearances by: Curt Skinner, Julie Danao, Shelly Nichols, Tobrina Danbuskirk, Linda Griffin, Arik Basso, Glenn Shiroma, William Lett, Julie Gray-Johnson. Producer/Director: Melanie Steensland. Proucer/ Writer: Barbara Zaneri. Lighting Director: Dick Sulprizio. Graphics Design: Claudio Mattia. Camera Operator: Victor Smith. Audio: Rawn Hairston. Editors: Carlos Lopez, Jeff Koss, Gary Ashton, Jan Schneider. Electronic Graphics: Mark Festen. Production Coordinators: Susan Nakamura, Janelle Ricksen. *Disneyland Promotions and TV Production Departments* Producer, Promotions: Lisa Cappel. Producer, TV Production: Gary Kurtz. Technical Supervisor: Chris Robinson. Production Coordinator: Melissa Boyer. Associate Producer: Robin Mensinger. Show Director: John Addis. Production Stage Manager: Julie Kirchen. Choreographer: Patty Columbo. Stage Manager: Tony Salvaggio. Gaffer: Mike Kennedy.

Electrics: Josh Griffin, Joyce Ehrenberg. Grip: John Clement. Operations Manager: Tom Jacobson. Board Operator: David Hatmaker. Aladdin Show Crew: Chris Lamarca, Mike Elliot, Dionia Hodge. Production Assistant: Arianne Glagola. A Production of The Wrightwood Group, Incorporated in association with Betty Productions.

MAKING OF DISNEYLAND'S INDIANA JONES ADVENTURE, THE
Produced by: David Jackson. Co-Produced by: Olivier Chaudet. Edited by: Doug Nichols. Director of Photography: Anghel Decca. Original Music Composed by: John Williams. Arranged by: Richard Bellis. Additional Music by: Laura Karpmann. Line Producer: Nicole Dintaman. Associate Producer: Bob Dahlin. Production Associate: Dave Cass. Casting Director: Nora Kariya. Production Coordinator: Cathie Christie. Post Production Supervisors: Ted Garvey, Andy Pierce. Additional Photography: Michael Negrin. Gaffer: Eric Foster. Sound: Rob Scott. Boom: Huck Canton. Key Grip: Ken Wheeland. Video Engineer: Mike Shaheen. Art Director: Dan Butts. Props: J.P. Jones. Special Effects: Tom Bellissimo. Make-up: Debbie Zoller. Hair: Alyson Murphy. Costume Designer: Verkina Flower Crow. On-line Editors: Mary Holland, Deron Warner. Re-Recording Mixer: Tim Carpenter. Digital Effects: Robby Vignado. Supervising Producers: Jean-Michel Michenaud, Charles Duncombe, Jr. Executive Producers: George Zaloom, Les Mayfield. ZM Productions.

MAKING OF THE NHL'S MIGHTY DUCKS, THE
Produced by: Tom Murray, Josh Kaplan. Produced and Written by: Tom Murray, Josh Kaplan, W. Scott Henry. Associate Producer: W. Scott Henry. Photographers: Victor Smith, Jodie Mena, Scott Moulton. Editors: Josh Kaplan, Jodie Mena, Josh Bradford, Cliff Armstrong. On-line Editors: Cliff Armstrong, Jeff Koss, Garry Ashton. Graphics Manager: Margaret Bassett. Electronic Graphics: Daniel Storm, Alan Pfister. Acknowledgments: National Hockey League, University of Maine, ESPN, CBC. *Closing Credits Music* Written and Performed by: Bob Moline. Arranged by: Edo Guidotti.

MAKING OF TOY STORY, THE
Produced, Directed, and written by: Suzan Joregensen-Torgerson. Coordinating Producer: Carrie Stewart Baker. Written by: Suzan Joregensen-Torgerson, Carrie Stewart Baker, Wil Shriner. Production Director: Melanie Steensland. Production Coordinator: Susan Nakamura. Production Assistant: Janet Glenny. On-Line Editors: Garry Ashton, Edward Lapple, Carlos Lopez, L.J. Davenport. Camera: Alex Calder, Chris Torgerson, Victor Smith, John Vincent. Audio: Jamal Banks, Mark Young. Supervising Field Engineer: Victor Smith. Graphic Design Director: Mike Radogna. Graphic Artists: Bruno Bruhwiler, Lisa Carcone, Johann Shearer. Announcer: Toby Browning. Business & Legal Affairs: Hugo Rossiter. KCAL 9 News: John Corcoran, Mike Waco. *Buena Vista Pictures Marketing* Richard Cook, Terry Press, Charles Nelson, Kellie Allred, Arlene Ludwig, Sheri Sedlik, Renee Stauffer, Sarah Steinberg, Michael Vollman. *Disney-MGM Studios* Matt Kahn, Rob Ryan, Jim DeRusha, Peter Downing, Carole Munroe. *Disney's Funhouse* Lylie Breier, Bob Gault, John Nelson. *Thinkway Toys* Gidget Leung *The Disney Store* Kristin Bacon, Debbie Bohnett, Michelie Clift *Disney Promotional Products* Julie Singletary, Wil Simpson.

MICKEY AND NORA
Produced by: Paul Bogart, Marcia Govons. Written by: Andrew Bergman. Directed by: Paul Bogart. Executive Producers: Michael Lobell, Andrew Bergman. Director of Photography: Bill Klages. Art Director: John C. Mula. Editor: Bill Petty. Associate Director: Carol Scott. Stage Manager: Mikki Capparelli. Theme Song *Back in the Mainstream* Words and Music by: Cheryl Wheeler. Casting by: Eileen Knight, C.S.A. Costumes Designed by: Tom Bronson. Costumes: Sharon Day. Costumer: Libby Carlton. Property Master: Bill Wall. Make-up: Dulcie Smith. Hair Stylist: Michele Payne. Associate Producer: Stephen P. Reagan. Production Continuity: Sandy Broadway. Audio: Sam Mollaun. Additional Music by: John Beasley. A Lobell/Bergman Production in association with Touchstone Pictures.

MICKEY'S CHRISTMAS CAROL
Prepared for Television by: Marc Stirdivant. With the Voice Talents of: Wayne Allwine (Mickey Mouse), Hal Smith (Goofy), Clarence Nash (Donald Duck). Drawings by: Michael Peraza, Jr. Production Coordinator: V. Renée Toensing. Additional Music by: John O'Kennedy. Selected Background Music by: Paul J. Smith. *Oliver & Company, The Little Mermaid* and *The Rescuers Down Under* Behind the Scenes Footage by: Asta Productions. *Additional credits for the 1994 version: Disney's Animal Actors Segment* Produced by: The Wrightwood Group, Inc. *Additional credits for the 1995 version: What Animates an Animator* Written by: Barbara Toennies. Produced by: Gary Allen. Supervising Producer: Kellie Allred. Edited by: Todd Roisman. Production Manager: Michèle Bornheim.

MIRACLE CHILD
Co-Producer: Irwin Marcus. Co-Executive Producer: Cecily Truett. Music by: Craig Safan. Editor: Millie Moore, A.C.E. Production Designer: Dan Lomino. Director of Photography: Mark Irwin. Produced by: Barry Bernardi. Based on the book *Miracle at Clement's Pond* by: Patricia Pendergraft. Teleplay by: Gerald DiPego. Directed by: Michael Pressman. Executive Producer: Steve White. Unit Production Manager: Irwin Marcus. 1st Assistant Director: Rob Corn. 2nd Assistant Director: Laura Petticord. Casting by: Francine Maisler. Casting Associate: Kathy Driscoll. Gaffer: Jay Yowler. Sound Mixer: Bayard Carey. Key Grip: Loren Corl. Set Decorator: Stephen Davis. Prop Master: David Harshbarger. Costume Design: Shawn Barry. Stunt Coordinator: Kim Kahana. Make-up: Paula Sutor. Hair Dresser: Nina Paskowitz. Florida Casting: Lori Wyman. Music Administrator: Kinda Koci. Location Manager: Liz Matthews. Production Coordinator: Millie Kline. Assistant Editor: Lareine Johnston. Sound Editors: Frank Serafine, L. Mo Weber, Phil Raves. Re-recording Mixers: Dennis Patterson, Randy Honaker. Transportation Coordinator: Edward Flotard. Production Accountant: Jenny Fitzgibbons. Assistant to the Producer: Sara Mata. Script Supervisor: Maxine Bergen. Associate Producer: Chris deFaria. Steve White Productions in association with Walt Disney Television.

MOM FOR CHRISTMAS, A
Casting by: Susan Glicksman, C.S.A. Co-Producer: Ric Rondell. Music by: John Farrar, Sean Callery. Edited by: Les Green, A.C.E., Andrew Cohen. Production Designer: Glenda Ganis. Director of Photography: Ron Lautore. Produced by: Barry Bernardi. Based on the novel *A Mom by Magic* by: Barbara Dillon. Teleplay by: Gerald DiPego. Directed by: George Miller. Executive Producer: Steve White. Associate Producer: Chris Defaria. Unit Production Manager: Ric Rondell. 1st Assistant Director: Steve Lofaro. 2nd Assistant Director: Peter Graupner. Costume Designer: Jai Galati. Art Director: Richard D. Bluhm. Set Decorator: Jacqueline Sartino. Location Manager: Elizabeth Matthews. Make-up by: Wayne Massarelli. Special Effects Make-up: Dale Brady. Hair by: Bonnie Walker. Wardrobe Supervisor: Randall Thropp. Gaffer: Walter Stewart. Key Grip: Ken Wheeland. Camera Operator: Philip Schwartz. Property Master: David Harshbarger. Local Casting: Kathy Binns. Script Supervisor: Maxine Bergen. Production Coordinator: Cydney Bernard. Transportation Coordinated by: Edward Flotard. First Assistant Editor: Gael Chandler. 2nd Assistant Editor: Josh Muscatine. Supervising Sound Editor: Jeremy Hoenack MPSE, C.A.S. Sound Editors: Melissa Peabody, Sabrina Stephenson. Production Accountant: Bernice B. Moschini. Assistant to the Executive Producer: Linda Koci. Assistant to the Producer: Renee du Pont. Production Assistant: M. Phil Senini. Acknowledgments: Lazarus Department Store, Vogue International, Koala Blue. Steve White Productions.

MONSANTO NIGHT PRESENTS WALT DISNEY'S AMERICA ON PARADE
Produced by: Jack Sobel. Directed by: Clark Jones. Written by: Red Skelton. Special Musical Material: Jack Lloyd. Associate Producer: Anthony Masucci. Associate Director: J.D. Lobue. Choreographer: Barnette Ricci. Assistant to the Producer: Jan Cornell. Production Assistants: Paula Levenback,

Robyn Lewis. Executive Gofer: Robert Lettin. Production Executive: Hannah Sobel. Lighting Director: Jeff Engel. Audio Director: Andrew Bloch. Pre-recording Audio Consultant: Ami Hadani. Stage Managers: Rick Locke, Don Barnhart, Bruce Coine. Music Director: Tom Bahler. Production Secretary: Sarah Wetherall. Make-up: Joe Cranzano, Ben Nye, Jr., Joy Zapata. Wardrobe: Frank Novak, Joe Rovetto, Jack Muhs. Videotape Editors: Carlo De Leo, Joe O'Dowd. Technical Supervisor: John Whitman. Technical Director: Bob Masters. Video: Mark Sanford, John Field. Cameramen: Mike Keeler, Hank Geving, Dean Hall, Larry Heider. Walt Disney World Second Tape Unit: Emerson Lawsom, Bob Chandler, Charles Felder, Tony Singleton, Doug McDaniel, Stu Triebwasser, Bob Buckner. Live production of *America on Parade* Conceived & Produced by the Entertainment Division, Disneyland/Walt Disney World. Produced by York Enterprises, Inc.

MUPPETS CELEBRATE JIM HENSON, THE
Produced and Directed by: Don Mischer. Co-Produced by: Martin G. Baker, David J. Goldberg. Written by: Jerry Juhl, Sara Lukinson, Bill Prady. Associate Producer: Ritamarie Peruggi. The Muppet Performers: Dave Goelz (Gonzo, Beauregard, Bunsen Honeydew, Zoot), Jerry Nelson (Robin, Ma Bear, Camilla, Lew Zealand, Floyd), Richard Hunt (Scooter, Beaker, Statler, Janice), Steve Whitmire (Rizzo the Rat, Bean Bunny, Lips), Kevin Clash (Clifford), Kathy Mullen, Frank Oz (Miss Piggy, Fozzie Bear, Sam the Eagle, Animal), Carol Spinney (Big Bird), Pam Arciero, Jim Martin, Fran Brill, Peter MacKennan, Camille Bonora, Carmen Osbahr, Joe Mazzarino, Martin P. Robinson, David Rudman. Clip Segments by: David Gumpel, Sara Lukinson. Music: Larry Grossman. Scenic Designer: Lyndon Mosse. Lighting Designer: John Rook. Assistant to the Producer: Maureen Kelly. Production Manager: Glenn Stickley. Associate Producer: Hank Neimark. Script Supervisors: Jana Panarites, Pat Nugent. Production Associates: Jonathan Murphy, David Blacker, Chris Barry, Michele McGrath, Caroljean Nowak. Design Assistants: Brian Hess, William Wiggins, Richard Velleu. Technical Director: Tom Guadarrama. Audio: Jim Anderson, Blake Norton. Cameras: Bob Keyes, Shaun Harkins, Larry Solomon. Clip Clearance: Jeanne Gottschalk. Editors: Girish Bhargava, David Gumpel. Post Audio: Ken Hahn, Pam Bartella. Jim Henson Productions, Don Mischer Productions.

MUSICAL CHRISTMAS AT WALT DISNEY WORLD, A
Executive Producer: Jeff Margolis. Producers: Gloria Fujita-O'Brien, Mick McCullough. Directed by: Jeff Margolis. Written by: Stephen Pouliot. Associate Producer: Benn Fleishman. Talent Executive: Susan Abramson. Music by: Dennis McCarthy. Lighting Designer: Jeff Engel. Production Designer: Jimbo Marshall. Choreographer: Dee Dee Wood. Costume Designer: Ret Turner. Associate Director: Julie Miller. Stage Managers: Peter Margolis, R.A. Clark. Script Coordinator: September George. Production Manager: Hugh Camargo. Production Coordinator: Don Harary. Talent Coordinator: Joette Phillips. Unit Manager: Amy Storti. Location Manager: Virgil Fabian. Assistant to the Producer: Jennifer Bures. Technical Director: Keith Winikoff. Audio Mixer: Paul Sandweiss. Camera Operators: David Eastwood, Dave Hilmer. Videotape Operator: Joe Aroesty. Lighting Director: Larry Kaster. Staging Supervisor: Dennis Langston. Head Utility: Charlie Fernandez. Audio Assistant: Dale Whealton. Utility: Al Bogart, Kevin Burke. Rigging Gaffer: Rick Summers. Best Boy: J.R. Roberson. Rigging Best Boy: Russell Curtis. Edited by: Alan Carter. Assistant Editor: Davy Weller. Graphics: Bob Gautieri. Post Production Audio: Jamie Ledner. Acknowledgment: Orlando Opera Children's Company. Jeff Margolis Productions, Inc.

NBC SALUTES THE 25TH ANNIVERSARY OF "THE WONDERFUL WORLD OF DISNEY"
Executive Producer: Ernest Chambers. Produced by: Rocco Urbisci. Directed by: Art Fisher. Writing Supervised by: Hal Kanter. Written by: Rick Kellard, Bob Comfort, Dennis Landa, Tom Adair, Rocco Urbisci, Ernest Chambers, Hal Kanters. Part 2 Opening Segment Written by: Bob Comfort, Rick Kellard, Rocco Urbisci, Ernest Chambers. Special Lyrics by: Tom Adair. Executive in Charge of Production: Jack Watson. Art

Director: Romain Johnston. Music Conducted by: Jack Elliott, Allyn Ferguson. Choreographer: Jerry Jackson. Costume Design: Nolan Miller. Disney Sequences Prepared for Television by: Bill Reid, Gary Graf. Choral Conductor: Marvin Laird. Production Manager: F. Dean Reed. Unit Manager: Will Oborn. Assistant Art Director: Mark Batterman. Associate Director: David Grossman. Assistant to the Producer: Mamie Mitchell. Production Assistant: Lyn McDowell. Production Associates: Terrell Greene, Peggy Pancoe, Ali Chambers, Earl Meneweather II. Technical Director: Bob Holmes. Lighting Director: John Freschi. Audio: Joe Ralston. Video: Ray Olsen. Stage Managers: Ted Baker, Gordy Morris. Video Tape Editors: Rex Bagwell, Bill Breshears, Tony Hayman. Make-up: Harry Blake. Hair Design: Mari Loshin. *For Walt Disney Productions* Producer for Disney: Nicholas Clapp. Film Editors: Roy M. Brewer, Jr., Toby Brown, A.C.E., Jim Love, Gregg McLaughlin, A.C.E., Ernie Milano, A.C.E., Normal R. Palmer, A.C.E., Steve Pfahler, Lloyd L. Richardson, A.C.E. Production Associates: James Ashton, Gary Graf, George Petlowany, Charles L. Richardson, David Saxon. True-Life Adventure Segments Photographed by: Alfred G. Milotte, Elma Milotte, N. Paul Kenworthy, Robert H. Crandall, Herb and Lois Crisler, Dick Borden, James R. Simon, Tom McHugh, Cleveland P. Grant, Murl Deusing, Lloyd Beebe. Song *You Can Fly:* Sammy Cahn, Sammy Fain.

NEW KIDS ON THE BLOCK AT DISNEY-MGM STUDIOS: WILDEST DREAMS
Executive Producer: Brad Lachman. Co-Executive Producer: Dick Scott. Produced by: G. Thomas Sills. Directed by: Jim Yukich. Segment Directors: Lynn Goldsmith, Scott Kalvert, Michael Peters. Written by: A. Whitney Brown, Jim Cahill. Co-Producer: Paul Flattery. Coordinating Producer: Tzvi Small. Associate Producer: Craig Fanning. Talent Executive: Maggie Barrett. Director of Photography: Toby Phillips. Lighting Director: Bob Dickinson. Production Designer: Jimbo Marshall. Editor: Alan Carter. Choreography by: Michael Peters. Production Supervisor: Angela Fairhurst. Production Supervisor "Fantasy Segments" Allen Newman. Talent Coordinator: Michael Levitt. Associate Director: Greg Fera. Stage Manager: Bob Staley. Unit Production Manager: M. Ackerman. 1st Assistant Director: Kelly Schroeder. 2nd Assistant Director: J. Whitman. Costume Designer: Tom Bronson. Script Supervisors: Christine Klages, Teresa McKnight. Production Coordinator for "New Kids on the Block": Cathy McGlaughlin. Production Coordinators: Ann King, Marci Bokash, Dan Shaheen, Tom Nolan, Vernon Whitaker. Assistant Choreographer: Bill Holden, Jr. Assistant Art Director: Jim Weathers. "New Kids on the Block" Band: Derek Antunes, Kevin Antunes, David Dyson, Yasko Kubota, Rob Sachs. Senior Audio: Ed Greene. Senior Video: Doug Barry. Technical Director: Jerry Behrens. Videotape: Mike Sherwood. Automated Lighting Design: Tom Littrell, Lisa Gilhousen. Make-up and Hair: Brad Bowman, Pat Pattens. Videotape Editor: Dave Williams. Re-Recording Mixer: David Fleur. "New Kids on the Block" Documentary Footage: MDS Audio Visions, Inc. Producer: Bruno Artero. Brad Lachman Productions, Inc.

NEWSIES! NEWSIES! SEE ALL ABOUT IT
Directed by: Gayle Hollenbaugh. Written by: Rick Sublett. Produced by: Suzanne McCafferty. Associate Producer: Heidi Wenzel. Director of Photography: Steven Wacks. Camera Assistant: Mark Anderson. Videographer: Chris McBrier. Sound Mixer: Gary Woods. Sound—Video Shoots: Jerry Nulte, Ed Riley, Bob Slater. Gaffer: Joe Alvarado. Boom: Tom Johnson. Best Boy: John Beyers. Key Grip: Chris Kennard. Make-Up: Mike Germain. Hair: Charlene Johnson. Tutor: Sharon Sacks. Teleprompter: Dan Nelson. Edit Supervisor: Kurt Tiegs. Online Editor: John Carroll. Title Animation: Bob Engelsiepen. Harry Artist: Marco Bacich. Telecine Operator: Howard Cisco. Production Assistants: Susan Androus, Karen Coleman, Katen Beth Davidson, Kenneth Funk, Mallorie Salomon, Sarah Sher. ASTA Productions.

ONE HOUR IN WONDERLAND
Written and Produced by: Bill Walsh. Directed by: Richard Wallace. Musical Score: Paul Smith. Photography: Lucien An-

driot. Settings by: Ernst Fegte. Special Process: Ub Iwerks. Film Editor: Richard Farrell. Sound Director: C.O. Slyfield. Assistant Director: Joe Lefert.

ONE MORE MOUNTAIN

Music by: J.A.C. Redford. Edited by: Anita Brandt-Burgoyne. Art Director: Rick Roberts. Director of Photography: Frank Tidy, BSC. Producers: John Kuri, Anne Hopkins. Executive Producer: Marian Rees. Teleplay by: Gerald DiPego. Story by: John Kuri, Gerald DiPego. Based on an article by: John Kuri. Directed by: Dick Lowry. Unit Production Manager: Grace Gilroy. First Assistant Director: Peter D. Marshall. Second Assistant Director/Unit Manager: Kathy Gilroy-Sereda. Casting by: Phyllis Hoffman (U.S.), Stuart Aikins, C.D.C. (Canada). Costumes by: Heidi Kaczemski. Make-up Artist: Suzanne Benoit. Costume Department Supervisor: Joanne Hansen. Set Decorator: Janice Blackie-Godine. Property Master: Dean Goodine. Hair Stylist: Iloe Flewelling. Camera Operator: Armin Matter. Key Grip: Ivan Hawkes. Location Manager: Tom Benz. Head Wrangler: John Scott. Gaffer: Jim Gregor. Production Sound Mixer: William Flick. Location Casting: Bette Chadwick. Production Coordinator: Rhonda Legge. Special Effects Coordinator: Michael Vezina. Script Supervisor: Anne Melville. Post Production Supervisor: Cindy Golin. Music Editing: Michael Hooser. Sound Supervisor: Joe Melody. Re-Recording Mixers: John Reitz, C.A.S., Gregg Rudloff, C.A.S., David Campbell, C.A.S. Marian Rees Associates Production.

OPERATION WONDERLAND

Written and Produced by: Bill Walsh. Directed by: Robert Florey. Assistant Director: Joe Lefert. Music Composed by: Oliver Wallace. Music Arranged by: Ed Plumb.

OUR PLANET TONIGHT

Executive Producers: Jerry Zucker, David Zucker. Co-Executive Producer: Rich Markey. Produced by: Mark Grossan. Directed by: Louis J. Horvitz. Written by: David Zucker, Jerry Zucker, Don Novello, Rich Hall, Lane Sarasohn, Peter Farrelly, Bennett Yellin, Matt Neuman, Rich Markey. Segment Directors: David Zucker, Jerry Zucker, Mark Grossan. Associate Producer: Hugh Arian. Production Designer: Bob Keene. Casting by: Richard Pagano, C.S.A., Sharon Bialy. Music Director: Evan M. Greenspan. Director of Photography: Chuck Cohen, Steve Confer, Mackenzie Waggaman, Clay Harrison. Production Consultant: Jim Abrahams. Associate Director: Christopher A. Berry. Stage Managers: Peter Bright, Gil Castro. Choreographer: Ted Lin. Lighting Director: Olin Younger. Segment Producer: Carolyn DeRigg. *Leisure Ware* Segment Produced by: Rich Hall. Lighting Coordinator: Robert Nicholas Lo Cash. Production Coordinator: Janet Levy. Location Manager: Gino Apicella. Assistants to the Producers: Tammy Hoffman, Bianca Pur. Costume Supervisor: Ellen Greenberg. Make-up Supervision: Lorraine Polak. Property Master: Patty Schmidt. Post Production Supervisor: David Basinski. Editors: Alys Pitt, Rob Golbeaux. Assistant Editor: Arlyn Schirmer. Technical Supervisor: Bill Conroy. Technical Director: Ray Conners. Sound Mixer: Edward L. Moskowitz, C.A.S. Cameras: Dean Hall, Ritch Kenney, Dave Levisohn, Jack Chisholm. Video: Andy Dickerman. Videotape Editor: Charley Randazzo. Re-Recording Mixer: Peter Cole. Production Accounting: Zeiderman/Oberman, Assoc. Post Production Facilities: The Post Group. Sister to the Producers: Susan Breslau. Morgan Fairchild's and Martha Quinn's Wardrobe Designed by: Margi Kent Studios. Executive in Charge of Almost Everything: Edward R. Horowitz. A Zucker Bros. Production.

OUR SHINING MOMENT

Co-Producer: Justis Greene. Produced by: Mark H. Ovitz. Written by: Patrick Hasburgh. Directed by: Mark Tinker. Executive Producer: Patrick Hasburgh. Original Music by: Peter Bernstein. Director of Photography: Laszlo George, C.S.C. Production Designer: David Willson. Editor: Michael Berman, A.C.E. Unit Production Manager: Justis Greene. First Assistant Director: Lee Knippelberg. Second Assistant Director: Ani Baravyan. Casting by: Beth Hymson Casting, C.S.A. Costume Design: Grace Anderson. Set Decorator: Michael O'-

Connor. Property Master: Wayne McLaughlin. Make-up Artist: Margaret Solomon. Hair Stylist: Malcolm Marsden. Production Coordinator: Sandra Palmer. Script Supervisor: Christine Wilson. Location Manager: Janice Frome. Camera Operator: Paul Birkett. Gaffer: Duncan MacGregor. Key Grip: J. Dillard Brinson. Sound Mixer: Frank Griffiths. Canadian Casting: Sid Kozak. Transportation Coordinator: Bob Bowe. Production Accountant: Elizabeth Pontsa. Additional Editing: Joe Fuller. Patrick Hasburgh Productions in association with Walt Disney Television.

PLYMOUTH

Original Music by: Brad Fiedel. Edited by: John W. Wheeler, A.C.E. Production Designer: Michael Baugh. Director of Photography: Hiro Narita. Executive Producer: Ralph Winter. Produced by: Ian Sander. Written and Directed by: Lee David Zlotoff. Executive Producer: Lee David Zlotoff. Unit Production Manager: Dennis L. Judd II. First Assistant Director: Janet Davidson. Second Assistant Director: Robin Winter. Casting by: Mary V. Buck, C.S.A., Susan Edelman, C.S.A. Costumes Designed by: Tom Bronson. Set Decorator: Robert Checchi. Key Costumer: Dawn Jackson. Make-up: Ronnie Specter. Hair Stylist: Leslie Anne Anderson. Art Director: Frank Richwood. Property Master: Barbara Adamski. Script Supervisor: Marion Cronin. Production Coordinator: Ann Ashcraft. Visual Effects Supervisor: Richard Mosier. Visual Concept Artist: James Hegedus. Production Associate: Rick Singer. Production Sound Mixer: Steve Nelson. Post Production Sound by: Ken Polk, Gerry Lentz, Patrick M. Griffith, Lew Goldstein. Music Editing by: Ken Weiss. Video Supervisor: Rauf Glasgow. Special Effects by: Darrell Pritchett. Video and Graphic Displays by: Video Image. Vehicle Fabrication by: Image Design and Marketing. Conceptual Illustrations by: Pat Rawlings. Visual Concepts Concepts Consultant: Eagle Aero Space, Inc. Architectural Consultant: Bell & Trotti. Special Visual Effects by: Perpetual Motion Pictures. Acknowledgments: NASA, The Lyndon B. Johnson Space Center, Mark Craig, Dr. Wendell Mendell, Dr. Mark Cintala. Zlotoff, Inc. in association with RAI-UNO and Touchstone Television.

POLLY—COMIN' HOME!

Choreography by: Debbie Allen. Original Score by: Joel McNeely. Edited by: Jim McElroy, Kelly Snyder. Art Director: Peter Clemens. Director of Photography: Isidore Mankofsky, A.S.C. Co-Producer: James Pulliam. Produced by: Frank Fischer. Written by: William Blinn. Based on Characters from the Novel *Pollyanna* by: Eleanor H. Porter. Directed by: Debbie Allen. Executive Producer: William Blinn. Unit Production Manager: Irwin Marcus. First Assistant Director: Leslie Jackson Houston. Second Assistant Director: Rodney Allen Hooks. Casting by: Peg Halligan, C.S.A. Costumes Designed by: Tom Bronson. Set Decorator: Jennifer Polito. Property Master: Lavar Emert. Key Costumers: Dallas D. Dornan, Charmain Nash Simmons. Make-up: Jack Wilson. Hair Stylist: Gloria Montemayor. Location Manager: Marta Ball. Script Supervisor: Hope Williams. Production Coordinator: Dot Stovall-Mallard. Production Sound Mixer: Bruce Bisenz, C.A.S. Sound Editing by: Echo Film Services, Inc. Music Editing by: Jamie Gelb, Craig Pettigrew. Songs Arranged and Conducted by: Harold Wheeler. Music Supervisor: Maureen Crowe. *Songs Coming Home* Words and Music by: Jim Cox. *You've Got a Family* Music by: Harold Wheeler. Words by: Robert Lorick. *What a Gentleman Does* Words and Music by: Andrew Gold. *Hot 'Lanta, Ga.* Words and Music by: Larry Riley. *A Distinct Possibility* Music by: Harold Wheeler. Words by: Robert Lorick. *I Can't Hear My Heart* Words and Music by: Michael Cruz. *Show Us the Way* Music by: Harold Wheeler. Words by: Robert Lorick. *The Wedding Waltz, Celebrate the Good Times* Music by: Harold Wheeler. Words by: Robert Lorick. Songs Recorded by: Gary Lux. Assistant Choreographer: Eartha Robinson. Echo Cove Productions in association with Walt Disney Television.

QUEEN: THE DAYS OF OUR LIVES

Directed by: "The Torpedo Twins," Rudi Dolezal, Hannes Rossacher. Producers: Jim Beach, Rudi Dolezal. Co-Producer: Joe Novello. Associate Producer: Rhonda Martyn. Editors: Klaus Hundsbichler, Geoff Kleindorfer, Michael Hudecek,

Jim McQueen. Graphics: Gerald Prangl. Cameras: Dick Pope, Nick Noland, Herman Dunzendorfer, David Seman. Audio: John Yaworsky. Post Production Audio: Charles McDanial. Assistant Director: Stephanie Wagner. Production Assistant: Eva Deutinger. A DoRo Production with Queen Films in association with Buena Vista Television.

REGIS AND KATHIE LEE: MOM'S DREAM COME TRUE
Executive Producer: Michael Gelman. Associate Producer: David A. Mullen. Directed by: David C. McGrail. Segment Producers: Barbara Fight, Dolores Spruell Jackson, Cindy MacDonald, Joanne Saltzman. Technical Director: Brian Chapman.

REGIS & KATHIE LEE: SPECIAL EDITION
Director: Brooke Bailey Johnson. Executive Producer: Michael Katz. Senior Producer: Michael Gelman.

RESTLESS SEA, THE
Associate Producer: Ken Peterson. Written by: William Bosché. Directed by: Les Clark. Acknowledgments: Dr. Kenneth O. Emery, Dr. Columbus Iselin, Dr. Bernard Pipkin, Dr. Roger Revelle, Dr. F.G. Walton Smith. Art Direction: A. Kendall O'Connor. Directing Animators: Robert Cannon, Joshua Meador. Music: George Bruns. Animation: Jack Boyd, Robert Youngquist. Background: Frank Armitage. Song: Richard M. Sherman, Robert B. Sherman. Narrated by: Lawrence Dobkin. Special Effects: Eustace Lycett. Film Editor: Jim Love. Sound: Robert O. Cook.

ROCKETEER: EXCITEMENT IN THE AIR
Executive Producers: Dan Boothe, Stu Schreiberg. Producer: Stephen Kroopnick. Director: Douglas Burnet. Coordinating Producer: Stacy Ryono. Director of Photography: Larry Gaudette. Editor: Jeff Caldwell. Camera Operators: Van Carlson, Dennis Gerber, Scott Judy, Uli Kretchmar. Aerial Photography: John D. Sarviss, Jim Stimpson. Sound: Gary Bacon, Bill Kennedy, Rick Simonton. Post Production Audio: Gary Coppola. Production Coordinator: Joanie Burton. Film Researcher, National Archives: Bonnie Rowan. *The Rocketeer* Original Score Composed by: James Horner. Music Supervisor *Excitement in the Air:* Greg Philippi. Original Music for *Excitement in the Air:* Greg Philippi, Paul Antonelli. Additional Music for *Excitement in the Air:* Music Cumlaude, Lindsay Tomasic, William Ashford. Hair & Make-up: Rene Caruso. Videotape Editors: Rick Bryan, Leroy Weaver. Acknowledgments: Kellie Allred, Katie Chin, John S. Hall, Jennifer Nestegard. Produced by: Wrightwood Group, Inc.

ROGER RABBIT AND THE SECRETS OF TOON TOWN
Directed by: Les Mayfield. Producer: George Zaloom. Co-Producers: William Rus, Mark Cowen. Executive Producers: Frank Marshall, Kathleen Kennedy. Editor: Michael Greer. Written by: Michael Greer, Greg Czech, Mark Cowen, William Rus. Directors of Photography: Nick Struthers, Mark Zavad, Hank Holton, Ed Barger. Unit Production Managers: Allyson Scheu, Joseph Finneran, Tom Shelly. Film Clip Research: Maureen Cowen. Post Production Supervisors: Daniel Gillett, John Pace. Casting by: Fenton, Feinberg & Taylor. Feature Score by: Alan Silvestri. Assistant Director: Alec Griffith. Production Associates: Craig Davenport, Shana Hagan, Lisa Chowdhury, John Benz. Film Clip Consultant: Leonard Maltin. Assistant Camera: Paul Bernard. Re-Recording Mixer: Mike Perricone. Sound Mixers: John Vincent, David Jones, John Boles. Acknowledgments: Warner Bros. Inc., Ed Bleier, Roger Mayer, Jim Warren, Jeanne Romano, Bonne Radford, Mary Radford, Mark Punswick. Location Provided by: Universal Studios Tour. ZM Productions Inc.

SANDY IN DISNEYLAND
Executive Producer: Marty Pasetta. Produced by: Bernard Rothman, Jack Wohl. Directed by: Marty Pasetta. Written by: Bernard Rothman, Jack Wohl, George Bloom, Audrey Tadman, Gary Ferrier. Musical Sequences Staged by: Ron Field. Associate Producer: Jack Thompson. Production Designer: Ray Klausen. Music Conducted and Arranged by: Eddie Karam. Choral Arranger and Conductor: John Baylor. Costume Designer: Bill Hargate. Assistant to Producer: Mimi

Seawell. Talent Coordinator: Danette Herman. Technical Supervisor: Bill Hogan. Associate Directors: Anthony Chickey, Bob Lally. Stage Managers: Tom Trbovich, Peter Barth. Lighting Designer: Carl Gibson. Pre-recording: Ami Hadani. Audio: Larry Stephens. Video: Mark Sanford. Set Decorator: Paul Galbraith. Make-up: Larry Abbott. Video Tape Editor: Jerry Greene. Audio Facilities Furnished by: Wally Heider. Pasetta Productions, Inc. in association with Roth/Wohl Productions.

SHAGGY DOG, THE (TV VERSION)
Music by: Mark Mothersbaugh, Denis M. Hannigan. Film Editor: Jeff Gourson. Art Director: Peter Clemens. Director of Photography: Russ Alsobrook. Produced by: Joseph B. Wallenstein. Executive Producers: George Zaloom, Les Mayfield, Scott Immergut. Teleplay by: Bill Walsh, Lillie Hayward, Tim Doyle. Based on the Screenplay by: Bill Walsh, Lillie Hayward. Based on Characters from *The Hound of Florence* by: Felix Salten. Directed by: Dennis Dugan. Coordinating Producer: Irwin Marcus. Unit Production Manager: Irwin Marcus. First Assistant Director: Mike Kusley. Second Assistant Director: John Isabeau. Casting by: Allison Jones. Costume Designer: Tom Bronson. Set Decorator: Brenda Meyers-Ballard. Property Master: Cliff Bernay. Script Supervisor: Susan Bierbaum. Production Coordinator: Millie Kline. Costumers: Emma Trenchard, Jay Caplan. Make-up: Kathryn M. Kelly. Hair Stylist: Cheri Ruff. Location Manager: Lisa Stewart. Production Sound Mixer: Jacques Nosco. Optical Effects by: Magic Box, Inc. Animals Supplied by: Jungle Exotics. ZM Productions, Inc.

SHE STOOD ALONE
Co-Producer: John Flynn. Co-Executive Producer: Bruce Franklin Singer. Music by: Michael J. Lewis. Edited by: Jim Oliver. Production Designer: Trevor Williams. Director of Photography: Tom Burstyn. Produced by: Barry Bernardi. Written by: Bruce Franklin Singer. Directed by: Jack Gold. Executive Producer: Steve White. Casting by: Mary V. Buck, C.S.A., Susan Edelman, C.S.A. Unit Production Manager: John Flynn. 1st Assistant Director: Debbie Dell'Amico. 2nd Assistant Director: Bryan Denegal. Location Manager: Steve Housewright. Sound Mixer: Ken Ross. Gaffer: Tom Wholey. Camera Operator: Don Fauntelroy. Key Grip: Mike Smith. Costume Designer: Marianna Elliott. Property Master: David Harshbarger. Set Decorator: Donald Elmblad. Construction Coordinator: Dan Bickel. Make-up by: Harriette Landau. Hair by: Vicky Phillips. Script Supervisor: Sidney Gilner. Production Coordinator: Carol Ann Thomas. Midwest Casting by: Carrie Houk. Post Production Supervisor: Chris Defaria. Assistant Editor: Mickey Sarama. Supervising Sound Editor: Richard Taylor. Rerecording Mixer: Gary Montgomery. Transportation Coordinated by: Edward Flotard. Music Administration: Linda Koci. Assistant to the Producer: Sarah Mata. Research Consultant: Dr. Dorothy G. Singer. Production Accountant: Jenny Fitzgibbons. Acknowledgments: Missouri Department of Natural Resources, St. Louis Film Commission, City of St. Charles and St. Louis. A Steve White Production.

SISKEL & EBERT: FUTURE OF THE MOVIES, THE
Executive Producer: Larry J. Dieckhaus. Produced by: Jim Murphy. Co-Producer: Andrea Gronvall. Associate Producers: Stuart Cleland, Susan Malone, Carie Lovstad. Directed by: Jim Murphy. Editor: Joe Langenfeld. Assistant Editor: Robert Churchill. Make-up: Carrie Angland, Deborah Howell, Nancy Cohen, Nancy Stanley. Audio: Mike Mihavics. Camera: Jessica Klimovitz, Karen Korr, Jim Mulqueeny, Bob Skorup, Brian Donitz, Ed Fabre, Lynn Rabren, Larry Johnson. Technical Director: Mike Pennella. Audio/Video: Tom Paweko, Jeff Edrich, Bob Meleta, Ned Hall, Kenny Kosar, Paul Oppenheim. Lighting: Peggy Sheffield. Stagehands: Alfie Klein, Augusta Medina, Willie Reed. Videotape: Tom Mayahara, Gil Munoz. Graphic Designers: Tim Miecznikowski, John Truckenbroud, Sandy Webster.

SISKEL & EBERT: IF WE PICKED THE WINNERS
Executive Producer: Larry J. Dieckhaus. Producer: Andrea Gronvall. Directed by: Don DuPree, Jim Murphy, Don Voight. Associate Producers: Sue Malone, Stuart Cleland, Carie Lovs-

tad. Assistant Producer: Janet La Monica, Linda Weseman. Art Directors: Jimbo Marshall, Bill Moore, Jr. Production Assistant: Carie Lovstad. Floor Director: Gordon Hannan. Stage Set Design: John Derdall. Technical Directors: Pete Court, Joy Grow, Roger Santschi. Lighting Directors: Peggy Friedrich, Jay Grinrod, Todd Nichols. Audio: Mike Mihavics. Audio Mixers: John DeRussey, Jim Fay. Video: Tom Pawelko. Camera Operators: Rudy Anderson, Richie Banales, John Bender, Jim Coglianese, Kevin Garrison, Pete Janin, Roger Lynch, Steve Martyniuk, Jim Mulqueeny, Dick Palmer, Bob Skorup, Melissa Wright. Remote Crew: Les Howard, Jeff Hand, Nils Warren. Audio Utilities: Curt Coniglio, Jim McCabe, George Moshonas, Dan Pyne, Jack Somerville, Dale Wheaton. Media Supervisors: Al Sauzer, Sam Walker. Videotape Operators: Rico Garibay, Gary Jones, Tom Mayahara, Gil Munoz, Mike Staben, Steve Stribling, Bill Thomas, Ric Weatherbee, Jim Weathers. Video Control: Craig Bulmer, Vinnie Vezzi, Ric Wetherbee. Video Utilities: Eric Bills, Al Bogart, Warren Jones, Lisa Moye, Chip Swetnam, Dave Treiber, Linda Tutten, Brent Wilson. Crane Operators: Kevin Burke, Ray Detore, Alan Solomon. Stage Manager: Buzz Hannan. Teleprompter: David Schmidt, Carl Stevens. Make-up: Patsy Clayton, Regina Peron, Nancy Stanley, Carol Whitaker. Gaffers: Mike Gooseman, Jay Grindrod, Dennis Hus. Board Operator: Mike Gooseman. Key Grips: Gary Bristow, Jay Grindrod. Electricians: Steve Arnold, David Bowling, Russell Curtis, Paul Goodstein, Heath Goodwin, Steve Gryna, Pat Knowles, Terry Neudecker, Warren Jones, Arnold Tucker. Spot Operators: Pat Meng, Russell Curtiss. Edited by: Jeff Palmer, Sam Patterson. Assistant Editors: Rob Mobley, Ted Roseman, Gary Wood. Off-Line Editor: John Carbo. Post Production Editor: Joe Langenfeld. Graphics: Eddie Pasquarello, Sandy Weber. Audio Mixing: Rob Hill, Dorrie Batten. Assistant Editor: Tom Heckbert. *Disney-MGM Studios* Engineers in Charge: Larry Gaetano, Gary Jones, Ray Lego, Ric Wetherbee. Studio Unit Manager: Lydia Wickham. Production Coordinators: Jim Campbell, Maria Caccavo. Production Assistants: Andrew Baird, Karen Baker, Lisa Haskins, JK Karless, Stacey Kennington, Mary Kay Minelli, Sue Nelson, Mindy Ott, Jeff Ratajczak, Jeanie Sorenson, Jonathan Taylor. Audio Band Mixer: Andre Herring, Doug Morris, Jeff Rupe. Walt Disney World Marketing: Kathleen Glasser, Toni Moody.

SISKEL & EBERT SPECIAL, THE
Executive Producers: Mitchell Cannold, Jan S. Rifkinson. Directed by: Jan S. Rifkinson. Segment Producers—*Happy Endings:* Ken Fink. *Hamlet, Adults Only:* David Lowe. *Kathleen Turner:* Martha Spanninger. *Clint Eastwood:* Martyn Burke. For *Siskel & Ebert Syndication* Larry Dieckhaus. Coordinating Producer: Mary Kane. Associate Producer: Patti Vine. Production Coordinator: Lois Otto Nalepka. Director of Photography: Don Lenzer. Art Director: Mitchell Greenberg. Graphics: Scott Miller. Talent Coordinator: Sally Marshall. Music: Greg Arnold. Segment Editors: Mark Raudonis, Pamela Birkhead, Ken Levis. Post Production Editor: Richard Duke. Production Associate: Lisa Batsu. Production Research: Ann Damato. Film Clearance: Sue Malone. Camera: John Else, Tom Krueger, Christopher Lanzenberg, Gary Steele, Bob King. Assistant Camera: Dave Dubank, Sam Henriques, Doug Hurt, Paul Marbury, Gerry O'Malley, Mark Trottenberg, Tom Yatsko. Technical Director: Richie Wirth. Video Operator: Paul Ranieri. Audio: Todd Miller, Mark Miller. Tape Operator: Allen Buckner. Lighting Director: Bruce Ferris. Script P.A.: Roslyn Davis. Stage Manager: Rose Riggins. Assistant Editor: Luis Blanco. Production Assistants: Megan Eng, Monica Eng, Steve Forlano, Patrick O'Hanian, Matt Ransom, Carie Lovstad. Post Production Audio: George Meyer. A Buena Vista Entertainment Production in association with Bogart's Daddy Inc.

SNOW WHITE LIVE
Produced by: Robert F. Jani. Associate Producer for Television: William T. Watts. Directed by: Kirk Browning. *For the Stage Production* Directed and Choreographed by: Frank Wagner. Written by: Joe Cook. Executive Musical Director: Donald Pippin. Production Executive: John J. Moore. Musical Conductor: Don Smith. Associate Conductor: Elman Anderson. Choreographers: Dru Davis, Howard Parker. Scenic Designer:

John William Keck. Costume Designer: Frank Spencer. Lighting Designer: Ken Billington. Mask Design & Animal Costumes: Joe Stephen. Special Effects: John Lovelady. Music: Frank Churchill. Lyrics: Larry Morey. Additional Music: Jay Blackton. Additional Lyrics: Joe Cook. Queens Presentation Arranged by: Ronald Melrose. Orchestrations: Philip J. Lang. Choral Arrangements: Jay Brackton, Donald Pippin. Orchestra Administrator: Robert L. Swan. Audio Consultant: Ed Santini. Stage Manager: Joe Lorden. Assistant Stage Manager: Jack Giannino. Associate Production Executive: Jeff Hamlin. *For the Television Production* Lighting Director: Ferd Manning. Associate Director: Michael O'Nofrio. Stage Manager: Alfreda Diggs Aldridge. Production Assistants: Leonard Roberts, Rob Bertram, Robert Underwood. Make-up Supervision: Frances Kolar. Technical Director: Marty Begley. Video: Dick Sens. Audio: Aaron Baron. Cameramen: Juan Barrera, Mel Becker, John Feher, Manny Gutierrez, Jay Millard, Jake Ostroff. Videotape Editor: Frank C. Cernese. Technical Producer: Maury Beaumont. A Production of Radio City Music Hall Television Productions, Inc. in association with Walt Disney Productions.

SOUNDS OF AMERICA, THE
Produced by: Henry Jaffe Enterprises for the Bell Telephone System. Executive Producer: Barry Wood. Produced and Directed by: Sid Smith. Words and Music by: Gordon Jenkins. Dance Creations by: Hermes Pan. *The Train to Yesterday* and *An Island, a Treehouse and a Cave* Sound Essays Directed by: Irving Jacoby. Costume Designer: Grady Hunt. Associate Producer: Ed Cosgrove. Associate Director: Drew Handley. Unit Manager: Chris Kochoff. Technical Director: Charles Schmidt. Lighting Director: Del Jack. Audio Director: Willis Freitag. Cinematographer: Joel Colman. Editors: George Brand, Richard Scovel.

STEVEN BANKS SHOW, THE
Co-Producers: Douglas McGrath, Susan Dietz. Supervising Producer: Mark Brull. Written by: Steven Banks, Douglas McGrath. Based on the Play *Home Entertainment Center* by: Steven Banks. Directed by: Tom McLoughlin. Executive Producer: Bob Young. Director of Photography: Vince Conterino. Production Designer: John C. Mula. Editor: Marco Zappia. Associate Director: Lex Passaris. Stage Manager: L.H. Grant. Casting by: Mary Buck, C.S.A., Susan Edelman, C.S.A. Original Score by: Gary Stockdale. Original Songs by: Steven Banks. Associate Producer: David Z. Sacks. Set Decorator: James Walter. Property Master: Rich Hobaica. Script Supervisor: Lisa Knox. Production Coordinator: Millie Kline. Costume Designer: Tom Bronson. Key Costumers: Bill Tiegs, Gail Viola. Make-up: Annie Maniscalco. Hair Stylist: Ariel Bagdadi. Technical Director: Len Uslaner. Audio: Jim Mylenek. Video: Tom Tcimpidis. Music Mixer: Avi Kipper. Re-Recording Mixers: David Fluhr, Rick Himot.

TAG TEAM
Produced by: Ric Rondell. Written by: Robert L. McCullough. Directed by: Paul Krasny. Executive Producers: Robert L. McCullough, Bruce Sallan. Original Score by: Jay Ferguson. Director of Photography: James Roberson. Art Director: Bryan Ryman. Editors: Richard E. Rabjohn, James W. Miller. Unit Production Manager: Ric Rondell. First Assistant Director: Stephen J. Fisher. Second Assistant Director: W. Alexander Ellis. Executive Consultant: Michael Rachmil. Casting by: Rhonda Young. Costumes Designed by: Tom Bronson. Associate Producer: Beth Peterson. Set Decorator: Robin Peyton. Property Master: Kenny Orme. Key Costumers: Joe McCloskey, Marcy Lavender. Make-up: Frederic J. Doria. Hair Stylist: Lynn Del Kail. Production Coordinator: Nancy Malone Claycomb. Script Supervisor: Judy Redlin. Location Manager: George W. Spicer. Stunt Coordinator: Burt Marshall. Special Effects Coordinator: Jim Hart. Sound Mixer: Bill Teague. Sound Design by: Biggart Production Services, Inc. Music Editing by: Steve McCrosky. The IndieProd Company in association with Touchstone Television.

THRILLS, CHILLS & SPIDERS: MAKING OF ARACHNOPHOBIA, THE
Written and Directed by: John Schultz. Executive Producer: Frank Marshall. Produced by: Michael Doqui, George Za-

loom, Les Mayfield. Edited by: Paula Einstein, Joe Weiss. Re-Recording Mixer: Michael Perricone. Music Editor: David Palmer. Sound Effects Editor: Jim Henderson. Research Supervisor: Marie Snyder. Post Production Supervisor: Kevin H. Lillestol. *Host Segment* Line Producer: Jean-Michael Michenaud. Production Manager: Chuck Duncombe. Director of Photography: Marc Reshovsky. Production Design: Bryan Jones. Art Director: Susan Richardson. Gaffer: Joel Unangst. Entomology Consultant: Steven Kutcher. Stylist: Jamie Burrows. Make-up: Dina Ousley-Carone. *Arachnophobia Behind-the-Scenes Footage* Director: Mark Cowen. Production Manager: Leslie Jett. Production Coordinator: Catherine Meyers. Director of Photography: Shawn Maurer. Sound Mixer: Richard Mortillaro. Acknowledgments: Mary Radford, Katie Chin. Produced by: ZM Productions, Inc. and Buena Vista Television.

TICKETS, PLEASE
Produced by: George Sunga. Written by: Charlie Peters. Directed by: Art Dielhenn. Executive Producers: Bill Dial, Charlie Peters. Director of Photography: Richard Hissong. Art Director: John C. Mula. Edited by: Judith A. Burke. Associate Director: Nancy Heydorn. Stage Manager: Stu Goldman. Music by: David Benoit. Casting by: Bonnie Pietilla. Costumes Designed by: Tom Bronson. Costumers: Philip Signorelli, Elaine Maser. Property Master: Steve Hill. Make-up: Jerry Cash. Hair Stylist: Ariel Bagdadi. Fox-Tape Unit Manager: Cindy Brody. Script Coordinator: Lorraine Sevre Kenney. Production Coordinator: Cheri Tanimura. Technical Director: Len Uslaner. Audio: Sam Mollaun. Acknowledgment: Metro-North Commuter Railroad. Charlie Peters Films, Inc. in association with Touchstone Television.

TO MY DAUGHTER, WITH LOVE
Music by: Branford Marsalis. Edited by: Lance Luckey. Production Designer: Veronica Hadfield. Director of Photography: Christopher Taylor. Co-Producer: Terence A. Donnelly. Produced by: Barry Bernardi. Written by: Michael de Guzman. Directed by: Kevin Hooks. Executive Producers: Steve White, Sheri Singer. Unit Production Manager: Terence A. Donnelly. First Assistant Director: Steve Lofaro. Second Assistant Director: Nancy King. Costume Designer: Jill M. O'Hanneson. Casting Director: Julie Mossberg. Post Production Supervisor: Steven Tyler Sahlein. Location Manager: Joanna Guzzetta. Script Supervisor: Heidi Sturdevant. Key Make-up: E. Larry Day. Key Hair Stylist: Jaqueline Bordeaux. Costume Supervisor: Marychris Mass. Camera Operators: Harry K. Garwin, Philip D. Schwartz. Set Decorator: Sean Kennedy. Property Master: John A. Pearson-Denning. Sound Mixer: Randy Gable. Gaffer: Adam Jones. Key Grip: Bruce Lawson. Transportation Coordinator: Edward Flotard. Production Coordinator: Brian Tanke. Balloon Coordinator/Owner: John Cox. Music Supervisor: Linda Koci. Music Editor: David Bondelevitch. Assistant Editors: Patrick Magee, Jon Altschuler. Production Accountant: Jenny Fitzgibbons. Assistant to the Producer: Sara Mata. Re-Recording Mixers: John Brasher, Marty Hutcherson. Sound Editors: Charlie Crutcher, Sarah Brady, Doug Reed. Steve White Productions.

TOAST OF THE TOWN
Written by: Ed Sullivan, Bill Walsh. Filmed Portions of this show Directed by: Bill Walsh. Assistant Director: Alvin Ganzer. Cameraman: Guy Roe, A.S.C. Film Editor: Al Teeter. Voice of Donald Duck: Clarence Nash. Gaffer: Vic Jones. Best Boy: Jim Eddy. Lighting: Henry Zabel. Produced by: Marlo Lewis, Ed Sullivan. Orchestra: Ray Bloch. Settings by: Nelson Baumé. Direction and Choreography: John Wray.

TURNER & HOOCH   (TV version)
Producer: Raymond Wagner. Produced by: Terry Morse. Teleplay by: Jeffrey C. Sherman, Stephen Metcalfe. Story by: Stephen Metcalfe. Based on Characters Created by: Dennis Shryack, Michael Blodgett. Directed by: Donald Petrie. Executive Producer: Daniel Petrie, Jr. Music by: Charles Gross. Director of Photography: Tom Sigel. Production Designer: John DeCuir, Jr. Editor: Don Brochu. Unit Production Manager: Terry Morse. First Assistant Director: Gary Strangis. Second Assistant Director: Carla Corwin. Beasley is owned

and trained by: Clint Rowe. Casting by: Matt Casella, C.S.A. Costumes Designed by: Tom Bronson. Set Decorator: Sharon Thomas. Property Master: Frank Irving. Key Costumers: Dawn Jackson, Richard Mahoney. Make-up: Del Armstrong. Hair Stylist: Lynn Del Kail. Production Coordinator: Miriam Holder Jacobs. Script Supervisor: Patience Thoreson. Location Manager: Joanna Guzetta. Stunt Coordinator: Ernie Orsatti. Special Effects: Bruce Mattox. Sound Mixer: Russell Fager. Sound Editing by: Rainbow Sound/Samuel C. Crutcher, MPSE. Music Editing by: Steve McCroskey. Touchstone Television.

U.S. JUNIOR TOURNAMENT WORLD JUNIOR TENNIS TOURNAMENT
Produced by: Sheldon Saltman. Directed by: Andrew Young. Executive Producers: Stan Moger, Jordan Ringle. Syndicated by SFM Media Corporation.

U.S. JUNIOR TOURNAMENT WORLD JUNIOR TENNIS TOURNAMENT #2
Produced by: Sheldon Saltman. Directed by: Andrew Young. Executive Producers: Stan Moger, Jordan Ringle. Syndicated by SFM Media Corporation.

WACO & RHINEHART
Editors: Stanford Allen, Rod Stephens, A.C.E. Art Director: Charles Hughes. Director of Photography: George Koblasa. Supervising Producer: Richard Briggs. Written by: Lee David Zlotoff. Directed by: Christian I. Nyby, II. Executive Producers: Daniel Petrie, Jr., Lee David Zlotoff. Unit Production Manager: Joe Boston. First Assistant Director: Jerram Swartz. Second Assistant Director: Joseph Paul Moore. Music Design: Cinemascore. *Waco & Rhinehart* Title Theme: Mark Vieha, Cliff Magness, Tom Bahler. Original Score: Joel Rosenbaum, Chris Boardman, Randy Kerber, Bruce Miller. Casting by: Mary V. Buck/Susan H. Edelman Casting Company. Costume Designer: William Ware Theiss. Set Decorator: Thomas Michael Cost. Property Master: Lavar Emert. Key Costumers: Aida Swinson, Milton G. Mangum. Make-up: Edouard F. Henriques III. Hair Stylist: Ramsey. Location Manager: James "Tad" Tadevic. Script Supervisor: Sally J. Roddy. Production Coordinator: Jeannie S. Jeha. Stunt Coordinator: Gary Jensen. Technical Advisor: Cheryl Hunt, U.S.M.S. Production Sound Mixer: Patrick Mitchell. Sound Editing by: Horta Editorial. Music Editing by: Else Blangsted. Acknowledgment: The United States Marshals Service.

WALT DISNEY CHRISTMAS SHOW, THE
Produced and Written by: Bill Walsh. Directed by: Robert Florey. Musical Score: Paul Smith. Photography: Guy Roe. Settings by: Ernst Fegte. Special Process: Ub Iwerks. Film Editor: Richard Farrell. Sound Director: Harold J. Steck. Assistant Director: Joe Lefert.

WALT DISNEY—A GOLDEN ANNIVERSARY SALUTE
Produced by: Bernie Kukoff, Jeff Harris. Directed by: Lou Tedesco. Written by: Christopher Finch, Linda Rosenkrantz, Jeff Harris, Bernie Kukoff. Associate Producer: Bill Martin. Lighting Director: Steve Burum. Production Assistant: Wendy Charles. A Production of Harry Stoones, Inc.

WALT DISNEY PRESENTS SPORT GOOFY'S OLYMPIC GAMES SPECIAL
Song *You Can Always Be No. 1*: Words and Music by: Dale Gonyea. Syndicated by SFM Media Corporation.

WALT DISNEY WORLD CELEBRITY CIRCUS
Produced and Directed by: Marty Pasetta. Written by: Bruce Vilanch, Tom Perew. Talent Executive: Wolf R. Kochmann. Associate Producer: Michael Petok. Production Designer: Robert W. Rang. Music Arranged and Conducted by: Bruce Healey. Lighting Designer: Bob Dickinson. Choreographer: Barnette Ricci. Assistants to the Producer: Pat Eyerman, Karen Apple. Associate Producer: Greg Pasetta. Stage Managers: Gary Hood, Electa Brownn, Hank Neimark. Production Assistant: Lee Maloney. Production Coordinators: Debi Giudice, Michael Svetina. Production Manager: Buck Allen. Assistant to Mr. Pasetta: Lynne Osborne. Production Associ-

ates: Greg Bohnert, Mike Callan, David Rossmaur. Lighting Directors: Simon Miles, Todd Nichols. Circus Assistant: Danny Costoldi. Lighting Coordinator: Max Brenner. Audio: Doug Nelson. Editor: Bruce Motyer. Re-Recording Mixer: David Fluhr. Assistant Editor: Doug Gibbs. *For Walt Disney World* Unit Manager: Matt Sites. Entertainment Supervisor: Del Shilling. Entertainment Operations: Michael Fletcher, Dora Franklin, Bill Brown, Larry Lee. Park Operations: Wayne Culver, Judi Daley. Talent Coordinator: Sonya Smith. Production Coordinators: Laura Broome, Jim Campbell, Jack Somerville. Character Coordinator: Julie Kirchen. Facilities Manager: Scooter Huller. Wardrobe: Patty Dunne, Sandy Ciupak. Production Associates: Fran Falcone, Rich Weed, Joel Kostuch, Amy Storti, Elaine Leslie, Brad Moore, Kim Lynch, Don Mascheri, Heather Peterson. Pyrotechnics: Tylor Wymer, John Albert, Bernie Durgin, Paula Craig. Flight Coordinator: Doug Dinkel. Acknowledgments: Colonial High School, Lake Mary High School. Helicopter & Stunt Coordinator: Helistar 1000. Production Executive: Gregory Sills. A Pasetta Production in association with Walt Disney Television.

WALT DISNEY WORLD JOURNEY INTO MAGIC

Executive Producer: Tim Klein. Producers: Hank Duderstadt, Jim Felber, Deborah Havens, John Perugini. Associate Producer: Jim Crane. Unit Manager: Diane Royal. Production Assistant: Amy Parbury. Music: Tony Battaglia, Tim Coons. Director: Tim Klein. Wraps Director: Richie Banales. Camera: Richie Banales, John Bender, Mark Lynch, Melissa Lynch, Roger Lynch, Dick Palmer. Audio: Dan Pyne, Don Young. Walt Disney World Promotions: Tom Kennington. Post Production: *The Post Group* Tom Heckbert, Calvin Kesterson, Jim Mancini, Eddie Pasquarello, Don Rogozinski, Kurt Wagner, Pete Yelverton. Walt Disney Imagineering: Mark Rhodes. Administrative Assistant: Lori Willson. Cue Cards: Tom Postel. A Walt Disney Co. Production.

WALT DISNEY WORLD: 20 MAGICAL YEARS

Producer: Tim Klein. Consulting Producer: Deborah Havens. Segment Producers: Hank Duderstadt, Deborah Havens, Tim Klein, John Perugini. Announcer: Bill Logan. Segment Writers: Steve Birnbaum, Hank Duderstadt, Deborah Havens, Tim Klein. Editors: Art David, Eddie Johnson, Grace Machado Arnold, James Mancini, Jeff Palmer, Sam Patterson. Assistant Editors: Kathy Beyers, Tom Heckbert, Rob Mobley, Jeff Olm, Bob Scarborough, Gary Wood. Videographers: Richie Banales, John Bender, Les Howard, Hank Johnson, Dick Palmer. Audio Technicians: Dan Pyne, Jim McCabe. Graphics and Effects Director: Hank Duderstadt. Graphics Artist: Eddie Pasquarello. Post Production Audio: Dorrie Batten, Rob Hill, Brad Simpson, Kurt Wagner. A Walt Disney Co. Production. Creative Concept: Tim Klein. In Memory of Steve Birnbaum.

WALT DISNEY WORLD 4TH OF JULY SPECTACULAR (1988 VERSION)

Executive Producer: Don Ohlmeyer. Produced by: Linda Jonsson. Directed by: Don Ohlmeyer. Associate Producer: H. "Screech" Washington. Associate Directors: Ellen Brown, Liz Plonka. Stage Managers: Suzan Marciona, Barbara Paresi. Assistants to the Producer: Roberta Savold, Dru Rafkin. Production Coordinator: Kim Moses. Location Coordinator: Clay Newbill. Talent Executive: Carole Propp. Production Supervisor: Buck Allen. Segment Producers: David Forman, Eric Scholtz. Technical Supervisor: Paul Boykin. Lighting Designer: Todd Nichols. Audio Supervisor: Steve Huntley. Technical Director: Joy Grow. Editors: Jeff Palmer, Stan Kellam. Researchers: Drew Ohlmeyer, Matthew Nelson. Musical Supervisor: Steve Skorija. Sandi Patti's Music Arranged by: David Clydsdale. Production Staff: Stuart Alpert, Angela Fairhurst, Tracy Kogut, Julie Spielman, Linda Sweeney. *For Walt Disney World* Show Supervisor: Gary Paben. Project Manager: Douglas May. Character Voices: Barnette Ricci. Ohlmeyer Communications Company.

WALT DISNEY WORLD 4TH OF JULY SPECTACULAR (1989 VERSION)

Executive Producer: Don Ohlmeyer. Produced by: Linda Jonsson. Written & Directed by: Don Ohlmeyer. Associate Producer: Kim Moses. Associate Director: Liz Plonka. Assistant

to the Producer: John M. Best. Unit Manager: Clay Newbill. Associate Producer/Technical: Chris Wolff. Stage Managers: Suzan Marciona, Keith Richmond. Production Coordinator: Linda S. Cormany. Talent Coordinators: Bruce Hanawalt, Julie Spielman. Segment Producers: David Forman, Eric Schotz. Segment Director: Liz Plonka. Art Director: Jimbo Marshall. Technical Supervisor: Paul Boykin. Lighting Designer: Todd Nichols. Audio Supervisor: Dave Mourey. Technical Director: Joy Grow. Editors: Jeff Palmer, Art David. Researchers: Chris Ohlmeyer, Drew Ohlmeyer. Production Staff: Angela Aiello, Ketti Kollin, Tracey Levine, Amy Storti, Dean Tendrich, Gary A. Turchin. Sandi Patti's Music Arranged by: David Clydsdale. *For Walt Disney World* Stage Show Development: Gary Paben. Musical Supervisor: Steve Skorija. Project Manager: Tony Peugh. Choreographers: Pam Killinger, Robbi Mackey, Wayne Bascomb, Patty Columbo. Ohlmeyer Communications Company.

WALT DISNEY WORLD 4TH OF JULY SPECTACULAR, THE (1990 VERSION)

Executive Producer: Don Ohlmeyer. Produced by: Linda Jonsson. Written and Directed by: Don Ohlmeyer. Associate Producers: Kim Moses, Carlos Torres. Segment Director: Liz Plonka. Associate Directors: Liz Plonka, Allan Kartun. Assistants to the Producer: Paula Shugart, Linda Pryor. Unit Manager: Clay Newbill. Segment Producer: Stephen Kroopnick. Stage Managers: Dency Nelson, Buck Allen, Craig Factor. Production Coordinators: Jim Campbell, Tracey Levine, Amy Storti. Talent Executive: Kim Swann. Talent Coordinators: Julie S. Linden, Jamie Keyser. Art Director: Jimbo Marshall. Technical Supervisor: Paul Boykin. Lighting Designer: Todd Nichols. Gaffer: Rick Campbell. Audio Supervisor: Dave Mouery. Audio Mixers: Doug Nelson, Jim Fay. Technical Directors: Joy Grow, Doug Ramsey. Editors: Ron Bar, Jeff Palmer. Researcher: Michael X. Ferraro. Production Staff: Rigo Ardon, Andrew Baird, Chris Muehlberger, Julie Robertson. *For Walt Disney World* Stage Show Directors: Gary Paben, Judy Lawrence. Musical Supervisor: Steve Skorija. Consultant: Cooper Williams. Choreographers: Roy Luthringer, Robbie Mackey. Assistant Choreographer: Betsy Glover. *For Disneyland* Project Managers: Dale Lanier, Brad Tallman. Musical Supervisors: Jim Dellas, Bruce Healy. Technical Supervisor: Chris Robinson. Announcer: Mark Elliott. Ohlmeyer Communications Company.

WALT DISNEY WORLD HAPPY EASTER PARADE (1985 VERSION)

Executive Producer: Walter C. Miller. Produced by: Tom Elrod. Directed by: Paul Miller. Written by: Don Wells. George Burns Material Written by: Hal Goldman. Associate Producer: Robert M. Allen. Associate Director: Rick Locke. Stage Manager: Andi Copley. Production Consultant: Gregory Sills. Assistants to the Producers: Pam McKissick, Maureen O'Donnell. Talent Coordinators: Sonny Anderson, Tisha Fine. Production Coordinators: Jim Moroney, Bon Williams. Production Associates: Kim Gunther, Grace Machado, Diane Royal, Matt Sites, Sonya Smith, Beth Townsend, Roni Weiners. Lighting Director: Todd O. Nichols. Lighting Consultant: Red McKinnon. Set Designer: Jeff Chandler. Costumes Designed by: Bill Campbell. Gaffer: Michael Gooseman. Key Grip: Beth Gillette. Camera: Rich Banales, Les Howard, Roger Lynch, Wayne Orr, Dick Palmer, Hector Ramirez, Melissa Wright. Audio: Gary Baldassari, James Glass, Cliff Harbin, Dave Mouery, Bill Tomlinson. Video Tape Editor: Bill Breshears. Re-Recording Mixer: Jerry Clemans. Graphics: Jim Cooper. Wrangler: Mike Leslie. Parade Production: Tom Craven, Dennis Despie, Greg Emmer, Darlene Faber, Julie Kirchen, Ron Logan, Mike O'Grattan. Choreographers: Judy Lawrence, Jay Smith. Technical Supervisor: Jim Pare. Parade Music: Jack Eskew, Tony Peluso, Ted Ricketts, Steve Skorija. Props: Betina Buckley, Cindy Ravetto. Grips: John Bender, Rick Campbell, Eric Dellacioppa, Jay Grinrod, Mark Lynch, John Peters, Jody Roberson, Brent Stayer, Tony Wikner. Maintenance Coordinators: Marty Ebersbach, Ed Hopping, Scooter Huller, J.R. Rutcho, Jerry Stripling, Phil Transue. Operations: Jim Athanis, Diane Black, Wayne Bush, Bill Burns, Norm Doerges, Bill Sullivan. Announcer: Dick Tufeld. Produced by Parade Productions in association with Walt Disney World Co.

WALT DISNEY WORLD HAPPY EASTER PARADE (1987 VERSION)

Executive Producer: Tom Elrod. Producers: Bruce Brown, Lisa Yee. Supervising Producer: Robert M. Allen. Associate Producer: Bob Williams. Writer: Lisa Yee. Director: Julio Fernandez. Production Manager: Matt Sites. Production Coordinators: Clay Newbill, Sonya Smith. Segment Production: Bruce Brown, Nina Graham, Hank Johnson, Dick Palmer, David Pool, Bob Williams, Melissa Wright. Program Consultant: Doug Cody. Lighting Designer: Todd Nichols. Advertising: Chip Eickmann. Publicity: John Dreyer. Talent Coordinators: Sonny Anderson, Bobbi Colquitt, Nancy Eskew. Administrative Affairs: Maureen O'Donnell. Post Production Supervisor: Gary Jones. Post Production: Edward E. Johnson, Jeff Palmer, Grace Machado. Musical Director: Ted Ricketts. Technical Supervisor: Jim Pare. Technical Director: Joy Grow. Engineering: Larry Gaetano, John Rochie, Al Taylor. Audio: Gary Baldassari, Dave Mouery, Allen Slansky, Bill Tomlinson, Steve Weber. Graphics: Wanda J. Collis, Gary Jones, John Samaha. Video: Tom Gamble, Bob Hunter, Cliff Wright. Set Designer: Jeff Chandler. Camera: Nina Graham, Les Howard, Mark Lynch, Roger Lynch, Dick Palmer, Melissa Wright. Steadicam: Rich Banales. Grips: John Bender, Rick Campbell, Jim Fay, Mike Gooseman, Jay Grindrod, R.E. Lanier, David Miller, Terry Neudecker, Chuck Smith. Crane Operators: J.L. Parker, Jody Roberson. Floor Manager: Buck Allen. Production Assistants: Laura Broome, Michael Forchetti, Kim Gunther, Jake Poore, Jack Somerville, Jim Wilson. Parade Concept: Judy Lawrence. Staging Directors: Judy Lawrence, Jay Smith. Parade Production: Michael O'Grattan, Darlene Kennedy, Julie Kirchen. Satellite Transmission: Tom Cormier, Bruce Bryson. Acknowledgments: Sue Arena, Dave Beck, Willy Brahn, Bettina Buckley, Bill Burns, Kenny Britton, Cliff Galloway, Jeff Crutchfield, Mike Davis, Jaime Davis, Norm Doerges, Jim Flynn, Mike Head, Penny Holtzclaw, Scooter Huller, Donald Jones, Chris Kanton, Laurie Kelley, John L. Kimbrough, James Krapps, Jim Macphee, Holly McCammack, Kristin McCracken, Deb Muenchow, Bruce Nierenberg, Jim Richardson, Sandy Richardson, Gail Schmidt, Linda Stayer, Sheri Solomon, Elaine Thomas, Debbie Toole, Katie Warner, Russ Wheeler, Laurel Wrigley, Captain D. Chilas and crew of the Starship Oceanic. Produced by: TELX Entertainment in association with Walt Disney World.

WALT DISNEY WORLD HAPPY EASTER PARADE (1988 VERSION)

Executive Producer: Tom Elrod. Supervising Producer: Debra Muenchow. Produced by: Bruce Brown, David Pool. Writer: Lisa Yee. Director: Julio Fernandez. Associate Producer: Clay Newbill. Segment Producer: Barbara Phillips. Segment Directors: Nina Graham, Dick Palmer, Melissa Wright, Roger Lynch. Post Production Supervisor: Gary Jones. Editors: Edward E. Johnson, Jeff Palmer, Grace Machado. Advertising: Chip Eickmann. Production Coordinators: Laura Broome, Jim Campbell, Diane Royal, Jack Somerville. Talent Coordinator: Sonya Smith. Lighting Designer: Jay Grinrod. Assistant Director: Dan Nabors. Musical Direction: Ted Ricketts, Dan Stamper, Jack Eskew. Technical Supervisor: Bruce Bryson. Technical Director: Joy Grow. Engineering: Marvin Kale, Terry McIntyre. Audio: Steve Weber, Bill Tomlinson, Dave Mouery, Jim Fay, Allen Slansky. Video: Al Chestelson, Gene Mikell. Videotape: Cliff Wright. Graphics: Wanda J. Collis, Gary Jones. Set Designer: Jeff Chandler. Camera: Nina Graham, Mark Lynch, Roger Lynch, Dick Palmer, Melissa Wright, Kim Nordquist. Steadicam: Rich Banales. Grips: John Bender, Terry Neudecker, Gerry Banales, Rick Campbell, Chuck Smith. Electricians: Franz Vonn Mann, Don White, Scott Smith, Gary Ware, Patty Crisp, Lenny Cooper. Utility Crew: Bruce Blackman, Mike Laninfa, Buddy Leavitt, Bob Gobel. Crane Operators: Mike Gooseman, Jody Roberson. Stage Manager: Doug Ramsey. Production Assistants: Maria Caccavo, Jerome Ravenna, Tracy Veler. Publicity: John Dreyer, Tom Brinkmoeller. Talent Booking: Sonny Anderson, Bobbi Colquitt, Nancy Eskew. Parade Staging Directors: Jay Smith, Judy Lawrence. Parade Production: Michael O'Grattan, Darlene Kennedy, Julie Kirchen. WorldLink Satellite Services: Tom Cormier, Bruce Bryson. Administrative Affairs:

Maureen O'Donnell. Acknowledgments: Gloria Beck, Carl Berczek, Willy Brahn, Bill Burns, Pam Carver, Paul Chiaravalle, Jeff Crutchfield, Sandy Dilello, Mike Fletcher, Teri Hamel, Dee Hansford, Rick Harbin, Sandi Hawkins, Penny Holtzclaw, Bob Horton, Scooter Huller, Donald Jones, James Krapps, Jim MacPhee, Sharon Madill, Debra Muenchow, Ray Phares, Gail Schmidt, Chris Schomagle, Kathy Shaffer, Jim Simmons, Stuart Sponger, Linda Stayer, Philip Steinbacher, Meri Tortorice, Jack Wagner, Anita Wilson, Lynda Wilson, Clovis West High School, Jefferson High School, Lake Mary High School. Produced by: TELX Entertainment in association with Walt Disney World. Announcer: Dick Tufeld.

WALT DISNEY WORLD HAPPY EASTER PARADE (1989 VERSION)

Executive Producer: Tom Elrod. Producer: Debra Muenchow. Supervising Producer: Jim DeRusha. Writer: Barbara Phillips. Director: Chico Fernandez. Segment Producers: Barbara Phillips, Jim DeRusha, Dave Pool. Associate Producer: Clay Newbill. Advertising: Chip Eickmann, Allen Humphrey, Anna Souza. *Easter Cruise Segment* Director: Peter Israelson. Director of Photography: Michael Negrin. *Main Street Hop Segment* Supervising Producer & Writer: John A. Lee. Director: Lee Ollerton. Line Producer: Dale Lanier. Staging Director & Choreographer: Marilyn Magness. Additional Segment Directors: Dick Palmer, Roger Lynch, Les Howard. Assistant Directors: Jeff Palmer, Dan Nabors. Editors: Jeff Palmer, Eddie Johnson, Grace Machado. Lighting Directors: Jay Grinrod, Ed Rowe. Stage Manager: Doug Ramsey. Set Design: Jeff Chandler, Jim Marshall. Production Coordinator: Jim Campbell. Producer's Assistant: Kim Lynch. Production Assistants: Chris Congdon, Brad Moore, Trish Ferdon, Jamie Keyser, Alison Swanson, Mark Schnallinger, Jack Somerville. Camera: Dick Palmer, Roger Lynch, Rich Banales, Melissa Wright, Mark Lynch, David Treiber, John Bender, Les Howard, Ron Bates, Erin Parish. Technical Directors: Joy Grow, Marty Krzyskoski. Engineering Supervisor: David Jones. Audio: Dave Mouery, Bill Tomlinson, Gerard Kane. Satellite Coordinator: Tom Cormier. Musical Director: Ted Ricketts. Character Department Supervisors: Julie Kirchen, Sharon Madill. Parade Supervisors: Heidi Vogel, Connie Willis. Staging Assistants: Molly Bergeson, Chris Hoffner, Suzie Lalone, Christine Schornagle, Meri Tortorice, Tom White-Spunner, Connie Willis. Acknowledgments: Jim Van Winkle, Don Youngs, Alan Alexander, Bruce Blackman, Annie Bornhurst, Ray Detori, John Cummings, Ken McCabe, Stacy Howen, Mark Rabinowitz, Gary Jones, John Atkinson, Jennifer Montegue, Charity Armbrister, Charles McKenzie, Judy Lawrence, Sonny Anderson, Rick Campbell, Terry Neudecker, Bruce Merwin, Digger Wilson, Pat Knowles, Ken Yochum, Gary Corbet, John DeRussey, Brien casey, Dan Pyne, Ric Weatherbee, Laurel Thompson, Scooter Huller, Susan Campbell, Brenda Reed, Bill McClancey, Vicky Daniel, Alan Johns, Elizabeth Rogers, Amanda Chevalier, Steve Ingram, Steve Kippert, Jennifer Carver. ABC Operations Manager: Bob Braunlich. Main Street Hop Segment Produced in association with Video West Entertainment. Announcer: Dick Tufeld.

WALT DISNEY WORLD HAPPY EASTER PARADE (1990 VERSION)

Executive Producer: Tom Elrod. Producer: Debra Muenchow. Supervising Producers: Dave Pool, Jim DeRusha. Writer: Barbara Phillips. Director: Chico Fernandez. Assistant Director: Doug Ramsey. Advertising: Chip Eickmann. Segment Producer: Barbara Phillips. Entertainment Show Director: Forrest Bahruth. Segment Director: Jeff Palmer. *That Dancin' Guy* Segment Produced by: Peter Israelson. *From Disneyland* Supervising Producer: Brad Tallman. Producers: Joel Johnston, Todd Komarnicki. Associate Producer: Nicole Ludwig. Production Directors: Booey Kober, Rick Squire. Line Producer: Dale Lanier. *From Walt Disney World* Business Affairs: Maureen O'Donnell. Promotions: Caroline Nicholas. Unit Manager: Jim Campbell. Unit Production Manager: Tricia Ferdon. Talent Coordinators: Janie Unger, Sonya Weathers. Stage Managers: Maria Caccavo, Marsha Groome, Diane Royal. Production Stage Manager: Joe Forton. Music Director: Ted Ricketts. Choreographers: Doug Jack, Betsy Glover, Cory Benedict. Parade Production Supervisor: Simon Penny. Character Supervisors: Sandy Hawkins, Lynda Wilson. Acknowledgment: James Madison University Marching Royal Dukes, Director: Pat Rooney. Production Secretary: Stacey Howen. Editors: Art David, Grace Machado-Arnold, Pat Clancey, Jim Mancini. Engineering Supervisor: David Jones. Satellite Operations: Tom Cormier. Technical Director: Joy Grow. Chyron: Margaret Mack. Show Timer: Jerry Johns. Video: Ray Lego, Ric Wetherbee. Videotape Operators: Pat Caudle, Gary Jones, Scott Miller, Cliff Wright. Audio Mixers: Dave Mouery, Steve Weber. Audio Assists: Linda Burns, John DeRussey, Jim Fay, Stan Johnson, Shawn McFail, George Moshonas, Steve Puryea, Dan Pine, Allen Slansky, Don Youngs. Camera Operators: Rich Banales, Les Howard, Mark Lynch, Roger Lynch, Steve Martyniuk, Dick Palmer, Dave Treiber, Melissa Wright. Camera Utilities: Eric Bills, K.C. Lee, Jerry Meibos, Lisa Moye, Peter Perez, John Tegethoff. Set Designer: Jimbo Marshall. Teleprompter: Bill Lulow. Lighting Director: Jay Grindrod. Gaffer: Bruce Blackman. Electricians: Gary Bristow, Dwight Brown, Rick Campbell, Bob Harper, Warren Jones, Todd Kramer, Don Lamont, Mark Malacane, Del Moody, Terry Neudecker, Frank Sleeman, Scott Smith, Lee Thomas, Gary Ware. Crane Operators: Rey DeTorre, Alan Soloman. Crane Assists: Greg Kelly, Kenny Rivenbark. Grips: Don Chiara, John Cristadelou, Zayd Darwish, Fred Lowery. Production Assistants: Mike Larsen, Jerome Ravenna, Chip Swetnam, JoAnn Santulli. Acknowledgments: John Atkinson, Bob Austin, Robert Braunstein, Mike Briggs, Kenny Brittan & Crew, Bill Bunting, Glenn Burdette, Jefferson Crutchfield, Linda Beach, John Cummings, Joe Danes, Tiersa Dennis, Ed Disney & Crew, Jane Gilane, Mike Head, Linda Heller, Scooter Huller, Hank Johnson, Linda Lenzen, Heidi Macklin, Jim Mooney, Todd Nichols, Laura Nilon, Gino Pelliciotta, Tony Picerno, Di Pittman, Bob Lamb, Eileen Rahman, John Rogers, George Spires, Ron Thompson, Margaret Thornton, Keith Unger, Ivy Vasquez, Tim Wolters, John Wilson, Cynthia Pollock & Crew. Announcer: Dick Tufeld.

WALT DISNEY WORLD HAPPY EASTER PARADE (1991 VERSION)

Executive Producer: Tom Elrod. Producer: Debra Muenchow. Supervising Producers: Jim DeRusha, Dave Pool. Writer: Barbara Phillips. Director: Chico Fernandez. Segment Producer: Barbara Phillips. Assistant to the Producers: Andrea Patrizzi. *For Walt Disney World Creative Entertainment* Show Producer: Doug May. Show Director: Forest Bahruth. Production Manager: Jim Heffelfinger. Music Directors: Ted Ricketts, Dan Stamper. Production Designer: Cindy White. Head Choreographer: Pam Killinger. International Festival Program: Paul Chiaravalle. *For Disneyland* Supervising Producer and Writer: Brad Tallman. Director: Gary Kurtz. Technical Director: Chris Robinson. Choreographer: Keri Keaney. Character Department Supervisors: Sandy Hawkins, Linda Wilson. Parade Production Supervisors: Cathy Arnott, Simon Penny. Business Affairs: Maureen O'Donnell. Promotions: Caroline Nicholas, Terri Gallagher. Editors: Jeff Palmer, Art David, Eddie Johnson, Sam Patterson. Graphic Design: Eddie Pasquarello. Unit Manager: Sonya Weathers. Stage Manager: Trish Weinstock. Talent Coordinator: Janie Unger. Art Direction: Jeff Chandler, Jim Sheridan. Chief Engineer: Larry L. Gaetano. Engineer: Ray Lego. Technical Director: Joy Grow. Electronic Graphics: TL Grant. Video: Jeff Court, Mike Sherwood. Videotape Operators: Tom Galloway, Rick Wetherbee. Show Timer: Wendy Dawson. Audio Mixers: Jim Fay, Steve Weber. Director of Photography-Video: Jay Grindrod. Cameras: Rich Banales, Nina Bartlett, Eric Bills, Mark Lynch, Roger Lynch, Dick Palmer, Dave Treiber, Melissa Wright. Studio "D": Bill Tomlinson, Len O'Bannon, Joe Fanelli, Cliff Harbin, James Glass. Production Assistant: Brad Moore. Teleprompter: Bill Lulowe. Acknowledgments: Scooter Huller & Crew, Main Street Operations, Mid-Florida Dalmation Club, U.S. Military. Announcer: Dick Tufeld.

WALT DISNEY WORLD HAPPY EASTER PARADE (1992 VERSION)

Executive Producer: Tom Elrod. Producer: Debra Muenchow. Supervising Producers: Jim DeRusha, Barbara Phillips, Jeff Palmer. Writers: Barbara Phillips, Greg Ehrbar. Director: Chico Fernandez. Segment Producer: Ann Patrizzi. *For Walt*

Disney World Creative Entertainment Show Producer: Doug May. Show Director: Sherilynn Draper. Production Manager: Jim Heffelfinger. Music Director: Steve Skorija. Orchestrations: Greg Smith, David Volpi. Music Coordinator: Dan Stamper. Production Stage Manager: Nancy Hart. Production Assistant: Lori Stephens. Art Director: Rhonda Counts. Choreographers: Denise Case, Gary Coburn, Gina Vaughn, Tom Murphy. Guest Talent Program: Paul Chiaravalle, John Torrito. Costumes: Creative Costuming. Character Department Supervisors: Sandy Hawkins, Lynda Wilson. Parade Production Supervisors: Cathy Arnott, Sue Ellen Collins. Staging Assistants: Corey Benedict, Meri Tortorice, Molly Piveral, Cheri Wells, Beth Scammon, Philip Steinbacher, Tom White Spunner. *From Disneyland* Producers: Brad Tallman, Gary Kurtz, T. Dale Lanier, Howard Barish. Director: Richard Squire. Editor: Kevin Miller. Business Affairs: Maureen O'Donnell. Promotions: Lori Smith, Bob Kane. Publicity: Jennie Hess, Bill Logan. Advertising: Ginger Watters, Julie Woodward, Linda Weekes. Editors: Sam Patterson, Art David, Eddie Johnson, Tom Heckbert. Graphic Design: Eddie Pasquarello. Unit Manager: Maria Caccavo. Production Coordinators: Laura Broome, Brad Moore. Talent Coordinator: J.B. Himmer. Stage Managers: Trish Weinstock, Jim Weathers. Booth P.A.: Wendy Dawson. Graphics: TL Grant. Teleprompter: Bill Lulow. Art Directors: Jeff Chandler, Sharon Dawn Tamaian. Engineering Supervisor: Larry Gaetano. Engineers: Ray Lego, Spike Jones, Ric Wetherbee, Pete Dahlstrom. Broadcast Coordinator: Hank Johnson. Technical Director: Joy Grow. Video: Vince Vezzi, Nick Cap. Videotape Operators: Bill Thomas, Tom Galloway. Audio Mixers: Steve Weber, Jim Fay. Camera Operators: Mark Lynch, Melissa Lynch, Dick Palmer, Jim Coglianese, Nina Bartlett, Steve Marty Nuik, Rick Pearrow, Kevin Garrison. Lighting Director: Jay Grindrod. Studio "D": Bill Tomlinson, Len O'Bannon, Alan Springer, John Sanborn. Acknowledgments: Dave Pool, Scooter Huller and Company, Main Street Operations, Carla Webb, Lydia Wickham. Announcer: Dick Tufeld.

WALT DISNEY WORLD HAPPY EASTER PARADE (1993 VERSION)

Executive Producer: Tom Elrod. Producer: Debra Muenchow. Supervising Producers: Jim DeRusha, Barbara Phillips, Jeff Palmer. Writers: Barbara Phillips, Dennis Chalifour. Director: Chico Fernandez. Assistant Producer: Maria Caccavo. Business Affairs: Maureen O'Donnell. Promotions: Caroline Nicholas, Chris Congdon. Advertising: Ginger Watters, Julie Woodward, Virginia Frederick. Publicity: Carole Monroe, Jennie Hess, Wallace Sears. *For Walt Disney World Creative Entertainment* Senior Show Producer: Douglas May. Show Director: George Koller. Production Manager: David Malvin. Music Director: Steve Skorija. Art Director: Rhonda Counts. Art Assistant: Cheryl Johnson. Choreographers: Corey Bendict, Gary Coburn, Deena Freeman, Rennie Gold, Gina Vaughn. Production Assistant: Lori Stephens. Editors: Tom Heckbert, Sam Patterson. Tape Operators: Kathy Beyers, Andy Ebert, Pete Yelverton, Lonnie Blackburn, Beth Brizio-Bufano. Graphic Designer: Eddie Pasquarello. Post Production Audio: Kurt Wagner, Rob Hill. Manager of Magic Kingdom Characters: Darlene Kennedy. Parade Production Supervisors: Cathy Arnott, Mike Wharton. Character Supervisors: Sandy Hawkins, Lynda Wilson. Staging Assistants: Jodie Gergley, Suzie Lalone, Beth Scammon, Kathy Shaffer, Meri Tortorice, Lori Linamen, Tom White-Spunner, Christine Schornagle. Guest Talent Programs: Paul Chiaravalle, Dan Stamper, Jim Simmons, John Torrito. Unit Production Manager: Tricia Ferdon. Production Coordinator: Kristan Kosh. Talent Coordinator: Louise Claiborne. Stage Managers: Brad Moore, Trish Weinstock. Production Secretary: Stace Howen. Production Designer: Jeff Chandler. Set Decorators: Sharon Tannian, Jean Lloyd. Production Assistants: Chris Debeic, Jean Barley, Jason Grey, Jim Weathers. Lighting Director: Jay Grinrod. Gaffer: Terry Neudecker. Electrics: Pat Knowles, Pat Meng. Engineer: Ray Lego. Technical Director: Joy Grow. Video Operators: Dennis Michels, Gary Jones. VTR Operators: Pete Court, Bill Lorenz. Chyron Operator: T.L. Grant-Harper. Teleprompter Operator: Bill Lulowe. Cue Cards: Tom Postel. Camera Operators: Richie Banales, Nina Bartlett, Rick Pearrow, Mark Lynch, Jim Coglianese, Dick Palmer, Steve

Martynuik. Aerial Photography: Preston Ewen, George Schaassma. Audio Supervisor: Dave Mouery. Audio: Jim Fay, Steve Weber, Cliff Harbin, Matt Gordon, Sharon Larson, Steve Puryea, Dan Pyne, Don Youngs, Fed Wetherbee, George Moshonas, Jack Somerville. Utilities: Eric Bills, K.C. Lee, Warren Jones, Brent Wilson. Crane Operators: Ray Dettore, Kevin Burke, Christopher Nye, Larry Shure. Cam-Remote Technician: Kenny Rivenbark. Hair and Make-up: Paulette Joiner-Schoen, David Polin, Winslow White. Wardrobe: Tracey Ferrena, Michelle Fischer. Studio "D": Bill Thomlinson, Joe Fanelli, Len O'Bannon, John Sanborn, Alan Springer.

WALT DISNEY WORLD HAPPY EASTER PARADE (1994 VERSION)

Executive Producer: Tom Elrod. Producer: Debra Muenchow. Supervising Producers: Jim DeRusha, Barbara Phillips, Jeff Palmer. Writers: Barbara Phillips, Dennis Chalifour. Segment Producers: Maria Caccavo, Jimmy Huckaby, Kitt McCleod. Creative Consultant: Peter Israelson. Business Affairs: Maureen O'Donnell. Promotions: Caroline Nicholas, Sue Nelson, Chris Congdon. Publicity: Wallace Sears, Jennie Hess. Advertising: Julie Woodward, Virginia Frederick. *For Walt Disney World Creative Entertainment* Senior Show Producer: Douglas May. Show Director: George Koller. Production Manager: David Malvin. Production Assistant: Miguel Berrios. Music Directors: Steve Skorija, Dan Stamper. Art Directors: Rhonda Counts, Cheryl Johnson. Choreographers: Judy Lawrence, Corey Bendict, Gary Coburn, Jim E. Ames, Denise Case, Deena Freeman, Doug Jack. Editors: Sam Patterson, Pete Opotowsky, Grace Machado, Robert Douglas. Tape Operators: Kathy Beyers, Andy Ebert, Pete Yelverton, Lonnie Blackburn, Calvin Kesterson, Beth Brizio-Bufano. Graphics Design: Vince Pedulla. Chyron: T.L. Harper. Post Production Audio: Kurt Wagner, Dave Howe, Dorrie Batten, Anthony Renda, Fred Venaglia. Parade Production Supervisors: Mike Wharton, Connie Willis. Unit Production Manager: Tricia Ferdon. Production Coordinator: Kristan Kosh. Talent Coordinator: Susan Garra. Stage Manager: Brad Moore. Production Designer: Jeff Chandler. Set Decorators: John DePiro, Sharon Tannian, Michel Norris, Bill Little. Production Assistants: Jason Grey, Mary Kay Minelli, Sundy Morgan, Tom Postel, Jim Weathers. Talent Assistants: Lisa Cassidy, Karen Kosh, Dan Severson. Lighting Directors: Jay Grinrod, Terry Neudecker. Electrics: David Bowling, Chip Neufield, Heath Goodwin. Engineers in Charge: Ric Wetherbee, Gary Jones. Technical Director: Joy Grow. Video Operators: Linda Tutten, Mike Rubin, Ray Lego. Camera Operators: Mark Lynch, Nina Bartlett, Melissa Lynch, Les Howard. Audio Mixers: Jim Fay, Dan Pyne. Audio Technicians: Jim McCabe, Don Youngs, George Moshonas, Curt Coniglio, Tim Stringfellow, Bow Owens, Jack Somerville. Utilities: Paul Skipper, Rick Foti, Lisa Moye, Chris Nye, Al Bogart, Jerry Meibos. Crane Operator: Ray Dettore. Crane Assist: Mike Larson. Cam-Remote Technician: Christopher Nye. Hair and Make-up: Paulette Schoen, Doug Marvaldi, Yolanda Winters, Hubert Kennedy. Wardrobe: Cathy Cox, Lori Loftis, George Milstead, Frankie Robinson. Announcer: Dick Tufeld.

WALT DISNEY WORLD HAPPY EASTER PARADE (1995 VERSION)

Executive Producer: Tom Elrod. Producer: Debra Muenchow. Supervising Producers: Jim DeRusha, Barbara Phillips, Jeff Palmer. Directed by: Chico Fernandez. Written by: Barbara Phillips. Executive in Charge of Production: Tom Boles. Segments Directed by: Peter Israelson, L. David Irete, Jeff Palmer. Talent Executive: Eileen Rahman. Production Designer: Jimbo Marshall. Production Supervisor: Emily Zolten. Talent Coordinator: Suzy Garra. Segment Coordinator: Mark Krumper. Set Decorator: Sharon Tannian. Post Production Coordinator: Jim Weathers. Production Coordinator: Laurie Zuckerman. Talent Assistants: Delise DelFavero, Susan Janis-Mashayekhi, M. Elizabeth Sachs. Production Assistants: Penny Renee Gerstenslager, Dan Severson, James Stuart. *For Walt Disney World Creative Entertainment* Producer: Douglas May. Parade Show Created by: George Koller. Production Manager: David Malvin. Production Assistant: Lori Stephens. Art Director: Cheryl Johnson. Music Producer: Dan Stamper. Guest Talent Programs: Paul Chiaravalle. Choreog-

raphers: Corey Benedict, Deena Freeman, Laura Kelly, Tom White-Spunner, Valerie Raskin, Meri Tortorese, Gina Puglese, Valerie Weld, Suzie Lalone, Russell Sultzbach, Christine Schornagle. Float Audio: Doug Larsen. Character Department Supervisors: Heidi Macklin, Suzanne Burton, Mike Wharton. Associate Director: Jeff Palmer. Stage Managers: Buck Allen, Dave Cove. Location Coordinator: Brad Moore. Technical Director: Stacy Rothwell. Engineering Supervisor: Larry Gaetano. Engineer in Charge: Ric Wetherbee. Engineer: Gary Jones. Video Control: Hans Muster, Al Bogart. Videotape Operator: Bill Thomas. Cameras: John Atkinson, John Bender, Neal Gallagher, Bill Giglio, L. David Irete, Mark Lynch, Melissa Lynch, Dick Palmer. Underwater Camera: Jordan Klein. Camera Remote Technicians: Steve Martyniuk, John Pivovarnick. Camera Utilities: Mark Austin, Eric Bills, Tom Jandersit, Lisa Moye, Chris Nye, Charles Oettel, Linda Tutten, Fed Wetherbee. Infinit!: T.L. Grant Harper. Lighting Director: Nick Woolfolk. Gaffers: John Peters, J.R. Roberson. Best Boy: Mike Gooseman. Electrics: Tim McGuire, Del Moody, Terry Neudecker. Audio Supervisor: Dave Mouery. Audio Mixer: John deRussy. Assistant Mixer: Don Youngs. P.A. Mixers: Don Mutschler, Curt Coniglio. A-2: Pat Ayotte, George Moshonas, Steve Puryea, Jack Somerville, Tim Stringfellow, Nils Warren. Studio D Audio: John Sanborn, Cliff Harbin, Joe Fanelli. Truck Maintenance: Steve Webber, Greg Belotte, Bill Morris. Editors: Kathy Beyers, Pete Opotowsky, Sam Patterson, Gary Wood. Tape Operators: Lonnie Blackburn, Calvin Kesterson, Paul Whidden, F. Doug Harley. Post Production Audio: Kurt Wagner, Brad Simpson. Key Costumer: Cathy Cox. Wardrobe Assistants: Lori Loftis, George Milstead. Hair/Make-up: Mark Fonzi, Hubert Kennedy, Paulette Schoen, Yolanda Winters. Business Affairs: Larry Haber. Promotions: Bob Gosselin. Publicity: Wallace Sears, Jennie Hess. Advertising: Julie Woodward. Announcer: Dick Tufeld.

WALT DISNEY WORLD HAPPY EASTER PARADE (1996 VERSION)

Executive Producer: Debra Muenchow. Producer: Barbara Phillips. Supervising Producer: Jeff Palmer. Directed by: Glenn Weiss. Written by: Judy Katschke. Executive in Charge of Production: Mark Rains. Segments Directed by: David Irete, Jimmy Huckaby. Associate Director: Gregg Gelfand. Music Producer: Marc Ellis. Production Designer: Jimbo Marshall. Production Supervisor: Stephanie J. Rondeau. Production Managers: Kristan Kosh, Susan Janis-Mashayekhi. Script Coordinator: Kasha Rafkin. Talent Supervisor: Karen Tasch-Weiss. Post Production Coordinator: Doug Harley. Production Coordinator: Tina Ostermeyer. Assistant to the Producer: Emily Zolten. Production Secretary: Lynn Antoniak. Production Assistants: Sharon Boehm, Dave Cundiff, Deanna Easterday, Jose Hernandez, Louie Iturri, Chip Monk, Iris Pearson, Steve Plastow, Geno Teofilo, Stephanie Purdy, Whitney Quillin, Colleen Tomlinson. Talent Assistants: Toni-Marie Martinez, Timothy Ovorachek, Delise Del Favero. *Walt Disney Attractions Entertainment* Producer: Matt Conover. Entertainment Director: George Koller. Assistant to the Director: Corey Benedict. TV Choreographer: Kenneth Green. Production Manager: Wayne Gagne. Production Stage Manager: Michael Harrod. Production Assistants: Bruce Wolfe, Angela Story-Krug. *Magic Kingdom Entertainment* Parade Management Team: Gene Harding, Miguel Berrios, Winnie Clark, Heidi Macklin. Props: Patti Smith. Magic Music Days: Carol Liberti. Parade Audio: Keith Miller, Jeff Parker, Leno O'Bannon, Joe Knapp. Costumer: Marion Barnum. Assistant Costumer: Frankie Robinson. Assistant Art Director: Sharon Tannian. Stage Managers: Dave Cove, Wendy Dawson, Vicki Hladik, Jeff Palmer. Technical Director: Eric Becker. Engineering Supervisors: Lisa Moye, Ric Wetherbee. Video Control: Paul Ranieri, Linda Tutten. Videotape Operators: Kathy Beyers, David E.R. Harper, Carlos Torres, Paul Whidden. Cameras: John Atkinson, Richie Banales, Mike Breece, Bob Del Russo, Neal Gallagher, Tom Galloway, Pat Gleason, Tommy Hildreth, Mike Lacey, Melissa Lynch, Jake Ostroff, Bob Van Dorn, Easter Xua. Lighting Director: Jay Grindrod. Audio Mixer: Jim Fay. Assistant Mixers: Gary Baldassari, Jim Van Winkle. Assistant Audio: Curt Coniglio, George Moshonas, Tom Muczio, Kenneth Neeley, Jack Somerville,

Nils Warren, Tim Wilson, Don Youngs. LMG-Teleprompter: Jennifer Schemm. Editors: Jeff Palmer, Sam Patterson, Mike Willets. Assistant Editor: Doug Harley. Post Production Audio: Rob Hill, Kurt Wagner. Wardrobe: Lori Loftis. Hair/-Make-up: Mark Fonzi, Hubert Kennedy, Regina Perron, Paulette Schoen, Yolanda Winters. Business Affairs: Larry Haber, Eileen Rahman. Promotions: Bob Gosselin. Publicity: Wallace Sears, Mark Jaronski, Amber Morris. Advertising: Patrick Grinnals. Announcer: Dick Tufeld.

WALT DISNEY WORLD VERY MERRY CHRISTMAS PARADE (1983 VERSION)
Directed by: Chico Fernandez. Narration Written by: Doug Cody. Production Consultant: Tom Elrod. Parade Production: Dennis Despie. Field Production: Robert M. Allen. Acknowledgments: James Mathis, Emmett Depoy, Mike Mathis, David Depoy, Chip Bickmann, Jack Eskew, Michael Hurley, Ron Logan, Pam McKissick, Maureen O'Donnell, Barnette Ricci. Produced by Broadcast Communications Inc. in Cooperation with Walt Disney World Company in association with BCI Television. Distributed by SFM.

WALT DISNEY WORLD VERY MERRY CHRISTMAS PARADE (1984 VERSION)
Produced by: Broadcast Communications, Inc. In Association with: Walt Disney World Co. Executive in Charge of Production: Thomas Elrod. Associate Production Executive: Robert M. Allen. Written by: Doug Cody, Dee Hansford. Directed by: Julio Fernandez. Production Coordinator: Bob Williams. Advertising: Chip Eickmann. Parade Production: Dennis M. Despie. Acknowledgments: Sonny Anderson, Gary Baldassari, Rich Banales, John Bender, Jeff Chandler, Bobbi Colguitt, Tom Cormier, Greg Emmer, Nancy Eskew, Beth Gillette, Mike Gooseman, Nina Graham, Cliff Harbin, Les Howard, Hank Johnson, Gary W. Jones, Judy Lawrence, Ron Logan, Mark Lynch, Roger Lynch, Jim Mathis, Mike Mathis, Pat McKissick, Jim Moroney, Dave Mouery, Todd Nichols, Maureen O'Donnell, Gary Paben, Jim Pare, Ted Ricketts, Judy Roberson, Diane C. Royal, Jay Smith, Rich Taylor, Bill Tomlinson, Melissa Wright.

WALT DISNEY WORLD VERY MERRY CHRISTMAS PARADE (1985 VERSION)
Produced by: Robert M. Allen. Directed by: Julio Fernandez. Written by: Doug Cody, Dee Hansford. Assistant Producer: Doug Cody.

WALT DISNEY WORLD VERY MERRY CHRISTMAS PARADE (1986 VERSION)
Executive Producer: Tom Elrod. Produced by: Robert M. Allen, Doug Cody. Associate Producers: Bruce Brown, Bob Williams. Written by: Lisa Yee. Director: Julio Fernandez. Production Coordinator: Matt Sites. Segment Production: Robert M. Allen, Bruce Brown, Doug Cody, Dee Hansford, Lisa Yee. Lighting Designer: Todd Nichols. Advertising: Chip Eickmann. Publicity: John Dreyer. Talent Coordination: Sonny Anderson, Bobbi Colguitt, Nancy Eskew. Administrative Affairs: Maureen O'Donnell. Post Production: Edward Johnson, Gary Jones, Jeff Palmer. Musical Director: Ted Ricketts. Technical Supervisor: Jim Pare'. Technical Director: Joy Grow. Engineering: Larry Gaetano, Eddie Perez, John Roche. Audio: Gary Baldassari, Dave Mouery, Allen Slansky, Bill Tomlinson, Steve Weber. Electronic Graphics: Wanda Collis. Video: Wayne Parker, R. E. Lanier, Cliff Wright, Leo Boucher, Bob Hunter. Set Designer: Jeff Chandler. Camera: Nina Graham, Les Howard, Hank Johnson, Roger Lynch, Mark Lynch, Dick Palmer, Doug Ramsey, Melissa Wright. Steadicam: Rich Banales. Crew Lead: Mike Gooseman. Grips: John Bender, Rick Campbell, Jim Fay, Jay Grindrod, Terry Neudecker, Wayne Parker, Jody Roberson, Chuck Smith. Production Assistants: Kim Gunther, Ray Marchant, Clay Newbill, Sonya Smith, Dave Ousley. Parade Concept: John Dreyer, Dennis Despie, Barnette Ricci. Staging Directors: Judy Lawrence, Jay Smith. Parade Production: Michael O'Grattan, Darlene Faber, Julie Kirchen. Uplink: Bruce Byson, Tom Cormier. Acknowledgments: Linda Affhalter, Buck Allen, David Atchison, Mark Baker, Jerry Banales, Tom Bisignano, Kenny Britton, Bill Burns, Cliff Callaway, Jim Cambell, Robert Carlton, Jeff

Crutchfield, Mike Davis, Doug Dinkel, Norm Doerges, Robert Garrett, Richard Halpern, Bobby Hopps, Penny Holtzclaw, Jimmy Huckaby, Scooter Huller, David Justice, Derek Johnson, Scott Linder, Grace Machado, Jim Macphee, Holly McCammack, Robin McCullough, Deb Muenchow, Rose Saumell, Terry Schwartz, Charley Posner, Jack Somerville, Susan Sims, Bill Sullivan, Rich Taylor. Produced by: Broadcast Communications, Inc. in association with Walt Disney World. This Program is Dedicated to the Memory of James B. Mathis. Announcer: Dick Tufeld.

WALT DISNEY WORLD VERY MERRY CHRISTMAS PARADE (1987 VERSION)
Executive Producer: Tom Elrod. Produced by: Bruce Brown, Lisa Yee. Supervising Producer: Robert M. Allen. Writer: Lisa Yee. Directed by: Julio Fernandez. Associate Producer: Matt Sites. Segment Producer: David Pool. Segment Directors: Rich Banales, Hank Johnson, Dick Palmer, Melissa Wright. Post Production Supervisor: Gary Jones. Editors: Edward E. Johnson, Jeff Palmer, Grace Machado. Advertising: Chip Eickmann. Production Coordinators: Sonya Smith, Clay Newbill. Lighting Designers: Todd Nichols, Jay Grinrod. Assistant Director: Dan Nabors. Musical Director: Ted Ricketts. Technical Supervisor: Bruce Bryson. Technical Director: Joy Grow. Engineering: Marvin Kale, Terry McIntyre, Joe Stovcsik. Audio: Steve Weber, Bill Tomlinson, David Mouery, Gary Baldassari, Jim Fay, Allen Slansky, Len O'Bannon. Video: Al Chestelson, Mike Dunn. Videotape: Cliff Wright. Graphics: Wanda J. Collis, Bob Krawczyk, Jim Noble, H.R. Russell. Set Designer: Jeff Chandler. Camera: Nina Graham, Les Howard, Mark Lynch, Roger Lynch, Dick Palmer, Melissa Wright, Stuart Allen. Steadicam: Rich Banales. Technicians: John Bender, Rick Campbell, Mike Gooseman, R.E. Lanier, David Miller, Terry Neudecker, Chuck Smith, Jerry Banales, Bruce Blackman. Drivers: Sam Rackham, Charles Monroe. Crane Operators: Mike Gooseman, Jody Roberson, Joe Grenon, Mike Laninfa. Stage Manager: Buck Allen. Production Assistants: Laura Broome, Jim Campbell, Joel Kostuch, Jack Somerville, Don Mascheri. Publicity: John Dreyer, Tom Brinkmoeller. Talent Booking: Sonny Anderson, Bobbi Colguitt, Nancy Eskew. Parade Staging Directors: Jay Smith, Judy Lawrence. Parade Production: Michael O'Grattan, Darlene Kennedy, Julie Kirchen. WorldLink Satellite: Tom Cormier, Bruce Bryson. Administrative Affairs: Maureen O'Donnell. Acknowledgments: Mary Barnett & Crew, Willy Brahm, Bill Burns, Paul Charvielle, Jeff Crutchfield, Jamie Dixon, Mike Davis, Mike Fletcher, Dee Hansford, Rick Harbin, Penny Holtzclaw, Scooter Huller, Paulette Joiner, Donald Jones, Laurie Kelley, Jim MacPhee, Holly McCammack, Debra Muenchow, Gail Schmidt, Jim Simmons, Linda Stayer, Murray Summerville, Joanne Wabisca, Tedd Wright. This Parade is Dedicated to the Memory of Robert C. Allen. Produced by TELX Entertainment in association with Walt Disney World.

WALT DISNEY WORLD VERY MERRY CHRISTMAS PARADE (1988 VERSION)
Executive Producer: Tom Elrod. Produced by: Debra Muenchow. Supervising Producer: David Pool. Writer: Barbara Phillips. Directed by: Chico Fernandez. Unit Manager: Clay Newbill. Segment Producers: Barbara Phillips, David Pool, Jim DeRusha. *Caribbean Segment* Director: Peter Israelson. Director of Photography: Michael Negrin. *At Disneyland* Supervising Producer: Ron Kollen. Segment Producer: John A. Lee. Producer: Steve Carroll. Writer: Dave Lancashire. Staging Director/Choreographer: Barnette Ricci. *Walt Disney World* Show Directors: Gary Paben, Jay Smith. Project Manager: Bettina Buckley. Musical Director: Ted Ricketts. Choreographers: Ronnie DeMarco, Robbie Mackey. Parade Production: Sharon Madill. Assistant Director: Dan Nabors. Segment Directors: Rich Banales, Roger Lynch, Dick Palmer. Post Production Supervisor: Jeff Palmer. Editors: Eddie Johnson, Grace Machado, Jeff Palmer. Advertising: Chip Eickmann, Alan Humphrey. Production Coordinators: Jim Campbell, Laura Broome, Jack Somerville. 2nd Unit Manager: Linda Lenzen. Celebrity Talent Coordinator: Sonya Weathers. Lighting Designers: Jay Grinrod, Danny Harvey. Engineering Supervisor: David Jones. Technical Supervisor: Larry Gaetano. Maintenance Engineering Support: Bill Morse, Dean Pearson. Tech-

nical Director: Joy Grow. Audio: David Mouery, Steve Weber. Walt Disney World Production Crew: Cathy Arnott, Gary Baldassari, Jerry Banales, Rich Banales, John Bender, Tom Berger, Bruce Blackman, Roger Braunstein, Tom Brinkmoeller, Kenny Brittain, Bruce Brown, Bill Burns, Maria Caccavo, Rick Campbell, James Carter, Jim Fay, Eric Carr, Les Goldberg, Pat Caudle, Gary Gorbet, Jeff Chandler, Nina Bartlett, Chris Congdon, Chris Henry, Tom Cormier, Scooter Huller, Jeff Crutchfield, Hank Johnson, John Cummings, Jeff Kaufholz, Ray Detori, Mark Lynch, Pat Knowles, Roger Lynch, Patrick Logan, Bruce Merwin, Polly Ann Mattson, Lee Thomas, Maureen O'Donnell, Jimmy Van Winkle, Dick Palmer, Gary Ware, Doug Ramsey, Charlie Weaver, Allen Slansky, John Stevens, Joseph Stovcsik, Abby Smith, Amy Storti, Cliff Wright, Mary Schmidt, J.R. Roberson, Bill Tomlinson, Stu Sponger, Melissa Wright, Frank Wynn. Announcer: Dick Tufeld. Produced by: TELX Entertainment in association with Walt Disney World.

WALT DISNEY WORLD VERY MERRY CHRISTMAS PARADE (1989 VERSION)
Executive Producer: Tom Elrod. Produced by: Debra Muenchow. Supervising Producer: Jim DeRusha. Writer: Barbara Phillips. Directed by: Chico Fernandez. Assistant Director: Jeff Palmer. Segment Producers: Jim DeRusha, Barbara Phillips, David Pool. Associate Producers: Sharon Dusley, Stanise Richardson. Entertainment Show Director: Douglas May. Segment Directors: Peter Israelson, Richie Banales, Dick Palmer. From Disneyland Supervising Producer/Writer: John A. Lee. Producer: Al Henderson. Line Producer: Dale Lanier. Director: Lee Ollerton. Business Affairs: Maureen O'Donnell. Unit Managers: Jim Campbell, Clay Newbill. Stage Managers: Laura Broome, Maria Caccavo. Advertising: Chip Eickmann. Promotions: Caroline Nicholas. Show Timer: Jerry Johns. Talent Coordinator: Sonya Weathers. Production Coordinators: Tricia Ferndon, Jack Somerville. Project Manager: Ken Harris. Production Stage Manager: Nancy Hart. Music Director: Ted Ricketts, Dan Stamper. Choreographers: Doug Jack, Pam Killinger, Sheri Lyn Draper, Robbie Mackey. Magic Kingdom Entertainment: Mike O'Grattan, Darlene Kennedy. Production Assistants: Louise Clairborne, Marsha Groome, Lisa Haskins, Brad Moore, Alison Swanson. Art Director: Jimbo Marshall. Production Secretary: Stacey Howen. Video Editors: Art David, Eddie Johnson, Jeff Palmer, Grace Machado. Video Graphics: Eddie Pasquarello. Engineering Manager: David Jones. Satellite Operations: Tom Cormier. Video: Ric Wetherbee, Ray Lego, Jim Pare. Video Tape: Gary Jones, Pat Caudle, Cliff Wright. Technical Director: Joy Grow. Chyron: Margaret Mack. Remote Engineers: Marvin Kale, Terry McIntyre. Parade Production: Sharon Madill. Assistant Director: Dan Nabors. Staging Director/Choreographer: Barnette Ricci. Walt Disney World Show Directors: Gary Paben, Jay Smith. Project Manager: Bettina Buckley. Cameras: Les Howard, Dave Treiber, Melissa Wright, Richie Banales, Steve Martyniuk, Paul Klekotta, Bill Papp, Dick Palmer, Roger Lynch, Mark Lynch, John Bender, Mike Gorentlo, Ken Kavanaugh, Joe Kelman. Teleprompter: Bill Lulow. Lighting Director: Jay Grinrod. Electrics: Warren Jones, Arnold Tucker, Arnie Smith, Gill Richardson, Gary Bristow, Clay McMillan. Camera Utilities: Chip Neufeld, John Tegethoff, Lee Thomas, Billie Mead, Lisa Moye. Crew Chief: Terry Hilton. Utility Grips: James Carter, Dan Cornett, Bobby Taylor, Todd Kramer, Don Gillis. Crane Operators: Ray Dettore, Alan Solomon. Crane Assistants: Steve Grnya, K.C. Lee, Kenny Rivenbark. Audio Supervisor: David Mouery. Audio Mixers: Steve Weber, Andy deGanahl. Audio Utilities: Don Youngs, Kris Barns, Dan Pyne, Tom Lewis, Allen Slansky, Buddy Levett, Jim Fay, Len O'Bannon, Brian Casey, Bill Tomlinson, John DeRussey, George Moshonas. Acknowledgments: John Atkinson, Paul Bosch, Robert Braunstein, Kenny Brittain, Bull Burns, Bill Bunting, Glen Burdette, John Cummings, Ed Disney, Debby Donarski, Jane Gilane, Scooter Huller, Gary Jennings, Hank Johnson, Patrick Logan, Vernon McGugan, Cal McWhorter, Ray Phares, Di Pittman, Joann Santulli, Ethelyn Spires, George Spires, Stu Sponger, Ben Taylor, Margaret Thornton, Casey Yadon, Jerome Ravenna.

WALT DISNEY WORLD VERY MERRY CHRISTMAS PARADE (1990 VERSION)
Executive Producer: Tom Elrod. Producer: Debra Muenchow. Supervising Producer: Jim DeRusha. Writers: Barbara Phillips, Merrily Terry. Directed by: Chico Fernandez. Segment Producers: Wayne Stuart, David Pool, Dan O'Loane, Ruth Gaskin. Assistant to the Producers: Andrea Patrizzi. Segment Director: Peter Israelson. For Walt Disney World Creative Entertainment Show Director/Producer: Doug May. Production Manager: Ken Harris. Music Directors: Ted Ricketts, Dan Stamper. Production Stage Manager: R.K. Little. Lead Choreographer: Pam Killinger. Character Supervision: Simon Penny. Parade Supervision: Heidi Macklin, Mike Wharton. For Disneyland Production Executives: Henry Caroselli, Jackie Schneider. Supervising Producer: Brad Tallman. Director: Rick Squire. Producers: Dale Lanier, Royce Steele. Business Affairs: Maureen O'Donnell. Promotions: Caroline Nicholas, Terri Gallagher. Production Secretary: Stace Howen. Editors: Jeff Palmer, Art David, Sam Patterson, Jim Mancini, Grace Machado-Arnold. Assistant Editors: Scott Miller, Tom Heckbert, Rob Mobley, Mike Coe. Unit Production Managers: Sonya Weathers, Jim Campbell. Production Coordinator: Trish Weinstock. Show Timer: Jerry Johns. Talent Coordinator: Janie Unger. Stage Manager: Laura Broome. Hair/Make-up: Angela Hewitt, Paulette Joiner, Penny Johnson, Tish Simpson. Production Designer: Jeff Chandler. Art Director: Jim Sheridan. Set Decorators: Jim Weather, John Cox, Jay Weber, Miquel DeJesus, John DePiro. Chief Engineer: Larry Gaetano. Engineers: Doug Berry, Mike Jones, Ray Lego. Technical Director: Joy Grow. Electronic Graphics: T.L. Grant. Video: Craig Bulmer, Jeff Court. Videotape Operators: Bill Thomas, Ric Wetherbee. Audio Supervisor: Dave Mouery. Audio Mixers: Jim Fay, Steve Weber. Audio Assists: John DeRussey, Jim McCabe, George Moshonas, Dan Pyne, Allen Slansky, Don Youngs. Cameras: Rich Banales, John Bender, Les Howard, Mark Lynch, Roger Lynch, Bruce Merwyn, Dick Palmer, Bill Papp, David Treiber, Melissa Wright, Steve Martyniuk. Studio "D": Bill Tomlinson, Len O'Bannon, Joe Fanelli, Cliff Harbin, James Glass. Lighting Directors: Todd Nichols, Jay Grindrod. Key Grip: Rick Campbell. Electricians: Gary Bristow, Terry Neudecker. Crane Operator: Ray Detorre. Crane Assists: Steve Grnya, Kenny Rivenbark, Alan Soloman. Production Assistants: Brad Moore, Kristan Kosh, Jerome Ravenna, Suzanne LaFace, John Rogers, Chris Debiec, Tracy Veler-Grindrod. Production Scheduler: Lydia Wickham. Acknowledgments: Stephanie Allen, Jim Ashe, John Atkinson, Tim Wolters, Bill Bunting, Djuan Rivers, Linda Beach, Iiersa Dennis, Di Pittman, Anita Wilson, Gary Edmonsen, Trish Ferdon, Scooter Huller, Bob Lamb, John Moss, Ed Disney & Crew, Van Bunting, Darryl Stokes, Karen Martin, Kenny Brittan & Crew, Robert Braunstein, U.S. Central Command in Dhahran, Saudi Arabia.

WALT DISNEY WORLD VERY MERRY CHRISTMAS PARADE (1991 VERSION)
Executive Producer: Tom Elrod. Producer: Debra Muenchow. Supervising Producers: Jim DeRusha, Barbara Phillips, Jeff Palmer. Writers: Barbara Phillips, Greg Ehrbar. Director: Chico Fernandez. Segment Producers: Ann Patrizzi, Brad Tallman, Gary Kurtz, Rod Madden. For Walt Disney World Creative Entertainment Senior Show Producer: Doug May. Associate Producer: Ken Harris. Show Director: Sherilyn Draper. Production Managers: Nancy Hart, Angie Howard. Musical Directors: Ted Ricketts, Dan Stamper. Choreographers: Gary Coburn, Denise Case. Art Director: Rhonda Counts. Audio Designer: Bob Owens. Production Assistants: Melinda Bell, Lisa Riley. Character Supervision: Sandy Hawkins, Darlene Kennedy, Lynda Wilson, Carl Bond, Mike Wharton. Staging Assistants: Beth Grayson, Suzie Lalone, Molly Piveral, Philip Steinbacher, Meri Tortorice, Cheri Wells, Tom White-Spunner. Business Affairs: Maureen O'Donnell. Promotions: Caroline Nicholas, Terri Gallagher. Advertising: Ginger Watters, Mark McNealy. Production Secretary: Stace Howen. Editors: Jeff Palmer, Art David, Grace Machado, Jim Mancini, Sam Patterson, Tom Heckbert. Assistant Editors: Kathy Beyers, Rob Mobley, Jeff Olm, Bob Scarborough, Gary Wood. Graphics: Eddie Pasquarello. Audio: Kurt Wagner, Rob Hill,

Brad Simpson, Dorrie Batten. Unit Production Manager: Sonya S. Weathers. Production Coordinators: Maria Caccavo, Kristen Kosh, Brad Moore. Talent Coordinator: Tracy Grindrod. Stage Manager: Trish Weinstock. Production Designer: Jeff Chandler. Set Decorators: Sharon Tannian, Tony Gabriel. Lighting Director: Jay Grindrod. Technical Supervisors: Larry Gaetano, Ray Lego. Technical Director: Joy Grow. Electronic Graphics: T.L. Grant. Video: Jeff Court, Dennis Michels. Videotape: Bill Thomas, Ric Wetherbee. Audio Supervisor: Dave Mouery. Audio Mixers: Jim Fay, Steve Weber, Andy DeGanahl. Camera Operators: Rich Banales, John Bender, Roger Lynch, Vince Vezzi, Steve Martyniuk, James Neihouse, Mark Lynch, Melissa Wright. Hair & Make-up: Paulette Joiner, Angela Raper, Yolanda Winters, Regina Perron. Production Assistants: Wendy Dawson, Sonja Jones, Jeanette Alderman, Alan Levi. Studio "D": Bill Tomlinson, Joe Fanelli, James Glass, Len O'Bannon, Cliff Harbin. Announcer: Dick Tufeld.

WALT DISNEY WORLD VERY MERRY CHRISTMAS PARADE (1992 VERSION)

Executive Producer: Tom Elrod. Producer: Debra Muenchow. Supervising Producers: Jim DeRusha, Barbara Phillips, Jeff Palmer. Writers: Barbara Phillips, Dennis Chalifour. Director: Chico Fernandez. Segment Producers: Maria Caccavo, Ann Patrizzi. Research: Greg Ehrbar. Business Affairs: Maureen O'Donnell. Promotions: Caroline Nicholas, Chris Congdon. Advertising: Ginger Watters, Julie Woodward, Virginia Frederick. *For Walt Disney World Creative Entertainment* Senior Show Producer: Douglas May. Show Director: Sherilyn Draper. Production Manager: Nancy Hart. Production Stage Manager: Angie Howard. Musical Directors: Ted Ricketts, Steve Skorija. Art Director: Rhonda Counts. Choreographers: Denise Case, Gary Coburn, Gina Vaughn. Production Assistants: Lori Stevens, Cheryl Johnson. Editors: Art David, Tom Heckbert, Ed Johnson, Grace Machado, Jim Mancini, Sam Patterson. Tape Operators: Kathy Beyers, Andy Ebert, Rob Mobley, Gary Wood, Calvin Kesterson, Beth Brizio-Bufano, Pete Yelverton. Graphic Design: Eddie Pasquarello. Post Production Audio: Kurt Wagner, Don Rogozinski. *For Disneyland* Supervising Producer: Brad Tallman. Producer: Gary Kurtz. Parade Production Services: Tom Cundiff, Mike Wharton. Character Supervision: Sandy Hawkins, Lynda Wilson. Staging Assistants: Jody Bergley, Suzie Lalone, Kathy Shaffer, Tom White-Spunner. Guest Talent Programs: Paul Chiaravalle. Unit Production Managers: Sonya S. Weathers, Tricia Ferdon. Technical Supervisors: Larry Gaetano, Ray Lego. Production Coordinator: Kristan Kosh. Talent Coordinator: Janie Unger. Stage Managers: Trish Weinstock, Jim Weathers, Brad Moore. Production Secretary: Stace Howen. Production Designer: Jeff Chandler. Set Decorators: Sharon Tannian, Jonna Schneeman. Production Assistants: Chris Debeic, Vanessa Rose Ioppolo, Gina Williams, Gerald Wu. Lighting Director: Jay Grindrod. Gaffer: Rick Campbell. Best Boy: Pat Knowles. Electrics: Steve Grnya, Gary Bristow. Engineers: Lynn Peggs, Bill Morse. Technical Director: Joy Grow. Video Operators: Vince Vezzi, Ric Wetherbee. Videotape: Ryals Thomas, Bill Moore, Jr. Chyron Operator: T.L. Grant-Harper. Teleprompter Operator: Bill Lulowe. Camera Operators: Richie Banales, Eric Bills, Les Howard, Mark Lynch, Melissa Lynch, Dick Palmer, Steve Martyniuk. Aerial Photography: Ken Sanborn. Audio Supervisor: Dave Mouery. Audio Mixers: Jim Fay, Steve Weber. Audio: John DeRussey, Dan Pyne, Jim McCabe, Don Youngs, Sharon Larson, Don Munschler, Gary Baldassari, Alan Slansky, George Moshonas. Utilities: Bill Mead, K.C. Lee, Jerry Meibos, Lisa Moye, Fed Wetherbee. Crane Operators: Ray Dettore, Kevin Burke. Cam-Remote Technician: Chris Nye. Hair & Make-up: Paulette Joiner-Schoen, Angela Raper, Regina Perron. Wardrobe: Kathy Cox, George Milstead. Studio "D": Bill Tomlinson, Cliff Harbin, Joe Fanelli, Len O'Bannon, John Sanborn, Alan Springer.

WALT DISNEY WORLD VERY MERRY CHRISTMAS PARADE (1993 VERSION)

Executive Producer: Tom Elrod. Producer: Debra Muenchow. Supervising Producers: Jim DeRusha, Barbara Phillips, Jeff Palmer. Writers: Barbara Phillips, Dennis Chalifour. Director: Chico Fernandez. Segment Producers: Maria Caccavo, Ann Patrizzi. Creative Consultant: Peter Israelson. Business Affairs: Maureen O'Donnell. Promotions: Caroline Nicholas, Chris Congdon. Publicity: Pam Brandon, Wallace Sears, Tom Lowe. Advertising: Ginger Watters, Virginia Frederick. Senior Producer: Douglas May. Show Director: Sherilyn Draper. Production Manager: David Malvin. Musical Directors: Steve Skorija, Ted Ricketts. Orchestrator: Gordon Goodwin. Art Director: Rhonda Counts. Associate Art Director: Cheryl Johnson. Talent Booking: Patti Craven. Choreographers: Denise Case, Gary Coburn, Betsy Glover, Rennie Gold, Robbie Mackey. Creative Costuming: Douglas Enderlee, Cathy Cox, Frankie Robinson, Hune DeBott, Susan Rovacik, Rasha Carney, Susan Schmideler, George Milstead. Production Assistant: Lori Stevens. Editors: Art David, Sam Patterson, Eddie Johnson, Gary Wood, Kathy Beyers, Pete Opotowsky. Tape Operators: Andy Ebert, Rob Mobley, Calvin Kesterson, Pete Mobley, Beth Brizio-Bufano. Graphic Design: Vince Pedulla, Tony Plett. Post Production Audio: Rob Hill, Dorrie Batten. Post Production P.A.: Jim Weathers. Post Production Scheduling: Christine Biondo. Parade Production Services: Gene Harding, Mike Wharton. Character Department: Darlene Kennedy, Sandy Hawkins, Lynda Wilson. Staging Assistants: Laura Kelly, Michelle Krallinger, Molly Piveral, Tom White-Spunner. Guest Talent Programs: Paul Chiaravalle. Unit Manager: Trish Ferdon. Production Coordinator: Kristan Kosh. Talent Coordinator: Suzy Garra. Stage Managers: Trish Weinstock, Brad Moore, Laura Roberson. Booth P.A.: Wendy Dawson. Production Designer: Jeff Chandler. Set Decorators: Jean Lloyd, Sharon Tannian, Jonna Schneeman. Production Assistants: Jason Grey, Chris Debeic, Colleen Tomlinson. Talent Assistants: Gina Mouery, Lisa Cassidy, Robert Teinowitz. Lighting Director: Rick Campbell. Gaffer: J.R. Roberson. Best Boy: Del Moody. Electrics: John Peters, Arnold Tucker, Lance Parrish, Tim McGuire. Engineers: Gary Jones, Larry Gaetano, Bill Morse, Lynn Peggs. Microwave Engineers: Bill Moore, Jr., Gene Mikell, Karl L. Smith, Charles Salvato. Technical Director: Joy Grow. Video Operators: Vince Vezzi, Ric Wetherbee. VTR Operators: Bill Thomas, Kevin McCabe. Chyron Operator: T.L. Grant-Harper. Teleprompter: Bill Ludlowe. Camera Operators: Richie Banales, Rick Pearson, Les Howard, Mark Lynch, Melissa Lynch, John Bender, Dick Palmer, Steve Martyniuk. Audio Supervisor: Dave Mouery. Audio Mixers: Steve Weber, Jim Fay. Assistant Mixer: John DeRussey. Audio Technicians: Jim McCabe, Don Youngs, George Moshonas, Dan Pyne, Don Munschler, Tim Stringfellow. Utilities: Demetrius Lewis, K.C. Lee, Mike Navage, Lisa Moye, Al Bogert, Fed Wetherbee. Crane Operators: Ray Dettore, Mike Larson. Crane Assists: Larry Shure, Jerry Meibos. Cam-Remote Tech: Christopher Nye. Hair/Make-up: Mark Fonzi, Paulette Schoen, Hubert Kennedy, Winslow White, Yolando Winters. Studio "D": Bill Tomlinson, Joe Fanelli, Cliff Harbin, Len O'Bannon, John Sanborn, Alan Springer. Announcer: Dick Tufeld.

WALT DISNEY WORLD VERY MERRY CHRISTMAS PARADE (1994 VERSION)

Executive Producer: Tom Elrod. Producer: Debra Muenchow. Supervising Producers: Jim DeRusha, Barbara Phillips, Jeff Palmer. Directed by: Chico Fernandez. Written by: Steve Pouliot. Executive in Charge of Production: Tom Boles. Segments Directed by: Peter Israelson, Jimmy Huckaby, L. David Irete. Segment Producer: Gary Turchin. Production Designer: Jimbo Marshall. Talent Executive: Eileen Rahman. Production Managers: Tricia Fedon, Charles Dafoe. Technical Supervisor: Larry Gaetano. Talent Coordinator: Suzy Garra. Script P.A.: Emily Zolten. Booth P.A.: Wendy Dawson. Set Decorator: Sharon Tannian. Production Coordinator: Kristan Kosh. Post Production Coordinator: Jim Weathers. Production Secretaries: Delise Delfavero, Laurie Zuckerman. Talent Assistants: Lisa Haskins, Susan Janis. Production Assistants: Suzie Lalone, Robert Fleming, Jason Grey, Dan Severson. *For Disneyland* Supervising Producer: Brad Tallman. Disneyland Parade Segments Directed by: Michael Garciulo. Producer: Gary Kurtz. Production Coordinator: Melissa Boyer. *For Walt Disney World Creative Entertainment* Producer: Ken Harris. Parade Show Directed by: Sherilyn Draper. Production Manager: Angie Howard. Music by: Steve Skorija, Gordon Goodwin. Art Director: Rhonda Counts. Scenic Designer: Cheryl

Johnson. Guest Talent Program: Paul Chiaravalle. Choreographers: Denise Case, Gary Coburn, Rennie Gold. Character Department Supervision: Heidi Macklin. Parade Production Services: Tom Angermeier, Mike Wharton. Audio: Joe Knapp, Bob Owens. Staging Assistants: Denise Ahlert, Laura Kelly, Michele Krallinger, Tom White-Spunner. Production Assistant: Trina Elder. Associate Director: Jeff Palmer. Stage Managers: Dave Cove, Jim Maroney. Engineering: Ray Lego, Bill Morse, Lynn Peggs. Technical Director: Joy Grow. Audio Mixers: Steve Weber, John DeRussey. Video: Linda Tutten, Ric Wetherbee. Electrics: Arnold Tucker, Tom Moench, David Wilson, Tim McGuire. Electronic Graphics: Fern Hoppenstand. Editors: Sam Patterson, Art David, Pete Opotowsky, Andy Ebert, Gary Wood. Tape Operators: Beth Brizio-Bufano, Lonnie Blackburn, Calvin Kesterson, Pete Yelverton, Todd Garman. Post Production Audio: Kurt Wagner, Dorrie Batten, Rob Hill, Todd Beals. Graphic Design: Vince Pedulla. Studio D: Joe Fanelli. Hair/Make-up: Paulette Schoen, Mark Fonzi. Wardrobe: Marion Barnum. Business Affairs: Larry Haber. Promotions: Bob Gosselin. Publicity: Wallace Sears. Advertising: Julie Woodward, Virginia Frederick.

WALT DISNEY WORLD VERY MERRY CHRISTMAS PARADE (1995 VERSION)
Executive Producer: Debra Muenchow. Producer: Barbara Phillips. Supervising Producer: Jeff Palmer. Directed by: Gary Halvorson. Written by: Judy Katscke. Executive in Charge of Production: Ricky Kirshner. Musical Director: Harold Wheeler. Segments Directed by: Peter Israelson, L. David Irete, Jeff Palmer. Associate Producer: Cisco Henson. Segment Producers: Kitt McLeod, Bart Roen. Production Designer: Jimbo Marshall. Unit Manager: Kristan Kosh. Production Supervisor: John M. Best. Associate Director: Christine Bradley. Talent Coordinator: Suzy Garra. Script Supervisor: Kelly Hernacki. Art Decorator: Sharon Tannian. Production Coordinators: Lyn Rappaport, Susan Janis-Mashayekhi. Post Production Supervisor: James Weathers. Office Coordinator: Delise Del Favero. Assistant Talent Coordinator: Lance Parrish. Assistant to the Producer: Emily Zolten. Production Assistants: Marc Caldwell, Robert Fleming, Jose Hernandez, Mike Licata, Whitney Quillin, Dan Severson, Mindy Spang, Suzy Spang, James Stewart, Gerald Wu. Business Affairs: Larry Haber. Business Manager: Eileen Dzwill Rahman. *For Walt Disney World Creative Entertainment* Producer: Nancy Hart. Show Director: Sherilyn Draper Rook. Production Managers: Kristine Zajkowski, Sherri Underwood. Production Assistant: Lori Stephens. Art Director: Deborah Smith. Music Producer (Christmas Parade/Toy Story): Dan Stamper. Guest Talent Programs: Paul Chiaravalle, Jim Simmons. Choreographer (Christmas Parade/Toy Story): Denise Case. Choreographers: Sloah Suhy, Robby Mackey, Tara Anderson, Betsy Glover, Pauline Locsin. Staging Assistants: Corey Benedict, Kathy Shafer. Cindy Bonnet, Cheri Wells, Tom White-Spunner, Lisa Pactovis. Parade Production Supervisors: Gene Harding, Heidi Macklin, Darlene Kennedy, Mike Wharton. Float Audio: Joe Knapp. Parade Central: Keith Miller, Jeff Parker, Leno O'Bannon, Jim Dotson. *Toy Story Parade* Producer: Matthew H. Conover. Show Director: Peter J. Downing. Production Manager: Rob Ryan. Art Director: Cindy White. Production Assistant: Bobby Gemellaro. Staging Assistants: Beth Scammon, Denise Ahlert, Robert Hargrove, Christine Schornagle. Parade Production Supervisors: Jan Jacobson, Kaohu Mookini. Stage Managers: Dave Cove, Wendy Dawson, Jim Moroney, Vicki Hladik, Jeff Palmer. Technical Director: Joy Grow. Video Control: Paul Ranieri, Linda Tutten. Videotape Operators: Bill Lorenz, L.W. Scott. Electronic Graphics: Fern Hoppenstand Loory. Camera Operators: Miguel Armstrong, Ted Ashton, John Atkinson, Richie Banales, Jim Coglianese, Ray Detorre, Eddie Fucell, Neal Gallagher, Bill Giglio, Tom Hildreth, David Irete, Bob Keys, Kenny Kraus, Mark Lynch, Melissa Lynch, Rick Parrow, Ronnie Smith. Camera Utilities: Max Beck, Al Bogart, David Chapiro, Nathan McMahon, Jason Imbs, Jon Myers, Lisa Moye, Bob Nealy, Ching Oettel, Alan Soloman, Fed Wetherbee, Dave Wilson. Lighting Director: Jay Grindrod. Gaffer: Stuart Hall. Electrics: John Peters, Alan Soloman, Arnold Tucker. Audio: Steve Webber, John DeRussey, Don Youngs, Gary Baldesari. Audio Assistants: Gary Armstrong, Pat Ayotte, Curt Coniglio, George Moshonas, Don Muenchler, Tim Stringfellow, Nils Warren. Post Production Assistant: Doug Harley. Graphics: Ron Wissing, Vince Pedulla, Lillian Brue. Editors: Sam Patterson, Pete Opotowsky, Andy Ebert, Gary Wood. Assistant Editors: Kathy Beyers, Ron Mobley, Calvin Kesterson, Lonnie Blackburn. Post Production Audio Mixers: Kurt James Wagner, Dorrie Batten. Post Production Audio Assistants: Rob Reinbolt, Anthony Renda. Teleprompter: Jerry Farnam. Cue Cards: Teresa Franklin. Promotions: Bob Gosselin. Publicity: Wallace Sears, Jennie Hess.

WALT DISNEY'S MICKEY AND DONALD PRESENTS SPORT GOOFY
Direction: Jack Kinney. Animation: Wolfgang Reitherman, John Sibley, Ed Aardal, Jack Boyd. Story: Jack Kinney. Music: Oliver Wallace. Layout: Al Zinnen. Background: Merle Cox. Song *You Can Always Be No. 1:* Words and Music by: Dale Gonyea. Syndicated by SFM Media Corporation.

WALT DISNEY'S MICKEY AND DONALD PRESENTS SPORT GOOFY #2
Direction: Jack Kinney. Animation: John Sibley, Hugh Fraser, Ed Aardal, George Nicholas. Effects Animation: Jack Boyd. Story: Milt Schaffer, Dick Kinney. Layout: Al Zinnen. Zinnen. Background: Ray Huffine. Music: Paul Smith. Song *You Can Always Be No. 1:* Words and Music by: Dale Gonyea. Syndicated by SFM Media Corporation.

WALT DISNEY'S MICKEY AND DONALD PRESENTS SPORT GOOFY #3: WINTER SPORTS
Direction: Jack Kinney, Jack Hannah. Animation: Jack Boyd, Hal King, John Sibley, Milt Kahl, Bill Justice, Hugh Fraser, Andy Engman. Story: Bill Berg, Dick Kinney, Milt Banta. Layout: Don DaGradi, Yale Lacey. Background: Art Riley, Maurice Greenberg. Music: Paul J. Smith, Oliver Wallace. Song *You Can Always Be No. 1:* Words and Music by: Dale Gonyea. Syndicated by SFM Media Corporation.

WALT DISNEY'S MICKEY, DONALD, AND SPORT GOOFY: GETTING WET
Song *You Can Always Be No. 1:* Words and Music by: Dale Gonyea. Syndicated by SFM Media Corporation.

WALT DISNEY'S MICKEY, DONALD, AND SPORT GOOFY: HAPPY HOLIDAYS
Song *You Can Always Be No. 1:* Words and Music by: Dale Gonyea. Syndicated by SFM Media Corporation.

WALT DISNEY'S MICKEY, DONALD, AND SPORT GOOFY: SNOWTIME
Song *You Can Always Be No. 1:* Words and Music by: Dale Gonyea. Syndicated by SFM Media Corporation.

WE'LL TAKE MANHATTAN
Executive Producers: Paul Junger Witt, Tony Thomas. Supervising Producer: Richard Vaczy, Tracy Gamble. Director: Andy Cadiff. Written by: Richard Vaczy, Tracy Gamble. Music: George Aliceson Tipton. Costume Designer: Judy Evans. Costumers: Helaine Bruck, Murshel Lewis. Make-up: Art Harding. Hairstyles: Joyce Melton Conroy. Casting: Bonnie Shane, Ellen Meyer & Associates. Associate Directors: Patrick Maloney, Harold McKenzie. Stage Managers: Doug Tobin, Lance Lyon. Production Coordinator: Gwen McCracken. Production Associate: Dona Cassella. Post-Production Manager: Richard J. Powell. Music Coordinator: Scott Gale. Executive Consultant: Stevan A. Vail. Consultant: Jackée. Production Assistant: Hayden Hilscher. Production Staff: Charles Carpenter, Danny Filous, Bill Ghaffary, Jordan Goodman, Ray Kolasa, Denise Porter, David Z. Sacks, Maria Schmidt, Dorothy Wong. Technical Director: Jim Horkey. Lighting: Dalton Roger. Audio: Edward L. Moskowitz. Video: Randy Johnson. Camera Operators: Jack Chisholm, Chester Jackson, Stephen A. Jones, Bruce Oldham. Property Master: Bob Church. Gaffer: Robert Dick. Carpenter Supervisor: Paul Wadian. Technical Manager: Bill Conroy. Sound Rerecording Mixer: Craig Porter. Production Executives: David Amico, Susan Palladino, Susan. Witt/Thomas Productions in association with Touchstone Television.

WINNIE THE POOH, AND CHRISTMAS TOO

Producer/Supervising Director: Ken Kessel. Producer: Jamie Mitchell. Director: Jamie Mitchell. Written by: Karl Geurs, Mark Zaslove. Assistant Producers: Donna Alcock Smith, Traci Tolman. Storyboard Designers: Holly Forsyth, George Goode, Hank Tucker. Storyboard Revisions: Roy Shishido, Phil Weinstein. Key Layout Design: Dennis Greco, Ed Ghertner. Character Design: Kenny Thompkins, Len Smith. Prop Design: Dennis Greco. Background Styling: Gary Eggleston, Bill Lorencz. Color Stylists: Robin Draper, Yolanda Rearick. Supervising Timing Director: Marlene Robinson May. Timing Director: Brian Ray. Script Coordinator: Leona Jernigan. Archives Supervisor: Krista Bunn. Art Coordinators: Karen Silva, William Waggoner. Talent Coordinators: Lynne Batchelor, Jamie Thomason. Post Production Manager: Sara Duran. Post Production Supervisor: Joseph Hathaway. Sound Dubbing Supervisor: Christopher Keith. Post Production Coordinators: Jeffrey Arthur, John Royer. Track Reader: Skip Craig. Post Production Assistant: Nanci Batetelle. Production Assistants: Michelle Robinson, Paul Fabela, Johanne Beaudoin. Shipping Coordinator: Craig Simpson. Managing Film Editor: Rich Harrison. Supervising Editor: Charlie King, M.P.S.E. Sound Editors: Rick Hinson, M.P.S.E., David Lynch, Jerry Winicki. Dialogue Editors: Jenny Harrison, Andy Rose. ADR Editor: Tally Paulos. Assistant Editors: James N. Harrison, Robb S. Paulsen. Music by: Steve Nelson, Thom Sharp. Animation Production by: Walt Disney Animation (France) S.A. Producers: Paul Brizzi, Gaetan Brizzi. Layout Director: Zoltan Marcos. Layout: Bolhem Bouchiba, Jean Duval, Vincent Massy, Pascal Pinon. Background Supervisor: Pierre Pavlov. Backgrounds: Olivier Adam, Jean-Paul Fernandez, Helene Godefroy, Patricia Millereau, Vincent Misser, Nathalie Nicolas, Michel Pisson, Frederique Reignier. Animation Directors: Gary Perkovac, Stephane Sainte Foi. Animation: Jean-Luc Ballester, Moran Caouissin, Sylvain Deboissy, Patrick Delage, Marc Eoche-Duval, Pierre Fassel, Alain Costa, Arnold Gransac, Javier Guittierez, Matias Marcos, Dominique Montferry, Catherine Poulain, Jean-Christophe Roger, Pascal Ropars, Mireille Sarrault, Ventura R. Vallejo. Animation EFX: Thierry Chaffoin, Peter Hausner. Assistant Animation: Laurence Adam, Philippe Balmossiere, Philippe Beziat, Patrizia Brizzi, Marie Cabo, Antonio Campiglio, Jean Deleani, Rene Dieu, Dina Gellert, Pierre Girault, Thierry Goulard, Karine Hjort, Isabelle Lelubre, Pierre Lyphoudt, Gizella Maros, Lieve Miessen, Florence Monceau, Gilles Noll, Sylvie Penege, Odile Perrin, Christian Simon, Xavier Villez, Karel Zilliacus. Inbetween: Philippe Ferrin, Ivan Kassabov, Christine Landes, Pierre Lecomte, Ludovic Letrun, Andre Nekkar, Daniela Tigano, Marc Tosolini, Christiane Van Der Casseven. Checking Supervisor: Bruno Gaumetou. Checking: Nathalie Devriese, Sylvie Fauque, Pierre Sucaud. Camera: Evariste Ferreira. Assistant Director: Raphael Vicente. Line Producer: Jean-Luc Florinda. Assistant to the Line Producer: Etienne Longa. Ink & Paint and Camera Services: Sunwoo Animation. Produced by: Walt Disney Television Animation. *Additional credits for the 1991 version: Hockey Champ* and *Bearly Asleep* Animation, Story, Backgrounds, Layouts and Artwork by Members of the Motion Picture Screen Cartoonists, Local 839. *Beauty and the Beast* Sequence Produced by: The Wrightwood Group, Inc. Producer: Joanie Burton. On-Line Editor: Tom Klemsrud. *Additional credits for the 1992 version: The Making of The Muppet Christmas Carol* Produced by: The Wrightwood Group, Inc. *Additional credits for the 1993 version: The Making of Aladdin: A Whole New World* Segment Hosted by: John Rhys-Davies. Director: Steve Kroopnick. Written by: John Culhane. A Production of The Wrightwood Group, Inc. in association with Betty Productions. *Additional credits for the 1995 version: The Magic Earmuffs* Producer/Director: Karl Geurs. Story Editor: Mark Zaslove. Assistant Story Editor: Carter Crocker. Story by: Terrie Collins, Mark Zaslove. Teleplay by: Carter Crocker. *The Making of Toy Story* Directed by: Mike Bonifer. Producer: Jonathan Bogner. Coordinating Producer: Kellie Allred. Editors: Gary Allen, La Rhonda Morris. Production Manager: Leslie Anne Shevick.

WINNIE THE POOH AND TIGGER TOO

The following credits are for the 1-hour version: *Bee on Guard* Direction: Jack Hannah. Animation: Bob Carlson, Bill Justice, George Kreisl, Volus Jones. Effects Animation: Blaine Gibson. Story: Nick George, Bill Berg. Layout: Yale Gracey. Background: Thelma Witmer. Music: Oliver Wallace. *Pluto and the Gopher* Direction: Charles Nichols. Story: Dick Kinney, Milt Schaffer. Animation: George Kreisl, George Nicholas, Hugh Fraser, Phil Duncan. Effects Animation: Josh Meador. Layout: Karl Karpé. Background: Art Landy. Music: Oliver Wallace. *In the Bag* Direction: Jack Hannah. Animation: John Sibley, Bob Carlson, Al Coe, George Kreisl. Effects Animation: Dan MacManus. Story: Dave Detiege, Al Bertino. Layout: Yale Gracey. Background: Ray Huffine. Music: George Bruns.

WONDERFUL WORLD OF DISNEY, THE: 40 YEARS OF TELEVISION MAGIC

Directed by: Frank Martin. Produced by: Jean-Michel Michenaud, John Caldwell. Written by: Glenn Berenbeim, Charles W. Hayes. Co-Producers: Olivier Chaudet, Frank Martin. Segment Producers: Harry Arends, Phil Savenick. Director of Photography: Anghel Decca. Editors: Terry Blythe, George Waite, Jonathan Siegel. Associate Producer: Daniel Gillett. Associate Director: Michael Kelly. Stage Managers: Doug Smith, Rey Vicenty. Line Producer: Nicole Dintaman. Original Music Composed by: Laura Karpman. Additional Editing: Dan Fouts, Bruce Bailey. Production Coordinator: Meghan Stephan. Talent Coordinators: Holly Breaux Schwartz, Joyce Estrin. Production Consultant: Rita Katsotis. Cameramen: Shawn Maurer, Rick Pendleton, Bryan Duggan, Harris Done, Bob La Russa, Mark Hunter, Patrick Stewart. Sound Mixers: Marc Gilmartin, Mark Burton. Field Producers: Holly Breaux Schwartz, Lisa Caruso. Video Technician: Barry Weissman. Art Director: Mindy Hahn. Costume Supervisor: Kelly Conway. Set Decorators: Lisa Thompson, Oliver French, Will Stahl. Gaffers: Jim McEachen, Kevin Brennan. Key Grip: Smokey Woodard. Script Supervisor: Cheryl Mallet. Make-up for Kirstie Alley: Francesca Tolot. Hair for Kirstie Alley: Mitch Stone. Make-Up & Hair: James Higgins. Assistant Editor: Tajuan Mercer. Production Assistants: Luke Ellis, Helen De Vivien, Garth Hammers, Brenna Shenkin, Scott Kowalchyk. Title Design: Jim House. On-Line Editors: Bruce Ochmanek. Deron Warner, Mary Holland, David M. Blum. Re-recording Mixer: Kenneth Novak. Archival Research: Bill Cotter. Executive Producers: George Zaloom, Les Mayfield. Walt Disney Television in association with ZM Productions.

CHAPTER 4

Anthology Series Episode Descriptions

ABSENT-MINDED PROFESSOR, THE (TV VERSION)
Executive Producers: Richard Chapman, Bill Dial. Produced by: Ric Rondell. Developed for Television by: Richard Chapman, Bill Dial. Based on Characters Created by: Samuel W. Taylor. Written by: Richard Chapman, Bill Dial. Directed by: Robert Scheerer. Executive Producer: William Blinn. "Albert" Designed and Performed by: Jay Johnson, Harry Anderson. Original Score Written and Performed by: Tom Scott. Director of Photography: King Baggot. Art Director: Cameron Birnie. Editor: Jerry Temple. Unit Production Manager: Paul Deason. First Assistant Director: Ken Collins. Second Assistant Director: Steve Cohen. Casting by: Robert W. Harbin, C.S.A., Beth Hymson, C.S.A. Costumes Designed by: Tom Bronson. Set Decorator: Ethel Robins Richards. Property Master: Lavar Emert. Key Costumers: Terrence K. Smith, Kendall Errair. Make-up: Carol Schwartz. Hair Stylist: Gregg Mitchell. Location Manager: Denis J. McCallion. Script Supervisor: Alleen N. Nollmann. Production Coordinator: Nancy Malone Claycomb. "Robin" the Dog Owned and Trained by: Grisco's Animals. Computer Assistance: John Mounsour Electronics, Bright Star Technology. Special Effects Coordinator: Alan E. Lorimer. Production Sound Mixer: William Teague, C.A.S. Sound Editing by: Soundbusters. Music Editing by: Chris Brooks. Visual Effects by: Buena Vista Visual Effects Group. Echo Cove Productions in association with Walt Disney Television.

ABSENT-MINDED PROFESSOR, THE: TRADING PLACES
Produced by: Neil T. Maffeo. Developed for Television by: Richard Chapman, Bill Dial. Based on Characters Created by: Samuel W. Taylor. Teleplay by: Richard Chapman, Bill Dial. Story by: Richard Chapman, Bill Dial, Harry Anderson. Directed by: Bob Sweeney. "Albert" Produced and Performed by: Jay Johnson, Harry Anderson. Original Score Written and Performed by: Tom Scott. Director of Photography: Isidore Mankofsky, A.S.C. Art Director: Frank Pezza. Editor: Tom Stevens. Unit Production Manager: Robin Chamberlin. First Assistant Director: Ken Collins. Second Assistant Director: Steve "Stevo" Danton. Costumes Designed by: Tom Bronson. Set Decorator: S. Lynn Smart. Property Master: Rudy Reachi. Key Costumers: Milton Mangum, Sandy Jordan. Make-up: Tony Lloyd. Hair Stylist: Gregg Mitchell. Script Supervisor: Alleen N. Nollmann. Production Coordinator: Pamela Hoffman. "Scruffy" The Dog Owned and Trained by: Frank Inn, Inc. Location Manager: Steve Share. Computer Assistants: John Monsour Electronics, Bright Star Technology. Special Effects Coordinator: Robbie Knott. Production Sound Mixer: Joe Kenworthy, C.A.S. Sound Editing by: Echo Film Services. Music Editing by: Segue Music, Inc. Magical Consultants: Harry Anderson, Jim Steinmeyer. Robotics by: Eric Allard, All Effects Company. NIK 7500 Developed and Executed by: Brenton Fletcher. Visual Effects by: Buena Vista Visual Effects Group. Echo Cove Productions in association with Walt Disney Television.

ADIOS EL CUCHILLO
Directed by: William Witney. Teleplay by: Bob Wehling. Based on the *Zorro* stories by: Johnston McCulley. Produced by: Bill Anderson. Associate Producer: Louis Debney. Director of Photography: Lucien Ballard, A.S.C. Art Director: Marvin Aubrey Davis. Film Editor: Basil Wrangell. Music: William Lava. Matte Artist: Peter Ellenshaw. Sound: Robert O. Cook. Set Decoration: Emile Kuri, William L. Stevens. Costumer: Chuck Keehne. Make-up: Pat McNalley. Hair Stylist: Ruth Sandifer. Fencing Master: Fred Cavens. Unit Manager: Roy Wade. Assistant Director: Vincent McEveety.

ADVENTURE IN ART, AN
Directed by: Wilfred Jackson and C. August Nichols. Sequence Directors: Hamilton S. Luske, Samuel Armstrong, Robert Cormack. Teleplay by: Dick Huemer. Cartoon Story by: Richmond Kelsey, Lee Blair. Animation: Jerry Hathcock, Les Clark, Don Lusk, Cy Young, Dan MacManus, Joshua Meador. Layout: McLaren Stewart, A. Kendall O'Connor, John Hench. Backgrounds: Dick Anthony, Art Riley, Joe Stahley. Camera: Kenneth Peach, A.S.C. Art Director: Marvin Aubrey Davis. Film Editors: Edward Sampson, Samuel Horta. Music: Joseph S. Dubin, Oscar Rasbach, Charles Wolcott. Lyrics: Joyce Kilmer, Ray Gilbert. Special Processes: Ub Iwerks, A.S.C. Sound: Robert O. Cook. Set Decorator: Fred MacLean. Costumer: Chuck Keehne. Make-up: Pat McNalley. Assistant Director: Vincent McEveety. Production Supervisor: Harry Tytle. Acknowledgments: Leopold Stokowski and the Philadelphia Orchestra, Dinah Shore, Fred Waring and his Pennsylvanians, Tania Riabouchinska and David Lichine.

ADVENTURE IN COLOR, AN (AND) MATHMAGIC LAND
Directed by: Hamilton S. Luske. Sequence Directors: Wolfgang Reitherman, Les Clark, Joshua Meador. Story: Bill Berg, Larry Clemmons, Joe Rinaldi, Otto Englander, Milt Banta, Dr. Heinz Haber. Art Styling: McLaren Stewart. Music: Buddy Baker. Songs: Richard M. Sherman and Robert B. Sherman. Animation: Ward Kimball, Hal King, Frank Thomas, Eric Larson, Cliff Nordberg, Milt Kahl, John Lounsbery, Ollie Johnston, Bob McCrea. Effects Animation: Jack Boyd. Layout: Joe Hale, Al Zinnen, Don Griffith, Basil Davidovich. Background: Art Riley, Al Dempster. Film Editors: Donald Halliday, Lloyd L. Richardson, A.C.E. Special Effects: Eustace Lycett. Sound: Robert O. Cook.

ADVENTURE IN SATAN'S CANYON
Director of Photography: Robert Sparks. Written by: James Douglass West. Narration Written by: Shane Tatum. Produced and Directed by: William Beaudine, Jr. Art Director: George Troast. Film Editor: Norman Palmer, A.C.E. Second Unit Director: Thomas A. Beemer. Music: Robert F. Brunner. Song *A Million Miles*: Shane Tatum. Sung by: Michael Dees. Sound: Herb Taylor. Assistant to the Producer: Scottie Cummings. Costumes: Oscar Rodriguez. Make-up: Loren Cosand.

Assistant Director: Richard Del Ruth. Acknowledgment: The U.S. Department of Agriculture, Forest Service.

ADVENTURE IN THE MAGIC KINGDOM, AN
Directed by: Hamilton S. Luske. Narration Written by: Larry Clemmons. Animation: Cliff Nordberg, Bob McCrea, Jack Boyd. Layout: Al Zinnen, Thor Putnam. Cameraman: Charles P. Boyle, A.S.C. Film Editor: Lloyd L. Richardson, A.C.E. Music: Buddy Baker. Special Processes: Eustace Lycett. Sound: Robert O. Cook. Assistant Director: Horace Hough. Production Supervisor: Harry Tytle.

ADVENTURE IN WILDWOOD HEART
Directed by: Hamilton S. Luske. Produced by: Winston Hibler. Written by: Jack Speirs, Winston Hibler. Photography: Kenneth Peach, A.S.C., N. Paul Kenworthy, Jr., Roy Edward Disney, Joel Colman, Walter Perkins, William Ratcliffe. Music: Joseph S. Dubin. Production Coordinator: Roy Edward Disney. Art Director: Marvin Aubrey Davis. Film Editors: Grant K. Smith, Jack L. Atwood. Set Decoration: Vin Taylor. Animation Effects: Joshua Meador. Special Processes: Ub Iwerks, A.S.C. Sound: Robert O. Cook. Assistant Director: Vincent McEveety. Production Supervision: Harry Tytle. Acknowledgments: U.S. Forest Service, U.S. Fish and Wildlife Service, Utah Fish and Game Department.

ADVENTURE STORY, THE
Directed by: Wolfgang Reitherman. Sequence Director: Jack Kinney. Story: Bill Peet, Dick Kinney, Brice Mack. Music: Paul Smith, Joseph S. Dubin, Oliver Wallace. Animation: Eric Cleworth, Dick Lucas, Bill Keil, Amby Paliwoda, John Sibley. Layout: Basil Davidovich, Dale Barnhart, Vance Gerry, Lance Nolley. Backgrounds: Richard H. Thomas, Al Dempster, Claude Coats. Film Editor: Roy M. Brewer, Jr. Special Processes: Ub Iwerks, A.S.C. Sound: Robert O. Cook. Production Supervision: Harry Tytle.

ADVENTURES IN FANTASY
Directed by: Bill Justice. Sequence Directors: Clyde Geronimi, Wilfred Jackson, Jack Kinney. Story: Bill Peet, Bill Cottrell, Erdman Penner. *Little Toot* from the book by Hardie Gramatky. With the talents of: The Andrews Sisters and Sterling Holloway. Art Styling: Xavier Atencio. Music: Oliver Wallace, Eliot Daniel, Ken Darby, Paul Smith. Animation: Cliff Nordberg, Eric Larson, Marc Davis, Ollie Johnston, Les Clark, Earl Combs. Layout: McLaren Stewart, Don DaGradi. Backgrounds: Al Dempster, Dick Ung, Ralph Hulett. Film Editor: Jim Love. Special Processes: Ub Iwerks, A.S.C. Sound: Robert O. Cook. Production Supervision: Harry Tytle.

ADVENTURES OF BULLWHIP GRIFFIN, THE
Project Florida Produced by: James Algar. Narration Written by: James Algar, Bill Bosché. Film Editor: Gordon Brenner. Music: Buddy Baker. Photography: Peter J. Barton Productions, Inc.

ADVENTURES OF CHIP 'N DALE, THE
Directed by: Bill Justice. Story: Bill Berg, Nick George, Milt Schaffer, Dick Kinney. Animation: Cliff Nordberg, Bob Carlson, George Kreisl, Volus Jones, Hal King. Effects Animation: Dan MacManus, Blaine Gibson. Layout: Xavier Atencio, Yale Gracey. Backgrounds: Dick Ung, Ray Huffine, Thelma Witmer. Film Editor: Jim Love. Music: George Bruns. Song *We Are Chip 'n Dale*: Gil George, Oliver Wallace. Sound: Robert O. Cook. Special Processes: Eustace Lycett. Production Supervision: Harry Tytle.

ADVENTURES OF MICKEY MOUSE
Credits for 1955 broadcast: Adapted for Television by: Hamilton S. Luske, Carl Cons, Lloyd L. Richardson, Harry Tytle. Credits for 1980 broadcasts: Direction: Jack Hannah, Bill Roberts. Animation: Hugh Fraser, Bob Carlson, Murray McClellan, Blaine Gibson, Wolfgang Reitherman, John Lounsbery, John Sibley, Jack Campbell, George Rowley. Story: Harry Reeves, Rex Cox, Homer Brightman, Ted Sears, Eldon Dedini. Music: Oliver Wallace, Paul Smith. Songs: Ray Nobel, Ray Gilbert, Arthur Quenzer, Paul Smith. *The Beanero* by:

Oliver Wallace. Layout: Yale Gracey, Al Zinnen, Hugh Hennesy, A. Kendall O'Connor, John Hench. Background: Thelma Witmer, Art Riley, Brice Mack, Claude Coats, Ralph Hulett. *Disney's Wonderful World* Theme: John Debney, John Klawitter.

ADVENTURES OF POLLYANNA, THE
Executive Producer: William Robert Yates. Produced by: Tom Leetch. Director of Photography: Jack A. Whitman, Jr. Based on the novel *Pollyanna* by: Eleanor H. Porter. Written by: Ann Beckett. Directed by: Robert Day. Music by: Jerrold Immel. Art Director: Mark Mansbridge. Editor: Ernie Milano, A.C.S. Unit Production Manager: Gary Credle. Assistant Director: Skip Beaudine. Second Assistant Director: Paul Moen. Casting: Bill Shepard, Virginia Higgins. Set Decorator: Norman Rockett. Sound: Bob Hathaway. Music Editor: Jack Wadsworth. Costumes: Jack Sandeen, Bill Thomas. Make-up: Robert J. Schiffer, C.M.A.A. Hair Stylist: Julia Walker.

ADVENTURES WITH MICKEY
Direction: Jack Hannah, Bill Roberts. Animation: Hugh Fraser, Bob Carlson, Murray McClellan, Blaine Gibson, Wolfgang Reitherman, John Lounsbery, John Sibley, Jack Campbell, George Rowley. Story: Harry Reeves, Rex Cox, Homer Brightman, Ted Sears, Eldon Dedini. Music: Oliver Wallace, Paul Smith. Songs: Ray Noble, Ray Gilbert, Arthur Quenzer, Paul Smith. *The Beanero*: Oliver Wallace. Layout: Yale Gracey, Al Zinnen, Hugh Hennesy, A. Kendall O'Connor, John Hench. Background: Thelma Witmer, Art Riley, Brice Mack, Claude Coats, Ralph Hulett.

ALICE IN WONDERLAND
Directed for Television by: Bill Walsh. Edited for Television by: Al Teeter.

ALL ABOUT MAGIC
Directed by: Hamilton S. Luske. Sequence Directors: James Algar, Jack Hannah. Story: Milt Banta, Erdman Penner, Perce Pearce, Ralph Wright. Music: Paul Smith. Face in the Mirror: Hans Conried. Special Processes: Ub Iwerks, A.S.C. Art Director: Marvin Aubrey Davis. Animation: Milt Kahl, Marc Davis, Fred Moore, Bill Justice. Layout: Al Zinnen, Tom Codrick, A. Kendall O'Connor, Yale Gracey. Backgrounds: Claude Coats, Art Riley. Set Decorator: Emile Kuri. Photography: Gordon Avil, A.S.C. Film Editor: Lloyd Richardson. Sound: Robert O. Cook. Assistant Director: Russ Haverick. Production Supervision: Harry Tytle.

ALONG THE OREGON TRAIL
Directed by: William Beaudine. Written by: James Algar. Music: George Bruns. Songs: *Westward Ho the Wagons!*: George Bruns and Tom Blackburn, *Pioneers' Prayer*: Gil George and Paul Smith. Photography: Charles P. Boyle, A.S.C. Art Director: Marvin Aubrey Davis. Film Editor: Norman Palmer, A.C.E. Matte Artist: Peter Ellenshaw. Set Decoration: Emile Kuri. Wardrobe: Chuck Keehne. Make-up: David Newell. Special Processes: Ub Iwerks, A.S.C. Sound: Robert O. Cook. Assistant Director: William Beaudine, Jr. Production Supervision: Harry Tytle. Additional Photography by: Stewart Jules.

AMBUSH AT LAREDO
Directed by: Harry Keller. Written by: Frank D. Gilroy, Albert E. Lewin, Burt Styler. Produced by: James Pratt. Director of Photography: Walter H. Castle, A.S.C. Art Director: Marvin Aubrey Davis. Film Editor: Robert O. Stafford. Music: Buddy Baker. Song: Stan Jones. Sound: Robert O. Cook. Set Decorators: Emile Kuri, Vin Taylor. Costumer: Chuck Keehne. Make-up: Pat McNalley. Assistant Director: Austen Jewell.

AND CHASE THE BUFFALO
Directed by: Lewis R. Foster. Television Story and Teleplay by: David Victor. Based on the book *Daniel Boone* by: John Bakeless. Produced by: Bill Anderson. Assistant Producer: Ron Miller. Director of Photography: Ray Rennahan, A.S.C. Art Director: Marvin Aubrey Davis. Film Editor: Basil Wrangell. Music: Oliver Wallace. Song: George Bruns, David

Victor. Sound: Robert O. Cook. Set Decoration: Emile Kuri, William L. Stevens. Costumer: Chuck Keehne. Make-up: Pat McNalley. Hair-stylist: Ruth Sandifer. Unit Manager: Roy Wade. Assistant Director: Joseph L. McEveety.

ANDY'S FIRST CHORE
Directed by: Lewis R. Foster. Teleplay by: Tom Blackburn. Based on a Novel by: Stewart Edward White. Music: George Bruns. Songs: *The Saga of Andy Burnett, Ladies in the Sky:* George Bruns, Tom Blackburn. Photographer: Walter H. Castle, A.S.C. Art Director: Carroll Clark. Matte Artist: Albert Whitlock. Film Editor: Cotton Warburton, A.C.E. Set Decoration: Emile Kuri, Fred MacLean. Costumes: Chuck Keehne. Make-up: Pat McNalley. Sound: Robert O. Cook. Assistant Director: Russ Haverick. Production Supervisor: Harry Tytle.

ANDY'S INITIATION
Directed by: Lewis R. Foster. Teleplay by: Tom Blackburn. Based on a Novel by: Stewart Edward White. Music: George Bruns. Songs: *The Saga of Andy Burnett, Ladies in the Sky:* George Bruns, Tom Blackburn. Photographer: Walter H. Castle, A.S.C. Art Director: Carroll Clark. Matte Artist: Albert Whitlock. Film Editor: Cotton Warburton, A.C.E. Set Decoration: Emile Kuri, Fred MacLean. Costumes: Chuck Keehne. Make-up: Pat McNalley. Special Processes: Ub Iwerks, A.S.C. Sound: Robert O. Cook. Assistant Director: Russ Haverick. Production Supervisor: Harry Tytle.

ANDY'S LOVE AFFAIR
Directed by: Lewis R. Foster. Teleplay by: Tom Blackburn. Based on a Novel by: Stewart Edward White. Music: George Bruns. Songs *The Saga of Andy Burnett, Ladies in the Sky, The Mountain Hoedown:* George Bruns, Tom Blackburn. Photographer: Walter H. Castle, A.S.C. Art Director: Carroll Clark. Matte Artist: Peter Ellenshaw. Film Editor: Cotton Warburton, A.C.E. Set Decoration: Emile Kuri, Fred MacLean. Costumes: Chuck Keehne. Make-up: Pat McNalley. Sound: Robert O. Cook. Choreographer: Jack Regas. Assistant Director: Russ Haverick. Production Supervisor: Harry Tytle.

ANTARCTICA—OPERATION DEEPFREEZE
Produced and Directed by: Winston Hibler. Written by: Ted Sears, Winston Hibler. Photographers: Lloyd Beebe, Elmo G. Jones. Additional Photography: Bill Fortin. Music: Joseph S. Dubin. Film Editors: Grant K. Smith, Hugh R. Chaloupka. Production Coordinator: William Redlin. Special Processes: Ub Iwerks, A.S.C., Eustace Lycett. Animation Effects: Joshua Meador. Sound: Robert O. Cook. Production Supervision: Erwin L. Verity, Harry Tytle. Acknowledgments: Antarctic Topographical Model by Allen-Shaw. Filmed with the cooperation of the Department of Defense, U.S. Navy, U.S. Air Force, U.S. Coast Guard. Narrated by: Winston Hibler.

ANTARCTICA—PAST AND PRESENT
Produced and Directed by: Winston Hibler. Written by: Ted Sears, Jack Speirs, Winston Hibler. Music: Joseph S. Dublin. Production Supervision: Erwin L. Verity, Harry Tytle. Photography by: Elmo G. Jones, Lloyd Beebe. Film Editor: Hugh R. Chaloupka. Special Processes: Eustace Lycett, Joshua Meador. Sound: Robert O. Cook. Acknowledgments: United States Navy, United States Coast Guard, Department of Defense.

APACHE FRIENDSHIP
Directed by: Harry Keller. Story by: Maurice Tombragel, Cyril Hume. Teleplay by: Maurice Tombragel. Produced by: James Pratt. Director of Photography: William Snyder, A.S.C. Art Director: Stan Jolley. Film Editor: Robert Stafford. Music: Oliver Wallace. Sound: Robert O. Cook. Set Decoration: Emile Kuri, William L. Stevens. Costumer: Chuck Keehne. Make-up: Pat McNalley. Hair Stylist: Ruth Sandifer. Unit Manager: Roy Wade. Assistant Director: Joseph L. McEveety.

ASK MAX
Original Score: Robert Folk. Supervising Producer: John Garbett. Executive Producers: Brian Grazer, Gil Grant. Teleplay by: Andy Guerdat, Steve Kreinberg, Gil Grant. Story by: Andy Guerdat, Steve Kreinberg. Directed by: Vincent McEveety.

Director of Photography: James Michael Swain. Art Director: William Elliott. Editor: Robert E. Pew. Unit Production Manager: Steve Barnett. First Assistant Director: Paul Deason. Second Assistant Director: Joseph Paul Moore. Casting: Linda Francis. Costume Designer: William Ware Theiss. Set Decorator: Ethel Robins Richards. Property Master: Lavar Emert. Key Costumers: Margo Baxley, Nick Mezzanotti. Make-up: Michael F. Blake. Hair Stylist: Gregg Mitchell. Location Manager: Ryan Rosenberg. Script Supervisor: Tom Moore. Associate Producer: Michael Sheehy. Production Coordinator: Lorna Neal. Production Sound Mixer: Patrick Mitchell. Sound Editing by: Dimension Sound/Michael Hilkene. Music Editing by: Robert E. Post. *Playing to Win* Words and Music by: John Farnham, Graham Goble. Performed by: Jess Harnell. *Walking on Sunshine* Words and Music by: Kimberly Rew. Performed by: Andrea Robinson. *What You Need* Words and Music by: Andrew Farriss, Michael Hutchence. Performed by: Tommy Funderburk. Skybike Provided by: Uni-Bmx, Appollo Cycles. A Gil Grant Production and Imagine Production in association with Walt Disney Television.

AT HOME WITH DONALD DUCK
Directed by: Jack Hannah. Sequence Director: C. August Nichols. Animation: Al Coe, Jerry Hathcock, Bob Carlson, George Kreisl, Bill Justice, Volus Jones, George Nichols, Dan MacManus. Story: Davy Detiege, Albert Bertino, Nick George, Bill Berg, Milt Schaffer, Dick Kinney. Music: Joseph S. Dubin, Oliver Wallace. Layout: Yale Gracey, Karl Karpé. Backgrounds: Ray Huffine, Ralph Hulett. Production Supervision: Harry Tytle. Film Editor: Tom Acosta. Special Processes: Ub Iwerks, A.S.C. Sound: Robert O. Cook.

ATTA GIRL, KELLY!
Co-producer: James Algar. Written by: Albert Aley. Directed by: James Sheldon. Director of Photography: William Snyder, A.S.C. Art Directors: Carroll Clark, William H. Tuntke. Film Editor: Norman Palmer, A.C.E. Set Decorators: Emile Kuri, William L. Stevens. Second Unit Director: Arthur J. Vitarelli. Music: Franklyn Marks, Willis Schaefer, Mullendore. *World of Color* Theme: Richard M. Sherman, Robert B. Sherman. Costumer: Chuck Keehne. Make-up: Gordon Hubbard. Hair Stylist: La Rue Matheron. Sound: Robert O. Cook. Special Effects: Eustace Lycett. Assistant Director: John C. Chulay. Animal Supervision: William R. Koehler. Program Co-ordinator: Jack Bruner. Produced with the co-operation of: The Seeing Eye, Inc., Morristown, N.J. Technical Advisor: G.W. Debetaz.

ATTORNEY AT LAW
Directed by: Christian Nyby. Written by: Maurice Tombragel. Produced by: James Pratt. Director of Photography: Lucien Ballard, A.S.C. Art Director: Stan Jolley. Film Editor: Edward Sampson, Jr. Music: Franklyn Marks. Song: Rich Dehr, Frank Miller. Sound: Robert O. Cook. Set Decorators: Emile Kuri, Vin Taylor. Costumer: Chuck Keehne. Make-up: Pat McNalley. Assistant Director: Arthur J. Vitarelli.

AULD ACQUAINTANCE
Directed by: James Neilson. Teleplay by: Bob Wehling. Based on the Zorro stories by: Johnston McCulley. Produced by: Bill Anderson. Associate Producer: Louis Debney. Director of Photography: Edward Colman, A.S.C. Art Director: Marvin Aubrey Davis. Film Editor: Robert Stafford. Music: Buddy Baker. Song: Richard M. Sherman, Robert B. Sherman. Sound: Robert O. Cook. Set Decoration: Emile Kuri. Costumer: Chuck Keehne. Make-up: Pat McNalley. Hair Stylist: Ruth Sandifer. Assistant Director: Joseph L. McEveety.

BACKSTAGE PARTY
Teleplay by: Larry Clemmons. Directed by: Jack Donohue, Hamilton S. Luske. Based on the Operetta *Babes in Toyland* by: Victor Herbert, Glen McDonough. Music by: George Bruns. Special Lyrics by: Mel Levin. Director of Photography: Edward Colman, A.S.C. Art Direction: Carroll Clark, Marvin Aubrey Davis. Film Editor: Lloyd L. Richardson, A.C.E. Art Styling: McLaren Stewart. Choreographer: Tom Mahoney. Set Decoration: Emile Kuri, Hal Gausman. Costumes Designed by: Bill Thomas. Costumers: Chuck Keehne, Gertrude Casey. Special Effects: Eustace Lycett. Toy Sequence: Bill Justice,

Xavier Atencio. Make-up: Pat McNalley. Hair Stylist: Ruth Sandifer. Sound: Robert O. Cook. Assistant Director: John Chulay. Assistant to the Producer: Louis Debney.

BALLAD OF HECTOR THE STOWAWAY DOG, THE

Teleplay by: Lowell S. Hawley. Story by: Homer Brightman. Based on the book *Hector, The Stowaway Dog* by: Kenneth Dodson. Published by: Little, Brown & Co. Directed by: Vincent McEveety. Associate Producer: Harry Tytle. Director of Photography: Amerigo Genarelli. Art Director: Aurelio Crugnola. Film Editor: Robert Stafford, A.C.E. Music: Oliver Wallace. Portuguese Songs: Manuel Viegas. *Hector* Theme Song: Richard M. Sherman, Robert B. Sherman. Sung by: "The Yachtsmen." Production Supervisor: Orazio Tassara, IFS, Roma. Costumer: Adriana Berselli. Make-up: Vittorio Biseo. Hair Stylist: Adriana Cassini. Sound: Robert O. Cook. Animal Trainers: Paul Le Royer, John Darlys. Assistant Director: Franco Cirino. Program Co-ordinator: Jack Bruner. Acknowledgments: The Government of Spain, The Barcelona Police Department.

BALLERINA

Co-producers: Bill Anderson, Peter V. Herald. Teleplay by: Casey Robinson and Robert Westerby (Part 1), Robert Westerby (Part 2). Story by: Casey Robinson (Part 1), Peter Schnitzler and Norman Thomson (Part 2). Directed by: Norman Campbell. Director of Photography: Günther Anders. Art Directors: Werner Schlichting, Isabell Schlichting. Film Editor: Alfred Srp. Original Music: Heinz Schreiter. *World of Color* Theme: Richard M. Sherman, Robert B. Sherman. Choreography for Walt Disney Productions: Norman Thomson. Wardrobe: Leo Bei, Laila Teisen. Make-up: Jupp Paschke, Joachim Schmalor. Unit Managers: Klaus Gotthardt, Gert Stachowski. Danish Location Manager: Finn Aabue. Sound: Robert O. Cook, Bernhard Reicherts. Camera Operator: Kai Borsche. Second Unit Photography: Rolf Ronne. Production Managers: Paul Waldherr, Waldemar Runge-Wasa. Assistant Director: Wieland Liebske. Danish Production Coordinator: Mogens Skot-Hansen. Program Co-ordinator: Jack Bruner. Acknowledgment: The Directors of The Royal Theater, Copenhagen.

BARRY OF THE GREAT ST. BERNARD

Executive Producer: Ron Miller. Produced by: Harry Tytle. Teleplay by: Sheldon Stark, Ann Udell. Adaptation by: Tom Seller. Narration by: Joe Ansen. Based on the book by: Adolf Fux. Directed by: Frank Zuniga. Director of Photography: Atze Glanert. Art Director: Wolfgang Hundhammer. Editor: Gregg McLaughlin, A.C.E. Matte Artist: P.S. Ellenshaw. Music: Robert F. Brunner. Sound: Herb Taylor. Costumes: Claudia Stitch. Make-up: Alfred Rasche. Unit Production Manager: Peter Spoerri. Assistant Directors: Stefaan Schieder, Edi Hubschmid. Production Assistant: Clint Rowe (animal trainer). Narrator: Brad Crandall. Filmed on location in Switzerland.

BASEBALL FEVER

Executive Producer: Ron Miller. Prepared for Television by: Lou Debney, Frank Brandt, Ed Ropolo, Dennis C. Vejar. Direction: Jack Kinney, Jack Hannah. Animation: Bob Carlson, Bill Justice, Volus Jones, Judge Whitaker, John Sibley, Wolfgang Reitherman, Dan MacManus, Ed Aardal, Blaine Gibson, Eric Larson, Cliff Nordberg, Hugh Fraser, George Rowley, Harvey Toombs, Fred Moore, Charlie Nichols, George Nicholas, Jack Boyd. Story: Nick George, Bill Berg, Dick Kinney, Milt Schaffer, Brice Mack, Eric Gurney, Homer Brightman. Layout: Yale Gracey, Al Zinnen, Hugh Hennesy, Bruce Bushman. Background: Thelma Witmer, Merle Cox, Dick Anthony, Al Dempster, Ralph Hulett. Music: Oliver Wallace, Ken Darby, Joseph S. Dubin, Paul J. Smith. With the Voice Talents of: Gary Owens, Jerry Colonna. *Disney's Wonderful World* Theme Song: John Debney, John Klawitter.

BATTLE FOR SURVIVAL

Written and Directed by: James Algar. Produced by: Ben Sharpsteen. Music: Paul Smith. Consulting Biologists: Rutherford Platt, Tilden W. Roberts. Time Lapse Photography by: John Nass Ott Jr., Stuart V. Jewell, William M. Harlow, Vincent J. Schaefer, Rex R. Elliott. Photographed by: Stuart V. Jewell, Robert H. Crandall, Murl Deusing, George and Nettie MacGinitie, Tilden W. Roberts, William A. Anderson, Jack C. Couffer, Claude Jendrusch, Arthur Carter, Fran William Hall, Roman Vishniac, Donald L. Sykes. Production Manager: Erwin L. Verity. Special Processes: Ub Iwerks, A.S.C. Sound: Robert O. Cook. Film Editor: Anthony Gerard.

BAYOU BOY

Produced by: James Algar. Written by: Louis Pelletier. Directed by: Gary Nelson. Associate Producer: Tom Leetch. Director of Photography: William Cronjager. Art Directors: John B. Mansbridge, Ed Graves. Film Editor: Lloyd L. Richardson, A.C.E. Set Decorator: Emile Kuri. Music: Buddy Baker. Song: Terry Gilkyson. Costumes: Chuck Keehne. Make-up: Robert J. Schiffer. Sound: Robert O. Cook. Assistant Director: Michael Dmytryk. Unit Manager: Austen Jewell. Program Co-ordinator: Jack Bruner.

BEAVER VALLEY (AND) CAMERAS IN AFRICA

Directed by: Winston Hibler, James Algar. Written by: Winston Hibler, Ted Sears, Lawrence Edward Watkin, Jack Speirs. Music: George Burns (Television), Paul Smith *(Beaver Valley)*. Photography: Alfred G. Milotte. Additional Wildlife Photography: Karl H. Maslowski, Murl Deusing. Film Editors: Robert Belcher, Norman Palmer. Special Processes: Ub Iwerks. Sound: C.O. Slyfield.

BEHIND THE CAMERAS IN LAPLAND (AND) ALASKAN ESKIMO

Directed by: Winston Hibler (Television), James Algar *(Alaskan Eskimo)*. Written by: Dwight Hauser (Teleplay), Ted Sears and Winston Hibler *(Alaskan Eskimo)*. Produced by: Ben Sharpsteen. Music: Joseph S. Dubin (Television), Oliver Wallace *(Alaskan Eskimo)*. Production Supervision: Harry Tytle. Film Editors: Harry Reynolds (Television), Anthony Gerard *(Alaskan Eskimo)*. Special Processes: Ub Iwerks, A.S.C. Sound: Robert O. Cook. Narrator: Winston Hibler.

BEHIND THE SCENES WITH FESS PARKER

Directed by: Francis Lyon. Produced by: Lawrence Edward Watkin. Written by: James Algar, Dwight Babcock, Lawrence Edward Watkin. Music: Paul Smith. *Sons of Old Aunt Dinah*: Music: Stan Jones. Lyrics: Lawrence Edward Watkin. Photography: Charles Boyle, A.S.C., Jack Whitman, Sr. Art Director: Carroll Clark. Film Editor: Stanley Johnson, A.C.E. Matte Artist: Peter Ellenshaw. Set Decoration: Emile Kuri. Production Supervision: Harry Tytle. Special Processes: Ub Iwerks, A.S.C. Sound: Robert O. Cook. Assistant Director: Robert Shannon. Production Manager: Russ Haverick.

BEHIND THE TRUE-LIFE CAMERAS (AND) OLYMPIC ELK

Directed by: Winston Hibler (Television), James Algar *(Olympic Elk)*. Written by: Jack Speirs, Ted Sears, Winston Hibler. Music: George Burns (Television), Paul Smith *(Olympic Elk)*. Production Supervision: Harry Tytle. Special Art Work: Joshua Meador, Art Riley, John Hench. Photography: Herb and Lois Crisler *(Olympic Elk)*, Charles P. Boyle, A.S.C. (Television). Film Editors: George Nicholson, Anthony Gerard. Special Processes: Ub Iwerks. Sound: Robert O. Cook. Acknowledgments: National Park Service, Olympic National Park, Mt. Rainier National Park.

BEN AND ME (AND) PETER AND THE WOLF

Directed by: Hamilton S. Luske *(Ben and Me)*, Clyde Geronimi *(Peter and the Wolf)*. Story by: Bill Peet *(Ben and Me, based on the book by: Robert Lawson, Dick Huemer and Eric Gurney *(Peter and the Wolf)*. Music: Oliver Wallace *(Ben and Me)*, Serge Prokofieff, as adapted by: Edward Plumb *(Peter and the Wolf)*. Narrated by: Sterling Holloway. Additional Voices: Hans Conried (Thomas Jefferson), Dal McKennon (Benjamin Franklin). Animation: Wolfgang Reitherman, Ollie Johnston, John Lounsbery, Eric Larson, Ward Kimball, Hal King. Layout: Al Zinnen, Thor Putnam, Charles Philippi, Hugh Hennesy. Background: Claude Coats, Al Dempster. Sound: Robert O. Cook. Program Co-ordinator: Jack Bruner.

BEST DOGGONED DOG IN THE WORLD, THE

Old Yeller Sequence Directed by: Robert Stevenson. Teleplay by: James Algar, Lee Chaney. Music: Oliver Wallace. Photographers: Charles P. Boyle, A.S.C., Ray Fernstrom, A.S.C., Jack Couffer. Art Director: Carroll Clark. Film Editors: Norman Palmer, A.C.E., Anthony Gerard. Set Decoration: Fred MacLean. Sound: Robert O. Cook. Assistant Director: Robert G. Shannon. Production Supervision: Harry Tytle. *Arizona Sheepdog Sequence.* Produced and Directed by: Larry Lansburgh. Written by: Janet Lansburgh, Bill Walsh. Music: William Lava. Narrator: Rex Allen. Photographer: Gordon Avil, A.S.C. Film Editor: John Link. Sound: Mac Dalgleish. *Credits for 1961 version* Directed by: Robert Stevenson. Teleplay by: James Algar, Lee Chaney. Produced by: Bill Walsh. Directors of Photography: Edward Colman, A.S.C., Jack Couffer. Art Director: Carroll Clark. Film Editor: Donald Halliday. Set Decoration: Emile Kuri. Sound: Robert O. Cook. Assistant Director: Arthur J. Vitarelli.

BEYOND WITCH MOUNTAIN

Executive Producer: William Robert Yates. Director of Photography: Jack A. Whitman, Jr. Produced by: Jan Williams. Based on Characters Created by: Alexander Key. Teleplay by: Robert Malcolm Young, B. W. Sandefur, Hal Kanter. Story by: Robert Malcolm Young. Directed by: Robert Day. Music by: George Duning. Art Director: Mark Mansbridge. Editor: Gordon D. Brenner, A.C.E. Unit Production Manager: Paul Wurtzel. Assistant Director: Skip Beaudine. Second Assistant Director: Doug Metzger. Casting: Bill Shepard, Virginia Higgins. Sound: Bob Hathaway. Sound Effects Editor: Ben Hendricks. Music Editor: Ralph Hall. Costumes: Jack Sandeen. Make-up: Robert J. Schiffer, C.M.A.A. Hair Stylist: Ginger Grieve. Set Decorator: Mary Swanson. Stunt Coordinator: Bob Harris. Special Effects: Michael Reedy.

BIG COUNCIL, THE

Directed by: Lewis R. Foster. Teleplay by: Tom Blackburn. Based on the novel by: Stewart Edward White. Photographer: Walter H. Castle, A.S.C. Art Director: Carroll Clark. Film Editor: George Gale, A.C.E. Music: George Bruns. Songs: *The Saga of Andy Burnett:* Tom Blackburn. *Ladies in the Sky:* George Bruns. *Molly:* George Bruns. Matte Artist: Peter Ellenshaw. Sound: Robert O. Cook. Set Decoration: Fred MacLean. Costumer: Chuck Keehne. Make-up: Pat McNalley. Assistant Director: Robert G. Shannon. Production Supervisor: Harry Tytle.

BIG SWINDLE, THE

Co-producer: Ron Miller. Teleplay: Maurice Tombragel. Based on the book by: Richard Harding Davis. Directed by: Jeffrey Hayden. Film Editor: Cotton Warburton. Assistant to the Producer: Joseph L. McEveety. Director of Photography: William Snyder, A.S.C. Art Directors: Carroll Clark, William H. Tuntke. Set Decorators: Emile Kuri, Frank R. McKelvy. Song: Richard M. Sherman, Robert B. Sherman. Costumes: Chuck Keehne. Make-up: Pat McNalley. Hair Stylist: La Rue Matheron. Sound: Robert O. Cook. Assistant Director: Tom Leetch. Program Co-ordinator: Jack Bruner.

BIGFOOT

Original Score by: Bruce Rowland. Editor: Howard Kunin, A.C.E. Art Director: Cameron Birnie. Director of Photography: Frank Flynn. Produced by: Michael S. McLean. Written by: John Groves. Directed by: Danny Huston. Unit Production Manager: Lynn H. Guthrie. First Assistant Director: John M. Poer. Second Assistant Director: John N. Whittle. Casting by: Allison Jones. Costume Designer: William Ware Theiss. Associate Producer: Harvey Marks. Set Decorator: Toby Considine. Property Master: Chris Eguia. Key Costumers: Cecil Bud Clark, Francis Harrison Hayes. Make-up: Carol Schwartz. Hair Stylist: Edie Panda. "Bigfoot" Design: Robert J. Schiffer, Lance Anderson. Additional Photography: Harry Mathias. Location Manager: Binnie Rubin. Script Supervisor: Sonny P. Filippini. Production Coordinator: Robin E. Birnie. Production Sound Mixer: Donald F. Johnson. Sound Editing by: Stephen J. Cannell Productions, Michael O'Corrigan. Music Editing by: The Music Design Group, Chris Ledesma.

BIRTH OF THE SWAMP FOX, THE

Directed by: Harry Keller. Teleplay by: Lewis R. Foster. Based on the book by: Dr. Robert D. Bass. Produced by: James Pratt. Director of Photography: Philip Lathrop. Art Director: Marvin Aubrey Davis. Film Editor: Robert Stafford. Music: William Lava. Songs: Lew Foster, Buddy Baker. Sound: Robert O. Cook. Set Decoration: Emile Kuri, Hal Gausman. Costumer: Chuck Keehne. Make-up: Pat McNalley. Hair Stylist: Ruth Sandifer. Assistant Director: Robert G. Shannon.

BLUEGRASS SPECIAL, THE

Executive Producer: Ron Miller. Produced by: James Algar. Director of Photography: Duke Callaghan. Teleplay by: Sheldon Stark. Based on a story by: James Algar. Directed by: Andrew V. McLaglen. Art Directors: John B. Mansbridge, Al Roelofs. Editor: Gordon D. Brenner. Set Decorator: Frank R. McKelvy. Matte Artist: P.S. Ellenshaw. Music: Buddy Baker. Sound: Herb Taylor. Costumes: Chuck Keehne. Make-up: Robert J. Schiffer. Hair Stylist: La Rue Matheron. Unit Manager/Assistant Director: Michael Dmytryk. Second Assistant Director: Dorothy Kieffer. Animal Supervision: Jay Fishburn, Don Spinney.

BOOMERANG, DOG OF MANY TALENTS

Produced by: Harry Tytle. Teleplay by: Rod Peterson, Orma Wallengren. Story by: Harry Tytle, Orma Wallengren. Directed by: John Newland. Director of Photography: Frank Phillips, A.S.C. Art Director: Carroll Clark. Film Editor: Norman Palmer, A.C.E. Set Decorators: Emile Kuri, Hal Gausman. Music: Buddy Baker. Songs: Mel Leven. *World of Color* Theme Song: Richard M. Sherman, Robert B. Sherman. Costumer: Chuck Keehne. Make-up: Gordon Hubbard. Hair Stylist: La Rue Matheron. Sound: Robert O. Cook. Second Unit Director: Arthur J. Vitarelli. Assistant Director: Christopher Hibler. Animal Supervision: William R. Koehler, Lionel Comport. Program Co-ordinator: Jack Bruner. Vice President in Charge of Television: Ron Miller.

BORN TO RUN

Director of Photography: Geoff Burton, A.C.S. Art Director: David Copping. Costume Designer: Judith Dorsman. Editor: Peter Boita. Additional Photography: Bill Grimmond, A.C.S. Camera Operator: John Seale. Production Manager: Sue Milliken. Assistant Director: Mark Egerton. Continuity: Lyn McEnroe. Production Co-ordinator: Pom Oliver. Casting: Sandra McKenzie. Make-up and Hairdressing: Patrica Cunliffe. Production Management in Australia: Samson Productions Pty. Ltd. Production Accountant: Fred Harding. Animal Trainer: Jim Prine. Stunt Co-ordinator: Heath Harris. Camera Assistants: David Williamson, David Burr. Sound Editor: Peter Best. Sound Recordists: Don Connolly, Ken Barker. Music Composed and Conducted by: Ron Goodwin. Production Supervision: Hugh Attwooll. Executive Producer: Ron Miller. Screenplay by: Ed Jurist. Based on the book *The Boyds of Black River* by: Walter D. Edmonds. Produced by: Jerome Courtland. Directed by: Don Chaffey. Filmed on location in Australia and Re-recorded at Pinewood Studios, London, England.

BOY AND THE BRONC BUSTER, THE

Produced by: Ron Miller. Television Story and Teleplay by: Herman Groves. Based on a book by: Will James. Directed by: Bernard McEveety. Director of Photography: Emmett Bergholz. Art Directors: John B. Mansbridge, Walter M. Simmonds. Film Editor: Marsh Hendry. Set Decorator: Bill Calvert. Music: Robert F. Brunner. Animal Supervision: Mel Ballard. Sound: Herb Taylor. Costumes: Chuck Keehne. Make-up: Robert J. Schiffer. Hair Stylist: La Rue Matheron. Assistant Director: Ted Schilz.

BOY CALLED NUTHIN', A

Produced by: Bill Anderson. Teleplay by: Lowell S. Hawley, James Leighton. Based on the book *Nuthin'* by: Harry E. Webb. Directed by: Norman Tokar. Director of Photography: William Snyder, A.S.C. Art Directors: Carroll Clark, John B. Mansbridge. Film Editor: Robert Stafford, A.C.E. Matte Artist: Alan Maley. Set Decoration: Emile Kuri, Frank R. McKelvy. Costumer: Chuck Keehne. Make-up: Gordon Hubbard. Hair

Stylist: La Rue Matheron. Music: George Bruns. Songs: Richard M. Sherman, Robert B. Sherman. Unit Manager: Art Vitarelli. Assistant Director: Bud Grace. Sound: Robert O. Cook. Program Co-ordinator: Jack Bruner.

Boy Who Flew with Condors, The

Co-producer: James Algar. Teleplay by: Homer McCoy. Based on a Story by: Ken Nelson. Narrator: Leslie Nielsen. Film Editor: Gordon Brenner. Music: Buddy Baker. *World of Color* Theme: Richard M. Sherman, Robert B. Sherman. Production Manager: Erwin L. Verity. Sound: Robert O. Cook. Program Co-ordinator: Jack Bruner. *For Ken Nelson Productions* Field Producer: Ken Nelson. Photographers: Ken Nelson, John Morrill. Additional Condor Photography: Ed N. Harrison. Acknowledgments: The Soaring Society of America, Inc., National Aeronautics and Space Administration, The National Audubon Society.

Boy Who Stole the Elephant, The

Produced by: Winston Hibler. Teleplay by: William Robert Yates, John McGreevey. Based on the book by: Julilly H. Kohler. Directed by: Michael Caffey. Associate Producer: William Robert Yates. Director of Photography: Emmett Bergholz. Art Director: John B. Mansbridge. Film Editor: Ray de Leuw. Set Decorators: Emile Kuri, Frank R. McKelvy. Music: Buddy Baker. Sound: Robert O. Cook. Costumer: Chuck Keehne. Make-up: Robert J. Schiffer. Hair Stylist: La Rue Matheron. Assistant Director: John Clarke Bowman. Program Co-ordinator: Jack Bruner.

Boy Who Talked to Badgers, The

Produced by: James Algar. Director of Photography: Gilbert Hubbs. Teleplay by: Sheldon Stark. Based on the book *Incident at Hawk's Hill* by: Allen W. Eckert. Directed by: Gary Nelson. Narrated by: Denver Pyle. Art Directors: John B. Mansbridge, Leroy G. Deane. Film Editor: Gregg McLaughlin, A.C.E. Set Decorator: John Irwin. Music: Buddy Baker, Franklyn Marks. Sound: Herb Taylor. Costumes: Chuck Keehne. Make-up: Robert J. Schiffer. First Assistant Director: Tom McCrory. Second Assistant Director: Martin Walters. Animal Supervision: George Toth, Carl Miller, Helena Walsh. Filmed entirely in Alberta, Canada.

B.R.A.T. Patrol, The

Original Score by: Jonathan Tunick. Editors: Glenn Farr, Barbara Dixon. Art Director: Raymond G. Storey. Director of Photography: Fred J. Koenekamp, A.S.C. Produced by: Mark H. Ovitz. Written by: Chris C. Carter, Michael Patrick Goodman. Directed by: Mollie Miller. Unit Production Manager: Robin S. Clark. First Assistant Director: John M. Poer. Second Assistant Director: John Whittle. Casting: Junie Lowery. Casting Associate: Joanne Koehler. Costume Designer: William Ware Theiss. Set Decorator: Gary Moreno. Property Master: Barbara Adamski. Key Costumers: Gene Ashman, Pam Wise. Make-up: Robert A. Sidell, S.M.A. Hair Stylist: Adele Taylor. Assistant to Mr. Ovitz: Cheryl Denise Edwards. Second Unit Director: R. A. Rondell. Location Manager: Bruce Lawhead. Script Supervisor: Nancy Banta Hansen. Production Coordinator: Susan Powers-Cullen. Production Sound Mixer: Glenn Anderson. Sound Editing by: Stephen J. Cannell Productions, Michael O'Corrigan/Cliff Bell, Jr. Music Editing by: Robert E. Post. Re-Recorded at: The Burbank Studios. *Wipe Out* Words and Music by: Robert Berryhill, Patrick Connoly, James Fuller, Ron Wilson. Performed by: Randall Crissman. A Mark H. Ovitz Production. Acknowledgment: United States Marine Corps.

Brand New Life: Above and Beyond Therapy

Created by: Chris Carter. Music: Steve Tyrell. Supervising Producer: Eric Laneuville. Produced by: George W. Perkins. Written by: John J. Strauss. Directed by: Eric Laneuville. Executive Producer: Chris Carter. Associate Producer: Elissa Rashkin. Casting by: Barbara Remsen, C.S.A., Ann Remsen Manners. Director of Photography: Jack Whitman, A.S.C. Art Director: Tommy Goetz. Film Editor: George Hively, A.C.E. Unit Production Manager: David H. Menter. First Assistant Director: Gary Law. Second Assistant Director: Ricardo Mendez Matta. Costume Supervisor: Wingate Jones. Set Decorator: Fred Winston. Property Master: Frank C. Irving. Construction Coordinator: John G. Heath. Barbara Eden's Makeup: Richard R. Blair. Barbara Eden's Hair: Danne D. Long. Script Supervisor: Patience Thoreson. Production Auditor: Maria Hunt. Production Coordinator: Rosie Dean. Assistant Production Coordinator: Kathy "Sam" Menteer. Camera Operator: William R. Whitman. Chief Lighting Technician: William Huffman. Key Grip: Vern Matthews. Sound Mixer: Charles Knight. Assistants to Executive Producer: Leslie Frishberg, Ray Hoese. Assistant to Producer: Lisa Lange. Assistant to Director: Marchella Liles. Location Manager: Bob Maharis. Transportation Coordinator: Mike Doyle. Sound Supervision: Sync-Pop, Inc. Music Editors: Doug Lackey, Marty Wereski. Assistant Film Editor: Christopher Notarthomas. Consultant: Gene Schwam. *Brand New Life* Theme Written by: Steve Tyrell, Stephanie Tyrell, Guy Moon. Performed by: Jill Colucci. Post Production Supervisor: Dorothy J. Bailey. Executive in Charge of Production: William F. Phillips, NBC Productions.

Brand New Life: Children of a Legal Mom

Created by: Chris Carter. Music: Steve Tyrell. Supervising Producer: Eric Laneuville. Produced by: George W. Perkins. Written by: Chris Carter. Directed by: Steve Robman. Executive Producer: Chris Carter. Associate Producer: Elissa Rashkin. Casting by: Barbara Remsen, C.S.A., Ann Remsen Manners. Director of Photography: Jack Whitman, A.S.C. Art Director: Tommy Goetz. Film Editor: George Hively, A.C.E. Unit Production Manager: David H. Menter. First Assistant Director: Gerry Walsh. Second Assistant Director: Ricardo Mendez Matta. Costume Supervisor: Wingate Jones. Set Decorator: Mark Hite. Property Master: Frank C. Irving. Construction Coordinator: John G. Heath. Barbara Eden's Makeup: Richard R. Blair, Dulcie E. Smith. Barbara Eden's Hair: Danne D. Long. Key Hair Stylist: Shanon Ely. Script Supervisor: Tom Moore. Production Accountant: Maria Hunt. Camera Operator: William R. Whitman. Chief Lighting Technician: William Huffman. Key Grip: Vern Matthews. Sound Mixer: Charles Knight. Location Manager: Bob Maharis. Transportation Coordinator: Mike Doyle. Production Coordinator: Rosie Dean. Assistant Production Coordinator: Kathy "Sam" Menteer. Assistants to Mr. Carter: Leslie Frishberg, Ray Hoese. Assistant to Mr. Perkins: Lisa Lange. Assistant to Mr. Laneuville: Marchella Liles. Sound Supervision: Sync-Pop, Inc. Music Editor: Marty Wereski. Assistant Film Editor: Christopher Notarthomas. Consultant: Gene Schwam. *Brand New Life* Theme Written by: Steve Tyrell, Stephanie Tyrell, Guy Moon. Performed by: Jill Colucci. Post Production Supervisor: Dorothy J. Bailey. Executive in Charge of Production: William F. Phillips. NBC Productions.

Brand New Life: I Fought the Law

Created by: Chris Carter. Music: Steve Tyrell. Supervising Producer: Eric Laneuville. Produced by: George W. Perkins. Written by: Duane B. Clark, Steven Wilde. Directed by: Steven Robman. Executive Producer: Chris Carter. Associate Producer: Elissa Rashkin. Casting by: Barbara Remsen, C.S.A., Ann Remsen Manners. Director of Photography: Jack Whitman, A.S.C. Art Director: Tommy Goetz. Film Editor: J. Benjamin Chulay. Unit Production Manager: David H. Menter. First Assistant Director: Gerry Walsh. Second Assistant Director: Ricardo Mendez Matta. Costume Supervisor: Wingate Jones. Set Decorator: Fred Winston. Property Master: Frank C. Irving. Construction Coordinator: John G. Heath. Paintings by: Norma Topa Gross. Barbara Eden's Make-up: Richard R. Blair. Barbara Eden's Hair: Danne D. Long. Script Supervisor: Patience Thoreson. Production Auditor: Maria Hunt. Production Coordinator: Rosie Dean. Assistant Production Coordinator: Kathy "Sam" Menteer. Camera Operator: William R. Whitman. Chief Lighting Technician: William Huffman. Key Grip: Vern Matthews. Sound Mixer: Charles Knight. Assistants to Executive Producer: Leslie Frishberg, Ray Hoese. Assistants to Producer: Lisa Lange, Marchella Liles. Location Manager: Bob Maharis. Transportation Coordinator: Mike Doyle. Sound Supervision: Sync-Pop, Inc. Music Editors: Doug Lackey, Marty Wereski. Assistant Film Editor: Jan Wesley. Consultant: Gene Schwam. *Brand New Life* Theme Written by: Steve Tyrell, Stephanie Tyrell, Guy

Moon. Performed by: Jill Colucci. Post Production Supervisor: Dorothy J. Bailey. Executive in Charge of Production: William F. Phillips. NBC Productions.

BRAND NEW LIFE: PRIVATE SCHOOL
Created by: Chris Carter. Music: Steve Tyrell. Supervising Producer: Eric Laneuville. Produced by: George W. Perkins. Written by: Dori Pierson. Directed by: Eric Laneuville. Executive Producer: Chris Carter. Associate Producer: Elissa Rashkin. Casting by: Barbara Remsen, C.S.A., Ann Remsen Manners. Director of Photography: Jack Whitman, A.S.C. Art Director: Tommy Goetz. Film Editor: Steven Polivka. Unit Production Manager: David H. Menteer. First Assistant Director: Gary Law. Second Assistant Director: Ricardo Mendez Matta. Costume Supervisor: Wingate Jones. Set Decorator: Fred Winston. Property Master: Frank C. Irving. Construction Coordinator: John G. Heath. Barbara Eden's Make-up: Richard R. Blair, Dulcie E. Smith. Barbara Eden's Hair: Danne D. Long, Shanon Ely. Script Supervisor: Patience Thoreson. Production Auditor: Maria Hunt. Camera Operator: William R. Whitman. Chief Lighting Technician: William Huffman. Key Grip: Vern Matthews. Sound Mixer: Charles Knight. Location Manager: Bob Maharis. Transportation Coordinator: Mike Doyle. Production Coordinator: Rosie Dean. Assistant Production Coordinator: Kathy "Sam" Menteer. Assistants to Mr. Carter: Leslie Frishberg, Ray Hoese. Assistant to Mr. Perkins: Lisa Lange. Assistant to Mr. Laneuville: Marchella Liles. Sound Supervision: Sync-Pop, Inc. Music Editor: Marty Wereski. Assistant Film Editor: William Turro. Consultant: Gene Schwam. *Brand New Life* Theme Written by: Steve Tyrell, Stephanie Tyrell, Guy Moon. Performed by: Jill Colucci. Post Production Supervisor: Dorothy J. Bailey. Executive in Charge of Production: William F. Phillips. NBC Productions.

BRAND NEW LIFE: THE HONEYMOONERS
Music by: Steve Tyrell. Edited by: Allan Jacobs, Steven Polivka. Art Director: Tommy Goetz. Directors of Photography: Branley B. Six, A.S.C., Jack Whitman, A.S.C. Supervising Producer: Eric Laneuville. Produced by: George W. Perkins. Written by: Chris Carter. Directed by: Eric Laneuville. Executive Producer: Chris Carter. Associate Producer: Elissa Rashkin. Co-Producer: Marvin Miller. Casting by: Barbara Remsen, C.S.A., Ann Remsen Manners. Unit Production Managers: Marvin Miller, David H. Menteer. First Assistant Directors: John A. Liberti, Gary Law. Second Assistant Directors: Michael J. Schilz, Ricardo Mendez Matta. Costume Design: Clifford L. Chally. Set Designer: Martha Johnston. Set Decorators: Bruce Kay, Fred Winston. Property Master: Frank Irving. Construction Coordinator: John G. Heath. Costume Supervisors: Wingate Jones, Maureen Gates. Barbara Eden's Make-up: Richard R. Blair. Barbara Eden's Hair: Danne D. Long. Camera Operators: Gordon Paschal, William R. Whitman. Sound Mixers: James La Rue, Charles Knight. Script Supervisor: Patience Thoreson. Chief Lighting Technicians: Ben Graham, William Huffman. Key Grips: Robert Blair, Vern Matthews. Transportation Coordinator: Mike Doyle. Production Assistants: Marilyn Tasso, Maria Hunt. Production Coordinators: Elaine Dysinger, Rosie Dean. Assistant to Executive Producer: Leslie Frishberg. Assistant to Producer: Lisa Lange. Assistant to Director: Marchella Liles. Production Assistant: David J. White II. Sound Supervision: Sync-Pop, Inc. Music Editor: Doug Lackey. Assistant Film Editors: Robert Hernandez, Charles Simmons. Re-Recording Mixers: Robert L. Harman, C.A.S., Jim Williams, Allen L. Stone. Consultant: Gene Schwam. *Brand New Life* Theme Written by: Steve Tyrell, Stephanie Tyrell, Guy Moon. Performed by: Jill Colucci. Post Production Supervisor: Dorothy J. Bailey. Executive in Charge of Production: William F. Phillips. NBC Productions.

BRIDE OF BOOGEDY
Original Score by: John Addison. Editor: Duane Hartzell, A.C.E. Art Director: James Shanahan. Director of Photography: King Baggot. Produced by: Oz Scott, Michael Janover. Written by: Michael Janover. Directed by: Oz Scott. Associate Producer: Carey Melcher. Unit Production Manager: Steve Barnett. First Assistant Director: Bob Rolsky. Second Assis-

tant Director: Lawrence J. Lipton. Casting by: Reuben Cannon & Associates, Monica Swan, C.S.A. Costume Designer: William Ware Theiss. Set Decorator: Ethel Robins Richards. Property Master: Lavar Emert. Key Costumers: Margo Baxley, Nancy Martinelli. Make-up: Rick Stratton. Hair Stylist: Lynn Masters. Script Supervisor: Nina Hibler. Production Coordinator: Lorna Neal. Special Effects: Robbie Knott. Special Photographic Effects: Richard Mosier, Allen Gonzales, Bill Kilduff. Production Sound Mixer: Charles M. Wilborn. Sound Editing by: Echo Film Services, Joseph Melody. Music Editing by: The Music Design Group/James Burt. A Michael Janover/Oz Scott Production.

BRIMSTONE, THE AMISH HORSE
Teleplay by: Bill Bryan. Based on a Story by: Larry Lansburgh. Produced and Directed by: Larry Lansburgh. Production Supervisor: Robert Baron. Photographer: Edward P. Hughes. Film Editor: Lloyd L. Richardson, A.C.E. Narrator: George Fenneman. Race Caller: Stan Bergstein. Music: William Lava. *World of Color* Theme Song: Richard M. Sherman, Robert B. Sherman. Sound: Robert O. Cook. "Brimstone" Trained by: Jay Sisler. Technical Assistance: Mrs. John B. Hannum, M.F.H. Wardrobe by: Brittany. Program Co-ordinator: Jack Bruner. Vice President in Charge of Television: Ron Miller.

BRISTLE FACE
Co-producer: Bill Anderson. Teleplay by: Maurice Tombragel. Based on the book by: Zachary Ball. Directed by: Bob Sweeney. Associate Producer: Louis Debney. Director of Photography: William Snyder, A.S.C. Art Directors: Carroll Clark, John B. Mansbridge. Film Editor: Robert Stafford, A.C.E. Set Decorators: Emile Kuri, Frank R. McKelvy. Music: George Bruns. Songs: Richard M. Sherman, Robert B. Sherman. Costumes: Chuck Keehne. Make-up: Pat McNalley. Sound: Robert O. Cook. Assistant Director: John C. Chulay. Program Co-ordinator: Jack Bruner.

BROTHER AGAINST BROTHER
Directed by: Harry Keller. Teleplay by: Lewis R. Foster. Based on the book by: Dr. Robert D. Bass. Produced by: James Pratt. Director of Photography: Philip Lathrop. Art Director: Marvin Aubrey Davis. Film Editor: Robert Stafford. Music: William Lava. Songs: Lew Foster, Buddy Baker. Sound: Robert O. Cook. Set Decoration: Emile Kuri, Hal Gausman. Costumer: Chuck Keehne. Make-up: Pat McNalley. Hair Stylist: Ruth Sandifer. Assistant Director: Robert G. Shannon.

CALL IT COURAGE
Teleplay by: Ben Masselink. Based on the book by: Armstrong Sperry. Narration by: Gerald Pearce. Produced and Directed by: Roy Edward Disney. Narrator: Don Ho. Film Editor: Toby Brown. Music: Robert F. Brunner. Sound: Herb Taylor. Production Manager: Erwin L. Verity. *For Cangary Limited* Field Producer: Milas Hinshaw. Photography: David E. Jackson. Production Assistant: Carmen Ribera. Underwater Photography: William "Bumpy" Bell. Production Staff: Brian Burton, Albert Walker Levy, Fabian Mataihau, Tom Hinshaw.

CAMERAS IN SAMOA (AND) THE HOLLAND STORY
Directed by: Winston Hibler. Written by: Jack Speirs, Winston Hibler. Music: Joseph S. Dubin. Production Supervision: Harry Tytle. Special Art Work: Joshua Meador, Art Riley. Photographed by: Samoa Sequence: Herbert and Trudi Knapp. Holland Sequence: Profilti. Film Editor: Grant K. Smith. Special Processes: Ub Iwerks, A.S.C. Sound: Robert O. Cook.

CAPTAIN EO BACKSTAGE
Produced and Directed by: Muffett Kaufman. Written by: Jeff Walker, Joshua Alper, Douglass Ross, Matthew Cohen, Muffett Kaufman. Associate Producer: Douglas Ross. Edited by: Joshua Alper. Director of Photography: Robert E. Collins. Cameraman: Michael Chevalier. Sound Men: Bruce Bisenz, John Glasscock, Garry Cunningham, John Vincent. Camera Assistants: John Abbene, Rod Blackie, Dan Dayton, Greg Schmidt. Gaffers: Howard Ex, John Reynolds, Scott Buttfield. Assistant Editor: Christopher Kassas. Production Assistants: Todd Crossley, Gary DePew, Matthew Cohen, Katie Morgan. Transcription: Julie Reed. Videotape Editors: Ron Menzies,

Alex Gimenez. Assistant Videotape Editors: Larry Peake, Robert Berryman, Thomas Haigh. Re-Recording Mixer: David Fluhr. Sound Editor: Ross Davis. Production Accountant: Barbara Pearlman. Electronic Graphics: Carol Phillips. *Captain Eo credits:* Cast: Michael Jackson (Captain Eo), Anjelica Huston (Witch Queen), Dick Shawn (Commander Bog), Tony Cox (Hooter), Gary DePew (Major Domo), Debbie Carrington (Geex), Cindy Sorenson (Geex). Executive Producer: George Lucas. Directed by: Francis Coppola. *Another Part of Me* by: Michael Jackson. *We Are Here to Change the World* by: Michael Jackson, John Barnes. Produced by: Rusty Lemorande. Choreography by: Michael Jackson, Jeffrey Hornaday. A Presentation of MKD Productions in association with Three DDD Productions, Inc.

CARLO, THE SIERRA COYOTE
Teleplay by: Homer McCoy. Based on the book *Sierra Outpost* by: Lila Loftberg, David Malcolmson. Produced and Directed by: James Algar. Narrator: Robert Fuller. Voice of John Muir: Walker Edmiston. Film Editor: Gordon Brenner. Music: Buddy Baker. Sound: Herb Taylor. Production Co-ordinator: Robert F. Metzler. *For Arcane Films Inc.* Field Producer: Hank Schloss. Photography: Hank Schloss, Derek Scott. Additional Photography: John Emerson. Animal Supervision: Hubert Wells. Production Assistant: Robert Misiorowski. Acknowledgments: U.S. National Park Service, U.S. Department of Agriculture, Inyo National Forest.

CARNIVAL TIME
Directed by: Hamilton S. Luske. Story by: Joe Rinaldi, Bill Berg. Art Styling: McLaren Stewart. Animation: Ward Kimball, Art Stevens, Julius Svendsen, Bob McCrea. Effects Animation: Jack Boyd. Layout: Joe Hale. Background: Al Dempster, Bill Layne. With the talents of: Paul Frees. Music: George Bruns. Songs: Richard M. Sherman and Robert B. Sherman. Film Editor: Lloyd L. Richardson, A.C.E. Sound: Robert O. Cook. New Orleans Mardi Gras Photographed by: J. P. Carson Productions. Rio de Janeiro Carnival Photographed by: Herbert Richers Productions.

CASE OF MURDER, A
Co-producer: Ron Miller. Teleplay: Maurice Tombragel. Based on the book by: Richard Harding Davis. Directed by: Jeffrey Hayden. Assistant to the Producer: Joseph L. McEveety. Director of Photography: William Snyder, A.S.C. Art Directors: Carroll Clark, William H. Tuntke. Film Editor: Marsh Hendry. Set Decorators: Emile Kuri, Frank R. McKelvy. Music: Bob Brunner. Song: Richard M. Sherman, Robert B. Sherman. Costumes: Chuck Keehne. Make-up: Pat McNalley. Hair Stylist: La Rue Matheron. Sound: Robert O. Cook. Assistant Director: Tom Leetch. Program Co-ordinator: Jack Bruner.

CASE OF TREASON, A
Directed by: Louis King. Teleplay by: Lewis R. Foster. Based on the book by: Dr. Robert D. Bass. Produced by: James Pratt. Director of Photography: Floyd Crosby, A.S.C. Art Director: Marvin Aubrey Davis. Film Editor: Cotton Warburton, A.C.E. Music: Buddy Baker, Joseph S. Dubin, Franklyn Marks. Sound: Robert O. Cook. Set Decoration: Emile Kuri, Hal Gausman. Costumer: Chuck Keehne. Make-up: Pat McNalley. Hair Stylist: Ruth Sandifer. Unit Manager: Roy Wade. Assistant Director: Ray Gosnell, Jr.

CASEBUSTERS
Supervising Producer: John Garbett. Executive Producers: Erwin Stoff, Paul Aaron. Teleplay by: George Arthur Bloom, Donald Paul Roos. Story by: Donald Paul Roos. Directed by: Wes Craven. Music by: David Frank. Director of Photography: George Koblasa. Art Director: James Shanahan. Editor: Duane Hartzell. Unit Production Manager/Associate Producer: Gordon Wolf. First Assistant Director: Jack Cummins. Second Assistant Director: Emmitt-Leon O'Neil. Casting by: Judith Holstra, C.S.A., Marcia Ross, C.S.A. Costume Designer: William Ware Theiss. Set Decorator: Carl Biddiscombe. Property Master: Anthony C. Thorpe. Key Costumers: Sandra Berke Jordan, Gene Deardorff. Make-up: Michael F. Blake. Hair Stylist: Eddie M. Barron. Location Manager: Ryan Rosenberg. Script Supervisor: John C. Dutton. Production Co-

ordinator: Vera Martin. Production Sound Mixer: Dean Vernon. Sound Editing by: Echo Film Service/Joseph Melody. Music Editing by: Robert E. Post. Songs: *Burn Down the Night* Performed by: Rose Banks. *Eat It* Performed by: Geoff Koch. *Dare Me* Performed by: Phyllis St. James. *Lucky Star* Performed by: Gail Lennon.

CAVALCADE OF SONGS
Directed by: Wilfred Jackson, Peter Godfrey. Written by: Erdman Penner, Joe Rinaldi. Musical Score: Oliver Wallace. Songs from *Lady and the Tramp* by: Peggy Lee, Sonny Burke. Additional songs by: Frank Churchill, Larry Morey, Allie Wrubel, Ray Gilbert. Photography: Charles Boyle, A.S.C. Special Processes: Ub Iwerks. Film Editor: John Young. Sound Director: C.O. Slyfield. Special Art Work: Ken Anderson, Jay Gould. Assistant Director: Russ Haverick.

CHANDAR, THE BLACK LEOPARD OF CEYLON
Produced by: Harry Tytle, Winston Hibler. Teleplay by: William Robert Yates. Based on the book *Black Lightning* by: Denis Clark. Narration by: Gerald Pearce. Narrated by: Ben Wright. Film Editor: Gregg McLaughlin. Music: Robert F. Brunner. Production Manager: Erwin L. Verity. Production Co-ordinator: Robert F. Metzler. Sound: Herb Taylor. *For Cangary Limited* Field Producers: Norman Wright, Peter B. Good. Photographers: Paul Hipp, Peter B. Good, Dennis Grisco, Somapala Dharmapriya, Willie Blake. Production Assistants: Jean Wright, Ronald Bourne, Charles Nugara, Leslie Abeysekera. Animal Supervision: John and Carol Weinhart, Marky Schumacher. Elephant Technical Advisor: Lynn Dassenaike. Acknowledgment: Government of Sri Lanka (Ceylon).

CHANGO, GUARDIAN OF THE MAYAN TREASURE
Produced by: Roy Edward Disney. Teleplay by: Gerald Pearce. Based on a book by: B. F. Beebe. Narrator: Ricardo Montalban. Film Editor: Norman R. Palmer, A.C.E. Music: Robert F. Brunner. Sound: Herb Taylor. Production Manager: Erwin L. Verity. Program Co-ordinator: Jack Bruner. *For Pisces Productions, Inc.* Field Producer: Frank Zuniga. Photography: Roberto Cedeno, Rene Reyna. Assisted by: Carlos Ancona. Production Assistant: Vicente Valjalo. Animal Supervision: Tom Shivers. Filmed entirely in Yucatán, Mexico. Acknowledgments: Mexican National Tourist Council, Mexican Historical and Archaeological Dept.

CHARLIE CROWFOOT AND THE COATI MUNDI
Produced by: Harry Tytle. Written by: Rod Peterson. Narrator: Elliott Reid. Film Editor: Ernie Milano. Music: Robert F. Brunner. Production Manager: Erwin L. Verity. Sound: Herb Taylor. Program Co-ordinator: Jack Bruner. *For Cangary Limited* Field Producer: Peter B. Good. Production Assistant: Ronald Bourne. Photographers: Peter B. Good, Dennis Grisco. Animal Supervision: Clint Rowe, Charley Blank. Acknowledgments: The Forest Service, U.S. Department of Agriculture for portions filmed in the Coronado National Forest, The University of Arizona, Department of Anthropology.

CHEROKEE TRAIL, THE
Executive Producer: Douglas Netter. Music by: Jerrold Immel. Director of Photography: Jack A. Whitman, Jr. Story by: Louis L'Amour. Teleplay by: Michael Terrance, Keith Merrill. Directed by: Keith Merrill. Art Director: Mark W. Mansbridge. Edited by: Ernest Milano, A.C.E. Unit Production Manager: Paul Wurtzel. Assistant Director: Douglas Wise. Second Assistant Director: Doug Metzger. Casting: Pam Polifroni, Virginia Higgins. Set Decorator: Norman Rockett. Sound: Bob Hathaway. Costumes: Jack Sandeen. Make-up: Robert J. Schiffer, C.M.A.A. Sound Editor: Ben F. Hendricks. Music Editor: Ralph Hall. Post Production Supervisor: John Copeland. In Association with Douglas Netter Productions.

CHESTER, YESTERDAY'S HORSE
Story by: Larry Lansburgh. Teleplay by: William H. Anderson. Produced and Directed by: Larry Lansburgh. Film Editor: Robert Stafford, A.C.E. Music: Richard Shores. Songs Sung and Written by: Randy Sparks. Sound: Herb Taylor. Production Manager: John Wilson. Production Assistant: Brian Lansburgh. Acknowledgments: United States Forest Service of

Umpqua National Forest and Roque River National Forest, Oregon, The Bohemia Lumber Company.

CHICO, THE MISUNDERSTOOD COYOTE
Produced and Narrated by: Winston Hibler. Teleplay by: Albert Aley. Additional Narration Written by: Roy Edward Disney. Based on a Story by: Ernest Thompson-Seton. Directed by: Walter Perkins. Film Editor: Lloyd L. Richardson, A.C.E. Music: Paul Smith. Production Coordinator: Robert F. Metzler. Sound: Robert O. Cook. *For Perkins Films, Inc.* Photographers: Walter Perkins, Charles L. Draper. Technical Advisors: Garry Kenwood, Tom Boutross.

The voices for several of the actors were dubbed as follows: Ray Teal (Rancher), Joe DeRida (Ranch Hand), Ford Rainey (Frank Miller).

CHILD OF GLASS
Art Directors: John B. Mansbridge, Leroy G. Deane. Editor: Lloyd L. Richardson, A.S.C., Danny Lee. Set Decorator: Ruby Levitt. Production Manager: John Bloss. Unit Production Manager/Assistant Director: Michael Dmytryk. Second Assistant Director: Dorothy Kieffer. Sound Supervisor: Herb Taylor. Sound Mixer: Lee Strosnider. Costumes: Chuck Keehne, Emily Sundby. Make-up: Robert J. Schiffer. Hair Stylist: Eddie Barron. Sound Editor: Ben F. Hendricks. Music Editor: Jack Wadsworth. Music by: George Duning. Director of Photography: William Cronjager, A.S.C. Executive Producer: Ron Miller. Produced by: Jan Williams, Tom Leetch. Teleplay by: Jim Lawrence. Based on the novel *The Ghost Belonged to Me* by: Richard Peck. Directed by: John Erman.

CHRISTMAS AT WALT DISNEY WORLD
Executive Producers: Ron Miller, Steve Binder. Directed by: Steve Binder. Written by: Danny Simon, Doug Beckwith, Avery Schreiber, Steve Binder, Robert Shields. Produced by: Phil May. Associate Producers: Patti Person, Vincent Poxon. Art Directors: Gene McAvoy, Tom Meleck. Musical Director: Dennis McCarthy. Musical Director for Shields and Yarnell: Norman Mamey. Choreographer: Paul DeRolf. Ballet Choreographed by: Patrice McCoy. Costumes by: Molly Harris Campbell. Associate Director: Cristina Saffer. Assistant to the Producer: Robin Westphall. Production Assistants: Dean Barnes, Kathy Baltimore, Nick Fearnley. Technical Director: Gene Growe. Lighting Directors: William Knight, Carl Vitelli. Production Services Co-ordinator: C.B. Chisam. Audio: Bruce Burns, Dennis Drake. Video: Don Clagett. Videotape Editor: Terry Climer. Aerial Photography: Ron Sheldon. Cameramen: Ron Sheldon, Bob Keyes, Wayne Orr. Stage Manager: Peter Barth. Make-up: Sheryl Leigh Shulman. Hair Stylist: Renata. Acknowledgment: The Entire Staff of Walt Disney World Co. A Steve Binder Production in association with Walt Disney Productions.

CHRISTMAS STAR, THE
Original Score by: Ralph Burns. Edited by: Andrew London, Joe Ravetz. Production Designer: Michael Bolton. Art Director: Eric Fraser. Director of Photography: Paul Lohmann. Executive Producer: Franklin R. Levy. Produced by: Alan Shapiro, Jeffrey White. Teleplay by: Alan Shapiro, Carol Dysinger. Story by: Alan Shapiro. Directed by: Alan Shapiro. Unit Production Manager: Fitch Cady. First Assistant Director: Robert Cowan. Second Assistant Director: Peter Dashkowytch. Casting by: Joyce Robinson, C.S.A., Penny Ellers, C.S.A. Costume Designer: Madeline Ann Graneto. Set Decorator: Peter Hinton. Property Master: James H. Chow. Costume Coordinator: Stephanie Nolin. Key Costumer: Wendy Foster. Make-up: Sandy Cooper. Hair Stylist: Sherry Linder. Casting Toronto: Stuart Aikens Casting. Casting Vancouver: Lynne Carrow. Location Manager: Stewart Bethune. Script Supervisor: Lara Fox. Production Coordinator: Sandra Palmer. Production Sound Mixer: Douglas Arnold. Sound Editing by: Superior Sound Inc., David Yewdall, Steve Rice. Music Editing by: Allan K. Rosen. Lake Walloon Productions, Inc. Catalina Production Group, Ltd.

CITY FOX, THE
Teleplay by: Homer McCoy, James Algar. Television story by: Sam Thomas. Based on a book by: John Kieran. Produced and Directed by: James Algar. Narrator: Rex Allen. Film Editor:

Gordon Brenner. Music: George Bruns. Sound: Herb Taylor. Production Manager: Erwin L. Verity. Program Co-ordinator: Jack Bruner. *For Charles Draper Productions, Inc.* Field Producer: Charles L. Draper. Photography: Charles L. Draper, Costa Nichols, Chris Malkiewicz. Animal Supervision: Gary Kenwood, Doug Bundock. Production Assistant: Don McMeekin. Acknowledgment: San Francisco Parks and Recreation Department.

COME FLY WITH DISNEY
This episode was aired without production credits.

CONCHO, THE COYOTE WHO WASN'T
Co-producer: James Algar. Narration Written by: Jack Couffer, Inez Cocke. Based on the Book *Coyote Come Home* by: B. F. Beebe. Narrator: Rex Allen. *World of Color Theme:* Richard M. Sherman, Robert B. Sherman. Music: Buddy Baker. Film Editor: Gregg McLaughlin. Production Manager: Erwin L. Verity. Sound: Robert O. Cook. Program Co-ordinator: Jack Bruner. *For Grey Owl Productions, Inc.* Field Producer: Jack Couffer. Photographers: Jack Couffer, Gary Kenwood. Production Manager: Pieter Hubbard. Wildlife Supervisors: Al Niemela, Mike Guinn. Acknowledgment: U.S. National Park Service, Sacred Mountain Trading Post.

COUNTRY COYOTE GOES HOLLYWOOD, A
Co-producer: Winston Hibler. Story by: Jack Speirs, Winston Hibler. Teleplay by: Jack Speirs. Narrator: Rex Allen. Production Manager: Erwin L. Verity. Production Co-ordinator: Robert F. Metzler. Film Editor: George Gale, A.C.E. Music: George Burns. Orchestration: Walter Sheets. Song *When The Neon Is In Bloom* by: Jack Speirs, George Bruns. Music Editor: Evelyn Kennedy. *World of Color* Theme: Richard M. Sherman, Robert B. Sherman. Sound: Robert O. Cook. Program Co-ordinator: Jack Bruner. *For Grey Owl Productions, Inc.* Field Producer: Jack Couffer. Photographers: Jack Couffer, Gary Kenwood. Wildlife Supervisors: Al Niemela, Mike Guinn. Production Manager: Tom Boutross. Vice President in Charge of Television: Ron Miller.

Not credited, but used in the show, was the song *A Country Coyote* by George Bruns.

COYOTE'S LAMENT, THE
Directed by: C. August Nichols. Story: Lance Nolley, Milt Schaffer, Dick Kinney, Eric Gurney. Animation: John Lounsbery, Cliff Nordberg, Robert Youngquist, Bill Keil, Eric Larson, George Nicholas, George Kreisl, Phil Duncan. Layout: Erni Nordli, Karl Karpé. Backgrounds: William Layne, Ralph Hulett. Animation Research: Bob McCrea. Film Editor: Tom Acosta. Music: George Bruns, Oliver Wallace, Paul Smith. Lyrics: C. August Nichols. Sound: Robert O. Cook.

CRISLER STORY, THE (AND) PROWLERS OF THE EVERGLADES
Directed by: James Algar. Produced by: Ben Sharpsteen. Teleplay written by: Dwight Hauser. *Prowlers of the Everglades* Written by: James Algar. Narrated by: Winston Hibler. Music: Paul Smith. Photographed by: Herb and Lois Crisler, Alfred G. Milotte. Film Editors: Edward Sampson, Anthony Gerard. Animation Effects: Joshua Meador, John Hench, Art Riley. Special Processes: Ub Iwerks, A.S.C. Sound: Robert O. Cook. Production Supervision: Harry Tytle, Erwin L. Verity. Acknowledgments: National Park Service, Everglades and McKinley National Parks.

CRISTOBALITO, THE CALYPSO COLT
Produced by: Roy Edward Disney. Written by: Norman Wright. Narrator: Ulises Brenes. Film Editor: Norman R. Palmer, A.C.E. Music: George Bruns. Song: Norman Wright, George Bruns. Production Manager: Erwin L. Verity. Sound: Robert O. Cook. Program Co-ordinator: Jack Bruner. *For Norman Wright Productions, Inc.* Field Producer: Norman Wright. Photography: Jack R. Steely. Production Manager: Charles A. Gibbs. Business Manager: Jean Wright. Acknowledgments: Federacion del Deporte de Caballos de Paso Fino de Puerto Rico, Dr. Arnaldo Monroig, Presidente, San Juan National Historic Site, National Park Service, Department of the Interior.

CRUSADING REPORTER
Co-producer: Ron Miller. Written by: Maurice Tombragel. Based on the book *Gallegher* by: Richard Harding Davis. Directed by: Joseph Sargent. Assistant to the Producer: Jerome Courtland. Director of Photography: William Snyder, A.S.C. Art Directors: Carroll Clark, William L. Campbell. Film Editor: Jack Vandagriff. Set Decorators: Emile Kuri, Bill Calvert. Music: Willis Schaefer. *World of Color* Theme: Richard M. Sherman, Robert B. Sherman. Costumer: Chuck Keehne. Make-up: Vivienne Zavitz. Sound: Robert O. Cook. Assistant Director: Paul L. Cameron. Program Co-ordinator: Jack Bruner.

DAD, CAN I BORROW THE CAR?
Produced and Directed by: Ward Kimball. Written by: Ted Berman. Narrated by: Kurt Russell. With the Talents of: Spencer Quinn (car salesman), Jesse White (father), Pete Renoudet, June Foray, Larry Cloege. Assistant to the Producer: Louis Debney. Film Editor: Lloyd L. Richardson, A.C.E. Music: George Bruns. Theme Song *Wheels* by: The Kaleidoscope. Animation: Art Stevens. Layout: Joe Hale. Graphic Design: John Emerson, Ed Garbert. Sound: Robert O. Cook. Program Co-ordinator: Jack Bruner. Field Producers: Walter Perkins, John O'Connor. Additional Photography: Rolf Darbo, Nick Iuppa, John Kimball, Jim Talbot. Acknowledgments: State of California, Department of Motor Vehicles, California Show Cars, Creative Playthings, Inc.

DAILY PRESS VS. CITY HALL, THE
Co-producer: Ron Miller. Teleplay: Maurice Tombragel. Based on the book by: Richard Harding Davis. Directed by: Jeffrey Hayden. Assistant to the Producer: Joseph L. McEveety. Director of Photography: William Snyder, A.S.C. Art Directors: Carroll Clark, William H. Tuntke. Film Editor: Marsh Hendry. Set Decorators: Emile Kuri, Frank R. McKelvy. Music: Bob Brunner. Song: Richard M. Sherman, Robert B. Sherman. Costumes: Chuck Keehne. Make-up: Pat McNalley. Hair Stylist: La Rue Matheron. Sound: Robert O. Cook. Assistant Director: Tom Leetch. Program Co-ordinator: Jack Bruner.

DAVY CROCKETT AND THE RIVER PIRATES
Directed by: Norman Foster. Produced by: Bill Walsh. Written by: Tom Blackburn, Norman Foster. Art Director: Feild Gray. Music: George Bruns. Set Decoration: Bertram Granger, Emile Kuri. Matte Artist: Peter Ellenshaw. Costumes: Carl Walker. Make-up: Phil Sheer, David Newell. Photography: Bert Glennon. Film Editor: Stanley Johnston, A.C.E. Special Processes: Ub Iwerks. Sound: Robert O. Cook. Assistant Director: Ivan Volkman. Production Manager: John Grubbs. Songs: *The Ballad of Davy Crockett* and *Yaller, Yaller Gold:* George Bruns, Tom Blackburn.

DAVY CROCKETT AT THE ALAMO
Directed by: Norman Foster. Produced by: Bill Walsh. Written by: Tom Blackburn. Art Director: Marvin Aubrey Davis. Music: George Bruns. Set Decorator: Emile Kuri. Matte Artist: Peter Ellenshaw. Costumes: Norman Martien. Photography: Charles Boyle, A.S.C. Camera Operator: Harvey Gould. Film Editor: Chester Schaeffer, A.C.E. Special Processes: Ub Iwerks. Sound Director: C. O. Slyfield. Assistant Director: James Judson Cox. Songs: *The Ballad of Davy Crockett:* Tom Blackburn, George Bruns. *Farewell:* Davy Crockett, George Bruns.

DAVY CROCKETT GOES TO CONGRESS
Directed by: Norman Foster. Produced by: Bill Walsh. Written by: Tom Blackburn. Music: George Bruns. Matte Artist: Peter Ellenshaw. Photography: Charles Boyle, A.S.C. Camera Operator: Harvey Gould. Editor: Chester Schaeffer, A.C.E. Special Processes: Ub Iwerks. Sound Director: C. O. Slyfield. Unit Production Manager: Henry Spitz. Assistant Director: James Judson Cox. Acknowledgment: State of Tennessee. Song: *The Ballad of Davy Crockett:* George Bruns, Tom Blackburn.

DAVY CROCKETT—INDIAN FIGHTER
Directed by: Norman Foster. Produced by: Bill Walsh. Written by: Tom Blackburn. Music: George Bruns. Photography: Charles Boyle, A.S.C. Editor: Chester Schaeffer, A.C.E. Special Process: Ub Iwerks. Sound Director: C. O. Slyfield. Special Art Work: Joshua Meador, Art Riley, Ken Anderson. Unit Production Manager: Henry Spitz. Assistant Director: James Judson Cox. Acknowledgments: Members of the Cherokee Nation residing on the Qualla Reservation, N.C., U.S. Department of the Interior for sequences photographed in the Great Smoky Mountain National Park, State of Tennessee. Song: *The Ballad of Davy Crockett:* George Bruns, Tom Blackburn.

DAVY CROCKETT'S KEELBOAT RACE
Directed by: Norman Foster. Produced by: Bill Walsh. Written by: Tom Blackburn, Norman Foster. Art Director: Feild Gray. Music: George Bruns. Set Decoration: Bertram Granger. Matte Artist: Peter Ellenshaw. Costumes: Carl Walker. Make-up: Phil Sheer. Photography: Bert Glennon. Film Editor: Stanley Johnson. Special Processes: Ub Iwerks. Sound: Robert O. Cook. Assistant Director: Ivan Volkman. Production Manager: John Grubbs. Songs: *The Ballad of Davy Crockett* and *King of the River:* George Bruns, Tom Blackburn.

DAVY CROCKETT: LETTER TO POLLY, A
Produced by: Frank Fischer. Supervising Producer: Mark H. Ovitz. Developed by: William Blinn. Written by: Paul Savage. Directed by: Harry Falk. Executive Producer: William Blinn. Associate Producer: Frank Merwald. Original Score by: Joel McNeely. Director of Photography: Isidore Mankofsky, A.S.C. Art Director: Ian Thomas. Editor: Edward Salier. Unit Production Manager/Associate Producer: Justis Greene. First Assistant Director: Ken Collins. Second Assistant Director: Robert Petrovicz. Casting by: Peg Halligan, C.S.A. Costumes Designed by: Tom Bronson. Set Decorator: Chris August. Property Master: Grant Swain. Key Costumers: Christopher Ryan, Linda Lee Langdon. Make-up: Joanne Smith. Hair Stylist: Ian Ballard. Vancouver Casting: Lynne Carrow. Location Manager: Janice Frome. Script Supervisor: Susan Weir. Production Coordinator: Catherine Howard. Stunt Coordinator: John Scott. Production Sound Mixer: Garry Cunningham. Sound Editing by: Stephen J. Cannell Productions. Music Editing by: Craig Pettigrew. Acknowledgments: The Province of British Columbia, Ministry of Parks, Golden Ears Provincial Park. Echo Cove Productions in association With Walt Disney Television.

DAVY CROCKETT: NATURAL MAN, A
Produced by: Frank Fischer. Supervising Producer: Mark H. Ovitz. Developed by: William Blinn. Written by: Steven Baum, Neil Alan Levy. Directed by: Charles Braverman. Executive Producer: William Blinn. Associate Producer: Frank Merwald. Original Score by: Joel McNeely. Director of Photography: Isidore Mankofsky, A.S.C. Art Director: Ian Thomas. Editor: Andrew Cohen. Unit Production Manager/Associate Producer: Justis Greene. First Assistant Director: Richard Peter Schroer. Second Assistant Director: Robert Petrovicz. Casting by: Peg Halligan, C.S.A. Costumes Designed by: Tom Bronson. Set Decorator: Chris August. Property Master: Grant Swain. Key Costumers: Christopher Ryan, Linda Lee Langdon. Make-up: Joanne Smith. Hair Stylist: Ian Ballard. Vancouver Casting: Sid Kozak. Location Manager: Janice Frome. Script Supervisor: Shelley Crawford. Production Coordinator: Catherine Howard. Stunt Coordinator: John Scott. Production Sound Mixer: Garry Cunningham. Sound Editing by: Stephen J. Cannell Productions. Music Editing by: Craig Pettigrew. Additional Editing by: Jeff Hodge. Acknowledgments: The Province of British Columbia, Ministry of Parks, Golden Ears Provincial Park. Echo Cove Productions in association With Walt Disney Television.

DAVY CROCKETT: RAINBOW IN THE THUNDER
Original Score by: Joel McNeely. Edited by: Andrew Cohen. Art Director: Ian Thomas. Director of Photography: Isidore Mankofsky, A.S.C. Produced by: Frank Fischer. Supervising Producer: Mark H. Ovitz. Written by: William Blinn. Developed by: William Blinn. Directed by: David Hemmings. Executive Producer: William Blinn. Associate Producer: Frank Merwald. Unit Production Manager/Associate Producer: Justis Greene. First Assistant Director: Tom Rowe. Second

Assistant Director: Ron French. Casting by: Al Onorato, C.S.A., Jerold Franks, C.S.A. Costumes Designed by: Tom Bronson. Set Decorator: Chris August. Property Master: Grant Swain. Key Costumers: Christopher Ryan, Linda Lee Langdon. Make-up: Jayne Dancose. Hair Stylist: Ian Ballard. Vancouver Casting: Sid Kozak. Location Manager: Janice Frome. Script Supervisor: Christine Wilson. Production Coordinator: Catherine Howard. Stunt Coordinator: John Scott. Production Sound Mixer: Ralph Parker. Sound Editing by: Stephen J. Cannell Productions. Music Editing by: Craig Pettigrew. Acknowledgments: The Province of British Columbia, Ministry of Parks, Golden Ears Provincial Park. Echo Cove Productions in association With Walt Disney Television.

DAVY CROCKETT: WARRIOR'S FAREWELL
Produced by: Frank Fischer. Supervising Producer: Mark H. Ovitz. Developed by: William Blinn. Written by: William Blinn. Directed by: James J. Quinn. Executive Producer: William Blinn. Associate Producer: Frank Merwald. Original Score by: Joel McNeely. Director of Photography: Isidore Mankofsky, A.S.C. Art Director: Ian Thomas. Editor: Andrew Cohen. Unit Production Manager/Associate Producer: Justis Greene. First Assistant Director: Patrice Leung. Second Assistant Director: Robert Petrovicz. Casting by: Peg Halligan, C.S.A. Costumes Designed by: Tom Bronson. Set Decorator: Chris August. Property Master: Grant Swain. Key Costumers: Christopher Ryan, Linda Lee Langdon. Make-up: Joanne Smith. Hair Stylist: Ian Ballard. Vancouver Casting: Sid Kozak. Location Manager: Janice Frome. Script Supervisor: Shelley Crawford. Production Coordinator: Catherine Howard. Stunt Coordinator: John Scott. Production Sound Mixer: Garry Cunningham. Sound Editing by: Stephen J. Cannell Productions. Music Editing by: Craig Pettigrew. Acknowledgments: The Province of British Columbia, Ministry of Parks, Golden Ears Provincial Park. Echo Cove Productions in association With Walt Disney Television.

DAY IN THE LIFE OF DONALD DUCK, A
Directed by: Jack Hannah. Story: Albert Bertino, Dave Detiege. Music: Oliver Wallace. Layout: Yale Gracey. Animation: Volus Jones, George Kreisl, Al Coe, Don Lusk, Dan MacManus. Art Director: Feild Gray. Production Supervision: Harry Tytle. Set Decorator: Bertram Granger. Photography: Charles Boyle, A.S.C. Film Editor: Tom Acosta. Special Processes: Ub Iwerks, A.S.C. Sound: Robert O. Cook. Assistant Director: Bill Beaudine, Jr. With the talents of The Mouseketeers, Jimmie Dodd, Roy Williams, Clarence Nash. *Drip-Dippy Donald* Sequence: Directed by: Jack King. Animation: Don Towsley, Paul Allen, Ed Aardal, Sandy Strother. Story: Nick George. Layout: Don Griffith. Background: Howard Dunn.

DAY OF RECKONING
Directed by: Louis King. Teleplay by: Lewis R. Foster. Based on the book by: Dr. Robert D. Bass. Produced by: James Pratt. Director of Photography: Gordon Avil, A.S.C. Art Director: Marvin Aubrey Davis. Film Editor: Cotton Warburton, A.C.E. Music: William Lava. Songs: Lew Foster, Buddy Baker. Sound: Robert O. Cook. Set Decoration: Emile Kuri, Hal Gausman. Costumer: Chuck Keehne. Make-up: Pat McNalley. Hair Stylist: Ruth Sandifer. Assistant Director: Ron Miller.

DEACON STREET DEER, THE
Produced by: David Bombyk. Written by: James Allen Mangold. Directed by: Jackie Cooper. Music by: Mark Snow. Director of Photography: King Baggott. Art Director: Ray Storey. Editor: John Wright. Unit Production Manager/Associate Producer: Bruce Hendricks. First Assistant Director: Anderson House. Second Assistant Director: Joseph Paul Moore. Casting by: Mary Gail Artz. Costume Designer: William Ware Theiss. Set Decorator: Bob Zilliox. Property Master: Lavar Emert. Key Costumers: Aida Swinson, Thalia C. MacArthur. Make-up: Carol Schwartz. Hair Stylist: Gregg Mitchell. Director-Second Unit: Skott Snider. Location Manager: Ronald L. Carr. Script Supervisor: Sally J. Roddy. Production Coordinator: Lorna Neal. Production Sound Mixer: Patrick Mitchell. Sound Editing by: Dimension Sound. Supervising Sound Editor: Michael Hilkene. Music Editing by: Ken Johnson.

DEACON, THE HIGH NOON DOG
Produced by: Roy Edward Disney. Written and Directed by: Norman Wright. Told and Sung by: Roger Miller. Film Editor: Lloyd L. Richardson, A.C.E. Music: Buddy Baker. Sound: Herb Taylor. Production Manager: Erwin L. Verity. Production Coordinator: Robert F. Metzler. *For Norman Wright Productions, Inc.* Field Producer: Norman Wright. Photography: Les Meek, Jack Steely. Production Manager: Jean Wright. Technical Advisors: Hubert Wells, Helena Walsh. Acknowledgments: The Wild Bunch, Tombstone, Arizona; Death Valley National Monument, U.S. Department of Interior; Bureau of Land Management, Boise, Idaho.

DESPERADO FROM TOMBSTONE
Directed by: Harry Keller. Story by: Maurice Tombragel, Cyril Hume. Teleplay by: Maurice Tombragel. Produced by: James Pratt. Director of Photography: William Snyder, A.S.C. Art Director: Stan Jolley. Film Editor: Robert Stafford. Music: Oliver Wallace. Sound: Robert O. Cook. Set Decoration: Emile Kuri, William L. Stevens. Costumer: Chuck Keehne. Make-up: Pat McNalley. Hair Stylist: Ruth Sandifer. Unit Manager: Roy Wade. Assistant Director: Joseph L. McEveety.

DIAMONDS ON WHEELS
Produced by: Ron Miller. Television Story and Teleplay by: William Robert Yates. Based on the book *Nightmare Rally* by: Pierre Castex. Directed by: Jerome Courtland. Associate Producer: Hugh Attwooll. Director of Photography: Michael Reed, B.S.C. Art Director: Vetchinsky. Film Editor: Peter Boita. Set Decorator: Arthur Taksen. Music: Ron Goodwin. Production Manager: Robin Douet. Assistant Director: Anthony Wayne. Make-up: Roy Ashton. Hair Styling: Eileen Warwick. Special Effects: Cliff Culley. Sound: Herb Taylor. Filmed on Location and at Pinewood Studios, London, England.

DISNEY ANIMATION: THE ILLUSION OF LIFE
Executive Producer: William Robert Yates. Director of Photography: Otto Nemenz. Produced by: Bob King, Phil May, William Reid. Narration Written by: William Reid. Story by: Bob King, Phil May. Directed by: William Reid. Editors: Norman R. Palmer, A.C.E., Jack Sekely. Production Manager: Ted Schilz. Assistant Director: Christopher D. Miller. Sound Supervisor: Herb Taylor. Costume Supervisor: Jack Sandeen. Make-up: Robert J. Schiffer, C.M.A.A. Sound Editor: Ben F. Hendricks. Music Editor: Robert E. Post. Set Decorator: Roger M. Shook. Acknowledgments: Directors Guild of America, Writers Guild of America, Screen Actors Guild, International Alliance of Television Stage Employees, American Federation of Musicians. Special thanks to Frank Thomas and Ollie Johnston for the research material provided in their book, *Disney Animation: The Illusion of Life.*

DISNEY CHRISTMAS GIFT, A
Executive Producer: William Robert Yates. Prepared for Television by: Ed Ropolo, Frank Brandt, Darryl Sutton, Joan Spollino. With the Talents of: Bobby Driscoll, Verna Felton, Frances Langford, Ilene Woods. Song *You Can Fly:* Sammy Cahn, Sammy Fain. Additional Music by: John Debney. *On Christmas Morning* Lyrics by: Linda Laurie, Music by: John Debney. Toys from the collection of the Walt Disney Archives.

DISNEY GOES TO THE OSCARS
Produced by: Andrew Solt, Susan F. Walker. Written by: Elayne Boosler, Sam Serlin, Andrew Solt. Directed by: Andrew Solt. Co-Producers: Mark Hufnail, Jim Milio. Segment Producers: Donna Egan-Kaplan, Kevin Miller. Associate Producer: Greg Vines. Unit Production Manager/First Assistant Director: Ira Shulman. Second Assistant Director: Sandi Hauch. Director of Photography: Stan Lazan. Art Directors: Molly Joseph, John Shaffner. Edited by: Donna Egan-Kaplan, Booey Kober, Kevin Miller, Mark West. Additional Music by: John Debney. Songs and Music by: Richard M. Sherman, Robert B. Sherman, Irwin Kostal, John Barry, Paul J. Smith, Mark Ishman, Wendy Carlos. Technical Consultant: Leonard Maltin. Talent Coordinator: Carole Propp. Production Coordinator: Laurie Eagle. Post Production Supervisor: Wayne

Hudgins. Assistant Editors: Daryl Baskin, Sidney Mandell, Greg Steinberg. Post Production Audio: Allen Patapoff. Title Graphics: Jim House. Additional Graphics: Lee Scott. Script Supervisor: Marilyn Bagley. Production Staff: James P. Axotis, Vickie Hilty, Doug Sloan, Sandra Williams. Production Executive: Rachelle Katz. Acknowledgment: Academy of Motion Picture Arts and Sciences. An Andrew Solt Production in association with Walt Disney Television.

DISNEY HALLOWEEN, A
Executive Producer: William Robert Yates. Prepared for Television by: Ed Ropolo, Frank Brandt, Bill Pentland. Featuring: Bing Crosby relating *The Legend of Sleepy Hollow*. From the Original Story by: Washington Irving. Ichabod Songs by: Don Raye, Gene De Paul.

DISNEY ON PARADE
Executive Producer: Ron Miller. Produced by: Michel M. Grilikhes. Directed by: Stan Harris. This telecast of the First Edition of Disney on Parade is from performances of the cast of the Australasian Tour with Joe Giamalva as Mowgli. Creative Staff of the First Edition of *Disney on Parade:* Stage Producer: Bob Jani. Choreographer: Miriam Nelson. *Jungle Book* Choreographer: Tom Hansen. Disney Character Costume Design: Bill Justice. Costume Design: Jack Muhs. Art Styling: Roland Crump. Music Supervisor: Buddy Baker. Sound: Herb Taylor. Program Co-Ordinator: Jack Bruner. Special Material: Tom Adair, Al Bertino, Chuck Corson, Ward Kimball, Alan Wakeling, Roy Williams and Mark Wilson. Production Staff for Australasian Tour, First Edition of *Disney on Parade:* Dances Re-created by: Bob Squire. Assistant: Darina Devens. Supervising Stage Manager: James Karr. Costume Consultant: Frank Marblo. Production Assistant: Helen Gorman.

DISNEY STORYBOOK, A
Dumbo Credits: Based on the book by: Helen Aberson, Harold Pearl. Special Sound Effects by: Sonovox. Supervising Director: Ben Sharpsteen. Screen Story by: Joe Grant, Dick Huemer. Story Direction: Otto Englander. Sequence Directors: Norman Ferguson, Wilfred Jackson, Bill Roberts, Jack Kinney, Sam Armstrong. Animation Directors: Vladimir Tytla, Fred Moore, Ward Kimball, John Lounsbery, Art Babbitt, Woolie Reitherman. Story Development: Bill Peet, Aurie Battaglia, Joe Rinaldi, George Stallings, Webb Smith. Character Designs: John P. Miller, Martin Provenson, John Walbridge, James Bodrero, Maurice Noble, Elmer Plummer. Music: Oliver Wallace, Frank Churchill. Lyrics: Ned Washington. Orchestration: Edward Plumb. Art Direction: Herb Ryman, Terrell Stapp, Al Zinnen, Dick Kelsey, Ken O'Connor, Don DaGradi, Ernest Nordli, Charles Payzant. Backgrounds: Charles Coats, Al Dempster, John Hench, Gerald Nevius, Ray Lockrem, Joe Stahley. Animation: Hugh Fraser, Harvey Toombs, Milt Neil, Hicks Lokey, Howard Swift, Don Towsley, Les Clark, Claude Smith, Berny Wolf, Jack Campbell, Walt Kelly, Don Patterson, Cy Young, Ray Patterson, Grant Simmons, Josh Meador, Bill Shull, Art Palmer.

DISNEY VACATION, A
The Rescuers Musical Score Composed and Conducted by: Artie Butler. *The U.S. Air Force* by: Robert Crawford. Songs: *You Can Fly:* Sammy Cahn, Sammy Fain. *Let's Get Away From It All:* Tom Adair, Matt Dennis.

DISNEY VALENTINE, A
The Jungle Book inspired by the Rudyard Kipling "Mowgli" Stories. *The Bare Necessities* Sung by: Phil Harris. Songs and Music: Richard M. Sherman, Robert B. Sherman, Sammy Fain, Jack Lawrence, Terry Gilkyson, Paul Smith. *Be My Valentine* Lyrics by: Galen R. Brandt. Music by: John Debney. Special Valentine Cards by: C. Robert Moore.

DISNEY'S ALL-AMERICAN SPORTS NUTS
Executive Producer: Ted Eccles. Directed by: Chep Dobrin. Written by: Phil Hahn, Tom Perew, Joseph Maurer, Hennen Chambers, Jack Wohl. Co-Producers: Richard Kaufman, Ashraf Wassef, Moe Ginsberg, Cynthia Convery, Stuart Jay Weiss, Ken Ashe, Richard Squire. Production Supervisors: Todd Komarnicki, Joel Johnston, Jim Damalas, Bart Herbst-

man. Associate Producer: Lesley Maynard. Stage Managers: Peter Bright, Carlos Torres. Production Designer: John C. Mula. Art Director: Kevin Pfeiffer. Videotape Editor: Richard Jacobson. Original Music by: Hopkins Hallman. Talent Coordinator: Robin Eccles. Set Decorator: Dorean Callari. Costume Designer: Larry Velasco. Property Master: Chris Circosta. Technical Director: Cal Slater. Lighting Director: Ken Dettling. Audio Mixer: Tom Ancell. Video: Steve Berry. Post Production Coordinator: Matthew Hintlian. Acknowledgments: Paul Bonnette, Steve Brown, Roger Berger, David Cantu, Arturo Escobar, John Fortino, Shawn Griffin, Walt Louie, Lori Martin, Simon Murton, Timm Nett, Wendy Polson, Shana Post, Apryl Prose, Alan Rich, Dave Romeo, Lynn Ross, Richard Russel, Brian Russo, Nancy Russo, Art Rutter, Mike Sachs, Tim Stack, Judy Toll, Don Woodard, Steve Young, Todd Young. New Wave Productions in association with Walt Disney Television.

DISNEY'S GREATEST DOG STARS
Produced by: Ron Miller. Prepared for Television by: George Petlowany, Bob King, Phil May, Lloyd L. Richardson, Willis Schaefer, Al Kasha, Joel Hirschhorn.

DISNEY'S GREATEST VILLAINS
Produced by: Ron Miller. Prepared for Television by: George Petlowany, Bob King, Jim Love, Irwin Kostal. Song *Trust in Me:* Robert B. Sherman, Richard M. Sherman. Song *My Favorite Dream:* Ray Noble, Bill Walsh.

DISNEY'S HALLOWEEN TREAT
Executive Producer: William Robert Yates. Prepared for Television by: Ed Ropolo, Frank Brandt, Darryl Sutton. With the Talents of: Bobby Driscoll, Peggy Lee. Featuring: Bing Crosby relating *The Legend of Sleepy Hollow*. From the Original Story by: Washington Irving. Songs and Music: Sammy Cahn, Sammy Fain, Don Raye, Gene De Paul, Paul Smith. Additional Music by: John Debney. *Disney's Halloween Treat* Lyrics by: Galen R. Brandt. Music by: John Debney.

DISNEY'S OSCAR WINNERS
Executive Producer: Ron Miller. Narrated by: John Forsythe. Written by: William Reid, Michael Russell. Directed by: William Reid. Editor: Walt Hekking. Songs and Music: Richard M. Sherman, Robert B. Sherman, Irwin Kostal, Sammy Fain, Carol Connors, Paul J. Smith, Ayn Robbins, Artie Butler, Jim Stafford. Additional Music by: John Debney, Walter Sheets. Acknowledgments: Directors Guild of America, Writers Guild of America, Screen Actors Guild, International Alliance of Television Stage Employees, American Federation of Musicians, Academy of Motion Pictures Arts and Sciences. *Disney's Wonderful World* Theme: John Debney, John Klawitter.

DISNEY'S SPORTS SPECIAL
This episode was aired without production credits.

DISNEY-MGM STUDIOS THEME PARK GRAND OPENING, THE
Directed by: Jeff Margolis. Produced by: Hildy Parks. Written by: Robert Arnott, Lane Sarasohn, Dutch C. Chadwick. Musical Numbers Conceived and Arranged by: Glen Roven. Production Designer: Brian Batholomew. Costumes by: Alvin Colt. Musical Numbers Staged and Choreographed by: Walter Painter. Coordinating Producer: Howard G. Malley. Associate Producer: Nina Lederman. Production Coordinator: Paula M. Shugart. Assistants to the Producer: Jerianne Burnette-Keaney, Mary Madeline Franco. Associate Directors: Terry McCoy, Liz Plonka. Stage Managers: David Wader, Leon Robinson. Clip Segments Produced by: Phil Savenick. Talent Coordinator: Robin Mathiesen. Assistant to the Executive Producer: Gail Rosenblum. Script Coordinator: Betsy Krouner. Lighting Designers: Simon Miles, Kirk Witherspoon. Art Director: Keaton S. Walker. Set Decorator: Linda Heller. Hair: Joe DiMaggio, Roberto Fernandez. Make-up: Joe Cranzano. Costumer: Sharon Smith. Assistant Choreographers: Charlene Painter, Michael Chambers. Talent Consultant: Gus Schirmer. Production Coordinators for Disney-MGM: Laura Broome, Heather Caetano, Matt Sites. Technical Su-

pervisor: John B. Field. Audio: Doug Nelson. Video: Keith Winikoff. Videotape Editor: Jon Aroesty. Cameras: Larry Heider, Dave Levisohn, Bill Philbin, Hector Ramirez, Dave Hilmer, David Irete. Utility: Dan Andresen, Charlie Fernandez, John Mayon, Mike Wilson. Audio Assistants: Jeff Fecteau, Murray Siegel. Set Assistants: Jennifer Heller, Vicki Wilson. Edited by: Kris Trexler, Terry Climer, Jeff Palmer. Digital Effects: Limelite Video West, Patrick Marty, Matt Mooney, Jana Fetner. *For Walt Disney Attractions—Opening Weekend Pageant Segments:* Directed by: Rick Locke. Associate Producer: Eddie October. Executive Producer: Ron Logan. Producer: Doug Strawn. Creation and Show Development: Gary Paben. Project manager: Scott Powhatan. Musical Arranger: Steve Skorija. Choreographers: Pam Killinger, Robbie Mackey. Re-Recorded by: Bob Manahan, C.A.S., Bob Douglass. Videotaped at the Disney-MGM Studios, Lake Buena Vista, Florida. Remote Facilities by: Greene, Crowe & Co., Unitel. Post Production Facilities by: Pacific Video-L.A., The Post Group-Orlando. Lech Walesa Segment Produced by: Marek Wosko. Executive Producer: Alexander H. Cohen.

DISNEYLAND AFTER DARK
Written by: Larry Clemmons. Directed by: Hamilton Luske, William Beaudine. Director of Photography: Gordon Avil, A.S.C. Film Editor: Lloyd L. Richardson, A.C.E. Art Styling: McLaren Stewart. Decorations: Emile Kuri. Special Effects: Eustace Lycett. Sound: Robert O. Cook. Assistant Director: Bernard McEveety.

DISNEYLAND AROUND THE SEASONS
Co-producer: Harry Tytle. Narration Written by: Larry Clemmons. Directed by: Hamilton Luske. Production Associate: McLaren Stewart. Director of Photography: William Snyder, A.S.C. Film Editor: Lloyd L. Richardson, A.C.E. Talent Co-ordinator: Tommy Walker. Music: Franklyn Marks. *World of Color Theme* and *It's a Small World:* Richard M. Sherman, Robert B. Sherman. Assistant Director: Joseph L. McEveety. Sound: Robert O. Cook. Program Co-ordinator: Jack Bruner.

DISNEYLAND: FROM THE PIRATES OF THE CARIBBEAN TO THE WORLD OF TOMORROW
Co-producer: Harry Tytle. Narration Written by: Martin A. Sklar. Directed by: Hamilton S. Luske. Production Associate: McLaren Stewart. Director of Photography: Gordon Avil, A.S.C. Film Editor: Lloyd L. Richardson, A.C.E. Music: Franklyn Marks. Songs: *Yo Ho:* Xavier Atencio, George Bruns. *World of Color* Theme Song: Richard M. Sherman, Robert B. Sherman. Assistant Director: Michael Moder. Sound: Robert O. Cook. Program Co-ordinator: Jack Bruner. Additional Photography by: Norman Wright Productions, Inc.

DISNEYLAND GOES TO THE WORLD'S FAIR
Narration Written by: Charles Shows. Directed by: Hamilton Luske. Animation Director: Ward Kimball. Cartoon Story: Bill Berg. Production Assistant: McLaren Stewart. Animation: Art Stevens, Julius Svendsen, Charlie Downs, Jack Boyd. Layout: Don Griffith, Joe Hale. Background: Jimi Trout. Film Editor: Lloyd L. Richardson, A.C.E. Music: Franklyn Marks. Songs: Richard M. Sherman, Robert B. Sherman. *The History of Fairs:* Written by: Mel Leven. Sung by: The Hi-Lo's. Associate Producer: Harry Tytle. Director of Photography: William Snyder, A.S.C. Assistant Director: Joseph L. McEveety. Sound: Robert O. Cook. Program Co-ordinator: Jack Bruner.

DISNEYLAND SHOWTIME
Produced by: Ron Miller. Co-producer: Tom Leetch. Written by: John Bradford, Jim De Foe, Bill Richmond, Ed Haas. Directed by: Gordon Wiles. Director of Photography: Frank Phillips, A.S.C. Film Editor: Lloyd L. Richardson, A.C.E. Music: Buddy Baker. Sound: Robert O. Cook. Costumer: Chuck Keehne. Make-up: Robert J. Schiffer. Hair Stylist: La Rue Matheron. Assistant Director: Christopher Hibler. Program Co-ordinator: Jack Bruner.

DISNEYLAND '61 (AND) OLYMPIC ELK
Directed by: Hamilton S. Luske. Narration Written by: Larry Clemmons. Music: Buddy Baker. Songs: Richard M. Sherman, Robert B. Sherman. Film Editor: Lloyd L. Richardson, A.C.E.

Olympic Elk credits: Directed by: James Algar. Written by: Winston Hibler, Ted Sears. Music: Paul Smith. Photographers: Herb and Lois Crisler. Sound: Robert O. Cook. Acknowledgment: National Park Service, Olympic National Park.

DISNEYLAND STORY, THE
Written and Produced by: Bill Walsh. Directed by: Robert Florey, Wilfred Jackson. Musical Score: George Bruns. Photography: Charles Boyle, A.S.C. Settings: Bruce Bushman. Film Editor: Al Teeter. Special Processes: Ub Iwerks. Effects: John Hench, Les Clark. Sound Director: C. O. Slyfield. Production Co-ordinator: Hal Adelquist. Assistant Directors: Russ Haverick, Michael Holoboff.

DISNEYLAND 10TH ANNIVERSARY
Special Material by: Bill Berg. Directed by: Hamilton S. Luske. Production Associate: McLaren Stewart. Director of Photography: Frank Phillips, A.S.C. Film Editor: Lloyd L. Richardson, A.C.E. Set Decoration: Emile Kuri. Disneyland Co-ordinator: Tommy Walker. Music: Buddy Baker, George Bruns, Franklyn Marks. *Anniversary Song:* Richard M. Sherman, Robert B. Sherman. Choreographer: Tom Mahoney. Assistant Director: Joseph L. McEveety. Costumes: Chuck Keehne. Make-up: Pat McNalley. Sound: Robert O. Cook.

DISNEYLAND, THE PARK (AND) PECOS BILL
Television Sequences Directed by: Hamilton S. Luske. *Pecos Bill* Directed by: Clyde Geronimi. Narration Written by: Larry Clemmons. Animation Story by: Erdman Penner, Joe Rinaldi. Music: Buddy Baker, Paul Smith. Animation: Ward Kimball, Milt Kahl, John Sibley, Joshua Meador. Layout: Hugh Hennesey, Lance Nolley. Backgrounds: Claude Coats. Photographer: Charles P. Boyle, A.S.C. Film Editor: Lloyd Richardson. Special Processes: Ub Iwerks, A.S.C. Sound: Robert O. Cook. Assistant Director: Horace Hough. Production Supervision: Harry Tytle.

DISNEYLAND'S ALL-STAR COMEDY CIRCUS
Produced by: Saul Ilson. Directed by: Stan Harris. Written by: Jeffrey Barron, Turk Pipkin, Saul Ilson. Associate Producer: Allan Baumrucker. Art Director: Robert Keene. Original Music by: Antony Marinelli, Brian Banks. Lighting Director: Bob Dickinson. Casting by: Vince Calandra. Costume Designer: Ret Turner. Choreographer: Dee Dee Wood. Associate Director: Laura Lyons. Assistants to the Producer: Roberta Savold, Amy Stober, Paul Hoen. Production Coordinator: Darla Blake. Stage Managers: Michael Kelly, Greg Pasetta, Terri McCoy, Leon Robinson. Make-up: Robert Ryan. Hair: Gail Rowell. Technical Director: John B. Field. Audio: Doug Nelson. Video: John Palacio. Cameras: Ted Ashton, Larry Heider, Sam Drummy, L. David Irete, Dean Hall, David Levisohn. Editor: Bill Breshears. *For Disneyland* Production Supervisor: Del Shilling. Project Manager: Dale Lanier. Technical Manager: Chris Robinson. Production Coordinator: Tim O'Day. Costuming Coordinator: Andy Gordon. Operations Supervisor: John Cameron. Character Supervisor: Tracy Nash. Maintenance Supervisor: George Cardwell. Production Consultant: Gregory Sills.

DISNEYLAND'S 35TH ANNIVERSARY CELEBRATION
Directed by: John Landis. *Cheers* Sketch Directed by: James Burrows. *Ernest* Sketch Directed by: John Cherry. Written by: Joe Guppy, Nancy T. Harris, Joie Albrecht, Scot Garen. *Pigerella* Sketch Written by: Bill Prady. *Ernest* Sketch Written by: Daniel Butler, Glenn Petach. Executive Producer: Debra Hill. Co-Executive Producer: Leslie Belzberg. Director of Photography: Robert Primes. Art Director: Dan Lomino. Edited by: Dale Beldin. Original Score by: Christopher L. Stone. Costumes Designed by: Tom Bronson. Unit Production Manager: Roger Joseph Pugliese. First Assistant Directors: Scott Thaler, Rey Vincenty. Second Assistant Director: Michele Solotar. Production Coordinator: Pam Cornfeld. Stunt Coordinator: Rick Avery. Special Effects: Gary Zink. Additional Editing by: Andrew S. Eisen. Post Production Supervisor: Howard Taksen. Pop-up Card by: Michael Bavaro. Production Sound Mixer: Jim Webb. Acknowledgments: Paramount Pictures Television, Jim Burrows, Glen & Les Charles, The Cast and

Crew of *Cheers*, George Lucas. A Hill/Landis/Belzberg Production in association with Walt Disney Television.

DONALD AND JOSE, OLÉ!

Executive Producer: William Robert Yates. Prepared for Television by: Ed Ropolo, Frank Brandt, Bill Pentland. Featuring: Aurora Miranda of Brazil, Carmen Molina of Mexico.

DONALD DUCK STORY, THE

Directed by: Jack Hannah, Robert Florey. Story by: Jack Hannah, Ted Berman, Albert Bertino. Music: George Bruns. Photography: Wilfred Cline, Charles Boyle. Settings: Feild Gray, Yale Gracey. Film Editor: John Young. Special Processes: Ub Iwerks. Sound Director: C.O. Slyfield. Special Animation: Bob Carlson, Bill Justice, Don Lusk, Al Coe.

DONALD LOVES DAISY

Prepared for Television by: Dennis Landa, V. Renee Toensing, Fausto Sanchez. *Mickey, She's Got a Crush on You.* Song by: Michael & Patty Silversher. Music Video by: Jymn Magon. Narrated by: Rick Dees.

DONALD TAKES A HOLIDAY

Prepared for Television by: George Petlowany.

DONALD'S AWARD

Directed by: Jack Hannah. Sequence Director: Jack King. Story: Dave Detiege, Albert Bertino, Bill Berg, Nick George, Roy Williams. Music: Paul Smith, Oliver Wallace, Joseph S. Dubin. Animation: Volus Jones, George Kreisl, Al Coe, Ken Hultgren, Roy Jenkins, Bob Carlson, Bill Justice. Layout: Yale Gracey. Backgrounds: Ray Huffine, Thelma Witmer. Film Editor: Tom Acosta. Special Processes: Ub Iwerks, A.S.C. Sound: Robert O. Cook. Production Supervision: Harry Tytle.

DONALD'S SILVER ANNIVERSARY

Direction: Hamilton S. Luske. Story: Bill Berg, Larry Clemmons. Layout: McLaren Stewart. Animation: Bob McCrea. Backgrounds: Art Riley. Music: Buddy Baker. Film Editor: Anthony Gerard. Sound: Robert O. Cook.

DONALD'S VALENTINE DAY SALUTE

Executive Producer: Ron Miller. Prepared for Television by: Frank Brandt, Dennis C. Vejar, Bill Pentland, Lou Debney. Direction: Charles Nichols, Clyde Geronimi, Jack Kinney, Jack King, David D. Hand, Wolfgang Reitherman, Hamilton Luske. Directing Animators: Frank Thomas, Norman Wright, John Lounsbery, Eric Larson, Les Clark. Animators: Hugh Fraser, George Kreisl, Don Towsley, Fred Kopietz, George Nicholas, Phil Duncan, Tom Massey, Sandy Strother, Preston Blair, John Sibley, Milton Kahl, Jack Boyd, Harry Holt, George Rowley, Fraser Davis, Jerry Hathcock, Ed Aardal, Ken O'Brien. Stories by: Roy Williams, Joe Rinaldi, Milt Banta, Brice Mack, Perce Pearce, Erdman Penner, Fraser Davis, Jerry Hathcock, Dick Kinney, Larry Morey, Ward Greene, Felix Salten, T. H. White, Charles Perrault. Music: Oliver Wallace, George Bruns, Frank Churchill, Edward Plumb, Paul Smith, John Debney. Songs by: Lorenz Hart, Richard Rodgers, Peggy Lee, Sonny Burke, Richard M. Sherman, Robert B. Sherman, Mack David, Al Hoffman, Jerry Livingston. *Disney's Wonderful World* Theme Song: John Debney, John Klawitter.

DONALD'S WEEKEND

Directed by: Jack Hannah. Sequence Director: Jack King. Story: Dave Detiege, Albert Bertino, Roy Williams, Bill Berg, Ralph Wright, Jack Kinney. Animation: Volus Jones, George Kreisl, Al Coe, Roy Jenkins, Bob Carlson, Harvey Toombs, Bill Justice. Layout: Yale Gracey. Backgrounds: Ray Huffine. Music: Joseph S. Dubin, Oliver Wallace, Paul Smith, Edward Plumb. Film Editor: Tom Acosta. Sound: Robert O. Cook. Production Supervision: Harry Tytle.

DONOVAN'S KID

Executive Producer: Ron Miller. Produced by: Christopher Hibler. Director of Photography: Al Francis, A.S.C. Teleplay by: Harry Spalding. Story by: Peter S. Fischer. Directed by: Bernard McEveety. Art Directors: John B. Mansbridge, Rodger Maus. Editor: Ray de Leuw, A.C.E. Production Manager: John

Bloss. Assistant Director: Paul "Tiny" Nichols. Second Assistant Director: Christopher D. Miller. Music: Jimmie Haskell. Animals Trained by: George Toth. Set Decorator: Frank R. McKelvy. Sound: Herb Taylor. Costumes: Chuck Keehne. Make-up: Robert J. Schiffer, C.M.A.A. Hair Stylist: Norma Lee.

DOUBLE AGENT

Original Score by: Alf Clausen. Editor: Dennis Virkler. Production Designer: John F. DeCuir, Jr. Director of Photography: Fred J. Koenekamp. Produced by: Mark H. Ovitz. Teleplay by: Steven Long Mitchell, Craig W. Van Sickle, Howard Friedlander, Ken Peragine. Story by: Howard Friedlander, Ken Peragine. Directed by: Mike Vejar. Unit Production Manager: Albert J. Salzer. First Assistant Director: David Menteer. Second Assistant Director: Scott Cameron. Casting by: Junie Lowry/Marcy Carriker. Associate Producer: Cheryl Denise Edwards. Costume Designer: William Ware Theiss. Set Decorator: Rochelle Moser. Property Master: Lavar Emert. Key Costumers: Richard Butz, Dawn Jackson. Make-up: Marvin G. Westmore. Hair Stylist: Gregg Mitchell. Location Manager: James "Tad" Tadevic. Script Supervisor: Sally J. Roddy. Production Coordinator: Diane Katz. Production Sound Mixer: William R. Teague. Sound Editing by: Stephen J. Cannell Productions/Michael O'Corrigan. Music Editing by: Seque Music Inc./Jim Harrison. *Secret Agent Man* Words and Music by: P.F. Sloan, Steve Barri. Song Performed by: Kipp Lennon. A Mark Ovitz Production in association with Walt Disney Television.

DOUBLE SWITCH

Songs Composed and Produced by: Jeffrey Hornaday, Charles Hornaday. Original Score by: Michel Colombier. Edited by: John Wright. Production Designer: John DeCuir, Jr. Director of Photography: Fred J. Koenekamp, A.S.C. Produced by: Mark R. Gordon. Teleplay by: John McNamara. Story by: Peter Noah. Directed by: David Greenwalt. Unit Production Manager: Robin S. Clark. First Assistant Director: Mike Kusley. Second Assistant Director: Bruce Solow. Casting by: Matt Casella. Choreography by: Jerry Evans. Set Decorator: Bruce Gibeson. Property Master: Barbara Adamski. Key Costumer: Pat Welch. Make-up: Lynn F. Reynolds. Hair Stylist: Gregg Mitchell. Script Supervisor: Sally J. Roddy. Song Vocalist: Kipp Lennon. Location Manager: Jim "Tad" Tadevic. Production Coordination by: Susan Powers. Production Sound Mixer: Pat Mitchell. Additional Editing by: Michael Tronick, Walter Hekking. Sound Editing by: Dimension Sound/Michael Hilkene. Music editing by: Michael Tronick.

DUCK FLIES COOP

Directed by: Jack Hannah. Story: Dave Detiege, Albert Bertino. Animation: Volus Jones, Al Coe, Roy Jenkins, George Kreisl, Bob Carlson, Bill Justice. Effects Animation: Jack Boyd, Dan MacManus. Layout: Yale Gracey. Backgrounds: Ray Huffine, Thelma Witmer. Film Editor: Tom Acosta. Music: Paul Smith, Oliver Wallace. Sound: Robert O. Cook. Production Supervision: Harry Tytle.

DUCK FOR HIRE

Direction: Jack Hannah. Story: Albert Bertino, Nick George, Dave Detiege, Bill Berg. Music: Oliver Wallace, Paul Smith. Animation: George Kreisl, Carlo Vinci, Roy Jenkins, Al Coe, Volus Jones, Jerry Hathcock, Bill Justice, Bob Carlson. Layout: Yale Gracey. Backgrounds: Ray Huffine, Thelma Witmer. Film Editor: Tom Acosta. Special Processes: Ub Iwerks, A.S.C. Sound: Robert O. Cook. Production Supervision: Harry Tytle.

DUCKTALES VALENTINE!, A

Producer/Supervising Director: Bob Hathcock. Director: Mircea Mantta. Story Editor: Tad Stones. Written by: Ken Uhley. With the Voice Talents of: Miriam Flynn, Linda Gary (Aphroducky), Ken Mars (Vulcan), Chuck McCann (Duckworth), Terence McGovern (Launchpad McQuack), Russi Taylor (Huey, Dewey, Louie, Webby), Alan Young (Uncle Scrooge McDuck). Voice Direction: Andrea Romano. Assistant Producer: Liza-Ann Warren. Art Director: Skip Morgan. Key Layout Stylist: Joe Pearson. Storyboard Design: Viki Anderson, Rich Chidlaw, Jim Mitchell, Wendell Washer, Ryan Anthony. Key Background Styling: Fred Warter. Color Key Styling: Robin Draper. Overseas Animation Supervisor: Brian Ray. Supervising Timing Director: Marlene Robinson May. Timing Directors: Richard Trueblood, Bob Shellhorn, Marsh Lamore, Mircea Mantta. Track Reading: Skip Craig. Production Assistants: Stephanie Elliott, Scott Wolf, Wade Nassir. Script Coordinator: Marie Sager. Talent Coordinator: Olivia Miner. Archive Supervisor: Krista Bunn. Art Coordinator: Karen Silva. Post Production Manager: Sara Duran. Post Production Coordinators: Barbara Beck, Jeffrey Arthur. Managing Editor: Rich Harrison. Supervising Editor: Charlie King. Special Effects Editor: Rick Hinson. Assistant Editors: David Lynch, Thomas Needell, Craig Paulsen. *DuckTales* Theme Composed by: Mark Mueller. Original Music Composed and Conducted by: Ron Jones. Animation Production by: Wang Film Productions Co., Inc, Cuckoos' Nest Studio.

EARTH*STAR VOYAGER
Original Score by: Lalo Schifrin. Visual Effects Produced by: Richard Edlund, A.S.C. Editors: Edward A. Biery, A.C.E., Edward Nassour. Production Designer: John F. DeCuir, Jr. Director of Photography: Robert Stevens. Co-Producer: Dennis E. Doty. Produced by: Howard Alston. Written by: Ed Spielman. Directed by: James Goldstone. Executive Producer: Martin Starger. Unit Production Manager: Justis Greene. First Assistant Director: Patrice Leung. Second Assistant Director: Sandra Mayo. Casting: Sally Dennison, C.S.A., Julie Selzer, C.S.A. Associate: Wendy Kurtzman. Vancouver Casting: Lynne Carrow. Art Director: Ian Thomas. Set Decorator: Linda Vipond. Property Master: Wayne McLaughlin. Costume Designers: Tom Bronson, Monique Stranan. Key Costumers: Thomas Pankiewich, Linda Lee Langdon. Make-up: Ilona Herman. Hair Stylist: Donna Bis. Script Supervisor: Pattie Robertson. Production Coordinator: Sandra Palmer. Production Sound Mixer: Eric Batut. Shell Design: Robert J. Schiffer, Lance Anderson. Stunt Coordinator: Paul Baxley. Visual Effects and Miniatures by: Boss Film Corporation, Los Angeles. Visual Effects Designer: Terry Windell. Motion Control Camera: Mat Beck. Production Supervisor: Donald R. Fly. Visual Effects Editor: Dennis Michelson. Optical Supervisor: Chris Regan. Model Shop Supervisor: Mark Stetson. Special Projects Supervisor: Garry Waller. Chief Engineer: Gene Whiteman. Video and Graphic Displays by: Video Image. Sound Editing by: Echo Film Service/Joseph Melody. Music Editing by: John Mick. Additional Editing by: Walter A. Hekking. Matte Paintings, Titles and Opticals by: Buena Vista Visual Effects Group. Acknowledgments: Roland Canada Music Ltd., Roland DG Canada, Inc., People of the Province of British Columbia. Marstar Productions, Inc. in association with Walt Disney Television.

EL BANDIDO
Directed by: William Witney. Teleplay by: Bob Wehling. Based on the *Zorro* stories by: Johnston McCulley. Produced by: Bill Anderson. Associate Producer: Louis Debney. Director of Photography: Lucien Ballard, A.S.C. Art Director: Marvin Aubrey Davis. Film Editor: Basil Wrangell. Music: William Lava. Matte Artist: Peter Ellenshaw. Sound: Robert O. Cook. Set Decoration: Emile Kuri, William L. Stevens. Costumer: Chuck Keehne. Make-up: Pat McNalley. Hair Stylist: Ruth Sandifer. Fencing Master: Fred Cavens. Unit Manager: Roy Wade. Assistant Director: Vincent McEveety.

END OF THE TRAIL
Directed by: James Neilson. Teleplay by: David P. Harmon. Produced by: Bill Anderson. Associate Producer: Ron Miller. Director of Photography: Edward Colman, A.S.C. Art Director: Marvin Aubrey Davis. Film Editor: Basil Wrangell, A.C.E. Music: Oliver Wallace. Sound: Robert O. Cook. Set Decoration: Emile Kuri. Costumer: Chuck Keehne. Make-up: Pat McNalley. Unit Manager: Roy Wade. Assistant Director: Joseph L. McEveety.

EPCOT CENTER: THE OPENING CELEBRATION
Executive Producers: Gary Smith, Dwight Hemion. Produced by: Ron Miziker. Directed by: Dwight Hemion. Written by: Buz Kohan. Special Musical Material by: Earl Brown. Associate Producer: Michael B. Seligman. Associate Director: Wenda Fong. Musical Director: Ian Fraser. Choreographer: Jim Bates. Costumes Designed by: Pete Menefee. Lighting by: Fred MacKinnon. Production Associate: Nikki Nash. Production Manager: Judith Zaylor. Production Assistant: Syngehilde Schweikardt. Assistant Choreographer: Judy Bates. Musical Arrangements: Bill Byers, Chris Boardman. Film Sequences: Bob Garner. Technical Director: Gene Crowe. Audio: Ed Greene. Video: Keith Winikoff. Video Tape Editor: Andy Zall. Camera Operators: Joe Epperson, David Johnson, Ron Sheldon. Stage Manager: Charles Gayton III. Make-up: Robert J. Schiffer, C.M.A.A., Ralph Gulko. Hairdresser: Gail Rowell. Facilities by: Greene, Crowe and Company, and TCS Productions. Production Assistance and Air Transportation Provided by Eastern Airlines. Acknowledgment: A special thanks to the entire cast of Epcot Center. A Smith-Hemion Production in Association with Walt Disney Productions.

ESCAPADE IN FLORENCE
Teleplay by: Maurice Tombragel, Bob Wehling. Based on a book by: Edward Fenton. Co-producer: Bill Anderson. Directed by: Steve Previn. Associate Producer: Harry Tytle. Director of Photography: Kurt Grigoleit, C.D.K. Film Editors: Lloyd L. Richardson, A.C.E., Alfred Srp. Dialogue Coach: Kent McPherron. Music: Buddy Baker. Songs: Richard M. Sherman, Robert B. Sherman, Franklyn Marks. Sound: Robert O. Cook. Program Co-ordinator: Jack Bruner. Italian Production Organization by International Film Service, Rome: Set Decorator: Andrea F. Antacci. Production Supervisor: Orazio Tassara. Art Director: Gastone Medin. Costumer: Annalisa Nasalli Rocca. Assistant Director: Ottavio Oppo. Make-up: Amato Garbini. Hair Stylist: Gabriella Bonzelli.

ESCAPE TO PARADISE (AND) WATER BIRDS
Escape to Paradise: Teleplay by: Larry Clemmons. Produced by: Bill Anderson. Music: Buddy Baker. *Swiss Family—Calypso* and *Limbo* by: Richard M. Sherman, Robert B. Sherman. *My Heart Was an Island* by: Terry Gilkyson. Production Supervisor: Bob Porter. Director of Photography: John Harris. Film Editor: Lloyd L. Richardson, A.C.E. Music Editor: Evelyn Kennedy. Sound: Robert O. Cook. Production Manager: Basil Keys. *Water Birds:* Directed by: Ben Sharpsteen. Written by: Ted Sears, Winston Hibler, William Otis. Music: Paul Smith. Photography: Alfred G. Milotte, Olin Sewall Pettingill, Jr., Alfred M. Bailey, Ed N. Harrison, Frances F. Roberts, John H. Storer. Film Editor: Norman Palmer, A.C.E. Special Processes: Ub Iwerks, A.S.C. Acknowledgments: National Audubon Society, Denver Museum of Natural History.

EXILE
Music Composed by: Peter Bernstein. Editor: Stanford C. Allen. Production Designer: Michael Nemirsky. Director of Photography: Jose Mignone. Produced by: Mark H. Ovitz. Co-Produced by: Justis Greene, Jonathan Lemkin. Written by: Jonathan Lemkin. Directed by: David Greenwalt. Executive Producer: Patrick Hasburgh. Associate Producer: Jodi Rothe. Casting by: Robert W. Harbin, C.S.A., Beth Hymson, C.S.A. Unit Production Manager: Robin Chamberlin. First Assistant Director: Jamie Freitag. Second Assistant Director: Jeffrey Ellis. Art Director: Sandy Getzler. Set Decorator: Cecilia Rodarte. Men's Costumer: Bill Tiegs. Women's Costumer: Yvonne Kubis. Make-up Artist: Rick Sharp. Hairdresser: K.G. Ramsey. Location Manager: Gary DeGalla. Script Supervisor: Theresa Banks. Post Production Supervisor: Erik Hasburgh. Transportation Coordinator: Craig Pinkard. Production Coordinator: Pamela Hoffman. Production Accountant: Nicole Furia. Camera Operator: Dusty Blauvelt. Stunt Coordinator: Gil Combs. F/X Coordinator: Jan Aaris. Key Gaffer: Alex Skvorzov. Key Grip: Bob Blair. Sound Mixer: David Ronne. A Patrick Hasburgh Production. Walt Disney Television.

FAMILY BAND, THE
Produced by: Bill Anderson. Television Story and Teleplay by: Lowell S. Hawley. From the book *Nebraska 1988* by: Laura Bower Van Nuys. Published by: University of Nebraska Press. Directed by: Michael O'Herlihy. Director of Photography: Frank Phillips, A.S.C. Art Directors: Carroll Clark, Herman Allen Blumenthal. Film Editor: Cotton Warburton, A.C.E. Set

Decorators: Emile Kuri, Hal Gausman. Matte Artist: Alan Maley. Costumes Designed by: Bill Thomas. Music and Lyrics: Richard M. Sherman, Robert B. Sherman. Music Supervised, Arranged and Conducted by: Jack Elliot. Choreography by: Hugh Lambert. Sound: Robert O. Cook. Costumer: Chuck Keehne. Make-up: Gordon Hubbard. Hair Stylist: La Rue Matheron. Unit Manager: Joseph L. McEveety. Assistant Director: Paul L. Cameron. Program Co-ordinator: Jack Bruner.

FANTASY ON SKIS
Associate Producer: Hamilton S. Luske. Teleplay by: Larry Clemmons. Based on a story by: Fred Iselin. Directed by: Fred Iselin. Film Editor: Lloyd L. Richardson, A.C.E. Music: Buddy Baker. Animation Effects: Joshua Meador. Sound: Robert O. Cook. *For Fred Iselin Productions* Photographer: Michael Murphy. Acknowledgment: The People of Aspen, Colorado.

FARAWAY PLACES—HIGH, HOT, AND WET (SIAM)
Produced by: Ben Sharpsteen. Narration Written by: Dwight Houser, Jack Speirs. *Siam* Script by: Ralph Wright, Winston Hibler, Ted Sears, Cecil Maiden. Photographed by: Herbert Knapp. Music: Oliver Wallace. Narrator: Winston Hibler. Film Editors: Harry Reynolds, Jack L. Atwood. Animation Effects: Joshua Meader, Art Riley. Special Processes: Ub Iwerks, A.S.C. Sound: Robert O. Cook. Production Supervisor: Erwin L. Verity, Harry Tytle.

FEATHER FARM, THE
Produced by: Harry Tytle. Teleplay by: John McGreevey. Story by: Rod Peterson. Narration by: Jack Speirs. Narrator: Rex Allen. Film Editor: Ernie Milano. Music: Buddy Baker, Franklyn Marks. Production Manager: Erwin L. Verity. Production Co-ordinator: Robert F. Metzler. Sound: Robert O. Cook. Program Co-ordinator: Jack Bruner. *For Hank Schloss Productions, Inc.* Field Producer: Hank Schloss. Photography: Hank Schloss, Lloyd G. Kenwood. Production Assistant: Gordon Perry. Technicians: Ronald Bourne, John Koester, Gerald Tyra.

FERDINAND THE BULL AND MICKEY
Executive Producer: William Robert Yates. Prepared for Television by: Dennis Landa, Bill Pentland, Darryl Sutton.

FIFTY HAPPY YEARS
Produced by: Ron Miller. Prepared for Television by: Bob King, Ed Ropolo, Gabe Essoe, Donavan Moye. Songs: Sammy Fain, Jack Lawrence: *Once Upon a Dream.* Roger Miller: *Oo-De-Lally.* Richard M. Sherman, Robert B. Sherman: *Jolly Holiday, Chim Chim Cheree, I Wan'na Be Like You, Supercalifragilisticexpialidocious.* Narrated by: Danny Dark.

FIGHTING CHOICE, A
Music by: Brad Fiedel. Editor: Stanford C. Allen. Art Director: Jan Scott. Director of Photography: Robert E. Collins. Produced by: Nelle Nugent. Written by: Craig Buck. Directed by: Ferdinand Fairfax. Unit Production Manager/Associate Producer: Bruce Hendricks. First Assistant Director: Ira Shuman. Second Assistant Director: Joseph Paul Moore. Casting by: Michael Fenton, Jane Feinberg, Judy Taylor, C.S.A. Costume Designer: William Ware Theiss. Set Decorator: Mary Ann Good. Property Master: Lavar Emert. Key Costumers: Aida Swinson, Thalia C. MacArthur. Make-up: Gary Liddiard, C.M.A.A. Hair Stylist: Gregg Mitchell. Location Manager: Ronald Carr. Script Supervisor: Al Greedy. Production Coordinator: Lorna Neal. Producer's Staff Assistant: Myra Model. Production Sound Mixer: Patrick Mitchell. Sound Editing by: Blue Light Sound. Music Editing by: Curtis Roush/Segue Music. Technical Assistants: Peter Reiss, John I. Mosley, M.D., Linda Klein.

FIRE CALLED JEREMIAH, A
Produced by: James Algar. Narration Written by: Dwight Hauser. Narrator: Lawrence Dobkin. Film Editor: Norman Palmer, A.C.E. Music: Oliver Wallace. Sound: Robert O. Cook. *For Ken Nelson Productions* Field Producer: Ken Nelson. Photographers: Ken Nelson, Gene Petersen, Don McIntosh. Filmed with the cooperation of: United States Forest Service, Aerial Fire Depot, Missoula, Montana, Montana State Forester, California State Division of Forestry, Los Angeles County Fire Department.

For the 1966 repeat, the show was re-edited to incorporate *Donald's Fire Survival Plan,* a 1956 animated fire safety short starring Donald Duck and Walt Disney. The credits for that short are as follows: Produced by: Walt Disney. Associate Producer: Ken Peterson. Film Editor: Jim Love. Director: Les Clark. Art Director: A. Kendall O'Connor. Story: William R. Bosché. Backgrounds. Frank Armitage. Music: George Bruns. Animation: Cliff Nordberg, Jack Boyd, Bill Keil. With the talents of: Clarence Nash, Richard Bakalyan, The Firehouse 5 Plus 2. Acknowledgments: Azusa Fire Department, California Fire Chiefs Association, National Fire Protection Association.

FIRE ON KELLY MOUNTAIN
Produced by: James Algar. Teleplay by: Calvin Clements, Jr. Based on the book *The Mallory Burn* by: Pete Pomeroy. *For Robert Clouse Associates, Inc.* Directed by: Robert Clouse. Photographers: Mike Jones, Keith Kelsay. Production Associate: William Redlin. Film Editor: Gordon Brenner. Production Co-ordinator: Robert F. Metzler. Music: Buddy Baker. Narrator: Blake Todd. Sound: Herb Taylor. Acknowledgment: Filmed in the Eldorado National Forest with the co-operation of the U.S. Department of Agriculture, Forest Service, the State of California, Division of Forestry.

FLASH, THE TEENAGE OTTER
Directed by: Hank Schloss. In Charge of Production: James Lebenthal. Photographers: Douglas Cox, Jack F. Ferrucci, Wallace M. Kammann, Wallace Kirkland, Austin McKinney. Technical Advisors: Mabel and Tom Beecham, Niles Fairbairn. With the Cooperation of the Wisconsin Conservation Department. Produced and Narrated by: Winston Hibler. Teleplay by: Albert Aley. Additional Narration by: Roy Edward Disney. Story by: Rutherford Montgomery. Based on a book by: Emil Liers. Production Co-ordinator: Robert F. Metzler. Film Editor: George Gale, A.C.E. Music: Oliver Wallace. Sound: Robert O. Cook.

FLIGHT OF THE GREY WOLF, THE
Produced by: Roy Edward Disney. Director of Photography: William Cronjaeger. Teleplay by: Clavin Clements, Jr. Based on the book *Flight of the White Wolf* by: Mel Ellis. Directed by: Frank Zuniga. Art Director: John B. Mansbridge. Film Editor: Norman R. Palmer, A.C.E. Music: Robert F. Brunner. Sound: Herb Taylor. Costumes: Chuck Keehne. Make-up: Robert J. Schiffer. Unit Production Manager/First Assistant Director: Frank Beetson, Jr. Second Assistant Director: Miles Tilton.

FLY WITH VON DRAKE
Directed by: Hamilton S. Luske. Sequence Director: Jack Kinney. Story: Bill Berg, Ward Kimball. Art Styling: McLaren Stewart. Animation: Art Stevens, Ward Kimball, Julius Svendsen, Jack Boyd. Layout: Joe Hale, A. Kendall O'Connor, Don Griffith. Background: Jimi Trout, Al Dempster, William Layne. Music: George Bruns, Oliver Wallace. With the Talents of: Paul Frees. Film Editor: Tom Acosta. Sound: Robert O. Cook. Program Co-ordinator: Jack Bruner. Map of the Heavens by: National Geographic Society.

FOOTLOOSE GOOSE, THE
Teleplay by: Homer McCoy. Based on the book *Wild Goose, Brother Goose* by: Mel Ellis. Produced and Directed by: James Algar. Narrator: Andrew Duggan. Film Editor: Gordon Brenner. Music: Buddy Baker. Production Manager: Erwin L. Verity. Sound: Herb Taylor. *For Arcane Film Inc.* Field Producer: Hank Schloss. Photography: Hank Schloss, Dave McMillan. Technical Advisors: Harvey Pengelly, Hubert Wells. Acknowledgments: Birdwing Farm, Minnesota, The Jack Miner Migratory Bird Foundation, Ontario, Canada.

FOR THE LOVE OF WILLADEAN
Co-producer: Ron Miller. Teleplay by: Arnold and Lois Peyser. Based on a story by: Borden Deal. Directed by: Byron Paul. Director of Photography: William Snyder, A.S.C. Art Directors:

Carroll Clark, Marvin Aubrey Davis. Film Editor: Robert Stafford, A.C.E. Set Decorators: Emile Kuri and Frank R. McKelvy. Music: Franklyn Marks (Part 1), Bob Brunner (Part 2). Costumes: Chuck Keehne. Make-up: Pat McNalley. Sound: Robert O. Cook. Assistant Director: Tom Leetch. Program Co-ordinator: Jack Bruner.

FOUR DOWN AND FIVE LIVES TO GO
Written and Directed by: Norman Foster. Produced by: James Pratt. Director of Photography: William Snyder, A.S.C. Art Director: Stan Jolley. Film Editor: Edward Sampson, Jr. Music: Buddy Baker. Songs by: Rich Dehr, Frank Miller. Matte Artist: Peter Ellenshaw. Sound: Robert O. Cook. Set Decorators: Emile Kuri, Armor E. Goetten. Costumer: Chuck Keehne. Make-up: Pat McNalley. Assistant Director: Vincent McEveety.

FOUR FABULOUS CHARACTERS
Directed by: Hamilton S. Luske. Sequence Directors: Jack Kinney, Wilfred Jackson. Story by: Bill Peet, Winston Hibler, Dick Kinney, Dick Huemer, Homer Brightman. Music: Clifford Vaughan, Paul Smith, Oliver Wallace, Ken Darby. Animation: Milt Kahl, John Sibley, Eric Larson, Ollie Johnston. Layout: MacLaren Stewart, Don DaGradi, Lance Nolley, Hugh Hennesy. Backgrounds: Claude Coats, Ray Huffine, Art Riley, Ralph Hulett. Photographer: Ray Fernstrom, A.S.C. Art Director: Bruce Bushman. Film Editor: Lloyd Richardson, A.C.E. Set Decoration: Emile Kuri. Special Processes: Ub Iwerks, A.S.C. Sound: Robert O. Cook. Assistant Director: Vincent McEveety. Production Supervision: Harry Tytle.

FOUR TALES ON A MOUSE
Directed by: Hamilton S. Luske. Story: Bill Berg, Nick George. Layout: Al Zinnen, Thor Putnam. Backgrounds: Jimi Trout. Film Editor: Lloyd L. Richardson, A.C.E. Sound: Robert O. Cook. Production Supervisor: Harry Tytle. Christmas Sequence *(Pluto's Christmas Tree):* Director: Jack Hannah. Animation: George Kreisl, Fred Moore. Layout: Yale Gracey. Backgrounds: Thelma Witmer.

14 GOING ON 30
Original Score by: Lee Holdridge. Editor: Richard A. Harris. Art Director: Raymond G. Storey. Director of Photography: Fred J. Koenekamp, A.S.C. Produced by: Susan B. Landau. Executive Producers: James Orr, Jim Cruickshank. Teleplay by: Richard Jefferies. Story by: James Orr, Jim Cruickshank. Directed by: Paul Schneider. Unit Production Manager: Paul Deason. First Assistant Director: Stephen Lofaro. Second Assistant Director: Jeffrey M. Ellis. Casting by: Allison Jones. Costume Designer: Tom Bronson. Set Decorator: Linda Spheeris. Property Master: Kent H. Johnson. Key Costumers: Terrence K. Smith, Kendall Errair. Make-up: Edwin Butterworth. Hair Stylist: Rita Bordonaro. Location Manager: James "Tad" Tadevic. Script Supervisor: Sally J. Roddy. Production Coordinator: Mary Kay Kelly. Production Sound Mixer: John Glascock, C.A.S. Sound Editing by: Dimension Sound. Music Editing by: Segue Music, Inc. Special Effects: Isadoro Raponi. Visual Effects Supervisor: Allen Gonzales. Visual Effects by: Buena Vista Visual Effects Group. *What You See* Music by: Lee Holdridge. Lyrics by: Mark Mueller.

FOURTH ANNIVERSARY SHOW, THE
Directed by: Sidney Miller, Hamilton S. Luske. Producer *Fourth Anniversary Party:* Bill Walsh. Teleplay: Albert Duffy. Music: Buddy Baker. Photography: Ray Terstrom, A.S.C. Art Director: Bruce Bushman. Film Editor: Al Teeter. Set Decoration: Emile Kuri. Choreographer: Tom Mahoney. Special Processes: Ub Iwerks, A.S.C. Sound: Robert O. Cook. Assistant Director: Dolph M. Zimmer. Production Supervision: Harry Tytle. *Peter and the Wolf:* With the Music of Serge Prokofieff. Directed by: Clyde Geronimi. Story: Dick Huemer. Layout: Charles Philippi. Backgrounds: Claude Coats. Animation: Eric Larson, Ward Kimball, Ollie Johnston, John Lounsbery. Narrated by: Sterling Holloway.

FRANK CLELL'S IN TOWN
Directed by: James Neilson. Teleplay by: Maurice Tombragel. Produced by: Bill Anderson. Associate Producer: Ron Miller.

Director of Photography: Edward Colman, A.S.C. Art Director: Marvin Aubrey Davis. Film Editor: Robert Stafford. Music: Buddy Baker. Sound: Robert O. Cook. Set Decoration: Hal Gausman. Costumer: Chuck Keehne. Make-up: Pat McNalley. Unit Manager: Roy Wade. Assistant Director: Joseph L. McEveety.

FRIENDLY ENEMIES AT LAW
Directed by: William Beaudine. Written by: Barney Slater. Produced by: James Pratt. Director of Photography: Lucien Ballard, A.S.C. Art Director: Stan Jolley. Film Editor: Basil Wrangell. Music: Franklyn Marks. Sound: Robert O. Cook. Set Decoration: Emile Kuri, William L. Stevens. Costumer: Chuck Keehne. Make-up: Pat McNalley. Hair Stylist: Ruth Sandifer. Unit Manager: Roy Wade. Assistant Director: Ivan Volkman.

FROM AESOP TO HANS CHRISTIAN ANDERSEN
Directed by: Clyde Geronimi. Story by: Bill Peet. Music: Oliver Wallace. Animation: Wolfgang Reitherman, John Sibley, Dan MacManus. Special Art Work: Tom Codrick, Dick Anthony, Basil Davidovich, Al Dempster, Ray Huffine, Collin Campbell. Editor: Donald Halliday. Special Processes: Ub Iwerks. Sound Director: C.O. Slyfield.

FROM ALL OF US TO ALL OF YOU
Directed by: Jack Hannah. Story: Albert Bertino, Dave Detiege. Styling: John Hench. Animation: Volus Jones, Al Coe, Les Clark, Bob McCrea. Layout: Yale Gracey. Backgrounds: Ray Huffine. Film Editor: Tom Acosta. Music: Paul Smith. Song *You Can Fly:* Sammy Cahn, Sammy Fain. Special Processes: Eustace Lycett. Sound: Robert O. Cook. Production Supervision: Harry Tytle. Acknowledgment: "This special holiday program has been made possible by the combined talents of the entire Walt Disney Studios. It is our way of saying 'Merry Christmas from all of us to all of you.' "

FUZZBUCKET
Music: Peter Bernstein. Supervising Producer: Richard Briggs. Executive Producer: John Landis. Written, Produced, and Directed by: Mick Garris. Director of Photography: Robert Stevens. Art Director: Mark Mansbridge. Editor: Michael S. Murphy. Unit Production Manager/Associate Producer: Bruce Hendricks. First Assistant Director: Mike Kusley. Second Assistant Director: Joseph Paul Moore. Casting: Johanna Ray. Costume Designer: William Ware Theiss. Set Decorator: Rochelle Moser. Property Masters: Lavar Emert, Martin L. Emert. Key Costumers: Aida Swinson, Milton G. Mangum. Make-up: Lance Anderson. Hair Stylist: Gregg Mitchell. Fuzzbuckets Created by: Robert J. Schiffer, Kevin Yagher. Location Manager: Ron L. Carr. Script Supervisor: Judi Brown. Production Coordinator: Lorna Neal. Production Sound Mixer: Patrick Mitchell. Sound Editing by: Echo Film Services/G. Michael Graham. Music Editing by: Robert E. Post.

GALLEGHER
Co-producer: Ron Miller. Teleplay: Maurice Tombragel. Based on the book by: Richard Harding Davis. Directed by: Byron Paul. Associate Producer: Louis Debney. Director of Photography: William Snyder, A.S.C. Art Directors: Carroll Clark, John B. Mansbridge. Film Editor: Robert Stafford, A.C.E. Set Decorators: Emile Kuri, Hal Gausman. Music: Bob Brunner. Song: Richard M. Sherman and Robert B. Sherman. Costumes: Chuck Keehne. Make-up: Pat McNalley. Sound: Robert O. Cook. Assistant Director: Tom Leetch. Program Co-ordinator: Jack Bruner.

GERONIMO'S REVENGE
Directed by: Harry Keller. Written by: David P. Harmon. Produced by: James Pratt. Director of Photography: William Snyder, A.S.C. Art Director: Stan Jolley. Film Editor: Robert Stafford. Music: Oliver Wallace. Song: David Harmon, Buddy Baker. Sound: Robert O. Cook. Set Decoration: Emile Kuri, William L. Stevens. Costumer: Chuck Keehne. Make-up: Pat McNalley. Hair Stylist: Ruth Sandifer. Unit Manager: Roy Wade. Assistant Director: Joseph L. McEveety.

GHOST OF CYPRESS SWAMP, THE

Executive Producer: Ron Miller. Produced by: Christopher Hibler. Director of Photography: Leonard J. South, A.S.C. Teleplay by: Harry Spalding. Based on the book *Weakfoot* by Linda Cline. Directed by: Vincent McEveety. Art Directors: John B. Mansbridge, Frank T. Smith. Editor: Gordon D. Brenner. Unit Production Manager/1st Assistant Director: Paul "Tiny" Nichols. Second Assistant Director: Bud Grace. Set Decorator: Lucien M. Hafley. Sound Supervision: Herb Taylor. Sound Mixer: Bill Teague. Costumes: Chuck Keehne. Make-up: Robert J. Schiffer. Hair Stylist: Judy Alexander. Sound Editor: Raymond Craddock. Music Editor: Jack Wadsworth. Animals Technical Supervisor: George N. Toth. Music: Jimmie Haskell. Orchestration: Walter Sheets.

GHOSTS OF BUXLEY HALL, THE

Executive Producer: William Robert Yates. Produced by: Jerome Courtland. Director of Photography: Leonard J. South, A.S.C. Teleplay by: Sy Gomberg, Rick Mittleman. Story by: Sy Gomberg. Directed by: Bruce Bilson. Art Directors: John B. Mansbridge, Ward Preston. Editor: Norman R. Palmer, A.C.E. Music by: Frank De Vol. Production Manager: John Bloss. Assistant Director: Howard Grace. Second Assistant Director: Don Newman. Special Effects: Art Cruickshank, A.S.C., Danny Lee. Set Decorators: Norman Rockett, Roger M. Shook. Sound: Herb Taylor. Costumes: Jack Sandeen. Make-up: Robert J. Schiffer, C.M.A.A. Hair Stylist: Eddie M. Barron. Portrait Artists: David Mattingly, Constantine Ganakes.

GIRL WHO SPELLED FREEDOM, THE

Music Composed and Conducted by: Mark Snow. Editor: Michael Jablow. Production Designer: Tracy Bousman. Director of Photography: Frank Watts, B.S.C. Executive Producer: Judith A. Polone. Co-Producer: David A. Simons. Produced by: R.W. Goodwin. Written by: Christopher Knopf, David A. Simons. Directed by: Simon Wincer. Executive in Charge of Production: Dennis A. Brown. Casting by: Mike Fenton, C.S.A., Jane Feinberg, C.S.A., Judy Taylor, C.S.A. Canadian Casting: Sid Kozak. Additional Casting: McCorkle Casting Ltd. Production Manager: Fitch Cady. 1st Assistant Director: Rob Cowan. 2nd Assistant Director: Casey Grant. Production Coordinator: Catherine Howard. Location Manager: Stewart Bethune. Production Accountant: Linda Jeffery. Art Director: David Hiscox. Set Decorator: Kim MacKenzie. Wardrobe Head: Stephanie Nolin. Hairdresser: Sherry Linder. Make-up Artist: Sandy Cooper. Transportation Coordinator: Drew Neville. Director of Photography/Second Unit: Michael Ferris. Camera Operator/Steadicam Operator: Robert C. Crone, C.S.C. Additional Camera Operators: Bob Ennis, Paul F. Birkett, Ron McManus. Prop Master: John Stooshnov. Gaffer: John Bartley. Key Grip: Dave Gordon. Sound Mixer: Claude Hazanavicius. Script Supervisor: Lara Fox. Translator/Production Assistant: Sourdsey Sinn. Los Angeles Production Controller: Tink Ten Eyck. Los Angeles Coordinator: Sandra V. Naiman. Assistant to Mr. Goodwin: Jolie Shartin. Assistant Editor: Vaune Kirby. Post Production Supervisor: Tim Myers. Supervising Music Editor: Dan Garde/Segue Music. Supervising Sound Editor: Vince Gutierrez. Supervising Re-Recording Mixer: Gordon Day. A Knopf/Simons Production in association with ITC Productions, Walt Disney Pictures.

GOLDEN DOG, THE

Executive Producer: Ron Miller. Produced by: Harry Tytle. Director of Photography: Robert F. Sparks. Teleplay by: William Canning. Narration written by: Norman Wright. Based on a story by: Harry Tytle. Directed by: William Stierwalt, Fred R. Krug. Editor: Gregg McLaughlin, A.C.E. Music: Robert F. Brunner. Sound: Herb Taylor. Unit Production Manager/Assistant Director: Morris R. Abrams. Second Assistant Director: Reuben Watt. Production Supervisor: William Redlin. Narrator: Douglas Fowley. *For Fred R. Krug Productions, Inc.* Photography: Peter B. Good, Lynn Ellsworth. Production Assistants: Ron Foreman, John Chesko, Clint Rowe. Acknowledgment: Fleetwood Airedales.

GOLDEN HORSESHOE REVUE, THE

Written by: Larry Clemmons. Directed by: Ron Miller. Associate Producer: Louis Debney. Director of Photography:

William Snyder, A.S.C. Art Director: Carroll Clark. Film Editor: Robert Stafford, A.C.E. Set Decorator: Emile Kuri. Costumer: Chuck Keehne. Make-up: Pat McNalley. Hair Stylist: Ruth Sandifer. Music: Buddy Baker. Songs *Mr. Piano Man* and *Hang a Lantern in Your Window* by: Richard M. Sherman, Robert B. Sherman. *Do the Buffalo Roundup:* Bob Jackman, Frank Worth. *Pecos Bill:* Johnny Lange, Eliot Daniel. Sound: Robert O. Cook. Assistant Director: Arthur J. Vitarelli.

GOOFY SPORTS STORY, THE

Directed by: Wolfgang Reitherman. Animation: Eric Cleworth, John Sibley, Harry Holt, Dick Lucas, Amby Paliwoda. Story: Jack Kinney, Dick Kinney. Music: Oliver Wallace. Layout: Don Griffith, Basil Davidovich, Al Zinnen. Backgrounds: Ray Huffine, Al Dempster, Don Peters, Merle Cox. Production Supervision: Harry Tytle. Film Editor: Roy M. Brewer, Jr. Special Processes: Ub Iwerks, A.S.C. Sound: Robert O. Cook.

GOOFY SUCCESS STORY, THE

Directed by: Jack Kinney, Wolfgang Reitherman. Written by: Jack Kinney. Music: Oliver Wallace. Production Supervision: Harry Tytle. Layout and Background Artists: Don Griffith, Dale Barnhart, Vance Gerry, Joe Hale, Eyvind Earle, Ray Huffine, Vera Ohman. Animators: Eric Cleworth, Harry Holt, George Goepper, Dick Lucas, Bob McCrea. Photography: Bert Glennon. Film Editor: Roy M. Brewer, Jr. Special Processes: Ub Iwerks. Sound: Robert O. Cook.

GOOFY'S CAVALCADE OF SPORTS

Directed by: Wolfgang Reitherman. Sequence Director: Jack Hannah. Animation: Dick Lucas, Amby Paliwoda, Bill Keil, Bill Justice. Story: Jack Kinney, Bill Berg. Music: Oliver Wallace. Layout: Basil Davidovich, Dale Barnhart, Vance Gerry, Yale Gracey. Backgrounds: Richard H. Thomas, Tom O'Loughlin, Donald Peters, Maurice Greenberg. Production Supervision: Harry Tytle. Film Editor: Roy M. Brewer, Jr. Special Processes: Ub Iwerks, A.S.C. Sound: Robert O. Cook.

GO WEST, YOUNG DOG

Produced by: Roy Edward Disney. Director of Photography: Michael Watkins. Written by: Barry Clark. Narration by: Milas Hinshaw. Directed by: William Stierwalt. Narrated by: Roger Miller. Editor: Lloyd L. Richardson, A.C.E. Music: George Duning. Sound: Herb Taylor. Unit Production Manager/Assistant Director: Morris R. Abrams. Second Assistant Director: Craig Huston. Production Supervisor: William A. Redlin. *For Milas Hinshaw Productions, Inc.* Field Producer: Milas Hinshaw. Photography: Kim Friese, Brian Burton. Coordinator: Camen Ribera. Technical Advisor: Harold K. Packer. Production Assistants: Milas E. Hinshaw, Tom Lynch, Mary Friese.

GREAT CAT FAMILY, THE

Directed by: Clyde Geronimi. Sequence Directors: Wilfred Jackson, Jack Hannah. Animation: John Sibley, Eric Cleworth, Eric Larson, Ward Kimball, John Lounsbery, Don Lusk. Story: Bill Peet, Winston Hibler, Ted Sears. Music: Oliver Wallace. Layout: Tom Codrick, Erni Nordli, McLaren Stewart. Backgrounds: Dick Anthony, Ray Huffine, Claude Coats, Production Supervision: Harry Tytle. Film Editor: Donald Halliday. Special Processes: Ub Iwerks, A.S.C. Sound: Robert O. Cook.

GREAT MOMENTS IN DISNEY ANIMATION

Produced by: Andrew Solt, Jim Milio. Written by: Jim Milio, Andrew Solt, Susan F. Walker. Directed by: Andrew Solt. Supervising Producer: Susan F. Walker. Co-Producers: Mark Hufnail, Philip Savenick. Associate Producers: Suzy Friendly, Greg Vines. Segment Producers: Donna Egan-Kaplan, Kevin Miller. Unit Production Manager/First Assistant Director: Ira Shuman. Second Assistant Director: Joseph Moore. Director of Photography: William Klages. Art Director: Molly Joseph, John Shaffner. Edited by: Donna Egan-Kaplan, Kevin Miller. Additional Music by: John Debney. Ms. Burnett's Gown by: Bob Mackie. Technical Consultant: Steve Gerbson. Talent Coordinator: Carole Propp. Camera Operator: Bill Philbin. Songs and Music: Richard M. and Robert B. Sherman, Elmer Bernstein, Sonny Burke, Sammy Cahn, Sammy Fain, Irwin

Kostal, Peggy Lee, Paul J. Smith. Make-up by: Joe Blasco. Hair by: Jerry Brennan. Script Supervisor: Cynnie Troup. Videotape Editors: Frank Mazzaro, Mark West. Post Production Supervisor: Wayne Hudgins. Assistant Editors: Daryl Baskin, Sidney Mandell, Greg Steinberg. Post Production Audio: Larry Sullivan. Title Graphics: Jim House. Additional Graphics: Lee Scott. Production Staff: James P. Axotis, Frank Hall, Vickie Hilty, Doug Sloan. *Mickey Mouse* from *Myths* copyright Andy Warhol, 1981. Production Executive: Rachelle Katz. An Andrew Solt Production.

GRETA, THE MISFIT GREYHOUND
Teleplay by: Janet Lansburgh. Produced and Directed by: Larry Lansburgh. Narration and Vocals: Rex Allen. Music: William Lava. Production Assistant: Jay Sisler. Photographer: Larry Lansburgh. Orchestration: Irving Gertz. Music Editor: Tom Downing. Song: Richard M. Sherman, Robert B. Sherman. Sound: Robert O. Cook. Program Co-ordinator: Jack Bruner.

GRISWOLD MURDER, THE
Directed by: Christian Nyby. Written by: Maurice Tombragel. Produced by: James Pratt. Director of Photography: Lucien Ballard, A.S.C. Art Director: Stan Jolley. Film Editor: Stanley Johnson, A.C.E. Music: Buddy Baker. Song: Rich Dehr, Frank Miller. Sound: Robert O. Cook. Set Decorators: Emile Kuri, Vin Taylor. Costumers: Chuck Keehne, Gertrude Casey. Make-up: Pat McNalley. Hair Stylist: Ruth Sandifer. Assistant Director: Joseph L. McEveety.

GUS TOMLIN IS DEAD
Directed by: William Beaudine. Story by: Arthur Orloff. Teleplay by: Fred Freiberger. Produced by: James Pratt. Director of Photography: Lucien Ballard, A.S.C. Art Director: Stan Jolley. Film Editor: Basil Wrangell. Music: Franklyn Marks. Sound: Robert O. Cook. Set Decoration: Emile Kuri, William L. Stevens. Costumer: Chuck Keehne. Make-up: Pat McNalley. Hair Stylist: Ruth Sandifer. Unit Manager: Roy Wade. Assistant Director: Ivan Volkman.

HACKSAW
Story by: Larry Lansburgh. Teleplay by: Dick Spencer III. Produced and Directed by: Larry Lansburgh. Photographed by: Edward P. Hughes. Film Editor: Bob Bring. Music: Franklyn Marks. Special Songs Written and Sung by Randy Sparks: *Hacksaw, Race Song* and *Love Song*. Sound: Herb Taylor. Location Sound: James Camery. Production Supervisor: William C. Davidson. Assistant Director: Terry Nelson. Associate in Production: Jay Sisler. Hacksaw Trained by: Glenn Randall. Program Coordinator: Jack Bruner. Acknowledgment: Forestry Service of Kootenay National Park, British Columbia, Canada.

HALLOWEEN HALL O' FAME
Produced by: Ron Miller. Director of Photography: Frank Phillips, A.S.C. Continuity Material Written by: George Petlowany. Directed by: Arthur J. Vitarelli. Art Director: John B. Mansbridge. Editor: Ernie Milano, A.C.E. Set Decorator: Frank R. McKelvey. Assistant Director: Randy Carter. New Music by: Richard Bowden. Sound: Herb Taylor. Costumes: Chuck Keehne. Make-up: Robert J. Schiffer. Animation Sequence Directors: Clyde Geronomi, Jack Hannah. Animation: Frank Thomas, Bill Justice, George Kreisl, Don Lusk, John Sibley, Wolfgang Reitherman, Eric Cleworth. Story: Erdman Penner, Joe Rinaldi, Winston Hibler, Ralph Wright, Bill Peet. Color Styling: Mary Blair, Don DaGradi, Claude Coats. Layout: Tom Codrick, Yale Gracey, Ernie Nordli. Background: Dick Anthony, Art Riley, Brice Mack. Music: Oliver Wallace, Paul Smith. Song *The Headless Horseman* by: Don Raye, Gene De Paul.

HAMAD AND THE PIRATES
Produced by: Roy Edward Disney. Teleplay by: Gerald Pearce. Based on a story by: Richard H. Lyford. Narrator: Michael Ansara. Film Editor: Toby Brown. Music: Robert F. Brunner, Franklyn Marks. Production Manager: Erwin L. Verity. Sound: Robert O. Cook. Program Coordinator: Jack Bruner. *For RHL*

International Films Field Producer: Richard H. Lyford. Photography: Richard H. Lyford. Production Managers: Khalifah Shaheen, Moray Foutz. Production Staff: Robert Gregory, Ann Crawford, Jack Madvo, Mubarek Buzaid, Sean Hickey, Ali Isa Isa. Acknowledgment: His Highness Sheik Isa Bin Sulman Al-Khalifah, Ruler of Bahrain.

HANS BRINKER OR THE SILVER SKATES
Associate Producers: Hamilton S. Luske, Norman Foster. Teleplay by: Norman Foster. Based on the book by: Mary Mapes Dodge. Narration Written by: Otto Englander. Directed by: Norman Foster. Directors of Photography: Gunnar Fischer, Lars G. Björne. Art Director: Per A. Lundgren. Film Editor: Jack L. Atwood. Production Manager: Gustav Roger. Music: Oliver Wallace. Special Art Work: Joshua Meador. Sound: Stig Flodin. Make-up: Carl M. Lundh. Assistant Director: Katherine Faragó.

HELP WANTED: KIDS
Music by: Craig Safan. Editor: Kaja Fehr. Art Director: Jan Scott. Director of Photography: King Baggot. Written and Produced by: Stephen Black, Henry Stern. Directed by: David Greenwalt. Executive Producer: Stan Rogow. Unit Production Manager/Associate Producer: Bruce Hendricks. First Assistant Director: Ira Shuman. Second Assistant Director: Joseph Paul Moore. Casting by: Marc Schwartz & Associates. Casting Associate: Vicki Huff. Set Decorator: Mary Ann Good. Property Master: Lavar Emert. Key Costumers: Aida Swinson, Thalia C. MacArthur. Make-up: Anthony S. Lloyd. Hair Stylist: Gregg Mitchell. Costume Designer: William Ware Theiss. Location Manager: Ronald L. Carr. Script Supervisor: Sally J. Roddy. Production Coordinator: Lorna Neal. Production Sound Mixer: Patrick Mitchell. Sound Editing by: Sam Horta. Music Editing by: Music Design Group. *Burnin' Down the House* Performed by: Kipp Lennon. *Jump* Performed by: David Morgan. A Stan Rogow Production in association with Walt Disney Television.

HERO IN THE FAMILY
Music: William Goldstein. Editors: Stanford C. Allen, Rod Stephens, A.C.E. Production Designer: Michael Bolton. Art Director: Eric Fraser. Director of Photography: Paul Goldsmith. Produced by: John Drimmer. Supervising Producer: Richard Briggs. Executive Producer: Les Alexander. Written by: John Drimmer, Geoffrey Loftus. Directed by: Mel Damski. Unit Production Manager: Justis Greene. First Assistant Director: Rob Cowan. Second Assistant Director: Patrice Leung. Set Decorator: Kim MacKenzie. Property Master: James H. Chow. Costume Coordinator: Stephanie Nolin. Key Costumers: Wendy Foster, Dan Bronson. Make-up: Sandy Cooper. Hair Stylist: Sherry Linder. Casting/Vancouver: Sid Kozak. Casting/Los Angeles: Mary Gail Artz. Stunt Coordinator: Chuck Waters. Stunt Coordinator/Vancouver: John Scott. Special Effects Coordinator: John Thomas. Vander Veer Photo Effects: Tom Andersen. Animal Supplier/Coordinator: Steve Berens. Animal Trainers: Ken Decroo, Mark Watters. Location Manager: Stewart Bethune. Script Supervisor: Lara Fox. Production Coordinator: Catherine Howard. Production Sound Mixer: Richard Patton. Sound Editing by: Stephen J. Cannell Productions, Larry Mann. Music Editing by: The MX Design Group. Space Sequence Designed by: Paul Peters. Acknowledgment: The National Aeronautics and Space Administration. Barry & Enright Alexander Productions in association with Walt Disney Television.

HIGH FLYING SPY, THE
Produced by: Ron Miller. Co-producer: Tom Leetch. Television Story and Teleplay by: William Robert Yates. Based on the book *High Spy* by: Robert Edmond Alter. Directed by: Vincent McEveety. Director of Photography: Frank Phillips, A.S.C. Art Directors: John B. Mansbridge, Al Roelofs. Film Editor: Cotton Warburton, A.C.E. Set Decorators: Emile Kuri, Harry Gordon. Matte Artist: Alan Maley. Special Effects: Eustace Lycett, Art Cruickshank, A.S.C., Danny Lee. Balloon Technical Consultant: Bill Berry. Music: George Bruns. Sound: Herb Taylor. Costumes: Chuck Keehne. Make-up: Robert J. Schiffer. Assistant Director: Christopher Hibler.

HIGHWAY TO TROUBLE
Directed by: Jack Hannah. Sequence Director: C. August Nichols. Story: Al Bertino, Dave Detiege, Nick George. Animation: Al Coe, Volus Jones, George Kreisl, Roy Jenkins, Bill Justice. Layout: Yale Gracey, Lance Nolley. Backgrounds: Ray Huffine. Film Editor: Tom Acosta. Music: Buddy Baker. Animation Research: Bob McCrea. Sound: Robert O. Cook. Special Processes: Eustace Lycett. Production Supervision: Harry Tytle.

HOG WILD
Produced by: Ron Miller. Teleplay by: Gabe Essoe. Based on the book by: Julia Ridle Mathieu. Co-produced and Directed by: Jerome Courtland. Director of Photography: Frank Phillips, A.S.C. Art Directors: John B. Mansbridge, Walter Tyler. Film Editor: Bob Bring. Set Decorator: Hal Gausman. Music: Franklyn Marks. Costumes: Chuck Keehne. Make-up: Robert J. Schiffer. Hair Stylist: La Rue Matheron. Sound: Herb Taylor. Unit Production Manager/Assistant Director: Michael Dmytryk. Animal Supervision: Hank Cowl.

HOLIDAY FOR HENPECKED HUSBANDS
Directed by: Wolfgang Reitherman. Sequence Directors: Eric Cleworth, Jack Kinney, Eric Cleworth, Bill Peet. Animation: John Sibley, Cliff Nordberg, Ted Berman, Dick Lucas, Ed Aardal, Hugh Fraser. Layout: Basil Davidovich, Dale Barnhart, Al Zinnen. Background: Ralph Hulett, Bill Layne, Dick Anthony. Music: Franklyn Marks, Joseph S. Dubin. Film Editor: Jim Love. Sound: Robert O. Cook.

HOLIDAY TIME AT DISNEYLAND
Directed by: Hamilton S. Luske. Narration Written by: Larry Clemmons. Art Styling: McLaren Stewart. Production Assistant: Louis Debney. Music: Buddy Baker, Franklyn Marks, George Bruns, Oliver Wallace. Song: Richard M. Sherman, Robert B. Sherman. Special Effects: Eustace Lycett. Film Editor: Lloyd L. Richardson, A.C.E. Sound: Robert O. Cook. Program Co-ordinator: Jack Bruner.

HOLSTER FULL OF LAW, A
Directed by: James Neilson. Teleplay by: David P. Harmon. Produced by: Bill Anderson. Associate Producer: Ron Miller. Director of Photography: Edward Colman, A.S.C. Art Director: Marvin Aubrey Davis. Film Editor: Basil Wrangell, A.C.E. Music: Joseph S. Dubin. Sound: Robert O. Cook. Set Decoration: Emile Kuri. Costumer: Chuck Keehne. Make-up: Pat McNalley. Unit Manager: Roy Wade. Assistant Director: Joseph L. McEveety.

HORSE OF THE WEST, THE
Produced and Directed by: Larry Lansburgh. Written by: Janet Lansburgh. Music: William Lava. Associate in Production: Katy Peake. Photographed by: Larry Lansburgh. Film Editor: Warren Adams. Sound by: Mac Dagleish.

HORSE WITH THE FLYING TAIL, THE
Teleplay by: Janet Lansburgh. Narration written by: Bill Bryan. Produced and Directed by: Larry Lansburgh. Told by: George Fenneman. English Commentator: Doriam Williams. Music: William Lava. Photography: Hannis Staudinger, Werner Kurz, Robert Carmet, James Bauden, Sidney Zucker, Larry Lansburgh. Film Editor: Warren Adams. Sound: Robert O. Cook. Program Co-ordinator: Jack Bruner. Acknowledgment: The United States Equestrian Team.

HORSE WITHOUT A HEAD, THE
Teleplay by: T.E.B. Clarke. Based on *A Hundred Million Francs* by: Paul Berna. Directed by: Don Chaffey. Associate Producer: Hugh Attwooll. Director of Photography: Paul Beeson, B.S.C. Additional Photography: Michael Reed. Camera Operator: David Harcourt. Art Director: Michael Stringer. Film Editor: Peter Boita. Costumes: Margaret Furse. Set Decorator: Vernon Dixon. Production Manager: Peter Marley. Unit Manager: Basil Appleby. Music: Eric Rogers. Song *Knights of the Headless Horse:* Richard M. Sherman, Robert B. Sherman. Animal Trainer: Jimmy Chipperfield. Assistant

Director: Denis Bertera. Make-up: Geoffrey Rodway. Hair Stylist: Florrie Hydes. Sound: Robert O. Cook. Continuity: Marjorie Lavelly. Casting: Maude Spector. Sound Director: C.C. Stevens. Sound Editor: Les Wiggins. Program Co-ordinator: Jack Bruner. Filmed at Pinewood Studios, London, England.

HORSEMASTERS, THE
Directed by: William Fairchild. Teleplay by: Ted Willis, William Fairchild. From the book by: Don Stanford. Associate Producer: Hugh Attwooll. Director of Photography: Frederick Francis, B.S.C. Art Direction: Michael Stringer, Norman Dorme. Film Editor: Peter Boita. Set Decoration: Martin Atkinson. Costume Design: Margaret Furse. Music: Alun Hoddinott. Conducted by: Muir Mathieson. *The Strummin' Song:* Richard M. Sherman, Robert B. Sherman. Assistant Director: Eric Rattray. Make-up: Freddie Williamson. Hair Stylist: Joyce James. Sound Recordist: Buster Ambler.

HORSES FOR GREENE
Teleplay and Directed by: Lewis R. Foster. Based on the book by: Dr. Robert D. Bass. Produced by: Bill Anderson. Associate Producer: Ron Miller. Director of Photography: Lucien Ballard, A.S.C. Art Director: Marvin Aubrey Davis. Film Editor: Robert Stafford. Music: Joseph S. Dubin. Songs: Lew Foster, Buddy Baker. Sound: Robert O. Cook. Set Decoration: Emile Kuri, William L. Stevens. Costumer: Chuck Keehne. Make-up: Pat McNalley. Hair Stylist: Ruth Sandifer. Unit Manager: Roy Wade. Assistant Director: Joseph L. McEveety.

HOW THE WEST WAS LOST
Directed by: Hamilton S. Luske. *Pecos Bill* sung by: Roy Rogers and the Sons of the Pioneers. Sequence Directors: Jack Kinney, Clyde Geronimi. Television Story: Ted Berman, Otto Englander. Production Associate: McLaren Stewart. Animation: Hal Ambro, Eric Larson, John Lounsbery, Bob McCrea, Ward Kimball, Wolfgang Reitherman, John Sibley, Ed Aardal. Layout: Tom Codrick, Al Zinnen. Background: Jimi Trout, Claude Coats. Music: Franklyn Marks, Paul Smith. Songs: Mel Leven. *World of Color* Theme Song: Richard M. Sherman, Robert B. Sherman. Film Editor: Edward R. Baker. With the talents of: Bill Thompson (oldtimer). Sound: Robert O. Cook. Program Co-ordinator: Jack Bruner.

HOW TO RELAX
Directed by: Wolfgang Reitherman. Sequence Director: Jack Kinney. Story: Albert Duffy, Dick Kinney, Milt Schaffer, Bill Berg, Al Bertino. Music: Franklyn Marks, Paul Smith, Joseph S. Dubin, Oliver Wallace. Animation: Dick Lucas, Eric Cleworth, Ted Berman, Amby Paliwoda, Bill Keil, Al Statter, John Sibley. Layout: Lance Nolley, Vance Gerry, Al Zinnen. Backgrounds: Richard H. Thomas, Art Riley. Film Editor: Norman Carlisle. Sound: Robert O. Cook. Production Supervision: Harry Tytle.

HUNTING INSTINCT, THE
Directed by: Wolfgang Reitherman. Sequence Directors: Eric Cleworth, Jack Hannah. Story: Otto Englander, Joe Rinaldi, Ted Berman, Bill Berg. Animation: Frank Thomas, Cliff Nordberg, John Sibley, Bill Justice, Volus Jones, Judge Whitaker. Layout: Basil Davidovich, Dale Barnhart, Yale Gracey. Background: Bill Layne, Thelma Witmer. Music: Buddy Baker, Oliver Wallace. Film Editor: Jim Love. Sound: Robert O. Cook.

HURRICANE HANNAH
Co-producer: James Algar. Story: James Algar. Narration Written by: Jason Wingreen. Film Editor: Norman Palmer, A.C.E. Music: Franklyn Marks. Narrator: Robert P. Anderson. Sound: Robert O. Cook. Filmed with the co-operation of: U.S. Weather Bureau National Hurricane Center, Miami, U.S. Navy "Hurricane Hunters," National Aeronautics and Space Administration, U.S. Air Force, U.S. Coast Guard, The American Red Cross. *For Ken Nelson Productions* Field Producer: Ken Nelson. Photographers: Ken Nelson, Jack Ferrucci, Larry Smith, Douglas Cox, Robert Jacobs.

I Captured the King of the Leprechauns
Directed by: Robert Stevenson, Harry Keller. Written by: Larry Watkin. Production Supervision: Hamilton S. Luske. Music: Oliver Wallace. Songs: Lawrence Edward Watkin, Oliver Wallace. Director of Photography: Winton C. Hoch, A.S.C., William Snyder, A.S.C. Art Director: Carroll Clark. Film Editor: Lloyd L. Richardson, A.C.E., Stanley Johnson, A.C.E. Special Photographic Effects: Peter Ellenshaw, Eustace Lycett. Sound: Robert O. Cook. Set Director: Fred MacLean. Assistant Director: R. W. Miller.

The footage from *Darby O'Gill and the Little People* was directed by Robert Stevenson, with Harry Keller directing the footage filmed specifically for this episode.

I-Man
Music: Craig Safan. Editor: Lovel Ellis. Production Designer: Michael Bolton. Director of Photography: Frank Watts. Supervising Producer: Richard Briggs. Written and Produced by: Howard Friedlander, Ken Peragine. Directed by: Corey Allen. Executive Producer: Mark H. Ovitz. Production Manager: Fitch Cady. First Assistant Director: Robert Cowan. Second Assistant Director: David Rollin Webb. Casting by: Joyce Robinson, C.S.A., Penny Ellers, C.S.A. Costume Designer: William Ware Theiss. Set Decorators: Sandie Arthur, Kim MacKenzie. Property Master: James H. Chow. Key Costumers: Stephanie Nolin, Wendy Foster. Make-up: Sandy Cooper. Special Make-up: Robert J. Schiffer. Hair Stylist: Sherry Linder. Casting-Canada: Sid Kozak. Location Managers: Stewart Bethune, Murray Ord. Script Supervisor: Lara Fox. Stunt Coordinator-U.S.: Gary McLarty. Stunt Coordinator-Canada: Jacob Rupp. Animal Trainer: Debra J. Coe. Production Coordinator: Catherine Howard. Assistant to Mr. Ovitz: Cheryl Edwards. Second Unit Director: Ric Rondell. Production Sound Mixer: Lars Ekstrom. Sound Editing by: Echo Sound Services, Joseph Melody. Music Editing by: Ken Johnson, Steve Livingston. Acknowledgment: Royal Roads Military Academy of Victoria, British Columbia. A Mark H. Ovitz Production in association with Walt Disney Television.

Ida, The Offbeat Eagle
Co-producer: Winston Hibler. Teleplay by: Jack Speirs, Homer McCoy. Story by: Rutherford Montgomery. Narrator: Winston Hibler. Production Co-ordinator: Robert F. Metzler. Production Manager: Erwin L. Verity. Film Editor: George Gale, A.C.E. Music: Paul Smith. Sound: Robert O. Cook. Program Co-ordinator: Jack Bruner. *For Charles Draper Productions, Inc.* Field Producer: Charles L. Draper. Photographers: Charles L. Draper, Frank Zuniga. Wildlife Supervisors: Gary Young, Joe Way, Norman Nelson, Allen Woodrow. Production Assistant: Hank Huisman. Art Styling: Robert Becker. Technical Advisors: Morlan Nelson, Ed Durden. Acknowledgments: United States Fish and Wildlife Service, State of Idaho Fish and Game Department, Idaho Power Company.

In Shape with Von Drake
Directed by: Hamilton S. Luske. Sequence Director: Jack Kinney. Story: Bill Berg. Art Styling: McLaren Stewart. Animation: Julius Svendsen, Art Stevens, Ollie Johnston, Bob McCrea, Wolfgang Reitherman, John Sibley. Layout: Joe Hale, Al Zinnen. Background: Jimi Trout, Merle Cox. Music: Franklyn Marks. With the Talents of: Paul Frees. Film Editor: Tom Acosta. Sound: Robert O. Cook. Program Co-ordinator: Jack Bruner.

Inky, The Crow
Produced by: Harry Tytle. Written by: Rod Peterson. Narrator: Olan Soulé. Film Editor: Gregg McLaughlin. Music: George Bruns. Production Manager: Erwin L. Verity. Production Co-ordinator: Robert F. Metzler. Sound: Robert O. Cook. Program Co-ordinator: Jack Bruner. *For Charles Draper Productions, Inc.* Field Producer: Charles Draper. Photography: Charles Draper, Ivan Craig, Ron Foreman. Animal Supervision: John Herod, Charles Hammond. Production Assistants: Charles Lyons, Robert Becker.

Inside Donald Duck
Directed by: Hamilton S. Luske. Sequence Directors: Jack King, Jack Kinney. Story by: Larry Clemmons, Bill Berg, Roy Williams. Art Styling: McLaren Stewart. Layout: Joe Hale, Don Griffith. Background: Walt Peregoy, Ralph Hulett. Animation: Ollie Johnston, Eric Larson, Bob McCrea, Ed Aardal, Milt Kahl, Julius Svendsen, Don Towsley, John Sibley. Effects Animation: Jack Boyd. Music: Buddy Baker, Oliver Wallace. Film Editor: Anthony Gerard. Sound: Robert O. Cook.

Inside Outer Space
Directed by: Hamilton S. Luske. Sequence Director: Ward Kimball. Story: Bill Berg, William Bosché, John Dunn. Art Styling: McLaren Stewart. Animation: Julius Svendsen, Art Stevens, Bill Justice, Charles Downs, John Sibley, Eric Cleworth. Layout: Joe Hale, A. Kendall O'Connor. Backgrounds: Ralph Hulett, Jimi Trout, William Layne. Music: George Bruns. With the Talents of: Paul Frees. Film Editors: Tom Acosta, Lloyd L. Richardson, A.C.E. Sound: Robert O. Cook. Program Co-ordinator: Jack Bruner.

It's Tough to Be a Bird
Teleplay by: Ted Berman. Produced and Directed by: Ward Kimball. Narrator: Richard Bakalyan. Animation: Art Stevens, Eric Larson. Layout: Joe Hale. Film Editor: Lloyd L. Richardson, A.C.E. Music: George Bruns. Songs: Mel Leven. Soprano: Ruth Buzzi. Bird Fanciers: John Emerson, Hank Schloss, Jim Swain, Walter Perkins, Ann Lord, Rolf Darbo. Sound: Robert O. Cook. Program Co-ordinator: Jack Bruner. With the co-operation of: Huntington Library, National Audubon Society, U.S. Department of the Interior, Fish and Wildlife Service, U.S. Department of Agriculture, Forest Service.

Jiminy Cricket Presents Bongo
Directed by: Hamilton Luske. Written by: Winston Hibler, Jack Speirs. Music: Oliver Wallace. Special Art Work: Al Zinnen, Milt Banta, Jimi Trout. Photography: Bert Glennon. Film Editor: Lloyd Richardson. Special Processes: Ub Iwerks. Sound: Robert O. Cook. Narrated by: Cliff Edwards.

Johnny Shiloh
Co-producer: Bill Anderson. Teleplay by: Ronald Alexander. Based on a novel by: James A. Rhodes, Dean Jauchius. Directed by: James Neilson. Assistant to the Producer: Louis Debney. Director of Photography: William Snyder, A.S.C. Art Directors: Carroll Clark, John B. Mansbridge. Film Editor: Robert Stafford, A.C.E. Set Decoration: Emile Kuri, Charles S. Thompson. Music: Buddy Baker. Song: Richard M. Sherman, Robert B. Sherman. Costumes: Chuck Keehne. Make-up: Pat McNalley. Hair Stylist: Ruth Sandifer. Sound: Robert O. Cook. Special Effects: Robert A. Mattey. Assistant Director: John Chulay. Program Co-ordinator: Jack Bruner.

Johnny Tremain
Adapted for television by Wilfred Jackson, Albert Duffy, Grant K. Smith and Harry Tytle.

Joker, The Amiable Ocelot
Co-producer: Winston Hibler. Teleplay by: Rod Peterson. Story by: Albert Aley. Narration Written by: Jack Speirs. Narrator: Winston Hibler. Production Co-ordinator: Robert F. Metzler. Production Manager: Erwin L. Verity. Film Editor: George Gale, A.C.E. Music: Paul Smith. *World of Color* Theme: Richard M. Sherman, Robert B. Sherman. Sound: Robert O. Cook. Program Co-ordinator: Jack Bruner. *For Charles Draper Productions, Inc.* Field Producers: Charles L. Draper, Robert Becker, Jan McNabb. Photographers: Charles L. Draper, Gary B. Young. Wildlife Supervisors: John Herod, Joe J. Way, Carol Draper, Art Matthews. Production Assistant: Hank Huisman. Acknowledgments: U.S. Fish and Wildlife Service, Arizona Game and Fish Department.

Journey to the Valley of the Emu, The
Written by: Barry Clark. Narration by: Norman Wright. Produced and Directed by: Roy Edward Disney. Narrator: Paul Ricketts. Editor: Toby Brown. Music: Robert F. Brunner. Sound: Herb Taylor. Production Supervisor: Erwin L. Verity. *For Coronado Productions, Inc.* Field Producer: Ron Brown. Photography: Ken Ball, Bill Grimmond, Peter Layden. Production Staff: Ken Beebe, Geof Bartram, Chris Shaw, Roy

Patrick Disney. Acknowledgments: Northern Territory Reserves Board, Commonwealth Scientific and Industrial Research Organization, Division of Wildlife Research, Royal Flying Doctor Service, Alice Springs Hospital.

JUSTIN CASE
Original Score by: Henry Mancini. Editor: Robert Pergament. Production Designer: James Shanahan. Director of Photography: Isidore Mankofsky, A.S.C. Executive Producer: Blake Edwards. Produced by: Tony Adams. Teleplay by: Blake Edwards. Story by: Jennifer Edwards, Blake Edwards. Directed by: Blake Edwards. Associate Producer: Trish Caroselli. Unit Production Manager: Denny Salvaryn. First Assistant Director: Joan Van Horn. Second Assistant Director: Carol L. Vitkay. Production Supervisor: Elton MacPherson. Casting by: Allison Jones. Costume Designer: Tom Bronson. Set Decorator: Ethel Robins Richards. Property Master: Anthony C. Thorpe. Key Costumers: Dan Bronson, Nancy Martinelli. Make-up: Nadia. Hair Stylist: Gregg R. Mitchell. Script Supervisor: Betty Abbott-Griffin. Location Manager: James "Tad" Tadevic. Production Coordinator: Mary Kay Kelly. Stunt Coordinator: Joe Dunne. Special Effects: Robbie Knott. Visual Effects Supervisor: Phil Huff. Production Sound Mixer: Charles M. Wilborn. Music Editing by: Stephen A. Hope, S.M.E. Visual Effects by: Buena Vista Visual Effects Group. The Blake Edwards Company in association with Walt Disney Television.

JUSTIN MORGAN HAD A HORSE
Produced by: Harry Tytle. Teleplay by: Calvin Clements, Jr., Rod Peterson. Based on the book by: Marguerite Henry. Directed by: Hollingsworth Morse. Director of Photography: Richard A. Kelley, A.S.C. Art Directors: John B. Mansbridge, William J. Creber. Film Editor: Bob Bring. Set Decorators: Emile Kuri, Robert Benton. Matte Artist: Alan Maley. Music: Franklyn Marks. Song *The Four Seasons:* Rod Peterson, Franklyn Marks. Sound: Herb Taylor. Costumes: Chuck Keehne. Make-up: Robert J. Schiffer. Hair Stylist: La Rue Matheron. Assistant Director: Paul L. Cameron. Program Co-ordinator: Jack Bruner. Acknowledgments: American Morgan Horse Association, Inc., University of Vermont, Morgan Horse Farm.

KENTUCKY GUNSLICK
Directed by: Harry Keller. Written by: David P. Harmon. Produced by: James Pratt. Director of Photography: William Snyder, A.S.C. Art Director: Stan Jolley. Film Editor: Robert Stafford. Music: Buddy Baker. Song: David Harmon, Buddy Baker. Sound: Robert O. Cook. Set Decoration: Emile Kuri, William L. Stevens. Costumer: Chuck Keehne. Make-up: Pat McNalley. Hair Stylist: Ruth Sandifer. Unit Manager: Roy Wade. Assistant Director: Joseph L. McEveety.

KIDS IS KIDS
Directed by: Hamilton S. Luske. Sequence Director: Jack Hannah. Story: Bill Berg. Art Styling: McLaren Stewart. Animation: Hal King, Milt Kahl, Eric Larson, Bob McCrea, Volus Jones, Bill Justice, Bob Carlson, George Kreisl. Layout: Joe Hale, Yale Gracey. Background: Art Riley, Ralph Hulett. With the talents of: Paul Frees. Music: Buddy Baker. Film Editor: Anthony Gerard. Sound: Robert O. Cook.

KIDS WHO KNEW TOO MUCH, THE
Executive Producer: Ron Miller. Produced by: Kevin Corcoran. Director of Photography: Jack A. Whitman, Jr. Teleplay by: Gail Morgan Hickman, David E. Boston. Based on the novel *Whisper in the Gloom* by: Nicholas Blake. Directed by: Robert Clouse. Art Directors: John B. Mansbridge, Leroy G. Deane. Editor: Lloyd L. Richardson, A.C.E. Music: Buddy Baker. Production Manager: John Bloss. Assistant Director: Michael Dmytryk. Second Assistant Director: William R. Poole. Stunt Coordinator: Reg Parton. Set Decorators: R. Chris Westlund, Roger M. Shook. Sound Supervisor: Herb Taylor. Sound Mixer: Art Names. Costumes: Jack Sandeen. Make-up: Robert J. Schiffer, C.M.A.A. Hair Stylist: Joan Phillips. Sound Editor: Ben F. Hendricks. Music Editor: Jack Wadsworth. *Disney's Wonderful World* Theme Song: John Debney, John Klawitter.

KILLERS FROM KANSAS
Directed by: Harry Keller. Written by: Frank D. Gilroy. Produced by: James Pratt. Director of Photography: William Snyder, A.S.C. Art Director: Marvin Aubrey Davis. Film Editor: Robert Stafford. Music: Franklyn Marks. Song: Stan Jones. Sound: Robert O. Cook. Set Decorators: Emile Kuri, Bertram Granger. Costumer: Chuck Keehne. Make-up: Pat McNalley. Assistant Director: Austen Jewell.

KILLERS OF THE HIGH COUNTRY
Directed by: Tom McGowan. Production Manager: William Redlin. Production Assistant: Thomas Boutress. Photographers: Robert Brooker, Lloyd Beebe. Technical Advisor: Milt Holt. Acknowledgment: The Utah State Department of Fish and Game. *For Walt Disney Productions* Produced by: Winston Hibler. Story by: Rutherford Montgomery, Arnold Belgard. Narration Written by: Donn Hale Munson. Narrated by: Winston Hibler. Film Editor: George Gale, A.C.E. Music: Buddy Baker. Sound: Robert O. Cook. Production Supervisor: Harry Tytle.

KILROY I
Co-producer: Ron Miller. Teleplay by: John Whedon. Based on the story by: Betty Fernandez. Directed by: Robert Butler. Director of Photography: Edward Colman, A.S.C. Art Directors: Carroll Clark, Marvin Aubrey Davis. Film Editor: Cotton Warburton, A.C.E. Set Decorators: Emile Kuri, Hal Gausman. Music: Buddy Baker. Costumes: Chuck Keehne. Make-up: Pat McNalley, La Rue Matheron. Sound: Robert O. Cook. Assistant Director: Joseph L. McEveety. Program Co-ordinator: Jack Bruner.

KILROY II
Co-producer: Ron Miller. Teleplay by: John Whedon. Based on a story by: Lee Pape. Directed by: Robert Butler. Director of Photography: Edward Colman, A.S.C. Art Directors: Carroll Clark, Marvin Aubrey Davis. Film Editor: Cotton Warburton, A.C.E. Set Decorators: Emile Kuri, Hal Gausman. Music: Bob Brunner. Costumes: Chuck Keehne. Make-up: Pat McNalley, La Rue Matheron. Sound: Robert O. Cook. Assistant Director: Joseph L. McEveety. Program Co-ordinator: Jack Bruner.

KILROY III
Co-producer: Ron Miller. Teleplay by: John Whedon. Based on the story *Empty Seven* by: Bart Burns. Directed by: Norman Tokar. Director of Photography: Edward Colman, A.S.C. Art Directors: Carroll Clark, Marvin Aubrey Davis. Film Editor: Robert Stafford, A.C.E. Set Decorators: Emile Kuri, Hal Gausman. Music: Buddy Baker. Costumes: Chuck Keehne. Make-up: Pat McNalley, La Rue Matheron. Sound: Robert O. Cook. Assistant Director: Tom Leetch. Program Co-ordinator: Jack Bruner.

KILROY IV
Co-producer: Ron Miller. Teleplay by: John Whedon. Based on the story *Empty Seven* by: Bart Burns. Directed by: Norman Tokar. Director of Photography: Edward Colman, A.S.C. Art Directors: Carroll Clark, Marvin Aubrey Davis. Film Editor: Robert Stafford, A.C.E. Set Decorators: Emile Kuri, Hal Gausman. Music: Bob Brunner. Costumes: Chuck Keehne. Make-up: Pat McNalley. Sound: Robert O. Cook. Assistant Director: Tom Leetch. Program Co-ordinator: Jack Bruner.

KING OF THE GRIZZLIES
Produced by: Winston Hibler. Teleplay by: Jack Speirs. Adaptation by: Rod Peterson, Norman Wright. Based on the book *The Biography of a Grizzly* by: Ernest Thompson Seton. Robert Lawrence Sequences Directed by: Ron Kelly. Associate Producers: Erwin L. Verity, Robert F. Metzler. Film Editor: Gregg McLaughlin. Narrator: Winston Hibler. Matte Artist: Alan Maley. Music: Buddy Baker. Song *The Campfire Is Home:* Jack Speirs. Sound: Robert O. Cook. *For Robert Lawrence Productions, Toronto, Ontario, Canada* Director of Photography: Reginald Morris. Set Decoration: Wilf Culley. Costumes: Roger Palmer. Make-up: William Morgan. Production Assistants: William Morgan, Don Hall. Wildlife and Grizzly Bear Sequences Filmed by Cangary Limited. Field Producer: Lloyd Beebe. Assisted by: William Bacon III, Bob

Rowland, Terry Rowland, Al Niemela, Marinho Coreia, Dell Ray. Acknowledgment: The Stoney Indian Nation.

KIT CARSON AND THE MOUNTAIN MEN
Executive Producer: Ron Miller. Produced by: Winston Hibler. Director of Photography: Andrew Jackson, A.S.C. Written by: Harry Spalding. Directed by: Vincent McEveety. Associate Producer/Second Unit Director: Christopher Hibler. Art Directors: John B. Mansbridge, Frank T. Smith. Editor: Bob Bring, A.C.E. Unit Production Manager/Assistant Director: Paul "Tiny" Nichols. Second Assistant Director: Bud Grace. Set Decorator: Charles R. Pierce. Matte Artist: P.S. Ellenshaw. Music: Buddy Baker. Song *Kit Carson:* Jay Livingston, Ray Evans, Buddy Baker. Sound: Herb Taylor. Costumes: Chuck Keehne. Make-up: Robert J. Schiffer. Acknowledgment: United States Forest Service, Inyo National Forest.

LAND OF ENEMIES, THE
Directed by: Lewis R. Foster. Teleplay by: Tom Blackburn. Based on the novel by: Stewart Edward White. Photographer: Walter H. Castle, A.S.C. Art Director: Carroll Clark. Film Editor: George Gale, A.C.E. Music: George Bruns. Song *The Saga of Andy Burnett:* Tom Blackburn, George Bruns. Matte Artist: Peter Ellenshaw. Sound: Robert O. Cook. Set Decoration: Fred MacLean. Costumer: Chuck Keehne. Make-up: Pat McNalley. Assistant Director: Robert G. Shannon. Production Supervisor: Harry Tytle.

LAST ELECTRIC KNIGHT, THE
Co-Producer: Sally Baker. Supervising Producer: John Garbett. Executive Producer: Michael L. Weisbarth. Written and Produced by: Dan Gordon. Directed by: James Fargo. Music Composed and Performed by: David Kurtz, James Roberts. Director of Photography: George Koblasa. Art Director: Jim Shanahan. Editor: Bill Brame. Unit Production Manager/Associate Producer: Dan Franklin. First Assistant Director: Jack Cummins. Second Assistant Director: Emmitt-Leon O'Neil. Casting by: Mary V. Buck, C.S.A., Susan H. Edelman, C.S.A. Set Decorator: Carl Biddiscombe. Property Master: Anthony C. Thorpe. Key Costumers: Sandra Berke Jordan, Gene Deardorff. Make-up: Michael F. Blake. Hair Stylist: Robert L. Stevenson. Costume Designer: William Ware Theiss. Location Manager: Ryan Rosenberg. Script Supervisor: Joyce Heftel. Production Coordinator: Vera Martin. Production Sound Mixer: Dean Vernon. Sound Editing by: Horta Editorial. Music Editing by: Music Design Group. Music Supervisor: Suzanne Coston. A Motown Production in association with Walt Disney Pictures Television.

LAW AND ORDER, INCORPORATED
Directed by: Christian Nyby. Written by: Maurice Tombragel. Produced by: James Pratt. Director of Photography: William Snyder, A.S.C. Art Director: Stan Jolley. Film Editor: Edward Sampson, Jr. Music: Joseph S. Dubin. Song: Rich Dehr, Frank Miller. Matte Artist: Peter Ellenshaw. Sound: Robert O. Cook. Set Decorators: Emile Kuri, Bertram Granger. Costumer: Chuck Keehne. Make-up: Pat McNalley. Assistant Director: Vincent McEveety.

LAWMAN OR GUNMAN
Directed by: Christian Nyby. Written by: Maurice Tombragel. Produced by: James Pratt. Director of Photography: William Snyder, A.S.C. Art Director: Stan Jolley. Film Editor: Edward Sampson, Jr. Music: Franklyn Marks. Song: Rich Dehr, Frank Miller. Sound: Robert O. Cook. Set Decorators: Emile Kuri, Bertram Granger. Costumer: Chuck Keehne. Make-up: Pat McNalley. Assistant Director: Vincent McEveety.

LEFTOVERS, THE
Original Score by: Tom Scott. Editors: Norman Holly, Dick Darling, A.C.E. Art Director: James Shanahan. Director of Photography: Fred J. Koenekamp, A.S.C. Executive Producer: Susan B. Landau. Teleplay by: Gen LeRoy. Story by: Steve Slavkin, Gen LeRoy. Directed by: Paul Schneider. Unit Production Manager: Albert J. Salzer. First Assistant Director: John M. Poer. Second Assistant Director: John N. Whittle. Casting by: Allison Jones. Costume Designer: William Ware

Theiss. Set Decorator: Rochelle Moser. Property Master: Charles C. Eguia. Key Costumers: Dawn Jackson, Joseph Markham. Make-up: Don L. Cash. Hair Stylist: Eddie Barron-Smith. Location Manager: Geoffrey R. Smith. Script Supervisor: Sally J. Roddy. Production Coordinator: Diane L. Katz. Production Sound Mixer: William Teague. Sound Editing by: Stephen J. Cannell Productions, Michael O'Corrigan, Cliff Bell, Jr. Music Editing by: Seque Music, Christopher Brooks. *New Song* Words and Music by: Howard Jones. Performed by: Geoff Koch.

LEFTY, THE DINGALING LYNX
Written by: Jack Speirs. Produced and Directed by: Winston Hibler. Narrator: May Nutter. Film Editor: Gregg McLaughlin. Music: Franklyn Marks. Production Co-ordinator: Robert F. Metzler. Production Manager: Erwin L. Verity. Sound: Herb Taylor. Program Co-ordinator: Jack Bruner. *For Cangary Limited* Field Producers: Lloyd Beebe, Ron Brown. Photographers: Lloyd Beebe, Robert Rowland. Animal Supervision: Marinho Correia, Terry Rowland, Dell Ray, Alfred Robb.

LEGEND OF EL BLANCO, THE
Co-producer: Roy Edward Disney. Teleplay by: Jack Speirs, Homer McCoy. Based on a story by: Rutherford Montgomery. Directed by: Arthur J. Vitarelli. Song Words and Music: Mel Leven. Narration Spoken and Sung by: Los Tres Con Ella, Pepe Callahan. Director of Photography: Edward Colman, A.S.C. Art Director: Carroll Clark. Film Editor: Lloyd Richardson, A.C.E. Set Decorator: Emile Kuri. Production Co-ordinator: Robert F. Metzler. Music: Franklyn Marks. *World of Color* Theme: Richard M. Sherman, Robert B. Sherman. Sound: Robert O. Cook. Program Co-ordinator: Jack Bruner. Location Companies: Ralph Chandler Productions, Hank Schloss Productions, Tom McGowan Productions. Photographers: William G. Hewitt, Robert Brooker, Hank Schloss, Frank Zuniga. Art Styling: Robert Becker. Mexican Government Supervisor: Matilde Landeta. Location Co-ordinator: Pablo Huston Albarran.

LEGEND OF SLEEPY HOLLOW, THE
Narrated by: Bing Crosby. Directed by: Clyde Geronimi. Written by: Bill Peet, Clyde Geronimi. Music: Oliver Wallace. Production Supervisor: Harry Tytle. Layout and Background Artists: Tom Codrick, Dick Anthony, Thor Putnam, Basil Davidovich. Animators: George Kreisl, Donald Lusk, Dan MacManus. Photography: Bert Glennon. Film Editor: Donald Halliday. Special Processes: Ub Iwerks. Special Effects: Bob Ferguson. Sound: Robert O. Cook. Voice of Washington Irving: John Dehner. *Ichabod* Songs by: Don Raye, Gene De Paul.

LEGEND OF TWO GYPSY DOGS, THE
Written, Photographed and Directed by: Dr. Istvan Homoki-Nagy. Adapted for television by: Roy Edward Disney. Narrated and Sung by: John van Dreelen. Music: George Bruns. Song: George Bruns, Roy Edward Disney. Film Editor: Lloyd L. Richardson, A.C.E. Sound: Robert O. Cook. Program Co-ordinator: Jack Bruner.

LEGEND OF YOUNG DICK TURPIN, THE
Co-producer: Bill Anderson. Teleplay by: Robert Westerby. Directed by: James Neilson. Associate Producer: Hugh Attwooll. Director of Photography: Michael Reed. Production Designer: Don Ashton. Film Editor: Peter Boita. Costume Designer: Anthony Mendleson. Matte Artist: Peter Ellenshaw. Music: Ron Grainer. Ballad *The Legend of Young Dick Turpin:* Lyrics: Robert Westerby, Norman Newell. Music: Ron Grainer. Sung by: Val Doonican. *World of Color* Theme: Richard M. Sherman, Robert B. Sherman. Second Unit Director: Alan Maley. Make-up: Harry Frampton. Hair Stylist: Helen Bevan. Sound: Dudley Messenger, C. LeMessurier. Program Co-ordinator: Jack Bruner. Filmed at Pinewood Studios, London, England.

LIBERTY STORY, THE
Directed by: Hamilton S. Luske, Robert Stevenson. Teleplay by: James Algar. *Ben and Me.* Story by: Bill Peet. Based on the Book by: Robert Lawson. Narrated by: Sterling Holloway.

Johnny Tremain: From the Screenplay by: Tom Blackburn. Based on the book by: Esther Forbes. Music: George Bruns, Oliver Wallace. Animation: Bob McCrea, Wolfgang Reitherman, Ollie Johnston. Layout: Al Zinnen, Thor Putnam, Ken Anderson. Backgrounds: Jimi Trout, Irv Wyner, Claude Coats. Photographer: Charles P. Boyle, A.S.C. Art Director: Carroll Clark. Film Editor: Lloyd Richardson. Set Decoration: Emile Kuri. Special Processes: Ub Iwerks, A.S.C. Sound: Robert O. Cook. Assistant Director: William Beaudine, Jr. Production Supervision: Harry Tytle.

LIBERATORS, THE
Music by: Joe Harnell. Editor: Alan Marks, A.C.E. Art Director: Raymond G. Storey. Director of Photography: George Koblasa. Supervising Producer: Ed Lahti. Produced by: Jeanne Marie Byrd. Written and Directed by: Kenneth Johnson. Executive Producer: Kenneth Johnson. Unit Production Manager: William Zborowsky. First Assistant Director: Steve Fisher. Second Assistant Director: Izidore Musallam. Casting by: Peg Halligan, C.S.A., Stuart Aikins (Toronto), Lucy Robitaille (Montreal). Costume Designer: Lynda Kemp. Set Decorator: Jacques Bradette. Property Master: Ken Clark. Key Costumers: Stacey Coker, Bruce Mellott. Make-up: Barbara Palmer. Hair Stylist: Malcolm Tanner. Additional Photography: Philip Lathrop. Location Manager: Fred Kamping. Script Supervisor: Alleen Nollmann. Production Coordinator: Sandy Webb. Production Sound Mixer: Peter Shewchuk. Edited by: Jeff Zacha. Sound Editing by: Echo Film Service/Joseph Melody. Music Editing by: Steve Livingston/Ken Johnson. Acknowledgments: The St. Lawrence Parks Commission, The Province of Ontario, The City of Hamilton. A Kenneth Johnson Production in association with Walt Disney Television.

LIFESTYLES OF THE RICH AND ANIMATED
Executive Producer: Robert Heath. Producer: Marijane Miller. Written by: Kenny Wolin. Edited by: Hank Polonsky. Original Music by: Charlotte Lansberg. On-Line Editor: M.T. Badertscher. Re-recording Mixer & Sound Effects: Bob Manahan. Audio Post Supervisor: Gary Coppola. Graphic Design: David Henry, Ian Dawson, Marco Bacich. Acknowledgments: Les Perkins, Paula Sigman. Robert Heath Inc.

LIKE FATHER, LIKE SON
This episode was aired without production credits.

LITTLE DOG LOST
Co-producer: Winston Hibler. Teleplay by: Catherine Turney. Based on a book by: Meindert de Jong. Narration by: Winston Hibler. *For Perkins Films, Inc.* Directed by: Walter Perkins. Production Co-ordinators: Robert F. Metzler, Roy Edward Disney. Film Editor: George Gale, A.C.E. Music: Oliver Wallace. Sound: Robert O. Cook. Program Co-ordinator: Jack Bruner. *For Perkins Films, Inc.* Photographed by: Walter Perkins, Charles L. Draper. "Candy" Trained by: Douglas Bundock.

LITTLE SHEPHERD DOG OF CATALINA, THE
Written by: Rod Peterson. Produced and Directed by: Harry Tytle. Narrator: Mike Parker. Associate Producer: Rod Peterson. Film Editor: Ernie Milano. Music: Franklyn Marks. Production Manager: Erwin L. Verity. Sound: Herb Taylor. *For Arcane Films, Inc.* Field Producer: Hank Schloss. Production Assistant: Ronald Bourne. Photographer: Ivan Craig. Animal Supervision: Hubert Wells, Clint Rowe. Acknowledgment: The Santa Catalina Island Company.

LITTLE SPIES
Music: Peter Bernstein. Editor: T. Battle Davis. Art Director: James Shanahan. Director of Photography: Isidore Mankofsky, A.S.C. Produced by: Joseph Stern. Teleplay by: Stephen Greenfield, Stephen Bonds. Story by: John Greg Pain, Stephen Bonds, Stephen Greenfield. Directed by: Greg Beeman. Casting by: Allison Jones. Unit Production Manager: Albert J. Salzer. First Assistant Director: Anderson G. House. Second Assistant Director: George Fortmuller. Costume Designer: William Ware Theiss. Set Decorator: Rochelle Moser. Property Master: Charles C. Eguia. Key Costumers: Dawn Jackson, Richard "Dick" Butz. Make-up: Carol Schwartz. Hair

Stylist: Eddie M. Barron. Location Manager: James "Tad" Tadevic. Script Supervisor: Alleen N. Nollmann. Production Coordinator: Exa Durham. Animals Supplied by: Ray Berwick, Inc. Animal Trainers: Steve Berens, Joe McCarter. Production Sound Mixer: Bill Teague. Sound Editing by: Stephen J. Cannell Productions/Michael Corrigan. Music Editing by: Seque Music/Kathy Durning. *We Got the Beat* Words and Music by: Charlotte Caffey. Performed by: The Go-Go's.

MAD HERMIT OF CHIMNEY BUTTE, THE
Directed by: Jack Hannah. Sequence Director: Jack Kinney. Story: Dave Detiege, Albert Bertino, Nick George, Bill Berg. Animation: Volus Jones, George Kreisl, Al Coe, Bill Justice, Bob Carlson, John Sibley, Dan MacManus. Layout: Yale Gracey. Backgrounds: Ray Huffine, Thelma Witmer. Film Editor: Tom Acosta. Music: Joseph S. Dubin, Oliver Wallace. Sound: Robert O. Cook. Production Supervision: Harry Tytle.

MAGIC AND MUSIC
Directed by: Hamilton S. Luske. Sequence Director: Jack Kinney. Story: Milt Banta, Otto Englander, Mary Blair. Animation: Jack Boyd, Eric Larson, Ward Kimball, Joshua Meador, Fred Moore. Layout: Al Zinnen, Thor Putnam, A. Kendall O'Connor, Ken Anderson. Backgrounds: Claude Coats, Art Riley, Ray Huffine. Camera: Ted McCord, A.S.C. Art Director: Bruce Bushman. Film Editor: Lloyd L. Richardson, A.C.E. Music: Joseph S. Dubin, Edward Plumb. Face in the Mirror: Hans Conried. Special Effects: Eustace Lycett, Art Cruickshank. Sound: Robert O. Cook. Set Decorator: Armor E. Goetten. Costumer: Chuck Keehne. Make-up: Pat McNalley. Assistant Director: Vincent McEveety. Production Supervisor: Harry Tytle. We gratefully acknowledge the assistance of: Leopold Stokowski and the Philadelphia Orchestra, Freddy Martin and his Orchestra, Frances Langford.

MAGIC HIGHWAY U.S.A.
Produced and Directed by: Ward Kimball. Story and Narration Written by: Larry Clemmons. Cartoon Story by: Charles Downs, John Dunn. Animation: Julius Svendsen, Jack Boyd, Charles Downs, John Dunn. Layout Design: A. Kendall O'Connor, John Brandt, Jacques Rupp, Tom Yakutis. Background Paintings: Gordon Legg, Irv Wyner, Barbara Begg, Al Dempster. Music: George Bruns. Film Editors: Lloyd L. Richardson, A.C.E., Lionel A. Ephraim. Narrator: Marvin Miller. Special Processes: Eustace Lycett. Sound: Robert O. Cook. Production Supervisor: Harry Tytle. Acknowledgments: Automotive Safety Foundation, California Division of Highways, Archives—Ford Motor Co.

MAGIC OF WALT DISNEY WORLD, THE
Produced by: Ron Miller. Written by: Tom Leetch. Narration by: Bill Bosché. Directed by: Tom Leetch. Narrator: Andrew Duggan. Director of Photography: John M. Stephens. Film Editor: Lloyd L. Richardson, A.C.E. Music: Buddy Baker. Sound: Herb Taylor. Assistant Director: Ronald R. Grow.

MAGICAL DISNEY CHRISTMAS, A
Executive Producer: William Robert Yates. Prepared for Television by: Ed Ropolo, Frank Brandt, Bill Pentland. This Special Holiday Program has been made possible by the combined talents of the entire Walt Disney Studios. With the Talents of: Bill Baucom, Verna Felton, Peggy Lee, Lee Millar, Larry Roberts, Bill Thompson, Ilene Woods. Special Lyrics by: Galen R. Brandt. Additional Music by: John Debney. *The Small One* based on the book by: Charles Tazewell.

MAGICAL WORLD OF DISNEY, THE
Executive Producer: Ted Eccles. Directed by: Max Fader. Written by: Peter Elbling, Steven Kunes, Gladys Glover, Charles Bogel, Harry Anderson. Segment Producers: Richard Kaufman, Moe Ginsberg, Cynthia Convery, Stuart Jay Weiss, Ashraf Wassef, Ken Ashe, Cord Keller, Douglass M. Stewart. Associate Director: Kent Weed. Stage Manager: Steve Burgess. Talent Consultants: Carole Propp, Eileen Bradley. Talent Co-ordinator: Robin Eccles. Lighting Director: Simon Miles. Art Director: Robert Keene. Edited by: John Chambers. Original Music by: Hopkins Hallman. Additional Music by: Christo-

pher L. Stone. Special Choreography Material by: Otis Sallid. Script Supervisor: John M. Best. Make-up: Bob Ryan. Hair: Gail Rowell. Assistant Art Director: Robert Coltrin. Assistant to the Choreographer: Dana White. Special Lighting Facilities: The Klages Group. Production Coordinators: Lynn Ross, Simon Murton, Tony Palermo, Art Rutter, Joel Johnston, Tim Nett. Production Assistants: Paul Hoen, Jerry Field, Elaine Feuer, Darren Foreman, Cheryl Rhoads. "Albert" Designed and Performed by: Jay Johnson and Harry Anderson. "Albert" Technician: John Monsour. Acknowledgments: ZM Productions, George Zaloom, Les Mayfield, Mark Cowen, Michael Greer, John Schultz, Mark Zavad, John Vincent. *Disneyland* Del Schilling, Chris Robinson, Andy Gordon, Tracy Nash, Walt Ward, Barnette Ricci. Buena Vista Television in association with New Wave Productions.

MAGNIFICENT REBEL, THE

Written by: Joanne Court. Directed by: Georg Tressler. Production Supervisor: Peter V. Herald. Studio Representative in Europe: Harry Tytle. Director of Photography: Goeran Strindberg, A.L.C. Art Directors: Werner Schlichting, Isabell Schlichting. Film Editor: Alfred Srp. Music Selected from Works By: Ludwig van Beethoven. Music Supervisor: Frederick Stark. Music Advisor and Incidental Music: Heinz Schreiter. Sound: Kurt Schwarz. Costumers: Leo Bei, Ernie Kniepert. Make-up: Rudolf Ohlschmidt, Leopold Kuhnert. Dialogue Coach: Marlene Felton. Production Manager: Heinz Abel. Assistant Director: Rudolph Nussgruber. Camera Operator: Hugo Schott. Program Co-ordinator: Jack Bruner.

MAJOR EFFECTS

Written and Directed by: Nicholas Harvey Bennion. Produced by: Philip A. May. Executive Producer: Ron Miller. Art Director: John B. Mansbridge. Film Editor: Ernie Milano. Music: Albert Stern. Arranged by: Al Capps. Production Manager: John Bloss. Associate Director: Terry W. Greene. Assistant Director: Joseph Paul Moore. Assistant to Producer: Fred R. Wardell. Disney Montages: George Petlowany. Special Effects: Danny Lee. Stunt Coordinator: Loren Janes. Set Decorators: Norman Rockett, Roger M. Shook. Sound: Herb Taylor. Costumes: Jack Sandeen. Make-up: Robert J. Schiffer, C.M.A.A. Hair Stylist: Julia Walker. Camera Wizard Sequence: Mike Jittlov, Deven Chierighino. Paper Moon Sequence: Frank and Caroline Mouris. Lighting Director: Jeff Engles. *For Compact Video Systems, Inc.* Video Tape Editor: Terry W. Greene. Video Tape Operator: Jacki-Ann Robison. Camera: Hang Geving, Ken Tamburri. Video: Keith Winikoff, Bill Feightner. Sound: Michael T. Gannon. Technical Operations: Brad Weyl. Sound Mixer: Jerry Clemans. Acknowledgments: Directors Guild of America, Writers Guild of America, Screen Actors Guild, International Alliance of Theatrical Stage Employees, The Stuntmen of Hollywood, American Federation of Musicians. *Disney's Wonderful World* Theme Song: John Debney, John Klawitter.

MAN AND THE MOON

Produced and Directed by: Ward Kimball. Written by: Bill Bosché, John Dunn, Ward Kimball. Music: George Bruns. Layout Design: A. Kendall O'Connor, Frank Armitage. Cartoon Animation: Julius Svendsen, Arthur Stevens, Joe Hale, Jack Boyd, Charles Downs, Conrad Pederson. Space Paintings: Al Dempster, William Layne. Technical Advisor: Dr. Wernher von Braun. Rocket Ship Crew: Frank Gerstle, Richard Emory, Frank Connor, Leo Needham. Production Supervision: Harry Tytle. Photography: Edward Colman, A.S.C., Charles Boyle, A.S.C. Art Director: Marvin Aubrey Davis. Set Decorator: Bertram Granger. Assistant Director: Robert H. Justman. Special Processes: Ub Iwerks, Eustace Lycett. Special Instruments: Maxwell Smith. Models: Wathel Rogers. Film Editors: Lloyd Richardson, Sam Horta. Sound: Robert O. Cook. Acknowledgments: Griffith Observatory, Douglas Aircraft Company, Inc., Bill Jack Scientific Instrument Co., Protection, Inc.

MAN FROM BITTER CREEK, THE

Directed by: Harry Keller. Written by: David P. Harmon. Produced by: James Pratt. Director of Photography: William Snyder, A.S.C. Art Director: Marvin Aubrey Davis. Film Editor:

Robert Stafford. Music: Franklyn Marks. Sound: Robert O. Cook. Set Decorators: Emile Kuri, Bertram Granger. Costumer: Chuck Keehne. Make-up: Pat McNalley. Assistant Director: Robert G. Shannon.

MAN IN FLIGHT

Directed by: Hamilton S. Luske. Sequence Director: Jack Kinney. Story: Milt Banta, Dr. Heinz Haber. Music: Oliver Wallace. Animation: Jack Boyd, Al Severns, Jack Campbell, Jane Fowler, Jack Buckley, Ward Kimball. Layout: Al Zinnen, Thor Putnam, Don DaGradi. Backgrounds: Jimi Trout, Irv Wyner, Ray Huffine. Film Editor: Lloyd Richardson. Special Processes: Ub Iwerks, A.S.C. Sound: Robert O. Cook. Production Supervision: Harry Tytle. Acknowledgments: The Armed Forces of the United States, The American Aviation Industry.

MAN IN SPACE

Produced and Directed by: Ward Kimball. Written by: Ward Kimball, William Bosché. Cartoon Story by: Julius Svendsen. Music: George Bruns. Orchestration: Ed Plumb. Layout Design: A. Kendall O'Connor, Donald Griffith, Jacques Rupp. Animation: Julius Svendsen, Arthur Stevens, Jack Boyd, John Sibley, Eric Cleworth, Harvey Tombs, John Dunn. Backgrounds: Claude Coats, Donald Peters, Anthony Rizzo, George DeLado, Art Riley. Scientific Advisors: Willy Ley, Dr. Heinz Haber, Dr. Wernher Von Braun. Photography: William Skall, A.S.C. Editor: Archie Dattlebaum. Narrator: Dick Tufeld. Special Processes: Ub Iwerks, Robert Ferguson. Sound: C.O. Slyfield. Assistant Director: Russ Haverick. Art Director: Feild Gray. Set Decorator: Emile Kuri. Models: Wathel Rogers. Acknowledgments: U.S. Air Force, American Rocket Society, Inc., California Institute of Technology, Jet Propulsion Lab, Glenn L. Martin Co., Douglas Aircraft Co., Inc., Curtiss Wright Corp.

MAN IS HIS OWN WORST ENEMY

Directed by: Hamilton S. Luske. Sequence Directors: C. August Nichols, Jack Kinney. Story: Joe Rinaldi, Bill Berg. Art Styling: McLaren Stewart. Animation: Ward Kimball, Julius Svendsen, Art Stevens, Bob McCrea, Jerry Hathcock, John Sibley, Ed Aardal, Jack Boyd. Layout: Joe Hale, Erni Nordli. Background: Art Riley. With the Talents of: Paul Frees. Music: Buddy Baker, Franklyn Marks. Film Editor: Tom Acosta. Sound: Robert O. Cook. Program Co-ordinator: Jack Bruner.

MAN ON WHEELS

Directed by: Hamilton S. Luske, Les Clark. Sequence Director: Ward Kimball. Story: Bill Berg, William R. Bosché. Associate Producer: Ken Peterson. Animation: Hal King, Fred Kopietz, Cliff Nordberg, Bob Youngquist, Bob McCrea, Julius Svendsen. Effects Animation: Joshua Meador, Jack Boyd. Art Directors: McLaren Stewart, A. Kendall O'Connor. Layout: Don Griffith, Ray Aragon. Background: Art Riley, Frank Armitage, Walt Peregoy, Bill Layne. Music: Buddy Baker, George Bruns. Songs and Rhymes: Mel Leven. *World of Color* Theme: Richard M. Sherman, Robert B. Sherman. With the Talents of: The Mellomen. Special Effects: Eustace Lycett. Sound: Robert O. Cook. Program Co-ordinator: Jack Bruner.

MAN'S HUNTING INSTINCT

Executive Producer: William Robert Yates. Prepared for Television by: Ed Ropolo, Frank Brandt, Bill Pentland.

MARS AND BEYOND

Produced and Directed by: Ward Kimball. Story by: William Bosché, John Dunn, Charles Downs, Con Pederson, Ward Kimball. Music: George Bruns. Layout Design: A. Kendall O'Connor, John Brandt, Tom Yakutis. Cartoon Animation: Julius Svendsen, Arthur Stevens, Jack Boyd, Charles Downs, John Dunn. Space Paintings: William Layne, Gordon Legg. Technical Advisors: Dr. Ernst Stuhlinger, Dr. Wernher Von Braun, Dr. E. C. Slipher. Models: Wathel Rogers. Film Editors: Lloyd Richardson, A.C.E., Lionel A. Ephraim. Narration: Paul Frees. Special Processes: Eustace Lycett. Sound: Robert O. Cook. Production Supervision: Harry Tytle. Acknowledgment: Lowell Observatory.

MEDITERRANEAN CRUISE

Directed by: Hamilton S. Luske, Steve Previn. Sequence Director: Ben Sharpsteen. Cartoon Story by: Otto Englander, Ted Berman. Art Styling: McLaren Stewart. Animation: Cliff Nordberg, Hal King, Eric Larson, John Lounsbery. Effects Animation: Jack Boyd. Layout: Joe Hale. Background: Jimi Trout. Music: Buddy Baker, Franklyn Marks, Oliver Wallace. Song: Richard M. Sherman, Robert B. Sherman. With the Talents of: Paul Frees. Film Editors: Anthony Gerard, Renzo Lucidi. Sound: Robert O. Cook. Photography: Amleto Fattori, Filmeco, Rome, Italy, Raymond Bricon, Amerigo Gengarelli. Assistant Director: Giorgio Gentili. Program Co-ordinator: Jack Bruner. Italian Dances with the cooperation of: E.N.A.L., Rome, Regione Siciliana, Palermo.

MEET THE MUNCEYS

Executive Producers: Chris Carter, Dori Pierson. Produced by: Michael S. McLean. Written by: Dori Pierson, Chris Carter. Directed by: Noel Black. Original Score by: Stephen Lawrence. Director of Photography: Gil Hubbs. Art Director: Marjorie Stone McShirley. Editor: Donald R. Rode. Unit Production Manager: Denny Salvaryn. First Assistant Director: Richard A. Wells. Second Assistant Director: Rodney Allen Hooks. Casting by: Vicki Rosenberg & Associates. Costume Designer: Tom Bronson. Set Decorator: Mark Hite. Property Master: Tracy Farrington. Key Costumers: John Casey, Sharon Swenson. Make-up: Robin Dee LaVigne. Hair Stylist: Edie Panda. Location Manager: Geoffrey Ryan. Script Supervisor: Doris Moody Chisholm. Production Coordinator: Patty McManus. Production Sound Mixer: David Ronne. Sound Editing by: Stephen J. Cannell Productions. Music Editing by: The Music Design Group.

MENACE ON THE MOUNTAIN

Produced by: Ron Miller. Co-producer: Tom Leetch. Teleplay by: Robert Heverly. Based on the book by: Mary A. Hancock. Directed by: Vincent McEveety. Director of Photography: William Snyder, A.S.C. Art Directors: John B. Mansbridge, Russell Menzer. Film Editor: Ray de Leuw. Set Decorators: Emile Kuri, Frank R. McKelvy. Music: Buddy Baker. Sound: Robert O. Cook. Costumer: Chuck Keehne. Make-up: Robert J. Schiffer. Hair Stylist: La Rue Matheron. Assistant Director: Philip L. Parslow. Program Co-ordinator: Jack Bruner.

MICHAEL O'HARA THE FOURTH

Produced by: Ron Miller. Co-producer: Joseph L. McEveety. Written by: Joseph L. McEveety. Directed by: Robert Totten. Director of Photography: Andrew Jackson, A.S.C. Art Director: John B. Mansbridge, Earl Hedrick. Film Editor: Ray de Leuw. Set Decorators: Emile Kuri, Frank J. Rafferty. Music: George Bruns. Assistant Director: Robert Webb. Costumes: Chuck Keehne. Make-up: Robert J. Schiffer. Hair Stylist: La Rue Matheron. Sound: Herb Taylor. Program Co-ordinator: Jack Bruner.

MICKEY AND DONALD KIDDING AROUND

Music: Buddy Baker.

MICKEY MOUSE ANNIVERSARY SHOW, THE

Written and Produced by: Ward Kimball. Live Action Directed by: Robert Stevenson. Friends of Mickey Mouse: Les Clark, Dick Huemer, Ken O'Connor, Joe Hale, Art Stevens, Nick Iuppa, Eustace Lycett, Otto Englander, Larry Clemmons, John Emerson, Jay Gould, Jim Swain. Film Editor: Ernie Milano. Assistant to the Producer: Louis Debney. Music: George Bruns. World of Color Theme Song: Richard M. Sherman, Robert B. Sherman. Sound: Robert O. Cook. Assistant Director: Paul L. Cameron. Program Co-ordinator: Jack Bruner. Vice President in Charge of Television: Ron Miller.

MICKEY'S 50

Executive Producer: Ron Miller. Produced by: Phil May. Written by: Nicholas Harvey Bennion, Phil May. Director of Photography: Leonard J. South, A.S.C. Art Director: John B. Mansbridge. Film Editor: Lloyd L. Richardson, A.C.E. Production Manager: John Bloss. Music by: Richard Bowden, Will Schae-

fer. (The Whole World Wants to Wish You) Happy Birthday Mickey Mouse: Words and Music by: Marty Cooper. Video Supervisor: Nicholas Harvey Bennion. Videotape Editor: Terry Green. Video Coordinator: Chuck Staley. Stop-Action Sequences: Mike Jittlov, Deven Chierighino. Set Decorator: Roger M. Shook. Sound: Herb Taylor. Costumes: Chuck Keehne. Make-up: Robert J. Schiffer, C.M.A.A. Acknowledgments: Black Inc. A.G. for permission to use Gold Rush. Birthday performed by the Beatles.

MICKEY'S HAPPY VALENTINE SPECIAL

Produced by: Joie Albrecht, Scot Garen. Written and Directed by: Scot Garen, Joie Albrecht. Edited by: Mark Cole, Mark Hebdon, Tim Powel. On-line Editor: Brent Carpenter. Original Score by: Christopher L. Stone. Post Production Supervisor: Howard Taksen. Assistant Editor: Craig Kitson. Production Coordinators: Lindanne Martin, Terry Chupak. Assistant to the Producers: Diana Valentine-Stricklin. Production Assistant: Rocky Kendall. Main Title Designer: Michael Bavaro. Paint Box Artist: Jerry Pojawa. Character Voices: Corey Burton, Wayne Allwine (Mickey Mouse), Tony Anselmo (Donald Duck), Joie Albrecht. Re-recording Mixer: David Fluhr, C.A.S. Garen-Albrecht Productions in association with Walt Disney Television.

MICKEY'S 60TH BIRTHDAY

Directed by: Scott Garen. Written by: Joie Albrecht, Scot Garen. Produced by: Scot Garen, Joie Albrecht. Associate Producers: Michael Petok, Denny Salvaryn. Original Score by: Christopher L. Stone. Director of Photography: Robert Primes. Art Directors: Bruce Ryan, Ira Diamond. Editor: Mark Hebdon. Choreographer: Kenny Ortega. Unit Production Manager: Denny Salvaryn. First Assistant Director: Paul Deason. Second Assistant Director: Nancy Green. Associate Director: Debbie Liebling. Stage Manager: Peter Bright. New Animation Supervised by: Sam Cornell. New Animation Production by: Murakami Wolf Swenson, Inc. Costumes Designed by: Tom Bronson. Magic, It's All Up to You Written by: Bob Esty, Joie Albrecht, J.C. Cole. Additional Editing by: Adam "Chip" Pauken. Production Coordinators: Lindanne Martin, Nancy Hobson. Post Production Supervisor: Howard Taksen. On-line Assembly: Brent Carpenter. Post Production Coordinators: Craig Shapiro, Craig Kitson. Assistants to the Producers: Terry Chupak, Krista Molter. Stop Action Animation by Dole Productions: Kevin Dole, Bill O'Neil, Don Waller, John Higbie, Jim Auperle, Ramone Alfonso. Acknowledgments: Paramount Pictures Television, Jim Burrows, Glen & Les Charles, The Cast and Crew of Cheers, Gary David Goldberg, The Cast and Crew of Family Ties, Steven Bocho, The Cast and Crew of L.A. Law, 20th Century-Fox Television, Stephen Cannell, The Cast and Crew of Hunter. Garen-Albrecht Productions in association with Walt Disney Television.

MILLION DOLLAR DIXIE DELIVERANCE, THE

Art Directors: John B. Mansbridge, Jack T. Collis. Editor: Jack Sekely. Production Manager: John Bloss. Unit Production Manager/Assistant Director: Bill Lukather. Second Assistant Director: Louis S. Muscate. Assistant to the Producer: Lawrence Montaigne. Sound Supervisor: Herb Taylor. Sound Mixer: Bill Teague. Special Effects: Danny Lee. Stunt Coordinator: Glenn Wilder. Animal Supervisor: James A. Prine. Technical Advisor: General Dent Meyer. Technical Assistant: Frank Rickman. Costumes: Chuck Keehne. Make-up: Robert J. Schiffer. Hair Stylist: Denise Kennedy. Sound Editor: Ben F. Hendricks. Music Editor: Evelyn Kennedy. Music: Irwin Kostal. Director of Photography: Rick Anderson. Executive Producer: Ron Miller. Produced by: Jerome Courtland. Teleplay by: Lawrence Montaigne, based on his story. Directed by: Russ Mayberry. Acknowledgments: The State of Georgia, The Community of Westville, The U.S. Forest Service, Chattahoochie and Sumter National Forests.

MINADO, THE WOLVERINE

Co-producer: James Algar. Teleplay by: Homer McCoy. Based on the book Minado by: Erle Wilson. Narrator: Sebastian Cabot. Music: Buddy Baker. World of Color Theme: Richard

M. Sherman, Robert B. Sherman. Film Editor: Norman Palmer, A.C.E. Production Manager: Erwin L. Verity. Sound: Robert O. Cook. Program Co-ordinator: Jack Bruner. *For Cangary, Ltd.* Field Producer: Lloyd Beebe. Photographers: Lloyd Beebe and William Bacon III. Acknowledgment: Canadian Wildlife Service, The.

Mr. Boogedy
Music by: John Addison. Supervising Producer: Ed Lahti. Produced by: Steven North. Written by: Michael Janover. Directed by: Oz Scott. Director of Photography: Robert Stevens. Art Director: Ray Storey. Editor: Duane Hartzell. Unit Production Manager/Associate Producer: Bruce Hendricks. First Assistant Director: Ira Shuman. Second Assistant Director: Joseph Paul Moore. Casting by: Allison Jones. Costume Designer: William Ware Theiss. Set Decorator: Robert L. Zilliox. Property Master: Lavar Emert. Key Costumers: Aida Swinson, Milton G. Mangum. Make-up: Rick Stratton. Hair Stylist: Carolyn Jean Ferguson. Location Manager: Ron L. Carr. Script Supervisor: Sally J. Roddy. Production Coordinator: Lorna Neal. Production Sound Mixer: Pat Mitchell. Sound Editing by: Echo Film Services/Joseph Melody. Music Editing by: Music Design Group/James Burt.

Monsters of the Deep
Directed by: Hamilton Luske, Peter Godfrey. Written by: Winston Hibler, John Lucas, Ted Sears, Jack Speirs. Music for Television: George Bruns. Photography (Television): Charles Boyle. Additional Photography: Jack Couffer, Conrad Hall, LaVerne Pederson, Harry Pederson, Stuart Jewell. Film Editor: George Nicholson. Special Processes: Ub Iwerks. Sound Director: C.O. Slyfield. Special Art Work: Al Zinnen, Joshua Meador, Jimi Trout. Acknowledgments: The National Geographic Society, The Allan Handcock Foundation, University of Southern California.

Moochie of Pop Warner Football
Directed by: William Beaudine. Written by: Ellis Marcus. Produced by: Bill Anderson. Associate Producer: Louis Debney. Director of Photography: Walter H. Castle, A.S.C. Art Director: Marvin Aubrey Davis. Film Editor: Basil Wrangell. Music: William Lava. Sound: Robert O. Cook. Set Decoration: Emile Kuri, William L. Stevens. Costumer: Chuck Keehne. Makeup: Pat McNalley. Unit Manager: Roy Wade. Assistant Director: Joseph L. McEveety. Acknowledgment: Members of National Pop Warner Conference.

Moochie of the Little League
Directed by: William Beaudine. Written by: Ellis Marcus. Production Coordinator: Louis Debney. Director of Photography: Walter H. Castle, A.S.C. Art Director: Hilyard Brown. Film Editor: Cotton Warburton, A.C.E. Music: William Lava. Sound: Robert O. Cook. Set Decoration: Emile Kuri, William L. Stevens. Costumer: Chuck Keehne. Make-up: Pat McNalley. Assistant Director: Ron Miller. Acknowledgments: Little League, Inc., The California State Director.

Mooncussers, The
Co-producer: Bill Anderson. Teleplay by: Lowell S. Hawley. Based on the book *Flying Ebony* by: Iris Vinton. Directed by: James Neilson. Assistant to the Producer: Louis Debney. Director of Photography: William Snyder, A.S.C. Art Directors: Carroll Clark, Marvin Aubrey Davis. Film Editor: Robert Stafford, A.C.E. Set Decoration: Emile Kuri, Armor E. Goetten. Music: George Bruns. Song: Richard M. Sherman, Robert B. Sherman. Costumer: Chuck Keehne. Make-up: Pat McNalley. Hair Stylist: Ruth Sandifer. Sound: Robert O. Cook. Assistant Director: John Chulay. Program Co-ordinator: Jack Bruner.

More about the Silly Symphonies
Directed by: Clyde Geronimi. Story: Nick George, Bill Berg. Music: Joseph S. Dubin. Animation: Jack Campbell, Bob Carlson. Layout: Erni Nordli, Lance Nolley. Backgrounds: Dick Anthony. Art Director: Marvin Aubrey Davis. Photographer: Charles P. Boyle, A.S.C. Set Decorator: Emile Kuri. Film Editor: Donald Halliday. Special Processes: Ub Iwerks, A.S.C. Sound: Robert O. Cook. Assistant Director: Russ Haverick. Production Supervision: Harry Tytle.

Mother's Courage, A: The Mary Thomas Story
Executive Producers: Ted Field, Robert W. Cort. Co-Executive Producers: Patricia Clifford, Kate Wright. Co-Producer: Chet Walker. Produced by: Richard L. O'Connor. Written by: Jason Miller. Directed by: John Patterson. Music by: Lee Holdridge. Director of Photography: King Baggot. Art Director: Michael Merritt. Edited by: Richard A. Harris. Production Manager: Joe Boston. First Assistant Director: Eric Jewett. Second Assistant Director: John Roman. Casting by: Al Onorato, C.S.A., Jerold Franks, C.S.A. Chicago Casting by: Jane Heitz Casting. Set Decorator: Bill Arnold. Property Master: Aaron Holden. Costume Designer: Cathy Newport-Logan. Wardrobe Supervisor: Gina Panno. Make-up/Hair Supervisor: Lillian Toth. Hair Stylist: Ron Scott. Transportation Coordinator: George DiLeonardi. Production Sound Mixer: Glenn Williams. Script Supervisor: Dru Anne Carlson. Location Manager: Joe Doyle. Production Coordinator: Debra Oyer. Sound Editing by: Dimension Sound. Music Editing by: Allan K. Rosen. *Sooner or Later* and *Goin' & Growin'* Written by: T.C. Carson. Chet Walker Enterprises, Inc. and Interscope Communications, Inc. in association with Walt Disney Television.

Mountain Born
Teleplay by: Homer McCoy. Based on the book by: Elizabeth Yates. Produced and Directed by: James Algar. Narrator: Mayf Nutter. Film Editor: Gordon Brenner. Music: Buddy Baker. Song *Mountain Born:* Sam Austin. Sound: Herb Taylor. Production Manager: Erwin L. Verity. Program Co-ordinator: Jack Bruner. *For Hank Schloss Productions* Field Producer: Hank Schloss. Photography: Hank Schloss. Production Assistant: Bob Misiorowski. Animal Supervision: Carl Bradford.

Mouseketeer Reunion, The
Executive Producer: William Robert Yates. Producers: Ron Miziker, Phil May. Directed by: Tom Trbovich. Written by: Rod Warren. Musical Director: Peter Matz. Special Music & Choral Direction: Tom Bahler. Choreography by: Dee Dee Wood. Art Director: John B. Mansbridge. Costume Designer: Jack Sandeen. Creative Consultant: Lonnie Burr. Assistant to the Producers: Suellen Wagner. Production Manager: John Bloss. Associate Directors: David Grossman, Kac Young. Technical Director: Gene Crowe. Video: Keith Winikoff. Audio: Bruce Burns. Mixer: Tom Huth. Stage Managers: Sandy Prudden, Larry Roslaw. Make-up: Robert J. Schiffer, C.M.A.A. Assistant Choreographer: David Rodriguez. Videotape Editor: Terry Green. Film Editor: Ernie Milano, A.C.E. Tap Consultant: Sharon Baird.

Mouseketeers at Walt Disney World, The
Executive Producer: Ron Miller. Produced by: Ed Ropolo. Written by: Tedd Anasti, David Talisman, Tom Adair. Directed by: John Tracy. Associate Producer: Bob Sutton. Associate Director: Shelley Jensen. Videotape Editor: Terry Green. Musical Supervisor: Robert F. Brunner. Choreography: Marilyn Magness, Judy and Jim Bates. Songs by: Frances Adair, Tom Adair, Tedd Anasti, Robert F. Brunner, Peter Martin, Marc B. Ray, David Talisman. Make-up: Guy del Russo. Hair Stylist: Irene Aparicio. Production Assistant: Joyce Van Brummelen. Technical Supervisor: Steve Dever. Technicam Director: Terry Green. Lighting Director: Al Reiners. Video: Mark Sanford, Dave Fruitman. Audio: John Berry. Video Facilities by: Compact Video Systems, Inc.

Move Along, Mustangers
Directed by: George Sherman. Written by: Maurice Tombragel. Produced by: James Pratt. Director of Photography: Lucien Ballard, A.S.C. Art Director: Stan Jolley. Film Editor: Basil Wrangell. Music: Franklyn Marks. Song: Maurice Tombragel, Franklyn Marks. Sound: Robert O. Cook. Set Decoration: Emile Kuri, Hal Gausman. Costumer: Chuck Keehne. Make-up: Pat McNalley. Hair Stylist: Ruth Sandifer. Assistant Director: Ivan Volkman.

Muppets at Walt Disney World, The
Produced by: Diana Birkenfield, Martin G. Baker. Directed by: Peter Harris. Written by: Jerry Juhl. The Muppets: Jim Henson, Frank Oz, Dave Goelz, Jerry Nelson, Richard Hunt, Steve Whitmire, Kevin Clash, David Rudman, Rickey Boyd,

Rick Lyon, Camille Bonora. Music Producer: Phil Ramone. Production Designer: Victor DiNapoli. Lighting Consultant: Phil Hawkes. Production Manager: Clay Newbill. Associate Director: Roberta Savold. Stage Manager: Tracy Eskander. Production Coordinator: Sonya Weathers. Muppet Workshop: Joanne Green, Mark Zeszotek, Henri Ewaskio, Larry Jameson. Costume Design: Polly Smith, Stephan Rotandaro. Art Director: Jeff Chandler. Musical Arrangements: Larry Schwartz, Charlie Camorata, Mark Radice, Merrill and Rubicam. Technical Supervisor: Kevin Hamburger. Video: Bob Kaufman. Audio: Doug Nelson. Cameras: Bob Minges, Richard Banales. Gaffer: Rick Campbell. Assistant to Producers: Jill Colley. Videotape Editor: Jeff Palmer. Videotape Facilities Provided by: Video One, Inc. Post Production by: The Post Group at the Disney-MGM Studios. Executive Producer: Jim Henson.

MUSIC FOR EVERYBODY
Prepared for Television by: Director: Hamilton S. Luske. Story: Joe Rinaldi. Art Styling: McLaren Stewart. Animation: Eric Larson, Ward Kimball, Charlie Downs, Julius Svendsen, Art Stevens. Layout: Joe Hale. Background: Jimi Trout. Music: Franklyn Marks. *World of Color* Theme: Richard M. Sherman, Robert B. Sherman. Film Editor: Edward R. Baker. With the talents of: Paul Frees. Sound: Robert O. Cook. Program Co-ordinator: Jack Bruner.

The end credits for this episode included the following: Walt Disney has presented: Nelson Eddy, Dinah Shore, Benny Goodman, Ethel Smith, Riabouchinska and Lichine. *Clair de Lune* Conducted by: Leopold Stokowski and Played by: The Philadelphia Orchestra.

MUSTANG!
Written by: Calvin Clements, Jr. Produced and Directed by: Roy Edward Disney. Narrator: Ricardo Montalban. Film Editor: Norman R. Palmer, A.C.E. Music: Robert F. Brunner. Production Manager: Erwin L. Verity. Production Co-ordinator: Robert F. Metzler. *For Cangary Limited* Field Producer: Frank Zuniga. Photography: Michael Lonzo. Assisted by: Carlos Ancona. Production Assistants: Joe Orlando, John Chesko, Tom Buchan, Sandy Alsobrook. Sets and Locations: Ron Foreman. Head Wrangler: Jack Conners. Assisted by: Roy Hunicutt, Dick McGuire. Additional Photography: Russ Alsobrook.

MUSTANG MAN, MUSTANG MAID
Directed by: George Sherman. Written by: Maurice Tombragel. Produced by: James Pratt. Director of Photography: Lucien Ballard, A.S.C. Art Director: Stan Jolley. Film Editor: Basil Wrangell. Music: Franklyn Marks. Song: Maurice Tombragel, Franklyn Marks. Sound: Robert O. Cook. Set Decoration: Emile Kuri, Hal Gausman. Costumer: Chuck Keehne. Make-up: Pat McNalley. Hair Stylist: Ruth Sandifer. Assistant Director: Ivan Volkman.

MY DOG, THE THIEF
Produced by: Ron Miller. Co-producer: Tom Leetch. Teleplay by: William Raynor, Myles Wilder. Based on a story by: Gordon Buford. Directed by: Robert Stevenson. Director of Photography: William Snyder, A.S.C. Art Director: John B. Mansbridge. Film Editor: Cotton Warburton, A.C.E. Set Decorators: Emile Kuri, William Stevens. Second Unit Director: Arthur J. Vitarelli. Special Effects: Eustace Lycett. Music: Buddy Baker. Song *That Dog, Barrabas:* Terry Gilkyson. Sound: Robert O. Cook. Costumer: Chuck Keehne. Make-up: Robert J. Schiffer. Assistant Director: Christopher Hibler. Program Co-ordinator: Jack Bruner.

MY FAMILY IS A MENAGERIE
Co-producer: Roy Edward Disney. Teleplay by: Ward Hawkins, Jack Speirs. Based on a story by: Sally Patton. Narrator: Rex Allen. Film Editor: Lloyd L. Richardson, A.C.E. Music: George Bruns. *World of Color* Theme Song: Richard M. Sherman, Robert B. Sherman. Production Manager: Erwin L. Verity. Sound: Robert O. Cook. Program Co-ordinator: Jack Bruner. *For Hank Schloss Productions, Inc.* Field Producer: Hank Schloss. Photography: Hank Schloss, Ivan Craig. Production Aide: Robert Dickson. Technical Consultant: Hubert Wells.

MY TOWN
Music: Craig Satan. Producer: John Garbett. Written by: Gil Grant. Directed by: Gwen Arner. Director of Photography: George Koblasa. Art Director: James Shanahan. Editor: Michael S. Murphy. Unit Production Manager/Associate Producer: Gordon Wolf. First Assistant Director: Mike Kusley. Second Assistant Director: Emmitt-Leon O'Neil. Casting by: Linda Francis, C.S.A. Costume Designer: William Ware Theiss. Set Decorator: Carl Biddiscombe. Property Master: Anthony C. Thorpe. Key Costumers: Sandra Berke Jordan, Gene Deardorff. Make-up: Michael F. Blake. Hair Stylist: Eddie M. Barron. Location Manager: Ryan Rosenberg. Script Supervisor: Alleen N. Nollmann. Production Coordinator: Vera Martin. Assistant to Executive Producer: Esther Caporale. Production Sound Mixer: Bill Teague. Sound Editing by: Echo Film Services/Joseph Melody. Music Editing by: Jack Wadsworth. *Crazy for You* performed by: Gail Lennon. Gil Grant Productions.

MYSTERY IN DRACULA'S CASTLE, THE
Produced by: Bill Anderson. Written by: Sue Milburn. Directed by: Robert Totten. Director of Photography: Charles F. Wheeler, A.S.C. Art Directors: John B. Mansbridge, Malcolm C. Bert. Film Editor: Hugh Chaloupka, A.C.E. Special Visual Effects: Alan Maley, Art Cruickshank, A.S.C., Danny Lee. Set Decoration: John A. Kuri. Music: Richard Shores. Sound: Herb Taylor. Costumes: Chuck Keehne. Make-up: Robert J. Schiffer. Hair Stylist: La Rue Matheron. Assistant Director: Robert Webb.

MYSTERY OF EDWARD SIMS, THE
Produced by: Ron Miller. Written by: Herman Groves. Based on a character created by: Richard Harding Davis. Directed by: Seymour Robbie. Assistant to the Producer: Tom Leetch. Director of Photography: William Snyder, A.S.C. Art Directors: Carroll Clark, Robert E. Smith. Film Editors: Marsh Hendry, Norman Palmer, A.C.E. Set Decorators: Emile Kuri, Hal Gausman. Music: Willis Schaefer. *World of Color* Theme Song: Richard M. Sherman, Robert B. Sherman. Costumer: Chuck Keehne. Make-up: Gordon Hubbard. Hair Stylist: La Rue Matheron. Sound: Robert O. Cook. Assistant Director: Paul L. Cameron. Program Co-ordinator: Jack Bruner.

NASHVILLE COYOTE, THE
Written by: Jack Speirs. Produced and Directed by: Winston Hibler. Narrated by: Mayf Nutter. Songs and Background Music by: Jack Speirs, Buddy Baker. *Hangin' on the Fringe:* Jack Speirs, Franklyn Marks. Film Editor: Gregg McLaughlin. Production Manager: Erwin L. Verity. Production Co-ordinator: Robert F. Metzler. Sound: Herb Taylor. Program Co-ordinator: Jack Bruner. *For Cangary Limited* Field Producer: Ron Brown. Photographers: Herb Smith, Ken Ball. Production Assistant: Harold Clifton. Animal Supervision: Bill Rowland, John Gillespie.

NATURE'S BETTER BUILT HOMES
Story by: Ted Berman. Narration Written by: Mel Leven. Directed by: Ward Kimball, Hamilton S. Luske. Narrator: Olan Soulé. Production Associate: McLaren Stewart. Animation: Eric Larson, Bob McCrea. Layout: Joe Hale. Background: Bill Layne. Music: Franklyn Marks. Songs: Mel Leven. *World of Color* Theme Song: Richard M. Sherman, Robert B. Sherman. Film Editor: Lloyd L. Richardson, A.C.E. Sound: Robert O. Cook. Program Co-ordinator: Jack Bruner.

NATURE'S CHARTER TOURS
Story by: Ted Berman. Narration Written by: Mel Leven. Directed by: Hamilton S. Luske, Ward Kimball. Production Associate: McLaren Stewart. Animation: Cliff Nordberg, Eric Larson, Bob McCrea, Charlie Downs, Hal King, Jack Boyd. Layout: Joe Hale. Background: Jimi Trout. Songs—Music and Lyrics: Mel Leven. Music: Franklyn Marks. *World of Color* Theme Song: Richard M. Sherman, Robert B. Sherman. Special Effects: Eustace Lycett. Film Editor: Anthony Gerard. Sound: Robert O. Cook. Program Co-ordinator: Jack Bruner.

NATURE'S STRANGEST ODDBALLS
Directed by: Les Clark, Hamilton S. Luske. Sequence Directors: Wolfgang Reitherman, Bill Roberts. Story: Otto Englan-

der, Ted Berman, Bill Peet. Animation: Cliff Nordberg, Bob McCrea, Bob Youngquist, John Lounsbery, Frank Thomas. Layout: A. Kendall O'Connor, Basil Davidovich, Herb Ryman. Background: Bill Layne, Frank Armitage, Ralph Hulett, Al Dempster. Music: Franklyn Marks, George Bruns, Paul Smith. Song *Nature Calypso:* Buddy Baker, Otto Englander. Film Editor: Anthony Gerard. Sound: Robert O. Cook. Program Co-ordinator: Jack Bruner.

NINE LIVES OF ELFEGO BACA, THE
Written and Directed by: Norman Foster. Produced by: James Pratt. Director of Photography: William Snyder, A.S.C. Art Director: Stan Jolley. Film Editor: Edward Sampson, Jr. Music: Franklyn Marks. Songs by: Rich Dehr, Frank Miller, Norman Foster, William Lava. Matte Artist: Peter Ellenshaw. Sound: Robert O. Cook. Set Decorators: Emile Kuri, Armor E. Goetten. Costumer: Chuck Keehne. Make-up: Pat McNalley. Assistant Director: Vincent McEveety.

NIOK
Directed by: Clyde Geronimi. Produced by: Ben Sharpsteen. Narration Written by: Larry Clemmons. Director of Photography: Walter H. Castle, A.S.C. Art Director: Marvin Aubrey Davis. Set Decorator: Emile Kuri. Film Editor: Harry Reynolds. Narrated by: Winston Hibler. Sound: Robert O. Cook. Production Supervision: Harry Tytle.

NOSEY, THE SWEETEST SKUNK IN THE WEST
Produced by: Roy Edward Disney. Written by: Gerald Pearce. Narrator: Rex Allen. Film Editor: Toby Brown. Music: George Bruns. Sound: Herb Taylor. Production Manager: Erwin L. Verity. *For Cangary Limited* Field Producer: Richard H. Lyford. Photography: Richard H. Lyford. Production Assistant: Patricia O'Rourke Foutz. Production Staff: Mac A. Child, Thomas Shivers, Bob Bradshaw, Sharon Lyford.

NOT SO LONELY LIGHTHOUSE KEEPER, THE
Co-producer: James Algar. Story and Teleplay by: Jack Couffer. Narration Written by: Homer McCoy. Narrator: Roy Barcroft. Film Editor: Gordon Brenner. Music: Buddy Baker. *World of Color* Theme Song: Richard M. Sherman, Robert B. Sherman. Production Manager: Erwin L. Verity. Sound: Robert O. Cook. Program Co-ordinator: Jack Bruner. *For Grey Owl Productions, Inc.* Field Producer: Jack Couffer. Photographer: Lloyd G. Kenwood. Production Assistant: Pieter Hubbard. Wildlife Consultants: Al Niemela, Mike Guinn. Acknowledgment: The United States Coast Guard.

OFFICER AND A DUCK, AN
This episode was aired without production credits.

OMEGA CONNECTION, THE
Director of Photography: Godfrey Godar. Aerial Photography: Peter Allwork, B.S.C. Art Director: Jack Shampan. Supervising Editor: Peter Boeta. Editor: Mike Campbell. Production Supervisor: Basil Rayburn. Casting Director: Maude Spector. Assistant Art Director: Alan Cassie. Unit Manager: Robert Lynn. Sound Editor: Dino di Campo. Assistant Director: Richard Hoult. Continuity: Phyllis Townshend. Camera Operator: Jack Lowin. Stunt Co-ordinator: Alan Stuart. Make-up: Freddie Williamson. Hairdressing: Betty Glasow. Sound Recordists: Ken Osborne, Ken Barker. Music Composed and Conducted by: John Cameron. Recorded at: Anvil Studios. Associate Producer: Hugh Attwooll. Executive Producer: Ron Miller. Produced by: Jan Williams. Teleplay by: Gail Morgan Hickman, David E. Boston. Story by: Gail Morgan Hickman, David E. Boston, David Assael, Joshua Brand, Martha Coolidge. Directed by: Robert Clouse. Filmed on location and re-recorded at Pinewood Studios, London, England.

ON VACATION
Directed by: Jack Hannah. Pluto and Gum Sequence Director: C. August Nichols. Animation: John Sibley, Al Coe, George Kreisl, Bob Carlson, Volus Jones, Bill Justice, Phil Duncan, Hugh Fraser, Jack Boyd, Dan MacManus. Story: Dave Detiege, Al Bertino, Ralph Wright, Riley Thompson, Milt Schaffer, Eric Gurney. Music: Oliver Wallace, Paul Smith. Layout: Yale Gracey, Karl Karpé. Backgrounds: Art Riley, Brice Mack. Art

Director: Marvin Aubrey Davis. Set Director: Emile Kuri. Film Editor: Tom Acosta. Sound: Robert O. Cook. Production Supervision: Harry Tytle. Photography: Charles Boyle, A.S.C. Special Processes: Ub Iwerks, A.S.C. Assistant Director: Gordon McLean.

ONE DAY AT TETON MARSH
Co-producer: James Algar. Teleplay by: James Algar. Based on the book by: Sally Carrighar. Narrator: Sebastian Cabot. Music: Buddy Baker. Film Editor: Norman Palmer, A.C.E. Production Manager: Erwin L. Verity. Sound: Robert O. Cook. Program Co-ordinator: Jack Bruner. *For Ken Nelson Productions* Field Producer: Ken Nelson. Photographers: Ken Nelson, Gene Petersen, Erik Daarstad, Gordon B. Eastman. Additional Photography by: Dick Borden. Wildlife Consultants: D'Arcy Humphries, Jay Sisler. Acknowledgments: National Park Service, Grand Teton National Park, Wyoming Game and Fish Commission, U.S. Fish and Wildlife Service, U.S. Forest Service.

ONE DAY ON BEETLE ROCK
Co-producer: James Algar. Teleplay by: Homer McCoy. Based on the book by: Sally Carrighar. Narrator: Sebastian Cabot. Film Editor: Gordon Brenner. Music: Buddy Baker. *World of Color* Theme Song: Richard M. Sherman, Robert B. Sherman. Production Manager: Erwin L. Verity. Sound: Robert O. Cook. Program Co-ordinator: Jack Bruner. *For Hank Schloss Productions, Inc.* Field Producer: Hank Schloss. Photography: Hank Schloss and Ivan Craig. Additional Photography: Jack Ferrucci. Wildlife Consultants: Ronald Bourne, Frank Treuting, George Toth. Acknowledgment: Sequoia National Park, Sequoia National Forest.

101 PROBLEMS OF HERCULES, THE
Co-producer: Harry Tytle. Teleplay by: Rod Peterson. Based on a story by: Tom McGowan. Production Manager: Erwin L. Verity. Film Editor: Lloyd Richardson, A.C.E. Music: Paul Smith. *World of Color* Theme: Richard M. Sherman, Robert B. Sherman. Narrator: Hugh Cherry. Sound: Robert O. Cook. Program Co-ordinator: Jack Bruner. *For Tom McGowan Productions* Field Producer: Tom Boutross. Photography: Tom Quayle. Production Assistant: Nancy Loper. Photographed in Utah with the co-operation of the State Department of Fish and Game and American Sheep Producers Council, Inc.

OPERATION UNDERSEA
Directed by: Winston Hibler, Hamilton Luske. Written by: Winston Hibler, Ted Sears, John Lucas. Cartoon Story by: Milt Banta, Bill Berg. Music: George Bruns. Cartoon Settings: Al Zinnen, George Delado. Photography: M. LaVerne Pederson, Jack Whitman. Film Editors: Lynn Harrison, A.C.E., Grant Smith. Special Processes: Ub Iwerks. Sound Director: C.O. Slyfield. Special Animation: John Sibley, Ed Aardal.

OTTER IN THE FAMILY, AN
Written and Co-produced by: Roy Edward Disney. Narrator: Rex Allen. Music: George Bruns. Film Editor: Lloyd L. Richardson, A.C.E. Production Manager: Erwin L. Verity. Sound: Robert O. Cook. Program Co-ordinator: Jack Bruner. *For Richard Lyford Productions, Inc.* Field Producer: Richard Lyford. Photographers: Richard Lyford, Jean Mickelson. Production Manager: Moray Foutz.

OUR FRIEND THE ATOM
Directed by: Hamilton S. Luske. Scientific Development: Dr. Heinz Haber. Teleplay by: Milt Banta. Music: Oliver Wallace. Art Director: Marvin Aubrey Davis. Animation Art Styling: Claude Coats, John Hench. Animation: Jack Boyd, Cliff Nordberg, John Lounsbery, Jack Campbell, Jack Buckley, Ed Parks. Layout: Al Zinnen, Thor Putnam. Backgrounds: Jimi Trout, Irv Wyner. Set Decorator: Emile Kuri. Photography: Walter H. Castle, A.S.C. Film Editor: Lloyd Richardson. Special Processes: Ub Iwerks, A.S.C., Eustace Lycett. Sound: Robert O. Cook. Assistant Director: Vincent McEveety. Production Supervision: Harry Tytle.

OUR UNSUNG VILLAINS
Directed by: Hamilton S. Luske. Written by: Carl Cons, Hamilton S. Luske. Music: Oliver Wallace. Face in the Mir-

ror: Hans Conried. Art Director: Marvin Aubrey Davis. Production Supervision: Harry Tytle. Photography: Gordon Avil, A.S.C., Bert Glennon. Film Editor: Lloyd L. Richardson. Set Decorator: Bertram Granger. Assistant Director: Gordon McLean. Special Processes: Ub Iwerks, A.S.C., Eustace A. Lycett. Sound: Robert O. Cook. Cartoon sequences from *Song of the South* and *Peter Pan:* Directed by: Wilfred Jackson, Hamilton S. Luske. Story: William Peet, Ralph Wright. Music: Paul Smith, Oliver Wallace. Animation: Milt Kahl, John Lounsbery, Ollie Johnston, Eric Larson, Wolfgang Reitherman, Les Clark, Bob Carlson. Layout: Ken Anderson, A. Kendall O'Connor. Backgrounds: Claude Coats, Ray Huffine.

Outlaw Cats of Colossal Cave, The
Produced by: Harry Tytle. Director of Photography: Robert F. Sparks. Written by: Rod Peterson. Directed by: Hank Schloss, William Stierwalt. Narrator: Leslie Nielsen. Film Editor: Ernie Milano, A.C.E. Music: Franklyn Marks. Songs *Home's Not Home Anymore* and *The Outlaws of Colossal Cave:* Rod Peterson, Franklyn Marks. Sound: Herb Taylor. Field Producer: Hank Schloss. Photography: Tom Koester. Unit Production Manager: Morris R. Abrams. Second Assistant Director: William R. Poole. Production Supervisor: William Redlin. Technical Advisors: William Redlin, Jr., Mindy Schloss, R.W. Torgerson. Dioramas by: Rick Shaw Productions. Photographed at Colossal Cave, Tucson, Arizona.

Owl That Didn't Give a Hoot, The
Produced by: Roy Edward Disney. Teleplay by: Otto Englander. Narration by: Gerald Pearce. Based on the book *The World of the Great Horned Owl* by: G. Ronald Austing, John B. Holt, Jr. Narrator: Steve Forrest. Film Editor: Lloyd L. Richardson, A.C.E. Music: Robert F. Brunner. *World of Color* Theme Song: Richard M. Sherman, Robert B. Sherman. Production Manager: Erwin L. Verity. Sound: Robert O. Cook. Program Co-ordinator: Jack Bruner. *For Pisces Productions, Inc.* Field Producer: Frank Zuniga. Photography: Michael Lonzo. Production Assistant: Irvin Park. Animal Supervision: Dennis Grisco. Assisted by: Rose Grisco, Mike Pociecha, Ramon Vega, Jr. Vice President in Charge of Television: Ron Miller.

Pablo and the Dancing Chihuahua
Co-produced and Narrated by: Winston Hibler. Teleplay by: Paul Lucey. Story by: Homer Brightman. Narration Written by: Jack Speirs. *For Perkins Films, Inc.* Directed by: Walter Perkins. Photography: Frank Zuniga. Recording: Tom Harvey. Animal Handling: Janice Chachin, Carol Darlington. Production Co-ordinator: Robert F. Metzler. Production Manager: Erwin L. Verity. Film Editor: Gregg McLaughlin. Music: George Bruns. *World of Color* Theme Song: Richard M. Sherman, Robert B. Sherman. Sound: Robert O. Cook. Program Co-ordinator: Jack Bruner.

Pacifically Peeking
Story: Bill Berg. Narration Written by: Mel Leven. Directed by: Ward Kimball, Hamilton S. Luske. Production Associate: McLaren Stewart. Animation: Ward Kimball. Globe Effects: Les Clark, Jack Boyd. Layout: Joe Hale. Background: Elmer Plummer. Songs—Music and Lyrics: Mel Leven. Music: Franklyn Marks. *World of Color* Theme Song: Richard M. Sherman, Robert B. Sherman. Special Effects: Eustace Lycett. Film Editor: Edward R. Baker. With the Talents of: Paul Frees (Moby Duck), George Walsh (narrator). Sound: Robert O. Cook. Program Co-ordinator: Jack Bruner. Vice President in Charge of Television: Ron Miller.

Pancho, The Fastest Paw in the West
Produced by: Roy Edward Disney. Teleplay by: Norman Wright, Tom Sellers. Narration by: Norman Wright. Based on the book *Pancho, A Dog of the Plains* by: Bruce Grant. Narrator: Rex Allen. Film Editor: Toby Brown. Music: Franklyn Marks. Song: Mel Leven. *World of Color* Theme Song: Richard M. Sherman, Robert B. Sherman. Production Manager: Erwin L. Verity. Sound: Robert O. Cook. Program Co-ordinator: Jack Bruner. *For Norman Wright Productions, Inc.* Field Producer: Norman Wright. Photography: Jack Steely, Ivan Craig. Production Assistant: Jean Wright. "Pancho" Trained by: Ray-

mond Hubbard. Animal Handler: Ronald Bourne. Portions of this picture were filmed in the Coronado National Forest and Ghost Town, Madrid, New Mexico. Acknowledgment: Forest Service, U.S. Department of Agriculture.

Parent Trap III
Produced by: Henry Colman. Producer: Jill Donner. Teleplay by: Jill Donner. Story by: Deborah Amelon, Jill Donner. Based in part on characters from the book *Das Doppelte Lottchen* by: Eric Kästner. Directed by: Mollie Miller. Original Score by: Joel McNeely. Director of Photography: Isidore Mankofsky, A.S.C. Art Director: Raymond G. Storey. Edited by: Howard Kunin, A.C.E., Duane Hartzell, A.C.E. Unit Production Manager: Robert M. Rolsky. First Assistant Director: Fredric B. Blankfein. Second Assistant Director: John Joseph Eyler. Casting by: Kathleen Letterie, C.S.A. Costumes Designed by: Tom Bronson. Set Decorator: Ethel Robins Richards. Property Master: Tracy Farrington. Key Costumers: Dawn Jackson, Bill Tiegs. Make-up: Pete Altobelli. Hair Stylist: Faith C. Vechio. Location Manager: Gary DeGalla. Script Supervisor: Pamela Alch. Production Coordinator: Teri Christopher. Production Sound Mixer: Joe Kenworthy, C.A.S. Sound Editing by: Todd-Ao/Glen Glenn Sound. Music Editing by: Segue Music, Inc.

Parent Trap Hawaiian Honeymoon
Original Score by: Joel McNeely. Edited by: Art Stafford, Karen I. Stern. Production Designer: Rodger Maus. Director of Photography: Michel Hugo, A.S.C. Co-Producer: John McNamara. Produced by: Charles Milhaupt, Richard Luke Rothschild. Written by: John McNamara. Based on Characters Created by: Deborah Amelon, Jill Donner. Based in part on Characters from the book *Das Doppelte Lottchen* by: Eric Kästner. Directed by: Mollie Miller. Unit Production Manager: Paul Deason. First Assistant Director: Stephen Lofaro. Second Assistant Director: Sandra M. Middleton. Casting by: Allison Jones. Casting Associate: Jeffrey Newman. Costumes Designed by: Tom Bronson. Set Decorators: Wally White, Lynn Smart. Property Master: Barbara Adamski. Key Costumer: Linda A. Matthews. Make-up: Carol Schwartz. Hair Stylist: Monica Hart Helpman. Location Managers: Sherry Spangler, Laura L. Brown. Script Supervisor: Nancy Banta Hansen. Production Coordinator: Nancy Malone Claycomb. Production Sound Mixers: Stan Gordon, Joe Kenworthy, C.A.S. Music Editing by: Segue Music, Inc.

People and Places—Tiburon, Sardinia, Morocco (and) Icebreakers
Directed by: Winston Hibler. Written by: Ted Sears, Winston Hibler, Jack Speirs. Music: Joseph S. Dubin. Production Supervision: Harry Tytle. Special Art Work: Joshua Meador, Art Riley. Photography: William Neil Smith, William Fortin, Elmo G. Jones, Chief Photographer, U.S. Coast Guard, Amleto Fattori, Raymond Bricon, Charles Hoyle, A.S.C. Film Editors: Grant K. Smith, Harry Reynolds. Special Processes: Ub Iwerks. Sound: Robert O. Cook. Acknowledgments: The United States Coast Guard, The United States Navy, The Department of Defense, The University of Arizona, The Wenner Gren Foundation for Anthropological Research.

People of the Desert
The Blue Men of Morocco: Directed by: Ralph Wright. Produced by: Ben Sharpsteen. Narration Written by: *The Blue Men of Morocco:* Ralph Wright, Winston Hibler, Harrison Negley. *Navajo Adventure:* Frank Cocrell, Dwight Hauser. Music: Oliver Wallace. Photographed by: *The Blue Men of Morocco:* Raymond Bricon. *Navajo Adventure:* Joe O'Connor. Film Editors: *The Blue Men of Morocco:* Jack M. Vandagriff. *Navajo Adventure:* Harry Reynolds. Music Editor: Evelyn Kennedy. Animation Effects: Joshua Meador, Art Riley. Narrated by: *The Blue Men of Morocco:* Winston Hibler. *Navajo Adventure:* Bill Ewing. Special Processes: Ub Iwerks, A.S.C. Sound: Robert O. Cook. Production Supervision: Harry Tytle.

Perilous Assignment
Directed by: Hamilton S. Luske. Narration Written by: Dwight Hauser. Produced by: William H. Anderson. Moun-

tain Unit Director and Guide: Gaston Rebuffat. Film Editor: Harry Reynolds. Music: Franklyn Marks. Song *Climb the Mountain:* By Dunham and Franklyn Marks. Cameramen: Georges Tairraz, August Julen, Pierre Tairraz. Matte Artist: Peter Ellenshaw. Sound: Robert O. Cook. Zermatt Liaison: Bernhardt Biner. Location Supervisor: Bob Porter. Production Supervisor: Alan L. Jaggs. Acknowledgment: The People of Zermatt, their Guides and the Guides of Chamonix.

PETER TCHAIKOVSKY STORY, THE
Directed by: Charles Barton. Produced by: Clyde Geronimi. Teleplay by: Otto Englander, Joe Rinaldi. Director of Photography: Walter H. Castle, A.S.C. Art Director: Marvin Aubrey Davis. Film Editors: George Gale, A.C.E., Donald Halliday. Music: George Bruns. Song *Once upon a Dream:* Sammy Fain, Jack Lawrence. Sound: Robert O. Cook. Special Processes: Eustace Lycett. Set Decoration: Emile Kuri, Hal Gausman. Costumer: Chuck Keehne. Make-up: Pat McNalley. Assistant Director: Vincent McEveety. Production Supervision: Harry Tytle.

PIGEON THAT WORKED A MIRACLE, THE
For Perkins Films, Inc. Directed by: Walter Perkins. Narrated by: George Fenneman. Photography: Walter Perkins, Wolf Lauter, Ray Jewell. Production Co-ordinator: William Redlin. Producer: Winston Hibler. Teleplay by: Otto Englander. Based on the book *Pigeon Fly Home* by: Thomas Liggett. Film Editor: Robert Stafford. Music: Paul Smith. Sound: Robert O. Cook. Production Supervisor: Harry Tytle. Acknowledgment: The Santa Barbara—Ventura Racing Pigeon Combine, A.U.

PLAUSIBLE IMPOSSIBLE, THE
Directed by: Animation: Wilfred Jackson. Live Action: William Beaudine. Story by: Dick Huemer. Music for Television by: Oliver Wallace. Art Director: Marvin Aubrey Davis. Production Supervision: Harry Tytle. Animation: Volus Jones, Vladimir Tytla, Ward Kimball, Jack Parr, Jack Campbell, Dan MacManus. Layout and Styling: Kay Nielsen, Al Dempster, Yale Gracey, Tom Codrick, Terrell Stapp. Backgrounds: Fil Mottola, Claude Coats. Set Decorator: Emile Kuri. Photography: Walter H. Castle, A.S.C. Film Editor: Samuel Horta. Special Processes: Ub Iwerks, A.S.C. Sound: Robert O. Cook. Assistant Director: Vincent McEveety.

PLUTO AND HIS FRIENDS
Food for Feudin' and *The Simple Things* Music by: Paul Smith.

PLUTO'S DAY
Directed by: Wolfgang Reitherman. Sequence Director: C. August Nichols. Animation: Eric Cleworth, Amby Paliwoda, Al Stetter, Marvin Woodward, Phil Duncan, Fred Moore. Story: Jack Kinney, Milt Schaffer, Bill Berg. Music: Franklyn Marks, Paul Smith. Lyrics: Gil George. Layout: Dale Barnhart, Karl Karpé, Lance Nolley. Backgrounds: Richard H. Thomas, Merle Cox, Ed Starr. Film Editor: Roy M. Brewer, Jr. Special Processes: Ub Iwerks, A.S.C. Sound: Robert O. Cook. Production Supervision: Harry Tytle.

POLLY
Choreography by: Debbie Allen. Original Score by: Joel McNeely. Edited by: Jim McElroy. Art Director: Peter Clemens. Director of Photography: Isidore Mankofsky, A.S.C. Produced by: Frank Fischer. Teleplay by: William Blinn. Based on the Screenplay by: David Swift. From the Novel *Pollyanna* by: Eleanor H. Porter. Directed by: Debbie Allen. Executive Producer: William Blinn. Associate Producer: James Pulliam. Unit Production Manager: Nick Smirnoff. First Assistant Director: Leslie Jackson Houston. Second Assistant Director: Rodney Allen Hooks. Casting by: Peg Halligan, C.S.A. Costumes Designed by: Tom Bronson. Set Decorator: Ethel Robbins Richards. Property Master: Lavar Emert. Key Costumers: Dallas Dornan, Nanrose Buchman. Make-up: Jack Wilson. Hair Stylist: Gloria Montemayor. Location Manager: Marta Ball. Script Supervisor: Hope Williams. Production Coordinator: Lark Bernini. Production Sound Mixer: Bruce Bisenz, C.A.S. Sound Editing by: Stephen J. Cannell Productions. Music Editing by: Chris Ledesma. Songs Arranged and Conducted by: Harold Wheeler. Supervising Music Consultant: Maureen Crowe. Assistant Choreographer: Eartha Robinson. Songs: *Stand Up* Words and Music by: Debbie Allen, Norman Nixon. *Shine a Light* Words and Music by: Jim Cox. *By Your Side* Words and Music by: Alan Menken, Jack Feldman. *Honey Ain't Got Nothin' on You, Something More* Words and Music by: Steve Nelson, Thom Sharp. *Rainbow Maker* Words and Music by: Michael Ruff. *Sweet Little Angel Eyes* Words and Music by: Michael Silversher, Patty Silversher. Songs and Score Recorded by: Gary Lux. Echo Cove Productions in association with Walt Disney Television.

POSTPONED WEDDING, THE
Directed by: James Neilson. Teleplay by: Bob Wehling, Roy Edward Disney. Based on the *Zorro* stories by: Johnston McCulley. Produced by: Bill Anderson. Associate Producer: Ron Miller. Director of Photography: Walter H. Castle, A.S.C. Art Director: Marvin Aubrey Davis. Film Editor: Robert Stafford. Music: Buddy Baker. Songs: Richard M. Sherman, Robert B. Sherman. Set Decoration: Emile Kuri. Costumer: Chuck Keehne. Make-up: Pat McNalley. Hair Stylist: Ruth Sandifer. Fencing Master: Fred Cavens. Unit Manager: Roy Wade. Assistant Director: Joseph L. McEveety.

PRAIRIE (AND) SEAL ISLAND
Directed by: James Algar, Richard Bare. Written by: Winston Hibler, Ted Sears, James Algar. Music: Oliver Wallace, Paul Smith. Special Orchestration: Edward Plumb. Photography: *Seal Island:* Alfred Milotte. Television: Wilfrid Cline, A.S.C. Additional Wildlife Photographers: Tom McHugh, James Simon, Dick Borden, Cleveland Grant, N. Paul Kenworthy, Jr., Lloyd Beebe, Murl Duesing, Herb Crisler. Editors: Anthony Gerard, Robert Belcher. Special Processes: Ub Iwerks. Sound Director: C.O. Slyfield.

PRE-OPENING REPORT FROM DISNEYLAND, THE (AND) TRIBUTE TO MICKEY MOUSE, A
Director—Cartoon Sequences: Wilfred Jackson. Written by: Milton M. Raison, Lee Chaney. Produced by: Bill Walsh. Production Supervisor: Al Teeter. Music: George Bruns. Photography: Travers Hill, Stuart Jewell. Film Editor: Lee Huntington. Special Processes: Ub Iwerks. Special Effects: Bob Ferguson. Sound: Robert O. Cook. Animation Effects: Joshua Meador, Art Riley.

PRESENT FOR DONALD, A
Credits for the 1954 broadcast: Adapted for Television by: Bill Walsh, Al Teeter. Director of Patzcuaro, Veracruz and Acapulco Sequences: Harold Young. Featuring: Aurora Miranda, Carmen Molina, Dora Luz, Donald Duck, Joe Carioca and Panchito. Music: George Bruns, Ed Plumb.

PRINCE AND THE PAUPER, THE
Screenplay by: Jack Whittingham. From the story by: Mark Twain. Directed by: Don Chaffey. Associate Producer: Hugh Attwooll. Director of Photography: Paul Beeson, B.S.C. Additional Photography: Ray Sturgess. Supervising Art Director: Michael Stringer. Art Director: Norman Dorme. Film Editor: Peter Boita. Set Decoration: Vernon Dixon. Costume Design: Margaret Furse. Music Composed and Conducted by: Tristram Cary. Special Photographic Effects: Wally Veevers. Special Art Work: Joshua Meador. Production Manager: Teresa Bolland. Make-up: Harry Frampton. Hair Stylist: Barbara Ritchie. Continuity: Phyllis Crocker. Sound Editor: Les Wiggins. Sound Recordists: Norman Bolland, Red Law. Casting: Maude Spector. Assistant Director: Dennis Bertera. Filmed at Shepperton Studios, England.

PROGRESS REPORT, A (AND) NATURE'S HALF ACRE
Directed by: Television: Winston Hibler, Al Teeter. Nature's Half Acre: James Algar. Written by: Winston Hibler, Ted Sears, James Algar, Jack Speirs. Music: Television: George Bruns. Nature's Half Acre: Paul Smith. Photography: Stuart V. Jewell, Travers Hill, Murl Deusing, Tilden W. Roberts, Karl H. Maslowski, Arthur A. Allen, Alfred G. Millotte, Joseph Heidenkamp Jr., Tom and Arlene Hadley, Olin Pettingill Jr., William Norman Jupe, John Nash Ott, Jr. Biologist Consultant: Tilden W. Roberts. Animation Effects: Joshua Meador,

John Hench. Special Processes: Ub Iwerks. Editors: Robert Belcher, Norman Palmer. Sound Director: C.O. Slyfield.

PROMISED LAND, THE
Teleplay and Directed by: Lewis R. Foster. Based on the book *Daniel Boone* by: John Bakeless. Produced by: Bill Anderson. Associate Producer: Louis Debney. Director of Photography: Edward Colman, A.S.C. Art Director: Marvin Aubrey Davis. Film Editor: Cotton Warburton, A.C.E. Music: Frank J. Worth. Song: David Victor, George Bruns. Matte Artist: Jim Fetherolf. Sound: Robert O. Cook. Set Decoration: William L. Stevens. Costumer: Chuck Keehne. Make-up: Pat McNalley. Unit Manager: Roy Wade. Assistant Director: Joseph L. McEveety.

PROUD BIRD FROM SHANGHAI, THE
Teleplay by: William P. Canning. Based on the book *The War Lord* by: Virginia C. Holmgren. Narration by: Joe Ansen. Produced and Directed by: Harry Tytle. Narrator: Marvin Miller. Film Editor: Ernie Milano. Music: Franklyn Marks. Special Art Work: Mel Shaw. Sound: Herb Taylor. Production Manager: Erwin L. Verity. *For Cangary Limited* Field Producer: Fred R. Krug. Photography: Ivan A. Craig, Fred R. Krug. Pheasant and Animal Supervision: Dennis R. Grisco. Production Assistants: Michael D. Arnold, Ian MacDonald. Acknowledgment: Washington State Department of Game.

RACE FOR SURVIVAL
Executive Producer: Ron Miller. Produced by: James Algar. Teleplay by: Jack Couffer. Based on a story by: Marshall Thompson. Directed by: Jack Couffer. Narrator: Peter Graves. Editor: Steve Pfahler. Music: Buddy Baker. Sound: Herb Taylor. *For Grey Owl Pictures, Inc.* Photography: Jack Couffer, A.S.C. Production Assistants: S. van der Laan, Dick Thomsett. Lion Supervised by: Monty Cox. Dog Trained by: Hubert Wells. Acknowledgments: Kenya National Wildlife and Management Department, The Pokot Tribe.

RAG, A BONE, A BOX OF JUNK, A
Directed by: Bill Justice. Story and Styling by: Xavier Atencio, T. Hee. Animation: Eric Larson, Cliff Nordberg, Les Clark, Art Stevens, Julius Svendsen, Fred Hellmich. Layout and Background: Dale Barnhart, Ralph Hulett. Songs: Richard M. Sherman, Robert B. Sherman, Mel Leven. Music: George Bruns, Camarata, Buddy Baker. Vocal Talent: Paul Frees, Jeanne Gayle, Jerome Courtland, Gloria Wood, James Macdonald, Skip Farrell, Billy Storm. Technical Assistants: Jim Love, Ed Sekac. Sound: Robert O. Cook. Program Co-ordinator: Jack Bruner.

RANGE WAR AT TOMBSTONE
Directed by: Harry Keller. Written by: David P. Harmon. Produced by: James Pratt. Director of Photography: William Snyder, A.S.C. Art Director: Marvin Aubrey Davis. Film Editor: Robert Stafford. Music: William Lava. Song: David Harmon, Buddy Baker. Sound: Robert O. Cook. Set Decoration: Emile Kuri, Hal Gausman. Costumer: Chuck Keehne. Make-up: Pat McNalley. Hair Stylist: Ruth Sandifer. Assistant Director: Arthur J. Vitarelli.

RANGER OF BROWNSTONE, THE
Directed by: Hamilton S. Luske. Sequence Directors: Jack Hannah, C. August Nichols. Story: Ted Berman, Dave Detiege, Al Bertino. Production Associate: McLaren Stewart. Animation: Art Stevens, Julius Svendsen, Bob McCrea, Bill Justice, Bob Carlson, Al Coe, John Sibley, Volus Jones. Layout: Joe Hale, Yale Gracey. Background: Jimi Trout, Ray Huffine. Music: Franklyn Marks, Oliver Wallace. Songs: Mel Leven. *World of Color* Theme Song: Richard M. Sherman, Robert B. Sherman. Film Editor: Edward R. Baker. With the talents of: Bill Thompson (Ranger's voice). Sound: Robert O. Cook. Program Co-ordinator: Jack Bruner.

RANGER'S GUIDE TO NATURE, A
Directed by: Hamilton S. Luske. Story: Ted Berman. Art Styling: McLaren Stewart. Animation: Charlie Downs, Bob McCrea, Cliff Nordberg. Layout: Joe Hale. Background: Elmer Plummer, Jimi Trout. Music: Franklyn Marks, Paul Smith. Songs: Mel Leven. *World of Color* Theme: Richard M. Sher-

man, Robert B. Sherman. Wildlife Photography: Stuart V. Jewell, Robert H. Crandall, Lloyd Beebe, Karl H. Maslowski, Murl Deusing. Special Effects: Eustace Lycett. Film Editor: Edward R. Baker. With the talents of: Bill Thompson (Ranger's voice). Sound: Robert O. Cook. Program Co-ordinator: Jack Bruner.

RAPIDS AHEAD (AND) BEAR COUNTRY
Directed by: William Beaudine. Teleplay by: James Algar. Director of Photography: Gordon Avil, A.S.C. Art Directors: Carroll Clark, Hilyard Brown. Film Editors: Norman Palmer, A.C.E., Cotton Warburton, A.C.E. Sound: Robert O. Cook. Set Decoration: Emile Kuri. Costumer: Chuck Keehne. Make-up: Pat McNalley. Assistant Director: Russ Haverick.

REDCOAT STRATEGY
Directed by: Louis King. Teleplay by: Lewis R. Foster. Based on the book by: Dr. Robert D. Bass. Produced by: James Pratt. Director of Photography: Floyd Crosby, A.S.C. Art Director: Marvin Aubrey Davis. Film Editor: Cotton Warburton, A.C.E. Music: Frank J. Worth. Song: Lew Foster, Buddy Baker. Sound: Robert O. Cook. Set Decoration: Emile Kuri, Hal Gausman. Costumer: Chuck Keehne. Make-up: Pat McNalley. Hair Stylist: Ruth Sandifer. Unit Manager: Roy Wade. Assistant Director: Ray Gosnell, Jr.

RETURN OF THE BIG CAT
Director of Photography: Frank Phillips, A.S.C. Produced by: Ron Miller, James Algar. Television Story and Teleplay by: Herman Groves. Based on the book *The Year of the Big Cat* by: Lew Dietz. Directed by: Tom Leetch. Associate Producer: Christopher Hibler. Art Directors: John B. Mansbridge, Walter Tyler. Film Editor: Ray de Leuw, A.C.E. Set Decorator: Hal Gausman. Matte Artist: Alan Maley. Second Unit Director: Christopher Hibler. Music: Buddy Baker. Sound: Herb Taylor. Costumes: Chuck Keehne. Make-up: Robert J. Schiffer. Hair Stylist: La Rue Matheron. Assistant Director: Irby Smith. Second Assistant Director: Dorothy Kieffer. Animal Supervision: Henry Cowl, Ron Oxley. Acknowledgment: United States Forest Service, Inyo National Forest.

RETURN OF THE SHAGGY DOG, THE
Music by: David Bell. Editors: Michael F. Anderson, A.C.E., Dennis C. Duckwall, Jack Harnish. Art Director: Ian Thomas. Director of Photography: Fred J. Koenekamp, A.S.C. Executive Producer: Michael S. McLean. Produced by: Harvey Marks. Written by: Diane Wilk, Paul Haggis. Directed by: Stuart Gillard. Associate Producer/Unit Production Manager: Justis Greene. First Assistant Director: Patrice Leung. Second Assistant Director: Sandra Mayo. Costume Designer: Tom Bronson. Casting by: Liberman-Hirschfeld Casting, Irene Cagen. Vancouver Casting: Lynne Carrow, Sid Kozak. Set Decorator: Linda Vipond. Property Master: Debbie Erhardt. Costume Supervisor: Christopher Ryan. Key Costumers: Wendy Foster, Danise Lee. Make-up: Jayne Dancose. Hair Stylist: Donna Bis. Animals Trained by: Jungle Exotics. Location Manager: Colleen Nystedt. Script Supervisor: Christine Wilson. Production Coordinator: Catherine Howard. Second Unit Director: Fred Waugh. Production Sound Mixer: Ralph Parker. Sound Editing by: Stephen J. Cannell Productions, Dick Wahrman. Music Editing by: Segue Music Inc./Kathy Durning. Special Make-up Effects by: Greg Cannom. Assistants to Greg Cannom: Earl Ellis, Larry Odien, Linda Notaro, Josephine Turner, John Vulich.

RICHEST CAT IN THE WORLD, THE
Music by: Peter Bernstein. Editor: Stanford C. Allen. Art Director: James Shanahan. Director of Photography: George Koblasa. Supervising Producer: John Garbett. Produced by: Andy Rose, Alexander Gorby. Executive Producer: Les Alexander. Teleplay by: Alfa-Betty Olsen, Marshall Efron. Story by: Les Alexander, Steve Ditlea. Directed by: Greg Beeman. Unit Production Manager/Associate Producer: Gordon Wolf. First Assistant Director: Mike Kusley. Second Assistant Director: Emmitt-Leon O'Neill. Casting by: Joyce Robinson, C.S.A., Penny Ellers, C.S.A. Costume Designer: William Ware Theiss. Set Decorator: Carl Biddiscombe. Property Master: Anthony C. Thorpe. Key Costumers: Sandra Berke Jordan, Gene Deardorff. Make-up: Michael E. Blake. Hair Stylist: Bar-

bara Lampson. Location Manager: Ryan Rosenberg. Script Supervisor: Alleen N. Nollmann. Production Coordinator: Vera Martin. Owner and Trainer of Palmer: Ray Berwick. Animals Supplied by: Ray Berwick Inc. Animal Trainers: Steve Berens, Bryan Renfro. Production Sound Mixer: Bill Teague. Sound Editing by: Echo Film Services/Greg Schorer. Music Editing by: Segue Music/Kathy Durning. Les Alexander Productions.

RIDE A NORTHBOUND HORSE
Produced by: Ron Miller. Co-produced by: Tom Leetch. Teleplay by: Herman Groves. Based on the book by: Richard Wormser. Directed by: Robert Totten. Director of Photography: Robert Hoffman. Art Directors: John B. Mansbridge, LeRoy G. Deane. Film Editor: Marsh Hendry, Cotton Warburton, A.C.E. Set Decorators: Emile Kuri, Hal Gausman. Costumer: Chuck Keehne. Make-up: Otis Malcolm. Music: George Bruns. *World of Color* Theme Song: Richard M. Sherman, Robert B. Sherman. Assistant Director: Paul L. Cameron. Sound: Robert O. Cook. Program Co-ordinator: Jack Bruner.

RINGO, THE REFUGEE RACCOON
Associate Producer: Ken Peterson. Written by: Barry Clark. Produced and Directed by: Roy Edward Disney. Narrator: Rex Allen. Film Editor: Toby Brown. Music: Robert F. Brunner. Sound: Herb Taylor. Production Manager: Erwin L. Verity. *For RHL International Films* Field Producer: Richard H. Lyford. Photography: Richard H. Lyford. Production Assistant: Patricia O'Rourke Foutz. Production Staff: Mac A. Child, Gary Kenwood, Timothy Barger.

ROBBER STALLION, THE
Directed by: Harry Keller. Written by: Fred Freiberger. Produced by: James Pratt. Director of Photography: William Snyder, A.S.C. Art Director: Marvin Aubrey Davis. Film Editor: Robert Stafford. Music: Frank J. Worth. Sound: Robert O. Cook. Set Decoration: Emile Kuri, Hal Gausman. Costumer: Chuck Keehne. Make-up: Pat McNalley. Hair Stylist: Ruth Sandifer. Assistant Director: Arthur J. Vitarelli.

ROCK 'N' ROLL MOM
Original Score by: Lee Ritenour. Music Consultant: David Kershenbaum. Editor: Conrad M. Gonzalez. Art Director: Mark W. Mansbridge. Director of Photography: Isidore Mankofsky, A.S.C. Produced by: Stan Rogow. Written by: Gen Le Roy. Directed by: Michael Schultz. Unit Production Manager: Denny Salvaryn. First Assistant Director: Joan Van Horn. Second Assistant Director: Linda Montanti. Casting by: Joyce Robinson, C.S.A., Penny Ellers, C.S.A. Costume Designer: Tom Bronson. Set Decorator: Ethel Robins Richards. Property Master: Kent H. Johnson. Key Costumers: John Casey, Donna Roberts Orme. Make-up: Edwin Butterworth. Hair Stylist: Ramsey. Executive Consultant: Vince Gannon. Location Manager: Gary De Galla. Production Co-ordinator: Jessica Griffin. Music Coordinator: Sid James. Script Supervisor: Marcia (Mavis) Girard. Production Sound Mixer: David Ronne. Sound Editing by: Echo Film Service. Music Editing by: The Music Design Group. Choreographer: Otis Sallid. *Devil with a Blue Dress On* Words and Music by: Frederick Long, William Stevenson. Song Performed by: Peter Hix.

RUNAWAY ON THE ROGUE RIVER
Teleplay by: Larry Lansburgh, Jr., Brian Lansburgh. Original Story by: Larry Lansburgh. Produced and Directed by: Larry Lansburgh. Film Editor: Ray de Leuw, A.C.E. Photography: Edward P. Hughes. Production Supervisor: Charles B. Mulvehill. Music: Richard Shores. Song *Sunshine Day* by: Shane Tatum. Sung by: Michael Dees. Song *Bucky's Song* by: Larry Lansburgh. Sound Supervision: Herb Taylor. Animal Supervision: Bucky Steele, Jr.

RUN, LIGHT BUCK, RUN
Co-producer: James Algar. Narration Written by: James Algar, Robert F. Metzler. Adaptation by: Dwight Hauser. Based on the book by: B. F. Beebe. Narrator: Roy Barcroft. Music: Buddy Baker. *World of Color* Theme: Richard M. Sherman, Robert B. Sherman. Film Editor: Gregg McLaughlin. Production Manager: Erwin L. Verity. Sound: Robert O. Cook. Program Co-ordinator: Jack Bruner. *For Grey Owl Productions, Inc.* Field Producer: Jack Couffer. Photographers: Jack Couffer, Gary Kenwood. Wildlife Supervisors: Al Niemela, Mike Guinn. Acknowledgments: Arizona Game and Fish Department, Montana Department of Fish and Game.

RUSTY AND THE FALCON
For Paul Kenworthy Productions Producer-Director: N. Paul Kenworthy, Jr. Production Manager: John W. Young. Photographer: Maitland Stewart. Film Editor: Ford Beebe. Music: William Lava. Song *A Boy Is a Curious Thing:* William Lava, Gil George, Winston Hibler. Falconry by: Morlan Nelson. *For Walt Disney Productions* Producer: Winston Hibler. Teleplay by: Ralph Wright, Winston Hibler. Based on the book *The White Falcon* by: Charlton Ogburn. Sound: Robert O. Cook. Production Supervisor: Harry Tytle.

SALTY, THE HIJACKED HARBOR SEAL
Written by: Rod Peterson, Orma Wallengren. Narration by: Irve Tunick, Rod Peterson. Produced and Directed by: Harry Tytle. Narrated by: Olan Soulé. Film Editor: Ernie Milano. Music: Robert F. Brunner. Production Co-ordinator: Robert F. Metzler. Production Manager: Erwin L. Verity. Sound: Herb Taylor. Program Co-ordinator: Jack Bruner. *For Cangary Limited and Charles Draper Productions, Inc.* Field Producer: Milas C. Hinshaw. Photographers: Russ Alsobrook, W. G. "Bumpy" Bell. Production Assistants: James T. Flocker, Brian Burton. Additional Wildlife Photographers: Charles Draper, Lloyd G. Kenwood. Acknowledgments: Y.M.C.A., Alameda County, California, The California Fish and Game Department.

SALUTE TO ALASKA, A
Co-producer: Harry Tytle. Narration Written by: Norman Wright. Directed by: Hamilton S. Luske. Animation Director: Ward Kimball. Cartoon Story: Bill Berg. Animation: Art Stevens, Charlie Downs, Jack Boyd. Layout: Joe Hale. Background: Elmer Plummer. Production Associate: McLaren Stewart. Production Manager: Erwin L. Verity. Film Editors: Anthony Gerard, Edward R. Baker. Music: Robert F. Brunner, George Bruns. *World of Color* Theme: Richard M. Sherman, Robert B. Sherman. With the Talents of: Paul Frees, George Walsh. Sound: Robert O. Cook. Program Co-ordinator: Jack Bruner.

SALUTE TO FATHER, A
Directed by: Wolfgang Reitherman. Sequence Director: Eric Cleworth. Story: Otto Englander, Joe Rinaldi. Animation: John Sibley. Effects Animation: Dan MacManus. Layout: Dale Barnhart. Backgrounds: Al Dempster. Music: Buddy Baker. Film Editor: Jim Love. Sound: Robert O. Cook.

SAMMY, THE WAY-OUT SEAL
Co-producer: Winston Hibler. Written and Directed by: Norman Tokar. Director of Photography: Gordon Avil, A.S.C. Art Directors: Carroll Clark, Marvin Aubrey Davis. Film Editor: Grant K. Smith, A.C.E. Set Decoration: Emile Kuri, Armor E. Goetten. Costumer: Chuck Keehne. Music: Oliver Wallace. Make-up: Pat McNalley. Hair Stylist: Ruth Sandifer. Sound: Robert O. Cook. Assistant Director: John D. Bloss. "Sammy" Trained by: Bennie Kirkbride. Program Co-ordinator: Jack Bruner. Acknowledgment: The Zoological Society of San Diego, California.

SANCHO, THE HOMING STEER
Produced by: Winston Hibler. Teleplay by: Homer McCoy. Television Story by: Fred Gipson, Rutherford Montgomery. Based on a story by: J. Frank Dobie. Narration Written by: Robert F. Metzler. Directed by: Tom McGowan. Narrator: Rex Allen. Production Coordinator: Robert F. Metzler. Film Editor: George Gale, A.C.E. Music: Franklyn Marks. Song *Tortillas:* Gil George, Winston Hibler, Jaime Mendoza-Nava. Song *Sancho:* Gil George, Winston Hibler, William Lava. Sound: Robert O. Cook. *For Tom McGowan Productions* Production Assistants: Ted Sizer, Thomas Boutross. Production Managers: Warren Brown, Ralph Butterfield. Art Styling: Robert Becker. Photographer: Robert Brooker.

SCARECROW OF ROMNEY MARSH, THE
Co-producer: Bill Anderson. Teleplay by: Robert Westerby. Based on *Christopher Syn* by: Russell Thorndike, William Buchanan. Directed by: James Neilson. Associate Producer: Hugh Attwooll. Director of Photography: Paul Beeson, B.S.C. Additional Photography: Ray Sturgess. Art Director: Michael Stringer. Film Editor: Peter Boita. Costumes: Anthony Mendleson. Set Decorator: Peter James. Make-up: Harry Frampton. Hair Stylist: H. Montsash. Continuity: Pamela Mann. Casting: Maude Spector. Music Composed and Conducted by: Gerard Schurmann. *The Scarecrow Song:* Terry Gilkyson. Production Manager: Peter Manley. Assistant Director: John Peverall. Camera Operator: David Harcourt. Sound Director: Robert O. Cook. Sound Editor: Les Wiggins. Sound Recordists: C.C. Stevens, C.F. LeMessurier. Program Co-ordinator: Jack Bruner. Filmed at Pinewood Studios, England.

SEARCHING FOR NATURE'S MYSTERIES
Directed by: Winston Hibler. Written by: Dwight Hauser. Produced by: Ben Sharpsteen. Music: Oliver Wallace. Abridged Version of Maurice Ravel's *Bolero* Conducted by: Frederick Stark. Art Director: Marvin Aubrey Davis. Production Supervision: Harry Tytle, Erwin L. Verity. Set Decorator: Emile Kuri. Photographed by: Stuart V. Jewell, John Nash Ott Jr., Murl Deusing, Robert H. Crandall, Charles P. Boyle, A.S.C. Film Editor: Edward Sampson. Special Processes: Ub Iwerks, A.S.C. Sound: Robert O. Cook. Assistant Director: Horace Hough.

SECRET OF BOYNE CASTLE, THE
Produced by: Ron Miller. Television Story and Teleplay by: Herman Groves. Based on a novel by: Lockhart Amerman. Directed by: Robert Butler. Associate Producer: Hugh Attwooll. Director of Photography: Michael Reed. Additional Photography: Ray Sturgess. Art Director: Albert Witherick. Film Editor: Peter Boita. Music: Buddy Baker. Orchestration: Walter Sheets. *World of Color* Theme Song: Richard M. Sherman, Robert B. Sherman. Costume Design: Beatrice Dawson. Make-up: Harry Frampton. Hair Stylist: Eileen Warwick. Sound Recordists: David Price, Ken Barker. Assistant Director: Barrie Melrose. Production Manager: Peter Crowhurst. Location Manager: Robin Douet. Camera Operator: Alec Mills. Continuity: Tilly Day. Casting: Maude Spector. Sound Editor: Christopher Lancaster. Program Co-ordinator: Jack Bruner. Filmed in Ireland and at Pinewood Studios, London, England.

SECRET OF LOST VALLEY, THE
Executive Producer: Ron Miller. Produced by: Christopher Hibler. Director of Photography: Leonard J. South, A.S.C. Teleplay by: Paul A. Golding. Story by: David Irving, Paul A. Golding. Directed by: Vic Morrow. Art Directors: John B. Mansbridge, Jack T. Collins. Editor: Ray de Leuw, A.C.E. Music: Jerrold Immel. Unit Production Manager: Christopher Hibler. Assistant Director: Randy Carter. Second Assistant Director: Christopher D. Miller. Production Manager: John Bloss. Animal Trainer: George Toth. Set Decorator: Norman Rockett. Sound: Herb Taylor. Costumes: Chuck Keehne. Make-up: Robert J. Schiffer, C.M.A.A. Hair Stylist: Eddie M. Barron. Acknowledgment: Deschutes National Forest. *Disney's Wonderful World* Theme: John Debney, John Klawitter.

SECRET OF OLD GLORY MINE, THE
Produced by: Harry Tytle. Teleplay by: William P. Canning. Story by: Winston Hibler. Narration Written by: Joe Ansen. Directed by: Fred R. Krug. Narrator: Rex Allen. Film Editor: Ernie Milano, A.C.E. Music: Franklyn Marks. Song *Winnin' the West* by: Jay Livingston, Ray Evans. Sound: Herb Taylor. Production Supervisor: Erwin L. Verity. Production Co-ordinator: Robert F. Metzler. *For Coronado Productions, Inc.* Field Producer: Fred R. Krug. Photography: Ivan A. Craig, Fred R. Krug. Production Assistant: Ron Foreman. Photographed at Corona de Tucson, Arizona.

SECRET OF THE POND, THE
Produced by: James Algar. Director of Photography: Leonard J. South, A.S.C. Teleplay by: Calvin Clements, Jr. Based on *The Pond* by: Robert Murphy. Directed by: Robert Day. Art Directors: John B. Mansbridge, Jack T. Collis. Film Editor: Gordon D. Brenner. Set Decorator: Hal Gausman. Associate Producer: Christopher Hibler. Music: Buddy Baker. Song *There's a Place for You* Composed and Performed by: Stephen B. Gillette. Sound Supervisor: Herb Taylor. Unit Production Manager: Austen Jewell. First Assistant Director: Irby Smith. Second Assistant Director: Scott Adam. Costumes: Chuck Keehne. Make-up: Robert J. Schiffer. Technical Supervisor: George Toth.

SECRETS OF THE PIRATE'S INN
Produced by: Ron Miller. Co-producer: Tom Leetch. Television Story and Teleplay by: Herman Groves. Based on a book by: Wylly Folk St. John. Directed by: Gary Nelson. Director of Photography: Frank Phillips, A.S.C. Art Directors: John B. Mansbridge, Russell Menzer. Film Editor: Cotton Warburton, A.C.E. Set Decorators: Emile Kuri, Hal Gausman. Music: Robert F. Brunner. Sound: Robert O. Cook. Costumer: Chuck Keehne. Make-up: Robert J. Schiffer. Assistant Director: Christopher Hibler. Program Co-ordinator: Jack Bruner.

SEEMS THERE WAS THIS MOOSE
Produced by: Roy Edward Disney. Co-produced by: Jack Speirs. Written by: Jack Speirs. Directed by: Roy Edward Disney. Narrator: Rex Allen. Film Editor: Gregg McLaughlin, A.C.E. Music: Buddy Baker, Franklyn Marks. Sound: Herb Taylor. Production Manager: Erwin L. Verity. Wildlife Photography: Lloyd Beebe. *For RHL International Films* Field Producer: Richard H. Lyford. Photography: Richard H. Lyford. Production Assistant: Patricia O'Rourke Foutz. Production Staff: Mac A. Child, Bill Hochstrasser, Timothy Barger, Wally Thomas.

SHADOW OF FEAR
Executive Producer: Ron Miller. Produced by: Jerome Courtland. Director of Photography: Tak Fujimoto. Teleplay by: Gerry Day. Based on the book *The Healer* by: Daniel P. Mannix. Directed by: Noel Nosseck. Art Directors: John B. Mansbridge, William J. Creber. Editor: Bob Bring, A.C.E. Second Unit Director: Michael Dmytryk. Unit Production Manager: Christopher Seit. Assistant Director: Nick Smirnoff. Second Assistant Director: Bob Mayberry. Production Manager: John Bloss. Music: George Duning. Special Effects: Eustace Lycett, Art Cruickshank, A.S.C., Danny Lee. Animals Trained by: George Toth. Set Decorator: Norman Rockett. Sound: Herb Taylor. Costumes: Chuck Keehne. Make-up: Bob Schiffer, C.M.A.A. Hair Stylist: Eddie Barron.

SHOKEE, THE EVERGLADES PANTHER
Co-produced by: Ken Peterson. Written by: Barry Clark. Produced and Directed by: Roy Edward Disney. Narrator: Michael Ansara. Film Editor: Toby Brown. Music: Robert F. Brunner. Sound: Herb Taylor. Production Manager: Erwin L. Verity. *For Coronado Productions, Inc.* Field Producer: Peter B. Good. Photography: Wolfgang Obst. Acknowledgments: Game and Fish Commission, Tallahassee, Florida, Lykes Bros., Inc., Florida.

SHOWDOWN AT SANDOVAL
Directed by: Harry Keller. Written by: Frank D. Gilroy, Maurice Tombragel. Produced by: James Pratt. Director of Photography: William Snyder, A.S.C. Art Director: Marvin Aubrey Davis. Film Editor: Stanley Johnson, A.C.E. Music: Joseph S. Dubin. Song: Stan Jones. Sound: Robert O. Cook. Set Decorators: Emile Kuri, Bertram Granger. Costumer: Chuck Keehne. Make-up: Pat McNalley. Assistant Director: Austen Jewell.

SHOWDOWN WITH THE SUNDOWN KID
Co-producer: Ron Miller. Written by: Maurice Tombragel. Based on the book *Gallegher* by: Richard Harding Davis. Directed by: Joseph Sargent. Assistant to the Producer: Jerome Courtland. Director of Photography: William Snyder, A.S.C. Art Directors: Carroll Clark, William L. Campbell. Film Editor: Marsh Hendry. Set Decorators: Emile Kuri, Bill Calvert. Music: Willis Schaefer. *World of Color* Theme: Richard M. Sherman, Robert B. Sherman. Costumer: Chuck Keehne.

Make-up: Gordon Hubbard. Hair Stylist: Vivienne Zavitz. Sound: Robert O. Cook. Assistant Director: Paul L. Cameron. Program Co-ordinator: Jack Bruner.

SILVER FOX AND SAM DAVENPORT, THE

Produced and Narrated by: Winston Hibler. Teleplay by: Albert Aley. Based on a book by: Ernest Thompson Seton. Narration Written by: Roy Edward Disney. Production Coordinators: Robert F. Metzler, Roy Edward Disney. Film Editor: George Gale, A.C.E. Music: Buddy Baker. Sound: Robert O. Cook. Program Coordinator: Jack Bruner. *For Hank Schloss Productions* Field Producer: Hank Schloss. Production Assistant: Jon Hedberg. Photographer: Jack R. Ferrucci. Production Staff: Lloyd G. Kenwood, Carlajean Stovall, John Wessell, Joe Murray.

SKY HIGH #1

Music Composed by: Peter Bernstein. Director of Photography: John Bartley. Production Designer: Michael Nemirsky. Editor: Michael Berman, A.C.E. Co-Producer: Justis Greene. Produced by: Mark H. Ovitz. Part 1 Written by: Rueben Gordon, Steven Schoenberg. Part 2 Written by: Glen Merzer. Part 1 Directed by: James Whitmore, Jr. Part 2 Directed by: James Fargo. Executive Producer: Patrick Hasburgh. Associate Producer: Jodi Rothe. First Assistant Director: Patrice Leung. Second Assistants Directors: Sandra Mayo, Bob Olden. Casting by: Robert W. Harbin, C.S.A., Beth Hymson, C.S.A. Costume Designer: Christina McQuarrie. Set Decorators: Sandy Arthur, Roger Dole. Property Master: Dan Sissons. Make-up Artist: Connie Parker. Hair Stylist: Malcolm Marsden. Location Manager: Janice Frome. Script Supervisors: Kelly Moon, Theresa Eubanks. Post Production Supervisor: Erik Hasburgh. Transportation Coordinator: Jake Callihoo. Production Coordinator: Carol Schafer. Production Accountant: Kathryn Drew. Camera Operator: Paul Birkett. Key Gaffer: Duncan MacGregor. Key Grips: Dave Gordon, Glenn Forrieter. Aerial Unit Director/Cameraman: Peter McLennan. Aerial Unit Coordinator: Steve Wright. Waco Pilot: Rod Ellis. Additional Editing by: Joe Fuller, Jon Koslowsky, A.C.E. Assistant Editor: Rob Robinson. Music Editing by: Patricia Carlin. Sound Mixer: David Lee. A Patrick Hasburgh Production.

SKY HIGH #2

Produced by: Mark H. Ovitz. Co-Producer: Justis Greene. Written by: Rueben Gordon, Steven Schoenberg. Directed by: James Whitmore, Jr. Executive Producer: Patrick Hasburgh. Associate Producer: Jodi Rothe. Music Composed by: Peter Bernstein. Casting by: Robert W. Harbin, C.S.A., Beth Hymson, C.S.A. Director of Photography: John Bartley. Production Designer: Michael Nemirsky. Editor: Michael Berman, A.C.E. First Assistant Director: Patrice Leung. Second Assistant Director: Sandra Mayo. Assistant Editor: Joe Fuller. Costume Designer: Christina McQuarrie. Set Decorator: Sandy Arthur. Property Master: Dan Sissons. Make-up Artist: Connie Parker. Hair Stylist: Malcolm Marsden. Location Manager: Janice Frome. Script Supervisor: Kelly Moon. Post Production Supervisor: Erik Hasburgh. Transportation Coordinator: Jake Callihoo. Production Coordinator: Carol Schafer. Production Accountant: Kathryn Drew. Camera Operator: Paul Birkett. Key Gaffer: Duncan MacGregor. Key Grip: Dave Gordon. Aerial Unit Director/Cameraman: Peter McLennan. Aerial Unit Coordinator: Steve Wright. Waco Pilot: Rod Ellis. Additional Editing by: Joe Fuller, Jon Koslowsky. Assistant Editor: Rob Robinson. Music Editing by: Patricia Carlin. Sound Mixer: David Lee. A Patrick Hasburgh Production.

SKY'S THE LIMIT, THE

Produced by: Ron Miller. Co-produced by: Tom Leetch. Director of Photography: Andrew Jackson, A.S.C. Teleplay by: Harry Spalding. Based on a story by: Larry Linville. Directed by: Tom Leetch. Art Directors: John B. Mansbridge, Al Roelofs. Film Editor: Bob Bring, A.C.E. Set Decorator: Hal Gausman. Special Effects: Danny Lee. Music: George Duning. Sound: Herb Taylor. Costumes: Chuck Keehne. Make-up: Robert J. Schiffer. First Assistant Director: Robert M. Webb. Second Assistant Director: William R. Poole. Assistant to the Producer: Kevin Corcoran.

SKY TRAP, THE

Acknowledgment: United States Customs Service. Second Unit Director: James W. Gavin. Second Unit Photography: Frank Holgate. Second Unit Assistant Director: Randy Carter. Set Decorator: Norman Rockett. Technical Advisor: Bill Aronson. Sound Supervisor: Herb Taylor. Sound Mixer: Martin R. Bolger. Costumes: Chuck Keehne. Make-up: Robert J. Schiffer, C.M.A.A. Hair Stylist: Dorothie Long. Sound Editor: Ben Hendricks. Music Editor: Jack Wadsworth. Music by: Will Schaefer. Production Manager: John Bloss. Assistant Director: Jon Triesault. Second Assistant Director: Christopher D. Miller. Editor: Bob Bring, A.C.E. Art Directors: John B. Mansbridge, David Marshall. Director of Photography: Rexford Metz. Executive Producer: Ron Miller. Teleplay by: Jim Lawrence. Based on a book by: D. S. Halacy, Jr. Produced and Directed by: Jerome Courtland.

SLAUGHTER TRAIL, THE

Directed by: Harry Keller. Written by: David P. Harmon. Produced by: James Pratt. Director of Photography: William Snyder, A.S.C. Art Director: Marvin Aubrey Davis. Film Editor: Stanley Johnson, A.C.E. Music: Frank Worth. Sound: Robert O. Cook. Set Decorators: Emile Kuri, Bertram Granger. Costumer: Chuck Keehne. Make-up: Pat McNalley. Assistant Director: Robert G. Shannon.

SMOKE

Produced by: Ron Miller. Co-producer: Tom Leetch. Teleplay by: John Furia, Jr. Based on the book by: William Corbin. Directed by: Vincent McEveety. Director of Photography: William Snyder, A.S.C. Art Directors: John B. Mansbridge, Russell Menzer. Film Editor: Robert Stafford, A.C.E. Set Decorators: Emile Kuri, Hal Gausman. Second Unit Director: Arthur J. Vitarelli. Music: Robert F. Brunner. Sound: Robert O. Cook. Costumer: Chuck Keehne. Make-up: Robert J. Schiffer. Hair Stylist: La Rue Matheron. Assistant Director: Robert M. Webb. Program Coordinator: Jack Bruner.

SNOW BEAR

Produced by: Harry Tytle. Written by: Rod Peterson, Tom Seller. *For Cangary Limited* Directed by: Gunther Von Fritsch. Second Unit Supervision: Hank Schloss. Field Manager: William Redlin. Photographers: John Koester, Tibor Vagyoczky, Hank Schloss, John Bailey, Gordon Perry. Production Assistants: Jim Enochs, Edna MacLean, Pierre d'Hoste. Narrator: John McIntire. Film Editor: Ernie Milano. Music: George Bruns. Production Manager: Erwin L. Verity. Production Coordinator: Robert F. Metzler. Sound: Robert O. Cook. Program Coordinator: Jack Bruner. Acknowledgments: Klant's Zoo and Training School, Valkenburg, Netherlands, Alaska Department of Fish and Game.

SOLOMON, THE SEA TURTLE

Produced by: James Algar. Teleplay by: Sam Thomas. Based on the book *The Windward Road* by: Archie Carr. Narrator: Sebastian Cabot. Film Editor: Gordon Brenner. Music: Buddy Baker. Song *Solomon* by: Sam Thomas, Mel Leven. *World of Color* Theme Song: Richard M. Sherman, Robert B. Sherman. Production Manager: Erwin L. Verity. Sound: Robert O. Cook. Program Coordinator: Jack Bruner. *For Ken Nelson Productions* Photography: Ken Nelson, Robert Gondell. Production Assistant: Hal Schwartz. Jaguar and Baby Turtle Sequences filmed by Charles Draper Productions, Inc. Acknowledgments: United States Navy, The Government of Costa Rica.

SPLASH, TOO

Original Score by: Joel McNeely. Edited by: Dennis M. Hill, Bobby Wyman. Art Director: Raymond G. Storey. Director of Photography: Fred J. Koenekamp, A.S.C. Produced by: Mark H. Ovitz. Written by: Bruce Franklin Singer. Based on Characters Created by: Bruce Jay Friedman. Directed by: Greg Antonacci. Unit Production Manager: Max A. Stein. First Assistant Director: James M. Freitag. Second Assistant Directors: Barry K. Thomas, Melanie M. Grefé. Casting by: Cathy Henderson, C.S.A., Michael Cutler. Costume Designer: Tom Bronson. Set Decorator: Linda Spheeris. Property Master: Lavar Emert. Key Costumers: Terrence K. Smith, Karen Bellamy. Make-up: Pete Altobelli. Hair Stylist: Edie Panda.

Florida Casting by: Barbara DiPrima. Location Manager: Denis McCallion. Script Supervisor: Marcia (Mavis) Girard. Production Coordinator: Patty McManus. Underwater Photography by: Jordan Klein. Dolphin Propmaker: Donald Pennington. Production Sound Mixer: David Ronne. Sound Editing by: Stephen J. Cannell Productions. Music Editing by: Charles Martin Inouye. *We Got Love* Written and Produced by: Lenny Macaluso. *Ocean of Love* Words and Music by: Thomas & Pamela Morrison. Visual Effects by: Buena Vista Visual Effects Group. Acknowledgment: The Dolphin Research Center. Mark H. Ovitz Productions in association with Walt Disney Television.

Spy in the Sky
Co-producers: Bill Anderson, Ward Kimball. Teleplay by: Maurice Tombragel, William Bosché, Ward Kimball. Cartoon Story: James Dunn. Directed by: Harmon Jones, Ward Kimball. Associate Producer: Ron Miller. Directors of Photography: Walter H. Castle, A.S.C., Lucien Ballard, A.S.C. Art Directors: Carroll Clark, Marvin Aubrey Davis. Film Editors: Lloyd L. Richardson, A.C.E., Robert Stafford, A.C.E. Set Decoration: Emile Kuri. Special Effects: Eustace Lycett. Costumer: Chuck Keehne. Make-up: Pat McNalley. Music: George Bruns. Song: Richard M. Sherman, Robert B. Sherman. Sound: Robert O. Cook. Assistant Director: Robert G. Shannon. Animation: Charles Downs, Fred Hellmich, Julius Svendsen, Arthur Stevens. Layout: A. Kendall O'Connor. Paintings: J. Gordon Legg. Effects Animation: Jack Boyd. Technical Consultant: Dr. Irving P. Krick. Narrator: Paul Frees.

Square Peg in a Round Hole, A
Directed by: Hamilton S. Luske. Sequence Directors: Wolfgang Reitherman, Jack Hannah, Jack Kinney. Story: Otto Englander, Ted Berman, Dave Detiege, Al Bertino. Art Styling: McLaren Stewart. Animation: Bill Justice, Bob Carlson, Phil Duncan, Jack Boyd, Bob McCrea, Cliff Nordberg. Layout: Joe Hale, Yale Gracey. Backgrounds: Ervin Kaplan, Al Dempster. Music: George Bruns, Buddy Baker. With the talents of: Paul Frees. Film Editor: Tom Acosta. Sound: Robert O. Cook. Program Co-ordinator: Jack Bruner.

Storm Called Maria, A
For Ken Nelson Productions Directed by: Ken Nelson. Photographers: John F. Stanton, Les Thomsen. Associate Producer: James Algar. Teleplay: James Algar, Larry Clemmons. Based on the book *Storm* by: George R. Stewart. Narrator: Don Holt. Film Editor: Norman Palmer, A.C.E. Music: Joseph S. Dubin. Song *Storm:* Stan Jones. Sound: Robert O. Cook. Production Supervision: Harry Tytle. Acknowledgments: Pacific Telephone and Telegraph Company, Pacific Gas and Electric Company, California Division of Highways, California Highway Patrol, Southern Pacific Company, United States Weather Bureau, United States Coast Guard.

Story of Dogs, A
Directed by: Clyde Geronimi, C. August Nichols, Robert Florey. Story: Clyde Geronimi, Tom Adair, Erdman Penner. Music: George Bruns. Photography: Charles Boyle, A.S.C. Art Director: Field Gray. Editors: Lynn Harrison, A.C.E., George Nicholson. Special Process: Ub Iwerks. Sound: C.O. Slyfield. Animation for Television: George Nicholas, George Kreisl. Special Art Work: Joe Rinaldi, Don DaGradi, Ken Anderson, Tom Codrick.

Story of the Animated Drawing, The
Animation Directed by: Wilfred Jackson. Live Action Directed by: William Beaudine. Written by: Dick Huemer, McLaren Stewart. Music: Joseph S. Dubin. Production Supervision: Harry Tytle. Animation Art Work: McLaren Stewart, Jay J. Gould. Photography: Charles Royle, A.S.C. Film Editor: Everett Dodd. Assistant Director: Gordon McLean. Film Research: Robert Sunderland. Special Processes: Ub Iwerks. Sound: Robert O. Cook. Acknowledgment: The Academy of Motion Picture Arts and Sciences.

Story of the Silly Symphony, The
Directed by: Clyde Geronimi. Written by: Bill Peet. Music: Bill Lava. Production Supervision: Harry Tytle. Layout and

Background Artists: Tom Codrick, Basil Davidovich, Dick Anthony. Animators: Dan MacManus, Marc Davis. Photography: Charles Boyle, A.S.C. Film Editor: Donald Halliday. Special Processes: Ub Iwerks. Sound: Robert O. Cook.

Strange Monster of Strawberry Cove, The
Produced by: Ron Miller. Co-producer: Tom Leetch. Television Story and Teleplay by: Herman Groves. From the story by: Bertrand R. Brinley. Directed by: Jack Shea. Director of Photography: Frank Phillips, A.S.C. Art Directors: John B. Mansbridge, William J. Creber. Film Editor: Robert Stafford, A.C.E. Set Decorators: Emile Kuri, Frank R. McKelvy. Music: George Bruns. Assistant Director: Ted Schilz. Costumes: Chuck Keehne. Make-up: Robert J. Schiffer. Hair Stylist: La Rue Matheron. Sound: Robert O. Cook. Program Co-ordinator: Jack Bruner.

Stub, The Best Cow Dog in the West
Original Story: Larry Lansburgh. Teleplay by: Janet Lansburgh, William C. Anderson. Produced and Directed by: Larry Lansburgh. Narrator: Rex Allen. Photographed by: Edward P. Hughes. Film Editor: Norman R. Palmer, A.C.E. Music: William Lava, Richard Shores. Location Sound: James Camery. Assistant Director: Frank Baur. Production Associate: Katy Peake.

Student Exchange
Original Score by: Phil Marshall. Editors: Paul Dixon, John Woodcock, A.C.E. Art Director: Raymond G. Storey. Director of Photography: Fred J. Koenekamp, A.S.C. Produced by: Charles Milhaupt. Teleplay by: William Davies, William Osborne. Story by: Debra Frankel. Directed by: Mollie Miller. Production Manager/Associate Producer: Richard Luke Rothschild. First Assistant Director: Paul Deason. Second Assistant Director: Karen Gaviola. Casting by: Steven Jacobs. Costume Designer: Tom Bronson. Set Decorator: Sam Gross. Property Master: Steve Westlund. Key Costumers: Terrence K. Smith, Dorothy Baca Wasserman. Make-up: Pete Altobelli. Hair Stylist: Rita Bordonaro. Choreography by: Susan Scanlon. Dialect Coach: Paul René St. Peter. Location Manager: James "Tad" Tadevic. Production Coordinator: Nancy Rae Stone. Production Sound Mixer: Bruce Bisenz, C.A.S. Sound Editing by: Stephen J. Cannell Productions. Music Editing by: Segue Music Inc.

Sultan and the Rock Star
Executive Producer: Ron Miller. Produced by: Jerome Courtland. Director of Photography: Mike Sweeten. Teleplay by: Steve Hayes. From the novel *Sandy and the Rock Star* by: Walt Morey. Directed by: Ed Abroms. Art Directors: John B. Mansbridge, Frank Swig. Editor: Dennis A. Orcutt. Music: Artie Butler. Production Manager: John Bloss. Assistant Director: Jan R. Lloyd. Second Assistant Director: Joseph Paul Moore. Technical Advisor: Ralph Helfer, Gentle Jungle. Set Decorator: R. Chris Westlund, Roger M. Shook. Sound: Herb Taylor. Costumes: Jack Sandeen. Make-up: Robert J. Schiffer, C.M.A.A. Song *Deeper in Love:* George Thomas Charouhas, Steven B. Furman. *Disney's Wonderful World* Theme: John Debney, John Klawitter.

Sunday Drive
Original Score by: Brad Fiedel. Editor: Duane Hartzell, A.C.E. Art Director: James Shanahan. Director of Photography: King Baggot. Executive Producers: Joe Wizan, Todd Black. Produced by: Joseph Stern. Written by: Larry Brand. Directed by: Mark Cullingham. Unit Production Manager: Steve Barnett. First Assistant Director: Paul Deason. Second Assistant Director: Larry Lipton. Casting by: Peg Halligan. Costume Designer: William Ware Theiss. Set Decorator: Ethel Robins Richards. Property Master: Lavar Emert. Key Costumers: Margo Baxley, Paul Siragusa. Make-up: Carol Schwartz. Hair Stylist: Gregg Mitchell. Assistant to Mr. Black and Mr. Wizan: Betty Buckley Gumm. Animal Supplier and Trainer: Birds and Animals Unlimited/Karen Dew. Location Manager: Binnie Ruben. Script Supervisor: Alleen N. Nollmann. Production Coordinator: Lorna Neal. Production Sound Mixer: Patrick Mitchell. Film Editor: Joe Ravetz. Sound Editing by: Stephen J. Cannell Productions, Larry Mann. Music Editing

by: Segue Music/Jamie E. Gelb. Re-Recorded at: Compact Sound Services. Wizan TV Enterprises, Inc.

SUPER DUCKTALES
Produced by: Walt Disney Television Animation. Producers: Bob Hathcock, Ken Koonce, David Wiemers. Director: James T. Walker. Written by: Ken Koonce, David Wiemers, Jymn Magon. Assistant Producer: Liza-Ann Warren. Art Director: Skip Morgan. Kay Layout Stylists: Joe Pearson, Derek Carter. Storyboard Design: Viki Anderson, Warren Greenwood, Paul Gruwell, Dale Schott, Dave Smith, Keith Tucker, Wendell Washer. Key Background Styling: Fred Warter. Color Key Styling: Marta Skwara. Overseas Animation Supervisors: Mike Reyna, Bruce Pedersen. Supervising Timing Director: Dave Brain. Timing Directors: Brad Case, Joan Case, Rick Leon, Mircea Mantta, Jamie Mitchell, Mitch Rochon, James T. Walker. Track Reading: Skip Craig. Production Assistants: Jeffrey Arthur, Stephanie Elliott, Scott Wolf. Script Coordinator: Marie Sager. Talent Coordinator: Olivia Miner. Production Archive Administrator: Krista Bunn. Art Coordinator: Karen Silva. Post Production Manager: Sara Duran. Post Production Coordinator: Barbara Beck. Managing Editor: Rich Harrison. Supervising Editor: Charlie King. Sound Effects Editor: Rick Hinson. Assistant Editors: David Lynch, Thomas Needell, Craig Paulsen. *DuckTales* Theme Composed by: Mark Mueller. Music Composed and Conducted by: Ron Jones. Animation Production by: Wang Film Productions Co., Ltd., Cuckoos' Nest Studio.

SUPERSTAR GOOFY
This episode was aired without production credits.

SURVIVAL IN NATURE
Directed by: Winston Hibler. Written by: Jack Speirs, Winston Hibler, Clinton Macaulay. Music: Joseph S. Dubin. Art Director: Marvin Aubrey Davis. Production Supervision: Harry Tytle. Photography: Charles Boyle, A.S.C., N. Paul Kenworthy, Jr., Robert H. Crandall, Jack C. Couffer, Alfred G. Milotte, Karl H. Maslowski, Stuart V. Jewell, Dick Bird, Olin Sewall Pettingill, Jr., Roman Vishniac, Tilden W. Roberts, William Fortin. Film Editor: Norman Palmer, A.C.E. Set Decorator: Bertram Granger. Assistant Director: Gordon McLean. Special Processes: Ub Iwerks, A.S.C. Sound: Robert O. Cook.

SURVIVAL OF SAM THE PELICAN, THE
Written by: Ben Masselink. Narration Written by: Norman Wright. Produced and Directed by: Roy Edward Disney. Told and Sung by: Michael Dees. Film Editor: Toby Brown. Music: Robert F. Brunner. Sound: Herb Taylor. Production Supervisor: Erwin L. Verity. *For Coronado Productions, Inc.* Field Producer: Milas Hinshaw. Photography: Milas Hinshaw. Location Manager: Brian Burton. Underwater Photography: William "Bumpy" Bell. Production Staff: Casey Hotchkiss, Curtis Burton, Mary Friese.

TALE OF TWO CRITTERS, A
Executive Producer: Ron Miller. Written and Produced by: Jack Speirs. Narrated by: Mayf Nutter. Editor: Gregg McLaughlin, A.C.E. Music: Buddy Baker. Orchestration: Walter Sheets. Song *Travelin' On* by: Erika Borgeson, Buddy Baker, Jack Speirs. Music Editor: Evelyn Kennedy. Production Supervisors: Erwin Verity, Rolf Darbo. Sound: Herb Taylor. Sound Editor: Raymond Craddock. For Olympic Game Farm: Field Producer: Lloyd Beebe. Associate Field Producer: Ron Brown. Technical Supervision: Marinho Correia, Terry Rowland, Alfie Robb. Wildlife Photographers: Bob Rowland, Lloyd Beebe, Ken Beebe, Bill Bacon.

TALES OF THE APPLE DUMPLING GANG
Executive Producer: William Robert Yates. Director of Photography: Dennis Dalzell. Produced by: Tom Leetch. Based on Characters Created by: Jack M. Bickham. Written by: Robert Van Scoyk. Directed by: E. W. Swackhamer. Music by: Frank De Vol, Tom Worrall. Art Director: Mark Mansbridge. Editor: Ernest Milano, A.C.E. Unit Production Manager: William L. Young. Assistant Director: Christopher D. Miller. Second Assistant Director: Doug Metzger. Casting: Bill Shepard, Virginia Higgins. Set Decorator: Norman Rockett. Sound:

Bob Hathaway. Sound Editor: Ben Hendricks. Music Editor: Jack Wadsworth. Costumes: Jack Sandeen. Make-up: Robert J. Schiffer, C.M.A.A. Hair Stylist: Ginger Grieve.

TATTOOED POLICE HORSE, THE
Original Story by: Larry Lansburgh. Teleplay by: Janet Lansburgh. Produced and directed by: Larry Lansburgh. Director of Photography: Edward P. Hughes. Film Editor: Herman Freedman. Narrator: Keith Andes. Races Called by: Stan Bergstein. Music: William Lava. *World of Color* Theme Song: Richard M. Sherman, Robert B. Sherman. In Charge of Production: Robert Baron. Sound: Robert O. Cook. Program Co-ordinator: Jack Bruner. Acknowledgments: The Harness Racing Institute, Lt. John Lynch and the men of Division 16, Boston Police Department.

TENDERFOOT, THE
Co-producer: Ron Miller. Teleplay by: Maurice Tombragel. Based on the book *Arizona in the '50s* by: James H. Tevis. Directed by: Byron Paul. Associate Producer: Louis Debney. Director of Photography: William Snyder, A.S.C. Art Directors: Carroll Clark, John B. Mansbridge. Film Editor: Robert Stafford, A.C.E. Set Decorators: Emile Kuri, Hal Gausman. Music: George Bruns. Song: Richard M. Sherman, Robert B. Sherman. Costumes: Chuck Keehne. Make-up: Pat McNalley. Sound: Robert O. Cook. Assistant Director: Tom Leetch. Program Co-ordinator: Jack Bruner.

TEXAS JOHN SLAUGHTER
Directed by: Harry Keller. Written by: Albert E. Lewin, Burt Styler. Produced by: James Pratt. Director of Photography: Walter H. Castle, A.S.C. Art Director: Marvin Aubrey Davis. Film Editor: Robert Stafford. Music: Joseph S. Dubin. Song: Stan Jones. Matte Artist: Peter Ellenshaw. Sound: Robert O. Cook. Set Decorators: Emile Kuri, Vin Taylor. Costumer: Chuck Keehne. Make-up: Pat McNalley. Assistant Director: Austen Jewell.

THANKSGIVING PROMISE, THE
Music by: Bruce Broughton. Editor: James T. Heckert. Production Designer: Ida Random. Director of Photography: Fred J. Koenekamp, A.S.C. Executive Producer: Mel Ferrer. Produced by: Mark H. Ovitz. Teleplay by: Glenn L. Anderson, Peter N. Johnson, Blaine M. Yorgason, Craig Holyoak. Based on the Novel *The Thanksgiving Promise* by: Blaine and Brenton Yorgason. Directed by: Beau Bridges. Unit Production Manager: Stephen J. Barnett. First Assistant Director: Ira Shuman. Second Assistant Director: Joseph Paul Moore. Casting: Joyce Robinson, C.S.A., Penny Ellers, C.S.A. Costume Designer: William Ware Theiss. Set Decorator: Ethel Robins Richards. Property Master: Lavar Emert. Key Costumers: Margo Baxley, Ron Caplan. Make-up: Lance Anderson. Hair Stylist: Gregg Mitchell. Assistant to Mr. Ovitz: Cheryl Denise Edwards. Animals Owned and Trained by: Birds & Animals Unlimited, Gary Gero/Mark Jackson. Second Unit Director: R.A. Rondell. Location Manager: Ryan Rosenberg. Script Supervisor: Bonnie Prendergast. Production Coordinator: Lorna Neal. Production Sound Mixer: Patrick Mitchell. Sound Editing by: Dimension Sound/Val Kuklowsky. Music Editing by: A. David Marshall. A. Mel Ferrer, Beau Bridges and Mark H. Ovitz Production in association with Walt Disney Television.

THIS IS YOUR LIFE DONALD DUCK
Directed by: Jack Hannah, C. August Nichols. Sequence Director: Jack Kinney. Story: Albert Bertino, Dave Detiege, Nick George. Animation: Volus Jones, Roy Jenkins, George Kreisl, Bill Justice, Al Coe. Layout: Yale Gracey. Backgrounds: Ray Huffine, Ralph Hulett. Film Editor: Tom Acosta. Music: Joseph S. Dubin. Animation Research: Bob McCrea. Sound: Robert O. Cook. Production Supervision: Harry Tytle. Acknowledgments: Ralph Edwards and *This Is Your Life.*

THREE ON THE RUN
Produced by: Bill Anderson, William Beaudine, Jr. Director of Photography: Robert Sparks. Written by: Robert Schaefer, Eric Freiwald. Directed by: William Beaudine, Jr. Editor: Lloyd L. Richardson, A.C.E. Associate Producer: Tom Beemer. Assistant Director: Richard Del Ruth. Music: Buddy Baker.

Sound: Herb Taylor. Assistant to the Producer: Scottie Cummings. Dogs Handled by: Rudd Weatherwax, Sam Williamson, Robert Weatherwax. Bear Supervised by: Lloyd Beebe. Acknowledgment: U.S. Department of Agriculture, Forest Service.

THREE TALL TALES
Directed by: Hamilton S. Luske. Sequence Directors: Les Clark, Jack Kinney, C. August Nichols. Story: Joe Rinaldi, Lance Nolley. Styling: McLaren Stewart, Eyvind Earle, Ernie Nordli, Tom Oreb. Animation: Julius Svendsen, Art Stevens, Cliff Nordberg, Bob McCrea, John Sibley, George Nicholas, Fred Moore, Jack Boyd. Layout: Joe Hale, Homer Jonas. Background: Art Riley, Walt Peregoy. With the talents of: Paul Frees, Rex Allen. Music: George Bruns, Franklyn Marks, Oliver Wallace. Lyrics: Tom Adair, C. August Nichols. Vocals: The Mellomen and Sons of the Pioneers. Film Editor: Tom Acosta. Sound: Robert O. Cook. Program Co-ordinator: Jack Bruner.

THREE WITHOUT FEAR
Produced by: Roy Edward Disney. Teleplay by: Ben Masselink. Narration by: Roy Edward Disney. Based on a book by: Robert C. DuSoe. Narrator: Hugh Cherry. Film Editor: Norman R. Palmer, A.C.E. Music: George Bruns. Production Manager: Erwin L. Verity. Sound: Robert O. Cook. Program Co-ordinator: Jack Bruner. *For Pisces Productions, Inc.* Field Producer: Frank Zuniga. Photography: Milas Hinshaw, Dennis Grisco. Additional Photography: Russ Alsobrook. Production Assistant: Vicente Valjalo. Production Manager: Irvin Paik. Acknowledgments: The Mexican National Tourist Council, The Baja California Bureau of Tourism.

TIGER TOWN (AND) STAR TOURS
Star Tours preview credits: Cast: Gil Gerard, Ernie Reyes, Jr., George Lucas, Anthony Daniels (C-3PO). Produced by: Brad Lachman. Directed by: Walter C. Miller. Written by: Jeffrey Barron. Supervising Producer: Milt Hoffman. Director of Photography: Bob Dickinson. Art Director: Rene Lagler. Videotape Editors: Russell Srole, David Foster, Jerry Bixman. Costume Designer: Rickie Hansen. Music by: Dennis McCarthy. Associate Producer: Steven Ligerman. Talent Coordinator: Debra Towsley. Associate Director: Emm-Jay Trokel. Script Supervisor: Pat Brannon Wise. Production Associates: Paul Hoen, Christine Jardine. Film Research: Drew Brown. Production Coordinator: Kent Weishaus. Post Production Coordinator: Kevin Gershan. Technical Director: John B. Field. Stage Managers: Peter Bright, Steven Ligerman. Audio: Larry La Sota. Post Production Audio: Jerry Clemans. Camera Operators: Hector Ramirez, Dave Levison, Hank Geving. Make-up: Judith Silverman, Wynona Price. Hair Stylist: Judith Tiedemann. Technical Manager: Kevin Hayes. Brad Lachman Productions, Inc.

TITLE MAKERS, THE (AND) NATURE'S HALF ACRE
Title Makers Directed by: Robert Stevenson. Special Material by: Lowell S. Hawley. *The Parent Trap* Written and Directed by: David Swift. Based on the book *Das Doppelte Lottchen* by: Erich Kastner. Songs by: Richard M. Sherman, Robert B. Sherman. *Nature's Half Acre* Directed by: James Algar. Written by: Winston Hibler, Ted Sears. Photography: Murl Deusing, Tilden W. Roberts, Karl H. Maslowski, Arthur A. Allen, Alfred G. Milotte, Joseph Heidenkamp, Jr., Tom and Arlene Hadley, Olin Sewall Pettingill, Jr., John Nash Ott, Stuart V. Jewell. Music: Paul Smith. Film Editor: Norman Palmer.

TO THE SOUTH POLE FOR SCIENCE
Produced and Directed by: Winston Hibler. Narration Written by: Ted Sears, Otto Englander. Photographed by: Lloyd Beebe, Jack C. Couffer, Elmo G. Jones, William Fortin. U.S. Navy Photographer: William W. Bristol, Ph.C. Music: Joseph S. Dubin. Film Editor: Grant K. Smith. Production Coordinator: William Redlin. Special Effects: Eustace Lycett, Joshua Meador, Ub Iwerks, A.S.C. Sound: Robert O. Cook. Production Supervision: Erwin L. Verity, Harry Tytle. Antarctic Topographical Model by: Allen-Shaw. Acknowledgments: The Department of Defense, U.S. Navy, U.S. Air Force, U.S. Army, U.S. Coast Guard, The Douglas Aircraft Company, Inc.

TOOT, WHISTLE, PLUNK, AND BOOM
Directed by: Wilfred Jackson. Sequence Directors: C. August Nichols, Ward Kimball, Bill Justice. Story: Dick Huemer, Dick Kinney, Roy Williams. Animation: Don Lusk, Hal Ambro, Dan MacManus, Julius Svendsen, Al Coe, Marc Davis. Animation Research: Bob McCrea. Layout: Joe Hale, A. Kendall O'Connor, Xavier Atencio. Backgrounds: Fil Mottola, Eyvind Earle. Film Editor: Samuel Horta. Music: Joseph S. Dubin. Songs: Paul Francis Webster, Sonny Burke, Jack Elliott, George Bruns, Billy Mills, Paul Mason Howard. Voice of Prof. Owl: Wm. H. (Bill) Thompson. Special Processes: Eustace Lycett. Sound: Robert O. Cook. Production Supervisor: Harry Tytle.

TORY VENGEANCE
Directed by: Louis King. Teleplay by: Lewis R. Foster. Based on the book by: Dr. Robert D. Bass. Produced by: James Pratt. Directed of Photography: Gordon Avil, A.S.C. Art Director: Marvin Aubrey Davis. Film Editor: Cotton Warburton, A.C.E. Music: William Lava. Songs: Lew Foster, Buddy Baker. Sound: Robert O. Cook. Set Decoration: Emile Kuri, Hal Gausman. Costumer: Chuck Keehne. Make-up: Pat McNalley. Hair Stylist: Ruth Sandifer. Assistant Director: Ron Miller.

TRACK OF THE AFRICAN BONGO, THE
Produced by: Roy Edward Disney. Written by: Harold Swanton. Narration by: Jack Speirs. Directed by: Frank Zuniga. Narrator: Michael Jackson. Editors: Norman R. Palmer, A.C.E., Toby Brown, A.C.E. Music: Robert F. Brunner. Sound: Herb Taylor. Production Supervisor: Erwin L. Verity. For Cangary Limited: Photography: Dick Thomsett. Production Assistant: Carmen Ribera. Animal Supervision: Seago-Parkinson. Production Staff: Max Alfonso, Mathew Kipion, Jean Hayes, Mike Richmond, Lissa Ruben, Diane Soash.

TRAGEDY ON THE TRAIL
Co-producer: Ron Miller. Written by: Maurice Tombragel. Based on a character created by: Richard Harding Davis. Directed by: James Sheldon. Assistant to the Producer: Jerome Courtland. Director of Photography: William Snyder, A.S.C. Art Directors: Carroll Clark, William L. Campbell. Film Editor: Roy Brewer. Set Decorators: Emile Kuri, Bill Calvert. Music: Willis Schaefer. *World of Color* Theme: Richard M. Sherman, Robert B. Sherman. Costumer: Chuck Keehne. Make-up: Pat McNalley. Hair Stylist: La Rue Matheron. Sound: Robert O. Cook. Assistant Director: Bud Grace. Program Co-ordinator: Jack Bruner.

TRAIL OF DANGER
Executive Producer: Ron Miller. Produced by: James Algar. Director of Photography: Duke Callaghan. Teleplay by: Calvin Clements, Jr. Based on the story *Open Winter* by: H. L. Davis. Directed by: Andrew V. McLaglen. Art Directors: John B. Mansbridge, LeRoy G. Deane. Editor: Gordon D. Brenner. Music: Buddy Baker. Sound: Herb Taylor. Costumes: Chuck Keehne. Make-up: Robert J. Schiffer. Unit Production Manager/First Assistant Director: Michael Dmytryk. Second Assistant Director: Wallace Jones. Animal Supervision: James A. Prine. Acknowledgments: State of Idaho, Cities of Mountain Home, Shoshone and Twin Falls, Bruneau Dunes State Park, Magic Valley Horseless Carriage Club, Bureau of Land Management, Boise National Forest.

TREASURE OF SAN BOSCO REEF, THE
Produced by: Ron Miller. Co-produced by: Tom Leetch. Written by: Maurice Tombragel. Directed by: Robert L. Friend. Director of Photography: Frank Phillips, A.S.C. Underwater Photography: Lamar Boren. Art Directors: Carroll Clark, Robert E. Smith. Film Editor: Marsh Hendry. Second Unit Director: Paul Stader. Set Decorators: Emile Kuri, Hal Gausman. Costumer: Chuck Keehne. Make-up: Otis Malcolm. Hair Stylist: La Rue Matheron. Music: Robert F. Brunner. *World of Color* Theme: Richard M. Sherman, Robert B. Sherman. Assistant Director: Paul L. Cameron. Sound: Robert O. Cook. Program Co-ordinator: Jack Bruner. Vice President in Charge of Television: Ron Miller.

TRIAL BY TERROR

Co-producer: Ron Miller. Written by: Maurice Tombragel. Based on a character created by: Richard Harding Davis. Directed by: James Sheldon. Assistant to the Producer: Jerome Courtland. Director of Photography: William Snyder, A.S.C. Art Directors: Carroll Clark, William L. Campbell. Film Editor: Marsh Hendry. Set Decorators: Emile Kuri, Bill Calvert. Music: Robert F. Brunner. *World of Color* Theme: Richard M. Sherman, Robert B. Sherman. Costumer: Chuck Keehne. Make-up: Pat McNalley. Hair Stylist: La Rue Matheron. Sound: Robert O. Cook. Assistant Director: Bud Grace. Program Co-ordinator: Jack Bruner.

TRIBUTE TO JOEL CHANDLER HARRIS, A

Directed by: William Beaudine, Clyde Geronimi. Produced by: Clyde Geronimi. Original Story: William Peet. Teleplay: Dwight Babcock. Music: Oliver Wallace. Art Directors: Marvin Aubrey Davis, Tom Codrick. Production Supervision: Harry Tytle. Set Decorator: Bertram Granger. Matte Artist: Peter Ellenshaw. Photography: Edward Colman, A.S.C. Film Editor: Stanley Johnson, A.C.E. Cartoon Editor: Donald Halliday. Special Processes: Ub Iwerks, A.S.C. Sound: Robert O. Cook. Assistant Director: Bill Beaudine, Jr. Unit Manager: John Grubbs. *The Tar Baby* Sequence: Directed by: Wilfred Jackson. Story: William Peet, Ralph Wright. Animation: Milt Kahl, Eric Larson, Marc Davis, Ollie Johnston. Layout: Ken Anderson. Backgrounds: Brice Mack. Songs: *Let the Rain Pour Down:* Ken Darby, Foster Carling. *That's What Uncle Remus Said:* Johnny Lange, Hy Heath, Eliot Daniel.

TRICKS OF OUR TRADE

Cartoon Director: Wilfred Jackson. Sequence Directors: James Algar, Hamilton S. Luske. Teleplay by: Dick Huemer. Cartoon Story: Ted Sears, Mel Shaw. Music: Joseph S. Dubin. Animation: Volus Jones, Dan MacManus, Ollie Johnston, John Lounsbery, Jerry Hathcock, Fred Moore. Art Styling: Al Dempster. Layout: Al Zinnen, A. Kendall O'Connor. Backgrounds: Dick Anthony. Photography: Charles P. Boyle, A.S.C. Film Editors: George Gale, A.C.E., Samuel Horta. Special Processes: Ub Iwerks, A.S.C. Sound: Robert O. Cook. Production Supervision: Harry Tytle.

TRIP THRU ADVENTURELAND, A (AND) WATER BIRDS

Directed by (Television): Winston Hibler. Directed by (Water Birds): Ben Sharpsteen. Written by: Ted Sears, Winston Hibler, Jack Speirs, William Otis. Music (Television): George Bruns. Music (Water Birds): Paul Smith. Production Supervision: Harry Tytle. Photography: Stuart V. Jewell, Alfred G. Milotte, Olin Sewall Pettingill, Jr., Alfred M. Bailey, Ed N. Harrison, Frances F. Roberts, John H. Storer. Film Editor (Television): Grant Smith. Film Editor (Water Birds): Norman Palmer. Special Processes: Ub Iwerks, A.S.C. Sound: Robert O. Cook. Acknowledgments: National Audubon Society, Denver Museum of Natural History.

TRIP TO TUCSON

Directed by: James Neilson. Teleplay by: Maurice Tombragel. Produced by: Bill Anderson. Associate Producer: Ron Miller. Director of Photography: Edward Colman, A.S.C. Art Director: Marvin Aubrey Davis. Film Editor: Robert Stafford. Music: George Bruns. Sound: Robert O. Cook. Set Decoration: William L. Stevens. Costumer: Chuck Keehne. Make-up: Pat McNalley. Unit Manager: Roy Wade. Assistant Director: Joseph L. McEveety.

TRUTH ABOUT MOTHER GOOSE, THE

Directed by: Hamilton S. Luske. Sequence Directors: Bill Roberts, Wolfgang Reitherman, Bill Justice. Story: Joe Rinaldi, Bill Peet, Homer Brightman. Art Styling: McLaren Stewart. Animation: Ward Kimball, Cliff Nordberg, Bob McCrea, John Lounsbery. Effects Animation: Dan MacManus. Layout: Joe Hale, Xavier Atencio, Basil Davidovich, A. Kendall O'Connor, Al Zinnen, Art Riley, Claude Coats. Music: George Bruns, Paul Smith, Oliver Wallace. Songs: Tom Adair, Bill Peet, George Bruns, Ray Nobel, Bennie Benjamin, Bill Walsh, George Weiss, Arthur Quenzer. With the talents of: Paul Frees. Film Editor: Anthony Gerard. Sound: Robert O. Cook. Program Co-ordinator: Jack Bruner.

TWISTER, BULL FROM THE SKY

Produced by: Bill Anderson, Larry Lansburgh. Teleplay by: Larry Lansburgh, Jr. Story by: Larry Lansburgh. Narration Written by: Jack Speirs. Directed by: Larry Lansburgh. Photography: Edward P. Hughes. Film Editor: Lloyd L. Richardson, A.C.E. Production Supervisor: Charles B. Mulvehill. Music: Richard Shores. Song *Country Days* by: Shane Tatum. Sung by: Richard McKinley. Sound Supervisor: Herb Taylor. Production Associate: Brian Lansburgh. Acknowledgments: Rodeo Cowboys Association of America, The Pendleton Roundup.

2 ½ DADS

Executive Producers: Fred Silverman, Gordon Farr. Written by: Gordon Farr. Produced and Directed by: Tony Bill. Music by: Robert Folk. Director of Photography: George Koblasa. Art Director: Jim Shanahan. Editor: Andy Blumenthal. Unit Production Manager/Associate Producer: Dan Franklin. First Assistant Director: Anderson G. House. Second Assistant Director: Emmitt-Leon O'Neill. Casting by: Joyce Robinson, C.S.A., Penny Ellers, C.S.A., April Webster, C.S.A. Set Decorator: Carl Biddiscombe. Property Master: Anthony C. Thorpe. Key Costumers: Sandra Berke Jordan, Gene Deardorff. Make-up: Michael F. Blake. Hair Stylist: Eddie M. Barron. Costume Designer: William Ware Theiss. Location Manager: Ryan Rosenberg. Script Supervisor: Joyce Heftel. Production Coordinator: Vera Martin. Production Sound Mixer: Dean Vernon. Sound Editing by: Blue Light Sound, Inc. Music Editing by: Curtis Roush/Segue Music. Twenty Paws Productions, Inc., Intermedia Entertainment Co. in association with Walt Disney Television.

TWO AGAINST THE ARCTIC

Produced by: James Algar. Teleplay by: James Algar. Based on the book *Icebound Summer* by: Sally Carrighar. Directed by: Robert Clouse. Narrator: Andrew Duggan. Production Manager: Erwin L. Verity. Film Editor: Gordon Brenner. Music: Buddy Baker. Sound: Herb Taylor. *For Robert Clouse Associates, Inc.* Photography: Gilbert Hubbs, Lynn Ellsworth. Technical Advisors: Lloyd Beebe, Terry Rowland. Production Co-ordinator: Steve Litt. Acknowledgments: Alaska Department of Fish and Game, University of Alaska.

TWO HAPPY AMIGOS

Direction: Jack Hannah, C. August Nichols. Story: Milt Banta, Bill Berg. Animation: John Sibley, Al Coe, Roy Jenkins, Cliff Nordberg, Jack Buckley. Layout: Yale Gracey. Backgrounds: Ray Huffine. Film Editor: Tom Acosta. Music: Joseph S. Dubin. Sound: Robert O. Cook. Production Supervision: Harry Tytle. Acknowledgment: Presented with the Talents of the Artists and Technicians of the Walt Disney Studios.

VALENTINE FROM DISNEY, A

Executive Producer: William Robert Yates. Prepared for Television by: Dennis Landa, Bill Pentland, Rick Piccini. *Pecos Bill* Sung by: Roy Rogers and The Sons of the Pioneers. *Johnny Fedora and Alice Blue Bonnet* Sung by: The Andrews Sisters. Additional Music: John Debney.

VARDA, THE PEREGRINE FALCON

Produced by: Roy Edward Disney. Teleplay by: Otto Englander. Narration by: Gerald Pearce. Based on the book *The Peregrine Falcon* by: Robert Murphy. Narrator: Hugh Cherry. Film Editor: Toby Brown. Music: George Bruns. Production Manager: Erwin L. Verity. Sound: Robert O. Cook. Program Co-ordinator: Jack Bruner. *For Pisces Productions, Inc.* Field Producer: Frank Zuniga. Photography: Michael D. Lonzo, Norman Nelson. Production Assistant: Irwin Paik. Falconry: Dennis Grisco. Assisted by: Robert McCallum, John M. Hall. Acknowledgments: Alaska Department of Fish and Game, Texas Department of Fish and Game, Florida Game and Fresh Water Fish Commission, National Audubon Society.

Von Drake in Spain

Associate Producer: Hamilton S. Luske. Directed by: Norman Foster. Photographer: Miguel Mila. Art Director: Gil Parrondo. Film Editors: Gordon Stone, Anthony Gerard. Original music from Spanish folk songs arranged by: Salvadore Ruiz de Luna. Additional Music: Buddy Baker. Song *Flamenco:* Mel Leven. Production Manager: Basil Somner. Assistant Director: Paul Ganapoler. Sound: Robert O. Cook. With the talents of: Paul Frees. Art Styling: McLaren Stewart. Story: Bill Berg, Joe Rinaldi. Animation: Eric Larson, Bill Justice, Cliff Nordberg, Ward Kimball. Effects Animation: Jack Boyd. Layout: Joe Hale. Backgrounds: Art Riley, Bill Layne.

Wacky Zoo of Morgan City, The

Produced by: Bill Anderson. Television Story and Teleplay by: Joseph L. McEveety. Based on the book *I'll Trade You an Elk* by: Charles A. Goodrum. Directed by: Marvin Chomsky. Associate Producer: Joseph L. McEveety. Director of Photography: John F. Warren, A.S.C. Art Directors: John B. Mansbridge, Russell Menzer. Film Editor: Bob Bring. Set Decorators: Emile Kuri, Jack H. Ahern. Music: George Bruns. Sound: Robert O. Cook. Costumer: Chuck Keehne. Make-up: Robert J. Schiffer. Hair Stylist: La Rue Matheron. Assistant Director: Jack Aldworth. Program Co-ordinator: Jack Bruner.

Wahoo Bobcat, The

Co-producer: Winston Hibler. Teleplay by: Louis Pelletier. Based on a book by: Joseph Wharton Lippincott. Narration written by: Robert F. Metzler, Jack Speirs. Narrator: Rex Allen. Production Co-ordinator: Robert F. Metzler. Production Manager: Erwin L. Verity. Film Editor: George Gale, A.C.E. Music: Buddy Baker. Sound: Robert O. Cook. Program Co-ordinator: Jack Bruner. *For Hank Schloss Productions, Inc.* Field Producer: Hank Schloss. Photographers: Hank Schloss, Frank Zuniga, Jack Ferrucci. Production Assistant: Jack Ferrucci. Technicians: Ron Dexter, Randy Gray, Darrell Hendricks, Gary Kenwood.

Walt Disney . . . One Man's Dream

Executive Producers: Gary Smith, Dwight Hemion. Produced by: Ken Welch, Phil May. Directed by: Dwight Hemion. Written by: Stan Hart, John McGreevey, Mitzie Welch. Associate Producer: Michael B. Seligman. Original Music and Lyrics by: Mitzie Welch, Ken Welch. Music Director: Ian Fraser. Art Director: Roy Christopher. Choreographer: Alan Johnson. Costumes Designed by: Pete Menefee, Ret Turner. Lighting by: Fred McKinnon, John Rook, George Riesenberger. Associate Director: Wenda Fong. Production Manager: Penelope Harrison. Assistants to the Producers: Sharon Taylor, Suellen Wagner. Production Assistant: Terrell Greene. Assistant Choreographer: Charlene Painter. Assistant Art Director: Bill Brzeski. Casting: Gus Schirmer. Music Arrangements: Billy Byers, Chris Boardman. Technical Directors: John B. Field, Len Uslaner. Audio: Ed Greene, Tom Durell. Video: John Palacio, Larry Brotzler. Video Tape Editor: Andy Zall. Cameramen: Larry Heider, Wayne Orr, Bill Philbin, Lou Adams. Camera Assistants: Marc Hunter, Jesse Wayne Parker. Stage Managers: Charles Gayton III, Ted Ray. Make-up: Ralph Gulko, Sheryl Shulman, Greg Nelson. Hairdressers: Jan Cook, Gail Rowell, Renate Leuschner. *The Collector* by: Mike Jittlov. Facilities provided by: Metromedia Square, Video Tape Associates. Post Production by: Complete Post. *Small World* sung by: The International Children's Choir. Acknowledgment: All the Disney Employees.

Walt Disney World's 15th Birthday Celebration

Executive Producer: Brad Lachman. Produced and Directed by: Marty Pasetta. Writing Supervised by: Jeffrey Barron. Written by: Bob Arnott, David Forman, Ken Welch, Mitzi Welch. Associate Producer: Michael Petok. Art Director: Robert Keene. Music Arranged and Conducted by: Dennis McCarthy. Special Music Material: Ken Welch, Mitzi Welch. Lighting Designer: Bob Dickinson. Choreographer: Barnette Ricci. Costume Designer: Alan Trugman. Assistants to the Producer: Laura Lyons, Roberta Savold. Associate Producer: Debbie Pasetta. Stage Managers: Terri McCoy, Steven J. Santos, David Wader. Production Assistants: Cecilia Aguilar, Lisa Gougas, Paige Rabban, Steven Schillaci, Karen Tasch. Talent Executives: Linda Ferris, Lillian Mizrahi. Production Coordinator: Rob Krueger. Production Managers: Kevin Berg, Larry Cohen. Lighting Directors: Simon Miles, Todd Nichols. Assistant Choreographer: Roy Luthringer. "Rollerskating" Segment Director: Neil Gordon. Assistant Art Directors: Griff Lambert, Batinna Buckley, David Ravetto. Lighting Coordinator: Max Brenner. Audio: Doug Nelson. Rerecording Mixer: David Fluhr. Assistant Editor: Matt Donato. Hair: Gail Rowell. Make-up: Sheryl Leigh Ptak. Gaffers: Dennis Rudge, Paul Bell. *In Florida:* Unit Manager: Jim "Mo" Moroney. Entertainment Coordinators: Bobbi Colquitt, Reggie Jarrett, Ronnie Rodriguez, Pam Killinger, Julie Kirchen. Audio: Dave Mouery. Production Assistants: Kim Gunther, Jack Somerville, Jim Campbell, Buck Allen. Acknowledgments: The Florida A&M University "Marching 100," Dr. William P. Foster, Director; St. Cloud High School Choir, Lake Brantley High School Choir, Walt Disney World Cast Choir, Florida Youth Symphony, Barbershoppers of Winter Park and Polk County. Dancers: Becky Cano, Jennifer Duke, Tami Fox, Deidre Lang, Robbie Mackey, Mickey Mance, Ken Passman, Vince Pesce, Louise Ruck, Randy Wojcik. Executive in Charge of Production: Gregory Sills. A Pasetta Production in association with Walt Disney Television.

Walt Disney's Mickey and Donald

Dude Duck music by: Paul J. Smith.

Walt Disney's Wet and Wild

This episode was aired without production credits.

Waltz King, The

Teleplay: Maurice Tombragel. Based on a Story by: Fritz Eckhardt. Directed by: Steve Previn. Associate Producer: Peter V. Herald. Director of Photography: Günther Anders. Art Directors: Werner Schlichting, Isabell Schlichting. Film Editor: Alfred Srp. The Music of Johann Strauss, Jr., Johann Strauss, Sr. and Jacques Offenbach Arranged and Conducted by: Helmuth Froschauer. Played by: The Vienna Symphony Orchestra. Music Advisor: Heinz Schreiter. Choreographer: Norman Thomson. Production Managers: Walter Tjaden, Robert Russ. Costumes: Leo Bei. Make-up: Rudolph Ohlschmidt, Leopold Kuhnert. Camera Operator: Robert Hofer. Dialogue Coach: Kent McPherron. Sound: Robert O. Cook, Herbert Janeozka, Kurt Schwarz. Assistant Director: Brigitte Liphardt. Program Co-ordinator: Jack Bruner. Produced at: Wien Film Rosenhügel Studios, Vienna, Austria.

Warrior's Path, The

Directed by: Lewis R. Foster. Television Story and Teleplay by: David Victor. Based on the book *Daniel Boone* by: John Bakeless. Produced by: Bill Anderson. Associate Producer: Ron Miller. Director of Photography: Ray Rennahan, A.S.C. Art Director: Marvin Aubrey Davis. Film Editor: Robert Stafford. Music: Oliver Wallace. Song: George Bruns, David Victor. Matte Artist: Peter Ellenshaw. Sound: Robert O. Cook. Set Decoration: Emile Kuri, William L. Stevens. Costumer: Chuck Keehne. Make-up: Pat McNalley. Hair Stylist: Ruth Sandifer. Unit Manager: Roy Wade. Assistant Director: Joseph L. McEveety.

Way Down Cellar

Produced by: Ron Miller. Co-produced by: Tom Leetch. Teleplay by: Herman Groves. Based on the book by: Phil Strong. Directed by: Robert Totten. Director of Photography: William Snyder, A.S.C. Art Directors: Carroll Clark, John B. Mansbridge. Film Editor: Marsh Hendry. Set Decorators: Emile Kuri, Frank R. McKelvy. Costumer: Chuck Keehne. Make-up: Gordon Hubbard. Hair Stylist: La Rue Matheron. Music: Willis Schaefer. *World of Color* Theme Song: Richard M. Sherman, Robert B. Sherman. Assistant Director: Paul Cameron. Sound: Robert O. Cook. Program Co-ordinator: Jack Bruner.

Welcome to the "World"

Produced and Directed by: Marty Pasetta. Written by: Sheldon Keller. Associate Producers: Michael Seligman, Ron Miziker. Music Conducted and Arranged by: Nick Perito.

Choreographer: Tommy Tune. Choral Arranger and Conductor: Alan Copeland. Assistant to the Producer: Danette Herman. Production Assistant: Nan Schwartz. Costume Designer: Jack Muhs. Technical Supervisor: Bill Hogan. Associate Director: Bob Bowker. Stage Manager: Gene Rowell. Lighting Director: Carl Gibson. Audio: Larry Stephens. Video: Mark Sanford. Make-up: Clay Lambert. Video Tape Editor: Bill Breshears. Production Executive: Bob Jani. In Association with Pasetta Productions, Inc.

WETBACK HOUND, THE
Produced and Directed by: Larry Lansburgh. Written by: Janet Lansburgh. Told by: Rex Allen. Music: William Lava. Photography: Carlos Carbajal. Production Associate: Hal Ramser. Film Editor: Warren Adams. Sound: Glen Glenn.

WHERE DO THE STORIES COME FROM?
Directed by: Jack Hannah. Raccoon Animation Director: C. August Nichols. Animation: Bill Justice, Volus Jones, Norm Ferguson, Bob Carlson, Marvin Woodward, George Kreisl, Jerry Hathcock, Dan MacManus. Story: Al Bertino, Dave Detiege, Ralph Wright, Bill Berg, Roy Williams. Music: Oliver Wallace, Paul Smith. Layout: Yale Gracey, Lance Nolley. Backgrounds: Art Riley, Merle Cox. Art Director: Marvin Aubrey Davis. Production Supervision: Harry Tytle. Set Decorator: Emile Kuri. Photography: Bert Glennon. Film Editor: Tom Acosta. Special Processes: Ub Iwerks, A.S.C. Sound: Robert O. Cook. Assistant Director: Gordon McLean.

WHITE MAN'S MEDICINE
Directed by: Lewis R. Foster. Teleplay by: Tom Blackburn. Based on the novel by: Stewart Edward White. Photographer: Walter H. Castle, A.S.C. Art Director: Carroll Clark. Film Editor: George Gale, A.C.E. Music: George Bruns. Song The Saga of Andy Burnett: Tom Blackburn, George Bruns. Second Unit Director: Yakima Canutt. Matte Artist: Peter Ellenshaw. Sound: Robert O. Cook. Set Decoration: Fred MacLean. Costumer: Chuck Keehne. Make-up: Pat McNalley. Assistant Director: Robert G. Shannon. Production Supervisor: Harry Tytle.

WHIZ KID AND THE CARNIVAL CAPER, THE
Produced by: Ron Miller. Co-producer: Tom Leetch. Director of Photography: Frank Phillips, A.S.C. Teleplay by: Herman Groves. Story by: Herman Groves, Tom Leetch. Based on characters created by: Clifford B. Hicks. Directed by: Tom Leetch. Art Directors: John B. Mansbridge, Al Roelofs. Film Editor: Cotton Warburton, A.C.E. Set Decoration: Frank R. McKelvy. Music: Richard Bowden. Sound: Herb Taylor. Costumes: Chuck Keehne. Make-up: Robert J. Schiffer. Hair Stylist: La Rue Matheron. Unit Production Manager: Michael Dmytryk. Second Assistant Director: Dorothy Kieffer. Carnival Arrangements: Bill Erickson. Assistant to the Producer: Jan Williams.

WHIZ KID AND THE MYSTERY AT RIVERTON, THE
Produced by: Ron Miller. Teleplay by: Herman Groves. Based on the books by: Clifford B. Hicks. Co-produced and Directed by: Tom Leetch. Director of Photography: Charles F. Wheeler, A.S.C. Art Directors: John B. Mansbridge, Robert Clatworthy. Film Editor: Ray de Leuw. Set Decoration: Hal Gausman. Costumes: Chuck Keehne. Make-up: Robert J. Schiffer. Hair Stylist: La Rue Matheron. Sound Supervisor: Herb Taylor. Music: Robert F. Brunner. Assistant Director: Jack Roe.

WILD BURRO OF THE WEST
For Perkins Films, Inc. Directed by: Walter Perkins. Photography: Walter Perkins, William R. Lieb, Richard Gunoff. For Walt Disney Productions Produced by: Winston Hibler. Written by: Albert Aley. Based on the book Dusty's Return by: Dorothy Childs Hogner. Narrated by: Winston Hibler. Film Editor: George Gale, A.C.E. Music: Oliver Wallace. Production Coordinator: Robert Metzler. Sound: Robert O. Cook. Production Supervisor: Harry Tytle.

WILD GEESE CALLING
Produced by: James Algar. Teleplay by: Homer McCoy. Narration by: James Algar. Based on the book by: Robert Murphy.

Narrator: Steve Forrest. Film Editor: Gordon Brenner. Music: Buddy Baker. Song Wild Geese Calling Me Home: Buddy Baker, Hal Blair. Production Manager: Erwin L. Verity. Sound: Robert O. Cook. Program Co-ordinator: Jack Bruner. For Charles Draper Productions, Inc. Field Producer: Charles L. Draper. Photographed by: Charles L. Draper. Wildlife Supervision: Lloyd Kenwood, Joe Way. Acknowledgment: U.S. Bureau of Sport Fisheries and Wildlife.

WILD HEART
Co-producer: James Algar. Teleplay by: Jack Couffer, Homer McCoy. Narration by: James Algar. Based on the book by: Emma-Lindsay Squier. Narrator: Leslie Nielsen. Film Editor: Gordon Brenner. Music: Buddy Baker. World of Color Theme: Richard M. Sherman, Robert B. Sherman. Production Manager: Erwin L. Verity. Sound: Robert O. Cook. Program Coordinator: Jack Bruner. For Grey Owl Productions, Inc. Directed by: Jack Couffer. Photography: Lloyd G. Kenwood. Production Manager: Pieter Hubbard. Wildlife Consultants: Mike Guinn, Joe J. Way.

WILD HORSE REVENGE
Directed by: Harry Keller. Written by: Fred Freiberger. Produced by: James Pratt. Director of Photography: William Snyder, A.S.C. Art Director: Stan Jolley. Film Editor: Robert Stafford. Music: William Lava, Frank J. Worth. Song: David Harmon, Buddy Baker. Sound: Robert O. Cook. Set Decoration: Emile Kuri, William L. Stevens. Costumer: Chuck Keehne. Make-up: Pat McNalley. Hair Stylist: Ruth Sandifer. Assistant Director: Joseph L. McEveety.

WILD JACK (#1)
Supervising Producer: Garner Simmons. Produced by: Michael S. McLean. Created by: Brian Rehak. Teleplay by: William Blinn. Story by: Brian Rehak, William Blinn. Directed by: Harry Harris. Executive producer: William Blinn. Original Score by: Phil Marshall. Director of Photography: King Baggot. Art Director: Ira Diamond. Editor: Howard Kunin, A.C.E. Unit Production Manager: Ron Mitchell. First Assistant Director: Irwin Marcus. Second Assistant Director: Claudia Sills. Casting by: Peg Halligan, C.S.A. Costumes Designed by: Tom Bronson. Set Decorator: Sam Gross. Property Master: Tracy Farrington. Key Costumers: Nancy McArdle, Bill Tiegs. Make-up: Jim McCoy. Hair Stylist: Gregg Mitchell. Location Manager: Peter M. Robarts. Script Supervisor: Alleen N. Nollmann. Production Coordinator: Lark Bernini. Special Effects Coordinator: Bruce Mattox. Stunt Coordinator: Ernie Orsatti. Animals Owned by: Dennis Grisco. Trained by: Jungle Exotics. Production Sound Mixer: Joe Kenworthy, C.A.S. Sound Editing by: Dimension Sound. Music Editing by: Segue Music, Inc. Echo Cove Productions in association with Walt Disney Television.

WILD JACK (#2)
Supervising Producer: Garner Simmons. Produced by: Michael S. McLean. Created by: Brian Rehak. Written by: Garner Simmons. Directed by: James Quinn. Executive producer: William Blinn. Original Score by: Phil Marshall. Director of Photography: King Baggot. Art Director: Ira Diamond. Editor: Diane Adler. Unit Production Manager: Ron Mitchell. First Assistant Director: Joan Van Horn. Second Assistant Director: Claudia Sills. Casting by: Peg Halligan, C.S.A. Costumes Designed by: Tom Bronson. Set Decorator: Ethel Robins Richards. Property Master: Tracy Farrington. Key Costumers: Nancy McArdle, Bill Tiegs. Make-up: Jim McCoy. Hair Stylist: Gregg Mitchell. Location Manager: Peter M. Robarts. Script Supervisor: Alleen N. Nollmann. Production Coordinator: Lark Bernini. Special Effects Coordinator: Bruce Mattox. Stunt Coordinator: Ernie Orsatti. Animals Owned and Trained by: Jungle Exotics. Production Sound Mixer: Joe Kenworthy, C.A.S. Sound Editing by: Dimension Sound. Music Editing by: Segue Music, Inc. Echo Cove Productions in association with Walt Disney Television.

WILD JACK (#3)
Supervising Producer: Garner Simmons. Produced by: Michael S. McLean. Created by: Brian Rehak. Teleplay by:

William Blinn. Written by: Garner Simmons. Directed by: Harry Harris. Executive Producer: William Blinn. Original Score by: Phil Marshall. Director of Photography: King Baggot. Art Director: Ira Diamond. Editor: Howard Kunin, A.C.E. Unit Production Manager: Ron Mitchell. First Assistant Director: Irwin Marcus. Second Assistant Director: Claudia Sills. Casting by: Peg Halligan, C.S.A. Costumes Designed by: Tom Bronson. Set Decorator: Ethel Robins Richards. Property Master: Tracy Farrington. Key Costumers: Nancy McArdle, Bill Tiegs. Make-up: Jim McCoy. Hair Stylist: Gregg Mitchell. Location Manager: Peter M. Robarts. Script Supervisor: Alleen N. Nollmann. Production Coordinator: Lark Bernini. Special Effects Coordinator: Bruce Mattox. Stunt Coordinator: Ernie Orsatti. Animals Owned and Trained by: Jungle Exotics. Production Sound Mixer: Joe Kenworthy, C.A.S. Sound Editing by: Dimension Sound. Music Editing by: Segue Music, Inc. Echo Cove Productions in association with Walt Disney Television.

WILDERNESS ROAD, THE
Teleplay and Directed by: Lewis R. Foster. Based on the book *Daniel Boone* by: John Bakeless. Produced by: Bill Anderson. Associate Producer: Louis Debney. Director of Photography: Edward Colman, A.S.C. Art Director: Marvin Aubrey Davis. Film Editor: Cotton Warburton, A.C.E. Music: Buddy Baker. Song: David Victor, George Bruns. Matte Artist: Albert Whitlock. Sound: Robert O. Cook. Set Decoration: Emile Kuri. Costumer: Chuck Keehne. Make-up: Pat McNalley. Unit Manager: Roy Wade. Assistant Director: Joseph L. McEveety.

WILLIE AND THE YANK
Co-producer: Bill Anderson. Written by: Harold Swanton. Directed by: Michael O'Herlihy. Assistant to the Producer: Louis Debney. Director of Photography: Frank Phillips, A.S.C. Art Directors: Carroll Clark, William H. Tuntke. Film Editors: Cotton Warburton, A.C.E., Robert Stafford, A.C.E. Set Decorators: Emile Kuri, Bill Calvert. Music: George Bruns. *World of Color* Theme: Richard M. Sherman, Robert B. Sherman. Costumer: Chuck Keehne. Make-up: Pat McNalley. Hair Stylist: La Rue Matheron. Sound: Robert O. Cook. Assistant Director: John C. Chulay. Program Co-ordinator: Jack Bruner.

WOMAN'S COURAGE, A
Teleplay and Directed by: Lewis R. Foster. Based on the Book by: Dr. Robert D. Bass. Produced by: Bill Anderson. Associate Producer: Ron Miller. Director of Photography: Lucien Ballard, A.S.C. Art Director: Marvin Aubrey Davis. Film Editor: Robert Stafford. Music: Buddy Baker. Songs: Lew Foster, Buddy Baker. Sound: Robert O. Cook. Set Decoration: Emile Kuri, William L. Stevens. Costumer: Chuck Keehne. Make-up: Pat McNalley. Hair Stylist: Ruth Sandifer. Unit Manager: Roy Wade. Assistant Director: Joseph L. McEveety.

WONDERS OF THE WATER WORLD
Produced, Narrated and Directed by: Winston Hibler. Narration Written by: Roy Edward Disney. Photography: William Carrick, Karl H. Maslowski, Dick Borden, Lloyd Beebe, Al Hanson, Harry Pederson, Verne Pederson, William H. Anderson, Cecil Rhode and the Disney Staff of Naturalist Photographers. Production Supervision: Erwin L. Verity. Film Editor: George Gale, A.C.E. Music: Paul Smith. Sound: Robert O. Cook. Acknowledgment: Marine Studios, Marineland, Florida.

YELLOWSTONE STORY (AND) BEAR COUNTRY
Directed by: James Algar. *The Yellowstone Story* Directed by: James Algar. Narration Written by: James Algar, Lee Chaney. Music: Oliver Wallace. Photographer: Stuart Jewell. Narrator: James Algar. Film Editor: Anthony Gerard. *Bear Country* Narration Written by: James Algar. Music: Paul Smith. Photographers: Alfred G. Milotte, James R. Simon, Tom McHugh. Narrator: Winston Hibler. Film Editor: Lloyd Richardson. Special Processes: Ub Iwerks, A.S.C. Sound: Robert O. Cook. Production Supervision: Harry Tytle. Acknowledgments: National Park Service, Yellowstone National Park, Montana Fish and Game Department.

YOU RUINED MY LIFE
Original Score by: Jonathan Tunick. Editors: Arthur Schmidt, Barbara Dixon. Art Director: Jack DeShields. Director of Photography: Ric Waite, A.S.C. Executive Producers: Alex Winitsky, Arlene Sellers, Robert Kosberg. Produced by: Mark H. Ovitz, Dylan Sellers. Written by: Robin Swicord. Directed by: David Ashwell. Unit Production Manager: Albert J. Salzer. First Assistant Director: David Menteer. Second Assistant Director: Scott Cameron. Los Angeles Casting by: Marci Liroff. Costume Designer: William Ware Theiss. Set Decorator: Rochelle Moser. Property Master: Roger Pancake. Key Costumers: Dawn Jackson, Joseph Markham. Make-up: Don L. Cash. Hair Stylist: Eddie Barron Smith. Assistant to Mr. Ovitz: Cheryl Denise Edwards. Las Vegas Casting by: Eddie Foy. Location Manager: Geoffrey R. Smith. Script Supervisor: Janna Stern. Production Coordinator: Diane Katz. Production Sound Mixer: William R. Teague. Sound Editing by: Stephen J. Cannell Productions, Michael O'Corrigan. Music Editing by: Robert E. Post. Location Site and Accommodations Provided by: Caesar's Palace. A Lantana/Kosbery and Mark H. Ovitz Production.

YOUNG AGAIN
Music Composed and Conducted by: James Di Pasquale. Edited by: Ron Wisman. Art Director: Tony Hall. Director of Photography: Laszlo George, CSC. Teleplay by: Barbara Hall. Story by: Steven H. Stern, David Simon. Produced and Directed by: Steven H. Stern. Ballet dancers appear courtesy of the Royal Winnipeg ballet. Stunts: R.L. (Bobby) Hannah, Alan Angus. Production Supervisor: John Danylkiw. 1st Assistant Director: Michael Zenon. 2nd Assistant Director: Rocco Gismondi. 3rd Assistant Director: David Flaherty. Casting—Toronto: Stuart Aikens. Casting—Los Angeles: Judith Holstra. Set Decorator: Sean Kirby. Assistant Film Editor: Stephen Humble. Sound Editors: Jim Hopkins, Charles Bowers. Music Editor: Else Blangsted. Assistant Editors: Cathy Hutton, Michele Cook, Jan Nicolichuk. Location Manager: Sherry Cohen. Production Co-ordinator: Sandra Webb. Costume Designer: Lynda Kemp. Wardrobe Mistress: Madelaine Stewart. Make-up: Linda Gill. Hair Stylist: David Beecroft. Script Supervisor: Elaine Yarish. Props Master: John "Frenchie" Berger. Production Sound Mixer: Richard Lightstone. Sound Re-recording: Jack Heeren. Transportation Co-ordinator: Stuart Hughes. Colour Timer: Chris Hinton. Title Design: Vlad Goetzelman. *Burning Up* and *Luckystar* Words and Music by: Madonna Ciccone. Performed by: Gail Lennon. *I'll Fall in Love Again* Words and Music by: Sammy Hagar. Performed by: Tommy Funderburk. *Life in One Day* and *Things Can Only Get Better* Words and Music by: Howard Jones. Performed by: Kipp Lennon. *The Search Is Over* Words and Music by: Jim Peterik, Frankie Sullivan. Performed by: Gene Miller. *Shout* Words and Music by: O. Kelly Isley, Ronald Isley, Rudolph Isley. Performed by: Jim Gilstrap. A Sharmhill Productions Inc. Film.

YOUNG HARRY HOUDINI
Original Score by: Lee Holdridge. Editors: Norman Hollyn, Robert Estrin, A.C.E. Art Director: James Shanahan. Director of Photography: Paul Lohmann. Producers: James Orr, Jim Cruickshank. Executive Producer: Susan B. Landau. Written by: James Orr, Jim Cruickshank. Directed by: James Orr. Unit Production Manager: Lynn H. Guthrie. First Assistant Director: John M. Poer. Second Assistant Director: John N. Whittle. Casting by: Joyce Robinson, C.S.A., Penny Ellers, C.S.A. Costume Designer: William Ware Theiss. Set Decorator: C. Michael Korian. Property Master: Kent H. Johnson. Key Costumers: Frances Harrison Hays, Bud Clark. Make-up: Carol Schwartz. Hair Stylist: Edie Panda. Technical Advisor: Doug Henning Magic. Location Manager: Binnie Ruben. Script Supervisor: Alleen N. Nollmann. Production Coordinator: Robin E. Birnie. Production Sound Mixer: Pat Mitchell. Sound Editing by: Stephen J. Cannell Productions/Dick Wahrman. Music Editing by: Segue Music, Inc./Dan C. Garde.

YOUNG LONER, THE
Produced by: Bill Anderson. Teleplay by: Lowell S. Hawley. Based on *The Loner* by: Ester Wier. Directed by: Michael O'Herlihy. Directors of Photography: Frank Phillips, A.S.C.,

William Snyder, A.S.C. Art Director: Carroll Clark, Dean Tavoularis. Film Editor: Cotton Warburton, A.C.E. Associate Producer: Peter V. Herald. Set Decorators: Emile Kuri, Hal Gausman. Costumer: Chuck Keehne. Make-up: Otis Malcolm. Hair Stylist: La Rue Matheron. Music: George Bruns. Songs: Richard M. Sherman, Robert B. Sherman. Assistant Director: Paul L. Cameron. Sound: Robert O. Cook. Program Co-ordinator: Jack Bruner.

YOUNG RUNAWAYS, THE
Art Directors: John B. Mansbridge, Jack Senter. Editor: Bob Bring, A.C.E. Production Manager: John Bloss. Unit Production Manager/Assistant Director: Christopher Seiter. Second Assistant Director: Dan Steinbrocker. Set Decorator: Sharon Thomas. Sound Supervisor: Herb Taylor. Sound Mixer: Gregory Valtierra. Stunt Coordinator: Glenn Wilder. Costumes: Chuck Keehne, Emily Sundby. Make-up: Robert J. Schiffer. Hair Stylist: Donna Turner. Sound Editor: Ben F. Hendricks.

Music Editor: Jack Wadsworth. Music: Robert F. Brunner. Orchestration: Walter Sheets. Director of Photography: Charles F. Wheeler, A.S.C. Executive Producer: Ron Miller. Produced by: Jerome Courtland. Written by: Sy Gomberg. Directed by: Russ Mayberry.

YOUR HOST, DONALD DUCK
Directed by: Jack Hannah. Animation: Bob Carlson, George Kreisl, Al Coe, Roy Jenkins, Volus Jones, Bill Justice, Hal King. Story: Albert Bertino, Dave Detiege, Ray Patin, Bill Berg. Music: Joseph S. Dubin, Oliver Wallace, Paul Smith. Layout: Yale Gracey. Backgrounds: Ray Huffine, Claude Coats, Ralph Hulett, Thelma Witmer. Art Director: Marvin Aubrey Davis. Photographer: Charles P. Boyle, A.S.C. Set Decorator: Emile Kuri. Film Editor: Tom Acosta. Assistant Director: William Beaudine, Jr. Special Processes: Ub Iwerks, A.S.C. Sound: Robert O. Cook. Production Supervision: Harry Tytle.

CHAPTER 5

The Mickey Mouse Club

The large number of episodes makes it impossible to list here all of the credits for individual shows. Instead, the following list includes the official Studio summary of the credits. Although Walt Disney was never officially credited for his work on *The Mickey Mouse Club*, he was the Executive Producer.

Producer: Bill Walsh. Associate Producers: Mike Holoboff, Louis Debney, Tommy Walker, Malcolm Stuart Boylan. General Coordinators: Herbert Knapp, Hal Adelquist, Chuck Dargan. Directors: Sidney Miller, Dik Darley, Jonathan Lucas, William Beaudine Jr., Charles Haas, Larry Lansburgh, Charles Shows, Robert O. Shannon, R.G. Springsteen, Edward Sampson, Charles Barton, Bob Lehman, Fred Hartsook, Montie Montana, Charles Lamont, Hamilton S. Luske, Clyde Geronimi, Tommy Walker. Assistant Directors: Jack Cunningham, William Beaudine Jr., Dolph Zimmer, Russ Haverick, Horace Hough, Erich von Stroheim Jr., Vincent McEveety, Joseph L. McEveety, Tommy Foulkes, Les Gorall, Bill Finnegan, Les Philmer, Art Vitarelli, Gene Law. Cameramen (Directors of Photography): Gordon Avil A.S.C., Edward Coleman A.S.C., Walter H. Castle A.S.C., John Martin, W. W. Goodpaster, Karl Maslowski, Herbert Knapp, Frederick Gately, Al Runkie, Doane R. Hoag, Lloyd Mason Smith, Tad Nichols, J. Carlos Carbajal, Charles P. Boyle A.S.C., Arthur J. Ornitz. Film Editors: Cotton Warburton A.C.E., Al Teeter, Joseph S. Dietrick, George Nicholson, John O. Young, Lee Huntington, Robert Stafford, George Gale A.S.C., Jack Vandagriff, Ed Sampson, Jim Love, Wayne Hughes, Laurie Vejar, Edward R. Baker, Lloyd Richardson, Hugh Chaloupka Jr., Ernest Palmer, Carlos Savage, Ellsworth Hoagland A.C.E., Anthony Gerard, Stanley Johnson A.C.E., Bill Lewis, Paul Capon. Special Processes: Ub Iwerks A.S.C., Eustace Lycett. Music: Buddy Baker, Franklyn Marks, Joseph S. Dubin, William Lava, Joseph Mullendore, Paul Smith, Oliver Wallace, Herman D. Koppel, Clifford Vaughn, Frank Worth, Richard Aurandt, Jaime Mendoza Nava, Temple Abady, Edward Plumb. Songs: Jimmie Dodd, Gil George, Charles Shows, Tom Adair, Larry Orenstein, Bob Amsberry, Ruth Carrell, Stan Jones, Larry Adelson, Roy Williams, Martin Schwab, Imogene Carpenter, Oliver Wallace, Cliff Edwards, Franklyn Marks, Sam Sykens, Bob Russell, Ray Darby, George Bruns, Jack Speirs, Paul Smith, Muzzy Marceleno, Erdman Penner, Larry Morey, Elliot Daniel, Frances Jeffords, Sidney Fine, Ron Salt, Jeanne Gayle, Ed Penner, Mack David, Al Hoffman, Jerry Livingston, Marvin Ash, Ray Brenne, Bob Russell, Carl Sigman, Bob Jackman, Fess Parker, Buddy Ebsen. Conductor: Leo Damiani of the Burbank Symphony. Animation: Due to the numerous credits for the shorts aired on *The Mickey Mouse Club*, animation credits are not included. Sound: Robert O. Cook, Sid A. Manor. Re-Recording Editor: Reese Overacker. Choreography: Tom Mahoney, Burch Holtzman. Art Directors: Bruce Bushman, Marvin Aubrey Davis, Carroll Clark. Set Decoration: Bertram Granger, Fred Maclean, Emil Kuri, William L. Stevens, Vin Taylor, Armor E. Goetten. Costumes: Chuck Keehne. Make-up: Pat Mcnalley, Tom Bartholomew, David Newell, Joe Hadley. Facilities Coordinator: Ben Harris. Production Managers: Ben Chapman, Mike Holoboff, Douglas

Peirce. Production Supervisors: Mike Holoboff, Lou Debney, Perce Pearce, Alan L. Jaggs, Stirling Silliphant, Bill Park, Hal Ramser, Charles Shows, Ben Sharpsteen, Harry Tytle, Jack Cutting, Gene Armstrong, Larry Clemens. Technical Facilities: Mark Amistead TV, Inc. Writers: Lillie Hayward, Lee Chaney, Bill Cox, Jackson Gillis, John and Rosalie Bodrero, Astrid Henning, Charles Haas, Larry Clemens, Janet Lansburgh.

The Mickey Mouse Club Serials
FIRST SEASON 1955–1956

ADVENTURES OF SPIN AND MARTY, THE
Executive Producer: Walt Disney. Produced by: Bill Walsh. Assistant to the Producer: Louis Debney. Production Manager: Ben Chapman. Directed by: William Beaudine, Sr. Assistant Directors: Robert G. Shannon, William Beaudine, Jr., Vincent McEveety. Written by: Lillie Hayward. Teleplay by: Jackson Gillis. Based on the book *Marty Markham* by: Lawrence Edward Watkin. Directors of Photography: Edward Colman, A.S.C., Gordon Avil, A.S.C. Film Editors: Cotton Warburton, A.C.E., Al Teeter, A.C.E., George Nicholson, A.C.E., Joseph S. Dietrick. Art Directors: Bruce Bushman, Marvin Aubrey Davis. Theme Song: Bob Jackman, William Lava. Music: Paul Smith, Buddy Baker. Sound: Robert O. Cook. Set Decorators: Bertram Granger, Fred MacLean. Costumer: Chuck Keehne. Make-up: Joe Hadley.

ANIMAL AUTOBIOGRAPHY
Narration Written by: Charles Shows. Narrated by: Bob Johnson *(The Buffalo)*, Dallas McKennon *(The Coyote)*, June Foray *(The Black Bear)*, Richard Beals *(The Prairie Dog)*, Bob Johnson *(The King of Beasts, The Mountain Lion)*, Sterling Holloway *(The Giraffe)*.

BORDER COLLIE
Executive Producer: Walt Disney. Produced by: Bill Walsh. Written by: Bill Cox. Directed by: Larry Lansburgh. Music: William Lava. Sound: Robert O. Cook.

CHRISTMAS 'ROUND THE WORLD
Produced by: Bill Walsh. Narration Written by: Ray Darby. Directed by: Edwards Sampson.

CORKY AND WHITE SHADOW
Executive Producer: Walt Disney. Produced by: Bill Walsh. Directed by: William Beaudine, Sr. Written by: Lillie Hayward, William Beaudine. Director of Photography: John Martin, A.S.C. Art Director: Marvin Aubrey Davis. Film Editor: Cotton Warburton, A.C.E. Music: Paul Smith, Clifford Vaughan. Song: Gil George, Paul Smith. Sound: Robert O. Cook. Set Decoration: Bertram Granger. Costumer: Chuck Keene. Make-up: David Newell. Assistant Directors: William Beaudine, Jr., Jack Cunningham. Production Manager: Ben Chapman. Theme Song: William Lava.

ITALIAN CORRESPONDENT
Narration Written by: Ray Darby.

JAPANESE CORRESPONDENT
Narration Written by: Ray Darby.

LET'S GO SERIES
Executive Producer: Walt Disney. Produced by: Bill Walsh. Directed by: Al Teeter. Photographers: Lloyd Mason Smith, Lee Chaney, Tad Nichols, Duane R. Hoag. Narration Written by: Lee Chaney. Film Editors: John O. Young, Robert Stafford, Lee Huntington. Sound: Robert O. Cook.

MEXICAN CORRESPONDENT
Narration Written by: Janet Lansburgh. Directed by: Larry Lansburgh. Music: Juan Garcia Esquivel.

SAN JUAN RIVER EXPEDITION
Produced by: Bill Walsh. Director: Al Teeter. Narration Written by: Lee Chaney. Cameramen: Tad Nichols, Lloyd Mason Smith. Film Editor: Robert Stafford. Music: Franklyn Marks. Song: Bill Walsh, Al Teeter. Sound: Robert O. Cook. Production Supervisor: Al Teeter.

WHAT I WANT TO BE
Executive Producer: Walt Disney. Produced by: Bill Walsh. Written by: Stirling Silliphant. Directed by: Charles Haas. Theme Song: William Lava. Art Director: Marvin Aubrey Davis. Director of Photography: Edward Colman, A.S.C. Film Editor: Ellsworth Hoagland, A.C.E. Sound: Robert O. Cook. Assistant Director: Gordon McLean.

SECOND SEASON 1956–1957

ADVENTURE IN DAIRYLAND
Executive Producer: Walt Disney. Produced by: Bill Walsh. Directed by: William Beaudine. Written by: Lillie Hayward. Director of Photography: Walter H. Castle, A.S.C. Art Director: Marvin Aubrey Davis. Film Editor: Stanley Johnson. Music: William Lava. Songs: Rudy Burkhalter. Special Processes: Ub Iwerks, A.S.C. Sound: Robert O. Cook. Set Decoration: Fred MacLean. Costumer: Chuck Keehne. Make-up: Pat McNalley. Unit Manager: Russ Haverick. Assistant Director: William Beaudine, Jr.

ANIMAL AUTOBIOGRAPHY
Narration Written by: Charles Shows.

BOYS OF THE WESTERN SEA, THE
Voice Credits: Richard Beymer (Paul Brask), Paul Frees (Father, Carl and Sheriff), Billy Bletcher (Brenner, Pelican, Man with Cap, Skipper), Herbert Vigran (Salesman, Foreman, Team Leader), Mary Lee Hobb (Else), Tommy Kirk (Andy and Boy), Bob Ellis (Gordon and Boy), Bobby Burgess (Boy), Lonnie Burr (Boy), Tommy Cole (Boy), Kevin Corcoran (Mads), Parley Baer (Frederick and Grocer), David Stollery (Frank), Gail Bonney (Mother Karen), Bob Jackman (Boat Builder, Man with Cap), Cheryl Holdridge (Bridget).
    Written by: Astrid Henning-Jensen. Directed by: Bjarne Henning-Jensen. From the book Klit Per by: A.C. Westergaard. Music by: Herman D. Koppel. Photography: Arthur J. Ornitz, Jorgen Skov, Poul Petersen. Assistant Director: John Hilbert Larsen. Sound: Hans Olsson, Jens E. Hansen. Scriptgirl: Kirsten Schou. English Dialogue by: Ray Darby. Music: Herman D. Koppel.

CHILDREN OF THE WORLD, PART 1: CHILDREN OF THE ARCTIC
Directed by: Charles Shows. Photography by: Alfred and Elma Milotte. Narration Written by: Charles Shows.

CHILDREN OF THE WORLD, PART 2: CHILDREN OF SIAM
Directed by: Charles Shows. Photography by: Herbert Knapp. Narration Written by: Charles Shows.

CHRISTMAS 'ROUND THE WORLD
Narration Written by: Ray Darby. Directed by: Edwards Sampson.

EAGLE HUNTERS, THE
Directed by: C. August Nichols. Narration Written by: Lee Chaney. Produced by: Bill Walsh. Director of Photography: Gordon Avil, A.S.C. Art Director: Bruce Bushman. Film Editor: Lee Huntington. Music: Frank Worth. Sound: Robert O. Cook. Set Decoration: Fred MacLean. Costumer: Chuck Keehne. Make-up: Tom Bartholmew. Assistant Director: Dolph M. Zimmer.

FIRST AMERICANS, THE
Directed by: Charles Shows. Narration Written by: Charles Shows. Produced by: Bill Walsh. Special Art Work: Ken Hultgren.

FURTHER ADVENTURES OF SPIN AND MARTY
Executive Producer: Walt Disney. Produced by: Bill Walsh. Directed by: William Beaudine, Sr., Fred Hartsook. Screenplay by: Jackson Gillis. Based on the book Marty Markham by: Lawrence Edward Watkin. Associate Producers: Louis Debney, Tommy Walker. Production Manager: John Grubbs. Assistant Director: Russ Haverick. Art Directors: Marvin Aubrey Davis, Bruce Bushman. Cameraman: Gordon Avil, A.S.C., Walter H. Castle, A.S.C. Make-up: Dave Newell. Hair Stylist: Ruth Sandifer. Wardrobe: Chuck Keehne. Film Editors: Irvin "Cotton" Warburton, Joseph S. Dietrick, Jim Love. Set Decorators: Bertram Granger, Emile Kuri. Music: Buddy Baker, Joseph S. Dubin, William Lava, Franklyn Marks, Oliver Wallace. Theme: William Lava. Sound: Robert O. Cook. Assistant Directors: Jack Cunningham, Bill Finnegan, Tommy Foulkes, Russ Haverick, Gene Law, Eric Von Stroheim, Jr. Facilities Coordinator: Ben Harris. Production Coordinator: Charles Dargan.

JAPANESE CORRESPONDENT
Narration Written by: Ray Darby.

JUNIOR SAFARI TO AFRICA
Directed by: Edward Sampson. Narration Written by: Ray Darby. Produced by: Bill Walsh. Photography by: Walter Castle, A.S.C. Film Editor: Anthony Gerard.

MOUSEKATOUR TO SAMOA, A
Produced by: Bill Walsh. Narration Written by: Ray Darby.

MYSTERY OF THE APPLEGATE TREASURE, THE
Executive Producer: Walt Disney. Produced by: Bill Walsh. Directed by: Charles Haas. Teleplay by: Jackson Gillis. Based on The Tower Treasure by: Franklin W. Dixon. Assistant to the Producer: Lou Debney. Directors of Photography: Gordon Avil, A.S.C., Walter H. Castle, A.S.C. Art Directors: Bruce Bushman, Marvin Aubrey Davis. Film Editors: George Nicholson, Ellsworth Hoagland, A.C.E., Al Teeter, Joseph S. Dietrick. Music: Buddy Baker, William Lava. Theme Gold Doubloons and Pieces of Eight: Jackson Gillis (words), George Bruns (music). Special Processes: Ub Iwerks, A.S.C. Sound: Robert O. Cook. Sound Mixer: Dean Thomas. Set Decoration: Fred MacLean. Costumer: Chuck Keehne. Wardrobe: Carl Walker. Make-up: David Newell. Hair Stylist: Lois Murray. Assistant Director: Robert G. Shannon. Production Manager: Russ Haverick.

SECRET OF MYSTERY LAKE, THE
Directed by: Larry Lansburgh. Screenplay by: John and Rosalie Bodrero. From an Original Story by: Janet Lansburgh. Produced by: Bill Walsh. Executive Producer: Walt Disney. Art Director: Bruce Bushman. Photographed by: Karl Maslowski, W.W. Goodpaster. Music: William Lava. Sound: Robert O. Cook.

SIERRA PACK TRIP
Executive Producer: Walt Disney. Produced by: Bill Walsh. Directed by: William Beaudine. Narration Written by: Lee Chaney. Director of Photography: Walter H. Castle, A.S.C. Art Director: Bruce Bushman. Film Editor: Lee Huntington. Music: Franklyn Marks. Song Along the High Sierra Trail by: Lee Chaney, Al Teeter. Sung by: Jerry Courtland. Sound: Robert O. Cook. Set Decoration: Fred MacLean. Costumer: Chuck Keehne. Make-up: David Newell. Assistant Director: William Beaudine, Jr.

THIRD SEASON 1957–1958

ADVENTURES OF CLINT AND MAC, THE
Directed by: Terrence Fisher. Produced by: Bill Walsh. Teleplay by: Malcolm Stuart Boylan. Associate Producer: Alan L. Jaggs. Music: Temple Abady. Narrator: Tim Considine.

ANNETTE
Executive Producer: Walt Disney. Produced by: Bill Walsh. Directed by: Charles Lamont. Teleplay by: Lillie Hayward. Based on the book *Margaret* by: Janette Sebring Lowrey. Production Manager: John Grubbs. Assistant Director: Russ Haverick. Cameramen: Frederick Gately, A.S.C., Walter H. Castle, A.S.C. Art Directors: Marvin Aubrey Davis, Stan Jolly. Make-up: Pat McNalley. Hair Stylist: Eve Newing. Wardrobe: Chuck Keehne. Film Editors: Ed Sampson, Al Teeter, Wayne Hughes, Robert Stafford. Set Decorators: Emile Kuri, Armor E. Goetten. Music: Buddy Baker, Oliver Wallace, Joseph Mullendore. Theme Song: Jimmie Dodd. Song *Don't Jump to Conclusions:* Tom Adair, Buddy Baker. Songs: Tom Adair, Buddy Baker, Franklyn Marks, Bob Jackman, Bill Walsh. Sound: Robert O. Cook. Choreographer: Tom Mahoney. Assistant Directors: Russ Haverick, Dolph M. Zimmer, Arthur Vitarelli. Production Supervisor: Mike Holoboff.

MYSTERY OF GHOST FARM, THE
Executive Producer: Walt Disney. Produced by: Bill Walsh. Directed by: Robert Springsteen. Script by: Jackson Gillis. Based on Characters Created by: Franklin W. Dixon. Production Manager: John Grubbs. Assistant Director: Horace Hough. Art Director: Marvin Aubrey Davis. Cameraman: Gordon Avil. Sound Mixer: Dean Thomas. Make-up: Pat McNalley. Wardrobe: Chuck Keehne. Hair Stylist: Elaine Stone. Film Editor: Ed Sampson.

NEW ADVENTURES OF SPIN AND MARTY, THE
Executive Producer: Walt Disney. Produced by: Bill Walsh. Directed by: Charles Barton. Screenplay by: Lillie Hayward. Based on the book *Marty Markham* by: Lawrence Edward Watkin. Theme: William Lava. Music: Buddy Baker, Joseph Mullendore, Oliver Wallace. Songs: Tom Adair, Marvin Ash, Gil Bruns, Ray Darby, Jeanne Gale, Gil George, Stan Jones, Franklyn Marks, Sidney Miller, Paul Smith, Bill Walsh. Assistant Director: Art Vitarelli. Art Directors: Bruce Bushman, Marvin Aubrey Davis. Cameramen: Walter H. Castle, A.S.C., Gordon Avil, A.S.C. Film Editors: Joseph S. Dietrick, George Gale, A.C.E., Wayne Hughes, Ed Sampson, Robert Stafford, Al Teeter, Jack M. Vandagriff. Set Decorators: Armor E. Goetten, Emile Kuri. Costumer: Chuck Keehne. Make-up: Pat McNalley. Sound: Robert O. Cook. Assistant Directors: Arthur Vitarelli, Dolph M. Zimmer. Production Supervisor: Mike Holoboff.

FOURTH SEASON 1958–1959

ADVENTURE IN THE MAGIC KINGDOM, AN
Directed by: Hamilton S. Luske. Narration Written by: Larry Clemmons. Director of Photography: Charles P. Boyle, A.S.C. Film Editor: Lloyd L. Richardson, A.C.E. Music: Buddy Baker. Special Processes: Eustace Lycett. Sound: Robert O. Cook. Assistant Director: Horace Hough. Production Supervisor: Harry Tytle. Animation: Cliff Nordberg, Bob McCrea, Jack Boyd. Layout: Al Zinnen, Thor Putnam.

CHAPTER 7

The New Mickey Mouse Club

THE NEW MICKEY MOUSE CLUB
Directed by: John Tracy, Dick Amos, James Field, Dick Krown. Written by: Tedd Anasti, David Talisman, Marc B. Ray, Ron Bastone. Produced by: Ed Ropolo, Mike Wuergler. Associate Producer: Dick Krown. Art Directors: John B. Mansbridge, Leroy G. Deane. Set Decorator: Lucien M. Hafley. Costume Designer: Betty Pecha Madden. Make-up: Robert J. Schiffer. Hair Stylists: Eddie Barron, La Rue Matheron. Technical Supervisor: Randy Blim. Technical Director: Robert C. Jones. Lighting Directors: Jeff Chang, Christopher Lynch. Video Engineer: Chuck Reilly. Audio Engineers: Jack Tossman, Doc Siegel. Videotape Editors: Arthur Schneider, A.C.E., Chip Brooks, Mario DiMambro, Don Johnson, Jim Rose, Marco Zappia. Post-Production: Hank Saroyan. Talent Coordinator: Virginia Martindale. Associate Director: Shelley Jensen. Stage Managers: Gene Sultan, Neil Gordon. Production Coordinators: Sheila Gillis, Carol Kahl. Production Assistants: Bob Sutton, Sheila Gillis, Eddie Lui, Donovan D. Moye, Marjorie Wollman, Theme Animation: Bob McCrea. Songs: *Showtime Day:* Marc B. Ray, Peter Martin. *Discovery Day:* Gary Graf, Peter Martin (there was also another version by Al Kasha and Joel Hirschhorn). *The Who, What, Why, Where, When and How Day:* Marc B. Ray, Peter Martin. *Mouseketeer Surprise Day:* Gary Graf, Peter Martin. *Let's Discover Discovery Day:* Al Kasha, Joel Hirschhorn. *Let's Go Day:* Marc B. Ray, Peter Martin. Musical Supervisor: Robert F. Brunner. Music: Buddy Baker, Robert F. Brunner, Will Schaefer. Choreography: Norine Xavier, Judy and Jim Bates. Vocal Coach: Sheryl Ford. Teacher/Social Worker: Dick Wicklund. Videotape Facilities by: Pacific Video Industries, Inc. Executive Producer: Ron Miller.

MYSTERY OF RUSTLER'S CAVE, THE
Executive Producer: Ron Miller. Teleplay by: Harry Spalding. Based on an story by: Christopher Hibler, Michael Beche. Produced and Directed by: Tom Leetch. Director of Photography: William Cronjagger, A.C.E. Art Director: Kirk Axtell. Film Editor: Ray de Leuw, A.C.E. Set Decorator: Norman Rockett. Music: George Duning. Sound: Herb Taylor. Associate Producer: Kevin Corcoran. Costumes: Chuck Keehne. Make-up: Robert J. Schiffer. Hair Stylist: Mary Hadley. Unit Production Manager/Assistant Director: Michael Dmytryk. Second Assistant Director: Dorothy Kieffer.

CHAPTER 8

Zorro

Directed by: Charles Barton, Lewis R. Foster, Norman Foster, Harmon Jones, Charles Lamont, John Meredyth Lucas, Hollingsworth Morse, Robert Stevenson, William Witney. Teleplay by: Robert Bloomfield, Malcolm S. Boyland, Gene L. Coon, Antony Ellis, Lewis R. Foster, Norman Foster, Jackson Gillis, Lowell S. Hawley, Maury Hill, David Lang, John Meredyth Lucas, Robert B. Shaw, N.B. Stone, Jr., Bob Wehling. Television Story by: Joel Kane. Based on the *Zorro* stories by: Johnston McCulley. Story Editor: Lowell S. Hawley. Associate Producer: William H. Anderson. Produced by: William H. Anderson. Music: William Lava. Title Song *Zorro* by: George Bruns, Norman Foster. Songs: Gil George, Joseph S. Dubin, Tom Adair, Buddy Baker, Norman Foster, George Bruns, Jimmie Dodd, N.B. Stone, Jr., Lowell S. Hawley. Art Director: Marvin Aubrey Davis. Director of Photography: Gordon Avil, A.S.C. Film Editors: Roy Livingston, A.C.E., Hugh Chaloupka, Cotton Warburton, A.C.E., George Gale, A.C.E., Ed Sampson, Al Teeter, Robert Stafford. Set Decoration: Emile Kuri, Hal Gausman. Costumer: Chuck Keehne. Make-up: Pat McNalley. Matte Artists: Albert Whitlock, Peter Ellenshaw. Sound: Robert O. Cook. Unit Managers: Roy Wade, Russ Haverick. Fencing Master: Fred Cavens. Assistant Directors: Vincent McEveety, Russ Haverick, Joseph L. McEveety, Arthur J. Vitarelli, William F. Sheehan, R.W. (Ron) Miller, Robert G. Shannon. Production Coordinator: Louis Debney.

CHAPTER 10

The Mouse Factory

Produced and Directed by: Ward Kimball. Narration Written by: Jack Hanrahan, Tom Dagenais, Ted Berman. Associate Producer: Lou Debney. Directors of Photography: Andrew Jackson, A.S.C., Frank Phillips, A.S.C., Meredith Nicholson, A.S.C., Richard A. Kelley, A.S.C. Film Editors: Lloyd L. Richardson, A.C.E., Bob Bring, Ernie Milano. Art Directors: John B. Mansbridge, Al Roelofs, Leroy G. Deane. Music Supervisor: George Bruns. Set Decoration: John A. Kuri, Emile Kuri, Frank R. McKelvy, Hal Gausman. Make-up: Robert J. Schiffer. Costumes: Chuck Keehne. Sound: Herb Taylor. Assistant Directors: Michael Messinger, Robert Webb, Howard Kazanhian. Production Assistants: Dennis Landa, Jim Ashton, Joe Hale, Charlie Downs, Jack Boyd, John Emerson, Rick Corwin, George Probert, Dennis Vejar, John Emerson. Choreographer: Bobby Squire.

CHAPTER 11

The Limited Series

MEET ME AT DISNEYLAND

Disneyland Personnel: Producer: Tommy Walker. Writer: Larry Clemmons. Assistant to Producer: Charles Corson. Production Coordinator: Robert Allen. Sound Coordinator: Bob Matheison. Film: Lloyd Richardson, Gordon Brenner. Talent Coordinator (Show #6–13): Charles K. Dargan.

KTTV Personnel: Director: Buck Pennington. Technical Director: Dick Bowen. Floor Manager: John Richardson. Stage Manager: Bob Claypool. Camera: John Westbrook, Chuck LaForce, Ira Doud. Video: Bob Work. Audio: Wally Heider, Berni Campbell, Chuck Genser. Lighting: Dixson Fannon, Darrel Gilmore, Bill Gossman. Production Manager: Al Bowen. Operations Manager: Val Conte.

Sponsors: Stouffer's, Fritos, Chicken of the Seas, Hills Brothers.

HERBIE, THE LOVE BUG

Executive Producer: William Robert Yates. Produced by: Kevin Corcoran. Written by: Arthur Alsberg, Don Nelson, Don Tait. Directed by: Bill Bixby, Charles S. Dubin, Vincent McEveety. Music by: Frank De Vol, Tom Worrall. Supervising Producers: Don Nelson, Arthur Alsberg. *Herbie, My Best Friend* Sung by: Dean Jones. Words and Music by: Frank De Vol, Tom Worrall. Directors of Photography: Jack A. Whitman, Jr., Jack Swain, A.S.C. Art Directors: Mark Mansbridge, Peter Romero. Editors: Gordon Brenner, A.C.E., Marsh Hendry, William P. Magee, Rin Hanthaner. Unit Production Manager: Paul Wurzel. Assistant Directors: Skip Beaudine, Bud Grace, Gary Crillo. Second Assistant Directors: Doug Metzger, Debbie Love. Casting: Bill Shepard, Virginia Higgins. Developed for Television by: Don Nelson, Arthur Alsberg. Based on Characters Created by: Gordon Buford. Sound: Bob Hathaway. Sound Director: Ben Hendricks. Music Editors: Ralph Hall, Jack Lowry, Dennis Ricotta. Costumes: Jack Sandeen. Make-up: Robert J. Schiffer, C.M.A.A. Hair Stylists: Donna Barrett Gilbert, Edie Panda. Post Production Executive: John Elizalde. Set Decorators: Norman Rockett, Roger M. Shook, Mary Swanson. Stunt Coordinator: Bob Harris. Special Effects: Michael Edmundson.

SMALL & FRYE

Executive Producers: Jan Williams, William Robert Yates. Supervising Producer: Nick Arnold. Created by: George Schenck, Ron Friedman. Written by: Nick Arnold, Ron Friedman, Richard Penn, Leonard Ripps, Larry Siegel. Directed by: John Bowab, Ed Feldman, Mel Ferber, Les Martinson, James Sheldon. Executive Story Editor: Ron Friedman. Creative Consultant: Lenny Ripps. Directors of Photography: Travers Hill, Jack A. Whitman, Jr. Produced by: Jan Williams. Music by: Mike Post, Pete Carpenter. Additional Music by: Dennis McCarthy. Art Directors: Mark W. Mansbridge, Gene Harris, Paul Peters. Editors: Gordon D. Brenner, A.S.C., Dennis A. Orcutt, Bob Bring, A.C.E., Ernie Milano. Unit Production Managers: Paul Wurtzel, Ronald G. Smith. First Assistant Directors: Doug Metzger, Christopher D. Miller. Second Assistant Directors: Victoria Rhodes, Paul Moen. Set Decorator: Norman Rockett. Special Effects: Roland Tantin, R. J. Spetter. Sound Supervisor: Bob Hathaway. Sound Mixer: Art Names. Costume Supervisor: Jack Sandeen. Men's Costumers: Glenn T. Wright, John Lemons. Women's Costumer: Gilda Craig. Make-up Supervi-

sor: Robert J. Schiffer, C.M.A.A. Make-up: Robin LaVigne. Hair Stylist: Julia Walker. Special Visual Effects Supervised by: Don Vargas, Phil Meador, Eric Brevig. Opticals by: Van Der Veer Photo Effects (pilot episode). Video Composite Printing by: Las Palmas Productions, Inc. Music Editor (pilot episode): Richard S. Luckey. Casting: Bill Shepard.

GUN SHY

Executive Producer: William Robert Yates. Produced by: Eric Cohen, Tom Leetch. Written by: Peter Baldwin, Eric Cohen, Farnsworth Gallagher. Directed by: Peter Baldwin, Marc Daniels, Alan Myerson. Supervising Producer: Eric Cohen. Executive Story Consultant: Pat McCormick. Developed for Television by: Eric Cohen, Robert Van Scoyk. Director of Photography: Ron Vargas. Art Director: John B. Mansbridge. Editors: Ernie Milano, A.C.E., Dennis A. Orcutt. Unit Production Manager: Michael Dmytryk. First Assistant Directors: Michael Dmytryk, Charles E. Walker. Second Assistant Director: Doug Metzger. Set Decorator: Michele Harding-Hollie. Sound Supervisor: Bob Hathaway. Sound Mixer: Arthur Names. Costume Supervisor: Jack Sandeen. Men's Costumes: Steve Ellsworth. Women's Costumes: Gilda Craig. Make-up Supervisor: Robert J. Schiffer, C.M.A.A. Make-up: Jim Scribner. Hair Stylist: Edie Panda. Music by: Dennis McCarthy. Casting by: Bill Shepard, Virginia Higgins.

ZORRO AND SON

Developed for Television by: Eric Cohen. Executive Producer: William Robert Yates. Produced by: Kevin Corcoran. Supervising Producer: Eric Cohen. Written by: Nick Arnold, Eric Cohen. Directed by: Peter Baldwin, Gabrielle Beaumont, Alan Myerson. Director of Photography: Ron Vargas. Production Designer: John B. Mansbridge. Editors: Gordon D. Brenner, A.C.E., Dennis A. Orcutt, Ernie Milano, A.C.E. Unit Production Manager: Paul Wurtzel. First Assistant Directors: Doug Metzger, Ramiro Jaloma. Second Assistant Director: James M. Freitag. Set Decorator: Norman Rockett. Special Effects: Roland Tantin. Sound Supervisor: Bob Hathaway. Sound Mixer: Arthur Names. Creative Consultant: Nancy Larson. Costume Supervisor: Jack Sandeen. Men's Costumer: Milton Mangum. Women's Costumer: Karen Hytten. Make-up Supervisor: Robert J. Schiffer, C.M.A.A. Make-up: Robin LaVigne. Hair Stylist: Edie Panda. Music by: George Duning. Casting: Bill Shepard, A.S.C.D. *Zorro and Son* is produced with the cooperation of Gertz-Larson Productions.

WILDSIDE

Supervising Producers: Tom Greene, E. Arthur Kean. Produced by: William F. Phillips. Created by: Tom Greene. Written by: Walter Brough, Tom Greene, Steve Johnson, Joseph Jones, Jonathan Torp, W.M. Whitehead. Directed by: Harvey S. Laidman, Richard C. Sarafian. Associate Producer: Dorothy J. Bailey. Story Editor: W.M. Whitehead. Music by: Jack Elliott. Director of Photography: Roland "Ozzie" Smith. Art Directors: Bill Malley, Michael Baugh. Film Editors: Gregory Prange, Ernest V. Milano, A.C.E., Tom Pryor, William B. Stich, Michael J. Sheridan, Toby Brown, A.C.E. Unit Production Manager: Dan Franklin. First Assistant Directors: Craig A. Beaudine, Doug Metzger, Skip Beaudine. Second Assistant Directors: Dennis Capps, Gary P. Schilz. Supervising Film Editors: Gregory Prange, Robert Florio, A.C.E. Costumes Designed by: Robert Turturice. Second Unit Director: Gregory Prange. Set Decorators: Jim Duffy, Travis Nixon. Stunts: Wayne Van Horn, Diamond Farnsworth. Special Effects: Ken Speed. Property Masters: Bill Dietz, Jim Wagner, William Fannon. Script Supervisor: Rosemary Dorsey. Gaffer: Paul F. Petzoldt. Key Grip: Ted Harrison. Production Sound Mixers: Keith A. Wester, C.A.S., David Ronne. Sound Effects Editor: Keith Stafford. Music Editor: Jack Wadsworth. Ramrod: Richard A. Lundin. Men's Costumer: Milton G. Mangum. Women's Costumer: Karen S. Hytten. Make-up: Jim Scribner. Hair Stylist: Susan Schuler. Casting by: Pam Polifroni, C.S.A. Main Title Design (pilot episode): Conrad/Fox Productions. Transportation Coordinator: Dave Marder.

CHAPTER 12

Saturday Mornings and Disney Afternoons

DISNEY'S WUZZLES

Voices: Gregg Berger, Brian Cummings (Bumblelion, Flizard), Stan Freberg (Narrator), Henry Gibson (Eleroo), Kathleen Helppie (Butterbear), Steve Kramer, Tress MacNeille (Mrs. Pedigree), Alan Oppenheimer (Rhinokey, Croc, Pack-cat), Will Ryan, Bill Scott (Moosel, Brat), Frank Welker, Joanne Worley (Hoppopotamus).

Produced by: Walt Disney Pictures, Television Animation Group. Produced by: Fred Wolf. Directed by: Carole Beers, Fred Wolf. Story Editors: Tony Benedict, Ken Koonce, David Wiemers. Written by: Mark Evanier, Ken Koonce, Ted Perry, David Wiemers. Story by: Bob Rosenfarb. Associate Director: Tom Ruzicka. Art Director: Brad Landreth. Model Design: Keith Sargent. Key Background Styling: Paro Hozumi. Animation Supervisor: Vincent Davis. Production Manager: Olivia Miner. Assistant Director: Randy Chaffee. Animation Checker: Ann Oliphant. Post Production Coordinator: Ken Tsumura. Production Assistants: Aida Belderol, Leigh Anne Locke, Judy Zook. Track Reading: Skip Craig. Title Design: Sam Cornell. Casting Facilities: The Voicecaster. Post Production Supervisor: Rich Harrison. Supervising Editor: Charlie King. Editor: Marc Orfanos. Assistant Editors: Shelley Brown, Robert A. Martel. Music Coordinator: Chris Montan. *Wuzzles* Theme Composed and Performed by: Stephen Geyer. Music Composed and Performed by: Tom Chase, Steve Rucker. Animation Production: TMS Entertainment, Inc.

DISNEY'S ADVENTURES OF THE GUMMI BEARS

Voices: Billy Barty, Corey Burton (Gruffi Gummi—1986 onward, Toadie—1986 onward, Giggalin, Clutch), Hamilton Camp, Roger C. Carmel (Sir Tuxford—1986), Townsend Coleman, Gino Conforti, Peter Cullen, Brian Cummings (Artie Deco, Sir Tuxford—1987 onward, Chillbeard Sr., Knight of Gummadoon), Jim Cummings (Chummi Gummi, Zummi Gummi—1990, Tuck—1990), Barry Dennen, Aeryk Egan, Walker Edmiston (Sir Thornberry), David Faustino (Knight of Gummadoon, Cavin—1987), June Foray (Grammi Gummi, "The Most Peaceful Dragon in the World", Counselor Woodale, Mobile Tree), Linda Gary, Ed Gilbert, Dana Hill, Bob Holt (Giant with the Wishing Stone, Dom Gordo of Ghent), Christian Jacobs (Cavin—1985), Brett Johnson (Cavin—1986), Katie Leigh (Sunni Gummi, Mobile Tree), Tress MacNeille (Lady Bane, Great Oak, Marzipan, Mother), Jason Marsden (Cavin—1987 to 1990), Chuck McCann (Tadpole), Allan Melvin, Howard Morris (Sir Paunch), Lorenzo Music (Tummi Gummi, Bubble Dragon), Pat Musick (Ursa), Noelle North (Cubbi Gummi, Princess Calla, Mobile Tree), Alan Oppenheimer (Knight of Gumadoon), Pat Parris (Trina, Aquarianne), Rob Paulsen (Gusto Gummi), Will Ryan (Unwin, Gad, Zook, Ogres, King Carpie, Knight), Michael Rye (King Gregor, Duke Igthorn, Toadie, Ogre—1985, Sir Gowan, Malsinger, Troll, Knight, Horse, Nip), Bill Scott (Gruffi—1985, Angelo Davini, Sir Tuxford—1985, Ogre—1985, Toadie—1985), Hal Smith, Kath Soucie (Princess Marie), Andre Stojka, Les Tremayne, Lennie Weinrib (Zorlock), Frank Welker (Ditto the Boggle, Mervyns, Mother Griffin), R.J.

Williams (Cavin—1990 to 1991), Paul Winchell (Zummi Gummi, Toadie, Slumber Sprite, Giggalin, Tuck—1987 to 1989), Keone Young.

Produced by: Walt Disney Television Animation. Producers: David Block, Rich Fogel, Mark Seidenberg, Tad Stones, Arthur Vitello, Alan Zaslove. Associate Producer: Tom Ruzicka. Directed by: David Block, Arthur Vitello, Alan Zaslove. Story Editors: Rich Fogel, Jymn Magon, Mark Seidenberg, Tad Stones. Story by: Gordon Bressack, Terrie Collins, Rich Fogel, Kevin Hopps, Eric Lewald, Cliff MacGillivray, Jymn Magon, Richard Mueller, Bruce Reid Schaefer, Mark Seidenberg, Tad Stones, Len Uhley, Arthur Vitello. Teleplay by: Gordon Bressack, Terrie Collins, Doug Hutchinson, Kayte Kuch, Richard Mueller, Sheryl Scarborough, Bruce Reid Schaefer, Len Uhley, Rose G. Wong. Written by: Gordon Bressack, Alan Burnett, Duane Capizzi, Randall Case, Terrie Collins, Dianne Dixon, Rich Fogel, Richard Hoag, Bob Holt, Kevin Hopps, Steve Hulett, Douglas Hutchinson, Kayte Kuch, Bob Langhans, Eric Lewald, Mike Lyons, Cliff MacGillivray, Jymn Magon, Bruce Malek, Michael Maurer, Richard Mueller, Pat Parris, Jim Pasternak, Sheryl Scarborough, Bruce Reid Schaefer, Mark Seidenberg, Tad Stones, Bruce Talkington, Len Uhley, Arthur Vitello, Lennie Weinrib, Kimberly Wells, Marion Wells, Mark Zaslove. Voice Direction: David Block, Jymn Magon, Tad Stones. Assistant Producers: Randy Chafee, Barbara Ebel, Kent Holaday. Storyboard Designers: Kurt Anderson, Alvaro Arce, Bob Arkwright, Kathy Carr, Derek Carter, Liz Chapman, Yi-Chih Chen, Brian Chin, Thom Enriquez, Jill Colbert, Steve Gordon, Warren Greenwood, Bob Kline, Rob Laduca, Don Manual, Dave Prince, Roy Smith, Michael Swanagan, David Thrasher, Karl Toerge, Hank Tucker, Roy Wilson, Monte Young, Al Zegler. Key Layout Design: Derek Carter, Ed Wexler. Character Design: David Block, Liz Chapman. Key Background Stylists: James Gallego, Gary Eggleston. Additional Background Styling: Michael Humphries. Color Key Stylists: Janet Cummings, Britt Greko, Britt Teegarden. Assistant Producer: Barbara Brysman. Production Manager: Olivia Miner. Assistant Director: Kent Holaday, Randy Chaffee. Animation Checker: Ann Oliphant. Post Production Coordinator: Ken Tsumura. Production Assistants: Aida Belderol-Martin, Leigh Anne Locke, Judy Zook. Post Production Supervisor: Rich Harrison. Tokyo Animation Producer: Brian Ray. Animation Supervisors: John Ahern, David Block, Bob Zamboni. Overseas Animation Producers: David Block, Ken Kessel, Rob Laduca, Russell Mooney. Associate Director: Jamie Mitchell. Animation Director: Mitch Rochon. Supervising Timing Directors: Mitch Rochon, Mike Svayko. Timing Directors: Craig Armstrong, Norm Gottfredson, Mircea Mantta, Jamie Mitchell, Ron Myrick, Spencer Peel, Mitch Rochon, Mike Svayko, Bob Zamboni. Production Manager: Rich Harrison. Supervising Editor: Robert S. Birchard. Editors: Willy R. Allen, Craig Jaeger. Assistant Editors: Shelly Brown, Rick Hinson, Glenn Lewis, David Lynch, Robert A. Martel, Craig Paulsen. Sound Editors: Karen Doulac, Marc Orfanos. Track Reading: Skip Craig. Archives Supervisor: Krista Bunn. Art Coordinator: Karen Silva. Production Assistants: Peggy

Becker, Jacaleen Cotter, Nanci Battelle, Wade Zia Nassir. Talent Coordinator: Olivia Miner. Post Production Manager: Sara Duran. Post Production Supervisor: Barbara Beck. Post Production Coordinators: Jeffrey Arthur, Sara Duran. Music Coordinator: Chris Montan. *Gummi Bear* Theme Words and Music: Silversher and Silversher. Music Composed and Conducted by: Thomas Chase, Steve Rucker. Casting Facilities: The Voicecaster. Recording and Mixing Facilities: B & B Sound. Videotape Facilities: Complete Post Inc. Animation Production: TMS Entertainment, Inc., Walt Disney Television Animation Japan, Inc., Guimaraes Productions, Walt Disney TV Animation Australia.

Additional credits for *Disney's Gummi Bears/Winnie the Pooh Hour: Unbearable Fun* Words and Music by: Mark Mueller. Produced by: Robert Kraft.

DuckTales
Voices: Charles Adler (Filler Brushbill), Jack Angel (Quackerbill), Tony Anselmo (Donald Duck), Rene Auberjonois (Dr. Nogood), Billy Barty (King Brian), Richard Beals (Pig Woodchuck), Michael Bell (Lieutenant Garlic), Gregg Berger, Susan Blu (M'Lady, Babydoll Beagle, Robotica, Goldfeather), Steve Bulen, Corey Burton (Ludwig Von Drake), William Callaway (Thor, Old Man Ribbit), Hamilton Camp (Gizmoduck, Fenton Crackshell, TV Director, Overlord Kronk, Grand Kishki), Roger C. Carmel (Glomgold's henchman, Sultan, Emir of Somnambula), Victoria Carroll (Boom-Boom Beagle), Mary Jo Catlett (Cookie Blurf), Philip Clark, Gino Conforti (Benzino Gassolini), Peter Cullen (Admiral Grimitz, Bankjob Beagle, Joaquin Slowly, High Priest, Guide, Armstrong, Police Chief, Mad Dog McGurk, Lesdred, Purple Alien, King Blowhard, Duke Duggan, J. Gander Hoover, Jack the Tripper, The Phantom Blot), Brian Cummings (Doofus, Bebop Beagle, Robot Butler, Green Alien, Swamp Dweller, Barnacle Biff, Captain Tann), Jim Cummings (El Capitan), Barry Dennen (Moorloon, Black Knight), Jerry Dexter, George Dicenzo (Brigadier Broccoli), Richard Erdman (King Artie, Mayor Rufus B. Pinfeathers), Miriam Flynn (Gandra Dee), June Foray (Magica de Spell, Ma Beagle, Scrooge's Mother, Mrs. Featherby), Pat Fraley (Sir Guy Standforth, Young Scrooge), Kathleen Freeman (Mrs. Crackshell), Linda Gary (Aphroducky), Dick Gautier (Mr. Wolf), Joan Gerber (Mrs. Beakley, Mrs. Featherby, Glittering Goldie, Webra Walters, Schewebazade, Duchess of Swansylvania, Mrs. McGurk, Small Terri-Fermian, Anastasia, Gloria Swansong, Lady de Lardo), Ed Gilbert (Glomgold's Lawyer), Phil Hartman, Johnny Haymer (Bull Weevil), Don Hills (Bank Manager), Arte Johnson (Ludwig von Strangeduck, Count Ray), Aaron Kincaid, Bernie Kopell (Victor Luzer), Maurice LaMarche (Count Roy), Richard Libertini (Dijon), Marilyn Lightstone (Priestess), Tress MacNeille (Griselda, Shepherd Girl, Circe, Ariel, Commander of Microducks, Agnes, Feathers Galore, Millionaira Vanderbucks), Danny Mann (Backwoods Beagle), Ken Mars (Vulcan), Chuck McCann (Duckworth, Burger Beagle, Bouncer Beagle, Lord Battmountain, Bernardo, Percival, Terri-Fermian Coach, Dr. Horatio Bluebottle, Wildcat, Quacks, Mr. Webworth, Chief of Rippon Taro), Pat McCormick (Shepherd), Jim McGeorge, Terence (Terry) McGovern (Launchpad McQuack, Baby Face Beagle, Penguin Leader, Major Courage, Irwin Mallard, Burt Quackarach, Charles Upstart III, Dr. Kooncen Wiemers), Allan Melvin (Captain Bounty), Don Messick (Scrooge's Father), Haunani Minn (Cinnamon Teal, Sen-Sen), Michael Mish (Homer), Howard Morris (Djinni, Dr. Von Geezer, Dr. Von Swine), Larry Moss, Pat Musick (Bully Beagle), Nicholas Omana, Alan Oppenheimer (Colonel Beauregard DuBark, Tex Dogie, von Duckhausen), Patty Parris (Skittles), Rob Paulsen (Gladstone Gander, Robin Lurch, Sundowner), Brock Peters (Druid Chief), Charles Pierce (Prison Warden), Georgette Rampone, Peter Renaday (Captain Slattery, Uncle Catfish), Clive Revill (Shedlock Jones), Robert Ridgely (Ripcord McQuack, Bomber Beagle), Neil Ross, Joe Ruskin, Will Ryan (Dangerous Dan Sharkey, Dog-Face Pete, Black Pete, Flagship Captain, Caesar), Michael Rye, Ronnie Schell (Ping the Pitiless), Avery Schreiber (Older Huey, Dewey and Louie), Hal Smith (Gyro Gearloose, Flintheart Glomgold, Witlow, Yardarm, Warden of Aquatraz, Chief of Banana Island, Mr. Merriweather, John D. Rockefeather, Hijacker), Steve Susskind (Sergeant Squash), Mark Taylor (Ensign Plover),

Russi Taylor (Huey, Dewey, Louie, Webbigail Vanderquack, Gwen, TV Reporter, Birdy McQuack, Harp), Len Uhley, B.J. Ward (Loopy McQuack), Christopher Weeks, Frank Welker (Bubba Duck, Poe, Big Time Beagle, Baggy Beagle, Colonel Beauregard DuBark, King Terri-Fermian, Sirens, Captain Foghorn, Captain Mallard, J.R. Mooing, Fardarig, Prince Greydrake, Carl Sagander, Megabyte Beagle, Poupon), Stanley Wojno Jr., JoAnne Worley (Bouffant Beagle), Alan Young (Uncle Scrooge McDuck), Keone Young (Mung Ho).

Produced by: Walt Disney Television Animation. Supervising Producer: Fred Wolf. Producer/Supervising Directors: Bob Hathcock, Alan Zaslove. Associate Producer: Tom Ruzicka. Co-Producers: Alan Burnett, Ken Koonce, David Wiemers. Directors: David Block, Steve Clark, Vincent Davis, Jeff Hall, Terence Harrison, Bob Hathcock, Rick Leon, Mircea Mantta, Jamie Mitchell, Rich Trueblood, James T. Walker, Alan Zaslove. Story Editors: Tedd Anasti, Alan Burnett, Patsy Cameron, Jeff Hall, Ken Koonce, Jymn Magon, Rich Trueblood, David Wiemers. Script Consultants: Tedd Anasti, Patsy Cameron. Story by: George Atkins, Alan Burnett, Carl Barks, Patsy Cameron, Evelyn Gabai, Ken Koonce, Cliff MacGillivray, Jymn Magon, James A. Markovich, Tom Naugle, John Pirillo, Astrid Ryterband, Mark Seidenberg, Bruce Talkington, Brooks Wachtel, David Wiemers, Mark Zaslove. Teleplay by: Anthony Adams, Tedd Anasti, Gordon Bressack, Eleanor Burian-Mohr, Bruce Coville, Diane Duane, Evelyn Gabai, Jack Hanrahan, Doug Hutchinson, Michael Keyes, Ken Koonce, Jymn Magon, Richard Merwin, Bruce Reid Schaefer, John Semper, Bruce Talkington, Len Uhley, David Wiemers, Mark Young, Mark Zaslove, Judy Zook. Written by: Anthony Adams, Tedd Anasti, Gordon Bressack, Alan Burnett, Patsy Cameron, Sharman Divono, Jack Enyart, Rich Fogel, Evelyn Gabai, Don Glut, Dale Hale, Pamela Hickey, Doug Hutchinson, Sam Joseph, Michael Keyes, Ken Koonce, Earl Kress, Sam Locke, Randy L'Officier, Jymn Magon, Dennys McCoy, Richard Merwin, Francis Moss, Michael O'Mahony, Margaret Osborne, Frank Ridgeway, Manette Beth Rosen, Bruce Reid Schaefer, David Schwartz, Jeffrey Scott, Mark Seidenberg, Bruce Talkington, Len Uhley, Chris Weber, David Wiemers, Cherie Dee Wilkerson, Karen Willson, Mark Zaslove. Voice Direction: Jymn Magon, Andrea Romano, David Wiemers. Assistant Producers: Maia Mattise, Liza-Ann Warren. Art Directors: Skip Morgan, Brad Landreth. Associate Art Director: Skip Morgan. Model Design: Liz Chapman, Terry Hudson. Key Layout Stylists: Derek Carter, Ed Ghertner, Joe Pearson, Michael Peraza, Carol Police, Ed Wexler. Storyboard Design: Viki Anderson, Ryan Anthony, Elizabeth Chapman, Rich Chidlaw, Davis Doi, Thom Enriquez, Steve Gordon, Jan Green, Warren Greenwood, Paul Gruwell, Chuck Harvey, Rob LaDuca, Jim Mitchell, Marty Murphy, Elyse Pastel, Dale Schott, Michael Swanigan, Jill Trousdale, Hank Tucker, Wendell Washer, Roy Wilson, Jim Woodring, Monte Young, Al Zegler. Key Background Styling: Gary Eggleston, James Gallego, Paro Hozumi, Lisa Keene, Fred Warter. Color Key Styling: Jan Cummings, Robin Draper, Britt Greko, Debra Jorgensborg, Marta Skwara, Jill Stirdivant. Character Design: Ron Scholefield, Jill Colbert, Ed Gombert, Toby Shelton. Overseas Animation Supervisors: Bob Baxter, Bruce Pedersen, Sean Newton, Brian Ray, Mike Reyna, Dale Schott, Bill Wolf. Supervising Timing Directors: Dave Brain, Marlene Robinson May, Bob Shellhorn. Timing Directors: Robert Alvarez, Vonnie Batson, David Brain, Becky Bristow, Brad Case, Joan Case, Rick Collado, Vincent Davis, Jeff Hall, Marsh Lamore, Rick Leon, Mircea Mantta, Mitch Rochon, Ernie Schmidt, Bob Shellhorn, Mike Svayko, Bob Treat, Richard Trueblood, James T. Walker, Bob Zamboni. Dialogue Direction: Andrea Romano. Track Reading: Skip Craig. Production Manager: Olivia Miner. Assistant Director: Randy Chaffee. Production Assistants: Jeffrey Arthur, Nanci Battelle, Barbara Brysman, Krista Bunn, Stephanie Elliott, Wade Zia Nassir, John Royer, Jacaleen Veber, Scott Wolf, LuAnne Wood, Judy Zook. Script Coordinator: Marie Sager. Talent Coordinator: Olivia Miner. Archive Administrator: Krista Bunn. Art Coordinator: Karen Silva. Post Production Manager: Sara Duran. Post Production Coordinators: Jeffrey Arthur, Barbara Beck, Ken Tsumura. Managing Editor: Rich Harrison. Supervising Editors: Robert S. Birchard, Charlie King, M.P.S.E. Sound Effects Editors: Rick Hinson, M.P.S.E., Craig Jager, Marc Orfanos, Jerry Winicki. Assistant Editors: Rick Hinson, Glenn Lewis, David Lynch, Thomas Needell, Craig Paulsen. Apprentice Editors: Thomas Needell, Jennifer Harrison. *Duck-Tales* Theme Composed by: Mark Mueller. Music Composed and Conducted by: Ron Jones. Additional Music by: Tom Chase, Steve Rucker. Animation Production by: Wang Film Productions Co., Ltd., Cuckoo's Nest Studio, TMS Entertainment, Inc.

NEW ADVENTURES OF WINNIE THE POOH, THE
Voices: Hamilton Camp, Peter Cullen (Eeyore), Jim Cummings (Winnie the Pooh, Tigger), John Fiedler (Piglet), Jackie Gonneau, Michael Gough (Gopher), Tim Hoskins (Christopher Robin), Chuck McCann, Nicholas Melody (Roo), Laura Mooney, Nicholas Omana, Patty Parris (Kanga), Stan Ross (Eeyore), Tracy Rowe, Ken Sansom (Rabbit), Hal Smith (Owl), Paul Winchell (Tigger).

Produced by: Walt Disney Television Animation. Producers: Ken Kessel, Karl Geurs, Ed Ghertner. Co-Producer: Mark Zaslove. Supervising Director: Karl Kessel. Directors: Vincent Bassols, Carole Beers, David Block, Karl Geurs, Terence Harrison, Jamie Mitchell, Charles A. Nichols, Mike Svayko. Story Editors: Carter Crocker, Bruce Talkington, Mark Zaslove. Assistant Story Editors: Carter Crocker, Evelyn A-R Gabai, Bruce Talkington. Producer: Russell E. Mooney. Story by: Mark Cassut, Marley Clark, Terrie Collins, Carter Crocker, Jimmy Danelli, Lynn Feinermann, Rich Fogel, Evelyn A-R Gabai, Ken Kessel, Eric Lewald, Jymn Magon, Dev Ross, Bruce Reid Schaefer, David Silverman, Stephen Sustarsic, Bruce Talkington, Len Uhley, Arthur Vitello, Mark Zaslove. Teleplay by: Larry Bernard, Terrie Collins, Carter Crocker, Rich Fogel, Evelyn A-R Gabai, Douglas Hutchinson, Eric Lewald, Jymn Magon, Dev Ross, Bruce Reid Schaefer, Stephen Sustarsic, Bruce Talkington, Len Uhley, Mark Zaslove. Written by: Marley Clark, Terrie Collins, Carter Crocker, Eveleyn A-R Gabai, Karl Geurs, Libby Hinson, Eric Lewald, Julia Jane Lewald, Sindy McKay, Elen Orson, Michele Rifkin, Cliff Roberts, Dev Ross, Bruce Reid Schaefer, Mirith Schilder, Stephen Sustarsic, Larry Swerdlove, Bruce Talkington, Mark Zaslove. Animation Directors: David Block, Terence Harrison. Voice Direction: Karl Geurs, Andrea Romano, Mark Zaslove. Assistant Producers: Peggy Becker, Barbara Ferro, Selma Gladney, Donna Alcock Smith, Ken Tsumura. Art Director: Ed Ghertner. Assistant Producer: Randy Chaffee. Storyboard Designers: Kurt Anderson, Ryan Anthony, Ken Boyer, Kathleen Carr, Ron Campbell, Elizabeth Chapman, Rich Chidlaw, Don Christensen, Jill Colbert, Kurt Conners, Larry Eikleberry, Michael Fallows, John Flagg, Holly Forsyth, George Goode, Steve Gordon, Jan Green, Bob Kline, Rob Laduca, Lin Larsen, Jim McLean, Bruce Morris, Eduardo Olivares, David Prince, Rhoydon Shishido, Tom Sito, Robert Souza, Hank Tucker. Storyboard Revisions: Kathleen Carr, Elizabeth Chapman, Jeff Howard, Paulette King, Albert Ring, Robert Souza, Phil Weinstein. Key Layout Design: Ed Ghertner, Dennis Greco, Jim Schlenker. Character Design: Tom Bird, Toby Shelton, Leonard Smith. Additional Character Design: Kenny Thompkins. Prop Design: David Mink. Background Styling: Hye Coh, Paro Hozumi, Bill Lorencz. Additional Background Styling: Gary Eggleston. Color Stylists: Robin Draper, Yolanda Rearick, Marta Skwara, Jill Stirdivant. Additional Color Styling: Debra Jorgensborg. Supervising Timing Directors: Dave Brain, Mircea Mantta, Marlene Robinson May, Bob Shellhorn. Timing Directors: Robert Alvarez, Vonnie Batson, Carole Beers, Dave Brain, Brad Case, Joan Case, Terence Harrison, Marsh Lamore, Rick Leon, Mircea Mantta, Jamie Mitchell, Russell E. Mooney, Karen Peterson, Brian Ray, Mitch Rochon, Bob Shellhorn, Ernie Schmidt, Bob Shellhorn Mike Stribling, Mike Svayko, Bob Treat, Richard Trueblood, James T. Walker, Neal Warner, Woody Yocum, Bob Zamboni. Continuity Coordinators: Vonnie Batson, Myrna Bushman, Jim Finch, Kathrin Victor. Track Reader: Skip Craig. Script Coordinators: Laraine Arknow, Johanne Beaudoin, Leona Jernigan, Leigh Anne Locke, Judy Maxey, Marie Sager, Mirith Schilder, LuAnne Wood. Archives Administrator: Krista Bunn. Artwork Coordinator: Karen Silva. Overseas Animation Supervisors: Ken Kessel, Jamie Mitchell, Mike Reyna. Talent Coordinator: Lynne Batchelor, Olivia Miner. Post Production Manager: Sara Duran. Post Pro-

duction Supervisor: Joseph Hathaway. Sound Dubbing Supervisor: Christopher Keith. Post Production Coordinators: Jeffrey Arthur, Barbara Beck, Rick Finn, John Royer, Ken Tsumura. Post Production Assistant: Nanci Batetelle. Production Assistants: Jeffrey Arthur, Johanne Beaudoin, Nanci Battelle, Peggy Becker, Jacaleen Cotter, Stephanie Elliott, Leona Jernigan, Michelle Pappalardo, Michelle Robinson, John Royer, William Waggoner, LuAnne Wood, Wade Zia Nassir. Shipping Coordinator: Craig Simpson. Managing Film Editor: Rich Harrison. Supervising Editors: Charlie King, M.P.S.E., Elen Orson. Supervising Sound Editors: Rick Hinson, M.P.S.E., David Lynch, Jerry Winicki. Editors: Roy Braverman, Rick Hinson, M.P.S.E. Dialogue Editors: Jenny Harrison, Peggy McAffee, Andy Rose. Assistant Editors: James N. Harrison, Craig Paulsen, David Lynch, Glenn Lewis, Robb S. Paulsen. Apprentice Editors: Thomas Needell, Jennifer Harrison. Sound Effects Editor: Roy Braverman. Music Editor & Re-recording Mixer: Ed Barton. Re-recording: Jon Bavin. Songs Written and Produced by: Steve Nelson. Music by: Steve Nelson, Thom Sharp. Animation Supervisor: Dale Case. *Animation Production by:* Walt Disney Television Animation Australia. Animation Supervisor: Dale Case. Animation Directors: Gairden Cooke, Ian Harrowell, Henry Neville. Layout Director: Alex Nicholas. Layout Artists: Yosh Barry, Scott Bennett, Zhigiang Ding, John Hill, Victor Juy, Steve Lyons, Mark Mulgrew, David Skinner, Mark Mulgrew, Bun Ung, Kevin Wotton. Animators: Rowen Avon-Smith, Ty Bosco, Chris Bradley, Andrew Collins, Geoff Collins, Dick Dunn, Ariel Ferrari, Peter Gardiner, Warwick Gilbert, Gerry Grabner, Lianne Hughes, Dwayne Labbe, Morris Lee, Helen McAdam, Wally Micati, Kathie O'Rourke, Kevin Peaty, Carol Seidl, Richard Slapczynzki, Paulo Santo, Mike Stapleton, Andrew Szemenyei, Maria Szemenyei, Steven Taylor, Steven Trenbirth, Jean Tych, Kang-Lin Zhu. Assistant Supervisors: Janey Dunn, Mickie Cassidy, Di Rudder. Background Supervisor: Beverley McNamara. Background Artists: Barry Dean, Jerry Liew, Paul Pattie, Helen Steele, Ken Wright. Production Manager: Dan Forster. *Animation Production by:* Walt Disney Animation UK Limited. Directors: Clive Pallant, Vincent Woodcock. Assistant Director: Jeremy Springett. Animators: Gary Andrews, Caron Creed, Joe Ekers, Al Gaivoto, Teddy Hall, Ramon Modiano, Anna Saunders, Duncan Varley, Simon Ward Horner. Junior Animators: Jon Collier, Andrew Painter, Bob Wilk. Background Artists: Michael Hirsh, Colin Stimpson, Andrew McNab. Layout Artists: Neil Graham, Dave Elvin, Peter Bielicki, Clive Hutchings. Video Operator: Peter Jessett. Production Coordinator: Steve Hollowell. *Animation Production by:* Hanho Heung-Up Co., Ltd., TMS Entertainment, Inc.

CHIP 'N DALE'S RESCUE RANGERS
Voices: Gregg Berger (Wild Bill Hiccup), Susan Blu, Corey Burton (Zipper, Dale, Snout, Mole, Bud Snake, Moe, Poptop, Chief of the Kiwis, Normie Nimnul, Macduff, Brik, Roger Baskerville, Dr. Piltdown, Euripides, Davey, Jeebee, Stormy the Pi-rat, Wexler, Ratatouille, Robocat), Frank Buxton (Mr. Starfish), Ruth Buzzi (Ma), Hamilton Camp (Chief Beetlebreath), Pat Carroll (Koko the Gorilla), Victoria Carroll (Pomonoa), Carol Channing (Canina Le Fur), Peter Cullen (Monterey Jack, Meps, Officer Kirby, Officer Muldoon, Mr. Stanislavsky, Nemo, Voltaire, Chief Hermit Crab, Mr. Gribbish, Brak, Restaurant Owner, Pharoah's Demon, Mr. Hancock, Ratso Ratskiwatski), Brian Cummings (Arnold Mousenegger), Jim Cummings (Monterey Jack, Fat Cat, Wart, Sergeant Spinelli, Professor Norton Nimnul, Stan Blather, Jolly Roger, Spud, Conrad Cockatoo, Mr. Whizzer, Steggy, Clyde Cosgrove, Butch the Bulldog, Pepto Gizmo, Hubert, Elmer, Barnacle Bill, Lord Howie Baskerville, Mr. Quigley, Sir Colby, Rocco, Dr. Crockery, Hiram the Mummy, Chirp-Sing, Heinrich von Sugarbottom, Cheddarhead Charlie, Bubbles, Lou Spider, Dr. Hibbleman, Baby Thaddeus, Hoo You, Monsieur LeSewer), Bernard Fox, Kathleen Freeman (Ma), Danny Gans (Seymour the Travel Agent, Fry, Moose, Muscles, Sparky, Buzz, Groucho Marx Pigeon), Joan Gerber (Zsa Zsa Labrador), Tim Hoskins, Patti Howeth (Queen of the Banshees), Robert Ito (Chow Ming), Tress MacNeille (Chip, Gadget, Siamese Twins, Winifred, Cassandra the Fortune Teller, Mrs. Squirrel, Joy Rider, Spunky, Kismet, Existential Mouse,

Jeremy, Jimmy, Harriet Wolf, Lady Richmore, Mrs. Hancock), Jimmy Macdonald (Humphrey the Bear), Chuck McCann (Sugar Ray Lizard, The Red Badger of Courage), Sindy McKay (Queenie Bee, Irweena Allen, Su Lien, Elliott the Elephant, Female Panda, Desiree D'Allure), Michael Merton, Laura Mooney (Mandy), Howard Morris (Maltese Le Sade), Noelle North (Tammy Squirrel, Binky Squirrel), Alan Oppenheimer (Aldrin Klordane, Plato, Captain Kernel), Rob Paulsen (Flash the Wonder Dog, Detective Donald Drake, Percy, Frenchie, Police Chief, Darby Spree, Tito, Harry Wolf, Myron, Heebee, Don Quijole, Clarence Dudley, Emperor Dim Sun, Male Panda, Erol, Shaka-Baka, Captain Finn, Dirk Suave, Louie), Dev Ross, Fran Ryan (Camembert Kate), Will Ryan (Dale singing), Maureen Schrum, Pete Schrum (Sewernose de Bergerac, Chief Hubba-Hubba, Francis, Elemenopeio), Russi Taylor, Deborah Walley (Foxglove, Lahini, Buffy Ratskiwatski), Frank Welker (Todd, Ribit), Anderson Wong (Fu Manchow), Tom Wyner (Fat Cat singing), Diana Zaslove (Female human opera singer).

Produced by: Walt Disney Television Animation. Producers: Ken Koonce, Tad Stones, David Wiemers, Alan Zaslove. Supervising Director: Alan Zaslove. Directors: John Kimball, Rick Leon, Jamie Mitchell, Bob Zamboni. Supervising Story Editor: Tad Stones. Story Editors: Lymn Magon, Bryce Malek, Ken Koonce, Tad Stones, David Wiemers, Mark Zaslove. Story by: Buzz Dixon, Kevin Hopps, Ken Koonce, Sindy McKay, Bruce Reid Schaefer, Tad Stones, Larry Swerdlove, David Wiemers, David Wise, LuAnne Wood. Teleplay by: Buzz Dixon, Kevin Hopps, Ken Koonce, Julia Jane Lewald, Dev Ross, Bruce Talkington, David Wiemers, David Wise, Linda Woolverton. Written by: Burt Brown, Art Cover, Mark Edens, Michael Edens, Kevin Hopps, Doug Hutchinson, Ken Koonce, Eric Lewald, Jymn Magon, Bryce Malek, Lydia Marano, Sindy McKay, Michael Price Nelson, Julia J. Roberts, Dev Ross, Bruce Reid Schaefer, Dean Stefan, Tad Stones, Somtow Sucharikul, Larry Swerdlove, Bruce Talkington, Len Uhley, David Wiemers, David Wise, Mark Zaslove. Voice Direction: Andrea Romano, Dev Ross. Assistant Producer: Maia Mattise. Animation Designer: Toby Shelton. Key Layout Artists: Michael Spooner, Ed Wexler. Character Design: Ken Boyer, Kenny Thompkins. Prop Design: Terry Hudson, Rob Laduca, Marty Warner. Overseas Animation Supervisors: Dale Case, Russell Mooney, Bob Zamboni. Tokyo Animation Producer: Russell Mooney. Storyboard Design: Kurt Anderson, Barry Caldwell, Rich Chidlaw, Larry Eikleberry, Holly Forsyth, Sharon Forward, Jim Gomez, Jan Green, Warren Greenwood, Larry Latham, Michael O'Mara, John Norton, Frank Paur, Dave Schwartz, Rhoydon Shishido, David Smith, Robert Taylor, Lonnie Thompson, Keith Tucker, Byron Vaugns, Roy Wilson, Monte Young. Key Background Styling: Gary Eggleston, Bill Lorencz. Color Key Styling: Janet Cummings, Robin Draper, Debra Jorgensborg. Supervising Timing Director: David Brain. Timing Directors: Robert Alvarez, Vonnie Batson, Carol Beers, Becky Bristow, Myrna Bushman, Brad Case, Joan Drake, Jeff Hall, Terence Harrison, John Kimball, Marsh Lamore, Rick Leon, Mircea Mantta, Mitch Rochon, Ernie Schmidt, Bob Shellhorn, Mike Stribling, Mike Svayko, Bob Treat, Richard Trueblood, James T. Walker, Neal Warner, Bob Zamboni. Continuity Supervisor: Marlene Robinson May. Continuity Coordinators: Vonnie Batson, James Finch. Track Reading: Skip Craig. Script Coordinators: Marie Sager, LuAnne Wood. Production Assistants: Jeffrey Arthur, Jacaleen Cotter, Barbara Ebel, Wade Nassir. Production Archive Administrator: Krista Bunn. Art Coordinator: Karen Silva. Post Production Manager: Sara Duran. Post Production Coordinators: Barbara Beck, Rick Finn. Talent Coordinator: Olivia Miner. Managing Editor: Rich Harrison. Supervising Editors: Cecil Broughton, Charlie King. Sound Effects Editors: Brian Baker, Rick Hinson, Mark Orfanos, Jerry Winicki. Assistant Editors: Theressa Gilroy, David Lynch, Bob Martell, Thomas Needell, Craig Paulsen. *Chip 'n' Dale's Rescue Rangers* Theme Song Words and Music by: Mark Mueller. Music Composed and Conducted by: Glen Daum for Score Productions. Songs: Kevin Hopps, George Kahn, Silversher and Silversher, Tad Stones, Diana Zaslove. Animation Production by: A-1 Productions, Inc., Sun Woo Animation, TMS Entertainment, Inc., Wang Film Productions Co., Ltd., Cuckoos' Nest Studio.

TALE SPIN

Voices: Charlie Adler (Mad Dog), Jack Angel (Detective Thursday, High Marshal of Thembria), Michael Bell (Colonel Grogg, Mr. Perry), Sheryl Bernstein (Broadcast Sally), Brandon Bluhm, Scott Bullock (Ignatz, Howard Huge), Rodger Bumpass, Corey Burton, Hamilton Camp (Seymour, Whistlestop Jackson, Babyface Half-Nelson), Jodi Carlisle, Victoria Carroll (Pwincess Gwace), Dan Castellaneta (Prince Rudolph, Dr. Zhibaldo), Cam Clarke (Daring Dan Dawson), Townsend Coleman, Phil Crowley, Jim Cummings (Don Karnage, Louie, Trader Moe, Ape Goon, Macnee, Covington, Officer Malarkey, El Gato, Chancellor Trample of Macadamia, Aunt Louise, O'Roarke), Cam Clark (Daring Dan Dawson), Tim Curry (Klang), Gabriel Damon, Jennifer Darling (Ms. Snarly), Debi Derryberry, David Doyle (Sheriff), Ron Feinberg (Coolhands Luke), Pat Fraley (Wildcat), Ben Ganger (Oscar Vandersnoot), Linda Gary (Muffy Vanderschneer), Liz Georges (Mira), Ellen Gerstell (Katie Dodd), Ed Gilbert (Baloo), Dan Gilvezan, Patrick Gorman, Michael Gough (Colonel Spigot), Edan Gross (Bobbo), Phil Hartman (Ace London), Billie Hayes (Ma Nelson), Whitby Hertford (Ernie), Jerry Houser, Robert Ito (Wan Lo), Tony Jay (Shere Khan), Stan Jones, Richard Karron (Waldo), Maurice LaMarche (Owl Capone), David L. Lander (Mr. Weazell), Sherry Lynn, Tress MacNeille (Kitten Kaboodle), Danny Mann, Ken Mars (Heinlich Menudo, Buzz), Mitzi McCall (Una), Chuck McCann (Dumptruck, Rhino Mayor of Cape Suzette), Edie McClurg (Mrs. Vandersnoot), Jim McGeorge, Allan Melvin (Slammer), Janna Michaels (Molly Cunningham), Howard Morris (King Amok of Macadamia), Lorenzo Music (Sergeant Dunder), Alan Oppenheimer (Principal Pomeroy), Rob Paulsen (Ratchet), Patrick Pinney (Professor O'Bowens), Henry Polic III, Tony Pope, Hal Rayle, Pete Renaday (Captain Stansbury), Robert Ridgely, Alan Roberts (Kit Cloudkicker), Neil Ross (Reggie), Maggie Roswell, Ken Sansom, Susan Silo (Plain Jane), Hal Smith (Joe McGee), Kath Soucie (Clementine, Princess Lotta Lamour of Macadamia), John Stephenson (General Bucky Tumult, Krackpotkin), Sally Struthers (Rebecca Cunningham), Mark Taylor (Dougie Benson), Simon Templeman (Rick Sky), Susan Tolsky (Ms. Morrissey), Frank Welker (Buffy Vanderschneer, Wiley Pole, Sheriff), R.J. Williams (Kit Cloudkicker), Alan Young (Doc Cooper), Patric Zimmerman.

Produced by: Walt Disney Television Animation. Supervising Producer: Jymn Magon. Producers/Directors: Ed Ghertner, Larry Latham, Jamie Mitchell, Robert Taylor. Co-Producers: Jamie Mitchell, Mark Zaslove. Associate Producer: Ken Tsumura. Story Editors: Duane Capizzi, Karl Geurs, Ken Koonce, Jymn Magon, Bruce Talkington, Ken Tsumura, David Wiemers, Mark Zaslove. Written by: Alan Burnett, Carter Crocker, Jeremy Cushner, Martin Donoff, Mark Edens, Michael Edens, Karl Geurs, Libby Hinson, Ken Koonce, Eric Lewald, Julia Jane Lewald, Bruce Morris, Cathryn Perdue, Steve Roberts, Don Rosa, Dev Ross, Jeffrey Scott, Dean Stefan, Jan Strnad, Steve Sustarsic, Ellen Svaco, Colleen Taber, Bruce Talkington, Chuck Tately, Len Uhley, David Wiemers, Mark Zaslove. Post Production Producer: Larry Latham. Dialogue Direction: Ginny McSwain. Animation Directors: Terrence Harrison, John Kimball, Marsh Lamore, Mircea Mantta, Jamie Mitchell, Richard Trueblood, James T. Walker, Bob Zamboni. Assistant Producers: Donna Alcock, Barbara Donatelli, Stephanie Elliott, Barbara Ferro, Beth Gunn, Traci Tolman, Scott Wolf. Storyboard: Kurt Anderson, Viki Anderson, Ryan Anthony, Yi-Chih Chen, Rich Chidlaw, Victor Cook, John Dorman, Larry Eikleberry, Dan Fausett, Holly Forsyth, Sharon Forward, George Goode, Jan Green, Warren Greenwood, Bob Kline, Rob Laduca, John Norton, Eduardo Olivares, Frank Paur, Chris Rutkowski, David Schwartz, Swinton Scott, David Smith, Robert Souza, Lonnie Thompson, Vincent Trippetti, Hank Tucker, Keith Tucker, Wendell Washer, Roy Wilson. Key Layout Design: Derek Carter, Kelly Day, Paul Felix, Colette Van Mierlo, Carol Kieffer Police, Jim Schlenker, Michael Spooner. Character Design: George Goode, Skip Morgan, Toby Shelton, Len Smith, Tom Owens, Kenny Thompkins. Computer Animation: Kelly Day, Michael Peraza. Prop Design: Liz Chapman, Dennis Greco, Terry Hudson, Marty Warner. Key Background Stylists: Greg Battes, Gary Conklin, Gary Eggleston, Paro Hozumi, James Gallego, Bill Lorencz, Christie Maltese, Fred Warter. Color

Key Stylists: Janet Cummings, Robin Draper, Debra Jorgensborg, Yolanda Rearick, Marta Skwara, Jill Stirdivant. Overseas Animation Producers: Bob Baxter, Russell Mooney, Brian Ray. Supervising Timing Directors: Marlene Robinson May, Bob Shellhorn. Timing Directors: Vincent Bassols, Carole Beers, Marsh Lamore, Mitch Rochon, Bob Treat, Richard Trueblood, James T. Walker. Continuity Coordinators: Vonnie Batson, Jim Finch, Kathrin Victor. Track Reading: Skip Craig. Post Production Manager: Sara Duran. Post Production Supervisor: Joseph Hathaway. Sound Dubbing Supervisor: Christopher Keith. Post Production Coordinator: Jeffrey Arthur. Post Production Assistants: Nanci Battelle, Wade Zia Nassir, John Royer. Production Assistants: Johanne Beaudoin, Donna Alcock, Yolanda Valdez, Samantha Weerasinghe, Donna Weir, LuAnne Wood. Talent Coordinator: Olivia Miner. Script Coordinators: Leona Jernigan, Anita Lish, Marie Sager, Mirith Schilder. Archives Supervisor: Krista Bunn. Art Coordinator: Karen Silva. Managing Editor: Rich Harrison. Supervising Editor: Cecil E. Broughton, M.P.S.E. Sound Editors: Brian Baker, Mark R. Crookston, Paul Diller, M.P.S.E., Michael Gollom, Rick Hinson, Sam Horta, Marc Orfanos, Jerry Winicki. Music Editors: Thomas Harris, Brian F. Mars. Assistant Editors: Jennifer Harrison, David Lynch, Thomas Needell, Craig Paulsen. Foley Design: Ron Eng. Dubbing Mixer: Timothy J. Borquez. Original Music Composed and Conducted by: Christopher L. Stone. *Spin It* Theme Words and Music by: Silversher and Silversher. Produced by: Robert Kraft. *Animation Production by: Walt Disney Animation (France) S.A.:* Layout: Bolhelm Bouchiba, Jean Duval, Vincent Massy, Pascal Pinon, James Baker, Nicolas De Crecy. Animation Director: Stephane Sainte-Foi. Animators: Marc Eoche-Duval, Pierre Fassal, Dina Gellert-Nielsen, Arnold Gransac, Dominique Monfery, Jean-Christophe Roger, Pascal Ropars, Johnny Zeuten, Jean-Luc Balester, Moran Caouissin, Bruno Galmetou, Nicolas Marlet, Catherine Poulain, Christophe Villez, Peter Hausner, Claude Montfort, Mireille Sarrault. Background Director: Pierre Pavloff. Assistant Background: Isabelle Bourelly, Helene Godefroy, Vincent Miesser, Patricia Millereau, Nathalie Nicholas, Michel Pisson, Brigitte Reboux, Olivier Adam, Jean Paul Fernandez, Thierry Fournier, Didier Pinot, Colin Stimpson, Ande MacNab, Mike Hirsh. Line Producer: Sylvie Fauque. 2nd Producer Assistant: Ellene Longa. Camera Coordinator: Serge Conchonnet. Artistic Director: Jean-Christophe Poulain. 1st Assistant Director: Isabelle Quenet. *Sun Woo Animation, Wang Film Productions Co., Ltd., Walt Disney Animation (Japan) Inc.* Additional Production Facility: Hanho Heung-Up Co., Ltd. Animation Supervisor: Shigeru Yamamoto. Animation Directors: Takeshi Atomura, Ritsuko Notani. Directors: Saburo Hashimoto, Yukio Okazaki, Shigeru Kimiya, Yasumi Mikamoto, Rokoh Ogihara. Animator/Layout Artist: Tadakatsu Yoshida. Background Artist: Minoru Nishida.

DARKWING DUCK
Voices: Charlie Adler (Andy Ape, Konjo, Mikey McMack, Pint-sized Snake-eyed Kid), Jack Angel (The Liquidator, Molucolo McCawber, Mel), Rene Auberjonois (Museum Director, Venerable One), Alyce Beasley (Queen Teeya), Michael Bell (Dean Spector McHex, Quackerjack, Sir Veillance), Sheryl Bernstein (Isis Vanderchill), Don Bovingloh, Valerie Bromfield (Dr. Fernchew), Scott Bullock (Dr. Gary, Tom Lockjaw, Zeke), Jack Burns, Corey Burton (Rubber Chicken), Ruth Buzzi (Dottie Debson), Bill Callaway (Comet Guy, Lou), Joey Camen (Stegmutt), Hamilton Camp (Jock Newbody, Gizmoduck), Jodi Carlisle (Dr. Sara Bellum, FOWL High Command, Mrs. Howl), Darlene Carr (Jingle Girl #1), Victoria Carroll (Dr. Brute, D-2000, Lawn Monster), Dan Castellaneta (Megavolt, FOWL Agent, FOWL High Command Voice, Huckster TV Announcer, Johnny T. Rex, Newscaster, Sir Glumfield, Smarmy Vegas Announcer), Cathy Cavadini, Christine Cavanaugh (Gosalyn Mallard), Cam Clark (Dance Instructor, Taxi Driver), Townsend Coleman (Guard, Pat, Vid Voice), Jesse Corti (Police Captain, Swenlin Swine, Wisconsin Webfoot), Brian Cummings (Fireman, Male Bowler, Weasel Loman), Jim Cummings (Darkwing Duck, Drake Mallard, Barrada, Cousin Globby, Dragon, Herb Muddlefoot, Flipper, Guard, Gumbo, King, Pick-El, Professor Moliarity, Negaduck, Nerd Mole, Tour Guide, Warden, Darkwing Duck, Webwulf,

Astroduck), Tim Curry (Taurus Bulba), E.G. Daly (Heatwave), Jennifer Darling (Camille Chameleon, Dr. Rhoda Dendron), Eddie Deezen (Hoof), Patty Deutsch (Emily Duckinson), Mark Dodson, David Doyle (Judge), Paul Eiding (Sir Cumference), Laurie Faso (Hammerhead Hannigan), Ron Feinberg (Chief Agent Gryzlikoff), David Fenoy (Officer), Miriam Flynn (Housewives), John Frost (Thaddeus Rockwell), Teresa Ganzel (Fly Girl, Prina Lott, Shelly), Linda Gary (Mother, Principal Farnsworth, TV Reporter), Brian George (Guitar), Joan Gerber (Gertie, Space Cow), Ellen Gerstell (Ample Pine, FOWL Secretary, Police Officer), Barry Gordon (Dr. Fossil), Michael Gough (Cowboy Doug, Jambalaya Jake), Michael Greer (Mona Lisa's Mouth, Museum Curator), Dorian Harewood (Official Guy), Jess Harnell (Bleeb), Jonathan Harris (Fineas Sharp), Phil Hartman (Paddywhack), Billie Hayes (Granny Whammy), Dana Hill (Tank Muddlefoot, Boy Scout #2), Tom Holiday (Policeman), Kevin Crosby Hopps (Nerd), Jerry Houser (Ham String), Marty Ingles (Beelzebub/Lucifer), Tino Insana (Reggie Bushroot, The Log), Robert Ito (Goose Lee), Tony Jay (Death), Richard Karron (A.F. Erret, Nikto), Jean Kasem (Ms. McElroy), Phyllis Katz (Female Bowler, Receptionist), Katie Leigh (Honker Muddlefoot, Boy Scout #1), Marilyn Lightstone (Hairdryer), Nancy Linari (Secretary), David Lodge (Teenage Punk #1), Sherry Lynn (Brat, Human Girl, Lightwave), Tress MacNeille (Opal Windbag, Webra Walters), Danny Mann (J. Gander Hooter, Daisy, Egg Man #1, Firefly, Guard, Spike, The Wacko, Hotshot), Kenneth Mars (Tuskernini), Andrea Martin (Splatter Phoenix), Mitzi McCall (Ammonia Pine), Edie McClurg (Cordilia), Roddy McDowell (Sir Quackmire), Terry McGovern (Launchpad McQuack, Ripcord McQuack, Thug Neanderthal, Zack), Candi Milo (Bimbette, Counselor, Duk Ling, Lamont), Lorenzo Music (Moliarity's Henchman, Webster), Pat Musick (Fans), Ron Pallelo (Ordinary Guy), Stuart Pankin (Dr. Denton), Rob Paulsen (Flarg, Flex, Klaatu II, Pelican, Steelbeak, Teenage Punk #2), Patrick Pinney (King), David Prince (Winslow Meekers), Hal Rayle (Actor, Bear, Bigfoot, Bignasti, Bulldog, Copter Cats, Dragon, Dr. Slug, Ego Monster, Huge Jerk, Leading Man, Radio Announcer, Ranger, Studio Guard, Witch Doctor), Pete Renaday (Derek Blunt), Zelda Reubenstein (Negaduck's Wife), Neil Ross (Dan Gander, Nodoff, T.V., Quack Mallardson), Maggie Roswell (Juniper, Newscaster, Supergal), Pam Segal (Radiowave), Susan Silo (Neptunia), Hal Smith (St. Peter), Kath Soucie (Morgana McCawber, Aunt Nasty, Mrs. Boriskowski, Daphne Duckbill, Princess Amira), Dani Staahl (Splatter Phoenix), John Stephenson (Major Synapse), Andre Stojka (Comic Book Editor, Museum Curator), Tad Stones (Quackrinomicon), Mark Taylor (Crosby), Susan Tolsky (Binkie Muddlefoot, Aunt Trudie, Dippy Girl Fan, Fat Lady Fan, Female Guard, Mother, Saleswoman, Talleah), Brenda Vaccaro (Slim), Chick Vennera (Johnny T-Rex), Marcia Wallace (Clovis, Didi Lovelost, Female Dognose, Mrs. Cavanaugh), B.J. Ward (Gloria Swansong, Jingle Girl #2, Stewardess, Pat), Frank Welker (Archie, Bats, Beachgoer, Big Webfoot, Cats, Crab Leader, Dean Tightbill, Dizzy, Dogs, Dr. Lilliput, Eak/Squeak, Hedgie, Lester, Meraculo McCawber, News Anchor, Pat, Rosie, Spike), April Winchell (Bianca Beakley), Diz White (Professor Bumprock), Patric Zimmerman (FOWL High Command).

Produced by: Walt Disney Television Animation. Supervising Producers: Tad Stones, Alan Zaslove. Producers: Bob Hathcock, Ken Kessel, Russell E. Mooney, James T. Walker. Story Editors: Gordon Bressack, Duane Capizzi, Carter Crocker, Kevin Crosby Hopps, Doug Kangdale, Tom Minton, Steve Roberts, Tad Stones, Bruce Talkington. Written by: John Behnke, Gordon Bressack, Kevin Campbell, Victor Cook, Pat Corcoran, Carter Crocker, Jeremy Cushner, Peter Hastings, Steven Hilbert, Charles Howell IV, Rob Humphrey, George Johnston, Gary Kelin, Katye Kuch, Doug Langdale, Eric Lewald, Julia Jane Lewald, Michael Maurer, Bill Motz, Joe Olsen, Jim Peterson, Steve Roberts, Dev Ross, Robert Roth, Sheryl Scarborough, Bruce Reid Schaefer, Mirth Schilder, Gary Sperling, Dean Stefan, Tad Stones, Jan Strnad, Steve Sustarsic, Ellen Svaco, Brian Swenlin, Coleen Taber, Len Uhley, Matt Uitz, Marlowe Shawn Weisman, Marion Wells. Dialogue Direction: Ginny McSwain. Animation Directors: Vincente Bassols, Carole Beers, David Brain, Terrence Harrison, John Kimball, Marsh Lamore, Rick Leon, Mircea Mantta, Tom Ray, Mitch Rochon, Bob Shellhorn, Michael Svayko,

Bob Treat, Bob Zamboni. Storyboard: Kurt Anderson, Ryan Anthony, Elizabeth Chapman, Yi-Chih Chen, Rich Chidlaw, Jill Cobert, Larry Eikleberry, Sharon Forward, Steve Gordon, Jan Green, James McLean, John Norton, David Prince, Chris Rutkowski, David Schwartz, Dale Schott, Roy Shishido, Robert Souza, Hank Tucker, Curt Walstead, Wendell Washer. Storyboard Clean-up Artists: Ryan Anthony, Elizabeth Chapman, Yi-Chih Chen, Rich Chidlaw, Paulette King, Chris Rutkowski, Kathrin Victor. Art Director: Fred Warter. Key Layout Design: Derek Carter, Kelly Day, Paul A. Felix, Colette Van Mierlo, Jim Schlenker, Fred Warter. Supervising Character Designer: Toby Shelton. Character Design: Tom Bird, Tom Owens, Kexx Singleton, Kenny Thompkins, J. Tom Owens, Jr. Prop Design: Darrel Bowen, Dennis Greco, Jeff Howard, Terry Hudson, David Mink, Marty Warner. Key Background Stylists: Greg Battes, Brooks Campbell, Gary Eggleston, James Gallego, Paro Hozumi, Bill Lorencz, Raymond Zibach. Color Key Stylists: Janet Cummings, Robin Draper, Debra Jorgensborg, Yolanda Rearick, Marta Skwara, Jill Stridivant, Britt Teegarden. Overseas Animation Supervisors: Colin Baker, Michael Fallows, Brian Ray. Supervising Timing Director: Marlene Robinson May. Timing Directors: Vincente Bassols, David Brain, Rick Leon, Tom Ray, James T. Walker. Assistant Producers: Peggy Becker, Selma Gladney, Maia Mattise, Liza-Ann Warren. Continuity Coordinators: Vonnie Batson, Myrna Bushman, Jim Finch, Kathrin Victor. Track Reading: Skip Craig. Post Production Manager: Sara Duran. Post Production Supervisor: Joseph Hathaway. Sound Dubbing Supervisor: Christopher Keith. Revisions Coordinator: Traci Tolman. Post Production Coordinators: Jeffrey Arthur, John Royer. Post Production Assistants: Nanci Battelle, Wade Zia Nassir, John Royer. Talent Coordinator: Olivia Miner. Production Assistants: Johanne Beaudoin, Beth Ann Knutson, Michelle Robinson, Michelle Schlicht, William Waggoner, LuAnne Wood, Melinda Wunsch. Script Coordinators: Susan McElroy, Marie Sager, Mirith Schilder. Archives Supervisor: Krista Bunn. Art Coordinator: Marjorie Warman. Shipping Coordinator: Craig Simpson. Managing Film Editor: Rich Harrison. Supervising Editors: Cecil E. Broughton, MPSE, Charlie King, MPSE. Sound Editors: Rick Hinson, MPSE, David Lynch, Marc Orfanos, Jerry Winicki. Dialogue Editor: Craig Paulsen. Assistant Editors: Jenny Harrison, Jim Harrison, Thomas Needell. Music by: Philip Giffin. Theme by: Steve Nelson, Thom Sharp. Animation Production by: Hanho Heung-Up Co., Ltd., Sunwoo Animation, Walt Disney Television Animation (Australia) Pty, Limited, Walt Disney Television Animation (Japan) Inc.

Goof Trap

Voices: Charlie Adler (Art Humanities, Brimley, Willie), Franklin Ajaye, Michael Bell (Burt, Dog #1, Driver, Manny), Gregg Berger, Scott Bullock (Nails), Corey Burton (Burly Guy, "How-to" Narrator, Melvin, Ring Master, School Dean), Jodi Carlisle (Anchor Woman, Snooty Woman), Nancy Cartwright (Pistol, Battle-Axe Mom, Melvin), Dan Castellaneta (Coach Roach), Brian Cummings (Bystander, Grand Marshal, Radio Announcer), Jim Cummings (Pete, Baby Pete, Cow, Jack, Mayor, Police Officer), Jennifer Darling, Eddie Deezen (Skooch), Debi Derryberry (Rose), David Doyle, Connor Duffy (Coupe Hatchback), Patrick Duffy (Harold Hatchback), Bill Farmer (Goofy, Baby Goofy, Gooferamus, J.J., Man, Mayor, Petunia, Supporter #1), Pat Fraley (Wally), Teresa Ganzel (Denise), Brad Garrett, Joanie Gerber, Ed Gilbert (Judge), Michael Gough (Fester Swollen, LaStrade), Dorian Harewood (Buster Vessel), Jess Harnell (Technician #1), Dana Hill (Max), Jerry Houser (Butch, Duke, Spud), Tino Insana (Narrator), Richard Karron (Slick), Sherry Lynn (Bimbette), Andrea Martin (Mrs. Willoughby, Edie McClurg, Candy Milo (Tooth), Gary Owens (Mr. Hammerhead), Charles Nelson Reilly, Rob Paulsen (P.J., Cameraman, Dagger, Eddie, Hercules, Leech, Moe, Snibbs, Twinkmeyer), Diane Pershing (Old Woman), Joe Piscopo (Bulk, Tan Roadster), Zelda Rubenstein, Bob Ridgely (Great Garbonzo), Kathy Soucie (Carhop, Cynthia Snodrew, Debbie, Mother, Nurse), Jim Staahl (Dr. Howard), Bruce Talkington (Director), Jay Thomas (Fenton Sludge), Susan Tolsky (Mrs. Pennypacker, Brenda Vaccaro (Gilda), Frank Welker (Bubba, Cats, Chainsaw, Clown, Dan Blather, Digger, Doberman, Dog #2, Dr. Watson, Giblet the Clown, Goldfish, Go-

pher, Grizz, Guard Dog, Junior, Mouse, Ooze Monster, Prince Freddy, Sabre Toothed Tiger, Sammy the Racehorse, Shark, Tiny Tuba, TV Announcer, Waffles), April Winchell (Peg, Danielle Wrathmaker, Doris, Little Old Lady, Mallory, NASA Scientist, Supporter #2, TV Reporter, Woman), William Windom (General).

Produced by: Walt Disney Television Animation. Supervising Producer: Robert Taylor. Producers: Ken Kessel, Robert Taylor, Hank Tucker, Roy Wilson. Post Production Producer: Bob Hathcock. Story Editors: Carter Crocker, Rich Fogel, Karl Geurs, Jymn Magon, Mark Seidenberg, Dean Stefan, Bruce Talkington. Written by: Jim Carlson, Mirith J.S. Colao, Steve Cuden, Steve Edelman, Rich Fogel, Gary Greenfield, Libby Hinson, Bob Kushell, Steven Levi, Julia Jane Lewald, Susan Maddocks, Jymn Magon, Mark McCorkle, Terry McDonnell, Mark McKain, Dennis Melonas, Cathryn Perdue, Mike Ryan, Jeff Saylor, Robert Schooley, Jeffrey Scott, Bruce Reid Schaefer, Mirith Schilder, Mark Seidenberg, George Shea, Steve Smith, Dean Stefan, Jan Strnad, Bryan Sullivan, Steve Sustarsic, Carl Swenson, Bruce Talkington, Mallory Tarcher, Chuck Tately, Kent Wadsworth, Marion Wells. Dialogue Director: Ginny McSwain. Animation Directors: Vincente Bassols, Ron Campbell, Carole Beers, Terence Harrison, Marsh Lamore, Mircea Mantta, Russell E. Mooney, Charles A. Nichols, Mitch Rochon, Bob Shellhorn, Mike Svayko, Richard Trueblood, Woody Yocum, Bob Zamboni. Storyboard: Viki Anderson, Ryan Anthony, Gaetan Brizzi, Paul Brizzi, Kuni Bowen, Ron Campbell, Kathleen Carr, Shawna Cha, Jill Colbert, Floro Dery, Larry Eikleberry, Sharon Forward, Holly Forsyth, Robert Fuentes, George Goode, Jan Green, Kirk Hansen, Stark Howell, Llyn Hunter, Craig Kemplin, Denise Koyama, Lonnie Lloyd, Fred Lucky, Don MacKinnon, Enrique May, Jim McLean, Andre Von Morisse, Tom Nelson, John Norton, Nick Pill, Albert Ring, Chris Rutkowski, Swinton Scott, Roy Shishido, David Smith, Robert Souza, Vincenzo Trippetti, Hank Tucker, Andre Von Morisse, Curt Walstead, Wendell Washer, Phil Weinstein, David Williams, Roy Wilson. Storyboard Revisions: Carin-Anne Anderson, Mark Bierbaum, Shawna Cha, Karl Gnass, Elizabeth Holzman, Stark Howell, Paulette King, Andre Von Morisse, Thomas Nelson, John Norton, Albert Ring, Mitch Rochon, Mike Svayko, Curt Walstead, Phil Weinstein, Woody Yocum, Bob Zamboni. Layout Styling and Development: J. Michael Spooner. Key Layout Design: Utit Choomuang, Jim Schlenker, Kelly Day, Dennis Greco, Carol Police, J. Michael Spooner, Colette Van Mierlo, Paul A. Felix. Character Styling and Development: Alex Mann. Character Design: Alex Mann, Tom Bird, Kuni Bowen, Larry Eikleberry, Elizabeth Holzman, Ritsuko Notani, Thomas Nelson, J. Tom Owens, Jr. Computer Graphics by: Kelly Day. Prop Design: Terry Hudson, David Mink, Marty Warner. Key Background Stylists: Greg Battes, Hye Coh, Gary Eggleston, James Gallego. Color Key Stylists: Janet Cummings, Robin Draper, Yolanda Rearick, Britt Teegarden, Nancy Ulene. Cel Painter: Marie Boughamer. Animation Supervisor: Bob Baxter. Overseas Layout Supervisor: Pere Van Reyk. Overseas Animation Supervisors: Bob Baxter, Mike Fallows, Doug Johnson, Michael Longden, Pere Van Reyk. Supervising Timing Director: Marlene Robinson May. Timing Directors: Vincente Bassols, Carole Beers, David Brain, Jesse Cosio, Barbara Dourmashkin-Case, Jang-Gil Kim, John Kimball, Robert Kirk, Marsh Lamore, Rick Leon, Russell E. Mooney, Brian Ray, Bob Treat, Richard Trueblood, Woody Yocum. Assistant Producers: Lori Baio, Selma Gladney, Beth Ann Knutson, Maia Mattise, Zahra Dowlatabadi, Donna Alcock Smith, Melinda Wunsch. Continuity Coordinators: Vonnie Batson, Myrna Bushman, Barbara Donatelli, Jim Finch, Myoung Smith, Kathrin Victor. Track Reading: Skip Craig. Post Production Managers: Sara Duran, Cheryl Murphy. Post Production Supervisors: Joseph Hathaway, Jeffrey Arthur, Regina Brittle. Sound Dubbing Supervisor: Christopher Keith. Post Production Coordinators: Jeffrey Arthur, John Royer. Post Production Assistants: Nanci Battelle, Steve Werner. Talent Coordinators: Lynne Batchelor, Jamie Thomason. Production Assistants: Johanne Beaudoin, Greg Chalekian, Paul Fabela, Beth Ann Knutson, Laura Perrotta, Michelle Schlicht-Pniewski, Yolanda Valdez, William Waggoner. Script Coordinators: Connie Gombert, Leona Jernigan, Anita Lish, Mirth

Schilder. Archives Supervisor: Krista Bunn. Production Art Service Coordinators: John Hall, Jodey Kaminski, Yolanda V. Saylor, Karen Silva, William Waggoner. Shipping Coordinator: Craig Simpson. Managing Film Editor: Rich Harrison. Supervising Editor: Charles King, M.P.S.E. Sound Editors: Rick Hinson, M.P.S.E. Foley Editor: Ron Eng. Editorial Consultant: Sam Horta. Supervising Sound Editors: Brian F. Mars, Timothy J. Borquez, Timothy M. Mertens, Michael A. Gollom, Gregory LaPlante. Sound Editors: Timothy M. Mertens, Michael A. Gollom, Gregory LaPlante. Dialogue Editors: James N. Harrison, Jenny Harrison, Thomas Jaeger, Andrew Rose. Assistant Producer Music: Bambi Moé. Music by: Robert Irving, Mark Watters. Theme by: Randy Petersen, Kevin Quinn, Robert Irving. Title Theme Produced and Arranged by: John Beasley. Music and Dialogue Editing: Marc Perlman. Sound Effects Editing: Jim Hodson, Bill Koepnick. Re-Recording Mixers: Jim Hodson, Bill Koepnick. *Animation Production by: Walt Disney Television Animation (Australia) Pty. Ltd.* Animation Directors: Ian Harrowell, Henry Neville. Assistant Directors: Janey Dunn, Mickie Cassidy, Di Rudder. Animators: Kang Zhu, Jean Tych, Kevin Peaty, Lianne Hughes, Warwick Gilbert, Mike Stapleton, Gairden Cooke, Morris Lee, Andrew Collins, Steven Taylor, Ariel Ferrari, Steven Trenbirth, Dick Dunn, Wally Micati, Helen McAdam, Kathie O'Rourke, Dwayne Labbe, Alexs Sterderman, Mike Chavez, Ty Bosco, Josef Szekeres, Martin Coombe, Adam Murphy, Carol Seidl. Layout Supervisors: Alex Nicholas, John Hill. Production Manager: Barry Pearce. Layout Artists: Yosh Barry, Scott Bennett, David Skinner, Mark Mulgrew, Bun Ung, Kevin Wotton, Steve Cooper, Nick Pill. Animation and Backgrounds: Freelance Animators Pty, Ltd., New Zealand. Background Supervisor: Beverley McNamara. Background Artists: Barry Dean, Jerry Liew, Paul Pattie, Helen Steele, Felice Ferrer. Production Manager: Terry Smith. Production Management: Charm Wilson, Nerida Bennett, Robert Letteri, Fernando Letteri, Carole Salter, Jose Barrerios, Mark Evans, Gary Page. *Animation Production by Walt Disney Animation (Japan), Inc.* Animation Supervisor: Shigeru Yamamoto. Director: Saburo Hashimoto. Animation Direction: Animal House. Animators: Hiro Tsuji, Teruo Handa, Masakazu Ikeda, Kenichi Tsuchiya, Kenichi Shimizu, Ayumi Namiki. Backgrounds: Animal House. Additional Production Facility: Morning-Sun Studio. Ink & Paint Services: Pacific Rim Productions, Inc. *Animation Productions by: Kennedy Cartoons, Inc.* Animation Director: Glen Kennedy. Animators: Sang Jin Kim, Todd Sullivan, Zaldy Zuno, John Williamson, Troy Sullivan, Darren Vandenburg, Grant Lounsbury, James Straus, Sergio Mazzotta, Dan Lee, Stan Chiu, Stephen Baker, Yon Kun Noh, Mark Petlock, Etae Kim, Enzo Avolio, Won Sung Ku, Derek Bond, Zaldy Zuno, Doug Smith, Mike Stevens, Wendy Parkin. Layout: Ed Lee, Brian Poelhman, Eui-Sun Hwang, Nam Kook Lee, Owen Smith, Raymond Romero, Richmond Zuno. Production Managers: Sue Chung, Mari Herrera, Alan Kennedy, Rey Zuno. Assistant Animation: Bon Art Studios. Ink & Paint Services: Thai Wang Film Productions Co., Ltd., Kennedy Cartoons Manila, Inc. *Animation Production by: Wang Film Production Co., Ltd., Animation Production by: Walt Disney Animation (France) S.A.* Animation Directors: Jean-Christophe Poulain, Maros Zoltan. Layout Artists: Olivier Adam, Philippe Balmossiere, Bolhem Bouchiba, Jean Duval, Vincent Massy, Richard Poulain, Yoshimi Tamura, Zoltan Maros. Background Supervisor: Pierre Pavloff. Background Artists: Olivier Adam, Jean-Paul Fernandez, Patricia Millereau, Vincent Misser, Nathalie Nicolas. Animation Supervisor: Marc Eoche-Duval. Animators: Jean-Luc Ballester, Bolhem Bouchiba, Sylvain Deboissy, Patrick Delage, Marc Eoche-Duval, Pierre Fassel, Bruno Gaumetou, Arnold Gransac, Matias Marcos, Dominique Monfery, Catherine Poulain, Jean-Christophe Roger, Pascal Ropars, Stephane Sainte Foi. Effects Animation: Thierry Chaffoin. Assistant Director: Raphael Vicente. Production Manager: Etienne Longa. *Animation Production by: Sunwoo Animation* Directors: Park Dong Kwun, Byun Kang Moon, Yun Young Sang, Lee Sung Woo. Background: Kim Young Gu. Layout: Cho Se Jin. Animation: Kang Chul, Won Sung Goo, Lee Gun, Han Chul Hee, Lee Kyoung Ho, Kwon Hyuk Jae, Song Kyung Sik, Jung Kyoung Sub. Camera: Lim Chul Kyu. Manager of

Production: Choi Yong Kum. *Animation Production by: Guimares Productions. Animation Production by: Moving Images International, Inc.*

DISNEY'S THE LITTLE MERMAID

Voices: Jodi Benson (Ariel), Samuel E. Wright (Sebastian), Edan Gross (Flounder), Ken Mars (King Triton), Charlie Adler, Joe Alaskey, Jeff Bennett, Mary Kay Bergman, Sheryl Bernstein, Danny Cooksey, Jesse Corti, Dave Coulier, Brian Cummings, Jim Cummings, Tim Curry, Keene Curtis, Betty Ford, Linda Gary, Joanie Gerber, Edan Gross, Whitby Hertford, Tino Insana, Jordon Jacobson, Richard Karron, David Lander, Scott Menville, Alan Oppenheimer, Hal Rayle, Kimmy Robertson, Neil Ross, Kath Soucie, Cree Summer, Russi Taylor, Frank Welker.

Produced by: Walt Disney Television Animation. Producer/Director: Jamie Mitchell. Co-Producers/Story Editors: Tedd Anasti, Patsy Cameron. Written by: Tedd Anasti, Laraine Arkow, Peter S. Beagle, Patsy Cameron, Emily Dwass, Lynn Lefler, Tony Marino, James Markovich, Chuck Menville, Marie Sager, Alicia Marie Schudt, David Schwartz, Chris Weber, Karen Willson. Dialogue Directors: Jamie Thomason, Meg McSweeney. Director: Mircea Mantta. Animation Directors: Dale Case, Terence Harrison, Russell E. Mooney, Bob Shellhorn. Storyboard: Victor Cook, Floro Dery, Jaime Diaz, John Dorman, John Flagg, Holly Forsyth, George Goode, Todd Kurosawa, Lonnie Lloyd, Frank Nissen, Ritsuko Notani, Robert Souza, Phil Weinstein. Art Directors: Ed Chernter, Ron Dias. Key Background Stylists: Brooks Campbell, Hye Coh, David Darrow, Michael Humphries, Sai Ping Lok, Raymond Zibach. Character Design: Len Smith, Ritsuko Notani. Assistant Producer: Traci M. Tolman. Key Layout Design: Paul A. Felix, J. Michael Spooner. Effects Animation: Mark Dindal. Character Animation: Ritsuko Notani. Prop Design: Tom Foxmarnick, Bob Pauley, Marty Warner. Color Key Stylists: Debra Jorgensborg, Marta Skwara. Cel Painter: Marie Boughamer. Storyboard Revisions: Kuni Bowen, Shawna Cha, John Fox, Mircea Mantta, Ritsuko Notani, Albert Ring, Curt Walstead. Timing Directors: Barbara Dourmashkin-Case, Robert Kirk, Marsh Lamore, Rick Leon, Russell E. Mooney, Brian Ray, Bob Shellhorn, Woody Yocum. Effects Consultant: Mark Dindal. Continuity Coordinators: Vonnie Batson, Barbar Donatelli, Brian Ray, Myoung Smith, Kathrin Victor. Track Reading: Skip Craig, Theresa Gilroy Neilsen. Post Production Manager: Cheryl Murphy. Sound Dubbing Supervisor: Christopher Keith. Post Production Coordinator: John Royer. Post Production Assistants: Nanci Battelle, Steve Werner. Production Assistants: Paul Fabela, Johanne Beaudoin. Script Coordinator: Pamela Kincheloe. Archives Supervisor: Krista Bunn. Art Coordinators: Marjorie Warman-Allan, John Hall, Karen Silva. Shipping Coordinator: Craig Simpson. Associate Producer Music: Bambi Moé. Music by: Dan Foliart. Theme by: Alan Menken. *Songs Just a Little Love, You Got to Be You* Music by: Tom Snow. Lyrics by: Jack Feldman. *To the Edge of the Sea, In Harmony, Dis is De Life* Words and Music by: Silversher & Silversher. *The Lobster Mobster's Mob* Words by: Tedd Anasti, Patsy Cameron. Music by: Michael Silversher. *Da Beddie Bye Blues, Sing a New Song* Words and Music by: Randy Petersen, Kevin Quinn. Songs Produced and Arranged by: Robby Merkin, Steve Gelfand. Supervising Editors: Sam Horta, John O. Robinson III. Post Production Sound Supervisor: Timothy J. Borquez. Picture Editors: Timothy Mertens, Kevin D. Spears. Music Editors: Brian F. Mars, Alex Wilkenson. Sound Editors: Michael Collom, Timothy Garrity, Michael Geisler, Greg LaPlante. Dialogue Editors: Thomas Jaeger, Rich Freeman. Animation Production by Walt Disney Animation (Japan) Inc. Animation Supervisor: Shigeru Yamamoto. Directors: Saburo Hashimoto, Takashi Ui. Animation and Animation Direction: Animal House, JC Staff, Magic Bus, Tama Productions. Animation Directors: Takeshi Atomura, Madoka Yasue, Hisashi Wada, Hiroshi Kawamata, Shinichi Suzuki. Animators: Koichi Maruyama, Masaji Tada, Masaaki Kudo, Kiyomi Miyakawa, Mitsuko Ohtaku, Masumi Maeda, Miyuki Hoshikawa, Yoshiaki Matsuda, Heihachiro Tanaka, Yuri Handa, Yasuo Torii, Masakazi Ikeda, Kiyoshi Nakamura, Hiro Tsuji. Backgrounds: Animal House, Film Magic, JC Staff, Studio Fuga, Masumi Nose. Background Supervisor:

Masayoshi Banno. Background Artists: Michiko Taniguchi, Naomi Sakimoto, Kazushige Takato, Tachiko Kimura, Shuichi Hirowatari, Satoshi Matsudaira, Junzaburo Kaiho. Additional Production Facilities: Jade Animation Productions, Morning-Sun Studio, Nakamura Productions, Studio Robin, Studio Cats, Light Foot, Takahashi Productions.

RAW TOONAGE
With the Voice Talents of: Jack Angel, Rene Auberjonois, Jeff Bennett (Jitters A. Dog), Gregg Berger, Scott Bullock, Rodger Bumpass (Grumbles the Grizzly), Corey Burton (Ludwig Von Drake), Jody Carlisle, Nancy Cartwright (Fawn Deer), Christine Cavanaugh (Gosalyn Mallard), Brian Cummings, Jim Cummings (Bonkers D. Bobcat, Norman, Don Karnage, Roderick Lizzard), Bill Farmer (Goofy), David Fenoy, June Foray (Norman's aunt), Pat Fraley, Teresa Ganzel, Maurice LaMarche, Katie Leigh, Steve Mackall (Marsupilami), Tress MacNeille, Gail Matthius, Terry McGovern (Launchpad McQuack), Rita Moreno, Gary Owens (Badly Animated Man), Rob Paulsen, Joe Piscopo, Hal Rayle, Kath Soucie, Russi Taylor, Dave Thomas, Marcia Wallace, B.J. Ward, Frank Welker (Maurice), Samuel E. Wright (Sebastian), Alan Young (Scrooge McDuck).

Produced by: Walt Disney Television Animation. Supervising Producer: Larry Latham. Producers: Larry Latham (Bonkers, Host & Parody Segments), Dan Rounds (Song Segment), Ed Wexler (Marsupilami Segment). Story Editors: Kevin Crosby Hopps (Marsupilami Segment), Tom Minton (Host & Parody Segments), Ralph Sanchez (Bonkers Segment). Producer/Director: David Block (Song Segment). Written by: Laraine Arkow, John Behnke, Terrie Collins, Jeremy Cushner, Shari Goodhartz, Kevin Crosby Hopps, Rob Humphrey, Mina Johnson, Alan Katz, Tom Minton, Bill Motz, Jim Peterson, Kevin Rafferty, Mark Rhodes, Dev Ross, Bob Roth, Ralph Sanchez, Robert Schechter, Alicia Marie Schudt, George Shea, Gary Sperling, Richard Stanley, Len Uhley, Mark Zaslove. Dialogue Director: Ginny McSwain. Animation Directors: Carole Beers, William Houchins, John Kimball, Marsh Lamore, Rick Leon, Mircea Mantta, Bob Shellhorn, James T. Walker. Storyboard: Carine-Anne Anderson, Kurt Anderson, Rich Chidlaw, Victor Cook, Thom Enriquez, Will Finn, Holly Forsyth, George Goode, Antoine Guilbaud, Llyn Hunter, Denise Koyama, Larry Latham, Enrique May, Jim McLean, Thomas Nelson, Ritsuko Notani, David Prince, David Schwartz, David Smith, Robert Souza, Hank Tucker, Andre Von Morisse, Curt Walstead, Roy Wilson. Storyboard Revisions: Mark Bierbaum, Shawna Cha, John Fox, Stark Howell, Llyn Hunter, Craig Kemplin, Thomas Nelson, Albert Ring. Key Layout Design: Tom Bird, Brooks Campbell, Derek Carter, Utit Choomaung, Kelly Day, Thom Enriquez, Paul A. Felix, Dennis Greco, Carol Police, Jim Schlenker. Character Design: Tony Bancroft, Brian Ferguson, Carole Holliday, Ritsuko Notani, Len Smith, Kenny Thompkins. Character Animation: Tony Bancroft, Mike Surrey. Prop Design: Donovan Cook, Tom Foxmarnick, Dennis Greco, Greg Guler, Terry Hudson, Vadim Sokolov, Len Smith, Marty Warner. Key Background Stylists: Brooks Campbell, Bill Lorencz, Raymond Zibach. Color Key Stylists: Robin Draper, Debra Jorgensborg, Yolanda Rearick, Jill Stirdivant, Britt Teegarden. Cel Painter: Marie Boughamer. Overseas Animation Supervisor: Bob Baxter. Overseas Layout Supervisor: Pere Van Reyk. Supervising Timing Director: Marlene Robinson May. Timing Directors: Vincente Bassols, Jang-Gil Kim, Mitch Rochon, Bob Shellhorn, Woody Yocum. Assistant Producer: Michelle Pappalardo-Robinson. Continuity Coordinators: Vonnie Batson, Myrna Bushman, Barbara Donatelli, Jim Finch, Myoung Smith, Kathrin Victor. Track Reading: Skip Craig, Theresa Gilroy-Nielsen. Post Production Manager: Cheryl Murphy. Film Editors: Elen Orson, Susan Edmunson. Post Production Supervisors: Jeffrey Arthur, Regina Brittle, Joseph Hathaway. Sound Dubbing Supervisor: Christopher Keith. Post Production Coordinator: John Royer. Post Production Assistants: Nancy Battelle, Steve Werner. Talent Coordinator: Jamie Thomason. Production Assistants: Johanne Beaudoin, Michelle Schlicht-Pniewski. Script Coordinators: Laraine Arkow, Janna Bryan, Connie Gombert. Archives Supervisor: Krista Bunn. Art Coordinators: Jodey Kaminski, Karen Silva, Marjorie Warman-Allan. Shipping Coordinator: Craig Simpson. Post Production Sound: Roy Braverman (Marsupilami Segment). Dialogue Editing: Marc Perlman. Re-Recording Mixers: Jim Hodson, Bill Koepnick. Assistant Producer Music: Bambi Moé. Theme by: Patrick DeRemer. Additional Themes by: Patrick DeRemer, Ed Fournier, Mark Watters. Music by: Stephen James Taylor, Mark Watters. Songs by: Richard Levinson, Silversher & Silversher. Songs Produced by: John Beasley, Robby Merkin, Steve Gelfand. Animation Production by: Wang Film Production Co., Ltd.

DISNEY'S BONKERS
The following credits are only for those episodes produced for the *Bonkers* series and do not include the compilation episodes originally seen on *Raw Toonage*.

Voices: Charlie Adler (Toon Siren, Louie the Ghost, Mr. Doodles, Tiny), Joe Alaskey (Flaps), Wayne Allwine (Mickey Mouse), Jack Angel (Max Coody, Pencil), Tony Anselmo (Donald Duck), Ed Asner (Grumps), John Astin (The Mole), Rene Auberjonois, Jon Bauman (Bull Finch), Michael Bell (The Collector, Julio Calimari), Jeff Bennett (Jitters A. Dog, Bull Frog, Roderick Lizard, Meenie), Gregg Berger (Mr. McScam, Mr. Corkscrew, Pelican), Earl Boen (Police Chief Leonard Kanifky), Sorell Booke (Boss Hoss), Eileen Brennan (Lillith DuPrave), S. Scott Bullock (Mr. Big, Skunky Skunk, Mikey Muffin, Charles Quibble, Dirty Pencil), Rodger Bumpass (Grumbles Grizzly, Mean Ol' Wolf, Agent Tolson), Corey Burton (Professor Ludwig Von Drake, Gas Truck), William Callaway (Vic "Stiff-Lips" Sullivan), Hamilton Camp (Commercial Director, Pitts), Nancy Cartwright (Fawn Deer), Mary Jo Catlett, Marty Cohen, Jesse Corti, Robert Costanzo (Crunchy Potato Chip), Peter Cullen (Abominable Snowman, Mackey McSlime), Jim Cummings (Bonkers D. Bobcat, Lucky Piquel, Bull Dog, Mynie), Keene Curtis, Karla DeVito (Miranda Wright), Mark Dodson, David Doyle (W.W. Wacky), Louise Duarte (Baa-bara), Bill Farmer, David Fenoy, Danny Ferro (T.J. Finger), June Foray (Ma Parker), Pat Fraley (Bucky Buzzsaw, Barker Boy, Big Boom), Matt Frewer (Peter Blaine), Brad Garrett (Toon Louse, Fireball Frank), Linda Gary (Helga), Gilbert Gottfried (Grandpa Ernie, Two-Bits), Michael Gough, Erin Gray (Shirley Wright), Mark Hamill, Dorian Harewood (Alto, Officer Stark), Jess Harnell (Toon Bomb, Charlie), Pamela Hayden, Billie Hayes, Dana Hill (Timmy), Gordon Hunt, Tino Insana (Scatter Squirrel, Stew), Bob Ito (Sergeant Tetsuo), Lauri Johnson, Richard Karron, John Kassir, Julia Kato, Maurice LaMarche (Tuttle Turtle, Mr. Blackenblue, Smarts), Katie Leigh (Belle), Rene Levant (Marilyn Piquel, Catia Legs Go-on-a-lot, Maggie the Worm), Tress MacNeille (Cheryl Germ, Francine Kominsky), Kenneth Mars (Gloomy), Chuck McCann, Sam McMurray, Don Messick (Mayor), Pat Musick, Rita Moreno (Tanya Trunk), Joe Onesto, Alan Oppenheimer, Stuart Pankin (Pops Klock, Mammoth Mammoth), Rob Paulsen (Zoom), Ron Perlman (Sergeant Francis Q. Grating), Jan Rapsin, Hal Rayle, Bob Ridgely (Al Vermin, Brain Z-Bot), Alex Rocco, Roger Rose, Neil Ross (Dobie), Stanley Ralph Ross, Maggie Roswell, Susan Silo, Hal Smith (Santa Claus), Cree Summer (Saxophone), Rip Taylor (Wacky Weasel), Brian Tochi, Chick Venerra (Chick, Moe), B.J. Ward, Beau Weaver (Jingle), Frank Welker (Fall-Apart Rabbit, Toots, Toon Radio, Toon Handbag, Quark, Barker Boy, Elmo, Gentle Ben Butterman, Ghost), Diz White, April Winchell (Dylandra "Dil" Piquel), Anderson Wong.

Produced by: Walt Disney Television Animation. Supervising Producer: Bob Hathcock. Producers: David Block, Bob Hathcock, Gordon Kent, David Schwartz, Robert Taylor, Richard Trueblood, Hank Tucker. Directors: David Block, Larry Latham, Robert Taylor, Roy Wilson. Co-Producer: Duane Capizzi. Supervising Story Editor: Duane Capizzi. Story Editors: Carter Crocker, Karl Geurs, Kevin Crosby Hopps, Matt McCorkle, Ralph Sanchez, Robert Schooley, Bruce Talkington, Len Uhley. Written by: Laraine Ankow, Jordana Arkin, Irv Bauer, John Behnke, Kevin Campbell, Steve Cuden, Shari Goodhartz, Libby Hinson, Rob Humphrey, Stephen Levi, Fred Lucky, Kathryn Perdue, Jim Peterson, Dev Ross, Ralph Sanchez, Jeff Saylor, Robert Schechter, William Scherer, Gary Sperling, Richard Stanley, Dean Stefan, Steve Sustarsic, Ellen Svaco, Brian Swenlin, Carl Swenson, Colleen Taber, Bruce Talkington, David Titcher, Len Uhley, Marlowe S. Weisman, Marion Wells, Mark Zaslove. Dialogue Directors: Gordon Kent, Andrea Romano. Voice Director: Ginny McSwain. Supervising Animation Director: Karen Peterson. Animation Directors: Vincente Bassols, Carole Beers, Dale Case, Terrence Harrison, William Houchins, John Kimball, Marsh Lamore, Rick Leon, Mircea Mantta, Charles A. Nichols, Brian Ray, Mitch Rochon, Bob Shellhorn, Mike Svayko, Richard Trueblood, James T. Walker, Woody Yocum, Bob Zamboni. Storyboard: Carin-Anne Anderson, Kurt Anderson, Viki Anderson, Ryan Anthony, Mark Bierbaum, Ron Bierbaum, Kuni Bowen, Ron Campbell, Kathleen Carr, Shawna Cha, Rich Chidlaw, Jill Cobert, Victor Cook, Floro Dery, Larry Eikleberry, Holly Forsyth, Sharon Forward, John Fox, Robert Fuentes, Karl Gnass, George Goode, Steve Gordon, Jan Green, Paul Gruwell, Elizabeth Holzman, Stark Howell, Llyn Hunter, Craig Kemplin, Denise Koyama, Lonnie Lloyd, Enrique May, Jim McLean, Thomas Nelson, Frank Nissen, John Norton, David Prince, Debra Pugh, Albert Ring, Chris Rutkowski, David Schwartz, David Smith, Roy Shishido, Robert Souza, Vincenzo Trippetti, Curt Walstead, Wendell Washer, Sherilan Weinhart, Phil Weinstein, Roy Wilson, Kevin Wurzer. Storyboard Revisions: Carole Beers, Mark Bierbaum, Kuni Bowen, Shawna Cha, John Fox, Karl Gnass, Stark Howell, Llyn Hunter, Paulette King, Phil Weinstein. Layout Development: J. Michael Spooner. Key Layout Design: Derek Carter, Paul A. Felix, Dennis Greco, Paul Gruwell, Jim Schlenker, Robert St. Pierre, Colette Van Mierlo. Key Layout Design: Paul A. Felix, Dennis Greco. Animation Layout Supervisor: Andre Clavel. Animation Layout: Utit Choomuang, Andre Clavel, Michael Genz, Robert St. Pierre. Character Design: Tom Bird, Kuni Bowen, Elizabeth Holzman, Shawn Keller, Craig Kellman, Bob Kline, Dana Landsberg, Alex Mann, J. Tom Owens, Jr., Kexx Singleton, Len Smith, Kenny Thompkins, Kevin Wurzer. Character Animation: Jesse Cosio, Michael Genz, William Houchins. Prop Design: Tom Foxmarnick, Greg Guler, Terry Hudson, Elizabeth Holzman, David Mink, Marty Warner. Assistant Producer: Margot Pipkin. Unit Supervising Animation Director: Warren Marshall. Background Development: Gary Eggleston. Key Background Stylists: Greg Battes, Brooks Campbell, Hye Coh, Greg Drolette, James Gallego, Paro Hozumi, Bill Lorencz, Serge Michaels, Raymond Zibach. Color Key Stylists: Janet Cummings, Debra Jorgensborg, Robin Draper Koblin, Yolanda Rearick, Marta Skwara, Britt Teegarden, Nancy Ulene. Overseas Animation Supervisors: Michael Fallows, Michael Longden. Assistant Producers: Selma Gladney, Jessica Koplos-Miller, Matt Pook, Larry Smith. Supervising Timing Director: Marlene Robinson May. Cel Painters: Marie Boughamer, Eyde Sheppherd. Computer Animation: Kelly Day. Assistant Producer Music: Bambi Moé. Music by: Mark Watters. Title Theme Written, Produced and Arranged by: Randy Petersen, Kevin Quinn. *The Rubber Room* Words and Music by: Randy Petersen, Kevin Quinn. Song Produced and Arranged by: Randy Petersen, Kevin Quinn. Post Production Manager: Cheryl Murphy. Post Production Supervisor: Jeffrey Arthur. Sound Dubbing Supervisor: Christopher Keith. Talent Coordinators: Daniel Pensiero III, Jamie Thomason. Timing Directors: Vincente Bassols, Jesse Cosio, Barbara Dourmashikin-Case, Terence Harrison, William Houchins, Jang-Gil Kim, Robert Kirk, Marsh Lamore, Mircea Mantta, Brian Ray, Mike Svayko, Bob Treat, Woody Yocum. Supervising Final Check: Marlene Robinson May. Continuity Coordinators: Vonnie Batson, Myrna Bushman, Barbara Donatelli, Barbara Dourmashikin-Case, Jim Finch, Marlene Robinson May, Myoung Smith, Kathrin Victor. Track Reading: Skip Craig. Supervising Editor: Robert Fischer, Jr. Editors: Robert S. Birchard, Monte Bramer, Susan Edmunson, Elen Orson, Phil Resnick. Post Production Sound Supervisor: Timothy J. Borquez. Supervising Sound Editors: Robert Redpath, John O. Robinson III. Re-Recording: Sherry Klein, C.A.S., Robert Edmondson, Edward Suski. Supervising Picture Editor: Sam Horta. Supervising Music Editor: Brian F. Mars. Sound Editors: Neil Anderson, Rick Freeman, Timothy Garrity, Michael Geisler, Michael A. Gollom, Thomas Jaeger, Greg LaPlante, Nancy McLound, Brian McPherson, Sanford Ponder, John Reynolds, Kenneth Young. Music Editors: William Griggs, Marc Perlman, Alex Wilkinson. Dialogue Editors: Melissa Gentry, Jennifer Mertens, Craig Paulsen. Sound Effects Editing: Bill Koepnick, M.P.S.E., Jim Hodson. Re-Recording Mixers: Jim Hodson, C.A.S., Bill Koepnick. *Animation Production by: Sunwoo Animation.* Directors: Park Dong Kwun, Kin Jung Gon, Lin Jung Kyu, Byun Kang Moon, Lee Sung Woo. Background: Kim Young Gu, Yun Woo Sang. Layout: Cho Se Jin, Hong Jin Sunng. Animation: Bag Jong Chul, Kang Chul, Lee Gun, Lee Kyoung Ho, Choi Huon, Han Chul Hee, Kwon Hyuk Jae, Chung Nak Jin, Kim Chan Jo, Hong Jin Soo, Jung Kyoung Sub. Camera: Lim Chul Kyu. Manager of Production: Choi Yong Kum. *Animation Production by: Walt Disney Animation (Japan) Inc.* Animation Supervisor: Shigeru Yamamoto. Directors: Saburo Hashimoto, Hiro Tsuji. Animation Directors: Takeshi Atomura, Ritsuko Notani, Madoka Yasue, Hisashi Wada, Hiroshi Kawamata, Hiro Tsuji, Madoka Yasue. Animators: Banshu Fujiwara, Teruo Handa, Yuri Handa, Miyuki Hoshikawa, Masakazu Ikeda, Isamitsu Kashima, Kenji Kajiwara, Masaaki Kudo, Masumi Maeda, Koichi Maruyama, Yoshiaki Matsuda, Yuko Matsuo, Kiyomi Miyakawa, Hirofumi Nakada, Ayumi Namiki, Kiyoshi Nakamura, Mitsuko Ohtaku, Hiromasa Sato, Kenichi Shimizu, Masaji Tada, Heihachiro Tanaka, Kenji Tsuchiya, Yasuo Torii, Hiro Tsuji, Sachiko Wakabayashi, Kazue Yamanaka. Background Supervisors: Masayoshi Banno, Shunji Kimura. Background Artists: Michiko Taniguchi, Norimitsu Kobayashi, Masanori Yamamoto, Shuichi Hirowatari, Tachiko Kimura. Backgrounds: Jinzaburo Kaiho, Satoshi Matsudaira. Animation and Animation Direction by: Animal House, Tama Production. Backgrounds by: Film Magic, Tama Production. Additional Production Facilities: Nakamura Productions, Studio Robin, Light Foot, Studio Cats, Anime Room, Morning-Sun Studio, Takahashi Production, Jade Animation. *Animation Production by: Guimares Productions. Animation Production by: Walt Disney Television Animation (Australia) Pty. Ltd.* Animation Director: Chris Bradley. Assistant Directors: Janey Dunn, Mickie Cassidy, Di Rudder. Animators: Gairden Cooke, Kang Zhu Lin, Andrew Collins, Dick Dunn, Helen McAdam, Mike Stapleton, Morris Lee, Steven Taylor, Wally Micati, Marek Kochout, Andrew Brooks, Peter Candeland, Paul Newell, Dwayne Labbe, Carol Seidl, Ariel Ferrari, Lily Dell, Mac Monks, Warwick Gilbert, Ty Bosco, Ian White, Martin Coombe, Alexs Sterderman, Kevin Peaty, Nilo Santillan, Georges Abolin, Troy Saliba, Mike Chavez, Henry Neville, Lianne Hughes, Josef Szekeres, Adam Murphy, Oscar Perez, Murray Debus, Dave MacDougall, Chris Derochie, Stephen Grant. Layout Supervisors: Alex Nicholas, John Hill. Layout Artists: Yosh Barry, Kevin Wotton, Steve Cooper, David Skinner, Kevin Spill, Nick Pill, Bruce Pedersen. Background Supervisor: Beverley McNamara. Background Artists: Barry Dean, Paul Pattie, Felice Ferrer, Jerry Liew, Helen Steele, George Humphrey, Milana Borkert. Ink and Paint Supervisors: Ruth Edelman, Angela Bodini, Robyn Drayton, Christine O'Connor, Liz Lane. Production Manager: Terry W. Smith. Production Management: Dan Forster, Robert Letteri, Carole Salter, Mark Evans, Charm Lee, Fernando Letteri, Jose Barrerios, Gary Page. *Animation Production by: Kennedy Cartoons, Inc.* Animation Director: Glen Kennedy. Animators: Enzo Avolio, Stephen Baker, Joseph Balederas, Derek Bond, Reinier Cataylo, Stan Chiu, Rolando Delfino, Sandy de Ramos, Nong Ditan, Anthony Estrada, Anabelle Galvez, Linton Gonzaga, Yoon Young Kang, Sang Jin Kim, Charlie Lee, Dan Lee, Ferdie Lorena, Grant Lounsbury, Jose Miguel, Yon Kun Noh, Wendy Parkin, Mark Petlock, Val Ramirez, Mike Stevens, Todd Sullivan, Troy Sullivan, Zaldy Zuno. Layout: Gord Sinclair, Ed Lee, Paul Lee, Raymond Romero, Owen Smith, Richmond Zuno. Assistant Animation/Ink & Paint Services: Kennedy Cartoons Manila, Inc. Production Managers: Sue Chung, Alan Kennedy, Doris Moscardon, Rey Zuno. *Animation Production by: Toon City Inc. and Moving Images International, Inc.* Unit Director: Colin Baker. Layout: Jun Aoanan III, Ross de la Vega, Kinjo Estioko, David Gonzales, Mel Padolina. Animation: Alex Acayen, Bang Sung Chul, Dante Clemente, Luis Dimaranan, Akiblas Flores, Jun Flores, Romeo Garcia, Oh Han Gil, Don Juan, Hong Li, Alex Ragsac, Royce Ramos, Bang Sung Soo, Apollo Soriano, Lee Doo Suk, Nowell Villano. Backgrounds: Bobby Angeles, Valerio Bituya, Ruben Calimlim, Ferdinand Capistrano, Ruben Romanban, Cayot Valerio. Post Production Coordinator: John Royer. Post Production Assistants: Nanci Battelle, Jason

Spratt, Steve Werner. Production Assistants: Nanci Battelle, Johanne Beaudoin, Greg Chalekian, Jacaleen Cotter, Paul Fabela, Connie Gombert, Michael Gracey, Jodey Kaminski, Beth Ann Knutson, Anita Lish, Michelle Pappalardo-Robinson, Laura Perrotta, John Royer, Marie Sager, Richard Salazar, Karen Silva, Craig Simpson, William Waggoner, Steve Werner. Script Coordinators: Connie Gombert, Cricket Luke. Supervisor of Production Art Services: Krista Bunn. Production Art Services Coordinators: John Hill, Karen Silva. Shipping Coordinator: Craig Simpson.

MARSUPILAMI

With the Voice Talents of: Charlie Adler, Rene Auberjonois, Sheryl Bernstein, Dan Castellaneta (Stuie, Groom), Jim Cummings (Maurice, Norman), E.G. Daily, J.D. Daniels, Debi Derryberry, June Foray (Norman's Aunt), Brad Garrett, Bill Kopp, Steve Landesberg (Edúardo), Steve Mackall (Marsupilami, Man), Tress MacNeille (Woman), Danny Mann, Jason Marsden (Shnookums), Andi McAfee, Kathy McAuley, Michael Pace, Malachi Pearson, Hal Rayle, Ronnie Shell, Susan Tolsky, Darryl Tookes, Marcia Wallace, Frank Welker (Meat), Ken Williams, April Winchell, Samuel E. Wright (Sebastian).

Produced by: Walt Disney Television Animation. Producer Shnookums & Meat: Bill Kopp. Directors: Ed Wexler (Marsupilami), Bob Hathcock (Sebastian), Jeffrey M. DeGrandis (Shnookums & Meat). Story Editors: Kevin Crosby Hopps, Ken Koonce, Bill Kopp, Bill Matheny, Gary Sperling, David Wiemers. Written by: Laraine Arkow, John Behnke, Terrie Collins, Jeremy Cushner, Rob Humphrey, Gordon Kent, Ken Koonce, Bill Kopp, Bill Matheny, Tom Minton, Bill Motz, Jim Peterson, Dev Ross, Bob Roth, Mike Ryan, Bruce Reid Schaefer, Robert Schechter, David Schwartz, Gary Sperling, Len Uhley, Mark Zaslove. Voice Directors: Ginny McSwain, Jamie Thomason. Casting: Jamie Thomason. Animation Directors: Vincente Bassols, Carole Beers, Jeffrey M. DeGrandis, Eddy Houchins, William Houchins, John Kimball, Marsh Lamore, Bob Shellhorn, Richard Trueblood, James T. Walker, Woody Yocum. Timing Directors: Vincente Bassols, Carole Beers, Jeffrey M. DeGrandis, Marsh Lamore, Rick Leon, Russel E. Mooney, Kevin Petrilak, Brian Ray, Bob Treat. Directing Supervisor: Karen Peterson. Storyboard: Carin-Anne Anderson, Ryan Anthony, Ron Campbell, Shawna Cha, Rich Chidlaw, Tony Craig, Jeffrey M. DeGrandis, Thom Enriquez, Eddie Fitzgerald, Holly Forsyth, Karl Gnass, George Goode, Antoine Guilbaud, Llyn Hunter, Vicki Jensen, Denise Koyama, Larry Latham, Enrique May, Tom Nelson, J. Tom Owens, Jr., David Prince, Bradley Raymond, Chris Rutowski, David Schwartz, David Smith, Kenny Thompkins, Hank Tucker, Andre Von Morisse, Curt Walstead, Wendall Washer. Art Director Shnookums & Meat: Lynne Naylor. Character Design: Tom Bird, Lynne Naylor, J. Tom Owens, Jr., Len Smith, Kenny Thompkins, Kevin Wurzer. Key Layout Design: Brooks Campbell, Derek Carter, Thom Enriquez, Paul A. Felix, Dennis Greco, Bill Lorencz, Carol Police, Robert St. Pierre, Colette Van Mierlo, Raymond Zibach. Prop Design: Tom Bird, Tom Foxmarnick, Terry Hudson, J. Tom Owens, Jr. Key Background Stylists: Greg Battes, Brooks Campbell, Bill Lorencz, Raymond Zibach. Color Key Stylists: Robin Draper Koblin, Yolanda Rearick, Jill Stirdivant. Animation Layout Shnookums & Meat: Charlie Bean, Mark Kausler, Robert Sledge, J. Tom Owens, Jr. Character Animation: Tony Bancroft, Tom Bird, Carole Holliday, Mike Surrey. Assistant Producers: Michelle Pappalardo-Robinson, Matt Pook. Unit Supervising Animation Director: Bob Baxter. Unit Supervising Layout Director: Pere Van Reyk. Continuity Coordinators: Vonnie Batson, Barbara Donatelli, Jim Finch, Kathrin Victor. Storyboard Revisions: Kuni Bowen, Shawna Cha, Llyn Hunter, William Houchins, Stark Howell, Llyn Hunter, Denise Koyama, Jim McLean, Thomas Nelson, Bradley Raymond, Albert Ring, Bob Shellhorn, Kevin Wurzer. Cel Painter: Marie Boughamer. Talent Coordinators: Daniel Pensiero III, Jamie Thomason. Marsupilami Theme by: John Beasley, John Vester, Ed Fournier. Additional Themes by: Ed Fournier, Alan Menken, Drew Neumann. Music by: Drew Neumann, Stephen James Taylor, Mark Watters. Assistant Producer Music: Bambi Moé. Song by: Silversher & Silversher. Song Produced by: Robby Merkin, Steve Gelfand. Animation Production by: Wang Film Production Co., Ltd. Unit Layout Director: Chen Shyh Chang. Unit Background Directors: Arron Du, Henry S. Lee. Unit Animation Directors: Yang Chyi Jang, Yan Shuenn Fa. Unit Production Managers: Liou Shen Yen, Richard Pimm. Animation Production by: Walt Disney Animation (France) S.A. Directors: Gaetan Brizzi, Paul Brizzi. Art Director: Jean-Christophe Poulain. Animators: Bolhem Bouchiba, Sylvain Deboissy, Patrick Delage, Marc Eoche-Duval, Pierre Fassel, Bruno Gaumetou, Dominique Monfery, Catherine Poulain, Jean-Christophe Roger, Stephane Sainte Foi, Yoshimi Tamura. Layout Artists: Bolhem Bouchiba, Jean Duval, Vincent Massy, Richard Poulain. Background Supervisor: Pierre Pavloff. Background Artists: Olivier Adam, Jean-Paul Fernandez, Helene Godefroy, Patricia Millereau, Vincent Misser. Effects Animation: Thierry Chaffoin. Production Manager: Etienne Longa. Post Production Manager: Cheryl Murphy. Film Editors: Elen Orson, Susan Edmunson. Post Production Supervisor: Regina Brittle, Wendy J. Miller-Smith. Sound Dubbing Supervisor: Christopher Keith. Sound Effects Editing: Roy Braverman, Bill Koepnick, Jim Hodson, Robert Duran. Music Editing: Marc Perlman. Dialogue Editing: Melissa Gentry-Ellis. Re-Recording Mixers: Jim Hodson, Bill Koepnick. Track Reading: Theresa Gilroy-Nielsen. Administrative Coordinator: Johanne Beaudoin. Script Supervisor: Anita Lish. Script Coordinators: Nanci Battelle, Janna Bryan, Pamela Kincheloe Finck, Connie Gombert. Production Assistants: Laura Perrotta, Michelle Schlicht-Pniewski, Yolanda Valdez-Saylor, William Waggoner. Post Production Assistants: Jason Spratt, Steve Werner. Production Art Services Coordinators: Jodey Kaminski, Mercedes Sichon. Shipping Coordinator: Craig Simpson.

DISNEY'S ALADDIN

Voices: Charlie Adler (Mekanikles), Jason Alexander (Abis Mal, al-Bhatros), John Astin (Sydney), Rene Auberjonois (Nefir Hassanuf), James Avery (Haroud Hazi Bin), Michael Bell (Aziz), Jeff Bennett (Amin D'Moola, Mozenrath), Sheryl Bernstein, Val Bettin (Sultan), Sue Blu, Jonathan Brandis (Mozenrath), Julie Brown (Saleen), S. Scott Bullock, Rodger Bumpass, Corey Burton, Bonnie Cahoon, William Callaway, Hamilton Camp (Ayam Agool), Nancy Cartwright (Sprites), Dan Castellaneta (Genie, Frijheed), Christine Cavanaugh (Bud), Cam Clarke (Mekanikles, Villager), Jim Cummings (Akbar, Amal al-Kateeb, Dominus Trask, Farouk, Hamar, Mud Sultan, Rasoul, Sultan's grandfather, Wazou), Tim Curry (Amok-Mumra, Capok), E.G. Daily, J.D. Daniels (Little Kid), Jennifer Darling (Hipsodeth), Keith David (Minos, Zabar), Alex Dent, Debi Derryberry (Dondi), Michael Dorn (Brisbane), Hector Elizondo (Malcho), David Fennoy, Jonathan Freeman (Ding), Matt Frewer (Chaos), Linda Gary, Ed Gilbert (Fasir), Ron Glass (Mamud's Vizier), Gilbert Gottfried (Iago), Michael Gough, Benny Grant, Dorian Harewood (Murk, Sootennai), Haven Hartman (Little Kid), Whitby Hertford, Erv Immerman (Destiny Stone Guardian), Tino Insana (Prince Uncouthma), Robert Ito (Yin), Charity James (Fatima), Nick Jameson, Tony Jay (Khartoum), Michael Jeter (Runta), Carol Kane (Brawnhilda), John Kassir, Janice Kawaye, Kay Kuter, Deb LaCusta, Linda Larkin (Jasmine), Nancy Linari, Tone Loc (Magma), Tress MacNeille, Danny Mann, Mona Marshall, Bill Martin, Kellie Martin (Sadira), Scott McAfee, Malcolm McDowell (Shaman), Lynette Mettie, Candi Milo (Thundra), Iona Morris, Tahj Mowry (Tonti), Kate Mulgrew (Hipsodeth), Bebe Neuwirth (Mirage), Stuart Pankin (Pasta al-Dente), Valerie Pappas (Eden), Rob Paulsen (Omar, Worm), Malachi Pearson, Ron Perlman (Arbutus, General Gouda), Hal Rayle (Squirt), Pete Renaday (Village Elder), Neil Ross, Maggie Roswell (Woman), Justin Shenkarow, Kath Soucie (Mother), Mark Taylor, Russi Taylor, Dave Thomas (Makha-na), Brian Tochi (Yang), Susan Tolsky (Scara), Pappas Valery (Eden), Marcia Wallace (Umpa), B.J. Ward (Fortune Teller), Scott Weinger (Aladdin), Frank Welker (Abu, Faisal, Rajah, Xerxes), Bonnie Wyler.

Producers: Tad Stones, Alan Zaslove. Directors: Bob Hancock, Rob LaDuca, Toby Shelton, Alan Zaslove. Associate Producer: Maia Mattise. Story Editors: Duane Capizzi, Douglas Langdale, Mark McCorkle, Bill Motz, Bob Roth, Robert Schooley, Mark Seidenberg, Tad Stones. Story by: Bill Motz, Dev Ross, Bob Roth, Mike Ryan. Written by: Mirith J.S. Colao, Kevin Campbell, Tom Minton, Bill Motz, Steve

Roberts, Bob Roth, Mike Ryan, Bruce Reid Schaefer, Robert Schechter, Mark Seidenberg, Richard Stanley, Tad Stones, Jan Strnad, Brian Swenlin, Marlowe S. Weisman. Teleplay by: Thomas Hart. Voice Director: Ginny McSwain. Voice Casting: Jamie Thomason. Animation Directors: Gerard Baldwin, Carole Beers, Dale Case, Barbara Dourmashkin-Case, Terrence Harrison, Eddy Houchins, John Kimball, Marsh Lamore, Rick Leon, Mircea Mantta, Mitch Rochon, Bob Shellhorn, Mike Svayko, Steven Trenbirth, James T. Walker, Woody Yocum, Bob Zamboni. Assistant Directors: Janey Dunn, Mickie Cassidy, Di Rudder. Timing Directors: Vicente Bassols, Dale Case, Warwick Gilbert, Ian Harrowell, Rick Leon, Karen Peterson, Kevin Petrilak, Brian Ray, Bob Treat, Richard Trueblood, James T. Walker. Storyboard: Kurt Anderson, Ryan Anthony, Nancy Beiman, Kuni Bowen, Rich Chidlaw, Victor Cook, Floro Dery, John Dorman, John Flagg, Holly Forsyth, Sharon Forward, Warwick Gilbert, Karl Gnass, Craig Kemplin, Denise Koyama, Larry Latham, Lonnie Lloyd, Jim McLean, Enrique May, Cynthia Petrovic, Debra Pugh, Bradley Raymond, Albert Ring, Chris Rutkowski, Robert Souza, Hank Tucker, Monty Young, Wendell Washer, Phil Weinstein, David Williams. Character Design: Kuni Bowen, William Finn, Greg Guler, Shawn Keller, Dana Landsberg, Lawrence Leichliter, Ritsuko Notani, J. Tom Owens, Jr., Kenny Thompkins. Key Layout Design: Greg Battes, Derek Carter, Kelly Day, Paul A. Felix, Carol Police, Jim Schlenker, David Skinner, J. Michael Spooner, Robert St. Pierre, Colette Van Mierlo, Fred Warter. Prop Design: Tom Foxmarnick, Dennis Greco, Greg Guler, Terry Hudson, David Mink, Marty Warner. Key Background Stylists: Greg Battes, Hye Coh, James Gallego, Paro Hozumi, Bill Lorencz, Beverley McNamara, Raymond Zibach. Color Key Stylists: Janet Cummings, Marta Glodkowska, Debra Jorgensborg, Robin Draper Koblin, Jenny North, Jill Stirdivant, Marta Skwara, Britt Teegarden, Nancy Ulene. Storyboard Revisions: Carin-Anne Anderson, Shawna Cha, Jan Green, Stark Howell, Llyn Hunter, Craig Kemplin, Mark Kennedy, Judie Martin, Enrique May, Bradley Raymond, Albert Ring, Robert Souza, Melissa Suber, Phil Weinstein. Production Manager: Selma Gladney. Overseas Animation Supervisor: Brad Goodchild., Unit Supervising Animation Director: Bob Baxter. Unit Supervising Layout Director: Pere Van Reyk. Directing Supervisor: Karen Peterson. Continuity Coordinators: Vonnie Batson, Barbara Donatelli, Jim Finch, John Hill, Kathrin Victor. Cel Painters: Marie Boughamer, Yolanda Rearick, Eyde Sheppherd. Talent Coordinators: Julie Morgavi, Daniel Pensiero III. Music by: Danny Beckerman, Bruce Rowland, Mark Watters. Title Theme Written by: Howard Ashman, Alan Menken. Title Theme Produced and Arranged by: Bruce Rowland. Animation Production by: Jaime Diaz Producciones S.A., Guimarães Productions, Kennedy Cartoons, Inc., Moving Images International, Pacific Rim Productions, Inc., Sunwoo Animation Co., Toon City, Inc., Walt Disney Animation (Japan), Inc., Walt Disney Television Animation (Australia), PTY, Ltd., Wang Film Productions, Inc. Animation Directors: Ian Harrowell, Harold Guimarães Neto, Kevin Peaty, Yeun Young Sang, Kazuo Terada, Steven Trenbirth. Assistant Directors: Mickie Cassidy, Janey Dunn, Glen Kennedy, Di Rudder. Animation Supervisors: Jaime Diaz, Kim Jung Gon, Shigeru Yamamoto. Unit Directors: Colin Baker, Saburo Hashimoto, Takamitsu Kawamura, Sin Tae Yong. Animation: Alexander Acayen, Baek Sam Bong, Dante Clemente, Luis Dimaranan, Genoviz Pagani Filho, Akiblas Flores, Romeo Garcia, Kim Jung Ho, Don Juan, Kwon Hyuk Jae, Sam Hyun Jung, Park Don Kwon, Bae Jung Mee, Park Sang Mok, Jung Jae Ok, Paulo Proenca, Alexander Ragsac, Royce Ramos, Song Kyung Sik, Lee In Soo, Hong Jin Soo, Seo Myung Soo, Apollo Soriano, Arnold Taroy, Nowell Villano. Animation and Animation Direction: Animal House, Tama Productions. Unit Animation Directors: Takeshi Atomura, Yan Shuenn Fah, Yen Shung Fah, Hiroshi Kawamata, Masaaki Kudo, Kazuyoshi Takeuchi, Yang Chi Tzang, Hisashi Wada, Yang Chih Yarng, Madoka Yasue. Animators: Georges Abolin, Enzo Avolio, Juan Ayala, Rodolfo Badiola, Stephen Baker, Joseph Balderas, Manny Banados, Pablo Barenbena, Franco Bittel, Ty Bosco, Derek Bond, Chris Bradley, Andrew Brooks, Simon Brown, Peter Candeland, Reinier Cataylo, Luis Ceder, Mike Chavez, Stan Chiu, Ha Sung Chool, Andrew Collins, Gairden Cooke, Marten

Coombe, Stephen Cooper, Nestor Cordoba, Sanny De Ramos, Murray Debus, Rolando Delfino, Lily Dell, Chris Derochie, Nong Ditan, Dick Dunn, Anthony Estrada, Ariel Ferrari, Koji Fukuoka, Ubaldo Galuppo, Annabelle Galvez, Warwick Gilbert, Linton Gonzaga, Stephen Grant, Alberto Grisolia, No Chang Gun, Atsuhiko Hara, Lee Kyung Ho, Han Churl Hee, Miyuki Hoshikawa, Lianne Hughes, Hong Oh Hyun, Kim Kyung Ja, Isamitsu Kashima, Takanobu Katada, Jung Nak Keel, Sang Jin Kim, Marek Kochout, Won Sung Ku, Masaaki Kudo, Hideaki Kurakawa, Dwayne Labbe, Charlie Lee, Dan Lee, Morris Lee, Andres Leiban, Lisinho, Ferdie Lorena, Dave MacDougall, Koichi Maruyama, Yoshiaki Matsuda, Masayo Matsumoto, Yuko Matsuo, Helen McAdam, Wal Micati, Jose Miguel, Kiyomi Miyakawa, Mac Monks, Adam Murphy, Hirofumi Nakata, Ayumi Namiki, Paul Newell, Yon Kun Noh, Kazuhiro Ohmame, Mitsuko Otaku, Wendy Parkin, Oscar Perez, Val Ramirez, Joo Kyung Ran, Kristina Reay, Falin Rodriguez, Alejandro Rojas, Kazumi Sagawa, Troy Saliba, Nilo Santillan, Hiromasa Sato, Carol Seidl, Hyun Jong Sik, Mok Hak Soo, Mike Stapleton, Mike Stevens, Mok Hak Su, Lee Doo Suk, Todd Sullivan, Troy Sullivan, Jung Kyung Sup, Jozef Szekeres, Tadao, Yuri Takasaki, Heihachiro Tanaka, Osamu Tanihata, Steven Taylor, Manao Torii, Kenichi Tsuchiya, Hiro Tsuji, Yoshihiro Tsuji, Leesa Tynan, Rodrigo Velez, Sachiko Wakabayashi, Ian White, Kazue Yamanaka, Shinichi Yoshikawa, Kang Lin Zhu, Nat Zirul, Zaldy Zuno. Key Assistants: Nestor Acevedo, Monica Acosta, Pepe Acosta, Andres Diaz, Mila Gimenez, Luis Solis, Walter Yucca. Animation Clean Up: Jun Hyun Myung, Lee Hae Sook, Lee Young Sook. Unit Layout Director: Jorge Benedetti, Chern Shyh Chang. Layout Supervisors: John Hill, Alex Nicholas. Layout: Yeun Jung Ah, Jun Aonan III, Lee Sung Chan, Ross Dela Vega, Kinjo Estioko, Dave Gonzales, Yeun Suk Jeen, Park Tae Kwun, José Miguel Silva Lara, Ed Lee, Paul Lee, Huh Sun Mee, Mel Padolina, Lee Dong Que, Raymond Romero, Gord Sinclair, Owen Smith, Song Meen Uk. Layout Artists: Kelly Baigent, Yosh Barry, Oscar Dela, Jorge Freeno, Carlos Grueso, Omar Hetchenkoff, Margaret Parkes, Bruce Pedersen, Pilin, Nick Pill, David Skinner, Kevin Spill, Kevin Wotton. Unit Background Directors: Du Yah Luen, Du Yar Luing, Lee Hong Shang. Background Supervisors: Beverley McNamara, Toshiharu Mizutani. Backgrounds: Bobby Angeles, Cayot Bituya, Ruben Calimlim, Ferdie Capistrano, Hong Sung Dae, William Jones, Jr., Kim Young Ku, Ruben Romanban, Luis Rosso, Ramonchito Talens, Cayot Valerio. Camera: Lim Chul Kyu, Leem Churl Que. Clean Up Supervisor: Melba Besa. Background Artists: Masayoshi Banno, Milana Borkert, Barry Dean, Kiyomi Enomoto, Felice Ferrer, Studio Fuga, Akihito Fujimori, Shuichi Hirowatari, George Humphrey, Jinzaburo Kaiho, Tachiko Kimura, Emi Kitahara, Kazue Kudo, Jerry Liew, Satoshi Matsudaira, Toshihal Mizutani, Masumi Nose, Kumiko Ohno, Kumiko Ojima, Paul Pattie, Naomi Sakimoto, Helen Steele, Shunsuke Suzuki, Michiko Taniguchi, Ken Wright. Additional Production Facilities: Jade Animation, Kennedy Cartoons Manila, Inc., Light Foot, Nakamura Productions, Studio Cats, Studio Robin, Takahashi Productions, Unlimited Energee. Ink and Paint Supervisors: Angela Bodini, Robin Drayton, Liz Lane, Christine O'Connor. Unit Production Managers: Richard Pimm, Liou Chyi Yen. Production Managers: Sue Chung, Bill Diaz, Fabio Hotz Guimarães, Doris Moscardon, Terry W. Smith, Rey Zuno. Checker: Osvaldo Garcia. Production Management: Jose Barreiros, Mark Evans, Dan Forster, Fernando Letteri, Robert Letteri, Elias Macute, Gary Page, Carole Salter. Post Production Manager: Cheryl Murphy. Post Production Coordinators: Wendy J. Miller-Smith, John Royer. Post Production Supervisors: Jeffrey Arthur, Nancy Blair, Joseph Hathaway, Wendy J. Miller-Smith, Keith Yaeger. Sound Dubbing Supervisors: Christopher Keith, Mark Von Der Heide. Assistant Post Production Supervisor: Steve Werner. Supervising Editor: Robert S. Birchard. Film Editors: Monte Bramer, Tony Mizgalski, Elen Orson. Assistant Film Editors: Eric Daroca, Susan Edmunson, Christopher Gee, Jennifer Harrison, Philip Malamuth, Salvatore Nikolas Rocco, John Royer, Shannon Scudder. Track Reading: Christine Craig, Skip Craig. Post Production Sound Supervisor: Timothy J. Borquez. Supervising Sound: John O. Robinson III. Effects Editor: William Geisler. Sound Effects Editors: Christopher Aud, Thomas Betz, Robert

Duran, Tom Harris, Jim Hodson, Bill Kopenick, Peggy McAffee, Charlie Rychwalski, Kenneth Young. Supervising Music Editor: William Griggs. Music Editing: Ginger Avernades, Marc Perlman, Alex Wilkinson. Supervising Sound Editor: William B. Griggs. Sound Editors: Patrick Foley, Michael A. Gollom, Thomas Jaeger, Greg LaPlante, Timothy Mertens, Kenneth Young. Dialogue Editors: Melissa Gentry Ellis, Gary Freidman, Jennifer Mertens, Craig Paulsen, Stacy Saravo. Re-Recording Mixers: Jin Hodson, Mike Jiron, Bill Koepnick, Alan Stone. Recordists: Bill Olson, Lori Thomas. Supervising Music Editor: William B. Griggs. Music Editor: Cecil Broughton. Scoring Music Editor: Dominick Certo. Production Assistants: Natasha Easter, Jodey Kaminski, Beth Ann Knutson, Laura V. Perrotta, Tom Pniewski, Yolanda Valdez-Saylor, William Waggoner. Script Coordinators: Susan Gold, Susan McElroy. Art Coordinator: Michael Gracey. Production Secretary: Regina Dixon. Administrative Coordinator: Johanne Beaudoin. Script Supervisor: Anita Lish. Story Coordinators: Nanci Battelle, Nanci Schwartz. Post Production Assistants: Andrew Sorcini, Jason Spratt, Steve Werner, Keith Yeager. Shipping Coordinator: Craig Simpson.

GARGOYLES

Voices: Monica Allison (Beth Maza), Edward Asner (Hudson, Jack Danforth), James Avery (Shaman), Deidrich Bader (James Conover), Brigitte Bako (Angela), Michael Bell (Martin Hacker, Pal Joey), Roxanne Beckford (Beth Maza, Tea), Jim Belushi (Fang), Jeff Bennett (Brooklyn, Clive, Commando Leader, Luach, Magus, Owen Burnett, Young Macbeth), Gregg Berger (Leo), Xander Berkeley (Iago), Bictor Brandt (Janus), Avery Brooks (Nokkar), Clancy Brown (Hakon, Thomas Brod, Wolf), Ian Buchanan (Prince Chalvim/Constantine), Levar Burton (Anansi), Rocky Carroll (Derek Maza, Dr. Sevarius, Glasses, Talon), James Charity (Ekidna), Cam Clark (Young Gillecomgain), Scott Cleverdon (Chu Chullain, Jon Carter, Rory Dugan), Jesse Corti (Jade), Robert Culp (Halycon Renard), Jim Cummings (Dingo, Gillecomgain's Father, Hunter, Matrix, Mr. Acme, Thailog), Tim Curry (Dr. Anton Sevarius), J.D. Daniels (Gunther, Prince Canmore, Tom), Keith David (Goliath, Officer Morgan), Neil Dickson (Griff, Prince Duncan, Renaissance Hunter), Michael Dorn (Coldstone, Taurus), Sarah Douglas (Una), Amentha Dymally (Grandmother), Sheena Easton (Banshee/Crom-Cruach, Finella, Molly, Robyn Correy), Hector Elizondo (Zafiro), Bill Fagerbakke (Broadway), Jonathan Frakes (David Xanatos, Coyote), Patrick Fraley (Brendan, Jogger), Matt Frewer (Jackal), Elisa Pensler Gabrielli (Maria Chavez), Ed Gilbert (Bodhe, Captain), Gerrit Graham (Guardian), Richard Grieco (Anthony Dracon), Charlie Hallahan (Macduff, Travis Marshall), Dorian Harewood (Talos, Boreas), Thom Adcox Hernandez (Lexington), Michael Horse (Carlos Meza, Sergeant Peter Meza), Robert Ito (Doctor Sato), Tony Jay (Anubis), Clyde Kusatsu (Dr. Arnada. Kai), Bruce Locke (Yama), Terrence Mann (Oberon), James Marabina (Turquesa), Darren McGavin (Dominic Dracon, G.F. Benton), Roddy McDowall (Proteus), Colm Meaney (Mr. Dugan), Haunani Minn (Sora), Kate Mulgrew (Anastasia Renard, Titania), Nichelle Nichols (Diane Maza), Rob Paulsen (Helios), C.C.H. Pounder (Desdemona), Gregg Rainwater (Coyote Trickster, Natsilane), Don Reed (Fara Maku), Roger Rees (Prince Malcolm), Pete Reneday (Commander, Father, Fortress One Captain), John Rhys-Davies (Macbeth, Dr. Morwood-Smythe, Findlaech), Salli Richardson (Elisa Maza), James Saito (Taro), Emma Samms (Grouch), John St. Ryan (King Arthur), Ruben Santiago-Hudson (Gabriel), Peter Scolari (Preston Vogel), Tony Shalhoub (Emir), Charles Shaughnessy (Douglas Bader), Morgan Sheppard (Petros Xanatos), Marina Sirtis (Demona, Margot), Kath Soucie (Maggie the Cat, Ophelia, Princess Elena, Princess Katharine, The Weird Sisters), Brent Spinner (Puck), Cree Summer (Hyena), Rachel Ticotin (Captain Maria Chavez), B.J. Ward (Duane, Fleance), David Warner (Archmage), Scott Weil (Max Loew), Frank Welker (Bronx, Alexander, Banquo, Bear, Boudicca, Crom-Cruach, Gilgamesh, Kiron), Thomas F. Wilson (Matt Bluestone), Paul Winfield (Jeffrey Robbins), Ric Young (Hiroshi), Efrem Zimbalist, Jr. (Mace Malone).

Supervising Producers: Frank Paur, Greg Weisman. Producer: Bob Kline, Dennis J. Woodyard. Associate Producers: Brynne Chandler Reaves, Lisa A. Salamone. Story by: Eric Luke, Michael Reaves. Teleplay by: Diane Duane, Lydia C. Marano, Peter Morwood, Brynne Chandler Reaves, Michael Reaves. Written by: Cary Bates, Robert Cohen, Adam Gilad, Shari Goodhartz, Marty Isenberg, Lydia C. Marano, Steve Perry, Brynne Chandler Reaves, Michael Reaves, Robert H. Skir, Gary Sperling. Directors: Saburo Hashimoto, Takamitsu Kawamura, Bob Kline, Frank Paur, Yeun Young Sang, Kazuo Terada, Dennis J. Woodyard. Music by: Carl Johnson. Voice Director: Jamie Thomason.

SHNOOKUMS & MEAT FUNNY CARTOON SHOW, THE

Voice credits: Charlie Adler (Chafe), Jeff Bennett (Pith Possum, Tex Tinstar), Corey Burton (Ian, Krusty Rustnuckle), Jim Cummings (Tex Tinstar narrator), Brad Garrett (Commissioner Stress, Wrongo), Jess Harnell (Floyd the Rattler, Lieutenant Tension), Bill Kopp, Steve Mackall (Husband), Tress MacNeille (Wife), Danny Mann, Jason Marsden (Shnookums), Frank Welker (Meat), April Winchell (Doris Deer), Patric Zimmerman (Obediah, The Wonder Raccoon).

Produced by: Walt Disney Television Animation. Voice Director: Bill Kopp. Voice Casting: Jamie Thomason. Animation Directors: Daniel De La Vega, Eddy Houchins, Bob Shellhorn. Timing Directors: Carole Beers, Richard Collado, Daniel De La Vega, Eddy Houchins, Kevin Petrilak, Bob Shellhorn, Bob Treat, Richard Trueblood. Storyboard: G. Keith Baxter, Rich Chidlaw, Belto Clarke, Douglas A. Craig, Charles Daniel, Jeff DeGrandis, Eddie Fitzgerald, Joe Horne, Vicki Jensen, Douglas McCarthy, Brian Mitchell, J. Tom Owens, Jr., Albert Ring, Bryan Ruff, Chris Rutkowski, Marc Schirmeister, David Smith, Benen Stone, Wendell Washer. Art Director, Shnookums & Meat: Lynne Naylor. Character Design: Michael Fontanelli, J. Tom Owens, Jr., Kenny Thompkins. Key Layout Design: Kelly Day, Gary Mouri, Jim Schlenker, Cliff Voorhees, Raymond Zibach. Prop Design: Tom Foxmarnick, J. Tom Owens, Jr. Key Background Stylists: Brooks Campbell, Bari Greenberg, Rolando Oliva, Raymond Zibach. Color Key Stylists: Janet Cummings, Robin Draper Koblin. Animation Layout: Charlie Bean, Shavone Cherry, Mark Christiansen, Mark Kausler, Michael Milo, Leonardo Pinero, Robert Sledge, Carey Yost. Production Managers: Michelle Schlicht-Pniewski, Selma Edelman. Assistant Producer: Michelle Robinson. Storyboard Revisions: Eddie Fitzgerald, Michael Milo. Continuity Coordinators: Barbara Donatelli, Jim Finch, Kathrin Victor. Theme Written by: John Jorgenson. Theme Performed by: The Hellecasters. Music by: Drew Neumann, Nathan Wang. Animation Production by: Wang Film Productions Co., Ltd. Unit Supervising Animation Director: Bob Baxter. Unit Supervising Layout Director and Layout Director: Pere Van Reyk. Animation Directors: Yang Chyi Jang, David Marshall, Yen Shuenn Fa, Bunis Yang, Jack Yen. Layout Directors: Chen Shyh Chang, Coke Lee, Steve Chen. Background Directors: Henry Lee, Monica Yu. Production Managers: George Chang, John Liou, Richard Pimm. Animation Production by: Toonz Animation Ltd. Animation Director: Lily Dell. Production Managers: Doug Johnson, Shaun Bell. Production Assistants: Simon Potter, Amy Gosman, Leanne Hutchison. Checker: Kim Kelly. Pencil Test Operator: Leanne Lunam. Layouts: Mark Lawrence. Background Artists: Jim Mondares, Jeff Fowler. Animators: Dave Gosman, Andy Powell, Mark Saunders, Heath Gray, Mark Allen, Mark Lawrence. Assistant Animators: Catherine McElhannan, Niche Wilton, Anita Grieg, Claire DeZoete. Ink, Paint and Camera Production by: Gnome Productions Ltd. Camera Operator: Karen Downes. Production Assistants: Lucy Bell, Selena Ngan, Natasha McKillop, Jayne Perry. Painting Supervisors: Karen Cheeseman, Rachel Lehen. Post Production Manager: Cheryl Murphy. Supervising Film Editor: Susan Edmunson. Pre-Production Film Editors: Monte Bramer, Eric Daroca, John Royer. Film Editor: Shannon Scudder. Assistant Film Editors: Eric Daroca, Shannon Scudder, John Royer. Post Production Supervisor: Wendy J. Miller-Smith. Sound Dubbing Supervisor: Mark Von Der Heide. Post Production Assistants: Steve Werner, Keith Yeager. Track Reading: Theresa Gilroy-Nielsen. Sound Effects Editing: Bill Koepnick, Robert Duran, Michael Warner. Foley: Bill Koepnick, Phyllis Ginter. Music Editing: Marc Perlman. Dialogue Editing: Melissa Gentry-Ellis. Re-Recording Mixers: Jim Hodson, Bill Koepnick. Production Assistants: John Carrillo,

Natasha Easter. Script Coordinator: Connie Gombert. Art Coordinators: Melinda Cisneroz, Mercedes Sichon. Administrative Coordinator: Johanne Beaudoin. Script Supervisor: Anita Lish. Talent Coordinators: Julie Morgavi, Daniel Pensiero III. Story Coordinator: Nanci Battelle. Shipping Coordinator: Craig Simpson.

LION KING'S TIMON & PUMBAA, THE
Voice Talents: Charlie Adler (Irwin, Buttons, Rabbit, Ted), Dee Baker (Paperboy), Jeff Bennett (Angel, Anteleope, El Toro, Mel, Natives, Toucan Dan), S. Scott Bullock (Fred), Roger Bumpass (Leo the Lion), Corey Burton (Quint, Fronk, Speedy the Snail), Nancy Cartwright (Pumbaa, Jr.), Cam Clark (Simba), Townsend Coleman (Vulture Police), Brian Cummings (Pizza Delivery Man, Vulture Police), Jim Cummings (Ed, Announcer, Baby Bird, Bartholomew, Big Ron, Boudreaux, Bruce, Female Gorilla, Junior Ostrich, Lawyer, Lester, Nobi, Ostrich, Simon's Father, Wild Goose, Woody Woodeater), Debi Derryberry (Children), Quinton Flynn (Timon, Monty), Brad Garrett (Wonderful Rhino of Laws), Gilbert Gottfried (Woodpecker), Robert Guillaume (Rafiki), Jess Harnell (Bugs), Estelle Harris (Timon's Mother), Richard Karron (Eddie, Herman), John Kassir, Joyce Katz (Mother Eagle), Nathan Lane (Timon), Steve Mackall (Mr. Happy, Happy Dog, Thief), Tress MacNeille (Shenzi, Mother Ostrich, Wife), Tahj Mowry (Nefu), Rob Paulsen (Banzai, Husband, Male Squirrel, Martin Pardon, Ralph, Simon, Star-madillo), Ernie Sabella (Pumbaa, Bampuu), Kath Soucie (Lara, Rosebud), Frank Welker (Ned, Hippos, Panther Kitten, Zebra), April Winchell (Bar Girl, Female Squirrel, Frieda, Tigress).

Produced by: Walt Disney Television Animation. Produced and Directed by: Tony Craig, Jeff DeGrandis, Rob LaDuca, Roberts Gannaway. Music Video Directed by: Steve Moore, Darrell Van Citters. Music Video Produced by: Steve Moore, Ashley Quinn. Story Editor: Roberts Gannaway. Written by: Trey Callaway, Darrell Campbell, Kevin Campbell, Mirith J.S. Colao, Roberts Gannaway, Patricia Jones, Gordon Kent, Karey Kirkpatrick, Nancy Neufeld, Donald Reiker, Mark Saraceni, Byron Simpson, Bruce Talkington, Bobbi J.G. Weiss, David Cody Weiss. Story by: Heather C. Kenyon. Storyboard by: Carin-Anne Anderson, Ryan Anthony, Michael Bennett, Cullen Blaine, Ken Boyer, Ashley Brannon, Jill Colbert, Holly Forsyth, Sharon Forward, Todd Frederiksen, Ken Harsha, Joe Horne, Denise Koyama, Lonnie Lloyd, Ken Mitchrooney, Cynthia Petrovic, Jeffrey Siergey, Andrew Stanton, Mark Swan, Wendell Washer, Phil Weinstein. Associate Producer: Michelle Pappalardo-Robinson. Voice Casting & Dialogue Director: Jamie Thomason. Animation Directors: Eddy Houchins, John Kimball, Marsh Lamore, Rick Leon, Kirk Tingblad, Woody Yocum, Bob Zamboni. Timing Directors: Donovan Cook, Daniel de la Vega, Eddy Houchins, John Kimball, Marsh Lamore, Rick Leon, Mircea Mantta, Kevin Petrilak, Kirk Tingblad, Bob Zamboni. Character Design: Dana Landsberg, Michael Milo, Kexx Singleton, Kenny Thompkins. Key Layout Design: John Koch, Jim Schlenker, Tim Soman, Colette Van Mierlo, Cliff Vorhees. Key Background Stylists: Thomas Cain, James Gallego, Bari Greenberg, Stephen Lee, Donna Prince, Sy Thomas. Animation Layout: Charlie Bean, Shavonne Cherry, Mark Christiansen, David Fassett, David Fulp, Garrett Ho, Perry Kiefer, Dana Landsberg, Robert Logan, Michael Milo, Greg Peters, Leonardo Pinero, Kexx Singleton, Joe Suggs, Amber Tornquist, Brad Vandergrift, Deke Wightman, Carey Yost. Production Manager: Michelle Schlicht-Pniewski. Prop Design: Tom Foxmarnick, Derric Treece. Color Key Stylists: Suzette Darling, Robin Draper Koblin, Jill Stirdivant. Storyboard Revisions: Ryan Anthony, Michael Bennett, Cullen Blaine, Shawna Cha, Todd Frederiksen, Craig Kemplin, Lonnie Lloyd, Cynthia Petrovic, Louis Tate. Continuity Coordinators: Barbara Donatelli, Jim Finch. Music by: Stephen James Taylor. Main Title Theme *Hakuna Matata* Music by: Elton John. Lyrics by: Tim Rice. Theme Arranged and Produced by: Randy Petersen. *Animation Production by:* Walt Disney Animation (Australia) Pty. Ltd. Animation Directors: Ian Harrowell, Kevin Peaty, Steven Trenbirth. Assistant Directors: Mickie Cassidy, Manuk Chang, Janey Dunn, Di Rudder. Animators: Manny Banados, Ty Bosco, Andrew Brooks, Simon Brown, Andrew Collins, Gairden Cooke, Lily Dell, Bernard Derriman, Dick Dunn, Ariel Ferrari, Warwick

Gilbert, Randy Glusac, Stephen Grant, Lianne Hughes, Marek Kochout, Dwayne Labbe, Morris Lee, Dave MacDougall, Paul McAdam, Walter Micati, Mac Monks, Adam Murphy, Paul Newell, Kathie O'Rourke, Kristina Reay, Troy Saliba, Nilo Santillan, Alexs Stadermann, Mike Stapleton, Steven Taylor, Leesa Tynan, Rizaldy Valencia, Ian White. Layout Supervisors: Alex Nichols, John Hill. Layout Artists: Kelly Baigent, Yosh Barry, Abeth Dela Cruz, Margaret Parkes, Nick Pill, David Skinner, Kevin Wotton. Background Supervisor: Beverly McNamara. Background Artists: Milana Borkert, Barry Dean, Felice Ferrer, George Humphry, Jerry Liew, Paul Pattie, Helen Steele, Ken Wright. Digital Paint & Compositing: Cambridge Animation Systems. Production Manager: Terry Smith. Ink and Paint Supervisors: Robyn Drayton, Liz Lane, Jenny North, Christine O'Connor. Production Management: Amanda Allen, Jose Barreiros, Mark Evans, Matt Jones, Dan Forster, Fernando Letteri, Robert Letteri, Elias Macute, Gary Page. *Animation Production by:* Wang Film Productions Co., Ltd. Animation Directors: Bunis Yang, Jack Yen. Layout Director: Steve Chen. Head of Background: Henry Lee. Head of Camera: Fonzie Lin. Production Manager: John Liou. *Animation Production by:* Rough Draft Studios, Inc. Unit Director: Gregg Vanzo. Animation Directors: Bong Hee Han, Dong Kwon Park. Layout Director: Yoo Mun Jeong. Animators: Moon Su Hong, Chul Jae Jung, Nak Gil Jung, Chan Jo Kim, Shin Young Kim, Young Shik Kim, Du Suk Lee, Ho Sik Lee, Gil Man Na, Yeol Dong Paik, Jin Soo Park, Yang Ho Park, Yoo Bong Park, Jung Bok Wi, Kyu Dae Yeon, Eui Su Yoon. Layout Artists: Jae Bok Lee, Tae Soon Kim, Jae Bong Ko, Joon Young Seong, Dong Keun Won, Jung Ah Yoon. Background Painting: Young Il Kim, Eun Kyung Sung. Camera: Yong Hwan Choi, Chul Kyu Lim. *Animation Production by:* Toon City, Inc. Unit Director: Colin Baker. Unit Coordinator: Louie Jhocson. Layout Artists: Jun Aoanan III, Ross Dela Vega, Kinjo Estioko, Joseph Garcia, Dave Gonzales, Ronel Gravo, Rodel Gravo, Mel Padolina. Animation Supervisor: Romeo Garcia. Animation: Allan Abelardo, Joseph Balderas, Ric Bernardo, Eduardo Busmente, Ferminito Catalan, Dante Clemente, Jerome Co, Joselito Cruz, Rolando Delfino, Jocelyn Diaz, Luis Dimaranan, Noel Domingo, Akiblas Flores, Ronnie Fuentes, Annabelle Galvez, Romeo Garcia, Gino Gozo, Don Juan, Charlie Lee, Romeo Libunao, Robert Ocon, Alexander Ragsac, Royce Ramos, Teofilo Reynon, Raul Santos, Apollo Soriano, Jocelyn Sy, Arnold Taroy, Nelson Udaundo, Nowell Villano. Layout Artists: Jun Aoanan III, Quintin Estioko, Joeseph Garcia, Dave Gonzales, Mel Padolina, Ross Dela Vega. Special Effects: Tobee Barretto. Backgrounds: Geoffrey Abaya, Bobby Angeles, Cayot Bituya, Valerio Bituya, Roberto Bravante, Darwin Camero, Ferdinand Capistrano, Bobby Jesus Lopez, Francisco Madronio, Mark Redulla, Ramonshito Talens. Clean-Up Supervisor: Melba Besa. Inbetween Supervisor: Norman Baculi. Camera Supervisor: Frank Aguila. Additional Production Facilities: Golden Key Animation Co., Ltd., Moving Images International, Inc., Thai Wang Production Co., Ltd. *Animation Production by:* Jaime Diaz Producciones S.A. Layout Artists: Andres Klacik, J. Massarolli, Eduardo Savid. Animators: Carlos Aguero, Juan Ayala, Raul Barbero, Arnoldo Cirilli, Nestor Cordoba, Diego Gobbo, Alberto Grisolia, Silvia Nanni, Rafael Rodriguez, Alex Tempesta, Franco Vittolo. *Animation Production by:* Toonz Animation Ltd. Animation Director: Lily Dell. Layout Artists: Mark Lawrence, Simon Potter. Animators: Mark Allen, Marten Coombe, Xuan Feng, Stan Fong, Heath Gray, Roy Peredo, Mark Saunders, Mathew Wilson. Head of Background: Jim Mondares. Backgrounds: Jim Mondares, Wen Xiao Quan. Head of Camera: Shaun Bell. Camera: Steve Leggat, Tom Atkinson. *Ink, Paint and Camera Production by:* Gnome Productions Ltd. Supervising Film Editor: Susan Edmunson. Film Editor: Elen Orson. Assistant Film Editors: Christopher K. Gee, Jennifer Harrison, John Royer. Pre-Production Film Editor: Monte Bramer. Post Production Supervisor: Nancy Blair. Sound Dubbing Supervisor: Mark von der Heide. Track Reading: Skip Craig. Supervising Sound Editor: William B. Griggs. Sound Effects Editors: Bill Kean, Peggy McAffee, Kenneth D. Young. Dialogue Editors: Gary Freidman, Jennifer Mertens, Darleen Stoker. Re-Recording Mixers: Dick Alexander, C.A.S., Michael Jiron, Ken S. Polk, C.A.S., Alan Stone. Recordists: Bill Olson, Lori Thomas. Supervising Music Editor: Brian F. Mars. Sound Effects Editing: Bill Koepnick, Robert Duran. Foley: Ray Leonard, Phyllis Ginter. Music Editing: Marc Perlman. Dialogue Editing: Melissa Gentry-Ellis. Re-Recording Mixers: Jim Hodson, Bill Koepnick. Production Assistants: Deirdre Brenner, John Carrillo, Michael Gracey, Yolanda Valdez-Saylor. Graphic Design: DeeDee Uchiyamada. Script Coordinators: Connie Gombert, Leona Jernigan. Art Coordinator: Melissa Kuhn. Administrative Coordinator: Johanne Beaudoin. Talent Coordinator: Julie Morgavi. Script Supervisor: Anita Lish. Assistant Post Production Supervisor: Steve Werner. Post Production Coordinator: Keith Yeager. Post Production Assistant: Andrew Sorcini. Story Coordinator: Nanci Schwartz. Shipping Coordinator: Craig Simpson. Walt Disney Television.

DISNEY'S SING ME A STORY: WITH BELLE
Executive Producer: Patrick Davidson. Directed by: Steve Purcell. Producers: Bart Roen, Alan Silberberg. Written by: Patrick Davidson, Daniel Benton, Alan Silberberg. Music Producer: Andy Belling. Associate Producer: Timothy Gaydos. Associate Director: Jeff Palmer. Production Designer: Jimbo Marshall. Lighting Designer: Greg Brunton. Production Manager: Kathy Erickson. Production Supervisor: Rebecca S. Ancheta. Script Supervisor: Janie Scurti. Lighting Director: Jay Grindrod. Costumer: Cathy Cox. Stage Manager: Dave Cove. Unit Manager: Geriann Baker-Decker. Post Production Supervisor: Lori Margules. Casting Director: Pati Thomas-Robinson. Acting Coach: Chris Jorie. Script Coordinators: Sheila R. Lawrence, Suzy Garra. Clip Coordinator: Hildie Katibah Jacobson. Make-up/Hair: Connie Little, Hubert Kennedy, Janet Wolek. Set Decorator: Sharon Tannian. Propmaster: Mark Dillon. Edited by: Craig Anderson, Lisa Bianco, Randy Magalski, Pete Opotowsky, Sam Patterson. Audio Mixer: John DeRussy. Music and Audio Post Production: Jon Baker, Andy Waterman. Sound Design: Randall Coppinger. Assistant to the Executive Producer: Jennifer Shulman. Production Secretary: Jennifer Chase. Talent Assist: Cathy Schreiber. Production Assistants: Trevor Baierl, Dustin Paddock, Mark Lach, Jeff Ratajczak, Nicole Burlison. Educational Consultants: Hasmik Avetisian, Judy Ferkel, Melanie Gordon, Nellie Rios, Seeds University Elementary School. Puppets by: Animax Designs. Puppeteer: Jeff Conover. Puppet Consultant: Jeff Domke. Puppet Character Voices: Jim Cummings, Christine Cavanaugh, Jeff Conover. Songs and Music: *Morris The Midget Moose* Underscore Composed by: Jerry Styner. *Two Heads Are Better Than One* Words & Music by: Randy Petersen, Kevin Quinn. *Babes In The Woods* Underscore Composed by: Gordon Goodwin. *Together* Words & Music by: Andy Belling, Bryan Miller. *Which, Witch* Words & Music by: Andy Belling. *Paul Bunyan* Underscore Composed by: Richard Band. *Paul Bunyan* Words & Music by: Rick Dempsey. *The Wise Little Hen* Underscore Composed by: Jimmy Hammer. *Will You Help Me!* Words & Music by: Dave Kinnoin, Jimmy Hammer. *Three Little Pigs* Underscore Composed by: Richard Band. *Three Little Piggies* Words & Music by: Alan O'Day. *Keep on Trying* Words & Music by: Dave Kinnoin, Jimmy Hammer. *The Brave Engineer* Underscore Compose by: David Kates. *Casey Jones* Words & Music Composed by: Randy Petersen, Kevin Quinn. Patrick Davidson Productions. Buena Vista Television.

CHAPTER 13

The Disney Channel

The Disney Channel Series

ADVENTURES IN WONDERLAND

Executive Producer: Andi Copley. Producer: Stan Brodsky. Directors: David Grossman, Gary Halvorson. Head Writers: Daryl Busby, Tom Astle. Production Designer: AWest. Musical Director: Mark Mothersbaugh. Make-up Designer: Ron Wild. Costume Designer: Lois DeArmond. Animation: Will Vinton Productions. Art Director: Kelly Van Patter. Puppet Designers/Puppet Masters: The Chiodo Brothers. Educational Consultants: Ruth Bunyan, Professor Yvonne Chan. Produced by Betty Productions in association with The Disney Channel. 30-minute format. 65 episodes. First aired in 1992.

ANIMALS IN ACTION

Written and Produced by: James T. de Kay, Michael Linley. Associate Producer and Director: Colin Eldred. Executive Producer: Lord Aubrey Buxton. Executive in Charge of Programming: Victor Simpkins. A Survival Anglia, Ltd. Production. 30-minute format. 40 episodes. First aired in 1986.

AVONLEA

A Kevin Sullivan Production. Art Direction: Perri Gorrara, Nancey Pankiw. Director of Photography: Manfred Guthe, C.S.C. Costume Design: Martha Mann, Madeleine Stewart. Casting: Anne Tait. Edited by: Mairin Wilkinson, Gordon McCLellan. Music Composed by: Hagood Hardy, John Welsman. Written by: Heather Conkie, Suzette Couture, Fiona McHugh, Lori Fleming, Marlene Matthews, Janet McLean, Jerome McCann, Patricia Watson, Graham Woods, Charles Lazer. Executives in Charge of Production: Cathy Johnson (The Disney Channel), Deborah Bernstein (C.B.C.). Line Producers: David Shepherd, Len D'Agostino, Brian Leslie Parker. Executive in Charge of Production: Paul Quigley. Executive Producers: Trudy Grant, Kevin Sullivan. Directed by: Don McBrearty, Rene Bonniere, Bruce Pittman, Paul Shapiro, Harvey Frost, Dick Frost, Stuart Gillard, Allan King, James Lahti. Senior Story Editor: Deborah Nathan. Story Editors: Lucie Hall, Helen Asimakis. Production Managers: Brian Leslie Parker, Joseph Boccia. 1st Assistant Directors: Jeffrey Steven Authors, Libby Hodgson. 2nd Assistant Directors: David J. Vaughan, Randi Richmond. 3rd Assistant Directors: Rose Tedesco, Rick Kush. 2nd Unit Assistant Director: Eric Banz. Camera Operators: Gordon Langevin, Andy Chmura. Location Managers: Joseph Boccia, Arthur Clarke. Assistant Location Managers: Arthur Clarke, Dan Matthews. Script Supervisor: Elaine Yarish. 1st Assistant Art Directors: Nancey Pankiw, Kenneth M. Watkins, James Oswald. 2nd Assistant Art Directors: Susie Mah, Joan Parkinson. Drafting: Tom Doherty, Barbra Matis. Set Decorators: Dan Conley, Elena Kennedy, Jaro Dick, Ian Wheatley. Assistant Set Decorator: Terry Edwards. Set Buyer: Michael P. Harris. Set Decorator Driver: Matthew Garland. Construction Coordinator: Stuart Ennis. Property Masters: J. Tracy Budd, Greg Pelchat. Assistant Property Masters: Tory Bellingham, Ken Clark. Make-up Design: Linda L. Gill, Marilyn Terry. Assistant Make-up Artist: Marilyn Terry, Dorothy Smith. 2nd Assistant Make-up Artist: Dorothy Smith. Hair Design: Paul Elliott. Assistant Hairdressers: Kelly Brennan, Carol Marinoff. Second Unit Hairdressers: Carmen Dodaro, Carol Marinoff. Assistant Costume Designers: Madeline Stewart, Quita Alfred. Wardrobe Mistresses: Michele Harney, Karen Matthews Renaut. 1st Assistant Wardrobe: Karen Renaut, Traceylee Guerin, Stacey Coker, Rob Roberts. Cutter: Graham Docherty. Tailor: Carl Docherty. Head Cutter: Evan Ayotte. Seamstresses: Loreen Lightfoot, Francine Tanguay. Production Accountant: Ronald J. Gilbert. Assistant Accountants: Elaine Scott, Sara Holmes. Payroll Clerk: Margie Schneiderman. Assistant to the Producer: Julie Steiner. Production Coordinators: Susan Phillips, Heather Boyd. Production Secretaries: Dawn L. Sinko, Helene Valinsky. Production Assistants: Dan Matthews, Nancy Sorge. Trainee Assistant Directors: Grant Lucibello, Matthew Weinstein. 1st Assistant Camera: Kerry Smart. 2nd Assistant Camera: Wendy Walgate. Camera Trainees: Richard W. Brown, Michael Harding. 2nd Unit Director of Photography: Robert Saad. 2nd Unit Sound Recordist: Peter Shewchuk. Stills Photographer: Michaelin McDermott. Sound Mixer: Owen Langevin. Boom Operators: Ken Porter, Stephe Switzer. Sound Trainee: Denis Bellingham. Gaffer: Gary W. Deneault. Best Boys: Michael Galbraith, Gordon Eldridge. Electrics: Barry Goodwin, Jim Gash, R.L. Hannah, Richard Young. Generator Operator: Ian Foulds. Rigging Gaffers: Robert Condie, Dave Kellner. Key Grip: Randal Tambling. 2nd Grip: Mike Kirilenko. Dolly Grip: Ron Renzetti. Grips: Ron Renzetti, Robert Rice, Sam Turturici. Rigging Grip: James Kohne. Transportation Co-ordinator: Wilf Bell. Driver Captains: Bruce Raymer, Tim Hilts, Bill Jackson. Drivers: Gary Flanagan, Brian O'Hara, John Cocks, Harry Ross. Honeywagon Driver: Kevin Wilson. Animal Wrangler: Lionel Purcell. Dog Trainer: Bryan Renfro. Craft Service: Paul Temple, Sean Parker, Brad Gratkowski. Inventory Supervisor: Jennifer Winnick. Inventory Assistant: Patricia La Pianta. Extras Casting: Donna Dupere. Casting: Anne Tait. Casting Assistant: Laura James. Tutors: Laurel Bresnahan, Janice Cameron. Children's Co-ordinators: Laurie Farrance, Aeden Langevin. Stunt Co-ordinators: Dennis Christensen, Alison Reid. Special Effects Supervisor: Arthur Langevin. Special Effects: Brad Middleton. Construction Co-ordinator: Weits Jekel. Head Carpenters: Jacob Haak, Patrick McCaffery. Key Scenic Artist: Reet Puhm. Scenic Artists: Norman Kelner, Melissa Morgan-Kelner. Head Painter: Melissa Morgan. Post Production Co-ordinator: Alice M. Lake. Post Production Supervisor: Gregor Hutchinson. Post Production Assistant: Anne Cobban. Assistant Editor: Ben Wilkinson. Supervising Sound Editor: Jeremy MacLaverty. Dialogue Editor: Tim Roberts. Assistant Sound Editors: Kris Engel, Denis Blais. Assistant Picture Editor: Ben Wilkinson. Post Production Assistant: Paul Vu. Foley Artists: Donna Powell, Gary Daprato. Studio Sound Mixer: Daniel Pellerin. Assistant Sound Mixer: Todd B. Warren. Video Editors: Bernie Clayton, Frank Biasi. Colourist: Bill Ferwerda. Music Consultant: Anne Lederman. Music Conducted by: Hagood Hardy, Glenn Morley. Music Assistant:

Donald Qun. Music Recorded by: Hayward Parrott. Series Developed by: Fiona McHugh. Adapted from the novels *The Story Girl*, *The Golden Road*, *Chronicles of Avonlea* and *Further Chronicles of Avonlea* by: Lucy Maud Montgomery. Produced by Rose Cottage Productions Inc. in association with The Disney Channel, The Canadian Broadcasting Association and with the participation of Telefilm Canada. Sullivan Films. 1-hour format. Six seasons, thirteen episodes per season. First aired in 1990.

BIG BANDS AT DISNEYLAND

Produced by: Ron Miziker. Directed by: Jim Gates. Written by: Harvey Siders. Associate Producer: Susan Dobak. Production Manager: Erik Marsters. Associate Director: George Baldwin. Assistant to the Producer: Barbara Wallace. Audio by: Best Audio. Audio Consultant: Larry Estrin. Audio Mixer: Shawn Murphy. Lighting Director: Don Cohen. Technical Director: Chris Donovan. Videotape Operator: Bob Carr. Video: Al Bowen, Jon Bowen, Christopher Grey. Cameras: Larry Gaudette, Carl Schloetel, Mike Tribble, Malcolm Bhone. Videotape Editing: Mary Danly. Art Director: Clare Graham. Title by: William Teitelbaum. Historical Materials: The Hugh Turner Collection. Music Clearance: Jonell Associates. Production Assistants: CoCo Zellitti, Bob Miziker. A Showmakers Production. 1-hour format. 12 episodes. First aired in 1984.

COLLEGE BOWL '87

Executive Producers: Don Reid, Richard Reid. Produced by: Mary Oberembt. Directed by: Dennis Rosenblat. Set Designers: Anthony Sabatino, William H. Harris. Segment Producer: Jefferson Lanz. Produced by: Richard Reid Productions, Moses-Reid-Cleary Productions, College Bowl Company Productions. 30-minute format. First aired in 1987.

COMING ON!

Executive Producer: Jack Linkletter. Produced and Written by: Ian Bernard. Directed by: Bob Knight. Associate Producer: Winter D. Horton Jr. Production Coordinator: Adrienne Pettijohn. Talent Coordinator: Mara Lynn Conrad. Production Manager: Mark Glick. Production Assistants: Mike Linkletter, Cindy Kurtz. Technical Director: Robert Shapiro. Lighting Director: Doug Dale. Audio: Rex Lundy. Produced by: Linkletter Productions. 1-hour format. 24 episodes. First aired in 1983.

CONTRAPTION

Director: Kip Walton. Supervising Producers: Larry Gottlieb, Jonathan Debin. Producer: Barry Cahn. Writers: Clair Brush, Lisa Stewart, Bruce Kernohan. Production Manager: John Callas. Casting Director: Marilyn Granas. Art Director: Peter Clemens. Music: Robin Frederick. Technical Director: Bob Jones. Lighting Director: David Lewis. Audio: Tom Moore. Video: Sue Knoll. Associate Director: Camilla Dunn. Stage Manager: Bob Chic. Production Associate: Anna-Lisa Nilsson. Camera Operators: Bill Dickson, Larry Gaudette, Rick Caswell, Kenny Dahlquist, Dick Price. Gaffer: Ken Christiansen. Set Construction by: Hollywood Construction Service. Announcer: Miranda Frederick. Coaches: Kevin Bickford, Robin Shaw. Executive Producers: Donald Kushner, Peter Locke. An Acme Game Show, Inc. Production. 30-minute format. 40 episodes. First aired in 1983.

DANGER BAY

Written by: John T. Dugan, Don Balluck, Gilbert Shilton, Nancy Ann Miller, Rick Drew, Michael Mercer, Christopher Haddock, Peter L. Dixon, Janet MacLean. Teleplay by: H.G. Bearns. Story by: Nancy Ann Miller, H.G. Bearns. Directed by: Gilbert Shilton, Allan Eastman, Michael Berry, Stuart Marholin, Ken Jubenvill, Nick Kendall, Allan King, Deepa Mehta Saltzman, Alan Simmonds, Brad Turner. Executive Producer: Paul Saltzman. Executive Script Consultants: John T. Dugan, Lionel E. Siegel. Supervising Producers: Harold Tichenor, John M. Eckert. Post-Production Producer: Paul Quigley. Associate Producers: Gordon Mark, Elizabeth Pontsa. Line Producers: Mary Eilts, Ray Sager. Production Manager: Harold Tichenor. Executive Story Consultants: Jane Veverka, Sondra Kelly. Directors of Photography: Doug McKay, Bob

Ennis, C.S.C., Philip Linzey. Editors: Stephen Lawrence, David Leach, Sally Peterson, Stephen Withrow, David Goorevitch, Pia DiCiaula, Evan Landis. Supervising Editor: Stephen Lawrence. Art Directors: Tom Duquette, Graeme Murray, Jill Scott. Music Composed and Conducted by: Don Gillis. Music Supervised by: David Greene. Rock Music by: New Regime. 1st Assistant Directors: Tom Braidwood, Jacques Hubert, Gordon Mark, Brad Turner, Michael Steele, T.W. Peacocke. 2nd Assistant Directors: Peter Dashkewytch, Mick Mackay, Murray Ord, T.W. Peacocke, Jim Marshall. 3rd Assistant Director: Elaine McMurtrie. Unit Manager: Mary Guilfoyle. Location Managers: George Horie, Scott Mathers, Rob McLaren, Andrew McLean. Script Supervisors: Jean Bereziuk, Shelley Crawford, Candice Field, Susan Weir. Sound Recordists: Lars Ekstrom, Ralph Parker, Richard Patton, Martin Fossum, Rob Young. Wardrobe Head: Susan Molloy. Wardrobe Supervisors: Jane Grose, Trish Keating. Seamstress: Debbie Douglas. Make-up Artists: Linda A. Brown, Phyllis Newman, Connie Parker, Laurie Finstad. Hair Stylists: Ian Ballard, Tom McIntyre, Janet Sala. Pauline Trembley. Property Masters: Ian Belcher, Wayne McLaughlin, Dan Sissons, Mark Francis. Assistant Propes: Dan Sissons. Art Department Trainee: Janet Brown. Set Decorators: Lesley Beale, Rondi Johnson, Barry Kemp, Janet Clark. Camera Operators: Curtis Petersen, Neil Seale, Brendon Spencer, Armin Matter. 1st Assistant Camera: Joel Ransom. 2nd Assistant Camera: Gary Kennedy. Special Stills: Dilip Mehta. Location Sound Recordist: Rick Patton. Boom Operator: Clancy Livingston. Key Grip: Dave Humphreys. Best Boy Grip: Rick Stadder. Dolly Grip: Brian Kuchera. Gaffers: Ron Williams, Barry Reid. Best Boy: Einar Hansen. Construction Coordinators: Garry Brolly, Barry Brolly, Stuart Ennis. Transport Captain: George Grieve. Co-Captain: Michael Murphy. Driver: Sylvia Nablo. Transportation Coordinators: George Grieve, Bud Bowe, Sylvia Nablo. Casting: Trish Robinson, Diane Polley, Lynne Carrow, Mike Fenton. Production Coordinators: Alice Ferrier, Catherine Howard, Mary McSweeny, Judith Rubin, Valerie McNicol. Specialities Coordinator: Brian Ferstman. Creative Consultant: Peter Dixon. Co-created by: Peter Dixon, Paul Saltzman. Stunt Coordinator: Bill Ferguson. Animal Trainer: Debra J. Coe. Dialogue Editors: Penny Hozy, Sharon Lackie, Arnold G. Stewart, Anita St. Denis. Sound Effects Editor: Fred Brennan. Assistant Editors: Gillian Jones, Pia Di Ciaula, Alexandra Horsky, Jane Tattersall. Production Assistants: Robert McLaren, Garry Wice, Karen Fernandez, Scott McCrorie. Re-recording Engineer: Elius Caruso. On-Line Editor: Jim Goessinger. Supervising Sound Editor: Steven R. Mitchell. Story Editors: Sondra Kelly, Jana Veverka, Jeffrey Cohen. Assistant Story Editor: Nancy Ann Miller. Additional Photography: Pauline Heaton. Costume Designers: Jane Grose, Jane Still. Production Co-ordinator: Alice Ferrier. Toronto Co-ordinators: Irka M. Iwathiw, Diane Parson, Tina Grewal. Production Accountants: Elizabeth Pontsa, Carol Reid, Lisa Richardson. Assistant Accountants: Carol Reid, Sharon Kates. Publicity: Dixie Cutler, Karen Pidgarski. Boats: John Smith, Don Steele. Sound Editors: Fred Berman, Marc Chiasson, Barry Gilmore, Manse James, Michele Moses, David Templeton. Pilots: Greg McDougall, Steve Wright. Timing: Les Bori. Negative Cutter: May Bischof. Colourist: Erik Johannessen. Effects Editor: Tony Gronick. Executives in Charge of Production for the CBC: Nada Harcourt, Deborah Bernstein. Assistant to the Executive Producer: Mara McSweeny. Writers' Secretary: Peny Gibbs. Acknowledgments: Vancouver Public Aquarium, Mount Seymour Provincial Park. Produced in association with The Disney Channel and The Canadian Broadcasting Association with the participation of Telefilm Canada and Rogers Communications, Inc. Produced by Danger Bay Productions, Inc. 30-minute format. 122 episodes. First aired in 1985.

DISNEY FAMILY ALBUM

Produced by: Cardon Walker, Michael Bonifer. Directed by: Michael Bonifer, Larry Smoot. Written by: Jim Fanning, Jamie Brasher, William Reid, Thor Challgren. Edited by: Cardon Walker. Creative Supervisor: Art Swerdloff. Director of Photography: Ted Ashton. Sound: Jack Tossman. Music by: John Debney. Production Manager: Thor Challgren. Production Assistant: Brady Connell. Camera: Ted Ashton, Paul Babbin, Dave Ogelvie. Sound: Klaus Landsberg, Mike Gannon, Tom

Robinson, Larry LaSota. Videotape Editors: Chris Ogden, Jill Stanton. Mixing Supervisors: Ken Berger, Larry Sullivan. Assistant Videotape Editors: Jacki Robison, Tony Rastatter, Bruce Yang. Title Designed by: John Lasseter, Brian McEntee. Assistant Director: Marc Gaede. Produced by Mica Productions. 30-minute format. 20 episodes. First aired in 1984.

DR. JOYCE BROTHERS PROGRAM, THE
Associate Producer: Ron Weed. Directed by: Terry Kyne. Fashions for Dr. Joyce Brothers Provided by: David Hayes. Art Director: Bill Morris. Fred Tatashore Productions. 1-hour format. 16 episodes. First aired in 1985.

DONALD DUCK PRESENTS
The first 60 shows were produced by Left Coast Television and compiled by Frank Brandt. The second group of 65 shows was produced by Tom Cummins of No-g Productions. First aired in 1983.

DTV
Producer: Chuck Braverman. Supervising Editor: Tedd Herrman. Editors: Bob Boucher, Todd Goodman, Tedd Herrman, Michael Herzmark, Margareta Schiappa. Production Manager: David Fudge. Production Engineer: Wayne Griffith. Music Clearances by: The Clearing House, Ltd. First aired in 1984.

DUMBO'S CIRCUS
Directors: Donald R. Ham, Ron Mangham, Philip F. Messina. Teleplay: Lois Becker, Betty G. Birney, David Ehrman, Jackie Hirtz, Carolyn Neal, Mark J. Stratton. Additional Material Directed by: Frank Groby, Ron Mangham, David Parish. Choreographers: Joe Giamalva, Patty Maloney, Ron Mangham, Denise McKenna. Song Dumbo's Circus by: Phillip Baron. Songs by: Phillip Baron, Rex Benson, Dan Crow, Robin Frederick, Steve Gillette, Will Ryan. Master Puppeteers: Paul Fusco, Frank Groby, John Lovelady. Assistant Puppeteers: Charlie Edwards, Joe Giamalva, Richard Griggs, Patty Maloney, Tom Reed, Van Snowden, Bruce Swift. Director of Photography/Lighting Director: James Swift. Music Directors: John Debney, Mike Watts. Music Producer: Phillip Baron. Production Manager: George Cook. Production Coordinator: Suzie Galler. Production Assistants: Steve Heltsley, Bill Mitchell. Production Stage Managers: Bronius Acalinas, David Parish, Ricky Stoutland. Script Supervisors: Laurette Healy, David Parish, Noelle Rose, Pam Grizz, Susan Gish. Character Wardrobe Designed by: Kristin Nelson. Puppet Wardrobe by: Lizbeth Gower. Costume Supervisors: Elaine Levi, Juliann Smith, Bonnie Sinclair, Kristin Nelson. Costume Assistant: Lesle Bennett. Technical Supervisor: Randy Simper. Character Sculptors: Tim Lawrence, Judy Feeley. Mechanical Designer: Al Colter. Electronics Supervisor: Gordon Brandt. Costume Technician: George Ryan. Preprogrammer: David Parish. Art Direction/Set Designer: James Higginson. Scenic Artists: Kelle Schaefle, Tom Dankiewicz. Construction Supervisor: Dan Brown. Set Decorator: Tom Reed. Assistants: Jack Bennett, Ben Johnson. Miniatures & Models: Steve Koch. Video Control: Chris Gray. Video Tape Operators: Dexter Padgitt, Kirk Morri, Kas Carr. Cameramen: Michael Tribble, Paul Dillingham, Jim Velarde. Production Stage Crew: Bronius Acalinas, Charlie Edwards, Richard Griggs, Peter Wessel, Nick Cline, Bruce Swift. Utility: Hugo Trujillo. Recording Engineer: Carla Frederick. Assistant Engineer: Lenise Bent. Recording Coordinator: Betty McCahon. Recording Assistants: Jack Bennett, Susan Gish. Production Audio Engineer: Bill Watson. Characters Designed by: Ken Anderson, Bob Moore. Post Production Supervisor: Tom Potter. Post Production Coordinator: Susan Kydd. Post Production Assistant: Steve Heltsley. Post Production Sound: Phillip Baron, John Walker, Zoundfx, Steve Michael. Production Assistant: Bill Mitchell. Production Secretary: Carolyn Neal. Assistant Producer: Christine Gorewit. Associate Producer: David Ehrman. Producer: Caroline Hay. Executive Producer: Frank Brandt. A Left Coast Television, Inc. Production. 30-minute format. 120 episodes. First aired in 1985.

EDISON TWINS, THE
Directed by: Rene Bonniere, Zale Dalen, Steve DiMarco, Peter Rowe, Paul Shapiro, F. Harvey Frost, Don Haldene, Timothy Bond, Alan F. Simmonds, Mario Azzopardi, Allan Eastman. Teleplay by: J. Blum, David Carol, Zale Dalen, Patrick Loubert, Sondra Kelly, Ian McDougall, Peter Sauder, Paul Shapiro, Elaine Waisglass, David Young, Paul Ledoux, Scott Barrie, Steve DiMarco, J.B. Martin. Created by: Michael Hirsh, Patrick Loubert. Story by: Nelvana Limited. Executive Producers: Michael Hirsch, Patrick Loubert, Clive A. Smith. Executive in Charge of Production for the C.B.C.: Nada Harcourt. Producers: Ian McDougall, Brian Walker. Title Song by: Bob Segarini. Music by: John J. Weisman, Patricia Cullen. Directors of Photography: Douglas Kiefer, C.S.C., Rene Ohashi. Art Director: Carmi Gallo. Editors: Teresa Hannigan, Scott Barrie, Scott La Barge. Story Editors: Susan Snooks, Sondra Kelly. Assistant Story Editor: Guy Mullally. Rewrite Editors: Scott Barrie, Susan Snooks. Science Consultants: George Van der kuur. Production Managers: Michael MacDonal, Sally Dundas, Nicholas J. Gray. Senior 1st Assistant Directors: Dennis Chapman, David Robertson, Rita Picard, Howard Barish. Casting Director: Arlene Berman. Assistants: Deborah S. Palz, Barbara Bjornason. Extras: Peter Lavender. Unit/Location Managers: Adam S. Shully, David Hart, Michael MacDonald. Assistant Location Managers: Steven J.D. Wakefield. Unit Manager: Francis R. Mahony III. Assistant Art Directors: Ed Hanna, Andris Hausmanis. 2nd Assistant Directors: Felix Gray, Rita Picard, Donald Brough, Alan Goluboff, Ella Picard, Lydia Wazana. Continuity: Tannis Baker, Nancy Eagles, Janine Slover, Danielle Lowi-Benchitritt, Janet Kranz. Location Sound Mixer: Douglas Ganton. Gaffers: Ira Cohen, Maris Jansons. Key Grips: Mark Silver, Christopher Dean. Property Masters: Greg Pelchat, Ed Hanna, Laird McMurray. Costume Co-ordinator: Kathy Vieira. Set Dressers: Christopher Dutton, Ed Hanna, Gareth Wilson. Wardrobe Coordinators: Leonie Reid, Delphine White. Make-up Artists: Pipsan Ayotte, Sandi Duncan. Sound Recordist: Doug Ganton. Hair Dresser: G.E. "Freddie" Godden. Stillsmen: John F. Phillips, Rob McEwan. Assistant Cameramen: Cathryn Robertson, John Hobson. Boom Operators: Reynold Trudel, Jack Buchanan. Key Grip: Christopher Dean. Best Boy/Grip: Ian Henderson. Grip: Mark Silver. Best Boys: G.L. Phipps, Ira Cohen, John David Hynes, Bill Brown. Assistant Grips: Gord Forbes, Mark Silver. Generator Operator: Duane Gullison. Props Buyer: Don Bennett. Assistant Set Dressers: Kim Sleede, Christopher Dutton. Assistant Props: Jeffrey A. Melvin, Greg Pelchat. Wardrobe Mistress: Eileen Kennedy. Assistant Wardrobe: Jay Du Boisson, Maureen Gurney. Post Production Supervisor/Supervising Editor: Tom Joerin. 1st Assistant Editors: Gregor Hutchison, Sarah Peddle. 2nd Assistant Editor: Alison Fisher. Assistant Editors: Neil Grieve, Gregor Hutchison, Paul Fox, Tim Eaton. Sound Editors: Catherine Hunt, Martin Ashbee, Kevin Ward. Dialogue Editor: Catherine Hunt. Dialogue and Effects Editors: Marc Chiasson, Jane Tattersail. Music and Effects Editor: Debbie Horowitz. Re-recording: Austin Grimaldi, David Appleby. Re-Recording Engineer: Elius Caruso. Foley Editors: Peter McBurnie, Terry Burke. Dialogue Coach: George Polhilos. Production Controller: Irene Phelps. Production Comptroller: Lacia Kornyio. Production Accountant: Marr Morgan. Assistant Accountant: Beth Boigon. Production Coordinators: Greg van Riel, Nicole M. Webster, Susan Kavesh. Assistant to Producer: Denise Mulvey. Trainee Assistant Directors: Linda Pope, David J. Vaughan, Orest Haba, Bill Bannerman. Production Assistants: Roberta Mayer, Joanne Kraemer, Joanne McIntosh, Francis R. Mahony III, Garth Roerick, Deborah Tiffin. Driver Captains: Allen S. Kosonic, Jerome McCann. Head Drivers: A. Randy Jones, Allen Kosonic. Drivers: Tom Osmond, Cactus Simser, Jerome McCann. Trainee Props/Set: Lloyd Brown. Trainee Art Director: Linda De Simone. 2nd Assistant Camera: Joel Guthro. Trainee Camera: David Allman, Lynnie Johnston, David Perkins, Laurie Longstaff. Screenplay Consultant: Joan Besen. Animation Directors: Kate Shepherd, Lawrence Jacobs, Laura Shepherd. Assistant Director: Lesley Headrick. Animation Production: Beverly Newberg-Lehman, Debra Collis-Armstrong, Lesley Headrick, Glen Binmore, Margaret Donaldson, Alan Knappett, Kim Cleary, Alan Bunce, John Laurence Collins, Mary Eklund, Victoria Shepherd, Barb Sachs, Kate Shepherd, Susan Kapigian, Denis Gonzales, Diana Lyle, Regina Salman, Marie Carter, David Altman, Val Fraser, Peter Yamasaki, Glen Bin-

more. Produced by Nelvana Limited in association with the Canadian Broadcasting Corporation, The Disney Channel and Telefilm Canada. 30-minute format. First aired in 1984.

EMERALD COVE

Based on Characters Created by: Dennis Steinmetz. Written by: Dennis Steinmetz, Stuart Werbin. Directed by: Dennis Steinmetz. Supervising Producer: Jack Seifert. Executive Producer: Dennis Steinmetz. Senior Associate Producer: Bob Williams. Associate Producer: Bruce Anderson. Associate Director: Cameron Loring. Stage Managers: Virgil Fabian, Dave Cove, Kelly Hernacki. Art Director: Gentry Akens. Director of Photography: Nick Woolfolk. Script Supervisor: Janie Scurti. Production Coordinator: Samantha Berger. Location Office Coordinator: Sarah Novin. Production Accountants: Cathy Clouse, Mary Joy. Studio Coordinator: Maura Akos. Transportation Captains: Kirsten Cobb, John Wiegman. Producers' Assistants: Lexy Brewer, Ellen Dunn. Production Staff: Wade and Rita Burby, Shronda B. Caudle, Mark Cranisky, Jeff Hand, Julie Hanson, Lori Higgs, Mike Lawrence, Oscar Vidal, Gerald Wu. Art Department Coordinator: Leigh Shipley. Head Carpenter: John Ehrhard. Carpenter: Jim Dreggors. Stage Coordinator: George Siplin. Head Scenic Artist: Mike Brown. Scenic Artist: Cindy J. Collins. Set Decorator: Saryn Goodall. Set Dressers: Mark Baker, Craig Nesbitt, Bently Tittle. Prop Master: Rich Swim. Props: T.J. Mannarino, Rich West. Gaffer—Stage: J.R. Roberson. Gaffer—Location: John Peters II. Best Boy: Dell Moody. Electricians: Michael Gooseman, Tim McGuire, Arnold Tucker. Grips: Ray Dettore, Steve Gryna, Jr., John Hatchitt, Chris Nye. Video Control: Hans Muster. Camera Operators: Neal J. Gallagher, Mark Lynch. Utility: Mike Navage, Linda Tutten. Production Mixer: Jim Fay. Boom Operators: Ricky Alvarez, Jim Hope, Al McGuire. Audio Assistant: Sharon Larson. Makeup: Regina Perron, Yolanda Winters. Hair: Liz Lavallee, Renee McKenzie, Marilyn Yarborough. Costumes: Marion Barnum, Terri Binion. Editors: Eddie Johnson, Ned Weissman. Rerecording Mixers: John Anderson, Larry Benjamin, Ross Davis. Blue Wave Productions, Inc. in association with Les Choux Company. First aired as a *Mickey Mouse Club* serial in 1993 (11 episodes), 1994 (15 episodes), 1995 (44 episodes).

ENCHANTED MUSICAL PLAYHOUSE

Credits were only available for *The Velveteen Rabbit:*
Cast: Marie Osmond (Velveteen Rabbit/Fairy), Joshua Tenny (Little Boy), Janey Swenson (Nana), Nina Sherman (Ballerina), Teri Waite (Baby Doll).
Directed by: Tom Trbovich. Written and Produced by: Jeffrey C. Sherman. Based on the Story by: Margery Williams. Music & Lyrics: Richard M. Sherman, Robert B. Sherman. Production Supervisor: Chad D. Murdock. Executive in Charge of Production: William L. Waite III. Musical Directors: Denny Crockett, Ike Egan. Musical Coordinator: Kurt Bestor. Associate Producer: Steve Thompson. Art Director: Seven Nielsen. Choreographer: Craig Call. Lighting Director: Dave Stoddard. Marie's Wardrobe: Ret Turner. Costume/Wardrobe: Noreen Pollei. Production Coordinator: Johnny Whittaker. Make-up: Ralph Gulko. Assistant to Producer: Denalee Chapman. Editor: Richard Jacobson. Production Secretary: Dana B. Robison. Production Assistant: Donna Mae Butler. Created by: Jeffrey C. Sherman. Co-Executive Producer: James Osmond. Executive Producer: James Rich, Jr. Nightstar, Inc. 30-minute format. First aired in 1984.

EPCOT AMERICA! AMERICA!

Producers: Wayne Threm, Jeff Thompson. Producers—Epcot Center Sequences: John Cosgrove, Wayne Threm. Writers: Nancy Griffin, Joseph Broido. Field Producers: Paul Bockhurst, Barbara Fisher, Michael Scott, Harry Wiland. Editorial Supervisor: Chip Brooks. Segment Editors: Beverly Baroff, Valerie Blitz, Jim Foster, Fred Golan, John Stromp. On-line Editors: Jess Bushhead, Bob Grubic, David Arnold. Post Production Supervisor: David Arnold. Post Production Coordinators: Carolyn Inman, Michael Elliott, L. Mark Medernach. Assistants: Tom Ohliger, Melanie Plummer. Production Manager: Rolf Darbo. Camera: Don Hunt, Jim McCalmont, David G. Trulli. VTR/Sound: Luanne Cadd, Dennis Drinnon, Bill Stitt. Assistant Camera: Tom Ohliger. Research Supervisor: Cynthia Shapiro. Research: Annie Azzariti, Heidi Barbarick, Danny Biederman, Judy Bornstein, Caren Canter, Eleanor Coleman, Shari Cookson, Barbara Fisher, Liz Mitchell, Teresa Modnick, Carol Schoenfeld, Tom Silberkleit, Gary Tarpinian, Kirsten Tellez, Joanna Vassiliadis. Theme Music Composed by: Christopher L. Stone. Segment Music Consultant: John Ortarotti. Chief Engineer: Duane Dahlberg. Engineers: John Portune, Bob Tubb, Tim Rollenhagen, John Trautman. *Epcot Center Sequences* Associate Producer: Michael Dobson. Camera: Bob Richardson. Video: Jerry Cell. Production Assistant: Mary Hamilton. Cue Cards: Tom Ohliger. Computer Programming, Future Choice Theatre: Mike Edison, Jean Brooks. Staff Assistants: Randy Backus, Mia Blanc, Jacqueline Canter, Peter Diskin, Tim Evans, Paul Koplin, Holly Laemmle, Jefferson Lanz. Executive Producer: Dave Bell. A Dave Bell Associates, Inc. Production. 30-minute format. 13 episodes. First aired in 1983.

EPCOT MAGAZINE

Executive Producer: Bill Hillier. Producer: Lawrence Taymor. Associate Producer: Erica Gerard. Senior Producer: Giovanna Nigro-Chacon. Production Supervisor: Dan Boothe. Assistant Production Supervisor: Darice Roesner. Assembly Editors: Mike Dimich, Michael Kirk. Assembly Assistant Director: John Bravakis. Epcot Producers: Don Asquith, Ken Marangell, John Storer. Epcot Director: Susan Shippey. Talent Coordinator: Joy Dolce. Assignment Editor: Margaret Carbonell-Smith. Story Producers: Arlene Acker, Roxy Allessandro, Bruce Bailey, Eric Bloom, Laura Burke, Michael Gladych, Brammy Lewenstein, Ken Marangel, Amy Nabseth, John Schwartz, Kevin Slattery, Marcy Wineman. New York Production: Smith-Tomlin. N.Y. Coordinating Producer: Sue Butler. San Francisco Production: Steve Kotton. Great Ideas Producers: Neisha Cohen, Karen Good, Theresa Ward. Continuity Writer/Producer: Joseph Shields. Assistant Continuity Writer: Robert Bruce. New York producer: Sue Butler. Associate Segment Producers: Sherry Bard, Mark Nadone, Rosemary Reid-Smith, Michael Stoneall. Assistant Assembly Editors: John Bravakis, Rebecca Reber. Assistant Story Producers: Bruce Bailey, Sherry Bard, Paul Hettler, Tammy Leshin, Susan Michaels, Rosemary Reid-Smith. Researchers: Stephanie Anderson, R. Michael Stoneall, Paula Willins. Epcot Associate Director: Sammy Romeo. Epcot Production Assistants: Mark Cunningham, Mary Hamilton, Eva Holmstrum, Dede Rector, Sammy Romeo. Music Coordinator: Ken Chernove. Production Accountant: John Rios. Production Assistants: Lori Otelsberg, John Rios. Production Associates: Michael Chacon, Sally Durbin, Scott Epstein, Mark Gilman, Mark Nardone. Animation: Dave Basinski, Doud Film, Inc. Epcot Magazine Theme Song: Ken Chernove, Jeff Labes. A Production of Hillier Productions, Inc. Varying formats: 55 60-minute episodes, 40 30-minute episodes, 150 30-minute evening episodes, 20 30-minute weekend episodes. First aired in 1983.

FIVE MILE CREEK

Executive Producer: Doug Netter. Producer: Henry Crawford. Associate Producers: Graham Foreman, John Copeland. Directed by: George Miller, Frank Arnold, Di Drew, Chris Thompson, Michael Jenkins, Kevin Dobson, Brendan Mahr, David Stevens. Story Editor: Graham Foreman. Written by: Peter Kinloch, Gwenda Marsh, Sarah Crawford, Michael Joshua, Denise Morgan, Bob Caswell, Greg Millin. Production Managers: David Lee, Jan Bladier. 1st Assistant Director: Bob Donaldson. Continuity: Jackie Sullivan. Director of Photography: Kevan Lind. Production Designer: George Liddle. Composer: Bruce Smeaton. Editor: Tim Wellburn. Costumer: Jeny Arnott. Art Directors: Lisa Elvy, Igor Nay. American Casting: Loretta Crawford. Casting Director: Vicki Popplewell. Gaffer: Graham Rutherford. Grip: Brett McDowell. Sound: Syd Butterworth. Make-up: Jose Perez. Hair-dressing: Joan Petch. Horse Master and Stunt Coordinator: Heath Harris. Post Production Sound: Stuart Armstrong. Music Editor: Garry Hardman. Series concept inspired by Louis L'Amour's *The Cherokee Trail*. Made in association with The Disney Channel and The Seven Network Australia. A Valstar Pty. Ltd. Production. 60-minute format. 39 episodes. First aired in 1983.

GOOD MORNING, MICKEY!

Production Company: Left Coast Television. Executive Producer: Frank Brandt. Producers: Caroline Hay, Marc Gaede. Compiled by: Frank Brandt. 30-minute format. 80 episodes. First aired in 1983.

GOOD MORNING, MISS BLISS

Supervising Producers: David Garber, Bruce E. Kalish. Produced by: Marcia Govons. Created by: Sam Bobrick. Written by: Peter Engel, Howard Ostroff, Michael Poryes. Directed by: Burt Brinckerhoff, Gary Shimokawa. Executive Producer: Peter Engel. Executive Story Consultants: Jake & Mike Weinberger. Executive Story Editor: Michael Poryes. Creative Consultants: R.J. Colleary, Tom Tenowich. Story Editors: Susan Sebastian, Diana Ayers. Associate Producer: Franco E. Bario. Casting by: Shana Landsburg. Art Director: Ken Johnson. Costumes by: Elizabeth Bass. Title Design: Douglas Boyd. *These Are the Best of Times* Music by: Charles Fox. Lyrics by: Mark Meuller. Music Scored by: Charles Fox. Associate Directors: Don Barnhart, Rick Gough. Stage Managers: Vincent Poxon, Jane E. Seidler. Production Associate: Ellen Deutsch. Production Coordinator: Mark Fetterman. Script Coordinators: Wanda Armstrong, Mary Temkin. Senior Unit Managers: Chris Conte, Ruthanne Morris. Editor: Sam Patterson. Lighting Consultant: Richard Brown. Technical Director: Michael Higuera. Lighting Director: John Conti. Audio: Jeff Smith. Assistants to the Producers: Greg D'Auria, Deanna Bernal, Gisele Evans, Sue Feyk, Mickey Friedman, Marybeth Maloney, Gisele Lyans, Dan Sachoff, Jerry N. Siegel. Executive in Charge of Production: William F. Phillips. Peter Engel Productions in association with The Disney Channel and NBC Productions. 30-minute format. First aired in 1988.

HAPPY TRAILS

Producer: Chuck Braverman. Director: Marc Payton. Editor: Tedd Herrmann. Art Director: Kim Kofax. Lighting Director: Jeff Chang. 10 episodes.

HOLLYWOOD LIVES

Executive Producers: Wili Baronet, Mark Israel. Producer: Wili Baronet. Directed by: Mark Israel. Co-Producer: Marina Sargenti. Director of Photography: Mark Israel. Editor: David Bret Egen. *Hollywood Lives* Theme by: Mark Mothersbaugh. Casting Director: Paul Dahmen. Producer's Assistant: Kathleen Koffman. Research: Stephanie Smith, Rebecca Witt. Camera Operators: Mark Israel, Harris Done, John Rhode. Camera Assistant: Patrick Murphy. 2nd Unit Director/Cameraman: Steven Kochones. 2nd Unit Camera Assistant: Robert Stemwell. Grip: Frank Horn. Production Coordinator: Paul Dahmen, Jeannie Olander. Production Sound Mixers: Roberto Chiofalo, Brandon Kubisen. Production Assistants: Terri Lynn Janison, Kathleen Koffman, Jay Lavely, John Garcia-Shelton, Stephanie Smith, Robert Stemwell, Rebecca Witt. Wilmark Entertainment in association with Buena Vista Television. 30-minute format. 10 episodes. First aired in 1995.

JUST LIKE FAMILY

Co-Executive Producer: Stan Rogow. Supervising Producer: Steve Pritzker. Written by: Robert Illes, James R. Stein, Steve Pritzker, Michael Gordon, Jim Geoghan, Michael Kagen. Teleplay by: Steve Ptizker, Michael Kagen. Story by: Michael Kagen. Based on Characters Created by: Stephen Black, Henry Stern. Directed by: Phil Ramuno, Jim Drake. Executive Producers: James R. Stein, Robert Illes. Associate Producer: Michael Petok. Executive Script Consultant: Jim Geoghan. Executive Story Editors: Stephen Sustarsic, David Silverman, Jeanne Baruch, Jeanne Romano. Story Editors: Barbara Davilman, Michael Gordon. Directors of Photography: Charles Barbee, Richard Hissong. Art Director: David Sackeroff. Editor: Ken Denisoff. Associate Directors: Michael Dimich, Don Sullivan. Stage Manager: Daniel Harris. Original Score by: Mark Hudson, Steve Dudas, Craig Safan. Costume Designer: Tom Bronson. Set Decorator: Roger Shook. Property Master: David McGuire. Key Costumers: Karen Kaufman, Milton Mangum. Make-up: Larry Abbott. Hair Stylist: Shawn McKay. Script Supervisor: Jeanette Barnes. Production Coordinator: Carla Myres. Technical Directors: Allan Wells, Robert G. Holmes, Ken Shapiro. Audio: Russ Gary. Video: Eric Clay, Mark San-

ford. Stein & Illes Productions, Stan Rogow Productions in association with Walt Disney Television. 30-minute format. First aired in 1989.

JUST PERFECT

Produced by: William H. Shippey. Written by: William Gosnell. Directed by: Andy Tennant. Director of Photography: Bob Ebinger. Original Music: Bruce Hanifan. Production Designer: Susan Volk. Editor: Art Luciani. Production Manager: Jeffrey M. Zeitlin. 1st Assistant Director: Stephen Lillis. 2nd Assistant Director: Eric Jones. Casting Director: Matt Casella. Script Supervisor: Sibylle Aldridge. Auditor: Phil Rodak. Production Coordinator: Debra Spidell. Location Manager: Dennis Williams. Property Master: Tucker Johnston. Costume Designer: Robin Lewis. Wardrobe Supervisor: Sue Bub. Makeup Artist: Dori Randall. 1st Assistant Camera: Jay Coolidge. Steadicam Operator: Chris Squires. Gaffer: Dan Zarlengo. Key Grip: Mike Epley. Sound Mixers: Don Sanders, Randy Gable. Animal Trainers: Mathilde de Cagny, Cheryl Harris, Gary Gero, Shauna Skidmore. Transportation Coordinator: Paul Kowalczyk. Music Supervisor: Michael Welsh. Post Production Supervisor: Pamela Havens. A Cornerstone Production. 13 episodes. First aired as a *Mickey Mouse Club* serial in 1990.

KIDS, INCORPORATED

Executive Producer: Earl Glick. Produced by: Thomas W. Lynch, Gary P. Biller. Co-Producer: Kevin A. Berg. Coordinating Producer: Jimmy Cuomo. Associate Producers: Andrew Liskey, Lenny Shulman. Written by: George McGrath, Lenny Shulman, Jan Silver, Ann Elder, Andy Gordon, David Mirsky, Lou Chagaris, Thomas W. Lynch, Blake Snyder. Directed by: Jules Lichtman, Michael Dimich, Gary Halvorson, Marty Pasetta, Jr., Greg Fera, Thomas W. Lynch. Music: Al Kasha, Joel Hirshhorn. Music Director: Reg Powell. Music Coordinator: Lou Chagaris. Art Direction: Jimmy Cuomo. Choreography: Dorian Grusman, Lester Wilson. Lighting Consultant: Carl Gibson. Costume Designer: Garland W. Riddle. Production Designer: Jimmy Cuomo. Associate Director: Emm Jay Strokel. Gaffer: Frank Olavis. Production Executives: Allan Baumrucker, John Lynch. Production Supervisor: Joel Hatch. Casting: Cate Praggastis, Tina Sellers. Produced for The Disney Channel by Hal Roach Studios, Inc. and Lynch/Biller Productions. 30-minute format. First aired in 1986.

MATCH POINT

Produced by: William H. Shippey. Written by: Paul W. Cooper. Directed by: Max Reid. Director of Photography: Robert Ebinger. Original Music: Bruce Hanifan. Production Designer: Susan Volk. Editor: Art Luciani. Production Manager: Jeffrey M. Zeitlin. First Assistant Director: David Turchi. Second Assistant Director: Jerome Goldberg. Casting Director: Matt Casella. Script Supervisor: Sibylle Aldridge. 1st Assistant Camera: Jay Coolidge. Auditor: Phil Rodak. Production Coordinator: Debra Spidell. Location Manager: Pinki Ragan. Property Master: Pasco DiCarlo. Costume Designer: Linda Durso. Wardrobe Supervisor: Katherine Quinif. Makeup Artist: Ann Mayo. Sound Mixer: Don Sanders. Sound Editor: Sheri Klein. Gaffer: Danny MacCallum. Key Grip: Mike Epley. Music Supervisor: Michael Welsh. Post Production Supervisor: Mitch Goddard. Extras Casting: Julie Kuhlman. Transportation Coordinator: Paul Kowalczyk. A Cornerstone Production. 15 episodes. First aired as a *Mickey Mouse Club* serial in 1989.

MICKEY MOUSE CLUB, THE

Executive Producer: Steve Clements. Produced by: Joe Carolei. Directed by: Joe Carolei, Bill Davis, Allan Kartun. Writing Supervised by: Alan Silberberg. Written by: Steve Clements, Evan Gore, Tim Grundmann, Fred Newman, Glenn Rabney, Hillary Rollins, Karl Tiedemann, Stephen Winer, Jeff Zimmer. Produced by: Kim Dawson. Coordinating Producer: Margie Friedman. Executive in Charge of Production: Jean Wiegman. Associate Producers: Jim Moroney, Mark Rains, Bob Williams. Musical Segments Produced and Staged by: Barbara Epstein, Nancy Gregory. Choreography by: Wayne Bascomb. Music Arranged by: John Kavanaugh. Music Supervisor: Dana Salyers. Associate Producer: Jim Moroney. Music Video Directed by: David Seeger. Music Arranged by: Dan Sawyer. Segment Directors: Andrew Ames, Maria Baltazzi, Steve Bronstein, Karen Cadle, Chaz Crompton, Judi Elterman, Julian Goldberg, Jimmy Huckaby, David Seege. Segment Producers: Sharon Dudley, Diane Fredel, Sharon Dudley, Matthew Gaven, Karen Good, Jimmy Huckaby, Kathy O'Reilly, Kathee Yamamoto. Post Production Producer: Bart Roen. Art Directors: Jeff Chandler, Randy Foster. Lighting Director: Nick Woolfolk. Associate Directors: Kim Anway, Christine Clark, Rudi Corbett, Judi Elterman, Bart Roen. Stage Managers: John Aguirre, Joshua Berger, Nancy Cohen, Keith Richmond, Fred Witten. Set Designed by: Gerry Hariton, Vicki Baral. Lighting Designed by: Greg Brunton. Production Supervisor: Meredith Fox Stewart. Production Associates: Linda Argari, Kelly Ann Hernacki, Melissa Blessing Weiss. Production Assistant: Janie Ferguson. Script Supervisor: Kimber Smith. Property Masters: John Depiro, Ruth Mary Kahl. Property Assistants: Larry Bradford, Kelly Ann Hernacki, Deborah Witt. Acting Coaches: Maria Gobetti, Tom Ormeny. Talent Coordinator: Leslie Hans. Cast Coordinator: Patti Silveira. Assistant Art Director: Mickey DeJesus. Assistant Segment Producers: Sharon Dudley, Andrea Guidry, Jim Huckaby. Set Decorator: Jim Sheridan. Post Production Supervisors: Jon Boyer, Nancy Carlson, Annie Court. Post Production Assistants: Adam Berger, James Weathers. Field Production Supervisor: Christopher D. Silveira. Production Coordinators: John Aguirre, Tom Cavanagh, Jane H. Ferguson. Editors: Cheryl Campsmith, Art David, Jim Mancini, Jeff Palmer, Sam Patterson, Dennis Phillips, Mike Walker. Research Supervisor: Kitt McLeod. Researchers: E.W. Land, Kate Link, Matt Oppy, Kathy O'Reilly. Transportation Coordinators: Tom Cavanagh, Bill Henry, Glenn Rocha. Production Staff: Ray Bastin, Marci Bokash, Ken Bowles, Beth M. Brady, Tom Cavanagh, Cathy Clouse, Rafael Colon, Jim Davis, John Depiro, Jr., Elizabeth Donahue, Leigh Foster, Mike Hays, Bill Henry, Christopher Heyn, Alexis Jackson, John Joshua, Jill Murphy, Phyllis Rose Nastri, Josef V. Page, Julie Pine, Julie Robinson, Barry Schuch, Patti Menieta-Silveira, Vernon Whitaker, John Weigman, Jean Winkelseth. Wardrobe Supervisors: Mellissa Berry, Shirley G. Bird. Wardrobe: Terri Binion, Kathryn Bird, Ken "Boma" Bolden, Carolyn Dessert, Leda Gutierrez, Barbara Heath, Monica Posse. Hair: Liz Lavallee, Tish Simpson. Make-up: Reneé Homitz, Regina Perron, Debra Summers, Yolanda Winters. Camera Operators: Bill Akerlund, Ken Krause, Mark Lynch, Bruce Oldham, Jim Scurti, Bob Van Dorn, John Woodhead, Melissa Wright. Head Carpenter: Alan Bruun. Assistant Carpenters: Clinton Nuedecker, George Siplin. Unit Production Manager: Clay Newbill. Studio Production Assistant: Virgil Fabian. Studio Production Coordinator: Maria Caccavo. Engineer in Charge: Larry Gaetano. Technical Director: Pete Court. Video Control: Vince Vezzi. Videotape Operators: Pat Caudle, Ann Court, Mike Sherwood, Gary Thomas. Audio Mixer: Jim Fay. PA Mixer: John DeRussey. Audio Assistants: Annie Bornhurst, Brien Casey, Jim McCabe, Sean McFall, Ken Yocum. Post Production Audio: Rob Hill, Kurt Wagner. Gaffer: J.R. Roberson. Lighting Board Operator: Michael Gooseman. Key Grip: Steve Gryna. Electricians: Mike Laninfa, Mark Malacane, Chip Nuefeld, John Peters, Martin Rudder, Pat Stare. Grips: Valery Burger, Jerry Meibos, Terry Nuedecker, Martin Rudder, Frank Vila. Executive in Charge of Production for Blue Light Productions, Inc: George Paige. Blue Wave Productions, Inc. 30-minute format. First aired in 1989.

MOUSERCISE

Executive Producer: Bob Banner. Supervising Producer: Sam Riddle. Producer: George Taweel. Directors: Michael Dugan, Gordon Myers. Executive in Charge of Production: Vic Markman. Associate Producers: Dee Baker, Sandy Hauch. Production Supervisor: Sandy Hauch. Writers: Michael Dugan, Earl Kress. Research Consultants: Bryan Blackburn, Stanley Ottenstein. Exercise Choreographer: Eileen Blake. Musical Director: Joey Carbone. Music Supervisor: Gary LeMel. Art Director: John Shaffner. Lighting Consultant: Greg Brunton. Set Decorator: Lissa Kapstrom. Wardrobe: Toni Vitale. Assistants to the Producer: Allison L. Birne, Michael Dugan, Laurie Berman Eagle. Production Coordinator: Linda Pryor. Produc-

tion Assistants: Bill Bailie, Michael Dugan, Jonathan Glassner, Meredith Haglund, Linda Pryor, Jill Williams. Talent Coordinator: M.J. Shooner. Casting: Harv Selsby, M.J. Shooner. Lighting Directors: George Mills, David Schirle. Technical Directors: Phil Burghdorf, John Tweden. Unit Manager: Jane Began. Graphics: Tim Neil. Editor: Raymond M. Bush. Audio Mixers: Kent Gibson, Michael Krupnik, Roger Vonier. Produced by RJB Productions, Inc. 30-minute format. 60 episodes. First aired in 1983.

MOUSETERPIECE THEATER

Directed by: Mitchell Kriegman. Written by: Ayn Lesley, Tom O'Malley, Arthur Prager, Lois Rowley. Camera/Lighting: Robert Balton. Video Engineers: Barry Minnerly, Ken Wise. Video Assistant: David Stein. Audio: Ron Honsa, Gino Lombardo. Gaffer: Tony Pasento. Make-up: Jill Stockland. Continuity: Catherine Brabec, Laura Mannes. Production Assistants: Jill Cunniff, Annie Goldson, Rich Kirschner, Jim Ovitt. Video Editor: Phil Fallo. Videotape Operator: Mike Polito. Off-line Editors: Tony Oursler, Shelly Silver. On-line Editors: Phil Fallo, Rick Walter, David Fost, Kris Trexle. Post Production Supervisors: Wayne Barthelemy, Steve Goldsmith. Opening Sequence Designed by: Mitchell Kriegman. Director of Photography: Chris Balton. Video: Edward O'-Connor. Executive Producer: Robert Cunniff. An ESNE production. 30-minute format. 60 episodes. First aired in 1983.

MY LIFE AS A BABYSITTER

Produced by: William H. Shippey. Written by: James Howe. Directed by: Matt Casella. Director of Photography: Robert Ebinger. Original Music by: John Beasley. Production Designer: Douglas Johnson. Editor: Art Luciani. Production Manager: Jeffrey M. Zeitlin. First Assistant Director: Stephen Lillis. Second Assistant Director: Eric Jones. Casting Director: David Brymer. Script Supervisor: Veronica Flynn. Auditor: Phil Rodak. Production Coordinator: Tom Leonardis. Location Manager: Dennis Williams. Costume Designer: Robin Lewis. Wardrobe Supervisor: Vincent Lapper. Make-up Artist: Dori Randall. Property Master: Tucker Johnston. 1st Assistant Camera: David Riley. Steadicam Operator: Kirk Gardner. Gaffer: Rhett Fernsten. Key Grip: George Palmer. Sound Mixer: Don Sanders. Extras Casting: Catrine McGregor. Transportation Coordinator: Paul Kowalczyk. Post Production Supervisor: Pamela Havens. A Cornerstone Production. 12 episodes. First aired as a *Mickey Mouse Club* serial in 1990.

NEW! ANIMAL WORLD

Executive Producer: John Burrud. Producers: Betty Battino, Jerry Dhesse. Writers: Stephanie Anderson, Miriam Birch, Steven Bourne, Barry Clark, Barbara Farnworth, Thomas Knight, Gary Sogol. Original Music: Chris Currell, Luis Cabaza. Cinematography: Lubo Mikula, Wolfgang Bayer, Peter Good, J. Barry Herron, Fred Krug, Charles Sutton, Ralph White, Wolfgang & Sharon Obst. Production Staff: Teresa Hamann, Joni Indursky, Suzanne McMillan, Ray Peschke, Elizabeth Shaw, Vince Matsudaira. Video Tape Editors: Chris Painter, Rick Piccini. Acknowledgments: San Diego Wild Animal Park, Miami Seaquarium. Co-Executive Producer: Jack Arbib. A Bill Burrud Production. 30-minute format. 105 episodes. First aired in 1983.

SCHEME OF THINGS, THE

Executive Producers: Jules Power, Richard R. Rector. Producers: Ben Bayol, Janice Tunder. Project Director: Stanley G. Burford. Executive in Charge/Program Manager: Ronald L. Weaver. Coordinating Producers: Paul Colardo, Madeline Werner. Field Producer: Charles Rudnick, Paul Shain. Field Reporters: Monsita Ferrer, Dave Garrison, Nan Nelson, Cynthia Pollard, Michele Russell. Science Consultant: Dr. John McCosker. A Power/Rector Production. 30-minute format. 65 episodes. First aired in 1983.

SECRET BODYGUARD

Produced by: William Shippey, Sally Baker. Written by: M.C. Varley, Kris Young. Story by: Michael Janover. Directed by: William Shippey. Director of Photography: Bob Ebinger. Original Music: Scooter Pietsch. Production Designer: Rob Siss-man. Editor: Art Luciani. Production Manager: Jeffrey M. Zeitlin. 1st Assistant Director: Stephen Lillis. 2nd Assistant Director: Kaaren Ochoa. Casting: Ulrich-Dawson. Script Supervisor: Paula Barrett. Auditor: Phil Rodak. Production Coordinator: Heather McGrath. Location Manager: Dennis Williams. Costume Designer: Robin Lewis. Wardrobe Supervisor: Sue Bub. Make-up & Hair Artist: Patti Brand. Art Director: Tucker Johnston. 1st Assistant Camera: David Riley. Steadicam Operator: Kirk Gardner. Gaffer: Jim Gilson. Key Grip: William Paul. Sound Mixer: Robert Janiger. Extras Casting: Samuel Warren. Martial Arts Choreography: Ernie Reyes, Sr. Dance Choreography: Steve Messina. Transportation Coordinator: Paul Kowalczyk. Post Production Supervisor: Betsy Wallace. A Cornerstone Production. 15 episodes. First aired as a *Mickey Mouse Club* serial in 1991.

SECRET OF LOST CREEK, THE
Produced by: William H. Shippey. Written by: Paul W. Cooper. Directed by: Mark Jean. Director of Photography: Robert Ebinger. Original Music: Gary Schyman. Production Designer: Roger Crandall. Editor: Art Luciani. Production Manager: Jeffrey M. Zeitlin. 1st Assistant Director: Stephen Lillis. 2nd Assistant Director: Eric P. Jones. Casting Director: Matt Casella. Script Supervisor: Carol Hubbard. Auditor: Phil Rodak. Production Coordinator: Debra Spidell. Location Manager: Dennis Williams. Set Decorator: Gay Lauritzen. Property Master: Sean Markland. Costume Designer: Robin Lewis. Wardrobe Supervisor: David Buckley. Make-up Artist: Dori Randall. 1st Assistant Camera: Jay Coolidge. Sound Mixer: Don Sanders. Gaffer: Dan Zarlengo. Key Grip: Jason Fife. Music Supervisor: Michael Welsh. Post Production Supervisor: Carol Lea Pike. Extras Casting: Catrine McGregor. Transportation Coordinator: Paul Kowalczyk. A Cornerstone Production. 15 episodes. First aired as a *Mickey Mouse Club* serial in 1989.

STEVE ALLEN'S COMEDY ROOM
Executive Producer: Steve Allen. Producer: Fred Tatashore. Directed by: Terry Kyne. Writers: Steve Allen, Fred Tatashore. Associate Producer: Ron Weed. Music Director: Terry Gibbs. Art Director: Bill Morris. Lighting Consultant: Carl Gibson. Assistant to the Producer: India Van Voorhees. Talent Coordinator: Carolyn Baker. Production Assistant: Paula Lockner. Production Secretary: Deb Kennedy. Production Associate: Bill Boyd, Jr. Associate Director: Selig Frank. Set Decorator: Ken Neumar. Unit Manager: Jim Schwab. A Presentation of Meadowlane Enterprises, Inc. 1-hour format. 6 episodes. First aired in 1984.

STEVE ALLEN'S MUSIC ROOM
Executive Producer: Steve Allen. Producer: Fred Tatashore. Directed by: Frank Buxton. Written by: Steve Allen, Fred Tatashore. Associate Producer: Ron Weed. Musical Director: Terry Gibbs. Art Director: Bill Morris. Assistant to the Producer: India Van Voorhees. Talent Coordinator: Carolyn Baker. Researcher: Perri Chasin. Production Assistants: D.E. Angel, Janet Tannenbaum. Production Coordinator: Ken Fuchs. Lighting Consultant: Carl Gibson. Associate Director: Robin Felsen. Set Decorator: Ken Neumar. Unit Manager: Jim Schwab. Technical Director: Darryl Kuenzler. Lighting Director: Reg Leffler. Audio: Dick Sartor. Video: Dick Browning. Stage Managers: Craig Factor, John Pudelek. Videotape Editor: David Foster. A Presentation of Meadowlane Entertainment. 1-hour format. 6 episodes. First aired in 1984.

STILL THE BEAVER
Executive Producers: Brian Levant, Nick Abdo. Produced by: Richard Gurman. Developed by: Brian Levant. Based on the series *Leave It to Beaver* Created by: Joe Connelly, Bob Mosher. Written by: Brian Levant, Richard Gurman, George Tibbles, Jeffrey Pohn, Andrew Horowitz, Fred Fox, Jr., Richard Correll, Lawrence Gay, Michael J. DiGaetano, Joe Glauberg, Tom Tenowich, Tony Dow, Cindy Begel, Lesa Kite. Directed by: Norman Abbott, Nick Abdo, Bob Claver, Brian Levant, Jeffrey Ganz, Roger Ducjowny. Associate Producers: Marty Sadoff, Herbert H. Dow. Theme Arranged and Performed by: Walter Murphy. Music by: David Frank. Director of Photography: Peter Smokler. Art Director: Mary Ann Biddle. Film

Editor: Herbert H. Dow. Unit Production Manager: John H. Ward. First Assistant Director: Harriette Ames-Regan. Second Assistant Director: Warren Turner. Casting by: Melvin Johnson. Set Decorator: Sam Jones. Sound: Michael Moore. Sound Editor: Colin Mouat. Music Editor: James E. Morriss. Costume Supervisors: Patrick Norris, Mary Lou Reinbold. Assistants to Executive Producer: Frank Saperstein, Susan Chilcote. Assistants to the Producer: Cindy Weidler, Dan Harris, Harriet Golin. Universal Pay TV Programming, Inc. Sprocket Films, Inc. and Telvan Productions, Inc. 30-minute format. 26 episodes. First aired in 1984.

TEEN ANGEL
A Cornerstone Productions Production. Segment Director: Max Reid. Written by: Kris Young. Produced by: William H. Shippey. Director of Photography: Robert Ebinger. Art Director: Susan Volk. Editor: Art Luciani. Production Manager: Jeffrey M. Zeitlin. First Assistant Director: David Turchi. Second Assistant Director: Jerome Goldberg. Original Music by: Bruce Hanifan. Casting by: Matt Casella. Costumes Designed by: Linda Dorso. Script Supervisor: Sibylle Aldridge. 1st Assistant Camera: Jay Coolidge. Auditor: Phil Rodak. Production Coordinator: Debra Spidell. Location Manager: Pinki Ragan. Property Master: Pasco Dicarlo. Wardrobe Supervisor: Linda Durso. Make-up: Ann Mayo. Sound Mixer: Don Sanders. Sound Editor: Sheri Klein. Gaffer: Danny MacCallum. Key Grip: Mike Epley. Music Supervisor: Michael Welsh. Post Production Supervisor: Mitch Goddard. Extras Casting: Julie Kuhlman. Transportation Coordinator: Paul Kowalczyk. 12 episodes. First aired as a *Mickey Mouse Club* serial in 1989.

TEEN ANGEL RETURNS
Produced by: William H. Shippey. Written by: Kris Young. Directed by: Mark Jean. Director of Photography: Robert Ebinger. Original Music by: Bruce Hanifan. Production Designer: Roger Crandall. Editor: Art Luciani. Production Manager: Jeffrey M. Zeitlin. First Assistant Director: Stephen Lillis. Second Assistant Director: Eric Jones. Casting by: Matt Casella. Script Supervisor: Becca Poulos. Auditor: Phil Rodak. Production Coordinator: Karen A. Snizik. Location Manager: Dennis Williams. Set Decorator: Gay Lauritzen. Property Master: Sean Markland. Costumes Designed by: Robin Lewis. Wardrobe Supervisor: David Buckley. Make-up Artist: Dori Randall. Assistant Make-up Artist: Gina Homan. 1st Assistant Camera: Jay Coolidge. Sound Mixer: Don Sanders. Gaffer: Dan Zarlengo. Key Grip: Jon W. Tilton. Music Supervisor: Michael Welsh. Post Production Supervisor: Carol Lea Pike. Extras Casting: Catrine McGregor. Transportation Coordinator: Paul Kowalczyk. A Cornerstone Production. 13 episodes. First aired as a *Mickey Mouse Club* serial in 1989.

TEEN WIN, LOSE, OR DRAW
Produced by: Jay Wolpert. Directed by: Dan Diana, Jeff Goldstein. Written by: Joel Hecht. Production Designers: Anthony Sabatino, William H. Harris. Production Coordinator: Shannon Dobson. Talent Coordinator: Harriet S. Mauro. Contestant Coordinator: Kathy Ladd. GSN Production Assistant: Phred Tinampay. Associate Director: Jean Kaye. Stage Manager: Kathy Ladd. Researcher: Sharon Jones. Booth PA: Mike Bourgeois. Assistant Contestant Coordinator: Eric Ota. Art Director: Scott Storey. Production Staff: Marsha Groome, Sebastian Jones, Janie Unger. Music by: Tom Morrison. Caricature Artist: Dave Martin. Lighting Director: Nick Woolfolk. Engineer in Charge: Peter Gaetano. Technical Director: Peter Court. Audio: Dan Berlin, Dave Mouery. Video: Vince Vezzi. Videotape Operator: Alex Gimenez. Unit Manager: Matt Sites. Based on *Win, Lose or Draw*. Buena Vista Entertainment. Stone-Stanley Productions. 30-minute format. First aired in 1989.

WALT DISNEY WORLD INSIDE OUT (original version)
Executive Producers: Stu Schreiberg, Dan Boothe. Producers: Steve Feld, Dennie Gordon, Peter Israelson, James P. Taylor, Jr. Directed by: Philip F. Cohen. Written by: Michael E. Zack. Coordinating Producer: Stacy Ryono. Field Producer: James M. Smith. Segment Producers: Jonathan Dowdell, Brian Ross, James M. Smith. Editors: Mark Bement, Jeff Caldwell, Kelly

Coskran, Brian Ross, Ray J. Pages, Marcus Weise. Art Director: Jimbo Marshall. Post Production Supervisor: Eric Van Wagenen. Production Coordinators: Renee Mendoza, Susan Garra. Unit Manager: Amy Storti. Music: Michael Tavera. Opening Theme: Pete Fahey. Camera: Richard Davis, Bob "Roshie" Jones, Jordan Klein, Jr. Audio: John DeRussy, John McCabe, George Mochonas, Norman Seow. Prop Master: Nick Farrell. Gaffers: Gary Bristow, Rick Campbell. Key Grips: Gary Bristow, Rob Curschman, Gordy Jorian, Pat Knowles, Dennis Hus. Script Supervisors: Wendy Dawson, Wendy DeLouche. Hair/Make-up: Maria Cuetara. Wardrobe: Beverly Safier, Teresa Myerscough. Assistant Directors: Lance Parrish, Gerald Wu. Post Production Coordinators: Bart Astor, Michael Cronin. Camera Assistants: Charles "Ching" Oettel, Jason Imbs, J.C. Jennings. Researcher: Susan Janis. Key P.A.: Daniel P. Johnson, Lance Parrish. Production Assistants: Maxwell Beck, Mark Brisbin, Mark Craninksy, Kevin Davis, Delise Del Favero, Christopher Freeland, Susan Garra, Seth Harris, Ryan Henry, Jason Imbs, Daniel Johnson, Sean Linderman, Lance Parrish, Cameron Roberts, Mike Scanlon, Dan Severson, Lynn Tschosik. Prop Assistants: Michael Foerstner, Mark Dillon, John Denk, Mike Dougherty, Mike Norris. Executive in Charge of Production: John Bravakis. The Wrightwood Group, Incorporated. 30-minute format.

WALT DISNEY WORLD INSIDE OUT (second version)
Executive Producer: Brad Lachman. Producer: Garry Bormet. Coordinating Producer: Bill Bracken. Directed by: Dennis Rosenblatt, Rob Wilson. Written by: Richard Albrecht, Casey Keller. Associate Producer: John Foy. Segment Producers: Lee Bernhardi, Wayne Orr, Rob Wilson. Executive in Charge of Talent: Patricia Bourgeois. Theme Music by: George Duke. Music by: Alan Ett Music Group. Post Production Supervisors: Scott Kinnamon, Robb Wagner. Production Designers: Joe Stewart, John Shaffner. Production Manager: Libby Osborn. Art Director: Greg Hart. Script Supervisors: Wendy Delouche, James Rowley. Production Manager: Libby Osborn. Production Coordinator: Ann Lauterio. Orlando Unit Manager: Mark Cranisky. Assistant Art Dougherty. Script Coordinators: Penny Gerstenslager, Sheri Spitz, Courtney Williams. Edited by: Bill DeRonde, Ron Diamond, David Gibrick, Randy Magalski. Post Production Audio: Troy Smith, Dave Pascucci. Post Production Staff: Will Hall, Matt Kibble, Jean Railla. Researcher: Andrew Lachman. Stage Managers: Kelly Hernacke, Victoria Hladik. Lighting Director: Jay Grindrod. Cameras: Richard Davis, Neal Gallagher, Mike Hawkins, Mark Lynch. Audio: Curt Coniglio, Tim Wilson, Jim McCabe. Graphic Design: Bob Gautieri, Kelly Shelly. Props: Trey Butts, Brian Woodsen. Production Staff: Jim Amerian, Melissa Burby, Joe Rosenzweig. Make-up/Hair: Regina Peron. Wardrobe: Beverly Safier, Theresa Meyerscough. Orlando Production Staff: Tracy Anderson, James Dubose, Tim Dvoracheck, Emily Griffith, Lisa Hill, Lisa Marie Lewis, Toni Martinez, Chris Roberts, Judson Self, Alex Simao, Dave Van Houtte, Krissie Wentz, Andrea West. Brad Lachman Productions. 30-minute format. First aired in 1995.

WELCOME TO POOH CORNER
Directors: Gary B. Baker, Donald R. Ham, Philip F. Messina. Additional Material Directed by: Donald R. Ham, Mark Stratton. Teleplay: Betty G. Birney, Curtiss Clayton. Story Concept: Caroline Hay. Based on the books written by: A.A. Milne. Illustrated by: Ernest H. Shepard. Main Title Song and Closing Song by: Richard M. and Robert B. Sherman. Songs: Phil Baron, Dan Crow, Robin Frederick, Steve Gillette, Will Ryan, Richard M. and Robert B. Sherman. Assistant Director: Gary B. Baker. Associate Producers: Betty G. Birney, Mark Gaede, David Deutsch. Video Operators: Christopher Gray, Dexter Padgitt. Production Coordinator: Susan Gish. Choreographers: Joe Giamalva, Marilyn Magness, Denise McKenna. Assistant Choreographers: Joe Giamalva. Lighting Director: James Swift. Script Supervisors: Linda Arcari, Susan Kydd. Art Department: Nancy King, Jim Higginson, Eleanore Fahey, Mark Stratton. Cameramen: Bill Dickson, Paul Dillingham, David Golia, Jim Velarde. Production Stage Crew: Charlie Edwards, Christopher Morley, Gary Shaw, Bruce Swift. Audio Engineers: Lee Gutenberg, Mark King, Russell Schmitt. Post Production Sound: Phil Baron, Bill Koepnick, John Walker.

Video Editor: Tom Potter. Costumes: Alchemy II. Costume Supervisor: Kristin Nelson. Costumers: Elaine Levi, Lizbeth Gower. Costume Technicians: David Parish, Fred Yawnick. Post Production Supervisor: Don Asquith. Grips: Christopher Morley, Charlie Edwards, Gary Shaw, Bruce Swift. Editor: Tom Potter. Post Production Coordinator: Susan Kydd. Consultant: Shirley Gallardo. Art Director: Mark Stratton. King. Costumes Designed by: Ken Forsse. Stage Manager: Gary Baker. Editorial Supervisor: Don Kline. Production Assistant: Bill Anderson. Assistants to the Producers: Christine Gorewit, Susan Coffey. Associate Producer: Betty G. Birney. Producers: Caroline Hay, Mark Gaede. Executive Producer: Frank Brandt. A Left Coast Television, Inc. Production. 30-minute format. 125 episodes.

WISH UPON A STAR
Executive Producer: Arnold Shapiro. Produced by: Marcia Lewis. Production Supervisor: Steve Muscarella. Associate Producer: Bruce Rubinstein. "Wish" Coordinators: Doreen Ringer, Kerry Lenhart, Dona Friedberg, Cindy Hiller, Vicki Alexander. "Wish" Location Producers: Benjamin Sachs, Kip Norris, Susan Shippey, Preston Wilder, Brian Roberts, Neal Marsala. Written by: Jean O'Neill. Assistant to the Producer: Linda Weiss. Post Production Supervisors: Joshua S. Alper, Carl Byker, Victor Lowrey, Hank Capshaw. Video Consultant: David M. Blum. Post Production Coordinators: Michael Lorenzo, Toby Hancock. Production Assistants: Victor Shinmei, Danna Rosenthal. Director of Photography: Dale Dimmick. Audio: Steve Kiger. Make-up: June Kone. Graphic Designed by: GRFX Productions. Music Arranger: Harvey Truitt. An Arnold Shapiro Production. 30-minute format. 26 episodes. First aired in 1983.

YOU AND ME, KID
Produced by: William H. Shippey. Associate Producer: Helene Seifer. Directed by: Mel Charles, Charles Stark. Written by: William H. Shippey, Helen Seifer, Kathee Yamamoto, Ricci Mann. Consultants: Dr. Stevanne Auerbach, Bettye Caldwell, Dr. Dorothy Singer. Researcher: Elise Getz-Flagg. Production Manager: Dixie J. Capp. Field Producer: Patricia Bourgeois. Field Directors: Ron Underwood, Susan Shippey, Rick Miner. Field Cameramen: Peter Smokler, Virgil Harper, Joan Weidman. Field Crew: Rod Blackie, Bill Hankins, Yvonne Harper, Mark Peckler, Bob Wigley, Elze Marie Zamperelli. Activities Specialist: Ricci Mann. Make-up/Stylist: Lucia Mace-Castaneda, Elaine Ramirez. Prop Master: Tom O'Brien. Production Coordinator: Keiren Kasun. Production Secretary: Debra T. Smith. Set Designer: Griff Lambert. *Just You and Me, Kid* Music and Lyrics by: Robin Frederick. Technical Directors: Nick Sorkeim, Joan Wood. Camera: Don Davis, Kathy Kitoaka, Jim Tynes. Video Control: Bob Worden. Audio: Lou Edwards, Michael Danesky. Floor Manager: Noam D. Travail. Set Operations: Howard Burkons. Lighting Director: Lester Meisenheimer. Tape Operators: William H. Kennedy III, Joani Wood. Set Manager: Tom O'Brien. Additional Material: Toni Attell, Caleb Chung, Ricci Mann, Gary Schwartz. Editors: Margaretta Schiappa, Barbro Semmingsen, Lee Rhoads, Phil Content. Sound Editors: Arthur Klein, Sherry Klein. Post Production Coordinator: Gail Mancuso Cordray. Associate Directors: Tracy Abbott, Dona Marie, Tracy Marie, Robin Felsen. Casting: Lisa Kane. Production Assistants: Howard Burkons, Bill Kennedy, Joe Kondash, Walt Miller, Jeff Scharping, Debra Smith, Stephanie Torres. A Cornerstone Production. 30-minute format. 130 episodes. First aired in 1983.

The Disney Channel Specials
ACADEMY OF TELEVISION ARTS AND SCIENCES HALL OF FAME
Executive Producer: Gary Smith. Produced by: Gary Smith, Dwight Hemion. Directed by: Dwight Hemion. Written by: Stephen Pouliot. Executive in Charge of Production: Ricky Kirshner. Art Director: Cindy White. Music Director: Gregory Smith. Film Tributes Producer: Douglas M. Stewart, Jr. Lighting Designer: Shawn Richardson. Associate Director: Gene Crowe. Talent Coordinator: Carleen Cappelletti. Script Coordinator: Leslie Wilson. Supervising Editor: Dann Netter. Clip Talent & Music Clearance: Vicki Grimsland. Editors:

Jeff Savenick, Ray Miller. Film Tribute Supervisor: Vince Maynard. Film Coordinators: Stacey Jill Zacken, Mary Aim. Film Editors: Randy Phipps, Michael Gladych. Assistant Film Editor: Steven M. Roberts. Stage Manager: Doug Smith. Technical Director: Annette Mitchell. Audio Director: Ed Greene. Camera Operators: Richard Davis, Sam Drummy, Mary Lynch, Bill Philbin, David Plakos, Kevin Richardson, Ron Sheldon. Production Assistants: Cleo Gonzales, Jennifer Kunishima, Gerard Rojo, Ryan Westheimer. Announcer: John Harlan. *For Walt Disney World Creative Entertainment* Producer: Scott Powhatan. Associate Producer: Tom Bisignano. Senior Show Director: Gary Paben. Director of Special Events: Doug Strawn. Production Manager: Cindy Rosten. Production Coordinator: Trish Weinstock. *For the Academy of Television Arts and Sciences* President: Rich Frank. Executive Director: James L. Loper. Chair, Hall of Fame: Edgar J. Scherick. Chair, Show Committee: George Sunga. Production Coordinator: Carleen Cappelletti. Executive Producer: Gary Smith. Smith-Hemion Productions. 90-minute format.

ALADDIN: INSIDE THE MAGIC
Producers: Dan Boothe, Stu Schreiberg. Director: Stephen Kroopnick. Coordinating Producer: Stacy Ryono. Editors: Jeff Caldwell, Dave Hogan, Mike Andrews. Associate Director: Kathryn Douglas. Camera: Larry Gaudette, Rick Simonton, Jeb Bergh. Associate Producer: Joanie Burton. Field Producer: Andy Ames. Sound: Hank Fried. Post Production Audio: Alan Porzio, Craig Plachy. Graphics: Vikki North. Production Assistant: Julie York. The Wrightwood Group, Incorporated in association with Betty Productions. 30-minute format. First aired in 1992.

ANNE MURRAY IN DISNEY WORLD
Executive Producers: Leonard T. Rambeau, Sandra Faire. Written & Produced by: Sandra Faire. Directed by: Bill Davis. Additional Writing: Anne Murray, Leonard T. Rambeau. Line Producer: Brenda Lebedorf. Production Manager: Joy Barker. Production Designer: Judith Lee. Technical Producers: Raymond Beley, Karel Noordover. Lighting Design: Gil Densham. Music Coordination & Production: Peter Mann. Audio Engineer: Simon Bowers. Sound Effects: Peter Campbell. Edited by: Dino DiGregorio. Second Unit Director: Faith Feingold. Associate Directors: Trisa Dayot, Dale Turner McDuffie. Assistant Directors: Fred Nicolaidis, Michael Lewis. Location Manager: Steve Hyde. Choreographer: Wendy Nicholson. Costume Design by: Lee Kinoshita-Benington. Music Director for Anne Murray: Steve Sexton. Anne Murray's Band: Steve Sexton, Peter Bleakney, Gary Craig, Brian Gatto, George Hebert, Aidan Mason. Vocalists: Debbie Ankeny, Shirley Eikhard, Bill Hughes. Arrangements: Rick Wilkins, Steve Sexton. Music Director for Patti LaBelle: James "Bud" Ellison. Creative Consultant: Susanne Rostock. Associate Producers: Alison Armstrong, Beverly Mattewson, Victoria Radford. Assistant to Producer: Susan Edwards. Lighting Director: David Parsons. Switcher: Tony D'Agostino. Video: Charles Goldman. Cameras: Michael Gyll, Ross Menzies, Ross Murray, Dennis Sitar, Don Spence. Louma Crane: Stuart Allen, David Hagala, Andy Hingenbergs, Mark Milne. Lighting: Stephen Plotkin, Brad Dickson, Marvin Klein, Tom McGrath, Brian McNutt, Mike Still. Audio Assistants: Ian Dunbar, Mike Nazarec, Ray Jeffery. TV Assistants: Eric Glover, Rance Nakamura. Assistant Set Designer: Andrew Kinsella. Anne Murray's Make-up Artist: George Abbott. Anne Murray's Hairstylist: Sheila Yakimov. Make-up & Hair: Elaine Saunders, Tom Dipasquale, Daisy Bijac, George Morrison. Patti LaBelle's Hair Designer: Norma Harris-Gordon. Cue Cards: Seamus Caulfield, Ken Ansell. Electronic Titles: Kirsten Patterson, Penny English, Gary Stroud. Road Manager for Anne Murray: Maurice Cardinal. Stage Manager for Anne Murray: Stephen "Tex" Paquette. *For Walt Disney World* Unit Manager: Clay Newbill. Marketing: Tony Howard, Terri Farrentine. Program Assistants: Andrew Baird, Val Burger, Lisa Haskins, Jeff Jacobson, Kristan Kosh, Jonathan Taylor, Brent Wilson. Electricians: Brad Allen, Rich Campbell, Paul Caswell, Terry Crisp, Jay Gringrod, Pat Knowles, Denise Moss, Mitch Wells, Dixon Wikner. Second Unit Audio: Dan Pine, Anthony "Bubba" Morris. Scenic Artist: Mary Hartwig. Wardrobe: Frankie Robinson. Engineer:

Ray Lego. Drivers: Clint Hannen, Lorenzo Rawls, Dina Watson, Kevin Deans, Randy Jones. Deputy Creative Head Variety: Ed Robinson. Creative Head Variety: George Anthony. A Production of The Canadian Broadcasting Corporation in association with Balmur Ltd., Sandra Faire Productions and Buena Vista Television International. 1-hour format. First aired in 1991.

ART OF DISNEY ANIMATION, THE
Produced and Directed by: Robert Heath. Written by: Leonard Maltin. Edited by: Hank Polonsky. Associate Producer: Jean Wiegman. Art Director: Bill Bohnert. Graphic Designer: Ron Clark. Production Coordinator: Kevin Traxler. Director of Photography: Joe Epperson, Tony Zapata. Sound: Dan Newman, Murray Siegel. Gaffer: John Beaver, Randy Gomez. Wardrobe: Mary Paxton. Make-up: Nina Kent. Assistant Art Director: Melody Boyd. On Line Editor: Michael Polito. Post Audio: Bob Manahan. Tape Director: Steven Kamm. Acknowledgments: Kathleen Gavin, Dennis Edwards. A Production of Heath and Associates. 30-minute format. First aired in 1988.

ASHFORD AND SIMPSON: GOING HOME
Executive Producer: Les Haber. Directed by: Richie Namm. Co-Producer: Richie Namm. Associate Director/Post Production Supervisor: John M. O'Connell. Director of Photography: Nick Hutak. Concert Lighting Director: Alan Adelman. Choreographer: George Faizon. Creative Consultant: Andy Ames. Technical Director: Richie Wirth. Video Engineering: Paul Renieri, Tom Guadarrama. Audio: Bob Aldridge, Randy Ezrati, Tim Lester, Jimmy Simpson. Cameras: Bill Ackerland, Juan Barrera, Eddie Barber, Nick Hutak, Alain Onesto, Larry Solomon. VTR: Warren Arenstein, Jerry Steinberg. Editor: Rob Ortiz. Assistant Editor: Joseph Annechiarico. Audio Post Production: Ken Hahn. Production Coordinators: Beth Greenbaum, Andrea Marie Brenninkmeyer, Altamese Alston. Production Assistants: Brett Alan Haber, Cabrini Lepis, Kathy Orbach, Stephanie Phillips, Barry Shapiro, Kirk Strong, Lauren Ulanoff, Jay Delman, Kim Yvette Benn, Jeffrey Schwartz. Costume Design: Kevin Emard. Make-up and Hair: Finney. Band Members: Raymond Chew, Chandra Armsted, Francisco Centene, Vincent Della Rocca, Sammy Figueroa, Ivan Hampden, Joseph Joubert, Joe Mosello, Andrew Schwartz, Raymond Simpson. Talent Consultants: Scott Sanders, Patricia Kellert. Executive in Charge of Production: John Kelly. Haber Production Group, Inc. 1-hour format. First aired in 1988.

BACKSTAGE AT DISNEY
Produced by: Christopher D. Miller. Written by: John Culhane. Directed by: Tom Leetch. Associate Director: Bud Grace. Music Composed and Conducted by: John Debney. Video Tape Editor: Chris Ogden. Camera: Ted Ashton. Gaffer: Bernie Bayless. Key Grip: Dennis McLean. Dolly Grip: Mike Mendez. *Something Wicked This Way Comes* Sequence Prepared by: Bill Pentland, Dennis Rocotta.

BACKSTAGE DISNEY: THE AMERICAN ADVENTURE
Director of Photography: Mark Morris. Associate Producer: Sharon Lasky. Camera: Nina Graham, Dick Palmer, Robin Hirsh. Audio: Jeff Chandler. Editor: Richard Piccini. Audio Post Production: John Walker. First aired in 1987.

BACKSTAGE DISNEY: THE MAIN STREET ELECTRICAL PARADE
Musical Director: Don Dorsey. Senior Show Director: Barnette Ricci. Parade Designer: Ken Dresser. Parade Creator: Robert F. Jani. Technical Director: Jerry Hefferly. V.P. Entertainment: Dennis Despie. Photo Information Adviser: Joe Wisneski. Costume Designer: Jack Muhs. Operations Manager: Bob Gault. Parade Supervisor: Vini Reilly. Parade Builder: Troy Barrett. Produced by: Ron Miziker. Written and Field Produced by: Kevin Meagher. Associate Producer: Susan Dobak. Lighting Director: Don Cohen. Production Assistants: Colleen Kennedy, Dennis Meagher. Camera: Paul Babin, Bert van Munster, George Stephenson. Audio: Tony Lewis, Mark Sharret, Russ Simon, Brian Brunell. Videotape Editor: Dennis Phillips. Disneyland Coordinator: Dale Lanier. Chicago Pho-

tos by: Kee Chang, CACI. A Showmakers Production. 45-minute format. First aired in 1986.

BACKSTAGE PASS: DISNEY'S BEAUTY AND THE BEAST GOES TO BROADWAY

Produced by: Dan Boothe, Stu Schreiber. Written and Directed by: Dan Boothe. Associate Producer: Joanie Burton. Edited by: David W. Foster. On-Line Editor: Brian Ross. Art Director: Scott Storey. Director of Photography: Larry Gaudette. Re-Recording Mixer: Gary J. Coppola, C.A.S. Recordist: Scott Ralson. Location Sound: Doug Donald. Make-up: Renee Caruso. Key Grip: Robin Banando. Grips: Jeff Rosa, Jason Elian. Best Boy: Tom Seymore. Teleprompter: Joshua Mertz. Production Assistants: Kelli Mayman, Kristin Henry. Extras Casting: Jerry Conca. Extras: Brian Guest, Rob Anderson, James Holland, Natalie Reich. Graphic Design: Chris Williamson. *Pantages Theater Crew* Special Events Director: Dixie Burton. Carpenters: William Young, Richard Stephens. Electrician: Jeff Martel. Sound: George Velmer. Props: Jack Stephens, Matt Stephens. Flyman: Kyle Gray. *New York Production Unit* Producer: Joanie Burton. Director of Photography: Keith Silverman. Location Sound: Gary McCafferty. *Houston Production Unit* Cameras: Larry Gaudette, Robert Porter, Jim Bowman. Sound: Henry Miller. Video: Dale Lynn. Utility: Chris Phillips. Acknowledgments: ECTS Scenic Technology; Walt Disney Theatrical Productions Limited, Ron Logan President; Theater Under the Stars, Houston, Texas. A Production of The Wrightwood Group, Incorporated. 30-minute format.

BE OUR GUEST: THE MAKING OF DISNEY'S BEAUTY AND THE BEAST

Executive Producer: Patrick Davidson. Directed by: Joe Carolei. Written by: David Leaf. Coordinating Producer: Bob Gautieri. Editor: Ray J. Pages. Researcher: Bart Roen. Lighting Director: Simon Miles. Camera Operator: Larry Gaudette. Re-recording Mixer: Steve Barton. Production Coordinator: Michelle LeTarte. Post Production Supervisor: Don Stables. Main Title Design: Bob Gautieri. Executive in Charge of Production: Steve Ligerman. Blue Streak Productions. 30-minute format.

BEE GEES, THE: GOING HOME

Executive Producer: Brad Lachman. Supervising Producer: Garry Bormet. Producers: Brian Roberts, Lisa Bourgoujian. Lighting Designer-Interview Segments: Bob Dickinson. Associate Producer: Debbie Martin. Production Coordinator: Ann King. Production Assistant: Chris Smith. Editor: John Moore. Audio Mixer: David Fluhr. Acknowledgments: Gary Borman, Dick Ashby. Brad Lachman Productions, Inc. 90-minute format. First aired in 1991.

BEHIND THE SCENES: LOVE LEADS THE WAY

Written, Produced and Directed by: Patrick Davidson. Post Production Supervisor: Richard Audd. Cameraman: J. Edgar. Tape Operator: Steve Beeson. Production Assistants: Ann Esquer, Marcia Wood. Post Production Editors: Richard Audd, Dennis Phillips, Michael Walker. Post Production Sound: John Walker. Acknowledgments: Jimmy Hawkins, Suzy O'Hara. A Patrick Davidson Production. First aired in 1984.

BEHIND THE SCENES WITH D3: THE MIGHTY DUCKS

Executive Producers: Richard Kaufman, Michelle Jackino. Directors: Michelle Jackino, Christine Smith. Supervising Producer: Kellie Allred. Producer: Christine Smith. Line Producer: Jeffrey Lerner. Writers: Karon Aghotte-Rice, Michelle Jackino, Christine Smith. Director of Photography: Steve Clark. Editors: Emmett Malloy, Amy Weber, Gary Lister. Videographer: Randy Krehbiel. Sound: Mike Sakaniwa, Mike Bidese. Additional Camera: Monica Zakkay, Brian Hoodenpyle, Jeffrey Lerner. Production Coordinators: James Costigan, Michele Bornheim. Post Production Supervisors: Kit Mulligan-Chambers, Erik Thaler. Assistant Editors: Charlie Honess, Gordon Phillips, Greg Mandel, Sheila Moreland. Online Supervisors: Dale Carroll, Cara Enright. Online Editors: Steven E. Browne, Ed Molina. Finishing Assistant: Todd Buford. Tape Operators: David Mawhinney, Kurt Stearns. Audio Mixer: Lisa Haines. Audio Editorial: Arthur Payson, Bridgid

Neil, Adam Clarke. Graphics: Scott Williams, Bohnie Wallace, Toby Williams. Production Assistants: Keir Serrie, Brian Hoodenpyle, Jim Heatherly. New Wave Entertainment. 30-minute format. First aired in 1996.

BEYOND TRON

Executive Producer: Ron Miziker. Produced, Written and Directed by: Giovanna Nigro-Chacon. Associate Producer: Susan Dobak. Edited by: William Carlquist. Music Coordination: Ken Chernove. Photographed by: Duane Anderly. Location Sound: Roger Andrews. Lighting Director: Don Cohen. Additional Photography by: John Tomlin, Michael Dolan, Tom Beintema. Additional Sound by: Matt Cole, Vince Farrell. Post Production: Horizontal Editing Services, The Post Group. Main Title Design by: William Covacs, Wavefront Technologies. Main Title Software by: IMI500. Tempest by: Vibeke Sorensen, Tom DeWitt, Dean Winkler. A Showmakers Production. First aired in 1986.

CANDLELIGHT CHRISTMAS CEREMONY, A

Musical Conductor: Sheldon Disrud. Musical Arrangers: James Christiensen, Sheldon Disrud, Jack Eskew, Bruce Healey, Bob Krogstadt, Brent Pierce, Roger Wagner, Ken Whitcomb. Directed by: Morris Abraham. Produced by: Sandra Moiseeff. Executive Producers: Paul Abeyta, Peter Kaikko. A Production of RC Entertainment, Inc. 30-minute format. First aired in 1987.

CAROLE KING: GOING HOME

Executive Producer: Ira Koslow. Producer: Luke Thornton. Director: Tony Mitchell. Line Producer: Lynn Rose Higgins. Associate Producer/Unit Production Manager: Michael Riffle. Production Coordinator: Robert E. Higgins. Line Producer, New York: Elizabeth Silver. Editors: Sean T. Fullan, David Greenwald. Production Designer: Linda Burton. Script Supervisor: Cori Glazer. Camera Operators: Ed Stephenson, Romeo Tirone, Scott Kaye, John LeBlanc, Rick Bota, Scott Ressler, Dave Rudd. Head Camera Assistant: James Gucciardo. Camera Assistants: Ed Guttentag, Bruce Manning, Jerry Sidell, Samuel "Buddy" Fries, Art Martin, Sharon Alley. Second Camera Assistants: Roberto "Tito" Blasini, Marcia Tenny, Gary Tachell, Todd Slyapich. Key Grip Crane: James Cooper. Key Grip L.A.: Tim Pershing. Dolly Grip: J.D. Ault. Grips: Michael "Chubb" McFadden, Scott Hollander. Swingman: Rick Pratt. Crane Technician: Rick "Fuzzy" Favazzo. Sound Person: Bob Dreeban. Make-up (Carole King): Kate Donahue. Make-up (Band): Paul Best. Production Assistants: Sheri Jones, Ed Cathell III, Rob Smith, Rex Taylor Smith, Michael Badami, Ted Fatseas, Kenn Ferro, Devin Pollich. Music Producer: Rudy Guess. Recorded and Mixed by: James Farber. Recording Assistants: Guy Charbonneau, Dave Roberts. Sound Engineer: Jolin Herman. *Carole King Band* Ted Abdreadis (Keyboards, background vocals), Jerry Angel (drums), Sherry Goffin (background vocals), Rudy Guess (Guitar, background vocals), Brie Howard (Congas, percussion, background vocals), John Humphrey (Bass), Robbie Kondor (Keyboards), Danny Pelfrey (Saxophone, guitar, background vocals). *Carole King Crew* Tour Manager: Joe Cardosi. Carole King's Assistant: Lorna Guess. Production Manager: John Vanderslice. Assistant Production Manager: Rose Blagaich. Lighting Designer: Louis Mawcinitt. Lighting Director: Rob Zablow. House Mixers: Jack Maxson, Greg Ross-Smith. Monitor Mixer: Peter Buess. Guitar Tech: Mike Mayhue. Drum Tech: Danny De La Luz. Keyboard Tech: Bernard Alexander. Rigger: Billy Phillips. Sound Crew: Brent Brito. Light Crew: John Vogel, Jim Zoehrer. An Asher/Kroft Management & N. Lee Lacy Production. 1-hour format. First aired in 1990.

CELEBRATING WALT DISNEY'S SNOW WHITE AND THE SEVEN DWARFS: THE ONE THAT STARTED IT ALL

Produced by: Dan Boothe, Stu Schreiber. Written & Directed by: Dan Boothe. Coordinating Producer: Joanie Burton. Editors: David W. Foster, Terence Curren. Director of Photography: Larry Gaudette. Camera: Bob Mingus, Scott Kaye. Sound: Gary Bacon, Doug Donald. Post Production Audio: Ted Gordon. Graphics: Chris Williamson. Researcher: Peter Hrisko. Production Assistants: Tracy Roberson, Danny Duran. The Wrightwood Group, Inc. 30-minute format.

CHICAGO ON THE GOOD FOOT
Produced and Directed by: Terry Stegner. A Mainframe, Inc. Production.

COMING YOUR WAY
Produced by: Tom Wilhite. A Hyperion Entertainment, Inc. Production.

CONVERSATION WITH BETTY WHITE, A
Executive Producers: Carol Burnett, Marcia Brandwynne, Brad Lachman. Produced by: Brad Lachman. Directed by: Gary Halvorson. Executive in Charge of Production: Steve Ligerman. Production Designer: Rene Lagler. Director of Photography: Greg Brunton. Music by: Chase/Rucker. Production Consultant: Garry Bormet. Associate Director: Cricket Wheeler. Associate Producer: Jeffrey R. Coates. Production Coordinator: Jennifer Kurtz. Clearance Administrator: Renee Baer. Post Production Coordinator: Tom Draper. Production Assistant: David Keyes. Stage Manager: Mavis Davis. Technical Director: Terry Donohue. Audio Mixer: Paul Sandweiss. Edited by: Michael Polito. Sound Mixers: Allen Patapoff, Craig Porter. Kalola Productions and Brad Lachman Productions, Inc. 45-minute format. First aired in 1989.

CONVERSATION WITH BOB HOPE, A
Executive Producers: Carol Burnett, Marcia Brandwynne, Brad Lachman. Produced by: Brad Lachman. Directed by: Gary Halvorson. Executive in Charge of Production: Steve Ligerman. Production Designer: Rene Lagler. Director of Photography: Greg Brunton. Music by: Chase/Rucker. Production Consultant: Garry Bormet. Associate Director: Cricket Wheeler. Associate Producer: Jeffrey R. Coates. Production Coordinator: Jennifer Kurtz. Clearance Administrator: Renee Baer. Post Production Coordinator: Tom Draper. Production Assistant: David Keyes. Stage Manager: Mavis Davis. Technical Director: Terry Donohue. Audio Mixer: Paul Sandweiss. Edited by: Michael Polito. Sound Mixers: Allen Patapoff, Craig Porter. Kalola Productions and Brad Lachman Productions, Inc. 45-minute format. First aired in 1989.

CONVERSATION WITH CAROL, A
Executive Producers: Carol Burnett, Marcia Brandwynne. Produced by: Brad Lachman. Directed by: Roger Beatty. Associate Producer: Steve Ligerman. Production Designer: Rene Lagler. Director of Photography: Greg Brunton. Music Arranged and Conducted by: Peter Matz. Costumes by: Bob Mackie. Associate Director: Margaret Scott. Production Coordinators: Cricket Wheeler, Jeffrey R. Coates. Production Assistant: Carlinda Beatty. Production Secretaries: Jennifer Kurtz, Michele Dix. Stage Manager: James Smith. Unit Manager: Jim Moroney. Technical Director: Robert Bowen. Audio Mixer: Bob Houston. Make-up: Edward Helm. Production Assistants at the Disney-MGM Studios: Laura Broome, Gary McKachnie, Jorge Morales, Kim Lynch, Elizabeth Dorsey, Marsha Groome. Edited by: David Foster, Floyd Carver. Sound Mixers: Ross Davis, Craig Porter. Produced by: Kalola Productions and Brad Lachman Productions, Inc. 1-hour format. First aired in 1988.

CONVERSATION WITH GEORGE BURNS, A
Executive Producers: Carol Burnett, Marcia Brandwynne, Brad Lachman. Produced by: Brad Lachman. Directed by: Gary Halvorson. Executive in Charge of Production: Steve Ligerman. Production Designer: Rene Lagler. Director of Photography: Greg Brunton. Music by: Chase/Rucker. Production Consultant: Garry Bormet. Associate Director: Cricket Wheeler. Associate Producer: Jeffrey R. Coates. Production Coordinator: Jennifer Kurtz. Production Assistants: Tom Draper, David Keyes. Stage Manager: Mavis Davis. Technical Director: Terry Donohue. Audio Mixer: Paul Sandweiss. Edited by: Michael Polito. Sound Mixers: Allen Patapoff, Craig Porter. Kalola Productions and Brad Lachman Productions, Inc. 45-minute format. First aired in 1989.

DISKIDS
Executive Producer: Thomas W. Lynch. Producer: John D. Lynch. Supervising Producer: Paul Hoen. Co-producers: Sam

Ingraffia, Gary Stein. Music Director: Gary W. Friedman. Associate Producer: Steve Uhlenberg. Editor: Bart Roen. Assistant Director: Sean McNamara. Assistants to the Producers: Christine Nyhart Schultz, Rebecca S. Ancheta. Production Manager: Greg Bauhofer. Costumes: Pauline Serrano. Casting Director: Sherri Taylor. Audio: Larry Chong, Mike Lavallee. Cameras: Jeff Barnes, Marc Hunter, Rob Palmer. Lighting: Fred Martin, Donald Jones. Make-up: Geri Oppenheim, Kim Meyer, Stephanie Berens. Acting Coach: Ray Young. Studio Teacher: Ann Leithliter. Props: Scott Griffin, David Sewell. Cue Cards: Channel Q. Controller: Randi Shields. Production Associates: Victoria Lichtman, Geoffrey Moore, Jim Prentice, Sonny Premo. Graphics: GRFX. Lynch Entertainment. 1-hour format. First aired in 1990.

DISNEY CHANNEL CHRISTMAS, A
Prepared for The Disney Channel by Film Landa, Inc. 90-minute format. First aired in 1983.

DISNEY HALLOWEEN, A
Produced for The Disney Channel by: Film Landa, Inc. Producer: Dennis Landa. 90-minute format. First aired in 1983.

DISNEY STUDIO SHOWCASE
Executive Producer: Tom Wilhite. Supervising Producer: Chris Miller. 1-hour format.

DISNEYLAND SPORTACULAR: SPORT GOOFY—USTA NATIONAL JUNIOR TENNIS CHAMPIONSHIP
Executive Producers: Jordan Ringel, Stan Moger. Produced by: Sheldon Saltman. Directed by: Andy Young. Associate Producer: Suzy Friendly. Associate Director: Robert Katz. Coordinator for Walt Disney Productions: Robert King. Edited by: Peter Sternlicht. Post Production Sound by: Tom Huth. Graphics: Lynn Grossblatt. First aired in 1984.

DISNEYLAND STORY, THE
Executive Producer: Brad Lachman. Produced by: Garry Bormet. Coordinating Producer: Randy Bright. Directed by: Gary Halvorson. Written by: Turk Pipkin. Executive in Charge of Production: Steve Ligerman. Edited by: Michael Polito. Production Coordinator: Christiane Steffen. Post Production Coordinator: Tom Draper. Associate Producer: David Mumford. Lighting Director: Bob Dickenson. Art Directors: Joe Stewart, John Shaffner. Assistant to the Producer: Jordan Sellinger. Assistant to Executive Producer: Lisa McConnell. Researcher: Sherri Beissner. 45-minute format.

DISNEY'S ROOTIN' TOOTIN' ROUNDUP
Executive Producer: Robert Heath. Producer: Zila Clinton. Written by: Kenny Wolin. Editor: Hank Polonsky. On Line Editor: Michael A. Polito. Post Audio: Bob Manahan. Sound Editor/Sound Effects: Gary Coppola. Music Editor: Charlotte Lansberg. Production Coordinator: Cesar Sutil. Robert Heath Inc. 90-minute format. First aired in 1990.

DISNEY'S ACADEMY AWARD WINNERS
Narrated by: John Forsythe. Material from *Disney's Oscar Winners:* Directed by: William Reid. Written by: William Reid, Michael Russell. Editor: Walt Hekking. Acknowledgment: Academy of Motion Pictures Arts and Sciences. *Disney's Academy Award Winners* Prepared for The Disney Channel by: Happyfeets Company. Nature Photographers: Robert H. Crandall, Herb Crisler, Murl Deusing, Cleveland P. Grant, Karl H. Maslowski, Alfred G. Milotte, Olin Sewall Pettingill Jr., James R. Simon, John H. Storer, Hugh A. Wilmar. Songs and Music: Richard M. Sherman, Robert B. Sherman, Irwin Kostal, Paul J. Smith, Sammy Fain, Ayn Robbins, Carol Connors, Artie Butler, Jim Stafford. Additional Music by: John Debney, Walter Sheets. 90-minute format. First aired in 1987.

DISNEY'S COYOTE TALES
Executive Producer: Robert Heath. Produced by: Marijane Miller, Zilla Clinton. Written by: Kenny Wolin. Edited by: Hank Polonsky. Original Music by: Charlotte Lansberg. On Line Editor: Howard Scott Stein. Post Audio: Bob Manahan. Sound Editor/Sound Effects: Gary Coppola. Graphic Design:

Ian Dawson, David Henry, Marco Bacich, Gerit Vandenberg. Editorial Assistant: Jenny Krug. Robert Heath Inc. 90-minute format. First aired in 1991.

DISNEY'S "THE HUNCHBACK OF NOTRE DAME" FESTIVAL OF FUN MUSICAL SPECTACULAR

Buena Vista Pictures Distribution Event Production Team Executive Producer: Dick Cook. Event Manager: Lylle Breier. Event Stage Production Directed by: Barnette Ricci. Producer: Rick Buche. Musical Director: Bill Conti. V.P. Marketing/Synergy Programming: Michael Mendenhall. Production Stage Manager: Hollie Hopson. Technical Director: Tom McClain. Production Designer: Charles Lisanby. Operations: Bob Gault. Executive in Charge of Broadcast Publicity: Kellie Allred. *For the Television Broadcast:* Executive Producer: Brad Lachman. Directed by: Louis J. Horvitz. Written by: Garry Bormet. Line Producer: Bill Bracken. Associate Producer: John Foy. Graphics: Bob Gautieri, Kelly Shelly. *Event Production:* Line Producer: Michael Murphy. Audio Designer: Sean Glen. Lighting Director: Brian Gale. Chief Projection Engineer: Kevin Rosenberger. Head Choreographer: Tam Warner. Casting: Kevin Frawley. Head Costumer: Andy Gordon. Operations Managers: Greg Holleran, Dennis Jones. Orchestra Conductor: Nathan Kaproff. Announcer: Bill Rogers. Production Coordinator: Bill Kavanagh. Human Resources/Permits: Gary Weaver. Media Coordination: Linda Palmer. Counsel: Denise Brown. Script Supervisors: Christine Klages Staley, Kris Sheets. Production Manager: Melissa Kimberly. Associate Director: Allan Kartun. Stage Managers: Garry Hood, Dency Nelson. Script Coordinator: Paige Rabban Hadley. Production Coordinators: Morgan Clevenger, Mark Cranisky, Ann Lauterio, Nancy Osborne. Lighting Director: Lee Rose. Engineer in Charge: Tad Scripter. Technical Director: John B. Field. Audio Mixer: Paul Sandweiss. Cameras: John Burdick, David Eastwood, Tom Geren, Larry Heider, Charlie Huntley, Dave Levisohn, Kenneth A. Patterson, David Plakos, Hector Ramirez, Manny Rodriguez, Ron Sheldon, Ron Smith. Senior V.P. Synergy Programming: Cory O'Connor. V.P. of Creative Development: Howard Schneider. Executive Producer: Jim Davy. Director of Operations: Dan Osti. Senior V.P. Business Affairs: Fred Kuperberg. Brad Lachman Productions. First aired in 1996.

DISNEY'S YOUNG MUSICIANS SYMPHONY ORCHESTRA (1992 VERSION)

Executive Producers: Dwight Hemion, Gary Smith. Producer: Gail Purse. Written by: Marty Farrell. Directed by: Dwight Hemion. Smith-Hemion Productions in association with The Disney Channel and The Young Musicians Foundation. One-hour format.

DISNEY'S YOUNG MUSICIANS SYMPHONY ORCHESTRA (1993 VERSION)

Executive Producers: Dwight Hemion, Gary Smith. Producer: Gail Purse. Co-Producer: Patrick Davidson. Written by: Marty Farrell. Directed by: Dwight Hemion. Smith-Hemion Productions in association with The Disney Channel and The Young Musicians Foundation.

DISNEY'S YOUNG MUSICIANS SYMPHONY ORCHESTRA (1995 VERSION)

Executive Producers: Gary Smith, Dwight Hemion. Produced by: Gail Purse. Directed by: Dwight Hemion. Written by: Buz Kohan. Co-Produced by: Patrick Davidson. Executive in Charge of Production: Allan Baumrucker. Music Supervisor: Pete Rugolo. Production Designer: Rene Lagler. Lighting Designer: Bob Dickinson. Associate Producer: Robin Howington. Script Supervisor: Kristine Fernandez. Associate Director: Allan Kartun. Stage Managers: Doug Smith, Debbie Williams. Script Coordinator: September George. Music Coordinator: Richard Bowers. Project Coordinator: Felice Mancini. Assistant Project Coordinator: Stephenie Hope. Event Coordinator: Bea Sohni. Assistant to the Executive Producers: Joyce Lupo. Production Associates: Daniel Konate, Lee Smith, Katherine Hammond, Ted Goodman. Technical Director: Gene Crowe. Audio: Ed Greene. Video: John Palacio, Sr., Steve Berry. Cameras: Ted Ashton, Sam Drummy, Larry Heider, Dave Levisohn, Wayne Orr, Bill Philbin, Hector

Ramirez, Ron Sheldon. House PA Mixer: Gene Richards. Videotape Operator: Dexter Padgitt. Videotape Editor: Bruce Motyer. Main Title & Graphic Designs: Tom Kane. Executive Director for Young Musicians Foundation: Edye Rugolo. Orchestra Selection Board: Jung-Ho Pak, Delores Stevens, Lara Webber. Orchestra Manager: Trilla Ray. Violin Soloist Teacher: Robert Lippsett. Activities Director: Joe Petrovich. Music Coaches: Katey Brackney, Ian Donald, Michael Duckworth, Kerry Farrell, M.B. Gordy, John Hester, Cynthia Kelley, Matt Nabours, Cynthia Penderghast, Peter Santucci, Theresa Treuenfels, Bing Wang, Elizabeth Wright. Profile Segments Produced by: Bart Roen, Tim Gaydos, Michelle Letarte, Hildie Jacobson. Profile Segments Edited by: Chris Simpson. Cerritos Center for the Performing Arts: Victor Gotesman, Cynthia Doss, Millie Dixon, Walter Morlock, Doug Wendel. Smith-Hemion Productions.

DISNEY'S YOUNG PEOPLE'S GUIDE TO MUSIC: THE GREATEST BAND IN THE LAND

Produced by: Jerry Hughes. Directed by: William Cosel. Executive Producer and Writer: David Obst. Created by: Rachel Worby, David Obst. Musical Director: Rachel Worby. A Hughes Television Production. 30-minute format. First aired in 1990.

DISNEY'S YOUNG PEOPLE'S GUIDE TO MUSIC: A TUNE FOR A TOON

Produced by: Jerry Hughes. Directed by: William Cosel. Executive Producer and Writer: David Obst. Created by: Rachel Worby, David Obst. Musical Director: Rachel Worby. A Hughes Television Production. 30-minute format. First aired in 1990.

DONALD'S 50TH BIRTHDAY

Happy, Happy Birthday to You Song by: Michael & Patty Silversher. Music Video by: Jymn Magon. *Macho Duck* Song by: Tom Worrall. Music Video by: Frank Brandt. Prepared for The Disney Channel by: Film Landa, Inc. Edited by: Fausto Sanchez. 90-minute format. First aired in 1984.

DTV²: THE SPECIAL

Producer: Darryl Sutton. Editor: Richard Audd. Production Manager: Fran Chamberlain. Assistant to the Producer: Yvonne Ma. The Brighton Group. 30-minute format. First aired in 1989.

FALLING FOR THE STARS

Written and Produced by: Roger Galloway. Directed by: Neal Phillips. Director of Tape Photography: Jim Mathers. Director of Film Photography: Neal Reichline. Editor: John Peterson. Sound: John Lifavi, Doug Freeman. Production Coordinator: Alice Galloway. Theme Song Composed and Sung by: Ben Armstrong. Assistant Editor: Josh Touber. Assistant to the Producer: John Culver. A Caroge Production. 1-hour format. First aired in 1985.

FANTASIA: THE CREATION OF A DISNEY CLASSIC

Director: Robert Heath. Producer: Henry Kimmel. Written by: Leonard Maltin. Associate Producer: Zilla Clinton. Editors: Hank Polonsky, Peter White. Director of Photography: H.J. Brown. Camera: Joe Epperson, John Sharaf, Scott Levine. Sound: Dana McClure, Paul Oppenheim. Gaffer: Mike Rogers. Make-up/Hair: Nina Kent. Production Coordinators: Michael Fomil, Lindsey Paddor, Cesar Sutil. On Line Editor: Mike Polito. Post Audio: Robert Manahan. Assistant Editor: Charlotte Lansberg. Graphic Design: Ron Clark. Production Assistants: Stephen Markel, Margaret Black, Guy Distad. Acknowledgments: Tim Hauser, Peter Schneider, Rose Motzko. Restoration Footage and Interviews Courtesy of The Wrightwood Group. Robert Heath Inc. 40-minute format. First aired in 1990

FESTIVAL OF FOLK HEROES

Johnny Appleseed Voices: Dennis Day. Direction: Wilfred Jackson. Animation: Milt Kahl, Ollie Johnston, Eric Larson, Hal Ambro, Don Lusk, Harvey Toombs. Effects Animation: George Rowley. Story: Winston Hibler, Joe Rinaldi, Erdman Penner, Jesse Marsh. Music: Paul Smith. Color Styling: Mary

Blair. Layout: McLaren Stewart, Don DaGradi, Thor Putnam. Background: Claude Coats, Brice Mack. *Casey at the Bat* Direction: Jack Kinney. Music: Homer Brightman, Eric Gurney. Animation: John Sibley, Eric Larson, Cliff Nordberg, Hugh Fraser. Effects Animation: George Rowley. Music: Ken Darby. Layout: Hugh Hennesy. Background: Merle Cox, Ralph Hulett. *The Saga of Windwagon Smith* With the Talents of Rex Allen and The Sons of the Pioneers. Story: Lance Nolley, C. August Nichols. Production Design: Erni Nordli. Layout: Homer Jonas. Color Styling: Walt Peregoy. Animation: Julius Svendsen, Art Stevens. Effects Animation: Jack Boyd. Music: George Bruns. Lyrics: C. August Nichols. Directed by: C. August Nichols. *Paul Bunyan* Directed by: Les Clark. Story by: Lance Nolley, Ted Berman. Animation: John Sibley, George Nicholas, Bob Youngquist, George Goepper, Fred Kopietz, Ken Hultgren, Jerry Hathcock, Jack Parr. Effects Animation: Jack Boyd. Color Styling: Eyvind Earle. Character Styling: Tom Oreb. Layout: Homer Jonas, Jack Huber. Background: Walt Peregoy. Music: George Bruns. Lyrics: Tom Adair. Vocals: The Mellomen. *The Brave Engineer* Voices: Jerry Colonna, The King's Men. Based on *The Ballad of Casey Jones* by: T. Lawrence Seibert, Eddie Newton. Direction: Jack Kinney. Animation: Milt Kahl, Fred Moore, Al Bertino. Effects Animation: Andy Engman. Story: Dick Kinney, Dick Shaw. Musical Score: Ken Darby. Layout: Don DaGradi. Background: Ray Huffing. *Pecos Bill* Cast: Roy Rogers, Trigger, Sons of the Pioneers. Direction: Clyde Geronimi. Story: Erdman Penner, Joe Rinaldi. Animation: Ward Kimball, Milt Kahl, John Sibley, Marvin Woodward, Cliff Nordberg, Ken O'Brien. Effects Animation: Josh Meador, Ed Aardal. Music: Paul Smith. Layout: High Hennesy, Lance Nolley. Background: Claude Coats, Merle Cox, Brice Mack. First aired in 1983.

FLEETWOOD MAC: GOING HOME
Executive Producer: Mick Fleetwood. Produced and Directed by: Stephanie Bennett. Co-Directed and Edited by: Janice Engel. Delilah Music Pictured in association with The Disney Channel. 90-minute format. First aired in 1993.

FOR OUR CHILDREN: THE CONCERT
Executive Producer: Dawn Steel. Producer: Brad Lachman. Directed by: Louis J. Horvitz. Written by: Bruce Vilanch, Garry Bormet. Associate Producer: Tom Boles. Talent Executive: Debi Genovese. Production Designers: John Shaffner, Joe Stewart. Music Arranged and Conducted by: George Duke. Musical Numbers Choreographed by: Lester Wilson. Lighting Designer: Bob Dickinson. Executive in Charge of Production: Sharon Morrill. Associate Director: Allan Kartun. Production Supervisor: John M. Best. Production Manager: Benn Fleishman. Editor: Michael Polito. Script Supervisor: Michael Dempsey. Production Coordinators: Ann King, James Dubose. Production Associate: Jeffrey R. Rudeen. Talent Coordinators: Lisa Weisner, John Reed. Post-Production Supervisor: Scott Schwartz. Production Secretary: Diana Siegel. Staging Supervisor: John Bradley. Costume Designer: Tom Bronson. Production Consultant: Lester Wilson. Assistant Choreographer: Rick Rozini. Stage Managers: Dency Nelson, Rac Clark, Bron Galleron, Scott Schwartz. Technical Director: John B. Field. Audio Mixer: Ed Greene. Video: Keith Winikoff, John Palacio, Jr. Technical Supervisor: Kevin Hayes. Post Production Audio: Charlie McDaniel, Craig Porter, Erik Zobler. PAF Concert Coordinator: Cyd Wilson. *Paula Abdul Segment* Directed by: Jonathan Dark. Produced by: Pete Dusthimer, Bruce Meade. Director of Photography: Jamie Anderson. Editor: Rich Uber. Illustrator: Alan Hoffman. Dance Captains: Bill Bohl, Nancy O'Meara, Cindy Picker. Costumer: Helen Hiatt. A Coyote Pictures Production. Baby Sinclair: John Kennedy, Terri Hardin, Kevin Clash. Jim Henson's Creature Shop: Andrew Eio, Jane A. Gootnick, Patrick Halm, Quentin Plant, Mike Scanlan, John B. Wilson, Jr. Supervising Producer: Gregory Sills. A Steel Pictures Production in association with Brad Lachman Productions, Inc. Two-hour format. First aired in 1993.

FROM DISNEY, A SUPER HALF TIME
Produced by: Ron Miziker. Written by: Ken Marangell. Production Assistant: Susan Dobak. A Showmakers Production. 30-minute format. First aired in 1984.

Credits for the *Super Bowl XVIII Half-Time Show:* Producer: Dennis Despie. Associate Producer: Ron Logan. Line Producer: Tom Craven. Show Director: Gary Paben. Assistant Show Director: Jay Smith. Technical Director: Scott Powhatan. Production Coordinator: Carol Campbell. Music Director: Steve Skorija. Orchestration: Jack Eskew. Choreographers: Jay Smith, Judy Lawrence, George Koller, Paul Killingrer, Tara Anderson. Costume Design: Bill Campbell. Costumers: Rebecca Broderick, Barbara Straub, Pam Carver. Production Assistant: Allan Cramer. Finance Manager: Phil Denmark. Transportation Coordination: Gregg Emmer. Lighting Designer: John Haupt. Audio Designer: Bill Thrasher. Audio Coordination: David Bush. Pyrotechnic Design: John Albert. Scenic Design: Cindy Ravetto, Mike Kennedy, David Ravetto. Facilities Coordination: Scooter Huller. Communications Coordination: Robb Resler. Equipment Coordination: John Unger. Production Staff: Rich Taylor, Reggie Jarrett, Jerry Janesick, Rick Harbin, Steve Zimmerman, Jabrill Alexander. Props Coordination: Bettina Buckley. Special Effects Coordination: Tylor Wymer. WDW Character Coordination: Mike O'Grattan. Balloon Coordination: Glenn Brome. Production Secretaries: Sandy Shepherd, Rosemary Healy, Debbie Angell.

FROM DISNEY, WITH LOVE
Prepared for The Disney Channel by: Film Landa Inc. With the Talents of: Mary Costa, Bill Shirley, Ilene Woods. *Pecos Bill* Sung by: Roy Rogers and Sons of the Pioneers. *Johnny Fedora and Alice Blue Bonnet* Sung by: The Andrews Sisters. Songs and Music: Sammy Fain, Jack Lawrence, Paul Smith, John Debney. Narrator: Charles Aidman. 90-minute format. First aired in 1984.

FUTURE TENSE
Executive Producer: Tad Stones. Produced by: Ron Diamond. Directed by: Frank DePalma. *Prairie Sun* Written by Edward Bryant. *The Solitaire Creature* Written by: Ron Clements. *Fun With Mr. Future* Directed by: Darrel Van Citters.

GOOFY'S GUIDE TO SUCCESS
Executive Producer: Robert Heath. Producer: Zilla Clinton. Written by: K.B. Wolin. Edited by: Hank Polonsky. Original Music by: Charlotte Lansberg. On Line Editor: Michael A. Polito. Post Audio: Bob Manahan. Sound Editor/Sound Effects: Gary Coppola. Graphic Design: Leslie Mais, Dennis Bader. A Production of Robert Heath, Inc. 90-minute format. First aired in 1990.

GREAT AMERICAN DREAMOBILE, THE
Produced by: John Klawitter. Original Music by: John Klawitter, Steve Zuckerman. A Happyfeets Productions.

HANSEL AND GRETEL/VINCENT
Executive Producer: Julie Hickson. Designed and Directed by: Tim Burton. Produced by: Rick Heinrichs. Written by: Julie Hickson. Director of Photography: Victor Abdalov. Music by: John Costa. Technical Director: Stephen Chiodo. Model Sculpture by: Rick Heinrichs. Associate Producer: Geoff Bennett. Production Coordinator: Clark Hunter. Production Consultant and Puppets by: Kelly Kimball. Sound: Jon Huck. Film Editors: Chris Roth, Michael Stringer. Videotape Editor: Paul Dougherty. Sweetening: Bill Gazecki. Wardrobe: Linnea Olson. Make-up: Felice Fassnacht. Boom: Pete Weiss. Model Assistant: Catherine Hardwicke. Grips: Ken D'Eliso, Ro Rybkowski, Deborah Switzer. Additional Photography: Michael Griffin.

HAPPY BIRTHDAY MICKEY
(The Whole World Wants to Wish You) Happy Birthday Mickey Mouse Words and Music by: Marty Cooper. Stop Action Sequences: Mike Jittlov, Deven Chierighino. Narrator: Charles Aidman. Prepared for The Disney Channel by: Film Landa, Inc. 90-minute format. First aired in 1983.

HERE COMES SAM: THE MAKING OF AN OLYMPIC SYMBOL
Directed, Written and Produced by: John Klawitter. Animated Japanese Footage Provided Courtesy of: Densu Advertising. A Happyfeets Production. 60-minute format. First aired in 1984.

HERE'S TO YOU, MICKEY MOUSE

Producer: George Paige. Associate Producer: Kent Weishaus. Editor: Sueann Fincke. Production Coordinator: Karen Deal. New Animation Produced by: Kroyer Films. Director of Photography: Jerry Watson. Original Score by: Kevin Quinn, Randy Petersen, Robert Irving. Art Director: Bruce Ryan. Narrator: Richard Tufeld. Assistant to Producer: James Tumminia. Script Supervisor: Cricket Wheeler. Production Assistant: David Hurwitz. Additional Editor: Bruce Motyer. Gaffer: Richard Ingle. Camera Assistant: Ken Barrows. Key Grip: Lloyd Moriarty. Sound: Steve Halbert, Rick Schexnoyder. Make-up: Bob Ryan. Hair: Gail Rowell. Assistant Art Director: Preston Sharp. Unit Production Manager/First Assistant Director: John Liberti. Second Assistant Director: Alan Brent Connell. A George Paige Associates Production. First aired in 1988.

HOLIDAY SPLENDOR

Show Director: Forrest Bahruth. Choreographer: Pam Killinger. Music Director: Ted Ricketts. Conductor: Michael Mahr. Executive Producer: Jerry Hughes. Director: Hugh Downing. Associate Producer: Catherine Hughes. Lighting Director: David M. Clark. Associate Director: Jill Phipson. Production Coordinator: Patricia Yarborough. Production Associate: Susi Simons. Make-up: Jeff Jones. Technical Supervisor: David Crivelli. Technical Director: Tom Clark. Video: Lynn Peggs. Audio: Aaron Baron. Camera: Rege Becker, Michael Cabana, Brad Finnell, Gene Kelly, Paul Rambo, Steve Zinn. Stage Manager: Michael Boyle. Videotape: Mark Adelsheim, Paul Byers. Maintenance: Kevin Clifford. Audio Assistant: Bob Aldridge. Production Assistants: Thom Downing, Rich Thomas. Videotape Editor: Paul Byers. Post Production Sound: Bob Millslagle. Titles: Gayle Hess. For Walt Disney World Costumes: Bill Campbell. Lighting: Ken Harris, Todd Nichols, Jody Roberson. Audio: Michael Potyrai, Shawn Brady. Scenic Design: Mike Kennedy. Special Effects: Tylor Wymer. Production Stage Managers: Mike Bucco, Gale Field, Michael Fletcher, Gene Rowell. Crane Operators: John Bender, Mike Gooseman. Utilities: James Crisp, Terry Crisp, Mickey DeJesus, Lee Thomas. Acknowledgments: Bill Anoka, Bob Austin, Mary Barnett, Bettina Buckley, Dan Burmester, Rich Burt, Wayne Busch, Dan Crudele, Susan Calhoun, Bobbi Colquitt, Carol Donegan, Bill Foster, John Haupt, Laura Haynes, Steph Henderson, Glen Howard, Larry Huff, Scooter Huller, Eric Larsen, Ron Logan, Alexandra Luna, Danni Mikler, Dave Ousley, Di Pittman, Velda Roddy, Nancy Rugh, Pam Santiago, Cathy Schiffauer, Cyd Stoll, Vince Tristram. A Hughes Television Production. First aired in 1987.

INTERNATIONAL CIRCUS STARS OF TOMORROW

Executive Producer and Director: Marty Pasetta. Producer: Wolf Kochmann. Associate Producer: Mick McCullough. Tape Segment Producer: David Forman. Associate Directors: Marty Pasetta, Jr., Debbie Pasetta. Production Manager: Philippe Leclercq. Lighting Designer: Francois Pailleux. Music Coordinator: Lee Maloney. Stage Manager: Greg Pasetta. Production Coordinator: Larry Cohen. Production Assistants: Vickie LaBrie, Drew Ogier, Steven Schillaci. Make-up: Muriel Martin. Technical Supervisors: Kevin Hayes, Keith Winikoff. Audio: Yves Jaget, Vincent Pitras. Cameramen: Ted Ashton, Antoine Gallet, Jean Yves Lemener. Lighting Control: Patrice Dorado. Telescan: Christophe Ducret, Jean Yves Morvan. Electricians: Bernard Bajard, Jean Philippe Harant, Olivier Wermuth. Videotape Editors: Michael Kelly, Bruce Motyer. Assistant Editors: Matt Donato, Keith Fernandez, Mark Humphrey. Acknowledgments: Dominque Montclair, The Staff of L'Association Francise du Cirque de Demain, Alexis Gruss, The Staff and Crew of Cirque Gruss.

IT ALL STARTED WITH A MOUSE: THE DISNEY STORY

Acknowledgments: Roy E. Disney, Etienne de Villiers, John Elia, Horace Bishop, Howard Green. Graphic Design: Pat Gavin, Andrew Brownlow. Main Title: G-Man Productions. Rostrum Camera: Ken Morse. Dubbing Editor: Nigel M. Parkes. Dubbing Mixer: David Old. Film Cameraman: Geoff Harrison. Film Sound: Reg Mills. Film Research: Trevor Hear-

ing. Production Assistant: Pamela Burke. Research: Steve Jenkins. Film Editor: Frank Webb. Video Tape Editors: Patrick Clancey, Stan Kellam. Produced & Directed by: Alan Benson. Edited by: Melvyn Bragg. Packaged for The Disney Channel by: G-Man Productions. Narrated by: Mason Adams. 90-minute format. First aired in 1989.

JIMINY CRICKET: STORYTELLER

Compilation Produced by: Kevin Reem, Julie Jenkins. Executive Producer: Phil Catherall. The Voice of Jiminy Cricket: Eddie Carroll. Videotape Editor: Bruce Ogden. Assistant Videotape Editor: Dale D. Menagh. 90-minute format. First aired in 1986.

JUDY COLLINS: GOING HOME

Producer: Geoffrey Drummond. Director: Elliott Edwards. Line Producer: Bob Jason. Co-Executive Producer: Amy Divine. Associate Producers /Music: Lucy Simon, David Levine. Director of Photography: Denver John Collins. Editor: Larry Jordan. Production Design Consultant: Louis Nelson. Production Manager: Christine Ernst. Location Coordinator: David Laughren. Music Supervisor: Bonnie Greenberg. Stage Manager: Wayne Pleasants. 1st Assistant Director: Kim Thomas. Camera Operators: Abe Schrager, Don Bogart, Allen Powers. Assistant Cameras: Doug O'Kane, Greg Poshman. Sound Recordists: Scott Terhark, Lynn Bodely. Lighting Director: Mike Sapsis. Live Mix: Robin Gately. Gaffer: John Thomas. Electrician/best Boy: Brad Lipson. Electricians: Tom Osborne, Harly Stumbaugh, Ghan Rucinsky. Key Grip: Bob Shulman. Grips: Lynn Alverson, Bob Uveges, Lloyd Sobel, Rob Seidman. Video Engineer in Charge: Roger Crawford. Mobile Unit Manager: John Eulberg. Technical Director: John Atkins. Videotape Operators: John Goerner, Al Romero, Ken Miller. Audio Recording Engineer: Alan Silverman. Assistant Engineer: Garry Long. Technician: Tim McColm. Audio Stage Manager: Nick "Beemer" Basich. Wardrobe Stylist: Maria Pizzuro. Wardrobe: Valerie Johnson. Make-up/Hair Stylist: Susan Houser. Floral Design: Alyson Taylor. Production Assistants: Mary Sue Foard, Mike Rosser, Jeff Chadwick, Brad Bradley, Lincoln Terhark, Laura Belsi, Chris Denny, Ashley Gilbert. Assistant to Ms. Collins: Nancy Roof. Assistant to the Producer: Teal Derrer. A Geoffrey Drummond Production. 1-hour format. First aired in 1989.

KRAG, THE KOOTENAY RAM

Produced by: Ron Miller. Director of Photography: Charles L. Draper. Teleplay by: B.W. Sandefur, William P. Canning. Narration by: Barry Clark. Based on a story by: Ernest Thompson Seton. Directed by: Frank Zuniga. Narrator: John McIntire. Editor: Toby Brown, A.C.E. Music: Robert F. Brunner. Sound: Herb Taylor. Production Coordinator: Rolf Darbo. For Pisces Productions, Inc. Field producer: Frank Zuniga. Production Manager/Assistant Director: Phillip B. Patton. Second Assistant Director: Paul Tucker. Wildlife Photography: Bruno Engler, Bill Schmalz. Animal Supervision: Dennis Grisco, Steve Martin, Howard Lacey, Harold Lacey, Patty Baily. Animals furnished by: Okanagan Game Farm, Steve Martin's Working Wildlife. Acknowledgments: Banff National Park, Jasper National Park, Alberta Film Commission. First aired in 1985.

LAKE WOBEGON COMES TO DISNEY

Producer: Anthony Eaton. Director: Thomas Schlamme. A Production of Minnesota Public Radio in association with Tall Pony Productions, Inc. 90-minute format. First aired in 1986.

LAKE WOBEGON LOYALTY DAYS

Produced and Directed by: Phillip Byrd. Written by: Garrison Keillor. Original Music: Randall Davidson. A Production of Minnesota Public Radio in association with Bradenburg Productions, Inc. 90-minute format. First aired in 1989.

LIFESTYLES OF THE RICH AND ANIMATED

Executive Producer: Robert Heath. Producer: Marijane Miller. Written by: Kenny Wolin. Edited by: Hank Polonsky. Original Music by: Charlotte Lansberg. On Line Editor: M.T. Badertscher. Re-recording Mixer & Sound Effects: Bob Manahan. Audio Post Supervisor: Gary Coppola. Graphic Design:

David Henry, Ian Dawson, Marco Bacich. Acknowledgments: Les Perkins, Paula Sigman. Robert Heath Inc. 90-minute format. First aired in 1991.

LOCATION: ANNE OF AVONLEA
Produced and Directed by: Jim Davy. Video Camera: Jan Zuchlinski. Field Engineer: Jack Buchanan. Editor: Richard Piccini. 20-minute format. First aired in 1987.

LORETTA & CRYSTAL: GOING HOME
Executive Producer: Dick Clark. Supervising Producer: Gene Weed. Producer: Fred Tatashore. Directed by: Gene Weed. Written by: Fred Tatashore. Associate Producer: Ron Weed. Art Director: Jim Stanley. Associate Director: Mary Jo Blue. Production Supervisor: Bridget Weed. Assistant to the Producer: Phyllis Claver. Production Assistant: Colleen O'Connell. Stage Managers: Jody Karlovic, Connie Mansfield. Production Manager: David Yost. Musical Conductors: Alan Steinberger, Bruce H. Frazier. Production Coordinators: Patricia Branan, Debbie Wamsley. Production Associates: Stephanie Parker, Kirby Allen, Bill Halbert. Program Clearance Executive: Karen Smith. Contract Administrator: Len Hughes. Technical Director: Chris Donovan. Lighting Director: Mike Gillen. Staging Supervisor: Larry Schwartz. Audio Mixer: Mark Repp. Video Control: Don Clagett, Larry Bearden. Video Tape Operators: Robert Brittin, Kurt O. Wortmann, Pete Cooke. Cameras: Larry Copeland, Allen Fuqua, Ed Fussell, Pat Gleason. Audio: Stan Dacus, Dick Hargett, Johnnie Shankland, Alan Stokes. Engineer in Charge: Gaylon Holloway. Make-up: Vanessa Sellers, Genie Bellar, Mary Beth Felts. Hair Stylist: Julie Brendel. Wardrobe: Valerie Wise. Video Tape Editors: Stanley Perkins, Brian Schnuckel. Post Production Audio Mixer: Doug Latislaw. Audio Embellishment: Rick Himot. Executive in Charge: Fran LaMaina. Dick Clark Productions. 1-hour format. First aired in 1992.

LUDWIG'S THINK TANK
Prepared by: Bart Roen. Voice of Ludwig by: Wayne Allwine. Post Production Supervisor: Richard Audd. Video Tape Editors: Richard Audd, Peter Cohen. Audio Mixer: Ken Dahlinger. ARENDEE Productions. 90-minute format. First aired in 1985.

HAROLD AND HIS AMAZING GREEN PLANTS
Designer: Robert Peluce. Director: Bob Kurtz. Produced for Epcot Educational Media by Kurtz & Friends.

WALT DISNEY PRESENTS ADVENTURES IN MUSIC: TOOT, WHISTLE, PLUNK, AND BOOM
Story: Dick Huemer. Character Styling: Tom Oreb. Music: Joseph Dubin. Art Direction: A. Kendall O'Connor. Assistant: Victor Haboush. Color Styling: Eyvind Earle. Songs: Sonny Burke, Jack Elliott. Animators: Ward Kimball, Julius Svendsen, Marc Davis, Henry Tanous, Art Stevens, Xavier Atencio. Directors: C. August Nichols, Ward Kimball.

WINNIE THE POOH DISCOVERS THE SEASONS
Written by: Ronald Kidd. Music and Lyrics by: Steve Zuckerman. Voices: Kim Christianson (Christopher Robin), Ronald Fineberg (Eeyore), Ray Earlenborn (Rabbit), Laurie Main (Narrator), John Fiedler (Piglet), Hal Smith (Tigger and Owl). Music: Steve Zuckerman. Animation: Don Hasket, Tom Ray, Bob Bermiller, Joe Roman, Ed Love. Directing Animator: Ennis McNulty. Written by: Ronald Kidd. Directed by: Rick Reinhert. Rick Reinhert Productions for Disney Educational Productions.

COMETS: TIME CAPSULES OF THE SOLAR SYSTEM
Produced by Media Four Productions for Walt Disney Telecommunications and Non-Theatrical Company. Written and Directed by: Charles L. Finance. Photographed by: William Heffner, Charles L. Finance. Animation by: Sylvia Keulen, Graphic Films Corp. Consultant: Ray Newburn, Jr., Ph.D., Jet Propulsion Laboratory.

DONALD IN MATHMAGIC LAND
Story: Milt Banta, Bill Berg, Dr. Heinz Haber. Styling: John Hench, Art Riley. Music: Buddy Baker. Director of Photography: Edward Colman, A.S.C. Art Director: Stan Jolley. Film Editor: Lloyd L. Richardson, A.C.E. Special Processes: Eustace Lycett. Sound: Robert O. Cook. Assistant Director: Vincent McEveety. Layout: McLaren Stewart, Al Zinnen, Basil Davidovich, Vance Gerry. Backgrounds: Richard H. Thomas, Thelma Witmer, Jimi Trout, Collin Campbell. Animation: Jerry Hathcock, John Sibley, Bob Carlson, Eric Cleworth, Cliff Nordberg, Harvey Toombs, Bob McCrea. Effects Animation: Jack Boyd. Supervising Director: Hamilton S. Luske. Sequence Directors: Wolfgang Reitherman, Les Clark, Joshua Meador.

MAGIC KINGDOM CELEBRATION—LIVE!
Director: Dennis Rosenblatt. Producers: Paul Abeyta, Peter Kaikko. Co-Producer: Sandra Moiseff. Associate Producer: Frank Torres. Associate Director: J.R. Pasetta. Production Assistant: Andrea Marshall. Technical Director: Keith Winikoff. Stage Manager: Leon Robinson. Sound Mixer: Jack Tossman. Camera Operators: Rob Bonas, Kenny Patterson, Ron Sheldon, Warren Jones. RC Entertainment, Inc. 1-hour format. First aired in 1986.

MAGIC KINGDOM YULETIDE SPECIAL, A
Produced by: Ron Miziker. Directed by: Rudi Goldman. Associate Producer: Susan Dobak. Created and Staged by: Barnette Ricci. Musical Director: Jack Eskew. Voices by: Jack Wagner, Barnette Ricci. Art Directors: John Shaffner, Joe Stewart, Jeanette Oleska. Lighting Director: Don Cohen. Production Co-ordinator: Colleen Kennedy. Assistant to Producer: Julie Eilber. Associate Director: Bob Fitzpatrick. Stage Manager: Bob Andrade. Disneyland Co-ordinator: Doug McIntyre. Disneyland Prop Master: Marvin Rea. Assistant Choreographer: Roy Luthringer. Technical Director: Terry Donahue. Audio: Ed Moskowitz. Cameras: Hector Ramierez, Jim Rohrig, Dan Webb. Sound Mixing: Dick Hart, John Walker. Recording Engineer: Russell Schmitt. Video: Jay Griffith, Cheryl Thompson. Editor: Peter Sternlicht. A Showmakers Production. 30-minute format. First aired in 1985.

MAKING OF A GOOFY MOVIE, THE
Executive Producers: Dan Boothe, Stu Schreiberg. Producer: Dan Boother. Written by: Zach Elliot. Edited by: Eric Ridley, Brian Ross. Coordinating Producer: Stacy Ryono. Production Manager: Lori Hirsch. Art Director: Scott Storey. Director of Photography: Larry Gaudette. Camera: Bob Keys, Joe Mealy. Lighting Director: Robin Banando. Location Sound: Gary Bacon, Doug Donald, Bernie Kriegel. *France Production Unit* Director of Photography: John Sorapure. Location Sound: Alistair Widgery. Make-up: Barbara Byrne. Hair: Shirley Bryan. Production Coordinator: Richard Mendoza. Production Assistants: Michele Bornheim, Michael Cronin, Rick Locke, Jr., Tracy Roberson, Rod Sanchez, Sheri Sedlik. Graphic Design: Chris Williamson. Post Production Supervisor: Eric Van Wagenen. Acknowledgment: Andrew Sorcini. Executive in Charge of Production: John Bravakis. The Wrightwood Group. 30-minute format. First aired in 1995.

MAKING OF BLACK ARROW, THE
Produced by: Film Landa, Inc. Producer: Dennis Landa. 30-minute format. First aired in 1985.

MAKING OF DISNEY'S CAPTAIN EO, THE
Produced and Directed by: Muffett Kaufman. Associate Producer: Douglas Ross. Edited by: Joshua Alper. Written by: Jeff Walker, Joshua Alper, Douglas Ross, Matthew Cohen, Muffett Kaufman. Director of Photography: Robert E. Collins. Cameraman: Michael Chevalier. Sound Men: Bruce Bisenz, John Glasscock, Garry Cunningham, John Vincent. Camera Assistants: John Abbene, Rod Blackie, Dan Dayton, Greg Schmidt. Gaffers: Howard Ex, John Reynolds, Scott Buttfield. Assistant Editor: Christopher Kassas. Production Assistants: Todd Crossley, Gary DePew, Matthew Cohen, Katie Morgan. Transcription: Julie Reed. Videotape Editor: Ron Menzies. Assistant Videotape Editors: Larry Peake, Robert Berryman. Re-Recording Mixer: David Fluhr. Sound Editor: Ross Davis. Production Accountant: Barbara Pearlman. 60-minute format. First aired in 1987.

MAKING OF DISNEY'S RETURN TO TREASURE ISLAND, THE

Producer: Richard Price. Prime Time Entertainment. 30-minute format. First aired in 1986.

MAKING OF FIVE MILE CREEK, THE

Producer: Dennis Landa. A Film Landa Production. 30-minute format. First aired in 1983.

MAKING OF "HONEY, I SHRUNK THE KIDS," THE

Produced by: Bob Gautieri, Paul Hall. Written by: Bob Gautieri. Directed by: Bob Gautieri, Steve Purcell. Technical Directors: Steve Purcell, Charley Randazzo. Edited by: Charley Randazzo, David Pincus. Assistant Editor: Marty Rosenstock. Motion Control: Kevin Haug, John Rostado. Re-Recording Mixers: Troy Smith, John Walker, Steve Michel. Paintbox Artist: Laurie Resnick. Harry Animation: Helen Davis, Scott Milne. Title Design: Deborah Ristic. Graphic Design: Bob Gautieri. Ultimatte Camera: Sergio Rodriguez. Stock Footage: Dave Fishbein. Film Transfer: Julius Friede. G-Man Productions, Inc. 30-minute format. First aired in 1989.

MAKING OF POCAHONTAS, THE: A LEGEND COMES TO LIFE

Executive Producers: Dan Boothe, Stu Schreiberg. Written, Produced and Directed by: Dan Boothe. Line Producer: Stacy Ryono. Coordinating Producer: Lori Hirsch. Director of Photography: Larry Gaudette. Edited by: Eric Ridley, Marcus Weise. Production Coordinators: Richard Mendoza, Christopher Freeland. Camera: Van Carlson, Bowden Hunt, Geoff Schaaf. Audio Engineers: Doug Donald, Rob Scott. Associate Director: Danya Browder. Graphic Design: Chris Williamson. Art Director: Lisa Caperton. Post Production Supervisor: Eric Van Wagenen. Sound Mixer: Fred Tator. Production Assistants: Mike Angelo, Georgie Dunn, Seth Harris, Ramesh Iyer, Mike Maleski, Lynn Tschosik, Melissa Wallace. Acknowledgments: The Association for the Preservation of Virginia Antiquities; Tim Kolly; Jamestown Settlement. Executive in Charge of Production: John Bravakis. A Production of The Wrightwood Group, Incorporated. 30-minute format. First aired in 1995.

MAKING OF RUDYARD KIPLING'S THE JUNGLE BOOK, THE

Executive Producers: Dan Boothe, Stu Schreiberg. Written, Produced and Directed by: Dan Boothe. Edited by: Brian Ross, David W. Foster. Coordinating Producer: Glenn Stickley. Art Director: Richard Wienecke. Location Footage Directed by: Michael S. Baumohl, Michael Strout, David Castell. Director of Photography: Larry Gaudette. Location Cameramen: Jay Elyayam, Cory Lash. Location Sound: Doug Donald, Alan Stokes. Lighting Director: David Newman. Graphic Design: Chris Williamson. Make-up: Dominique Graham. Wardrobe: Erin Farrell. Production Manager: Mary Sue Foard. Production Coordinator: Christopher Freeland. Production Assistants: Seth Harris, Richard Mendoza, Sheri Sedlik, Patricia Valenzuela. Post Production Supervisor: Eric Van Wagenen. On-Line Editor: Ron Barr. Post Production Audio: Ron Miller. Telecine Supervisor: Shawn Stoner. Telecine Colorist: Mike Sowa. Executive in Charge of Production: John Bravakis. Produced for The Disney Channel in association with Wrightwood Entertainment, Inc. 30-minute format. First aired in 1994.

MAKING OF THE BLUE YONDER, THE

Writer, Director and Producer: Michael B. Gladych. Director of Photography: Martin Unversaw. Audio/Production Assistant: Scott Norlund. Original Score by: Christopher Stone. A Michael Gladych Production. 30-minute format. First aired in 1985.

MAKING OF THE DISNEY-MGM STUDIOS THEME PARK, THE

Executive Producer: Eric Schotz. Producer: Lisa Shaffer. Director: Eric Schotz. Segment Producers: Don Cambou, Paul Hall, Rob Kirk. Managing Editor: Michael Bonifer. Editor: Scott Reynolds. Associate Producer: Darci Fletchall. Video Camera: Bowdon Hunt, Steve Suggs. Sound Technicians: Eric Bourgoujian, Dave Bowen. Production Assistant: Mikel Androsky. Video Technicians: Victor Gonzaga, Joe Lewis. Main Title Graphics: Helen Davis. Acknowledgments: Cheryl Doherty, Kathryn Douglas, Stacy Ryono. Executive in Charge of Production: Carol Sherman. Narrator: Bill Ratner. LMNO Productions, Tri-Crown Productions. 1-hour format. First aired in 1989.

MAKING OF THE HUNCHBACK OF NOTRE DAME, THE

Executive Producers: Dan Boothe, Stu Schreiberg. Written, Produced and Directed by: Dan Boothe. Director of Photography: Larry Gaudette. Editors: Dave Basinski, Kelly Coskran, Eric Ridley. Associate Director: Seth Mellman. Production Manager: Renee Mendoza. Production Coordinator: Michele Bornheim. Production Designer: Scott Storey. Graphic Designer: Chris Williamson. Telecine Colorist: Mike Underwood. Telecine Supervisor: Sean Stoner. Sound: Doug Donald. Post Production Supervisors: Michael Cronon, Joe Keeper, Renee Stauffer. Gaffer: Dave Newman. Make-up: Suzi Pannebacker. Production Assistants: Jim Amerian, Tom Demko, Julie Donsky, Sheri Sedlik, Sarah Steinberg. Executive in Charge of Production: John Bravakis. Produced for The Disney Channel in association with Wrightwood Entertainment, Inc. 30-minute format. First aired in 1996.

MAKING OF THE LION KING, THE

Executive Producers: Dan Boothe, Stu Schreiberg. Produced and Directed by: Dan Boothe. Written by: Rex Lobo. Edited by: David W. Foster. Art Director: John Gilles. Camera: Randy Gomez, Mark Nelson. Location Sound: Rob Scott. Lighting Director: David Newman. Graphic Design: Chris Williamson. Make-up: Suzi Pannenbacker. Animal Trainers: Animal Actors of Hollywood. Production Coordinator: Troy Norton. Production Assistants: Kelli Mayman, Chris Freeland, Sean Linderman. Post Production Supervisor: Eric Van Wagenen. On-Line Editor: Mark Bement. Post Production Audio: Ron Miller. Telecine Supervisor: Renée Stauffer. Telecine Colorist: Mike Sowa. Executive in Charge of Production: John Bravakis. The Wrightwood Group, Incorporated. 30-minute format. First aired in 1994.

MAKING OF THE LITTLE MERMAID, THE

Produced and Directed by: Robert Heath. Written by: Henry Kimmel. Edited by: Hank Polonsky. Associate Producer: Zilla Clinton. Production Coordinators: Michael Fomil, Lindsey Paddor. Camera: Joe Epperson, Alan Brennecke, Scott Levine, John Sharaf. Sound: Peter Hliddal, Dan Newman, Paul Oppenheim. Gaffer: Mike Rogers. Wardrobe: Matt Van Dyne, Jeff Bryan. Make Up and Hair: Nina Kent. On Line Editor: Michael A. Polito. Post Audio: Robert Manahan. Graphic Designer: Ron Clark. Production Assistants: Stephen Markel, Margaret Black, Mitchell Ford, Charles Goubert. Acknowledgments: Nancy Parent, Stacey Slossey. A Production of Robert Heath, Inc. 30-minute format. First aired in 1989.

MAKING OF THE MIGHTY DUCKS, THE

Produced and Written by: Tom Murray, Josh Kaplan. Associate Producer: W. Scott Henry. Photographers: Victor Smith, Jodie Mena, Scott Moulton. Editor: Josh Kaplan. On-line Editors: Cliff Armstrong, Jeff Koss. Graphics Manager: Margaret Bassett. Electronic Graphics: Daniel Storm, Alan Pfister. Acknowledgments: National Hockey League, University of Maine, ESPN, CBC. *Closing Credits Music* Written and Performed by: Bob Moline. Arranged by: Edo Guidotti. KCAL-TV. 15-minute format. First aired in 1993.

MAKING OF THE THREE MUSKETEERS, THE

Produced by: Dan Boothe, Stu Schreiberg. Written and Directed by: Dan Boothe. Edited by: David W. Foster. Associate Producer: Joanie Burton. On-Line Editor: Jeff Caldwell. Production Assistant: Kelli Mayman. *Vienna Production Unit* Director of Photography: Larry Gaudette. Location Sound: Gary Bacon. *The Three Musketeers* Unit Publicist: David Linck. *Cornwall Production Unit* Director of Photography: Paul Bernard. Location Sound: Aidan Hobbs. Make-up: Paul Engelen. Camera Crane Operator: Rupert Lloyd-Parry. Location Manager: Bill Darby. Assistant Location Manager: Teresa Hidalgo De Caviedes. Horsemaster: Tony Smart. Armorer: Simon Atherton. Location Drivers: Sean Christie, Gary Rowe. *United States Production Units* Directors of Photography: Larry Gaudette, Scott Kaye, Van Carlson. Location Sound: Gary Bacon, Vince Singletary, John Scarpaci. Acknowledgments: One For All Productions, William W. Wilson III. Sword Fighters: Gary Bradford, Cynthia Bradford. Computer Graphics: Chris Williamson. Paintbox Graphics: Tom Kane. Dubner Graphics: Mark Festen. Post Production Audio: Gary Coppola. The Wrightwood Group, Incorporated. 30-minute format.

MAKING OF THE UNDERGRADS, THE
Producer: Steve Stern. Sharmhill Productions. 30-minute format. First aired in 1985.

MAKING OF TOY STORY, THE
Narrated by: Annie Potts. Written and Directed by: Mike Bonifer. Produced by: Jonathan Bogner. Editors: Eric Ridley, Berfin Haymes. Production Manager: Leslie Anne Shevick. Production Coordinators: Renne Stauffer, Tracy Roberson. Camera: Larry Gaudette, M. David Muellen, Jarid Johnson, Van Carlson. Location Sound: Marget Long, Jack Morris, Gary Bacon. Audio Engineers: Jim Corbett, Lou Thomas, Robert Corbett. Telecine Supervisor: Shawn Stoner. Telecine Colorist: Earl Adams. Music: Dan Radlauer. Graphics: Mike Goedeke. Production Assistants: Christian Raymond, Sheri Sedlik, Sarah Steinberg. Research Clip Clearance Supervisor: Kelann Michelle Collins. A Production of Bonifer/Bogner Media. 30-minute format. First aired in 1995.

MANHATTAN TRANSFER, THE: GOING HOME
Executive Producers: Brian Avnet, John Cutcliffe. Produced and Directed by: Ken Ehrlich. Associate Producer: Jeff Ross. Lighting Designer: Sid Strong. Assistant to the Producer: Pamela Cantori. Associate Director: Patti Vine. Stage Manager: Gregory Sills. Technical Director: Keith Winikoff. Audio: Don Worsham. Video: Mark Sanford. Cameras: Ted Ashton, Sam Drummy, Tom Geren, Ken Patterson, Bill Philbin, Ron Sheldon. *The Manhattan Transfer Staff* Tour Manager: Reginald Wiggins. Production Manager: Jack White. Lighting Director: Stan Crocker. House Sound Engineer: Dan Kasting. Monitor Engineer: Geoff Parker. Carpenter/Wrangler: Marc Engel. Stage Equipment: Rick Garcia. Audio Tech: Tom Martin. Lighting Tech: Ray Freeman. Hair & Make-up: Lee Garland. Wardrobe: Eileen Licitri. Wardrobe Assistant: Charlene Colon. Bus Driver: John Coons. Truck Drivers: Chuck Hadley, Gerry Nerrison. Merchandising: Scott Hawn. Talent Agents: Fred Lawrence, Bob Zievers. Executive in Charge of Production: Gregory Sills. K.E. Enterprises, Inc. First aired in 1988.

MATTER OF SURVIVAL, A
Directed by: John Stephen O'Neill. Produced by: John Stephen O'Neill, Robert Mills. Written by: Mary Anderson, John Stephen O'Neill. Edited by: Mitchell Sinoway. Cinematography by: Bruce Olinder. Music Composed and Performed by: Rick Johnston. Assistant Camera: Kris Roe, George Mooradian, Chuck Skinner. Recording Mixer: Jim Cypher. Audio Engineer: Bob Walter. Associate Producer: Thaya du Bois. Additional Photography: John Stephen O'Neill. Acknowledgments: Primarily Primates, Los Angeles Zoo, San Diego Zoo, San Diego Wild Animal Park, U.S. Fish and Wildlife Service.

MICHAEL ICEBERG IN CONCERT FROM DISNEYLAND
Executive Producer: Kevin Anderson. Produced by: Dave Hilmer, Robb Royer. Written by: Michael Iceberg, Robb Royer. Directed by: Danielle Kail. Associate Producer: Dee Baker. Production Coordinator for Disneyland: Mike Davis. Assistant to the Producers: Sharon Nagata. Lighting Director: Jeff Engel. Stage Managers: Doug McIntyre, Steve Gaskins. Video: Ron Stutzman, Mike Snedden. Audio: Dana McClure. Camera Operators: Bob Keys, Dave Levisohn, Hector Ramirez. Make-up: Lisa Pharren. Video Tape Editor: Jeff U'Ren. An Anderson & Associates Production. 30-minute format. First aired in 1985.

MICKEY GOES TO MOSCOW
Narrated by: Willard Scott. Produced by: Jerry Hughes. Written by: James C. Rogal. Editor: Catherine Hughes. Director of Photography: Rege Becker. Original Music Composed and Performed by: Michael Moricz. Production Coordinator: Masha Norbye. Camera: Michael Regan. Sound: Mark Adelsheim, Michael Boyle. Videotape: Mike Kobik. Soviet Support: Anatoly Valushkin, Jurij Pavlovitch, Lena Zhazkovskaya, Lena Shabanova. Videotape Editor: Paul Byers. Re-Recording Mixer: Bob Millslagle. Graphics: Gayle Hess. *The Marathon:* Byelorusfilm Animation Studio. A Hughes Television Production. 30-minute format. First aired in 1989.

MICKEY MOUSE CLUB FIRST ANNIVERSARY SPECIAL
Executive Producer: Steve Clements. Produced and Directed by: Joe Carolei. Writing Supervised by: Alan Silberberg. Written by: Steve Clements, Tim Grundmann, Hillary Rollins, Karl Tiedemann, Stephen Winer, Jeff Zimmer. Executive in Charge of Production: Jean Wiegman. Coordinating Producer: Margie Friedman. Musical Performance Segments Produced by: Nancy Gregory. Senior Segment Producer: Kathy O'Reilly. Associate Producer: Jim Moroney. Music Supervisor: Dana Salyers. Choreography by: Myles Thoroughgood. Vocal Director: Dan Sawyer. Segment Directors: Jimmy Huckaby, Cricket Wheeler. Segment Producers: Gerette Allegra, Jim Casey, Matthew Gaven, Cricket Wheeler. Art Director: Randy Foster. Lighting Director: Nick Woolfolk. Associate Director: Kim Anway. Stage Managers: Henry Z. Neimark, Keith Richmond, John Aguirre. Set Designed by: Gerry Hariton, Vicki Baral. Lighting Designed by: Greg Brunton. Acting Coach: Tom Ormeny. Talent Coordinator: Gerette Allegra. Production Associate: Janie Ferguson. Production Assistant: Kimber Smith. Script Coordinator: Jim Davis. Assistant Art Director: Mickey De Jesus. Set Decorators: Jim Sheridan, Deborah Witt. Property Master: John DePiro. Assistant Property Master: John Wiegman. Art Department Assistant: Christine Howard. Engineer in Charge: Larry Gaetano. Post Production Supervisor: Annie Court. Post Production Assistants: Beth M. Brady, James Weathers. Production Coordinator: Tom Cavanagh. Editors: Jim Mancini, Jeff Palmer, Sam Patterson. Research Supervisor: Kitt McLeod. Researchers: Debbie Green, Kate Link. Transportation Coordinator: Bruce Anderson. Production Staff: Marci Bokash, Andy Calandrino, Cammie Cavallin, Cathy Clouse, David Cove, Jo Etta Geralde, Christopher Heyn, Alexis Jackson, Jean Lloyd, Phyllis Rose Nastri, Julie Pine, Julie Robinson, Kathryn Waters, Jack Weber, Vernon Whitaker. Wardrobe Supervisor: Mellissa Berry. Wardrobe: Terry Binion, Ken 'Boma' Bolden, Carolyn Dessert, Leda Gutierrez, Marion Ellen Knackert, Betty Miller. Hair: Colleen Labaff, Liz Lavallee, Tish Simpson. Make-up: Regina Perron, Debra Summers, Yolanda Winters. Camera Operators: Gary Jelaso, Ron Smith, Bob Van Dorn, Jim Yockey. Head Carpenter: Alan Bruun. Assistant Carpenters: Clinton Neudecker, George Siplin. Studio Production Assistants: Maria Caccavo, Virgil Fabian. Technical Director: Pete Court. Video Control: Vince Vezzi. Videotape Operators: Mike Sherwood, William Thomas. Audio Mixer: Jim Fay. PA Mixer: Sean McFall. Audio Assistants: Kris Barnes, Brien Casey, Jim McCabe, Lori Stasko. Post Production Audio: Rob Hill, Kurt Wagner. Gaffer: J.R. Roberson. Board Operator: Michael Gooseman. Key Grip: Steve Gryna. Electricians: Mike Laninfa, Dell Moody, John Peters. Grips: Frank Vila, Jerry Meibos, Terry Neudecker. Production Executive: George Paige. Blue Wave Productions, Inc. 30-minute format. First aired in 1990.

MICKEY MOUSE CLUB STORY, THE
Narrated by: Frankie Avalon. Executive Producers: Dan Boothe, Stu Schreiberg. Written, Produced and Directed by: Dan Boothe. Line Producer: Stacy Ryono. Editors: Eric Ridley, Brian Ross. Segment Producers: Gerry Johnston, Renee Mendoza. Camera: Richard Davis, Scott Kaye, Duane Rude. Researcher: Teri Scott. Associate Director: Wendy Dawson. Stage Manager: John Bravakis. Art Director: Jimbo Marshall. Music by: Michael Tavera. Sound: George Moshonas, Rick Hayes. Post Production Supervisor: Eric Van Wagenen. Post Production Coordinators: Michael Cronin, Joe Keeper, Patricia Valenzuela. Sound Mixer: Larry Sullivan. Production As-

sistant: Lynn Tschosik. Creative Consultant: Lorraine Santoli. Acknowledgments: Harold Braun, Rick DeCroix. Executive in Charge of Production: John Bravakis. Produced for The Disney Channel by Wrightwood Entertainment, Inc. 1-hour format. First aired in 1995.

MICKEY: REELIN' THROUGH THE YEARS

Executive Producers: Dan Boothe, Stu Schreiberg. Written by: Michael E. Zack. Produced and Directed by: Dan Boothe. Director of Photography: Larry Gaudette. Edited by: David Foster, Brian Ross. Line Producer: Stacy Ryono. Coordinating Producer: Renee Mendoza. Production Manager: Christopher Freeland. Associate Director: Aviva Jacobs. Stage Manager: Seth Mellman. Art Director: Scott Storey. Camera: Bob Mingus. Location Audio: Doug Donald. Graphic Design: Chris Williamson. Post Production Supervisor: Eric Van Wagenen. Post Production Coordinators: Michael Cronin, Joe Keeper. Sound Mixer: Craig Plachy. Production Assistants: Seth Harris, Lynn Tschosik, Patricia Valenzuela, Damon Zwicker. Production Interns: Blaine Bensyl, Aaron Lindenthaler, Jesse Mitchell, Dave Palarmo. Executive in Charge of Production: John Bravakis. Produced for The Disney Channel by: The Wrightwood Group, Incorporated. 30-minute format. First aired in 1995.

MICKEY'S NUTCRACKER

Stage Show Production Team Executive Producer: Bob McTyre. Producer: Mike Davis. Directed by: Robert Jess Roth. Choreographed by: Matt West. Book by: Tom Child. Lyrics by: Tom Child, Jim Cox. Musical Director: Bruce Healey. Scenic Design: Stanley A. Meyer. Costume Design: Alya Klegg. Lighting Design: Norm Schwab. Production Stage Manager: Holly Hopson. *Disney Video Production Team* Director: Brad Ramsey. Supervising Producer: Brad Tallman. Producer: Gary Kurtz. Associate Director: Tim Powell. Production Coordinators: Rhonda Hays, Melissa Boyer. Editors: Bryan Hargrave, Dan Swietlik. Lighting Director: Dennis Rudge. Technical Support: Jim Henderson. EIC: Andrew Sabol. Video Engineer: Rich Rose. Audio Engineer: Stillman Kelly. Tape Operator: Steve Bires. Gaffer: Mike Boisclair. Camera Operators: Brad Zerbst, John Evans, David Hilmer. Electrics: Scott Linder, Bill Eastham, Roger Cole, Tim Garvey, Ernie Sweet, John Anderson, Doug Hatfield, Jim McFail, Paul Cadena, Greg Camacho, Fred Cuttler, Kevin Donahoe, Cathy Kubel, Michael Luth. Video Utility: Charlie Fernandez, Dean Plotnick, Sean Woodside. Crane Arm: Pete Mahoney. Dolly Grip: Gerald Bozian. *Disneyland Videopolis Stage Crew* Technical Director: Earle Greene. Assistant Technical Director: Rory Masseth. Crew Lead: Bev Stauger. PA Mixer: Hugh Healy. Stagehands: Jeff Carr, Nola Jackson, Sarah Shirley, Larry Charbonneau, Dean Howlett, John Pierce, Troy Romeo, Molly Runner, Ingrid Thronson, Bruce Rosen, Brent Thurston. A Disneyland Television Production. 30-minute format. First aired in 1992.

MIND'S EYE, THE: THE EXPERIENCE OF LEARNING

Written and Produced by: Terry Strauss. Directed and Edited by: Wendy Blair Slick. Director of Photography: Jerry Slick. Production Manager: Blanche Chase. Gaffer: Tom Schnitzler. Consulting Editor: Susan Crutcher. Music by: Bernie Krause, Gary Remal. A Terry Strauss Production.

MIRACLES OF SPRING—A TRUE-LIFE ADVENTURE

Prepared for The Disney Channel by: Film Landa, Inc. Photographers: Arthur A. Allen, Lloyd Beebe, Dick Bird, Dick Borden, Martin Bovey, Arthur Carter, Herb and Lois Crisler, Murl Deusing, Rex R. Elliott, Warren Garst, Cleveland P. Grant, Tom and Arlene Hadley, Fran William Hall, William M. Harlow, Joseph Heidenkamp, Jr., Stuart V. Jewell, William Norman Jupe, N. Paul Kenworthy, Jr., Tom McHugh, Karl H. Maslowski, Alfred G. and Elma Milotte, John Nash Ott, Jr., Olin Sewall Pettingill, Jr., Vincent J. Schaefer, James R. Simon. Music: Paul Smith, Oliver Wallace. First aired in 1984.

MMC IN CONCERT

Executive Producer: Dennis Steinmetz. Supervising Producer: Jack Seifert. Directed by: Dennis Steinmetz. Music Performance Producer: Sarah Elgart. Senior Associate Producer: Bob Williams. Additional Material Directed by: Jimmy Huckaby. Associate Director: Christopher A. Berry. Stage Managers: Virgil Fabian, Dave Cove, Carol Anne Miller, Buck Allen. Art Director: Gentry Akens. Director of Photography: Nick Woolfolk. Music Producer: Michael Egizi. Choreographer: Myles Thoroughgood. Vocal Music: Barbara Bentree. Music Coordinator: Jody Walker-Gordon. Associate Segment Producer: Bently Tittle. Production Associate: Janie Scurti. Production Assistant: Kirsten Cobb. Assistant Art Director: David Hughes. Art Department Coordinator: Holly Roarke. Set Decorator: Daryn Goodall. Set Dressers: Mark Baker, Greg Hale. Construction Coordinator: John Ehrhard. Construction Crew: Hank Lower, Jeff Gilbert. Head Scenic Artist: Michael Brown. Scenic Artists: Cindy J. Collins, Mary Jo Annan. Property Master: Rich West, Mark Cranisky. Stage Coordinator: George Siplin. Stage Hands: Jeff Britt, Johnny Ehrhard. Technical Director: Bill Moore. Video Control: Hans Muster. Audio Mixer: Pat Lucatorto. Videotape: Bill Thomas. Camera Operators: James Arminio, William Chaikowsky, Neal J. Gallagher, Mark Lynch, Melissa Lynch, Mike Navage, Jim Scurti. Utility Camera: Eric Bills, Al Bogert, Lisa Moye, Linda Tutten, Fed Wetherbee, John Wiegman. Studio Coordinator: Tiersa Dennis. Engineer-In-Charge: Ray Lego. Gaffer: J.R. Roberson. Vari-Lite Operator: Harry Sangmeister. Electricians: Russell Curtis, Michael Gooseman, Bruce Blackman, Tim McGuire, Pat Meng, Del Moody, John Peters, Arnold Tucker. PA Mixer: Curt Coniglio. Audio Department: Jim Hope, Sharon Larson, Jim McCabe, Al McGuire. Costume Supervisor: Mellissa Berry. Costume Department: Terri Binion, Marion Barnum, Claudia Combee, Leda Gutierrez, Lori Higgs, Jeanie Sturgeon. Make-up: Regina Perron, Yolanda Winters, Elaine Thomas. Hair: Liz Lavallee, Renee McKenzie, Tish Simpson, Marilyn Yarborough. Business Affairs Manager: Kristin Erickson. Production Accountants: Cathy Clouse, Jennifer Eveleth. Production Coordinators: Carole Beams, Samantha Berger. Producers' Assistants: Lexy Brewer, Tamara Brinkman, Melissa Resch. Audience Coordinator: Andy Calandrino. Audience Warm-up: Bill Timberlake. Transportation Coordinator: Shronda B. Caudle. Production Staff: Wade & Rita Burby, Michael Dougherty, Susan Neely, C. Chris Wright. Post Production Manager: Annie Court. Post Production Supervisor: Jim Weathers. Post Production Audio Supervisor: Nancy Blair. Post Production Associate: Amy Parbury. Editors: Pete Opotowski, Sam Patterson. Assistant Editors: Andy Ebert, Pete Yelverton. Post Production Audio: Rob Hill, Dorrie Batten, Kurt Wagner. Blue Wave Productions, Inc. in association with Les Choux Company. 1-hour format.

MMC ROCKS THE PLANET

Executive Producer: Dennis Steinmetz. Supervising Producer: Jack Seifert. Directed by: Dennis Steinmetz. Writing Supervised by: Tim Grundmann. Written by: Terrie Collins, Christine Ecklund, Keith Hoffman, Fred Newman, Troy Schmidt. Associate Producer: Bob Williams. Music Performance Producer: Sarah Elgart. Associate Director: Christopher A. Berry. Stage Managers: Virgil Fabian, Kelly Hernacki, Dave Cove, Wendy Dawson. Segment Producer: Kitt McLeod. Associate Segment Producer: Bruce Anderson. Art Director: Gentry Akens. Director of Photography: Nick Woolfolk. Acting Coach: Gary Spatz. Choreographer: Myles Thoroughgood. Music Supervisor: Michael Egizi. Vocal Music: Barbara Bentree. Music Coordinator: Melva Akens. Production Associate: Janie Scurti. Production Assistant: Cammille Cavallin. Script Supervisor: Kathleen Connolly. Script Department: Sarah Novin, Dinah Tompkins. Research Assistants: Laura Roberson, Kelli Traub, Heather Whittall. Business Affairs Manager: Leigh Foster. Production Coordinator: Samantha Berger. Production Accountant: Cathy Clouse. Studio Coordinator: Maura Hayes. Audience Coordinator: Jeff Hand. Audience Warm-up: Bill Timberlake. Transportation Coordinator: Kirsten Cobb. Production Staff: Lexy Brewer, Shronda Caudle, Ellen Dunn, Julie Hanson, Mary Joy, John Karliss, Mike Lawrence, Gerald Wu. Art Department Coordinators: Leigh Shipley, T.J. Mannarino. Set Decorator: Daryn Goodall. Set Dressers: Cheryl Johnson, Bently Tittle. Property Master: Rich Swim. Props: Rich West, Mark Cranisky. Stage Hand: George Siplin. Head Carpenter: John Ehrhard. Carpenter:

William Dreggors. Head Scenic Artist: Michael Brown. Scenic Artist: Cindy Collins. Technical Director: Bob Holmes. Video: Hans Muster. Audio Mixer: Jim Fay. Videotape: Bill Thomas, Ric Wetherbee. Camera Operators: James Arminio, Ed Fussell, Neal J. Gallagher, Mark Lynch, Ronnie Smith. Utility: Al Bogert, Rick Foti, Mike Navage, Linda Tutten, John Wiegman. Gaffer: J.R. Roberson. Electricians: Michael Gooseman, Steve Grnya, Jr., Tim McGuire, Del Moody, Steve Owens, John Peters, Arnold Tucker, Paul Vanwormer. PA Mixer: John DeRussey. Audio Department: Jim Hope, Sharon Larson, Jim McCabe, Gary Platt. Engineer-In-Charge: Gary Jones. Wardrobe Supervisor: Mellissa Berry. Wardrobe Department: Marion Barnum, Amy Lewfeldt, Leda Gutierrez, Lori Higgs, Claudia Combee, Trinidad Wilson. Make-up: Regina Perron, Yolanda Winters, Elaine Thomas. Hair: Liz Lavallee, Renee McKenzie, Tish Simpson, Marilyn Yarborough. Post Production Supervisor: Jim Weathers. Post Production Coordinator: Emilie Gibbs. Post Audio Coordinator: Paula S. Warner. Editor: Eddie Johnson. Assistant Editor: Rob Mobley. Post Production Audio: Bob LaMasney, Bob Manahan, Kurt Wagner. Music Production Audio: Gary Platt. Graphic Artist: Eddie Pasquarello. Mouseketeer Casting by: Matt Casella. Set Designed by: Gerri Hariton, Vicki Baral. Blue Wave Productions, Inc. 1-hour format.

Movie Show, The
Written, Produced and Directed by: Gary Rocklen, Jack Weinstein. Associate Producer: Tony Nasch. Edited by: Jeff Okun, Doug Jackson. Production Designer: Paul Peters. Main Title and Animation: Deborah Ross, John Kafka. Movie Palaces Sequence: Bill Morgan, Ken Rudolph. Production Manager/2nd Unit Director: Tony Nasch. Production Coordinator: Dan Zimbaldi. Assistant to the Producers: Kay Gallin. Director of Photography: Frank Harrell. Camera: Wayne Isham. VTR/Sound: Dam Zimbaldi, Tim Kitz. Gaffer: Patric Abaravich. Utility: Frank Morgan. Grip: Richard Perez. Assistant Camera: Chris Evans. Make-up: Andy Cervantes. Production Assistants: Kay Gallin, Mary Neema Barnette. On-line Editor: Steve Brown. Executive Producer: Christopher Miller.

Muppets Take to the High Seas, The: The Making of Muppet Treasure Island
Produced and Directed by: Suzanne McCafferty. Written by: Murray Cohen. Associate Producer: Jane H. Gross. Post Production Supervisor: Jule Green Williams. Production Coordinators: Reneé Stauffer, Chana Pierce. Director of Photography: Edward G. Dadulak. Production Designer: Cynthia Marks. Edited by: Deborah Liekkio. Production Assistants: Kimberly Krohn, Ross Sexson, Nicole Wrathall, R.K. Spencer, Sheri Sedlik, Sarah Steinberg. Make-up Artist: Debbie San Filippo. Audio Mixer: Bruce Peters. Re-recording Mixer: Terry Mader. Gaffer: Kelly Porterfield. Electricians: Jonas Lagunoff, Ashley Reid. Grips: Scott Putnam, Samuel James. Engineer: Bobby White. Video Control: Chuck Riley. Tape Operator: Richard Coniglio. Location Camera: Shawn Maurer. Location Sound: Rick Hays. Effects Editor: Brian Bogle. Graphics: Daniel Camejo. McCafferty & Company Productions Inc. 30-minute format. First aired in 1996.

National Family Safety Test, The
Directed by: Morris Abraham. Produced by: Sandra Moiseeff. Associate Producer: Jeff Shore. Set Designer: Bob Rang. Lighting Consultant: Jim Carne. Music by: Associated Production Music, Jerry A. Ranger. Graphic Designer: Elan Soltes. Associate Director: Allison L. Birnie. Assistant to the Producers: Pamela Cantori. Production Coordinator: Patricia Kavanagh. Stage Managers: Craig Factor, Dean S. Lawrence. Unit Manager: Shar Belanger. Technical Director: Dick Woodka. Audio Mixer: Tom Ancell. Lighting Director: Johnny Franco. Engineer in Charge: Cal Slater. Video Control: Richard Ward. Video Operator: Jack Hamilton. Cameras: Luis Fuerte, Ron Graft, Mike Keeler, Kenneth A. Patterson. Audio Assist: Gerald Zelinger. Set Decorator: John Orr. Property Master: Ralph Leslie. Lighting Utilities: Randy Gomez, Roy La Voise. Camera Utilities: Jim Parent, Andre Radford, Richard Rubalcava. Wardrobe: Jolene Porcaro. Make-up: Christy Newquist. Hair: Victor London. Chron Operator: Bob Anderson. ADDA Operator: Ed Freeman. Videotape Editors: Ron Barr, Cheryl Campsmith, Patrick Clancey. Assistant Videotape Editor: Marty Rosenstock. Re-Recording Mixer: Peter Cole. Acknowledgment: National Safety Council. Executive Producers: Paul Abeyta, Peter Kaikko. A Production of RC Entertainment Inc. 1-hour format. First aired in 1989.

New Vaudevillians, The
Executive Producer: Paul Abeyta. Producers: Peter Kaikko, Sandra Moiseeff. Co-producer: Steve Hansen. Producing Director: Sue Ann Hirschberg. Editors: Fred Raimondi, Larry Bordomaro. Directors of Photography: Ken Patterson, Rob Bonas. 90-minute format. First aired in 1986.

New Vaudevillians Too
Executive Producers: Paul Abeyta, Peter Kaikko. Producer: Sandra Moiseeff. Director: Morris Abraham. First aired in 1987.

New Vaudevillians III
Executive Producers: Paul Abeyta, Peter Kaikko. Produced by: Sandra Moiseeff. Directed by: Dennis Rosenblatt. Associate Producer: Pat Germann. A RC Entertainment Production. 60-minute format. First aired in 1988.

Odds & Ends
Produced by: Chris Miller.

Party All Nite Concert, The: Grad Nite at Walt Disney World
Executive Producer: Brad Lachman. Coordinating Producer: Tom Boles. Directed by: Gary Halvorson. Written by: Gary Bormet. Lighting Designer: Bob Dickinson. Art Director: Jimbo Marshall. Edited by: Michael Polito, Scott Jeffress. Associate Director: Kim Anway. Stage Manager: Buck Allen. Production Manager: Cisco Henson. Additional Music Material by: Alan Ett. Production Supervisor: Dorothy Wong. Script Supervisor: Becky Schraeger. Production Coordinator: Ann Lauterio. Production Assistant: Amy Storti. Production Staff: Grace Cooke, Mark Pineiro, John Karliss, Christine Eichers, Shane Evans, Michael Landry, James Moran, William Portalatin. Unit Manager: Tricia Ferdon. Technical Director: Keith Winikoff. Audio Director: Doug Nelson. Audio Mixers: Don Youngs, Jim McCabe, Murray Siegel. Video: Mark Sanford. Videotape Operator: John Cook. Cameras: Dave Irete, Ron Sheldon, Neil Gallagher, Mark Lynch, Al Camoin, Bob Vandoran. Location Lighting Director: Todd Nichols. Varilite Operator: John Morgan. Brad Lachman Productions, Inc. 1-hour format.

Party, The: In Concert
Executive Producer: Steve Clements. Produced & Directed by: Joe Carolei. Supervising Producer: Jean Wiegman. Associate Producer: Tom Boles. Art Director: Randy Foster. Lighting Designer: Olin Younger. Program Consultant: David Garfinkle. Associate Director: Judi Elterman. Choreographer: Jeff Andrews. Production Supervisor: Mellissa Blessing Weiss. Production Coordinators: Bruce Anderson, Hugh Camargo. Assistant Art Director: Tim Colohan. Stage Manager: Hank Niemark, Keith Richmond. Technical Director: Clay Jacobsen. Cameras: Ted Ashton, Bill Chaikowsky, Bob Keyes, Bruce Oldham, Kenny Patterson, Hector Ramirez. Camera Utilities: Dan Andreeson, Randy Gomez, Mike Wilson. Audio Mixer: Doug Nelson. Audio Assist: Jeff Fecteau. Video: Stuewe. Edited by: David Seeger. Additional Editor: Steve Ball. Graphic Artists: Terri Yarbrow, Today Person. Wardrobe Consultant: Mellissa Berry. Wardrobe Supervisor: Terri Binion. Music Consultant: Dana Salyers. Hair Stylist: Tish Simpson. Make-up Artist: Karen Knop. Production Staff: Damon Greenfield, Robert Kaufman. Production Accountant: Cathy Clouse. Additional Footage Provided by: Nancy Hale. Acknowledgments: Dennis Bickel, Jeanne Park, Patricia McCoy. Steve Clements Productions. 1-hour format. First aired in 1990.

Pop Quiz
Produced by: Amy Weintraub. Directed by: R.J. DeMaio. Written by: Richard Hadley. Weintraub Prods. 30-minute format. First aired in 1985.

PRAIRIE HOME COMPANION, A: THE SECOND ANNUAL FAREWELL PERFORMANCE
Executive Producer: Garrison Keillor. Executive Co-Producer: Art Wolff. Producers: Bill Siegler, Richard Kibler. A Production of Minnesota Public Radio in association with Radio City Music Hall Television and Silverlake Productions. 2-1/2 hour format. First aired in 1988.

THE THIRD ANNUAL FAREWELL PERFORMANCE
Producer: Geoffrey Drummond. A Production of Minnesota Public Radio in association with Geoffrey Drummond. 90-minute format. First aired in 1990.

PRESIDENTIAL INAUGURATION CELEBRATION FOR CHILDREN, THE
Executive Producers: Jerry Hughes, Patrick Davidson. Supervising Producer: Michael Petok. Directed by: Hugh Martin. Written by: Bill Prady. *Adventures in Wonderland* Sketch Written by: Daryl Busby, Tom J. Astle. Associate Producers: Susan McCoy, Danny Harris. Production Designers: Joe Stewart, John Shaffner. Lighting Designer: Bill Klages. Production Supervisor: Sandra Restrepo. Script Coordinators: Susan Leeds, Marie Yamamoto. Production Coordinators: Ann King, Alison Sherman. Associate Director: Lynn Klugman. Stage Managers: Richard Arthur Dampf, Mavis Davis, Dean Gordon, Marilyn Seabury, Debbie Williams. Talent Coordinator: Marisa Costa. Technical Director: Terry Donohue. Audio: Paul Sandweiss. Cameras: Rick Alexander, Alan Anesto, Juan Barrera, Chris Dahl, Pat Gleason, Manny Gutierrez, Mike Lieberman, Ron Washburn. Acknowledgment: The John F. Kennedy Center for The Performing Arts, John D. Wolfensohn, Chairman. Executive Producer for The Presidential Inaugural Committee: Markie Post. A Hughes Television Production in association with Brad Lachman Productions, Inc. One-hour format. First aired in 1993.

PRESIDENTIAL INAUGURAL CELEBRATION FOR YOUTH, THE
Executive Producer: Brad Lachman. Co-Executive Producer: Patrick Davidson. Supervising Producer: Michael Petok. Directed by: Paul Miller. Written by: Garry Bormet. Associate Producer: Danny Harris. Production Designers: Joe Stewart, John Shaffner. Lighting Designer: Bill Klages. Music Conducted and Supervised by: George Duke. Executive in Charge of Talent: Debi Genovese. Segment Producers: Andrew Lachman, Robin Sestero, Andy Thomas, Rob Wilson. Production Supervisor: Mary Braun. Script Coordinators: Daniela Davis, Marie Yamamoto. Additional Music Arranged and Produced by: George Duke. Production Coordinator: James Dubose, Ann King, Alison Sherman. Associate Director: Christine Clark. Stage Managers: Debbie Williams, Mavis Davis, Dean Gordon, Marilyn Seabury, Richard Arthur Dampf. *Mickey Mouse Club* Performance Staged and Choreographed by: Sarah Elgart, Myles Thoroughgood. Talent Coordinator: Lisa Weisner. Technical Director: Terry Donohue. Audio: Paul Sandweiss. Cameras: Rick Alexander, Juan Barrera, Chris Dahl, Pat Gleason, Manny Guttierrez, Mike Lieberman, Alain Onesto, Ron Washburn. Acknowledgments: The John F. Kennedy Center for The Performing Arts; James D. Wolfensohn. Executive Producer for the Presidential Inaugural Committee: Markie Post. First aired in 1993. 70-minute format.

PRETTY GOOD NIGHT AT CARNEGIE HALL, A
Produced by: Bill Siegler, Richard Kilbur. A Production of Minnesota Public Radio in association with Silverlake Productions. 90-minute format. First aired in 1989.

RED RIDING HOOD
Director of Photography: Tom Koester. Edited by: Toby Brown, A.C.E. Production Designed by: Ed Nunnery. Music by: Dan Kuramoto. Written by: Paul Lally. Produced by: Elizabeth Lynch-Brown, Catherine C. Rocca. Directed by: Harrison Ellenshaw. Costume Design by: Linnea Olson. Make-up Designed by: Felice Fassnacht. Assistant Director: Lynda Lemon. Post Production Supervisor: Christopher Keith. Sound Mixer: Walter S. Hoylman. Boom Operator: Mychal D. Smith. Re-recording Mixer: William L. Schlegal. Sound Editors: Sam Horta, Denise Horta. Gaffer: Donald Giroux. Key

Grip: Michael Molnar. Assistant Camera: Margaret Duke. Script Supervisor: Sheila Carter. Electrician: Clark Hunter. Best Boy: Stephen Shapiro. Set Construction: Jack McIntosh, Tim Sessions. Matte Artist: Alan Short. Production Assistant: Victor Bartholetti.

RICK NELSON: A BROTHER REMEMBERS
Written by: Phil Savenick. Directed by: David Nelson. Producer: Phil Savenick. Associate Producer: Sandra Perlstein. Edited by: Penny Johnson, Robert P. Schneider. Montage Sequences: Harry Arends. Clearance Administrator: Vicki Grimsland. *Casablanca Productions* Producer: Gary Geweniger. Stage Manager: Scott Luhrsen. Lighting Director: Tom Harvey. Set Designer: Allen Jones. Production Secretary: Holly Vega. Production Assistants: Eric Nelson, Lisa Boags. Researchers: James Austin, Ron Furmanek, Paul Surratt. Voice-over Narration: Chuck Woolery. Executive Producer: David Nelson. A Nelson Co./Casablanca Production. 60-minute format. First aired in 1987.

RINGO STARR: GOING HOME
Executive Producers: Ringo Starr, David Fishof, Hilary Gerrard. Produced and Directed by: Stanley Dorfman. A Roccabella Inc. Production in association with The Disney Channel and Barron Management Ltd. 1-hour format.

ROCK 'N TOONTOWN
Produced by: Patrick Davidson. Directed by: Steve Purcell. Written by: Troy Schmidt. Co-Producers: Sharon Nagata, Bart Roen. Associate Producer: Tim Gaydos. Art Director: Mark Laskowski. Choreographer: Nancy Gregory. Production Manager: John Foy. Talent Coordinator: David Perler. Production Coordinator: Michelle LeTarte. Costumer: Madeline Kozlowski. Videotape Editors: Ray J. Pages, Steve Purcell. Technical Director: Gene Crowe. Director of Photography: James L. Moody. Concert Lighting Designer: Jeff Ravitz. Lighting Director: Marc Meisenheimer. Camera Operators: Brian Pratt, Ted Ashton, Edgar de la Espriella, Bob Keys, Allen Merriweather, Dennis Turner, Jerry Watson. Stage Managers: Debbie Williams, Danny Harris. Audio: Toby Foster, Russ Simon, Sandy Fellerman. Video: John Palacio, Jr. Re-Recording Mixer: Troy Smith. Audio Assistant: Steve Michel. Production Assistants: Jonathan Stone, Troy A. Norton. Songs by: Craig Taubman, Michael Turner. Co-Executive Producer: Ken Fritz. Executive Producer: Patrick Davidson. Blue Streak Productions. 30-minute format.

ROOTS OF GOOFY, THE
Prepared for Television by: Frank Brandt, Ed Ropolo. *The Roots of Goofy* Music and Lyrics by: Galen Brandt. Video Tape Editor: Darryl Sutton. Post Production Supervisor: Don Asquith. Prepared Especially for Television by: Left Coast Television, Inc. 90-minute format. First used in 1984.

SAMANTHA SMITH GOES TO WASHINGTON . . . CAMPAIGN '84
Executive Producer: Arnold Shapiro. Produced by: Jean O'Neill. Consultant: Gerald Rafshoon. 90-minute format. First aired in 1984.

SEBASTIAN'S CARIBBEAN JAMBOREE
Director: Steve Purcell. Writers: Alan Silberberg, Jeff Zimmer. Producer: Tammara Wells. Lighting Directors: Todd Nichols, Nick Woolfolk. Head Cameraman: Lynn Rabren. Art Director: Jimbo Marshall. Editor: Steve Purcell. Choreographer: Nancy Gregory. Production Manager: Clay Newbill. Assistant Directors: Andy Felcher, Gary Rogers. Stage Manager: Josh Burger. Script Supervisor: Jonna Sherman. Camera Operators: Richie Banales, Rudy Carames, Bruce Dworsky, Tom Galloway, Kevin Garrison, Roger Lynch, Steve Martyniuk, Kim Scurti, Melissa Wright. Sound: Jim Fay, Ned Hall. Re-recording Mixer: Peter Cole. Production Coordinator: Maria Caccavo. Video Head: Larry Gaetano. Gaffers: Terry Neudecker, J.R. Robinson. Key Grip: Steve Gryna. Audio Re-recording: Troy Smith, Chris Trent, Mike Robie. Wardrobe: Carolyn Desert. Make-up/Hair: Paulette Joiner, Tish Simpson, Liz Spang. Additional Choreography: Julie Arenal. Main Title Design: Bob Gautieri. Casting: Ashley Dane Michaels.

Acknowledgments: Les Perkins, Paula Sigman. A One Heart Production. 30-minute format. First aired in 1991.

Sebastian's Party Gras
Executive Producer: Patrick Davidson. Directed by: Steve Purcell. Written by: Katharine Sloan. Associate Director: Steve Ligerman. Art Director: Jimbo Marshall. Edited by: Steve Purcell. Choreographer: Nancy Gregory. Lighting Directors: Todd Nichols, Nick Woolfolk. Head Camera Operator: Lynn Rabren. Audio: Ned Hall. Production Manager: Geriann Baker-Decker. Stage Manager: Dave Cove. Script Supervisor: Sharon Nagata. Camera Operators: Richie Banales, Nina Bartlett, Jim Coglinese, Mark Lynch, Roger Lynch, Keevan Saddock, Melissa Wright. Re-recording Mixer: Peter Cole. Audio Re-recording: John Walker, Troy Smith, Chris Trent. Production Supervisor: Michelle LeTarte. Production Coordinator: Maura Akos. Technical Director: Mike Rubin. Technical Supervisor: Larry Gaetano. Gaffers: Gary Bristow, Rick Campbell, Al Meyers. Wardrobe: Terri Binion. Make-up/Hair: Angie Margeson, Anita Polin, Luisa Williams, Yolanda Winters. Production Assistants: Bethany Berry, Stacy Kennington, Kurt Kulhanek, Heather Parker, Don Stables, Tobert Teinowitz, Steve Wein. Main Title Design: Bob Gautieri. All songs from *Sebastian's Party Gras*. Record Producer: Shepard Stein. Executive in Charge of Production: Steve Ligerman. Blue Streak Productions. 30-minute format. First aired in 1991.

Seeing Spots
Produced by: Willard Caroll. Produced by Hyperion Entertainment, Inc.

Smithsonian Salutes Disney Music, The
Music Director: David Bishop. Executive Producer: Jerry Hughes. Director: Paul Lally. Editor: Catherine Hughes. Associate Producer: Linda Blythe. Lighting Director: David M. Clark. Technical Supervisor: Doug Berry. Audio: Terry Kulcher. Camera: Rege Becker, Ed Crosby, Charlie Huntly, Ken Patterson, Fred Roth, Timothy J. Walbert. Videotape: Bill Lorenz, Mark Adelsheim. Production Coordinators: David Shack, Geoff Manifold. Production Assistants: Felicia Barkley, Nancy Shack, Quintin O'Brien. Videotape Editor: Paul Byers. Titles: Gayle Hess. Rerecording Mixer: Aaron Baron. *For the Smithsonian Institution:* Director, National Museum of American History: Roger G. Kennedy. Producer: Theodore S. Chapin. Stage Director: Susan H. Schulman. With: Renee Kortum, Anne Walton, B.J. Davis. Acknowledgments: Frank Nelson Doubleday Lecture-Performance Series, Bourne Music Publishing Co., National Park Service, National Capitol Region, United States Park Police. A Hughes Television Production. First aired in 1987.

Snow White: Singin', Dancin', Heigh Ho
Produced and Directed by: Steve Hirsen. Co-Producer: Edward Lammi. Associate Director: Kent Weed. Stage Managers: Steven J. Santos, Paul Forrest. Lighting Director: Olin Younger. Production Manager: Susan Ross. Production Supervisor: Karen Apple. Technical Director: Ken Shapiro. Video: Tom Tcimpidis. Cameras: Ted Ashton, Steve Conant, Larry Heider, Dave Hilmer, Kenneth A. Patterson. Audio: Doug Nelson. Videotape: Larry Meyers. Editor: Mike Polito. Production Secretary: Lisa Palazzo Liem. Production Assistant: Tom Vogel. Make-up: Nina Kent. *For Disneyland* Produced for the Stage by: Dennis Despie. Original Performance Created and Staged by: Barnette Ricci. Choreography by: Keri Keaney, Roy Luthringer, Tam Warner, Barnette Ricci. Music Director and Original Composition by: Bruce Healy. Costumes Designed by: Alyja Kalinich. Announcer: Jack Wagner. Hirsen Productions. 30-minute format. First aired in 1987.

So You're Afraid to Fly
Written and Directed by: Harrison Ellenshaw. Produced by: Harrison Ellenshaw, Christopher Keith. Camera: Ted Ashton. Gaffer: Steve Litt. Sound: Larry Lasota. Narrator: Byron Keith. Executive Producer: Christopher Miller. Videotape Editor: Joe Bella. Mixer: Larry Sullivan. Synthesizer: Dan Kuramoto. Animators: Dan Lasseter, Mike Show, Gary Trousdale, Pat Ventura. Animation Camera: Mike Beard, Douglas Eby. Production Assistant: Lynda Lemon. First aired in 1983.

Strange Companions
Executive Producer: Ron Miller. Director of Photography: John Hora. Teleplay by: Calvin Clements, Jr. Based on the book *Strange Companion: A Story of Survival* by: Dayton Hyde. Directed and Produced by: Frank Zuniga. Art Directors: Douglas Higgins, Keith Pepper. Editor: Toby Brown, A.C.E. Music: Robert F. Brunner. Unit Production Manager: Paul Tucker. First Assistant Director: Gordon Mark. Second Assistant Director: Bill Mizel. Assistant to the Producer: Marc Stirdivant. Production Coordinator: Rolf Darbo. Sound: Herb Taylor. Sound Mixer: Ralph Parker. Costumes: Christopher Ryan. Make-up: Phyllis Newman. Sound Editor: Ben F. Henricks. Music Editor: Jack Wadsworth. Special Effects: John Thomas, Cliff Wenger, Lee Routley. Field Producer: Pisces Productions, Inc. Animal Supervision by: Mark Weiner, Bob Bise, Madelyn Klein, Sam Vaughn. Animals Furnished by: Steve Martin's Working Wildlife, Bob Bise's Wild Wings. 90-minute format. First aired in 1987.

Time for Grandparents, A
Written and Produced by: Terry Strauss. Directed and Edited by: Wendy Blair Slick. Director of Photography: Jerry Slick. Gaffer: Tom Schnitzler. Production Manager: Blanche Chase. Sound: Steve Balick. Research Assistants: Nancy Rice, Stephanie Clark. Editing Assistant: Jenny Stein. Music: Andy Kuhlberg. Dramatic Performance and Vocals: Sarah Jane Norris. Sound: Eliot Mazer. Graphic Design: Kevin O'Farrell. Narrator: Sydney Walker. A Terry Strauss Production. One-hour format. First aired in 1984.

Too Smart for Strangers
Consultants: Michael W. Agopian, Ph.D., Hershel K. Swinger, Ph.D., Detective Gary Lyon, Find the Children, Inc. Writer: Betty G. Birney. *Winnie the Pooh* Sequences Produced by: Left Coast Television, Inc. Producer: Frank Brandt. Director: Philip F. Messina. Director of Photography/Lighting Director: James Swift. Choreographer: Denise McKenna. Production Manager: George Cook. Production Coordinator: Suzie Galler. Production Assistant: Steve Heltsley. Production Stage Manager: Ricky Stoutland. Script Supervisor: Laurette Healey. Costumes: Alchemy II. Character Wardrobe Designed by: Kristin Nelson. Costume Supervisors: Elaine Levi, Lizbeth Gower, Bonnie Sinclair. Technical Supervisor: Randy Simpler. Art Director: James Higginson. Art Department: Kelle Schaefle, Dan Brown, Tom Reed. Video Control: Christopher Gray. Video Tape Editor: Dexter Padgitt. Cameramen: Michael Tribble, Paul Dillingham. Production Stage Crew: Charlie Edwards, Peter Wessel, Bruno Acalinas, Nick Cline, Bruce Swift. Production Secretary: Carolyn Neal. Assistants to the Producer: Christine Gorewit, Susan Kydd, David Parish. *Live Action Sequences* Director: Ron Underwood. Director of Photography: Virgil Harper. Production Manager: Debra T. Smith. Art Director: Chava Danielson. Editor: Millie Paul. Video Engineer: Bob Worden. Assistant Camera: Tom Kantrud. Gaffer: Michael Bolner. Lighting Crew: Andy Roach, Ric Delgado, William W. Mann. Grips: Jack Tankard, Stephen B. Martinez. Boom Operator: Ed Palacios. Production Assistants: Leslie Ross Crane, John Beckman, Scott L. Rose. Music Composed by: Phil Baron, Robin Frederick, Will Ryan. Music Arranged by: John Debney. Casting: Universal Creative Management. A Cornerstone Production. Executive Producer: William H. Shippey. 1-hour format. First aired in 1985.

Tribute to Mom, A
Prepared for The Disney Channel by: Film Landa, Inc. Edited by: Fausto Sanchez. With the Talent of Ilene Woods. *Father's Day Off* Music: Paul Smith. Song *Your Mother and Mine:* Sammy Fain, Sammy Cahn. The song *The Bare Necessities* sung by: Phil Harris. Narrator: Charles Aidman. 90-minute format. First aired in 1984

Trisha Yearwood: The Song Remembers When
Director: Steve Purcell. Producer: Joseph Sassone. Director of Photography: Daniel Pearl. Musical Director: Garth Fundis. Executive Producer: Steven H. Galloway. Produced by: MCA Music Entertainment Group in association with The Disney Channel.

TWENTIETH CENTURY FADS
Produced by: Kevin Rafferty

VACATIONING WITH MICKEY AND FRIENDS
Produced by: Frank Brandt. Prepared for Television by: Left Coast Television, Inc. 90-minute format. First aired in 1988.

VIDEOPOLIS: STARTRACKS
Executive Producer: Brad Lachman. Associate Producers: Garry Bormet, Dan Dobson. Written by: Garry Bormet, Steve Ligerman. Directed by: Bill Davis, Gary Halvorson. Executive in Charge of Production: Steve Ligerman. Associate Producer: Dan Dobson. Talent Executive: Vince Calandra. Assistant to the Producers: Wayne Damore. Associate Director: Sharon Trojan. Edited by: Michael Polito. Post Production Audio: David Fluhr, Craig Porter. Post Production Coordinator: Tom Draper. Production Staff: Lisa McConnell, Robert Douglas. Segment Director: Paul Hoen. Stage Manager: Steve Ligerman. Brad Lachman Productions, Inc. 30-minute format. First aired in 1989.

WALT DISNEY COMPANY PRESENTS THE AMERICAN TEACHER AWARDS, THE
Produced by: Gary Smith, Dwight Hemion. Co-Produced by: Patrick Davidson. Directed by: Dwight Hemion. Written by: Buz Kohan, Gary Smith. Associate Producers: Bill Bracken, Ricky Kirshner. Production Designer: Rene Lagler. Musical Director: Ian Fraser. Choreographer: Jim Bates. Lighting Designer: Bob Dickinson. Costume Designers: Pete Menefee, Ret Turner. Talent Executive: Vince Calandra, Sr. Associate Director: Allan Kartun. *I Have Come to Learn* Music by: Larry Grossman. Lyrics by: Buzz Cohan. Profiles Narrated by: Mason Adams. Executive Producer: Gary Smith. Smith-Hemion Productions. 3-hour format.

1990 Presenters: Carol Burnett, Kirk Cameron, Tony Danza, Danny DeVito, Valerie Harper, Goldie Hawn, Edward James Olmos, Rhea Perlman, Pat Riley, Tom Selleck, Jon Voight, Robin Williams, Oprah Winfrey, Barbara Bush, Michael Eisner. Sylvia Anne Washburn, a third-grade teacher from Toledo, Ohio, was chosen as the teacher of the year. Ian Fraser, Bill Byers and J. Hill won an Emmy award for Music Direction for this Special.

1991 Presenters: Tony Danza, Melanie Griffith, Don Johnson, Michelle Lee, Jay Leno, Jason Priestly, Jane Seymour, Arnold Schwarzenegger, Ben Vereen, Jon Voight, Betty White, Michael Eisner. The winner was Edward M. Schroeder, an English teacher from Coolidge Junior High School in Granite City, Illinois.

1992 Presenters: Paula Abdul, Paul Anka, Johnny Carson, Tony Danza, Morgan Freeman, Melanie Griffith, Mark Harmon, Dustin Hoffman, Don Johnson, Jay Leno, Luke Perry, John Ritter, Michael Eisner. The winner was Rafe Esquith, an elementary school teacher from South Central Los Angeles.

1993 Presenters: Sean Astin, Patti Austin, Debby Boone, Susan Dey, Phil Donahue, Nancy Dussault, Melanie Griffith, Amy Irving, Don Johnson, Joey Lawrence, Ed McMahon, Bill Nye, Sinbad, Harry Smith, Marlo Thomas, Lindsay Wagner, Michael Eisner. During the show it was announced that the winner was Leta Andrews, an athletic coach. Afterwards, it was discovered that a voting error had occurred and general elementary teacher Patricia Ann "Pann" Baltz was named as co-winner.

1994 Presenters: Alan Alda, Debbie Allen, Anita Baker, Beau Bridges, Jackson Browne, Gabrielle Carteris, Cindy Crawford, Tony Danza, Jill Eikenberry, Melanie Griffith, Mel Harris, Marlee Matlin, Harry Smith, Michael Tucker, Janine Turner, Billy Dee Williams, Paula Zahn, Michael Eisner. The winner was Huong Tran Nguyen from Long Beach, California.

1995 Presenters: Jane Alexander, Gabrielle Carteris, Richard Dreyfuss, Hector Elizondo, Harrison Ford, Kathy Ireland, Richard Karn, Harry Smith, Paul Winfield, Paula Zahn, Vice President Al Gore. The winner was Richard Ruffalo from New Jersey.

WALT DISNEY WORLD: A DREAM COME TRUE
Co-Producers: Peter Kaikko, Sandra Moseef. RC Entertainment, Inc. 90-minute format. Aired on 10/04/86.

WALT DISNEY WORLD: PAST, PRESENT, AND FUTURE
Executive Producer: Patrick Davidson. Directed by: Joe Carolei. Written by: Mike Bonifer. Researcher: Bart Roen. Segment Producer: Bob Gautieri. Editor: Ray Pages. Production Manager: Geriann Baker-Decker. Production Coordinator: Michelle LeTarte. Script PA: Kimber Huckaby. Stage Manager: Kelly Hernacki. Production Assistants: Bethany Berry, Kurt Kulhanek, Don Stables, Steve Wein. Executive in Charge of Production: Steve Ligerman. Blue Streak Productions. 1-hour format. First aired in 1991.

WAPATULA
Directed by: Bruce Seth Green. Written by: Michael Bonifer, L.G. Weaver. Production Manager: Marc Gaede. Director of Photography: Ted Ashton. Casting Director: Dennis Cornell. Editor: John Blizek. Art Director: Peter Clemens. Location Manager: Lisa Shuart. Music: Bruce Kernohan. Script Supervisor: Sharon Hagen. Costume Designer: Taryn De Chellis. Talent Coordinator: Daryl Kass. Audio: Stu Fox. Researcher: Lisa Stewart. Still Photographer: Damon Webster. Property Master: Bruce Kernohan. Assistant Costumer: Jean Hart. 2nd Camera: Stan Taylor. Assistant Property: Lorraine Schweizer. Graphics: Paul Olsen. Controller: Karen Locke. Make-up: Julie Purcell. Hair: Ramona Joy. Key Grip: Steve Litt. Lighting Director: Richard Brown. Boom Operator: Michael Rizzolo. Assistant to the Producers: Barbara Dreyfuss. Production Assistants: David Levinson, Bob Johnson. Extra Casting: Judi's Casting. Special Effects: John Peyser. Transportation Captain: Phil Shaw. Executive in Charge of Production: Barry Cahn. Produced by: Peter Locke, Donald Kushner. An Acme Production. 30-minute format. First aired in 1985.

WHALE'S TOOTH, THE
Produced and Directed by: Roy Edward Disney. Written by: Ben Masselink. Narration by: Norman Wright. Narrated by: Don Ho. Editor: Toby Brown, A.C.E. Music: Robert F. Brunner. Sound: Herb Taylor. Production Coordinator: Erwin L. Verity. *For Milas Hinshaw Productions, Inc.* Field producer: Milas Hinshaw. Photography: Dick Thomsett, Casey Hotchkiss. Production Supervisor: Brian Burton. Location Manager: Carmen Ribera. First aired in 1986.

WHERE DID ALL MY MONEY GO?
Hosted by: Aljean Harmetz. Produced by: Bruce Franchini, Aljean Harmetz. Directed by: Sean Stapely. Written by: Richard S. Harmetz. Associate Producer: Esther Kwan. Director of Photography: Thomas Tucker. Technical Director: David Lezynzky. Editor: Norman Levy. Post Production Audio: Vance Frost. Production Assistant: Patricia St. Anthony. Gaffers: James Childers, Tom Farmer, Michael Railsback, Gary Sanders. Grip: Todd Sheets.

WHERE THE TOYS COME FROM
Written and Directed by: Theodore Thomas. Associate Producers: Kuniko Okubo, Paul Deason. Photographed by: Christopher Fryman, Ed Winkle. Edited by: Lisa Palattella. Music by: Akiko Yano. Music Arranged by: Ryuichi Sakamoto. Sound: Hiroshi Yamashita. Lighting: Masayuki Masuda, John Bonfield. Assistant Camera: Saburo Ueda, Clint Dougherty. Best Boy: Roger Sassen. Key Grip: John Savka. Production Assistant: Blaine Bartell. Assistant Editor: Nancy Richardson. Music Editor: Jack Tillar. Sound Effects and Recording: Neiman-Tillar Associates. Story Sketch: Joseph Griffith. Peepers and Zoom Customizing: Carla Fallberg. Special Effects: Larry Wright. *Omoocha No Cha Cha Cha* Composed by: Nobuyoshi Koshibe. English Lyrics by: Pete Barakan. Antique Toys from the Collection of Ward Kimball. Produced by: Theodore Thomas. Theodore Thomas Productions.

WHO'S IN CHARGE HERE?: THE RONN LUCAS SPECIAL
Produced and Directed by: Michael Fowlkes, Kin Dawson. Written by: Ronn Lucas. Special Written Material by: Richard Jamison, Bobby Herbeck. Associate Producer: Anne Avis. Consulting Producer: Jim Yukich. Directors of Photography: Richard Ocean, Lee Rose. Gaffer: Chris Phenpimon. Art Director: Ginni Barr. Editor: Howard Scott Stein. Original Music Composed and Recorded by: Parmer Fuller. Casting by: Bev-

erly Long & Associates. Stage Manager: Cameron Blake. Mr. Lucas' Costume Design by: Mary Openshaw. Wardrobe: Scott Barton. Set Designer: Alison Rupp. Make-up Artist and Hair Stylist: Wendy Hogan. Production Assistant: Peter Clark. Audio & Recording Engineers: Ed Greene, Barton Chiate. Video Control: Mark Sanford. Cameras: Hector Ramirez, Katherine Kitaoka, Dave Levisohn, Joseph Epperson, Bob Keys. Post Production Audio: Carroll Pratt. Curtis Theatre Coordinator: Scott Riordan. Executive Producer: Michael Clark. Corl Street Entertainment, Inc. 1-hour format. First aired in 1988.

WISE ONE, THE
Produced by: Roy Edward Disney. Director of Photography: William Mendenhall. Teleplay by: Gerald Pearce, Roy Edward Disney. Based on the book by: Frank Conibear, J. L. Walsh. Directed by: Frank Zuniga. Film Editor: Norman R. Palmer, A.C.E. Production Managers/Assistant Directors: Frank Beetson, Jr., Phillip B. Patton. Music: Robert F. Brunner. Sound: Herb Taylor. Production Coordinator: Rolf Darbo. Costumes: Pat Cummings. Make-up: Charlene Roberson. Animals Supplied by: Robert Bise, Steve Martin. Wildlife Material: Austin McKinney, John Chesko, Larry Secrist, Robert Keeston, Jeffrey Aas, Roy Patrick Disney. First aired in 1986.

The Disney Channel Films

ANNE OF AVONLEA: THE CONTINUING STORY OF ANNE OF GREEN GABLES
A Kevin Sullivan Production. Director of Photography: Marc Champion. Art Direction: Susan Longmire. Costume Design: Martha Mann. Casting: Diane Polley, Ann Tait. Based on the novels *Anne of Avonlea, Anne of the Island* and *Anne of Windy Poplars* by: Lucy Maud Montgomery. Executives in Charge of Production for Disney Channel: Cathy Johnson. For Wonderworks: Jay Rayvid. For CBC: Nada Harcourt. Executive Producers: Trudy Grant, Kevin Sullivan. Line Producer: Duane Howard. Edited by: Mairin Wilkinson, James Lahti. Music Composed and Conducted by: Hagood Hardy. Produced, Written and Directed by: Kevin Sullivan. Production Manager: David Shepherd. Set Decorator: Christine MacLean. Hair Design: Judi Cooper-Sealy. Make-up: Linda Preston. Unit/Location Manager: Sherry Cohen. 1st Assistant Director: David McAree. 2nd Assistant Director: Don Brough. 3rd Assistant Director: Myron Hoffert. Trainee Assistant Director: Chris Ball. Script Supervisor: Kathyrn Buck. Production Coordinator: Therese Paquette. Production Secretary: Brian Parker. Production Assistants: Xavier Villada, Paula Fleck. 1st Assistant Camera: Phillippe Champion. 2nd Assistant Camera: Chris Thompson. Camera Trainees: Phil Anderson, Anne Strange. Still Photography: Michaelin McDermott. 2nd Unit Photography: Robin Miller, Phillip Earnshaw, Barry Bergthorson. Steadicam: Bob Crone. Assistant Set Decorator: Jane Manchee. 2nd Assistant Set Decorators: Tom Reid, Ted Whelan. Prop Master: Ed Hanna. Assistant Props: Lee Wildgen. Construction Manager: John Banksone. Head Wardrobe Coordinator: Sherry McMorran. Wardrobe Mistress: Maggie Thomas. Wardrobe Assistants: Julia Jones, Anita Simard, Kim Sisson, Margaret Forsyth, Eva Richter. Wardrobe Construction: Isabelle Kaczmarek. Assistant Make-up: Donald Mowat. Hair Dressers: Jenny Bennicke, Ivan Lynch. Sound Recording: Stuart French. Boom Operator: Alan Scarth. Gaffer: Roger Bate. Best Boy: David Fisher. Generator Operator: Geoffrey Wilkinson. Electrician: Thomas Bate. Key Grip: Ian Henderson. 3rd Grip: John Westerlaken. Transportation Coordinator: David Chudnovsky. Driver Captains: Jerome McCann, Tom Pinteric. Special Effects: Laird McMurray. Extras Casting: Rose Lewis. Livestock/Period Vehicles: Lionel Purcell. Assistant Editor: Ben Wilkinson. ADR Editor: Jeremy McLaverty. ADR Assistant Editor: Donna Powell. Foley Artist: Reid Atherton. Foley Assistants: Bonnie Sharrat, Mhairi Kerr. Sound Mixers: Wally Weaver, Daniel Pellbrin. Colorist: Kim Krause. Video Editor: Bernie Clayton. *Prince Edward Island Unit* Location Manager: Brian Ramsay. Wardrobe Dressers: Krista Wells, Sharon Pretty. Production Assistants: Tim Woolner, Randy McAndrew, Wendy Ader. Transportation Captain: George Brookins. Camera Assistant: Stuart Shikatani. Grip: Greg Palermo. Filmed on location at Penryn Park, Port Hope, Southern Ontario, and on Prince Edward Island, Canada. Produced by: Anne of Green Gables II Productions (1986) Inc., in association with The Disney Channel, PBS' *WonderWorks*, The Canadian Broadcasting Co., Channel Four and with participation of Telefilm Canada. 1-hour format. Four episodes. First aired in 1987.

BACK HOME
Screenplay by: David Wood. From the Book by: Michelle Magorian. Director of Photography: Witold Stok. Production Designer: Tim Hutchison. Costume Designer: Jenny Beavan. Edited by: Peter Coulson. Music Composed by: Ilona Sekacz. Executive in Charge of Production: Dickie Bamber. Co-Producer for Verronmead: Maureen Harter. Executive Producers: David R. Ginsburg, Graham Benson. Produced by: J. Nigel Pickard. Directed by: Piers Haggard. Development Executive for Citadel Entertainment: Tom Patricia. Executive in Charge of Production for The Disney Channel: Cathy Johnson. Casting U.K.: Anne Henderson. Casting U.S.: Victoria Burrows, Mark Tillman. Production Supervisor: Peter Lancaster. Location Managers: Nigel Gostelow, Sally Shewring. 1st Assistant Director: Chris Hall. 2nd Assistant Director: Rupert Ryle-Hodges. Script Supervisor: Angele Noakes. Production Co-ordinator: Margaret Adams. TVS Contact: Christine Morris. Producer's Assistant: Hilary Baverstock. TVS Script Executive: Corinne Cartier. Camera Operator: Rodrigo Gutierrez. Focus: Nick Lowin. Sound Recordist: Colin Charles. Boom Operator: David Pearson. Make-up and Hair: Sally Harrison, Stella O'Farrell. Wardrobe Master: Kenny Crouch. Art Director: Mark Raggett. Gaffer: Larry Prinz. Props: John Hogan, Daryl Series, Paul Taylor. Sound Editor: John Ireland. Assistant Editor: Angelica Landry. Dubbing Mixer: Brian Saunders. Stills: David Farrell, Tony Nutley. Special Effects: Effects Associates. Publicist: Brian Seeney. Production Accountant: Joan Murphy. Acknowledgment: Staff and Pupils of St. Crispin's School, Wokingham. Produced by TVS Films Verronmead in association with Citadel Entertainment and The Disney Channel for TVS Television. First aired in 1990.

BACK TO HANNIBAL: THE RETURN OF TOM SAWYER AND HUCKLEBERRY FINN
Original Score by: Lee Holdridge. Edited by: Richard E. Rabjohn. Production Designer: Robert J. Bacon. Director of Photography: James W. Roberson. Co-Producer: Thomas Lane. Produced by: Hugh Benson. Written by: Roy Johansen. Directed by: Paul Krasny. Casting Executive: Eddie Foy III. Unit Production Manager: Mitchell Gamson. 1st Assistant Director: Steven Fisher. 2nd Assistant Director: Alexander Ellis. Missouri Casting: Carrie Houk. Costume Designer: Donna Roberts. Set Decorator: W. Joseph Kroesser. Property Master: Kenneth Orme. Wardrobe Supervisor: Julene McKinney. Make-up & Hair Design: Lynn Del Kail. Key Make-up: Cheryl Ann Markowitz. Key Hair Stylist: Laura Connolly. Script Supervisor: Sally J. Roddy. Production Coordinator: Lisa Helfrich. Production Sound Mixer: Kim Ornitz. Stunt Coordinator: Burt Marshall. Production Accountant: Julianna Arenson. Casting Associate: Gennette Tondino. Post Production Supervisor: Richard E. Rabjohn. Assistant Editor: Grant Hoag. Music Editor: Stan Jones. Re-recording Sound Mixers: Walter Goss, Tom Beckert, Rex Slinkard. Acknowledgments: Operators of the Spirit of St. Louis Riverboat. Produced in association with WonderWorks. A Gay-Jay Productions Film. First aired in 1990.

BEJEWELLED
Editor: Belinda Cottrell. Designer: Bob Cartwright. Director of Photography: Ken Brinsley. Music: Ken Thorne. Teleplay by: Tom J. Astle. Based on the novel *Bejeweled Death* by: Marian Babson. Executive Producers: Graham Benson, Wendy Dytman, Paula Weinstein. Producers: John Price, J. Nigel Pickard. Director: Terry Marcel. Casting U.K.: Susan Whatmough, Kathleen Mackie. Casting U.S.: Eddie Foy. Children's Dialogue Coach: Brian Lidstone. Graphics: The Original Graphics Company. Production Manager: Mark Cooper. First Assistant Director: Glynn Purcell. Second Assistant Director: Michael Guthrie. Location Manager: Dennis Firminger. Wardrobe: Rita Angell, Lawrie Oxley. Make-up:

Judy Courtney. Art Director: Phil Murphy. Production Buyer: Mike Smith. Property Master: Darryl Series. Car Special Effects: Dave Bickers. Stunt Arranger: Marc Boyle. Continuity: Liz West. Production Secretary: Carol Barker. Production Secretary: Carol Barker. Camera Operator: Richard Muller. Focus Puller: Lee Mander. Grip: Joe Winnington. Gaffer Electrician: Ian Edwards. Second Unit Cameraman: Paddy Seale. Assistant Film Editor: Mark Sale. Sound Recordist: Geoff Neate. Dubbing Mixer: Peter Maxwell. Dubbing Editor: Steve Pitwell. Dialogue Editors: John Nuth, Howard Eaves. A TVS Television Production in association with PWD Productions for The Disney Channel and TVS Television. First aired in 1991.

BLACK ARROW

Photographed by: John Cabrera. Edited by: Geoffrey Foote. Music Composed & Conducted by: Stanley Myers. Screenplay by: David Pursall, Peter Welbeck. Based on the book by Robert Louis Stevenson. Associate Producers: Andres Vincente Gomez, Maria Rohm. Produced by: Harry Alan Towers, Michael-John Biber. Directed by: John Hough. Casting: Sue Watnough. Art Director: Jose Maria Alarcon. Assistant Director: Luis Valdivieso. Camera Operator: Ricardo Navarrete. Stunt Director: Jose Luis Cinchilla. Assistant Editor: Gary Dishman. Dubbing Editor: Michael Campbell. Assistant: Terry Busby. Sound Mixer: Aad Wirtz. Costumes: Bermans & Nathans. Production Assistant: Gerry Wheatley. A Panatlantic Picture. First aired in 1985.

BLUE YONDER, THE

Associate Producer: Jeffrey White. Music by: David Shire. Film Editor: Betsy Blankett. Editorial Consultant: Paul Hirsch. Production Designer: Mark Billerman. Director of Photography: Hiro Narita. Produced by: Annette Handley, Susan B. Landau, Alan Shapiro. Written and Directed by: Mark Rosman. Stunt Coordinator: Buck McDancer. Stunts: Sandra Gimpel, Alan Gibb. Consultant: Bobby Fine. Casting: Judith Holstra, Marcia Ross. Costume Designer: Richard Shissler. Aerial Coordinator: Art Scholl. Production Manager: Jeffrey White. 1st Assistant Director: Taylor Charles. 2nd Assistant Director: B.C. Cameron. 3rd Assistant Director: Paul Landau. Art Director: Rick Brown. Decorator: Maggie Martin. Property Master: Brian McPartlon. Set Dresser: Kay MacArthur. Set Artist: Margery Garbrielson. Assistant to Production Designer: Carol Bosselman. 1st Assistant Camera: Paul Marbury. 2nd Assistant Camera: Barbara Kloeppel. 2nd Unit Director: William Smock. 2nd Unit Camera Assistant: Mahlon Picht. Optical Unit Cameraman: Peter Collister. Sound Mixer: Agamemnon Adrianos. Sound Boom: Patrick Moriarty. Script Supervisor: Martha Wax. Assistant to the Producers: Susan Booker. 2nd Unit Aerial Director: Alan Shapiro. Principal Pilot: Art Scholl. Aerial Director of Photography: Jack Cooperman, A.S.C. Aerial Coordinator/Pilot: Chuck Wentworth. Airplane Mechanic: Richard Savell. Assistant Costume Designer: Maureen Hogan. Make-up: Marietta Engelbrecht. Hairdresser: Roxanne Yahyavi. Construction Coordinator: Richard Clot. Construction Foreman: Rodney Armanino. Leadman: Dwayne Grady. Gaffer: Greg Davies. Best Boy: Jani Vournas. Electricians: Tom Fox, Roger Dodd. Key Grip: Jeff Bane. 2nd Grip: Chris Kievman. Dolly Grip: Robie Price. Grip: Don Lind. 1st Assistant Editor: Joe Hutshing. Assistant Editor: David Brenner. Apprentice Editor: Teressa Longo. Visual Effects: Peter Donen. Optical Effects: Mark Dornfeld. Special Effects Supervisor: Dave Pier. Re-recording Mixer: Robert Glass, Jr. Supervising Sound Editors: James Troutman, Paul Carden. ADR Editor: Chris Jargo. Transportation Coordinator: Rich Ficara. Transportation Captain: Craig Patterson. Vintage Automobiles Mechanic: Guy Smith. Historical Consultant: Ed Linotti. San Francisco Casting: Patricia de Oliveira. Extra Casting: Audrey Grace. Location Auditor: Deborah Moore. Production Coordinator: Kerry Peterson. Assistant Production Coordinator: Lisa Cohn. Location Manager: Mary Ensign. Location Scouts: Maggie McCracken, Will McCracken. Caterers: Bruce Goldsmith, Polly Goldsmith, Martin Brown. Production Assistants: Greg Williams, Ellen Stapenhorst. Creative Advisor: Steven Fazekas. Filmed on location at Historical Railroad Square, Santa Rosa and in Sonoma County, California. First aired in 1985.

CHIPS, THE WAR DOG

Casting by: Julie Alter, Susan Young. Music by: David Michael Frank. Editor: Curtis Freilich. Art Director: Michael Marcus. Director of Photography: Kent Wakeford. Executive Producer: Fred Weintraub. Line Producer: Martin Hornstein. Produced by: Sandra Weintraub. Teleplay by: Michael Pardridge, Janice Hickey. Story by: Sandra Weintraub. Directed by: Ed Kaplan. Unit Production Manager: Martin Hornstein. First Assistant Director: Robert D. Simon. Second Assistant Director: Christopher Gerrity. Associate Producer and Military Technical Advisor: Captain James Monaghan, Ret. Animal Trainer: Karl Lewis Miller. Assistant Trainers: Theresa Miller, Glen Garner. Location Manager: Julie Duvic. Script Supervisor: Karen Thorndike. Production Coordinator: Luba Dmytryk. 1st Assistant Camera: Michael Gfelner. Set Decorator: Woody Crocker. Property Master: Frank Silva. Costume Designer: Ronald Leamon. Key Costumer: Henry Earl Lewis. Make-up: Katharina Hirsch Smith. Hair Stylist: Brenda Good. Gaffer: Michael Schuyler. Key Grip: Robert Beaumont. Production Sound Mixer: Robert Marts. Special Effects: Gene Grigg. Transportation Coordinator: Bruce Holland. Auditor: Maxwell Metzer. Additional Casting, Seattle: Dixon Casting. 2nd Unit Director: Karl Epstein. Director of Photography: Jerry Deane. Assistant Editor: Elizabeth Canney. Sound Editing by: Horta Editorial. Music Editing by: John La Salandra, S.M.E. Re-recorded at: Meredian Studios. Re-recording Mixers: Ken S. Polk, C.A.S., Robert Thirlwell, Dan Wallin, C.A.S. Acknowledgments: The Department of Defense; Department of the Army, Fort Lewis, Washington; Ltg. William H. Harrison, Commanding General I Corps, Fort Lewis; George S. Pollich, PAO; Washington State Film Board. W.G. Films, Inc. Animal trainer: Karl Miller. W.G. Films, Inc. First aired in 1989.

CHRISTMAS VISITOR, THE

Director of Photography: David Connell, A.C.S. Production Designer: Otello Stolfo. Editor: Tim Wellburn. Music Composed by: Bruce Rowland. Original Story and Screenplay: Jeff Peck. Produced by: Peter Beilby, Robert Le Tet. Directed by: George Miller. Production Manager: Helen Watts. Production Co-ordinator: Hilary May. Financial Control: Ian Smith. Production Accountant: Mandy Carter. 1st Assistant Director: Brian Giddens. 2nd Assistant Director: Jamie Leslie. 3rd Assistant Director: Jo Friesen. Continuity: Liz Perry. Casting: Adrienne Dolphin, Liz Mullinar, Greg Apps. Focus Puller: Warwick Field. Clapper Loader: Terry Howells. 2nd Unit: Ian McMillan. Sound Recordist: Andrew Ramage. Boom Operator: Scott Rawlings. Gaffer: Bob Young. Best Boy: Roy Pritchett. Electrics: Brett Hull. Key Grip: Geoff Full. 2nd Grip: David Nichols. Assistant Grip: Stuart Crombie. Art Director: Bernadette Wynack. Set Decorator: Trish Keating. Props Buyer/Dresser: Daryl Mills. Standby Props: Bryan Lang. Construction Managers: Bob Hern, Gerry Powderley. Carpenter: Hugh Bateup. Scenic Artist: Graeme Galloway. Special Effects: Peter Stubbs, Peter Armstrong. Make-up: Amanda Rowbottom. Hairdresser: Rochelle Ford. Costumes by: Rose Chong. Wardrobe Supervisor: Gail Mayes. Wig Maker: Cheryl Newton. Unit Publicist: Susan Elizabeth Wood. Location Manager: Murray Boyd. Unit Manager: John Suhr. Assistant Editor: Jeanine Chialvo. Sound Supervisor: Richard Brobyn. Dubbing Editors: Glenn Newnham, Gavin Myers. Assistant Dubbing Editor: Anne Carter. Re-recording Engineers: Andrew Jobson, Melita Jagic. Produced in association with The Disney Channel, PBS WonderWorks, Revcom Productions. First aired in 1987.

DANNY, THE CHAMPION OF THE WORLD

A Portobello Film for The Disney Channel and Wonderworks in association with Thames Television, British Screen and The Children's Film & Television Workshop. Co-producer: Robin Douet. Production Designer: Don Hamfray. Editors: Peter Tanner, Angus Newton. Director of Photography: Oliver Stapleton. Music by: Stanley Myers. Screenplay by: John Goldsmith. Produced by: Eric Abraham. Director: Gavin Millar. Production Manager: Joanna Gollins. First Assistant Director: Chris Newman. Costume Designer: Ann Sinclair. Chief Make-up Artist: Jennifer Boost. Chief Hairdresser: Patricia Kirkman. Art Director: Richard Hornsby. Set Dresser: Aly Burge. Prop Master: Barry Gibbs. Location Manager: Alan

Pinniger. Focus Puller: James Ainslie. Clapper Loader: Paul Grech. Key Grip: Teddy Tucker. Gaffer: Tony Hester. Camera Trainee: Swavek Zukowski. Sound Mixer: Tony Jackson. Boom Operator: Simon Hayter. Sound Trainee: Louise Machin. Production Co-ordinator: Caroline Hill. Producer's Assistant: Vanessa Lees. Script Supervisor: Angela Marks. Second Assistant Director: Keith Young. Third Assistant Director: Mark Challenor. Assistant Location Manager: Guy Tannahill. Production Runner: Nick O'Hagan. Wardrobe Master: Steve Hubbard. Assistant Make-up Artist: Ann McEwan. Casting Director: Debbie McWilliams. Unit Publicist: Zakiya Powell. Stills Photographer: John Timbers. Dubbing Editor: Philip Bothamley. Assistant Dubbing Editor: Dave Docker. Sound Editor: Mike Crouch. Assistant Sound Editor: Penny Woolley. First Assistant Editor: Bill Parnell. Music Editor: Michael Parkinson. Second Assistant Editors: Laura Evans, Tracy Sheffield. Footsteps Editor: Len Tremble. Dialogue Editor: Peter Elliott. Assistant Dialogue Editor: Duncan Elliott. Dubbing Mixer: Hugh Strain. Music Orchestrated by: Fiachra Trench. Construction Manager: Ken Marples. Dressing Props: Peter Bryant, Adam Blezard. Stand-by Props: Paul Bradburn, Daryl Paterson. Stand-by Carpenter: Steve Furneaux. Stand-by Painter: Jonathan Holbrook. Stand-by Rigger: Tony Rubini. Stand-by Stagehand: Peter Wells. Best Boy: Mark Hanlon. Generator Driver: Paul Slatter. Electrician: Gerry Connolly. Stand-in for Mr. Irons: James Linton. Stand-in for Samuel Irons: Simon Spaull. Pheasant Handler: Henry Plumridge. Assistant Handlers: David Bruce, Alison Hughes, Sheila Noake. Wildlife Camera: Michael Richards. Second Unit Cameramen: Wally Byatt, David Worley. Executive Producer for Thames Television: Alan Horrox. Executive Producers for The Disney Channel: Paulo de Oliveira, Carol Rubin. Executive Producers for Wonderworks: Jay Rayvid, Dale Bell. Executive Producer for British Screen: Simon Relph. Executive Producer for The Children's Film and Television Foundation: Monica Sims. Filmed on location in Oxfordshire. Acknowledgment: Stonor Park, Henley-on-Thames. First aired in 1989.

DISNEY'S RETURN TO TREASURE ISLAND

Written by: John Goldsmith. Executive Producer: Patrick Dromgoole. Produced by: Alan Clayton. Directed by: Piers Haggard. Associate Directors: Alex Kirby, Alan Clayton. Series Developed by: Robert S. Baker. Based on a storyline by: Ivor Dean. Title Music: Terry Oldfield, Tom McGuinness. Incidental Music: Terry Oldfield. Music Coordinator & Additional Music: Tom McGuinness. Music Supervisor: Ray Williams, Pollyanna Music and Film Co. Ltd. Director of Photography: Tony Impey. Production Designers: Doug James, Phil Williams. Costume Designer: Aideen Morgan. Film Editors: Tim Wallis, Bob Freeman. Supervisory Film Editor: Geoff Shepherd. Lighting Cameraman: Peter Thornton. Camera Operators: Robin Higginson, Mike Matthews, Howard Rockliffe. Sound Mixers: Alan Jones, Barrie White, Paul Gaydon. Art Directors: Richard Hornsby, Kate Barnett. Graphics: Rae Lambert. Production Buyers: Barry Greaves, Peter Smith, George Noonan. Production Accountant: David Aubrey. Make-up Supervisors: Barbara Southcott, Pam Mullins. Key Grip: Alan Imeson. Prop Man: Roger Grocott. Gaffer Electricians: Len Tyler, Ray Telling, Bill Usher. Chargehand Riggers: Paul O'Neil, Martin Duckett. Casting Director: Michael Barnes. Local Casting: Laura Cairns. Horse Manager: Maria Bisset. Armoury/Special Effects: Ken Lailey Studios. Stunt Arranger: Alf Joint. The Saracen: Square Sail. Assistant Film Editors: Simon Johnson, Tessa Harris. Dubbing Editors: David Scobbie, Richard Dunford, John Parr. Production Assistants: Carol Evans, Barbara Thomas. Location Manager: Alan Pinniger. Assistant Directors: Chris Dando, Paddy Carpenter, Tony Dyer. Production Managers: Peter Richardson, Dennis Morgan, Artie Thomas, Trevor Gittings. Production Secretaries: Cathy Long, Sarah Anderson. Production Controller: Dave Bartle. Assistant Producer: Manny Wessels. Produced by HTV (Harlech Television) in association with Primetime Television Ltd., The Disney Channel, and WWF (Germany). Ten 1-hour episodes or five 2-hour episodes. First aired in 1986.

DOWN THE LONG HILLS

Music by: Mark Snow. Film Editor: Warner E. Leighton. Art Director: Roger S. Crandall. Director of Photography: Reed Smoot. Executive Producers: Pat Finnegan, Sheldon Pinchuk. Produced by: Bill Finnegan. Teleplay by: John and Ruth Povare. Based on the book by: Louis L'Amour. Directed by: Burt Kennedy. Unit Production Manager: D. Scott Easton. First Assistant Director: Ray Marsh. Second Assistant Director: Benjamin Weiss. Casting by: Shari Rhodes, Liz Keigley. Casting Associate: Elyn Wright. Production Supervisor: Margaret E. Fannin. Production Executive: David Roessell. Property Master: Bill Shira. Costume Supervisor: Nina Padovano. Assistant Costumers: Kathleen O'Brien, Jeanne Mascia. Make-up: Karl E. Wessen. Cave Design/Construction: Doug Johnson. Location Manager: Carole Fontana. Script Supervisor: Arrah Thomsen. Key Grip: Arly Thomsen. Transportation Coordinator: Billy G. Arter. Production Auditor: Brian A. Williams. Extra Casting: Cate Praggastis. Special Effects: Rick Josephsen, Lynn Maughan. Assistant Editor: Margaret Webb. Assistants to Producer: Beau L'Amour, Marian Shambo. Production Sound Mixer: Doug Arnold. Sound Supervision: James Troutman & Associates. Music Editor: Ken Johnson. Stunt Coordinator: David Cass. Livestock Coordinator: Corky Randall. Horse Trainer, "Big Red": Rex Peterson. Bear: "Bart." Bear Stunts & Trainer: Doug Seus. Horse/Bear Stunt Trainers: Lynne Seus, Doug Seus. Snarling Wolf Trainer: Doug Seus. Wolves Owned & Trained by: Steve Martin's Working Wildlife. Acknowledgments: The American Humane Association, The State of Utah, Norman H. Bangerter, Governor, Utah Film Development Office, The People of Heber City, Utah. Filmed Entirely on Location in Utah. A Finnegan Company Production. First aired in 1986.

ERNEST GREEN STORY, THE

Original Music by: Mason Daring. Edited by: Jeff Freeman. Production Designer: Roy Amaral. Director of Photography: Felix Alcala. Executive Producers: Carol Abrams, Adrienne Levin. Produced by: Jean Higgins. Written by: Lawrence Roman. Directed by: Eric Laneuville. Unit Production Manager: Jean Higgins. 1st Assistant Director: Burt Burnam. 2nd Assistant Director: Nancy King. Casting by: Jaki Brown & Associates, Kimberly Hardin. Costume Designer: Enid Harris. Set Decorator: John Clark. Property Master: David McGuire. Key Costumer: Tangela Crawford. Costumer: Martin Brodfuerher. Make-up Artist: Coree Lear. Hairstylist: Joann Stafford-Chaney. Location Manager: Joe O'Har. Gaffer: Kevin Kelley. Key Grip: Tony Poston. Script Supervisor: Diane Newman. Production Auditor: Diana Johnson. Production Coordinator: Tamara Allen. Production Sound Mixer: Will Yarbrough. Location Casting: Sarah Tackett. Assistant Editor: Julie J. Webb. Music Editing by: Sharon Heather Smith. Title Design: Ernest Farino. AML Entertainment, Inc. First aired in 1993.

FOUR DIAMONDS, THE

Co-Producer: Todd Robinson. Music by: Phil Marshall. Production Designer: John DeCuir, Jr. Director of Photography: Neil Roach. Produced by: Jean Higgins. Executive Producers: Joe Byrne, Jeb Rosebrook. Teleplay by: Todd Robinson. Based on a Short Story by: Christopher Millard. Directed by: Peter Werner. Edited by: Corky Ehlers. Unit Production Manager: Jean Higgins. First Assistant Director: Eric Jewett. Second Assistant Director: Scott Metcalfe. Casting by: Judith Holstra, C.S.A., Kathryn Eisenstein. Visual Effects Supervisor: Diana Dru Botsford. Costume Designer: Enid Harris. Set Decorator: Karen McGaughey. Property Master: Lynda Reiss. Costume Supervisor: Bob Iannaccone. Make-up Artist: Lydia Milars. Hair Stylist: Susan Mills. Production Illustrator: Peter Mitchel Rubin. Location Manager: Robert Dohan. Script Supervisor: Elisabeth Myles. Production Coordinator: Tamara Allen. Location Casting: Katherine Wilson. Production Sound Mixer: Bruce Bisenz. 2nd Unit Director: Al Jones. Medical Advisor: Dr. Michael Gruber. Gaffer: James Rose. Key Grip: Benny Mendez. Transportation Coordinator: David Menapace. Animal Wrangler: Deanna Esmaeel. Assistant Editor: Marc Pollon. Music Editor: Sharon Smith. Sound Design: Rick Smith. Consultants: Charles and Irma Millard. O'Byrne Productions. First aired in 1995.

FRIENDSHIP IN VIENNA, A

Music by: Lee Holdridge. Director of Photography: Hanania Baer. Art Director: Tamas Banovich. Film Editor: Bert Glatstein. Associate Producer: Richard Alfieri. Co-Producer: Frederic Hunter. Produced by: Christopher Morgan. Executive Producers: Bill Finnegan, Patricia Finnegan, Sheldon Pinchuk. Teleplay by: Richard Alfieri. Based on the book *Devil in Vienna* by: Doris Orgel. Directed by: Arthur Allan Seidelman. Casting by: Jose Villaverde, C.S.A. Unit Production Manager: Maria Ungor. 1st Assistant Director: Gyula Kormos. 2nd Assistant Director: Pal Karpati. London Casting: Allan Foenander. Production Supervisor: David Roessell. Head of International Production-Mafilm: Sandor Toth. Film Commission-Hungarofilm: Istvan Gardos. Production Controller: Lori-Etta Taub. Production Controller, U.S.: Lisa Matsukawa. Property Master: Miklos Molnar. Costume Supervisor: Maria Horanyi. Make-up: Ottilia Pasztory. Hair: Janosne Kajtar. Script Supervisor: Eva Banhidi. Sound Mixer: Tim Himes. Location Manager: Helena Toth. Key Grip: Mikel Christiansen. Gaffer: Peter Sidlo. Music Editor: A David Marshall. Assistant Editor: Richard Boehm. Supervising Sound Mixers: David Hankins, Dave Weathers. Rerecording Sound Mixers: Andrew D'Addario, Dean Okrand, Dean Zupancic. Filmed in Budapest, Hungary. The Finnegan/Pinchuk Company. First aired in 1988.

GONE ARE THE DAYES
Music by: Jerrold Immel. Editor: Ernest Milano, A.C.E. Art Directors: John B. Mansbridge, William H. Miney. Director of Photography: Richard N. Hannah. Produced by: Tom Leetch. Written by: Bill Bleich, Jim Brecher. Directed by: Gabrielle Beaumont. Unit Production Manager: Paul Wurtzel. First Assistant Director: Xavier Reyes. Second Assistant Director: Patrick Regan. Casting Supervisor: Bill Shepard. Casting: Joe Scully. Costume Department Supervisor: Jack Sandeen. Men's Costumer: Milton G. Mangum. Women's Costumer: Sandy Berke-Jordan. Make-up Supervisor: Robert J. Schiffer, C.M.A.A. Make-up: Michael F. Blake. Hair Stylist: Julia Walker. Set Decorator: Norman Rockett. Property Master: Horst Grandt. Script Supervisor: Doris Moody Chisholm. Music Supervisor: Jay Lawton. Sound Supervisor: Bob Hathaway. Supervising Sound Effects Editor: Joseph Parker. Sound Effects Editors: George Fredrick, Wayne A. Allwine, David Horton, George Probert. Dialogue Editor: Al Maguire. Supervising Music Editor: Jack Wadsworth. Music Editor: Richard S. Luckey. Music Scoring Mixer: Shawn Murphy. Re-Recording Mixers: Richard Portman, Nick Alphin, Frank Regula, Tom Gerard. First aired in 1984.

GOOD OLD BOY: A DELTA BOYHOOD
Screenplay by: Paul W. Cooper. Based on the novel *Good Old Boy: A Delta Summer* by: Willie Morris. Original Music: Elliot Sokolov. Editor: Craig Tyree. Production Designer: Edward Gianfrancesco. Director of Photography: Ilie Agopian. Produced and Directed by: Tom G. Robertson. Executive Producer: Tom G. Robertson. Associate Producer/Development: Mary Kelly. Associate Producer: Peggy Doyle. Production Manager: Craig Tyree. Assistant Directors: R. Allen Haehnle, Maureen Arata. Camera Operator: Bernie Dwertman. Assistant Camera: Barry Allen Congrove. Costume Design: Jeanette Oleska. Wardrobe Assistant: Alexis Scott. Production Associate: Mandy Wheeler. Make-up & Hair: Catherin Mahlin. Sound: Will Gethin-Jones. Assistant Sound/Sound Effects Editor: Kent Meloy. Key Grip: Dale Emminger. Dolly Grip: Scott Porter. Electric: Doug Cribbs. Grips: Mark D. Oliver, Jamie Brown, Otis Dent. Assistant Production Designer: Taylor Morrison. Props/Set Construction: Hayden Petkovsek, Artie Peterson, Jim Willard, Phil Kerzner. Production Assistants: Dorease Priest, Dusty Cauthen. Drivers: Cliff McCarstle, Allen McCallister. Wrangler: Sammy Cauthen. Dog Trainers: Bill Berloni, Lane Haverly. Post Production: On-Line Editor: Jim Krob. Assistant: Gerry Cummings. Re-recording Mixer: Jay Petach. Filmed on location in Mississippi. Produced in association with The Disney Channel & PBS: WonderWorks. Multimedia Films, Inc. First aired in 1988.

GOODBYE, MISS 4TH OF JULY
Music by: Mark Snow. Director of Photography: Neil Roach. Production Designer: Charles C. Bennett. Editor: Jim Gross.

Executive Producers: Patricia Finnegan, Bill Finnegan, Sheldon Pinchuk. Producers: Christopher Seiter, Josephine Lyons, Peter Miller. Teleplay by: Kathy McCormick. Based on the book *Miss 4th of July, Goodbye* by: Christopher G. Janus. Directed by: George Miller. Casting by: Mary V. Buck, C.S.A., Susan Edelman, C.S.A. Unit Production Manager: Christopher Seiter. 1st Assistant Director: William L. Lukather. 2nd Assistant Director: Carole Keligian. Associate Producer: David Roessell. Tennessee Casting: Jo Doster. Costume Designer: Barbara Anderson. Set Decorator: John Levinge. Wardrobe: Diane Cornelius. Make-up Artists: Robert Jermaine, Rita Sabatini. Hair Stylists: Linle White, Frankie Campbell. Script Supervisor: Connie Collins. Sound Mixer: Tim Himes. Location Manager: Charles Baxter. Props: Batia Grafka, Cesar D. Alava. Gaffer: Dan Delgado. Key Grip: Scott Floren. Production Controller: Lori-Etta Taub. Facilities Coordinator: David A. Menapace. Production Coordinator: Marian Shambo. Assistant Editor: Terry Szostek. Music Editing: Stan Jones. Supervising Sound Editors: David Hankins, Dave Weathers. Rerecording Sound Mixers: Andrew D'Addario, Dean Okrand, C.A.S., Dean Zupancic. Acknowledgments: The Tennessee State Film Commission, The People of Jonesborough, Tennessee, The Cherokee National Forest. The Finnegan/Pinchuk Company. First aired in 1988.

GREAT EXPECTATIONS
Based on the Novel by: Charles Dickens. Production Designer: Keith Wilson. Director of Photography: Doug Milsome, B.S.C. Editor: Barry Peters. For Primetime Entertainment, Executive Producer: Michael Clark. Executive in Charge of Production for Primetime Television: Deirdre Simms. Executive Producer for The Disney Channel: Carol Rubin. Supervising Executive Producers for HTV: Patrick Dromgoole, Johnny Goodman. Screenplay by: John Goldsmith. Produced by: Greg Smith. Directed by: Kevin Connor. Casting by: Jose Villaverde, C.S.A., Allan Foenander. Production Supervisor: Terence Lens, G.F.P.E. Music Composed and Conducted by: Ken Thorne. Unit Production Manager: David Middlemas. First Assistant Director: Roy Stevens. 2nd Assistant Director: Andrew Wood. Location Manager: Micky Moynihan. Production Accountant: Gerry Wheatley. Wardrobe Supervisors: Tiny Nichols (Men), Joyce Stoneman (Women). Chief Hairdresser: Eithne Fennell. Chief Make-up: Eddie Knight. Sound Mixer: Laurie Clarkson. Art Director: Stephen Bream. Camera Operator: Derek Browne. Production Coordinator: Dione Orrum. Stills Cameraman: Stephen Morley. Sound Editor: Peter Horrocks. Dubbing Mixer: Bill Rowe. Music Editor: Bob Hathaway. Script Supervisor: Andrea Fontaine. Assistant Editor: Helen Eley. Unit Publicity by: Dennis Michaels. Filmed on Location at: Chatham Historic Dockyard, Chatham, Kent; The City of Rochester Upon Medway, Kent; Pinewood Studios. Produced by Primetime for The Disney Channel in association with HTV Limited and Tesauro Television (Spain). Three parts, each in a 2-hour format. First aired in 1989.

HEIDI
Costume Designer: Derek Hyde. Original Score by: Lee Holdridge. Edited by: Randy Jon Morgan. Production Designer: John Blezard. Director of Photography: Denis C. Lewiston. Line Producer: Nick Gillott. Produced by: Frank Agrama, Daniele Lorenzano. Executive Producer: Bill McCutchen. Written by: Jeanne Rosenberg. Based on the novel by: Johanna Spyri. Directed by: Michael Rhodes. U.S. Casting by: Jose Villaverde, C.S.A. Great Britain Casting by: Allan Foenander. Production Managers: Arie Bohrer, Andjelija Vlaisavljevic. 1st Assistant Director: Chris Newman. 2nd Assistant Director: Simon Moseley. Art Director: Vladislav Lasic. Set Decorator: Peter Manhardt. Property Master: Vladimir Stojanovic. Wardrobe Supervisor: Diane Murphy. Woman's Costumer: Marina Skundric. Men's Costumer: Zoran Savic. Key Make-up: Penny Bell. Key Hairdresser: Stephanie Kaye. Location Manager: Knut Losen. Unit Manager: Moidrag Stevanovic. Script Supervisor: Vesna Milic. Production Coordinator: Sylvia Pike. Production Accountant: Barbara Bergman. Production Associate: Alessia Pedrazini. Sound Mixer: Paul Le Mare. Assistant Editor: Amy Shorr. 2nd Assistant Editor: Karen Greene. Post Production Supervisor:

Tim King. Music Supervisor: John Caper, Jr. Orchestration by: Ira Hearshen. Re-recording Mixers: John Ross, C.A.S., Paul Berolzheimer, Patrick Giraudi. ADR Supervisor: Debbie Melford. Additional Sound by: Ahmed Agrama, Kent Harrison Hayes, Gerard Shadrick, Serge Perron. Title Design: Ernest Farino. Creative Executives: Carol Rubin, Norman Siderow. Filmed entirely in Salzburg and the East Tirol, Austria. A Harmony Gold Production in association with Bill McCutchen Productions, Inc., Silvio Berlusconi Communications and The Disney Channel. Two parts, 2-hour format each. First aired in 1983.

LANTERN HILL
Director of Photography: Brian Thomson. Costume Design: Martha Mann. Art Direction: Perri Gorrara. Casting: Anne Tait. Screenplay by: Fiona McHugh, Kevin Sullivan. From the novel *Jane of Lantern Hill* by: Lucy Maud Montgomery. Edited by: Mairin Wilkinson. Music Composed by: John Welsman. Line Producer: David Shepherd. Executives in Charge of Production: Cathy Johnson, Jim Burt, Jay Rayvid. Executive Producer: Trudy Grant. Produced and Directed by: Kevin Sullivan. Production Manager: James Goff Martin. First Assistant Director: Erika Zborowsky. Second Assistant Director: Francis R. Mahony. Third Assistant Director: Michael Johnson. Unit/Location Manager: Fred Kamping. Unit/Location Assistant: Kim Saltarski. Script Supervisor: Mimi Wolch. Story Editor: Lucie Hall. Set Decorator: Carol Lavoie. Head Set Dresser: Tom Alway. Set Dresser: Ron Hewitt. Property Masters: Tory Bellingham, John Tracy Budd. Make-up Design: Linda Gill. Make-up Artist: Linda Dowds. Hair Design: Paul Elliot. Hairdressers: Albert Paradis, Hazel Gordon. Assistant Wardrobe Manager: Ann Russell. Wardrobe Supervisor: Michele Harney. Head Cutter: Evan Ayotte. Wardrobe Assistants: Lynne MacKay, Deborah Weldon. First Assistant Art Director: Nancy Pankiw. Location Sound Recordist: Owen Langevin. Boom: Ken Porter. Camera Operator: Julian Chojnacki. First Assistant Camera: Brian Harper. Second Assistant Camera: Stewart Aziz. Stills Photographer: Michaelin McDermott. Construction Coordinator: Wietz Jekel. Head Carpenter: Jake Haak. Assistant Carpenter: Henry Ilola. Scenic Artist: Willie Holst. Head Accountant: Hannelore Biesinger. Assistant Accountant: Sherri Hunter. Production Coordinator: Therese Paquette. Production Secretary: Heather Ross. Gaffer: Gary Denault. Best Boy: Michael Galbraith. Electricians: Herb Reischl, James MacCammon, Barry Goodwin. Generator Operator: John Eldridge. Key Grip: Wayne Goodchild. Assistant Key Grip: Glen Goodchild. Grips: C.W. Goodchild, Roy Elliston. Special Effects Coordinator: Michael Kavanaugh. Stunt Coordinator: Ted Hanlan. Livestock Handler: Lionel Purcell. Dog Handler: Jane Conway. Picture Vehicle Coordinator: Eric Lynd. Transportation Coordinator: Wilf Bell. Driver Captain: William Leeking. Head Driver: Bruce Raymer. Honeywagon: Kevin Wilson. Craft Service: Jake Miller. Catering: Darren Schmidt. Production Assistants: Jeff Pope, Emily Wilkinson. Camera Trainee: Linda Watt. Art Department Trainee: Andrew Stearn. Trainee Assistant Director: Patrick Sisam. Children's Tutor: Janice Nutter. Publicity: Kim Luke, Lucie Hall. Assistant Editor: Rosemary Conte. Supervising Sound Editor: Jeremy MacLaverty. Dialogue Editor: Timothy Roberts. ADR Editor: Dale Sheldrake. Sound Assistants: Kris Engel, Richard Kelly. Foley Artist: Kelly Hall. Foley Assistant: Teresa Hannigan. Sound Mixer: Daniel Pellerin. Assistant Sound Mixer: Tony van den Akker. Timing: Chris Hinton. Negative Cutting: Erika Wolff. Video Editing: Bernie Clayton. Video Timing: Brian Lavery. Music Assistant: Donald Quan. Musical Orchestration by: John Welsman, Glenn Morley. Orchestra Conducted and Music Supervised by: Glenn Morley. Produced by: Lantern Hill Motion Pictures Inc. in association with The Disney Channel, The Canadian Broadcasting Corporation (CBC), Wonderworks and the Corporation for Public Broadcasting with the participation of Telefilm Canada. First aired in 1990.

LITTLE KIDNAPPERS, THE
Co-Producer: Gerald Testar. Original Score by: Mark Snow. Edited by Ron Wisman. Production Designer: Bill Brodie. Director of Photography: Miklos Lente, C.S.C. Executive Producers: Glenn R. Jones, Noel Resnick. Produced by: James Margellos, Coralee Elliott Testar. Based on the screenplay *The Little Kidnappers* and the short story *Scotch Settlement* by: Neil Paterson. Directed by: Donald Shebib. Casting: Karen Hazzard. U.K. Casting: Allan Foenander. The Disney Channel Executive in Charge of Production: Carol Rubin. CBC Executive in Charge of Production: Jim Burt. Production Manager: Peter d'Entremont. 1st Assistant Director: Don Buchsbaum. 2nd Assistant Director: Tim Reed. 3rd Assistant Director: Andrea Kikot. Costume Designer: Ruth Secord. Art Director: Mary Steckle. Set Decorator: Steve Shewchuk. Property Master: Simon LaHaye. Scenic Artist: Susan High. Key Make-up Artist: Ingrid Udine. Hair Stylist: Diane Memmott. Continuity: Maggie Thomas. Animal Coordinator: Gary Swim. Extras Coordinator: John Dunsworth. Production Sound Mixer: David Lee. Location Manager: Charlotte Harper. Production Coordinator: Robin Sarafinchan. Production Accountant: Lyn Lucibello. Gaffer: Gabriele Dichiara. Key Grip: Scott Brooke. 1st Assistant Camera: Michael Soos. Transportation Coordinator: James Ritchie. Transportation Captain: Bob Hicks. Assistant Film Editor: Stephen Humble. Sound Editor: Jim Hopkins. ADR Editor: Robin Leigh. Dialogue Editor: Penny Hozy. Music Editor: Bill Carruth. Re-recording Sound Mixers: Joe Grimaldi, Dino Pigat. Music Recording Engineer: Hayward Parrott. Wedding Dance Music Arranged and Performed by: The Barra MacNeils. Acknowledgments: Nova Scotia Film Office, the People of Halifax, Iona and Sherbrooke. A Jones Maple Leaf Production in association with The Canadian Broadcasting Corporation, Resnick/Margellos Productions and The Disney Channel. First aired in 1990.

LITTLE RIDERS, THE
Original Score by: Lee Holdridge. Editor: Barry Peters. Production Designer: Keith Wilson, B.F.D. Director of Photography: Willy Kurant, A.F.C. Executive Producer: Bill McCutchen. Produced by: David Anderson. Teleplay by: Gerald DiPego. Based on the novel by: Margaretha Shemin. Directed by: Kevin Connor. Unit Production Manager: Dirk Schreiner. First Assistant Director: Gary Robinson, Matthias Cleerdin. Second Assistant Director: John Withers. Art Director: Alistair Kay. Property Master: Hans Oosterhuis. Costume Designer: Diane Holmes. Chief Make-up and Hair: Christine Penwarden. Camera Operator: Seamus Corcoran. Production Accountant: Dorothy Precious. Location Manager: Lex Plas. Script Supervisor: Sue Field. Production Coordinator: Patsy de Lord. Construction Coordinator: Chris Gaerthe. Production Sound Mixer: Laurie Clarkson. Assistant Editor: Helen Eley. Supervising Sound Editor: Joe Melody. Re-recording Mixers: Larry Stensvold, Adam Jenkins, Don Digirolamo. Special Effects by: Harry Wiesenhaan. Casting by: Jose Villaverde, C.S.A. Additional Casting by: Margaret Crawford, U.K., Job Gosschalk. Executive for The Disney Channel: Carol Rubin. Produced by Signboard Hill Productions Inc. in association with Bill McCutchen Productions and The Disney Channel. First aired in 1992.

LOOKING FOR MIRACLES
A Kevin Sullivan Production. Director of Photography: Brian Thomson. Costume Design: Martha Mann. Art Direction: Carmi Gallo. Casting by: Anne Tait. Line Producer: David Shepherd. Story Editor: Lucie Hall. Screenplay by: Kevin Sullivan, Stuart McLean. Based on the book *A Memoir About Living* by: A.E. Hotchner. Edited by: James Lahti. Music Composed by: John Welsman. Executives in Charge of Production: Cathy Johnson, John Kennedy, Jay Rayvid. Executive Producer: Trudy Grant. Produced and Directed by: Kevin Sullivan. Production Manager: James Goff Martin. Unit/Location Manager: Fred Kaming. First Assistant Director: Erika Zborowsky. Second Assistant Director: Wendy Eidson. Third Assistant Director: Michael Johnson. Script Supervisor: Mimi Wolch. Camera Operator: Julian Chojnacki. First Assistant Camera: Brian Harper. Second Assistant Camera: Stewart Aziz. Sound Recordist: Owen Langevin. Boom Operator: Ken Porter. Set Decoration: Carol Lavoie. Set Dressers: Tom Alway, Ron Hewitt. Make-up Design: Linda Gill. Make-up: Linda Dowds. Hair Design: Carmen Dodaro. Hairdressers: Kelly Brennan, Hazel Gordon. Stills Photographer: Michaelin

McDermott. Props Master: Sean Kirby. Assistant Props: George Beck. Construction Coordinator: Wietz Jekel. Scenic Artist: Willie Holst. Head Carpenter: Jake Haak. Carpenter: Patrick McCafferty. Assistant Costume Designer: Lynda Kemp. Wardrobe Supervisor: Aleida MacDonald. Wardrobe Assistant: Michele Harney. Head Cutter: Evan Ayotte. Gaffer: Gary Deneault. Electricians: James MacCammon, George Yurkiv. Generator Operator: Hern Reischl. Best Boy: Michael Galbraith. Key Grip: Frank Teunissen. Best Boy Grip: Paul Sheridan. Grips: Matthew Pill, Scott MacDonald. Transportation Co-ordinator: Wilf Bell. Driver Captain: William Leeking. Head Driver: Bruce Raymer. Production Accountant: Hannelore Blesinger. Assistant Accountant: Janina Barrett. Stunt Coordinator: The Stunt Team, Ted Hanlan, T.J. Scott. Special Effects Co-ordinator: Michael Kavanaugh. Dialogue Coach: Jan Green. Horse Wrangler: Lionell Purcell. Snake Wrangler: Jim Lovisek. Extras Casting: Rose Lewis Casting Ltd. Trainee Assistant Director: Ron Oxley. Art Department Trainee: Valerie Kaelin. Camera Trainee: John Konye. Assistant Locations Managers: Patrick Sisam, Kim Saltarski. Assistant Art Director: Marian Wihak. Production Assistant: Marty Earl. Production Co-ordinator: Debbie Cooke. Production Secretary: Tina Grewal. Location Cooks: Darren Schmidt, Ian Thomson. Craft Service: John Leebosh. Assistant Picture Editors: Ben Wilkinson, Victoria Rose. Sound Effects Editor: Jeremy MacLaverty. Assistant Sound Effects Editor: Jerry Swallow. Foley Artist: Reid James Atherton. Foley Assistant: Denise Skuse. Sound Mixer: Daniel Pellerin. Video Editor: Bernie Clayton. Timing: Chris Hinton. Negative Cutting: Erika Wolff. Music Recording: Hayward Parrott. Orchestra Conducted and Music Supervised by: Glen Morley. Musical Orchestration by: John Weisman, Glen Morley, Martin Loomer. Filmed on location in Toronto, Haliburton, Minden and throughout Southern Ontario, Canada. Produced by Looking for Miracles Productions Inc. in association with The Disney Channel, Wonderworks, The Corporation for Public Broadcasting, The Canadian Broadcasting Company and with the participation of Telefilm Canada. First aired in 1989.

LOTS OF LUCK

Art Director: C. Robert Holloway. Music by: William Goldstein. Director of Photography: Reed Smoot. Edited by: Mark Melnick. Executive Producers: John D. Backe, Philip D. Fehrle. Producer: Shirley J. Eaton. Written by: Deborah Cavanaugh, Eric Loeb. Directed by: Peter Baldwin. Casting by: Caro Jones. Production Manager: Robert Bennett Steinhauer. 1st Assistant Director: Robin Chamberlain. 2nd Assistant Director: Dan Dugan. Assistant Cameraman: George Griner. 2nd Camera Assistant: Brent Loefke. Production Sound Mixer: Bill Teague. Set Decorator: Richard Villalobos. Script Supervisor: Paulette Pasternak. Costume Supervisor: Kathy Dover. Men's Wardrobe: Robert Bedford. Women's Wardrobe: Beth Holmes. Make Up Artist: Christine Boyer. Hair Stylist: Enid Arias. Gaffer: Ian Kincaid. Key Grip: Phil Sloan. Transportation Coordinator: Clive Henderson. Location Manager: Joe Hosking, Holloway's Eagle Scouts. Extra Casting: Extra Special People. Stunt Coordinator: Terry James. Production Office Coordinator: Fran Billos. Production Assistant: Anne Hart. Supervising Sound Editor: Vince Gutierrez. Music Editor: Curt Roush, The Music Design Group. Orchestrations: Alf Clausen. Assistant Film Editor: Keith Critchlow. First aired in 1985.

LOVE LEADS THE WAY

Music by: Fred Karlin. Edited by: Art Seid, A.C.E. Casting by: Hank McCann, C.S.A. Director of Photography: Gary Graver. Executive Producer: David Permut. Produced by: Jimmy Hawkins. Teleplay by: Henry Denker. Story by: Jimmy Hawkins, Henry Denker. Based on the book First Lady of the Seeing Eye by: Morris Frank, Blake Clark. Directed by: Delbert Mann. Associate Producer/Production Manager: Robert Charles Stroud. 1st Assistant Director: Donald Roberts. 2nd Assistant Director: Bart Roe. Production Coordinator: Anne Carlucci. Script Supervisor: Connie Barzaghi. Dog Trainer: Ron Bledsoe. Sound Mixer: Ronald Curfman. Boom Operator: Steve Bowerman. Steadicam: Frank Waldeck. Gaffer: Jono Kouzouyan. Key Grip: Douglas Wood. Property Master: Tommie Hawkins. Art Director/Nashville: Carolyn Ott. Set Decorator/Nashville: Fred Schwoebel. Art Director/Washington:

Dumas Production Service. Auditor: Don Hultman. Costumer: Dodie Shepard. Make-up: Cheryl Buttrey. Hair Stylist: Linda Conroy. Casting Associate: Tom Folino. Assistant Editor: Stuart Bass. Sound Editing: Echo Film Services. Supervising Sound Editors: Joseph Melody, Russ Tinsley. Music Editor: Ted Roberts. Titles and Opticals: Ray Mercer, Murray Naidich. Song Someone to Watch Over Me Music by: George Gershwin. Lyrics by: Ira Gershwin. Filmed on location in: Nashville, Tennessee and Leavenworth, Washington. Acknowledgment: The Seeing Eye, Inc., Morristown, NJ. Technical Advisor: Ned Myrose. A Hawkins/Permut Production, Inc. First aired in 1984.

MARK TWAIN & ME

Music by: Laurence Rosenthal. Edited by: Paul Lamastra, A.C.E. Production Designer: Bill Beeton. Director of Photography: Francois Protat. Executive Producers: Julian Fowles, Geoffrey Cowan. Written by: Cynthia Whitcomb. Based on the book Enchantment by: Dorothy Quick. Produced and Directed by: Daniel J. Petrie. Associate Producer/Unit Production Manager: John Danylkiw. 1st Assistant Director: David Warry-Smith. 2nd Assistant Director: Ken Smith. Art Direction: Jacques M. Bradette. Costume Designer: Lynda Kemp. Wardrobe Mistress: Gail Filman. Set Decorator: Joyce Liggett. Property Master: Ken Clark. Make-up Artist for Mr. Robards: Kevin Haney. Make-up Artist: Donald Mowat. Hair Stylists: Albert Paradis, Diana Ladyshewsky. Choreographer: Anne Wootten. Development Associate: Vikram Jayanti. Location Manager: Keith Large. Script Supervisor: Katherine Hart. Production Coordinator: Regina Robb. Production Accountant: Phil Rodak. Production Sound Mixer: David Lee. Assistant Editor: Chip Masamitsu. Sound Editor: Brad Stephenson. Music Editor: Roy Prendergast. Re-recording Sound Mixer: Elius Caruso. Chilmark Productions Inc. First aired in 1991.

MOTHER GOOSE ROCK 'N' RHYME

Produced by: Paula Marcus. Co-Produced by: Thomas Bliss. Teleplay by: Mark Curtiss, Rod Ash. From a Story by: Hilary Hinkle, Linda Engelsiepen. Directed by: Jeff Stein. Executive Producer: Shelley Duvall. Music Director: Van Dyke Parks. Stunt Coordinator: Donna Garrett. Music Coordinator: Glenn Jordan. Composed by: Stephen Bray. Executive in Charge of Production: Wayne Morris. Think Entertainment. First aired in 1990.

NIGHT TRAIN TO KATHMANDU, THE

Music Composed and Conducted by: Paul Baillargeon. Production Designer: Bill Bonecutter. Costume Design: Mary Etta Lang. Co-Producers: Marshall Wiemer, Steven B. Kalafer, S. Rogers Benjamin. Associate Producer: Carrie Frances-King. Executive Producers: Robert Wiemer, Ned Kandel. Edited by: James Eaton, Stephanie Ng. Director of Photography: Glenn Kershaw. Written by: Robert Wiemer, Ian Robert. Produced by: Glenn Kershaw. Directed by: Robert Wiemer. Casting: Danielle Eskinazi. Gaffer: Karen Bean. Best Boy: Ramiesh Rai. Electrician: Mahendra Lama. Key Grip: Gerry Polinsky. Best Boy: Bishnu Prasad. Grips: Butch Lee, Ronnie Bills. Swingmen: Wilford Caplayan, Karl Hawks. Assistant Cameraman: James Eaton. 2nd Assistant Cameraman: Raju Thapa. Sound Mixer: Marshall Wiemer. Boom Man: Gerry Beg. Make-up and Hair Design: Cochise Ochoa. Assistant Make-up and Hair: Ann "Breeze" Emmetsberger. Stunt Coordinator: Doc Charbonneau. Props and Set Decoration (Los Angeles): Hoagie K. Hill. Assistant Director: Michael Friedland. 2nd Assistant Director: Anil Shah. Production Office Coordinator: Donna Langley. Studio Services Manager: Kevin Wilson. Social Worker/Studio Teacher: Kenny Wolin. Assistant Editor: Roy Seeger. Sound Editors: James Eaton, Stephanie Ng, Roy Seeger. Re-recording Mixer: John Brady. Production Assistant: Gary Kwashige. Matte Artist: Mark Sullivan. Matte Photography: Robert Bailey. Title Design: Darryl F. Azzopardi. Transportation Captain: Vijay Shamsher Rai. H.M. Government of Nepal Liaison: Bala Ram Pant. Golden Tiger Pictures. First aired in 1988.

NIGHTJOHN

Executive Producer: David Manson. Co-Producers: John Landgraf, Bill Cain. Produced by: Dennis Stuart Murphy.

Teleplay by: Bill Cain. Based on the book by: Gary Paulsen. Directed by: Charles Burnett. Director of Photography: Elliot Davis. Music by: Stephen James Taylor. Costume Designer: Sharen Davis. Editor: Dorian Harris. Production Designer: Naomi Shohan. Casting by: Judith Holstra, C.S.A. Unit Production Manager: Dennis Murphy. First Assistant Director: Kris Krengel. Second Assistant Director: Donald Sparks. Sound Mixer: Veda Campbell. Art Director: Jim Hill. Set Decorator: Evette Siegel. Property Master: Melissa Matthies. Wardrobe Supervisor: Dana Hart. Costumer: Kelly O'Gurian. Hair Stylist: Kenneth Walker. Make-up Artists: Kris Evans, Sheryl Blum. Production Supervisor: Anne McCaffrey. Script Supervisor: Patti Fullerton. Production Accountant: Jyllel Dickerman. Atlanta Casting: Shay Griffin. Stunt Coordinator: David Sanders. Assistant to the Executive Producer: Joan Marie Churchill. Post Production Coordinator: Brynne Millrany. Historical Advisors: Beverly Robinson, Ph.D., Bernard Powers, Ph.D. Assistant Editor: Anthony Santiago. Music Editor: Liz Lachman. Music Supervisor: John Bidasio. Re-recording Mixer: Phillip Seretti. *Horse and Rider* Hymn Music: Todd Barton. Signboard Hill Productions, Inc., Hallmark Productions, Sarabande Productions in association with The Disney Channel. First aired in 1996.

NOT QUITE HUMAN

Music by: Tom Scott. Edited by: Ron Wisman. Production Designer: Elayne Ceder. Director of Photography: Ken Lamkin, A.S.C. Executive Producer: Steven H. Stern. Produced by: Noel Resnick. Written by: Alan Ormsby. Based on characters from the book series *Not Quite Human* by: Seth McEvoy. Directed by: Steven H. Stern. Unit Production Manager: Jim Margellos. First Assistant Director: Ray Marsh. Second Assistant Director: Dennis Ranke. Casting: Matt Casella. Local Casting: Darlene Wyatt. Costume Designer: Jana Stern. Set Decorator: Nigel Clinker. Property Masters: Elliot Ellentuck, Marcia Calosio-Foeldi. Costume Supervisor: Jean Aiken. Make-up/Hair: Rocky Frier, Ingrid Udine. Camera Operator: Monty Rowan. Gaffer: Jerry Workman. Key Grip: Mike Connors. Location Managers: Janet Nelson, Blake Hocevar. Script Supervisor: Lee Nowak. Production Coordinator: Pinki Ragan. Production Sound Mixer: Don Sanders. Assistant Film Editor: Stephen Humble. Sound Editors: Jim Hopkins, Charlie Bowers. Assistant Sound Editor: Michele Cook. Music Supervisor: David Franco. Music Editors: Ken Johnson, Steve Livingston. Sound Mixers: Joe Grimaldi, Don White. Prosthetics/Special Effects: John Harrington, John Rielly. Computer Consulting and Animation: Dan Stoneman, Rick Gessner. Live Musical Performance by: Major Figures. A Sharmhill Production Inc. Film. First aired in 1987.

NOT QUITE HUMAN II

Music by: Michel Rubini. Film Edited by: David Berlatsky. Production Designed by: Nilo Rodis. Director of Photography: Jules Brenner. Executive Producer: Noel Resnick. Produced by: James Margellos. From the book series *Not Quite Human* by: Seth McEvoy. Based on characters created by: Kevin Osborn. Written and Directed by: Eric Luke. Unit Production Manager: James Margellos. First Assistant Director: Anthony Brand. Second Assistant Director: Alisa Matlovsky. Casting: Matt Casella. Set Decorator: Susan Volk. Storyboard Artist: Phillip Norwood. Prop Master: Marcia Calosio. Costume Designer: Lynn Kizlin. Wardrobe Supervisor: Jean Aiken. Make-up Artist: Ingrid Udine. Hair Stylist: Diane Memmott. Special EFX: Mark Passarelli. Sound Mixer: Bob Wald. Camera Operator: Chris Schweibert. Gaffer: Danny Buck. Key Grip: Bob Fischer. Stunt Coordinator: Christine Baur. Script Supervisor: Sibylle Aldridge. Production Coordinator: Denise Zollman. Production Accountant: Julianna Arenson. Location Manager: Pinki Ragan. Visual Effects: Ted Rae. Assistant Editor: Bill Steinberg. Sound Editing: Echo Film Services, Joseph Melody. Music Editor: Brian Vessa. Re-recording Sound Mixers: Jerry Clemans, William Benton, Ray O'Reilly. Computer Animation Sync and Engineering: Steve Carpenter. Computer Graphics: Production Masters, Inc. A Resnick/Margellos Productions Film. First aired in 1989.

OLD CURIOSITY SHOP, THE

Based on the Novel by: Charles Dickens. Music Composed by: Mason Daring. Editor: Barry Peters. Production Designer: Keith Wilson, B.F.D. Director of Photography: Doug Milsome, B.S.C. Associate Producer: John Davis. Executive for The Disney Channel: Carol Rubin. Executive Producer: Robert Halmi, Jr. Screenplay by: John Goldsmith. Produced by: Greg Smith. Directed by: Kevin Connor. Casting by: Allan Foenander. Unit Production Manager: Kevan Barker. First Assistant Director: Martin O'Malley. Second Assistant Director: Marian Barlow. Costume Designer: Tiny Nicholls. Art Director: Alistair Kay. Set Decorator: Jim Harkin. Property Master: Daragh Lewis. Wardrobe: Jim Smith, Brian Cox. Chief Make-up: Ken Jennings. Chief Hairdresser: Bernie Dooley. Casting Assistant: Brian Jones. Production Accountant: Neil Chaplin. Location Manager: David Murphy. Script Supervisor: Jean Skinner. Camera Operator: Seamus Corcoran. Production Coordinators—Dublin: Anneliese O'Callaghan. London: Gail Bateman. Production Sound Mixer: Laurie Clarkson. Supervising Sound Editor: Michael C. Gutierrez. Re-recording Mixers: Thomas J. Huth, C.A.S., Craig M. Otte, David Weishaar, C.A.S. Music Editor: Sharon Smith. Assistant Editor: Helen Eley. Post Production Auditor: Sonja Solomun. Acknowledgments: Bunratty Heritage Folk Park; The Shannon Development Corporation; The National Museum of Ireland; Office of Public Works. Produced in Ireland by Curiosity Productions Ltd. for RHI Entertainment, Inc. and The Disney Channel. RHI Entertainment, Inc. in association with The Elstree Company and The Disney Channel. Two 90-minute parts. First aired in 1994.

OLLIE HOPNOODLE'S HAVEN OF BLISS

Written and Narrated by: Jean Shepherd. Directed by: Dick Bartlett. Executive Producer: Fred Barzyk. Producer: Olivia Tappan. Assistant to the Producer: Leigh Brown. Coordinating Producer: Bernice Olenick. Associate Producer: Ellen Locy. Director of Photography: D'Arcy Marsh. Production Designer: John Wright Stevens. Lighting Designer: Robert Tompkins. Costume Designer: Jeanette Oleska. Sound: Stacy Brownrigg, Alex Griswold, John Osborne. Editors: Dick Bartlett, Bill Anderson. Set Decorator: Margaret Peckham. Art Director: Gayle Wurthner. Prop Masters: David Gulick, Philip Shirey. Hairdressers: Steve Aturo, Patti Gowen. Make-up: Allison Levy, Nena Smarz. Art Assistants: Hal Hayes, Jennifer Lawson, Erika Peterson. Costume Assistants: Alexis Scott, Beba Shamash. Assistant Directors: Michael Dempsey, Andrew Doerfer. Second Assistant Director: Helen McGinn. Camera Assistants: Brwon Cooper, Barbara Hanania. Sound Editor: Stephanie Monroe. Assistant Editors: Andrew Doerfer, Jacques Weissgerber. Key Grip: Tom Doran, Greg Williams. Second Grip: Tom Davidson, Wayne Simpson. Second Electric: Neil de la Pena, Russell Towry. Third Electric: Karin Albano, Paris Gutierrez. Color Grading: Paul Broncar. Sound Mix: Richard Bock. Videotape Editors: Mary Fenton, Danda Stein, Judy Washington. Production Unit Manager: Scot Osterweil. Location Managers: Donna B. Brown, Kim Davis. Script Continuity: Inga Carboni, Pam Fuller. Production Assistants: Karen Kalbacher, Lisa Lewis, Anne Smith, Drew Stubbs. Production Consultant: Joe Dishner. Office Coordinator: Kathryn Kaycoff. Production Secretary: Genia Christine. Production Aides: Joe Binford, Jr., Chris Borden, Michael Lee, John Parish. Production Interns: Lance Cheatham, Scott Davis, Susan Gray-Haynes, Wanda Lewis, Peter Lovett, Gregory Narkunas, Jessica Pallington. Stock Footage Researcher: Kenn Rabin. Casting: Anne Baker (Boston), Rody Kent (Dallas), Lynne Kressel (New York). Music: Steve Olenick. Stunt Coordinator: Randy 'Fife.' Executive in Charge of Production: Alan W. Potter. An American Playhouse/The Disney Channel Production. First aired in 1988.

ON PROMISED LAND

Music by: Mason Daring. Costume Designer: Marsha Perloff. Editor: Robert P. Seppey. Production Designer: John Huke. Director of Photography: Denis Lewiston. Executive Producer: Robert Benedetti. Written by: Ken Sagoes. Directed by: John Tewkesbury. Unit Production Manager: Cleve Landsberg. First Assistant Director: Thomas J. Blank. Second Assistant Director: Jessica Kreps. Los Angeles Casting: Judith Holstra, C.S.A., Nikki Valko, C.S.A. Atlanta Casting: Shay Bentley-Griffin, C.S.A. T-Top Supplied by: The Lion. Trainers: Cindy James, Chuck Coulter. Co-Producer: Peter Stelzer. Visual Consultant: Peter Jamison. Set Decorator: Sally Nicolaou. Property Master: Scott Stephens. Make-up: Janeen Davis. Hair Stylist: Jennifer Bell. Costume Supervisor: Diane Cornelius. Location Manager: Gina Cascino. Script Supervisor: Lesley King. Production Coordinator: Katie Willard Troebs. Production Sound Mixer: Ed White. Gaffer: Rick Anderson. Key Grip: Billy Sherrill. Negative Cutter: Rick Downey. Post Production Supervisor: Benjamin Benedetti. Sound Editor: Michael Guttierez. Music Editor: Sharon Smith. Anasazi Productions. First aired in 1994.

PARENT TRAP II

Executive Producers: Alan Landsburg, Joan Barnett. Produced by: Joan Barnett. Music by: Charles Fox. Edited by: Corky Ehlers. Art Director: Dan Leigh. Director of Photography: Peter Stein. Based on characters from the book *Das Doppelte Lottchen* by: Erich Kästner. Written by: Stuart Krieger. Directed by: Ronald F. Maxwell. Unit Production Manager: David Kappes. First Assistant Director: Robert Bordiga. Second Assistant Director: Nikola Colton. Associate Producer: Edward R. Horwitz. Production Assistants: Anne Grace, Laura Petticord. Casting by: Lynn Kressel. Location Casting by: Liz Keigley, Shari Rhodes. Costume Designer: Susan Gammie. Property Master: Peggy Parker. Set Dressers: Robert H. Satterlee, John L. Geier. Wardrobe Supervisor: Lynda Foote. Key Make-up & Hair Stylist: Marie-Ange Ripka. Make-up & Hair: Toni Trimble. Production Assistant: Heidi Meitzler. Location Manager: Claire Parks. Script Supervisor: Dawn Freer. Production Coordinator: Wendi J. Haas. Assistant Production Coordinator: Kevin Franklin Gieb. Assistant to Mr. Landsburg: Marilyn Lassen. Assistant to Mr. Maxwell: David Holbrook. Second Unit Director: David Kappes. Assistant Editor: Ruben R. Munoz. First Assistant Camera: Jonathan Herron. Second Unit Photography: Kenneth Peterson. Boom Operator: Bob Anderson, Jr. Generator Operator: Michael Roy Graham. Production Sound Mixer: Rick Waddell. Sound Editing by: Echo Film Services. Music Supervision: Music Design. Titles and Opticals: Westheimer Company. Theme Song *Let's Keep What We've Got* Music by: Charles Fox. Lyrics by: Hal David. Performed by: Marilyn McCoo. *Nothing At All* Performed by: Andrea Robinson. *Stand Back* Performed by: Phyllis St. James. Executive in Charge of Production: Howard Lipstone. The Landsburg Company. First aired in 1986.

PERFECT HARMONY

Music Scored by: Billy Goldenberg. Edited by: Sidney Wolinsky. Production Designer: Ladi Wilheim. Director of Photography: Bob Yeoman. Executive Producers: Joe Wizan, Todd Black. Supervising Producer: Jean Higgins. Produced by: Mickey Borofsky. Written by: David Obst. Directed by: Will Mackenzie. Stunt Coordinator: Lonnie Smith. Stunts: Jeff Gripper, C.C. Taylor. Unit Production Manager: Jean Higgins. First Assistant Director: Randy Corday. Second Assistant Director: Chris Halle. Casting by: Fern Champion, C.S.A., Dori Zuckerman. Casting Assistant: Mark Paladini. Location Casting: Shirley Crumley. Art Director: Joe O'Har. Costume Designer: Timothy D'Arcy. Set Decorator: Kristen McGary. Property Master: Tom Garkowski. Key Costumers: Tracy Thornton, Deborah M. Davis. Make-up: Peggy Teague. Hair Stylist: JoAnn Stafford Chaney. Script Supervisor: Amy Blane. Production Auditor: Catherine Webb. Production Coordinator: Ginny Warner. Production Sound Mixer: Itzhak "Ike" Magal. Assistant Editor: Fabienne Rawley. Sound Editing by: John A. Larson. Music Supervisor: Harry Shannon. Music Editing by: Bunny Andrews, Allan K. Rosen. Filmed on location at: Berry College, Rome, Georgia. Sea Breeze Productions, Inc. First aired in 1991.

SAVE THE DOG

Composer: J.A.C. Redford. Editor: Norman Hollyn. Production Designer: Chester Kaczenski. Director of Photography: Jacques Haitkin. Producers: Jim Kouf, Lynn Bigelow. Executive Producers: Paul Aaron, Erwin Stoff. Supervising Producer: George W. Perkins. Written by: Haris Orkin, John Mc-

Namara. Directed by: Paul Aaron. Unit Production Manager: Arthur Seidel. First Assistant Director: Joseph Paul Moore. Second Assistant Directors: Jeffrey M. Ellis, Thomas Zapata. Second Unit Director/Stunt Coordinator: Ronnie R. Rondell. Second Unit Director of Photography: Layton Blaylock. Production Sound Mixer: Wayne Bell. Casting: Matt Casella. Costume Designer: Merril Greene. Make-up: Frances Mathias. Hair Stylist: Manny Millar. Set Decorator: Michael O'Sullivan. Property Master: William Tozer. Gaffer: Jon H. Lewis. Key Grip: Ferrell A. Shinnick. Script Supervisor: Leslie Park. Location Manager: Cecyle Rexrode. Location Casting: Jo Edna Boldin. SFX Coordinator: Tim J. Moran. Production Coordinator: Elaine Dysinger. Assistant to Mr. Aaron: Jim McLindon. Production Auditor: Dan Conora. Supervising Sound Editor: Michael O'Corrigan. Supervising Music Editor: Kathy Bennett. Re-Recorded by: Gary Bourgeois, Dean Okrand, Chris Carpenter. Produced by Elsboy Productions in association with The Disney Channel. 90-minute format. First aired in 1988.

SPIES

Music by: Ken Thorne. Edited by: Bill Blunden. Production Designer: Bernt Capra. Director of Photography: Doug Milsome, B.S.C. Executive Producer: Susan Landau. Produced by: Christopher Morgan. Written by: Thomas Hood. Directed by: Kevin Connor. Unit Production Manager: Morris Chapnick. First Assistant Director: David Anderson. Second Assistant Director: Mathew Dunne. Casting: Judith Holstra. British Casting: Allan Foenander. North Carolina Casting: Fincannon & Associates. Costume Designer: Enid Harris. Costume Designer: Enid Harris. Art Director: John Myhre. Property Master: Robert M. Beck. Key Costumer: Kelly Mitchell. Make-up: Rudolph Eavey III. Hair Stylist: Michelle Johnson. Location Manager: F. Stanley Pearse, Jr. Gaffer: James R. Tomaro. Key Grip: Gene Poole. Script Supervisor: Cornelia "Nini" Rogan. Production Accountant: Phil Rodak. Production Coordinator: Eleanor Hemingway. Production Sound Mixer: Richard Van Dyke. Assistant Editor: Les Butler. Post Production Supervisor: Mark Eiges. Re-recording Mixer: Phillip Seretti. Sound Effects Supervisor: John K. Adams. Dialogue Supervisor: John M. Dodge. Foley & ADR Supervisor: T.W. Davis. Sound Editors: Donald Murray, Stan Hope. The Christopher Morgan Company. First aired in 1992.

SPOONER

Music by: Anthony Marinelli, Brian Banks. Director of Photography: Tim Suhrstedt. Art Director: Joe Rainey. Editor: Jim Gross. Co-Producers: Peter Baloff, Dave Wollert. Executive Producers: Sheldon Pinchuk, Bill Finnegan, Patricia Finnegan. Written by: Peter Baloff, Dave Wollert. Directed by: George Miller. Casting by: Mary V. Buck, C.S.A., Susan Edelman, C.S.A. Associate Producer: Lindsley Parsons, Jr. Unit Production Manager: Chuck Murray. 1st Assistant Director: Rob Corn. 2nd Assistant Director: Jeff Rafner. Costume Design: Joan Hunter. Set Decorator: Leonard Spears. Property Master: David Harshbarger. Costume Supervisor: Harold O'Neal. Wardrobe: Patti Breen. Make-up Artist: Bill Myer. Hairstylist: Frankie Campbell. Production Controller: Lori-Etta Taub. Production Coordinator: Lisa Matsukawa. Script Supervisor: Connie Collins. Sound Mixer: Glenn Berkovitz. Location Manager: John-Steven Agoglia. Gaffer: Bob Field. Key/Dolly Grip: Shunil Borpujari. Associate Editor: Suzanne Hines. Music Editor: Stan Jones. Music Recording and Mixing: Mark Curry. Supervising Sound Editor: George H. Anderson. Rerecording Sound Mixers: Dean Okrand, Philip J. Flad, Jr., C.S.A., Mike Getlin. Wrestling Choreographed by Jon "Jake" Jacobmeier. Produced by: The Finnegan-Pinchuk Company. First aired in 1989.

SPOT MARKS THE X

Costume Designer: Madeline Ann Graneto. Music by: Patrick Williams. Flute Soloist: Hubert Laws. Film Editor: Michael A. Stevenson. Production Designer: David Fischer. Director of Photography: Kelvin Pike, B.S.C. Executive Producers: Franklin R. Levy, Gregory Harrison, Matthew Rushton. Produced by: Marc Rubel, Dori Pierson. Written by: Michael Jenning. Directed by: Mark Rosman. Unit Production Manager: Fitch Cady. First Assistant Director: Brad Turner. Second Assistant Director: Karen Robyn. Casting by: Joyce Robinson, C.S.A., Penny Ellers, C.S.A. Production Consultant: Clint Rowe. Casting Director (Canada): Lynne Carow. Camera Operator: Tony Westman. Set Decorator: Kim MacKenzie. Property Master: Bill Thumm. Costume Supervisor: Jean Murphy. Make-up: Sandy Cooper. Hair Stylist: Sherry Linder. Special Effects: Dean Lockwood. Stunt Coordinator: John Wardlow. Animal Trainers: Debra J. Cob, Barbara Ann Tyack. Publicist: Stuart Fink. Extras Casting: Extraordinary Casting. Location Manager: Stewart Bethune. Production Sound Mixer: Richard Patton. Transportation Coordinator: George Grieve. Key Grip: Jim Hurford. Script Supervisor: Lara Fox. Production Auditor: Jack Brubach. Production Coordinator (Canada): Linda J. Sheehy. Production Coordinator (USA): John Charles Thomas. Assistant to Executive Producers: Kevin Hall. Assistant to Producers: Jeffrey R. Lane. Assistant to Director: Naomi Janzen. Post-Production Sound: Compact Sound Services. Sound Editing by: Superior Sound, Inc. Music Editing by: Allan K. Rosen. Orchestration: Michael Moores, Edward Karam. Music Recording Mixer: Don Hahn. Post-Production Coordinator: Megan McConnell. Associate Editor: Dennis E. Lew. Filmed on location in Vancouver, British Columbia. First aired in 1986.

STILL NOT QUITE HUMAN

Music by: John Debney. Edited by: David Berlatsky, A.C.E. Production Designer: Mark Freeborn. Director of Photography: Ron Orieux. Executive Producer: Noel Resnick. Produced by: James Margellos. From the book series *Not Quite Human*. Based on Characters Created by: Kevin Osborn. Written and Directed by: Eric Luke. Stunt Coordinator: Brent Woolsey. Unit Production Manager: Warren Carr. First Assistant Director: Don Hauer. Second Assistant Director: Colleen Mitchel Neill. Casting Executive: Eddie Foy III. Casting Vancouver: Lynne Carrow. Art Director: David Willson. Set Decorator: Rose Marie McSherry. Property Master: Bill Thumm. Costume Designer: Larry S. Wells. Costume Supervisor: Nicola Ryall. Make-up Artist: Victoria Down. Hair Stylist: Ian Ballard. Production Sound Mixer: Larry Sutton. Camera Operator: Peter Woest. Special Effects Coordinator: Bill Orr. Conceptual Artist: Phillip Norwood. Gaffer: Stephen Jackson. Key Grip: David B. Gordon. Construction Coordinator: Mike Rennison. Transportation Coordinator: Dennis Houser. Transportation Captain: Rodney Beech. Transportation Co-Captain: Murray Mills. Location Manager: Kirk Johns. Production Coordinator: Padi Mills. Script Supervisor: Lara Fox. Production Auditors: Lynn Elston, Liz Staniforth. Assistant to the Director: Robert Hicks. Animal Trainer: Mark Wiener. Extras Casting: Coreen Mayrs. Visual Effects: Ted Rae. Visual Display Graphics: Robert J. Peppler. Lead Model Maker: Dennis J. Dale. Puppet Construction: Asao Goto. Seamstress: Wendy Polutanovich. Post Production Supervisor: David Berlatsky. Assistant Editor Los Angeles: Bill Steinberg. Assistant Editor Vancouver: Bruce Giesbrecht. Music Editor: Brian Vessa. A Resnick/Margellos Productions Film. First aired in 1992.

TIGER TOWN

Costume Designer: Gary Jones. Production Designer: Neil J. Spisak. Music: Eddy L. Manson. Film Editors: Richard A. Harris, John Link. Director of Photography: Robert Elswit. Writer: Alan Shapiro. Additional Material: Bobby Fine. Producer: Susan B. Landau. Directed by: Alan Shapiro. Production Associate: Forrest Murray. Production Manager: Joanne Mallas. Second Assistant Directors: Steve Novak, Mary Ellen Woods. Casting: Lynn Kressel (Detroit), Nancy Kelly (New York). Sound Mixer: Alan Byer. Sound Boom: Jeff Jones. First Assistant Camera: Frank Perl, Kim Marks. Camera Assistant: Michael Menlo. Still Photographer: Linda Soloman. Assistant to the Director: Evan Dunsky. Assistant to the Producer: Janice Yarbrough. Property Master: Michael Foxworthy. Props: Brian Hartley. Location Manager: Corinne Saaranen. Location Scout: Kimberly Conley. Storyboard Artist: Bill Bryan. Script Supervisor: Susan Malerstein. Location Auditor: Marianne Scanlon. Production Office Coordinator: Maria Petrella. Trainee: Elizabeth Wetzel. Technical Advisor: Gates Brown. Stunt Coordinator: Sandra Gimpel. Assistant Editor: Toni Morgan. Apprentice Editor: Pamela Easley. Post Production

Assistant: Mary Ellen Woods. Make-up and Hair: Felice Fassnacht. Casting Assistant: Jane Ann Lowther. Assistant to the Costume Designer: Anne Saunders. Costume Assistant: Michaelene Cristini. Sound Editors: Sound Flash, Inc. Supervising Sound Editor: Jim Troutman. Re-recording Mixers: Christopher L. Haire, John L. Anderson, Andy Bass. Music Editor: Ted Roberts. Gaffer: Robert Hayward. Grips: Gordon Connelly, William T. Strachan, Jr., Jim Troutman, Jack Tobin. Title Design: Dan Curry. Acknowledgment: The Detroit Tigers.

UNDERGRADS, THE

Edited by: Ron Wisman. Music by: Matthew McCauley. Production Designer: Bill Brodie. Director of Photography: Laszlo George, C.S.C. Screenplay by: Paul W. Shapiro. Story by: Paul W. Shapiro, Michael Weisman. Produced and Directed by: Steven H. Stern. Casting: Dierdre Bowen. Production Supervisor: John Danylkiw. First Assistant Director: Michael Zenon. Second Assistant Director: Elizabeth Halko. Third Assistant Director: Howard Tothschild. Art Director: Tony Hall. Draughtsman: Tom Doherty, Debra Gledem. Art Department Assistants: Birgit Siber, Caroline George. Location Manager: Jason Paikowsky. Production Co-ordinator: Ursula Korell. Production Secretary: Sandy Webb. Production Accountant: Rachelle Charron. Bookkeeper: Mary Robbie. Script Supervisor: Blance McDermaid. 1st Assistant Editor: Stephen Humble. 2nd Assistant Editor: Jan Nicolichuk. Sound Editor: Jim Hopkins. Assistant Sound Editor: Cathy Hutton. Foley: Charles Bowers. Sound Re-recording: Joe Grimaldi, David Appleby, Dino Pigat. Propmaster: Dan Wladyka. Assistant Props: John "Frenchie" Berger. Set Dresser: Tom Coulter. Assistant Set Dresser: Sean Kirby. Make-up: Linda Gill. Hair: Donna Bis. Assistant Hair: Malcolm Tanner. Wardrobe Designer: Olga Dimitrov. Wardrobe Mistress: Rose Mihalyi. Assistant Dresser: Jana Stern. Camera Operator: Henry Fiks. 1st Assistant Camera: Monty Rowan. 2nd Assistant Camera: David Makin. Stills: Chin Sugino. Gaffer: Brian Monta. Best Boy: Rae Thurston. Generator Operator: Norman O'Halloran. Key Grip: Michael Kohne. Dolly Grip: James Kohne. Sound Mixer: Richard Lightstone. Boom: Herb Heritage. Special Effects: Martin Malivoire. Stunts: Bobby Hanna. Transportation Co-ordinator: Jim Kennedy. Transportation Captain: Craig Kohne. Drivers: Frank Tenaglia, Pat Brennan, Rudy Bachuchi, Richard Moryn, Harry Ross. Motorcycle built by: Jack Innes. Craftservice: Stephen Payne. Director Observer/Trainee: Jeff Authors. Production Office Assistant: David Flaherty. Construction Supervisor: Alex Russell. Head Carpenter: Stanley Young. Scenic Artist: Fred Geringer. 2nd Carpenter: Paul Theodore. Labourer: William Johnston. Carpenter/Painter: Neil Grocut. Publicity: Prudence Emery. Music Engineer: Gary Gray. Additional Music Recording and Production: Tim McCauley. *Getaway* Performed by: Tamme Dakota. *Stayin' Alive* Written by: Barry Gibb, Maurice Gibb, Robin Gibb. Acknowledgment: Ontario Film Commission. A Sharmhill Production Inc. in association with The Disney Channel.

WHIPPING BOY, THE

Music by: Lee Holdridge. Costume Designer: Tiny Nicholls. Production Designers: John Blezard, Norbert Scherer. Edited by: Sean Barton. Director of Photography: Clive Tickner. Co-Produced by: Georges Campana. Executive Producers: Gerhard Schmidt, Glenn R. Jones, Philip D. Fehrle. Produced by: Ellen Freyer. Teleplay by: Max Brindle. Based on the Novel *The Whipping Boy* by: Sid Fleischman. Directed by: Syd Macartney. Casting Director, U.K.: Allan Foenander. Casting Director, U.S.: Barbara Baldavin, C.S.A. Casting Director, Germany: Horst D. Scheel. Executives in Charge of Production—The Disney Channel: Carol Rubin. Gemini Films: Frank Dohman. WDR Executive: Siegmund Grewenig. Line Producer, Gemini: Andreas Grosch. Line Producer, Jones: Marty Eli Schwartz. Unit Production Manager: Andreas Bodenstein. Production Coordinator: Dorothee Specht. Production Accountants: Uschi Schlieper, Bettina Bott. 1st Assistant Director: Marty Eli Schwartz. 2nd Assistant Director: Michael Rowitz. 3rd Assistant Director: Kathrin Braun. Continuity: Jean Bourn. Camera Operator: Jeremy Hiles. Camera Assistants: Henning Jessel, Britta Becker. Stills Photographer:

Astrid Wirth. Sound Mixer: Wolfgang Wirtz. Boom Operator: Raymond Meyer. Assistant Editors: Hansjorg Weissbrich, Andreas Lemke. Sound Editor: Lothar Segeler. ADR Editor: Bettina McCall. Foley Artists: Mel Kutbay, Jo Furst. Re-recording Sound Mixer: Max Rammler-Rogall. Set Decorator: Simon Wakefield. Prop Master: Eliane Huss. Assistant Art Director: Heike Jodicke. Scenic Artist: Rudolph Reinstadler. Make-up Supervisor: Linda Mooney. Make-up Artist: Birger Laube. Costume Assistant: Brian Cox. Wardrobe: Martina Schall, Sandra Fuhr. Gaffer: Klaus-Peter Venn. Electrician 1: Thomas Brugge. Electrician 2: Bernd Niggeschulze. Electrician 3: Andreas Theiner. Key Grip: Claus Dorner. Grip: Markus Spater. Orchestration by: Ira Hearshen. Music Coordinator: Paul Talkington. Recording Engineer: Keith Grant. Music Performed by: The Munich Symphony Orchestra. Color Timer: Hans-Gabriel Bergmann. *French Unit* Line Producer: Jean-Claude Marchant. Unit/Location Manager: Pascal Maillard. Assistant Unit/Location Manager: Margot Luneau. Transport Coordinator: Isabelle Gautier. Production Secretary: Carine Thevenet. Accountant: Anne-Marie Billon. 2nd A.D.: Elise Crosnier. Casting: Sylvie Brochere. Extras Casting: Sylvina Pieres. Filmed on location in North Rhine-Westphalia and Burgundy. Dedicated to: Hans Sandmair. Co-Produced in association with Le Sabre Group. A Gemini Films Production in association with Jones Entertainment Group, Ltd. and The Disney Channel. First aired in 1994.

CHAPTER 14

Touchstone Television and the Studio's Bid for the Big Time

SISKEL & EBERT & THE MOVIES
The credits for the series include the following: Executive Producer: Larry J. Dieckhaus. Supervising Producer: Jim Murphy. Producer: Andrea Gronvall. Assistant Producers: Linda Weseman, Susan Malone, Stuart Cleland. Directors: Don Voight, Jim Murphy. Scenic Designers: Michael Lowenstein, Mary Margaret Bartley.

LIVE! WITH REGIS & KATHIE LEE
Producer: Michael Gelman.

CHALLENGERS, THE
Created by: Rob Greenberg. Directed by: Morris Abraham. Co-producer: Janet Markowitz. Associate Producer: Chris Plourde. Dick Clark Prods. in association with Ron Greenberg Prods.

MIKE & MATY
Exec Prod: Tamara Rawitt, Kari Sagin. Senior Producers: Ray Giuliani, Michael J. Miller. Executive in Charge of Production: John Alexander. Director: Steve Grant. One-hour format. First aired on 4/11/94.

JUDGE FOR YOURSELF
Executive Producer: Kari Sagin. Supervising Producer: Laura Gelles. Director: Paul Casey. Producers: Elaine Bauer, Lisa Erspamer, Jessica Malloy, Shannon O'Rourke. Executive in Charge of Production: Jerry Jaskulski. Set Design: Rene Lagler. Produced by: Faded Denim Productions. One-hour format. Airdates: 9/12/94 to 4/07/95.

STEPHANIE MILLER SHOW, THE
Exec Prod: John Kalish, Anne Beatts. Director: Sandi Fullerton. Senior Producer: Ronnie Weinstock. One-Man Band: Hami. "The Rainbow Rep": James Stephens, Carlos Alazraqui, Karen Maruyama. Produced by: Lipshtick Productions Ltd. One-hour format. Airdates: 9/15/95 to 1/20/96.

DANNY!
Executive Producer: Velma Cato. Executive in Charge of Production: Jennifer Mullin. Contest Producer: Stephen Radosh. Produced by: Faded Denim Productions. One-hour format. Airdates: 9/11/95 to 2/02/96.

ELLEN BURSTYN SHOW, THE
Created by: Norman Steinberg, David Frankel. Executive Producer: Norman Steinberg. Written by: Robert Bruce, David Cohen, David Frankel, Cheryl Gard, Howard Abbott Gewirtz, Barry Gurstein, Bo Kaprall, Robert Keats, Jim Mulligan, Holly Nadler, Pamela Norris, David Pitlik, Bob Rosenfarb, Roger S.H. Schulman, Norman Steinberg, Martin M. Weiss. Directed by: Dolores Ferraro, Arlene Sanford, Norman Steinberg, Sam Weisman. Supervising Producers: Ronald E. Frazier, David Frankel. Produced by: David Frankel, Ronald E. Frazier. Associate Producer: Nick O'Gorman. Executive Story Editor: Bo Kaprall. Story Editors: David S. Cohen, Roger S. H.

Schulman, Robert Keats, Robert Bruce, Martin M. Weiss, Cheryl Gard. Casting: Meg Simon, Fran Kumin, C.S.A. Director of Photography: George Spiro Dibie. Production Designer: Herman Zimmerman. Unit Production Manager/First Assistant Director: Gene Sultan. Second Assistant Director: Jules Lichtman. Art Director: Gary Weist. Lighting Director: Leo Farrenkopf. Associate Director: Franklin Melton. Stage Managers: Steve Della Pietra, Barbara Ravis, Jill Frank. Editor: Jimmy B. Frazier. Music: Artie Butler. Theme Song *Nothin' in the World Like Love* Music: Artie Butler. Lyrics: John Bettis. Performed by: Rita Coolidge. Production Associate: Susan Diamant. Costume Designers: William Ware Theiss, Joan V. Evans. Set Decorator: Charles Pierce. Property Master: Charles Eguia. Key Costumers: Ruby K. Manis, Sandra Berke Jordan, Cindy Chock, Andrea Ross, Gracia Littauer. Make-up: Bill Tuttles, Arlette Greenfield, Lee Halls, Frances Kolar, Sajata Robinson. Hair Stylists: Kathy Blondell, Lillian Cvecich. Script Supervisor: Kristine Greco. Production Coordinators: Ann Ashcraft, Robin E. Chambers. Production Sound Mixer: Michael Ballin. Technical Directors: Abraham Kabak, Meryl Foster. Audio: Chuck Eisen. Video: John Monteleone.

HARRY
Developed by: Gary Jacobs. Written by: Ken Finkleman, Ben Gramin, Gary Jacobs, David Tyron King, Alan Mandel, Rich Orloff, H. Schireson. Directed by: Linda Day, Bill Foster, Steve Robman. Executive Producers: Barry Levinson, Mark Johnson. Co-Executive Producer: Alan Arkin. Supervising Producer: Gary Jacobs. Produced by: Don Van Atta, Shelley Zellman. Created by: Susan Kramer. Associate Producer: Phyllis J. Nelson. Executive Story Editor: David Axelrod. Story Editor: Harold Kimmel. Director of Photography: Richard Hissong. Art Director: Herman Zimmerman. Editors: Jimmy B. Frazier, Mark K. Samuels. Associate Director: Carol Scott. Stage Manager: Steve Burgess. Music by: Alf Clausen. Casting by: Rosenberg/Haberman & Associates. Set Decorator: Richard Spero. Property Master: William Fannon. Key Costumers: Joseph R. Markham, Elaine Maser. Make-up: Karen Kubeck. Hair Stylists: Lynn Masters, Ginger Grieve. New York Casting by: David Tochterman. Script Supervisor: Mattie Caruthers. Production Coordinator: Laura L. Garcia. Technical Directors: Ken Lamkin, Robert G. Holmes, Parker Roe. Audio: Larry Stephens. Video: Larry Huchingson.

SIDEKICKS
Executive Producers: Richard Chapman, Bill Dial. Creative Consultant: Bill Dial. Supervising Producer: Ric Rondell. Produced by: Ric Rondell, Thomas Perry, Jo Perry. Created by: Dan Gordon. Written by: Richard Chapman, Robert Comfort, Bill Dial, Elia Katz, Casey Kelly, John Kostmayer, Bill Luetscher, Chris Miller, W. Reed Moran, David Peckinpah, Jo Perry, Thomas Perry. Mike Piller, Gary Rosen, Steve Stoliar, Michael Sutton. Directed by: Jay Broad, Linda Day, Gil Gerard, Nick Havinga, Helaine Head, Victor Lobl, Kim Manners, Vincent McEveety, Sig Neufeld, Allen Reisner, Ric Rondell, Judy Vogelsang. Executive Producer for Motown: Michael L.

Weisbarth. Co-Producer: Sally Baker. Associate Producer: Janice Cooke-Leonard. Executive Story Consultant: Bob Comfort. Story Editor: W. Reed Moran. Executive Story Consultant: W. Reed Moran. Music by: Rareview. Theme Song *Just Trust Tomorrow* Music: Rareview. Lyrics: Mark Mueller. Song Performed by: Kipp Lennon. Director of Photography: F. Pershing Flynn. Art Director: Charles Hughes. Art Directors: Charles Hughes, Cameron Birnie. Film Editors: Domenic G. DiMascio, Jerry Temple, Bill Brame, A.C.E., Judith A. Burke, Steve Schultz. Unit Production Managers: Ric Rondell, Ira Shuman. First Assistant Directors: Richard Peter Schroer, Ira Shuman, Joseph Paul Moore, Kenneth D. Collins. Second Assistant Directors: Kenneth D. Collins, Steve "Stevo" Danton. Casting by: Fern Champion, C.S.A., Pamela Basker, C.S.A. Associate: Joanne Koehler. Set Decorators: Ira Bates, Robert L. Zilliox. Property Master: Ken Orme. Key Costumers: Nick Mezzanotti, Milton G. Mangum, Sandy Berke-Jordan, Sharon Day, Bob Christenson. Make-up: Michael F. Blake, John M. Norin, Carol Schwartz. Hair Stylist: Ariel Bagdadi. Costume Designer: William Ware Theiss. Stunt Coordinator: Mike Vendrell. Location Managers: M. Ryan Rosenberg, Peter M. Robarts, Stuart Ganong. Script Supervisors: Betty Goldberg, Roslyn Harris, Andrea Walzer, Gillian Murphy. Production Coordinator: Nancy Malone Claycomb. Production Sound Mixers: Richard Church, C.A.S., Bob Gravenor. Sound Editing by: Soundelux. Music Editing by: Music Design Group. Martial Arts Choreographer: Ernie Reyes, Sr. A Motown Production in association with Walt Disney Television.

DOWN AND OUT IN BEVERLY HILLS

Developed for Television by: Howard Gewirtz. Based on Characters from the Play *Boudu Sauvé Des Eaux* by: René Fauchois. Supervising Producer: Don Van Atta. Executive Producer: Howard Gewirtz. Written by: Al Aidekman, Robert Bruce, Howard Gewirtz, Terry Hart, Robert Keats, Rich Reinhart, Martin Weiss. Directed by: Peter Baldwin, Jeff Chambers, Linda Day, Bill Foster, Oz Scott. Co-Executive Producer: Richard Rosenstock. Associate Producer: Phyllis J. Nelson. Executive Story Editors: Robert Bruce, Martin Weiss, Harold Kimmel. Creative Consultant: Terry Hart. Story Editor: Joe Fisch. Director of Photography: Richard Hissong. Art Director: John C. Mula. Editor: Bill Petty. Associate Directors: Carol Scott, Franklin Melton. Stage Manager: Keith E. Richmond. Music by: David Frank. Casting by: The Casting Company, Denise Chamian, Peg Halligan, C.S.A. Set Decorators: Patricia Bruner, Rochelle Moser, Richard Spero. Property Master: Steve Johnson. Costume Designer: Emily Williams Draper. Key Costumers: Terrence K. Smith, Patricia Landis, Elaine Maser. Make-up: John Goodwin. Hair Stylists: Dianne Roberson, Ginger Grieve. Production Consultant: Clint Rowe. Script Supervisors: Susan Diamant, Gabrielle James. Production Coordinators: Robin Chambers, Bruce Tallerman, Cynthia Marquoit. Technical Directors: Tom Doak, John B. Field, Ken Lamkin, Jim Johnson. Audio: Larry M. Stephens, Michael T. Gannon, Neal Weinstein, Don Worsham, Russ Gary. Video: Larry Huchingson.

OLDEST ROOKIE, THE

Created by: Gil Grant, Ricahrd Chapman. Executive Producers: Richard Chapman, Gil Grant. Written by: Richard Chapman, Tom Chehak, Daniel Freudenberger, Gil Grant, Steve Johnson, Bill Luetscher, Larry Nesbitt, Jo Perry, Thomas Perry, Tom Shehak, Elliott Stern. Directed by: Roger Duchowny, F. Pershing Flynn, Harry Harris, Paul Krasny, Kim Manners, Vincent McEveety, Donald Petrie, Allen Reisner, Ric Rondell, Judith Vogelsang. Supervising Producers: Ric Rondell, Jo Perry, Thomas Perry, Tom Chehak. Produced by: Tom Chehak. Associate Producer: Jeanne Marie Byrd. Co-Producer: Janice Cooke-Leonard. Story Consultant: Daniel Freudenberger. Music by: Steve Dorff. Directors of Photography: Isidore Mankofsky, A.S.C., F. Pershing Flynn, Roland "Ozzie" Smith. Art Directors: Cameron Birnie, Al Rohm. Editors: Robert E. Pew, Judith A. Burke, Jerry Temple. Unit Production Manager: Ira Shuman. First Assistant Directors: Richard Peter Schroer, Kenneth D. Collins, Marty Eli Schwartz, Frederic B. Blankfein. Second Assistant Directors: Peter "Pistol" Choi, Steve "Stevo" Danton, Peter Jordan. Casting by: Fern Champion, C.S.A., Pamela Basker, C.S.A.,

Joanne Koehler. Set Decorators: Robert L. Zilliox, Rochelle Moser. Property Master: Lavar Emert. Costumers: Maureen Gates, Joseph L. Roveto. Make-up: Nadia, John M. Norin. Hair Stylists: Gregg R. Mitchell, Shawn McKay. Sound Mixer: Robert Gravenor. Script Supervisors: Nancy Malone Claycomb, Linda "Bunky" Conklin. Costumes Designed by: Tom Bronson. Costumers: Nick Mezzanotti, Karen Bellamy. Sound Mixer: William Teague. Stunt Coordinator: R.A. Rondell. Acknowledgement: Terry Cammack. Sound Editing by: Stephen J. Cannell Productions. Music Editing by: Music Design Group. Gil Grant Productions and Chapman Productions in association with Touchstone Television.

GOLDEN GIRLS, THE

1985–86 SEASON

Executive Producers: Paul Junger Witt, Tony Thomas. Produced by: Kathy Speer, Terry Grossman. Co-Produced by: Marsha Posner Williams. Created by: Susan Harris. Written by: Susan Beavers, James Berg, R.J. Colleary, Barry Fanaro, Terry Grossman, Susan Harris, Winifred Hervey, Christopher Lloyd, Mort Nathan, Liz Sage, Stuart Silverman, Kathy Speer, Stan Zimmerman. Directed by: Paul Bogart, Jim Drake, Terry Hughes, Jack Shea, Gary Shimokawa. Supervising Producer: Paul Bogart. Executive Story Consultant: Winifred Hervey. Executive Script Consultants: Mort Nathan, Barry Fanaro. Creative Consultant: Liz Sage. Production Designer: Edward Stephenson. Music by: George Aliceson Tipton. Casting by: Judith Weiner & Associates, Allison Jones. Costumes Designed by: Judy Evans. Associate Directors: Jon Sharp, Gary Shimokawa, Doug Smart. Stage Managers: Tom Carpenter, Doug Tobin. Production Associate: Robert Spina. Post Production Supervisors: Harold McKenzie, Lex Passaris. Production Assistant: Ellen Deutsch. Post Production Manager: Adria Horton. Music Coordinator: Scott Gale. Editorial Assistant: Lex Passaris. Videotape Editor: Frank Mazzaro. Assistant to the Executive Producers: Stacy Saltman. Production Staff: Jeffrey Goodman, Richard King, Jeannie Taylor, Anne Thomopoulos, Kit Wilkinson. Unit Manager: David Amico. Technical Manager: Ted Ashton. Technical Coordinator: Bill Conroy. Technical Directors: Joseph Epperson, O. Tamburri. Lighting: Alan Walker. Audio: Wolf Seeberg, Doc Siegel, C.A.S. Video: Andrew Dickerman. Cameras: Tony Balderama, Jack Chisholm, Tom Faigh, Dave Hilmer, Ritch Kenney, Ron Olson, Wayne Orr, Carol A. Wetovich. Property Master: Ken Dawson, Jasper Ehrig. Gaffer: Andy Kassan. Head Carpenter: Henry Petersen, Paul Wadian. Costumer: Rhoda Yarbrough. Make-up: Maurice Stein. Hair Stylist: Joyce Melton. Re-recording: Allan Patapoff. Production Executive: Susan Palladino. Production: Harry Waterson. A Witt Thomas Harris Production. Not listed in official credits: Theme song *Thank You for Being a Friend* Written by: Andrew Gold. Sung by Cindy Fees.

1986–87 SEASON

Produced by: Kathy Speer, Terry Grossman. Co-Produced by: Winifred Hervey, Mort Nathan, Barry Fanaro, Marsha Posner Williams. Created by: Susan Harris. Written by: Jeffrey Duteil, Barry Fanaro, Jan Fischer, Scott Spencer Gordon, Terry Grossman, Winifred Hervey, Christopher Lloyd, Russell Marcus, Mort Nathan, Bob Rosenfarb, Patt Shea, Kathy Speer, William Weidner, Harriett Weiss, Susan Harris Witt. Directed by: Terry Hughes, Jay Sandrich, David Steinberg. Executive Producers: Paul Junger Witt, Tony Thomas. Story Editor: Christopher Lloyd. Story Editor: Bob Rosenfarb. Associate Producer: Greg Giangregorio. Production Designer: Edward Stephenson. Music by: George Aliceson Tipton. Casting by: Sharon Siegel, Susan Vash. Original Casting by: Judith Weiner & Associates. Costumes Designed by: Judy Evans. Associate Directors: Gary Shimokawa, Lex Passaris, Lex Cohen. Post Production Supervisor: Lex Passaris. Stage Managers: Tom Carpenter, Jane Greene. Production Associate: Robert Spina. Production Assistant: Ellen Deutsch. Post Production Manager: Adria Horton. Music Coordinator: Scott Gale. Technical Coordinator: Ted Ashton. Editor: Harold McKenzie. Associate Designer: Michael Hynes. Production Staff: Jeffrey Goodman, Jackie Schaffner, Jeannie Taylor. Technical Director: O. Tamburri. Lighting: Alan

Walker. Audio: Edward L. Moskowitz, C.A.S., Dick Burns. Video: Bob Kaufman, John O'Brien. Cameras: Jack Chisholm, Ritch Kenney, Ken Tamburri, Carol A. Wetovich. Property Master: Ken Dawson. Gaffers: Ron Ruby, Robert Dick. Head Carpenter: Henry Petersen, Paul Wadian. Costumers: Rhoda Yarbrough, Julie Rhine. Make-up: Maurice Stein. Hair Stylist: Joyce Melton. Re-recording: Allan Patapoff. Production Executive: Susan Palladino. Production: Harry Waterson. A Witt Thomas Harris Production.

1987–88 SEASON

Co-Executive Producers: Kathy Speer, Terry Grossman. Supervising Producers: Mort Nathan, Barry Fanaro. Produced by: Winifred Hervey Stallworth. Co-Produced by: Marsha Posner Williams, Jeffrey Ferro, Fredric Weiss. Created by: Susan Harris. Written by: Jeff Abugov, Robert Bruce, Barry Fanaro, Jeffrey Ferro, Terry Grossman, Christopher Lloyd, Mort Nathan, David Nichols, Kathy Speer, Winifred Hervey Stallworth, Fredric Wiess, Martin Weiss. Directed by: Terry Hughes. Executive Producers: Paul Junger Witt, Tony Thomas, Susan Harris. Executive Story Consultants: Robert Bruce, Martin Weiss. Executive Script Consultant: Christopher Lloyd. Story Editor: Christopher Lloyd. Executive Story Editor: Jeff Abugov. Production Designer: Edward Stephenson. Music by: George Aliceson Tipton. Casting by: Jennifer J. Part, C.S.A. Original Casting by: Judith Weiner & Associates. Costumes Designed by: Judy Evans. Associate Directors: Michael Riolo, Lex Passaris, Harold McKenzie. Stage Managers: Tom Carpenter, Kent Zbornak. Production Associate: Robert Spina. Unit Manager: David Amico. Technical Manager: Bill Conroy. Post Production Manager: Adria Horton. Music Coordinator: Scott Gale. Choreographer: Carl Jablonski. Production Coordinator: Richard King. Associate Designer: Michael Hynes. Production Assistant: Jackie Schaffner. Editorial Assistant: Richard J. Powell. Production Staff: Jeannie Taylor, Esther F. Himbaugh. Technical Director: O. Tamburri. Lighting: Alan Walker, J. Kent Inasy. Audio: Edward L. Moskowitz, C.A.S. Video: Bob Kaufman, John O'Brian. Cameras: Dave Banks, Jack Chisholm, Stephen A. Jones, Steve Jones, Ritch Kenney, Ken Tamburri. Property Master: Ken Dawson, James Draper. Gaffers: Ron Ruby, Warren Bellamy, William Updegraff, Johnny Walker, Bill Updegraff. Head Carpenter: Paul Wadian. Costumers: Helaine Bruck, Barbara Yokooji. Make-up: Maurice Stein. Hair Stylist: Joyce Melton. Editor: Jim McElroy. Re-recording: Allan Patapoff. Production Executive: Susan Palladino. Production: Harry Waterson. A Witt Thomas Harris Production.

1988–89 SEASON

Co-Executive Producers: Kathy Speer, Terry Grossman, Mort Nathan, Barry Fanaro. Supervising Producer: Eric Cohen. Created by: Susan Harris. Written by: Kevin Abbott, Robert Bruce, Eric Cohen, Rick Copp, Barry Fanaro, David A. Goodman, Harriet B. Helberg, Sandy Helberg, Tracy Gamble, Terry Grossman, Christopher Lloyd, Mort Nathan, Kathy Speer, Winifred Hervey-Stallworth, Richard Vaczy, Martin Weiss. Directed by: Terry Hughes, Stephen Zuckerman. Executive Producers: Paul Junger Witt, Tony Thomas. Co-Produced by: Martin Weiss, Robert Bruce. Executive Script Consultant: Christopher Lloyd. Executive Story Editors: Richard Vaczy, Tracy Gamble. Associate Producer: David Amico. Production Designer: Edward Stephenson. Music by: George Aliceson Tipton. Casting by: Jennifer J. Part, C.S.A., Joanne Koehler. Original Casting by: Judith Weiner & Associates. Associate Directors: Lex Passaris, Peter D. Beyt. Stage Managers: Tom Carpenter, Kent Zbornak. Production Associate: Robert Spina. Post Production Manager: Adria Horton. Music Coordinator: Scott Gale. Production Coordinator: Nina Feinberg. Technical Manager: Bill Conroy. Production Associate: Jackie Schaffner. Production Staff: Kari Hendler, Bobbi JG Weiss. Editorial Assistant: Pamela Phelps. Technical Director: O. Tamburri. Lighting: Andy Kassan, Alan Walker. Audio: Edward L. Moskowitz, C.A.S. Video: John O'Brien. Cameras: Chester Jackson, Stephen A. Jones, Ritch Kenney, Ken Tamburri. Property Master: Robert Devicariis. Gaffer: William Updegraff. Head Carpenter: Paul Wadian. Costumers: Helaine Bruck, Barbara Yokooji. Make-up: Maurice Stein. Hair Stylist: Joyce Melton Conroy. Re-recording: Craig Porter. Production

Executive: Susan Palladino. A Witt Thomas Harris Production.

1989–90 SEASON

Co-Executive Producers: Marc Sotkin, Terry Hughes. Supervising Producers: Tom Whedon, Philip Jayson Lasker. Producers: Gail Parent, Martin Weiss, Robert Bruce. Supervising Producer: Eric Cohen. Created by: Susan Harris. Written by: Harold Apter, Robert Bruce, Marc Cherry, Tracy Gamble, Susan Harris, Philip Jayson Lasker, Gail Parent, Don Reo, Marc Sotkin, Eugene B. Stein, Richard Vaczy, Martin Weiss, Tom Whedon, Jamie Wooten. Directed by: Terry Hughes. Executive Producers: Paul Junger Witt, Tony Thomas, Susan Harris. Co-Produced by: Tracy Gamble, Richard Vaczy. Story Editors: Rick Copp, David A. Goodman, Marc Cherry, Jamie Wooten. Associate Producer: Nina Feinberg. Production Designer: Edward Stephenson. Music by: George Aliceson Tipton. Casting by: Ellen Meyer, C.S.A. & Associates, Bonnie Shane. Costumes Designed by: Judy Evans. Associate Directors: Lex Passaris, Peter D. Beyt. Stage Managers: Tom Carpenter, Kent Zbornak. Technical Manager: Bill Conroy. Production Associate: Robert Spina. Art Director: Michael Hynes. Post Production Manager: Richard J. Powell. Music Coordinator: Scott Gale. Production Assistants: Esther Himbaugh, Jackie Shaffner. Production Staff: Tim Donnelly, Jordan Goodman, Ray Kolasa, Daniel Levey, Todd Morris, Pamela Phelps, Denise Porter, David Sacks, Bobbie Shane, Andy Stone, Bobbi JG Weiss, Kari Hendler. Editorial Assistant: Pamela Phelps. Technical Director: O. Tamburri. Lighting: Alan Walker, Kent Inasy. Audio: Edward L. Moskowitz, C.A.S., Douglas Botnick, C.S.A. Video: Randy Johnson. Cameras: David Heckman, Chester Jackson, Stephen A. Jones, Ritch Kenney. Property Master: Robert Devicariis. Gaffers: William Updegraff, Warren Bellamy, Ron Ruby. Editor: Peter Beyt. Head Carpenter: Paul Wadian. Costumers: Helaine Bruck, Barbara Yokooji. Make-up: Art Harding. Hair Stylist: Joyce Melton Conroy. Original Casting by: Judith Weiner & Associates. Re-recording: Craig Porter. Production Executives: David Amico, Susan Palladino. Executives in Charge of Production: Susan Palladino, Ken Stump. A Witt Thomas Harris Production.

1990–91 SEASON

Executive Producer: Marc Sotkin. Co-Executive Producers: Tom Whedon, Philip Jayson Lasker. Supervising Producers: Gail Parent, Richard Vaczy, Tracy Gamble, Don Seigel, Jerry Perzigian. Created by: Susan Harris. Written by: Harold Apter, Marc Cherry, Tracy Gamble, Mitchell Hurwitz, Philip Jayson Lasker, Gail Parent, Jerry Perzigian, Don Seigel, Marc Sotkin, Robert Spina, Richard Vaczy, Jim Vallely, Tom Whedon, Jamie Wooten. Directed by: Robert Berlinger, Peter D. Beyt, Zane Buzby, Matthew Diamond, Lex Passaris, Judy Pioli. Executive Producers: Paul Junger Witt, Tony Thomas. Co-Produced by: Nina Feinberg. Executive Story Editors: Marc Cherry, Jamie Wooten. Story Editors: Jim Vallely, Mitchell Hurwitz. Production Designer: Edward Stephenson. Music by: George Aliceson Tipton. Casting by: Ellen Meyer, C.S.A., Bonnie Shane. Costumes Designed by: Judy Evans. Associate Directors: Lex Passaris, Peter D. Beyt. Stage Managers: Tom Carpenter, Tom Seidman, Tom Ohliger. Technical Manager: Bill Conroy. Production Associate: Robert Spina. Art Director: Michael Hynes. Post Production Manager: Fred Roth. Music Coordinator: Scott Gale. Production Coordinator: Denise Fleissner Barta. Production Assistant: Salli Shrewsbury. Production Staff: Brenda Bos, Laurie K. Parres, Pam Phelps, Denise Porter, Kurt Schindler. Original Casting by: Judith Weiner & Associates. Technical Directors: Ken Tamburri, Jim Horky. Lighting: Alan Walker, Roger Dalton. Audio: Edward L. Moskowitz, C.A.S. Video: Randy Johnson. Cameras: Ritch Kenney, David Heckman, Chester Jackson, Stephen A. Jones. Property Master: Robert Devicariis. Gaffers: William Updegraff, Robbie Dick. Head Carpenter: Paul Wadian. Costumers: Helaine Bruck, Barbara Yokooji. Make-up: Art Harding. Hair Stylist: Joyce Melton Conroy. *Thank You for Being a Friend* Words and Music by: Andrew Gold. Editors: Pamela Phelps, Peter D. Beyt. Re-recording: Craig Porter. Production Executive: David Amico. Executive in Charge of Production: Susan Palladino. A Witt Thomas Harris Production.

1991–92 SEASON

Co-Executive Producers: Marc Sotkin, Tracy Gamble, Richard Vaczy, Gail Parent, Tom Whedon. Supervising Producers: Don Seigel, Jerry Perzigian. Produced by: Nina Feinberg. Producers: Jamie Wooten, Marc Cherry, Mitchell Hurwitz. Created by: Susan Harris. Written by: Kevin Abbott, Marc Cherry, Tracy Gamble, Mitchell Hurwitz, Gail Parent, Jerry Perzigian, Don Seigel, Marc Sotkin, Robert Spina, Richard Vaczy, Jim Vallely, Tom Whedon, Jamie Wooten. Directed by: Peter D. Beyt, Lex Passaris. Executive Producers: Paul Junger Witt, Tony Thomas, Susan Harris. Co-Producers: John Ziffren, Mitchell Hurwitz, Jim Vallely, Kevin Abbott. Production Designer: Edward Stephenson. Music by: George Aliceson Tipton. Casting by: Ellen Meyer, C.S.A., Donna Larson. Costumes Designed by: Judy Evans. Associate Directors: Tom Carpenter, Peter D. Beyt. Stage Managers: Kent Zbornak, Danny Filous. Technical Manager: Bill Conroy. Production Associates: Robert Spina, Cindy Nexon. Associate Production Designer: Michael Hynes. Assistant Designers: Judy Lowey, Scott Latendresse. Post Production Executive: George Englund. Music Coordinator: Scott Gale. Original Casting by: Judith Weiner & Associates. Production Assistant: Salli Shrewsbury. Production Staff: Catherine Dunn, Alan Helfand, Brian Kahn, Todd Morris, Denise Porter, Richard King, Julie Thacker. Unit Manager: Audrey Joy Johnson. Technical Directors: Ken Tamburri, Wayne McDonald. Lighting: Darryl Palagi. Audio: Larry Lasota, C.A.S., Ed Epstein, C.A.S. Video: Randy Johnson. Cameras: Ritch Kenney, David Heckman, Chester Jackson, Stephen A. Jones. Property Masters: Robert Devicariis, John Blanco. Gaffer: Jim Orthel. Head Carpenter: Paul Wadian. Costumers: Barbara Yokooji, Patricia Byrne. Make-up: Art Harding. Hair Stylist: Paulette Pennington. Editor: Pamela Phelps. *Thank You for Being a Friend* Words and Music by: Andrew Gold. Re-recording: Craig Porter. Production Executive: David Amico. Executive in Charge of Production: Susan Palladino. A Witt Thomas Harris Production.

GOLDEN PALACE, THE

Executive Producer: Marc Sotkin. Supervising Producers: Mitchell Hurwitz, Jamie Wooten, Marc Cherry. Produced by: Jim Vallely, Nina Feinberg. Created by: Susan Harris. Written by: Marc Cherry, Michael Davidoff, Tony Delia, Susan Harris, Mitchell Hurwitz, Marco Pennette, Kevin Rooney, Bill Rosenthal, Jonathan Schmock, Marc Sotkin, Julie Thacker, Jim Vallely, Jamie Wooten. Directed by: Peter D. Beyt, Terry Hughes, Lex Passaris. Executive Producers: Paul Junger Witt, Tony Thomas, Susan Harris. Co-Producers: Marco Pennette, Michael Davidoff, Bill Rosenthal. Associate Producer: Sally S. Kleiman. Production Designer: Edward Stephenson. Music by: George Aliceson Tipton. Casting by: Kathleen Letterie, Nora Kariya. Costumes Designed by: Judy Evans. Associate Directors: Tom Carpenter, Harold McKenzie. Stage Managers: Kent Zbornak, Danny Filous. Production Associates: Robert Spina, Jennifer Reed. Associate Production Designer: Michael Hynes. Assistant Designer: Scott Latendresse. Post Production Executive: George Englund. Technical Manager: Bill Conroy. Production Assistants: Terre Alison, David Rosenberg. Production Staff: Catherine Dunn, Alan Helfand, Julie Manoogian, Sabrina Wind, Robin Weiner. Technical Director: Ken Tamburri. Lighting: Darryl Palagi. Audio: Ed Epstein. Video: Randy Johnson. Cameras: David Heckman, Chester Jackson, Stephen A. Jones, Ritch Kenney. Property Master: Robert Devicariis. Gaffer: Jim Orthel. Head Carpenter: Paul Wadian. Costumers: Barbara Yokooji, Patricia Byrne. Make-up: Art Harding. Hair Stylist: Mary Guerrero. *Thank You for Being a Friend* Words and Music by: Andrew Gold. Re-recording: Craig Porter. Production Executive: David Amico. Executive in Charge of Production: Susan Palladino. A Witt Thomas Harris Production.

EMPTY NEST

1988–89 SEASON

Executive Producers: Paul Junger Witt, Tony Thomas, Susan Harris, Gary Jacobs, Rod Parker, Hal Cooper. Supervising Producers: Arnie Kogen, David Tyron King. Producer: Susan Beavers. Co-Producer: Gilbert Junger. Created by: Susan Harris. Written by: Susan Beavers, Susan Harris, Kim Hill, Gary Jacobs, Mady Julian, Harold Kimmel, David Tyron King, Arnie Kogen, Rob LaZebnik, Rod Parker, Don Reo, David Sacks, Marie Therese Squerciatti. Directed by: John Bowab, Hal Cooper, Stephen Zuckerman. Directed by: Script Supervision: Rod Parker. Executive Story Editors: Marie Therese Squerciati, David Sacks, Rob LaZebnik. Associate Producer: David Amico. Production Designer: Edward Stephenson. Music by: George Aliceson Tipton. *Life Goes On* Written by: George Aliceson Tipton, John Bettis. Performed by: Billy Vera and the Beaters. Casting by: Ellen Meyer, C.S.A. Costumes Designed by: Judy Evans. Associate Directors: Doug Smart, Harold McKenzie. Stage Managers: Jeff Meyer, Doug Tobin, Jeffrey Goodman. Production Associate: Dona Cassella. Videotape Editor: Harold McKenzie. Post Production Manager: Adria Horton. Music Coordinator: Scott Gale. Associate Designer: Diane Yates. Technical Manager: Bill Conroy. Production Coordinator: Gwen McCracken. Medical Consultant: Jay N. Gordon, M.D., F.A.A.P. Animals Provided by: Birds and Animals Unlimited. Production Assistant: Jody Margolin. Production Staff: Jeffrey Goodman, Hayden Hilscher, Elise Ogden, Meredith Siler. Editorial Assistant: Charles Carpenter. Technical Director: Ken Tamburri. Lighting: Andy Kassan, Alan Walker. Audio: Edward L. Moskowitz, C.A.S., Ed Epstein. Video: George Palmer. Cameras: Jack Chisholm, Stephen A. Jones, Ritch Kenney, Jim Lunsford. Property Master: Bob Church. Gaffer: Ron Ruby. Head Carpenter: Paul Wadian. Costumers: Elizabeth Barber, Murshel Lewis. Make-up: Art Harding. Hair Stylist: Joyce Melton Conroy. Main Title Design: Castle/Bryant/Johnsen. Re-Recording: Craig Porter. Production Executive: Susan Palladino. A Witt Thomas Harris Production. Touchstone Pictures and Television.

1989–90 SEASON

Supervising Producers: Arnie Kogen, David Tyron King. Producers: Susan Beavers, Gilbert Junger. Created by: Susan Harris. Written by: Susan Beavers, Pat Dougherty, Gary Jacobs, Mitchell Hurwitz, Harold Kimmel, David Tyron King, Arnie Kogen, Rob LaZebnik, Neil Alan Levy, Toni Perling, David Sacks. Directed by: Andy Cadiff, Doug Smart, Steve Zuckerman. Executive Producers: Gary Jacobs, Paul Junger Witt, Tony Thomas. Executive Story Editors: Rob LaZebnik, David Sacks. Executive Story Consultant: Harold Kimmel. Story Editor: Pat Dougherty. Associate Producer: Gwen McCracken. Production Designer: Edward Stephenson. Music by: George Aliceson Tipton. *Life Goes On* Written by: George Aliceson Tipton, John Bettis. Performed by: Billy Vera and the Beaters. Casting by: Ellen Meyer, C.S.A. & Associates, Bonnie Shane. Costumes Designed by: Judy Evans. Associate Directors: Michael Riolo, Doug Smart, Harold McKenzie. Stage Managers: Doug Tobin, Lance Lyon. Production Associate: Dona Cassella. Art Director: Diane Yates. Post Production Manager: Richard J. Powell. Music Coordinator: Scott Gale. Technical Manager: Bill Conroy. Medical Consultant: Jay N. Gordon, M.D., F.A.A.P. Animals Provided by: Birds and Animals Unlimited, Joel Silverman. Production Assistants: Jody Margolin, Hayden Hilscher. Production Staff: Charles Carpenter, Greg Dolge, Tim Donnelly, Bill Ghaffary, Jonathan Glabman, Hayden Hilscher, Ray Kolasa, Ellen Moshein, Elise Ogden. Technical Director: Ken Tamburri. Lighting: Andy Kassan. Audio: Edward L. Moskowitz, C.A.S. Video: John O'Brien. Cameras: Jack Chisholm, Dave Heckman, Stephen A. Jones, Ritch Kenney. Property Master: Bob Church. Gaffer: Ron Ruby. Head Carpenter: Paul Wadian. Costumers: Murshel Lewis, Julie Rhine. Make-up: Art Harding. Hair Stylist: Joyce Melton Conroy. Main Title Design: Castle/Bryant/Johnsen. Re-Recording: Craig Porter. Production Executive: David Amico. Executive in Charge of Production: Susan Palladino. A Witt Thomas Harris Production. Touchstone Pictures and Television.

1990–91 SEASON

Supervising Producers: Arnie Kogen, Susan Beavers. Producers: Roger Garrett, Rob LaZebnik, David Sacks, Harold Kimmel, Gilbert Junger. Created by: Susan Harris. Written by: Susan Beavers, Sydney Blake, Bill Braunstein, Pat Dougherty, Roger Garrett, Gary Jacobs, Harold Kimmel, Arnie Kogen, Rob LaZebnik, Laura O'Hare, Paul B. Price, David Sacks, Meredith Siler, Miriam Trogdon. Directed by: Robert

Berlinger, Doug Smart, Steve Zuckerman. Executive Producers: Gary Jacobs, Paul Junger Witt, Tony Thomas, Susan Harris. Executive Story Editor: Pat Dougherty. Story Editors: Sydney Blake, Bill Braunstein. Associate Producer: Gwen McCracken. Production Designer: Edward Stephenson. Music by: George Aliceson Tipton. *Life Goes On* Written by: George Aliceson Tipton, John Bettis. Performed by: Billy Vera and the Beaters. Casting by: Ellen Meyer, C.S.A. & Associates, Bonnie Shane. Costumes Designed by: Judy Evans. Associate Directors: Doug Smart, Harold McKenzie, Tony Porter, Dona Casella Racine. Stage Managers: Doug Tobin, Greg Dolge. Production Associates: Dona Cassella Racine, Hayden Hilscher. Assistant Art Directors: Wendy Fine, Daniel Saks. Post Production Manager: Fred Roth. Music Coordinator: Scott Gale. Technical Manager: Bill Conroy. Medical Consultant: Jay N. Gordon, M.D., F.A.A.P. Animals Provided by: Birds and Animals Unlimited, Joel Silverman. Production Assistants: Hayden Hilscher, Dona Cassella Racine, Jonathan Glabman. Production Staff: Charles Carpenter, Bill Ghaffary, Jonathan Glabman, Jordan L. Goodman, Liza Persky, Heather Stewart. Technical Director: Ken Tamburri. Lighting: Andy Kassan. Audio: Ed Epstein. Video: John O'Brien, Randy Johnson. Cameras: Jack Chisholm, Dave Heckman, Stephen A. Jones, Ritch Kenney. Property Master: Bob Church. Gaffers: Ron Ruby, Jim Orthel. Head Carpenter: Paul Wadian. Costumers: Murshel Lewis, Julie Rhine. Make-up: Art Harding. Hair Stylist: Joyce Melton Conroy. Re-Recording: Craig Porter. Production Executive: David Amico. Executive in Charge of Production: Susan Palladino. A Witt Thomas Harris Production. Touchstone Pictures and Television.

1991–92 SEASON

Executive Producers: Fred Freeman, Lawrence J. Cohen. Co-Executive Producer: Arnie Kogen. Supervising Producers: Roger Garrett, Rob LaZebnik, Harold Kimmel. Producers: Pat Dougherty, David Richardson, Peter Gallay, Gilbert Junger. Created by: Susan Harris. Written by: Lawrence J. Cohen, Pat Dougherty, Fred Freeman, Peter Gallay, Roger Garrett, Harold Kimmel, Arnie Kogen, Sandy Krinski, Rob LaZebnik, Dinah Manoff, Lyla Oliver, David Richardson, Lisa Sanderson, Ed Sharlach, Steve Sullivan, Ursula Ziegler. Directed by: Doug Smart, Steve Zuckerman. Executive Producers: Paul Junger Witt, Tony Thomas. Story Editors: Steve Sullivan, Ursula Ziegler. Associate Producer: Joanne Diaz. Production Designer: Edward Stephenson. Music by: George Aliceson Tipton. *Life Goes On* Written by: George Aliceson Tipton, John Bettis. Performed by: Billy Vera and The Beaters. Casting by: Ellen Meyer, C.S.A., Donna Larson. Costumes Designed by: Judy Evans. Associate Directors: Doug Smart, Dona Cassella-Racine, Harold McKenzie, John Neal. Stage Managers: Doug Tobin, Greg Dolge. Technical Manager: Bill Conroy. Production Associate: Dona Cassella-Racine, Marcia Gould. Assistant Production Designer: Michael Hynes. Assistant Designer: Daniel Saks. Post Production Executive: George Englund. Production Assistant: Jonathan Glabman. Production Staff: Eric Black, Sherry Carter, Gary A. Gamble, Alan Helfand, Timothy Kestle, Richard King, Catherine Lepard, Kurt A. Schindler. Editors: Jerry Davis, Mary Holland. Technical Director: Ken Tamburri. Lighting: Andy Kassan. Audio: Leroy P. Castelina, Ed Epstein. Video: John O'Brien, Jean Mason. Cameras: Neal Carlos, Jack Chisholm, Dave Heckman, Stephen A. Jones, Ritch Kenney, Cathy Lewis. Property Master: Bob Church. Gaffer: Ron Ruby. Head Carpenter: Paul Wadian. Costumers: Murshel Lewis, Julie Rhine. Make-up: Art Harding. Hair Stylist: Joyce Melton Conroy. Animals Trained by: Birds and Animals Unlimited, Joel Silverman. Re-Recording: Craig Porter. Production Executive: David Amico. Executive in Charge of Production: Susan Palladino. A Witt Thomas Harris Production. Touchstone Pictures and Television.

1992–93 SEASON

Executive Producers: Arnie Kogen, Ron LaZebnik. Co-Executive Producer: Roger Garrett. Supervising Producers: Pat Dougherty, David Richardson, Peter Gallay. Produced by: Gilbert Junger. Created by: Susan Harris. Written by: Ross Abrash, Wendy Braff, Lawrence J. Cohen, Pat Dougherty, Fred Freeman, Peter Gallay, Roger Garrett, Cheryl Holliday, Tim

Kelleher, Arnie Kogen, Rob LaZebnik, Paul B. Price, David Richardson, Steve Sullivan, Ursula Ziegler. Directed by: Dinah Manoff, Doug Smart, Renny Temple, James Widdoes, Steve Zuckerman. Executive Producers: Fred Freeman, Lawrence J. Cohen, Paul Junger Witt, Tony Thomas. Associate Producer: Joanne Diaz-Koegl. Story Editor: Wendy Braff. Production Designer: Edward Stephenson. Music by: George Aliceson Tipton. *Life Goes On* Written by: George Aliceson Tipton, John Bettis. Performed by: Billy Vera and the Beaters. Casting by: Ellen Meyer, C.S.A., Grady Roberts. Costumes Designed by: Judy Evans. Associate Directors: Doug Smart, Art Kellner. Stage Managers: Doug Tobin, Charles Carpenter, Greg Dolge. Technical Manager: Bill Conroy. Production Associates: Dona Cassella-Racine, Jennifer Reed. Assistant Production Manager: Michael Hynes. Assistant Designer: Daniel Saks. Post Production Executive: George Englund. Production Assistant: Catherine Lepard. Production Staff: Eric Black, Sherry Carter, Cody Farley, Gary A. Gamble, Susan Gilbert, Richard King, Marta Knittel, Jennifer Saxon. Technical Director: Ken Tamburri. Lighting: Andy Kassan. Audio: Ed Epstein. Video: John O'Brien. Cameras: Dave Heckman, Chester Jackson, Stephen A. Jones, Ritch Kenney. Property Master: Bob Church. Gaffer: Ron Ruby. Head Carpenter: Paul Wadian. Costumers: Murshel Lewis, Julie Rhine. Make-up: Art Harding. Hair Stylist: Joyce Melton Conroy. Animals Trained by: Birds and Animals Unlimited. Re-Recording: Craig Porter. Production Executive: David Amico. Executive in Charge of Production: Susan Palladino. A Witt Thomas Harris Production. Touchstone Pictures and Television.

1993–94 SEASON

Co-Executive Producer: Nina Feinberg. Supervising Producers: Peter Gallay, Rick Newberger, Bob Tischler. Co-Producers: Ursula Ziegler, Steven Sullivan, Regina Stewart Larsen, Dennis Snee. Created by: Susan Harris. Written by: Ross Abrash, Susan Beavers, Cindy Chupack, Pat Dougherty, Cody R. Farley, Peter Gallay, Harold Kimmel, Regina Stewart Larsen, Kari Lizer, Rick Newberger, Greg Phillips, Paul B. Price, Ellen Sandler, Drake Sather, Dennis Snee, Steven Sullivan, Bob Tischler, Ursula Ziegler. Directed by: Dinah Manoff, Doug Smart, Steve Zuckerman. Executive Producers: Fred Freeman, Lawrence J. Cohen, Paul Junger Witt, Tony Thomas, Susan Harris. Story Editor: Paul B. Price. Associate Producer: Joanne Diaz-Koegl. Production Designer: Edward Stephenson. Music by: George Aliceson Tipton. *Life Goes On* Written by: George Aliceson Tipton, John Bettis. Performed by: Billy Vera. Casting by: Ellen Meyer, C.S.A., Grady Roberts. Costumes Designed by: Judy Evans. Associate Directors: Doug Smart, Tom Doke, Harold McKenzie. Stage Managers: Doug Tobin, Charlie Carpenter. Technical Manager: Bill Conroy. Production Associates: Dona Cassella-Racine, Hayden Hilscher-Ghaffary, Kate Wright. Assistant Production Manager: Michael Hynes. Assistant Designer: Daniel Saks. Post Production Executive: George Englund. Production Assistant: David Rosenberg. Music Coordinator: Nick South. Production Staff: Sherry Carter, Catherine Dunn, Cody R. Farley, Alan Helfand, Jennifer Saxon, Matt Stein. Technical Director: Ken Tamburri. Lighting: Andy Kassan. Audio: Ed Epstein. Video: John O'Brien. Cameras: Dave Heckman, Chester Jackson, Stephen A. Jones, Ritch Kenney. Property Master: Bob Church. Gaffer: Ron Ruby. Head Carpenter: Frank Stevens. Costumers: Murshel Lewis, Nancy Butts, Julie Rhine. Make-up: Art Harding. Hair Stylist: Joyce Melton Conroy. Animals Trained by: Birds and Animals Unlimited. Re-Recording: Craig Porter. Production Executive: David Amico. Executive in Charge of Production: Susan Palladino. A Witt Thomas Harris Production. Touchstone Pictures and Television.

1994–95 SEASON

Executive Producers: Nina Feinberg, Regina Stewart Larsen, Bob Tischler. Co-Executive Producer: Peter Gallay. Supervising Producers: Vince Cheung, Ben Montano. Producers: Dennis Snee, Steven Sullivan, Ursula Ziegler. Created by: Susan Harris. Written by: Jack Amiel, Michael Begler, Ron Bloomberg, Vince Cheung, Peter Gallay, Mark Grant, Andy Guerdat, Valerie Landsburg, Regina Stewart Larsen, Dinah Manoff, Ben Montano, Paul B. Price, David Rosenberg, Dennis Snee, Steven Sullivan, Bob Tischler, Ursula Ziegler. Directed by: Dinah Manoff, Doug Smart, Steve Zuckerman. Executive Producers: Paul Junger Witt, Tony Thomas, Susan Harris. Co-Producer: Paul B. Price. Associate Producer: Joanne Diaz-Koegl. Story Editors: Jack Amiel, Michael Begler. Production Designer: Edward Stephenson. Music by: George Aliceson Tipton. *Life Goes On* Written by: George Aliceson Tipton, John Bettis. Performed by: Billy Vera. Casting by: Camille H. Patton, C.S.A., Julie Pernworth, Vickie Beck. Costume Designer: Judy Evans. Associate Directors: Doug Smart, Danny White. Stage Managers: Lance Lyon, Charles Carpenter. Production Associate: Kate Wright. Production Assistant: David Rosenberg. Music Coordinator: Nick South. Technical Manager: Bill Conroy. Post Production Executive: George Englund. Production Staff: Catherine Dunn, Nikki Kessler, David Krovitz, Todd Morris, Matthew Singer, Matthew Stein. Technical Directors: Ken Tamburri, Jim Horky. Lighting Designer: Andy Kassan. Audio: Ed Epstein. Video: Doug Dessero. Cameras: Dave Heckman, Chester Jackson, Stephen A. Jones, Ritch Kenney. Property Master: Bob Church. Gaffer: Ron Ruby. Head Carpenter: Paul Wadian. Costumers: Murshel Lewis, Nancy Butts. Make-up: Art Harding. Hair Stylist: Joyce M. Conroy. Animals Trained by: Birds and Animals Unlimited. Re-Recording: Allen Patapoff, Craig Porter. Production Executive: David Amico. Executive in Charge of Production: Susan Palladino. A Witt Thomas Harris Production. Touchstone Pictures and Television.

HARD TIME ON PLANET EARTH

Created by: Jim Thomas, John Thomas. Written by: Bruce Cervi, Richard Chapman, Nick Corea, Daniel Freudenberger, E. Jack Kaplan, David Percelay, Michael Piller, Van Gordon Sauter, Michael Eric Stein, Rob Swigart, Jim Thomas, John Thomas, Rob Ulin, Edward Zuckerman. Directed by: Timothy Bond, James A. Contner, Bill Corcoran, Charles Correll, Roger Duchowny, Michael Lange, Robert Mandel, Ric Rondell, Al Waxman. Executive Producers: Jim Thomas, John Thomas, Richard Chapman, E. Jack Kaplan. Supervising Producers: Ric Rondell, Michael Piller. Produced by: Ric Rondell. Co-Producer: Janice Cooke-Leonard. Associate Producer: Edward E. McCobb. Executive Story Editors: Bruce Cervi, Daniel Freudenberger. Executive Story Consultant: Phil Combest. Composers: Thomas Chase, Steve Rucker. Original Score by: Joseph Conlan, Bill Thorpe. Directors of Photography: Fred J. Koenekamp, A.S.C., F. Pershing Flynn. Art Director: Joseph M. Altadonna. Editors: Byron "Buzz" Brandt, A.C.E., Anita Brandt-Burgoyne, Jerry Temple, Art Stafford. Unit Production Managers: Albert J. Salzer, Dennis L. Judd, II. First Assistant Directors: Marty Eli Schwartz, Richard Peter Schroer. Second Assistant Directors: Skip Surguine, Steve Cohen. Casting by: Junie Lowry, Elisa Goodman, Jean Sarah Frost, C.S.A. Set Decorators: Linda Spheeris, Rochelle Moser. Script Supervisors: Melady Preece, Marion Cronin. Make-up: Marvin G. Westmore, Edwin Butterworth. Hair Stylists: Gregg Mitchell, Rebecca DeMorrio, Stephen A. Elsbree. Property Masters: Roger Pancake, Lavar Emert, Mark E. Hollingsworth. Sound Mixers: Richard I. Birnbaum, C.A.S., William Teague, C.A.S. Special Effects: Alan Edward Lorimer. Costumes Designed by: Tom Bronson. Costumers: Terrence K. Smith, Karen Bellamy, Kendall Errair. Location Managers: Denis J. McCallion, John C. Armstrong. Production Coordinator: Nancy Malone Claycomb. Ramrod: Rudy Ugland. Stunt Coordinator: R.A. Rondell. Supervisor of Visual Effects: Jay Jacoby. Visual Effects by: Planet Blue. Visual Effects Compositer: Fred Raimondi. Digital Animation by: Maury Rosenfeld. Special Effects Coordinator: Larry Fioritto. Sound Editing by: Echo Film Services, Soundeluxe, Inc. Music Editing by: The Music Design Group. A Demos-Bard/Shanachie Production in association with Touchstone Television.

NUTT HOUSE, THE

Created by: Mel Brooks, Alan Spencer. Written by: Mel Brooks, Richard Day, Jim Geoghan, Alicia Marie Schudt, Alan Spencer. Directed by: Bruce Bilson, Bill Bixby, Roger Duchowny, Gary Nelson. Executive Producer: Bob Brunner. Producer: Alan Mandel. Produced by: Ronald E. Frazier. Creative Consultant: Leonard B. Stern. Executive Producers: Mel Brooks, Alan Spencer. Executive Story Editors: Mark Curtiss,

Rod Ash. Story Editors: Richard Day, Alicia Marie Schudt. Associate Producer: Jimmy B. Frazier. Original Score by: Lance Rubin. Directors of Photography: Gayne Rescher, A.S.C., Paul Lohman. Art Directors: Raymond G. Storey, Tommy Goetz. Editors: Jimmy B. Frazier, Janet Ashikaga. Unit Production Manager: Nick Smirnoff. First Assistant Directors: Carl Olsen, Joan Van Horn, Linda Montanti. Second Assistant Directors: Susan Norton, Brian Fong. Casting by: Cathy Henderson, C.S.A., Michael Cutler. Costumes Designed by: Tom Bronson. Set Decorators: Ethel Robins Richards, Rochelle Moser. Property Master: Ronald E. Greenwood. Key Costumers: Paul Lopez, Dawn Jackson, Terrence K. Smith, Marcee Smith. Make-up: Nadia. Hair Stylists: Frankie Bergman, Donna Turner Culver. Production Coordinator: Lark Bernini. Stunt Coordinators: Ed Ulrich, Edward J. Ulrich. Script Supervisors: Hope Williams, Alleen N. Nollman. Special Effects Coordinator: Jim Hart. Sound Mixers: Don Johnson, C.A.S., Bill Teague, C.A.S. Post Production Sound by: EFX Systems. Music Editing by: Steve McCroskey. Brooksfilms Television and Alan Spencer Productions, Inc. in association with Touchstone Television.

CAROL & COMPANY

The following production credits are for the episodes *Battle of the Exes, Bump in the Night, The Fabulous Bicker Girls, In Laws Should Be Outlawed, Jewel of Denial, Kruber Alert, Mother from Hell, Myna and the Messenger, Noah's Place, Reunion, Soap Gets in Your Eyes* and *Spudnik*: Produced by: Gayle S. Maffeo. Co-Producer: Marcia Brandwynne. Supervising Producer: Bob Tischler. Developed by: Matt Williams, David McFadzean. Written by: Marilyn Anderson, Darrel Campbell, Darrel Montgomery, Lynn Montgomery, Billy Riback, Mark St. Germain, Bob Tischler, Ken Welch, Mitzie Welch. Directed by: Asaad Kelada, Will Mackenzie, Dave Powers, Jay Sandrich, Jack Shea, Andrew D. Weyman. Co-Executive Producer: David McFadzean. Executive Producer: Matt Williams. Associate Producer: Gary S. Drews. Creative Consultants: Dennis Koenig, Robert Illes, James R. Stein. Story Editors: Lynn Montgomery, Marilyn Anderson, Billy Riback. Director of Photography: Daniel Flannery. Production Designer: David Sackeroff. Carol Burnett's Costumes Designed by: Bob Mackie. Associate Director: Marian Deaton. Stage Managers: Willie Dahl, Julie Meehan. Editors: Marco Zappia, Alex Gimenez. Casting by: Deborah Barylski, C.S.A., Robin Lippin, C.S.A. Theme by: Dan Foliart, Howard Pearl. Music by: Dan Foliart, Howard Pearl. Script Supervisors: Janet Kagan, Carol Summers. Production Coordinators: Jim Praytor, Frank McKemy. Set Decorators: Portia Iversen, Jennifer Polito. Property Master: Warren Shaffer. Costume Designer: Ret Turner. Key Costumer: Alan Trugman. Make-up: Deborah Lamia Denavér, Debbie Figuly, Brenda Todd. Hairstylists: Suzan Bagdadi, Michaeljohn, Renate Leuschner, Linda Trainuff. Technical Directors: Richard Edwards, Russell Reinsel, Allan Wells. Audio: Michael Gannon, Ed Greene, J. Mark King, Kerry Boggio. Video: Bob Kaufman, Mike Snedden. Kalola Productions and Wind Dancer Productions in association with Touchstone Television.

The following production credits are for the episodes *Diary of a Really Mad Housewife, Driving Miss Crazy, A Fall from Grace, For Love or Money, Goin' to the Chapel, Grandma Gets It On, Guns and Rosie, Here's to You, Mrs. Baldwin, High on Life, Intimate Behavoir, The Jingle Belles, Mom and Dad Day Afternoon, Momma Needs a New Pair of Shoes, No News Is Bad News, Overnight Male, Stiff Competition, Suture Self, Teacher, Teacher, That Little Extra Something, Trisha Springs Eternal* and *Turning Tables*: Produced by: Robert Wright. Co-Producer: Marcia Brandwynne. Developed by: Matt Williams, David McFadzean. Written by: Lauren Eve Anderson, Darrel Campbell, Dana Coen, Terrie Collins, Joyce Costanza, Larry Moskowitz, Ian Praiser, Billy Riback, Peter Tolan, David N. Weiss, Ken Welch, Mitzie Welch. Directed by: Marian Deaton, Andrew D. Weyman. Co-Executive Producer: Ian Praiser. Executive Producers: David McFadzean, Matt Williams. Associate Producers: Gary S. Drews, Steven Schott. Creative Consultant: Carmen Finestra. Executive Story Consultant: Lauren Eve Anderson. Executive Story Editors: Darrel Campbell, Billy Riback. Story Editors: Terrie Collins, Peter Tolan. Lighting Designer:

Kieran C. Illes. Director of Photography: Richard Hissong. Production Designer: David Sackeroff. Carol Burnett's Costumes Designed by: Bob Mackie. Associate Directors: Marian Deaton, Pat Maloney. Stage Manager: Paul Paolasso. Editors: Marco Zappia, Alex Gimenez. Casting by: Robin Lippin, C.S.A. Theme by: Dan Foliart, Howard Pearl. Original Score by: Dan Foliart, Howard Pearl. Costume Designer: Ret Turner. Key Costumers: Alan Trugman, Trudy Otterson. Set Decorator: Mel Cooper Fischer. Script Supervisor: Janet Kagan. Hairstylists: Michaeljohn, Renate Leuschner. Wigs by: Renate Leuschner. Makeup: Brenda Todd. Property Master: Marjorie Coster. Production Coordinator: Frank McKemy. Post Production Coordinator: Jim Praytor. Technical Director: Robert A. Bowen. Audio: Doug Nelson, Klaus Landsburg, Toby Foster. Video: Bob Kaufman. Kalola Productions and Wind Dancer Productions in association with Touchstone Television.

CAROL BURNETT SHOW, THE
Co-Executive Producers: Marilyn Suzanne Miller, Marcia Brandywnne. Produced by: Robert Wright. Directed by: Paul Miller. Written by: Barbara Allyn, Mike Armstrong, Vince Calandra, Jr., Susan Gauthier, Bill Applebaum, Stan Hart, Ron Hauge, Charlie Rubin, Linda McGibney, Jon Marans, Neal Marshall, Marilyn Suzanne Miller, Mark C. Miller, Marty Nadler, J.J. Paulsen, Bill Prady, Steve Rudnick, Leo Benvenuti, Rosie Shuster, Rocco Urbisci, Linda Wallem, Ken Welch, Mitzie Welch, Barry Harman, Dick Clair, Jenna McMahon. Supervising Producer: Marty Nadler. Producers: Marcia Brandynne, Rosie Shuster. Associate Producer: Steven Schott. Production Designer: Roy Christopher. Associate Director: Tony Csiki. Stage Managers: Willie Dahl, Dency Nelson. Lighting Designers: Red McKinnon, Kim Killingsworth. Music Arranged and Conducted by: Tom Scott. Musical Material by: Ken Welch, Mitzie Welch. Carol Burnett's Costumes by: Bob Mackie. Original Casting by: Liberman. Hirschfeld Casting, C.S.A. Art Director: Debe Hale. Set Decorator: Ron Olsen. Script Supervisor: Kristine Fernandez. Production Coordinator: Kim Tushinsky. Assistant to Ms. Burnett: Sara Recer. Assistant to Producer: Kathryn Davison. Writer's Assistants: Dawn Hernandez, Keith Hosman, Bernie Anchetta. Production Assistants: John Sokoloff, Robert Haworth, Bruce Williams. Talent Coordinator: Liza Hall. Choreographer: Don Crichton. Costume Designer: Ret Turner. Make-up: Brenda Todd. Hair Stylist: Michaeljohn. Wigs by: Renate Leuschner. CBS Production Supervisor: Mike McDaniel. Technical Directors: Steve Cunningham, Ervin Hurd. Audio: Paul Sandweiss. Videotape Editors: Frosty Oden, Robert Bernstein. Video: Allen Latter. Kalola PAU and Urbisci/Marshall Productions in association with Touchstone Television.

HULL HIGH
Supervising Producer: Peter Dunne. Co-Executive Producer: Kenny Ortega. Created by: Gil Grant. Written by: David Babcock, Gil Grant, Steven Hollander, Bruce Kirschbaum, Dennis E. Leoni, Shawn Schepps. Directed by: Bruce Bilson, James Keach, Kenny Ortega, Steven Robman, Paul Schneider, Bryan Spicer. *Figure of Speech* Music by: Tom Snow. Lyrics by: David Weiss. Produced by: Tom Snow, David Weiss. *Hanging on For Dear Life* Music by: Jon Lind. Lyrics by: Brock Walsh. Produced by: Jon Lind, Brock Walsh. *Speed of Light* Lyrics by: Brock Walsh. Music by: Brock Walsh, Andrew Gold. Produced by: Brock Walsh, Andrew Gold. *Sorry, Mr. Slovak* Lyrics and Music by: Brock Walsh. Produced by: Brock Walsh. *You'll Never Make Me Talk* Written by: Jim Cox, Brock Walsh. Produced by: Richard Gibbs, Mark Vieha. *Laws of Motion* Music by: George Duke, Brock Walsh. Lyrics by: Brock Walsh. Produced by: George Duke, Brock Walsh. *The Desert Song* Words and Music by: Brock Walsh. Produced by: Brock Walsh. *Rescue Me* and *Embraceable You* Produced by: Steve Tyrell. *Team Sandwich* Words and Music by: Brock Walsh. Produced by: Brock Walsh. *That's All Over now* Music by: Brock Walsh. Lyrics by: Brock Walsh. Produced by: Brock Walsh. *Undeniably Yours* Words and Music by: Brock Walsh. Produced by: Bill Elliott, Brock Walsh. *The Game of Life, Back to the Action* and *Goodnight Gracie* Words by: Brock Walsh. Music by: Steve Tyrell. *Whoa—Time Out* Music by: Steve Tyrell. *Life Among the Eaves* and *The Desert Song* Words and Music

by: Brock Walsh. Producers: Steven Hollander, Bruce Kirschbaum. Executive Producer: Gil Grant. Executive Story Editor: David Babcock. Associate Producer: Howard Taksen. Directors of Photography: Charles Minsky, Dennis T. Matsuda. Production Designer: Jeremy Railton. Editors: Norman Hollyn, Art Stafford, David Latham, Richard Harkness. Original Score by: Stanley Clarke, Richard Gibbs. Choreography by: Kenny Ortega. Unit Production Managers: Denny Salvaryn, Jan DeWitt. First Assistant Directors: Newton Dennis Arnold, Leslie Jackson Houston, Alan Brent Connell. Second Assistant Directors: Grant Gilmore, Bob Nellans. Casting by: Susan Shaw, C.S.A., Amy Lieberman. Music Supervisor: Maureen Crowe. Co-Choreographer: Peggy Holmes. Assistant Choreographer: Liz Imperio. Music Consultant: Brock Walsh. Music Coordinator: Marylata Elton. Assistant Art Director: Jocelyn Railton. Set Decorator: Greg Grande. Property Masters: John Klima, Richard A. Pine. Make-up: Ken Chase, Joe McKinney. Hair Stylists: Charlene Johnson, Vivian McAteer, Dale Miller. Costume Designer: Tom Bronson. Additional Casting: Gregg Smith. Key Costumers: Florie Kemper, Terrence Smith, Murray Lantz, Charmaine Nash Simmons. Script Supervisors: Pam Alch, Renate Schneuer. Location Manager: Denis McCallion. Special Effects: Greg Tippie. Production Coordinators: Jenny Campbell, Sandy Watterson, Beth Peterson. Assistant to Executive Producer: Jeffrey Lane. Executive Assistant to Executive Producer: Lynn Hostein. Sound Mixers: Bruce Bisenz, Kenn Michael Fuller, C.A.S. Music Editing by: Jamie Gelb. Post Sound by: Patrick M. Griffith, Gerry Lentz, Sherry Klein, Derrick C. Perkins, Bill Freesh, Richard Corwin. *Once in a Lifetime* Music by: Stanley Clarke. Lyrics by: Lawrence "G. Love E." Edwards. Chant Lyrics by: Kenny Ortega, Peggy Holmes. Produced by: Stanley Clarke. Sound Effects Editor: Derrick Perkins. Dialogue/ADR Editor: Richard Corwin. Additional Music by: Steve Tyrell. Rap Adaptations by: Lawrence "G. Love E." Edwards. Acknowledgement: Jim Henson. Gil Grant Productions in association with Touchstone Television.

LENNY
Created by: Don Reo. Supervising Producers: Judith D. Allison, Bill Richmond. Producers: Racelle Rosett Schaefer, Gilbert Junger. Written by: Judith D. Allison, Josh Goldstein, Brenda Hampton-Cain, William C. Kenny, David Landsberg, Jonathan Prince, Don Reo, Bill Richmond, Racelle Rosett Schaefer, J.J. Wall. Directed by: Andy Cadiff, Terry Hughes, Patrick Maloney. Executive Producers: Paul Junger Witt, Tony Thomas, Don Reo. Co-Producers: David Landsberg, Josh Goldstein, Jonathan Prince. Executive Script Consultants: William C. Kenny, Brenda Hampton-Cain. Program Consultant: Lenny Clarke. Associate Producers: Janet Grushow, Laura L. Garcia. Production Designer: Edward Stephenson. Main Title Written by: Dion, Bill Tuohy. Title Song Performed by: Dion. Music by: Mike Post, Frank Denson. Casting by: Kathleen Letterie. Costumes Designed by: Judy Evans. Associate Directors: Lex Passaris, Peter D. Beyt, Patrick Maloney, Richard J. Powell, Joe Bergen. Stage Managers: Tom Carpenter, Kent Zbornak, Gary Ramirez. Production Associates: Robert Spina, Esther F. Himbaugh. Art Director: Michael Hynes. Assistant Art Director: Daniel Saks. Post Production Managers: Richard J. Powell, Fred Roth. Music Coordinator: Scott Gale. Production Coordinators: Gwen Mc Cracken, Denise Fleissner Barta. Production Assistants: Wanda Armstrong, Eve Needleman. Production Staff: Danny Filous, Bill Ghaffary, Jordan Goodman, Ray Kolasa, Todd Morris, Ellen Moshein, Denise Porter, David Z. Sacks, Maria Schmidt, Dorothy Wong, Wendy Braff, Eve Needleman, Susan Tenney. Technical Director: Ken Tamburri, Bill Conroy, Jim Horky. Lighting: Kent Inasy, Alan Walker. Audio: Leroy P. Castelina, Edward L. Moskowitz, C.A.S., Pete San Filipo. Video: John O'Brien, John Palacio, Jr. Cameras: Jack Chisholm, Chester Jackson, Stephen A. Jones, Ritch Kenney, Neal Carlos, Corey Kimball, Jim Lunsford, Jeff Rifkin. Property Masters: Robert Devicariis, Gary Clayton. Gaffers: Ron Ruby, Tom Lindsay. Head Carpenter: Bob Berry. Costumers: Ron Hodge, Mary Taylor. Make-up: Art Harding, Diane Shatz. Hair Stylists: Joyce Melton Conroy, Faye Woods. Editors: Joe Bergen, Shoeless Joe. Re-recording: Craig Porter. Post Production Supervisor: Charles Carpenter. Production Executive: David Amico.

Executive in Charge of Production: Susan Palladino. Impact Zone Productions. A Witt/Thomas Production.

BLOSSOM

1990–91 SEASON
Created by: Don Reo. Executive Producer: Gene Reynolds. Supervising Producer: Paul Perlove. Producer: John Ziffren. Written by: Judith D. Allison, Nancy Beverly, Josh Goldstein, Brenda Hampton-Cain, William C. Kenny, David Landsberg, Paul Perlove, Jonathan Prince, Don Reo, Bill Richmond, Racelle Rosett Schaefer. Directed by: Zane Buzby. Executive Producers: Paul Junger Witt, Tony Thomas, Don Reo. Associate Producer: Susan Nessanbaum-Goldberg. Production Designer: Edward Stephenson. Music by: Frank Denson, Mike Post. Main Title Written by: Mike Post, Stephen Geyer. Main Title Performed by: Dr. John. Casting by: Ellen Meyer, C.S.A. & Associates, Bonnie Shane. Costumes Designed by: Sherry Thompson. Associate Directors: Jim Balden, Tony Porter, Nancy Sherman, Peter Beyt. Stage Managers: John J. Hill, Jeffrey Jacobs. Production Associate: Sorel Kaire. Assistant Art Director: Scott Latendresse. Post Production Manager: Fred Roth. Music Coordinator: Scott Gale. Technical Manager: Bill Conroy. Production Assistant: Wanda Armstrong. Production Staff: Nancy Beverly, Ellen Moshein, Terre Rigali, Emily Whitesell, Pamela Phelps. Technical Directors: Jim Horky, Kenneth Tamburri. Lighting: Roger Dalton. Audio: William H. Kennedy III. Video: Randy Johnson. Cameras: Neal Carlos, Chester Jackson, Corey Kimball, Jim Lunsford, Jeff Rivkin. Property Master: John P. Bozajian. Gaffer: Robert Dick. Head Carpenters: Paul Wadian, Bob Berry. Costumers: Renee Sacks, David Velasquez. Make-up: Diane Shatz. Hair Stylist: Faye Woods. Production Executive: David Amico. Executive in Charge of Production: Susan Palladino. Impact Zone Productions. A Witt/Thomas Production.

1992–93 SEASON
Created by: Don Reo. Co-Executive Producer: Judith D. Allison. Supervising Producers: Bill Richmond, Josh Goldstein, Jonathan Prince. Producer: Glen Merzer. Written by: Judith D. Allison, Josh Goldstein, Brenda Hampton, Portia Iversen, Shelley Karol, Glen Merzer, Eve Needleman, Jonathan Prince, Don Reo, Bill Richmond, Racelle Rosett Schaefer, Jonathan Schmock, Susan Tenney, J.J. Wall. Directed by: Bill Bixby, Ted Wass. Executive Producers: Paul Junger Witt, Tony Thomas, Don Reo. Associate Producers: Joe Bergen, Richard G. King. Executive Script Consultant: Brenda Hampton. Executive Story Editor: J.J. Wall. Story Editor: Jonathan Schmock. Production Designer: Edward Stephenson. Music by: Frank Denson. Main Title Written by: Mike Post, Stephen Geyer. Main Title Performed by: Dr. John. Casting by: Ellen Meyer, C.S.A., Grady Roberts. Costume Designer: Sherry Thompson. Associate Directors: Franklin Melton, Joe Bergen. Stage Managers: John J. Hill, Tom Ohlinger. Production Associate: Cindy Nexon. Associate Production Designer: Michael Hynes. Assistant Designers: Jerry Dunn, Roland Rosenkranz. Post Production Executive: George Englund. Technical Managers: Bill Conroy, Chris Neuman. Production Assistant: Eve Needleman. Production Staff: Dorie D'Amore, Brian Dorfman, Sherry Gallarneau, Beverly Hsiao, Gary McCarthy, William J. Murray III. Technical Directors: Charles Ciup, Jim Horky, Karl Messershmidt. Lighting: Robert Dick, Alan Walker. Audio: William H. Kennedy III. Video: James Lucas, John Palacio, Jr. Cameras: Jeff Barnes, Neal Carlos, Steve Casaly, Rocky Danielson, Mike Denton, David L. Hilmer, Bob Keys, Corey Kimball, Raymond Liu, Bryan W. McKenzie. Property Master: John P. Bozajian. Gaffer: Mark Bauer, Robert Dick. Head Carpenter: Carl Hicks. Costumers: Gregory Bolton, Marion Kirk, David Velasquez. Make-up: Vikki McCarter. Hair: Joyce Conroy. Re-Recording: Craig Porter. Production Executive: David Amico. Executive in Charge of Production: Susan Palladino. Impact Zone Productions. A Witt/Thomas Production.

1993–94 SEASON
Created by: Don Reo. Executive Producers: Judith D. Allison, Rob Lazebnik. Supervising Producer: Glen Merzer. Produced by: Kenneth R. Koch. Producers: Joe Bergen, Brenda Hampton.

Co-Producer: Jonathan Schmock. Written by: Judith D. Allison, Roger Garrett, Josh Goldstein, Brenda Hampton, Rob LaZebnik, Glen Merzer, Jonathan Prince, Don Reo, Bill Richmond, Jonathan Schmock, J.J. Wall. Directed by: Peter Baldwin, Joe Bergen, Bill Bixby, Ted Wass, John Whitesell. Executive Producers: Paul Junger Witt, Tony Thomas, Don Reo. Associate Producer: Sally S. Kleiman. Production Designer: Edward Stephenson. Music by: Frank Denson. Main Title Written by: Mike Post, Stephen Geyer. Main Title Performed by: Dr. John. Casting by: Ellen Meyer, C.S.A., Grady Roberts. Costume Designer: Sherry Thompson. Editor: Dennis Vejar. Associate Directors: Michael Conley, Selig Frank. Stage Managers: John J. Hill, Tom Ohlinger. Technical Managers: Bill Conroy, Chris Neuman. Production Associates: Sorel Kaire, Jody Margolin. Associate Production Designer: Michael Hynes. Assistant Designer: Jerry Dunn. Post Production Executive: George Englund. Production Coordinator: Robin Weiner. Production Assistant: Catherine LePard. Production Staff: Brian Dorfman, Paul Durant, Dionne Gordon, Katherine Eckert, Richard Matthews, William J. Murray III, Norman Schmoller. Technical Director: James Horky. Lighting: Alan Walker. Audio: William H. Kennedy III. Video: John Palacio, Jr. Cameras: Jeff Barnes, Steve Casaly, Mike Denton, Corey Kimball. Property Master: John P. Bozajian. Gaffer: Robert Dick. Head Carpenter: Carl Hicks. Costumes: Marion Kirk, Dan North. Make-up: Vikki McCarter. Hair: Joyce Conroy, Faye Woods. Music Coordinator: Todd Grace. Sword Choreography by: Tim Weske. Re-Recording: Alan Patapoff, Craig Porter. Production Executive: David Amico. Executive in Charge of Production: Susan Palladino. Impact Zone Productions. A Witt/Thomas Production.

1994–95 SEASON
Executive Producer: Allan Katz. Created by: Don Reo. Executive Producer: Judith D. Allison. Supervising Producer: Susan Seeger. Produced by: Kenneth R. Koch. Written by: Judith D. Allison, Dan Cohen, Dorie D'Amore, Brenda Hampton, Brian Herskowitz, Allan Katz, F.J. Pratt, Don Reo, Jonathan Schmock, Susan Seeger. Directed by: Gil Junger, Allan Katz, Ted Wass. Executive Producers: Paul Junger Witt, Tony Thomas, Don Reo. Story Editors: Dan Cohen, F.J. Pratt. Associate Producer: Robin Weiner. Production Designer: Edward Stephenson. Lighting Designers: Daryl Palagi, Alan Walker. Music by: Frank Denson. Main Title Written by: Mike Post, Stephen Geyer. Main Title Performed by: Dr. John. Casting by: Ellen Meyer, C.S.A., Gary Oberst. Associate Directors: Wendy Acey, Art Kellner. Stage Managers: Rusty Colemon, Marc Peterson. Production Associate: Sorel Kaire. Associate Producer: Tara Stephenson. Post Production Executive: George Englund. Music Coordinator: Simeon Speigel. Production Assistants: Sarah Distad, Jeff Rabin. Technical Managers: Bill Conroy, Chris Meuman. Production Staff: Cynthia Bain, Katy Ballard, Brian Dorfman, Jennifer Gillis, Wm. J. Murray, Mark A. Thomson, Tanya Ward. Technical Directors: James Horky, William B. Irwin. Head Carpenter: Bob Berry. Audio: William Kennedy. Video: Randy Johnson. Cameras: Jeff Barnes, Neil Carlos, Bob Keys, Corey Kimball, Ray Liu, Jeff Rifkin. Property Master: Scott Shepherd. Gaffer: Tom Lindsay. Costumers: Topaz, Rasmus Olsson. Make-up: Vikki McCarter. Hair: Faye Woods. Re-Recording: Alan Patapoff, Craig Porter. Production Executive: David Amico. Executive in Charge of Production: Susan Palladino. Impact Zone Productions. A Witt/Thomas Production.

FANELLI BOYS, THE
Created by: Barry Fanaro, Mort Nathan, Kathy Speer, Terry Grossman. Supervising Producers: Martin Weiss, Robert Bruce. Producer: Treva Silverman. Written by: Robert Bruce, Rebecca Carr, Michael Davidoff, Barry Fanaro, Howard Gewirtz, Terry Grossman, Tom Maxwell, Mort Nathan, Martin Pasko, Treva Silverman, Kathy Speer, Martin Weiss, Don Woodard. Directed by: Gary Brown, James Burrows, Jim Drake, J.D. Lobue, Jack Shea, David Steinberg, Andrew D. Weyman, Steve Zuckerman. Executive Producers: Kathy Speer, Terry Grossman, Mort Nathan, Barry Fanaro. Story Editors: Don Woodard, Tom Maxwell, Michael Davidoff. Associate Producer: Jill Andersen. Directors of Photography: Richard Brown, Richard Hissong, William R. Davis, Vincent

F. Contarino. Art Director: Jane Fletcher. Editors: Michael L. Weitzman, Mike Beltran. Associate Directors: Gary Shimokawa, Tom Doak, Christine Ballard, Jim Cox. Stage Managers: Julie Meehan, Paul Paolasso, Lance Lyon. Post Production Supervisor: Gary Brown. *Why Should I Worry* by: Dan Hartman, Charlie Midnight. Original Music by: Thomas Pasatieri, Scott Gale, Rich Eames. Lighting Consultant: Richard Brown. Casting by: Deborah Barylski, C.S.A. Costume Designer: Tom Bronson. Costumers: Sherry Thompson, Terrence K. Smith, Marcy Lavender, Richard E. Mahoney. Make-up: Ken Wensevic, Charles House. Hair Stylists: Ariel Bagdadi, Suzan Bagdadi. Set Decorators: Richard Decinces, Stewart Kane McGuire. Script Supervisors: Gabrielle James, Kathy Giangregorio. Production Coordinators: Kim Rozenfeld, Lisa Gougas-Aamoth. Props: Dave Crockett, Bill Dolan, Pat Moudakis. New York Casting Consultants: Chavanne/Mossberg. Assistants to the Executive Producers: Gail Haller, Alexandra Mulligan, Rebecca Sullivan. Script Coordinators: Gordon R. McKee, Jeannie Taylor, Dollie Tidwell. Technical Directors: Ken Tamburri, Chris Donovan. Audio: R. Steven Kibbons, Michael Ballin. Video: Jean Mason, Richard Edwards. Re-Recorded by: Dave Fluhr, Allen Patapoff, Craig Porter. Executive in Charge of Production for KTMB: Andrew J. Selig.

DISNEY PRESENTS THE 100 LIVES OF BLACK JACK SAVAGE
Music by: Mike Post. Co-Executive Producers: James Wong, Glen Morgan. Supervising Producers: Jo Swerling, Jr., Jack Bernstein. Co-Producers: Daniel Hugh Kelly, Alan Cassidy. Produced by: John Peter Kousakis. Created by: James Wong, Glen Morgan, Stephen J. Cannell. Written by: Jack Bernstein, Stephen J. Cannell, Glen Morgan, Gary Rosen, James Wong. Directed by: Tucker Gates, Bruce Kessler, Kim Manners, Jorge Montesi, David Nutter, James Whitmore, Jr. Executive Producer: Stephen J. Cannell. Story Editor: Gary Rosen. Director of Photography: Frank Johnson, A.S.C. Production Designer: Bill Malley. Unit Production Manager: Jan DeWitt. 1st Assistant Directors: Garry A. Brown, Tom Connors, Chris Griffin, Craig R. West. 2nd Assistant Directors: Melanie Grefé-Feder, Timothy Lonsdale. Film Editors: Howard Terrill, A.C.E., Larry D. Lester, Chris G. Willingham, Ron Spang, Argyle Coe Nelson, A.C.E., Larry Strong, A.C.E. Sound Effects Coordinator: Dick Wahrman. Sound Mixer: Bernie Blynder. Music Editor: Kay Kleinberg. Casting by: Lisa Miller. Miami Casting by: Ellen Jacoby, C.S.A. Camera Operator: Marty Mullin. Gaffer: Danny Eccelston. Key Grip: Barry Ryan. Property Master: Nick Romanac. Script Supervisors: Mark Lighterman, Amy Diamond. Set Decorator: Don Ivey. 2nd Unit Director/Stunt Coordinator: Ronnie Rondell. Marine Coordinator: Ransom Walrod. Special Effects: Kevin Harris. Costume Designers: Tom Bronson, Kristy Aitken. Costume Supervisor: Mary Lou Byrd. Make-up: Marie Del Russo. Hairstylist: Gary Walker. Casting Executive: Peter Golden, C.S.A. Location Managers: Colette Hailey, Valerie Schields. Transportation Coordinator: Larry Crenshaw. Production Coordinator: Mark LaFata. Assistant to Mr. Cannell: Grace Curcio. Special Photographic Effects by: Howard Anderson Co. Executive in Charge of Post Production for Stephen J. Cannell Productions: Gary Winter. Executive in Charge of Production for Stephen J. Cannell Productions: Matthew N. Herman. Stephen J. Cannell Productions in association with Walt Disney Television.

STAT
Created by: Tony Sheehan, Danny Arnold, Chris Hayward. Written by: Danny Arnold, John Bunzel, Chris Hayward, Barry Sandler, Samuel Shem, M.D., Andrew Smith. Directed by: Danny Arnold, Alan Bergman, Ron Glass. Executive Producer: Danny Arnold. Producers: Chris Hayward, John Bunzel. Director of Photography: Vincent F. Contarino. Production Designer: Tho. E. Azzari. Music: Jack Elliott. Casting: David Tochterman. Production Manager: Burt Bluestein. Associate Director: Jim Balden. Stage Managers: L.H. Grant, Barbara Roche, Tracy Eskander, Joe Hughes, Lynn McCracken. Supervising Editor: Homer Powell. Editors: Sherman Overton, Bradley Earle. Set Decorator: Greg Garrison. Costume Designer: Sharon Day Nye. Property Master: Richard Hobaica. Technical Advisors: Gary Sugarman, M.D., Lance Gentile, M.D. Make-up: Joe Blasco. Hair Stylist: Elaina Schul-

man. Script Supervisor: Margaret Scott. Production Sound: Boyd Wheeler. Sound Re-recording: David Fluhr. Technical Director: Bob Tubb. Senior Video: Michael Snedden. Gaffer: Brink Brydon. Key Grip: Richard Noack. Camera Operators: John Lee, Keeth Lawrence, Hank Geving, Ken Dahlquist, Diane Biederbeck, Tom Karnowski, Dean Hall, Dave Hilmer. A Tetragram Ltd. Production in association with Touchstone Television.

DINOSAURS

1990–91 SEASON
Performers: Earl Sinclair: Dave Goelz, Bill Baretta, Stuart Pankin (voice). Fran Sinclair: Allan Trautman, Mitchell Young Evans, Pons Maar, Jessica Walter (voice). Robbie Sinclair: Steve Whitmire, Leif Tilden, Jason Willinger (voice). Charlene Sinclair: Bruce Lanoil, Arlene Lorre, Michelan Sisti, Sally Struthers (voice). Baby Sinclair: John Kennedy, Kevin Clash (voice and puppeteer). Roy Hess: David Greenaway, Pons Maar, Sam McMurray (voice). B.P. Richfield: Steve Whitmire, Sherman Helmsley (voice). Ethyl: Kevin Clash, Brian Henson, Florence Stanley (voice). Additional Dinosaur Performers: Michael Earl, Tom Fisher, Terri Hardin, Brian Henson, Arlene Lorre, James Murray, David Rudman, Michelan Sisti, Jack Tate. Created by: Michael Jacobs, Bob Young. Supervising Producer: Bob Young. Co-Executive Producer: Brian Henson. Producer: Mark Brull. Written by: David A. Caplan, Tim Doyle, Victor Fresco, Andy Goodman, Michael Jacobs, Brian Lapan, Dava Savel, Kirk Thatcher, Rob Ulin, Bob Young. Directed by: Reza Badiyi, Bruce Bilson, William Dear, Jay Dubin, Patrick Johnson, Tom Trbovich. Executive Producer: Michael Jacobs. Co-Producers: Kirk Thatcher, Jeff McCracken. Associate Producer: Kim Rozenfeld. Executive Script Consultants: Rob Ulin, Victor Fresco, Dava Savel. Director of Photography: Robert E. Collins. Production Designer: John C. Mula. Editors: Marco Zappia, Howard S. Deane, A.C.E., Duane Hartzell. Supervising Editor: Marco Zappia. Unit Production Manager: Irwin Marcus. First Assistant Directors: Warren Gray, Joseph Paul Moore, Stephen Lofaro. Second Assistant Directors: Ricardo Mendez Matta, Ronnie Chong, Mark Glick. Theme by: Bruce Broughton. Music by: Bruce Broughton, Ray Colcord. Original Voice Casting by: Robin Lippin. Set Decorators: Brian Savegar, Jeannie Gunn, Robinson Royce. Property Masters: Joshua Meltzer, David L. McGuire. Make-up: Annie Maniscalco. Hair Stylist: Delree Todd. Script Supervisors: Patience Thoreson, Susan Bierbaum. Production Coordinator: Millie Kline. Production Sound Mixer: Avi Kipper. Special Effects: Gary D'Amico. Music Editing by: Patricia Carlin. Post Production Sound: Patrick M. Griffith, Gerry Lentz, Alan Howarth, Richard Corwin, Jason King, Chris Reeves. Harry Artist: Bob Engelsiepen. Dinosaur Designer: Kirk Thatcher. Dinosaurs by: Jim Henson's Creature Shop. Michael Jacobs Productions and Jim Henson Productions in association with Walt Disney Television.

1991–92 SEASON
Performers: Earl Sinclair: Mak Wilson, Tom Fisher, Bill Barretta, Stuart Pankin (voice). Fran Sinclair: Allan Trautman, Tony Sabin Prince, Jessica Walter (voice). Robbie Sinclair: Steve Whitmire, Leif Tilden, Jason Willinger (voice). Charlene Sinclair: Bruce Lanoil, Michelan Sisti, Sally Struthers (voice). Baby Sinclair: Brian Henson, John Kennedy, Kevin Clash (voice and puppeteer). Roy Hess: David Greenaway, Pons Maar, Sam McMurray (voice). B.P. Richfield: Steve Whitmire, Sherman Hemsley (voice). Ethyl: Brian Henson, Florence Stanley (voice). Additional Dinosaur Performers: Julianne Buescher, Kevin Carlson, Tom Fisher, Terri Hardin, Brian Henson, Pons Maar, Noel MacNeal, Sam McMurray, James Murray, Jack Tate, Star Townshend. Created by: Michael Jacobs, Bob Young. Producer: Mark Brull. Co-Executive Producer: Bob Young. Executive Producer: Brian Henson. Producers: Rob Ulin, Victor Fresco, Dava Savel. Written by: David A. Caplan, Richard Day, Tim Doyle, Victor Fresco, Andy Goodman, Bruce Lapan, Steve Pepoon, Dava Savel, Rob Ulin. Directed by: Bruce Bilson, Mark Brull, Tom Trbovich. Executive Producer: Michael Jacobs. Co-Producers: Kirk Thatcher, Jeff McCracken. Associate Producer: Kim

Rozenfeld. Executive Story Consultants: David A. Caplan, Brian Lapan. Story Editors: Tim Doyle, Andy Goodman. Director of Photography: Robert E. Collins. Production Designer: John C. Mula. Editors: Duane Hartzell, Larry Mills, A.C.E. Unit Production Manager: Irwin Marcus. First Assistant Directors: Joseph Paul Moore, Craig R. West. Second Assistant Director: Ronnie Chong. Supervising Editor: Marco Zappia. Theme by: Bruce Broughton. Music by: Ray Colcord. Original Voice Casting by: Robin Lippin. Staff Advisor: Tim Doyle. Set Decorators: Jeannie Gunn, Dwight Jackson, Robinson Royce. Property Master: David L. McGuire. Script Supervisor: Elizabeth C. Porter. Choreography by: Bill Barretta, Leif Tilden. Production Coordinator: Millie Kline. Production Sound Mixers: Avi Kipper, Jim Hill. Post Production Sound: Patrick M. Griffith, M.P.S.E., Gerry Lentz, Scott Wolf, Bruce Nazarian, Chris Reeves, The Sound Guys, Inc., Electronic Melody Studios, Inc. Post Production Coordinator: Steve Anker. Additional Editing by: Ron Menzies. Harry Artist: Bob Engelsiepen. Dinosaur Designer: Kirk Thatcher. Dinosaurs by: Jim Henson's Creature Shop. Michael Jacobs Productions and Jim Henson Productions in association with Walt Disney Television.

1992–93 SEASON
Performers: Earl Sinclair: Mak Wilson, Tom Fisher, Bill Barretta, Stuart Pankin (voice). Fran Sinclair: Allan Trautman, Tony Sabin Prince, Jessica Walter (voice). Robbie Sinclair: Rob Mills, Michelan Sisti, Leif Tilden, Steve Whitmire, Jason Willinger (voice). Charlene Sinclair: Bruce Lanoil, Michelan Sisti, Star Townshend, Sally Struthers (voice). Ethyl: Rickey Boyd, Julianne Buescher, David Greenaway, Brian Henson, Florence Stanley (voice). Roy Hess: David Greenaway, Pons Maar, Sam McMurray (voice). B.P. Richfield: Rob Mills, Steve Whitmire, Sherman Hemsley (voice). Spike: David Greenaway, John Kennedy, Christopher Meloni (voice). Baby Sinclair: Rickey Boyd, John Kennedy, Kevin Clash (voice and puppeteer). Additional Dinosaur Performers: Rickey Boyd, Julianne Buescher, Tom Fisher, David Greenaway, Terri Harden, Pons Maar, Rob Mills, Michelan Sisti, Jack Tate, Star Townshend. Created by: Michael Jacobs, Bob Young. Supervising Producer: Mark Brull. Co-Executive Producer: Bob Young. Executive Producer: Brian Henson. Producers: Dava Savel, David A. Caplan, Brian Lapan. Written by: Adam Barr, David A. Caplan, Tim Doyle, Mark Drop, Victor Fresco, Andy Goodman, Brian Lapan, Lawrence H. Levy, Richard Marcus, Peter Ocko, Dana Savel, Kirk Thatcher, Rob Ulin. Directed by: Bruce Bilson, Mark Brull, Jeff McCracken, Max Tash, Tom Trbovich. Executive Producer: Michael Jacobs. Co-Producers: Kirk Thatcher, Jeff McCracken, Peter Ocko, Adam Barr. Associate Producer: Kim Rozenfeld. Executive Script Consultant: Tim Doyle. Executive Story Editor: Andy Goodman. Director of Photography: Tony Cutrono. Production Designer: John C. Mula. Editors: Jeffrey Bass, Howard S. Deane, A.C.E., Larry Mills, A.C.E. Unit Production Manager: Irwin Marcus. First Assistant Directors: Joseph Paul Moore, Craig R. West. Second Assistant Director: Dirk Craft. Supervising Editor: Marco Zappia. Music by: Ray Colcord. Theme by: Bruce Broughton. Original Voice Casting by: Robin Lippin. Art Director: Kevin Pfeiffer. Set Decorator: Robinson Royce. Property Master: Joshua Meltzer. Script Supervisors: Patti Dalzell, Elizabeth C. Porter. Production Coordinator: Millie Kline. Animatronics/Puppets: Peter Abrahamson, Jane Kriesel Allen, Deborah Anne Ambrosino, Laura Baker, Jon Boyden, Mae Canaga, Marilee Canaga, Wanda E. Chenault, Andrew Clement, John Criswell, Andrew Eio, Charles W. Fetyko, Thomas Michael Ficke, Jeff Forbes, Jane A. Gootnick, Patrick Halm, Greg N. Hamlin, James Hayes, Tim Hawkins, Colleen Henry, David Barrington Holt, Tim Huchthausen, Marian Keating, Niki Lyons, Michael MacFarlane, Roger L. McCoin, Joelle McGonagle, Quentin Plant, Lisa Rocco, Mike 'Mud' Scanlan, Martin E. Simon, Jill K. Thraves, Ann Marie Timinelli, Alissa Warshaw, Jean-Guy White, John B. Wilson, Jr., Kenny Wilson, Julie Zobel. Production Sound Mixers: Jim Hill, Avi Kipper. Post Production Audio by: Bruce Nazarian, Stanley Johnston, Chris Reeves, M.P.S.E. Post Production Supervisor: Steve Anker. Effects Design: Bob Engelsiepen. Dinosaur Designer: Kirk Thatcher. Dinosaurs by: Jim Henson's Creature Shop.

Michael Jacobs Productions and Jim Henson Productions in association with Walt Disney Television.

1993–94 SEASON
Performers: Earl Sinclair: Mak Wilson, Bill Barretta, Stuart Pankin (voice). Fran Sinclair: Allan Trautman, Tony Sabin Prince, Jessica Walter (voice). Robbie Sinclair: Leif Tilden, Steve Whitmire, Jason Willinger (voice). Charlene Sinclair: Bruce Lanoil, Michelan Sisti, Sally Struthers (voice). Baby Sinclair: John Kennedy, Steve Whitmire, Kevin Clash (voice and performer). Additional Dinosaur Performers: Rickey Boyd, Julianne Buescher, Bob Gibson, Tom Fisher, David Greenaway, Jack Tate, Star Townshend. Created by: Michael Jacobs, Bob Young. Supervising Producer: Mark Brull. Co-Executive Producer: Bob Young. Executive Producer: Brian Henson. Producers: David A. Caplan, Tim Doyle, Mark Drop, Jane Espenson, Andy Goodman, Brian Lapan, Peter Ocko, Rick Tabach, Kirk Thatcher. Directed by: Mark Brull, Brian Henson, Jeff McCracken, Tom Trbovich. Executive Producer: Michael Jacobs. Producer: Jeff McCracken. Co-Producers: Ritamarie Peruggi, Peter Ocko, Adam Barr, Tim Doyle, Andy Goodman. Coordinating Producer: Irwin Marcus. Associate Producer: Kim Rozenfeld. Story Editor: Mark Drop. Director of Photography: Tony Cutrono. Production Designer: John C. Mula. Editors: Jeffrey Bass, Larry Mills, A.C.E. Unit Production Manager: Irwin Marcus. First Assistant Directors: Joseph Paul Moore, Craig R. West. Second Assistant Director: Dirk Craft. Supervising Editor: Marco Zappia. Music by: Ray Colcord. Theme by: Bruce Broughton. Original Voice Casting by: Robin Lippin. Art Director: Kevin Pfeiffer. Set Decorator: Robinson Royce. Property Master: George Tuers. Script Supervisor: Elizabeth C. Porter. Production Coordinator: Millie Kline. Animatronics/Puppets: Peter Abrahamson, Jane Kreiesel Allen, Deborah Anne Ambrosino, Laura Baker, Peter Brooke, Abigail Belknap, Mae Canaga, Wanda E. Chenault, Andrew Clement, John Criswell, Carol Dobrovolny, Andrew Eio, Bill Elliott, Jr., Thomas Michael Ficke, Jeff Forbes, John "Fraz" Frassrand, James A. Gootnick, Patrick Halm, James Hayes, Coleen Henry, David Barrington Holt, Sir Guy of Hudson, Marian Keating, Niki Lyons, Michael MacFarlane, Lisa Rocco, Mike 'Mud' Scanlan, Martin E. Simon, Jill K. Thraves, Anne Marie Timinelli, Alissa Warshaw, Jean-Guy White, John B. Wilson, Jr., Kenny Wilson, Julie Zobel. Production Sound Mixers: Jim Hill, Avi Kipper. Post Production Audio by: Bruce Nazarian, Stanley Johnston, Chris Reeves, M.P.S.E. ADR Mixer: John Reiner. Post Production Supervisor: Steve Anker. Henry Artist: Bob Engelsiepen. Dinosaur Designer: Kirk Thatcher. Dinosaurs by: Jim Henson's Creature Shop. Michael Jacobs Productions and Jim Henson Productions in association with Walt Disney Television.

SINGER & SONS
Created by: Michael Jacobs, Bob Young. Supervising Producer: Bob Young. Producer: Mark Brull. Written by: Michael Jacobs, Neil Alan Levy, Lisa Medway, Bob Young. Directed by: Steve Zuckerman. Executive Producer: Michael Jacobs. Associate Producers: Susan R. Nessenbaum-Goldberg, Janet Grushow. Director of Photography: Richard Hissong. Production Designer: John C. Mula. Editor: Marco Zappia. Associate Director: Michael Riolo. Stage Manager: Kimberly Sizemore. Theme and Original Music by: Ray Colcord. Casting by: Eileen Knight, C.S.A. Costume Designer: Tom Bronson. Set Decorator: Scott Heineman. Property Master: Joshua Meltzer. Key Costumers: Don Pike, Perri Kimono, Mindy Kurtz. Make-up: Annie Maniscalco, Patricia Bunch. Hair Stylist: Julia Walker. Script Supervisors: Carol McKechnie, Patti Passarelli. Technical Directors: Chuck Reilly, Bob Jones. Production Coordinators: Janet Grushow, Janice Minsberg. Audio: Klaus Landsberg. Video: Jean Mason. Camera: Randy Baer, Diane Biderbeck, Hank Geving, Marc Hunter, Mark La-Camera, Vince Singletary, Jeff Wheat. Production Staff: Joan Blankenship, Wendy Braff, John Fitzpatrick, Paul Freeman, Eric Blair, Doug George, English Heisser, Leslie Kirvin, Lynn McCracken, Marc Peterson, Yvette Plummer, Steve Solomon, Jannelle Wilde. Re-recording Mixers: David Fluhr, Rick Himot. Michael Jacobs Productions, Inc. in association with Touchstone Television.

HERMAN'S HEAD

1991–92 SEASON

Co-Executive Producers: Stephen Kurzfeld, David Landsberg. Co-Producers: Roberto Benabib, Karl Fink, David Babcock. Created by: Andy Guerdat, Steve Kreinberg. Written by: David Babcock, Roberto Benabib, Don DeMaio, Bill Freiberger, Karl Fink, D.B. Gilles, Andy Guerdat, Cheryl Holliday, Michael B. Kaplan, Steve Kreinberg, David Landsberg, Adam Markowitz, Rich Singer, Barry Stringfellow, Diane Wilk, Graham Yost. Directed by: Andy Cadiff, David Landsberg, J.D. Lobue. Executive Producers: Paul Junger Witt, Tony Thomas. Executive Story Editor: Michael B. Kaplan. Story Editors: Cheryl Holliday, Adam Markowitz, Bill Freiberger. Creative Consultants: Andy Guerdat, Steve Kreinberg. Associate Producer: Gwen McCracken. Production Designer: Edward Stephenson. Music by: Scott Gale, Rich Eames. Main Title Music by: Bill Bodine. Casting by: Cheryl Bayer, C.S.A. Costumes Designed by: Judy Evans. Associate Directors: Tom Doak, Danny White. Stage Managers: Peter Margolis, Charles Carpenter. Production Associate: Lisa Knox. Associate Production Designer: Michael Hynes. Assistant Designers: David Smith, Roland Rosenkranz. Post Production Executive: George Englund. Technical Managers: Bill Conroy, Chris Neuman. Production Assistant: Susan Tenney, Jamie Dinsmore. Production Staff: Deborah A. Bissell, Jill Condon, Jamie Dinsmore, Bill Ghaffary, Andy Glickman, Char Holliday, Mindy Pomper, Wendy Wotherspoon. Technical Director: Bill Irwin. Lighting: J. Kent Inasy. Audio: Doug Nelson, L.D. Gamel, William H. Kennedy III, Myles Weiner, Kerry Boggio. Video: John Palacio, Jr. Cameras: Jeff Barnes, Jack Chisholm, Michael Denton, Marc Hunter, Cathy Lewis, Vince Mack. Property Master: Steve Hill. Gaffer: Thomas Lindsay. Head Carpenters: David Lawton, Bob Berry. Costumers: Ron Hodge, John Patton, Julie Rhine. Make-up: Diane Shatz. Hair Stylist: Faye Woods. Re-Recording: Craig Porter. Production Executive: David Amico. Executive in Charge of Production: Susan Palladino. A Witt/Thomas Production. Touchstone Television.

1992–93 SEASON

Executive Producer: David Landsberg. Producers: Roberto Benabib, Karl Fink, David Babcock. Produced by: Nina Feinberg. Co-Producers: Michael B. Kaplan, Adam Markowitz, Bill Freiberger. Created by: Andy Guerdat, Steve Kreinberg. Written by: David Babcock, Roberto Benabib, Kent Black, Karl Fink, Bill Freiberger, Andy Glickman, Andy Guerdat, Keith Hossman, Michael B. Kaplan, Paul A. Kaplan, Steve Kreinberg, David Landsberg, Tim Maile, Adam Markowitz, Douglas Tuber. Directed by: J.D. Lobue. Executive Producers: Paul Junger Witt, Tony Thomas. Executive Story Editors: Adam Markowitz, Bill Freiberger. Story Editors: Douglas Tuber, Tim Maile. Creative Consultants: Andy Guerdat, Steve Kreinberg. Associate Producer: Gwen McCracken. Production Designer: Edward Stephenson. Music by: Scott Gale, Rich Eames. Main Title Music by: GNG Music. Casting by: Cheryl Bayer, C.S.A., Lisa Miller. Costumes Designed by: Judy Evans. Associate Directors: Tom Doak, Danny White. Stage Managers: Peter Margolis, Charles Carpenter, Greg Dolge. Production Associate: Lisa Knox. Associate Production Designer: Michael Hynes. Assistant Designer: Roland Rosenkranz. Post Production Executive: George Englund. Technical Managers: Bill Conroy, Chris Neuman. Production Assistant: Susan Youngman. Production Staff: Michael Begler, Carol Blankenship, Jill Condon, Catherine Dunn, Andy Glickman, Trevor Kirschner, Wendy Wotherspoon. Technical Director: Bill Irwin. Lighting: J. Kent Inasy. Audio: Dana Mark McClure. Video: John Palacio, Jr. Cameras: Gary Allen, Jeff Barnes, Michael Culp, Michael Denton, Corey Kimball, Vince Mack. Property Master: Steve Hill. Gaffer: Thomas Lindsay. Head Carpenter: Bob Berry. Costumers: Ron Hodge, Julie Rhine. Make-up: Diane Shatz. Hair Stylist: Faye Woods. Main Title by: Geoff Nelson. Re-Recording: Craig Porter. Production Executive: David Amico. Executive in Charge of Production: Susan Palladino. A Witt/Thomas Production. Touchstone Television.

1993–94 SEASON

Executive Producer: David Babcock. Co-Executive Producers: Mark Ganzel, Nina Feinberg. Supervising Producer: Michael B. Kaplan. Producers: Adam Markowitz, Bill Freiberger, Joel Madison. Created by: Andy Guerdat, Steve Kreinberg. Written by: Jack Amiel, David Babcock, Michael Begler, Alec Berg, Tim Doyle, Mark Drop, Bill Freiberger, Mark Ganzel, Andy Glickman, Keith Hossman, Michael B. Kaplan, Joel Madison, Tim Maile, Adam Markowitz, Jeff Schaffer, Douglas Tuber. Directed by: Greg Antonacci, Gary Halvorson, Gail Mancuso. Executive Producers: Paul Junger Witt, Tony Thomas. Executive Story Editors: Douglas Tuber, Tim Maile. Story Editors: Alec Berg, Jeff Schaffer. Associate Producer: Gwen McCracken. Production Designer: Edward Stephenson. Music by: Scott Gale, Rich Eames. Main Title Music by: Mark Nilan. Casting by: Cheryl Bayer, C.S.A., Lisa Miller. Costumes Designed by: Judy Evans. Associate Directors: Tom Doak, Danny White. Stage Managers: Anita Cooper-Avrick, Gregory Dolge. Production Associate: Jennifer Reed. Associate Production Designer: Michael Haynes. Assistant Designer: Scott Latendresse. Post Production Executive: George Englund. Technical Managers: Bill Conroy, Chris Neuman. Production Coordinator: Denise Porter. Music Coordinators: Russell Chan, Todd Grace. Production Staff: Michael Begler, Carol Blankenship, Jamie Dinsmore, Catherine Dunn, Andy Glickman, Todd Morris. Technical Director: Jim Horky. Lighting Designer: J. Kent Inasy. Audio: William Kennedy III. Video: John Palacio, Jr. Cameras: Jeff Barnes, Steve Casaly, Michael Denton, Chester Jackson. Property Master: Steve Hill. Gaffer: Thomas Lindsay. Head Carpenter: Bob Berry. Costumers: Bobbi Yokooji, Michael Lynn, Andrew Slyder. Make-up: Diane Shatz. Hair Stylist: Faye Woods. Main Title by: Geoff Nelson. Re-Recording: Craig Porter. Production Executive: David Amico. Executive in Charge of Production: Susan Palladino. A Witt/Thomas Production. Touchstone Television.

NURSES

1991–92 SEASON

Executive Producers: Susan Beavers, Tom Straw. Co-Executive Producer: Bob Underwood. Supervising Producers: Billy Van Zandt, Jane Milmore, Bruce Ferber. Produced by: Nina Feinberg. Producers: Andy Cadiff, Mitchell Hurwitz. Created by: Susan Harris. Written by: Susan Beavers, Cassandra Clark, Dianne Dixon, Bruce Ferber, Susan Harris, Mitchell Hurwitz, Jane Milmore, Debbie Pearl, David Rosenthal, Danny Smith, Tom Straw, Peter Tilden, Bob Underwood, Billy Van Zandt. Directed by: Andy Cadiff, Terry Hughes. Executive Producers: Paul Junger Witt, Tony Thomas, Susan Harris. Co-Producers: Debbie Pearl, Cassandra Clark, Eric Gilliland. Executive Story Editor: Danny Smith. Story Consultant: Racelle Rosett Schaefer. Associate Producer: Sally S. Kleiman. Production Designer: Edward Stephenson. Music by: George Aliceson Tipton. Casting by: Susan Vash, Debi Levine Nathan. Costumes Designed by: Julianne DeChaine. Associate Directors: Marian Deaton, Patrick Maloney. Stage Managers: Mark Cendrowski, Paul Paolasso. Technical Manager: Bill Conroy. Post Production Supervisor: Peter D. Beyt. Here I Am Written by: George Aliceson Tipton, John Bettis. Production Associate: Esther F. Himbaugh. Associate Production Designer: Michael Hynes. Assistant Designer: Tara Stephenson. Post Production Executive: George Englund. Original Casting by: Kathleen Letterie. Production Assistants: Gordon R. McKee, Robin Welch. Production Staff: Catherine Dunn, Kelly Durham, Cody Farley, Rob Des Hotel, Richard King, Georgia McCreery, Todd Morris, Kurt Schindler. Technical Directors: Jim Horky, Wayne McDonald. Lighting: Alan Walker, Roger Dalton. Audio: William H. Kennedy III. Video: Randy Johnson, Christopher Gray, John O'Brien. Cameras: Neal Carlos, Jack Chisholm, Cory Kimball, Bruce Oldham, Jeff Rifkin. Property Master: Gary Clayton. Gaffers: Jeffrey Chang, Bob Hallsworth. Head Carpenter: Keith Visona. Costumers: Donna Casey, Gina Dedomenico, Donna Fong, Rasmus Olsson, Lori Robinson. Make-up: Wendi Lynne Tolkin. Hair Stylist: Paulette Pennington. Editors: Joseph W. Bateman, Art Kellner. Production Executive: David Amico. Executive in Charge of Production: Susan Palladino. A Witt Thomas Harris Production.

1992–93 SEASON

Executive Producer: Tom Straw. Supervising Producer: Michael Kagan. Producer: Boyd Hale. Co-Producer: Danny

Smith. Produced by: Gilbert Junger. Created by: Susan Harris. Written by: Susan Beavers, Michael Davidoff, Steve Elkins, Boyd Hale, Michael Kagan, Mark Nutter, Tom Reeder, Bill Rosenthal, Danny Smith, Tom Straw. Directed by: Tom Berlinger, Peter Beyt, Gilbert Junger, Lex Passaris, Tom Straw. Executive Producers: Paul Junger Witt, Tony Thomas, Susan Harris. Executive Script Consultant: Tom Reeder. Supervising Producer: Michael Kagan. Executive Story Editor: Danny Smith. Story Editor: Mark Nutter. Associate Producer: Denise Fleissner Barta. Production Designer: Edward Stephenson. Music by: George Aliceson Tipton. Casting by: April Webster, C.S.A. Costumes Designed by: Julianne DeChaine. Associate Directors: Mark Cendrowski, Michael Conley, Jerry Davis, Selig Frank. Stage Managers: Mark Cendrowski, BJ Paul Paolasso, Julie Meehan. Technical Manager: Bill Conroy. Production Associates: Hayden Hilscher, Esther Himbaugh. Associate Production Designer: Michael Hynes. Assistant Designer: Tara Stephenson. Post Production Executive: George Englund. Production Assistant: Robin Welch. Production Staff: Eric Black, Diane Hamilton, Keith Hosman, Maxx Komack, Todd Morris, Denise Porter, Julie Thacker. Technical Director: William Irwin. Lighting: J. Kent Inasy. Audio: Kerry Boggio. Video: Christopher Gray. Cameras: Neal Carlos, Ray Liu, Bruce Oldham, Jeff Rifkin. Property Master: Gary Clayton. Gaffers: Bob Hallsworth, Robert Searcy. Head Carpenter: Keith Visona. Costumers: Penelope L. Larson, Rasmus H.P. Olsson. Make-up: Bruce Grayson. Hair Stylist: Faye Woods. Original Casting by: Kathleen Letterie. Re-Recording: Craig Porter. Production Executive: David Amico. Executive in Charge of Production: Susan Palladino. A Witt Thomas Harris Production.

1993–94 SEASON
Executive Producer: Tom Straw. Supervising Producer: Boyd Hale. Producer: Boyd Hale. Created by: Susan Harris. Written by: Boyd Hale, Mark Nutter, Tom Reeder, Danny Smith, Tom Straw, Barbara Wallace, Thomas R. Wolfe, Christine Zander. Directed by: Gilbert Junger, Tom Straw. Produced by: Gilbert Junger. Executive Producers: Paul Junger Witt, Tony Thomas, Susan Harris. Executive Script Consultant: Tom Reeder. Executive Story Editor: Mark Nutter. Story Editors: Barbara Wallace, Thomas R. Wolfe. Associate Producer: Denise Fleissner Barta. Production Designer: Michael Hynes. Original Production Designed by: Edward Stephenson. Music by: Frank Denson, Mike Post. Main Title Written by: Mike Post. Casting by: April Webster, C.S.A., Cydney McCurdy. Costumes Designed by: Julianne DeChaine. Associate Directors: Mark Cendrowski, Art Kellner. Stage Managers: Rusty Colemon, Bill Ghaffary. Technical Manager: Bill Conroy. Production Associate: Jolie Barnett. Post Production Executive: George Englund. Music Coordinator: Nick South. Production Staff: Eric Black, Jennifer Gillis, Jim Halkett, Diane Hamilton, Maxx Komack, Leslie Strain, Wendy Wotherspoon. Technical Director: Bill Irwin. Lighting: Andy Kassan. Audio: Ed Epstein. Video: Doug Dessero. Cameras: Neal Carlos, Ray Liu, Bruce Oldham, Jeff Rifkin. Property Master: Gary Clayton. Gaffer: Robert Searcy. Head Carpenter: Don Phillips. Costumers: Gabriel Espinosa, Penelope L. Larson, Rasmus H.P. Olsson. Make-up: Elizabeth Cooper. Hair Stylist: Kim Urgel. Original Casting by: Kathleen Letterie. Re-Recording: Allen Patapoff, Craig Porter. Production Executive: David Amico. Executive in Charge of Production: Susan Palladino. A Witt Thomas Harris Production.

PACIFIC STATION
Created by: Barry Fanaro, Mort Nathan, Kathy Speer, Terry Grossman. Co-Executive Producers: Robert Bruce, Martin Weiss. Co-Producer by: Gary Brown. Produced by: Rita Dillon, George Sunga. Written by: Robert Bruce, Michael Davidoff, Richard Day, Barry Fanaro, Terry Grossman, Tom Maxwell, Stephen A. Miller, Mort Nathan, Teresa O'Neil, Bill Rosenthal, Kathy Speer, Martin Weiss, Don Woodard. Directed by: Gary Brown, James Burrows, Art Dielhen. Executive Producers: Kathy Speer, Terry Grossman, Mort Nathan, Barry Fanaro. Executive Story Editors: Michael Davidoff, Bill Rosenthal, Don Woodard, Tom Maxwell. Story Editors: Gary Apple, Michael Carrington. Associate Producer: Jill Andersen. Director of Photography: Michael Berlin. Art Directors: Ed La Porta, Jane Fletcher. Editors: Michael L. Weitzman. Associate Director: Christine Ballard. Stage Managers: Julie Meehan, Lance Lyon. *Rescue Me* Performed by: Margo Thunder, Phaedra Butler, Rise Engermann. Original Music by: Scott Gale, Rich Eames. Casting by: Amy Lieberman, C.S.A., Jeff Oshen, C.S.A. Costume Designer: Tom Bronson. Costumers: Marcy Lavender, David Baca, Richard E. Mahoney. Make-up: Art Harding, Bruce Grayson. Hair Stylist: Dale Miller. Set Decorators: Ed McDonald, Nel Cooper Fischer. Script Supervisor: Kathy Giangregorio. Production Coordinator: Lisa Gougas-Aamoth. Property Master: Pat Moudakis. Assistants to the Executive Producers: Gail Haller, Rebecca Sullivan. Assistant to the Producer: Dollie Tidwell. Script Coordinators: Jeannie Taylor, Chris Brown. Technical Directors: Ken Tamburri, Dick Woodka. Audio: R. Stevens Kibbons, Carolyn L. Bowden, Greg Orrante. Video: Tom Tcimpidis, Rich Rose, Richard W. Edwards. Re-recorded by: Allen Patapoff, Craig Porter. KTMB, Touchstone Television.

HOME IMPROVEMENT

1991–92 SEASON
Producer: John Pasquin. Produced by: Gayle S. Maffeo. Created by: Carmen Finestra, David McFadzean, Matt Williams. Written by: Lauren Eve Anderson, Sheila M. Anthony, Carmen Finestra, Allison M. Gibson, Susan Estelle Jansen, David McFadzean, Rosalind Moore, Billy Riback, Marley Sims, Elliot Stern, B.K. Taylor, Peter Tolan, Matt Williams. Directed by: John Pasquin. Executive Producers: Carmen Finestra, David McFadzean, Matt Williams. Co-Producers: Billy Riback, Peter Tolan. Associate Producer: Frank McKemy. Executive Story Editor: Elliot Stern. Story Editors: Allison M. Gibson, Marley Sims. Executive Consultant: Tim Allen. Directors of Photography: Donald A. Morgan, Gary Scott. Production Designer: David Sackeroff. Editors: Marco Zappia, Alex Gimenez. Associate Director: Peter Filsinger. Stage Managers: Shawn Shea, Bill Shea. Original Music by: Dan Foliart. Casting by: Deborah Barylski, C.S.A., Julie Pernworth. Set Decorator: Rick Caprarelli. Property Master: Warren Shaffer. Script Supervisor: Carol McKechnie. Production Coordinator: Caterina N. Fiordellisi. Key Costumers: Rudolph Garcia, Nicole Gorsuch. Make-up: Diane Shatz, Wendy J. Weiss. Hair Stylists: Richard Sabre, Maria Valdivia. Opening Design by: Geoffrey Nelson. Post Production Coordinator: Jim Praytor. Staff: Geoff Addison, Tony Allegre, Steve Gabriel, Tamara Gregory, Brett Gregory, Tyler Jones, Helen MacDonald, Kathy O'Connell, Terrie Rigali, Robert Zappia. Technical Directors: Chris Donovan, Craig Shideler. Audio: Doug Nelson, Myles Weiner, Klaus Landsberg, C.A.S., Toby Foster. Video: Bob Kaufmann, Mark W. Sanford. Based on the Stand-up Comedy of Tim Allen. Wind Dancer Productions, Inc. in association with Touchstone Television.

1992–93 SEASON
Producer: John Pasquin. Produced by: Gayle S. Maffeo, Billy Riback. Created by: Carmen Finestra, David McFadzean, Matt Williams. Written by: Darrel Campbell, Carmen Finestra, Steve Gabriel, Howard M. Gould, Stacey Hur, Susan Estelle Jansen, Maxine Lapiduss, David McFadzean, Rosalind Moore, Howard J. Morris, Billy Riback, B.K. Taylor, Matt Williams, Robert Zappia. Directed by: Andy Cadiff, John Pasquin. Executive Producers: Carmen Finestra, David McFadzean, Matt Williams. Supervising Producers: Maxine Lapiduss, Billy Riback. Associate Producer: Frank McKemy. Executive Story Consultant: Howard M. Gould. Executive Story Editors: Howard J. Morris, Susan Estelle Jansen. Story Editor: Susan Estelle Jansen. Creative Consultant: Elliot Shoennan. Executive Consultant: Tim Allen. Directors of Photography: Donald A. Morgan, Gary Scott. Production Designer: David Sackeroff. Editors: Marco Zappia, Alex Gimenez. Associate Director: Peter Filsinger. Stage Manager: Shawn Shea. Original Music by: Dan Foliart. Casting by: Deborah Barylski, C.S.A. Set Decorator: Jeannie Gunn. Property Master: Warren Shaffer. Script Supervisors: Carol McKechnie, Susan Straughn Harris. Production Coordinators: Anthony Allegre, Caterina N. Fiordellisi. Key Costumers: Valerie Laven, Nicole Gorsuch. Make-up: Wendy J. Weiss. Hair Stylists: Sandra Rubin-Monk, Maria Valdivia. Opening Design by: Geoffrey Nelson. Post Production Coordinator: Jim

Praytor. Staff: Geoff Addison, Tony Allegre, Steve Gabriel, Tamara Gregory, Brett Gregory, Tyler Jones, Helen MacDonald, Kathy O'Connell, Terrie Rigali, Robert Zappia. Technical Directors: Chris Donovan, Kenneth R. Shapiro. Audio: Paul Sandweiss, Klaus Landsberg. Video: Bob Kaufmann. Based on the Stand-up Comedy of Tim Allen. Wind Dancer Productions, Inc. in association with Touchstone Television.

1993–94 Season
Produced by: Gayle S. Maffeo. Created by: Carmen Finestra, David McFadzean, Matt Williams. Executive Producer: Bob Bendetson. Supervising Producer: Bruce Ferber. Written by: Tim Allen, Bob Bendetson, Ron Bloomberg, Max Eisenberg, Art Everett, Bruce Ferber, Diane Ford, Matthew Miller, Rosalind Moore, Howard J. Morris, Barrie Nedler, Elliot Shoenman, Marley Sims, B.K. Taylor, Jon Vandergriff, Paul Wolff. Directed by: Andy Cadiff, Peter Filsinger. Executive Producers: Elliot Shoenman, Carmen Finestra, David McFadzean, Matt Williams. Co-Produced by: Frank McKemy. Consulting Producer: Billy Riback. Co-Producer: Howard J. Morris. Executive Story Editor: Rosalind Moore. Creative Consultant: Marley Sims. Executive Consultant: Tim Allen. Directors of Photography: Donald A. Morgan, Walter Glover. Production Designer: David Sackeroff. Editors: Marco Zappia, Roger Ames Berger. Associate Directors: Peter Filsinger, Tom Doak. Stage Manager: Shawn Shea. Original Music by: Dan Foliart. Casting by: Deborah Barylski, C.S.A. Set Decorator: Jeannie Gunn. Property Masters: Warren Shaffer, Gordon Fletcher. Script Supervisors: Susan Straughn Harris, Lani Robin Bergstein. Production Coordinator: Anthony Allegre. Costumers: Valerie Laven-Cooper, Nicole Gorsuch, Dayton C. Anderson. Make-up: Wendy J. Weiss, Sandy Reimer. Special Make-up: Steve LaPorte. Hair Stylists: Sandra Rubin-Munk, Maria Valdivia. Opening Design by: Geoffrey Nelson. Post Production Supervisor: Jim Praytor. Technical Directors: Chris Donovan, Cliff Miracle, Eric Becker. Audio: Klaus Landsberg, Richard Wachter. Video: Bob Kaufmann. Based on the Stand-up Comedy of Tim Allen. Wind Dancer Production Group in association with Touchstone Television.

1994–95 Season
Produced by: Frank McKemy. Consulting Producer: Gayle S. Maffeo. Created by: Carmen Finestra, David McFadzean, Matt Williams. Co-Executive Producer: Bruce Ferber. Producers: Andy Cadiff, Howard J. Morris. Written by: Bob Bendetson, Bruce Ferber, Carmen Finestra, Lloyd Garver, Neil Kramer, David McFadzean, Rosalind Moore, Howard J. Morris, Thad Mumford, Elliot Shoenman, Marley Sims, Ned Teitelbaum, Jon Vandergriff, Matt Williams, Paul Wolff. Directed by: Andy Cadiff, Peter Filsinger. Executive Producers: Elliot Shoenman, Bob Bendetson, Bruce Ferber, Carmen Finestra, David McFadzean, Matt Williams. Consulting Producer: Billy Riback. Co-Producers: Rosalind Moore, Jim Praytor. Associate Producer: Alan Padula. Creative Consultants: Marley Sims, Lloyd Garver. Story Editor: Jon Vandergriff. Executive Consultant: Tim Allen. Director of Photography: Donald A. Morgan. Production Designer: David Sackeroff. Editors: Marco Zappia, Roger Ames Berger. Associate Director: Peter Filsinger. Stage Managers: Shawn Shea, Guy Distad. Original Music by: Dan Foliart. Casting by: Deborah Barylski, C.S.A., Jonell Dunn. Set Decorator: Jeannie Gunn. Property Master: Warren Shaffer. Script Supervisors: Susan Straughn Harris, Kathy Giangregorio. Costume Supervisors: Valerie Laven-Cooper, Nicole Gorsuch. Make-up: Wendy J. Weiss. Hair Stylist: Maria Valdivia. Opening Design by: Geoffrey Nelson. Post Production Coordinator: Judy Rauh. Camera: Gary Allen, Randy Baer, Larry Gaudette, Victor Gonzales, Marvin Shearer. Booms: Steve Dichter, Dan Ortiz, Vic Ortiz. A-2: Gary Long. Leadman: Steve Jarrard. Gaffer: Bill Bryant. Key Grip: Mike Hagopian. Technical Directors: Craig Shideler, Kenneth R. Shapiro, Chris Donovan. Audio: Klaus Landsberg, Richard Wachter. Video: Bob Kaufmann. Based on the Stand-up Comedy of Tim Allen. Wind Dancer Production Group in association with Touchstone Television.

1995–96 Season
Produced by: Frank McKemy. Producer: Gayle S. Maffeo. Created by: Carmen Finestra, David McFadzean, Matt Williams.

Co-Executive Producers: Andy Cadiff, Howard J. Morris, Rosalind Moore. Written by: Ruth Bennett, Jennifer Celotta, Max Eisenberg, Bruce Ferber, Lloyd Garver, Rosalind Moore, Howard J. Morris, Teresa O'Neill, Elliot Shoenman, Marley Sims, Jon Vandergriff. Directed by: Peter Bonerz, Andy Cadiff, Richard Compton, Peter Filsinger, Geoffrey Nelson, Andrew Tsao. Executive Producers: Elliot Shoenman, Bob Bendetson, Bruce Ferber, Carmen Finestra, David McFadzean, Matt Williams. Consulting Producers: Billy Riback, Marley Sims. Co-Producer: Jim Praytor. Associate Producer: Alan Padula. Creative Consultants: Lloyd Garver, Teresa O'Neill, Ruth Bennett. Executive Story Editor: Jon Vandergriff. Executive Consultant: Tim Allen. Director of Photography: Donald A. Morgan. Production Designer: David Sackeroff. Editors: Marco Zappia, Roger Ames Berger. Associate Director: Peter Filsinger. Stage Managers: Shawn Shea, Guy Distad. Original Music by: Dan Foliart. Casting by: Deborah Barylski, C.S.A., Jonell Dunn. Set Decorator: Jeannie Gunn. Property Master: Warren Shaffer. Script Supervisor: Susan Straughn Harris. Technical Consultant: Brett Gregory. Production Coordinator: Jeff Sarver. Costume Supervisors: Valerie Laven-Cooper, Nicole Gorsuch. Make-up: Wendy J. Weiss. Hair Stylist: Maria Valdivia. Opening Design by: Geoffrey Nelson. Post Production Coordinator: Judy Rauh. Technical Director: Craig Shideler. Audio: Klaus Landsberg, Gary Long, Richard Wachter. Video: Bob Kaufmann. Based on the Stand-up Comedy of Tim Allen. Wind Dancer Production Group in association with Touchstone Television.

TORKELSONS, THE
Created by: Lynn Montgomery. Co-Producers: Wayne Lemon, Lynn Montgomery. Producer: Philip LaZebnik. Co-Executive Producer: Norma Safford Vela. Supervising Producers: Dawn Tarnofsky, Richard Christian Matheson, Thomas Szollosi. Producer: Arlene Sanford. Co-Producers: Arlene Grayson, Mitchell Bank. Developed by: Michael Banks. Written by: Diana "Jennie" Ayers, Virginia K. Hegge, Michael Jacobs, Philip LaZebnik, Wayne Lemon, Richard Christian Matheson, Lynn Montgomery, Connie Ray, Susan Sebastian, Thomas Szollosi, Christopher Vane, Norma Safford Vela. Directed by: Robert Berlinger, Arlene Sanford. Executive Producer: Michael Jacobs. Executive Story Editors: Susan Sebastian, Diane "Jennie" Ayers. Director of Photography: Richard Hissong. Production Designer: John C. Mula. Edited by: Jeffrey Bass, Marco Zappia. Supervising Editor: Marco Zappia. Unit Production Manager: Jan DeWitt. First Assistant Director: Chuck Gayton. Second Assistant Director: Shari Genser. Music by: Ray Colcord. Theme Song by: Michael Jacobs, Ray Colcord. Performed by: The Judds. Casting by: Robin Lippin, C.S.A., Allison Jones. Original Casting by: Mary V. Buck, C.S.A., Susan Edelman, C.S.A. Set Decorator: Rochelle Moser. Property Masters: Horst Grandt, Anne Reeves. Script Supervisor: Kit Wilkinson. Production Coordinator: Janice Minsberg. Technical Coordinator: Lauren Breiting. Costume Designer: Tom Bronson. Key Costumers: Mindy Kurtz, David Baca. Make-up: Bruce Grayson. Hair Stylist: Dale Miller. Production Sound Mixers: J. Mark King, Dana Mark McClure, Jessie W. Peck. Michael Jacobs Productions.

ALMOST HOME
Created by: Lynn Montgomery. Developed by: Michael Jacobs. Supervising Producer: Philip LaZebnik. Supervising Producer: Wayne Lemon. Producer: Arlene Grayson. Written by: Lisa A. Bannick, Michael Jacobs, Philip LaZebnik, Wayne Lemon, Mark Lisson, Patricia Nardo. Directed by: Bruce Bilson, Linda Day, Dennis Erdman, Patrick Maloney, Arlene Sanford, David Trainer. Executive Producers: Charlotte Brown, Michael Jacobs. Associate Producer: Karen MacKain. Creative Consultants: Lisa A. Bannick, Mark Lisson. Director of Photography: John Conti. Production Designer: John C. Mula. Editor: Marco Zappia. Associate Director: Nancy Heydorn. Stage Manager: Jonathan Weiss. Music by: Ray Colcord. Theme Song by: Michael Jacobs, Ray Colcord. Casting by: Judith Weiner, Megan McConnell. Set Decorator: Mel Cooper Fischer. Property Master: Marjorie Coster. Script Supervisors: Kathy Giangregorio, Carol McKechnie. Production Coordinator: Russell Dague. Costume Designer: Tom Bronson. Key Costumers: Mindy Kurtz, Gail Viola. Make-up: Annie Man-

iscalco. Hair Stylists: Lucia Mace Castaneda, Maria Valdivia, Catherine A. Marcotte. Production Staff: Pam Bileck, Christian Boudman, David Michael Ginsburg, Ann Johnson, Paul Lerner, Katy Penland, Jackie Schaffner, Larry Solomon. Technical Director: Craig Shideler. Audio: Michael T. Gannon. Video: Eric Clay. Michael Jacobs Productions.

GOOD & EVIL

Executive Producer: Tom Straw. Co-Executive Producer: Bob Underwood. Producers: Valerie J. Curtin, Bill Bryan, Gilbert Junger. Created by: Susan Harris. Written by: Bill Bryan, Valerie J. Curtin, Susan Harris, Tom Reeder, Tom Straw, Bob Underwood. Directed by: Terry Hughes. Executive Producers: Paul Junger Witt, Tony Thomas, Susan Harris. Associate Producers: Gwen McCracken, Denise Fleissner Barta. Production Designer: Edward Stephenson. Music by: George Aliceson Tipton. Casting by: Kathleen Letterie, Pat Melton. Fashion Stylist: Paul Sinclaire. Costumes Designed by: Julianne DeChaine. Associate Directors: Lex Passaris, Peter D. Beyt, Pat Maloney, Harold McKenzie. Stage Managers: Tom Carpenter, Kent Zbornak, C.J. Rapp Pittman, Rusty Colemon. Production Coordinator: Denise Fleissner Barta. Production Associates: Robert Spina, Hayden Hilscher. Associate Designers: Michael Hynes, Scott Latendresse. Production Associate: Salli Shrewsbury. Production Assistant: Robin Welch. Technical Manager: Bill Conroy. Post Production Executive: George Englund. Post Production Manager: Fred Roth. Music Coordinator: Scott Gale. Production Staff: Eric Black, Jeff Clinkenbeard, Rob Des Hotel, Gary A. Gamble, Bill Ghaffary, Bridget Johnson, Pamela Phelps, Denise Porter. Technical Directors: Ken Tamburri, William C. Irwin. Lighting: Alan Walker, William Updegraff. Audio: Edward L. Moskowitz, C.A.S., L.D. Gamel, C.A.S. Video: John O'Brien, Christopher Gray. Cameras: Neal Carlos, Dave Heckman, Chester Jackson, Stephen A. Jones, Ritch Kenney, Cathy Lewis, Bruce Oldham, Jeff Rifkin. Property Masters: Robert Devicariis, Daniel F. Beringhele. Gaffers: William Updegraff, Robert Searcey. Head Carpenters: Paul Wadian, Frank Stevens. Costumers: Donna Casey, Murshel Lewis, Pie Lombardi, Thomas Siegel. Make-up: Alfonso Goé Gonzalez, Angela A. Levin. Hair Stylists: Joyce Melton Conroy, Robert Ramos. Re-recording: Craig Porter. Production Executive: David Amico. Executive in Charge of Production: Susan Palladino. A Witt Thomas Harris Production. Touchstone Television.

WALTER AND EMILY

Created by: Paul Perlove. Executive Producer: John Rich. Supervising Producers: Ron Bloomberg, Larry Levin, Bruce Ferber. Producer: Gilbert Junger. Written by: Ron Bloomberg, Bruce Ferber, Michael Langworthy, Larry Levin, Paul Perlove, Jerry Ross. Directed by: John Rich. Executive Producers: Paul Perlove, Paul Junger Witt, Tony Thomas. Associate Producer: Denise Fleissner Barta. Production Designer: Edward Stephenson. Music by: George Aliceson Tipton, Jeff Koz, Dave Koz. Theme by: Jeff Koz, Dave Koz, Audrey Koz. Casting by: Kathleen Letterie, C.S.A. Casting Associate: Nora Kariya. Costume Designer: Judy Evans. Associate Directors: Bob Lahendro, Vince Humphrey. Stage Managers: Chris La Barbera, Anthony Rich, Tracy Eskender. Production Associate: Jennifer Reed. Associate Production Designer: Michael Hynes. Assistant Designers: Roland Rosenkranz, Diane Yates. Post Production Executive: George Englund. Technical Managers: Bill Conroy, Chris Neuman. Unit Manager: Audrey Joy Johnson. Production Staff: Eric Black, Michael C. Dixon, Cody R. Farley, Susan Leslie, Denise Porter, Christine Schultz. Technical Directors: Robert A. Bowen, William C. Irwin. Lighting: William Updegraff. Audio: Kerry J. Boggio, L.D. Gamel, William Kennedy. Video: Randolph D. Johnson, Christopher Gray. Cameras: Randy Baer, David Bushner, Neal Carlos, Roy E. Holm, Chester Jackson, Cathy Lewis, Bruce Oldham, John Repczynski, Jeff Rifkin. Property Masters: Dave Crockett, Hector Hermosillo. Gaffer: Dave Lechuga. Carpenter: Ron Leal. Costumers: Helaine Bruck Ross, Michael C. Lynn. Make-up: Angela A. Levin. Hair: Susan Lipson. Re-Recording: Craig Porter. Production Executive: David Amico. Executive in Charge of Production: Susan Palladino. A Witt/Thomas Production. Touchstone Television.

LAURIE HILL

Created by: Carol Black, Neal Marlens. Supervising Producer: Stuart Wolpert. Producer: Stephen Neigher. Produced by: Mark Grossan. Written by: Carol Black, Kim Friese, Rita Hsiao, Neal Marlens, Stephen Neigher, Hugh O'Neill, David Rosenthal. Directed by: L.G. Day, Neal Marlens, Steve Miner. Executive Producers: Carol Black, Neal Marlens. Co-Producer: Kim Friese. Story Editor: David Rosenthal. Associate Producer: Frank Merwald. Director of Photography: Robert F. Liu, A.S.C. Art Director: Greg Richman. Editor: Dennis C. Vejar, A.C.E. Production Manager: Neil Rapp. First Assistant Director: Charles W. Liotta. Second Assistant Director: Heide Gutman. Music: W.G. "Snuffy" Walden. Casting by: Randy Stone. Executive Consultant: Michael Becker. Original Casting by: Mary V. Buck, C.S.A., Susan Edelman, C.S.A. Technical Coordinator: David Owen Trainor. Set Decorator: Nancy Nye. Property Master: Scott L. London. Script Supervisor: Sandra Eustis. Production Coordinator: Scott Sites. Key Costumer: Wendy Range. Costumers: Melissa Merwin, Emily Jane Kitos. Leadman: Tom Kaltsas. Make-up: Dulcie Smith-Sorbo. Hairstylist: Michele Payne. Chief Lighting Technician: Randall Burak. Key Grip: Brian Smith. Camera Operators: Eric Anderson, Kurt Braun, Patrick McGinness, Gordon Paschal, Philip D. Schwartz. Best Boy/Electric: Rich Kamins. Best Boy/Grip: David Goode. Electricians: Michael Bailey, Scott Grinham, John A. Haskell. Grips: Emilio Anzures, Tim Arnold, David French. Camera Assistants: Scott Birnkrant, Steve Burnett, Bob Feller, Hunt Hibler, Peter Kowolski, Wally Sweeterman. Production Sound Mixer: Brentley Walton. Re-recorded by: Marti D. Humphrey, John Bickelhaupt, John L. Sisti. Assistant Editor: Jennifer Vejar-Bryan. Production Auditor: Debra Meek. Post Production Coordinator: Cynthia Uccello. Assistants to the Producer: Melissa Ferrell, Anji Sawant, Cynthia Uccello, Amy Jo Weinstein. Writers' Assistants: Teddy Tenenbaum, Latrice Williams. Production Assistants: Keith Barber, Mark Andrew, Kurt Bauerle, Eddie Fickett, Erik R. Press, Debra Russell, Judith Spivak, Terri Stadtmueller. The Black/Marlens Company.

WOOPS!

Created by: Gary Jacobs. Co-Executive Producers: Harold Kimmel, Ross Abrash. Co-Producer: Richard Day. Written by: Ross Abrash, Maria Brown, Bill Bryan, Richard Day, Gary Jacobs, Harold Kimmel, Tim Maile, Gary Murphy, Mark Nutter, Larry Strawther, Douglas Tuber. Directed by: Terry Hughes. Executive Producers: Gary Jacobs, Paul Junger Witt, Tony Thomas. Story Editors: Mark Nutter, Tim Maile, Douglas Tuber. Creative Consultants: Gary Murphy, Larry Strawther. Associate Producer: Drew Brown. Art Director: Ramsey Avery. Costume Designer: Erin Quigley. Lighting Designer: Daniel Flannery. Music by: GNG Music. Original Casting by: Molly Lopata, C.S.A. Original Production Design: Garvin Eddy. Associate Directors: Carl Lauten, Jimmy B. Frazier. Stage Managers: Paul Paolasso, Bill Ghaffary. Production Associate: Hayden Hilscher. Post-Production Executive: George Englund. Assistant Art Director: Rachel Hauck. Production Assistant: Jonathan Glabman. Production Staff: Emily Berke, Andrew Green, Gary A. Gamble, Elise Ogden, Kurt Schindler. Technical Manager: Bill Conroy. Technical Directors: Karl Messerschmidt, Jim Horky. Audio: Bill Kennedy. Video: Randy Johnson. Cameras: Neal Carlos, Raymond Liu, Bruce Oldham, Jeff Rifkin. Property Master: Dave Crockett. Gaffer: Dave Lechuga. Head Carpenter: Frank Stevens. Costumers: Lynda Pyka, Tom Siegel. Make-up: Robert Jermain. Hair Stylist: Susan Lipson. Re-Recording: Craig Porter. Production Executive: David Amico. Executive in Charge of Production: Susan Palladino. Heartfelt Productions and Witt-Thomas Productions.

WHERE I LIVE

1992–93 SEASON

Created by: Michael Jacobs, Ehrich Van Lowe. Co-Executive Producer: Ehrich Van Lowe. Supervising Producers: Dawn Tarnofsky, April Kelly. Produced by: Mitchell Bank. Written by: Alan Daniels, Gary Hardwick, Michael Jacobs, April

Kelly, Lore Kimbrough, Paula Mitchell Manning, Stan Seidel, Ehrich Van Lowe. Directed by: Arlene Sanford, Rob Schiller, David Trainer, Tom Trbovich. Executive Producer: Michael Jacobs. Co-Producers: Stan Seidel, Doug E. Doug, Kevin Brown. Associate Producer: Brian J. Cowan. Story Editors: Alan Daniels, Lore Kimbrough, G.A. Howard. Director of Photography: Donald A. Morgan. Production Designer: John C. Mula. Edited by: Marco Zappia. Associate Director: Patrick Maloney. Stage Manager: Barbara J. Roche. Music by: Ray Colcord. Casting by: Chemin Sylvia Bernard, C.S.A. Set Decorator: Robinson Royce. Script Supervisor: Kathy Giangregorio. Production Coordinator: Kevin Lillestol. Technical Director: Parker Roe. Costume Supervisor: Nanrose Buchman. Key Costumer: Terry Gordon. Costumer: Paulette Holmon. Make-up: Stephanie Cozart Burton. Hair Stylists: Ora Green, Ken Walker. Property Master: David McGuire. Audio: J. Mark King. Video: Bob Snyder. Michael Jacobs Productions.

1993–94 Season
Created by: Michael Jacobs, Ehrich Van Lowe. Co-Executive Producer: Ehrich Van Lowe. Supervising Producers: David A. Caplan, Brian Lapan. Producer: Stan Seidel. Produced by: Mitchell Bank. Written by: David A. Caplan, Allison M. Gibson, Gary Hardwick, Lore Kimbrough, Brian Lapan, Stan Seidel, Ehrich Van Lowe, Lynn Mamet. Directed by: Matthew Diamond, Tom Trbovich, Michael Zinberg. Executive Producer: Michael Jacobs. Consulting Producer: Dawn Tarnofsky. Co-Producers: Doug E. Doug, Kevin Brown. Associate Producer: Brian J. Cowan. Executive Story Editor: Lore Kimbrough. Story Editors: Allison M. Gibson, Gary Hardwick, Lynn Mamet. Director of Photography: Donald A. Morgan. Production Designer: John C. Mula. Edited by: Marco Zappia. Associate Director: Lauren Breiting. Manager: Kimberly Sizemore. Main Theme Song and Music by: Ray Colcord. Casting by: Chemin Sylvia Bernard, C.S.A. Set Decorator: Robinson Royce. Costume Supervisor: Nanrose Buchman. Key Costumer: Terry Gordon. Costumers: Jerry Ross, Jackie Quigley. Make-up: Stephanie Cozart Burton. Hair Stylist: Erman Kent. Property Master: David McGuire. Script Supervisor: Erma Elzy-Jones. Production Coordinator: Gregory Frampton. Technical Director: Parker Roe. Audio: J. Mark King. Video: Bob Snyder. Opening Design by: View Studios. Michael Jacobs Productions.

Cutters
Created by: Allan Burns, Burt Metcalfe, Howard M. Gould, Lindsay Harrison. Music by: Patrick Williams. Produced by: Patricia Rickey. Supervising Producer: Lindsay Harrison. Written by: Allan Burns, Howard M. Gould, Lindsay Harrison, Kerry Lenhart, Bill Levinson, Burt Metcalfe, John J. Sakmar. Directed by: Andy Cadiff. Executive Producers: Allan Burns, Burt Metcalfe, Howard M. Gould. Associate Producer: Geralyn Maddern. Production Designer: Tho. E. Azzari. Associate Director: Marian Deaton. Stage Managers: Tom Seidman, A.J. Johnson, Valdez Flagg, Joann Kamay. Casting: Shana Landsburg, C.S.A., Robin Joy Allan, C.S.A., Sharon Jetton. Costume Designer: Elizabeth P. Palmer. Director of Photography: Bill Williams. Set Decorator: Jennifer Polito. Property Master: Dan Beringhele. Script Supervisor: Esther F. Himbaugh. Production Associate: Hilton Smith. Production Coordinators: Betty Arnold, Alexis Genya, Meg Green. Assistants to the Producers: Craig Feeney, John French, Chris Cragnotti, Jason Porath, Maryann Raines. Technical Director: Jim Horky. Video Control: Ross Elliott. Camera Operators: Tom Conkwright, Ray Gonzales, George Loomis, Leigh Nicholson, Dick Price, Jeff Rifkin. Edited by: Ken Denisoff. Audio Supervisor: Michael T. Gannon. Re-recording: Tamara Johnson, Craig Porter, Rick Himot, John Bickelhaupt. Executive in Charge for Grant/Tribune: Alan Duke. A Turnaround Production. Grant/Tribune Productions.

Disney Presents Bill Nye the Science Guy
Executive Producers/Directors: Erren Gottlieb, Jim McKenna. Executive in Charge of Production: Elizabeth Brock. Production Manager: Hamilton McCulloh. Writers: Kit Boss, Melissa Gould, Michael Gross, Mark Ashton Hunt, Jim McKenna, Bill Nye, Ian Saunders, Jon Sherman, Ann Slichet. Senior Segment Producer: Scott Schaefer. Segment Producers: Adam Gross, Seth Gross. Associate Producers: Lauren Karpo, Nancy Mutzel. Senior Editors: Michael Gross, Darrell Suto. Editors: Greg Day, Michael Gross, Blake Hurley, Felicity Oram, John Reul. Key Costumer/Home Demo Coordinator: Christine Duncan. Property Mistress: Diane McGinn. Assistant Property Master: Scott Fogdall. Property/Wardrobe Assistants: Kimberly Talbert, Deanna Wiseman. Assistant Unit Manager: Shanna Thurston. Unit Production Manager: Jamie Hammond. Second Unit Producer: Simon Griffith. Second Unit Assistant Producers: Mark Hunt, Jennie Peabody. Directors of Photography: Mike Boydstun, Darrell Suto. Field Photographers: Karal Bauer, Greg Davis, Jennifer Moran, Pete Rummel, Arlo Smith, Tom Speer, Kevin Tomlinson, Valerie Vozza. Audio: Resti Bagcal, David Huddey, Jerry Neuman, Bob O'-Hearn, Myron Partman, Marion Smith. Production Designer: Bill Sleeth. Production Coordinators: Nancy Mutzell, Tessa Porterfield, Stacy "Sam" Rosen. Assistant Production Coordinators: Leanne Bunas, Alice Ikeda. Business Manager: Tula Urdaz-White. Educational Consultant: Susan Wood-Megrey. Science Researchers: Amy Axt-Hanson, Ian Saunders. Script Coordinator: Shannon Stapelton, Assistant Directors: Leslie Bloom, Steve Cammarano, Bill Predmore, Jen Todd. Assistant Editors: Steve Cammarano, Glenn Sterling. Assistant Producers: Greg Day, Lauren Karpo, Shannon Stapelton, Glenn Sterling. Make-up: Teresa Jones. Assistant to Bill Nye: Julia Miller. Lighting Director: Don Lange. On-Line Editors: Wistar D. Rinearson, Doug Lyons, David Shirmer. Graphic Designer: Lucy Woodworth, Lou Zumek, Tina Eastlake, Mitch Craig. Production Carpenter: Marc Brown. Produced by KCTS Television in association with the National Science Foundation and Rabbit Ears Productions, Inc. for Buena Vista Television.

Countdown at the Neon Armadillo
Executive Producer: Don Weiner. Written by: Tom Roland. Directors: Richie Namm, Kent Weed. Executive in Charge of Production: Jeff Kopp. Current Programming and Talent Executive: Tisi Aylward. Talent Coordinator: Steven Schillaci. Associate Directors: Tony Imparto, Greg Schowengerdt. Production Designer: Randy Foster. Art Designer: David Hoffman. Lighting Designer: Olin Younger. Production Supervisor: Risa Thomas. Script Supervisor: Amy Storti. Production Manager (Orlando): Gary Turchin. Production Manager (Los Angeles): Brad Hart. Choreographer: Kaylee Scott. Post Production Coordinator: Jordan Goodman. Financial Coordinator: Rock Birt. Produced by BIP Productions, Ltd.

Bakersfield P.D.
Created by: Larry Levin. Co-Executive Producer: Dennis Klein. Producers: Richard Dresser, Dean Parisot. Produced by: David Latt. Written by: Richard Dresser, Peter Giambalvo, Bryan Gordon, Dennis Klein, Larry Levin, Jeff Nathanson. Directed by: Michael Engler, Tim Hunter, Ken Kwapis, Nick Marck, Dean Parisot. Executive Producer: Larry Levin. Creative Consultant: Jeff Nathanson. Coordinating Producer: Barry M. Berg. Associate Producer: Jeff Henry. Director of Photography: Victor Goss. Production Designer: Waldemar Kalinowski. Edited by: Todd Busch, Suzanne Petit, Steven Weisberg. Unit Production Manager: Barry M. Berg. First Assistant Directors: James E. Lansbury, Gary Marcus, Leo Zisman. Second Assistant Directors: J.J. Linsalata, Marty Mericka. Casting by: Liberman/Hirschfield Casting, C.S.A. Music Supervisors: Karyn Rachtman, Mary Ramos. Music Composed by: Mark Mothersbaugh, Greg O'Connor, Joseph Vitarelli. Main Title Theme by: Carl Finch. Performed by: Brave Combo. Set Decorator: Florence Fellman. Property Master: Jeffrey Moore. Script Supervisor: Dawn Gilliam, Petra Joregensen. Production Coordinator: Yoli Poropat. Post Production Supervisor: Billy Redner. Costume Designer: Tom Bronson. Costume Supervisors: Donna Marcionne, M.J. Chic Gennarelli. Key Make-up: Lily Benyair-Gart, Alan Friedman, Mony Mansano. Key Hairstylist: Suzan Bagdadi, Dione Taylor. Location Manager: Kevin Halloran. Production Sound Mixer: Douglas B. Arnold. Sound Editors: Lew Goldstein, Doug Kent, Joel Valentine. Rock Island Productions in association with Touchstone Television.

SINBAD SHOW, THE

Created by: Gary Murphy, Larry Strawther, Sinbad. Developed by: Michael Jacobs, David A. Caplan, Brian Lapan. Written by: Gary Apple, Calvin Brown, Jr., David A. Caplan, Michael Carrington, Michael J. Eithorn, Ralph Farquhar, Michael Jacobs, Sharon D. Johnson, Orlando Jones, Arnie Kogen, Mike Langworthy, Brian Lapan, Gary Murphy, David Palladino, Sinbad, Marc Sotkin, Larry Strawther, Michael J. Weithorn, Tom Whedon. Directed by: Debbie Allen, Neema Barnett, Bob Berlinger, J. Burrows, Jim Drake, Michael Peters, Howard Ritter, Rob Schiller, David Trainer, Chuck Vinson. Executive Producer: Sinbad. Supervising Producers: Arnie Kogen, Daniel Palladino, Tom Whedon. Producers: David A. Caplan, Brian Lapan. Produced by: Michael Petok, Tim Steele. Executive Producers: Gary Murphy, Larry Strawther, Michael Jacobs, Ralph Farquhar, Marc Sotkin, Michael J. Weithorn. Creative Consultant: Judy Askins. Co-Producers: Gary Apple, Calvin Brown, Jr., Michael Carrington, Orlando Jones. Associate Producer: Brian Cowan, Paula S. Warner. Executive Story Editors: Michael Carrington, Gary Apple, Orlando Jones. Story Editor: Mike Langworthy. Creative Consultant: Gary Jacobs. Executive Consultant: Sinbad. Director of Photography: Mike Berlin. Art Director: Bruce Ryan. Editors: John Doutt, Mike S. Gavaldon, Marco Zappia. Associate Directors: Mattie C. Caruthers, Howard Ritter. Stage Manager: B.J. McCurdy. Theme by: Chuck Brown (original theme), Kurt Farquhar (second theme). Opening Design (first version) by: WYSIWYG. Opening Design (second version) by: Willie Harper, Stacy Peralta. Music by: Ray Colcord, Kurt Farquhar. Casting by: Eileen Knight, C.S.A., Monica Swann, C.S.A. Set Decorator: Melinda Ritz. Property Master: Gil Spragg. Script Supervisors: Jennifer Farmer, Carol Summers. Post Production Supervisors: Mitchell Bank, James Tripp-Haith. Production Coordinators: Natalia Matthews, Vesper Osborne. Costume Designer: Tom Bronson. Costumers: Paulette Holmon, Alfred Martin, Jr. Make-up: Sheila Evers, Beverly Jo Pryor. Hair: Erma Kent, Debbie Pierce. Technical Director: Bob Holmes. Audio: James Mylenek. Video: Steve Berry, Andrew Dickerman, Tom Tcimpidis. Post Production Mixers: Dennis Durante, Rick Himot. Michael Jacobs Productions, David & Goliath Productions, Gary Murphy/Larry Strawther Productions.

BOY MEETS WORLD

1993–94 SEASON

Created by: Michael Jacobs, April Kelly. Co-Executive Producers: April Kelly, Ed Decter, John J. Strauss. Producer: Arlene Grayson. Written by: Janette Kotichas Burleigh, Ed Decter, Mark Fink, Patricia Forrester, Michael Jacobs, Susan Estelle Jansen, April Kelly, Ken Kuta, Bill Lawrence, Jeff Mennell, Jeffrey C. Sherman, John J. Strauss. Directed by: John Tracy, David Trainer. Executive Producer: Michael Jacobs. Co-Producer: Susan Estelle Jansen. Associate Producer: Karen MacKain. Executive Script Consultant: Ken Kuta. Director of Photography: Richard Brown. Production Designer: John C. Mula. Edited by: Marco Zappia. Associate Director: Patrick Maloney. Stage Manager: Lynn McCracken. Theme Song and Music by: Ray Colcord. Casting by: Sally Stiner, C.S.A. Original Casting by: Allison Jones, Sally Stiner, C.S.A. Set Decorator: Robinson Royce. Property Master: David Glazer. Script Supervisor: Kathy Giangregorio. Production Coordinator: Russell Dague. Costume Designer: Tom Bronson. Key Costumers: Mindy Kurtz, Melissa Franz, Nanrose Buchman. Make-up: Annie Maniscalco, Francesca Maxwell. Hair Stylists: Laurel Van Dyke, Janet Medford. Production Staff: Christine Boudman, Bonnie Buckley, Janette Burleigh, Jillian Harris, Fred O. Herrman, Ann Johnson, Todd Zeldin. Technical Director: Craig Shideler. Audio: Michael L. Clark. Video: Eric Clay. Main Title Concept and Graphics Design: Barbara Eddy, Richard Probst, Bill Lebeda. Michael Jacobs Productions, Inc. Touchstone Television.

1994–95 SEASON

Created by: Michael Jacobs, April Kelly. Executive Producer: David Kendall. Supervising Producer: Glen Merzer. Producers: David Trainer, Susan Estelle Jansen. Produced by: Arlene Grayson. Written by: Mark Blutman, Eric Brand, Howard Busgang, Susan Estelle Jansen, Kevin Kelton, David Kendall, Robert Kurtz, Jeff Menell, Glen Merzer, Matthew Nelson, Michele Palermo, Jeffrey C. Sherman, Steve Young. Directed by: David Kendall, Jeff McCracken, David Trainer. Executive Producer: Michael Jacobs. Co-Producers: Howard Busgang, Mark Blutman. Associate Producer: Karen MacKain. Creative Consultant: Kevin Kelton. Story Editors: Jeff Menell, Jeffrey C. Sherman. Director of Photography: Richard Brown. Production Designer: John C. Mula. Edited by: Marco Zappia. Associate Director: Lauren Breiting. Stage Managers: Lynn McCracken, Steve Hoefer. Theme Song and Music by: Ray Colcord. Casting by: Sally Stiner, C.S.A. Original Casting by: Allison Jones, Sally Stiner, C.S.A. Set Decorator: Robinson Royce. Property Masters: David Glazer, Mark Papson. Script Supervisors: Kathy Giangregorio, Kit Wilkinson. Production Coordinator: Russell Dague. Costume Supervisor/Wardrobe Supervisor: Sara Markowitz. Key Costumers: Lisa Buchignani, Bob Morgan. Make-up: Annie Maniscalco, June Brickman. Hair Stylists: Laurel Van Dyke, June Brickman. Production Staff: Bonnie Buckley, Sonja Cannon, Didi Destefano, Erica Grissen, Ernest Hollingsworth, Ann Johnson, Scott Miles, Al Myers, Rich Tabach, Todd Zeldin. Technical Directors: Kenneth R. Shapiro, Craig Shideler, John Pritchett. Audio: Michael L. Clark. Video: Eric Clay. Michael Jacobs Productions, Inc. Touchstone Television.

1995–96 SEASON

Created by: Michael Jacobs, April Kelly. Executive Producer: David Kendall. Producers: Mark Blutman, Howard Busgang, Kevin Kelton. Produced by: Karen MacKain. Written by: Mark Blutman, Howard Busgang, Kevin Kelton, Jeff Mennell, Susan Meyers, Matthew Nelson, Jeffrey C. Sherman, Michael Swerdlick, Judy Toll, Donna Trujillo. Directed by: David Kendall, Jeff McCracken, John Tracy, David Trainer. Executive Producer: Michael Jacobs. Associate Producer: Steve Lamar. Executive Story Editor: Jeffrey C. Sherman. Story Editors: Jeff Menell, Matthew Nelson, Judy Toll, Susan Meyers. Director of Photography: Darryl Palagi. Production Designer: John C. Mula. Edited by: Marco Zappia. Associate Director: Lauren Breiting. Stage Managers: Steve Hoefer, Michael Shea. Associate Stage Manager/Florida: Jeffrey Gitter. Theme Song and Music by: Ray Colcord. Casting by: Sally Stiner, C.S.A. Associate: Barbie Block. Original Casting by: Allison Jones, Sally Stiner, C.S.A. Set Decorator: Robinson Royce. Property Master: David Glazer. Script Supervisor: Kathy Giangregorio. Production Coordinator: Russell Dague. Wardrobe Supervisor: Sara Markowitz. Key Costumers: Steven C. Hicke, Wanda Leavey. Make-up: Annie Maniscalco, Cory Jeen. Hair Stylists: Laurel Van Dyke, Terry Robbins. Production Staff: John D. Beck, Sonja Kaye Cannon, Carl Ellsworth, Angela Giannoni, Erica Grissen, Ernest Hollingsworth, Mark J. Kunerth, Christi Whitham, Todd Zeldin. Technical Director: Craig Shideler. Audio: Jim Mylenek. Video: Mike Snedden. Michael Jacobs Productions, Inc. Touchstone Television.

GOOD LIFE, THE

Created by: Jeff Martin, Kevin Curran, Suzanne Martin. Supervising Producer: Warren Bell. Producers: David Silverman, Stephen Sustarsic. Produced by: George A. Sunga. Written by: Warren Bell, Wendy Braff, Kevin Curran, Mark Driscoll, Holly Hester, Frank Lombardi, Jeff Martin, Suzanne Martin, Dana Reston, Leslie Rieder, David Silverman, Stephen Sustarsic. Directed by: Gerry Cohen, John Rich. Executive Producers: Jeff Martin, Kevin Curran. Co-Producer: Wendy Braff. Creative Consultant: Bruce Helford. Story Editor: Holly Hester. Co-Producers: Richard Baker, Rick Messina, Jimmy Miller. Executive Consultant: John Caponera. Directors of Photography: Richard Hissong, Tony Yarlett. Art Directors: Kevin Pfeiffer, Richard Improta. Edited by: Larry Harris. Associate Directors: Bob Lahendro, Steve Burgess. Stage Managers: Salvatore Baldomar, Jr., Chris La Barbera, Sean Mulcahy. Associate Producer: Cheri Tanimura. Casting by: Brian Chavanne, C.S.A. Music by: Jonathan Wolff. Set Decorators: Robinson Royce, Rochelle Moser. Property Masters: Dave Crockett, James A. Rathbun. Script Supervisors: Carol Summers, Lorraine Sevre Kenney. Costume Designer: Tom Bronson. Hair: Mary Guerrero, Maria Valdivia. Make-up: Bruce Grayson. Production Coordinator: Margien Burns. Technical Director:

Robert A. Bowen. Audio: Kerry Boggio, Christopher Banninger. Video: Eric Anthony Clay, Larry Brotzler. Opening Design by: Lynne Lussier. Production Staff: Wendell Anderson, Wanda Armstrong, Melissa C. Ferrell, Richard Finn, Melissa Gould, Mary Hidalgo, Joseph Martin, Melissa D. McDowell, Jody Jill McIntyre, Mary Elizabeth Stewart, Janet Viscome. Based on the Stand-up Comedy of John Caponera. Interbang, Inc.

MONTY

Executive Producer: Henry Winkler. Supervising Producer: Katie Ford. Producer: Ana Krewson. Created by: Marc Lawrence. Written by: George Beckerman, Robert Borden, Jane Espenson, Katie Ford, Marc Lawrence, Frank Lombardi, Caryn Lucas, Dana Reston. Directed by: Robby Benson, James Burrows, Linda Day, Matthew Diamond, Pat Fischer-Doak, Gail Mancuso, John Pasquin, Gene Reynolds. Executive Producer: Marc Lawrence. Associate Producer: Steve Lamar. Consulting Producer: George Beckerman. Creative Consultant: Bruce Helford. Story Editors: Caryn Lucas, Robert Borden. Directors of Photography: Dan Kuleto, Donald A. Morgan. Production Designer: David Sackeroff. Editor: Tony Porter. Associate Director: Pat Fischer-Doak. Stage Manager: Harriette Ames-Regan. Music by: Dan Foliart. Casting by: Allison Jones. Casting Associate: Linda Kohn. Set Decorator: Freddie Rymond. Property Master: Al Eisenmann II. Script Supervisors: Lisa Knox, Kit Wilkinson. Production Coordinator: Heidi Addison. Costume Designer: Tom Bronson. Key Costumers: Jennifer Lax, Linda Cormany. Make-up: Lisa Pharren, Marina Torpin. Hair: Michele Payne. Technical Directors: James Horky, Cliff Miracle, Parker Roe. Audio: Edward L. Moskowitz. Video: Larry Brotzler. Fair Dinkum, Inc. and Reserve Room Productions, Inc. in association with Touchstone Television.

THUNDER ALLEY

1993–94 SEASON

Produced by: Gayle S. Maffeo. Producer: Tim Doyle. Written by: Tim Doyle, Carmen Finestra, Steve Gabriel, Rita Hsiao, David McFadzean, Joey Murphy, John Pardee, Matt Williams, Robert Zappia. Directed by: Robby Benson, Andy Cadiff, Barnet Kellman, John Rago. Executive Producers: Carmen Finestra, David McFadzean, Matt Williams. Creative Consultants: Billy Riback, Marjorie Gross. Associate Producer: Caterina Fiordellisi Nelli. Directors of Photography: Donald A. Morgan, Walter Glover. Production Designer: David Sackeroff. Editors: Marco Zappia, Roger Ames Berger, Alex Trocker. Associate Directors: John Rago, Mimi Deaton. Stage Manager: Bill Shea. Post Production Supervisor: Jim Praytor. Original Music by: Howard Pearl. Casting by: Deborah Barylski, C.S.A. Set Decorator: Jeannie Gunn. Property Master: Michael C. Blaze. Script Supervisors: Christina Gunderson, Susan Straughn Harris. Production Coordinator: Stefen T. Maekawa. Costume Designer: Sarah Lemire. Key Costumer: Patti Taylor. Make-up: Leslie Lightfoot, Sandy Reimer-Morris. Hair Stylists: Maria Valdivia, Renee DiPinto. Re-Recording Mixers: Charlie McDaniel, John Bickelhaupt. Post Production Coordinator: Kathy O'Connell. Technical Director: Chris Donovan. Audio: J. Mark King. Video: Bob Kaufmann. Wind Dancer Production Group in association with Touchstone Television.

1994–95 SEASON

Produced by: Gayle S. Maffeo. Created by: Carmen Finestra, David McFadzean, Matt Williams. Supervising Producers: Bob Burris, Michael B. Kaplan, Lissa Levin, Michael Ware. Producer: Barry Gold. Executive Story Consultants: Jake Weinberger, Michael Weinberger. Written by: Bob Burris, Bill Freiberger, Steve Gabriel, Barry Gold, Michael B. Kaplan, Paul A. Kaplan, Lissa Levin, Debbie Pearl, Michael Ware, Jake Weinberger, Michael Weinberger, Robert Zappia. Directed by: Robby Benson, Pat Fischer-Doak. Executive Producers: Dan Guntzelman, Carmen Finestra, David McFadzean, Matt Williams. Consulting Producer: Billy Riback. Co-Producer: Debbie Pearl. Associate Producer: Caterina Fiordellisi Nelli. Edited by: Marco Zappia. Director of Photography: Donald A. Morgan. Production Designer: David Sackeroff. Compositing Editors: Mark Intravartolo, Alex Trocker. Associate Director:

Pat Fischer-Doak. Stage Manager: Bill Shea. Post Production Supervisor: Jim Praytor. Original Music by: Howard Pearl. Casting by: Deborah Barylski, C.S.A., Jonell Dunn. Set Decorator: Jeannie Gunn. Property Master: Michael C. Blaze. Script Supervisor: Christina Gunderson. Production Coordinator: Stefen T. Maekawa. Costume Designer: Sarah Lemire. Key Costumer: Patti Taylor. Make-up: Sandy Reimer-Morris. Hair Stylists: Clare Corsick, Renee DePinto, Maria Valdivia. Re-Recording Mixers: Charlie McDaniel, John Bickelhaupt, Tamara Johnson. Post Production Coordinator: Kathy O'Connell. Post Production Associate: Matthew Asner. Technical Director: Craig Shideler. Audio: J. Mark King, Russ Gary. Video: Bob Kaufmann. Wind Dancer Production Group in association with Touchstone Television.

THESE FRIENDS OF MINE (AND) ELLEN

1993–94 SEASON

Created by: Neal Marlens, Carol Black, David Rosenthal. Supervising Producer: David Rosenthal. Producer: Richard Day. Produced by: Mark Grossan. Written by: Warren Bell, Carol Black, Richard Day, Mark Driscoll, Neal Marlens, Suzanne Martin, David Rosenthal, Mark Wilding. Directed by: Andy Ackerman, John Bowab, Neal Marlens, Rob Schiller, Andrew D. Weyman. Co-Executive Producers: David Rosenthal, Warren Bell. Executive Producers: Carol Black, Neal Marlens. Associate Producer: Frank Merwald. Director of Photography: Thom Marshall. Production Designer: Bill Brzeski. Edited by: Dennis C. Vejar, A.C.E., Tony Hayman. Production Manager: Neil Rapp. First Assistant Director: Michael Looney. Second Assistant Director: Joanne Keene. Music by: W.G. Snuffy Walden. Casting by: Brian Chavanne, C.S.A., Lisa London, C.S.A. Original Casting by: Lisa London, C.S.A. Executive Consultant: Michael Becker. Technical Coordinator: David Owen Trainor. Set Decorator: Lynda Burbank. Property Master: Scott L. London. Script Supervisor: Dianne Sullens-Hoehing. Production Coordinator: Scott Sites. Script Coordinator: Teddy Tenenbaum. Costume Supervisor: Wendy Range. Key Costumers: Pie Lombardi, Janis Mekaelian, Lynda Pyka. Costumers: Melissa Merwin, Brian Cotton, Wendy Greiner. Make-up: Robin Dee LaVigne. Hair Stylist: Robert Hallowell. Chief Lighting Technician: Drain M. Marshall. Key Grip: Albert Cicolello. Camera Operators: Ed Neilsen, Jeff Miller, Charlie Young, Gene Talvin. Production Sound Mixers: Michael Ballin, Bill Stephens, Jr. Re-recorded by: Marti D. Humphrey. Production Accountant: Jeanne Andrews. Assistant Editor: Jennifer Vejar. Assistants to the Producers: Anji Sawant, Amy Jo Weinstein, Kathy Karlin, Jennifer Melchoir, Susan Kydd, Sam Froelich, Layne Kovach, Andrew Green, Taylor Bryon. Production Assistants: David Driver, Keith Wheeler, Adam Rosen, Cindy Linnick, Keiann Collins. Executive Consultant: Ellen DeGeneres. The Black/Marlens Company.

1994–95 SEASON

Created by: Neal Marlens, Carol Black, David S. Rosenthal. Supervising Producer: Richard Day. Producers: Vicki S. Horwits, Tracy Newman, Johnathan Stark. Produced by: Mark Grossan. Written by: Richard Day, Mark Driscoll, Pamela Eells, Holly Hester, Vicki S. Horwits, Sally Lapidus, Suzanne Martin, Tracy Newman, David S. Rosenthal, Maria Semple, Jonathan Stark. Directed by: Tom Cherones, David Owen Trainor. Executive Producers: Warren Bell, David S. Rosenthal. Associate Producer: Frank Merwald. Co-Producers: Mark Driscoll, Holly Hester. Executive Story Editors: Holly Hester, Maria Semple. Story Editors: Suzanne Martin, Maria Semple. Consultants: Suzanne Martin, Alex Herschlag. Director of Photography: Thom Marshall. Production Designer: Bill Brzeski. Edited by: Judith A. Burke. Production Manager: Neil Rapp. First Assistant Director: Richard Wells. Second Assistant Director: Joanne Keene. Music by: W.G. Snuffy Walden. Casting by: Tammara Billik, C.S.A. Production Coordinator: Scott Sites. Technical Coordinator: David Owen Trainor. Set Decorator: Lynda Burbank. Property Master: Scott L. London. Script Supervisor: Lorraine Kenney, Lorraien Sevre-Richmond. Costume Supervisors: Brett Barrett, Joyce Unruh. Key Costumer: Jennifer Soulages. Make-up: Robin LaVigne. Hair Stylists: Robert Hallowell, Gloria Ponce. Consultant: Bambi Breakstone. Assistants to the Producers: Cody Farley, Jennifer Fisher, Sam Froelich, Bud Robertson, Patrick Harrigan, Jennifer Hayes, Layne Kovach, Jenny Siff, Andrew Green, Keiann Collins, Chris DelConte, Matt Selman. Production Sound Mixer: Michael Ballin. Re-recorded by: Charles McDaniel III. Opening Design by: Lumeni Productions, Inc. Executive Consultant: Ellen DeGeneres. The Black/Marlens Company and Touchstone Television.

1995–96 Season
Created by: Neal Marlens, Carol Black, David S. Rosenthal. Executive Producer: Vic Kaplan. Co-Executive Producers: Tom Leopold, Dava Savel. Producers: Tracy Newman, Jonathan Stark, Lisa DeBenedictis, Daryl Rowland. Consulting Producer: Matt Goldman. Written by: Lisa DeBenedictis, Jennifer Fisher, David Flebotte, Matt Goldman, Eileen Heisler, DeAnne Heline, Alex Herschlag, Tom Leopold, Tracy Newman, Daryl Rowland, Dava Savel, Jonathan Stark. Directed by: Robby Benson. Executive Producers: DeAnn Heline, Eileen Heisler. Associate Producers: Lisa Helfrich, Lisa H. Jackson. Coordinating Producer: Ken Orenstein. Executive Story Editor: David Flebotte. Story Editor: Alex Herschlag. Director of Photography: Richard A. Brown. Production Designer: Bill Brzeski. Edited by: Kris Trexler. Unit Production Manager: Ken Ornstein. First Assistant Director: Richard Wells. Second Assistant Directors: Joanne Keene, Sandra Middleton. Music by: W.G. Snuffy Walden. Theme Composed by: John McElhone, Sharleen Spiteri. Performed by: Texas. Casting by: Tammara Billik, C.S.A. Set Decorator: Archie D'Amico. Costume Supervisor: Kathy Monderine. Make-up: Robin LaVigne. Hair Stylist: Kent Nelson. Production Coordinator: Scott Sites. Technical Coordinator: Ray de Vally, Jr. Property Master: Kelly H'Doubler Crowder. Script Supervisor: Lorraine Sevre-Richmond. Costumes by: Bambi Breakstone. Assistants to the Producers: Barbara Siebertz, Katrina Edwards, Anne Davis, Jennifer Boller, Lesly Lieberman, Matthew Seng, Robert B. Evans, Marshall Boone, Erik Marino, Chris D'Arienzo, Gabriel Gold, Sean Siska. Production Sound Mixer: Larry Stephens. Executive Consultant: Ellen DeGeneres. The Black/Marlens Company and Touchstone Television.

Someone Like Me
Created by: Bruce Helford. Co-Executive Producer: Ruth Bennett. Produced by: George A. Sunga. Written by: Eve Ahlert, Ruth Bennett, Drew Carey, Robert Cohen, Dennis Drake, Mark Driscoll, Bruce Helford, Holly Hester, Lona Williams. Directed by: Zane Buzby, Rob Schiller, John Whitesell. Executive Producers: Sandy Gallin, Gail Berman, Stuart Sheslow, Bruce Helford. Associate Producer: Cheri Tanimura. Creative Consultants: Marc Lawrence, Kevin Curran, Mark Driscoll. Executive Story Editors: Holly Hester, Robert Cohen. Story Editors: Dennis Drake, Eve Ahlert, Janice Jordan Nelson. Consultants: Drew Carey, Alexa Junge. Casting by: Steven Fertig. Original Casting by: Mary V. Buck, C.S.A., Susan Edelman, C.S.A. Director of Photography: Daniel Flannery. Production Designer: Garvin Eddy. Edited by: Larry Harris. Associate Director: Steve Burgess. Stage Managers: Salvatore Baldomar, Jr., John Hill. Music by: Jonathan Wolff. Set Decorator: Rochelle Moser. Consultant: Debra McGuire. Opening Design by: Castle Bryant/Johnsen. Hair: Clare Corsick, Maria Valdivia. Technical Directors: Craig Shideler, Robert Bowen. Audio: Ed Moskowitz, Kerry Boggio. Video: Larry Brotzler. Script Supervisor: Lorraine Kenney. Property Master: Dave McGuire. Production Coordinator: Salli Shrewsbury. Key Costumer: Diane Crooke. Costumer: Vicki Skinner. Make-up: JoAnn Kozloff, Allison Woody. Production Assistants: Wanda Armstrong, Joy Creel, Richard Finn, Sharon Klein, Melissa D. McDowell, Mary Ryther, James Spezialy, Janet Viscome, Christy Snell. Mohawk Productions, Inc. and Sandollar Television in association with Touchstone Television.

Hardball
Created by: Kevin Curran, Jeff Martin. Produced by: Bill Freiberger, George Sunga. Written by: Tracy Baldwin, Michael Barker, Kevin Curran, Bill Freiberger, Jeff Martin, Tracy Newman, Jonathan Stark, Matt Weitzman, Lona Williams. Directed by: Peter Baldwin, Gerry Cohen, Gil Junger, John

Whitesell. Executive Producers: Jeff Martin, Kevin Curran, Bill Bryan. Co-Producers: Tracy Newman, Jonathan Stark. Associate Producer: Cheri Tanimura. Director of Photography: Richard Brown. Art Director: Richard Improta. Edited by: Larry Harris. Associate Director: Howard Ritter. Stage Managers: Sal Baldomar, Jr., John Hill. Casting by: Brian Chavanne, Mary Hidalgo. Music by: Jonathan Wolff. Set Decorator: Leslie Frankenheimer. Property Master: Jim Samson. Script Supervisors: Janet Kagan, Carol Summers. Production Coordinators: Gregory A. Frampton, David Yrisarri. Costume Designer: Tom Bronson. Costumers: Michael Fitzpatrick, Steve Sharp. Hair: Sandra Munk. Make-up: Allison Woody. Production Staff: Wanda Armstrong, Neal Boushell, Melissa Ferrell, Mary Elizabeth Stewart, James Spezialy, Stephanie Silvestri, Jim Rhine, Helen Schorr. Audio: Richard J. Masci. Video: Bob Bowen. Interbang, Inc. Magic Beans, Inc. Touchstone Television.

All-American Girl
Created by: Gary Jacobs. Executive Producer: Gary Jacobs, Sandy Gallin, Gail Berman, Stuart Sheslow. Co-Executive Producer: Pat Dougherty. Supervising Producer/Co-Executive Producer: Clay Graham. Produced by: Bruce Johnson. Written by: Aline Brosh, Kell Cahoon, Dawn DeKeyser, Pat Dougherty, Charleen Easton, Clay Graham, Gary Jacobs, Jeff Kahn, Arnie Kogen, Tim Maile, J.J. Paulsen, Tom Saunders, Kurt Schindler, Jon Sherman, Douglas Tuber, Elizabeth Wong. Directed by: Terry Hughes, Arlene Sanford, Andrew D. Weyman. Co-Producers: Doug Tuber, Tim Maile. Associate Producer: Brian J. Cowan. Executive Story Editors: Stacey Hur, J.J. Paulsen. Director of Photography: Daniel Flannery. Production Designer: David Sackeroff. Editor: Jimmy B. Frazier. Associate Director: Mark Cendrowski. Stage Managers: Bill Ghaffary, Paul Paolasso. Casting by: Nikki Valko. Original Casting by: Mary V. Buck, C.S.A., Susan Edelman, C.S.A. Music by: George Englund, Nick South, Wendell Yuponce. Set Decorator: Freddie J. Rymond. Property Master: Jeff Ackerman. Script Supervisor: Jennifer Farmer, Marsha Gould. Consultant: Erin Quigley. Production Coordinator: Doeri Welch Greiner. Key Costumers: Lynda Pyka, Brian Cotton. Make-up: Adam Christopher. Hair Stylist: Yvonne De Patis-Kupka. Technical Director: Russ Reinsel. Audio: Larry Stephens. Video: Guy Jones, Mike Snedden. Based on the Standup Comedy of: Margaret Cho. Sandollar Television in association with Heartfelt Productions, Inc. Touchstone Television.

Unhappily Ever After

1994–95 Season
Supervising Producers: David A. Caplan, Brian Lapan. Co-Executive Producers: Marcy Vosburgh, Sandy Sprung. Written by: Alan Aidekman, J. Stewart Burns, David A. Caplan, Brian Lapan, Ron Leavitt, Christina Lynch, Arthur Silver, Sandy Sprung, Gabrielle Topping, Marcy Vosburgh, Kimberly Young-Silver. Directed by: Gerry Cohen, Linda Day, Sam W. Orender. Executive Producers: Ron Leavitt, Arthur Silver. Produced by: Harriette Regan. Created by: Ron Leavitt, Arthur Silver. Program Consultants: J. Stewart Burns, Christina Lynch. Associate Producer: Cathy Rosenstein. Director of Photography: Mark Levin. Art Director: Richard Improta. Edited by: Larry Harris. Associate Director: Selig Frank. Stage Managers: Salvatore Baldomar, Jr., John J. Hill. Casting by: Tammara Billik, C.S.A., Justine Jacoby, C.S.A. Theme Music by: Jonathan Wolff. Set Decorator: Larry Wiemer. Property Master: Bobby Cardenas. Script Supervisor: Janet Kagan. Production Coordinator: Carmen Herrera. Costume Supervisor: Peter Flaherty. Costumers: Maryann Bozek, Liza Stewart. Hair: Dottie McQuown, Michelle Payne, Cynthia P. Romo, Barry Rosenberg. Make-up: Patty Bunch, Diane Shatz. Technical Directors: John Pritchett, Ken Tamburri. Audio: Christopher Banninger, Richard Masci. Video: Eric Clay, John Palacio, Jr. Producers' Assistants: Carol Croland, Liz Jaworski, Lisa Lang, Antoinette Stella.

1995–96 Season
Co-Executive Producers: David A. Caplan, Brian Lapan. Written by: J. Stewart Burns, David A. Caplan, Bobcat Goldthwait, Brian Lapan, Matt Leavitt, Christina Lynch, Arthur Silver,

Sandy Sprung, Gabrielle Topping, Allan Trautman, Marcy Vosburgh, Kimberly Young-Silver. Directed by: Gerry Cohen, Linda Day, Sam W. Orender. Executive Producers: Marcy Vosburgh, Sandy Sprung, Ron Leavitt, Arthur Silver. Produced by: Harriette Regan. Created by: Ron Leavitt, Arthur Silver. Story Editors: J. Stewart Burns, Christina Lynch. Associate Producer: Cathy Rosenstein. Director of Photography: Mark Levin. Art Director: Richard Improta. Edited by: Roger Ames Berger, Leland Gray, Larry Harris. Associate Directors: Selig Frank, Salvatore Baldomar, Jr. Stage Managers: Salvatore Baldomar, Jr., John J. Hill, Tom Ohlinger. Casting by: Tammara Billik, C.S.A., Justine Jacoby, C.S.A. Theme Music by: Jonathan Wolff. Set Decorator: Larry Wiemer. Property Master: Bobby Cardenas. Script Supervisor: Pamela Cantori. Production Coordinator: Carmen Herrera. Key Costumer: Christy Ito-Waller. Costumers: T. Baxter, Claudia Wick. Hair: Lana Heying, Terry Robbins, Michael White. Make-up: Eryn Krueger, Tania McComas. Technical Director: Chuck Abate. Audio: Toby Foster. Video: Victor Bagdadi. Producers' Assistants: Liz Jaworski, Eric Kornick, Lisa Lang, Beth Sherman, Antoinette Stella.

GEORGE WENDT SHOW, THE
Created by: Peter Tolan, Lew Schneider. Producer: Lew Schneider. Supervising Producer: Daphne Pollon. Co-Executive Producers: Dan O'Shannon, Michael Petok. Produced by: Michael Petok. Written by: Mike Martineau, Gordon R. McKee, Daphne Pollon, David Regal, Lew Schneider, Peter Tolan. Directed by: Robby Benson, Rick Beren, Terry Hughes. Executive Producer: Peter Tolan. Co-Producer: Donald Capen. Creative Consultants: Ray Magliozzi, Tom Magliozzi, Doug Berman. Executive Story Editor: Mike Martineau. Director of Photography: Richard A. Brown. Art Director: Ken Johnson. Editor: Kris Trexler. Unit Production Manager/First Assistant Director: Irwin Marcus. Second Assistant Director: Barbara Gelman. Music by: Fred Kaz. Casting by: Liberman/Hirschfeld Casting, C.S.A., Michael A. Katcher, C.S.A. Technical Director: Chris Brougham. Set Decorator: Melinda Ritz. Property Master: Gilbert L. Spragg. Script Supervisor: Christine Nyhart. Production Coordinator: Wanda Armstrong. Costume Designer: Tom Bronson. Costumers: Linda S. Cormany, Bob Iannaccone. Make-up: Dale Bach-Siss. Hair Stylist: Linda Trainoff. Production Sound Mixer: Ed Moskowitz. Post Production Mixer: Dennis Durante. Post Production Supervisor: Jennifer Velo-Stewart. Opening Design by: Nick Newton. The Cloudland Co. Touchstone Television.

PRIDE & JOY
Executive Producer: Marc Lawrence. Supervising Producers: David Pollock, Elias Davis. Producers: Caryn Lucas, Robert Borden, Arleen Sorkin, Paul Slansky. Produced by: Ana Krewson. Created by: Marc Lawrence. Written by: Robert Borden, Wil Calhoun, Leslie Eberhard, Katie Ford, John Frink, Marc Lawrence, Caryn Lucas, Don Payne. Directed by: Michael Lembeck, Tom Moore, Arlene Sanford, Thomas Schlamme. Associate Producer: Steve Lamar. Creative Consultants: Katie Ford, Larry Spencer. Directors of Photography: Mike Berlin, Gerald Perry Finnerman, A.S.C. Production Designer: Bill Brzeski. Edited by: Tony Porter. Unit Production Managers/First Assistant Directors: Stephen Lofaro, Bill Cosentino. Second Assistant Director: Wendy Ikeguchi. Music by: Bennett Salvay, Jesse Frederick. Casting by: Allison Jones, C.S.A. Production Assistants: Sandy Berry, Jennifer Brown, Sarah Dohrmann, Carl Ellsworth, Monica Gelardo, Greg Guzik, Vince Robinette, Leslie Strain, Suzanne Villandry. Production Coordinator: Heidi Addison. Technical Coordinator: Tommy Thompson. Set Decorator: Jennifer Polito. Property Master: Al Eisenmann II. Script Supervisors: Jan Corey, Diane Sullens-Hoehing. Costume Designer: Tom Bronson. Costumers: Jennifer Stone, Michael Fitzpatrick. Make-up: June Brickman, Bonita DeHaven. Hair Stylists: Terry Robbins, Christina Raye. Production Sound Mixer: Edward L. Moskowitz, C.A.S. Reserve Room Productions, Inc. Touchstone Television.

NOWHERE MAN
Produced by: Peter Dunne. Supervising Producer: Joel Surnow, Art Monterastelli. Co-Executive Producer: Joel Surnow. Created by: Lawrence Hertzog. Written by: Erica Byrne, Peter Dunne, David Ehrman, Jane Espenson, Lawrence Hertzog, Schuyler Kent, Art Monterastelli, Joel Surnow, Jake Weinberger, Michael Weinberger. Directed by: Reza Badiyi, Greg Beeman, Mel Damski, James Darren, Tobe Hooper, Tim Hunter, Michael Levine, Guy Magar, Steven Robman, Stephen Thomas Stafford, Ian Toynton, James Whitmore, Jr., Thomas J. Wright. Executive Consultant: Stan Rogow. Executive Producers: Lawrence Hertzog, Stan Rogow. Coordinating Producer: Jan Dewitt. Associate Producer: Marianne Canepa. Director of Photography: James Chressanthis, Ric Waite. Production Designers: Bill McAllister, James Shanahan. Art Director: James Shanahan. Editors: Peter Basinski, Andrew Cohen, A.C.E., James S. Giritlian, A.C.E., Josh Muscatine, Gene Ranney. Unit Production Manager: Jan Dewitt. First Assistant Directors: Richard W. Abramitis, Richard Denault, Rodney Hooks, Tyrone L. Mason, Craig West. Second Assistant Directors: Suzanne C. Geiger, Nancy Green. Music by: Mark Snow. Casting by: Beth Hymson-Ayer, C.S.A. Portland Casting by: Nannette Troutman. Set Decorators: Sal Bydenburgh, Sean Kennedy. Property Master: Greg McMickle. Script Supervisor: Patience Thoreson. Location Managers: Joanna Guzzetta, Eric Hedayat, Marjie Lundell, Ty Nelson, Kirk Steppe. Production Coordinator, Portland: Gwyn Lustenberger, Laura "L.T." Tateishi. Production Coordinator, Los Angeles: Stacey Kosier. Costume Designer: Tom Bronson. Costume Supervisor: Ron Leamon. Key Costumers: Michele Dunn, Earl L. Lewis. Make-Up/Hair Supervisor: Martin "Vinnie" Hagood. Make-Up: Jo Jo Myers Proud. Hairstylist: Sami Mattias. Stunt Coordinator: Vince Deadrick, Jr. Choreography: Smith Wordes. Video Supervisor: Bob Moregnorth. Production Sound Mixers: Robert Marts, Glen Micallef, Douglas Tourtelot. Music Editor: Marty Wereski. Lawrence Hertzog Productions in association with Touchstone Television.

MAYBE THIS TIME
Created by: Michael Jacobs, Bob Young, Susan Estelle Jansen. Executive Producers: Bob Young, Michael Jacobs. Supervising Producer: Susan Estelle Jansen. Producer: David Trainer. Produced by: J. Cowan. Written by: Amy Engelberg, Wendy Engelberg, Andrew Green, Susan Estelle Jansen, Michael Jacobs, Chip Keyes, Heather MacGilvray, Linda Mathious, Peggy Nicoll, Rick Singer, Bob Young, Steve Young. Directed by: David Trainer. Associate Producer: Jill Andersen. Creative Consultants: Chip Keyes, Ehrich Van Lowe, Danny Kallis. Executive Consultants: Karl Engemann, Brian Blosil. Director of Photography: Walter Glover. Production Designer: John C. Mula. Edited by: Marco Zappia. Associate Director: Lynn McCracken. Stage Manager: Merv Hawkins. Music by: Ray Colcord. Casting by: Melinda Gartzman, C.S.A., Greg Orson. Set Decorator: Robinson Royce. Key Costumers: Sara Shaw, Sonya Ooten. Make-up: Bob Jermain, Shannon Engemann. Hair Stylists: Mary Guerrero, Katherine Kotarakos. Property Master: Jim Samson. Script Supervisor: Jennifer Farmer. Production Coordinator: Greg Frampton. Costumes by: Simon Tuke. Assistants to Producers: Carlos Aragon, Bonnie Buckley, Barbara Feldman, Pamela Hall, Andrew Hayes, Aaron Kemp, Al Myers, Michelle D. Robinson, Geralyn Schaefer, Leslie Strain. Technical Director: Parker Roe. Audio: Bruce Peters. Video: Eric Clay. Michael Jacobs Productions, Inc.

BROTHERLY LOVE
Created by: Jim Vallely, Jonathan Schmock. Executive Producers: Paul Junger Witt, Tony Thomas, Gary Levine, Jonathan Schmock, Jim Vallely. Written by: Pamela Eells, Eddie Gorodetsky, Jim Halkett, Craig Hoffman, John Levenstein, Jonathan Schmock, Jim Vallely, Michele J. Wolff. Directed by: Terry Hughes. Supervising Producer: Pam Eels. Producers: Michele Wolff, Craig Hoffman. Co-Executive Producer: Nina Feinberg. Co-Producers: Eddie Gorodetsky, Donna Lawrence, Joe Lawrence. Consultant: Rob LaZebnik. Associate Producer: Denise Porter. Associate Director: Mark Cendrowski. Stage Managers: Doug Tobin, Bill Ghaffary. Production Designer: Ed LaPorta. Assistant Art Director: Jeff Hall. Production Coordinator: Dionne Kirschner. Post Production Manager: Trevor Kirschner. Editor: Danny White. Editorial Assistants: Bill Murray, Todd Morris. Composer/Sound Coordinator: George Englund. Lighting Designer: Kent Inasy.

Casting: Cami Patton, Julie Pernworth. Costume Designer: Julianne Dechaine. Make-up: Kathleen Crawford, Bob Jermain. Hair Stylists: Mary Guerrero, Jennifer Guerrero. Produced by Witt-Thomas Productions in association with Touchstone Television.

IF NOT FOR YOU

Created by: Larry Levin. Executive Producer: Dennis Klein. Produced by: David Latt. Written by: Leslie Caveny, Dennis Klein, Larry Levin. Directed by: Robert Berlinger, Dennis Erdman, Barnet Kellman, John Rich, Thomas Schlamme. Executive Producer: Larry Levin. Associate Producer: Billy Redner. Co-Producer: Maria Semple. Creative Consultants: Mike Reiss, Al Jean. Story Editor: Wil Calhoun. Director of Photography: Peter Smokler. Production Designer: Waldemar Kalinowski. Editor: Briana London, A.C.E. Unit Production Manager/First Assistant Director: Richard Allen. Second Assistant Director: Molly Muir. Music by: Mark Mothersbaugh, Tito Larriva. Theme Composed by: Bob Dylan. Performed by: Valerie Carpenter with Tito and Tarantula, Victoria Williams, World Party. Music Supervisors: Karyn Rachtman, Dondi Bastone. Set Decorator: Florence Fellman. Key Costumers: Lynda Pyka, Brian J. Cotton. Make-up: Barbara Fonte Byrne. Hair Stylist: Faye Woods. Technical Coordinators: Jeff Wheat, Ray DeVally. Property Masters: Art Shippee, Joanne Hicks. Script Supervisor: Rosemarie Clemente-Johnstone. Production Coordinator: Linda Ota. Costumes by: Kathryn Morrison. Production Sound Mixer: Bill Remhild. Rock Island Productions. Touchstone Television.

LAND'S END

Executive Producers: Fred Dryer, Victor Schiro, Brian K. Ross, Jim Reid. Producers: Ron Frazier, Jefferson Kibbee. Co-Producer: John Clarkson. Coordinating Producer: Diana Young. Created by: Fred Dryer, Victor Schiro, Peter Gethers, David Handler. Written by: John Clarkson, Fred Dryer, Peter Gethers, David Handler, Tom Hazelton, Karen Kevner, Lincoln Kibbee, Peter Koper, Norman and L. Lee Lapidus, John Le Masters, Geoffrey Lewis, Gene Miller, Alphonso H. Moreno, Victor A. Schiro, Elliot Stern. Directed by: Paul Abascal, James Bruce, Christian Faber, John Huneck, Jefferson Kibbee, Geoffrey Lewis, Paul Lynch, Martin Pasetta, Jr. Camera: Garrett Griffin. Editors: Terry Blythe, Jason Freeman. Production Design: Michael Clausen. Sound: Mike Hogan, Craig Clark. Music: Marco Beltrami, Chris Beck. Script Supervisor: Colette Panah. Fred Dryer Productions and Skyvision Partners in association with Buena Vista Television.

MISERY LOVES COMPANY

Supervising Producer: David Trainer. Co-Executive Producer: Sandy Frank. Executive Producer: Bob Young. Created by: Michael Jacobs, Bob Young, David Trainer. Produced by:

Mitchell Bank. Written by: Harry Dunn, Sandy Frank, Andrew Green, Rich Halke, Michael Jacobs, Charlie Kaufman, Heather MacGillvray, Linda Mathious, Rick Singer, David Trainer, Bob Young. Directed by: John Tracy, David Trainer. Executive Producer: Michael Jacobs. Associate Producer: Cheri Tanimura. Co-Producer: Charlie Kaufman. Executive Story Editors: Rich Halke. Story Editors: Andrew Green, Rich Singer, Harry Dunn. Program Consultants: Linda Mathious, Heather MacGillvray. Director of Photography: Walter Glover. Production Designer: John C. Mula. Edited by: Marco Zappia. Associate Director: Kevin Tracy. Stage Managers: Paul Coderko, Nancy Jacobs. Music by: Ray Colcord. Casting by: Melinda Gartzman, C.S.A., Nora Kariya. Set Decorator: Robinson Royce. Property Master: Paul Oannizzotto. Script Supervisor: Dianne Sullens-Hoehing. Production Coordinator: Stephanie Silvestri. Costume Supervisors: Paul DeLucca, Patti B. Taylor. Make-up: Annie Maniscalco. Hair Stylist: Laurel Van Dyke. Production Staff: Rachel Bendavid, Bonnie Buckley, Blanca Conchas, David Kemker, Fred Lewis, Barry Safchik, Paulette Sharen, Jana Wallace. Technical Director: Parker Roe. Audio: Richard Masci. Video: Eric Clay. Opening Design by: Nick Newton Design. Michael Jacobs Productions, Inc. Touchstone Television.

BUDDIES

Produced by: Gayle S. Maffeo. Created by: Matt Williams, David McFadzean, Carmen Finestra. Written by: Trish Baker, Bob Burris, Lisa DeBenedictis, Art Everett, Carmen Finestra, Sharon D. Johnson, Steve Gabriel, Richey Jones, Todd Jones, David McFadzean, Daphne Pollon, Daryl Rowland, Mark St. Germain, Peter Tolan, Michael Ware, Matt Williams, Robert Zappia. Directed by: Andy Cadiff, Paul Lazarus, John Pasquin, Andrew Tsao. Executive Producers: Bob Burris, Michael Ware. Supervising Producers: Billy Riback, Daphne Pollon. Producer: John Pasquin. Executive Producers: Matt Williams, David McFadzean, Carmen Finestra. Co-Produced by: Caterina Fiordellisi Nelli. Associate Producer: Stefen T. Maekawa. Executive Story Consultant: Art Everett. Story Editors: Stephen Gabriel, Robert Zappia, Todd Jones, Richey Jones. Lighting Designer: Donald A. Morgan. Production Designer: David Sackeroff. Edited by: Marco Zappia. Associate Director: Kevin Sullivan. Stage Managers: Jay Zabriskie, Anthony Rich. Post Production Supervisor: Jim Praytor. Music by: Brian Bennett. Theme by: Derrick Perkins. Casting by: Deborah Barylski, C.S.A., Jonell Dunn. Set Decorator: Jeannie Gunn. Property Master: Red Fletcher. Script Supervisor: Mary Valente. Production Coordinator: Nell Uhry. Costume Supervisor: Nanrose Buchman. Key Costumer: Jackie Quigley. Make-up: Sandy Reimer-Morris. Hair Stylists: Linda Flowers, Sandra Rubin Munk. Post Production Coordinator: Jodie Baba. Technical Director: Craig Shideler. Audio: J. Mark King. Video: Bob Kaufman. Wind Dancer Production Group in association with Touchstone Television.

THE WONDERFUL WORLD OF DISNEY

The Wonderful World of Disney, one of television's most beloved Sunday night traditions, has returned to the ABC primetime schedule, with a spectacular lineup of programming to be watched and enjoyed by viewers of all ages. The series—which made its original debut on ABC more than four decades ago—airs Sunday nights.

Michael Eisner, CEO of The Walt Disney Company, continues his role as host for *The Wonderful World of Disney*. Mr. Eisner has hosted Disney's telefilm presentations for *The Disney Sunday Movie*, which aired on ABC in 1986, and for NBC's *The Magical World of Disney* in 1988.

The series showcases more than 30 films, with broadcast premieres of some of Disney's biggest theatrical hits in recent box office history, including *Toy Story*, *Pocahontas*, and *The Santa Clause*.

The series also features an exciting roster of all-new made-for-television films created by Walt Disney Television especially for this franchise. These original movies range from whimsical comedies to compelling dramas, and star some of Hollywood's most recognizable faces.